An Englishman's Adventures on the Santa Fe Trail (1865-1889)

An Englishman's Adventures on the Santa Fe Trail (1865-1889)

Larry Phillips

Copyright © 2019 by Larry Phillips.

Library of Congress Control Number:		2019903168
ISBN:	Hardcover	978-1-7960-2208-7
	Softcover	978-1-7960-2207-0
	eBook	978-1-796-02206-3

All rights reserved. No part of this book may be reproduced or transmitted in any form or by any means, electronic or mechanical, including photocopying, recording, or by any information storage and retrieval system, without permission in writing from the copyright owner.

This is a work of fiction. Names, characters, places and incidents either are the product of the author's imagination or are used fictitiously, and any resemblance to any actual persons, living or dead, events, or locales is entirely coincidental.

Any people depicted in stock imagery provided by Getty Images are models, and such images are being used for illustrative purposes only.
Certain stock imagery © Getty Images.

Print information available on the last page.

Rev. date: 04/27/2019

To order additional copies of this book, contact:
Xlibris
1-888-795-4274
www.Xlibris.com
Orders@Xlibris.com
792930

This book is dedicated to the frontiersmen, traders, freighters, teamsters, bull whackers, soldiers, pioneers and settlers who forged ahead on the Santa Fe Trail during its prominence as the highway of commerce in the 1800s. And special thanks to part-time editor and friend Brett Mellington. The pioneering spirit still lives and enriches the High Plains of Western Kansas, Southeastern Colorado and the Texas and Oklahoma Panhandles.

He could hear the crackling of low embers – the smoky stench burning his nostrils. He couldn't open his eyes, but the metallic taste of blood and dirt in his mouth hinted he was still alive.

"I'm sure this is my home, but what is happening?" he thought to himself.

Then it hit him.

He immediately sat upright but fell over to one side on his elbow. His eyes tried focusing through the cloud-like haze as he glanced from side to side.

"Matty?" he creaked, his lungs full of ashes and smoke. "Matty, can you hear me?"

The scenes started rushing back in his mind: The two men hitting him with their rifle butts, another also putting his boots to his rib cage. The other two men had Matty down, one using his knife to shred her buckskin smock from her body, and her terrified screams filled his head.

"Matty, where are you?" he yelled again, this time sounding more like himself as he tried crawling over on his knees – his left wrist unable to hold his weight. He could see tendons and raw muscle sticking out of the knife slash, but he didn't sense the bone was broken. He grabbed his neckerchief and tied it off above the cut, using his teeth as another hand.

As he tried to push himself up with the other arm, he slipped in the huge pool of blood on the old stone base of the fireplace.

His vision was clearing as he crawled toward where the front door had been, as there was no roof.

"God, please don't let them take Matty," he whispered.

"Matty, please Matty, talk to me," he cried out.

He reached over to what remained of the front wall, a three-foot tall burned out section – there was no door. In fact, as he looked around, there were only pieces of the house here and there.

He couldn't believe the fire had burned almost everything down to the ground, especially considering the back half of the home was a dugout. Only the stone fireplace at the back of the house stood with the pool of blood at its base where he had been left for dead.

His eyes shifted to his left where the bed had stood. Everything was charred and smoke wafted from the ashes. He stumbled over to it and froze as he realized the ashes were his beloved Matty.

She had been stripped naked and there were burnt rope strands around her ankles and wrists. They had tied her to the bed posts after he had passed out from the blows. Part of her belly and chest had been cut out, as if they were cleaving apart a buffalo looking for its liver.

Adkin Yates fell to his knees and started weeping.

"Oh God, Matty. I'm so sorry, but I will find those who did this to you – so help me, God Almighty."

...

Adkin Maxwell Yates had been born July 30, 1846, to Arthur Adam and Annag Elspeth (Craig) Yates in Olney, England.

His father had been born in the Midlands north of Olney, (pronounced Oh-knee) and learned the art of blacksmithing from his father before him.

Adkin's father, Arthur, at the age of 20 and just married, got an offer for the position of blacksmith at the Bull Inn in Olney, a carriage town on the trail to London. He immediately gathered up his new bride, "Anna," as he called her, and headed south to Olney, excited to be the head blacksmith of such a famous carriage inn. It sat at the last major stop on the road heading south into London from central England.

Once settled in, Arthur truly enjoyed taking care of all the horses and mules that were stabled at the Bull, hooking up coaches, shoeing horses and taking care of the guests and travellers that stopped for maintenance work on their rigs with the young blacksmith.

Anna was soon helping the kitchen and household staff caring for guests, even helping with feeding and watering the livestock.

Their small room was above the stables, which could house up to 20 head of horses and mules. It was one year almost to the date of their arrival in Olney that Anna gave birth to their first son, Adkin Maxwell Yates. It was Anna, born of Scottish heritage, that named the boy.

Adkin was a Scottish pet name for Adam amongst the Midlanders of England. Maxwell was the name of Arthur's father.

At a few months old, Adkin was Christened at St. Peter and St. Paul Angelican Church that sat on the River Great Ouse on the south end of the village. The church had been built of locally quarried stone and was completed in 1325. The Yates were almost as proud of their church as they were of their newborn son, Adkin.

An Englishman's Adventures on the Santa Fe Trail (1865-1889)

In January of 1848, the couple had another son, George William. Arthur was fond of royalty and their names, as were thousands of Brits.

Charles Alfred came along in May of 1850. Arthur and his eldest son, Adkin, had their hearts set on a girl and a sister, but Charlie was an immediate hit with the family.

By this time, Arthur was helping Sidney Overstreet, the owner of the Bull Inn, with nearly all the day-to-day business. Shortly after Charles' birth, Overstreet called Arthur into his office in his living quarters.

"Arthur, I'm getting old and my health is failing. You're a strong and Godly man – now with three sons – and a hard-working wife," Sidney said, while gazing down at his ledger on the desk. "As you know, I have no children – the good Lord just didn't see it our way."

He paused and looked up at the now-26-year-old blacksmith.

"How would you like to purchase the business?"

As Arthur's mouth gaped, and a startled look sent a shadow across his eyes, Sidney spoke again.

"I'll make you a fair deal, and you can pay it off over the next few years. The physician says I should move to the southeast of England and avoid the cold damp here in the south of Buckinghamshire."

It was a short conversation between Arthur and Anna that evening. They immediately agreed it was the opportunity they had often prayed about – not taking over the Bull Inn, necessarily – but having faith in God they would be able to improve their lot with hard work and faith in the Almighty.

Adkin never forgot that day when his father told him they were now the owners of the Bull Inn, and Adkin would have to start learning not only the blacksmith trade but how to handle all the other chores involved with running a carriage house.

The 6-year-old suddenly felt much older and bigger, even though he had been helping wherever his father had allowed him prior to the news.

Sixteen months later, the Yates finally welcomed a baby girl – Eliza Francis in September of 1852. Her name had been chosen when Anna discovered her condition prior to Adkin's birth years before. But George and Charlie had postponed the Christening.

•••

Business at the Bull was booming. Travellers and others came from all over central England – even a few from London – to see the new anvil Arthur had forged. Rather than the two round-horned anvils that were popular at the time, Arthur had put a short square horn opposite the long round-pointed horn.

It gave him more flexibility in creating flat springs and other straight-angled, machinery pieces.

With business doing well, Arthur was able to send a little more money to Overstreet in his quarterly payments. Arthur double checked his ledger shortly after Charlie's 4th birthday and proudly announced Overstreet would be paid off by Christmas 1854, nearly a year quicker than the four years they agreed upon.

Meanwhile, 8-year-old Adkin was learning things about the business that would forever influence his life. His father had even let him ride alongside in the coach seat on a few trips to London and back. With good weather they could make it to London in six hours. They would stay at Aurthur's livery at Paddington Station and return with passengers or freight the next day.

The Bull Inn had established a small stable at Paddington long before Aurthur and Anna arrived. Three to five horses would be traded out every other week or so. A man who worked with one of the other freighters took care of the animals for a small stipend.

Arthur would make at least two trips a week, and Adkin wanted to go on every trip, but he wasn't allowed. His father kept telling him one day he would be making runs by himself, but Adkin thought that day would never come.

"I'll be an old man before father lets me drive a team to London," Adkin complained to his mother.

"Be patient, Adkin. Remember, patience is a virtue, and the ability to wait for something without getting angry or upset is a valuable quality in a person."

It made sense, but Adkin was sure he could handle a team all by himself. He worked with the horses every day. He had an innate way of calming the beasts – a simple touch of his hand on their nose or neck would bring them to a calm stance – no head tossing or turning from the hackamore bridles.

He hardly ever had trouble pulling a horse leg up for hoof cleaning, trimming or shoeing. In fact, he shod his first horse, a reliable Morgan that was twice Adkin's age, when he was but 6. Of course, it helped that the boy was tall and wiry strong. His size belied his age – he looked closer to 10 or 11 then.

His father was a big man at about six feet tall and very muscled over large, big bones. His hands could engulf a normal man's hand, yet he could swing a hammer on hot-pink iron as deftly as a surgeon wields a knife.

Anna often stared at young Adkin and could see her husband in the boy's figure and manners. He would be taller than his father, she often teased Arthur.

Christmases came and passed, and then three days after New Year in 1858, tragedy marred the wonderful bliss the Yates family had been experiencing in life and business.

Arthur had traded out New Year with another of his coach drivers so Arthur could spend Christmas with his family. That meant he had to take the coach to London on New Year's eve – three passengers just had to get there that day.

That meant Arthur had to make the return trip on New Year's Day, but he had no passengers and all the freight agents were closed for the holiday. He was told he could get freight or possibly travellers the following day.

He stayed over another night and found some freight to take back to Bucks Lace Factory in Olney. Bucks being short for Buckinghamshire, the shire where Olney was located.

After arriving late Jan. 2, Arthur was tired the next morning and asked Adkin to take care of the animals and check the shoes on the team he had just taken to London.

Anna was preparing breakfast as Adkin got his work clothes on and headed out the side door of their quarters. The door opened next to the first set of stables in the yard that sat behind the double wooden gates that opened onto the dirt road in front of the Bull. There were four horse stalls in that first yard.

He swung the gate back half open and marched into the stable grounds. He didn't notice that his sister, Eliza, had followed him into the stable yard. As he opened the stall gates, he allowed the four horses out into the yard. As he turned toward the yard, he heard a scream, and then a horse started neighing and stomping the ground with heavy thuds.

Just as he ran to reach the horse, he noticed the small twisted body of Eliza, still wearing her sleeping gown and her tiny rain boots, lying lifeless on the cold hard ground.

Later, the constable and physician told the family she had at least two fatal blows to her head. They said she probably died with the first kick.

Eliza was only 5-years and four-months-old, and the family, as well as the villagers, were devastated. Arthur and Anna had grown into not only good citizens of Olney, but had been accepted and loved by the villagers as if they had been born there.

Adkin thought he might die from the pain in his body – he blamed himself for not closing the side gate when he entered the yard. His mother consoled him, but it was watching his father break down at the services in the small cemetery that surrounded the parish church that brought him out of his self pity.

He had never seen his father cry. He had not seen him do a lot of things he had witnessed in other men. Arthur would never swear, he never drank or used tobacco. Adkin often wondered if his father was really a human, or if he was an angel sent down by God just to look after this family.

Adkin walked to his father and they both hugged and cried together in each other's arms. No person went near them, as everyone slowly cleared the cemetery – Anna leading George and Charles by the hand back down the lane to the Bull – leaving the man and his 11-year-old son standing together in the gloom of a dreary winter day.

•••

For the next few weeks, things had changed around the Bull. Adkin sensed nothing would ever be the same again. Without Eliza's little squeals and giggles, the place seemed forlorn, even as the guests and customers continued to grow in numbers and were constantly in every other room or in the stable yards or in the dining room eating.

Adkin didn't suffer from his guilt pangs as much – he was most concerned with his father's trance-like existence. The man seemed to be moving about like a mechanical machine.

Adkin's mother had told him to be patient with his father. Adkin hadn't realized how much his father had wanted and prayed for a little girl to fill out their family.

One day, about mid-morning, some hunters stopped at the Bull for lunch and were quite excited about the two red foxes they had taken just west of Olney.

"That's it," Adkin thought. "I'll get father to take me hunting – we can get away for a few days – just us men."

Arthur had taught Adkin about guns and shooting as far back as Adkin could remember. Arthur had several black powder pistols, as well as several muskets. Arthur's pride and joy was a Sharp's rifle made in America that hung over the fireplace in his personal quarters.

Arthur had traded some gold coins and blacksmith work for the gun with one of the tradesman that lived near Paddington Station in London. It was a Model 1853 breech loader with a 32-inch barrel and fired a .52 caliber lead bullet "about as far as a man could see," his father bragged.

Adkin remembers almost falling down the first time his father let him fire the gun when he was only 8. Had it not been for his large size and his father's quick grasp, Adkin would have surely dusted his backside on that first shot.

Waiting until after the evening meal, which was usually taken with a few of the guests in the Bull's long dining room, Adkin waited for his father to sit back in his favorite rocker near the fireplace. His mother gently rocked in her chair to Arthur's left, deftly knitting a wall tapestry depicting the 185-feet spire of their parish church.

"Father," Adkin said. "Why don't' we check with Lord Colchester and see if we can hunt a few days on his manor?"

There, it was out.

Adkin waited to see if his father would take his gaze from the flickering flames of the fireplace.

Anna spoke up, "That sounds like fun. You two need to get away for a few days and get some rest. You've both been doing nothing but work.

"Danny Boy and his brother can look after things here at the Bull," she added."

Arthur slowly turned his head and looked at Adkin.

An Englishman's Adventures on the Santa Fe Trail (1865-1889)

"I overheard those hunters that came in to eat midmorning about hunting at Colchester Manor," Adkin spoke hurriedly now. "They used the hounds and got two red foxes, but they said they saw a lot of stags."

"We could use some venison, Arthur," Anna jumped in. "The last we had was from the Verger before Christmas."

Arthur blinked a few times, as if he was just awakening, "You know, that's not a bad idea, Adkin"

Adkin almost cried when his dad started smiling.

"That's a great idea, son."

His mother smiled as she gave Adkin a sly wink.

"I'll send a messenger to Colchester House this evening and see when we can go out to the manor," Arthur said.

Colchester House was centered in about 10,000 acres of land called Colchester Manor that was a gift from the King of England many centuries ago. The Colchester family had controlled that land and paid taxes and profits to the Crown from its farm animals, crops and other products, like its saddlery shop. Colchester saddles and tack were some of the finest in all of Buckinghamshire.

The manor house itself was surrounded by a tall rock wall and inside the wall lived the servants and employees in their separate small but tidy homes. Adkin had heard that 50 people lived inside the manor walls.

The outer reaches of the property were enclosed and separated by huge hedge rows that were centuries old. The hedges were also used to break up lots of land for different uses within the manor, such as crops or pasture land.

Lord Colchester had been one of Arthur's first acquaintances when he and Anna had moved to Olney. They hit it off immediately and became good friends. Colchester had even offered to loan Arthur the money when the owner of the Bull Inn had suggested selling it to Arthur.

Arthur had hunted as a guest at the manor even before Adkin was born, and Lord Colchester never allowed Arthur to ever pay for using a hunting cabin – there were four or five – or for the servants who helped them with cooking meals or cleaning wild game. Adkin had been taken hunting for years when he was smaller. But it had been nearly a year or more since he had been to the manor.

Late that night, the messenger had returned from his 10-mile round trip.

"Lord Colchester would be very pleased if you would come to hunt red stag two days hence," the messenger read from his piece of paper.

He handed it to Arthur and Arthur saw the small, red seal pressed into the wax – the seal of Colchester House Manor.

Even though the two were only gone three days, the trip had done wonders for Arthur. Adkin saw his father slowly come back to the smiling, friendly man he had known all his life. Who teased Adkin when the boy missed a shot at a large hedge hog only meters away.

But Adkin knew his father was back to himself when Adkin dropped a huge red stag at nearly 400 meters on their last morning at the manor. Arthur had pulled up the rear elevation sight on the Sharp's rifle and told Adkin to squeeze it off while slowly exhaling. Adkin did just as they had practiced the morning they first got to Colchester's.

"Boom."

The big stag jumped and ran about 10 paces and fell dead.

Adkin could see the pride in his father's eyes. That and his father's hug was worth 100 red stags to Adkin.

•••

A couple of years later, Adkin had the chance to meet a seafaring captain who came to Olney to learn about another captain who had been the Curate of St. Peter and St. Paul Angelican Church – Pastor John Newton.

Newton had been a slave trader and found God when his ship nearly sank and spent the rest of his life serving the Lord. He had been the Rector at the Yates' family church in the mid to late 1700s.

Captain Ned Dearing was writing a book about famous English captains and he was researching Newton in Olney. He stayed six weeks at the Bull Inn during the summer of 1860.

Adkin had never met a man who, as his father said, "Is truly a man of the world."

Dearing took to young Adkin quickly, as he saw the boy's eagerness to learn, especially about distant lands and peoples. Though Adkin had received most of his learning from the classes at church and from his parents, they seldom reached out across oceans and other continents.

Dearing did most of his studies at the Cowper Museum, studying the writings of William Cowper, a poet and hymnist who collaborated with Newton on, literally, hundreds of hymns and poems. Newton was considered the author of the hymn, Amazing Grace, and the two men published the start of the hymn in a book in 1779 titled "The Olney Hymns."

Dearing was also fortunate enough to find several people in the shire who had known Newton when he lived in Olney, and they were children.

When Dearing returned each day to the Bull, Adkin would always be waiting for him – if Adkin wasn't on a trip to London or working in the blacksmith shop.

"Tell me more about America," Adkin would plead.

Though the lad had heard about the native headhunters on the Island of Borneo, riding hump-backed camels along the Nile River in Egypt and the aborigines in Australia, it was America that fascinated Adkin. It was "The New World."

An Englishman's Adventures on the Santa Fe Trail (1865-1889)

Dearing told the boy he had sailed the Atlantic many times, but his most adventurous trip to the Americas had been when they sailed to the port of New Orleans.

They unloaded their cargoes and were looking for goods to return to England; such as furs, tobacco, sugar cane, cotton and other goods, when a merchant offered them a chance to take building materials, weapons and munitions to St. Louis on a steam boat – "up the mighty Mississippi River," as Dearing put it.

Adkin loved hearing about the alligators in the swamps of Louisiana, the timber as far as the eye could see, and especially the American Indians that attacked the boat coming and going.

"They would paddle their boats next to us and sling arrows from their bows and throw spears at us. They painted bright colors on their faces and gave out war chants – yells and screams, actually," Dearing said. "They didn't stay long after we sprayed them with some cannonades loaded with mace."

While the adventures were appealing, it was the unknown that stayed in Adkin's mind.

"I met men who had loaded up wagons in Independence, Missouri – not far from St. Louie – up the Missouri River – and headed off into the great plains of the west for hundreds of miles – and lived to return," Dearing said. "A great road called the Santa Fe Trail takes people into the west of the United States into Mexico where few white men have travelled.

"It's supposed to be the home of wild Indians, wild desperados who carry guns on their belts and huge herds of wild game that cover the landscape as far as one can see. Herds of elk and deer and buffalo – unlike African Buffalo, but big, hairy, burly animals that can kill a man in an instant."

It was that "great road" that took one into the hinterland of the great "unknown," that struck a nerve with Adkin.

The Santa Fe Trail.

When he said it aloud, it almost tickled when it rolled off his tongue.

"I'm going there someday – I'm going to go down that trail and see where it takes me," Adkin promised himself.

Shortly after Adkin celebrated his 14th birthday, Dearing was preparing to head off to London. He wanted to catch a ship to the Caribbean Islands to do some more of his writing.

"Sitting on a sandy, white beach with turquoise waters lapping at her shoreline is preferable over these miserable dank and dreary winters in England," Dearing explained, with a big laugh.

"Remember laddie, if you still have your heart set on travelling the Sante Fe Trail, go through New Orleans, and when you get there, seek out my friend," Dearing said to Adkin as he prepared to load into a carriage for

9

London. Here is his name and address. Remember his name reads strange, but it's pronounced Car-bo-no – he is of the French-Creole people."

The note read:

Captain Jean Carbeauneaux

110 Rue Toulouse

New Orleans

Dear Jean, Please take care of this lad should he present this letter to you. He is a countryman and a good lad from a good God fearing family.

Truly yours,

Capt. Ned Dearing

Adkin looked at the note and then smiled to Dearing. He wanted to hug the man, but Dearing simply reached out his hand and shook Adkin's hand – as grown men greet each other.

As an equal.

"Take care laddie, and with God's will, we shall cross paths again in His wonderous world."

As the carriage set out with Dearing waving out the window, Adkin handed the note to his mother, who was also seeing Dearing off, as well as several other people he had befriended during his stay.

"Mercy, I wish he wouldn't encourage those wild dreams of yours Adkin," Anna said. "You're much too young to be thinking of such foolishness."

"I know," Adkin said, as he took back the note and squeezed it into his vest pocket.

But he secretly knew he would go there – eventually – even if he had to wait a few years.

"The Meyers boy was allowed to go off to university in France just last week, and he was only 16," Adkin said to himself. "I can jolly well wait several more years."

When Adkin got up to his room, he straightened the note and slid it into his Bible. He seldom used his personal Bible except during his time when reading alone in his room. He used a pew Bible at the parish church on Sundays.

•••

For the next few years, Adkin tried to find as much as he could about America and the Santa Fe Trail. In London, he found a small book printed by a New York City, New York, publishing house that cited William Becknell of Missouri as the man who first established the trail to Santa Fe, Mexico, in 1821.

The book said, "The Santa Fe Trail (aka, Santa Fe Road) was an ancient passageway used regularly after 1821 by merchant-traders from Missouri who took manufactured goods to Santa Fe, New Mexico, to exchange for furs and other items available there.

Mexican traders also provided caravans going to western Missouri in this international trade."

He heard a tale from one of the tradesmen at Paddington Station who told Adkin he was crazy to think he could make it on the Santa Fe Trail. The man said his brother had died on the trail in 1855 while crossing the section in western Kansas called the Jornada Route – or Jornada de Muerte – journey of death.

It was a desert-like stretch of the route that didn't have a consistent supply of water for about 70 miles, the man explained.

"For all his adventure, he ended up dying of thirst in a desert – at the age of 25," the man said, as he scowled and walked away.

That had to be a very rare occurrence in Adkin's mind. He was sure all the great herds of wild animals couldn't be living in a desert. The dead man had surely been unprepared for such an undertaking.

In early 1861, most of the talk in London concerned the troubles brewing in America over slavery. Many were predicting big problems between the pro-slavery south and anti-slavery forces in the north.

Many wealthier Brits had servants from their numerous colonies around the world who lived and worked in England. Adkin had never considered them anything but working labor.

"Are some of Lord Colchester's servants slaves Mother?" Adkin asked one day.

"Not really, Adkin," she answered. "They live there on their own free will, but many can't save enough money to go out on their own. They are fairly dependent on the goodness of Lord Colchester.

"Besides, most are quite happy to have a roof over their head and food aplenty."

Then one day, Adkin ran across a seaman at the marketplace near Paddington Station who was selling trinkets and small books near the new train station they were building beside Paddington.

Adkin ask him if he had anything from America. The man said he had many things from America. He had lived there six years and had to return to family in England because he went broke and money lenders were looking for him still. He had a ring, a necklace, an U.S. Army canteen and some real Indian beads, so claimed the man.

"Anything else?" Adkin asked.

The man pulled out a small flyer from a book and handed it to Adkin. It was preaching the virtues of buying land around Ft. William – or Bent's Fort – in Colorado territory.

Adkins eyes flew open as he read: "Bent's Fort was established in 1834 as a fur trading post on the upper Arkansas River on the Santa Fe Trail."

Adkin couldn't believe it – across the bottom of the bulletin was a irregular line marking the trail and a few side trails from Independence, Missouri, to Santa Fe.

There it was. A Santa Fe Trail map with what looked like river crossings and small dots with mostly illegible names printed next to them. The flyer had been folded and rolled so many times, much of the map was somewhat invisible.

"How much," Adkin barked at the man.

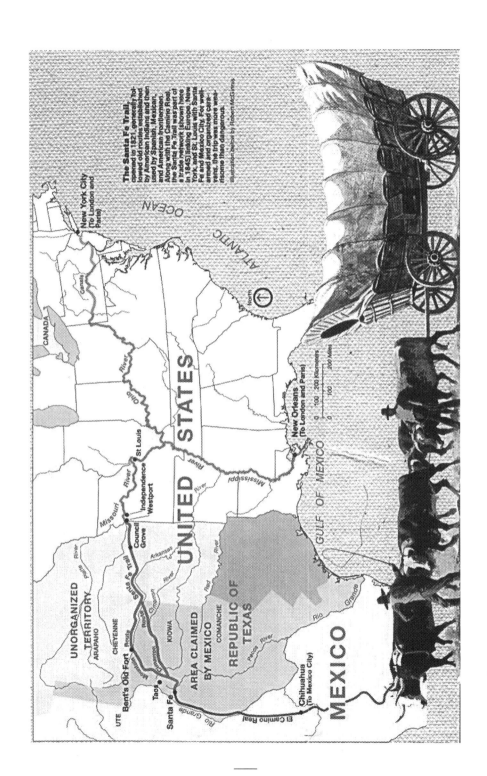

"Easy lad," the man said. "Howse 'bout one pound?"

"One pound?" Adkin yelled.

"OK, 10 shillings," the man said, eager to accept half his original price.

"Here's 2 pounds and God be with you," Adkin said, as he flipped the coins to the man and ran off.

...

"You best get aboard, lad," the burly first mate said to Adkin as he walked by, telling others the same thing.

"Goodbye Mother," Adkin said as she nearly took his breath away with her hug. As she backed away from him with her hands still resting upon his shoulders, Adkin could see her tears welling up.

"I know. I promised not to cry, but..." her voice withered as she turned away.

George William, 16, and Charles Alfred, 15, had accompanied Adkin and his parents on the carriage to Liverpool to say their goodbyes.

"Georgie, you and Charlie had better take care of Mother," Adkin scolded softly.

Both promised they would as they hugged their big brother and kissed his cheeks.

"God be with you Adkin," Char- lie said, as tears started leaking from the corners of his big blue eyes.

"Be very careful Adkin," Arthur said as he hugged his eldest son.

"I will father, I assure you."

Adkin saw a tear slide down his father's cheek, but the big man smiled as he pushed Adkin away.

"Now get going son. Get aboard lest they leave you behind, and make sure you keep God close in your heart."

As Adkin waved farewell to his family on the docks, his mind was already looking across the expanse of the Atlantic and what lay ahead of him in America. He would miss his home greatly, but the Santa Fe Trail was calling him.

As the ship's remaining sails were hoisted, they billowed with a soft wind, and the ship moaned as it started a turn to the southwest out of the bay at Liverpool. Adkin had been waiting forever – in his mind – for this adventure, but the war between the states had set him back only a few years.

As his blues eyes scanned the dark-blue swells on the horizon, his long blonde hair waved in the salty breeze as he leaned into the rushing wind with his muscled 6- feet-4 frame.

"I never imagined the air could smell so different but so pleasant," he thought to himself.

It was the first of July, 1865, and if all went well, he might celebrate his 19th birthday in New Orleans, or at worst, he was hoping by the time they reached the Spanish colony of Cuba.

Plans called for the ship to make a stop in Havana to deliver some goods and take on additional cargo for New Orleans, "If the winds be blessed to us," Captain Wares had told him on boarding.

...

Not much happened the first week or so aboard the Euterpe, a 35-foot, 3-masted sailing ship. Ad- kin loved it because it had an iron hull, something he was familiar with being a master blacksmith. He was comforted by its strength.

All was going well, even though several of the passengers had been stricken by sea sickness. Adkin had succumbed as well the second day, but seemed to be "getting his sea legs," according to Barnsworth, Captain Ware's first mate.

Barnsworth had indicated he was originally from Sunderland, a village in the far north of England. He had said being born in a fishing village on the 55th parallel made him the perfect seaman. Plus the fact he claimed he was sailing before he could walk.

Most of the people Adkin had met from northern England usual- ly had an Irish, Scottish or Welsh accent, but he couldn't quite hear any distinction from Barnsworth. Adkin did feel warmly for the man. Barnsworth seemed to be a genuine fellow, if he trusted you.

The Euterpe had been a cargo ship since it was built in 1863, but had been caught up in a sea battle along the African coast and hit with cannon from friendly fire. She made it back to England, but the owners had repaired her back as new and sold her.

Captain Terrence Wares had purchased her and refitted her for not only carrying cargo but the occasional passengers. The ship had several staterooms. Captain Wares' prospects were soaring since news of the Civil War ending in the Colonies, as he liked to call America.

"Why is you want to go to New Orleans?" Barnsworth asked. "That's a pretty rough place, even though the war is over."

"Well, I have a letter of introduction to a seafaring captain there, and I'm hoping he can help me get to St. Louie," Adkin replied as the two men stood looking to the west off the bow.

"You mean St. Louis?" Barnsworth asked with an uplifted eye brow. "That's quite a ways up the Mississipi. I've never been up that river, but I hear it's a dangerous trip."

"I've got to go that way in order to reach the start of the Santa Fe Trail," Adkin smiled. "I intend to travel west on that mythical road and see where it takes me."

Barnsworth shook his head as he turned away.

"Good luck, lad," he said, as he mumbled to himself, "He's going to need it."

Adkin's biggest worry was his belongings. He only carried two tote bags – one a long carpet bag which held the Sharp's rifle his father had given him and clothing. The other a large square-shaped leather bag, which had his Bible, additional clothing and a short Remington carriage gun. He had purchased the gun from a trader at Paddington Station just six months earlier. It was a double-barrel 12 gauge shot gun.

•••

Sailing time to Havana had been estimated to take three weeks, "In good weather," Captain Wares had said.

"Just my luck I'd be one of Captain Wares' few passengers to sur- vive 35-feet seas in the storm we hit two weeks out of England," Adkin said to himself as he watched the palm trees in the distance grow nearer.

One month to here was okay with him. He was alive and had never prayed so much since the death of his baby sister. Adkin had repeated Psalm 55:22 over and over for nearly 15 hours: "Cast the burden upon the Lord, and he shall sustain thee: He shall never suffer the righteous to be moved."

"I can now see how Captain John Newton – the slave trader – swore his allegiance to the Lord and became the Vicar of our parish church 100 years ago," Adkin said to Barnsworth the day following the storm.

Barnsworth had never heard of Newton, but he was impressed after Adkin filled him in.

"Aye, I can believe that myself," Barnsworth said, shaking his head with wide eyes.

Adkin wondered if maybe that was the first time Barnsworth had ever battled 35-foot swells for 15 hours, as well.

Adkin and the other passengers, all eight of them, were not allowed off the ship at Havana.

"We'll only be docked for about four hours unloading and loading cargo," Captain Wares said. "There's too many pirates around here, and you might just disappear on me."

There was a variety of races and costumes of people crowding the docks. He heard some rough looking men walk by speaking what sounded like German or Dutch to him, and then there were men, and some women, of all colors of brown – from a light ochre to dark chocolate.

He saw men in heavy clothing to some wearing nothing but small breechcloths and feathers. His sense of adventure was definitely reinvigorated after doubts had arisen during the storm.

"America, here I come," he smiled to himself.

•••

It would take at least another two weeks to reach New Orleans. The Euterpe stopped in St. Augustine, Florida, and Adkin got to disembark with the others to roam the small but bustling village. There was an old fort the Spaniards had built that he walked over to. He thought it was still imposing, being 200 years old.

Barnsworth later said it was now called Fort Marion, and that the Union Army had controlled it most of the time during the Civil War. He said the old timers still called it Castillo de la San Marcos.

But it was in the market place along the docks that amazed Adkin. The aromas of foods laying out on small tables or in grand cooking pots were overwhelming and produced an excitement that surprised him.

"I've got to try some of this," he said to himself.

He saw an attractive dark-skinned woman toiling away over a pot of hot oil pulling out pieces of golden fried something or other and laying them on papers. He noticed she had a large amount of knobby colorful shells all around her little station among the hordes of vendors.

"Do you speak English?" he asked her.

"Si," she said, adding "Yes, yes. I speaka da anglis."

"What is that?" Adkin asked pointing to the piles of freshly fried pieces.

"Eee's conch," she said, smiling.

"What?"

"Conch. Eee's the heart of a conch."

Adkin wasn't sure this was going anywhere. He had no idea of what "konk" was.

She grabbed two large sea shells and held them up.

"Conch."

Adkin shook his head a little. She turned, reached into a wet, brown woven sack and pulled out a live conch. She then slammed it onto her table and started using one of the other shells to pound on the one she had removed from the bag. She was using the pointed end to break open a spot on the other one that Adkin guessed was its backside.

Once cracked, she grabbed a small iron tool that looked like a huge plank nail with a sharp end and started prying and twisting the tool in circular motions. She then turned the shell back to its open side, reached in the thin slot and pulled out a piece of white meat.

Then she dropped it into her pot of hot oil. It startled Adkin when it immediately started hissing and sizzling from the heat of the oil.

"Conch," she said, handing him a piece that was already fried.

"You try."

Adkin figured it may be in the oyster family, and he had eaten oysters before in Paddington Station.

He loved conch immediately.

As he was eating it, he reached into his pocket and pulled out a few shillings and handed it to her. She smiled broadly and picked up a wide bladed leaf, waxy and bright green, and wrapped up three more pieces of conch and handed it to him.

"Thank you very much, it's very delicious," he said.

"Gracias senior, tank you."

Adkin made his way through the throngs of people. He had never dreamed so many different types of people and cultures could fit in such a narrow lane which stretched down the entire length of the docks behind the cargo road by the bay.

The goods were amazing, too.

Handmade knives, and tools caught his eye at an elderly blacksmith's place. It was good work, but Adkin knew he could do better, and he was only 18 years old. He was buoyed because the old man seemed to be selling quite a few pieces, and Adkin planned on making his living doing the same thing.

Clothing, carvings, candles, a myriad of sea shells, beads, jewelry – and all the foods – you name it, Adkin saw it.

After about three hours, he headed back to the Euterpe.

As he approached the gangplank at the dock, he noticed a tall, scroungy-looking man scurrying down the plank half- dragging a large square-shaped leather bag. The man was swivelling his head rapidly side to side and fore and aft.

Adkin jolted to a halt.

"Hey, that's my bag," he shouted at the man. "Stop right there."

Barnsworth was at the rail on the ship when he heard Adkin.

"Hey, you there, stop," Barnsworth stammered, realizing what was going on. Barnsworth headed down the gangplank

The man started trying to run with the bag, but its hefty weight was not allowing him a lengthy gait.

In about 30 feet, Adkin overcame the man and slammed him to the ground when he jumped on his back.

The man stumbled to his feet and squared around to face Adkin who was trying to find his legs and also stand.

The man reached into his waistband and pulled out a knife with a 10-inch blade. He cussed Adkin and lunged at the young man.

Adkin just managed to move his torso in time to avoid a direct hit with the blade. It caught his shirt above his waist and it broke the man's momentum as the vagabond tried to loosen it from Adkin's shirt.

As he moved back to his left, Adkin swung his right arm and caught the man in his left temple area with his fist. There was a loud thud, and the man dropped to the ground as if he had been shot through the heart. He lay there on his side, completely knocked out.

Barnsworth grabbed Adkin's shoulder, and Adkin reflexively drew his right fist back again.

"It's me," Barnsworth said. "Don't hit me."

Adkin relaxed and looked down at the thief. The man still wasn't moving, and blood was oozing out his nose, his mouth and his ear.

"Good God man, I'll bet he never tries to rob from a ship again," Barnsworth said. "I'll wager he were loading the hides when he decided to visit some staterooms and found your bag."

Barnsworth kneeled down as the man lay quietly on his side.

"He's a scallywag for sure – stinks to high heaven," Barnsworth said. "I believe he's going to have a bad headache when he awakes."

Two men dressed like soldiers with long guns heft over their shoulders approached, and the tall one barked, "What's going on here?"

"This cur tried to steal this lad's bag from the Euterpe here," Barnsworth answered, pointing back toward the ship. "Young Yates here clobbered him with one to the ear, and you should've heard the thump."

The men informed Adkin and Barnsworth they were U. S. Army, and they patrolled the streets. And, they growled, "We don't put up with trouble along the docks."

Barnsworth was grinning ear-to-ear.

The soldiers were not smiling.

The tall man leaned over and put his hand on the downed man's chest, while the short one started berating Adkin for fighting.

"But your honor," Barnsworth interrupted. "The man's a thief. That's young Yates bag right there, and that's the knife he pulled on Yates."

The other soldier said, "I don't think this man is breathing."

The short one squatted down and felt for a pulse in the man's neck area. He then bent over, putting his ear to the man's bloodied mouth.

He then looked at the other, and they both looked up to Adkin.

"This man is dead," the short one said.

"Dead?" Adkin whispered.

"Yes, dead."

"You don't know what you're talking about," Barnsworth squealed. "You're no doctor."

Both soldiers stood and pointed their rifles at them.

"You're both under arrest."

•••

Ironically, the old fort he had admired earlier in the day, the Castillo de la San Marcos, was now his bane. He and Barnsworth were placed with about 40 others in a small iron-walled room that could hardly hold 20.

Adkin was scared and angry, but the words of his mother kept repeating themselves in his mind: "Be patient, Adkin. Remember, patience is a virtue, and the ability to wait for something without getting angry or upset is a valuable quality in a person."

His emotions swirled as Barnsworth was bragging about Adkin's strength to any who would listen.

"The lad's a simple blacksmith," Barnsworth said loudly. "I 'spect he could lift the horse if needed be."

One man in the cell said, "He's not stronger than the hangman's noose." Several others laughed.

Adkin remembered his conch, and reached into his pocket and pulled out the leafy package and shared with Barnsworth.

News of the arrests reached Captain Wares as soon as the soldiers marched Barnsworth and Adkin off to the fort. It wasn't long he and several witnesses he had found who had seen the incident walked to the front gate asking for the commander.

U.S. Army Colonel Henry D. Wallen was the post commander. He was 46 and had seen a lot of action in the Civil War – fighting on the Union's side. He had only been appointed commander in May.

And even in two months, he had seen a lot of misfits and troublemakers living in St. Augustine. Seems the town attracted the best and the worst.

Once Captain Wares and the others had their turns and the soldiers made their report, Wallen found in Adkin's favor and both men were turned over to Wares with instructions Adkin and Barnsworth were never to disembark in St. Augustine again while he was commander.

As they made their way across the catwalk above the old moat of the Castillo, four men with revolver-style pistols in their breech belts stopped them. They looked like pirates and brigands who had been at sea for months.

A large red-bearded man stepped directly in front of Wares. The man had his hand on one of his pistols.

"We want that man," he said, pointing to Adkin.

"He killed my brother, and I don't care what Colonel Wallen says, he's a murderer."

"He killed a thief – accidently, but the man had it coming trying to steal all the belongings the lad owns and then trying to knife him," Wares growled. "You should have taught you brother proper behavior."

Wares held his ground, eye-to-eye with the heavier man, as if daring the man to try something. Wares wasn't one to be pushed around either. He stood 6-feet tall and weighed around 260 pounds himself. He had won his way to being a captain the hard way.

"I didn't mean to kill that man," Adkin spoke up. "I only swung at him after he tried to use a knife on me."

"Stand back Yates," Wares commanded. "We're headed to sea."

Wares took one step to the side of the red-bearded man and began walking toward the docks. The four men stepped back and allowed Wares and the seven others pass by.

"Don't worry lad, you haven't seen the last of me. I'll catch up with you sometime when your mother isn't protecting you."

They kept on walking.

Once aboard the Euterpe, the crewmen said the dead man was rumored to be the younger brother of the captain of the Erie, an infamous pirate ship once owned by Nathaniel Gordon.

Gordon was the first and only American slave trader to be tried, convicted, and executed "for being engaged in the Slave Trade" in accordance with America's Piracy Law of 1820. He was hanged in 1862.

His son, Samuel "Gutsy" Gordon was now the Erie's captain, and rumors were there were rewards for his capture from several European fleet owners and was wanted by the Italian government for piracy.

The crew said "Gutsy" Gordon was a large, barrel-chested man with a flowing red beard and always carried two pistols in his belt.

"I'm off to a pretty bad start here in the Americas," Adkin thought to himself.

•••

When the Euterpe sailed into New Orleans, they had been aboard the ship for nearly two months altogether. Getting to New Orleans proved somewhat risky, as well.

They had to sail through what seemed like hundreds of little islands through East Bay – the giant delta area of the great Mississippi River – and the shallows abounded everywhere. The silt carried out the Mississippi River kept even the best navigators alert.

Several crewmen acted as soundmen, dropping weights with markers on their ropes to check for water depths. They worked both sides on the prow of the ship all day shouting out the water's depths. The helmsmen had to rotate out about every hour with so much maneuvering.

Not much room to turn about a sailing vessel – iron hull or not.

Captain Wares had dropped anchor in the early afternoon as to not get "trapped in the maze," as Barnsworth had called it, after dark.

The next day they were sailing the Mississippi, and it was a busy waterway with crafts of all types – from canoes to steam ships – travelling to and fro.

As crewmen were tying up at the docks of New Orleans, Adkin felt his emotions rising within him – like a volcano, and he wasn't sure if he was going to cry or scream with joy.

He was now 19, and he let out a sigh that was overwhelming – and loud enough to attract the attention of Barnsworth.

"Well lad, You're finally here," Barnsworth said. "Was it worth it?"

"Yes indeed, Mr. Barnsworth. "Yes indeed."

Without notice, Adkin turned and grabbed Barnsworth's shoulders and then hugged him so hard, Barnsworth let out a grunt.

"You're breaking my ribs lad."

"I'm sorry," Adkin said, releasing Barnsworth. "It's just you've been a good friend to me and watched my back and gave me solid advice throughout our trip."

"Well lad, we've shared some rough times together," Barnsworth said. "I have to tell you, I've never rode out a storm like the one we survived – and I've sailed the seas for 20 years. I knew it was only a matter of time, but it's nervewracking all the same.

"Then you go and kill a man with a single fist to the head ... I'm teasing you lad. Did think – for just a moment – we might be in the brig for quite awhile," Barnsworth said, laughing.

"It's why I'm a sailor, lad," he continued, more solemnly. "Journeys can be short, or long, or easy or dangerous, but I see my crew – and the occasional passengers – grow and learn about themselves like they can never learn on land. Like I've seen you mature more in two months than you probably would in two years.

"What's more gratifying is I get to grow and learn more about myself from all of you on each and every trip. I'm truly blessed," Barnsworth added.

They shook hands and said nothing more.

Adkin hefted his bags and walked down the gangplank. He needed to try and find one Captain Jean Carbeauneaux, who at one time lived at 110 Rue Toulouse in New Orleans.

•••

The Euterpe had docked just east of a large market near the numerous piers and bulkheads along the river. After his goodbyes to his small band of friends – especially Barnsworth – he eagerly headed up the docks to the market. As he approached, he asked a man sorting fresh fish into baskets where he could find 110 Rue Toulouse.

The man pointed west and said, "Just follow the cargo road, it's called Decatur. Once you pass Jackson Square on your right, it will be the next street on your left, turn back down toward the river, it's in those plank houses somewhere."

"Thanks."

Adkin was in awe of the hustle and bustle along the docks. There was every type of water vessel – small canoes or row boats squeezed in among schooners, caravels and clippers. There was even a five-masted steamer taking up what looked like 200 feet of the river front.

Adkin was elated. He felt like he was now truly in America. His brief feelings of excitement of arriving on the continent in Florida had fizzled the very first day he had set foot in the country.

He was taking in every sight and scene possible as he walked west on Decatur. When he got to what he presumed was Jackson Square, he could see a large pewter-colored statue of a man straddling a rearing horse and waving his hat in the air in the center of a large garden area. Behind the horseman was a majestic cathedral-looking building with a towering steeple.

It immediately reminded him of the steeple on his parish church back home – half a world away.

A few yards further down the road, Adkin saw the corner street sign that read "rue Toulouse." He gazed down toward the river, and there seemed to be all types of plank buildings. Some looked to be 20- or 30-feet tall, like rooms and rooms built atop each other as to house or warehouse as many people as possible in such little space available. It reminded him of the old stone multi-level buildings along the docks in Liverpool, but these were wooden.

It was not impressive, and the people walking or working about – or sitting on stairs in front of the shacks – seemed unwashed and impoverished.

"This is probably where a lot of the dock workers and their families live," Adkin thought to himself.

He stopped a youngster running by with friends.

"Where's 110 Toulous?"

He quickly pointed behind Adkin and ran off.

Adkin turned to look at a set of plank stairs – No. 110 was painted in small letters above the doorway. He went up five steps to an open door, noticing a hallway with rooms on each side. Some doors were closed, others open. Several children scuttled through the hall and voices could be heard talking, laughing and even yelling throughout the building.

A large burly woman stepped out into her doorway.

"Whoos ya lukin fer lad?" she asked.

Startled, Adkin slowly said, "Captain Jean Carbeauneaux. Car-Bo-No."

"Aye, I knows him. He lives at the end of the hall, but ya won't be findin' him there," she said, matter-of-factly. "He'll be at the Napoleon House. It's a bar on Chartres Street."

"Shar – what," Adkin repeated.

"Char-tray," she said. "Go left two blocks on Decatur and turn right. Ya can't miss it."

"Thank you madam."

"Humph," she grunted.

As Adkin made his way up from the river front, the air seemed to be cooling a little as the sun settled toward the western horizon. He was still trying to get comfortable with the heat and humidity of the western hemisphere since arriving in Cuba last month.

"Was it only a month ago?" Adkin asked himself, then smiling at his mind's question.

As he made his way to the Napoleon House, Adkin panicked for a brief moment.

"Where is my letter of introduction from Captain Dearing?" he asked himself.

He let out a sigh remembering it's still stuffed into the pages of his Bible.

"Oh Lord, let me find Captain Carbeauneaux, as I'm not sure what I will do if he's unable to help."

A few yards up Shar-tray, Adkin saw the street sign spelling of Chartres Street. Adkin then saw a large painted sign with "Napoleon House" that had "Welcome" painted under it on a high rock wall next to a fancy wrought iron gate. He sat down one bag and lifted the gate handle and swung it open. Stepping inside, he saw a beautiful garden area around the house with tables full of people eating and drinking on the grass in the open.

He reached back and swung the gate shut with a clanking sound as it latched. A couple of patrons looked his way at the noise.

He walked up the steps of the main house and then entered. There was a long mahogany bar on his left that ran the length of the huge room. Men and a few women huddled along the front of the bar, busy with conversation and jollity.

Adkin stopped at the front end of the bar near the door and put his bags at his feet. Since leaving Saint Augustine, Adkin had rarely been out of sight of his worldly belongings for more than a few minutes.

"Would you like something to drink or eat?" a slim mustachioed barkeep asked him.

"Yes. A cup of tea if you please," Adkin answered.

"We have tea from the far east, South America, the West Indies ..."

"How about an English tea?" Adkin interrupted.

"Fine, English tea it is."

As he looked around the room, Adkin was trying to determine who looked like a seafaring man, a Captain, but it was impossible to tell. Some seemed to be dressed as successful bankers, others could be Captains, crewmen or even pirates, as far as Adkin could ascertain.

An Englishman's Adventures on the Santa Fe Trail (1865-1889)

"Here's your tea, let me know iffin' you want somethin' to eat," the bartender said. "That'll be 10 cents."

Adkin dug into his pocket and pulled out a few English coins and opened his hand to the man. The bartender grabbed a two pence.

"Pardon, but do you know a Captain Jean Carbeauneaux?" Adkin asked him.

"Aye, dat's him over dare on the back side of the poker table."

"Thanks."

The man at the table looked to be middle-aged, but healthy and stout. His face was clean-shaven, but he wore his thick, white sideburns down to his jawline. He wore a large black tricon hat with a 2-feet long ostrich feather dangling off the back of it. His black waistcoat had a high collar and brass buttons down it's front.

"He looks like a pirate," Adkin thought. "A well-dressed pirate."

Lifting both bags with one hand, Adkin picked up his cup of tea and worked his way through the crowd to the poker table.

"Excuse me sir, would you be Captain Jean Carbeauneaux," Adkin asked the man at the back of the table.

"That would be me sir," Carbeauneaux said, raising one bushy white eyebrow to gaze upon the tall, muscled young man with long golden hair folded behind his ears.

"I'm very pleased to make your acquaintance sir. My name is Adkin Yates. I'm from Olney, England."

"Never heard of it," Carbeauneaux said, shaking his head.

"I suppose not, but I met a friend of yours when he came to Olney and stayed about six weeks at my family's carriage house. His name is Captain Ned Dearing, and I have a letter of introduction written to you from him."

"Dearing you say?"

"Yes sir."

"My God son, why didn't you tell me that sooner," Carbeauneaux said as he kicked his chair back and stood.

"Take care of my chips," he said to the house dealer.

He came about and grabbed Adkin by both shoulders, nearly knocking the tea cup from Adkin's hand. He looked up to Adkin's face.

"How is Ned doing mon chéri? The old pirate – is he still wondering the world? Is your village on the coast?

"No sir, we're north of London near the Midlands."

"Come, come. Let's get us a table so we can visit," Carbeauneaux said, dragging Adkin hastily through the room to an empty table.

After they sat down, Adkin reached into the bag, pulled out his Bible, and leafed through it until he came upon the letter. He handed it to Carbeauneaux.

The captain opened it and slowly read it aloud, embarrassing Adkin a little.

Captain Jean Carbeauneaux

110 Rue Toulouse
New Orleans
Dear Jean, Please take care of this lad should he present this letter to you. He is a countryman and a good lad from a good God fearing family.
Truly yours,
Captain Ned Dearing

"Well I'll be. It's written in his hand for sure. I've known him 20 years, but haven't seen or heard from him in over two years," Carbeauneaux said, longingly.

The two men had crewed together on several ships throughout the West Indies and back to Europe in their early years.

Adkin filled Carbeauneaux in on what Dearing had been doing in England – and answered Carbeauneaux's question: "What was he doing landlocked for six weeks?"

"He has always kept writing logs of almost everything he's done," Carbeauneaux said. "He must have figured out a way to make a little money from such foolishness."

"He didn't stay as long as I would have liked." Adkin said. "And he left to get back to the sea. Said he was going to the Caribbean – the West Indies – and sit in the sun."

Carbeauneaux laughed and finally got around to asking Adkin what could he do for him.

"Well sir, I'm wanting to travel the Santa Fe Trail, and Captain Dearing said you may be able to help me find my way to St. Louis."

"It will be my pleasure, mon chéri. If Ned thinks so much of you, you're as good as family."

Carbeauneaux and Adkin sat at the Napoleon House until nearly 1 in the morning. They talked about Dearing's interest in Vicar John Newton. How Dearing had been to St. Louie, as Dearing liked to call it, and about Adkin's desire to travel the Santa Fe Trail.

Carbeauneaux explained that had he a ship, he would gladly ply the waters of the Mississippi, as he had numerous times over the last decade.

"I'm presently without a ship," Carbeauneaux said. "Let's just say I lost her in an argument that nearly turned deadly when a gentleman pulled a pistol on me and put it against my forehead.

"The gentleman just happened to be the manager for the fleet owner and had decided I was too contrary to his plans. He wanted to run contraband between here and the West Indies," he added with a bellowing laugh. "I refused and immediately accepted his request for me to resign."

They ate their evening meal there; roasted slabs of what Carbeauneaux called red drum, with fresh poached scallops along side – all sitting on a bed of colorful rice and covered with a savory gravy called remoulade sauce. They sopped the sauce off their plates with buttered crunchy cornbread.

Adkin had never tasted anything so wonderful in his life. He was thinking maybe this was all a dream.

Carbeauneaux drank numerous rum concoctions, and didn't seem to mind when Adkin refused alcohol, even wine. Carbeauneaux finally explained that mon chéri was a term of endearment; as my darling, or my son. The captain also couldn't believe Adkin had just turned 19 the following month.

"I have to say, you look a little older," Carbeauneaux said, smiling.

He sympathized with the young man's trouble in Saint Augustine, saying he had killed two men himself – also accidently – while trying to repair wind-damaged rigging on a ship.

"You never get over it, mon chéri, but you can't carry a dagger around in your heart for the rest of your life, either," Carbeauneaux explained.

Finding a steamer to St. Louis would be no problem, according to Carbeauneaux, but passage costs were a concern.

Adkin explained he had a promissory note from the Bank of London, and had planned on using it once he got to St. Louis. He didn't tell Carbeauneaux how much it was worth, and Carbeauneaux didn't ask.

"Mon chéri, I'm very close with the Bank of New Orleans president. We play cards together," Carbeauneaux said. "We'll stop by there tomorrow, if you like, and he'll cash it all out for you or see you get enough to get you to St. Louis.

"Whatever you wish," he said, with a wink.

"He's a good man and," as Carbeauneaux cupped his hand near his mouth and whispered closely to Adkin's ear, "His bank is where I keep my little nest egg."

The two finally made their way back to Carbeauneaux's room at the boarding house. He explained there was an extra straw mattress in the room for sailor friends who only stay in town a night or two.

His room was barren, with plank floors, plank walls and a planked ceiling – with two small oil lamps.

It contained a round table with five rickety chairs – probably used for playing cards, Adkin thought; a long, waist-high shelf that had a few beer bottles on it and several ash pails with cigar butts; a spittoon; a small dais with a water bowl atop and a mirror on the wall above it where a razor strop hung; the straw mattress in the corner, a small chest of drawers; and Carbeauneaux's small cot with a large, woolen U.S. Army blanket on it.

Adkin placed his bags near the wall next to the straw mattress and started fishing around for his nightshirt. Carbeauneaux had already collapsed in his bed sans hat but fully clothed.

"You get some sleep, and we'll make haste tomorrow," Carbeauneaux muttered, as he kicked off his shoes. "See you in the morning and put out the lamps will you."

Adkin lowered the lamp wicks and then laid back on the straw sack. He could see a half moon through a thinly-curtained window above his head. A soft cool breeze lightly ruffled the curtains. Carbeauneaux was already snoring in his bed.

"Thank you God for steering me to Captain Carbeauneaux," Adkin whispered softly. "His kindness washes away the pain of my struggles encountered on the first leg of my journey.

"I promise, Lord, I will keep you close in my heart," he added, remembering his father's loving admonition.

•••

Carbeauneaux was like a youngster the next morning. Though a little pudgy with short legs – Adkin guessed the man was only about 5 feet, 8 inches – and was probably 50 to 60 years old. But on this morning, Carbeauneaux had a spring in his step.

He took Adkin to a small stall with several little tables and chairs under a tarpaulin at the corner of Jackson Square where they had strong coffee (Carbeauneaux insisted Adkin pass on tea this one time) and ate small French pastries called beignets. (ben-yays)

From their spot at the square, Adkin saw the Euterpe was still docked east of the market. He asked Carbeauneaux if the Captain would like to meet Captain Wares and Adkin's friend, first mate Barnsworth, later in the day, and Carbeauneaux was agreeable.

"Aye, aye, of course" he said.

They headed away from the river front, and the Captain was well known. He was constantly introducing Adkin to all his acquaintances, and Adkin felt very humbled. Everyone had big smiles and hugs for "Capitanne," as most called him – in the French way.

Carbeauneaux told Adkin about another Captain, Alaine Broussard, a fellow French-Acadian like Carbeauneaux, who was a Fleet Captain of a 270-foot steamer called the Mississippi Delta Queen. It was a triple decker and used a steam engine driving a paddle wheel for power.

He told Adkin that Broussard had once been Captain of the Natchez VI, also a steamer. After Union invaders captured Memphis, Tenn., the boat was moved to the Yazoo River.

In 1863, the Natchez VI was burned – either by accident or to keep it out of Union hands.

Broussard knew the truth, Carbeauneaux said with raised eyebrows, but had never whispered a word about it.

Carbeauneaux discovered Broussard and the Queen would be returning to New Orleans in the next five to eight days, according to the manager of the local Cunard Steamship office.

Passage, Carbeauneaux told Adkin, would be $30 to St. Louis.

"But they feed you twice a day," he smiled.

Adkin asked if they could talk with the banker. They marched about eight blocks, with Carbeauneaux introducing Adkin to all he knew along the way.

Once inside the bank, Adkin reached into his waistband and pulled out a small slip of paper, He gently unfolded it several times and handed it to Carbeauneaux's friend. He explained it was money he had been saving since he was 13 years old and a stipend from his father.

"That's a lot of money," the man said. "Would you like it all in cash, or would you like a little cash and another promissory note for the balance?"

Carbeauneaux looked at Adkin mysteriously. He hadn't wanted to know how much the young man had – he was afraid someone might overhear their conversation. It could result in Adkin becoming a marked man.

"How much would it total in American currency if I cashed it all?" Adkin asked.

"Well let's see. It's 100 British pounds," the banker said, while scribbling in a notebook. "That would come out to $220 U.S. dollars and change."

"That is a troubling amount, mon chéri," Carbeauneaux spoke up immediately. "There's scofflaws around here that'd cut a man's head off for $10. I know you're a big, strong young man, but I'd suggest taking a small amount and keeping the rest on a note that can be easily hid from those who would create mischief."

"I agree, thank you Capitanne," Adkin said, smiling.

They walked out of the bank with Adkin pocketing $40 U.S. cash to go along with the two or three pounds in coins he still had on his person from England. He had discovered early people will accept pounds, pence and shillings anywhere in the world, it seemed. He had been buying his and his benefactor's meals with it.

Now he could hide the balance note – now drawn on the St. Louis National Bank – in the hidden pouch inside the waistband of his trousers his mother had sewn in for just such purposes.

•••

"First thing we need to do is get you a proper hat, mon chéri – to keep all that ... that," pointing to Adkin's mane, "out of your eyes. You could get killed if that flew into your eyes at the wrong moment," he explained with a chuckle.

They stopped at what Carbeauneaux called a mercer's shop. It was full of men's clothing. One wall was full of hats, all kinds of hats. Carbeauneaux, of course, said he should purchase a tricon or a captain's hat.

"But don't get a grey one, people up north will think you're a Reb, and they just lost the war," Carbeauneaux said with a smile.

The wall was full of captains' hats, straw hats, floppy cotton hats, wool derbies and even coon skin hats and beaver skin top hats. There was also an odd assortment of various Union and Confederate military hats. Adkin wondered had some of these hats been taken from dead men.

"Do men in the West wear these?" Adkin asked, holding up a raccoon skin hat with a long striped coon tail attached.

"Yes, but I'd advise against it. They attract lice and other vermin," Carbeauneaux said, with a sour look on his face.

Adkin picked up several straw hats that had broad brims all the way around. He liked them – some of the farm hands around Olney, especially at Colchester Manor, wore similar hats in the summer. They protect well from rain and sun with the large brims.

After trying on several different kinds, he decided on one that had a high rounded crown and had a brim about 5 inches around. It's crown wasn't too high, and it felt comfortable.

They took it to the store clerk and Adkin asked how much.

"That will be a dollar America," the man said, recognizing Adkin was English with that accent.

"Whew," Adkin sighed.

"How about 50 cents?" Carbeauneaux interjected.

"Try it on," said the clerk while turning a small mirror sitting on the counter around so Adkin could look at himself.

Adkin bent over and looked into the mirror. He moved his head side to side, then turned around to Carbeauneaux and asked. "How's it look?" with a big smile.

"It looks like you like it, and that's good enough for me," Carbeauneaux answered.

"Seventy-five cents," the clerk countered.

"Sold," Adkin responded.

Carbeauneaux didn't tell Adkin he looked like a sodbuster from Pennsylvania, but it did keep his hair out of his face.

They eased back to the river front and went down to where the Euterpe had been docked, but she was gone.

A stevedore nearby said Captain Wares decided to leave a day early and left before dark so he could be at the delta by daylight on the high tide.

"A sound and learned captain," Carbeauneaux said.

An Englishman's Adventures on the Santa Fe Trail (1865-1889)

Walking along Decatur, Adkin was feeling a little sad not getting to see Barnsworth again, and he was starting to reevaluate his Santa Fe Trail plans. New Orleans was such a colorful place – full of excitement and adventure.

"It is definitely alluring," Adkin said to himself.

•••

The two spent the next five days seeing the sights of New Orleans. They went to music halls, dance halls, several theatres, gambling halls and eateries. Some places offered them all under one roof.

Back at the "Napoleon House" on the second night, two young women came over to their table. Both wrapped themselves around Adkin, one on each side with arms across his shoulders.

"My what a handsome rascal, Capitanne. Wherever have you been keeping this lad hidden?" said one with long black hair, her full bosoms nearly exposed.

"Now Carla, don't go frightening my newfound friend. His name is Adkin Yates, from England," Carbeauneaux said, with a laugh.

Adkin was fairly startled, trying to appear soberly but very uncomfortable at the moment.

"Eee's adorable," the one with curly brown hair said, brushing Adkin's cheek with her fingers.

"This is Dawn, Adkin. She's not as silly as she's acting at the moment," Carbeauneaux said. "She's Irish."

"Nice to meet you ladies," Adkin took a deep breath. "But I really do have some important business to discuss with Capitanne. Perhaps we can visit later, though."

"Sure Adkin, sure," Dawn said.

"Just whistle," Carla added.

"A very kind way to rid yourself of those two," Carbeauneaux said, after they walked away. "They're really not that bad, just working girls trying to make a living like everybody else."

"I understand, and I think no less of them in any way," Adkin said. "It's just a vow I have made with my Lord to wait until I wed before I bed a woman."

"Hope you don't think me too strange," he added.

Adkin felt as if Carbeauneaux were staring a hole through him.

"Why no," he finally replied. "It takes a lot of willpower to hold to those beliefs, especially when a young man has your appeal with the ladies.

"No, no. Bless you mon chéri, you'll do well in this crazy world."

Adkin had discovered he was becoming addicted to the creole food Carbeauneaux introduced to him. He was surprised he actually liked the creole spices. He wasn't particularly partial to the spices in the east Indian food he had tried at Paddington Station in London.

But the creole food was something out of this world to Adkin, and he was developing a real taste for shell fish of all types. Especially since his encounter with conch in Florida.

Carbeauneaux teased him that he wouldn't find those kinds of meals in the desert on the Santa Fe Trail.

"No, mon chéri. You will only be able to eat desert rats and snakes and cactus stew," he would laugh.

On the morning of day five, the Delta Queen arrived at dock that afternoon.

"She's here mon chéri," Carbeauneaux said excitedly, as he approached Adkin sitting on a bench at Jackson Square. Adkin had been sitting there admiring the statue after learning the lore of Andrew Jackson.

"I just talked with Brussard, and he said by the time they are unloaded, re-supplied, loaded and ready to head out, they will be sailing day after tomorrow," Carbeauneaux said, smiling broadly.

Adkin threw his head back and stared into the soft blue sky and sighed. His dreams of the Santa Fe Trail blossomed brightly in his mind's eye.

"I'm ready for my next adventure Lord, Thank you for your blessings."

•••

Carbeauneaux walked with Adkin along Decatur after the two retrieved Adkin's belongings from Carbeauneaux's room.

Adkin handed his new dear friend an envelope with the name of Aurthur Yates written on it and an address in Olney, England.

"Would you post this for me Capitanne," Adkin asked.

"Of course I will, mon chéri."

Adkin wanted to let his family know what had transpired thus far, but he found it impossible to relate the incident in Florida. He felt ashamed, and he didn't want his family to feel the same way. It would also worry them, reinforcing his mother's thinking that America was full of savages.

While walking down Decatur, Carbeauneaux was chattering away with all kinds of safety tips:

"Don't trust any of the gamblers aboard the Queen. They travel back and forth every trip and scalp naive card players."

"I don't gamble."

"Well just in case you change your mind."

Then on Adkin's heading into Indian Territory:

"The red devils will sneak aboard at night to rob staterooms, or even worse, kill you."

Reminding Adkin can get additional cash on his promissory note at the federal bank:

"Remember, it's the St. Louis National Bank. It's the only reputable one up there."

A warning to keep an eye on those boarding at the stops along the river.

"Lots of bandits board at small villages and try robberies where they can then jump ship at places they have tied up horses just downstream."

He finally admitted, "Brussard runs a tight ship, and he does have several gunmen onboard to keep the peace. But damn it, just be careful, Adkin," Carbeauneaux pleaded.

They approached the gangplank, and Captain Broussard was there greeting passengers with two other men who wore leather gun belts with large revolvers. Adkin had seen several men armed the same way while in New Orleans. They looked like a Remington model Adkin had already seen at Paddington Station in London.

Carbeauneaux carried a small pistol in his pocket and suggested Adkin do the same.

"You can't pull out that Sharps or a shotgun with any haste," Carbeauneaux had said.

Carbeauneaux hailed Broussard and both men shook hands earnestly while laughing together.

"Would you like to haul some slaves from Arruba, Capitanne?" Broussard bellowed, teasing Carbeauneaux about his current unemployment.

"You're a worthless rascal, Alaine," Carbeauneaux laughed.

"So that is why Carbeauneaux had been threatened by the fleet manager," Adkin thought to himself. Carbeauneaux had only said he refused to haul "contraband." Adkin hadn't pried any further.

"I want you to look after mon chéri here for me," Carbeauneaux said, while patting Adkin on the shoulder. "This is the young man I told you about. He's from England, and he's mon ami. His name is Adkin Yates"

"Say no more," Brussard said reaching out to shake Adkin's hand.

"You might find him useful, too. He's a master blacksmith – a third generation he tells me," Carbeauneaux said.

"Great. We actually have a small smitty's shop below deck near the boiler room. We've got a forge, an anvil and a steam powered firing fan," Brussard said. "Our engine man is not a true blacksmith, but he does' know the ins and outs of that old boiler and the power train."

"I'll show it to you once we get up the river some," he added.

"I'd love to see it," Adkin answered.

"Well, mon ami, 'tis time to say goodbye for now," Carbeauneaux said. "Have a happy and safe trip.

"And think of me when your eating desert rats," he added, laughing.

Brussard could see how much the old salt liked the boy when they hugged. It looked like a grisly old pirate with his head under the chin of a tall sun-kissed farm boy.

•••

For a day and a half, Adkin had spent most every waking minute exploring the huge ship. He couldn't believe her size, and it seemed there must be 200 people aboard. No way to get to know everybody like he did on the Euterpe. Plus, they were scheduled to reach St. Louis in about 12 to 14 days.

The scenery was much like what he had experienced around New Orleans, and Florida, to the extent he didn't wander far from St. Augustine and the Fort Marion jail.

But leaving New Orleans, the woods seemed much more intense and thick. The gargantuan cypress trees were everywhere with their hanging moss draped throughout their canopies. He also noticed elms, maples and numerous evergreens, including pine trees that seemed to reach 100 feet in the air.

Adkin figured there was enough timber north of New Orleans to provide wood for the world forever.

He also got to see an alligator on his first day aboard the Queen. A young boy on the second deck had shouted, "There's a big 'gator, mama," pointing port side.

Adkin watched as the ancient-looking creature slowly moved toward shore, his tail swishing gently side to side.

A man next to him said, "That one's about 10 feet, and they got bigger ones, too."

A crewman was walking the decks telling passengers our first stop would be in one hour, at a port called Baton Rouge.

It turned out to be quite a busy little river port. The docks could easily handle several large ships, and the town was built up mainly on the east side of the riverbank, though there were small docks and piers on the opposite bank, as well.

"Get those lines ready," Captain Brussard shouted from the door of the wheelhouse. He stepped back inside and yelled at someone, and the Queen gently slowed to a stop, and her paddle wheel reversed itself. Her stern gently shifted sideways and snuggled up to the dock.

"The man's done this more than once," Adkin thought.

Two men with canvas bags and a travelling chest boarded, and it looked like two entire families – children and all – scurried off the ship.

In only a few moments, billowing clouds of steam and smoke belched through the stacks atop the Queen, and she was under way again.

"Seven more stops to make," Adkin mumbled to himself. He had been told she would stop at least eight times, more if hailed for an emergency, before reaching St. Louis. Captain Brussard had called the river: "The major artery of the United States – everyone is going somewhere or returning to somewhere."

On the fifth day, Adkin ran into Brussard on the lower deck as the Captain was scurrying aft in a hurry.

"Oh Yates, I'll show you our forge after lunch," Brussard said. "Sorry, but it's been hectic since we departered – having some mechanical problems. Might get your input on it. Come to the wheelhouse at 1."

'Yes sir," Adkin responded, as Brussard scuttled away. "But I'm no mechanic ..."

Brussard didn't hear him.

•••

"This here boiler was built just two years ago, and she's been fairly trouble-free – just regular maintenance – but that's a lot," Brussard said, as they hopped down the steps below deck.

"Heinz, this is Yates," Brussard said. "He's a master blacksmith. I'd like him to look at that drive sleeve.

"This is Heinz Guderian, he's our engineer and engine room chief," he said, turning to Adkin.

"I don't need a smitty to tell me how to fix a drive sleeve," Guderian snarled.

"Just let him look," Brussard said, giving Guderian a hard stare.

He finally stepped to the side and pointed at several long rocking arms attached to huge rods that moved back to the large drive wheels attached to the paddle wheel gears. The rods looked similar to those on a railroad engine as they circled around the rods from the steam boiler.

Adkin could see where one of the rods had parted where the sleeve held the rod to the drive arms.

"We're having trouble keeping this sleeve on – it's cracked, and we can't get a new one until we get to St. Louis," Brussard said. "It's like we're flying with one wing."

"If you have some 1-inch iron rod and some flat steel sheets, I might be able to build a clamp, which might get you to St. Louis," Adkin said.

"I'm telling you, Captain, I don't need his help," Guderian said forcefully.

"You take him to the smitty shop, and let him try," Brussard said. "I'll be back later to check on what he's come up with."

Guderian, Adkin and two other engine room crewmen went down the railed walkway and entered an area that had a forge, piles of coal and timber, an anvil stand and the steam powered fire fan.

"There's all kinds of iron over there," Guderian said, pointing to an open storage area piled high with metal.

One of the men fired the forge and started pushing coal up to the main flame, where coke was being made. The other man opened a small valve and steam started turning the fire fan faster and faster.

Adkin was impressed with this floating blacksmith shop.

He went to work pulling iron rods out, placing ends into the coke flame. As he worked each rod around the horn of the anvil with a hammer, his bends got tighter and tighter. It was clang, clang, clang and then the steaming hiss of pink-hot metal being submerged in cool water.

He soon had four horseshoe shaped rods. He went back to the shaft and used a piece of twine to measure its outside diameter.

Guderian kept right on his heels, mumbling to the others, "This boy doesn't know what he's doing."

Adkin then went back to the forge and started bending a sheet of thick metal plate. He burned, and chisled to get the shape and size he wanted.

Within an hour, Adkin said it was ready.

"Go get the captain," Guderian told a crewman.

Within minutes, Brussard was there, and Adkin told him how it would work.

"Once we get the metal sleeve over the connector joint, we can place the U-clamps over it and tighten their extended ends with steel wire. They should hold the sleeve secure – there's four of them," he said, looking up at Brussard.

"By damn, I think that will work," Brussard said.

"Start wrapping this up, and do as Yates says," he blurted at Guderian and the others.

"Thanks lad. We might make an engineer out of you, yet," he said as he turned away.

Feeling somewhat proud, Adkin lost that feeling as soon as he looked at Guderian. Seems Guderian didn't like another cook in his kitchen, Adkin thought.

"You made it, you put it together," Guderian told Adkin.

"I'll need help with the metal sleeves, and it will take a least two of us to tighten the ends of the U-clamps," Adkin said.

"I don't give a damn what you need," Guderian said, stepping forward and placing his face just inches away from Adkin's.

"Back away, Guderian," Adkin said, not feeling terribly afraid of this squat German who looked to be at least 40 years old, even though he was thick as one of those big cypress trees.

Just as Adkin was sizing him up, Guderian hit him right between the eyes. Adkin stumbled backwards and hit his head and back on several pipes. Had it not been for that, Adkin would've hit the deck.

As he was trying to get his bearings, Guderian hit him again in the jaw.

"I don't take any shit from a stinkin' limey," Guderian shouted.

Adkin was again stunned, but then he felt a red-hot rage stirring up from his stomach. He straightened himself up and stood erect, seething and raised his fists.

It was then Adkin saw through a haze the red haired man with a knife in his hands in St. Augustine. He was standing there, as real as when it actually happened.

Adkin froze. His eyes were glazed over unable to swing at the man.

"I didn't mean to kill you," Adkin mumbled softly. "I didn't mean to kill you."

"You won't be killing no body," the bulldog German yelled, and pounded Adkin again and again and again.

Adkin fell backward to the ground – out like the flame of a candle, and Guderian pounced on him like a jackal. He slugged him over and over and as a few crewmen tried to pull him off Adkin, he got in a few kicks to Adkin's ribs and stomach as well.

As Adkin was drifting into the netherlands, he could see the redheaded man standing over him as Adkin faded into total darkness.

•••

When Adkin awoke, he found himself in his little stateroom with a young girl sitting in the room's only chair at the end of the bed.

"What happened," he muttered softly through bandages covering most of his head.

"Thank God. You're alive," the girl sputtered, then ran from the room.

As Adkin was trying to clear his thoughts, one of the ship's officers stepped into the room.

"How are you feeling, Yates," the man asked. "My name is Wilson. Dr. Benjamin Wilson. I'm the ship's medical officer. You took a pretty bad beating young man. You're lucky to be alive."

"Something happened in the engine room, didn't it?" Adkin asked.

"You don't remember?"

"Not all of it. I remember Guderian and a redheaded man."

"Guderian was involved, but I don't know of any redheaded man," Wilson said. "Guderian was the one who beat you, and all the witnesses say you started it when you pushed him against the bulkhead."

"I don't remember that at all," Adkin said. "I don't start fights, I never have."

"Well whatever, Guderian just about killed you with his bare knuckles," Wilson said. "You've been out for four days."

"What does he look like?" Adkin asked wryly.

"Fine. They said after Guderian landed the first punch, you never got a lick in."

"That makes no sense," Adkin said, trying to clear the cobwebs away.

The girl Adkin had seen when he awoke brought him some soup that evening. She looked to be 13 or 14.

"You know, scuttlebutt among the crew is you never fought back – at all," the girl said. "By the way, My name is Elizabeth – most call me Liz. I'm a nurse's aide."

"Is that right?

"Oh and thank you, Liz, for looking after me" Adkin said as he pondered what she had said.

Just then, Captain Brussard knocked as he walked through the open door.

"Glad to hear your coming along, Yates," he said. "We was worried quite a bit there for a few days. Your breathing wasn't too good with those broken ribs. Doc says you probably have two or three banged up fairly bad, but he says they'll heal in time."

"Can you tell me your side of what happened?" Brussard asked.

"It's kind of fuzzy, but I remember Guderian hitting me, and I got really angry," Adkin stammered. "I know this, Captain. I didn't push him or anybody.

"I hate to admit this, but the last thing I remember seeing is a redheaded man – the same one I accidently killed in St. Augustine, Flori …"

"Carbeauneaux told me all about that unfortunate incident the moment he greeted me when we docked in New Orleans," Brussard interrupted. "I never brought it up because Carbeauneaux said it had bothered you quite a bit."

"Yes sir. It did."

"I think I understand what's happened, and I wouldn't put it past Guderian to lie about it – and to get his crew to back him up, as well," Brussard said. "He's been warned that I won't tolerate that kind of behavior in the future.

"I'm sorry for your injury, Yates, but you're going to have to deal with what happened in Florida or you will end up dead – for sure."

"Yes, sir," Adkin said. "You remind me of what my father always said, 'Life's lessons are often painful.' I won't forget it sir."

"By the way, your clamp is working fine, just fine – good job," Brussard said, reaching out to shake Adkin's hand

Liz helped Adkin for a few more days, fetching his meals and washing his clothes. She was the daughter of a couple that worked on the Queen – the mother a cleaning woman and her father worked as a dealer in the gambling hall. She said the entire crew on the Queen totaled 75 people.

"No wonder they charge $30 a person," Adkin thought. "That's a lot of salaries to pay."

She happily accepted a tip from Adkin, saying, "God Bless, and be careful, Mr. Yates."

An Englishman's Adventures on the Santa Fe Trail (1865-1889)

A few days out from St. Louis, Adkin made his way back on the decks to watch the people and see the sights. The countryside had changed to dryer habitat. The cypress had been replaced with large oak trees, hackberry, maple and cottonwoods. He also noticed there was more hedge-like brush around and large grassy clearings.

Adkin was almost sad they hadn't seen any wild Indians, though. They had encountered some on day four – what one man called "tame Indians" – who came alongside the Queen and begged for food and money. Some of the passengers threw them things wrapped in little scarfs or rags.

"That's the man the engine room chief beat in a fight," a young boy said to his friend at the rail one morning.

"Yeah, I heard crewmen saying he fought like a girl. That he didn't even get a punch in on the chief."

Adkin wondered what kind of person brags on beating someone who is down and knocked out. Not much of a real man, in Adkin's mind. He had developed a real distaste for the arrogant German.

On the morning of day 13, Adkin awoke to foot stomps, excited conversations and children laughing and running down the outer deck.

"Prepare to dock in St. Louis in 30 minutes," a crewman yelled as he walked down the planking.

Adkin had stowed most of his gear in his bags the night before, knowing St. Louis was close at hand. He put on a clean shirt and packed away his nightshirt and finished dressing. Making sure his promissory note was still in his waistband.

He made his way toward the front gangplank as Brussard shouted orders for docking. As the Queen nestled along the pier and lines were being tied off fore and aft, Adkin noticed Guderian was standing near the starboard prow with a large canvas bag at his feet, with several crewmen around him in their uniforms. Apparently, Guderian was going to disembark immediately upon landing.

Adkin walked over slowly and laid both his bags on the deck. He looked up slowly with shade from his hat brim covering the anger in his eyes.

"Mr. Guderian, I want to thank you for the lesson you gave me," Adkin said.

"Get out of my sight or I'll bludgeon you agai…

He never finished his sentence.

Others would later say the thud sounded like someone bashing an oak tree with a canoe paddle.

One shot to the jaw from Adkin's right fist caused Guderian to fly over backward, his feet clearing the 2-feet high roped rail.

Splash.

Guderian was floundering about in the river gurgling, "Help, help me."

Adkin looked up at the wheelhouse, and Brussard had seen it all. He shook his head but saluted, and Adkin saluted back. He picked up his bags and made his way to the gangplank.

"I'm still on my way to Santa Fe," he said to himself, with a broad grin.

•••

As Adkin walked up to the main road that paralleled the riverfront, he noticed it was paved and looked similar to macadam roads in London. A Scottish engineer, John Loudon McAdam, had developed the roadway covering, and Adkin had even noticed a few of them in New Orleans, as well.

He had spent an unlucky 13 days aboard the Queen, and with days lost to recovering from his beating, he hadn't found a chance to ask how he was going to get to Independence, Missouri.

Carbeauneaux had told him there were all kinds of boats that he could find passage on – and he could ask the dock master.

Finding a place to stay a few days was what Adkin wanted right now. That would buy him time to search out the best deal to get to Independence.

'Excuse me, sir," a man said as he tapped Adkin on the shoulder from behind. "My name is Sanderson, Jared L. Sanderson."

He offered his hand, and Adkin shook it.

"I'm Adkin Yates, pleased to meet you."

"When I was disembarking the Delta Queen, I couldn't help notice you struck a man and put him in the river quite efficiently."

"Well, I'm sorry about that, but there was a score to settle," Adkin said. "I shouldn't have let my temper go like that, but …"

"No. No. I know all about it," Sanderson said. "You were quite the talk on the Queen. Everybody was hoping you would recover quickly after what the chief engineer did to you. The truth got out he lied about you starting the fight, then he had the audacity to continue beating you when you passed out.

"There were enough people at the front gangplank who saw what you just did, that I won't doubt you will again be the point of conversation at a few eateries tonight in St. Louis," Sanderson said, chuckling. "In fact, I would be honored to buy you a whisky right now."

"Well, I really don't drink alcohol that much," Adkin said. "But I could use a spot of tea."

"Great, I'll flag us a coach. I'm staying at the Jefferson Hotel," Sanderson said.

After paying the coach driver, Sanderson hurried Adkin up the steps to the stately front of the hotel. To Adkin, it resembled a large ornate house, much like the plantation homes in New Orleans.

An Englishman's Adventures on the Santa Fe Trail (1865-1889)

"Take this to Room 212, please," Sanderson said to a young black man tending the doorway as Sanderson handed him a large leather satchel.

"And watch these for the gentleman," he added, pointing to Adkin's bags.

"That's fine, I'd prefer to carry them with me, if you don't mind," Adkin said.

"Come, let's go to the saloon."

The saloon was in an ornate dining hall that could probably seat 100 people, Adkin guessed, and it was about half full. Sanderson pulled out a chair for him at a table near the windows overlooking a busy street.

"Rumor aboard the Queen was you are a master blacksmith," Sanderson began. Adkin nodded.

He went on to tell Adkin he was a co-owner of a coach line and they were looking to staff several new stops along the stage lines in Missouri, Kansas and even Colorado.

"And we're always needing blacksmiths," Sanderson added.

Adkin immediately started grinning from ear-to-ear.

"What's so humorous, Mr. Yates?"

"Mr. Sanderson, my father owns a coach line in England," Adkin beamed. "I was born into a carriage house and have been a coachman since I was old enough to grab the reins."

"It's pure fate, Mr. Yates. Pure fate," Sanderson bellowed loudly.

"Call me Adkin."

"Call me J.L."

Adkin learned Sanderson had been born in Vermont in July, the same month as Adkin. He was 45 years of age, 26 years older than Adkin, and as a youngster, Sanderson had apprenticed with a carriage maker. He began working for a stage company at 20 and began by first taking care of livestock, and later, started driving teams out of Burlington, Vermont.

Adkin filled Sanderson in about his own experiences since birth with handling livestock and repairing and driving carriages.

The two men could hardly believe how alike their lives had been – as if they had been brothers, only on two different continents.

Sanderson told Adkin he started out driving teams out of Burlington, but the railroads crippled the stage business in the Northeast. It was in 1860 Sanderson moved to St. Louis and started a new stage company.

Adkin about passed out with excitement when Sanderson told him, "I'm a partner in the Barlow and Sanderson Overland Stage Company that operates over the Santa Fe Trail and other routes on the Plains. My partner is Bradley Barlow."

Adkin felt tears trying to well up in his eyes as he explained his dreams of the Santa Fe Trail to Sanderson.

Both men were also experienced with the Concord Stagecoaches built by the Abbot Downing Company in Concord, New Hampshire. Adkin's father had purchased one in 1860, and it was a top of the line coach. Even in 1860, Concords were being sold around the world; Europe, Australia, Africa and South America.

Sanderson had been in New Orleans finalizing financing for two new Concords that were being delivered to him in St. Louis in a few days.

"They cost us $2,000 apiece, and I could use a good man to help me drive them to Leavenworth, Kansas.

"Would you like a job, Adkin?" Sanderson asked.

"I'd be honored, J.L."

The men talked for hours, only pausing long enough for a meal of beef steaks and small boiled red potatoes and fresh green beans. Sanderson asked for a slice of onion to be added to his order when the waiter brought an uncut loaf of warm bread and creamy butter to the table. Sanderson had a couple of glasses of red wine, and Adkin had another cup of tea.

Though Sanderson was much older than Adkin, Sanderson was stocky and looked as strong as a mule. He was definitely a man in his prime. He wore cheek whiskers and was nattily attired, and seemed to have a penchant for expensive wool derbies.

He stopped at the front desk and ask the manager to give Adkin a room and put it on his bill.

"I'll meet you for breakfast at 9," Sanderson said.

"Fine, see you then – and J.L., thank you, truly."

"It's pure fate, Adkin. Pure fate."

•••

At breakfast, Sanderson told Adkin they would take a coach to the stockyards near the Calvary Cemetery on the north side of town. They would meet up with a horse wrangler to discuss the purchase of several teams to drive to Kansas.

Adkin was curious where Leavenworth was?

"It's where Fort Leavenworth is," Sanderson said, spreading his arms apart. "It the biggest and most important U.S. Army post west of the Alleghenys. Everything the U.S. government does from here to California goes through there."

"I see. I was under the impression I had to start on the Santa Fe Trail in Independence, Missouri," Adkin said.

"We'll drive these coaches and teams right through Independence on the Santa Fe Trail and stay on the trail until we cross the Kansas River at Kansas City," Sanderson said. "Technically, we get on the trail a stone's throw south of Franklin, Missouri – that's 90 miles before we get to Independence. Franklin is where the famous William Becknell started his run in 1823 or '24, I can't remember exactly."

"He made his first trip in 1821," Adkin said.

An Englishman's Adventures on the Santa Fe Trail (1865-1889)

"Well all right, you know your Santa Fe Trail history," Sanderson said, with a smile. He really liked this big, strong kid. "Our trip takes us along the Boone's Lick Trail through Jefferson City, and then we'll hit the Santa Fe Trail at Franklin and head along the Missouri River crossing just south of Kansas City. Leavenworth is just a two-day ride after that. We should be able to make 20 miles a day, and it's around 260 miles – so about 13 days."

Adkin didn't like hearing 13 again, even though he never considered himself to be superstitious.

Sanderson haggled with the wrangler and finally settled on a price for 16 head. Of those, the wrangler assured Sanderson eight were trained coach animals.

"We'll see about that soon enough," Sanderson said as they walked away.

The two Concords were expected to be arriving the next day, or the day after, depending on when the ship carrying them from the northeast had arrived in New Orleans.

"I arranged to have them loaded onto a cargo ship – a steamer – that doesn't make stops on its way to St. Louis," Sanderson explained to Adkin. "They were supposed to hit New Orleans about 3 or 4 days after we departered on the Delta Queen."

...

"Telegraph for Mr. J.L. Sanderson. Mr. J.L. Sanderson," a young boy yelled at the entrance to the dining room at the Jefferson Hotel. "Telegraph for Mr. J.L. Sanderson."

"Over here boy – I'm Sanderson."

The young man hopped over to their table and Sanderson took the piece of paper and handed him a coin.

"We're moving into the modern world, Adkin. This telegraph will soon allow us to communicate from coast to coast," Sanderson said, shaking his head. "Can you believe it?"

"It's even being used in England and the continent," Adkin replied.

"Says here our stagecoaches will be landing in the morning," Sanderson said. "If we get prepared, we could probably hit the trail by noon tomorrow or shortly thereafter."

Adkin said the first thing he needed to do was stop by the St. Louis National Bank and cash out his promissory note. It was only four blocks away, and Sanderson said he would stay and make out the list of supplies they would need.

Adkin was only gone about 20 minutes and returned to the saloon.

"Got squared away did you?" Sanderson asked.

"Sure did, I'm itching to get on the trail," Adkin said, smiling

Sanderson's plans for the horses included each coach using six in harness with two lashed behind each coach to be ready in case one or more in the team had any problems.

They then left the hotel in one of its small dearborn wagons to gather supplies, stopping at a big general store.

Sanderson told the store clerk they needed some extra horseshoes, nails, farrier's hammer and a hoof pick. He also told him to include six sacks of oats, even though there would be plenty of natural grasses along the trail.

"Put together two complete bed rolls with two oilskin tarps," he said, as the wiry man hurriedly scribbled on a small pad.

Sanderson then remembered and handed the man his own list.

"We'll need three or four water bags, hard tack, jerky, flour, salt, sugar, lard, coffee, a coffee pot, couple of skillets and eating utilities for two – everything we'll need for two weeks on the trail. Oh, and don't forget some extra rope so we can make hobbles."

"Yes sir, Mr. Sanderson," the man said. "I'll have this together in about 20 minutes."

"Let's go next door and have a refreshment, Adkin," Sanderson said.

As they walked out onto the elevated wooden walkway around the corner store, five men stood out front in the dusty street.

"Vell, vell, vell. If it isn't dat stinkin' limey, Yates," Guderian said sarcastically, as he looked up at Adkin and Sanderson.

Guderian didn't quite look like himself, and it pleased Adkin; the whole left side of his face was still a little swollen – even after two days – and it was all darkish blue-black and purple. He was standing there with four other men, one slapping an oak axe handle into his palm.

"Vee've been luking for you," Guderian said.

Sanderson looked at Adkin and smiled, "I forgot to tell you, there is a substantial population of Germans here in St. Louis.

"What do you think we should do?" Sanderson asked.

"I think we should try to avoid trouble, and walk away," Adkin said.

"I don't," Sanderson said, still smiling. "I think it's better to show these boys there's right and wrong. We'd be doing them an injustice by putting off such an important lesson in life."

"Then I want Guderian," Adkin said, now grinning himself as both men started down the steps to the street. Sanderson had removed his waistcoat as they set foot on the dry, sandy dirt and tossed it onto the hitching rail.

•••

After the dust settled, Guderian was laying in the dirt moaning, totally incapable of speaking clearly. Adkin had only hit him twice after ducking Guderian's first wild swing – once with a right to the same area on his left jaw and a hard, quick left directly under Guderian's nose.

As soon as the punch landed, Guderian spit blood and three teeth into the air. He was finished and fell to his knees, wobbled a little and fell face down in the street.

Sanderson had wrestled with two immediately, one trying to hold his arms from behind his back, but Sanderson stomped on his foot in time to break his hold and turned to pound a solid fist into the other's face, knocking him backward several steps.

Sanderson then turned back to the man who had been holding him and kicked him square in the crotch. That man was quickly down, as well.

After dropping Guderian, Adkin turned in time to block an overhand swing by the man with the axe handle. Adkin grabbed his arm, spun him around and with one steel grip on the man's wrist and another grip on his elbow, Adkin smashed it over his knee.

The man dropped the club, went to his knees and started screaming, "You broke my arm, you sons-a-bitch."

Adkin silenced him with a powerful right fist to the forehead. The man's eyes rolled back in their sockets, and he fell over backward, staring blankly into the netherlands.

After Sanderson had kicked the one man in the family jewels, he hopped toward another with both fists up high, his arms cocked. Adkin thought he looked like one of those dandy prizefighters he'd seen on posters in London.

Thump, thump, thump … Sanderson punched the man in the face five or six times in what seemed like a split second, one hand after the other. Adkin had never seen someone that could punch that fast with that much power.

As the man stumbled backward 10 or 12 steps before falling down with blood flowing from his nose and mouth, the last German took off running down the street. He apparently had seen enough.

It was all over in less than a minute. A small crowd assembled, but no one went to the Germans' aid. Guderian was still down, gurgling, as was the man who had been kicked – he was groaning. The man with the broken arm was still staring into the sky – splinters of his arm bones glistened in the sunlight, as blood dribbled into the sandy soil.

"This is what happens to people who don't fight fairly," Sanderson bellowed to no one in particular. He reached for his waistcoat.

"What say we finish preparing for our adventure, Adkin?

"I'm with you J.L."

Both men headed for the saloon next to the store, and neither had a mark on him.

•••

As Adkin repacked his bags early the next morning, he kept going over in his mind everything they needed to head out on the trail. To Adkin, it seemed they would need much more in the way of supplies, but Sanderson had assured him they weren't heading out into the wilds of the Santa Fe Trail, yet – and the road to Kansas City, the Boone's Lick Trail, was well traveled.

Sanderson did suggest Adkin purchase a few more munitions for his guns; .52 caliber balls, powder charges and firing caps for his Sharps breech loader and more 12-gauge shot shells.

Sanderson told him from now on, most of their meat would be from kills along the trails, especially after they departed Leavenworth.

"And don't worry about supplies, we can replenish everything at our warehouse in Leavenworth."

Adkin learned once Sanderson and his partner, Barlow, started their line, Barlow was able to finally obtain a contract with the U.S. Army to help ship supplies between Fort Leavenworth and a few of the western military forts, and if things worked out, the Barlow and Sanderson Overland Stage Company would soon be hauling the U.S. mail throughout the west.

"That's where the big money is right now," Sanderson told Adkin. "And, of course, helping out the Army pays well, too. We've heard President Andrew Johnson and Congress has declared war on all the Indians of the west. Barlow has even heard the Army plans on building more forts out there, but we're keeping that quiet for now."

Barlow, Sanderson said, had been a member of the Vermont House of Representatives from 1845 to today and has contacts throughout Washington.

"He's also a banker," Sanderson said, with a wink. "And owns an interest in a railroad back East."

The two knew each other in Vermont, and when Sanderson decided to head west, he approached Barlow with his plans. They decided to put in $5,000 each at $1 per share, and it would be a 50-50 partnership, even though Sanderson did most of the work, like setting up an office in St. Louis in 1860 and buying their first four freight wagons and two small coaches. It was Barlow's political contacts, though, that were paying off.

"We kind of struggled during the war years, but the Union Army kept us afloat," Sanderson said. "Then last year, as we reached an agreement for hauling goods and selected mail routes for the Army out of Fort Leavenworth, we moved our operations there and have started to make a little money.

"We did set up a line with stations in early 1861 to Santa Fe, but all was abandoned once the war broke out," he continued. "None of those stations are still in existence, and we don't even know if any of those contacts are still out there.

An Englishman's Adventures on the Santa Fe Trail (1865-1889)

"But mark my words, Adkin, our dreams, coupled with hard work, are going to pay off someday – but good," Sanderson said laughing. "They better or I'm going to have to beg to be let through the doors of the poor house."

•••

An hour after daybreak on Aug. 22, Adkin and Sanderson slapped the reins on their teams of six in harness pulling two brand new high-dollar Concord Stagecoaches with two horses each in tow – their supplies stacked inside the coaches and some lashed atop.

Adkin was thrilled.

Sanderson was thrilled.

"Just follow me," Sanderson hollered. "We'll head due west to Chesterfield and then pick up Boone's Lick Trail along the Missouri."

That trail, according to Sanderson, had been named after Daniel Boone's two sons, Nathan and Daniel Morgan Boone. Seems they had a business delivering salt from their home just south of Franklin, Mo., and hauled it to St. Louis for sale.

"Their home area was called 'Boone's Lick,' thus the road they made was named 'Boone's Lick Trail,'" Sanderson explained.

When Adkin thought about explorers like William Becknell and Daniel Boone, it made the hair on the back of his neck stand up.

There was something about men of those stripes Adkin found appealing. He couldn't explain it thoroughly, but he saw it in Sanderson, and he believed, Sanderson could see it in him – that eagerness to explore the unknown.

"Thank you for your bounty Lord," Adkin whispered as the coaches glided along. "What a sweet ride."

About an hour before dark, Sanderson pulled his team over near a high bank on the Missouri. Adkin followed suit.

"We'll spend the night here," Sanderson said, as he stood up from his carriage seat and stretched his arms out to the sky.

"I don't think any highwaymen can sneak up behind us from this cliff.

"I think we've made close to our goal of 20 miles," he added, smiling.

Sanderson started unloading the tarpaulins and bed rolls from the carriage, while Adkin instinctively started unhooking the horses.

"There's plenty of nice grass here," Adkin said.

"Yeah, but we should give them a few oats, too, after they've been hobbled and curried," Sanderson said.

"My thoughts exactly."

In a short while, camp was pitched, a fire had been started, coffee was on and Sanderson was clanging around in a sack of pots and pans.

"How about some fried sweet corn cakes and jerky tonight," Sanderson asked, as he pulled out a large skillet.

"I have the lard right here," Adkin responded.

Sanderson couldn't help but feel like Adkin was a little brother. They had never set camp together before, but they both took on chores to get it done with absolutely no duplication or getting in each other's way.

"We make a good team, Adkin," Sanderson said. "I've felt that from the moment I met you."

"I feel the same way, J.L.," Adkins aid. "Seems like you're thinking what I'm thinking at any moment."

They both laughed and set about fixing their meal.

While sitting back on their bed rolls and enjoying coffee and tea, Adkin sighed as he noticed the silence of the night.

The enjoyment came because it was not silence. Though he and J.L. had stopped talking, he listened to the crackle of the fire as its embers jutted off and disappeared into the darkness, how the crickets sang to the moon, the hoots of a far off owl – even the gutteral calls of frogs down at the river's edge.

'I believe this is what heaven is like, J.L.," Adkin interrupted the evening's orchestra. "If a man could experience this daily, I can't see where troubles could ever bring him down."

"I know exactly what you mean, Adkin," Sanderson sighed. "That's why I'm here. I told Barlow, let's get the money together, and I'll gladly push the company across the prairies – plus, make us some money."

"I've been reluctant to bring this up J.L., but … do you think there is any way I could invest in your adventure?" Adkin asked.

"You're already in, Adkin. Like I said, I'll pay you your first month's salary when we get to Leavenworth," Sanderson said. "You're going to be one of our top hands, I have no doubt."

"I'm not talking about the job – investing my time. I'm asking if I can buy some shares of Barlow and Sanderson Overland Stage Company," Adkin said. "And, of course, I'll still do whatever job you wish me to do, as well – and for as long as you want."

"I see." Sanderson said. "I'll tell you what I'll do. Let me think on it a few days."

"Okay."

"It's not that I'm saying no in any way, Adkin. It's just I don't think Barlow will sell any of his stock, and if I sell you some of mine, I would become the minority partner. See what I mean?"

"Oh, I see," Adkin responded. "I really don't know how these stock things work, I just know this is something I want to be involved with – even up to my eyes, if you understand."

An Englishman's Adventures on the Santa Fe Trail (1865-1889)

"Let me ask you, Adkin, how much are you wanting to invest?"

"Well, I have $180 U.S., but I was thinking about investing $100. That way, I would still have $80 to spend on particulars.

"One of my dreams is to have my own freight wagon to use on the Santa Fe Trail – you know, so I can pay my way," Adkin continued. "I've been figuring, I could help you set up the stagecoach stops all the way to Colorado, and then I could use my freighter and haul for you, too. That way you're getting to haul more for the Army, and we could split that charge for my wagon however you feel is fair."

"My God, Adkin. I swear I'm going to have to ask my pappy back in Vermont if there are any Yates in our ancestry," Sanderson said with a laugh. "It's scary how much we think alike.

"I'll figure out something by the time we reach Leavenworth," he continued, shaking his head. "We will make it work somehow, I promise."

"Thanks J.L."

•••

On Day 5, they rolled into Jefferson City, a pretty little town, and everyone was very friendly, especially the children They came running alongside the two Concords shouting and laughing.

"They don't have any passengers," one boy informed the others.

"They must've got kilt by Injuns," another yelled.

"Those sure are a pretty red, look as shiny as a newborn baby," another crowed.

Sanderson rolled to a stop at the stables next to the livestock corrals.

"Whoa," he grunted, as an aproned farrier stepped out from under a partial roof covered with tin. "Could we use your forge? We need to fit some shoes on a few horses."

"Sure," the man said. "I can help if you need it.

"That's fine, it won't take us long, and we'll get back on the trail."

Adkin was already dismounting from his coach and retrieving a bag of shoeing supplies. He followed the farrier into the shade and saw his anvil and forge. The man still used old goat skins as a bellows to force air into the fire pit. A young boy of about 8 or 9 sat in a small chair next to the pit. Adkin figured he handled the goatskins.

"You the bellows operator?" Adkin asked the boy.

"Sure am," he squealed, jumping up and feeling important that this man knew how important his job was. "I've been helpin' my pa since I was 4."

"Well, it's good to have an experienced hand," Adkin said, with a wink to the boy.

"You sure you don't want any help?" the man asked, with a dour look in his eyes.

"We'll see," Adkin said, looking over to Sanderson. Sanderson reflexively knew what Adkin was saying with that look: The man needs the money, and if they do all their own heating, hammering, shaping, nailing and filing, he isn't getting paid.

"I'll tell you what, mister… mister…"

"Lamming. The name's Anthony Lamming, and this here's my son, Lawrence – we call him Larry."

"I'll tell you what, Mister Lamming, how about I pay Larry here $3 to keep the bellows going and you can help wherever you want as Yates here gets to work," Sanderson said.

Lamming's face lit up.

"Why, yes sir, that'd be fine with me."

Lamming helped Sanderson untie three of the horses that were tethered to the coaches and bring them over to the hitching post.

"Fine horses," Lamming said. "And beautiful stages."

"Taking them to Leavenworth where we're expanding stagecoach services throughout Kansas along the Santa Fe Trail," Sanderson said, with some pride.

"Name's J.L. Sanderson," he said as he shook hands with Lamming. "This here is Adkin Yates, one of my partners."

Adkin paused, then turned and looked at Sanderson, who was smiling.

"Where's the telegraph office, Mister Lamming," Sanderson asked, and Lamming pointed down the street. "You fellas take care of things, I have to send a telegram to our other partner in Vermont."

Adkin and Lamming started removing the old shoes, some cracked. Two were completely missing. Larry started pumping the goat skins and pushing coals up to the fire pit.

They were about finished when Sanderson came back carrying a small bag.

"Sorry to take so long, had to go find a place that had tins of pemmican," Sanderson said. "It's something I forgot to buy in St. Louis."

"What's pemmican?" Adkin asked.

Sanderson, Lamming and Larry all froze and stared at Adkin.

"Well its canned meat and was first invented by the Indians," Sanderson said. "Now we've learned how to duplicate it, and it lasts forever without rotting. Perfect for the trail."

"Everybody knows what pemmican is," Larry said.

"Shush, Larry. He's not from these parts," Lamming interrupted.

"That's right, Larry. That accent of Mister Yates is from England – he's an Englishman," Sanderson interjected. "I hadn't realized Mister Yates had never had pemmican. My apologies, Adkin."

Feeling a little embarrassed, Adkin said, "No problem. If you like it, I'll be fine."

"It's really good, 'specially if it has berries in it," Larry smiled.

"I know some Germans and I-tal-yons," he added.

"Shush."

•••

They pushed out of town with about four or five hours of daylight left. Sanderson had explained by noon the next day they should be near Franklin and Boones Lick – the eastern terminus of the Santa Fe Trail.

That evening, after the horses had been taken care of and hobbled close to camp, Sanderson handed Adkin his usual cup of tea, poured himself some coffee and sat back on his bed roll.

"You haven't asked about the telegram, Adkin," Sanderson said, with mischief in his voice.

"I figured you'd tell me when you were ready," Adkin smiled.

"I asked Barlow to have an additional 100 shares issued to the company to be certified under your name at $1 a share," Sanderson said. "If he agrees, then you'll have to wire the money to him, and the share certificates will be issued – with your name on them – as owner of said shares."

"I really don't know what to say, J.L. I'm literally speechless," Adkin smiled.

"Well, it's not a done deal yet," he responded. "Barlow has to agree to it and agree the shares should still be valued at $1 per share. If he balks and says they're worth $2, you'll only get 50 shares.

"But the way I calculated it, we only broke even, after expenses, last March – you know, finally earned enough to pay off our original investment. And that took nearly 5 years," Sanderson explained. "So I'm satisfied the shares are fairly valued at our original investment price when we incorporated the company."

"I don't know about all that, I'm just ecstatic I have the possibility of owning a piece of your's and Barlow's adventure," Adkin said. "I feel very blessed."

"Well, we'll know something by the time we reach Leavenworth, I told him to wire me there. I will tell you this, it was the longest telegraph I've ever sent anybody. It was fairly wordy," Sanderson said, and they both laughed.

•••

"Well, Adkin, this is Hardemen's ferry, and that's Franklin on the other side of the river," Sanderson said as he pulled up the reins on his coach. "Where we're stopped is actually what's known as the Boones Lick area, and this is the start of the world-famous Santa Fe Trail."

Adkin just sat there trying to take it all in. He wasn't sure what to expect. It was so simple, no sign post or roadway marker, not even a rock-piled cairn – or anything – to signify such a majestic road that crosses the continent. Maybe he has concocted more of an adventure than what is real.

"You look a little sad, Adkin. I thought you'd be excited," Sanderson said.

"I am, it's just it seems so plain or drab. There is not even a marker recognizing William Becknell, and he's been dead since April 25, 1856. He was buried in Red River County, Texas," Adkin rattled off the facts he knew so well.

"Hey don't feel let down, this is the civilized end of the trail. You'll see plenty of adventure once we get down the Military Trail and join back up with the Santa Fe," Sanderson reassured him and slapped the reins. "Let get going. yee haw."

As they topped a small knoll in the road, Sanderson pulled up his team and Adkin eased alongside. It was a couple of hours until sunset.

"How would you like to sleep in a bed tonight, Adkin?" Sanderson asked, pointing ahead to a good-sized town about five miles out. "That's Independence, my friend, and that's Kansas City on the horizon – see that big bend in the Missouri there."

"I don't necessarily need a bed, but I would love to walk around Independence some," Adkin said, smiling back at Sanderson's big grin. He didn't get much of a chance to see a lot in St. Louis. He wanted to see that city's wagon factories he had heard about.

"Yee haw."

As they slowly rolled into town, Adkin noticed a sign post saying, "Welcome to Independence, Missouri," and the road turned from dirt to macadam. He soon noticed the street signs had Independence Avenue painted on them, though streets leading off the avenue were dirt on both sides.

The obvious jumped out immediately. Store fronts with signs, "Blacksmith Service." "We will iron anything." "Wheelwright," "Mule or Ox Wagon Parts," "We Make Chains, Hooks and Iron Wheels," "Blacksmith On Call."

Adkin was taking in everything and almost ran over Sanderson's team as they slowed to turn off the avenue. He pulled over about a block down at a livery stable. Adkin parked next to him.

"Will leave the teams here," Sanderson said.

"Welcome Señor Sanderson," a tall, lanky man said as he ran up to the coaches. "I see you finally got your hands on the new Concords – bueno. Was it a good treep, Señor?"

"Si, Jesus, muy bueno," Sanderson said. Adkin just stared. Sanderson hadn't got around to telling him he spoke Spanish, too.

"An amazing man," Adkin thought to himself.

He would also have to ask J.L. what kind of hat was that man wearing – it's brim was at least 2-feet wide.

"We'll need to leave the teams and coaches with you for the night, Jesus. Make sure you push those coaches into the back and lock the doors – I don't want to loose them now," Sanderson said.

"Si, Señor, Jesus will take muy good care of dem, and de caballos."

The men grabbed their personal bags, Adkin leaving his long bag well hidden under supplies in the coach, but retrieved his leather bag which housed his shotgun.

"You can see by the wheelwright's shops and blacksmiths, they cater to Santa Fe travelers, don't they?" Adkin asked.

"They sure do," Sanderson responded. "Last I heard, there were around 65 blacksmiths in town, and four or five wagon builders. You can see my interest when I heard you were a blacksmith on the Queen. The wagon manufacturers from here to Kansas City actually run 'For Hire' advertisements in newspapers back east for blacksmiths."

Sanderson led the way as they walked back to the avenue and two blocks further into town. There stood a wooden building with a large sign on the second floor above the entrance that had swinging slatted doors. The sign read, "Cattleman's Cafe: Hotel & Saloon."

They walked through the doors and turned left into an alcove where a suited man stood behind a counter with small key and mail boxes lining the wall behind him.

"Mister. Sanderson, welcome back to the Cattleman's Cafe. How have you been?" the man asked.

"Fine George, just fine. But my friend and I are needing two rooms with a bath," Sanderson said, as he signed the register book on the counter.

"You can have the two suites at the top of the stairs, Mister Sanderson. Rooms 7 and 8, and they both have tubs," George said. "I'll have the boys start bringing up hot water right now, if you like."

"I like," Sanderson said. "You like, Adkin?"

"Sounds great, J.L."

"Meet you back down here in the dining room in about a hour, if that's OK," Sanderson said.

"See you then."

•••

Both men walked out of their hotel rooms at almost the same moment. Sanderson just shook his head; the similarities in their mannerisms, timing, thoughts were scary at times.

"You feel like a nice meal?" Sanderson asked.

"Sounds fine with me."

They made their way to the dining room and found a table near a window. It was just getting dark, and, like New Orleans, a city worker was going from lamp post to lamp post lighting the kerosene lanterns.

Adkin was always mesmerized by city lights. Olney had its charm at night, with a few street lanterns – mostly around the Market Place in the centre of the village, but when you see what seems like hundreds of glowing lanterns across the skyline of a large city, it was riveting.

"Will we have time to look around tomorrow," Adkin asked.

"We will make time," Sanderson said. "If we can get across the Kansas River by noon tomorrow – and it's only about 3 miles from here – we'll be in Leavenworth by Friday evening. Only one more night on the road."

"What I'd like to do is visit some of the wagon builders here. I've read that Independence has all the tack rooms, saddle makers, wagon and carriage builders one can find – all right here," Adkin said.

"There's quite a few places for preparing for the Santa Fe Trail – and all points west – and we've purchased goods and equipment from several local merchants that can be trusted," Sanderson said. "I'll show you them first thing after breakfast."

The men enjoyed a meal of roasted lamb with jelly sauce, sweet potatoes and turnip greens. Adkin hadn't eaten lamb since Christmas 1864, and he started smiling to himself.

"What's so funny? Sanderson asked.

"Oh I was just thinking, I hadn't had lamb since last year's Christmas dinner in Olney. It seems like an eon ago, but it's only been nine months," Adkin said, breaking into a loud chuckle.

Sanderson started laughing hard, as well. Neither cared they were causing attention.

They laughed and laughed heartily.

•••

At breakfast, Sanderson explained he does business with Hiram Young when it comes to freight wagons.

"He's a former slave that bought his freedom and started a yoke and wagon business back in '54," Sanderson said. "He started out as a carpenter, and he's had a few partners now and then. He had to move up to Leavenworth when the war broke out, but he moved back here last May. He puts out thousands of yokes, and he probably makes the best wooden-axle freight wagon around, and he's reasonable."

"What's reasonable J.L.?" Adkin asked.

"He's got used wagons for around $50 to $80, but his new ones are around $120 to $150, depending how much freight you want to haul," Sanderson answered. "There are also other lesser-known builders here that specialize in ox carts and dearborns and small carriages, or surreys. Last I heard, here in Jackson County, which goes all the way west to Kansas City, there were 24 carriage and wagon-making establishments."

"Whew," Adkin exhaled. "I was under the illusion I could get a new freighter for $80 to $90."

"Oh you can, but that's the down payment," Sanderson chuckled. "If you have a written contact with a reliable merchant who is putting together a caravan to Santa Fe, the builder will often give it to you if you sign his contract for balance due upon returning to Independence or Leavenworth for that matter."

"What if you don't come back or show up?"

"When word gets out on the trail you broke your word to a wagon builder, you're considered to be driving a 'stolen' wagon. That makes you a marked man," Sanderson said, with a stern expression. "Bandits or scurrilous businessmen virtually have an open license to kill you. Then they'll sell your merchandise, and then the wagon in Santa Fe – for often twice what it's worth.

"There's no law out there, Adkin, and what law there is, is isolated to just a handful of towns," Sanderson said. "And we're talking 900 miles of trail."

They finished their meal of fried potatoes and a chunk of flame-grilled ham with bread, butter and jam. Sanderson sent a boy to the hotel's livery to fetch a buggy, telling him to meet them out front.

It was a beautiful morning as they walked on the walkway. From around the corner of the building, Sanderson saw the buggy.

"Here he comes, Adkin. Now we'll stop wherever you wish and maybe some places I'd like you to see, But let's not get hasty and buy something we may find a better deal on later, because I want to show you some things just outside of Kansas City at a crossroads called Westport," Sanderson said, holding his palm up.

"I realize we've only known each other 13 days, but you should know I'm not a frivolous man or prone to irrationality," Adkin said, smiling.

"You're right. Sorry about that partner," Sanderson said, while slapping Adkin on the back. "Let's get going."

•••

They pulled up an a side street with wooden fencing all around a big yard full of all kinds of wagons – big and small freighters, hay wagons, even hay sleds, dearborns, drays, buggies and oxen yokes. Yokes were piled row after row. There were at least several hundred.

Adkin was impressed.

The large sign at the wide gate introduced the place as "YOUNG'S WAGONS" with "You Can Trust a Young Wagon on the Trail" written underneath.

They parked in front of a large warehouse looking building and walked inside.

"Well, Hello, J.L.," a large black man said as he reached out his hand.

"Good to see you, Hiram, it's been awhile," Sanderson said, shaking hands with the man.

"Adkin, this is Mister Hiram Young, one of the best wagon builders in Missouri," Sanderson said. "Hiram, I'd like you to meet Adkin Yates. He's a master blacksmith originally from England."

"Both men shook hands and simultaneously said, "Pleased to meet you, and laughed at their timing and each using the exact words.

"I pay good money for a master blacksmith, Mister Yates, if you're looking for work," Young said. "I badly need an ironer, right now."

It was a term for a blacksmith that could put iron strips on a wooden wagon wheel in order to roll across the ground and not destroy the wood, as well as ironing metal on the ends of axles.

"Easy Hiram, he works for me at the moment," Sanderson said, laughing. "In fact, I'm in the process of making Adkin a partner."

"I see. Nevertheless, if J.L. doesn't treat you well, you can always work here," Young said with a wink and a smile.

Young was wearing work coveralls, but he looked tidy, his hair, though tightly curled, was parted on the left side of his head, and his features were chiseled. With traces of white sneaking into his hair, he looked to be in his mid-50s.

"A handsome-looking man," Adkin thought to himself.

"It didn't take you long to get set back up here in Independence," Sanderson said, looking around.

There were sounds of power saws, hammering activities and what sounded like a forge through an open door off the front office where they were standing.

"Let me show you around, J.L.," Young said as he turned to the open door into his factory. "You looking for some more freighters?"

"Not really. We're expanding our stagecoach service to Colorado. I've got two new Concords and two teams over at Jesus' livery stable right now. We're on our way to Leavenworth today, but I wanted to show Adkin your place.

"He's actually the one looking to get a wagon of his own so he can make a little money hauling merchandise on the trail.

"I see. You looking to buy, or you shopping?" Young asked Adkin.

"Just trying to get a feel for what I really need to pay my way on the trail," Adkin responded.

"Ah, shopping," Young said, winking at Sanderson.

Adkin explained his dreams of travelling the trail and how he met up with Sanderson and decided to help him expand their stagecoach services.

"Well J.L. is a good one to hook up with. I've known him for five years now, and they alway keep to their word and pay cash," Young said. "Now that fellow

Barlow, I've only met him once and he's kind of slippery, if you know what I mean – being a politician and such."

Young patted Sanderson on the back while chuckling.

Young showed Adkin his best freight wagon which was rated at 6,000 pounds.

"This one costs $150," Young said. "I still believe in strong wooden axles – they're flexible when compared to iron axles, and it keeps my manufacturing costs down. Those steel-axle wagons made in St. Louis and Westport can carry up to 7,000 to 10,000 pounds, but they'll cost you about $250 to $300."

"What about used wagons?" Adkin asked.

"Freighters?"

"Yes, that's all I'd be interested in," Adkin answered.

"Well, I have them from $50, $60 to $100 depending on use, or if you're wanting to re-band the wheels yourself or take them as-is – depends," Young replied. "But if you're going all the way to Santa Fe, you'll most likely only get that one trip out of it."

"OK, I'll keep that in mind, Mr. Young." Adkin said. "I appreciate that information and your help."

"Just remember – and J.L. can tell you – if I take a shine to someone, I'll bend over backwards to work with them and help them with their financing," Young said. "And you're okay in my books, especially if you're running with this man."

The two shook hands with Young and said they'd be in touch. They hopped in the buggy and headed back into the main part of town.

They stopped at a blacksmith's shop that specialized in finishing wagons. Sanderson explained this was part of the "outfitter's trade" in Missouri.

"Outfitters do everything from finishing the iron work on wagons to providing all the tack for draft animals – or even providing draft animals from oxen, mules and horses," Sanderson said. "The outfitters trade also includes all the merchants who provide goods for freighters to haul to Mexico – from firearms and ammunition to clothing, saddles and foodstuffs.

"The outfitters trade probably brings more money into Jackson County than wagon manufacturing," Sanderson said, as he jumped out of the buggy. "I guarantee there are at least 100 forges in this county, alone."

Inside the building, Sanderson introduced Adkin to its owner, blacksmith James C. Mason.

"Jim here has banded a few wheels for us," Sanderson said, referring to banding the wooden wheels with iron. "This is Adkin Yates, Jim. He's a blacksmith."

"Is he looking for work?" Mason asked.

"No, no. He's from England and working for the Barlow and Sanderson Overland Stage Company," Sanderson said. "I wanted to show him what you do, as he'll be headed out onto the Santa Fe Trail helping us set up stage stops for our expanded coach lines."

Mason slowly took them through his factory. He explained he had 22 workers and utilized three forges between them.

"Most of the wagon makers only handle the wood work, and they bring them to us outfitters to finish them up," Mason said. "We band the wheels, of course, and manufacture axles, axle-trees, axle clouts, skeins and lynch pins, various hooks and chains. There's certain swivels we put on drop down tongues, as well as the yoke ring. You name it, if it needs iron on the wagon, we handle it.

"We can earn $50 to $75 dollars a wagon," Mason boasted, without being asked. "Those big freighters similar to the Murphy Monsters built in St. Louis, have those huge 6- to 7-feet wheels and can be up to 8-inches wide. Good money.

"Trouble is, more and more wagon manufacturers are putting in their own forges and hiring every blacksmith from here to Pittsburg, Pennsylvania, so they can finish their wagons in one building," Mason said, as he shook his head. "Hell, a few people have even started building wagons in Santa Fe now. It used to be you could buy a wagon for $150, load it with goods, take it to Santa Fe and earn four of five times as much on your goods, and then – you could sell the wagon for $700 if you wanted to.

"You can still make money on selling wagons out there, but it's not as profitable as it used to be," he added. "We also build small parts and pieces for all the tack used on draft animals. You know, bridle bits, rings, things like that.

"You sure you want to go down the trail? I pay good money for a smitty," he offered with a laugh.

"That's the second offer he's had today," Sanderson said, with a chuckle. "Hiram wanted to hire him, too. I think I better get him to Kansas before I lose him."

•••

As Sanderson was paying Jesus, Adkin was checking the horses, their hooves and shoes, and the tack gear, after the three of them had hooked up the teams. It was a little after 10 and Sanderson had one more stop he wanted to make in Westport, just outside of Kansas City.

It seems Westport was not only home to a famous wagon manufacturing factory, Sanderson said the town played a vital role in keeping the Confederacy from taking Fort Leavenworth, the town, and in extension, putting Kansas under control of the South.

"Confederate Major General Sterling Price invaded Missouri in the fall last year with 12,000 men," Sanderson said. "When he was thwarted in the eastern part of the state, he decided to turn westward toward Kansas City and Leavenworth.

"Major General Samuel R. Curtis was the Post Commander at Fort Leavenworth then, and he decided to place his units on the Kansas-Missouri border, which took position southeast of Kansas City," he continued. "Curtis defeated Price on October 23, 1864, at the battle of Westport."

"Price's retreat ended the Confederate threat to the Kansas frontier," Sanderson added. "But I want you to see Minor T. Graham's steam wagon factory. He uses steam powered equipment to manufacture wagons. It's very impressive."

Both men climbed onto the driver's bench of the Concords, and Sanderson shouted, "Let's move out, we want to be in Kansas by noon.

"Yee haw."

About 3 or 4 miles down the road, Adkin saw large plumes of steam and smoke arising from an industrial-looking area. It was the steam factory.

As the men rolled into Westport, Adkin couldn't help but think about the men that had probably died right where he was sitting during the battle.

"That was less than 11 months past," Adkin thought to himself.

Sanderson drove through the expansive gates and parked at the front office. Adkin followed.

"Graham's factory turns out 50 wagons a month," Sanderson said as they dismounted the coaches.

"Whew," Adkin responded.

Inside, they were steered to an office at the back wall and Adkin was introduced to Graham.

"Nice to meet you, Yates," Graham said. "And what kind of mischief have you been up to J.L.?"

"Not much, Minor. Adkin and I are delivering our new Concords to our Leavenworth station," Sanderson said. "He's going to help us establish some new stations out west – we're expanding our stagecoach lines."

"Well congratulations and good luck – to both of you," Graham said.

He led the pair into his factory. It was divided into four separate departments, and he said he was presently employing 35 men.

His steam-powered machines could produce mortices, bolsters, tongues, grooves, scrolls, etc.

"This machine will make all the mortices for the hubs on a wagon in 18 minutes," Graham said. "It would take a man all day, and his work wouldn't be as precise."

Adkin saw machines that planed, lathed, drilled, sawed and even turned grind stones.

After the tour, they gave Graham their thanks and shook hands. As they prepared to mount the coaches, Sanderson said, "Rumor has it Graham is going out of business."

"That's hard to believe," Adkin said. "It's the most impressive factory I've seen yet."

"The problem is he has too many unsettled accounts," Sanderson said. "Too many people have not paid him for his good works. I've even heard he's mortgaged the factory to keep his head above water."

"Sounds as if he has too big a heart and has been taken advantage of," Adkin said, while shaking his head.

"There's a lesson there, Adkin." Sanderson said.

"I know, J.L.," Adkin said.

•••

As they approached a large bridge, Sanderson signalled Adkin to come alongside. As he did, they stopped their coaches.

"This is the Kansas River, and it meets the Missouri over there, Sanderson said, pointing to his right. "Once we're over the bridge, we're in Kansas and the beginning of the Great Plains, a frontier like few men get to see, let alone be a part of."

Adkin could see the look on his face and the glow in his eyes that only explorers would appreciate. Adkin could see the geat frontier in his mind's eye. He could feel it. He felt he could almost smell it, too.

"Tomorrow afternoon, Adkin, we'll be in Leavenworth.

Both men were grinning from ear to ear.

"Yee haw."

Shortly after noon on September 4, 1865, the coaches were hugging the rutted road along the southwest side of the Missouri as it made a gradual bend northward. Ahead, lay a fairly good-sized city.

"There she is," Sanderson yelled, smiling, pointing ahead. "It's headquarters, and my home, if you can say I have one."

They rolled into Leavenworth, and Adkin could see the town was definitely a supply town. The signs offered everything one would need on the trails heading into the west. As they rolled north, Sanderson finally pulled into a fenced yard with several barns, stables and livestock pens. They stopped.

Adkin could see several blocks ahead were two long, two-story buildings that had the look of barracks.

"That's Fort Leavenworth," Sanderson said, as he noticed Adkin staring at the expanse of buildings through the trees. "This is the western home of the Barlow and Sanderson Overland Stage Company."

A man ran out of the nearest barn heading right for them.

"Mister Sanderson, We've been expecting you. You said 13 days in your telegram, and here you are."

"It's good to be here, Earl," Sanderson said, as he stepped down from his coach seat. "Earl, this here is Mister Adkin Yates, the one I mentioned in my telegram."

"Pleased to meet you, Mister Yates," Earl said.

"Please, call me Adkin."

"Good enough ... Adkin," Earl said as he moved over to the team harnessed to Sanderson's Concord.

"We'll take care of these teams right away, Mister Sanderson," Earl said, then yelled, "Robert, get out here and help."

A young black man came running from the stables.

"Come, Adkin, I want you to meet the rest of the crew."

Sanderson hadn't said much about the actual operations of "Headquarters," as J.L. called it. He did mention a man called Tyler Ryan. Sanderson said he was one his drivers and could handle any animal ever used to pull a load.

Inside the front section of the barn they entered was a large office area walled off from the barn except for a large door at the back that was shut. There were stairs and a handrail on the south wall that led to a small doorway into a room above the office.

Several small table and shelves were situated around the office, with a couple of desks with one having two full baskets of paper leaflets.

"I see I need to pay some bills," Sanderson said, as he sat down at the desk with the full baskets.

A tall man then entered the front door. He was nearly as tall as Adkin, but more wiry. His face was weathered and browned from the sun. He wore a small-brimmed straw hat with the brim pulled down in the front and back. "He also wore leather chaps with pointed-toe boots. Adkin had first seen those in New Orleans. Carbeauneaux had called them cowboy boots.

"Hey Boss, good to have you back. The Concords look beautiful."

"Hello, Tyler," It's good to be home," Sanderson said. "This is Adkin Yates. Adkin this is Tyler Ryan. Tyler is our foreman here in Leavenworth, but you'll find out he can handle about anything comes his way."

"Pleased to meet you. Mister Yates, Ryan said, as he reached out his hand.

"Please, call me Adkin."

"Fine, a lot of folks just call me Ryan," he said with a smile as they shook hands.

"Lord knows we need good hands," Ryan said, as he looked back to Sanderson. "I think you did well hiring this man."

"Me, too," Sanderson said, relaxing a little because he wasn't sure how Tyler would accept the younger man. Tyler was 30 and had been born along the Missouri River in what is now Kansas City. And there would be another possible friction when Tyler finds out Adkin may become a partner in the business. Tyler had been one of Sanderson's first hires in 1860, as Tyler was an experienced teamster, horseman and wrangler.

"I'll cross that bridge when I get to it," Sanderson thought to himself.

"I'm sure glad you got back, Boss," Ryan said. "The Army has called a meeting day after tomorrow for freight bids. They didn't say what exactly, but rumor has it some big shots are going to need supplies for a caravan to a pow wow with some Indian tribes in central Kansas.

"Some kind of peace treaty or something," Ryan continued. "We've got six freighters ready to go, and our other one is down at Lawrence. Darrell should be back with that one tomorrow."

"Good. Do you know who the big wigs are?" Sanderson asked.

"None other than retired Major General William S. Harney, Commander of the Department of the West – and Indian Agent Colonel Jesse H. Leavenworth," Ryan said, with eyebrows raised and his hands on his hips.

"That is big," Sanderson said, looking toward Adkin. "Harney is well respected with the Indians, though he cusses like a sailor. And Jesse is the son of General Henry Leavenworth, whom this fort is named after.

"You're right, Tyler, something big is going down," Sanderson said. "Find out the exact time and which office so we can be there. All three of us will go to the meeting."

Sanderson showed Adkin around the buildings and their blacksmith's shop. Adkin thought he might convince Sanderson to allow him to make an anvil like his father made in England. It opens up so much more that can be constructed out of steel having the one end squared.

In each of the barns, the second floor space typically used for feed and hay storage, had been partitioned into living quarters with six to eight bunks in each with a stove for cooking and heating as well as tables and means to cook. They were essentially small cabins.

"Impressive," Adkin said.

"Well, we have mattresses and additional bedding in that warehouse building, and travel chests you can use to store your personal things," Sanderson said. "I'll have Tyler take you over there and get whatever you need and bring it back over to this barn here.

"Just pick out one of those empty bunks and make yourself at home," he added. "There won't be any more of those fancy hotels like we stayed at in St. Louis and Independence for some time."

At breakfast the next morning, the smell of bacon awoke Adkin. He was somewhat surprised to see Ryan at the stove with a large skillet in hand.

"Did you get a good sleep, Adkin?" Ryan asked.

"Yes sir, I sure did," Adkin said as he stood and stretched. "That mattress is much better than a simple bed roll on the ground or on a stagecoach bench."

"Don't get used to it," Ryan said, smiling. "If we get in on this caravan, we'll be back on the ground in a few days – won't be any room in the wagons.

"Wake up, Earl," Ryan hollered, as Adkin fished out a shirt from his new clothes chest, and stowed away his nightshirt.

"Does not Robert sleep here as well?" Adkin asked seeing the four other cots with a mattress and bedrolls, still tidy and neat.

"Oh, once in awhile," Ryan responded. "His folks live just down the street – he's only 16 – and he usually stays with them until we have several jobs to get ready for, like loading wagons or getting supplies together for a long haul."

Ryan volunteered three other "hands" lived there "once in awhile:" Darrell Holmes, Carl Long and Ray Dee Rinehart.

"Ray Dee's a squat little German, but strong as a mule and twice as contrary when he gets too much liquor in him," Ryan said. "He's a good hand when he's sober, though."

Adkin had met a "squat tough German," already, he thought to himself.

"Hope I get along better with this one than I did with Guderian," he mumbled under his breath.

"Carl is a genuine cowboy, come up from Texas a few years ago with a cattle drive to Kansas City – decided to stay.

"We also have hands that live on some of the stage routes – like the one from here to Fort Scott," Ryan said. "We also have routes such as Fort Larned, Kansas, to Fort Lyon, Colorado.

"Darrell, who lives here, is making a run to Lawrence, like I said, and Carl and Ray Dee probably stayed at the saloon last night," Ryan said. "They have an attraction to some of the ladies down there, and they just got their pay on the first – if you get my drift.

"They should be here soon to start their chores," Ryan said, as he put a tin plate with fried chunks of bacon and potatoes in front of Adkin. He then put some utensils on the table and a loaf of cold bread.

"I've had mine already. Eat up, enjoy," Ryan said, with a warm smile. "Coffee is in the pot, I've got to get over to the fort."

"Might as well have coffee until I can put my tea makings together," Adkin thought.

Shortly, Long and Rinehart came into the barn. Adkin introduced himself, saying he was a new hand hired by Sanderson in St. Louis.

"Nice to meet you, Yates," Long said, as he stretched out his hand.

"Please, call me Adkin."

"Humph," Rinehart grunted, as he also shook Adkin's hand.

"Oh boy, here we go again," Adkin thought to himself as Rinehart turned and went up the stairs mumbling something about needing coffee.

"Don't pay any attention to him," Long said. "He had a little too much to drink last night. He's a little grumpy right now, but he's a good hand.

"Where's Tyler?" Long asked, as he looked around.

"He saddled a horse and rode over to the fort," Adkin said. "Seems they're going to be bidding out wagons for a caravan for some kind of peace treaty with the Indians."

"Yeah, that was some of the talk at the saloon last night," Long said. "Seems some big shots with the government are already coming into Leavenworth – some soldiers were talking about it.

"I heard James R. Meade just arrived," Long continued. "He's a famous hunter and Indian Agent out west. Owns several ranches across Kansas."

Long was a medium-built man, looking around 40 or so, with a short brown beard with a few streaks of white in it. His hands were calloused and rough, probably been a driver or wrangler for a long time, Adkin was thinking.

"Is the Boss around?" Long asked, referring to Sanderson.

"I haven't seen him," Adkin said. "Does he stay above the office?"

"Sometimes. He also has a small house a few blocks away," Long responded.

Long went up the stairs saying he needed to change into some work clothes.

Adkin decided to go outside and walk around a bit. He noticed there were three different stables, one containing at least 20 head of horses, another with about a dozen mules and a separate corral with at least two dozen oxen – all white as clouds, with no distinguishing marks at all.

"He saw Rinehart making his way to the barn next to the oxen.

"Need any help?" Adkin yelled.

Surprised, Rinehart thought a moment and then replied, "Sure, I never have been one to refuse help."

The two grabbed pitchforks and started throwing grass into the hay feeders off the side of the corral. The oxen crowded up to the feeders, knowing it was time for breakfast.

"Someone likes all white oxen, it appears," Adkin tried to make small talk.

"Ugh," Rinehart coughed.

Once the feeder was filled with hay, Rinehart turned and said, "Thanks Yates – er I mean … Adkin is it?

"Yes."

Rinehart stared at him a bit, Adkin not knowing what he was thinking about.

"You see, a lot of caravans like to use oxen teams that are all alike," Rinehart explained. "It makes them identifiable at long distances – whose wagons they belong to.

"Plus, I think there is a little vanity for some who like to show off – especially if they have 5 to 10 yokes of oxen that are all white and spotted brown – things like that," Rinehart said.

"I see, it does sound impressive," Adkin said.

"You sound British," Rinehart said.

"Well, Adkin is Welsh for Adam – my mother's side – but I was born in the Midlands of England with a English father," Adkin responded.

"My mother was English, as well," Rinehart said, with a smile. "Welcome to the wild west."

"I'm living my dream," Adkin said.

"Me, too," Rinehart said, laughing. "It's a hell of a place."

Adkin was relieved he was communicating with the stoutly German. Rinehart seemed to be closer to his age than the others. Adkin guessed Rinehart to be about 25 years old. He was about 5-feet, 8- or 9-inches tall and weighed probably 200 pounds.

Though his work clothes were a little shabby, Rinehart's face took on a pleasant oval shape when he smiled and laughed.

...

Adkin helped out with the chores, watering and feeding the animals. About mid-morning, Sanderson came riding up on a big roan, dismounted in front of the office and tied the mare to the hitching post.

"Adkin, I need to talk with you," he said, as he motioned for Adkin to come over from the nearest outbuilding.

"Come, I have news for you," Sanderson said, as he put his arm on Adkin's shoulder and led him through the office door. "Have a seat."

"Well, I have a telegram right here from Barlow," he said, while waving it back and forth in the air. "Barlow is on board.

"You are now a minority partner in the company," he said. "Of course, it won't be official until you wire the money and the new shares are issued."

"I can't believe it, J.L., That's great news. I very much appreciate your and Barlow's faith in me," Adkin said. "I don't know what else to say. I feel like I'm dreaming, and I might awake and discover I'm in my bed at the Bull Inn in Olney."

"Well, we're going to work you hard Adkin, but I know you'll be just fine with that," Sanderson said. "Is Tyler back from the fort yet?"

"No, but Carl said they heard soldiers at the saloon last night say a Mister James Meade had rode into town yesterday?" Adkin said.

"Jim Meade you say?" Sanderson asked. "I've only met him once, but he is an agent for all the Wichita Indian Tribes.

"Quite a guy," he continued. "He came out here in '59 and settled out on the Saline River in the middle of Indian country, freighted hides and meat back to Leavenworth – and still has his scalp."

"By the way, here's your first month's pay – $30," Sanderson said.

"Thanks J.L. It's greatly appreciated."

"You've earned it, and you'll earn every dollar you make in this country," Sanderson said, with a chuckle.

Just at that moment, Ryan came riding into the yard.

"Tomorrow morning at 9," Ryan panted, as he dismounted and tied his horse up. "That's when they want to talk to everybody about their caravan needs."

"Rumor has it they're going to need to leave by September 15 for the Little Arkansas River for a pow wow with the major tribes of Kansas."

"That would include thousands of Indians," Sanderson said. "Of course, many of them live throughout the entire southwest plains – from Mexico to the Dakotas."

"Sounds big," Ryan said. "Wish we had more freight wagons."

"You ready to buy your own freighter, Adkin?" Sanderson asked, looking at Adkin.

"Not sure I have the money, J.L.," he responded. Ryan had a small frown on his face, as he was wondering why Adkin was getting such an offer.

"Tyler, I want you to tell the men the company will finance any wagon they want to buy," Sanderson said, beaming. "You can all pay it back free of interest. We need as many wagons as we can put together – and you know we can double tang them and beef up the teams to handle the loads.

"I believe we can all make enough on this one trip to set us up for real expansion," he added. "Go tell them now, and let Darrell know when he gets in, too."

"Wow, that's a unbelievable offer, J.L.," Adkin said, as Ryan bolted out the door yelling, "Men, get over here, now."

"I sent a telegram first thing to Barlow, and had to wait two hours for his reply – beside the one that was already there approving you becoming a partner," Sanderson said. "Barlow said he's heard the government is going to try this treaty with numerous tribes, and if it doesn't work out, all hell will break loose, because the Army has been given orders to wipe out the 'hostiles' if this doesn't work.

"And they have definite plans to build more forts to protect westward expansion," he added with a grin. "Barlow's bank has guaranteed the company a $10,000 line of credit to help us get in on this pow wow caravan.

"We could double or triple that investment if we play it right, and you men can make some extra cash for yourselves, as well.

"I was wondering if you would allow me a little more time before I tell the men you're a minority partner, Adkin," Sanderson said. "I think it will come easier for them after they get to know you a little better, especially Tyler. He's been with us the longest.

"That's your call J.L.," Adkin responded.

The men came crowding through the door.

"What's this about, Boss?" Long asked.

"The company will help finance wagons for each of you," Sanderson said. "There won't be any finance charge, but the catch is you will have to pay the company 25 percent of any load you haul until the wagon is paid off."

They looked back and forth to each other and Adkin. He was the first to speak up.

"I'm in," Adkin said.

"Me, too," Rinehart and Ryan piped up.

"I'm not sure about this," Long said. "I'm getting older, and I figured I only need to make a couple of more trips to Santa Fe, and I can buy myself a little farm near Kaw Point.

"I'm looking to settle down Boss," he added. "But I sincerely thank you."

"No problem, Carl," Sanderson said, as he patted Long on his back. "That's a royal plan. I'll help you any way I can, too."

"Well it's settled, get out there and find some wagons. Remember, a good used wagon will get you there and there's a prospect you'll be able to sell it and pay it off in one trip – and make some money, too," Sanderson said.

•••

The room was full of teamsters, merchants and caravan organizers all sitting in chairs that were lined up like those in a large courtroom. A long table was against the far wall with several empty chairs behind it.

"Ah-ten-hut!" A young soldier yelled near a door in the back corner of the room as it swung open.

In marched several officers and men in old uniforms with medals adorning their breasts and civilians.

One of the officers walked to the center of the table as the others took a seat behind it on each side of him.

"Gentlemen, could I have your attention, please. I'm Commander Major General Samuel R. Curtis, and I have several gentlemen and commissioners to introduce to you," Curtis said. "Over here, we have Mister James R. Meade of Towanda, Kansas, Indian Agent for the U.S. Department of the West; next to him is Brevet Major General John B. Sanborn, Commander of the Upper Arkansas District; Colonel Jesse H. Leavenworth, Indian Agent of the Kiowas and Comanches in the Indian Territory; Major General William S. Harney, Commander of the Department of the West; Thomas Murphy, Commissioner of Indian Affairs and Indian Affairs Commissioner James Steele.

"I would like to turn this meeting over to Brevet Major General William S. Harney," Curtis said.

"Gentlemen, The Department of Indians Affairs has arranged a meeting of numerous plains tribes in the pursuit of a peace treaty with the Indians," Harney said loudly.

There were some mumblings and foot shuffling among those in the crowded room.

"This meeting is scheduled to occur on the banks of the Little Arkansas River just north of its confluence into the Arkansas – in Sedgwick County," Harney continued. "Others representing the Indian Affairs Commission will meet us there, including Brigadier General Christopher "Kit" Carson and Santa Fe trader William W. Bent.

"This meeting will occur during the first or second week of October," Harney concluded.

Men in the crowd started whispering and jabbering among each other.

"That's more than 200 miles," Sanderson whispered to his men, all realizing that could be a 15- to 20-day trip, depending on the size of the caravan.

"Gentlemen," Harney interrupted. "Our purpose is to ask you for bids – and there should be enough damn work to enjoin the services of most of you."

All mumbling ceased, as Harney's bark quieted the room.

He was a domineering man, and Adkin guessed he was at least 6-feet, 4-inches tall with a big barreled chest and wide shoulders. His wavy white hair and a face full of white mustache and beard demanded attention.

His large round head was encapsulated by white hair which was in stark contrast to his deep blue uniform coat with 18 parallel brass buttons in front with black velvet sleeve cuffs and neck collar. Each shoulder carried the brass rectangular box enclosing two brass stars.

He was the most impressive man Adkin had met yet in America. Adkin later learned Harney was 65 years old, a former cavalry officer and a vicious Indian fighter.

Meade, spoke up and said rather than using his own trail through El Dorado to Towanda, which would reduce the trip by two or three days, it was not usually travelled by large freight wagons.

He said the caravan could follow the Santa Fe Trail to just south of Cottonwood Crossing at a place called Turkey Creek, then head south to reach the Little Arkansas River and down to about six miles north of its mouth where it flowed into the Arkansas River.

The crowd was told the U.S. Army would be transporting at least 20 troop wagons and three ambulances, and the Army would also be providing those troops most of their provisions, However, the caravan would need an additional 300,000 pounds of provisions and goods.

"We're going to need everything from basic foodstuffs to ammunition and powder," Leavenworth said.

"Sounds like they're going to war instead of a peace treaty pow wow," Ryan said. "That'll require about 60 to 70 wagons – fully loaded."

"Gentlemen, here is a pile of lists of the various goods we will need for the caravan," Harney said, pointing to a stack of papers at the end of the table.

Sensing the entire crowd may be feeling like Ryan, Meade spoke up, "Gentlemen, we're attempting to eliminate the bloodshed that has permeated the plains since the war's end. Indian raids have increased in relation to the numbers of settlers escaping the ruins of their homelands during the war who have decided to move west."

"We keep intruding on the Indians' hunting lands and removing them from their traditional seasonal settlements," Leavenworth interjected. "If we can reach a mutual agreement with their concerns, it can save many lives."

There was still muttering among those being asked to help with this meeting; many knowing the Indians could be the most ruthless murderers on earth. Some of them would probably never consider peace with the Indians.

"We would like to have your available services and costs submitted to us in two days," Harney said, as several grumbled about the shortness of time to get their bids put together.

"We want to depart September 15th," he added.

It was September 6, 1865.

Adkin was stunned. He realized he had only left England 68 days ago, and in another nine days, he would be easing down the Santa Fe Trail as a participant in a caravan headed into an adventure that will expose them all to thousands of wild Indians.

"Lord, I will always hold you close to my heart," Adkin said to himself, as a big smile spread across his face.

•••

Once Sanderson and his men got back to the office, they huddled over the list of the Army's caravan needs.

"We can bid the new coaches – says here, 'means of passage for officers and commissioners,'" Sanderson said, as he scribbled on a piece of ledger paper. "Of course, we'll bid goods that we can get discounts on from our friends.

"And men, if there are things you want to purchase for resale, make sure your list it kept separately from the company's purchases for Army supplies. We'll make sure our accounting is inscrutable," he added. "Make sure you don't duplicate anything between each other – work together."

Sanderson made out lists of various goods and supplies and gave each of the men one of them, and told them to head out and negotiate the best prices they could get from area merchants for those particular items.

"Adkin, you and I will go look for some more horses and mules. We'll have to double tang at least three loads, so that will mean pulling around 10,000 to 12,000 pounds behind a team," Sanderson said. "Let's get going men, yee haw."

The following day Sanderson submitted their bid at the fort, while Ryan huddled together with Adkin, Rinehart and Holmes – Holmes had returned the day before from Lawrence – to report on purchasing personal wagons.

There were no real wagon factories in Leavenworth, but several area manufacturers had sales yards with inventories of used wagons and even new models available.

"Men, I stopped by Studebaker Brother's wagon yard, yesterday, and told their manager what I was looking for and about the opportunity the company is giving us," Ryan said. "And he suggested we come in together, and he'd give us a big discount if they can meet all our needs and buy all the wagons from him.

"I propose we put our ideas together and check out several wagon yards to see where we can get the best deal," he continued.

"Sound good to me, Tyler," Rinehart said.

"Me, too," Holmes said, with the other two nodding assent.'

Besides the Studebaker Brothers, which built their wagons in Great Bend, Kansas, on the Santa Fe Trail and were said to handle the rough trail better than some; their was a Young yard, some wagons offered by Murphy and wagons by Espenschied, also of St. Louis, had a local yard.

After several days, the men settled on Studebakers. Ryan and Holmes found used wagons they liked and were determined the wagons would make the haul and still be in good enough shape to sell them for a profit after the caravan reached the treaty sight.

Rinehart and Adkin decided to gamble and purchase brand new wagons, even though they were $160 each. The Studebakers had triangulated uprights with additionals bracing, and they had nearly straight or vertical ends, which made them ideally suited to tandem hookups. They also had sidewalls at 38 inches – higher than most others

The new wagons they had on hand in the yard had 5-inch axles with a 12-feet long beds, and were rated to haul 8,000 pounds each.

"We can lease the company's oxen – at least a 12-yoke team – and work them together," Rinehart said to Adkin. He also pointed out the bid for hauling was by the hundred-weight, and the more one can get in a wagon, the more money made, especially if the two are pulled in tandem.

Adkin was in.

"Let's do it, Ray Dee," Adkin said reaching out his hand.

"Done, Adkin," Rinehart said with a big smile while pumping Adkin's arm.

The men started working together to see who was going to make personal investments of supplies for resale.

"I'm buying $50 worth of coffee," Rinehart said. "You can never have too much coffee. What about you Tyler?"

"I'm thinking about sugar or flour," Ryan said.

"I was wanting to buy about $40 worth of whisky," Holmes said.

"Boss won't like that, Darrell, if you're planning to sell it to the Indians," Ryan said. "Or the troops, for that matter."

"Yeah, you're probably right," Holmes said. "And you, Adkin?"

"I was wanting to have items to sell to the Indians, or to trade with them," he said, sheepishly. "But I'm not sure exactly what that should be."

"That's a good idea Adkin," Ryan spoke out. "They don't have a lot of money, but you could bring back hides and furs – that could make big bucks back here."

"They like calicos, colorful cotton cloth, beads, iron knives and iron for arrowheads, things like that," Rinehart interrupted. "I'll pitch in $40 with you, if that's OK with you."

"Will you help me pick out what we need, Ray Dee?" Adkin asked.

"Sure."

"Also, I'm think about buying myself a sidearm," Adkin said.

"We can all help you with that one," Ryan said, while the others laughed and Rinehart said, "It wouldn't hurt to have one where we're going."

•••

On September 10, the Barlow and Sanderson Overland Stage Company received notice from two soldiers on horseback its bid for caravan services had been accepted.

The letter of approval noted: "Both Concord stagecoaches will be utilized with the provision each coach will be driven by a Barlow and Sanderson Overland Stage Company employee, while the U.S. Army will provide an armed guard riding each coach."

The letter also noted five other merchants and operators were accepted, and gave notice to all to be ready to pull out at noon September 15 from the fort's yard with all wagons – 60 in all – fully loaded and ready to roll.

"We've got five days to fill these orders gentlemen," Sanderson said. "Holmes, you and Long need to head out right away to pick up these supplies in Westport, there's not enough in Leavenworth.

"You should be able to make it in four days at worst," he continued. "The rest of you need to start pulling these wagons around picking up all the supplies we've contracted for here. That includes you, Earl and Robert.

"It's all hands on deck for the next five days," Sanderson added. "And no staying over at the saloon. We have to be at it by daybreak each day."

Everybody took off with their appointed lists and wagons.

As one of the wagons came back to the yard, Earl and Robert would get to work sorting and stacking the supplies with precision. Robert would list the supplies and number of crates or bags as Robert shouted out the inventory.

"Four cases of firing caps. Fifteen bags of corn … " he would yell, as he kept fitting the items into the smallest space available.

Adkin and Rinehart filled nearly a quarter of one of their wagons with their personal purchases; not only the colorful cloths and calicos, but with all kinds of knives and numerous tools, like several hand saws, hatchets, axes, hammers, nails and even a large foot-powered grinding stone with a wooden stool attached.

They had spent $40 each and hoped to double their investments. Of course, this meant they would not be earning the hauling rate of a full load with one wagon. But both the young men were full of adventure with no thoughts of failure. They just hoped the Army book keepers didn't estimate the weight of their personal goods too high.

•••

After getting Army approval of the loads – each wagon was inspected and lists of the goods were confirmed, Sanderson told his men he had made a deal with them to be fed by Russell, Majors & Company. Their outfit would be the largest hauler on this caravan, providing 35 wagons and one ambulance – besides the Army ambulance – and two chuckwagons. The Army also was going to provide two chuckwagons to feed their troops.

"Remember, men, help out and volunteer with the hunting parties," Sanderson said. "I told Russell we'd help put meat in the pot during the trip so he'd give us a good contract for cooking and providing other particulars."

The Barlow-Sanderson line had to hire six additional men to be teamsters and bullocks – or bullwhackers – to help with the oxen, mules and horses. All the draft animals had been refitted with shoes where needed, including the oxen.

"We'll be lining up behind their train, which puts our wagons about midway in the caravan," he continued. "The Army's wagons will be split up with half leading and the others bringing up the rear."

The entire caravan would probably include a total of 80 to 90 wagons when they eventually hit the trail, according to Sanderson, who admitted this was his first large foray into freight hauling.

"But, this is helping us expand," Sanderson said. "I've already ordered four more stagecoaches for what we want to do in Colorado. And if we pull this off, we should be able to order four more when we get back."

•••

A soft, cool breeze was coming in off the Missouri River on the morning of September 15, 1865. Adkin had noticed the mornings were getting more fall-like, yet the days were still warm, but not nearly as uncomfortable as it was in Florida and New Orleans.

He couldn't believe the amount of wagons, animals and men surrounding the fort positioned in its large grassy fields. Before he had mounted one of the new Concords, Ryan had told him, "I've seen caravans on the Santa Fe Trail that included 150 wagons – near twice this size."

A single soldier approached Sanderson shortly before noon and asked him and Adkin to follow him with their Concords to the front of the adminstration building to pick up their passengers.

Several men and a few soldiers were walking down to the front road on a cobblestone walkway.

Harney, Steele and Murphy loaded into Sanderson's coach, while Meade, Leavenworth and Sanborn got into Adkin's Concord.

A soldier with a breechloader rifle, a holstered revolver and a battle sword each climbed up to the driver's seats and introduced themselves to Adkin and Sanderson.

The coaches were led by the horseback soldier to the front of the caravan. Harney opened the door on Sanderson's coach, leaned out on the step of the coach and signaled about 20 mounted soldiers with a wave.

"Let's get this sumbitch rolling, Captain," he bellowed.

One of the mounted soldiers raised a bugle and blew a series of blasts that gave Adkin goosebumps.

"We're on our way to the Santa Fe," Adkin said to himself.

•••

It didn't take long until the young army soldier riding shotgun with Adkin began talking. He was a tall lanky man who didn't look much older than Adkin, yet he had a look in his dark brown eyes that belied his life's experiences.

"The name's Lieutenant Samuel Oscar Phillips," he said, as he offered his hand to Adkin.

"Adkin Yates – you can call me Adkin, Lieutenant,' he said as he shook the man's hand. The man had a strong wiry grip and only one side of his mouth smiled, but it seemed genuine. "Pleased to make your acquaintance."

The two made small talk for a few miles, and Phillips pried.

"You sound British," he said.

"Yes, I'm from a small village north of London, England," Adkin said.

Both smiled.

Adkin asked Phillips how long he had been in the Army.

Phillips went on to explain he had joined the Union Army when he had just barely turned 17 earlier that year.

"My grandfather and his father-in-law fought the British – no offense – in the Revolutionary War," Phillips said. "I always wanted to be in the military.

"I was raised in Perry County, Ohio, and after enlisting, I was assigned to the Ohio Heavy Artillery Regiment, Company K," Phillips continued. "We made our way down to Tennessee, fighting several skirmishes along the way.

"The Rebs were scattering with rumors of losses at several battle sites, but we pushed through," he continued. "We received erroneous scouting reports near Knoxville that indicated the Rebs had abandoned an armory stockpile, and we marched right into an ambush.

"They had 12 cannon hidden under brush piles on the hill behind the armory, and they opened up on us at close range," Phillips said, with a sad look on his face. "We lost a lot of men that first volley and officers were screaming, 'Retreat, retreat.'"

"We were running back to a tree line when something caught me in the right thigh, and I stumbled and fell. I was able to crawl though and made it into the trees.

"I had been hit with chain shrapnel, but it fortunately wasn't much more than a flesh wound," Phillips said. "We were able to move up our cannon and unleashed return fire until dark.

"By morning, our officers had worked up a circular offensive when an Army scout rode up on horseback and told us the war was over.

"As we tried to call out to the Rebs under a white flag, we discovered they had hightailed it out of there during the night.

"It was June 3 – just 15 weeks ago," he continued. "My leg was starting to fester a little, and we went into Knoxville and they took us wounded to the local hospital where our doctor could assist us.

"I was treated for an abscess," Phillips said matter-of-factly. "We stayed there another day and refreshed our supplies and made haste to return north to Ohio. On the next day, an official team of officers wearing the new Army Uniforms of the United States intercepted us and gave us details of the war's end.

"Seems the Rebs' President Jefferson Davis was captured on May 10 and their Departments of Florida and South Georgia, commanded by Confederate Major General Samuel Jones, surrendered the same day – and essentially, it ended the war, because Lee had also surrendered at Appomattox," Phillips said. "I couldn't help but shed a tear over my comrades that had died three days earlier – even though hostilities supposedly had ended. It would be very hard on their families knowing that, as well.

"They died in spite of the fact we had already won that damn war," Phillips said, as he stared down at his boots. "I'm goin' turn 19 in January."

An Englishman's Adventures on the Santa Fe Trail (1865-1889)

"Well, Lieutenant, how did you end up at Fort Leavenworth?" Adkin asked. "I would think after being wounded by shrapnel, you would want to get home to security and family."

Phillips then looked up at Adkin, and with that crooked smile, said, "I'm full of adventure Adkin. I've always wanted to see the west, and when those Army officers offered all of us in the company enlistment bonuses to stay in the new U.S. Army – I volunteered and was promoted to Lieutenant."

Adkin smiled at Phillips, knowing exactly how Lieutenant Phillips was looking at the world. He felt an immediate bond with the 18-year-old Civil War veteran.

Adkin was only too happy to tell Phillips his dreams and how he had been longing for the war to also end – but because it meant he could then leave England on his own adventure.

•••

The first night, the train made camp about 20 miles out of Leavenworth. The officials and several officers and troops set up their own camps about 50 yards from where Adkin and Sanderson parked the Concords and hobbled their teams. The Barlow and Sanderson men made their way to their camp as soon as they took care of their animals.

The main Army camps were set at the head and tail of the train.

Adkin learned from Sanderson they were traveling the "Fort Riley Military Road" trail to Topeka and then south to the Santa Fe Trail.

Fort Riley was opened in 1853, whereas Fort Leavenworth had been established in 1827, just a few years after Becknell opened the famed trading route to Mexico and the vast riches of the west.

Fort Riley was formed at a site between the Oregon trail which passed to its north and the Santa Fe Trail which headed west some miles south of the fort. It housed U.S. Army Cavalry troops for quick responses to threats along either of the great trails.

The government wanted to help protect the eastern traders from hostiles, which included Indians, bandits and "renegades of all sorts."

The Fort Riley Military Road intercepted the Santa Fe near a place called Wilmington, which was just west of several stagecoach stations and the Dragoon Creek Crossing on the Santa Fe.

It was on the second day when a voice inside the coach yelled up at Adkin and Phillips.

"Hey Lieutenant, could I take your seat for a while?"

Phillips looked down to his left and said, "Of course Mister Meade," then signaled Adkin to stop by raising his hand.

Phillips jumped down, and Meade crawled up on the seat next to Adkin.

"Jim Meade, young man, and your name is ?"

"Adkin Yates. Pleased to make your acquaintance."

"Are you British, Yates?"

"Why, yes sir – British," Adkin said. "I've only been in your wonderful country for about eight weeks, sir."

"Grand, sounds as if you like it here so far," Meade said quizzically.

"Yes sir. It's been a dream of mine since I was 13 years old to travel the Santa Fe Trail," Adkin said, smiling.

"And how old are you now, if I may ask?"

"Turned 19 on July 30."

"Great, we need you young, strong people to help us tame this part of the world," Meade said, smiling. "It's so vast and dangerous, but it's also the greatest place on Earth.

"But then, I am wholly biased," he added with a big laugh.

Meade had an average build with narrow shoulders, but his face and eyes could be very stern until he flashed a genuine smile, and the crow's feet blossomed around his brown eyes. His hair was light brown and wavy, but not as blonde as Adkin's. He had a high forehead and a small mustache on his upper lip.

Adkin found out later Meade was only 31 years old himself, but he had also lived a lot of life since coming to Kansas from Iowa where he was raised on the banks of the Mississippi River.

He learned Meade took off for Kansas in 1859, one day after his 23rd birthday. He was also looking for adventure, for he didn't want to be a farmer and a preacher, as was his father. But his arrival in Kansas left him wondering, initially, what he had gotten himself into.

"My feelings on first setting foot on the soil of Kansas were various," Meade told Adkin. "We had a feeling of insecurity; that we had left the land of law and order and got among outlaws and desperados.

"This feeling, however, wore away soon," Meade continued. "I felt we had entered a land where an important scene in my life's history was to be enacted out and – perhaps my lot cast for life."

"I feel the same way, Mister Meade," Adkin said. "I feel this land is my lot as well."

"Please, Yates, call me Jim."

"Feel free to call me Adkin."

"I prefer Yates, the way it rolls off my tongue," Meade said, smiling. "That's if you don't mind."

"Fine with me."

When Meade left Iowa, he told Adkin he had one wagon with a team, a horse and a few companions.

An Englishman's Adventures on the Santa Fe Trail (1865-1889)

A week after they had camped outside of Fort Leavenworth in early June, Meade said, "The young men who had come with me got homesick and wanted to see their mammas."

They divided the teams and what game and furs they had harvested and left for home.

"But I was much too delighted with the new and beautiful country to think of returning and set out to see something more of it."

Meade also explained to Adkin he didn't like sitting in the stuffy coach even though he said it was much more comfortable than a normal wagon – or an ambulance.

"I love the wind in my face and the smell of Mother Nature in my nostrils," he said, more than once during the trek.

...

Late on the third day, they camped about 2 miles west of a small town named Topeka after an Indian term meaning "where we dug potatoes." It had been named the state capital in 1862 after Kansas had become a state the year before. During the war, it had been in the territory known as "Bleeding Kansas."

It was also the site where the trail headed due west to Fort Riley, though they would traverse a trail southwest to Wilmington.

That night, Adkin filled in Sanderson on his talks with Meade. Sanderson had noticed Meade spending a lot of time in the driver's bench visiting with Adkin.

"He's a brilliant man,"

Sanderson said. "He's lived and hunted alone on the upper Saline River where no white man has ever hunted – and lived to not only tell about it, but made a good living at it and made friends with numerous tribes throughout Kansas. He now owns a ranch up there west of Salina called Meade's Ranch. He also owns ranches and trading posts in Burlingame and Towanda, where he is the local postmaster.

"I've even heard he's filed on lands in the Osage Trust Lands near where we're going," Sanderson continued. "Some say he and others are going to build a new town in there somewhere.

"You should feel honored he has taken a liking to you, Adkin, He is a man of his word, and he knows what's going on in this part of the country as well as most," he added. "I would feel free to tell him about our stagecoach expansion plans and see if he has any advice – you know like staging locations, trails, where the Indians will leave us alone – things like that."

After breakfast on the fourth day, Meade spoke up to those near their dying campfire.

"General Harney has asked me to put a couple of hunting parties together," Meade said. "Would you like to go, Yates? Any of you men want to participate, as well?"

More than a dozen men threw their arms in the air, and Meade chuckled.

"I don't blame you all, but we only need about five men per party," he said, then started pointing at others and asking if they had a ride. He then turned to Phillips and said, "Lieutenant, go fetch three saddled mounts with rifle scabbards and lariats – for me, Yates … and yourself."

"Yes sir!" Phillips shouted, as he took off behind the coaches.

"Get your things together men, we'll set off in 15 minutes," Meade yelled. He turned to Adkin, "Hey Yates, you might wear that new pistol you told me about, never know what you might encounter over the next hill."

"He's talking about wild-ass Indians," Sanderson whispered to Adkin, as Adkin pulled his Sharp's rifle out of his bag along with a western style gun belt holstering a used Colt 1860 Army percussion pistol in .44 caliber. He paid $9 for the complete package from a gunsmith in Leavenworth.

He also grabbed a few boxes of bullets, firing caps and paper cartridges for the Colt.

Sanderson told one of the hired teamsters to drive Ryan's team while Ryan moved over to handle the Concord.

As the hunting party started gathering, the train headed out again with dust rising for nearly half a mile into a willowy sky just turning soft blue in the west. Wagons were five abreast at some points, trying to avoid the swirling dust.

•••

Meade's party, including Adkin and Lieutenant Phillips, headed northwest from the trail, while the others took off south. Within minutes, the parties had disappeared out of sight, the gentle rolling hills belying the appearance of flatness. Adkin was amazed how in just under a mile, everything behind them seemed to have completely fell off the earth.

They rode outward for about three or four miles in Adkin's estimate, with rolling hills of beautiful buffalo grass turning somewhat gold near the tops. There were also some outcroppings of white limestone that easily caught the eye at a great distance.

They didn't gallop, but just eased along in a walking gait. Meade was eyeing every direction as they went along, as well as searching the ground for sign when they crossed every game trail.

As they approached a creek line that could be discerned by the trees and bushes that snaked along it's life of water, Meade held up his hand, motioning them to stop.

"You men go around to the east of that bowl," Meade said, pointing ahead toward the creek. "You two come with me."

As Meade, Adkin and Lieutenant Phillips moved off to their left, Meade stared intently into the willows and elms that surrounded the "bowl" he had pointed at.

He pulled up the reins sharply on his mount and pointed ahead.

"Dismount," he said, adding, "There is several deer in there and they're getting ready to bolt. Pull out those rifles now."

Meade had his out and was aiming it across his saddle before the others had their's fully removed from their scabbards.

Boom.

Meade released a shot that startled Adkin.

"Shoot," Meade said as he readied his rifle for another shot. Five or six deer shot out of the trees headed north, quartering away from them.

Several other rifles from the other two in the party rang out as they shot, also. Adkin brought his sight around on the lead buck which was near 150 yards away and squeezed the trigger. The animal stumbled and fell after four of five more feeble bounds.

Boom.

Lieutenant Phillips released a volley just as Adkin's deer was falling.

"I got 'er," Phillips shouted, with a huge grin. He had dropped a doe at the rear as she came out of the brush.

"Good shooting men," Meade said. "Let's go see what we got."

As the neared the trees and plum bushes from the west, there were two more quick shots, indicating two men had discharged their weapons almost simultaneously. The horses whinnied and jumped at the nearness of the shots.

Once the men started riding over to the animals they had dropped, Adkin realized Meade had killed a big buck, just at the edge of the bowl. Adkin never saw it as he was still pulling his rifle from its scabbard when Meade shot.

He now realized why Meade had such a reputation as a great hunter – he was quick and deadly. Adkin realized he was going to have to practice more than what little he had in Leavenworth with Ryan and Rinehart.

Adkin's buck was about 50 yards out into the tall flowing buffalo grass and he tied a rope around it's head and started dragging it back to the trees.

In all, within only a few minutes, they had harvested two bucks, three does and two turkeys – the men from the other party had shot the turkeys when they got into the brush.

It didn't take long for the men to field dress their game under the guidance of Meade, who showed them a quick and easy way to gut them. They then tied the deer over the backs of their horses behind their saddles.

"Well men, You have shown yourselves to be not only good hunters, but men who have shown an ability to use your time efficiently, as well," Meade said, laughing. "Let's catch up with the caravan."

They slowly moved off to the southwest chattering like school boys full of pure enjoyment.

•••

They were well greeted once they caught up with the train. Several soldiers, teamsters and bullwhackers helped unload the animals and throw them in the small drays being pulled by the chuckwagons. They also helped with skinning and butchering while cooks bellowed orders

"Well, I'll be God damned," Harney shouted loudly from the window of his stagecoach. "You sumbitches are full of piss and vinegar alright. I'm ready for some fresh venison this evenin'."

The man cusses worse than the old salts Adkin had met at sea and at the various docks he had visited.

Sanderson told Adkin to go ahead and ride horseback the rest of the afternoon, as Ryan was just settling in driving the Concord team. Horses can get used to new drivers, but it takes a little time for them to adjust to new voices and the way a driver handles the reins.

"Well, that didn't take long," Sanderson said, as Adkin rode alongside Sanderson's coach. "You harvested all that and are back by 3 – can't beat that."

"That Meade is some shot," Adkin said. "He was off his horse, aiming and killing a buck before I could get my rifle out of its scabbard."

"I told you," Sanderson said, smiling. "Did you bag anything?"

"Yes, I got the smaller buck, but at least I hit him – he was bounding away, and I was afraid I'd miss, especially since Meade was standing there reloading and watching me."

"Well, good for you."

"By the way, Meade said if we want to start stagecoach business to Pueblo, we should definitely use the Mountain Route of the Santa Fe Trail to Bent's Fort – or Fort Wise? – at La Junta, Colorado? And then there is a fairly decent trail along the Arkansas River to Pueblo," Adkin said.

"I was thinking that myself, but if Meade says that's the way, I'm definitely agreeable," Sanderson said, smiling.

The hunting party that headed out southward that morning didn't arrive until sundown, just as the caravan was halting and gathering wagons and animals together. But they were dragging a travois made of rough-hewn cedar poles behind one of the horses. Adkin had heard of an Indian travois, but had never seen one.

It was carrying a large gutted buffalo.

The animal was more amazing than Adkin had dreamed. He went up to it while all nearby were talking and laughing. Its head was absolutely huge – looking as if it could weigh more than a hundred pounds alone. And with its massive horns, it was, indeed, a terrifying animal. Its shoulders were gigantic, and he couldn't help but reach out and gently touch its curly mane.

He could only imagine the fear one would have if it was charging you – as he had heard they would do if given the opportunity.

"Whew," Adkin exhaled softly, as a shiver went through his whole body.

The party also brought in four deer, two antelope and six turkeys. Several of the cooks – Army and company cooks – were shouting orders as men were butchering and laughing.

"Cookie, break out a ration of brandy for the men," Harney shouted at the Sergeant who was apparently the head Army cook.

"A ration is one cup of brandy for each man," Sanderson explained to Adkin. "If he's in a real good mood, he'll break out a ration of whisky for the men. That's one coffee cup full of whisky. I've heard Harney has two wagons completely full of barrels of just whisky."

"You know what J.L.? I think I'll have a brandy on this grand day," Adkin said, with a chuckle. "It's been a magnificent day, indeed."

"I'll drink to that," Sanderson said, slapping Adkin on the back.

"You think it's possible I could try some of that buffalo meat?" Adkin asked.

"You bet, partner."

As soon as he spoke, Sanderson realized Ryan was standing there, and Ryan gave Sanderson a puzzled look. He knew he was going to have to tell Ryan and the rest of his crew about Adkin's status with the company.

"First thing in the morning," Sanderson told himself, not wanting to dampen anyone's merriment for the evening. He wasn't sure how Ryan would take it but it had to be aired one way or another.

As the men were returning their tin breakfast plates to the chuckwagon. Sanderson took Ryan to the side and asked him if he would assemble the Barlow and Sanderson men together for a meeting.

In a few moments, Sanderson was standing behind one of the Concords.

"Gather 'round men," Sanderson said. "I know some of you are on contract for this caravan, and some are company men, but I wanted all of you to hear this.

"Adkin Yates, here, asked to buy into the company, and Barlow and I approved his request," Sanderson said. "He is now an official minority partner of the Barlow and Sanderson Overland Stage Company. He still follows order from me or Barlow, and he has not been promoted to be a supervisor over anyone.

"I want you to know, we have a lot of faith in Adkin's abilities, as a blacksmith and since he was raised in a carriage business which his father owns in England.

He is going to help us set up stage stations to expand our services to Colorado, and possibly, even to California – if everything works out."

"But, he is still just a hand like anybody else," Sanderson said, looking around at his men. "Any questions?"

No one said a word, though they were looking back and forth at each other.

"Well. I say congratulations Adkin," Long said, reaching out his hand to Adkin. "If you're that crazy to want to be a part of this crew, you're okay with me."

Several laughed and someone said, "You must have mental problems."

Most congratulated Adkin and most were laughing. Ryan shook hands with Adkin and said congratulations, too, but he then turned and quietly walked away.

"Well, let's get rolling," Sanderson shouted, as men headed off to their wagons and teams.

Meade had slipped up on the meeting as he was preparing to load his group in the Concord.

"Couldn't help but overhear what you were telling your men, J.L.," Meade said. "My feelings are you made a good choice in hooking up with this young man – he appears to be an honest and good man."

"Thanks, Jim, I feel the same way," Sanderson responded.

"All aboard, let's get going," Meade yelled. "We should be in Wilmington by dark."

The following morning, they were, again, officially on the Santa Fe Trail headed westward. Adkin still felt as if he were in a wonderful dream. The trail was very wide in some places with wagon ruts in the sandstone or grasslands five- to six-wagons wide in some areas.

At mid-day, they passed another wagon train of about 50 wagons being pulled almost exclusively by mules heading to Westport Landing's docks in Kansas City. They were returning from Santa Fe and had at least 20 wagons completely loaded with salted buffalo and elk hides.

"We probably won't see many more large caravans returning eastward from now on," Sanderson told Adkin that night at their campfire. "It's late in the season and most of the big trains of trade goods finish up before winter sets in. There are still small trains of traders but most prefer to travel in the large caravans during the summer for safety reasons, naturally. Plus, the Army will send troops with the larger caravans, too."

That night, Adkin and most of the camp was awaken with several gunshots ringing out, followed by shouting and three or four more shots booming into the darkness.

Men started jumping up out of their bedrolls and reaching for various pieces of clothing and guns. Adkin saw one man near the campfire hopping on one booted foot while trying to hold his other boot in one hand and his rifle in the other. The man fell down and almost landed in the campfire embers.

An Englishman's Adventures on the Santa Fe Trail (1865-1889)

"What the hell is going on Captain?" Harney yelled from the commissioners' tent.

"Sir, it looks like Indians have stolen some mules from Robert's teams," the officer shouted. "There were three or four of them."

Another soldier ran up to Harney and panted, "A boy, young Parkinson, was seriously injured General – not by the Indians, it happened when several other mules stomped him when they were trying to get out of their hobbles.

"He was trying to calm them," the soldier said. "He's bad hurt, General."

"Get the God damn doctor over there, Captain," Harney barked.

Adkin and others ran over to where several men were kneeling around a body writhing on the ground moaning.

"Hold him down," someone said. "Easy son – take it easy. The Doc is on his way."

Adkin looked over the man's shoulder and saw the large open wound on the boy's forehead. The gash was about 4-inches wide starting just above his eyes and went back over his left ear. The skull was crushed open and tissue behind the bone could be seen in the dim light. Several men with torches and lanterns had crowded around the kneeling men.

Adkin immediately flashed back to seeing his little Eliza lying lifeless in the stable yard at the Bull Inn. A wave of heart-wrenching pain shivered through him.

"He can't live with that wound," Adkin silently thought to himself.

The boy was still groaning, but stopped twitching and softly whimpered, "Pa... Pa...?"

The boy went limp and his head rolled to the side with his eyes wide open, staring into the netherlands.

He was dead.

"Where is he?" a panicked voice shrieked from the crowd.

"He's over here, Parkinson."

The men parted as Daniel Parkinson Sr. dropped to his knees near the body of his 15-year-old son. The man lifted him to his cheek and started hugging him and crying, "No, no, God no."

One of the other teamsters was telling everyone they had heard the mules crying out and three or four headed over to check them and see what was going on, thinking maybe it was wolves or a mountain lion. That's when they saw three or four mounted Indians start whooping and pulling several mules away from camp with lariats, disappearing into the darkness. The men fired several rounds at them to no avail.

The man said Parkinson Jr. was trying to calm the other mules when he got caught between a couple of them and they knocked him to the ground. They were rearing up their hobbled front legs and trying to bust free.

The doctor arrived with his ambulance and several men had to pull Parkinson from his son and place the boy's body in the wagon.

Adkin helped gently pry Parkinson Sr.'s hands from his boy and stood him up looking into the anguish in the man's teary eyes. Instinctively, Adkin hugged the man as he burst into wailing cries.

"God, don't take my boy," he sobbed.

The pain of Adkin's own memories shot through him like a bolt of lightning through his heart. Silent tears ran down Adkin's cheeks as he held the shaking man.

Most of the men slowly turned to leave the scene in total quietness. Someone in the dark muttered, "Those filthy Indians are to blame. We should hunt them down and kill the bastards."

Several others grunted their assent.

Parkinson Sr. later made the decision to wait until they reached Cottonwood Crossing in order to bury his son "in some kind of semblance of civilization."

As they neared Council Grove the next afternoon, an Army messenger was riding through the wagons telling everyone the caravan would be forming three wagon circles with about 30 wagons per circle for the night's camp. And that they could park double wide if desired, but there was one important stipulation.

"Make sure all your animals are hobbled inside the circles," the soldier shouted. "The general doesn't want to see one ox, mule or horse outside that circle. Understand?"

After watching all those teams and wagons form three huge circles and start unharnessing animals, Adkin was again in awe. It was as if every teamster, bullwhacker and driver automatically knew what to do or where to go for lining up. The circles must have covered about 40 acres in Adkin's estimation.

Camp fires were beginning to fire up while teamsters were yelling at each other.

"Get those mules away from my horses or I'll shoot the bastards," one called out in the dimming light.

Sanderson told Adkin, the talk was the Indians had probably been following the other caravan heading east, but saw an ideal opportunity when the Army's train stopped with so many animals – and they were hobbled outside of a secure circle.

Indians were the best horse, mule or oxen thieves in the world, according to everything Adkin had heard. They preferred horses because they could run them faster when escaping. But they preferred to sell mules.

As Sanderson's crew began preparing for a meal from Robert's chuckwagon, Adkin noticed Ryan had been keeping to himself the last few days – ever since Sanderson told the men he was a partner. Adkin wasn't sure just how to handle the situation, mainly because he didn't know exactly why Ryan would be bothered by the deal.

"Hopefully, time will heal any wrongs he may be feeling," Adkin thought to himself. "I still consider him a friend."

Sanderson sat down next to him with a plate of stewed venison and corn bread with beans.

"I hear another hunting party is going out in the morning," Sanderson said. "But there will be plenty of volunteers, you don't have to go."

"I would love to go," Adkin said.

"I know, so would about 100 other men," Sanderson replied. "Everyone wants to break up their routines and enjoy some hunting, but it's going to become more and more dangerous from here out."

"What do you mean?"

"The reason we're circling the wagons is because scouts have most likely seen additional Indians out hunting, too," Sanderson said. "Or looking for places to raid and steal animals, food – whatever they can get their hands on – like they did last night.

"I would imagine the scouts have seen more than one band out there roaming around, that's why they don't want any animals hobbled outside the wagons – it's just too much of an invitation for thieving Indians," he continued. "And they don't want any trouble before we get to the pow-wow. Our men are ready to shoot any Indian they see after last night."

"How far is it to the pow-wow site?" Adkin asked.

"I'm not sure, I haven't been south of the trail in this part of the country," Sanderson answered. "But we'll head south at Turkey Creek in a couple of days. People are saying it's only about two or three days after that."

As the morning sun crept upward creating a golden glow on the horizon, Adkin noticed the beauty around this area called Council Grove. Sanderson had told him traders often gathered here to form larger caravans for safety when heading west. In the 1820s – Sanderson couldn't remember the exact date – the Osage Indians signed a treaty to ensure safe travel for traders "through these parts."

Three or four creeks emptied into the Neosho River here, and plant life was fully abundant – live oaks, hackberry and walnut trees, plum bushes filling the drainage sloughs to the creeks, towering elms, huge cottonwood trees and bright green willows everywhere. Even some wild flowers were still blooming along the river bank.

On the west side of the Neosho, a nice little village had been developed, and numerous traders had intercepted the soldiers yelling out they had goods to sell or trade. Sanderson said the town actually had a newspaper. Adkin could see a small church spire. The sight comforted him.

He could fully understand why the traders called this place "Prairie Eden." Before the caravan got rolling, Harney stepped over to Adkin's coach.

"Hey Jim, if you're going to be on that bench so much, would you mind carrying a God damn gun with you, since Lieutenant Phillips is carrying his inside?" Harney asked. "I don't want a sumbitchin' Indian riding straight in and putting an arrow in your ass."

"I've got a belly pistol, General," Meade said, folding his waist coat back to show Harney the pearl handled grip.

"I'm not talking about a God damned pee shooter, Jim. You need a long gun that will reach out there and stop the bastards."

"I've got a shotgun I can get, General," Adkin spoke up. "It's a Remington double barrel 12 gauge – a coach gun."

"That's more like it," Harney smiled and turned back to Sanderson's coach. "And keep that sumbitch handy, Yates."

Adkin crawled over the bench and onto the top of the Concord. He opened his leather bag and pulled out the Remington and a box of shells. He handed them to Meade as he got back on the reins.

He placed the shotgun next to his thigh and smiled at Meade.

Meade smiled back and nodded.

The train made several short stops along the trail to replenish water and ensure all water barrels were topped off. The first water out of Council Grove was at Diamond Spring, then again at Lost Spring.

Adkin couldn't help but think back to the street peddler at Paddington Station in London who said his brother died of thirst on the Santa Fe Trail.

"This is paradise, with more sweet-tasting water than a man could ever use," Adkin thought to himself as a smile grew across his face and the coach rolled along.

On the evening of the ninth day since departing Ft. Leavenworth, the caravan was nearing Cottonwood Crossing and the North Cottonwood River. It was home to the place called Moore's Ranche.

"It was made a U.S. Post Office in 1861," Meade told Adkin as they were looking ahead from atop the Concord. "A man named Shreve ran the ranch until earlier this year when he died. His daughter runs it now. It's a well established boarding house and trading post.

"It's only been attacked by Indians one time – a hundred of them, and only one man was wounded – by a spear," Meade said, with a smile.

Adkin shivered.

"Those clouds rolling in from the north don't look inviting," Meade said looking back to his right. "No sir, this could slow us down."

Adkin was intrigued by the pure white tops of the clouds which were shaped like a giant anvil spreading out away from the dark blue-gray clouds along the horizon – and heading directly toward them. Lightning cracked and thundered through the black clouds.

Sure enough, within about 15 minutes, and with the Moore Ranche in sight about 2 miles ahead, the wind started picking up and it turned icy cold within minutes.

As dust and weeds started kicking up in the air, horseback soldiers were riding up and down the lines yelling "Circle up – circle up, now."

This time, the circular maneuver wasn't as smooth as it had been the evening before. Wind was spooking animals here and there, and men were having to yell at the top of their lungs to be heard over the howling wind coming in from the north. As teams and wagons tried to get in their positions, the hail hit – the stones were the size of silver dollars.

Something tore into Adkin's cheek, just as he was trying to size up the situation. He automatically reached up to rub his cheek and noticed blood on his glove.

Meade yelled, "Take cover Adkin," as he set the brake and swiveled off the coach to his left and clamored into the side door of the Concord as the passengers were pulling down the window curtains.

Adkin pulled his hat down further and reined hard to his left to get behind a yoked team of oxen – their bullwhackers already scrambling under the two wagons the team was harnessed to.

Several of the stones were pounding Adkin's head as he set the brake and jumped off to his right and pulled the door to the coach open. The passengers almost tore his shirt off as they grabbed him and whisked him inside.

"Are you okay?" Leavenworth asked, as he noticed blood running off Adkins right cheek. He handed Adkin a kerchief to stem the blood.

"Yes sir, I think I'm okay – thank you sir."

"This shouldn't last long," Meade said, sounding more hopeful than confident.

The pounding was loud and Adkin found himself somewhat worried. He had never seen such weather. He had read about hail and heard stories, but he was totally unprepared for this savagery.

He was mostly concerned with his horses, which kept crying out and trying to jerk the coach ahead. He could hear other animals as well – bellowing oxen and mules screaming out in pain.

Within a few minutes, the pounding stopped – almost as fast as it had started. The loud banging was replaced by the swish of heavy wind-blown rainfall.

They pulled up the leather side guards on the windows, and everyone was looking out as the sky seemed to open as if releasing an ocean of water. Adkin couldn't even see the teams he knew were parked 20 or 30 feet from them.

And the sky was turning black, as if the sun has suddenly disappeared far behind the horizon. Yet he knew it was at least two hours before sunset.

"Well men, We'll probably be mired here at Cottonwood Crossing for at least a day or two," Meade said, while the others shook their heads in agreement.

After about 15 minutes, Adkin said he wanted to check the horses, and eased out of the coach, the rain still falling in sheets, sometimes coming at him sideways.

He started on the right side, checking the harnesses and running his hands down the sides and backs of the horses while talking to them and telling them to take it easy.

"I'm here girl, you'll be okay," he told them as he moved from horse to horse. They quit shaking and twitching and seemed to settle down and accept the pouring rain.

They were closing their eyes and breathing more evenly. One of them had a huge knot above her right eye, the swelling already the size of a man's fist.

Adkin jumped up in the seat and re-engaged the brake. He could see the bullwhackers under the wagons in front of his team. They waved as if to let him know they were okay, even as water was running around them like they were boulders in a creek.

Adkin thought about opening his leather bag lashed to the roof of the coach to get his new buckskin jacket with the leather fringe for warmth, but he was afraid everything in the bag would end up soaked. He jumped back down and into the coach, shivering to the bone.

•••

Some 30 minutes later, the rain had slowed to a drizzle and the sky was clearing blue along the horizon to the north. It was blowing over and men were starting to crawl out from under wagons, ease out of wagons that had their canvas coverings up, which included most of the freighters.

Only about half the caravan had been able to position themselves in some kind of resemblance of a circle before the storm hit. Now men were pulling on harnesses and pushing and pulling on the spokes of wheels to move the wagons into the preferred security rings, while water was rushing here and there.

But the mud was everywhere. Adkin could not believe hard dusty earth had been there less than an hour ago. Now it was a river of gelatinous mud – most of it sludging toward Moore's Ranche and the river behind it.

"I'll bet that norther dropped at least 6-inches of rain," Meade said as he stood looking around at the wagons, men and animals trying to situate themselves for nightfall.

A few minutes later, a horse rider approached from the ranch and yelled out to the stages, which Adkin only now realized had been about 20 yards apart.

"My name is Jarvis – Joel Jarvis," he shouted. "I work for Miss Charity at Moore's Ranche. She wanted me to tell you we have an Indian healer, a squaw, staying at the ranch, and she can help if you need her. If you do. I'll go fetch her right away."

'Thank you Jarvis," Harney bellowed, after walking up near Adkin's coach. "We have a doctor and ambulances, but we're not sure what needs we have. We're processing our damages as we speak.

"But tell Miss Charity we are grateful for her offer of assistance. I'm General William S. Harney, and please pass along our appreciation."

"We were told you were with the caravan, General," Jarvis said. "Two of your scouts are warm and toasty at the ranch as we speak.

"Miss Charity also ask me to invite you and your party to sup with her this evening – if at all possible."

"Why thank you Jarvis," Harney said. Adkin couldn't believe the General hadn't cursed yet. Harney could hardly get out one sentence without using curse words or using the Lord's name in vain. "We'll be there in one hour."

Jarvis reined his horse and went galloping off to the ranch.

"Get these sumbitches straightened out Captain," Harney barked to an officer who had walked up while Harney pointed at the men and animals currently in chaos. "Get everyone in the circles and have those God damned animals hobbled inside."

Harney then checked with Adkin's passengers and they all made small talk. Adkin couldn't tell what they were saying. Harney then walked back to Sanderson's coach and climbed inside, yelling, "Let's get over there, J.L.," pointing to the north circle forming.

Adkin's group climbed back in and he jumped onto his bench, grabbed the reins and turned his team to follow Sanderson. Phillips leaped up just as he was snapping the reins.

•••

About an hour after sunset, both stagecoaches and four horse soldiers pulled up to the main house at Moore's Ranche. Adkin noticed a small boarding house, a barn and stables and what looked like a trading post with a porch the length of the log building. All the buildings were made of logs with sod chinking to seal them from the weather. The roofs looked like sod as well, with grasses growing on them.

Jarvis and another man helped hold the harnesses while everyone climbed down from the coaches.

"You men set up a perimeter," Harney huffed to the soldiers on horseback. "And make sure you keep your God damned eyes open – you hear?

"J.L., you and Adkin come along with us," he added, surprising both men.

Lieutenant Phillips and his counterpart stayed on the coaches while being led over to the stables where they were being parked.

"Welcome General Harney," a woman's soft voice said as they approached the steps to the house. "Welcome to Moore's Ranche."

Harney came face to face with the young woman at the doorway, where lights from inside lit up her face.

"Well God Almighty. It's little Cherry," Harness said in surprise. "It didn't connect when I heard Miss Charity."

Charity Shreve stood on her tiptoes as she hugged the big man.

"Good to see you, too, Uncle Bill. Come on in. Men, welcome," she told the others and held her arm toward the front sitting room.

After introductions, Harney shared his sympathy about William Shreve's death a few months earlier.

"I met your father in 1861, shortly after the Moore brothers, Abraham and Ira, hired him to run the place," Harney said, with a gentle smile Adkin had never witnessed on the man before. "He was a fine gentleman. I enjoyed his company – and your's – for the three days I was here waiting on troops.

"But you were only about 12 or 13 – skinny as a half-starved mule," Harney said, laughing.

"That's the sweet talker I have grown to know," Adkin thought to himself.

"I stopped by here two years ago when they were shipping me off to Washington to sit behind a God damn desk, but your father said you were off to school or somewhere," Harney said.

"I spent two school years in Topeka," Charity said. "But the summer months I still helped father here at the ranch. I remember father telling me Uncle Bill Harney stopped by to see me. I was tickled, but I knew that was father's way to make me feel special."

Adkin was taken by this 18-year-old girl who carried herself as a much more mature woman – a woman running a ranch and trading post this size out in the wilds of Kansas. She was impressive – and pretty.

She was taller than most women, but slim and shapely. Her eyes were blueish-gray with light brown hair tied up in a curl on the back of her head and a ribbon bow above one ear. Her skin was browned from hours of working in the outdoors in the hot summer sun, but her hands were slender and dainty.

The first thing Harney brought up was the death of young Parkinson Jr., and his father's request the boy be buried at the Moore's Ranche.

"Why of course, Uncle Bill," Charity said. "We'll put him in our family plot, bless his soul. That way his family will know where he is, and they can move him later if they wish.

"Just have poor Mister Parkinson bring him over in the morning," she said. "I'll have the hands digging his grave by daybreak. How is Mister Parkinson?"

"I guess he's doing as well as can be expected," Harney said with a dour expression on his face.

Everyone then started talking about the storm, and it was Meade who brought up the fact Adkin had been hit in the face with a sizable hail stone.

"Yates here got whacked right in the cheek – tore it open pretty good," Meade said. "Had to have the doc patch him up."

"So that's the reason for the bandage," Charity asked Adkin. "I hope it was not too severe a wound."

Adkin sat there for an awkward moment. He hadn't said a word except for "Nice to meet you, Miss Charity."

Now everyone, including this lovely woman, was staring at him – waiting for him to say something.

"No Maam," he stuttered. "I mean, it was not too severe a wound."

"Good God, I sound like a parrot – echoing other's speech," Adkin thought to himself.

"I mean, I'm doing fine – just fine," he said, his face flushing red with embarrassment.

"Well good," she said, smiling and seeming to know he was flaying about like a fish out of water. "Let's eat. Rosita has the table ready, I believe."

The dining room sat off to the west side of the sitting room and the table was about 20-feet long. It had be hewn from a large cottonwood trunk. It easily handled Charity and her eight guests. Rosita and two other Mexican men began placing stoneware plates in front of the guests with silver eating utensils.

The main meal centered around buffalo. That was fine with Adkin, he had already decided there was no finer meat in the world than the American Buffalo. This salted meat had been finished by roasting over an open flame. There were also boiled corn ears and squash and biscuits with fresh-churned butter. Rosita was also filling glass steins with a red wine.

"Try some of this sauce on your buffalo, Mister Yates," Charity said, as she handed a small gravy boat across the table to Adkin. "It's a specialty of Rosita's – she calls it chili con carne sauce."

Adkin took it and used the ladle to spoon some of the reddish sauce onto his meat.

"So what brings you to our part of the world Uncle Bill?" Charity asked. "Let me preface that question with the rumors I've heard that you're working on a peace treaty with the Plains Indians."

She smiled devilishly at Harney.

"Damn it Cherry, you're as bright and direct as your Pa." Harney said, laughing. "You should be in the business of spying."

"We're hoping to quell some of the violence that's rearing its ugly head since the end of the war," Meade interrupted.

"Yes, we think most of the tribes are ready to consider our offers of food and shelter on reservations in exchange for peace – especially with winter coming on," Leavenworth added.

"That's fine, gentlemen," Charity said stoically. "But there are some that will never make peace with the white man or live in an enclosed reservation.

"There are a couple of instances I doubt some Indians will ever forget or forgive," she continued. "Take the Sand Creek Massacre last November in Colorado. Colonel Chivington and his 700 men killed more than 100 Indians, I heard, and most of them were women and children.

"Don't get me wrong, I believe Chivington was vicious because he has learned to fight fire with fire," Charity explained. "The White Man is going to have to learn how to be as vicious in warfare as the Comanches and Cheyennes if we are ever to conquer this land."

She seemed to be looking directly at Meade and Leavenworth. Though all the officials and commissioners favored bending over backward to assist the Indians, according to talk among a lot of the men in the caravan. It was those two who were considered almost dangerous when it came to dealing with Indians.

"Also last year, as you're well aware, our friend Kit Carson nearly lost his life and three companies trying to kill the Comanches at Adobe Walls," she continued. "I may be a pessimist, but the Cheyenne, Kiowa and Comanche – especially the Comanches – should never be trusted. The Comanches are the most terrifying and vicious Indians on Earth."

Wow, Adkin thought. This young woman knows what she's talking about, according to what he's been learning since arriving at Fort Leavenworth.

"We agree there are problems ahead, Miss Charity, but that's why we're attempting to reach out," Meade said. "We're hoping to save the lives of many decent Indians. We know there are those that live by the sword, and they will die by the sword. We want to help those who choose to live with the White Man."

Charity apologized for turning the discussion "to politics" and said her father always begged her to not involve herself with men's business.

"But, as you know, Uncle Bill, if I'm asked, I volunteer my thoughts – however silly," she said, in a little-girl way.

Charity informed them it was most likely they wouldn't be able to cross the river in the morning.

"After that much rain, that North Cottonwood will most likely be out of its banks for a day and moving very rapidly," she said.

Talk continued about local events, how the area was growing and the economy. The Moore Ranche was doing well financially. Charity said, since more and more farmers were moving into the area. They were in the process of building a local school and had approved and enacted a tax on commerce to fund it.

With so many people in the area now, Charity said they had organized a militia that could depend on about 40 armed men to be assembled in about 30 minutes or less.

"We ring the new alarm bell we have that will eventually be placed in the new school," Charity said, chuckling. "I think that's why these small Indian raiding bands leave us alone. Plus, most of the Indians around here are of the peaceful Kaw tribe, and they live here permanently."

Harney asked about his caravan scouts, and Charity admitted once they saw the stagecoaches approaching, they took off north from the stables. She mentioned she had four other travelers staying in the boarding house, and one was a Pennsylvania doctor on his way to Santa Fe to set up a practice.

"Now that it's part of the United States," Charity added. "He may end up spending the winter with us if he can't get on with another caravan heading west."

The discussion turned to the storm again.

"Your timing is fortunate, Uncle Bill," Charity said. "Most of our watermelon growers – it's our largest local crop now – just finished putting up their melons for shipment. I'm sure they would allow your men to salvage whatever melons they can find tomorrow that were still in the field and have been damaged by the storm."

Everyone laughed, but Harney said, "We'll take them up on that, Cherry."

On the way back to camp, Meade sat atop with Adkin, which had become his habit.

"That's the kind of woman you need to pursue, Adkin, if you're going to be happy out here on the Plains," he said, almost sadly. "I have been successful out here as a hunter, trader and – not regretting my life. But it was completed when I met and fell in love with Agnes Barcome of Montreal, Quebec, four years ago.

"I've dragged that poor woman through the wilds of the Saline Valley to Towanda, where she's at now with my son and daughter, and she has never said a negative word through all the hard times and Indian scares.

"Young Charity reminds me of Agnes in many ways," he said, turning to look at Adkin.

"Well, she is a striking woman, Jim, but I need to make my way first – much like you did," Adkin said.

"You're probably right, Adkin," Meade said, while patting Adkin on the back.

•••

At daylight, several wagons and riders on horseback and mules started with Parkinson Sr. and his son toward Moore's Ranche. There were at least three dozen men who had decided to attend the boys burial. An Army Chaplain rode next to Parkinson Sr. as he reined the team westward through the mud.

Adkin decided to stay and help his crew, as he didn't have enough emotional strength after hugging the boy's Pa. It dug at his innards like when he had hugged his own father at his little sister's burial in Olney years ago.

The hail did less damage than Adkin would have guessed. Maybe because of the cut he sustained and the two large knots on his head. He had decided last night driving back to camp his straw hat was finished as his choice of headwear. He would be searching for one of those cowhide hats that would hold up to heavy rain and hail.

Several men had also been cut and hit hard enough to seek the doctor's help. Only one animal had to be put down – a mule – as she had been blinded in one eye with a hail stone, and they couldn't stop the bleeding sufficiently during the storm. She had collapsed on the ground by the time the rain ceased and had to be shot.

Numerous animals, though, had welts, a few cuts and knots on their heads, but considering the size of the stones, most were going to be okay.

Scouts had returned by breakfast to inform the commissioners crossing the North Cottonwood River would not be possible anytime soon. It was about a quarter of a mile wide and out of its banks below and above the crossing.

"The rapids are fast enough to carry away a 10-yoke team of oxen," one of them said. "Jarvis said he would take us to the melon farmers nearby to see if we can salvage any watermelons."

Harney directed one of his soldiers to gather two crews and two drays and see what they could find. He also assigned four riflemen to ride guard on horseback to protect them.

Officers went about checking with the freighters to see if repairs were needed. One wagon had broken an axle when the hail storm hit and the mules bolted sideways and entangled the wagon among some deadfall off the trail. There were also several holes in some of the wagon covers that had to be patched.

Adkin offered to help repair the axle and "iron" it if needed, but he was told one of the Army's wagons was carrying six extra axles for just such emergencies. It dawned on Adkin that being prepared out here in the wilds was a key to survival.

Most of the men were in fairly good spirits, not minding the wait for the river to recede. Some cleaned their guns, checked the tack on their teams, replaced harnesses, some washed their clothes. Others sat around drinking coffee and playing cards. The camp was taking on a relaxed feeling like everyone was on a Sunday picnic.

By late afternoon, the drays had returned with mud covering their wheels and the soldiers looking very tired – and muddy up to their knees. But both wagons were full of damaged or whole watermelons and men were laughing and giggling like children as they passed around melons and everyone was feeding like swine at a trough.

Even old Harney laughed at the sight, along with the commissioners as they all sat in chairs under the huge awning on the front of their walled tent. Several soldiers brought pieces of melons to them, and they, too, buried their faces into the sweet meat while laughing.

"This really does resemble a picnic," Adkin thought to himself.

As the sun was setting, Jarvis and Miss Charity pulled up to the commissioners' tent in a small buckboard being pulled by a single pony. Adkin hadn't realized Harney had invited Charity to eat with them. He had been wondering all day if they would return to the Moore's Ranche. He found himself fascinated with this bright, brave woman living out here so far from civilization.

Unfortunately, he and J.L. were not invited to supper for the evening, so he only got to see her walk into the big tent holding Harney's left arm. Her hair was down this evening, and the lighting in the tent made it gleam as she threw back her head, laughing at whatever Harney had said to her.

Sanderson and his crew enjoyed themselves around their camp fire, telling stories and yarns. Ryan still sat near them, yet he didn't engage in any of the discussions. He was aloof, and Adkin worried things could go bad between them. But, he refused to let himself accept their relationship would sour. He was determined to stop that – somehow, someway.

Several soldiers walking by said the river was dropping and most likely, the caravan would be departing in the morning. Some of the men grumbled, but the jokes and stories resumed and laughter filled the night air again.

They were still at least a day and a half away from departing the Santa Fe Trail and heading south into the lands of the Wichita Tribes.

•••

It was mid-day on September 28 when two scouts rode up to Sanderson's Concord and yelled for General Harney.

"General, Turkey Creek is about four miles ahead, but there is a small band of Caddos camping there. It's only a hunting party, but there are at least a dozen," the scout said.

Adkin had learned that many of the scouts in this caravan were full blooded Ute Indians that dressed as soldiers, with exception of their hair feathers hanging from under their soldiers' hats. Adkin had only had a couple of glances of them during the entire trip, as they would come into camp late – if they came in at all – and departed before daylight.

"General, I most likely know these Indians, as the Caddos live down this valley all the way to the Big Arkansas and below to Texas," Meade spoke up. "Most of them around here trade with me at my Towanda trading post."

"Good," Harney said. "Because I don't want any damn problems with these bastards at this point in the game."

"Don't worry, I speak Caddo and am well versed in sign," Meade responded sarcastically.

Many of the civilians in the caravan considered the commissioners a bunch of "rosewater dreamers" when it came to dealing with the Indians – especially Meade and Leavenworth.

Adkin had heard some of these "rosewater dreamers" in the Indian Office blame the White Man for everything the Indian does.

"If the Army is successful, it's an Indian massacre, if the Army isn't successful, it's a bunch of imbeciles running the operations," said a teamster at camp one night. "All these people back east have no clue as to what the Indians are capable of and how deadly they are – and blame everything on us Whites.

"The farther east these people live, the more devoutly they believe that bull shit," he added, to much agreement from the men sitting near the campfire.

Sanderson had confirmed many of these men on the caravan were grizzled traders and Indian fighters who have experienced the ways of true Indian warriors. Adkin had already heard blood-curdling stories and didn't doubt what these men were saying or how they felt.

Now, he apparently was going to see some of these wild Indians – eye-to-eye so to speak. Turkey Creek was straight ahead.

Harney signaled Adkin to lead the train into the Caddo band's camp as they neared Turkey Creek. Meade was sitting next to Adkin at the ready. As soon as they got within ear-shot, Meade stood and yelled "Koo-ah-aht," with his right hand raised palm forward.

"Koo-ah-aht," one of the Caddos said, also raising his arm. He stepped forward as the coach pulled to a stop.

"Koo-ah-aht Jim Meade," he said again, with a broad smile.

"Koo-ah-aht John Wilson," Meade said, as he jumped down to the ground. Both men gripped each others shoulders and grinned.

They said several things back and forth as everyone watched. Adkin found it strange Meade called him John Wilson, which hardly seemed "Indian" to Adkin.

This Wilson was an imposing figure, though. He had headgear that included a bright red feathers down the middle of his head sticking out about five inches out of his brown hair that had been cut back from his ears. And, there was a dead bird's head at the front above his forehead.

He wore large, round, hammered silver earrings and had a small half-moon silver plate under his nose. There were red painted streaks on the bare skin above his ears and he was dressed in fancy beaded deerskins.

Harney had walked up and Meade gladly introduced him to

"John Wilson." There it was, again, Wilson had to be the man's English name, Adkin thought.

The man said, "Koo-ah-aht" to Harney and shook his hand like a White Man. Adkin learned later that meant "good to see you or hello."

They chatted a little, Adkin unable to hear exactly what they were discussing, but soon Harney was signalling to one of his captains who ran off into the caravan after Harney whispered something in his ear.

The other Indians were dressed similar to Wilson but not wearing the same headdress, but their head was partially shaven as his was. They all stood and kept roving eyes on everything around them. They carried long bows and quivers of arrows. Their ponies wandered freely behind them eating green grass along the creek bank.

The Captain came driving up on a wagon and dismounted and ran to the back and started dragging sacks out. It looked to Adkin that Harney was giving Wilson sacks of flour, sugar and coffee, Wilson signaled several of his warriors who took the sacks from the Captain at the back of the wagon and stacked them near their camp fire.

A few minutes later, Harney headed back to Sanderson's coach and Meade grabbed Wilson by the shoulders again and said loudly, "Tie-bow-ah John Wilson."

"Tie-bow-ah, Jim Meade," Wilson responded, and turned to his warriors as Meade came back and climbed up to take the seat next to Adkin.

"Let's get this sumbitchin' caravan headed south," Harney bellowed from his coach window.

•••

Meade had climbed back up the coach sitting with Adkin as the train made its way south along Turkey Creek.

"Was that Indian's name really John Wilson," Adkin asked.

"Sure is," Meade said. "He's only a quarter Caddo, but he has refused to ever learn any other language. He may know more, but he will never talk to anybody if it isn't in Caddo. He's also part French and half Delaware Indian.

"He's originally from Texas, but the government forced his tribe to relocate into the Indian Territories when he was 19 or 20 years old," Meade continued. "He's considered a medicine man, and has much respect among his people."

"What did he say?" Adkin was curious.

"They were on a hunt and wanted to see if they could bargain with any traders on the Santa Fe Trail – they had come up this way anyway," Meade explained. "He was happy they ran into us – got some valuable goods for just camping at the trail here at Turkey Creek. He's no fool.

"Also, he knows where we're going and will be there for the pow wow, as well," Meade said. "He said the word is out and many, many tribes will be there, too."

By late afternoon, the caravan had reached a large clearing which Adkin could see had been used by previous travellers. There were even a few old rock camp fire enclosures which had been somewhat overgrown by weeds and tall grass.

"This is the site of the 1825 Kaw Peace Treaty," Meade said as they reined up with commands from Harney to make camp – and make circular camps, at that. "Indians and hunters have used this site through the years. Buffalo migrate through here during the spring, and the creek has good water here."

As soldiers went through the standard routine of pitching the huge white canvas tents for the commissioners and officers, Adkin asked Sanderson just how many tribes are the commissioners talking about when they say 'Many tribes will be here.'"

"I'm not really sure, Adkin," Sanderson said. "I would imagine five or six, probably. I would guess they have invited the Kiowa, Comanche, Cheyenne, Arapaho and some lesser ones.

"I guess we'll find out when we get there," he added.

•••

The next morning was cool and brisk. Temperatures were surely dropping as fall approached. Adkin could see leaves on some of the trees turning a light gold, especially in the cottonwoods, which seemed to clack together a little louder in the breeze.

The train moved out and wagons spread apart as well. Some five abreast. As they rounded a big bend in Turkey Creek, there were some Indian lodges ahead – about 30 tipis in all. Meade called out to halt, and he quickly changed places with Lieutenant Phillips. Phillips was already being called "His Majesty" by other soldiers and teamsters because he was always riding in the coach with the commissioners and not on the driver's seat.

"Ok, let's head out," Meade said to Adkin. "These are Osage Indians – they come up here on their fall hunts. They don't number as many as they did a few years ago. They have probably spilt up to establish several hunting parties, but this group has their women and children with them."

Sanderson's coach pulled over briefly and Harney ordered more sacks of food stuffs to be unloaded and given to an Osage Chief. Adkin didn't hear his name, but Meade was right there in the middle, translating and waving his arms and hands as he deftly communicated with the Indians.

Most of the Osage – men and women – wore tufts of small colorful red feathers atop their head with a lone eagle feather sticking nearly straight into the air. It looked as if it were a contest to see who had the longest feather, Adkin thought to himself.

The train moved on in short order.

"This is why it's going to take two days to get to the treaty site," Meade said after jumping on the bench next to Adkin. "They just said there is another camp of Creek Indians about 15 miles south of here."

It dawned on Adkin that had to be the reason the Army wanted bids on about 300,000 pounds of goods to supply this caravan. Gifts to the Indians was definitely a major part of the plan.

Meade explained once they get to the Little Arkansas River, they would be running into numerous lodges where tribes had established semi-permanent quarters all the way to the treaty site.

"There's the Kickapoos, the Delawares, the Wichitas, many Shawnee, Wacos, Ionis, Tawakonis, Kechis and others," Meade said.

Adkin sighed to himself, "That's more than five or six tribes."

Meade explained many of the small tribes that lived along the river "had cultivated gardens with scaffolds covered with sliced pumpkins, beans and corn drying for winter use – with plenty of melons, which are a feast to visiting brethren."

"How many Indians do you think will attend the meeting?" Adkin asked.

"Well, there's more than a thousand that live along the river now, and I will represent their concerns as the Indian Affairs Agent of the Wichita Tribes," he answered. "I would suspect we should see another 1,000 show up, as well."

Adkin shook his head in disbelief.

"Two thousand Indians, and I've only been in Kansas less than a month," he said to himself.

He had already seen the weapons these people carried – the spears, bows and arrows, tomahawks, knives and various guns. That reminded him he would take up Rinehart's offer to sell him a hunting knife.

"Whew," Adkin exhaled loud enough for Meade to hear.

Meade just smiled and patted Adkin on the shoulder.

•••

The caravan made camp where Turkey Creek emptied into the Little Arkansas River the following evening. Word was it was one day to the pow wow site, which had been selected 6 miles north of where the Little Arkansas ran into the Big Arkansas River in Sedgwick County – not far from where Meade lives at Towanda.

"It will be a long day, if we stop at every Indian Camp along the way," Sanderson said as they ate around the night's campsite.

"Meade told me Harney has given orders to tell the Indians we encounter tomorrow to follow us to the treaty site to receive goods from our Big Father in Washington." Adkin said.

"You're getting along well with Meade, aren't you Adkin?" Sanderson asked.

"Yes, I am. He's a fascinating man," Adkin responded. "He's teaching me some Indian words and how to use sign language – which, according to him, most Indians know regardless if they speak only a few Indian dialects.

"Hey Ray Dee, you still wanting to sell me that hunting knife you showed me in Leavenworth?" Adkin asked. "The more I see of your American Indians, the more I believe it may be in my best interest to be well armed."

"Sure, Adkin, let me go fetch it," Rinehart said, as he stood and walked to their wagons. Rinehart and two bullwhackers had been handling his and Adkin's tandem wagons of goods and Army supplies. Adkin was happy to be in a small partnership with the stout reliable German.

"Here you go," Rinehart said as he handed Adkin a skinning knife with a 10-inch blade and cherry-wood grip. The quillions were made of brass and curled out from the handle about an inch on each side. The sheath was light tan cow hide with a leather strip on bottom to tie it to one's leg. "That'll be $2."

"That's fine with me," Adkin said, laughing.

"You know, with that pistol and belt holster, your new buckskin shirt and – if you get a real leather hat – you'd look like a real American Indian fighter," Rinehart said, with a chuckle. "And with that scar on your cheek, you can tell the ladies you've escaped death at the hands of a savage. Hell, you could tell them you fought off a dozen of them – the ladies love to hear those kinds of tales."

Several of the men laughed, including Adkin.

"I'll leave the story telling to you Ray Dee," Adkin said, still laughing. "And what's wrong with my hat?"

"You can't tell the ladies you're an Indian fighter when you look like a farm boy," Rinehart laughed, and that brought another round of hoots from the men.

"I agree," Adkin said. "This straw hat almost got me killed in that hail storm. Thank God I have a thick skull."

"Hey men, what's so funny?" Meade asked, as he and Leavenworth walked up to their campfire.

"Seems my straw hat doesn't fit the image of an Indian fighter," Adkin said.

"Well, let's hope you don't ever have to become an Indian fighter," Meade said. Several men stood up and huffed away, mumbling something to effect they needed to check on the stock. Adkin recognized one of them as the one who called Meade and the other commissioners "rosewater dreamers."

"Hey J.L., we're wanting to let all the caravan leaders know that tomorrow, we're going to be asking the Indians we meet along the way to the treaty site to follow us onto that area to camp with us," Leavenworth said. "If any approach your men on their wagons, they're to tell them, 'Follow us' and simply wave like this."

That's not difficult sign language, Adkin thought as he watched Leavenworth raise his arm and swing it forward.

An Englishman's Adventures on the Santa Fe Trail (1865-1889)

"We also wanted to let you know Harney sent ahead two scouts to Fort Zarah on the upper Arkansas the morning we crossed the North Cottonwood River," Meade said. "The General has ordered a company from the fort to meet us at the treaty site. They're to be there by October 5th.

"Harney said the scouts have heard Indians are accumulating from all over the Plains – we may see 3,000 Indians in attendance," Meade added. "Harney wants another hundred men available, in case there's any mischief."

"Who all is invited to this pow wow, Jim?" Sanderson asked. "Well, several Comanche and Kiowa chiefs, including Satanta – and there will be Black Kettle. Little Raven and Seven Bulls," Meade said. "We're not sure just who will all show, but we're hoping for more. The word is out across the Plains."

"I've heard Satanta has personally killed at least 40 white men," Sanderson said. "Why would we want to deal with someone like that? Why wouldn't he be taken into custody instead?"

"Well, arresting him during an invitation to talk peace just isn't done," Meade said. "It would most likely cause many, many more deaths – and quickly. Actually, immediately.

"Besides, I know the man personally," Meade said, as he sat back against a log and sighed. "He was at my home for several days just last June. Let me tell you about the Satanta I know.

"He is a war chief, and he told me he has been at war with the whites for many seasons," he began, as one of the men poured cups of coffee for Meade and Leavenworth, who sat back to listen as well. "He is a perfect specimen of manhood, both mentally and physically. His brawny breast is covered with scars, mementos of many a battle and adventure.

"He came to my home with the Arapahoe Chief and Medicine Man Heap of Bears – perfectly unconcerned for their own safety – because they wanted to hold council with the government agent and signified their desire to make a treaty of peace," Meade continued. "I intimated the fact there was a squad of soldiers stationed about an hour's ride distant, and they were on the watch for wild Indians. I intimated that the soldiers might get after them. Satanta laughed and said he was not afraid of soldiers; that he had plenty of fights with them on the Plains.

"They remained several days and, as they did not appreciate white man's food, I killed a beef for their entertainment," Meade said. "They found this a very satisfactory change and cooked it after their own fashion, roasting it before a fire.

"This battled-scarred warrior, Satanta, took my little baby boy, Bunnie, on his knee and talked and played with him as I presume he did with his own little children at his distant prairie home, showing that at least he had one tender spot in his heart that was not calloused by a long life of war, rapine and murder on the Plains."

With that, Meade said nothing more and sipped his coffee. All were quiet as Meade's words sank in and wormed their way through the men's minds. Listening to Meade, one sensed maybe there was goodness in some Indians, even war chiefs who fought and slaughtered Whites.

"Well men, we better get going and talk to the others," Leavenworth spoke up. "Remember to wave along any Indians that contact you directly tomorrow. That way we should make our next camp at the treaty sight. Then we'll be able to call that place home for a couple of weeks – or however long it takes."

"Good night, Jim, Colonel ... thanks." Sanderson said.

"Night, J. L., Adkin. Men," Meade said as he rose and strode into the darkness with Leavenworth.

A few hours later, Sanderson awaken shortly after he had fallen asleep. He was sure he'd heard some kind of noise, like several horses whinnying in fear. He sat upright and strained his ears. Nothing.

He had decided to check out noises since the night the mules were stolen and young Parkinson had died. He slipped into his coat and eased over to where they had their stock hobbled. One of his crew would be on watch, but he wasn't sure who had duty at the moment.

"Who is that?" A voice boomed out of the darkness.

"It's me, J.L."

"Is that you Ryan?

Sanderson responded.

"Yeah Boss, over here."

"Were the horses acting up a few moments ago?" Sanderson asked.

"Yeah, a fox came running through here and spooked several of them," Ryan said. "Scared me, too. At first I thought it was a wolf."

"Okay. It woke me," Sanderson said. "Guess I'm a little jumpy after the other night."

"I know what you mean," Ryan said. "Speaking of the other night, Boss. Did you see when Adkin helped them remove young Parkinson from his Pa's arms?"

"No, I didn't. Why do you ask?"

"Well, Boss he started crying when he hugged Parkinson Senior," Ryan said. "Never seen anything like it – it puzzled me. He didn't know the boy at all."

"Well, Tyler, there's something you don't know about Adkin," Sanderson said. "When he was only about 11 or 12, his little 5-year-old sister got killed by a rearing horse kicking her in the head in their family's stable yard. He's told me that was about the worst thing that ever happened to him in his life.

"I think he still blames himself some because he had left the gate open, and she followed him to help without him seeing her," Sanderson continued. "He told me the real tragedy was his father has never been the same man as he was before the accident. He feels guilt about that as well.

"I would suspect when he saw young Parkinson dying from a kick to the head, he saw his little sister lying there as well," he concluded.

"I see," Ryan said, standing there looking at his boots. Ryan didn't say another word.

"You might want to try and get to know the man a little better, Ryan," Sanderson said. "He's a good man, a lot like you."

Ryan stood motionless and quiet.

Sanderson finally told him to stay alert and keep an eye on the animals as he headed back to his bed roll.

"We're getting deep into Indian territory and the hills are full of them for this pow wow," Sanderson reminded Ryan as he walked away.

•••

On the morning of October 1, 1865, 17 days after departing Fort Leavenworth, the caravan made its way along the east bank of the Little Arkansas River. Indian camps and their lodges were showing up everywhere along both sides of the river.

"They're almost stacked upon one another," Adkin remarked to Meade, who was at his usual position beside him.

"Some of these, like the Wichitas, the Wacos and Kechis, are semi-permanent villages for the Indians at this time of year. Some will then spread out to roam the Plains after spring comes and the huge buffalo herds start their migrations," Meade said.

At a large clearing on both sides of the river, Sanderson's lead Concord reined to a stop and Harney stood on the step of the coach's open door – with the calvary soldiers halting was well.

"Captain Pierce, this is our new home," Harney yelled, as he jumped to the ground. "Now spread out, God damn it."

Adkin pulled up beside Harney and stopped.

"Men, I want the river to be used to cover our asses, and the wagons placed in an arc that's out far enough away from the river to contain all our animals and camps within," Harney bellowed as the commissioners and officers started stepping out of the coaches. "And make sure there's enough room for the Second Colorado Cavalry from Fort Zarah and our guests Carson and Bent."

"Well, we're here," Meade said, as he pointed at about 50 tipis further south along the river. "That looks like some of the Comanches down there, probably the Nokonis or Kotsotekas."

"How can you tell Jim?" Adkin asked, bewildered.

"It's the way different tribes or inter-tribal bands design their tipis," Meade said. "The Kiowas are usually the most decorative with bands of paintings around the bases and some up near the top where the camp fire flue opens.

"See those three there," he said pointing at the Comanche camp. "Those tipi poles are at least 25-feet tall and they represent the lodges of chiefs or a powerful medicine man. The others are about 12- to 15-feet tall – they're shorter, see?

"Ironically, its the women and female children that carry and drag all the tipi poles and hides – usually on foot – and set up and take down every camp they ever establish," Meade continued. "The females are the true industry of Indian life."

As the afternoon wore on and men and soldiers were preparing the site, positioning wagons, pitching all the tents, unharnessing animals and, more and more Indians were coming into the valley. Some were erecting their tipi lodges across the river on the west bank. Adkin had heard there was a low water crossing about a half mile further south on the Little Arkansas. About 6 miles farther, it dumped into the Big Arkansas.

That evening, camp fires sparkled throughout the valley – some by the river banks and other spread throughout the hills away from the river.

On the morning of Oct. 3. the Second Colorado calvary arrived from Fort Zarah with its company of 100 men, with a few wagons and four small howitzer canons on two-wheeled carts. They settled in on the northern end of the Army camp, then busied themselves with pitching their tents – two large walled tents for officers and then the small, white two-man tents for soldiers.

Meade announced he was going to leave the site, but only for a couple of days. He and one of the scouts took horses and headed out at daybreak due east toward Towanda, where Meade's trading post and family home was. He had established the trading post in 1863. He had said it was less than a day's ride, and he would return the next night.

"I just want to make sure my wife and children are doing well," he had said.

Just a year earlier, Meade had also established a post four miles south of where they were camped. Meade said Indians come and go from there and there were even a few Caddos who had built permanent lodges there.

Meanwhile, the treaty site was becoming – what looked to Adkin – like a summer picnic. Men had brought along some musical instruments, like a banjo and a fiddle – and were dancing among themselves by campfire light.

Some had also apparently been cacheing away some whisky and beer until reaching the site. No one seemed to think about how many Indians kept coming into the valley. On the fourth day, Army scouts were reporting to the commissioners there were probably already 2,000 Indians along the river.

Several had already came over to introduce themselves to the commissioners. According to camp talk, they had heard from Oh-has-tee (Southern Arapaho

Chief Little Raven); and Moke-ta-ve-too'o (Cheyenne Chief Black Kettle). He said several others, including Satanta were expected any day.

Meade arrived back at camp on the evening of Oct. 4. He reported his family was well.

"It's amazing how one's mental being improves after sleeping a night in one's own bed."

"Having your wife in that bed also helps, I bet," Rinehart joked, after being told what Meade had said.

On October 5, a certain excitement buzzed through the camps, Colonel Christopher "Kit" Carson and Colonel William Bent and their parties were just a couple of hours out from camp. The two well-respected men had met up at Bent's Fort to complete the journey to the treaty site.

Adkin just sat there for a moment after hearing the news. He had read about Carson and Bent. His old faded, wrinkled map had Bent's Fort on it along the Santa Fe Trail. He had carried that map with him since he was 13 years old. Adkin felt as if he were dreaming. He couldn't conceive that he might get to meet these men.

Scouts said Carson had come down the Big Arkansas from his home in New Mexico with "an Army officer's ambulance and army wagons, with teamsters, a cook and an escort of six soldiers. The scouts said "he was well equiped with tents, provisions, etc."

They reported the famous Cheyenne trader, Bent, "had come down from his fort on the big river up toward the mountains."

Meade explained Col. Bent actually lived in a huge house in Westport along the Missouri River after he leased his fort to the Army, and they had renamed it Fort Wise.

"Col. Bent still makes a trip or two out to the fort each year – he's the purchasing agent for trade goods – and we all still call it Bent's Fort," Meade said, laughing.

"Make sure you put those two camps right here," Harney barked pointing next to the commissioners' big walled tent. "Those two will be very important to our efforts to reach a treaty."

About an hour before dusk, Carson and Bent rolled into camp. Everyone was helping them situate their wagons and aid in setting their tents next to the commissioners' camp site.

Adkin and Sanderson watched the hoopla from horseback. Sanderson had asked Adkin if he would like to take a ride and see how the valley was filling with Indian camps. They had saddled two horses and rode about a mile east to a rise on a hill.

They could see nearly two miles of the valley in each direction, and already camp fires were igniting all along the river and its small adjacent hills and within clumps of trees. Tipis were scattered everywhere as far as the eye could see from their point on the hill.

"I remember being laid up recovering from Guderian's beating on the Delta Queen and finding out I missed seeing the wild Indians that approached the boat," Adkin reminisced. "I was very disappointed. Now look, there's more than 2,000 of them camping in the same valley as I am now living within."

"This is a remarkable experience," Sanderson said. "Something we both will not soon forget."

"Let's get down there and see how our visitors fared and if they have any important news about the Indians or the treaty," he added, as they reined their horses and headed back to camp.

Once they unsaddled the horses and one of Sanderson's teamsters led them away, the two men walked a short distance over to the camp fire near Robinson's chuckwagon. Men were getting their plates filled and grabbing cups filled with strong black coffee.

The two got a plate of stew, beans and chunks of cold hard bread, which when sopped in the stew made the bread fairly tasty. They sat on a couple of wooden stools that were around the fire. Since they had settled in, stools, chairs, even small benches had been pulled out of the wagons to help make camp seem more home-like.

"Anyone heard any news from Carson or Bent?" Sanderson asked the men.

"No, haven't heard anything yet," Rinehart spoke up. "They've all been laughing it up in the commissioners' tent. But no scuttlebutt has yet escaped their quarters."

Several men laughed.

"We're as bad as old women," someone said, and more laughter rang out.

"Well, hopefully, they bring no bad news, and the treaty can begin soon with no immediate problems," Sanderson said, with several grunts of approval and an "Amen."

The following day, news spread throughout the valley some of the Indian heavy-weights had reached the valley during the night. The principle Kiowa Chief Lone Wolf (Mamay-day-te – actually Lone Wolf III); and his war chief and main spokesman for the Kiowa, Chief Dohasan and his War Chief Satanta, had arrived with their powerful Medicine Man Black Horse. The oldest Kiowa Chief Satank was also there.

Cheyenne Chief Seven Bulls, and several chiefs of the Comanche Bands: Chief Rising Sun, of the Yampirica band; Chief Buffalo of the Pennetaka Band and Chief Silver Brooch, head chief also of the Pennetaka Band.

By the time the talks began in ernest, which Adkin couldn't remember exactly if it is was Oct. 8 or 9, he had learned, as everyone else had, that a little more than 3,000 Indians were camped in the valley, and tribes included the Arrapahoes, Comanches, Cheyenne, Kiowas and the Kiowa-Apaches.

An Englishman's Adventures on the Santa Fe Trail (1865-1889)

•••

Adkin's main memory of the entire pow wow was etched indelibly in his mind on the morning of Oct. 12, 1865.

"He had awakened early, as was his habit, and decided to walk down to the river to wash off in the cold water and brisk air. He knew it would invigorate his body and mind for the day's events. Harney had said a major obstacle had been removed and a treaty could be signed within a day or two.

He had invited several Indian spokesmen, Chiefs and negotiators to a feed for that night, and ordered two head of cattle to be butchered so as to "entertain the Indians," as Meade put it.

As Adkin walked a little north of camp and neared a steep embankment, he heard a woman's muffled squeals and cries. He was startled and didn't see anything until he took another step forward and saw below him on the narrow band between the slope and the water, two men were wrestling with a small Indian girl.

Another Indian woman looked to be either knocked out or dead lying on the beach with a man crawling atop her with her calico skirt pulled up to her waist. The other two men were grappling with the girl he had heard – one of them was holding his hand over her mouth and was hoisting her into the air as she struggled and flayed with both legs.

The other man, recognizable as one of the teamsters, had ripped open her tan, beaded blouse and was trying to pull her skirt down.

"You there, halt," Adkin yelled as everything his eyes were telling him finally registered in his mind. "What do you think you're doing?"

As he screamed, "Let her go," he leapt from the bank and landed on the back of the man trying to remove her skirt and groping her breasts. The four of them fell into the shallow water along the bank.

"Adkin was on his feet before any of them could stand. He hit the nearest man, the groper, with a hard right fist to the side of the man's head. It knocked him onto his back into the water, and he was trying to get his hands under him when the other man lunged at Adkin with a silver-bladed knife in his hand.

Adkin swerved left and avoided the blade and hit the man between the eyes with his left fist. He, too, fell backward into the water.

By then the man who had been writhing atop the girl who was unconscious, stood and came at Adkin. Adkin kicked him in his left knee and as the man stumbled pass, Adkin hit him in the back of the head with another blast with his powerful right fist.

The first man that was slugged finally crawled up and stood to face Adkin, and as he pulled back his arm, Adkin busted him with a left to the right side of his head. He again stumbled backward and fell into the water.

Boom!

Adkin dodged and winced at the ear-splitting crack of a rifle shot.

"Just hold it right there," a voice behind Adkin hollered. "You make another move, I'll kill you where you stand."

Adkin turned to see Ryan standing on the bank with his trusty Spencer aimed at the nearest man to Adkin's right.

"Drop the knife," Ryan hollered.

During the scuffle, the Indian girl who had been fighting the men had reached her friend and was holding her head in her lap crying while trying to pull her own torn blouse over her breasts. Her face was bruised and her lip was bleeding. She was pulling the older woman's dress down to cover her, as well.

"You men better not move or … I swear to God, I'll shoot you like the rabid dogs you are," Ryan growled at the men, who were soaking wet and bleeding from their mouths – and one from his ear as well as a cut in his eyebrow.

Five or six other men ran up behind Ryan and examined the scene. Two pulled out their pistols.

"I think we need to take these men to General Harney," Ryan commanded.

"Come with us," said one of the men with a pistol as he got behind the men below the bank.

Adkin had noticed the girl looked to by maybe 12 or 13 years old. He placed his hand on her shoulder as she was crying over her friend. She screamed and pulled away.

"I won't hurt you," Adkin said, knowing she probably didn't understand him. He pulled off his shirt and put it around her shoulders. She winced but quickly pulled it completely around her in order to hide her small breasts.

As she attended to covering herself, Adkin lifted the woman up in his arms. The young girl said something and Adkin could tell she was again alarmed. He tried to smile gently as he said softly, "Come," and he motioned with his head several times. "Come, come, we need to take her to the surgeon. Come."

He drudged up the bank and she followed, still sobbing lightly and mumbling something he could not understand. He kept walking, a little quicker as he headed for the commissioners' tents. The ambulance was there as well as the Army doctor.

By now, the entire camp was alive with soldiers and men running back and forth, some worried Indians would soon know what had happened and all hell could break loose.

Meade met Adkin as they walked up: Ryan and the other men leading the assaulters at gunpoint and the small girl following Adkin, trembling like a small tree in a cold, blustery wind.

Meade started talking to the girl as the surgeon took the woman from Adkin and laid her in the back of his ambulance.

The young girl was excited to converse with someone that understood her. She chattered away.

"Her name is Mah-aht-tay," Meade said as she continued to chirp faster and faster. "She's the daughter of Black Horse, the Kiowa Medicine Man.

"Captain Pierce, do you know where Satanta's camp is" Harney barked, as Pierce nodded he knew. "Go fetch him and Black Horse. The sooner we get this settled the better off we'll all be. God damn it."

"Mah-aht-tay said they were down at the river to wash some of their clothes for tonight's feast," Meade said. "They wanted to do their chores early so they wouldn't take any chances in coming into contact with the Whites."

She squeaked out a few more words – somewhat softly – and then went down to her knees and started sobbing into her hands again.

"She thinks those men killed her friend, and she wasn't able to save her – she's her aunt, Black Horse's sister," Meade said, as he gently placed his hand on the crying girl's shoulder. "This could prove most troublesome, General."

"You're tellin' me," Harney said. "Put those men in irons and lash them to the wheels of that freighter over there.

"You sorry sumbitches," he added.

The surgeon hastly approached and said, "General, the woman's alive – she was only knocked out. She has an ugly bruise to her jaw, but she'll live."

He leaned closer to Harney and almost whispered, "Sir, she was violated, though."

"Shit, this is going to call for an immediate trial, Jim, and even though they aren't military, I'm going to be forced to make a life or death decision," Harney said, shaking his head. "And soon."

Harney ordered Lieutenant Phillips to find out who the assaulters worked for and to bring their boss to him "at once."

News of what happened was spreading through camp like wildfire, and people were getting nervous about what the Indians would do. When all the other Indians hear that the sister of the Kiowa's Medicine Man has been raped and his daughter had also been attacked, it could be very dangerous.

"There's 3,000 wild Indians in this valley, and we only have 200 soldiers and four howitzers," someone in the crowd said. "That ain't good odds to me."

Several commissioners heard the man, and Leavenworth and Commissioner Steele stepped toward the crowd.

"Men, let's not do anything in haste," Leavenworth yelled. "It's okay to be prepared, but let's not do anything stupid."

"Being stupid is why we're in this situation," Steele added. "Let's not complicate it any more than what it currently is."

"Now, let's get to taking care of regular duties while we Commissioners delve into possible solutions," Leavenworth said.

•••

It didn't take long to find the man the perpetrators worked for. It was John Kissick, the son of wagon builder Samuel Kissick, who had a factory just outside of Independence, Mo.

John runs the Missouri plant and had won part of the bid to put together 15 wagons for the caravan.

When he met Harney and the commissioners and heard what had happened, he wanted to talk with his men. After about 15 minutes, he returned to report to Harney that the men had been drinking all night and saw the Indian girls heading to the river with their baskets. They followed and Raines, the man who raped the older woman, was the instigator.

"He started it, and he admitted he raped the woman," Kissick said. "The other two claim they just wanted to have some fun but didn't plan on raping the young girl. Raines was leading the attack on the youngun'."

"Well you know damned well the Indians are going to want to kill them," Harney told Kissick. "This is the family of Black Horse, Satanta's Medicine Man, and Satanta is one of the most violent and ferocious warriors on the Plains today."

"What the hell are we supposed to do, Kissick?" Harney asked.

"I don't know, General," Kissick That's not difficult sign language, Adkin thought as he watched Leavenworth raise his arm and swing it forward.

"We also wanted to let you know Harney sent ahead two scouts to Fort Zarah on the upper Arkansas the morning we crossed the North Cottonwood River," Meade said. "The General has ordered a company from the fort to meet us at the treaty site. They're to be there by October 5th."

"Harney said the scouts have heard Indians are accumulating from all over the Plains – we may see 3,000 Indians in attendance," Meade added. "Harney wants another hundred men available, in case there's any mischief."

"Who all is invited to this pow wow, Jim?" Sanderson asked. "Well, several Comanche and Kiowa chiefs, including Satanta – and there will be Black Kettle. Little Raven and Seven Bulls," Meade said. "We're not sure just who will all show, but we're hoping for more. The word is out across the Plains."

"I've heard Satanta has personally killed at least 40 white men," Sanderson said. "Why would we want to deal with someone like that? Why wouldn't he be taken into custody instead?"

"Well, arresting him during an invitation to talk peace just isn't done," Meade said. "It would most likely cause many, many more deaths – and quickly. Actually, immediately."

"Besides, I know the man personally," Meade said, as he sat back against a log and sighed. "He was at my home for several days just last June. Let me tell you about the Satanta I know.

"He is a war chief, and he told me he has been at war with the whites for many seasons," he began, as one of the men poured cups of coffee for Meade and Leavenworth, who sat back to listen as well. "He is a perfect specimen of manhood, both mentally and physically. His brawny breast is covered with scars, mementos of many a battle and adventure.

"He came to my home with the Arapahoe Chief and Medicine Man Heap of Bears – perfectly unconcerned for their own safety – because they wanted to hold council with the government agent and signified their desire to make a treaty of peace," Meade continued. "I intimated the fact there was a squad of soldiers stationed about an hour's ride distant, and they were on the watch for wild Indians. I intimated that the soldiers might get after them. Satanta laughed and said he was not afraid of soldiers; that he had plenty of fights with them on the Plains.

"They remained several days and, as they did not appreciate white man's food, I killed a beef for their entertainment," Meade said. "They found this a very satisfactory change and cooked it after their own fashion, roasting it before a fire.

"This battled-scarred warrior, Satanta, took my little baby boy, Bunnie, on his knee and talked and played with him as I presume he did with his own little children at his distant prairie home, showing that at least he had one tender spot in his heart that was not calloused by a long life of war, rapine and murder on the Plains."

With that, Meade said nothing more and sipped his coffee. All were quiet as Meade's words sank in and wormed their way through the men's minds. Listening to Meade, one sensed maybe there was goodness in some Indians, even war chiefs who fought and slaughtered Whites.

"Well men, we better get going and talk to the others," Leavenworth spoke up. "Remember to wave along any Indians that contact you directly tomorrow. That way we should make our next camp at the treaty sight. Then we'll be able to call that place home for a couple of weeks – or however long it takes."

"Good night, Jim, Colonel … thanks." Sanderson said.

"Night, J. L., Adkin. Men," Meade said as he rose and strode into the darkness with Leavenworth.

A few hours later, Sanderson awaken shortly after he had fallen asleep. He was sure he'd heard some kind of noise, like several horses whinnying in fear. He sat upright and strained his ears. Nothing.

He had decided to check out noises since the night the mules were stolen and young Parkinson had died. He slipped into his coat and eased over to where they had their stock hobbled. One of his crew would be on watch, but he wasn't sure who had duty at the moment.

"Who is that?" A voice boomed out of the darkness.

"It's me, J.L."

"Is that you Ryan?

Sanderson responded.

"Yeah Boss, over here."

"Were the horses acting up a few moments ago?" Sanderson asked.

"Yeah, a fox came running through here and spooked several of them," Ryan said. "Scared me, too. At first I thought it was a wolf."

"Okay. It woke me," Sanderson said. "Guess I'm a little jumpy after the other night."

"I know what you mean," Ryan said. "Speaking of the other night, Boss. Did you see when Adkin helped them remove young Parkinson from his Pa's arms?"

"No, I didn't. Why do you ask?"

"Well, Boss he started crying when he hugged Parkinson Senior," Ryan said. "Never seen anything like it – it puzzled me. He didn't know the boy at all."

"Well, Tyler, there's something you don't know about Adkin," Sanderson said. "When he was only about 11 or 12, his little 5-year-old sister got killed by a rearing horse kicking her in the head in their family's stable yard. He's told me that was about the worst thing that ever happened to him in his life.

"I think he still blames himself some because he had left the gate open, and she followed him to help without him seeing her," Sanderson continued. "He told me the real tragedy was his father has never been the same man as he was before the accident. He feels guilt about that as well.

"I would suspect when he saw young Parkinson dying from a kick to the head, he saw his little sister lying there as well," he concluded.

"I see," Ryan said, standing there looking at his boots. Ryan didn't say another word.

"You might want to try and get to know the man a little better, Ryan," Sanderson said. "He's a good man, a lot like you."

Ryan stood motionless and quiet.

Sanderson finally told him to stay alert and keep an eye on the animals as he headed back to his bed roll.

"We're getting deep into Indian territory and the hills are full of them for this pow wow," Sanderson reminded Ryan as he walked away.

•••

On the morning of October 1, 1865, 17 days after departing Fort Leavenworth, the caravan made its way along the east bank of the Little Arkansas River. Indian camps and their lodges were showing up everywhere along both sides of the river.

"They're almost stacked upon one another," Adkin remarked to Meade, who was at his usual position beside him.

"Some of these, like the Wichitas, the Wacos and Kechis, are semi-permanent villages for the Indians at this time of year. Some will then spread out to roam the Plains after spring comes and the huge buffalo herds start their migrations," Meade said.

At a large clearing on both sides of the river, Sanderson's lead Concord reined to a stop and Harney stood on the step of the coach's open door – with the calvary soldiers halting was well.

"Captain Pierce, this is our new home," Harney yelled, as he jumped to the ground. "Now spread out, God damn it."

Adkin pulled up beside Harney and stopped.

"Men, I want the river to be used to cover our asses, and the wagons placed in an arc that's out far enough away from the river to contain all our animals and camps within," Harney bellowed as the commissioners and officers started stepping out of the coaches. "And make sure there's enough room for the Second Colorado Cavalry from Fort Zarah and our guests Carson and Bent."

"Well, we're here," Meade said, as he pointed at about 50 tipis further south along the river. "That looks like some of the Comanches down there, probably the Nokonis or Kotsotekas."

"How can you tell Jim?" Adkin asked, bewildered.

"It's they way different tribes or inter-tribal bands design their tipis," Meade said. "The Kiowas are usually the most decorative with bands of paintings around the bases and some up near the top where the camp fire flue opens.

"See those three there," he said pointing at the Comanche camp. "Those tipi poles are at least 25-feet tall and they represent the lodges of chiefs or a powerful medicine man. The others are about 12- to 15-feet tall – they're shorter, see?

"Ironically, its women and female children that carry and drag all the tipi poles and hides – usually on foot – and set up and take down every camp they ever establish," Meade continued. "The females are the true industry of Indian life."

As the afternoon wore on and men and soldiers were preparing the site, positioning wagons, pitching all the tents, unharnessing animals and, more and more Indians were coming into the valley. Some were erecting their tipi lodges across the river on the west bank. Adkin had heard there was a low water crossing about a half mile further south on the Little Arkansas. About 6 miles farther, it dumped into the Big Arkansas.

That evening, camp fires sparkled throughout the valley – some by the river banks and other spread throughout the hills away from the river.

On the morning of Oct. 3. the Second Colorado calvary arrived from Fort Zarah with its company of 100 men, with a few wagons and four small howitzer canons on two-wheeled carts. They settled in on the northern end of the Army camp, then busied themselves with pitching their tents – two large walled tents for officers and then the small, white two-man tents for soldiers.

Meade announced he was going to leave the site, but only for a couple of days. He and one of the scouts took horses and headed out at daybreak due east toward

Towanda, where Meade's trading post and family home was. He had established the trading post in 1863. He had said it was less than a day's ride, and he would return the next night.

"I just want to make sure my wife and children are doing well," he had said.

Just a year earlier, Meade had also established a post four miles south of where they were camped. Meade said Indians come and go from there and there were even a few Caddos who had built permanent lodges there.

Meanwhile, the treaty site was becoming – what looked to Adkin – like a summer picnic. Men had brought along some musical instruments, like a banjo and a fiddle – and were dancing among themselves by campfire light.

Some had also apparently been cacheing away some whisky and beer until reaching the site. No one seemed to think about how many Indians kept coming into the valley. On the fourth day, Army scouts were reporting to the commissioners there were probably already 2,000 Indians along the river.

Several had already came over to introduce themselves to the commissioners. According to camp talk, they had heard from Oh-has-tee (Southern Arapaho Chief Little Raven); and Moke-ta-ve-too'o (Cheyenne Chief Black Kettle). He said several others, including Satanta were expected any day.

Meade arrived back at camp on the evening of Oct. 4. He reported his family was well.

"It's amazing how one's mental being improves after sleeping a night in one's own bed."

"Having your wife in that bed also helps, I bet," Rinehart joked, after being told what Meade had said.

On October 5, a certain excitement buzzed through the camps, Colonel Christopher "Kit" Carson and Colonel William Bent and their parties were just a couple of hours out from camp. The two well-respected men had met up at Bent's Fort to complete the journey to the treaty site.

Adkin just sat there for a moment after hearing the news. He had read about Carson and Bent. His old faded, wrinkled map had Bent's Fort on it along the Santa Fe Trail. He had carried that map with him since he was 13 years old. Adkin felt as if he were dreaming. He couldn't conceive that he might get to meet these men.

Scouts said Carson had come down the Big Arkansas from his home in New Mexico with "an Army officer's ambulance and army wagons, with teamsters, a cook and an escort of six soldiers. The scouts said "he was well equipped with tents, provisions, etc."

They reported the famous Cheyenne trader, Bent, "had come down from his fort on the big river up toward the mountains."

Meade explained Col. Bent actually lived in a huge house in Westport along the Missouri River after he leased his fort to the Army, and they had renamed it Fort Wise.

"Col. Bent still makes a trip or two out to the fort each year – he's the purchasing agent for trade goods – and we all still call it Bent's Fort," Meade said, laughing.

"Make sure you put those two camps right here," Harney barked pointing next to the commissioners' big walled tent. "Those two will be very important to our efforts to reach a treaty."

About an hour before dusk, Carson and Bent rolled into camp. Everyone was helping them situate their wagons and aid in setting their tents next to the commissioners' camp site.

Adkin and Sanderson watched the hoopla from horseback. Sanderson had asked Adkin if he would like to take a ride and see how the valley was filling with Indian camps. They had saddled two horses and rode about a mile east to a rise on a hill.

They could see nearly two miles of the valley in each direction, and already camp fires were igniting all along the river and its small adjacent hills and within clumps of trees. Tipis were scattered everywhere as far as the eye could see from their point on the hill.

"I remember being laid up recovering from Guderian's beating on the Delta Queen and finding out I missed seeing the wild Indians that approached the boat," Adkin reminisced. "I was very disappointed. Now look, there's more than 2,000 of them camping in the same valley as I am now living within."

"This is a remarkable experience," Sanderson said. "Something we both will not soon forget.

"Let's get down there and see how our visitors fared and if they have any important news about the Indians or the treaty," he added, as they reined their horses and headed back to camp.

Once they unsaddled the horses and one of Sanderson's teamsters led them away, the two men walked a short distance over to the camp fire near Robinson's chuckwagon. Men were getting their plates filled and grabbing cups filled with strong black coffee.

The two got a plate of stew, beans and chunks of cold hard bread, which when sopped in the stew made the bread fairly tasty. They sat on a couple of wooden stools that were around the fire. Since they had settled in, stools, chairs, even small benches had been pulled out of the wagons to help make camp seem more home-like.

"Anyone heard any news from Carson or Bent?" Sanderson asked the men.

"No, haven't heard anything yet," Rinehart spoke up. "They've all been laughing it up in the commissioners' tent. But no scuttlebutt has yet escaped their quarters."

Several men laughed.

"We're as bad as old women," someone said, and more laughter rang out.

"Well, hopefully, they bring no bad news, and the treaty can begin soon with no immediate problems," Sanderson said, with several grunts of approval and an "Amen."

The following day, news spread throughout the valley some of the Indian heavy-weights had reached the valley during the night. The principle Kiowa Chief Lone Wolf (Mamay-day-te – actually Lone Wolf III); and his war chief and main spokesman for the Kiowa, Chief Dohasan and his War Chief Satanta, had arrived with their powerful Medicine Man Black Horse. The oldest Kiowa Chief Satank was also there.

Cheyenne Chief Seven Bulls, and several chiefs of the Comanche Bands: Chief Rising Sun, of the Yampirica band; Chief Buffalo of the Pennetaka Band and Chief Silver Brooch, head chief also of the Pennetaka Band.

By the time the talks began in ernest, which Adkin couldn't remember exactly if it is was Oct. 8 or 9, he had learned, as everyone else had, that a little more than 3,000 Indians were camped in the valley, and tribes included the Arrapahoes, Comanches, Cheyenne, Kiowas and the Kiowa-Apaches.

•••

Adkin's main memory of the entire pow wow was etched indelibly in his mind on the morning of Oct. 12, 1865.

"He had awakened early, as was his habit, and decided to walk down to the river to wash off in the cold water and brisk air. He knew it would invigorate his body and mind for the day's events. Harney had said a major obstacle had been removed and a treaty could be signed within a day or two.

He had invited several Indian spokesmen, Chiefs and negotiators to a feed for that night, and ordered two head of cattle to be butchered so as to "entertain the Indians," as Meade put it.

As Adkin walked a little north of camp and neared a steep embankment, he heard a woman's muffled squeals and cries. He was startled and didn't see anything until he took another step forward and saw below him on the narrow band between the slope and the water, two men were wrestling with a small Indian girl.

Another Indian woman looked to be either knocked out or dead lying on the beach with a man crawling atop her with her calico skirt pulled up to her waist. The other two men were grappling with the girl he had heard – one of them was holding his hand over her mouth and was hoisting her into the air as she struggled and flayed with both legs.

The other man, recognizable as one of the teamsters, had ripped open her tan, beaded blouse and was trying to pull her skirt down.

"You there, halt," Adkin yelled as everything his eyes were telling him finally registered in his mind. "What do you think you're doing?"

As he screamed, "Let her go," he leapt from the bank and landed on the back of the man trying to remove her skirt and groping her breasts. The four of them fell into the shallow water along the bank.

"Adkin was on his feet before any of them could stand. He hit the nearest man, the groper, with a hard right fist to the side of the man's head. It knocked him onto his back into the water, and he was trying to get his hands under him when the other man lunged at Adkin with a silver-bladed knife in his hand.

Adkin swerved left and avoided the blade and hit the man between the eyes with his left fist. He, too, fell backward into the water.

By then the man who had been writhing atop the girl who was unconscious, stood and came at Adkin. Adkin kicked him in his left knee and as the man stumbled pass, Adkin hit him in the back of the head with another blast with his powerful right fist.

The first man that was slugged finally crawled up and stood to face Adkin, and as he pulled back his arm, Adkin busted him with a left to the right side of his head. He again stumbled backward and fell into the water.

Boom!

Adkin dodged and winced at the ear-splitting blast of a rifle.

"Just hold it right there," a voice behind Adkin hollered. "You make another move, I'll kill you where you stand."

Adkin turned to see Ryan standing on the bank with his trusty Spencer aimed at the nearest man to Adkin's right.

"Drop the knife," Ryan hollered.

During the scuffle, the Indian girl who had been fighting the men had reached her friend and was holding her head in her lap crying while trying to pull her own torn blouse over her breasts. Her face was bruised and her lip was bleeding. She was pulling the older woman's dress down to cover her, as well.

"You men better not move or ... I swear to God, I'll shoot you like the rabid dogs you are," Ryan growled at the men, who were soaking wet and bleeding from their mouths – and one from his ear as well as a cut in his eyebrow.

Five or six other men ran up behind Ryan and examined the scene. Two pulled out their pistols.

"I think we need to take these men to General Harney," Ryan commanded.

"Come with us," said one of the men with a pistol as he got behind the men below the bank.

Adkin had noticed the girl looked to by maybe 12 or 13 years old. He placed his hand on her shoulder as she was crying over her friend. She screamed and pulled away.

"I won't hurt you," Adkin said, knowing she probably didn't understand him. He pulled off his shirt and put it around her shoulders. She winced but quickly pulled it completely around her in order to hide her small breasts.

As she attended to covering herself, Adkin lifted the woman up in his arms. The young girl said something and Adkin could tell she was again alarmed. He tried to smile gently as he said softly, "Come," and he motioned with his head several times. "Come, come, we need to take her to the doctor. Come."

He drudged up the bank and she followed, still sobbing lightly and mumbling something he could not understand. He kept walking, a little quicker as he headed for the commissioners' tents. The ambulance was there as well as the Army doctor.

By now, the entire camp was alive with soldiers and men running back and forth, some worried Indians would soon know what had happened and all hell could break loose.

Meade met Adkin as they walked up: Ryan and the other men leading the assaulters at gunpoint and the small girl following Adkin, trembling like a small tree in a cold, blustery wind.

Meade started talking to the girl as the doctor took the woman from Adkin and laid her in the back of his ambulance.

The young girl was excited to converse with someone that understood her. She chattered away.

"Her name is Mah-aht-tay," Meade said as she continued to chirp faster and faster. "She's the daughter of Black Horse, the Kiowa Medicine Man."

"Captain Pierce, do you know where Satanta's camp is" Harney barked, as Pierce nodded he knew. "Go fetch him and Black Horse. The sooner we get this settled the better off we'll all be. God damn it."

"Mah-aht-tay said they were down at the river to wash some of their clothes for tonight's feast," Meade said. "They wanted to do their chores early so they wouldn't take any chances in coming into contact with the Whites."

She squeaked out a few more words – somewhat softly – and then went down to her knees and started sobbing into her hands again.

"She thinks those men killed her friend, and she wasn't able to save her – she's her aunt, Black Horse's sister," Meade said, as he gently placed his hand on the crying girl's shoulder. "This could prove most troublesome, General."

"You're tellin' me," Harney said. "Put those men in irons and lash them to the wheels of that freighter over there."

"You sorry sumbitches," he added.

The doctor hastly approached and said, "General, the woman's alive – she was only knocked out. She has an ugly bruise to her jaw, but she'll live."

He leaned closer to Harney and almost whispered, "She was violated, though."

"Shit, this is going to call for an immediate trial, Jim, and even though they aren't military, I'm going to be forced to make a life or death decision," Harney said, shaking his head. "And soon."

Harney ordered Lieutenant Phillips to find out who the assaulters worked for and to bring their boss to him "at once."

News of what happened was spreading through camp like wildfire, and people were getting nervous about what the Indians would do. When all the other Indians hear that the sister of the Kiowa's Medicine Man has been raped and his daughter had also been attacked, it could be very dangerous.

"There's 3,000 wild Indians in this valley, and we only have 200 soldiers and four howitzers," someone in the crowd said. "That ain't good odds to me."

Several commissioners heard the man, and Leavenworth and Commissioner Steele stepped toward the crowd.

"Men, let's not do anything in haste," Leavenworth yelled. "It's okay to be prepared, but let's not do anything stupid."

"Being stupid is why we're in this situation," Steele added. "Let's not complicate it any more than what it currently is."

"Now, let's get to taking care of regular duties while we Commissioners delve into possible solutions," Leavenworth said.

•••

It didn't take long to find the man the perpetrators worked for. It was John Kissick, the son of wagon builder Samuel Kissick, who had a factory just outside of Independence, Mo.

John runs the Missouri plant and had won part of the bid to put together 15 wagons for the caravan.

When he met Harney and the commissioners and heard what had happened, he wanted to talk with his men. After about 15 minutes, he returned to report to Harney that the men had been drinking all night and saw the Indian girls heading to the river with their baskets. They followed and Raines, the man who raped the older woman, was the instigator.

"He started it, and he admitted he raped the woman," Kissick said. "The other two claim they just wanted to have some fun but didn't plan on raping the young girl. Raines was leading the attack on the youngun'."

"Well you know damned well the Indians are going to want to kill them," Harney told Kissick. "This is the family of Black Horse, Satanta's Medicine Man, and Satanta is one of the most violent and ferocious warriors on the Plains today.

"What the hell are we supposed to do, Kissick?" Harney asked.

"I don't know, General," Kissick said, shaking his head. "I do hate to see the boys that didn't rape anyone die. I don't think that's fair.

"But as for Raines, I don't give a damn what you do with him – that's inhuman in my opinion, whether she's an Indian or my White neighbor in Missouri," Kissick said.

Harney turned to see Captain Pierce leading about a dozen Indians riding horseback into camp. At the front were both Satanta and Black Horse.

Black Horse was the first to jump off his mount as his daughter ran into his arms crying. He hugged the girl for a few moments and then turned her toward the other Indians.

Satanta dismounted as she ran by his horse. Both men approached the officers and commissioners and greeted Harney and Meade by name.

Satanta was a sturdy man, tall – at least six feet, and he had a barrel of a chest with his black hair parted down the middle and a big round face. His eyes were stark, like those of an eagle – sharp and piercing. The edges of his mouth turned down slightly, giving him a sinister look.

After a few words Adkin couldn't make out, Meade led Black Horse to the doctor's ambulance. Harney led Satanta and the others into the big walled tent. Meade and Black Horse followed into the tent a few minutes later.

The other Indians didn't dismount, and one had pulled Mah-aht-tay onto his horse behind him. She looked so small and frail sitting behind the tall warrior, still clutching Adkin's shirt around her along with a blanket.

While all the Whites kept an eye on the Indians, very little talking or mumbling could be heard. There was an eerie silence that seemed to envelope the entire valley. Adkin shivered, and he was sure he wasn't the only one with those feelings.

It was a volatile situation indeed, he thought to himself.

•••

It only took about 30 minutes before they all came out from the tent. Harney escorted Satanta and Black Horse over to see the three accused men. Harney pointed out Raines and said something Adkin could not make out. Meade then led Black Horse over to the ambulance.

"Men, a verdict has been agreed upon concerning the savagery these men have inflicted upon our Indian friends," Harney shouted. "The boys will spend two years imprisoned at Fort Leavenworth and will remain in irons until such time as they are delivered to the brig.

"Raines ... he will be shot at sunrise tomorrow by a military firing squad," he continued. "His actions betray everything we value as Christians, regardless if the sumbitch was drunk or not. Let this be a warning that contrary behavior in the duration of this U.S. Army caravan will not be tolerated while I'm in command.

"Tonight's planned feast is, regrettably, postponed until tomorrow evening," Harney said. "That is all, dismissed."

Several men grumbled as the crowd dispersed, and Adkin was sure those were men who despised Indians regardless if a woman had been senselessly ravaged. Adkin had not developed a hate or liking of Indians, and he didn't plan on it, either. He had always been raised to treat people by how they treated him.

But, he felt no pity for Raines, because there are consequences men must pay for their actions. He terrorized and eternally shamed a woman and traumatized a little girl.

"I heard Black Horse's sister had a husband who was killed in a battle not long ago against soldiers on the edge of the Llano Estacado in the Texas Panhandle," Sanderson said as they walked back to their camp. "If he had still been alive, he would have wanted to kill Raines himself in the Indian way; a fight to the death with knives and tomahawks.

"Raines is actually lucky he's being shot," he added. "A Kiowa warrior would have made him suffer, probably would have scalped him while he was still alive and then would torture him slowly."

"Well, Raines has only himself to answer to – besides his maker – for what he did," Adkin said. "It was a ghastly sight."

"Well, you're the talk of the town, again," Sanderson said, grinning. "Seems your fist fighting is becoming legendary."

As they walked into camp, Ryan was standing there.

"I want to thank you, Tyler," Adkin said, as he reached out his hand to Ryan. "I could've been killed, and you stopped them before they could gather themselves and attack in force."

Ryan shook his hand, and smiling, he said, "You're welcome, Adkin. I consider you a friend, and I was glad to be able to help."

"Your friendship means more to me than you know," Adkin said, pumping Ryan's arm. "How was it you came along there?" Adkin asked.

"I was on the 3 to 7 watch there on the north end of camp – that's why I was carrying my Spencer," Ryan said. "I heard some noises, and I once I saw what was happening, I decided to save those ass holes' lives – you would've killed them all."

They both started laughing and then Sanderson broke into a chuckle himself. The other men nearby stared at all three men as they laughed harder and louder. They didn't understand all that laughter was the release of weeks of hidden stress and angst.

•••

While Adkin was dressing the next morning, he decided beside his buckskin outer shirt, he would strap on his holster with the Colt pistol. After the events yesterday, he had decided it was time to keep himself armed at most times. He also placed his knife sheath on his belt and tied the leather strap to his thigh.

Just at sunrise, nearly 100 Indians rode into the Army's camp. Harney had not told everyone he had invited Black Horse and Satanta to attend the execution of Raines, but most understood he had to.

As they approached, Adkin noticed Mah-aht-tay was astride a pony riding bareback. She didn't look as tiny while sitting a horse when she was by herself.

Adkin wondered why Black Horse would bring his daughter, who had been attacked, to an execution. It almost seemed morbid to Adkin, but he reasoned it might be cathartic as well.

"Maybe she needs to see her demons put to death," he thought to himself. "Poor little thing."

As a crowd gathered – and it wasn't as big as yesterday's judgement announcement – Meade hollered at Adkin.

"Yates, come here, please," Meade said, waving at Adkin.

Adkin gently pushed through the men and walked up to Meade. Several of the Indians had dismounted and walked up to Meade, Harney and the commissioners. Adkin recognized Satanta and Black Horse from the day before.

"Chief Satanta – Black Horse – this is Adkin Yates," Meade said. "Yates, these men wanted to meet you and thank you for stopping the trouble yesterday."

Both Indians grunted and nodded their heads and held out their hands as White Men greet.

Adkin was stunned but he shook hands with Black Horse who was nearest and said, "Pleased to meet you."

"Black Horse thanks you … Yates," Black Horse said.

As Adkin was going through the same greeting with Satanta, he didn't see Black Horse motioning to his daughter.

"Pleased to meet you," Adkin said to Satanta.

"Yes. Yes. Pleased to meet you Adkin Yates," Satanta said in a loud voice. "You are brave man who help my people."

Black Horse said something to Meade as Mah-aht-tay appeared at his side.

"His daughter wants to thank you, as well," Meade said to Adkin. "And she wants to present you with a gift."

She bowed her head and whispered, "Thank you, Yates," as she handed Adkin his shirt and a beaded head band, similar to what he had seen on numerous Indians. It was immaculately designed with an eagle's head in the front made of colorful beads. Small leather thongs were on the ends to secure it according to size.

"Thank you Mah-aht-tay," Adkin said, bowing his head as well. He had heard Meade say her name several times.

An Englishman's Adventures on the Santa Fe Trail (1865-1889)

It startled her when she heard Adkin say her name. She looked up immediately with big brown eyes, and a smile – although slight – crept across her round face. She wore long, braided pig tails on each side of her head, and they were wrapped with some kind of fine, short brown animal fur.

She then turned and walked back to her pony and sprang upon its back without much effort for a small girl. Meade would later tell him even girls were taught to ride horses at an early age, especially a daughter of Black Horse's.

"She is his princess because he has yet to sire a son," Sanderson added.

Harney then interrupted and began with another pronouncement of Raines' guilt and the punishment that was agreed upon.

With little fanfare, Raines was unstrapped from the wagon wheel and walked toward the river bank and turned so his back was to the river. Eight soldiers fanned out in a short line about 15 steps away from him.

An Army Chaplain briefly prayed for Raines' soul and asked if he had any last words. Raines shook his head and said, "No." He was then blindfolded and Captain Pierce commanded the squad.

"Ready, aim … fire."

The bullets ripped through Raines' torso, lifting him backward about 3 feet where he collapsed.

It was over, but the sounds of rifles echoed throughout the valley.

Then all was quiet, and Satanta and Black Horse mounted their horses and rode slowly away with the others, saying not a word.

The same was true with the soldiers and White Men in attendance. Everyone quietly walked away with heads hung in silence.

•••

Hundreds of Indians started arriving at noon, their regular meeting times the last few days. The commissioners were still eager to strike a deal with the chiefs and negotiators.

For the time being, Adkin thought the reason the Indians seemed so eager, was they were receiving all kinds of goods; food, flour, sugar, coffee – all the basics – most every day now from the freight wagons under the supervision of Army logistic officers and book keepers.

For the meetings, the Indians formed up around the commissioners' and officers' tents and a chief would stand in the center and talk about what he and his tribe wanted in return for peace. Several spoke English, though broken English at times. Others preferred using their own languages, like the Caddos or some Arapahoes. Either Meade, Carson or Bent would translate for them.

The Indians felt secure in knowing the meaning of their words would not be changed with men like Carson, Bent, Meade – and especially Harney – overseeing the negotiations.

Harney was probably the most influential White Man in attendance, with possibly Carson as well. Harney was a noted and feared Indian fighter, and was an engaging story teller.

He had spent his entire life in the Army, fought in the Mexican-America War, soldiered in Kansas in the mid-1850s, been the commander of the Department of Oregon in the late 1850s and had been named commander of the Department of the West in 1860.

Meade had openly commented about Harney's oratory skills: "It is said that his temperament is revealed in a large vocabulary of expletives upon which he draws liberally at the slightest provocation."

Satanta was one of the boldest of the Indian speakers and quite eloquent at times. Adkin was also impressed by an old Comanche Chief, Ten Bears, chief of the Yamparika band of Comanches, whose band – Adkin learned – had battled Kit Carson at Adobe Walls in Texas late last year.

Various commissioners would stand and talk after an Indian speech, assuring them if they would move to reservation settlements, they would be fed and clothed and not have to worry about starving to death in the winter or having to fight soldiers.

Their biggest concern, in Adkin's opinion, was the Big White Chief in Washington didn't want travellers, such as traders or settlers, to be attacked on the westward trails, especially the Santa Fe Trail.

With the Civil War ended, many more Whites wanted to expand westward without threats to their lives and possessions.

This concern was also a major Indian concern: The Whites pouring into the Plains were killing their buffalo, building towns near their water holes and generally crowding out the camps of the nomadic tribes, which included almost all of them.

Late in the afternoon, as the Indians were making their way back to their lodges, word went out a treaty would be signed tomorrow, Oct. 14, but Harney said it was not quite the end of negotiations.

"Men, the commissioners, negotiators and I want to explain the conclusion of the day's talks," he shouted. "The Cheyennes and the Arapahoes have agreed to terms and will sign a treaty with the U.S. Government at noon tomorrow.

"Other tribal leaders are still contemplating offers and counter-offers," he added. "Everyone is invited to the feast tonight, but proper behavior is commanded and disruptions of any kind will not be tolerated.

"I would also ask you men who have personal trade goods for the Indians hold off with your dealings for another day, as we still have gifts for our Indian friends.

Harney may have initially demanded no trading with the Indians until they were finished with negotiations, but Adkin had seen several teamsters quickly loading up animal hides from travois the Indians had dragged into their camps.

"And Captain, have Cookie break out a round of brandy this evening," Harney said, to rounds of yelps and laughter.

Soldiers, teamsters, bullwhackers and cooks all made preparations. Men were pulling out fancy waistcoats, blazers, jackets and fancy woolen derbys – brushing the dust off shoes and boots. There was only about two hours to be ready. Soldiers and cooks were already roasting large quarters of beef on spits over dugout fire pits inside the Army's main camp.

Large urns and brass cooking vats were being placed over other fire pits and burning logs.

Sanderson's men were also preparing for the feast, donning clothes a little finer than their usual work duds.

Adkin was straightening his leather fringed shirt jacket as Sanderson walked up.

"You know, you're looking like a true Plainsman," Sanderson said.

"With that pistol and holster and a knife off the other hip."

Ryan walked up wearing his Texas hat and a tan jacket with sheep hide lining and sized up Adkin.

"Why don't you put that straw hat aside tonight, Adkin," he said.

"Wear that new beaded head band that little gal gave you. It'll keep all that blonde mane out of your face."

Sanderson laughed, "Tyler is right, you can throw that straw hat away now that you have a genuine Kiowa head band."

Adkin laughed, too, and tied off the head band and looked in the shaving mirror on the side of the wagon.

"It is colorful at that," Adkin said, admiring the craftsmanship of such a young girl.

As men made their way to the chuckwagons that had assembled near the Army's main camp. One could smell the aromas of roasted beef, beans, biscuits and venison stew. It smelled delicious to Adkin.

Indians were arriving and Meade and the other commissioners were busy attending and welcoming their guests.

Suddenly, Meade looked back into the crowd accumulating.

"Yates, are you here?" he shouted, rising on his toes and searching the crowd. "Someone find Yates and tell him to get over here."

"I'm over here, Jim," Adkin waved. He suddenly noticed Black Horse whispering in Meade's ear as he worked his way toward Meade.

"Ryan, Tyler Ryan. I need you over here, as well," Meade yelled again.

Adkin looked back a few feet and waved to Ryan.

"Come, he wants you over there, too," Adkin said.

As they approached, Black Horse was talking to Meade, Leavenworth and Harney with a crowd of Indians behind them.

Meade made the customary introductions again, mainly for the benefit of Ryan, who had a bewildered look on his face, wondering why he was being singled out. Everyone shook hands and bobbed heads.

"Men ... Black Horse and Satanta wish to offer gifts to you," Meade said, grinning.

Black Horse stepped forward and Adkin noticed he had reins in his left hand and there was a large black horse attached to the reins and an Indian harness behind him.

"This for you," Black Horse said, looking at Adkin and handing him the reins. "His name Diablo. He is strong, powerful horse, but still very young."

"That means he's not well broken," Meade tried whispering in Adkin's ear.

"No, not well broke," Black Horse repeated, smiling mischievously.

Adkin took the reins and paused, speechless. He just stood there for a lingering moment.

"Thank you, Chief Black Horse," he finally stuttered and then rattled off, "You didn't have to do this, it was my duty as a man to help your family. It's the way I was raised."

Black Horse looked to Meade, who spoke some Indian words and used his hands some, as well.

Black Horse then nodded his head to Adkin and smiled and stepped back.

Satanta then stepped forward. He pulled out a small leather pouch from his waistband and reached inside.

"This for you, so Indians know Tyler Ryan is brave man who helped the Kiowa People," Satanta said, handing Ryan a necklace with a large bear claw in the middle of a leather strand with about 10 colorful beads on each side of the claw.

Now it was Ryan's turn to be dumbfounded.

Finally, "Thank you Chief Satanta," Ryan muttered. "I will treasure this gift always."

"And this for you Adkin Yates," Satanta handed Adkin a necklace as well. "Wear this and all tribes will know you are man of honor and friend of the Kiowa-Apaches – and that you are a brother of Satanta and should not be disturbed ... as long as you not take up arms against Indians.

"Your Kiowa name will now be known as P'ahy-Ch'i, as well, But I shall still call you Yates when we greet each other," Satanta said, again with a nod.

Adkin was aghast. The necklace also had a huge bear claw in the middle, then three beads on each side and a beaver's tooth on each side, curling inward and almost circling the claw. Additional beads went out further on the strand after each tooth.

"Thank you Chief Satanta,"

Adkin said softly, feeling very emotional and sincerely touched by this mighty warrior's gratitude. "I will keep it close to my heart, always, as I do my God."

Meade said a couple of Indian words to Satanta, and he, too, smiled and nodded his head in agreement.

"Now we feast, yes?" Satanta bellowed.

As all headed to the chuckwagons and mingled together, Meade pulled Ryan and Adkin to the side.

"It's customary when receiving any kind of gift from an Indian that you also offer a gift in return," Meade said, barely audible.

"I see," Adkin said. "By the way, what does P'ahy-ch'i mean in Kiowa?"

"Literally, it is Moon Man," But it's more like man with moon colored – or blonde – hair," Meade said, smiling.

Adkin and Ryan looked at each other and without another word hurriedly walked off to their freight wagons – Adkin pulling the rope reins of his new black stallion who didn't particularly like being rushed through a crowd and reared a couple of times.

"What are you going to give them?" Ryan asked, as Adkin tied Diablo to the wagon.

"I was thinking I would give Black Horse a knife or a hatchet."

"Give him a hatchet, and I'll give him a knife," Ryan said. "That way we don't duplicate. What about Satanta?"

"I think I'll give him the grinder wheel," Adkin said.

"I'll give him a hatchet then, is that OK?" Ryan asked.

"Sure," Adkin said. "You know what, I need to have something for Mah-aht-tay, too. I'll give her one of our brass cooking pots."

They gathered their booty and headed back to the main camp.

Meade led them over to where Black Horse and Satanta were sitting in chairs with several other Chiefs and Harney and Carson.

Ryan handed over his gifts and Adkin sat down the sharpening wheel with attached stool and the large brass pot. He then pulled out the knife – handing it to Black Horse and then hoisted the other hatchet, telling them it and the sharpening wheel were for Chief Satanta.

Meade spoke a couple of Indian words.

"This is how it works," Adkin said as he sat on the stool and started using his legs to turn the grinding wheel. As it spun faster and faster, Adkin touched the edge of the hatchet to the stone and sparks flew everywhere.

Grunts, ahs and laughter erupted from some of the Indians, and Satanta stood and clapped while laughing.

"Thank you, Yates," Satanta said, while slapping Adkin on the back. "Thank you."

Adkin then handed the brass pot to Black Horse and said, "This is for Mah-aht-tay. Please give it to her for me."

Black Horse, too, laughed and nodded to Adkin.

"Thank you."

•••

The feast went well, but the following morning, they heard there was some more drinking during the night. This time, some Arapahoes got into it with a few Indians that belonged to a Comanche band. Only one Indian got hurt, and it was only a minor cut with a knife.

"Meade said, 'There was alcohol involved,'" Sanderson reported.

"You reckon?" Ryan asked, sarcastically.

Then at mid-forenoon, rumors hit camp that Indians that were supposedly making their way to the treaty had been attacked by soldiers on the Santa Fe Trail north of them – and that 13 Indians had been killed. At once, all hell was breaking loose.

"About an hour later, Meade stopped at Sanderson's camp and said it was just rumors and that things were settling down.

"Carson and Bent have tempered the uproar," Meade said. "I was sitting with Carson and Charley Rath when we were told of the rumor. Carson instantly said emphatically, 'I don't believe a word of it. Those Indians could not possibly have been there at that time.' He looked at me and added, 'But if the rumor is true, the treaty is gone to hell. I had six soldiers coming down and would need a hundred going back.'"

As the furor subsided, Indian chiefs and negotiators gathered again at noon and began their pontifications, as usual. This time, it was the concerns of Apaches and some of the smaller bands of the Cheyenne and Arapahoe that hadn't signed anything the day before. They didn't want to give up their lands to the north and some southwest of the area, as well.

That day, Oct, 17, those three finalized their treaty with the government, which then put pressure on the two tribes who were still holding out and arguing for more guarantees from the Feds – the Comanches and Kiowas.

That evening, Harney sent out word if any privateers had trading to do with the Indians, they should do their best to conclude their business in the next couple of days.

"That means they think the Comanches and Kiowas are nearing terms," Sanderson said.

"You fellas best make haste if you want to get all your goods traded."

Rinehart had told Adkin the evening before he had been letting certain Indian traders know what he and Adkin had to offer and what they wanted in trade – hides and furs mainly.

An Englishman's Adventures on the Santa Fe Trail (1865-1889)

On the morning of Oct. 18, there were as more Indians in camp as there were freighters and soldiers. Indians were bringing in travois full of hides, and there were wagons, carts and pack mules brimming with Indian goods for trade. The place reminded Adkin of the fish and produce market in New Orleans. People throughout camps were dickering and loading and unloading goods.

As the final negotiating group of Kiowa and Comanches rode in for treaty talks, Rinehart asked Adkin to go to their wagons with him. There stood several Indians with a complete wagon full of hides and furs. There were also several travois hooked to horses with more of the same and some bundles.

Help me get these bolts of cloth and calicos out of the wagon," Rinehart said, breathlessly – but with a huge grin. "We've got to get all these hides and trinkets loaded."

"Good Lord, Ray Dee, what are we looking at in trade values," Adkin asked, his eyes wide with amazement of all the goods the Indians had brought with them.

Rinehart, pulled Adkin to the side of their tandem wagons and spoke in a soft voice.

"We're ending up with 30 buffalo hides that will fetch $5 each;, 20 elk hides at $3 a piece, at least $100 worth of Beaver and mink furs; around $60 or $70 worth of lesser furs, you know; fox, wolf, otters, skunks," Rinehart said, without taking a breath. "And there's maybe $20 or $30 in beaded shirts, vests, moccasins and necklesses.

"We could end up getting about $400 for all this stuff," he panted. "Can you believe it?"

Adkin was stunned. He didn't know what to say – he just stood there.

"Everyone that brung things are doing well, too," Rinehart said. "I'm just glad not as many thought like we did, huh?

"I even got an offer for the wagons, but I told them we had to have them to get all this back to Leavenworth," Rinehart added, shaking his head.

"Whew, let's get this stuff loaded," Adkin said, grinning from ear to ear.

Shortly after 3, on October, 18, 1865, Harney made a public – and rather boisterous – announcement that the Kiowas and attending Comanches had signed a treaty. He didn't give any details other than thanking "Our friends – the Indians of the Great Plains and Comancheria."

As Satanta, Black Horse and several Comanche chiefs rode north out of camp, Harney turned to Pierce again, and yelled, "A round of brandy for the men this evening, Captain. This God Damn caravan will be heading for home in the morning."

...

Before the evening meal – and a cup of brandy – Sanderson called his men together for a meeting. The men who had made some investments, however meager, for goods to trade with the Indians were excited at their returns.

"Men, I have something we need to discuss and see what we can do to further enhance the opportunities this endeavor has created," Sanderson said, silencing the small talk. "I brought this up with Adkin earlier today because a lot of the plan would incur his cooperation.

"He has agreed to ride horseback under the security of the Second Calvary back to Fort Zarah and from there, to ride west through the winter establishing stagecoach stations to Pueblo, Colorado," Sanderson continued. "What I need is another man who will volunteer to travel with Adkin – it's a dangerous task, even with two men, once they depart La Junta on the trail to Pueblo.

"I have discussed this with Kit Carson and Colonel Bent, for they will be traveling together this same route on the Santa Fe Trail.

"I will also need several teamsters to take over the teams to get all our wagons and goods back to Leavenworth," he added. "And someone to volunteer to drive a Concord back, as well."

The men eyeballed each other, and Ryan suddenly stepped forward.

"Boss, I'd like to accompany Adkin," he said. "I've traveled the Santa Fe Trail through that area, and I think I could be of help.

"Rinehart could handle my duties back in Leavenworth," he added, knowing Sanderson relied on his ability as foreman at headquarters.

"I can handle that J.L.," Rinehart spoke up.

"I can handle a four-team coach, Boss, you know that," Long shouted out, making it known he wanted to drive the Concord coach.

Another experienced teamster said he could handle the extra driving, and they could tandem up another set of wagons like the rig Rinehart would be driving back to Leavenworth.

"OK, then. I thank you all, and there will be an extra bonus when we get home for each and every man," Sanderson said, with a big smile. "This has been a very profitable trip, and we can save six months by having Adkin and Tyler start expansion work now rather than waiting until next spring.

"I'll confirm our arrangements with the others that Adkin and Tyler will be traveling with them to La Junta."

•••

That evening, the caravan leaders, including Sanderson, were invited to eat with the commissioners, where Harney and others related how they would return to Fort Leavenworth. They would use the trails through Towanda to El Dorado to Bazaar and then northeast to Emporia – they would bypass south of Cottonwood

Falls – and then up through waterloo and on to Burlington to Lawrence and into Fort Leavenworth.

"With most of the wagons empty, we can redistribute the loads and make all of them lighter. Plus ... that will make all the damn river and creek crossings easier," Harney said. "And, it will knock off maybe three days of travel."

All agreed, and after eating and sipping some more brandy, Sanderson talked with Carson and Bent, as well as Fort Zarah Commander Major Don Hatfield, about his plans to send Yates and Ryan along with their caravans north and west.

"Would you mind if my men rode with you gentlemen?" Sanderson asked. "They will be no burden, as they will travel lightly and be fully self-sustained."

"I have no problems," Hatfield spoke up immediately.

Initially, Bent was going to travel with Harney and return home, but he learned from Leavenworth that building supplies were on their way to Fort Wise for more construction. Bent got worried and decided to spend part of the winter at his fort to oversee any construction additions.

Bent said, "They are welcome to ride with us – right Kit?"

"That's fine with me ... they are indeed welcome," Carson sided in. "It won't hurt to have them riding with us. They may be our best security, now that they're wearing big medicine from Satanta."

Several laughed at the reference to Yate's and Ryan's new necklaces Satanta gave them.

"Yeah, who will be protecting who?" Meade asked.

"You realize you'll be on your own after you leave the Santa Fe Trail at La Junta, don't you?" Bent asked.

"Yes, Colonel, they are well aware," Sanderson answered. "But I have a lot of faith in these two. They're intelligent – and tough when need be."

"That's apparent," Carson said with a chuckle. "They helped immensely in getting this treaty signed by taking care of those violators."

Sanderson thanked everyone and told Harney and the commissioners his teams would be ready at sunrise.

Back at his camp, Sanderson told Adkin and Ryan things were a go, and they should make sure their horses and pack horses were ready for an early departure.

"Well, there's something you should know, Boss," Ryan said. "That Diablo isn't ready for the trail, yet."

Sanderson looked to Adkin.

"What's the problem?" he asked.

"Well, he's put me on my backside twice this evening already," Adkin answered, sheepishly.

"That's a nice way of saying Adkin's ass is black and blue already," Ryan interrupted, with a laugh.

"Black Horse was correct when he told us Diablo 'Not broke,'" Adkin said. "But I'm going to work with him some more now that we've had our supper."

"Well, if he's not ready by morning, you'll have to pick out another to take along," Sanderson said.

"Okay, J.L.," Adkin said, as he headed back to where the big stallion was tied up. They had roped off an area in the trees along the river to construct a small corral.

"I'll go and make sure our supplies are laid out and ready to pack in the morning, Adkin," Ryan said. "Good Luck."

Adkin untied Diablo, and the horse whinnied and reared up. Adkin started talking to him again softly while rubbing his neck. Adkin knew he was close to gaining the horse's trust.

Diablo had been ridden before, but Adkin felt the horse had never been given enough time to gain the trust of a rider or the consistency of one man's voice that made him feel comfortable.

Rather than mount him again, Adkin walked him around with the saddle on for nearly an hour. Adkin told the horse his life's story about where he was born, how he was raised and how he came to Kansas. The horse kept twitching his ears and constantly looking at Adkin as the man talked and talked.

Adkin would stop every now and then and rub Diablo's hide. He would rub down his legs, across his withers, both sides of his neck – his nose and forehead. Then he would again start walking him around the makeshift corral.

At about 10 o'clock, Adkin stopped the horse, unsaddled him and hobbled his hind legs, He also removed Diablo's hackamore bridle and told the horse "Good night, Diablo."

Ryan had noticed several times Adkin walking the horse, but never saw Adkin try to mount him again.

"Did you not try to get in the saddle again, or did I miss seeing you hit the ground again?" Ryan asked, chuckling.

"No, I decided to let him know I am his friend, and he can trust me," Adkin said, with a wink. "He'll be fine."

"Well, I have found you another good saddle horse if he's not," Ryan said. "I'm going to sleep."

Good night, Tyler," Adkin said. "Me, too."

•••

While the sky was just turning gray the next morning, Adkin was walking to the makeshift corral when he heard someone call his name.

"Yates, could I talk with you a moment" Meade asked, as he strode toward Adkin.

"Sure Jim, I was going to come over after I had a meeting with my new horse," Adkin said, smiling. "He's a little contrary having not been ridden much."

"I just wanted to say I am very pleased to make your acquaintance and to be able to spend much quality time with you on this caravan," Meade said. "You have a knack for getting along with men – Indians and Whites – that will serve you well in your endeavors."

"If you are ever in these parts again, please feel free to stop and meet my family," Meade continued, while handing Adkin a map with an X marked Towanda Trading Post on Walnut Creek. "It is due east about 25 miles."

'I am truly honored to meet you, Jim, as well, and I consider it a Blessing I can call you a friend," Adkin responded. "I hope we cross paths many more times in our lifetimes."

Meade stuck out his hand, and Adkin shook it vigorously.

"See you later, Yates," Meade said as he turned away.

"See you," Adkin answered.

Adkin walked over to Diablo and started talking to him again as he slid on the bridle. Ryan sat up about the moment Adkin placed the saddle on Diablo and cinched it up. The horse looked at ease, but Adkin hadn't jumped in the saddle yet.

As Adkin spoke softly, he put a foot in the stirrup and slowly eased up and sat down. Adkin purposely didn't tense up – he sat there at ease, knowing the horse could sense any nervousness in its rider.

Diablo just stood there and as Adkin leaned the reins against the horses neck on the right side, Diablo took a slow turn to his left. Adkin barley nudged him with his heels and Diablo started walking ahead, as Adkin said, "Let's go boy."

He walked Diablo around the corral and turned him left and right. Adkin then nudged him a little harder with his lower legs and knees and Diablo started loping in circles. Adkin continued to talk to the horse, saying things like, "Okay boy, a little faster."

"He's teaching that horse word commands," Ryan said to himself after witnessing something he would remember a long time. "I've never heard of breaking a horse by talking to him for hours on end."

Adkin rode Diablo over to the wagons and dismounted and tied him off.

"Hey Tyler, would you help me untie the ropes we used to make the corral?" Adkin asked, with a proud smile on his face.

"Sure thing, Adkin," Ryan said, with a wink and a nod.

The camp was coming alive and there was a charge in the air: Teamsters, bullwhackers, soldiers – even the animals – seemed to be excited about going home, wherever that was.

Sanderson walked over to Adkin and Ryan while they were lashing their packs of supplies onto the backs of two horses they would be trailing behind their mounts.

"Well men, I wish you God's speed and hope you suffer no hardships along the trail," Sanderson said. "By the time you get to Fort Dodge on the Big Arkansas, they should have the telegraphs lines completed to there. The Army is aiding in laying lines all along the Santa Fe Trail. When you find a place offering service, telegraph me and let me know your status. Plus I can then cable more money to you if they have a reputable bank there or an U.S. Army bank.

"Please be safe and watch each other's back," Sanderson said, shaking both men's hands.

"See you tamed that horse enough to ride," he added, looking at Adkin.

"Don't worry about us, Boss," Ryan said. "We'll have us stagecoach stations all the way to Pueblo by Spring."

"Yeah, see you in the Spring, J.L.," Adkin said. "You be safe, too."

Sanderson and Long had their teams in harness and Sanderson signaled Long to follow him over to the Commissioners' tents that were being torn down by soldiers.

"We need to go load up the brass," Sanderson said to Long, who nodded in agreement.

With that, Adkin and Ryan mounted their horses and tied the rope leads from their pack horses to their saddle horns and headed toward the Second Colorado Calvary's caravan, where Carson and Bent were also gathering their teams.

"Headed back to the Santa Fe Trail," Adkin thought to himself. "Thank you Lord – for everything."

•••

Adkin's and Ryan's caravan was first to depart camp, heading north along the route they came in on initially. Someone had said they would cross the Little Arkansas River about 15 miles north and go west until they hit the Big Arkansas. They would then travel that trail on the east side of the river to where it intersects the Santa Fe Trail, and that is where the new Fort Zarah is located.

By most accounts, it should only take them two days to reach the fort.

That first evening, Adkin and Ryan were invited to stay in Carson's tent with he and Bent.

"Thanks, but we need to get in the habit of sleeping near our horses and supplies, since we'll be on our own later," Adkin said, stoically.

Carson laughed, "No sense doing that until you absolutely have to, Yates. Might as well be comfortable until then."

"You're right Mr. Carson," Ryan spoke up. "We'd be more than happy to share your tent."

Sanderson had told Adkin that Carson was a well-known Indian fighter and the subject of dime novels back east. But to Adkin, Carson seemed a simple man and somewhat short for a noted Indian fighter. Adkin guessed he was maybe 5-feet, 5- or 6-inches tall with stout short legs and arms attached to a barrel-chested man with a smooth-skinned face.

Carson's hair was silky and hung to his shoulders and his eyes looked almost red with rays running from his pupils like spokes in a wheel. He also looked fierce, while at the same time he could look kind and unassuming. Someone had mentioned he had married into the Arapaho and Cheyenne tribes early in his life and had been married several times with numerous offspring.

Bent, on the other hand, was as dark as an Indian with black piercing eyes and a large, hooked Roman nose. Sanderson had told Adkin he was married to two Indian women – sisters – at individual times, and his children were educated in White schools. He had also said Bent knew every substantial Indian from Kansas to the Rocky Mountains.

The next morning, Adkin had pains up and down his legs and lower back. Ryan noticed him trying to stretch out and pump his legs a couple of time.

"It will get better," Ryan said, with a chuckle. "When you haven't been accustomed to riding in the saddle all day, you discover sore muscles you didn't know existed. I've got a few myself."

It took the caravan another day and a half to reach Fort Zarah. Major Hatfield had informed Adkin and Ryan some of the history of the fort since its beginning in 1853.

He said Brevet Major Robert H. Chilton and his Company B, First Dragoons, had left Fort Leavenworth for the soon-to-be abandoned Fort Atkinson on the Arkansas. Accompanying them down the Santa Fe Trail were "teams and citizen teamsters to transport the government property from the Arkansas to the new military camp near the mouth of Walnut Creek."

The fort had been called Camp Dunlap at one time and was officially named Fort Zarah in July 1864 by Gen. Samuel R. Curtis and named for his son, Maj. H. Zarah Curtis, who had been killed in the Baxter Springs Massacre Oct. 6, 1863.

Hatfield said his Second Colorado Calvary arrived in February nearly nine months ago and had built an addition to the fort; an octagonal blockhouse of stone. Also, a small building with a walkway across the top was built. The location of this building was north of the crossing of the Walnut Creek.

And to Adkin's delight, it sat on the Santa Fe Trail.

Ryan had suggested this area may be a good place to locate a stagecoach station as they would establish one for Barlow and Sanderson Overland Stagecoach Company back east on the trail near the other stagecoach lines' stations, such as the Havana lines, the McGee-Harris Stagecoach Station and Simmons Point Stagecoach lines.

"There's safety in numbers staying close together heading west from here," Ryan said, adding they should look around for some nearby property or a local farmer tomorrow morning.

At daybreak, the caravan headed west and Ryan and Adkin had told Carson and Bent to go ahead and the two would catch up, hopefully, by camp that night.

Hatfield had informed them William Allison and Francis Booth had established a trading ranch at the Walnut Creek Crossing in the 1850s, selling supplies and provisions to travelers on the Santa Fe Trail. The Kiowa called the creek Tsodalhente-da Pa, or Armless Man's Creek, for Allison, who had only one arm.

Hatfield said after old man Allison died, it was taken over by another trader named Peacock, who got killed by Indians.

"We know all about Peacock, Adkin said. "It was Satanta who killed him."

Hatfield nodded and then said a man named Rath took it over.

"Charles Rath, and he was at the treaty – don't know if you met him, but a man named Booth operates it for him," Hatfield said.

"Did y'all meet Charley Rath?" Bent asked Adkin and Ryan.

"No, can't say we did," Ryan said after Adkin nodded negatively.

•••

Ryan and Adkin rode north.

Rath's place was idea for a station – it had an outbuilding that looked like a storage warehouse, a small corral and barn with a large sod house with a grass roof. There was a parapet built atop the house used as a lookout.

They made their pitch to Louie Booth and he was fully on board. He confirmed that Charles Rath did indeed own the trading post now, though he had took off across the Plains a couple of years earlier after his wife left him.

Booth had recently hired a new hand and $30 a month from Barlow and Sanderson Overland Stagecoach Company would alleviate his financial strain.

Booth had been trying to re-establish their trading post since traffic fell off when Rath set up a toll to use the bridge they had built at the Walnut Creek Crossing. Freighter and settler traffic was really picking up on the Santa Fe Trail now that the war was over, and this would further their opportunities.

Ryan and Adkin assured him they would bring horses and supplies in the Spring. They asked him to sign a temporary contract and gave him $90 cash as pre-payment to keep him over until their coaches and supplies arrived.

"If we're late, we'll make sure you receive back-pay," Ryan assured him.

"Don't worry, Charley has given me complete authority to handle everything here," Booth said. "Oh by the way, Charley's brother, Chris Rath, just established a trading post on the Santa Fe Trail at the Aubrey Cutoff if his location suits your station needs."

"Thanks, we'll look him up when we get there," Adkin said.

They shook hands with Booth and headed back to the trail to catch up with the caravan.

"That was easy enough," Adkin said.

"Hopefully, it's a good omen, and I don't think our necklaces hurt either," Ryan said, smiling. "Did you see Booth staring at them? He couldn't take his eyes off them. I have a feeling he knows they're gifts from the Kiowas."

"Either that or we killed some Kiowa chiefs and took them," he added, laughing.

Adkin laughed, too.

•••

By noon, they had overcome Carson's caravan and hadn't hurried their horses in any way. The caravan had reached Fort Zarah, where Hatfield and his troops would end their journey. From there, it would be Carson, Bent and the stagecoach men travelling west. They departed Fort Zarah the following morning.

As they were approaching Pawnee Rock along what Carson called, "The Dry Route" of the Santa Fe Trail, and he added they should be at Fort Larned by dark.

At Pawnee Rock, Adkin and Ryan carved their names into the sandstone rocks near the base of the promontory along with hundreds of other names left by decades of Santa Fe Trail travellers.

Fort Larned had been established originally as the Camp on Pawnee Fork on October 22, 1859, to protect trail traffic from hostile American Indians along the Santa Fe Trail. In May 1860, it was moved 3 miles west of the Pawnee Fork and renamed Camp Alert.

A month later, it was renamed Fort Larned in honor of Colonel Benjamin F. Larned, the paymaster general of the United States Army at the time the post was established.

They learned, ironically, that Colonel Larned never set foot in Kansas during his lifetime.

Everyone made sure their water containers – and a few extra empty potato barrels – were full of water before departing Fort Larned. Carson had informed them it was a three-day trip to Fort Dodge, and this was called the "Dry Route" for a reason.

Ryan told Adkin, they should be on the lookout for another station site as they neared Fort Dodge, as a stagecoach could travel the same distance they would in at least three to four days compared to their five to six days.

The second day out of Fort Larned, Adkin got to witness one of the sights he had only heard about. As they approached the top of a long grassy knoll, the plains opened before them for miles and miles.

And there before them were several thousand buffalo slowly meandering south. Their numbers were such they looked like a dark brown horde of ants crawling over the yellowing grasslands.

"They're headed to the Big Arkansas," Carson said, as they all stopped to watch the herd. "You can bet there are Indian hunting parties nearby."

"Let's go kill one for meat but keep an eye out for Indians – and don't shoot at anybody unless they release a volley at us first," Carson said. "As long as they see we're only taking one for our own subsistence, there should be no problems."

"I'll stay with the wagons," Bent said, looking at Carson, Ryan and Adkin. "I'll take care of your pack animals."

Carson yelled at two soldiers that were traveling with him and as they galloped up, he shouted, "Let's go men," and the five of them headed southwest toward the huge heard of animals – a sight Adkin would not forget the rest of his life, he said to himself.

It was only a matter of minutes they reached the first line of buffalo who were starting to run, and Carson waved the soldiers to his right and motioned Adkin and Ryan to his left, as he was pulling a rifle from its scabbard. Both Ryan and Adkin had pulled their rifles from their scabbards as well.

Adkin watched as Carson neared one of the beasts and raised his rifle with one hand while at a full gallop.

Boom!

A big buffalo with large black and white-tipped borns hit the ground and flipped over in a dusty heap as it died from Carson's bullet. The other buffalo turned west nearly in perfect unison at a full run.

Adkin could feel the earth rumbling beneath he and his horse. It was unlike anything he could imagine or describe.

They all reined in and turned to Carson and his harvest. At that moment, a dozen Indians came riding up from a draw southwest of them, yelping and whooping it up. Adkin had heard some similar sounds from the Indian camps at the treaty site.

But these Indians were not making sounds of merriment.

They rode in fast as Carson turned his horse and halted by the buffalo. He held up his right hand as they pulled up in a cloud of dirt and dust, his rifle laying across his lap.

Carson said something, and the leader of this little band smiled and said, in English, "Hello Colonel Kit Carson."

Carson smiled and said, "Happy to see you, Little Skunk."

They both dismounted and held each others shoulders briefly and said some more words in Indian.

An Englishman's Adventures on the Santa Fe Trail (1865-1889)

"You men start skinning this beast, and we'll go fetch a wagon," Carson said, as he and Little Skunk and his warriors rode back to the caravan, which was less than a mile away.

Adkin was still breathless.

"Things happen so fast in this country," he said to Ryan. "It's definitely not for the meek or weak of heart."

"You got that right," Ryan said, shaking his head, as he dismounted and pulled out his butcher knife.

Adkin got down and unsheathed his knife as well and started helping Ryan and the soldiers.

He had never seen such a huge beast. Its shoulder reached nearly as high as Adkin's waist – and it was lying on its side.

Two other soldiers came out with a small dray and they loaded the skinned and butchered quarters into the wagon and headed back.

Carson introduced Ryan and Adkin to the Indians, explaining they were of the Yampirica band of Comanches under Chief Rising Sun. They had not attended the pow wow because they had been looking for this herd of buffalo for three weeks, knowing the herd would be heading south from the upper Saline River area this time of year.

"They only crossed the buffaloes' path yesterday and have taken about a dozen but will need more than twice that to take home with them to the Texas Panhandle," Carson said. "I have invited them to eat with us this evening and assured them we will only take this one animal."

Adkin noticed several of Little Skunk's warriors pointing at Adkin's necklace and whispering to each other. Adkin realized they knew its significance or knew it was a sign from Chief Satanta. It gave him a sense of calm in a way.

•••

The train got under way the next morning, and there was an icy feeling in the blustery wind coming out of the north.

"Smells like snow to me," Ryan said as they sat in their saddles, their hips slowly shifting back and forth with the horses' easy gaits.

Within the hour, Ryan's nose proved to be nascent; small specs of ice started blowing in on a medium wind.

"Doesn't look good over there," Adkin said to Ryan, as he pointed to the north. Dark gray clouds hovered on the horizon. After only about 15 minutes, the wind slowed to a light breeze, but the small ice chips had turned into large, soft snowflakes. They danced on the shifting wind and were the size of a half dollar.

The caravan was scheduled to reach Fort Dodge by nightfall, but snow was already sticking to the ground and the temperatures had dropped substantially.

"If this keeps up, we'll have to find a place to camp before long," Carson said from his horse. Carson had let it be known he preferred riding horseback, though he wasn't dismissive of sitting on a wagon bench, either.

The train trudged westward, as men pulled their coat collars up over their ears. Adkin was pleased the wind wasn't blowing as hard as it did in the hail storm at Cottonwood Springs.

By noon, Adkin's mood had changed as had the wind. It was whistling a little harder and the snow flakes were just as large, but the amount of snow had reduced visibility to less than half a mile.

Carson stopped his horse, stood in his stirrups and pointed ahead just left of the trail.

"Let's head for that grove of trees, men," he yelled loud enough for most within 50 feet to hear. He spurred his horse and galloped ahead. Adkin and Ryan did likewise, and the front wagon driver snapped his reins several times.

"Yee haw," he shouted at his team.

They pulled up into the grove of Cottonwoods, Carson helping gather the Army wagons and his ambulance into a box-like formation in order to use it similar to a corral to protect the animals.

Carson had a strong leadership quality that Adkin admired, and the man was spry, as he vaulted from his saddle and gave orders to his men. Bent was also barking orders and within about 30 minutes, a camp had quickly been set. Carson's soldiers had even pitched four tents, while Bent's men had done so as well.

The animals had been released inside the perimeter of wagons but were not hobbled. Several men were trying to build small fires in front of some of the tents, but to no avail. The wind and damp firewood retrieved wasn't cooperating.

Everybody finally dove into tents with Adkin and Ryan jumping in with Carson and Bent.

"Sure you don't want to sleep out on the ground to watch your horses and supplies, Adkin?" Bent asked, breaking into laughter.

"I'm happy to pass on that experience, Colonel Bent," Adkin answered, chucking with the others.

The men made small talk about what they would do depending on the snow storm – how long it lasts, or how deep it gets.

Adkin remembered Meade telling him Carson wasn't one to discuss himself – unless asked, but Adkin was curious about the tales of his exploits in the Texas Panhandle.

"I keep hearing about this Llano Estacado, Colonel Carson," Adkin said. "Would you mind explaining what it is?"

Carson sat there for a moment and scratched his head.

An Englishman's Adventures on the Santa Fe Trail (1865-1889)

"Well, Adkin, it's at the edge of what was our known universe when I came out here as a teenager," he started. "The explorer Coronado named it Llano Estacado, which means palisaded plains.

"It's an area more than 200 hundred miles long and nearly as wide," he continued. "It's where the Great Plains climb into great valleys of rock turrets, canyons and cliffs between 200 to 1,000 feet of sandstone, limestone and sheer rock – a place which is a pure haven to the country's most hostile Indians on the continent."

"Is that where Adobe Walls is located?" Adkin asked softly.

"Well, Adobe Walls is actually just out of the canyons on the north end of Llano Estacado, where the Canadian River comes out onto the lower plains," Carson responded. "You have, no doubt, heard about my exploits at Adobe Walls?"

"I have, Colonel Carson," Adkin said. "I have heard only parts about the battle you fought there."

Carson laughed loudly.

"The old place was originally built by Bent here and his brothers as a trading post," Carson said, looking over to Bent. "When was that Colonel, '48 or '49?"

"It was in 1848, but we could never keep it manned – the Indians killed everybody we hired to run it," Bent answered, matter-of-factly.

Adkin later learned Carson had actually worked as a hunter for the Bent brothers when he was 19, and some years later, as well.

"It wasn't so much a battle, Adkin, as it was an old fashioned ass kickin'," Carson said. "And it my ass – and those of my men."

"What do you mean?" Adkin pressed.

Carson shifted on his stool next to his cot.

"Well, to put things into perspective, there was an incident in October a year ago, called the Elm Creek raid," Carson began with a sigh. "Comanche Chief Little Buffalo led about 700 warriors of Comanches and Kiowa that were camped on the upper Canadian River down the valley, and they crossed the Red River about 10 miles north above Fort Belknap and attacked a settlement of about 60 houses in the creek bottoms just south of the Red.

"They burned and killed, stole cattle and horses and forced some settlers to retreat to a small stockade called Fort Murrah," he continued, solemnly. "Well, in short order, the cavalry came riding in to save the day.

"Calvary from where?" Adkin interrupted.

"They were from Fort Belknap, and it was actually only 14 state militiamen," Carson answered. "They ran slap into the middle of about 300 mounted warriors. Five soldiers died immediately, several were wounded and those escaping to Fort Murrah were said to be riding double on horses that looked like pincushions – with so many arrows stuck in them.

"After some time, the Indians lost interest and left the area, never to be found or even pursued," Carson added. "The tally was 11 settlers, five soldiers killed, and seven women and children carried off."

"Unbelievable," Adkin said. "There was never any retribution?"

"Well, not exactly," Carson said. "About month later, the ranking Army officer for the Territory of New Mexico – one Brigadier General James H. Carleton – decided retribution was called for. He didn't like the fact Indians were terrorizing whites in his territory.

"Now this man was quite unique, and it's important to know his temperament," he continued. "He was a button-down New Englander, a prig and a stubborn know-it-all with a large ego. He decided he was going to use me to stop this killing in his area."

"Why you, if you don't mind me asking?" Adkin said.

"Well, I had recently forced about 8,000 Navajos onto a reservation after cornering them in Canyon de Chelly in New Mexico," Carson said, adding no more details.

"He dispatched me November 12, 1864, to find and attack any and all Indians who did not surrender along the eastern side of the Llano Estacado, where few white men had dared to travel," he continued. "I had 14 officers, 321 enlisted men and a screen of 72 Apache and Ute scouts and two Mountain Howitzers.

"We knew it was that time of year when most Plains Indians made winter camps along rivers, and I had reason to believe Comanches and Kiowas were camping along the Canadian River there in the Panhandle," Carson said. "Well, after 12 days, our scouts finally spotted Comanche and Kiowa lodges in the Canadian River Valley. That night, we rode silently and in darkness into the valley with strict orders not to talk or smoke. We finally stopped, dismounted and stood motionless in heavy frost until gray streaks appeared in the eastern sky.

"We rode forward at dawn, and it was difficult dragging those howitzers along the river bottom over logs and such," Carson said. "They fired 12-pound payloads of either case shot or canister."

"What is the difference," Adkin asked.

"Well, spherical case shot is a round iron shell filled with 82 musket balls packed in sulphur with a small bursting charge of gunpowder," Carson explained. "The canister shells spew 148 .69-caliber musket balls in every shot. It's like a giant shotgun.

"When the case shots are fired, there's the initial explosion, then it explodes again," he continued. "The Indians had never seen anything like it up to that time, and we learned later, they named it 'the gun that shot twice.'

"At about 8:30 in the morning, we swept into a village that had 170-some lodges and got the upper hand with surprise," Carson said, looking more stern than normal. "The Warriors fought hard trying to cover the retreat of their

women and children, and then they, too, retreated down the river. There were only a few casualties in the skirmish, among them four blind and crippled old Kiowas who had their heads cloven with axes wielded by our Ute squaws.

"We pressed onward toward the much larger Comanche camp, which was located about four miles ahead, finally stopping at the ruins of Bent's old trading post known throughout the frontier as Adobe Walls," he said, with his eyes getting wider. "It was there, around 10 a.m., that we engaged some 1,600 Comanches and Kiowas."

"Whew," Adkin said, looking over to Bent and Ryan, who sat in silent awe.

"Well actually, the initial battle did not last long," Carson continued. "We had positioned the howitzers on a small hill nearby and fired. Those Indians charging furiously saw the case shot explode and then explode again, and they ceased their advance at once. They stood high in their stirrups, watched and then cut out of there as fast as they could ride. By the fourth shot, there was not an enemy within range of a howitzer.

"So that's the battle of Adobe Walls?" Adkin asked, looking puzzled.

"No, Yates, that was the beginning," Carson said, exhaling a long breath. "I decided to not pursue the enemy but rather let my men rest. After all, they had been marching or fighting for more than 30 hours. We ate, refreshed our water supplies and grazed our horses.

"Just as I was about to resume the chase, Indians had started to amass on open ground in front of the old adobe ruins, and once again, we heard the sharp, quick whiz of the Indians' rifle balls. And then they had a bugler blaring opposite signals of our bugler. It was the damndest thing," Carson said. "But then the battled resumed, only this time, they had figured out that grouping together was dangerous with howitzers aimed at them, so they spread out. Hundreds of warriors got off their horses and laid down withering fire from the grass where they lay on their bellies – all the while mounted warriors swooped in front firing rifles from under the necks of their horses.

"The battle raged on until mid-afternoon when we noticed more and more groups of warriors were coming up the valley, probably from another larger camp," Carson continued, while others in the tent were mesmerized. "My Captain, George Pettis, figured there were 3,000 Indians engaged in battle. Finally, at 3:30 p.m., I decided to fall back and gave the order to do so immediately, even though I had officers opposed to my decision.

"I sent out skirmishers on both flanks and very carfully retreated back up the valley while Indians continued to attack on all sides," he said. "I intended to go back to the smaller Kiowa village, burn it and then move out. When we got to it just before sundown, it was again full of Indians. Now we're surrounded by a full force of Indians, which meant about 10 to 1 odds.

"Looking back, there was no reason we survived – but for our lethal howitzers," Carson said. "We dragged them up on a small sand hill behind the Kiowa village – firing case and cannister and running them out of the village. We then plundered it – their lodges were full of coveted buffalo robes – but we burned the village down, while firing deadly case shot through the twilight air.

"One round hit squarely amid some 30 to 40 Indian riders," he said, shaking his head. "Darkness fell, and we continued our retreat.

"The story many know nothing of is – the battle was still not over," Carson said, looking to the others in the tent. "The Indians followed us and threatened us for four more days before ceasing their harassment.

"I ended up losing seven men, one Indian and six soldiers, with 21 wounded" he continued. "We had fought one of the largest battles ever fought on the Great Plains, and gentlemen, if it were not for the howitzers, few would have been left alive to tell the tale."

With that, Carson fell quiet, and he looked as if he had lifted a weight off his shoulders. Adkin wondered if he had ever told the whole story before this evening.

"How remarkable," Adkin thought to himself.

"Well men, how about some hard tack and bacon?" Bent interrupted the silence.

"I'll have some when I get back," Carson said, somberly. "I'm going to go check the animals."

He put on his Buffalo hide overcoat and untied the tent flaps. Snow blew inside as he stepped out into the blustery wind, and then he closed the flaps.

"That's the most I've heard him say at one sitting in many a year," Bent said, as he dug through a duffle bag searching for dried foods. "I think he knows how close he was to losing almost every man he had – including his own life, though he's not afraid of death. I think it's good he got it off his chest.

"You know, those damn dime store novelists have made that fight out to be some kind of heroic battle that Colonel Kit Carson won by badly defeating the savage Indians," Bent continued. "He knows better, and now you do, too. Like he said, it was a butt whippin,' and they were lucky to escape.

"I know one thing, he loves those little howitzers," Bent added, laughing.

•••

A few minutes later, Carson returned and dusted snow off his hat and coat and retied the tent flaps.

"Not going anywhere tonight, gentlemen," Carson said, looking more like himself now. "Hopefully, it will be finished by morn. As hard as it's blowing, it should move on through during the night."

Bent handed Carson some hard tack and a piece of raw bacon fat, as a voice at the tent front hollered, "Colonel Carson, it's Private Crawford, sir."

Carson motioned his head and Bent stood and opened the flaps. Crawford stepped inside with his arms full of small firewood logs.

"Here's your wood, and I'll have more stacked by the front as soon as possible," Crawford said.

"Thank you soldier," Carson said, as Crawford shuffled back into the storm.

"Yates, will you and Ryan go fetch the stove?" Carson asked. "I found it, and it's in the second wagon to your right when you exit the tent."

"Sure Colonel," Yates answered.

Both men donned their coats and leaned into the storm as they headed to the wagon. It was the first chance they had to see what the storm had done in the last hour or so.

"Look at those drifts," Ryan yelled above the howling wind.

Snow had drifted to about four feet on the south sides of what wagons they could see from their position. The wagons on the north side were not visible, though Adkin knew they were only about 60 or 70 yards away.

They opened the canvas on the second wagon, and a tent stove was right there. They grabbed it and sat it down to tie the covering closed on the wagon. It was a small stove, but Adkin guessed it weighed around 100 pounds or so, they both heft it up and scrambled sideways back to their tent, yelling to Bent and Carson, "We're here."

The tent flaps opened and they stepped inside. Carson had them position it near the back wall and turned to Yates.

"We'll need the pipe flue as well, Yates," Carson said, with a perplexed look. "It should be right next to where the stove was sitting."

"Oh yeah," Adkin said as he headed back to the wagon, worried Carson probably thought he was a complete dunderhead.

After Adkin returned, it was only a few minutes until the flue had been attached to the flute flap on the back wall near the top of the tent. Bent stuffed several logs and some tender in the stove and quickly had a fire going. The warmth spread through the tent immediately, and they all smiled broadly.

"That's going to improve the night's sleep considerably,"

Carson said, beaming.

• • •

Carson had correctly predicted the storm's movement, as by morning, it was calm with bright blue skies and very cold. Ice crystal were already forming on men's moustaches as they scurried about trying to dig out paths in front of wagons. The snow had drifted as high on the lee side of everything as high as it was.

Some men had found shovels in the remaining goods in the wagons, but there wasn't enough for everybody. Some were using poles to help pull sideways – a man on each end moving 6- to 8-inches at a time.

"I think we can try to move out by noon," Carson said, with Bent grunting approval.

Adkin noticed both men worked well together, most likely from knowing each other for 25 years. They were both in their mid-50s, but still handled chores like younger men.

"This will set us back another day," Carson said.

"Crawford, come over here, please," Bent yelled at the Private, as he dragged himself through the foot of snow.

"Make sure all the men know we'll be camping one more night before we can make it to Fort Dodge," Bent said. "Tell them to ration their water supplies, unless they want to start melting snow for their coffee."

Since the caravan decided to travel the Dry Route of the Santa Fe Trail there were no water locations for the entire 61 miles between Fort Larned and Fort Dodge. It had been termed by traders as Jornado del Muerte, or the Journey of Death because of the lack of water.

"There is another Jornado del Muerte on the original Cimarron Route to Santa Fe," Bent explained.

The present trip was usually three days, but with the snow storm, it would take them four, but it was lucky in a way that snow could be used for water when gathered and melted.

The caravan finally started out shortly after the noon meal, with men and animals full of energy and a zeal to get going.

But the going was sluggish in many areas, especially where hillocks and tree groves were near the trail. The scouts out front often broke trail around such demarcations to try and stay on open ground where the snow depth was only a foot or so.

Around 5 p.m., Carson ordered the caravan to make camp, despite a few grunts from some of the men.

"We'll set up a warm camp, have a good hot meal and get a good night's rest," Carson explained his reason for stopping early. "That way we can get an early start and be in Fort Dodge by noon tomorrow."

Adkin was glad to stop early, he and Ryan had been fighting their pack horses most of the way, and it was slow going. They had also helped push a couple of wagons through some tough spots where they slid off into holes or creek beds that had drifted over. Even Diablo seemed to be ready to take a break and get some oats.

Once a small clearing had been kicked and shoveled out, they set the tent and grabbed the stove. This time, the chuckwagon and cook could set up and start a large cooking vat boiling with buffalo meat and potatoes. Adkin could smell the odor of biscuits cooking in a cast iron Dutch oven as he helped secure the tent's ropes to stakes.

An Englishman's Adventures on the Santa Fe Trail (1865-1889)

After their evening meal, Adkin thought it important he tell his traveling partners his story, especially since Carson had bared his soul about the Battle of Adobe Walls, where he had been a so-called hero and victor.

Adkin shared how he discovered the existence of the Santa Fe Trail and his obsession with collecting more information on the trail throughout his young life. How he saved and prepared for the journey, and of course, the adventures he encountered on his trip to where he was today.

He even brought up the incident in St. Augustine, and his brief imprisonment. He rightfully figured the men in his company would understand his predicament at that time.

"That's one thing men on the frontier will not tolerate, Adkin, that's theft – especially theft of a man's possessions which could – and often does – sentence someone to death," Bent said, with a grunt of agreement from the others.

"Would you mind telling me how it came to be that you would build a trading post so far out on the frontier, Colonel Bent?" Adkin asked.

"Well, I had traveled the Santa Fe Trail west, much like all of us – looking for adventure," Bent began, with a sigh. "I had decided I wanted to be a hunter, trader and get involved with the fur trade, as it was quite lucrative.

"It didn't take me long to meet a French aristocrat by the name of Ceran de Hault de Lassus de St. Vrain, who happened to be a fur trader and trapper. His father had been a big shot with the French Navy during the French Revolution.

"Anyway, we just called him Ceran St. Vrain," Bent continued. "He and I formed the Bent, St. Vrain and Company in 1830. Our trade with Mexico grew rapidly in company stores in Santa Fe and Taos, then a part of Mexico, where our wagon trains made deliveries of goods shipped from Independence and Westport, Missouri. We traded cloth, glass, hardware and tobacco for silver, furs, horses, and mules.

"In 1833, we decided to build a trading post – actually it was a rather large fort – on the Big Arkansas River in Southeast Colorado along the Santa Fe Trail," he continued. "That's also about the time my brother, Charles – I had three other brothers – came on board to help us. We did well, but had to always deal with the Mexican government officials and, of course, the Indians, where we were very successful overall.

Adkin learned later from Carson, like he, Bent had also married an Indian; Owl Woman, the daughter of White Thunder, a Cheyenne chief and medicine man, in 1835, then later, her sister, Yellow Woman.

"Charles got caught up in an Indian uprising in 1847 in Taos and got killed," Bent said, looking down at the floor. "But my brothers, George and Robert helped out with the business.

"We had our ups and downs, especially when General Kearny and his Army of the West was returning from taking Santa Fe," he continued. "He and his

1,600 men decided to rest up at the old fort without paying a dime. They used up everything, including all the pasture grazing we had.

"The Army wanted to buy the fort, and I said $16,000 would do it for me," Bent said. "They said they'd only pay $12,000.

"On top of that, with the California Gold strike in 1849, travel along the trail increased substantially, and with them, they brought the cholera," Bent said, looking saddened. "So, we salvaged everything of value, hauled it out and set it on fire near a barrel of powder I left behind and blew the damn thing to hell.

"We then moved our headquarters north to Fort Saint Vrain on the South Platte until 1952.

"When we returned south in 1852, we relocated our trading business to a log trading post at Big Timbers, 38 miles downstream on the Arkansas.

"Later, in the fall of 1853, we began building a stone fort on the bluff above Big Timbers. In 1860, we leased our fort to the United States government, and they renamed it Fort Wise. It had been called Old Fort Lyon earlier," Bent said. "By 1855, Ceran had relocated to Mora County, New Mexico, and I had no surviving brothers by then, either. Ceran built a flour mill and became a newspaper publisher."

"His ability to negotiate with Indians – giving them respect, yet fighting against injustice from either side, is Colonel's Bent's gift to the nation," Carson interjected.

"Thank you Colonel Carson," Bent said, sheepishly, then laughed.

•••

At daylight the next morning, Adkin realized the air wasn't freezing his nostril hairs – it seemed to have returned to the briskness of a fall morning.

Within about three hours, the caravan intersected the Wet Route of the Santa Fe Trail on a bluff near the Arkansas River. Adkin enjoyed the sight of the river as they approached the intersection. He had learned from the others, this was an ambush location the Indians had used for years, once they figured out travelers on the dry Route would often hole up here for a day or two to refresh themselves and their animals.

The actual intersection was highly visible on this day as it looked as if thousands of hooves had cleared all snow from the trail. One of the scouts came riding up to the riders at the lead.

"Colonel Carson, it looks as if about 200 head of cattle moved through here yesterday," the scout said. "They came in from the south, and they're in Fort Dodge, too. The fort is just over that hill."

"The government probably purchased enough beef to feed the soldiers at the new Fort Dodge, and maybe Fort Aubry through the winter," Carson reasoned. "They might also have some Indian bands wintering at the forts."

Though the trail was virtually cleared several hundred yards wide, the warmer temperature was creating boggy areas here and there, but the fort was just over the next hill.

As they approached the new fort, the cattle were immediately visible as they filled the pastures on the north side of the dug outs, and men were busy constructing corral walls with timber poles.

It looked nothing like a fort to Adkin, as there were no walls and only a sod building stood about 100 yards north of the Arkansas River. A U.S. Flag flew on a lone wooden pole above the small building, and Adkin guessed it was the officers' quarters.

The fortifications were crude earth dugouts excavated along the high north bank of the river.

The soldiers had to use the available materials, grass and earth, to create about 70 sod dugouts. Adkin noticed the dugouts looked to be about 10- by 12-feet in circumference and 7-feet deep into the bank. A door of canvas or planks, in some places, faced the river to the south, and a hole in the roof admitted air and light.

"Some fort," Adkin thought to himself. "Poor devils."

As they rolled in, Carson greeted the official guards standing near a tiny guardhouse made of mud and grass and announced his intensions.

"Sentries, would you please inform Captain Henry Pierce that Colonel's Christopher Carson and William Bent would like to visit with him?" Carson spoke loudly.

"Please come on in Colonel Carson," one of the sentries said. "We've been expecting your return."

"Colonel Bent, Yates and Ryan, come with me," Carson said, waving them to follow him to the hitching posts in front of the sod office. "You men set up camp over there on the west side of the dugouts along the river."

As they dismounted, the sentry said, "We'll take care of your horses, gentlemen."

"Thank you Private," Carson said, as he walked up to the front door. Before he could reach for the door handle, it flew open and an officer stepped out.

"Welcome Colonel Carson and Colonel Bent," the man said, as he shook hands with Bent and Carson. "We had heard the peace treaty was successful, and you were headed this way.

"Who do we have here," he asked, looking to Adkin and Ryan.

"Captain Henry Pierce, this is Adkin Yates and Tyler Ryan," Carson said. "They are with the Barlow and Sanderson Overland Stagecoach Company. They're securing coach layovers and stations for a new route to Pueblo."

"Nice to meet you Yates, Ryan. Please, gentlemen, come in," Pierce said as he moved to the side of the doorway.

The quarters were small indeed, and the captain's bed was in sight as there were no interior walls.

"As you can see, we're still in the process of trying to settle in," Pierce said, looking at Adkin and Ryan.

"The Captain here and his men only started building this fort in April, only about seven months ago," Carson explained.

"Yes, Major General Grenville M. Dodge, ordered this fort to be established in order to assist traders and settlers traveling the Santa Fe Trail," Pierce said. "There have been numerous preditations by the Indians in this area where the Dry Route meets back up with the Wet Route."

"We're in constant alert, and we've been busy this summer accompanying caravans between here and Fort Aubry and Fort Larned," he added. "We're hoping to have a little more time to work on settling in now that the busy season is coming – not a lot of freighters like to travel during winter.

"An Army train came through about a week ago loaded with construction supplies for additions at Fort Wise," Pierce said, "Unfortunately, we weren't able to retrieve many supplies from them. Their captain said our building supplies will come out next spring."

"That's what I'm going to keep an eye on," Bent said, with raised eyebrows. "And I assure you, Captain Pierce, if I have any remaining lumber, I will get it to you posthaste."

"The Army may be wanting to increase forts on the Plains, but they are cutting ranks left and right – probably mustered out 500,000 troops in the last six months," Carson added. "Hopefully, many will rejoin the new U.S. Army."

"What's with the cattle you've brought in?" Bent asked Pierce. "Would you like to sell us a few head?"

"I guess we could sell a couple," Pierce answered, with a chuckle. "That would get you to your fort without having to get off the trail to hunt among the Indian raiders that are still out there – and you know as well as I, they are out there, Colonel.

"We contracted with trader Jesse Chisholm two months ago for 200 head of cattle," Pierce said. "He is here now – planning on leaving as soon as the corrals are completed. His cowboys are helping build them, and there is not much timber around here, at all. We'll most likely have to use sod and rocks for all the posts, as you've probably seen when coming in."

"We know Jesse well, Colonel Bent and I do anyway," Carson said. "I met Jesse's good friend Jim Meade at the Little Arkansas Treaty. How did you hook up with Jesse? He's a big time trader in the Indian Territories mainly, or that's what I thought."

"Well, my procurement officer, Lieutenant Willow, is part Caddo Indian and knows Chisholm well," Pierce said. "Plus, Willow fought for the Confederacy, as most of my soldiers did, and he assured me we'd get a better deal from Chisholm – and we did."

"Confederates?" Adkin spoke up, without realizing he had said it out loud.

"Yes Yates, most of these men decided to join the U.S. Army after the war and fight Indians on the frontier rather than languish in prisons in the North," Pierce explained. "But, this is no Garden of Eden, either. My men sleep on banks of earth – not bunks – that sleep four to six men. The sanitation is poor and late spring rains flooded their dugouts. Many have suffered from pneumonia, dysentery, diarrhea and even malaria. This cold spell hasn't helped either.

"But these ex-Confederates are stubborn-headed and deadly Indian fighters," he continued. "The Indians are learning to fear them and their reputation to fight to the death.

"These men don't have much else, and I'm proud to be their commanding officer," Pierce added, with a stern look on his face.

Captain Pierce suggested they get their camp situated and invited them back for supper.

Carson, Bent, Adkin and Ryan showed up at Pierce's quarters at 6:30, having squared away their few wagons and made their animals comfortable. Bent had sent one of his men over to select two beeves from the Army's herd that they would take with the caravan for meat.

When they entered, Captain Pierce made introductions to a tall, white-haired man with high prominent cheekbones that looked much like an Indian warrior. It was Jesse Chisholm of Oklahoma – deep from the Indian Territories – and wearing tasseled buckskins from head to toe.

Before they left their camp for supper, Bent had told Adkin that Chisholm's father was a Scotsman and his mother was a full-blooded Cherokee Indian. Adkin could see the family ancestry without doubt.

Carson and Bent greeted Chisholm like an old friend with comments like, "Glad to see you still have your hair" and similar jokes about surviving the wild west. All three men were near identical ages – 55 to 57 years old.

As Captain Pierce poured the men a glass of whisky and set out a box of cigars, Adkin asked if he could have water.

"So, Yates, Ryan, where are you two from?" Chisholm asked. "I have not heard of you in my travels."

Yates explained they both represented Barlow and Sanderson Overland Stagecoach Company and their role in heading west to Pueblo.

"Your dialect sounds like an Englishman or Australian," Chisholm said.

Yates gave him a quick synopsis of his brief history in America after his departure from England, and Chisholm seemed impressed.

"When I saw your headband and the necklaces you both wear, I knew you to be protected in the brotherhood of the Kiowa tribe, that's why I was puzzled that I had never heard of you," Chisholm said. "And it looks like you, Yates, are the friend and brother of Chief Satanta – those beaver teeth are his sign. I am also a friend of Satanta"

"Young Yates helped protect the daughter of Satanta's medicine man, Black Horse, from severe harm at the Little Arkansas Treaty a week or so ago," Carson explained. "It helped substantially in coming to peaceful terms with the Kiowa and Comanches."

"That is good," Chisholm said, with a chuckle. "It never hurts to have a friend like Satanta in this part of the world. He can be a ruthless killer, but if he is your friend, he will not harm you – if you do not cross him.

"My fellow trader, Jim Meade, is also good friends with Satanta, and he has many tales about that Indian, as well as others he know well," he added. "Was old Chief Satank there?

"No, didn't see him anywhere," Bent said.

Several spoke up about Meade being instrumental at the peace treaty negotiations, and Chisholm was glad to hear it went well and that his friend, Meade, was back in Towanda.

"Let me tell you how contrary Satanta's old competitor Chief Satank can be, plus other Chiefs he knew well," Chisholm said. "Jim told me the story about how Satank killed old George Peacock back in '60 at old Allison's Ranch House on Walnut Creek.

"Back in the days when the Kiowa supreme Chief Dohäsan, died, there was a power struggle between Satank and Satanta, who was younger. But Satanta was already a big War Chief," Chisholm said. "Anyway, Mead told me an intersting story about Satank, how easy he could be set off.

"Peacock had taken over the trading post after One-Armed Allison had died," he continued. "Seems old Satank came to Peacock wanting a letter of introduction, because he was a chief of importance, and the letter would help Satank be treated civilly and entertained by freighters traveling on the trail.

"Well, Peacock wrote a letter – in English – saying that, "The bearer of this, Satank, is the dirtiest, laziest, lousiest vagabond on the Plains; if he comes to your camp, kick him out,'" Chisholm said, smiling. "Well, the very next caravan passing through, Satank showed them the letter – and to his surprise – he was treated with derision, contempt and abuse. Satank realized there was something wrong with the credentials he had from Peacock.

"He took the letter to his friend, Buffalo Bill – Bill Mathewson on Cow Creek, who truthfully translated the letter into Kiowa," he continued, laughing harder now. "Satank swore vengeance, and Bill sent word to Peacock to what he might expect, but Peacock scoffed at the warning.

"The killing was well planned. Peacock had a tall lookout on top of his trading post because he was selling liquor to the Indians and was afraid of troops. Well,

Satank and some of his men came by and told Peacock there were a lot of soldiers coming," Chisholm continued. "Peacock climbed to the top of his lookout to see, and Satank shot him dead. They also killed Peacock's clerk and a Mexican herder.

"As Jim told it, 'If Peacock had treated the Indians decently, he probably would not have been disturbed,'" he added, laughing. "Disturbed? Jim always did have a way with words.

"I surprised Satank wasn't there with Satanta at the treaty," he said.

The men laughed, and Adkin realized that death, honor, respect, vengeance – all had extreme meanings and extreme worth in this extreme world called the American Frontier.

After a meal of fresh beef roasted over flames, and cornmeal and watered-down gravy, the men settled back for more conversation; mostly about where Indians had disturbed the peace recently. Though nothing serious had erupted along the trail locally, they discussed some of the battles being fought throughout the Plains from Oklahoma down through Texas.

"Word is the Army is going to build many more forts throughout Comancheria to protect settlers," Carson said. "I've heard several forts will be used to stockpile lumber and building materials for the expansion in the coming year or so."

"It can't some soon enough," Pierce said. "My men deserve civilized quarters – to sleep in dry wooden barracks and sleep on solid warm bunks off the ground."

He informed the travelers the Army was currently increasing its presence at Fort Aubrey, which was about a three-day trip upstream.

"Two separate troop movements have passed through here in the last three weeks," Pierce said.

"We must have just missed them as we were coming down for the peace treaty," Carson said.

"The last re-enforcements came through Oct. 14 with Company "D," 13th Missouri Volunteer Cavalry, under the command of First Lieutenant T. J. Shinn," Pierce said. "He had 49 extra horses with him and adding his troops, there must be more than 300 soldiers at Fort Aubrey now."

"Sounds like the Army is fulfilling its promise to us traders to help protect us and the new settlers coming west," Bent said.

Ryan asked if anyone knew of a trader named Chris Rath nearby along the trail. Adkin told Pierce about signing a deal with Louie Booth, the manager of Charley Rath's trading post – Peacock's old post – at Walnut Creek.

Pierce said he did know Chris Rath – his place was just a mile north of the Dry Route-Wet Route intersection.

"He established a trading post on the Fort Hays Trail where it comes into the Santa Fe Trail," Pierce said. "You went just passed it."

"Chris Rath you say, Captain?" Bent spoke up. "I know Charley Rath. He worked for us in 1853 – a big dark-haired German."

"That's right, Colonel Bent, Chris is Charles' older brother – they own a post on the Fort Hays to Fort Riley Road, too," Pierce said.

"Charley's a good man, but I don't know his brother, Chris," Bent said.

"I know him and Charley," Carson said. "They stirred up quite a few folks when they built a toll bridge over Walnut Creek and made everybody on the trail pay to cross it.

"Even the Indians," he added, laughing.

Adkin and Ryan agreed they would ride back to see this Rath in the morning, and told Carson and Bent not to wait on them, they would catch up with the caravan, hopefully, by noon.

"Do you mind if I ride with you, Yates?" Bent asked. "I would like to meet Charley's brother"

"No problem, we'd enjoy your company," Adkin said.

Chisholm said he, too, would be departing Fort Dodge on the morning on his way back to Hughes County, Okla.

"And I'm going to stop in Towanda to see my old friend Jim Meade," he said, laughing. "Just to make sure he hasn't been 'disturbed' by irate Indians."

They all laughed.

•••

Early the next morning, with an icy wind pouring in from the north, Adkin, Ryan and Bent headed southeast on horseback along the trail to find Chris Rath's new trading post just north of a major intersection of the Santa Fe Trail's Dry Route and Wet Route and the new trail north to Fort Hays.

Adkin's and Ryan's pack horses were tied to the back of one of Carson's wagons headed west again.

Within a couple of miles, the riders recognized a small rarely used trail breaking off to the left. It hadn't been visible a few days earlier due to the snow-covered ground. As they topped a small sandhill about a mile north, they saw a small log house with a corral that had been thrown together from driftwood. Smoke rose from the rooftop and disappeared almost immediately to the south. There was also a barn-like building and numerous chickens were chasing insects across the pasture land near the house.

As they approached, a man came out the front door carrying a long gun.

"Would you be Chris Rath?" Bent bellowed, raising his arm as many Indians do upon greetings.

"I would be," Rath said. "And who would be looking for me?"

"I am Colonel William Bent of Colorado, and a friend of your brother, Charley," Bent said, as he, Adkin and Ryan dismounted.

"Ah yes, I be from that Rath family, and my brother speaks well of you, Colonel Bent," Rath said, reaching out his hand. "Welcome to our humble post."

Bent shook hands with Rath and introduced Adkin and Ryan. All were invited into the house where Rath offered them coffee and said he would be pleased to fry them some eggs if they were hungry.

"We've had our breakfast, but thank you Mr. Rath," Bent said.

"Please, Colonel, call me Chris," Rath said. "I feel as if I know you from all the glorious tales my brother has told me about the adventures you two have shared."

'They are only called adventures – if you are not killed," Bent said, with a chuckle. The others laughed, as well.

"How is it you are here?" Bent asked. "We spent time with Charley at the Little Arkansas Treaty north of Walnut Grove in mid-October. He never mentioned you and he had established a new post here."

"Well, Charley has had a lot on his mind the last few years," Chris said. "His heart is broken because he and his wife had to separate, and she has his daughter."

"A wife? A daughter?" Bent asked, looking surprised.

"Yes, you may know he married a Cheyenne woman in 1860, and they had a little girl a year later," Rath continued. "He had developed good relations trading with the Southern Cheyenne, the northern Comanche bands and the Kiowa after he took over Peacock's place at Walnut Creek."

"Yes, we stopped there," Bent said.

"Yes, but after a few years, tensions developed between white settlers and the Indians. He tried his best to keep the peace, but his trading post was raided several times, and his wife convinced him to divorce her for his own safety.

"He reluctantly agreed after nearly getting killed in one of the raids," Rath said, looking weary.

"Sorry to hear that," Bent said, shaking his head. "He didn't say a word about that to us."

"He's still hauling goods and hides all over Kansas and down into the Indian Territories in Oklahoma," Rath said, smiling again. "We decided to build this place and Charles has filed for ownership of trust lands along the Arkansas here and even some west of the new Fort Dodge – if you can call it a fort."

"Charley came out west to haul freight for me in 1853," Bent said. "I don't remember him saying too much about family other than he was originally from Germany and had come to America when he was 11 or 12 – said he had lived in Ohio, I believe."

"Yes, that's right," Chris said. "After that year with you, he sent for me in Ohio, and I came out to team up with him in late 1854. We built a gristmill on Mill Creek east of Fort Riley four years later, and it got wiped out by a flood as soon as we were ready to start operations."

"I remember hearing about that," Bent said. "But Charley always did have grit – he won't quit on life. He looked good when we saw him."

Bent filled Chris in on who Adkin and Ryan represented and what they were looking for.

"A stagecoach station?" Chris asked, more to himself than to the others. "Charles would love that, and so would I. Where do I sign?"

Adkin told Chris how they planned to establish the stations and supply them in the Spring of 1866 as operations would be up and running as soon as weather and stagecoach traffic cooperated.

As Adkin gave out more details, of where they were setting up stations, Adkin remembered to tell Chris about their contract with Louie Booth – and in extension, Charley and Chris Rath, too.

"That's great, so we have two stagecoach stations?" Chris said with a chuckle. "Let's all make some good money while we can. Word is the railroads will be moving through the High Plains within a few years. That's what Charley says anyway.

"Oh, they're coming, but we can all make a small fortune before that happens," Adkin said, with Ryan agreeing with a nod.

The men finished their business, and after the farewells, the three headed west to catch up with their caravan.

They stopped briefly in Fort Dodge and greeted Captain Pierce and reported the Rath brothers would be establishing a stagecoach station at their place, and it would be supplied by Barlow and Sanderson in the Spring.

After a cup of coffee, they took off west again, hoping to catch up with Carson in a couple of hours or so.

About 15 miles west of Fort Dodge, the men came across the ruins of the old abandoned Fort Atkinson.

"It closed down in about 1854," Bent said. "The soldiers had called it Fort Sod because it was built much like Fort Dodge – built of sod, covered with poles, brush, sod and canvas."

Just then from the top of a large sand dune, five Indians appeared on horseback and plunged down through the sand yelping at the top of their lungs and waving their bows in the air. Adkin didn't see any rifles.

They skidded to a dusty halt about 15 feet from Bent who turned his horse toward them and held up his right hand. He said something in an Indian language and gave Adkin and Ryan a stern look – as if to say be careful.

One Indian started speaking and Bent interrupted him with several words spoken in a mean, gutteral sound. Bent, again, gave the other two a look and a nod of his head toward the Indians.

Adkin looked at Ryan and Ryan, looked down at his pistol and nodded to Adkin as if to say, be prepared to pull their guns.

Several of the Indians started arguing with the lead speaker, who then turned back to Bent and started yelling and pumping his bow up and down with his left arm. Bent noticed the Indian ease his right hand toward the arrow quiver attached to the right side of the waistband of his deerskin breeches.

In a heartbeat, Bent pulled the small Remington pistol he carried in his waistband and shot the Indian right in the middle of his forehead. As the Indian fell backward off his mount, Bent had pulled his long-barrelled Colt from his holster with his other hand and aimed both at the rest of the Indians who sat there, momentarily frozen.

Adkin and Ryan pulled their handguns out and also aimed at the remaining Indians.

Bent said something again, in a low menacing voice, and the Indians turned and started kicking their ponies. Bent then yelled several more words at them and fired several rounds from both pistols in the air.

Adkin was still aiming his pistol at the horizon and at nothing in particular as Bent dismounted and kneeled next to the dead Indian, his blood soaking into the soft sand as he was sprawled on his back.

"They're Kwaharu Indians," Bent broke the silence. "They are a Comanche band known as the Antelope Eaters.

"They said they were going to kill us because I told them they couldn't have our horses," I told them who I was, who you were – protected friends of the Kiowa – and the others decided they didn't want any trouble," Bent explained. "But this one would hear nothing of it. While he was waving his bow he said he would put an arrow in me as soon as he could string it.

"So, I had to shoot him," Bent said. "It's too bad – he wanted our animals and was ready to kill for them. I had no choice."

"What were you yelling at those riding away?" Adkin asked.

"I told them if I ever saw them again I would kill them and then go kill their families as well," Bent said, matter of factly, as he remounted his horse. "They'll come back for him later, after we've been gone awhile. They're a hunting and raiding party and probably have stolen horses nearby, but the main band's lodges are most likely much further south of here at this time of the year.

"Raiding bands will sometimes stay out for four or five weeks from their main lodges, stealing and killing," Bent said, as he reined his horse westward. "This one chose the wrong people to try to kill today."

Adkin and Ryan fell in behind Bent as they headed west again on the Santa Fe Trail.

"It's one hell of a place," Adkin thought to himself. "Now I know what Bent means by defining 'adventure' as when one isn't killed."

About an hour and a half later, they spotted their caravan trudging through desolate sand hills sporadically spotted with sage brush, yucca and buffalo grass.

Adkin had noticed the countryside had turned into sand hills as far as the eye could see once they neared Fort Dodge a few days ago. Now, the hills were giving way to vast expanses of flatness, but the sandy soil still sucked at the hooves of animals, the wheels of wagons and even men's boots.

Carson halted the train as they approached and told everyone they would camp there for the night.

As camp was being set, Bent explained they had run into a "crazy, bloodthirsty Comanche," according to Bent's words. He told Carson how the others wanted no problems after hearing who they were.

"But this young warrior was hell-bent with his desire for more horseflesh," Bent said. "And when he reached for his quiver, I shot him."

"You're lucky he didn't have a gun," Carson said, while shaking his head. "He would have probably shot you the second he rode up."

"Believe me, I was ready for that, Colonel Carson," Bent said with a broad smile.

As they ate a meal of roasted beef from Captain Pierce's herd, Adkin told Carson they had succeeded in signing Chris Rath to a stagecoach station contract.

"He also signed his brother's name in his stead," Adkin added. "He said Charley would stand behind his decision to add him to the contract."

"Great, those guys will become a force in business out here," Carson said. "That German stubbornness and work ethic will do them well."

They went to bed early in order to get an early start. Carson said they should make Fort Aubrey in two more days, and he was anxious to see how much that fort had grown in only a month.

After supper the next evening, Bent asked Adkin if he could make a suggestion about the stage line. Adkin eagerly encouraged Bent to speak up, as both Bent and Carson had already given him and Ryan invaluable information about the trail, the various bands of Indians that haunted the Santa Fe Trail and its travelers.

"What's on your mind, Colonel Bent?" Adkin asked.

"Well Yates, I've noticed the average days' travel between your stations," Bent began. "I would like to work with you and the Barlow and Sanderson stage line and establish a station at my trading post just east of old Fort Lyon. Folks are calling it Bent's New Fort. From there, you probably would not require another location until your destination at Pueblo."

"How many days travel is it from your place to Pueblo?" Ryan asked.

"Well normally, it's about four days with a large caravan, but I'm guessing it's nearly half that with a stagecoach and four- to six-horse teams," Bent said.

"I also have a experienced trader that was a so-called partner with Francois Xavier Aubrey – a renowned freighter and trail blazer in these parts for many years. The trader's name is John O'Loughlin, and he now has a place where the

Aubrey Cutoff Trail to the Cimarron Route of the Santa Fe Trail – the original Santa Fe Trail – heads south," Bent continued. "After we pass the upper crossing of the trail, his place is the next post on the Arkansas, where Aubrey's cutoff heads to the southern route of the Santa Fe Trail."

"I think I know where he's talking about, but I haven't been through there in two years," Ryan said, looking back to Bent. "You know this O'Laughlin well, Colonel Bent?"

"Not well, but I knew his partner very well, and if Aubrey let him invest in his dealings, he has my respect," Bent said. "I knew Francois since he and my brother, Charles, first met in 1846 or '47. Some called him Colonel Aubrey or Auberry, but we called him Francois – he was French-Canadian. Later, newspaper writers and dime store novelists called him 'Skimmer of the Plains' because he set records traveling certain trails – many times.

"In 1848, he made it from Santa Fe to Independence in 14 days in a wagon," Bent said. "Later that year, he rode alone and made it in eight days and 10 hours."

"How could a man do that?" Adkin asked, with a slack-jaw.

"Francois was very creative," Bent continued. "He would set out fresh horses along the trail at various places, whether riding alone or with caravans. He also was good at breaking and setting trails to reduce time on the prairie.

"On one trip, Francois left Santa Fe and reached Cold Spring in the Oklahoma Panhandle. From there, he chose to leave the regular Santa Fe road about two miles northeast of the spring and attempted a new road running in an east-north direction," Bent said. "He was hoping to find a better trail to the Arkansas River. Francois hoped that by choosing a new route, the wagons could avoid the dreaded Jornada – a trip over the extreme dry area of the Cimarron Trail – and reach the river faster. But that trip was unsuccessful.

"But he didn't give up," Bent continued. "His next attempt in 1851 was successful. He told us, 'We traveled from 10 to 40 degrees east of north to the Arkansas, finding an excellent wagon road, well supplied with water and grass, and avoiding the Jornado and Cimarron Trail altogether.'

"Since that time, the trail has been aptly called the Aubrey Cutoff," he added.

"His friend O'Laughlin has set up a post where the cutoff intersects with the Santa Fe Trail," Bent said.

"Is Aubrey not alive?" Adkin asked.

"No, unfortunately, his fame for fast trips across the Plains got him killed – in a way," Bent said, looking sorrowful. "His exploits attracted the attention of a man who Francois thought was his friend. His name was Richard Weightman, and at the time, he was a reporter for an Albuquerque newspaper.

"He interviewed Francois about a successful sheep selling trip to California from Santa Fe. Francois had successfully herded thousands of sheep to California twice, and while he was out there during his last trip, he got word Weightman's article was apparently quite abusive of Francois' character and reputation, and it ridiculed his personal attractions," Bent continued. "Much like Satanta got mad at Peacock, Francois immediately returned to New Mexico, mad as a hornet.

"He soon found Weightman at Moncure's Saloon and the two started arguing. Someone threw a drink in Francois' face, and he pulled a pistol, and it went off," Bent said. "Some witnesses said the gun misfired, and Weightman wasn't hit, but he pulled a bowie knife and stabbed Francois, killing him.

"I know for a fact if Francois had been trying to shoot Weightman, that hack would be dead. Francois may have been only 5-feet, 4-inches and small framed, but he was a dead shot with a pistol – or a rifle. No one could out shoot him," Bent said, with anger in his voice.

"That was on August 20, 1854, and Francois was only 29 years old," Bent said. "Weightman was found not guilty because of self defense. But it was all politics. This Weightman was a West Point graduate, had fought in the Mexican War and served in Washington as a delegate to New Mexico.

"I thought about tracking him down myself several times and killing the coward, and I was pleased to hear of his death while he was commanding a division at the Battle of Carthage in 1861 in Missouri," Bent said, with a pleased look in his eyes.

"I've met O'Laughlin, Adkin, and I think you will find him an honorable man to do business with," Carson added.

"Well, I think your proposal sounds wonderful, Colonel Bent," Adkin said, looking at Ryan, who nodded his approval with a smile. "We would consider it an honor to have you as part of our line."

"I have another proposal, that can save you money and make me some cash, too," Bent said, smiling himself now. "I can procure all the horses for your stations from Pueblo to Fort Dodge – and have my men deliver them."

"That is an answer to my prayers, Colonel Bent," Ryan spoke up excitedly. "I've been dreading trying to move a large herd of good horses all the way from Fort Leavenworth to Colorado – considering our Indian friends' love of horse flesh."

They all started laughing.

•••

That evening, they camped at what was called Indian Mound, where a small wooded island sat midstream in the Arkansas River.

"You can see places up here on the mound where treasure hunters have been digging looking for valuable relics," Carson said, shaking his head. "Some believe this mound is a great burial ground where Indians from centuries ago and all their earthly goods were piled up like gold bars.

"Fool's gold is what it is," he added with a laugh. "But it does make for a good lookout – you can see for miles in every direction."

"That little island is named Chouteau's Island after a fur trader who got ambushed near here by 200 Pawnees," Bent interrupted, pointing south to the river. "His name was Auguste P. Chouteau, and he and his hunting party were attacked in 1816 and crossed over to the island to defend themselves. They survived, and the story goes he only lost one man.

"See how the water lines on the river banks are going down, especially around the island?" Bent asked. "That means winter has set up in the Colorado Mountains. As freezing temperatures increase, the water flow downstream decreases.

"That island was almost twice its size about 30 years ago," he continued. "A little more of it will erode away next spring when the snow runoff swells the river again."

Adkin noticed a team of men off the trail that were walking along on each side of a small wagon without canvas being pulled by two mules. The men on foot were bending over and throwing buffalo dung into the wagon. Ryan told him this was the main fuel out on the prairie where trees were seldom found.

"They've been using those chips for our cooking fires the last few days," Ryan said.

Adkin decided to keep his thoughts to himself and didn't respond.

After eating more beef, this time boiled with chunks of potatoes with flour stirred into the stew, Adkin laid back on his bed roll and tried to gather his thoughts.

First, he didn't notice the buffalo chips had changed the taste of his meal at all, and he was greatly relieved.

Then he realized he had departed Fort Leavenworth only 47 days ago, yet it had seemed like a lifetime. Even in his wildest dreams he could have never imagined the reality of traveling the trails and experiencing the Plains of Kansas.

His appreciation of adventurous men – and women – had become a daily part of his life. Everyone out here has that yearning to explore and to see what lies around the next bend in the trail or the rivers and creeks.

Tomorrow, they will arrive at Fort Aubrey and meet Bent's acquaintance, O'Laughlin. If he is everything Bent says, he and Ryan will have easy sailing into Pueblo, since Bent has offered to get involved and will establish a station at his fort.

"And I can't wait to see Bent's Fort," Adkin thought to himself. "He, Carson and all the others I have met are nothing less than extraordinary.

"Thank you God, and I will always hold you near to my heart," he prayed to himself. "And please watch over my family in England."

•••

About two hours after breaking camp, an Army scout came riding up. He, too was Indian but wore the usual hat and uniform shirt of a trooper. He wore his hair in long braids on each side, hanging down from under his hat.

He informed Carson an Army detail was over the hill behind him, led by Lieutenant Thomas Doyle. They were on their way to Fort Dodge to retrieve some cattle.

Two soldiers on horseback came into view ahead of them, riding in file with a freight wagon behind them. Trailing the wagon were 10 more troops, also on horses.

"Halt," a lead soldier said, raising his hand.

"Sirs, I am Lieutenant Thomas Doyle of Company 'K,' 13th Missouri Cavalry, at Fort Aubrey," he said to Carson and Bent with a salute.

Both men introduced themselves, and Adkin could tell the Lieutenant was impressed.

"Er ... nice to meet you ... Colonels – er ... pleased ... er"

"At ease, Lieutenant Doyle," Carson said, smiling, then introducing Adkin and Ryan as well.

"So you're on your way to Fort Dodge for some fresh beeves?" Carson asked.

"Yes sir," Doyle said. "We're charged with returning 50 head back to Fort Aubrey, sir."

"They're tasty beef," Bent said, pointing back at their lead wagon. "That's one of them over there tethered to that freighter."

"Well, you men be careful returning with all those beeves," Carson said. "We ran into a party of Kwaharu Comanches a ways back and had to kill one of them. They wanted our horses.

"They may still be in the area, if there are any buffalo around," Bent added.

"Yes sir, we'll be careful," Doyle said, and saluted again as Carson and Bent reined their horses westward while saluting back.

Adkin smiled to himself as he watched the soldiers just staring at Carson and Bent as they rode away. Undoubtedly, they were in awe of being in the presence of Colonels "Kit" Carson and William Bent.

The caravan rolled up to O'Laughlin's place about mid-day on Nov. 2, 1865. Adkin was impressed by O'Laughlin's accommodations.

The main house and barn were made of split cottonwood logs, which meant there had been an extra amount of tedious labor – the huge trees would have been cut down along the river banks, dragged by teams to the site, peeled of bark and using wedges and sledges, split in slabs about 4- to 6-inches wide and various lengths.

There was a small corral but large enough to keep a couple of dozen horses. The outbuilding was also somewhat small, but Adkin figured it was where O'Laughlin kept most of his trade goods, besides what storage the barn provided.

An Englishman's Adventures on the Santa Fe Trail (1865-1889)

The main building and outbuilding both had rock chimneys, and the firewood piles looked a little shy of inventory to Adkin, especially with winter coming on.

Bent was the first out of his saddle as he neared the front hitching posts.

"John, John," Where are you man?" Bent yelled as he hit the ground.

"I'm right here," O'Laughlin said, as he stepped out of the doorway and chuckled. "You don't have to bray like a mule."

Both men shook hands then grabbed each other's shoulders.

"I'm sorry we missed you when we came through last month," Bent said.

"I'm sorry, too," O'Laughlin said. "We were out gathering a few buffalo to salt away for the winter.

"And how are you, Colonel Carson," he asked, as he turned toward Carson and shook his hand, too.

"Fine, John, just fine."

Bent introduced Adkin and Ryan, and O'Laughlin invited them into the house, as the air was brisk and chilly, even though clear, blue skies and bright sunshine dominated the countryside.

O'Laughlin filled several clay goblets with wine and offered them to the men. Adkin went ahead and took one and sipped it lightly. He had discovered he didn't disagree with some of the alcohol he had tasted, but knew his partaking would only be a social gesture. He had learned people on the Plains – including Indians – didn't care for those who didn't appreciate hospitality.

They made small talk, discussing the troopers heading to Fort Dodge for some of Jesse Chisholm's cattle herd. O'Laughlin said they hadn't encountered any hostile Indians lately, and he mentioned how Fort Aubrey had increased in size within just a few months.

"We had some snow last week, but it didn't hold," O'Laughlin said. "But winter is definitely on its way – the Arkansas is down about a foot. Won't be long and most everything will be iced up."

"I noticed your firewood inventory looked somewhat low," Akin said. "I guess there's not that much timber around these parts, though."

"We'll scrounge up and down the river for more deadfall, but we also have two chip piles behind the barn," O'Laughlin said.

"Chip piles?" Adkin asked.

O'Laughlin looked back and forth at the others, smiling.

"He's from England and only been in Kansas a couple of months," Carson said, then turned to Adkin. "They go out in wagons and gather dried buffalo scat – we call 'em buffalo chips. They make a good, hot fire and burn for quite awhile.

"You may have noticed several piles of them behind the big rocks on the east side of the corrals they were building at Fort Dodge," he continued. "Those were chip piles."

"Without buffalo chips, half the new settlers out here wouldn't have made it through last winter," Bent added.

"Or even some soldiers," O'Laughlin said, with a chuckle.

"That's what I love about America," Adkin said, smiling. "You learn something new every day."

"You better learn, or the adventures will end – if you know what I mean," Bent said, with a wink.

They all laughed, knowing exactly what Bent meant.

The discussion turned to what Adkin and Ryan were looking for, and O'Laughlin jumped on board immediately.

"This place is situated in a very favorable location – to provide stagecoach service onward northwest to Pueblo, or to expand southwest down the Aubrey Cutoff to the Cimarron Route to Santa Fe – if desired at a later date," O'Laughlin said, enthusiastically.

"Plus, I've been wanting to build another warehouse attached to the barn and this will be a great motivation to get me off my arse and get it started."

They laughed again, and O'Laughlin filled their goblets with more wine.

"We've got one more night's salted beef left – the other is still on the hoof," Carson said. "What say we get the boys to cooking?"

"If you don't need us for anything, Adkin and I would like to go down to the river and get some more shooting practice in," Ryan said.

"No, you boys go ahead," Carson said. "You can never get too much practice."

Adkin and Ryan had decided to practice with their pistols the last two evenings after their encounter with the Comanches.

"You know, Tyler, I can handle my rifle well, but I need to know how to handle this pistol, too," Adkin had said to Ryan the afternoon Bent had shot the Indian dead.

"I'm in the same boat," Ryan said. "I'm comfortable with a rifle, but I have never really had to use my handgun, except maybe killing a rattlesnake or some varmint in camp."

"It's apparent that making life or death decisions have to be made quite fast," Adkin had said. "But if you're not a good shot, your decision doesn't count."

The two made their way down to a high bank of the river, and as the sun was nearing the horizon, he couldn't help but stop and take in the magnificent view up and down the valley.

"It's bloody beautiful out here, Tyler," Adkin said, silently asking for the Lord's forgiveness for cursing.

They picked out small targets along the bank – sticks or small logs jutting out of the moving water and fired round after round.

After shooting nearly a box of balls and caps, Adkin called it an evening as the sun had sunk half way below the purple and golden edge of the world.

"With all this practicing for three nights in a row," We're going to have to see if O'Laughlin has some shooting supplies for us," Ryan said, with a laugh. "I'm about out."

"I'm sure he does," Adkin responded, laughing, too.

The next morning, Adkin and Ryan purchased more ammunition for their pistols. Adkin was correct in thinking O'Laughlin's other outbuilding was being used as a warehouse. It was only about 15-feet long and 10-feet wide, but it contained shelves from the floor to the roof – and the shelves were full of various items and goods.

"Well, we best get moving gentlemen," Carson yelled as Adkin and Ryan walked out of the warehouse. "If you get to Taos, come see me, John."

"I will, Colonel Carson," O'Laughlin said, while saluting. "Be careful, Colonel Bent."

"God bless, John," Bent said half saluting as well.

Carson and Bent reined their horses westward with the small caravan falling in behind them.

"We should be in Fort Bent in two days men," Bent yelled to no one in particular.

...

Shortly after the caravan had stopped for lunch, two Indian scouts rode up and started talking in an Indian language with Bent. They didn't look like the Ute scouts Adkin had become familiar with. He would later learn they were Tonkawas – or Tonks – who hated Comanches.

Bent answered, then smiled and laughed with the scouts. Adkin could not make out what they were jabbering about, but Bent seemed happy.

"Colonel Carson, come here please. I've good news,"

Bent shouted back to Carson who was sitting near the cook's wagon on a stool. He rose and walked to Bent. They both started laughing and patting each other on the back.

The Tonks refused an offer for a meal and started loping off eastward toward O'Laughlin's trading post. Bent and Carson came back to the cook's wagon.

"Well men, looks like we're moving into the telegraph age sooner than expected," Carson said.

"Telegraph crews under Army protection are stringing wire along the Santa Fe Trail just a few miles ahead of us," Bent said, beaming. "They've already set up a telegraph station at Bent's Fort.

"The scouts said they started out of Santa Fe, New Mexico, and are working eastward, while crews are working westward and should be somewhere behind us by about a week or two," Carson said. "Seems the effort is a high priority and the crews are being supplied and protected by at least an Army Company at each end."

"I had seen many of these supplies being assembled at Fort Union last year," Bent said. "Didn't you, Colonel Carson?"

"Yes, but I didn't have much faith the Army would get it all together this soon," Carson answered. "It was President Lincoln's big dream to build a railroad and the telegraph from coast to coast, but he ain't alive to see it happening."

"Well, it's great news," Adkin and Ryan said, almost simultaneously, while smiling at each other.

"We may have to change our plans a little, Tyler," Adkin said to Ryan.

"I was thinking the same thing, Ryan said. "If we waited until the lines are completed in a week or two, we could get in touch with Sanderson and let him know what's been accomplished so far."

"Yes, and he could wire us some more funds – that's if you would honor a bank draft on the Barlow and Sanderson Overland Stagecoach Company, Colonel Bent."

Bent smiled and said, "I think I can trust a company I'm going to get involved with, gentlemen."

"This changes several things and could have us running coaches sooner than we expected," Ryan said, slapping Adkin on the back. "Partner, we must be doing something right."

"God has truly blessed us thus far, that's for sure," Adkin said, chuckling.

After sharing a few more light moments and laughs, Carson readied everyone again, shouting, "We're wasting daylight men," as he mounted his steed and waved westward.

Adkin pulled himself into the saddle on Diablo and patted the horse's coal black neck.

"Things are looking good, Diablo," he whispered close to Diablo's ear.

"You talk to that horse more than you do most people," Ryan said, chuckling. "And you're pretty chatty, too."

"He's getting used to my voice, and I'm training him more and more to voice and whistle commands," Adkin said. "When his reins are untied, I can say 'come' and he'll follow – for awhile anyway – he's getting better and better. He's the smartest stallion I've ever seen."

"He's the real thing, that's for sure, "Ryan agreed. "A beautiful beast at that. And he's from stock that's been bred for a hundred years by the Kiowa."

The caravan spotted the telegraph crews within about two hours. Adkin was somewhat surprised at how many men, wagons and soldiers were involved.

The crews were spread out about three-quarters of a mile. There were wagons with poles hewn from what looked like pine trees being unloaded, men were using picks to dig wide and deep holes, others were using block and tackle to raise the poles and slide them into the holes, then others tamping them down.

The wagons with wire had huge spools on them sitting astride fulcrums with men pulling off the wire as the wagon slowly moved along. Others were climbing the poles with the wire being lifted to them with long, thin push poles.

And the men: There must have been at least a hundred and most looked to be dark skinned, like the few Mexicans he had seen so far. Many wore the wide-brimmed sombreros, Adkin noticed.

Soldiers were everywhere, too. There were numerous wagons sitting about a hundred yards on each side of the workmen with soldiers all around with their long guns. There were also four howitzers on their two-wheeled carts at the ready.

"Looks as busy as an ant hill," Carson said. "Looks like they know what they're doing, too."

"Sure does," Bent said, as five cook's wagons and a couple of ambulances slowly moved ahead of the chaos with an Army escort of calvary on both sides.

"I bet this even impresses the Indians," Ryan said to Adkin. "And they don't have any idea how this is going to affect them when it's up and running. Communication between these forts will allow troops to be dispatched with a speed Indians will not believe."

"A deadly speed," Adkin said, with a frown on his brow.

•••

Two calvary riders came galloping up to the front of the caravan and saluted when they brought their steeds to a dusty halt.

"Greetings Colonel Bent and General Carson," a young-looking Lieutenant said.

"Hello, Lieutenant Campbell," both men said at the same time, smiling. "This is Adkin Yates and Tyler Ryan, representatives of the Barlow and Sanderson Overland Stagecoach Line from Leavenworth," Carson said. "Gentlemen, this is Lieutenant Weldon Campbell, with the New Mexico Volunteers of the U.S. Army."

"All the men nodded their heads with a few mumbled, "nice to meet you" comments thrown in.

"Captain Pettis would like to visit with you when possible," Campbell said, pointing over his left shoulder. "He's in that wagon over there with the two white stallions tied to the back."

"We'll be over shortly, Lieutenant," Carson said, saluting as they spurred their horses around back to the chaotic scene of workers, soldiers and wagons.

After Bent and Carson shouted commands to move their caravan north of the trail and around the linemen, Adkin spoke up.

"He called you General Carson?"

"Yeah, some Army hot shot in Washington decided I should be promoted earlier this year to Brigadier General of the Army,

Carson said, sheepishly. "I much prefer Colonel though, and that's what my friends call me. I don't pay much attention to that other bull."

As Carson turned his mount back to his personal wagon to freshen up, Bent started laughing.

"He's not too much on all that hoopla and things like promotions," Bent said. "He's just a good man – a great Indian fighter and Indian protector – very courageous at every turn. Plus, if he gives you his word, you can count on it til the day you die."

"Let's make ourselves presentable for Captain Pettis," Bent said, as he reined his horse back to the wagons.

•••

Two Army wagons had stopped and a few soldiers had set out wooden chairs and a small table. One man, Captain Pettis, Adkin guessed, was sitting down at the table as another trooper was putting out glasses on the table.

"How are you, Captain Pettis?" Carson laughed, as the four stopped and dismounted. "See you still have your hair."

"I'm doing well, General," Pettis said, chuckling while hugging his old commander.

"I told you not to use that title," Carson said, laughing.

Pettis greeted Bent, and Carson introduced Adkin and Ryan to the Captain. The men sat down as a soldier poured water into the glasses from a clay ewer.

"This here is Captain George Pettis, originally of the New Mexico Volunteers," Carson said. "He was my right-hand man for about a year and a half out of Santa Fe, Mexico, – and then Fort Lyon. We served under Brigadier General James H. Carleton."

"Captain Pettis was a big factor in saving the lives of our three companies at the battle of Adobe Walls," Carson added, smiling at Pettis. "Like I told you earlier."

"The true story is Colonel Carson's strategy to retreat from sure slaughter was the reason we all survived," Pettis said, looking at the others.

"But it was your howitzer troops that made that possible, Captain," Carson added.

"So, how is it you are guarding this telegraph crew? Carson asked, grinning. "Did you anger Carleton that bad?"

"No. I volunteered," Pettis said. "I didn't want to go on an assignment with Chivington, and preferred keeping these men safe. I do know a little about fighting Indians, thanks to you Colonel."

"Indeed you do, Captain," Carson said. "And I'm proud of your decision to avoid that dog Chivington and his dirty hounds after they shot down Cheyenne squaws and blew the brains out of innocent children at Sand Creek.

"J.M. Chivington is a former Methodist preacher who was a territorial officer out of Fort Lyon who massacred Chief Black Kettle's village at Sand Creek," Carson said, looking to Adkin and Ryan. "All but about 35 warriors were out hunting buffalo when Chivington charged the village of 600 women and children.

"Children were shot point-blank, babies were bayoneted – in all about 300 were slaughtered and they were all scalped and many were mutilated," Carson continued, with scorn written all over his face. "One man had cut out a woman's private parts and exhibited them on a stick.

"Chivington is no Christian as far as I am concerned," he added.

"That's one man that is due a killing," Bent said, a scornful look on his face.

Adkin wouldn't find out for another month when staying at Bent's Fort, that Bent's children, two sons and a daughter, were staying at Black Kettle's camp when attacked by Chivington. Another son had been forced at gunpoint to tell Chivington where Black Kettle's village was located.

That son later testified against Chivington in court, but no person or soldier was ever held to account for the massacre.

"There were even more horrors that came out later – with all the men bragging," Bent added, a painful ache glowing in his eyes. "What's really disgusting is Black Kettle had just signed a peace treaty with the soldiers."

After a few uncomfortable moments of silence, Pettis spoke up.

"So how did the Little Arkansas Treaty go? I've heard all the tribes signed except for the Comanche Quahadis."

"That's a fact, and I don't believe the Quahadis will ever sign an agreement with Whites," Carson said. "But everything else went fairly well."

He told Pettis of some of the details of where certain tribes were going to establish reservations, and then he went into how Adkin and Ryan had stopped the violation of a young Indian girl.

"I noticed those Kiowa necklaces right away," Pettis said. "Good for you to make friends with Satanta and Black Horse – powerful and dangerous warriors."

Pettis gave them an update on how the line crew was handling the terrain and the uncertainty of Indian raids.

"We haven't had any trouble, yet," Pettis said. "We've had to give away a little more trade goods to the Indians than we had planned on. But that's good for your business, Colonel Bent. We restocked with quite a few goods at your trading post."

"I'm sure the order for replenishing inventory has already been sent," Bent answered, chuckling. "We'll order more when this line is connected."

"How long until the crews will meet?" Ryan asked Pettis.

"If everything goes according to plans, it should be in another two to three weeks," he answered. "Barring any Indian raids or blizzards. Most of the Indian bands have headed to southern Comancheria and the Llano Estacado for the winter.

"The ones who haven't went south are settled outside your Fort Colonel," Pettis said, looking at Bent. "I'd say you have about 4,000 Indians camped around your fort – mostly Cheyenne and some Cherokee."

"What do you expect, my children are half-Cheyenne," Bent said. "After the first big blow, we'll have 10,000 surrounding the fort."

Adkin had heard from Ryan that many Indians friendly to Bent often spent winter months near the safety of Bent's Fort, especially now that the army had reinforced the fort with troops and additional supplies that could be traded for.

Bent looked to Adkin and Ryan, "A few weeks won't hurt your schedule, will it? We'll make you feel right at home at Bent's Fort during that time." He also explained to Pettis his arrangement with the Barlow and Sanderson Stagecoach Line.

"Well, get it while the gettin's good," Pettis said. "I've heard once they get the railroads running from coast to coast, the trails – the Oregon and the Santa Fe – will dry up. I've heard they're finishing up telegraph line on the Oregon Trail, too.

"But rail lines may take another 5 to 10 years," he added, laughing. "Western Union started planning this telegraph line at the end of 1861."

"That's our plan," Adkin spoke up, while Ryan nodded in agreement. "And we'd be glad to accept your offer of hospitality, Colonel Bent."

All agreed to make camp for the evening and sent out orders to the caravan and the line crews and soldiers.

Carson and Bent offered up fresh beef for the officers meal, and Pettis gave them a choice between wine or brandy. Adkin and Carson were the only two who tactfully explained fresh water was all they needed.

Adkin was amazed at the battle stories, the history – he hadn't realized Carson had actually worked for Bent and Bent's brothers as a meat hunter again at Old Bent's Fort in 1840.

For so many years in England, he had felt somewhat different than other boys his age. His wonderlust for adventure was rare amongst his peers – and their parents.

But now, here he was in the vast expanse of the Great Plains of Kansas, and it seemed everyone he meets is full of the same wonderlust he has.

"This is where God means for me to be," he silently said to himself. "We'll reach Bent's Fort tomorrow."

•••

The temperature was freezing when they awoke, small puddles of water had frozen and there were ice crystals on much of the equipment and wagons. Now at mid-forenoon, the temperature was probably about 35 to 40. One could still see the foggy breath of men and beasts.

An Englishman's Adventures on the Santa Fe Trail (1865-1889)

As the caravan approached Bent's Fort, there was what looked like a gray cloud hovering over the horizon, hardly moving, simply suspended with bright blue icy skies surrounding them as far as the eye could see.

"That's smoke from all the camp fires and tipi fires," Bent said as his horse walked alongside of Adkin and Ryan. "When it get this cold with no wind, it seems to trap the smoke like some kind of ceiling."

"There's probably 5,000 tipis and tents set up by now," Bent added with a smile.

Adkin could only shake his head slowly. He'd seen about 2,000 tipis at the Little Arkansas and a little more than 3,000 Indians. This fort must be something.

The sight of telegraph poles and the wire stretching through the air toward the fort was somewhat strange. Adkin felt as if it was piercing the frontier with manmade intrusions that didn't fit the prairie and its rolling hills and the on-and-off sights of the mighty Arkansas River.

Cresting a long, flat-top mesa, the sights of the valley exploded with the number of tipis, Indians on horseback and women and children milling about, smoke from fire pits and wagons lying about like small pieces of wood amongst the huge village.

Off to their left, the river meandering westward with large trees in abundance. Adkin would learn later this area was called Big Timbers by Indians and traders.

After scanning from side to side, Adkin caught sight of large tall walls of stones and some adobe. It was a huge fort, yet it looked small compared to the vastness of the villages surrounding its walls and along the river bend.

"It's almost as big as Fort Leavenworth," Adkin mumbled out loud.

"I'm pretty proud of what it took to get it to this stature," Bent answered, hearing Adkin mumbling. "It's 180-feet long and 135-feet wide, with 16-foot tall walls that are four-feet thick.

"There's cannons in the bastions at the southwest and northwest corners, and cactus was planted on the tops of the walls to discourage climbers," Bent added.

"The Army thinks they own it, but it's just a lease," he continued. "It's still my baby, even though there is a lot of blood and agony that my family has endured.

"This will probably be my last winter here," he added with a sigh.

As they followed the Santa Fe Trail, ruts and all – and now the telegraph poles, they started down the east side of the structure. Indians and a few traders mixed in, making way for Bent and Carson's small caravan. As the four rode up front, many were shouting out greetings to Bent and Carson. Several youngsters had shimmied up the telegraph poles waving and shouting, "Welcome Colonel Bent."

As they neared the massive front two-door gate made of thick timbers, Adkin noticed a couple of Indians pointing at his necklace and he heard one say, "Kiowa."

Adkin had a feeling of coming upon something like the Egyptian pyramids he'd seen in books of etchings in London. Out here on the Santa Fe Trail, the fort seemed magnificent yet imposing. Like they had reached another world after crossing the Great Plains.

Adkin would put down his thoughts late that night after his adrenalin had settled down.

A glorious November 4, 1865.

Arrived at Bent's Fort.

•••

Bent had made sure Adkin and Ryan got boarded in the guest quarters on the second floor above the long warehouse. Their horses were stabled just a few yards away from the stairs leading up to the quarters. Their pack horses were unloaded by men looking somewhat like Carson's Ute scouts and the goods piled against a wall in their bunkhouse.

There seemed to be maybe five or six doors along the bunkhouse, and their room had four wooden beds with straw-filled mattresses and a cook stove which was also used as a heating stove. A basket of small chunks of firewood sat nearby with more stacked at the bottom of the steps. A low fire had already been started for them.

A young Indian boy wearing a serape entered carrying a tin bowl of water and several hand towels.

"You clean now," he growled matter-of-factly. "Colonel Bent want you come down when clean."

With that he scrambled out the door and down the steps.

"Well, Mr. Ryan. I believe we have our orders," Adkin said as they both chuckled.

•••

When they got near the bottom of the steps, the young boy suddenly appeared before them waving his arms and barking orders, again.

"You follow me to Colonel Bent," he yelled.

They walked across the center of the yard, which was full of troops and traders, numerous wagons. It looked like the center of Independence or Westport when Adkin travelled through there looking at wagons and coaches with Sanderson.

Busy, busy, busy.

"Over here," Bent shouted as they walked through an ornate carved wooden door with elk antlers trimming the entrance.

"Antonio, mi jiho, Hohóo," Bent nodded to the boy.

"You welcome Colonel Bent," the boy responded, smiling from ear to ear and running out the door.

"Have a seat men," Bent waved an arm toward large chairs covered in leather in front of a rock fireplace.

"Is your room satisfactory," Bent asked.

"It's goin' beat sleeping on a bedroll on the ground next to a spittin' fire," Ryan answered with a chuckle.

They all laughed and in walked Colonel Carson.

"What's so funny?" he asked as he walked over and took a chair.

"Well the boys here figure they might enjoy sleeping in a real bed tonight," Bent answered.

"That's why I travel with wagons these days," Carson said "Too old to be sleeping on the ground anymore.

"Colonel Bent, I've decided I'm going to try and make it home before the big snows come," Carson said. "So I'll be leaving in the morning before daylight. I've got to try and get through Raton Pass before it gets snowed in. Plus I want to see our old friend, Uncle Dick."

Bent nodded his head in agreement, and the men started talking about what they'd like to eat, and Bent hinted Adkin and Ryan should contemplate spending the winter with him at the fort.

"That telegraph line ought to be connected in a few more days and you can make a lot of arrangements with Sanderson back at Leavenworth," Bent said.

They agreed to wait and see what Sanderson is thinking and how things are going with plans for the stages, equipment, and other concerns.

A large black man came in, dressed like a judge wearing a white shirt with black pants and a black vest and asked Bent what the men would like for supper.

"Buffalo stew with biscuits. Okay with you fellas?" Bent asked, with everyone shaking their head in approval.

Talk after dinner was somewhat subdued, as if everyone had finally reached a destination and were fatigued.

"How many civilian employes do they have here now Colonel Bent?" Carson asked.

"Oh, I think it's around 60 or 70, but we still have a commissary, medical hall, the dry goods warehouse and the blacksmith's place," Bent answered. "That's where I'd like you to look around Adkin and see if improvements could be made. I remember you talking about how your father developed a new-style anvil.

"I would be pleased to, Colonel," Adkin responded.

"Just doesn't seem to be like the old place, does it William?" Carson asked Bent with his head tilted to the side.

"Nope, it really never has, Kit," Bent said, with a heavy sigh. "Like I was tellin Adkin the other day, This is probably my last winter to be out here on the trail. Maybe even my last trip, who knows.

"I know what you mean," Carson said, rising to thank everyone and shaking hands with the others as they rose to bid farewell.

"Won't have a chance to say bye in the morning, leaving early," Carson said.

"A real honor to meet you and ride with you," Ryan said as he gripped Carson's hand.

"I consider it a treasured and pleasant experience," Adkin said.

"You English have a way with words, Adkin. Good luck to you and Ryan and the stage line," Carson said "Hope to see you on the trails again."

With that he turned and walked out the large wide door, making him look smaller and stockier than he already was.

•••

Adkin and Ryan fell into the fort's functions well, Adkin working with the blacksmith and helping design and make another anvil that works well with creating flat surfaces and angled pieces.

Ryan was more interested in the fort's political intrigue, as both had met the commanding officers and had a few drinks with some of the soldiers who seemed to love gossiping about who's coming or leaving or which officer's wife was flirting with enlisted men.

After about a week, news hit the fort that the telegraph operator had just received a message from Fort Dodge, and communications were open to Fort Leavenworth to Washington, D.C., and New York City.

It seemed the several hundred that lived inside the fort came out in the yard to celebrate, several traders started shooting pistols and rifles into the air until soldiers insisted they stop or be thrown in the brig.

There were thousands of Indians camped around the fort, even though it sat about a mile north of a big southernly bend in the Arkansas River. Most of the Indians were encamped in the Big Timbers along the river as it wound like a horseshoe around the fort.

The fort sat upon a big mesa above the river valley, and Ryan and Adkin had discovered there was an area traders had set up to practice shooting about a half mile north of the fort. They had used up their pocket cash and now had IOUs with Bent's store, mainly for bullets and powder. They practiced alot.

Adkin had made arrangements with Bent to attempt to contact Sanderson in Leavenworth the next day, but he had to wait an additional day for the telegraph to make its way to J.L. – by hand delivery – after travelling up the Western Union line.

When the telegraph from Sanderson arrived, a delivery boy ran into the blacksmith's shop and yelled, "Telegraph delivery for Mr. A. Yates."

It was lengthy, and Adkin ran up the stairs to their room and found Ryan before starting to read it. Sanderson wished them good health and went right into the business. He was very happy they had arrangements to Pueblo, even though they didn't have the contracts signed between Bent's Fort and Pueblo, yet.

Adkin had also assured J.L. they could provide horses from Pueblo to Fort Dodge

Sanderson said the railroad he and Barlow were major investors in was making lots of money, so they were planning on sending out six new coaches on the first big caravan out of Leavenworth in April or May. He wants to set a stageline route to Santa Fe, New Mexico, as well, where the trail splits at La Junta.

Adkin looked up at Ryan.

"We're set, Ryan. Looks like we'll be positively busy in the spring," he said and both laughed and shook hands.

Within about a week of telegrams going back and forth, Adkin learned he and Rinehart's joint venture of hauling hides and buffalo skins back to Leavenworth was very profitable. More profitable than Adkin could dream.

They had taken most of the trade goods to Westport docks and brought back their two empty Studebaker wagons with a gross profit of $1,100. Adkin's share, after paying back the $150 cost of the wagon, less $90 for oxen fees and initial investment of trade goods – he netted $310. Plus he had two months wages due, which brought his payment to $370.

Ryan's investments for the Arkansas Treaty haul – plus salary – actually came to $440. He had traded for more fine buffalo hides than Adkin and Rinehart.

Sanderson asked Adkin if he wanted the money wired to him at Bent's Fort or – J.L. made a suggestion – to purchase another wagon, load both with goods and bring them out with the spring caravan and the new coaches.

He hinted that Adkin and Ryan could get even more for goods at Santa Fe, and even sell the two wagons for three or four times their value. J.L. also pointed out a gallon of brandy in Leavenworth cost only $2, but that gallon sells for $25 in Santa Fe.

Ryan decided to purchase two more Studebakers and load his three wagons with $300 worth of goods and cover any excess in spending out of his salary.

Adkin chose to buy one more wagon and spend up to $300 on goods enough to fill two wagons and wire him $30, one month's pay. He asked Sanderson to keep his remaining $40 in the bank.

Sanderson also informed them he would wire salary's on the first of each month until told to do otherwise.

When Bent heard of their good fortune, he encouraged them to be shrewd when entering the trading business. He warned that too many buyers can be influenced by merchants with less than superior goods. He said that is still why he is the fort's major buyer, especially since living in Westport near its docks.

Adkin said he trusted Sanderson to look out for them. Ryan agreed. Bent confirmed J. L. was a good and decent man, and the two could make some serious money come springtime.

Another telegraph message was delivered to Adkin about a week later. It was from Sanderson, and he had forgot to mention earlier that Adkin's stock in the company had quadrupled in value in just three months, mainly due to securing more than two dozen new U.S. mail routes between train coverage and stageline routes. And Barlow had just been elected a Vermont State Senator (he had been a Vermont State Representative before that).

Then the Great Blow began.

•••

It was the week before Thanksgiving, and Adkin had finished with the new anvil, much to the delight of the fort's blacksmith, who discovered he was going to be much more versatile and efficient.

Shortly after lunch, the northwestern sky began turning dark blue and gray, reminding Adkin of the hail storm that left its mark on his cheek. He rubbed it unconsciously.

"Don't worry Adkin, that ain't a hail storm, that's a blue northern," Ryan exclaimed as they walked across the yard to the stables. "We're in for some snow, and it looks like a pretty big storm at that."

The cold breeze quickly enveloped everyone, soldiers started heading different directions, animals were being dragged to the stockade and forced inside. Traders and women gathered up children and headed inside their respective abodes.

The air temperature felt as if it had dropped 20 degrees in just a heartbeat. A shiver went through Adkin.

"It's coming in right off the Rockies," Ryan said. "Lets' get our animals secured."

Fifteen minutes later as they started for their rooms, small flakes of snow mixed with tiny pieces of ice were whirling around and settling on the ground.

It's goin' get cold, too," Ryan said, while Adkin was thinking he should have purchased that Buffalo-hide coat the old Indian woman had offered him near the gate a few days earlier when they rode out to target shoot.

"When the snow quits, I'm going to find that woman and buy that coat," Adkin thought to himself.

•••

Adkin heard men barking orders and others shoveling snow. He and Ryan had tried for three days to keep opening their door some to keep the snow from drifting so great as to block them in, but it buried them last night while they were sleeping. Ryan had fallen asleep while on watch just long enough to get them snowed in. The door wouldn't budge any more than an inch.

As the noise got closer, a shovel hit the door.

"Well have you out a moment," a man's voice boomed. "Are ya'all alright?"

"Yes, we're fine. Jolly good to hear you," Adkin yelled back.

While the storm raged, both men had made several trips down the stairs to the wood pile and fought the gales and blinding snow, having to sweep away snow to get to the pile. Several trips had kept the wood fairly easy to get to.

It was the door that kept presenting a problem from the drifting.

"Go ahead and push," the voice ordered. "There you go, Colonel Bent wanted to see you as soon as you can make it over to his quarters."

"Thanks Lieutenant," Ryan said as he shouldered the door a little more open.

"Wow, might take some time to get across the yard," Ryan said as Adkin came out into the waist-deep snow.

The fort was covered to the point of most sights were unrecognizable. Adkin scanned the areas around the fort, smoke vents were everywhere, but many tipis looked as if they had disappeared.

Several small trails led across the yard at various angles. The two started on the one directly to the main quarters, even though it was 4- to 5-feet deep and only two or three men had broken trail.

The sky was deep blue and there wasn't even a whisper of wind – dead still. That beautiful sunlight came at a price: The temperature was probably 20 to 30 below.

"Damn, it's cold," Ryan said as he huffed with each step through the tracks.

Adkin huffed directly behind him, both trying to find footing where others had stomped through. Soldiers were coming out and many were digging and using long poles in a sweeping way to find planked walkways, stairs to upper entrances to the warehouses and goods.

When they got to the front steps of the main quarters, several soldiers were on the porch, still clearing snow. Standing there, wrapped in buffalo hides were several Indians.

"Come on in, please, and warm up by the fireplace," a Lieutenant said as the door opened.

Inside, four more Indians were talking with the commander at his desk, while Bent and several other Indians were standing by the huge fireplace. Bent waved Adkin and Ryan over.

"Men, we don't have much time for pleasantries, we're mounting a relief effort with as many men as we can find for the moment," Bent said, hurriedly. "We're going to have to provide rations immediately. Our Indian brothers are dying as we speak. Reports so far are that as many as 30 or 40 people are already dead from cold and hunger."

•••

By the time a clearing could be provided to the front gate and while more soldiers were trying to clear an area of about 50-feet in radius in front, several hundred Indians had made their way to the fort. Some of them were also helping soldiers by kicking snow to the side.

An old squaw sat against the stone wall wailing and rocking back and forth as she clutched a small bundle in her arms. Adkin assumed it was a child, though he couldn't see it. He was sure it was dead considering her painful moans and cries.

Soldiers formed a line and were passing bags of flour, sugar, coffee and beans down the steps of the large warehouse.

As a wagon was filled to its top, a two-horse team of mules was hitched and they led the animals and wagon to the front gate and rolled into the clearing, Indians swarmed the wagon as soldiers handed and even tossed bags to them.

One soldier, an Indian in uniform, was urging calm by the tone of his voice and speaking their languages. He kept holding up one finger as if urging them to take one bag for the moment. Several Indians, though, took off with a bag under each arm slowly trudging away.

Adkin and Ryan were helping load wagons. When Adkin climbed up to help stack goods, he suddenly fell as a soldier barked, "Get going" to the driver, and the wagon lurched forward.

Adkin was fine and helped hand bags of food to the swarming crowd. It seemed to be getting more harried and worrisome.

As he handed a bag of flour over the side, two hands grabbed his wrists and yanked him out of the wagon. He landed face down, his forehead hitting rock-hard, frozen dirt, the bag now under his right arm by his side.

As he tried to clear his thoughts, a heavy blow to his head was the last thing he remembered until he awoke a few hours later in the medical dispensary.

"Can you hear me, Adkin?" Ryan asked.

"Do you see me?" he blurted, waving his hand in front of Adkin's eyes.

"I can hear and see you," Adkin said as he grabbed Ryan's hand to stop the waving.

Ryan laughed, "This hard-headed Englishman is okay, gentlemen."

Looking around, there were a couple of soldiers, the doctor, a rotund nurse, Colonel Bent, Ryan and three Indians crowding around wrapped in furs in the small room.

"Quite a gathering," Adkin said, as he reached for the back of his head. The doctor caught his arm and warned Adkin to check that out later.

"I want you to follow my finger," the doctor said, as he watched Adkin's eye movements from top to bottom, side to side.

"He's got a concussion for sure, but his eye movement hasn't been damaged too severely," he said stepping back. "That's a relief."

Bent moved to his side.

"Someone wanted your lucky charm," Bent said. "Looks like all he took was your necklace from Satanta. They didn't even touch your pistol."

"But he used a Buffalo club on you, and I imagine you could have a cracked skull, according to Doc, here, and he had to use numerous stitches to close the wound," Bent added.

"Your head dressing will have to stay on for several days," the doctor interrupted.

"These three Cheyenne are the ones that dragged you back to the front gate and handed you over to soldiers," Bent continued. "If they hadn't, you might have been trampled to death."

Adkin glanced at the Indians and nodded his head in respect. They nodded back.

"Did they see who it was?" Adkin asked Bent.

"No, they didn't see his face, but they got a look at his outer blanket, and they think he is a Sioux – a Dakota," Bent explained. "No one is getting out of here for at least week with these temperatures. Horses don't like struggling through 5-feet of snow at 30 below. If he's a Sioux, he's a little far south as a rule and should be easy to find, not many Sioux around here."

"Easy to find amongst 6,000 Indians buried in a blizzard?" Adkin asked trying to laugh, but wincing at the pain in his head.

They all laughed, except the three Indians.

Bent spoke Cheyenne to them and they laughed, too, which got everybody to laughing again.

"Colonel Bent, would you see to it they are rewarded for their grand effort in saving me," Adkin said. "Something very appropriate, and money is no obstruction."

"Sure, Adkin. Consider it done," Bent said. He turned and spoke to them again, and the three walked out of the room as Bent turned to Adkin.

"Take care to get well. Don't rush it – do what the doctor tells you to do. A cracked skull is not just an ordinary knot on the head."

"Thank you Colonel," Adkin said, as Bent left the room to catch up with the Cheyenne.

As the others departed, with Ryan repeating Bent's warning about the need to be patient as he walked out.

The nurse remained and came over to make sure Adkin's bedding was fitted and tucked away. When he reached for his head, she whispered, "Gently, gently."

His head was totally wrapped in medical gauze and bandages. She handed him a hand mirror and held up her first finger before her lips, going, "Shhhh."

When Adkin got the mirror properly fixed, he almost screamed.

"Shhhh," she repeated.

Most of his forehead was nothing but a big red knot the size of an apple. It was already turning blue and purple around the outer edges. All the skin around both his eyes were black and blue – completely encircling the entire eyes. His eyes were full of bright red veins – glowing like serpents, he thought to himself. There was a red scrape down the middle of his nose, and his chin was bandaged, covering some kind of cut.

He hardly recognized who was staring back at him. He started feeling more pain than ever.

"Bloody hell," he whispered to himself.

•••

Adkin was kept under doctor's care for two days, then released and told to stay in bed for another week. Back in his room, now with Ryan as his nursemaid, Adkin learned more about the big blow.

Nearly 40 Indians had died, mostly old and very young. Some of the older ones ran out of firewood before neighbors discovered their plight. Some of the babies just couldn't handle the relentless below temperature, even though in tipis with small fires.

Animals also faced destruction: More than 200 horses, some mules and many other small animals like sheep, calves and dogs.

"We've got people looking for the Sioux," Ryan said. "Nobody has tried to leave the area as of this morning. Snow is still too deep to make any trails, and outriders, including soldiers have found no tracks trying to leave.

"But that may change in the next day or so," he added. Temperatures are getting above freezing, but 5- to 8-feet of snow doesn't melt quick.

The day after Thanksgiving, which really didn't register too much in or around the fort, as President Lincoln had only made it a federal holiday the year before, Ryan came rushing into their room.

"Scouts found tracks of three ponies heading west out of the village about an hour ago," Ryan spit out rapidly. "They believe it may be Sioux Indians, who had been staying with an Arapaho family.

"One of them goes by Minninnewah, which is Sioux for Wild Wind," Ryan added. "We're getting a posse together to go after them."

"I'm going, too," Adkin said as he sat up in bed, reaching for his deerskin breeches. "If this is the same Indian, he's going to answer to me."

Adkin still had bandages around his head, and one of the scouts brought him a beaver hat that would fit over his bandages. It had long straps of hide hanging over each ear down to his side. Before he tied them together, Ryan teased him that it looked as if he had Indian braids.

Bent had offered two Indian Scouts to the posse, and the fort commander asked for two soldiers to volunteer, which quickly offered their help to Adkin and Ryan.

Once fully dressed, packing their handguns and rifles, the six headed out of camp following the tracks going westward along the Sante Fe Trail.

The Scouts figured they might be heading to La Junta, where Sioux were known to camp. But about five miles west of the fort, their trail turned north at Adobe Creek. The horses weren't having too much trouble with footing as the Indians ahead of them had found the bog holes and reversed around them, as well as avoiding the remaining deep drifts.

The Scouts estimated they were only about four or five miles behind them, and the posse was making better time by not having to break trail. They also said there was a natural camping site where Horse Creek entered Adobe Creek. They Sioux may stop there to rest their mounts or for an overnight camp.

Two hours later, one of the scouts spurred ahead to a small hill. Once he stopped and pulled out his telescopic eye glass, he raised his hand in a "halt" motion, then quickly turned his horse and came loping back.

"They're resting in the big grove at Horse Creek," he said. "Their smoke in visible, and I can see their ponies hobbled nearby. Looks like they may spend the night."

One of the posse soldiers spoke up.

"Yeah, it's only three hours til dark. Are we going to ride in where they can see us coming, or do we wait til dark and ride in and take them?"

Ryan looked to Adkin, who looked to the older scout.

"What do think is best?" he asked the scout.

"If we just ride in and it's them, they will most likely just start shooting – we have no advantage of surprise," he said.

"Let's wait til they go to bed," Adkin said, the others nodding in agreement.

They then backed off several hundred yards and dismounted near a large wallow of wild plum bushes where they tied their mounts.

"We're going to have to bundle up – no fire with smoke to tell them we're here," the scout warned.

They kicked snow away in a few areas and sat down.

•••

It had been dark for about two hours when they decided to make their move. Even as they all had taken turns walking around to warm up and keep the blood flowing, Adkin felt really stiff as he swung into Diablo's saddle.

A slight moon turned the countryside somewhat silver, and the lead scout followed the Indians' trail down into the river bottom. The fire glowed through the trees and bushes, and when they got about 100 yards away, one of their ponies neighed.

"As the blanketed lumps around the fire started to jump up, the scout spurred his horse and let out a blood-curdling scream, and they all followed him while raising their guns.

As the lead scout came into the glow of the fire ring, he halted his horse and yelled something in Indian, and they heard him say "Minninnewah." Then one the men said something and added "Minninnewah." All of them had pulled out their rifles at the disturbance.

The scout turned to Adkin and said, "That's him." And as Adkin walked Diablo into the dim light, he thought he recognized the man who admitted he was Minninnewah. And when Minninnewah saw, Adkin and the others walk their horses into the circle of light, his eyes got big and he looked startled as he recognized Adkin.

He immediately shouldered his rifle and sent a bullet right past Adkin's ear. Adkin had kept the man in his sights with his Colt. Diablo skittered to his left, and without any movement from Adkin, he shot Minninnewah three times in about two seconds from his hip, never once raising his arm to aim down the sights.

Then all hell broke loose, the Sioux started shooting at the same time the posse let loose. The posse members spread out – moving left and right and had the advantage of being on horseback. Adkin never shot again, he kept his hands on Diablo's reins as the big stallion whirled around in circles a few times.

In about 30 seconds, it was all over. The three Sioux lay dead, and no posse members were hit. One of the scouts' horses was nicked in the left shoulder, but it proved to be only a flesh wound, though the scout couldn't believe his good luck. It had passed between his leg and the horse, ripping a small slit in his breeches.

Adkin holstered his pistol, dismounted and slowly walked over to Minninnewah. He stood there just staring, not a word, no movement. All three bullets had hit him in the middle of his beaded breast plate. Blood was still spreading over his entire chest.

"Well, check if he has your necklace, Adkin," Ryan said.

Adkin just stood there, still and unmoving. Like he was in a trance.

Ryan walked over and tore back the breast plate to see a cotton shirt underneath, bloody red. He ripped that open, but there was no necklace.

Ryan then pulled at his waist strap, a colorful wide heavy cloth used as a belt. A small deerskin pouch fell out. Ryan opened it and shook out the necklace into his palm.

"Here it is, Adkin," he said as he held it up to Adkin. "Are you okay?"

Adkin just stood there.

Ryan stood up in front of him.

"Are you okay?"

Suddenly, Adkin started blinking his eyes and looked directly at Ryan, like he had just awaken from sleep.

"Yes," Adkin stuttered. "Thanks."

He took the necklace and retied its leather string around his neck, and turned away and walked over to Diablo.

Ryan and the others just stared at Adkin until he mounted Diablo and just sat in the saddle like a statue.

The lead scout gave some orders and the three Sioux were tied over the haunches of their ponies and they had gathered their guns and belongings and tied them to one of their horses. They also found a war club made from the leg of a buffalo. They brought it along with the other belongings.

"Are you sure you want to go back tonight?" the lead scout asked no one in particular.

"Let's try it, we can stop along Adobe Creek and rest if it gets too tiring," Ryan said.

They did stop for a couple of hours sleep on the banks of the creek with a big fire. The Sioux slept the sleep of the dead still tied on the backs of their hobbled ponies.

The lead scout told Ryan he figured the crazy Sioux Minninnewah either thought Adkin had killed a Kiowa to get that necklace, or he thought it had big medicine because it was the sign of the Kiowa war chief Satanta.

"Either way, he made a fatal mistake," he said. "Adkin is one helluva shot – and fast."

...

An Army commission was called together the day after they returned to the fort. Each man in the posse was asked to relate the actual events prior to and during the fire fight while the others waited in separate rooms so they couldn't hear the testimony of the others.

The events were remarkable similar with the exception of Adkin's testimony. He had trouble remembering just what happened after a bullet whined by his head and he responsively pulled the trigger as fast as he could.

Ryan swore to hitting maybe two of the Sioux, but couldn't swear exactly because his horse was "jumping quite a bit." And after emptying his pistol, he was able to pull his rifle from its scabbard, "… and I got off a couple more shots, but don't think I hit anyone," Ryan said.

Details were given postmortem by the camp surgeon, who said each Sioux had been hit multiple times: Minninnewah died of three bullets to his sternum; one was hit six times, the fatal most likely a bullet to the side of his head, according to the doc; and the last was hit twice, killed by a bullet to the face.

The commission found the incident justified with the fact testimony verified Minninnewah shot first at Adkin, the fact Adkin's necklace was in Minninnewah's possession and that the buffalo bone club had blood and blond hair on it, which the surgeon said the hair could belong to Adkin.

As people were clearing the hearing room, Bent took Adkin by the arm and whispered, "Adkin, would you please follow me, I need to visit with you."

The two men went into Bent's office, a small room off the main living area.

"Have a seat, please," Bent said. "I've noticed you have been somewhat aloof after your incident – no enthusiasm. Where is that gleam of adventure in your eyes I notice every time we meet?

"Tell me if I'm wrong, but I feel like killing that Sioux has disturbed you much," Bent said, sitting down behind his desk.

"I have been raised a Christian, with very strong beliefs in the Bible, Colonel Bent," Adkin said softly. "Now I have killed a second man, and I left home only eight months ago."

"I understand more than you know, Adkin," Bent said with a sigh. "I had to kill a man when I was 18. I and three of my brothers left our home in Missouri when I was 16 to trap furs on the upper Arkansas. We had met up that fall with St. Vrain and decided to work together to produce more furs for market. I had turned 17 in May, that spring.

"That next fall, we were finishing up our furs for market when we were attacked by Arapahoes and Cheyenne," Bent continued. "It was a good-sized raiding party, probably about two dozen of them. Fortunately, we had camped on a huge river embankment about 45 miles west of here, actually, and it forced them to attack us head-on, with no way to successfully attack us from the rear.

"I actually killed two Cheyenne that day, loading a bulky old Tennessee flintlock rifle," Bent said. "You know, I can still feel that agony today, it's something that stays with you forever. And it should, lest you become a hardened killer.

"But, killing to stay alive, when your attackers want you dead and only dead, it's your duty to stay alive, for your right to live in peace and be productive," Bent said. "I've had to kill many men, but you know how I feel about the Cheyenne People. I married two, they have bore my children. But, if a Cheyenne walked in right now and tried to kill me, I would kill him as fast as possible to save my own life.

"Do you see what I'm talking about?" he looked directly into Adkin's eyes.

"Yes sir, I believe I do," Adkin said.

"Good. Always remember why you had to kill or, even if it was an accident, like you told us of what happened in Florida, because if you bury it, it's very easy to turn into a murderer – I've seen it many times over the last 35 years," Bent said. "And realize that an instinct to live can very well be dependent upon a decision in a few seconds or less. You did well to keep alive and possibly save the men in your posse, too."

"Thanks, Colonel, I'd better get to work," Adkin said, as he rose from the chair.

"Make peace with God, Adkin, he forgives you," Bent said as Adkin turned away.

•••

Adkin got back to helping out at the blacksmith's shop, winter was a good time for equipment repairs, like re-strapping iron to wagon wheels – an ironer's duty – and other pieces having to be made from raw iron.

He and Ryan still practiced their marksmanship. Ryan worked very hard on shooting from the hip, as Adkin had done against the Sioux. Word of Adkin's aim and speed had quickly spread through the fort and the entire village. Some of the Indians had started calling him "English."

A few more storms hit the area but none to the extent of the Big Blow, as it became to be known. Adkin and Ryan had been communicating with Sanderson and making plans for the spring.

They had informed Sanderson they would move as early as possible on to Pueblo, then back to the Trail and down to Santa Fe. They had been informed of a man by the name of Smith Archibald Sayre would be a good contact for stagecoach stations.

They were told Sayre, basically a rancher, had received a forage contract with the Army at his trading posts at Red River and Willow Spring – in the Raton Pass areas. He would start providing hay and grasses for the military in the spring of 1866. They reasoned he might want a stage station or two, as well.

After they reach Santa Fe, they planned on coming back on the southern route, and depending on where the caravan with the coaches is located, they will either use the Aubrey Cut Off Trail to Fort Aubrey, or continue on to Fort Dodge to meet up with the incoming wagon train.

Sanderson had confirmed he would be driving one of he new coaches, but one would be dropped at Cottonwood Crossing on the North Cottonwood River. It was Charity Shreve's Moore's Ranche.

Another new Concord would be dropped at Chris Rath's place just a mile north of the Dry Route-Wet Route intersection outside of Fort Dodge.

Rath's station would be where the Fort Hays Road comes into the Santa Fe Trail.

Sanderson had wired Adkin that he had it from a top source at Fort Leavenworth that several hundred wagons of building materials were headed to Fort Dodge as soon as the spring weather allowed.

Plans for the other four coaches was to headquarter one at Bent's Fort). A fourth Concord would originate from Santa Fe. Two would be stored at Bent's Fort.

Sanderson had also confirmed he and his men, including the squat little German Ray Dee Rinehart, would be bringing Adkin's and Ryan's wagons full of trade goods. Sidekicks Darrell Holmes and Carl Long would be coming, as well.

All concerned with the company was excited at how the telegraph would save valuable time by being able to know what was happening and where that first big caravan would be at any given time. The advantage of knowing which rivers or creeks ahead were overflowing would also be immense. And where blizzards were occurring.

•••

Christmas came and they celebrated quietly. Ryan and Adkin exchanged gifts; A real beaver skin cowboy hat for Adkin, and Ryan received a new custom-made saddle that had "Tyler Ryan" etched into the back skirt of the saddle.

A leather worker at the fort did the tooling, plus he added Santa Fe Trail around the base of the horn. Adkin shelled out $20 for the gift, but he was proud to have Ryan as a partner and felt they were close as brothers now.

Bent surprised both of them when he gave them each a small 1858 Remington belly gun, a .44 caliber pistol like he used alarmingly quick against the Indian who wanted their horses near the ruins of the old abandoned Fort Atkinson.

"It's always good to have a concealed weapon, especially when someone wishing you harm is only watching your holstered pistol," Bent had told them.

He told them to forget it when they said they didn't have a gift for him.

"You two young men staying alive is gift enough for me," he said with a laugh.

Chores kept the men busy, but they had time to pick up a lot of Indian language, not only from Bent, but numerous people who worked for the camp, whether on the civilian side or for the Army, were Indians who spoke many languages.

When weather was fair, both continued their shooting practice. They definitely practiced how to remove a hidden belly gun and fire from the hip. Ryan was getting expert at handling handguns, but Adkin was better. He had a natural flow and instinct to hit what his eyes were focused on.

They also volunteered to go out on hunting parties, as well. One of the main targets was prairie antelope. Adkin loved hunting them, as it often took long shots as the animals were extremely wary of riders. The meat was a little gamey for Adkin's taste, but Ryan loved antelope.

It was on these hunting outings that Adkin first encountered the Mule Deer. He had seen and hunted whitetails throughout his trip to Bent's Fort. He had been told of them, but until he finally dropped one and examined it up close, he hadn't been prepared for the massive size of the creature, plus its huge antlers.

Though Mulies were beautiful and mighty, Adkin still preferred meat from the buffalo or the elk, which was the king of deer in his mind. Everyone at the fort called elk wapiti.

Another fine sport Adkin enjoyed was hunting prairie dogs, again because it took a sure shot to knock them off their dirt mounds with a kill shot. If wounded, they scuttled down their burrows never to be seen again.

The cooks liked to put six or eight of them, skinned and gutted, into a huge pot and stew them untill all the meat fell off the bones. They would then remove the bones, throw in potatoes, wild onions and carrots if they had them, add flour and boil until thickened. The meat was quite tasty to everyone when served with corn bread or biscuits.

•••

Celebrating the new year – 1866 – was uneventful, with the exception Adkin had been molested after the dinner celebration with Bent, the officers and their wives.

It seems Adkin had two brandies and was feeling quite giddy, and he hadn't realized one of the servants, a beautiful, raven-haired Indian girl, had taken a liking to him.

Ryan later told Adkin the girl was actually a Comanchero, and she had been trailing Adkin around from room to room. Adkin remembered seeing her, as she often asked if he needed anything from her tray. He didn't think much of it at the time.

It was when he and Ryan departed the party, around 1 in the morning, that she was waiting at the end of the planked porch. As the men approached, the girl stepped out of the shadows and stopped directly in front of them.

She rattled off some Spanish and said something about "amor." She then jumped up and flung her arms around Adkin's shoulders and kissed him right on the mouth. Just as quickly, she dropped, turned and ran down the steps and into the night.

Ryan teased Adkin for several days, telling him he should find the girl, as she was attractive and she could keep Adkin warm at night. Adkin was embarrassed at the whole affair, and reminded Ryan he wasn't that kind of man. Ryan had trouble understanding Adkin's rejection of pre-marital sex.

"The way you act, I bet that's the first time you ever kissed a girl," Ryan needled Adkin.

"No. it's not."

"You're fibbing, that was the first, wasn't it?" Ryan persisted.

"No, I actually had a girl back home I cared for very much," Adkin began. "Her name is Devon. She has long blond hair and the lightest blue eyes I have ever seen."

"Why Adkin, you never cease to amaze me," Ryan said. "I had no idea you were already a ladies' man."

"It wasn't like that. Devon is sweet and kind, and if I had stayed in Olney, we would probably be married and starting a family," he said, in a whisper."

"No kidding. Did you love her?" Ryan asked.

"I'm not really sure, and that's what makes me sad. She told me she loved me, but she knew from the time we met – when we were but 16 – that I was determined to come to America and travel the Sante Fe Trail," he explained. "She knew I was possessed with my plan, but I think she thought I would outgrow it – much like my Mum did."

"Wow, I'm sorry," Ryan said. "I think I understand how you must've felt leaving her."

"I still think of my sweet Devon from time to time, but I'm living my dream, and I can't explain it – how important it is to my life," Adkin said.

•••

In the first week of February, Adkin and Ryan received a telegram from Chris Rath at his station a few miles east of Fort Dodge. Chris had said he and his brother, Charley, wanted to open a stage line to Fort Hays.

Though they had met Charley Rath at the Little Arkansas Treaty, they didn't get to visit with him at all. But if he was sure a line between Fort Hays and his brother's location at the intersection of the Santa Fe Trail and the Fort Hays Road would be successful, it was good enough for them.

They did preface their approval that Sanderson had to approve the deal to make it official.

They telegraphed Chris the moment they received Sanderson's jubilant approval. This decision proved to be a valuable source of revenue in the future – the stage service from Fort Hays to Santa Fe, New Mexico, paid off well.

The weather had improved greatly, and Adkin and Ryan were eager to take off. They asked Bent, but he told them they shouldn't be fooled by the warm weather through those last two weeks of February. He called it folly – a false Indian Summer.

"You get out on the trail, and the next thing you know a blizzard traps you for several days, and you could die," Bent said. "Some of our worst weather has come as late as the end of March."

•••

By mid-March, temperatures had held and actually improved. It seemed like spring. Even several large Indian bands had moved out of the village, headed out with everything they owned. Adkin was in awe watching how the women took down the tipis, bundled the poles, strapped them to travois, stacked the buffalo hides. They did everything – all the work, while the men and older boys sat around smoking their pipes or riding their horses around the plateau, as if racing.

Bent told them it was a 50-50 chance that spring had truly arrived. They telegraphed Sanderson to see how things were going on that end. He reported they had just experienced a pretty strong snow storm, and plans for that first wagon train was for it to proceed west on April 10.

The Army was putting together more than 300 wagons, mostly of materials for construction at forts. It would meet up for additional supplies at the railhead of the Santa Fe Railroad, which had reached just east of Council Grove.

Sanderson told them the Army was planning on a second huge train to assemble and leave from Council Grove two weeks after that. He said they would ride with the first caravan, and he guessed they would reach Fort Dodge in about four to five weeks, if everything went well.

They would have to average about 12 miles a day to cover the 350 miles to Fort Dodge. Sanderson said a merchants' wagon train was leaving April 1, but he preferred to travel with the Army caravan for safety reasons.

He added everyone back there was eager to hit the trail. Sanderson said traffic should pick up considerably compared to 1865.

"Time to make some real money now that the war is over," he telegraphed.

Adkin, Ryan and Bent sat down and put the pencil to it and calculated that would give Adkin and Ryan time to travel to Pueblo, back down to the Santa Fe Trail and on into Santa Fe, New Mexico, in about four to five weeks.

Bent had already made a deal for two of his Indian guides to accompany the two men on their journey for 50-cents a day for the two guides. By riding horseback, even with two or three pack mules, they should be able to average 20 miles a day.

Bent figured it would only take them three to four weeks traveling the Cimarron route of the Santa Fe Trail back to Fort Dodge. They should arrive about May 15th. If they are behind the Army caravan, they could catch up in a day or two.

Adkin hurriedly telegraphed Sanderson they would leave the next day, March 15, and planned on being at Fort Dodge about the same time as Sanderson.

They would telegraph him when they were in Santa Fe and their planned departure time. There would be no telegraphs while they traveled the southern route – or the Journado de Muerte – as there were no telegraph lines, yet.

Sanderson sent back three words: "See you then," meaning mid-May.

Bent had made the horse deal with Sanderson and would provide an initial herd of about 40 head, but would only move them with large caravans.

"If I was to send out 40 horses with a half-dozen men, I'd lose the horses and probably get my men killed," Bent said. "Comancheros wouldn't let them get 20 miles from here."

The horses had been divided up where they would be stationed, and Bent would send some eastward when the Santa Fe caravans started heading east and send the others westward with large trains headed to Santa Fe. This would ensure their safety.

Sanderson also sold them a short-string of fresh saddle horses just for the four men; eight altogether in case they needed fresh rides or their main mounts broke a leg or became ill.

Sanderson had been busy telegraphing new station managers along the trail to see which ones needed horses, and which ones would provide their own stock, for a nominal fee.

Bent had also made contact with an old friend of his and Kit Carson's, a Mister Richens Lacy Wootton, originally from Virginia, who operated the toll road through Raton Pass on the Santa Fe Trail.

Everybody calls him "Uncle Wootton," even though he only in his late 40s," Bent had explained. "He obtained franchises from the territorial legislatures of Colorado and New Mexico in '64 and hacked, blasted, cut and filled nearly 30 miles of road from Trinidad to Red River."

The good news was Wootton was ready to sign a stagecoach station agreement with Barlow and Sanderson at his home and hotel on the north end of the road – where he made a handsome living charging travelers a toll to use his improved roadway.

"Everything on foot pays the toll," Bent had said. "Of course, except for Indians, especially the Utes, who considered the area their traditional grounds. "He never charges any posse chasing horse thieves, either, or some Mexicans."

With the names of a few people between La Junta and Pueblo, establishing stage stations should be an easy and quick endeavor all the way to Santa Fe, as Adkin and Ryan saw it.

On March 15, 1866, Adkin, Ryan, two Indian guides and two fully loaded pack mules and their string of horses left the fort at first light headed west on the Santa Fe Trail.

•••

On the third day, they passed by Old Fort Bent or what remained of it. Bent had torched every structure that would burn and most of the remnants were old adobe walls that erosion had nearly erased from sight.

"It feels eerie looking at what remains, especially after hearing the stories of its magnificence," Adkin said.

"It is a place of death," the guide Uribe said. "Many people died there from the cholera. I was but a boy when we heard of the death taking everyone who was at the fort. They burned out the cholera."

Adkin glanced at Ryan, as they had heard the other version of why the fort had been destroyed. But they kept silent.

"We never go back, and no one wants to go in there even today," Uribe added. "Bad medicine."

Uribe Mendosa was the talker of the two guides, who preferred to be called scouts. Adkin and Ryan had seen him now and then around the fort throughout the winter, but they never met him or had contact.

Uribe explained his father had been a Mexican soldier and his mother was a Ute squaw, who had been stolen several years before the outbreak of the Mexican-American war.

His father was killed in 1846 when Uribe was only 7. For years, his hate was aimed at not only Whites, but at Texans particularly. His father was killed in an ambush by Texas nationalists. He called them "Texicanos" or "Tejanos."

He explained his life changed dramatically when he met Kit Carson and was hired as a hunter and outrider when Carson took several thousand head of sheep to California when Uribe was about 17.

For being only about 26 or 27 years old, Adkin realized, Uribe had already lived a lifetime, and it showed in his weathered face. But not in his big, toothy grin, which was inviting.

Uribe had learned early how to ride and shoot like an Indian, his father having been an officer in the Mexican Calvary. He had been in "Mucho fights" he explained, with Indians, Comancheros and even White bandits – "Rebels," he said.

The other scout was named "Dusty." Though he had a strange, long Indian name and was a Timpanogo Indian, Uribe said he is only known as Dusty.

"He ride ahead of wagon trains for maybe two, three days scouting," Uribe said. "He come back after first trip for Colonel Bent, and he covered completely with dust – he look like White Man. So Colonel Bent name him Dusty."

It was through Kit Carson that Uribe met Bent. When Carson and the sheep herders returned from California, he wasn't able to keep Uribe on the payroll.

"Carson asked Colonel Bent to give me chance for work," Uribe said. "Colonel Bent very, very good man, and I die for him should he ask."

•••

That evening at camp. Adkin asked Ryan what he thought about the location of the old fort being a site for a stage station.

"You read my thoughts," Ryan said. "It's an idea place, and it wouldn't take much to repair those southern walls and building a nice station. There's plenty of workers around Fort Lyon and Bent's New Fort to do it.

"I'ts the perfect mileage wise, too," he added. "I'm sure Bent would like to be involved, being so close."

"We'll have to plan for that when we return back through."

Later that day after departing the old Fort Bent, clouds to the west disappeared from the horizon, and Adkin got his first view of the spine of snow-covered mountain crests called the Rockies.

"How majestic," Adkin said to himself. He had heard tales of the mountains but had not thought too much about them. But seeing them jutting above the sandy hills with ice and snow capping their peaks was something he could have never imagined. He found himself just staring and staring.

"They're beautiful, aren't they?" Ryan interrupted Adkin's silence.

"Absolutely lovely," Adkin whispered.

"Beauty that can kill a man a hundred different ways," Ryan responded, as they rode on silently.

They arrived at the Arkansas River crossing an hour or so before sunset, with the small village of La Junta just west of the crossing.

Once in La Junta, they quickly made contact with a man named Ablo Velasquez, who was an agent of Waldo, Hall & Co., the company which had received the first mail contract from the government in 1849 for U.S. mail delivery to Santa Fe, New Mexico.

Velasquez assured Adkin and Ryan his company wanted to run stage stations in Pueblo and any other places along the trail.

"We have trading post agents all over," Ablo said.

On the seventh day, they established a contract with Waldo, Hall & Co. through their Pueblo agent, Mello Velasquez, ironically, Ablo's brother.

Adkin still couldn't keep his eyes off the mountains. They looked so close one might be able to reach out and touch them. But he had been told it was still a good day's ride just to get to the foothills where they went nearly straight up into the sky.

Four days later, they were back to La Junta and headed west on the trail to reach Raton Pass and meet Uncle Dick Wootton. They stopped at the U.S. Post Office adobe hut in La Junta and telegraphed Sanderson on their success and to update their location.

Sanderson had responded a few hours later that his team was still scheduled to leave Fort Leavenworth April 10 and meet up with the others in Council Grove.

"Hopefully, we will not spend more than a day in Council Grove," he had telegraphed.

•••

Everything had been going smooth, with no problems other than a few rattle snakes that had crawled out of their holes to sun bathe and scared the animals. One of the mules bucked so hard she broke several knots loose on her load, and they had to refit their goods on her and lash them up again.

The string of horses had been untied from their leashes after the first couple of days and now plodded along with the crew, following the bell mare.

As they rode along in silence, Uribe pointed out two mountains pared in the western horizon. He said they are called Spanish Peaks. Adkin was impressed, as he had been since first seeing the Rocky Mountains. He felt as if they were riding right into the middle of its spine.

A few miles north of the Purgatoire River, Uribe pulled up the reins on his horse and shot his arm into the air. As they all stopped, they could see riders on horseback trotting toward them and kicking up dust. It looked to Adkin to be about five or six riders.

"Comancheros," Uribe hissed. "If they are bandidos, they may want our animals. Be ready."

Dusty had slid his Henry lever-action rifle out of its scabbard, Ryan unscabbarded his double barreled 12 gauge, Uribe laid his carbine over his lap and pulled his revolver. Adkin pulled out his Colt as they rode up to them.

One of them greeted Uribe in Spanish, Adkin thought that was the language, and Uribe said some words back that Adkin didn't understand, but he heard Uribe say Colonel Bent in the middle of a sentence of undistinguished words. Uribe sounded mad.

They kept their eyes on the six rag-tag riders that looked like some of the troublemakers in the Indian village at Bent's Fort. The lead man started talking tougher and nodding his head towards Ryan and Adkin.

Adkin heard Uribe say their names and a few words later he heard "Satanta" in a stream of louder talk from Uribe.

"They want our horses but would settle for our mules," Uribe said out of the side of his mouth, never taking his eyes off their leader. "This could get bad."

About then, two riders came galloping up the trail from the same direction the Comancheros had come. They looked like military Indian scouts to Adkin, wearing parts of uniforms and military hats.

"Uribe, is that you?" One of the men shouted as they rode up and halted their horses. The Comancheros looked startled, their eyes darting back and forth between the two new riders and Adkin's crew and their leader. Every man had a finger on a trigger of some type of weapon.

"Bueno, ees Uribe, Uribe of Bent's Fort," Uribe said, then realizing he knew the man. "Fransisco, buenas dias."

"Bueno," the man said. He then looked to the Comanchero leader and spoke in a language Adkin had heard before though he knew little of the meanings.

The Comanchero answered, then Uribe started speaking again, loudly, and he heard Uribe throw in Satanta and a few words later Colonel Bent.

There was some more arguing, and Adkin was getting nervous, but finally, the Comancheros' leader reined his horse around, and they spurred their mounts eastward along the trail.

"Fransisco, this is Adkin Yates and his partner Tyler Ryan," Uribe said as the Comancheros rode out. "We are headed to Santa Fe to set up stagecoach stations for Barlow and Sanderson Stagecoach Line.

"Fransisco and I have ridden together with Colonel Bent's freight caravans," Uribe added.

"Nice to meet you Señors," Fransisco said. "This is Polti. We are scouts riding for Señor Epifanio Aguirre. His freighters are just now leaving Trinidad behind us – more than 200 wagons accompanied by soldiers.

"I told the Comancheros the soldiers were only a few miles behind us," Fransisco continued. "Plus, I don't think they wanted to fight six-on-six and with a blood brother of Chief Satanta."

"Blood brother?" Adkin asked, looking to Uribe.

Uribe raised his shoulders, and put out his hands, palms up,

"Well, a little story help scare them, I tink. And they recognized your necklace as big medicine from Comanche chief."

...

Within three hours, they met the caravan commanded by Señor Aguirre. He pulled over his ambulance to talk briefly with Adkin and his crew while the freighters kept slowly rolling along, five wagons across at most places. It was the biggest caravan Adkin had seen yet.

Aguirre was a somewhat famous freighter who put together trade goods to take to Kansas City for sale. He had acquired quite a fortune and a reputation of a bold Indian fighter.

When told of the confrontation with the Comancheros, Aguirre was pleased no one got hurt.

"I don't tolerate any depredations by Indians or bandidos," he said in perfect English. "Comancheros were once good middle men to do business with the Indians, but they have become more and more bandidos than friends these days."

Aguirre wrote down several names for them to contact in Santa Fe and the villages a little further up the trail. One was his brother, a partner, and said they would like very much to provide a stagecoach station, as they ran stagecoach service south of Santa Fe to Old Mexico.

"We have the perfect place with a very nice hotel, a bar with gambling and a large stable – directly facing the Plaza," Aguirre said proudly. "Meet with my brother, Conrado, and give him this note. He will take care of you with whatever you need."

Adkin reached out and took the list of names and a small sealed envelope with the name Conrado scribbled on it.

With that Aguirre told his driver to get going.

"I'll tell Colonel Bent you are all well when we meet him," Aguirre said out the door window.

•••

As they crested a butte of red rock, they could see the small village of Trinidad below straddling the Purgatoire River as it meandered through the valley. A mountain on their left was called by Uribe as Raton Mountain. It was large, but different. It had two flat-topped mesas sitting atop its summit and no trees.

A few miles later, they spotted Uncle Dick Wootton's Ranch. Adkin was amazed again.

Wootton was the first one to run out and greet them as they approached a gate made of a long, thin piece of timber, raised by rope and a swivel.

The gate was right next to where Wootton's house had been built. The home had an addition which later proved to be the guest bunk house. Wootton called it the Raton Pass Hotel.

After he got the four riders settled into a large adobe room with six bunks, he invited them over to his home which was only a few paces. An adobe barn and stables were off to the south a short distance.

"Welcome to my humble abode," Wootton said to the men as he ask them to sit down in large buffalo hide chairs made of hand-carved timber.

"My dear friend Colonel Bent telegraphed me of your travels and intentions," he said. "I don't know if he told you, but Bent gave me my first job out here in the west. I even worked for him again in the '40s before I decided to raise buffalo for a living."

"Buffalo?" Adkin asked, as he was always interested in how to make money in these wild lands. He had seen how Bent had scraped and fought to build his wealth and respect.

"Yeah, I had hunted buffalo for the Army and the fort, along with Kit Carson, but they were getting harder and harder to find nearby, so I caught some and started breeding them," Wootton explained. "I finally had a decent herd put together and took them to Kansas City and sold them for a small fortune.

"That's how I was able to put this place together," he continued. "I got the rights from the government and then hired about 100 Utes through the year, and we used TNT to clear rock, hauled dirt and rock for filling holes and made a passable road through the pass.

"It used to take a full three of four days to get a wagon through here, if they dared it," he continued. "Now one can get down to Sayre's Willow Spring Station in two days, and that's about 25 miles from right where you're sitting."

Wootton kept the men busy for about an hour with stories of fighting Indians and trapping and hunting for a living. He was quite entertaining.

"Fact is, I'm nothing more than a mountain man and not ashamed of it in any way," he said with a huge smile.

He showed the men where to freshen up and told a Mexican youngster to make sure their horses were fed.

After a big meal of roasted chicken and boiled eggs, Uribe and Dusty went out to check on the horses and get away from "business talk," as Uribe put it.

Adkin and Ryan explained their plans for the stagecoach line and Wootton signed an agreement without asking one question. He did make the statement he would provide his own horses from his ranch, but wanted exchanges on either end of his runs.

"Done deal," Ryan said as he rolled up the paper.

The next morning, they rode off as Wootton waved adios and wished them safe travels on his toll road. Wootton had told them he gets $1.50 for one wagon and 25 cents per single horseman. He said he never charges Indians either, especially the Utes, the one who made his dream of a toll road come true.

Within two days, they were riding into Smith Sayre's Ranch at Willow Spring. He was very happy to sign a deal with Barlow and Sanderson, and also said his Red River station could be used as well, depending on how wore out the horses were after crossing through Raton Pass.

They departed Willow Spring that afternoon and made deals for stations at Cimarron with a contact suggested by Bent. A man named Swink hosted the four riders overnight at the Aztec Hotel, and treated them as guests.

One the morning of their 20th day since leaving Bent's Fort, they headed southward hoping to make it to Fort Union by late afternoon.

An incident nearly killed one of the pack mules at Rayado Creek. The mule apparently stepped into a hole and started pitching and lost a few boxes, and a bag of beans and a bag of sugar.

Dusty and Uribe rode down stream, one on each side, and finally recovered the lost cargo, but little could be saved of the sugar, and the beans were never seen again.

The incident delayed their travel, and it wasn't until darkness, around 9, when they arrived at Fort Union. The men could see the lanterns in the guard houses on the timbered walls. The had to speak up when confronted by guards near the main gate. The fort looked very large, even in the dark.

After telling the guards who they were, six soldiers exited the gate when both doors opened up. They greeted the four with rifles aimed at them, then slowly lowered them when Adkin's English accent confirmed they weren't bandidos.

They were escorted to Commander Brown's quarters, who greeted them warmly and invited them in for a meal, saying his cook had just removed plenty of leftovers that could be brought back out. After the Rayado Creek problem, they ate heartily.

Brown told them not to worry about supplies, his stores were aplenty, as his fort was the military's main supply depot for the Southwest area.

A soldier led them to guest quarters, and the four fell asleep as soon as they hit the cots, clothes and all.

The next morning, after a bountiful breakfast, Brown told them where to find a man Aguirre had recommended they contact. Brown knew him well and said he knew the Aguirre brothers quite well, too. He said this man, Antonio Aguilar, was a solid citizen of the area and gave them directions a short distance south of the fort.

Adkin and Ryan soon had Aguilar's agreement signed and departed Fort Union with grateful thanks to Commander Brown and his soldiers.

They were on the trail again by 11, and stopped for a late lunch at Watrous on the Sapello River. The small village was named after a famous freighter and trader on the Santa Fe Trail, Sam Watrous, who owned a general store there. It was located south of a small fort, called by locals Fort Barclay.

It was here the Cimarron Route connected with the Northern Route, with the southern trail coming into the village from the east. Adkin could tell from the usage on the trail most of the caravans were using the Southern Route – it was much wider and rutted with wagon wheels. Adkin had heard more caravans used that route because it cut the trip by about 7 to 10 days between Westport and Santa Fe.

The fort looked abandoned, and Uribe explained it was nothing more than a forage camp, or had been. The small building at front of the adobe enclosure had a faded Post Office sign nailed by the front door, which had rotted and broken apart, exposing nothing inside but a dirt floor.

On they trekked southward and reached a village called Las Vegas. Again, all the buildings were of adobe. They completed an agreement with another friend of Aguirre's and decided to sleep at the local blacksmith's stables.

The weather was rather chilling to Adkin at these altitudes, but he could smell the hot coals that were simmering in the smitty's shop. It reminded him of home.

He fell asleep thinking of his family back in Olney, especially his mum, she would be worried sick, as he had not written them since arriving at Fort Bent last winter. He was determined he would write them when they reached Santa Fe.

After deals made in San Miguel del Vado, they made their way into Santa Fe at 3 in the afternoon on Day 23, April 7.

The were ahead of their estimated travel time by about a week, and Adkin realized he needed to telegraph Sanderson as soon as possible, as he was leaving Leavenworth in four days.

•••

The Aguirre Brothers' place was on the Santa Fe Plaza, just two buildings from the "Palacio," the home of Mexico's government in the northern territories for more than two centuries.

Adkin asked for Conrado when they checked in at the Hotel Aguirre. The desk man said he was not there, but would be back in a few hours.

"But his brother Jose is here," the man interjected. "Could he help you Señor?"

"Yes, please," Adkin answered.

Jose was in a back office, and after greeting Adkin's crew, Adkin handed him Epifanio's note.

"How many rooms do you need Señor?" Joe asked hurriedly.

"Two would be good if we can sleep two per room," Adkin said, looking to the others, who nodded in approval."

"Dario, place these gentlemen in Suites 2 and 3, and prepare hot baths for the four," Jose barked at the desk man. "Make sure their belongings are put in their suites, then stable and feed their animals at once.

"Gentlemen, when you get comfortable, please come down and dine with me, say around 8?" he added.

Adkin was stupefied. It was Ryan who said, "Thank you," as he took Adkin by the arm and led him toward the stairway.

"Yes, thank you," Adkin suddenly said. Uribe and Dusty followed not saying a word.

"Once they got to their rooms, it was Ryan who said, "I don't know what that note said from Aguirre, 'but sire, this is the royal treatment,'" he said to Adkin, who laughed at Ryan's attempt to sound British.

A few hours later, they met with Jose at the bar next to the front door. He led them through the bar area and sat them all at a large round table in the corner, that had a red table cloth with a vase of colorful flowers and two candles.

The room windows had red velvet drapes on each side of the large, glass vanes. Several chandeliers hung throughout the room and bar area. Aguirre's claim he and his brothers had a "great place" to stay was not an exaggeration.

After suggesting beef steaks for all, Jose finally asked Adkin – after they had all eaten and were sipping brandy, – "So what can I and my brothers do for you?"

Adkin was dumbfounded again.

"Well, did your brother not say in his note?" Adkin asked.

"No Señor, the note only said, 'Treat these men as you would your brothers,'" he said flatly.

Adkin and Ryan laughed and thanked him for his hospitality and told him about the stagecoach line they were establishing.

"That's great, mis amigos," We're in the process of operating stagecoach lines to Mexico City ourselves," Jose said. "That will fit our business very well – being able to offer travel on north and eastward.

At that moment Conrado walked up to the table. After introductions, Jose quickly told Conrado the plans and showed him Epifanio's note.

Conrado smiled big and said, "Well, hermanos ... brothers ... let's go celebrate at the bar.

Adkin couldn't believe their luck in hooking up with these successful traders and brothers, all working to make the best of their lives. And he was especially moved that both Jose and Conrado treated Uribe and Dusty with full respect and honor as they had he and Ryan.

And Uribe and Dusty were thrilled with their treatment, having never been allowed into such a place in their lives. Even Uribe, who usually speaks enough for both of them hadn't chattered but a few words of "gracias."

When they we're walking to the bar, Uribe did whisper into Adkin's ear, "The stories we will have for our families and friends will not be believed."

...

After breakfast the next morning, Conrado showed them the stables and a stagecoach they already had. They also had several new ambulances, like the one Epifanio was travelling in.

"These make into wonderful beds when on the trail," Conrado said, pointing to the ambulance's bench seats. "These seats fold over, it's great – if the road is not too rough – but very good while camping at night."

He showed them around the plaza, and pointed to a plaque on the "Palacio" that said it was established in 1609. All the buildings around the plaza – and beyond – were adobe with beautiful large logs sticking out of the walls at roof heights.

The Hotel Aguirre was also adobe, but it was two stories with large cactus and flowering plants surrounding the front of the hotel. A raised wooden porch stretched the length of the building in front.

The stable area was made of hewn logs with huge corner posts made of trees nearly three-feet in diameter and six-feet tall. The partially enclosed stalls were also adobe.

Jose met up with them for lunch and made arrangements for Adkin and his crew to re-supply their food needs and any other sundries they needed at ... naturally, the Aguirre Brothers Trading Post.

Adkin asked where the telegraph office was, and the brothers led them across the plaza and onto the next road over. There flew an American Flag in front of an adobe building with painted letters above the wooden double doors, "U.S. Post Office and Telegraph." A tall pole stood behind the place with a telegraph line stringing off to the north and passing atop other posts.

Adkin noticed "and Telegraph" had been a new addition as it was fresher paint than the "U.S. Post Office."

"It's new," Conrado said. "We didn't have it operating until about two months ago."

Adkin and Ryan scribbled out a message to Sanderson and handed it to the operator who started clicking away. They were told a reply may take about an hour or so, as sometimes finding the recipient was troubling.

"It could take a day even," the operator told them. "But we'll deliver it to you. Are you staying at Aguirre's?"

Adkin said, "Yes," and thanked him, and pulled out a sealed envelope from his shirt pocket and handed it to the man.

"Could you see this gets posted in the mail? It's a letter for my family in England," Adkin said.

The man pulled out a chart, ran his finger down the lines and stopped.

"No problem, but that will be $5 sir?" the man said, smiling.

Adkin handed him five silver coins, and thanked him.

•••

After checking the supplies at the general store that had been laid aside, Uribe asked if they could get an additional bag of tobacco, as he and Dusty were born into smoking pipes.

"It's better than if we were to smoke peyote," Uribe said, smiling.

Adkin agreed to more tobacco, and he asked Jose if he had any paraffine paper. Jose said he did indeed. Adkin told him they wanted to double wrap all their stagecoach contracts in more waxed paper and seal them in a box, in case it fell off in a river.

Jose pointed out he had issued two extra water bags for each animal.

"Horses and mules have to get their water or they die," Jose said with a stern look. "Men can go a few days without water, but not the animals, especially travelling the Dry Route. You can fill these when you get to start of Jornada del Muerte."

Adkin thanked him, and then told Uribe he would notify he and Dusty as soon as they had heard back from Sanderson.

"If it's late today, we'll wait and depart early tomorrow," Adkin said.

"And if its before noon tomorrow, we'll leave as soon as the supplies are strapped down," Ryan added.

An Englishman's Adventures on the Santa Fe Trail (1865-1889)

Conrado offered to show Adkin and Ryan more of Santa Fe, and both accepted. He also shared with them that a small caravan of freighters had set out on the southern route about a week before Adkin and his crew had arrived.

"You will probably catch them in about 10 days or so," Conrado said. "But they were eager to start and so only found about 30 wagons of freight to partake the journey. They did get approval to be protected by 10 or 12 Army soldiers from Fort Union, though."

As they walked around the plaza, Conrado told them who owned the businesses – from small tack shops to cafes – Conrado knew everyone. Many often shouted greetings to him as the three made their way through the streets of Santa Fe.

Adkin was impressed with the town and its size. Even Ryan had said it had grown since he had been there nearly three years ago. Conrado confirmed it was growing and said they were looking to more growth since the end of America's Civil War. He and the Western freighters were eager to return to heavy trading like it was in the late 1850s.

There was a busy feel to everyone in the town. Adkin realized it was probably because it was the start of the freighting season, Santa Fe was awakening from its winter sleep, and it was time to start hauling goods to a hungry market back east. Conrado had already mentioned several small caravans and his brother's large wagon train had already departed east with trade goods.

As they passed a saddle shop, Adkin noticed a pair of leather leggings hanging in one of the windows. They had leather thongs tied down the outer sides with the tops edged with fur, He told Conrado he would like to talk with the store clerk about the leggings.

Adkin had seen these at various places along his journeys, and most had been worn by Indians and he had seen a few trappers, or mountain men, wearing them. They made perfect sense to Adkin – a way to protect one's lower legs in thickets and brush, especially when on horseback.

The store clerk, who happened to be the owner, greeted Conrado warmly and told Adkin the leggings were topped with wolf fur, and wolf fur was waterproof and warm in winter. Adkin held the leggings up beside his legs, and they looked to come up to just above his knees.

The clerk was extremely happy, saying they had been ordered by another very tall man about six months ago, but the would-be customer had been killed in an Indian raid shortly after the order was completed and the owner had already paid the Ute that made them.

The clerk admitted he had been wondering if he would ever sell them.

"They are normally five U.S. dollars, Señor, but today you are my good luck – only four dollars for you," the clerk said.

Adkin paid the man five dollars with a grin, and the ecstatic clerk rolled up the leggings and wrapped them in brown paper.

Once back at the hotel, Conrado and Jose formalized the stagecoach agreements for the family, and Conrado suggested they share a drink at the bar to celebrate.

Jose went outside and found Uribe and Dusty sitting on a bench on the front porch of the hotel and invited them in for a drink celebrating the agreement. Again, the two were awed, but eagerly jumped up and said "Si, si, gracias!"

While laughing and sharing a bottle of rum, with Adkin drinking tea, the telegraph operator came through the front door and hurriedly approached them.

"Got your reply Mister Yates," he said, proudly.

Adkin took the slip of paper, as Conrado handed the man a coin, saying, "Gracias, Señor."

Adkin read the words aloud,

"Departing tomorrow. Stop.

Congratulations on your success. Stop.

Will meet at Ft. Dodge. Stop.

J.L. Sanderson. Stop."

Adkin looked up smiling and said, "Men, we depart tomorrow morning at daylight."

All of them cheered and toasted each other.

"Another adventure on the Santa Fe Trail," Ryan said, patting Adkin on the back.

"It can be very much adventure on the Cimarron Route," Uribe added, with a wry smile as Ryan nodded in agreement.

Conrado jumped up and said he had a surprise for them.

"Let us attend the fandango a friend of ours is having tonight," Conrado said. "There is music and dancing, with food and drink."

"Let's go, men," Adkin said grinning.

They spent several hours at the fandango, where every class of citizen in Santa Fe was celebrating. From the peons to upper class women with dainty lace covering their faces were having fun together. There were tables of food and something to drink everywhere aound the plaza.

It was quite a night, and even Adkin had put down a few drinks he wasn't even sure what they were called.

Laying in bed, Adkin had trouble falling asleep – even with the alcohol in him. He was thinking about the stories he had heard about the long dry stretches on the Cimarron Route to Fort Dodge.

It would take maybe four weeks, but they wouldn't be hampered by signing deals with station owners and operators. And he was comforted by the fact Ryan had made the trek once before, and Uribe had covered the trail three or four times.

An Englishman's Adventures on the Santa Fe Trail (1865-1889)

"What an adventure I'm living," Adkin thought to himself. "I'm nearly 800 miles from Fort Leavenworth. He was glad he had written his family the first night they arrived in Santa Fe."

But then he suddenly remembered Kit Carson's and Colonel Bent's reminder that, 'It's only an adventure if you keep your scalp.'

•••

Conrado and Jose had hot coffee ready for the men when they came down the stairs around 6 and offered them a breakfast of sourdough bread, bacon chunks with fresh eggs, but Adkin asked if it would be okay to just take some bread with them.

"We appreciate your hospitality more than we could put into words, but we're very excited to hit the trail," Adkin explained.

"Some fresh bread would give us an excuse to stop in a few hours to make coffee and really enjoy it," Ryan said, with a big smile.

"So be it," Conrado said as they all walked out to the stables. Jose had made sure all their supplies had been securely lashed to the pack mules before the men came down from their suites.

After warm handshakes and best wishes, the four mounted their horses, with Uribe tying the bag of bread loaves to his saddle horn.

"Gracias por el fandango, Señors, "Uribe shouted, and they all laughed.

They then turned and headed through the plaza and back down the Santa Fe Trail. The sky was just beginning to lighten in the east, and a cool, grey light bathed the crew as they rode out of town.

Uribe had said they would return to Watrous and then head due east to take the southern route – or the Semarone (See-mah-roan) Route as some spelled it, and Uribe pronounced it.

"In two days, I'll be seeing new lands again," Adkin thought to himself, a slight smile crossing his face as Diablo slowly rocked back and forth in his leisurely stride.

•••

On the morning of the third day, the crew moved out of Watrous on the Cimarron Cut-off, as some called it. They all knew this would be the more dangerous route than the Mountain Route, due mainly to the facts there were long stretches between water holes, and it was a frequent target of Indian raids – the nearest fort was Fort Union north of this stretch.

They knew of Fort Nichols, or Camp Nichols. Kit Carson had told them about its location and why he personally oversaw its construction in May 1865, before he joined up with Bent for the trip to the Little Arkansas Treaty.

"It's a place near water, Cedar Springs, and to help increase your odds fighting Indian depredations," he had told them on their way to Fort Bent last Fall.

When they mentioned it to Conrado, he explained Fort Nichols had been abandoned in September 1865.

As this territory was dangerous, Dusty would outride for five to ten miles ahead each day, looking for Indians and shooting game now and then for food. They made sure to camp each evening in a place where they could see great distances, even if it was somewhat windy.

They always spent time building rock or timber firewalls and kept their flame as low as possible so it couldn't be seen by enemies – just enough to cook a little meat or make coffee.

On the third evening, the wind was ripping across the butte they wanted to camp on which forced them to go down the leeward side and camp in a small ravine. It barely had enough room for them and their hobbled animals. Adkin didn't sleep much and kept watch for all but three hours of the night. It was a vulnerable spot, offering easy ambush for someone wanting to kill them.

On the fifth day about mid-forenoon, they saw small wisps of black and gray smoke on the eastern horizon.

"That should be Cedar Springs and Camp Nichols," Uribe said. "I worry where Dusty is?

"I think we should stop here for awhile and wait for Dusty. If he knows what is happening, he will come back and report as soon as he can."

•••

Buzzards covered numerous bodies spread across the trail, pieces of burned wagons still simmered and smoked. Adkin's nostrils filled with the stench of death as he gazed over the scene.

Dusty had returned to the crew, his horse lathered up, shouting "Estan muertos. Estan muertos."

"Who is dead," Uribe asked.

"The caravan y the soldiers." he yelled.

After Uribe calmed Dusty, they found out he had seen the smoke and advanced cautiously up a small ravine and saw the aftermath of an Indian raid that had hit the caravan that had departed Santa Fe before they had. Adkin realized it was the one Conrado said only had about 30 wagons.

Dusty said the fort was abandoned, and the wagons had been ambushed when they neared the old fort, its walls already eroding and no roofs.

As they walked into the horror, they could see where several soldiers had been tied to wagon wheels. The Indians had cut off their hands and set the wagons on fire.

One soldier, who had been seated next to a wagon wheel, had his arms tied to the outer wheel and had his pants pulled down below his knees. His feet had been cut off. Adkin could see he had his testicles hanging out of his mouth, his burned upper body still simmering in the mid-forenoon sun.

Adkin saw a white woman who was obviously pregnant laying on the ground, her dress gathered up around her neck. She had been violated and then her body, even her unborn child, had been shot with more than a dozen arrows. She had also been scalped, her skull glistening amongst the dried blood splotches.

Bloated bodies were everywhere, covered with flies, there was the pervasive smell of burning bodies, a few mules and wagons. Items of trade goods were strewn everywhere, but what was on the ground had been burned or partially destroyed or was completely covered in blood. Dried black blood was everywhere.

"Those arrows belong to Jicarilla Apaches," Uribe said. "Most likely they were travelling with other tribes of the Comanches – probably close to a hundred or so."

Adkin's mind was numb as they slowly walked their horses through the carnage. All his senses felt violated.

"Jefe Adkin, what should we do?" Uribe asked. "Jefe Ryan?"

"We have to check every body here to see if any are still alive – with a heartbeat," Ryan spoke up.

"And count the dead," Adkin whispered. "Women, children, men, soldiers, animals."

"We will have to report every detail we can find when we get to Fort Dodge," Adkin said, sounding more in control of his senses.

"You want we should collect some arrows and lances?" Uribe asked.

Adkin nodded and Ryan said, "Yes, that's a good idea. We'll need to find out who did this."

•••

By evening, they had found the bodies of 10 soldiers; six men, apparently freighters or teamsters, two women, including the pregnant one – the other found under the wagon floor who was hiding and burned to death without the Indians ever seeing her; two dead mules, killed by misguided arrows; and the remains of only five wagons.

"The arrows show the Quahadis were here, too – another Comanche tribe," Uribe said. "There are some others I'm not sure, but the soldiers' scouts will know. We also found one battle shield and two broken spears."

"The Comanches took all the remaining wagons full of goods, all the surviving animals; horses, mules, probably some cattle and all the women and children," Ryan said. "We'll have to telegraph the freighters in Santa Fe who put this caravan together and find out who and how many were listed in the wagon train. There were no guns found anywhere.

"Also, every one of them have been scalped," Ryan continued. "And Uribe and I are guessing about 30 or more hostages were taken – teamsters, mule skinners and bullwhackers – to move the wagons south. They are overloaded with the goods from the wagons they destroyed.

"The hostages will most likely be killed once they get where they're headed, except for any women or children that are with them," Ryan added.

"The wagons and horse tracks head south, and the wagon tracks are deep from heavy loads," Uribe said. "Most likely the Comanches are headed to their normal winter grounds in the Llano Estacado – in Tejas, Texas – the northern end of the canyons is only two day's ride from here."

"Well, we need to gather the bodies. Use a horse and lariat if necessary, and move them over here," Adkin said, pointing to a low spot on the ground just above a small ravine. "We'll bury them in the morning. Cover them with our tarps for the night."

The other three glanced back and forth to each other, unsure if he was serious.

Adkin walked down to the spring and sat by its gurgling waters, contemplating how vicious man could be to another man – and woman. This horror was seared into his memory forever.

The next morning, since they didn't have a shovel, Adkin said they would use some partially burned planks from the remains of wagons and dig out a shallow trench long enough to place the 18 bodies side-by-side. He made a mark with his boot toe and paced 18 strides away and made another mark.

"This should do it," he said.

They used their hatchets to produce somewhat sharpened ends of the planks and to break up the ground's deadpan surface. It took the four of them six hours taking turns with three short pieces of planks and a wagon tongue.

Though the trench was only about three-feet deep, they covered the bodies in about an hour and placed rocks on top. Exhausted, they ate early and went to sleep before dark.

Dusty took the first watch.

•••

As they rose the following morning, all of them could feel their aching muscles from digging the hard clay earth with hatchets and pieces of wood.

"I want to pray for their souls before we depart," Adkin said, as he walked over to the makeshift mass grave. Uribe had made one small cross from some twisted branches to place in the middle of the lengthy mound.

As Adkin prayed that their souls be looked over by God, Dusty and Uribe started laying some stones on each end of the grave.

Adkin said, "Lord, these souls have been placed in your hands. Please take the best of care."

Seeing that Ryan and Adkin held their hats over their hearts, Uribe and Dusty did likewise, and they both made the sign of the Catholic Cross.

"Are the extra water bags filled?" Adkin asked.

"Si Señor," Uribe said.

"Well let's move out," Adkin said. "We need to get out of this hell-hole."

Uribe had said the next water hole would be at Flag Spring, or Upper Spring as some called it, and they should reach it by nightfall.

"It is at Point of Rocks, a beautiful place where the Indians say that Coronado, the Spaniard, camped hundreds of years ago.

•••

Three days later, they arrived at Point of Rocks, a great plateau high above the swirling muddy waters of the Cimarron River with nearby Middle Spring. The plateau's height apparently a safe place travellers camped many times or kept their lookouts. The river had recently flooded and backed up to the still spring, making it as nearly as muddy as the river.

Uribe suggested they camp a little below the top of Point of Rocks in order to build a fire and boil water. Their watch shifts could then be stationed further atop the plateau to guard against enemies.

Adkin agreed, enjoying hearing the normal chatter of men doing their chores to establish camp. The tragedy they had seen at Cedar Springs had kept talk to a minimum the last few days, as each man was quietly mulling the horror in their own ways.

Uribe and Dusty unpacked the mules and used one of them to haul bags of muddy water a few hundred yards from the spring to camp. Uribe said it was not just because of the mud, but many beaver lived along the river and boiling would help prevent disease and clean up the taste.

They poured the water into two large bean pots and brought ithem to a boil. Then they would use a small amount to rinse the bag and then fill it with the hot water and lay it on the ground. After about three hours – just before sunset, they had replenished about 20 gallons they had used from Cedar Springs.

"If we get to Lower Spring – Wagon Bed Spring – and it's dry, it's 60 to 70 miles to the Arkansas River, a day's ride west of Fort Dodge," Uribe explained. "These animals will need about five gallons of water a day, each one."

Adkin had noticed the days were getting longer and warmer. Plus the land was looking more featureless and flatter, much like that between Fort Dodge and Fort Aubry.

Taking the first watch, Adkin stood atop Point of Rocks and scanned the miles eastward and northward. He could see forever in his opinion, much like at sea.

"Somewhere out there is La Journado de Muerte," Adkin thought to himself – 70 miles of desert-like country that could kill man and beast.

He remembered the old man at Paddington Station in London who said his brother had died of thirst in a desert on the Santa Fe Trail.

"I wonder if he died near here?" Adkin silently asked himself.

•••

Just before sunrise, Adkin heard a rumbling, something akin to hundreds of horse hoofs trampling the ground. The others had, too. Dusty came riding down from the plateau, waving his arms and pointing south.

As they turned to look, Uribe shouted, "Buffalo."

Several thousand buffalo were trotting up to the south side of the Cimarron, the ones leading already belly-deep and lapping up the river's water, mud and all.

The ones behind them smelling the life-supporting fluid hurrying and running to crowd and shuffle to the water's edge. They were spreading out for more than a mile along the wandering river. Clouds of dust were rising into the sunlight, though the sun had barely reached the horizon.

"What do you think Adkin?" Ryan asked. "Think we ought to kill one for meat? They don't even know we're over here yet."

The crew was less than a half mile from the river, but they were on the north side. And their horses were still hobbled, except for Dusty's

"It would cost us another whole day, Ryan," Adkin answered. "Plus we have plenty of meat now."

"Too much work to pack all that meat through a high river today," Uribe said, shaking his head negatively. "There will be more coming up from Tejas now that it is Spring. The Comanches and other tribes like the Kiowa and Apaches will be following them."

"He's right," Adkin said. "Let's get packed and move out."

•••

It took them another day and a half to reach Lower Spring, or Wagon Bed Spring. The landscape had depressed Adkin. Its barren desert-like hostility was hard on the animals. It had warmed, especially considering last week, as well. Adkin's thermometer he carried with his compass, showed it to be 94 degrees F. when they arrived at the famous Wagon Bed.

An Englishman's Adventures on the Santa Fe Trail (1865-1889)

Travellers had removed the wheels and axle and placed a freight wagon bed in a dug-out area to allow spring water to be filtered into the bed and as a collection point.

But ... there was no water in it. In fact, only drying mud and fresh buffalo chips covered the area.

"The buffalo have wallowed throughout this entire area, Señor," Uribe broke the silence. "Mucho buffalo. They have covered the spring or there is no longer water coming from the spring."

"This is a problem," Ryan said, sitting on his horse next to Adkin and Diablo. "We probably don't have 30 gallons of water left, and it's 70 miles to the Arkansas."

After a long silence, Adkin asked, "Men, what should we do?"

"Even if we men didn't drink for the next three to four days, there's not enough to keep the animals alive," Ryan said.

"Maybe we look for spring right here," Uribe said. "We make spears from those small trees and maybe find water."

Dusty nodded his head emphatically, his look saying he dreaded going onward without water.

"Este es La Journada," Dusty said frightfully.

Uribe explained they could take some limbs, trim off the branches and sharpen the ends.

"We poke and dig in the ground and see if water comes up," he explained.

"We don't have much choice," Adkin said, with Ryan mumbling agreement.

There was a small grove of trees, not more than 10- to 12-feet tall a hundred paces from the wagon bed. They looked like young willows intermingled with several large cotonwoods.

Uribe used his hatchet to fell one and started shearing off the branches, at about 6-feet up, he cut the remaining wood off and made a sharp point with his knife. He then walked over near the mud surrounding the wagon bed and started stabbing the ground and wiggling the pole back and forth in the mud.

"Not here," he said looking to the others. "Make more poles, and we all have to cover the area mucho."

In short time, all four were working the area by sticking the pointed poles as far as they could into the ground and parting the mud to see if water would rise. After about an hour, Adkin suggested they go ahead and make camp on nearby dry ground.

It was nearing sunset, and after drinking their fill and watering the animals, they returned to the huge mud wallow around the wagon bed.

The area soon had at least a 100 holes, most within about two feet of each other.

"Why is the wagon bed there?" Adkin asked Uribe while pointing at it.

"The last time I here, a small pipe came from the ground and water spilled into the old wagon bed from the pipe," he said. "That kept the buffalo from wallowing in it, or it did most of the time."

"The bed would overflow and a small stream of water and mud followed down there near the trees and into the See-mah-roan," Uribe added.

Adkin walked to the bed and started poking around, he could feel no pipe or stir any water up. He was thinking maybe buffalo had moved the wagon bed away from the spring itself. He then stepped into the bed and fairly fresh mud came up nearly to the tops of his boots.

He raised his pole and stabbed into the wooden bed. A clunking sound resulted.

"Hope this doesn't offend fellow travellers, but I'm going to knock a hole in this wagon bottom," Adkin said, as he took his hatchet from his belt and started pounding the mud and the bed.

It soon gave way, and Adkin grabbed his pole. He drove it through the hole and into the ground as hard as he could and started shifting it back and forth. Suddenly, a gurgling spurt of water shot up through the mud.

'Ahyee,' Uribe shouted. "Agua."

Everybody had huge smiles on their faces, and Adkin stuck the pole in the flow even further and more water started filling the muddy wagon bed.

"We'll need to clean all this mud from the bed," Adkin said. "Grab some pots and we'll start cleaning this up."

Just as it was getting dark, the wagon bed looked like a small wooden pond, brimming with fresh cool water and overflowing into the small ravine again.

"Buffalo decided to wallow here and fighting for position in the mud, they must have buried that old pipe several feet down," Ryan said as they sipped coffee by the small fire they made. "Then enough dirt and mud – and the wagon bed – was pushed over the spring, and it just didn't have enough pressure to find daylight."

"I was very unsettled about what we were going to do," Adkin said in his English way. "Very unsettled."

The others laughed – with similar relief.

•••

At daylight, Uribe and Ryan had finished strapping water bags to the mules and horses along with their supplies. Dusty had already saddled his mount and was out-riding ahead of them.

The three headed out with nine bags of water and four full canteens. Dusty carried the maximum he could carry, too.

They were now headed into a desert, it seemed, with no dry river bed off to their right. The Cimarron River valley had turned off south, but it had at least provided some firewood and small game to shoot for meals. They were following the wagon tracks which had been carved into the hard red sandstone from thousands of wagons throughout the years.

"When I came this way three years ago, there had been big rain storms to the north of here and that dry river bed had raging water roaring through that valley at least a mile wide," Ryan said to Adkin as they rode along the trail. "I remember seeing wagon ruts at least a half-a-mile wide through this area."

"Well, there's nothing in a wagon's way in this desolate place," Adkin remarked. "No trees, creeks, bushes, rocks, barely any creatures. And I haven't even seen a lizard in the hour past."

Dust rose from every step of the animals' hooves, and it was 92 degrees at mid-forenoon when they stopped for a water break and 20 minutes of rest.

"Now that it's spring, the Plains Indians will be moving north with the buffalo," Uribe reminded them. "They look for small caravans to steal their horses.

"Or they seek fools like us," he added, with a crooked smile. "Maybe we get going soon."

"He's right, let's move on," Adkin said, remembering the horrors at Cedar Springs.

About an hour later, they came across the decaying body of a mule.

"It has not been long dead," Uribe said. "Maybe four or five days."

Buzzards and ravens were still picking the bones clean. They surmised maybe a mule escaped at Cedar Springs and tried to make it up the trail but died of thirst. Uribe rode over to the beast and dismounted. He covered the area around it. Suddenly a shot rang out.

"Ees a tarantula – most disagreeable to me," Uribe explained. He holstered his pistol and then got back in the saddle and rode back to the crew.

"No tracks, but wind may have blown any away, or possibly it just escaped from someone and died of thirst."

They had seen numerous bleached bone piles of mules or horses, they were difficult to distinguish once totally decayed. And there were also bones of oxen along the way, but none as fresh as the one they had suspected as coming from the massacre.

The nights during this stretch of the trail were the worst for Adkin, thinking what could happen if they were spotted by a large hunting or raiding party of Indians. Though the temperature was cool, worry sat heavy on his shoulders during his time at each night's watch.

Late on the fourth day, Dusty came loping back to meet them.

"Arkansas River one hour ahead," he shouted, smiling from ear-to-ear.

•••

"That was the longest four days in my life," Adkin thought to himself, even as he kept his head on a swivel for the next hour, looking for danger.

When they reached the river, all of them stayed on their horses and allowed all the animals to wade into the water and drink their fill.

"This is known as the Middle Crossing," Uribe announced. "We cross over there, and then it's another day to Fort Dodge."

At about that time, dust was rising on the horizon north of the river. Dusty spoke up, "It's either buffalo, Indians or soldiers. They're moving too fast for a wagon train."

The first thing that came into sight was two horsemen holding an American Flag and a Kansas Flag.

"It's calvary," Ryan said. "Thank God it's not 100 Indians."

Adkin shook his head in agreement. It looked like at least a company, or about 100 men. As they came down the shallow valley wall, they could see four supply wagons, two ambulances and two howitzers were behind the wagons.

They were in full gallop, and the front soldiers continued splashing through the river and bounding up to the crew. One raised his arm and yelled, Haa-aalt."

Two officers came riding forward across the river and stopped directly in front of Adkin and Ryan.

"Gentlemen, Could you please offer your names and business," the Captain asked. A Lieutenant was by his side.

"Wait, aren't you Adkin Yates," the Captain asked.

"I can scarcely believe my eyes," Adkin smiled. "How are you Lieut … I mean Captain Samuel Oscar Phillips?"

Phillips dropped from his saddle as the others quickly followed suit.

Adkin grabbed both arms and embraced Phillips, as Phillips said, "Wonderful to see you my English friend. "I didn't recognize you behind all that hair and beard."

He then grabbed Ryan, "You still riding with this bruiser, Tyler?"

"Yes, sir, and it's great to set eyes on you again," Ryan said. "Never thought I'd say it's a small world way out here."

"Lieutenant, dismount the troops and put them at ease for 20 minutes," Phillips barked. "Let their animals drink but be prepared to mount up in a moment's notice."

Adkin introduced Uribe and Dusty and Phillips asked them to have a seat on some sandstone outcroppings. He wanted to talk.

Phillips asked where they had travelled, and did they go through Cedar Springs last week.

"Why yes, Captain, we did," Adkin said. "I was just going to tell you about the massacre we came upon there."

"Believe it or not, that's where we're headed, Adkin," Phillips said. "There was one young bullwhacker that survived and rode out of that battle on a mule.

"He made it to Wagon Bed Spring and said it was only a mud hole. He tried to eat some of the mud for the water, and it nearly killed him.

"His mule died a few miles later and he was on foot when a dozen Comancheros came upon him," Phillips continued. "They were talking about killing him since he had nothing to trade or steal, but the youngster promised them $100 in gold if they would bring him to Fort Dodge.

"And, by God's will, they did," Phillips said. "The fort's commander ordered me to put together a company detail to see if we can hunt down the Comanches that did this. We believe there's about four or five women and as many children taken hostage.

Adkin and Ryan told Phillips about the dead woman and the others they found.

"We buried 18," Ryan said. "We figure they must have taken about 30 captives, and they will surely kill the men when they are finished with their services."

Adkin handed Phillips his notes and numbers of dead. He had Uribe and Dusty grab the bags with the belongings they took off the victims and the Indian pieces they gathered up. Phillips had his adjutant take them to the wagons.

'Well, we must hurry," Phillips said, excitedly. "We think it was Chief Ten Bears, and some other Comanche bands that follow him.

"They were headed south with about 20 wagons – to the Llano Estacado," Uribe said. "It will be easy to track them."

"That's what I'm worried about, Phillips said. "If they get down into those deep ravines and gulches, we'll never find them.

"I'm stationed at Fort Dodge now, Adkin. Hopefully, we can meet again, but for now, we have to get going," Phillips said, as he rose to his feet. "You shouldn't have any trouble into Fort Dodge, we didn't see any danger.

"Adkin quickly asked if Phillips had seen J. L. Sanderson with a large Army caravan, yet. Phillips said no, but they were scheduled to arrive fairly soon. He also told them Pierce was still the Fort Dodge Commander, but he was now a Colonel.

"Great to see you, and I wish we could've visited more," Phillips said to Adkin, then shaking all the men's hands. "Be careful."

"Jolly good to see you Captain Phillips," Adkin said. "Jolly good."

"Call me Sam from now on, English," Phillips said as he mounted his steed.

"Mount up, Lieutenant," he yelled.

As the calvary waded through the river, several men looked familiar to Adkin. Ryan mentioned the same thing.

"Maybe they're former Rebs that we saw when we went through there last Fall," Ryan said.

"That's good for Phillips, he's got some really tough Indian fighters with him, they're experienced.

"Well, let's find a camp site across the river," Adkin said. "Our last night before Fort Dodge."

•••

They could hardly believe their eyes as they crossed the bluff and looked down toward Fort Dodge. It looked like real fort, with a large redoubt surrounding several buildings; all made of adobe, rock and timber. It had only been about six months earlier when they passed through and there was only one building, Colonel Henry Pierce's lodgings.

Those quarters were still central to the fort, but there was another with long barracks, another large out-building, new stables and a corral.

As they approached the main gate, several soldiers opened it and one, a Sergeant, recognized Ryan immediately and Adkin, after a long glance-over. Adkin was telling them who they were when the sergeant said, "Welcome, welcome. Come on in. I'll let Colonel Pierce know you're here"

He ran off double-time to the old adobe office.

As they got off their horses in front of the officer's quarters, Pierce stepped onto the porch.

"Well, if it isn't the stagecoach agents Yates and Ryan," he shouted. "Welcome, glad to see you still have your scalps."

"We're glad to still have them as well, Colonel," Adkin said, laughing. "Good to see you, I assure you."

After introductions, Pierce invited the men for a glass of rum and water and fresh cigars. Adkin asked for just water, but took the cigar. He had tried rolled cigarettes and tobacco in pipes, but never a cigar. It smelled good, but the first puff reminded him why he detested rolled cigarettes and pipes.

Discussions began with the caravan that was massacred. Pierce told them it was put together by a famous Santa Fe trader named Franz Huning. He had been contacted by telegraph and reported to Pierce the manifest included 28 wagons, 50 sale mules, 43 teamsters and bullwhackers, 10 U.S. Army soldiers, five women and four children.

"Plus the oxen and mules pulling the wagons, and all the trade goods," Pierce said.

"Well, we buried 18, including one pregnant woman and all the soldiers," Adkin reported. "The others were taken hostage, we suspected to drive the wagons to the Llano Estacado.

"We have some arrows and a few broken lances for you to inspect," he added. 'We turned them over to Captain Phillips. We encountered him yesterday."

Pierce interrupted, "We're pretty sure it's Ten Bears' bands of Comanches. We're just hoping to catch up with them and save the hostages.

"But if they get down into Llano Estacado, the odds are against us," Pierce continued. "We'll have to let them go. Captain Phillips won't do anything stupid that would get his men ambushed."

"We know him well," Adkin said, as Ryan shook his head. "We travelled together from Fort Leavenworth to the Little Arkansas Peace Treaty last Fall."

"He's a good man," Pierce added. "Hopefully, the 'Comanch' will ask to trade hostages, and we'll get them back."

Pierce asked them what they thought about his new fort, and both expressed surprise. A large late Fall caravan brought building supplies and two hundred men to help get things going.

"By God, the Army Brass kept their word," Pierce said. "They then sent me 200 calvary just before Christmas. That's when Phillips arrived, and I was promoted."

Adkin asked about Sanderson.

"I realize we're early, we thought it would take us a little longer," Adkin said. "We left Fort Bent March 15th, made it to Santa Fe, and here we are May 2nd. We have travelled light and fast.

"That's probably why you still have your scalps," Pierce said, laughing. "We believe Indian depredations will only increase now that the buffalo herds are moving north."

Sanderson had telegraphed twice, once when they departed Leavenworth and just last week, saying they were at the Peacock Ranch Trading Post.

"They should be here in about a week," Pierce said.

"Good, they are ahead of schedule as well," Adkin said.

Pierce had them led to guest rooms at the end of the new barracks, barracks that could sleep 300 men if needed. They found out the other building was the mess hall and cook's kitchen.

"I'm happy those poor soldiers don't have to sleep in those cold, wet dugouts down by the river with canvas tarps hanging over the entrance," Ryan said.

"Amen," responded Adkin.

Within a few days, the crew was feeling fairly spoiled from living in civilization again. They were sleeping in beds with straw mattresses, eating big hot meals, not worrying about their animals.

"I didn't realize how hard those three weeks along the Cimarron Route had been on me, until now," Adkin told Ryan. "Being able to relax and not worry about Indian attacks has given me relief I can't quite understand."

"I know what you mean," Ryan said. "My memories of the scenes at Cedar Springs is only now becoming more bearable."

"The same for me," Adkin responded, softly.

Pierce suggested they telegraph Fort Larned and ask the commander there to inform Sanderson that Adkin and Ryan had safely arrived at Fort Dodge and were awaiting his arrival.

Later that day, the telegraph operator notified them their message had been received and they would tell Sanderson as soon as he arrived.

Meanwhile, the crew went about being lazy, Uribe actually complained there was nothing to do.

"Why don't you go over to the stables and hobble our animals, give them a good rub-down, run around the fort a couple of times and then go and unhobble them," Ryan teased.

"You joke, but I just might do that," Uribe said with a big laugh.

Adkin and Ryan found out where they could practice their pistol shooting, and Ryan noticed Adkin didn't hardly miss anything, especially when shooting from his hip.

Adkin decided to see the camp barber to "tidy up," as he called it. He had stopped trimming his hair after leaving Fort Bent. Then after leaving Pueblo, he had quit shaving as well.

He had the barber trim his beard to about 2-inches on his face and off his chin. He also lightly trimmed his hair but kept it just below his collar. It was still blond, but his blond-reddish beard made him look more like a redhead at times.

"It's that Scottish blood in me," he'd tell Ryan when his beard color was mentioned.

One day, Uribe and Dusty volunteered to go out with the fort's hunting party. It made his whole stay at the fort worthwhile. He chattered like a magpie for two days about how each of them had shot a deer.

"Mine was about 500 yards away," Uribe boasted, as Dusty rolled his eyes. "And Dusty dropped one about 400 yards out."

Dusty just grinned and then said, "It was muy grande to get back on a horse. I don't belong to a fort bunk."

They were all laughing when the telegraph operator burst in their room with a message from Sanderson. He was at Fort Larned and expected to arrive at Fort Dodge in two-and-a-half to three days.

"It won't be long, Dusty, until you're back in the saddle and heading for home," Adkin said.

Adkin went to sleep that night thinking about the fact he had departed England only 10 months ago, and he would turn 20 in two months.

He felt his life had exceeded an adventure and turned into a canvas which he would have the privilege of finishing the painting with his own decisions, actions and God' guidance and blessings – for the rest of his life. The Great Plains was now his home.

•••

An out-rider arrived at Fort Dodge mid-forenoon May 10th, announcing that the 8th Kansas Infantry was approaching Fort Dodge, less than 30 minutes out.

Adkin had been told by Pierce that the 8th Kansas Infantry, a volunteer regiment that fought in the war, had been mustered out of service at Fort Leavenworth on January 9, 1866. Many had re-enlisted in the new U.S. Army.

Pierce added not all the companies were coming west, but enough to start reinforcing Forts along the Santa Fe Trail.

As the wagon train approached, several soldiers, officers and a Barlow & Sanderson Overland Stage Company Concord swung out of the masses of wagons and men and raced to the front of the column.

Everyone started shouting greetings as J.L. Sanderson reined his four horses to a stop.

"Who is that with you Ryan?" were the first words out of his mouth. Then he started laughing, "By golly, you've turned into a real mountain man, Adkin Yates."

They all dismounted and embraced, Sanderson holding Adkin back at arms length and checking out his wardrobe from head to toe.

"Indian leggings, buckskin britches and buckskin shirt with long hair and a beard. My God, man, you look wonderful – and healthy," Sanderson said, shaking the tall muscular man in front of him.

He then reached out with an arm and pulled Ryan closer.

"You two are sure a sight for sore eyes," Sanderson said. "I hate to admit this, but I've been worried sick about both of you. Don't think I've worried about two people more in my life. I mean it."

"Well, we're sure happy to see you, too," Ryan said, while Adkin just grinned and shook his head in agreement.

"Let's get this caravan settled in," Sanderson said. "I've got so much news to tell you, and I'm sure you're going to like it."

•••

Once the large caravan circled their wagons in three or four places outside the fort's redoubts, Sanderson had the three remaining Concords pull into the main gate. That's when Ryan and Adkin got their glimpses of some of the old gang.

Waving and yelling greetings was the squat friendly German Ray Dee Rinehart, and Darrell Holmes and Carl Long were driving the other two.

"Great to see you partner," Adkin yelled to Rinehart, both grinning ear to ear.

All of them embraced and teased each other after parking the coaches in the stock yard, with permission from Pierce. All of them expressed delight at seeing Ryan and the young Englishman.

"You have turned into an American," Rinehart teased. "An American Indian fighter, I hear, too."

Adkin introduced Uribe and Dusty to the others and explained their relationships. They quickly joined the frivolity.

"We'll fill you in on all our adventures, you ragamuffin teamsters," Ryan yelled with laughter. "Let's go get some brandy to celebrate."

Everyone was toasting something when Sanderson asked Adkin and Ryan to have a chair in the rear of the mess hall.

"Gentlemen … let me change that. Dear friends, I can't tell you how impressed we all have been with your good work," Sanderson began. "You probably don't know this, but in January, Napoleon III ordered the withdrawal of his French troops from Mexico. It's going to be done in stages and should be finished by November.

"General Sheridan has been down in Texas and had put together more than 50,000 fighters, and that's why Napoleon is getting out," he continued. "Word is General Sherman is going to move Sheridan up here soon to quell the Indian raids, and do it with absolute force.

"Sherman means business and he's justifying his efforts to rid the west of any Indians in order to help get the railroads developed out here," Sanderson continued. "It was reported in the newspapers Sherman wrote a letter to Grant that said: 'We are not going to let a few thieving, ragged Indians check and stop the progress of the railroads.'"

"My point is, Barlow and I figure we may only have five to six years before rail lines are laid to Santa Fe," Sanderson explained. "So, we have to make good while we can and establish these outer areas to serve those who won't have rail service."

"We've already got the Raths wanting to get the Fort Hays to Santa Fe going," Adkin said. "His brother will be coming later this evening to talk with you."

"That's great, that's what I'm talking about," Sanderson said. "We may also want to look further into Colorado as we've heard people are finding valuable minerals out there, other than gold."

"We can do it Boss," Ryan said.

"I know you can, and I'm going to get you more help," Sanderson said. "Rinehart has agreed to stay out here with you for at least a year.

"I think it's because one of those ladies down at the saloon is pressuring him for marriage," he added with a big laugh.

Adkin and Ryan laughed, too.

"He's a good man, and I know he can help," Ryan said.

"I agree," Adkin echoed.

"Well, let's go celebrate for now," Sanderson said. "Because in the morning, we're moving out, and we can visit more on the trail about more details and ideas."

•••

Chris Rath showed up just at sunset to talk with Sanderson. As they discussed the strategies of the stagecoach line, Rath said he had talked with his brother, Charley, and they definitely wanted to handle the Fort Hays to the Santa Fe Trail line and points westward, as well. When Sanderson told him about the imminent threat that the railroads presented, he said they were well aware of the railroads progressing across Kansas.

"Charley told me, the damn railroads will destroy most every trading post along the Santa Fe Trail, but it wasn't going to stop them from making as much money as possible before that happened," Rath said.

Sanderson made arrangements for Rath to take one of the Concords with the new lettering painted on each side in gold with black trim in the morning.

"I'll drive it back to the wet-dry route junction, if you'll have a man accompany me for protection," Rath said.

"How about I go with you?" Adkin asked, smiling. "Diablo and I can catch up with the caravan by noon."

"Can I go, too?" Uribe asked.

"Sure," Adkin answered.

"Wonderful Yates," Rath responded, then shaking hands with all the Barlow and Sanderson crew.

"Only two more Concords to find homes for," Sanderson said, laughing.

•••

Once Chris Rath rolled the new Concord into his corral at the trading post and untied his horses from it, Adkin and Uribe dismounted and shook Rath's hand.

"Stay in touch, and tell Charley I said best wishes," Adkin said. "Get this Concord moving between here and Fort Hays as soon as you can so we an all make some money."

"Thanks Adkin, I truthfully believe this route will prove very profitable," Rath said as he waved goodbye. "Safe travels."

It didn't take but about two hours for Adkin and Uribe to catch up with the Army wagon train. Adkin rode past double-trained wagons being pulled by 12-teams of oxen, a young bullwhacker snapping his jip by the side of the leading yoked animals.

Driving the team was Ryan, who waved wildly.

"These are two of my Studebakers and I'm feeling richer already," Ryan yelled. "It feels good to sit down and relax a little."

Dusty was riding along with Ryan and Uribe eased alongside to visit with Dusty.

Adkin galloped further ahead and found Sanderson driving one of the Concords. Adkin rode up and asked Sanderson if he could spell him awhile?

"Sure," Sanderson said as he moved over a little and stopped the Concord. "Whoa."

Adkin tied Diablo to the back of the wagon and climbed up in the driver's seat with Sanderson now riding shotgun.

"Yee haw!" Adkin yelled as he snapped the reins on the four-horse team.

"This is a comfortable place for me," Adkin said. "It not only reminds me of our trip to the peace treaty, but it takes me back to my boyhood days of learning to handle a team with my father's kind instructions.

"I can't remember the first time I sat on a coach seat with my father," Adkin continued, with a laugh. "I must have been quite young."

"Probably a toddler," Sanderson said, laughing, too.

Sanderson started telling Adkin his plans: Sanderson was going to take his Concord to The Pueblo, taking Carl Long and Ryan along with him. He said he had already made plans for a dozen soldiers to accompany them.

"They are soldiers that will eventually be stationed at New Bent's Fort – the Army now calls it Fort Lyon," Sanderson said. "Long and Ryan will go with me while I explore other possible routes in Colorado. We may want to look into running a line north to Denver, too.

"I won't take longer than three or four weeks, then we'll head back to Bent's Fort where we'll hook up with you," he continued. "I want you to take Darrell Holmes and Rinehart with you to Santa Fe and get squared away with the Aguirre brothers. Rinehart needs to know them, as he'll be staying out here with you.

"I telegraphed Conrado Aguirre about the goods we're bringing, and he's very excited. He assures me we'll make a tidy profit.

"Between our employees and the company, we'll be delivering 12 wagons of goods, that's including your two wagons," Sanderson said. "I know you don't drink much, but I invested $20 of your money for 10 gallons of brandy. That should sell for $250 or a $230 profit."

"I don't mind selling alcohol at those kind of profits at all, J.L.," Adkin said laughing.

"Another thing I wanted to discuss is company stock," Sanderson said. "Barlow and I decided at the first of the year to give each employee that has been with us two years or more 10 shares of company stock.

"However, we decided you and Ryan should get a bonus for everything you have accomplished – it's short of miraculous," he continued. "We have issued you each 25 shares of stock. I haven't had the chance to tell Ryan, yet, so don't say anything, I want to tell him myself."

"I understand, J.L., and thank you very much," Adkin said. "It's funny, when I came to America, I was dreaming of travelling the Santa Fe Trail and making money – lots of money. But now, money is not as important to me as much as living this life and what every moment teaches you out here.

"It's amazing – you learn quickly that simply surviving is the most important thing about life," Adkin continued solemnly. "It's about living life and doing it well."

"Well, money may not be as important as you once thought it was, but you're doing okay my young partner," Sanderson said with a big smile. "If you decide to sell your Studebakers as well as your investment in goods, you could probably make about $3,000 to $3,500 dollars."

Adkin looked at Sanderson with wide eyes, "Are you serious?"

"Yep," Sanderson replied. "Oh, and by the way, your stock was worth $23 a share as of April 1."

Adkin was speechless. He just gazed across the plains adding up what he may be worth.

"I could have about $5,000 by the time we reach Santa Fe," he thought to himself. "That's a small fortune, and I haven't even been here a year."

"I don't know what to say J. L.," Adkin said. "But thanks for believing in me."

...

As they approached Aubrey Crossing, the train encountered another caravan coming up the trail. "An outrider soon advised the caravan ahead was organized by a veteran Santa Fe freighter, Charles Kitchen. He was leading 150 wagons to the railroad depot at Council Bluffs.

Word soon spread that Colonel William Bent was with Kitchen's caravan, too.

As they neared, Sanderson turned the Concord toward the ambulances in the middle of Kitchen's train and yelled as they approached. There were four of them amongst the freight wagons.

"Can you tell us where Colonel Bent is travelling?" Sanderson asked. The driver of the front ambulance said Bent was in the third one back, while waving his arm backward.

Bent must've heard Sanderson as he stuck his head out from the ambulance window and ordered his driver to pull over and stop.

Bent was stepping out of his ambulance as Sanderson reined his team to a stop.

"Fancy stagecoach there J.L.," Bent said, as Sanderson and Adkin got down from the driver's bench. They were embracing and shaking hands as Ryan pulled up in another Concord and dismounted.

"Good to see you young men made it through in good health," Bent said laughing. "And you still have your scalps."

They visited briefly, Sanderson thanking Bent for his help in lining up stations as well as selling the company horses and allowing Uribe and Dusty to aid the boys.

Bent explained he was going home to Westport with Kitchens, an old friend of Bent's

"I doubt I'll be back for some time," Bent said. "It's not the same as the old days, and the Army runs the fort a little different than I like. So, I'm going to go relax and only help with re-stocking orders and things like that.

"I need to retire," he added with a laugh.

"I was going to ask you Colonel, would you mind if we offered Uribe and Dusty a job with the company," Adkin asked, then looked to Sanderson who seemed surprised. "I was going to suggest we hire them, J.L., they're great hands and know the area like the back of their hands."

"They technically work for the Army, Adkin," Bent answered. "I think they'd make good hands, I've known them quite awhile.

"I'd just make them an offer and see what they say," Bent added.

"We'll do that Colonel," Sanderson responded, smiling at Adkin and Ryan. Everybody made their farewells and returned to their wagons.

"Come see me when you get to Westport," Bent said, waving goodbye.

The crew didn't realize it, but it would be the last they ever saw of Colonel William Bent again. He would die of pneumonia in Westport almost three years to the day later and four days before his 60th birthday.

He never did return to the famous fort he had originally built.

"That man and his brothers did more than anybody to help tame this part of the west," Sanderson said as they headed back to the Army caravan. "They were real mountain men and the most successful traders on the Santa Fe Trail."

•••

When the caravan reached Bent's Fort, Sanderson, Adkin and Ryan quickly asked to speak with the fort commander and tell him of their intentions to offer Uribe and Dusty jobs with Barlow & Sanderson.

The commander said he had no problems with that proposal, with one exception.

"Colonel Bent said you were going to pay 25-cents a day to each of these scouts for their services," he said. "We decided that money should go to the men. The Army gives up any claims for their services as long as you meet those conditions. Plus we'll give them their regular scout pay for that time.

"Give them all that money, and you might want to see if they'll have anything to do with y'all," he added laughing.

They departed his office and started figuring up how much they owed their scouts.

"Today is May 17, and we left here on March 15," Adkin said, curling up fingers while doing the math.

"That's 64 days," Ryan spoke up, smiling. "And at 50-cents a day, that's $32 divided by two. That's $16 each."

"I think if we're going to offer them a job, lets pay them $30 each for their services – nearly twice what they're thinking they'll get," Sanderson said

"Worth every penny, J.L.," Adkin said, with Ryan nodding approval.

"You know men, we really need to hire a couple of more full-time scouts out here," Sanderson said.

"Amen," Ryan said.

"I agree," Adkin added.

"Well, let's talk to Uribe and Dusty and see if they have any suggestions," Sanderson said as they headed to the stables. "We'll be leaving in the morning."

...

After Uribe and Dusty had been rounded up, Sanderson paid them in silver coins and told them about their plans for expansion throughout the Southwest and asked if they would like to hire on and work for Adkin and Ryan.

Uribe jumped at the offer, saying he had already been approached by his former girlfriend who still wants to marry.

"I like her charms, but I'm not good one for marry," he said. "I was made to roam these plains like the buffalo."

Dusty was a little hesitant, and he didn't say anything. He kept looking down at his boots, reluctant to answer.

"We will pay you $25 a month, and if you stay a year, we will raise that to $35 a month," Sanderson said, sensing Dusty may be wondering what the pay was. Uribe didn't even ask.

"Si, si Señor, I will be happy to work for these men – and you," Dusty spoke up, grinning from ear to ear.

"We'll need to go over what we may need, we're leaving in the morning," Sanderson said. "Ryan and I are going to Pueblo and seeking other routes in Colorado. Dusty, I would like for you to scout for us.

"Uribe, you go on with Adkin to Santa Fe and help sell our goods with the Aguirre brothers," he continued. "By the way Uribe, do you know any other scouts who know these plains and their trails? We need to find at least two more scouts that are trustworthy."

"My mother and family – I have three hermaños, brothers, and two sisters still alive in our village on the Purgatoire River," Uribe said excitedly. Plus my brother, he scouted for Captain Chivington one year north of here to all the way to Wyoming.

"The village is about half-a-day's ride off the trail before we get to La Junta. It's a small village but very honest people," Uribe added.

"When we near the Purgatoire, I can ride down and see if any in my family want to scout, or maybe a friend or cousin."

"Sounds good, we'll definitely see who you may find, but they must be able to be on the trails for maybe months at a time," Sanderson said.

"Si, I know," Uribe answered.

They all went over the plans again, who was going where and which wagons and teamsters and bullwhackers were heading to the markets in Santa Fe.

Uribe pulled Adkin to the side and whispered, "Dusty know mucho about Colorado territory. We are very happy to stay to scout with you and Ryan, Señor. Gracias."

"Don't forget our tobacco, Señor Sanderson," Uribe added with a big smile.

•••

The caravan made it to the Purgatoire River late the first day after leaving Bent's Fort. Uribe insisted on riding down to his village, knowing he wouldn't arrive until a few hours after dark.

"I know the trail very well," Uribe assured all and took off on his gelding.

The Army Captain ordered the train to continue along the Arkansas for about four or five more miles in order to camp at Las Animas, a small village where the Horse River empties into the Arkansas.

At daylight, the crew was up and unhobbling their animals after a quick breakfast of beans and bread loaves and strong, black coffee. Adkin, as usual, had heated water over the fire's pink coals and made his tea in his tin cup.

Adkin couldn't help but be impressed with this location along the Arkansas – and the little village. The area was teeming with timber – for the plains anyway – all kinds of berry bushes, flowers, plant life and several clearings of pure buffalo grass.

Before long, soldiers and others were all preparing to start moving, and Uribe was not back from his village.

"He'll catch up with us later today, I'm sure," Adkin said.

Right then, a shout blared through the cool air, "Mount up … Move out!

They were once again rolling down the trail. Adkin was amazed at how familiar some areas were, especially since he had only seen this area of the trail one time.

He realized how much a man can take in when he's being very careful "and a little scared at the same time," he thought to himself as a smile crept across his face that nobody saw.

•••

Late afternoon, they reached the east side of La Junta and halted to make camp for the night. Just as the wagons had been circled and animals were being unhooked and fed, Uribe and several riders came loping into camp and headed directly to the crew's camp.

"Oyé," Uribe shouted. "I arrive with my scalp and an empty stomach."

"If we feed you, will you give us your scalp?" Ryan hollered, as everybody started laughing.

Uribe had three men with him, and as they dismounted, he introduced them to the crew who had all gathered. They looked like regular fort Indians, yet they were not rough or unkempt. Adkin figured they were probably Utes like Uribe. One looked a lot like a heavier and thicker Uribe with long hair braided down each side of his face.

"This is my brother, Don Diego. He has scouted before, though he is a very old man now at 30, but he is very strong," Uribe said as several laughed, including Uribe and Don Diego.

"This is my cousin, Sanpete. His mother is also Ute, my mother's sister," Uribe said. "He is of the Caputa tribe of Utes, as I am as well."

Sanpete looked to Adkin to be only about 18 to 20 years old.

"But Sanpete scouted for Colonel Kit Carson two years ago when Carson captured 8,000 Navajos who had been battling Pueblos, Hopis, Zunis and Utes," Uribe said. "He is only 22 but has much experience, especially in fighting.

"This man is a childhood friend to me and Don Diego. His name is Fransisco, Uribe said. "He worked briefly for General Kearney several years ago – scouting and translating. A very good man who's wife died last fall. His two children were with her when their canoe overturned in the Purgatoire and all drowned.

"Fransisco is 29 years old," Uribe added.

"Very pleased to me you, gentlemen," Fransisco said, reaching out his hand and sounding like a school teacher.

"Nice to me you Fransisco, and you all, too," Sanderson said while shaking hands with Fransisco. "Well let's get camp set, and then we can sit down and enjoy a full meal and discuss our plans. That is if you gentlemen are agreeable to work with us?"

All shook their heads in approval.

After chores were finished, Uribe's new men met Ray Dee, Darrell, Carl and about a dozen teamsters and bullwhackers that worked for the company.

Sanderson reiterated he was going on with Ryan and Dusty to Pueblo and maybe several other places in Colorado. He wanted Don Diego and Fransisco to ride with them.

He told Uribe and Sanpete to ride with Adkin and the others.

"Long, Rinehart and Holmes, now that we have more help, I want y'all to go ahead with Adkin to help with the sale of our goods," Sanderson said.

In the morning, Sanderson's crew made a brief stop at Ablo Velasquez's place, the agent for Waldo, Hall & Co., and the place where they had set up a stagecoach station, so everybody could meet. Sanderson explained his plans for Colorado, and Ablo scribbled out several names of people to talk with in Pueblo.

"Is she our new stagecoach Señor?" Ablo asked Sanderson while pointing at the Concord.

"Yes she is, we'll be leaving her with your brother, and he'll make the first run back here to you. Then you can find customers to take to Pueblo."

"Wonderful, she is muy bonita – very beautiful. We are expecting mucho business, Señor. We hear they're finding new silver veins at the headwaters of South Clear Creek on Glacier Mountain," Ablo said. "Also silver has been discovered at the Belmont Lode, just above Georgetown on McClellan Mountain.

"The people I wrote down – and my brother, too – will be able to tell you more details," Ablo added.

"That's the kind of news we want to hear, Ablo," Sanderson said, smiling at his crew. "Thank you, and we'll see you after we come back from Pueblo. It may be about four or five weeks, so do not worry."

"Bueno, Señor," Ablo said. "Vaya con Dios."

"Gracias Ablo," Adkin spoke up.

"Adios," Ryan added.

As they turned back to the train, Uribe smiled at Adkin.

"You gringos are learning mucho Español," he said, turning and nodding to Ryan. "When you learn it well and all the Indian tongues, you maybe understand this country like Colonel Bent."

"I would be happy to learn half the languages Colonel Bent knows," Adkin said. "And I have already made this my country, too, in my heart."

"Me, too," Ryan added with a laugh.

"Well men, here is where we go our separate ways – for awhile anyway," Sanderson said. "I want all you men to haggle hard for the best prices for our goods. I'm sure the Aguirre brothers will be very fair, but we want the best prices possible.

"And remember, Adkin has the last word – what he says goes. Understand," Sanderson said, waiting until each man nodded in agreement or mumbled 'Yes sir.'

"We'll meet up, hopefully, about the end of June at Bent's Fort," Sanderson added. "Be careful and good luck."

With that he reined his coach team northwest up the Pueblo Trail. His riders and the 10 cavalry soldiers fell in behind him. Adkin turned Diablo and waved an arm for his crew so they could catch up with the main Army train that was rolling southwest on the Santa Fe Trail.

Adkin couldn't help but smile to himself as Diablo sauntered along.

•••

That evening, they had made it to Iron Spring. Adkin told the newcomers in his crew who had never been all the way to Santa Fe – which was everyone but he and Uribe – that the following day from there, they would be crossing the mountains at Raton Pass.

"You'll need to keep in single file and stay at least 50 yards between wagons in case one breaks down or the brake fails if it is stopped," Adkin said. "Uncle Wootton and his crew keep the road pretty clean, but he told us there are times when some boulders break loose and fall into the road. Most are easy to roll out of the way, but if your brakes don't hold, it could get messy – and deadly.

"If you do have to stop, either going up or coming down, it would be best if one man stay at the reins at all times while others, like bullwhackers, help remove any rocks," Adkin continued. "If it's a wheel problem on the wagon, chock all the others while stopped."

One of the men asked if they could get through the pass in one day.

"I'm not sure with this many wagons, ambulances and calvary troops," Adkin said. "We'll find out."

Even though the Army train had been whittled down to about 100 wagons and half the troops because of deliveries and reinforcements stationed at the various forts they had travelled through. But Adkin still didn't know if 100 wagons could get through Raton Pass in one day.

•••

Uncle Wootton was glad to see his first Army westward caravan of the Spring come up the pass, as the Army paid either in silver or gold. He also embraced young Yates when Adkin stopped to pay for the company's wagons and horseback crew.

"It's taken us 10 days from Bent's Fort," Adkin told Wootton. "Glad we only had 100 wagons remaining from there, they started with 300 and had whittled it down to about 170 by the time they reached Fort Dodge. Hopefully, we timed it just right so we can get everybody through today."

"Well, it's early enough, as long as no wagons break down under the loads," Wootton said. "Things going okay with the stagecoach line?"

Adkin had Ray Dee pull the last new Concord over so Ray Dee could meet Uncle Wootton, and Wootton could check out the new coach.

"This coach will be on your run, Uncle Wootton, but we're going to take it on to Santa Fe and the runs will start immediately," Adkin explained. "You'll have to check with telegrams to see if you need to run it on to La Junta or if they'll have a coach there ready to head to Pueblo."

"You and Ablo Velasquez, our station manager in La Junta – will have to coordinate the runs so we can move customers as quickly as possible," Adkin added.

"I know Ablo, and his brother, Mello, too. Good Mexicans," Wootton said. "That will be no problem, for sure."

Adkin introduced Ray Dee to Wootton, telling Wootton Ray Dee would be the region's field agent for Barlow & Sanderson.

"If you have problems with the Concord or need repairs or parts, telegraph me and Ray Dee at Bent's Fort," Adkin said. "That's if you can't handle it yourself, which I trust you can handle about anything that comes up, Uncle Wootton."

"You flatter me, son, and I love it, because I can handle about any damn thing that jumps up in front of me," Wootton said, laughing.

Adkin and Ray Dee laughed, too.

As Ray Dee got back on the driver's seat and they were pulling away, he told Adkin, "I guarantee that old bastard can take on anything and anybody."

"He's smart, ingenious and tough as the rock around here," Adkin said.

It took until mid-forenoon for the last mule to walk through Wootton's gate – 3 hours – but now there was still another 15 miles to get to the base of the pass where the upper Canadian River passed through. It was a small shallow river most of the time as it was very near the headwaters.

Adkin kept riding up and down the line of the company's wagons making sure everybody stayed in line and kept safe distances between the wagons. The crack of all the bull whips echoed throughout the canyons and valleys.

Many of the teamsters, including company men, were in awe of the vista and the Sangre de Cristo Mountains.

The caravan set for camp just south of the small village of Willow Springs. No wagons were damaged through the pass, but workers got busy greasing the axles and wheels after the animals were taken care of.

•••

The train got short and vulnerable after reaching Fort Union. That's where the Army ended it's caravan and dropped its last wagons and assigned its last troops. The wagon master, a Captain, did offer two dozen calvary troops to supply security for Adkin's group, as they would also return and be stationed at Fort Union for duty. Adkin was thankful for the help.

The remaining caravan was still two days out from Santa Fe, and Adkin realized he really missed his partner, Tyler Ryan. He didn't realize how close they had become. It's like brothers, Ryan nearly always could read his mind even before he spoke.

"We make a good team," Adkin thought to himself, and a smile crept across his face.

Uribe noticed.

"What so funny boss?" he asked.

"Oh, just missing that crazy Ryan," Adkin said. "We've been riding together since September last year."

"Si, I miss him, too," Uribe said. "He make me laugh."

"We'll all meet up in about four weeks," Adkin said.

"Wonder how much we can get for the wagons in Santa Fe?" Adkin asked himself. Ryan had said if they could make double, sell all three of his wagons. If not, sell the old wagon and keep the two new Studebakers.

That's what Adkin had decided to do as well. Keep the newer wagons if the price wasn't right and sell the old one that already had about 1,200 miles on it from going to the peace treaty on the Little Arkansas River.

Ryan had also told him to buy furs and silver goods if possible – up to $500 if the wagons didn't sell, so the goods could be cashed in at Westport or Council Grove.

Adkin was going to follow suit, and most of the decisions about returning wagons would determine how the trading goes down. He had made up his mind to go over all their wagons very thoroughly, even iron anything he needed to do once they got to the Aguirre's stables. They would let him use their blacksmith shop so they could get top dollar for the wagons.

•••

They rolled into Santa Fe on June 3, 1866, and crowds were forming on the north side of town waving, while children and dogs ran along side the lead wagons shrieking, "Bienvenidos" – welcome, the oxen lumbering along unsure what all the ruckus was about. Startled mules began dancing sideways as a teamster hollered, "Whoa. Whoa."

Adkin and Uribe spurred their mounts to the front and saw Jose and Conrado approaching on horseback waving.

"Good to see you mi amigos," Conrado said. Jose nodded.

"Have your men bring their wagons to our corral south of the hotel," Conrado said. "Follow us. We can stable the animals there and sort the goods."

Uribe turned his horse and kicked him, "Yah," and headed back to the Concord and the others driving the wagons belonging to Adkin, Ryan and the company.

"Follow us," Uribe shouted at Ray Dee, swinging his arm at the others behind Ray Dee.

"Pleased to see you gentlemen," Adkin said as he fell in next to the brothers. "Have you heard from Epifanio? How's he doing?"

"He telegraphed, and they reached Council Grove in good shape," Conrado said. "They then loaded all our trade goods onto rail cars and took them to the big buyers in Westport."

"He's on his way back now. It was a very profitable trip," Conrado added.

"I'm hoping what we have in these wagons is very profitable, too," Adkin said, smiling.

"It will be, Adkin. I assure you," Jose interjected.

•••

After unloading the wagons, and separating the piles according to the investors' manifests, Adkin told Conrado of his plans to inspect and repair the wagons before selling them.

"It shouldn't take more than two days," Adkin told him. "But we believe it will be worth the wait."

Conrado and Jose sent out messages that afternoon to several other buyers and traders to come first thing in the morning to haggle over the goods and make bids.

"We will buy much, but certain items we do not need at this moment, but our friends may need them and will also pay fair prices," Conrado explained to Adkin.

Adkin had already removed a wagon axle and re-ironed it before the evening meal.

As buyers gathered around the goods the next morning, Adkin was re-ironing a wheel rim on another wagon. He watched and listened as the bidding started.

The Aguirre brothers were outbidding most of the others early, but when it came to about 5 bales of calico, they weren't interested.

"We have much calico in inventory now," Conrado told Adkin.

Knives, plows, copper cooking pots and all metal things were selling good and at great prices. Adkin's two kegs of brandy – 5 gallons each – came on the block.

"$250," Conrado shouted to the auctioneer.

"$300," another buyer barked.

Conrado nodded his head to the man signifying he could have it at $300.

"I guess he needs it more than we do," Conrado said, smiling at Adkin. "That's good for you, though."

Adkin was thinking his investment of $10 per keg had paid off quite handsomely.

"Wish Sanderson had purchased more," he thought to himself.

It took about four hours to auction off all the goods, and the buyers started bringing in their wagons to haul their goods away. The Aguirres' bookkeeper was checking everything off and collecting the money in silver and gold coins.

Conrado told the buyers they would be auctioning five wagons – Studebakers made in Ohio the day after tomorrow at 8 a.m.

Adkin continued to remove axles, re-iron if necessary and always adding new grease. He replaced a couple of cracked wagon-bed planks with new boards and fixed a tongue connector. Coronado watched him work for several hours the following days, and then asked Jose to come out and look at what Adkin was doing.

At mid-forenoon on the second day, Coronado and Jose asked if Adkin would come to their office.

"Well, Señor Yates, your goods were sold for $1,900, and Ryan has earned $2,300 on his investments," Conrado said, smiling and pushing two leather bags forward on his desk. "This is your's and this bag is Ryan's – it's a little heavier.

"Goodness, how delightful," Adkin said. "You were right, it is very profitable."

"This is Sanderson's earnings – It comes to $5,400," Conrado said as he slid a large bag across the desk with a big smile.

"Now, we come to the wagons," Conrado said more seriously. "Jose and I have watched your repairs and are very impressed with the re-conditioning you have accomplished.

'We would like to offer you $1,300 for the newest Studebakers and $900 for the two older ones – in gold," Conrado said. "We know these will make good wagons to travel on south to Chihuahua many times, yet.

"We feel it is a good price, but you can wait til morning and see what auction prices will be, too" he continued. "It is up to you.

"But to sweeten the bid, we will pay your repair costs, too – planks, grease, sheet iron, pins, etcetera," Conrado said with a huge smile.

"I graciously accept your offer Señors," Adkin said. "Con mucho gusto."

They all laughed and shook hands.

Jose called in two young boys and ordered them to go about town and tell the buyers, no wagons would be on auction tomorrow as originally planned.

Conrado walked over to a tall safe sitting against the wall and opened it, grabbed two more bags, shuffled some gold coins and stuffed them into the bags. He walked over to Adkin and laid the bags next to the three others.

"Adkin's math finally came to him: He was walking away with $3,600 and Ryan was getting $5,800,

"We're rich," Adkin thought to himself. "Bloody rich."

•••

Adkin's problem now was trying to get in touch with Ryan and Sanderson, because the company had five wagons that would be returning to Leavenworth with only $2,000 worth of trade goods. Sanderson had instructed Ray Dee to spend $2,000 of their profits on furs and hides.

"Sanderson doesn't want to buy any mules, as mules weren't as profitable as they once were, plus you have to take care of them all the way back," Ray Dee had told Adkin. "He just wanted furs and hides, they're selling good at Westport."

The company's goods in those five wagons sold for $5,400, so Adkin and Ray Dee started trying to figure out how many furs and hides they could buy for two grand. Conrado and Jose helped them, and determined it would only fill about three to four wagons.

A telegraph was sent off immediately to Bent's Fort to see if they had heard any word from Sanderson.

A quick reply noted Sanderson was in Denver and had telegraphed for money, as Western Union had lines into Denver, as well. Money was actually sent with a promissory note – an IOU, in a sense. Bent's Fort guaranteed backing for the amount Sanderson wanted.

That note then could be handed to a bank or a fort's quartermaster. The money would then be sent via whatever transportation was available to that bank or fort for reimbursement. There was always a small percentage fee paid to who issued the note.

Adkin immediately sent a telegraph to Denver detailing the sale information, and if Ryan wanted to invest in any goods for shipment back east? He also asked Sanderson if he and Ryan could lease one wagon for the return trip?

The next morning, both had responded to Adkin; Sanderson approving filling his last wagon with goods, and Ryan saying to spend $1,000 of his profits on furs and hides as well.

The Aguirre brothers had been working with Ray Dee to find the furs and hides Sanderson wanted. Adkin interrupted to say he and Ryan wanted to fill the last wagon with like goods, and they would spend up to $2,000.

Conrado told Adkin his brother Epifiano had informed them sheared wool and sheep skins had been very profitable on his current trip.

"My suggestion is you lay about 20 buffalo hides in the bottom of your wagon, then layer about 100 sheep skins over that and lay sheared wool bales on top," Conrado said.

Adkin agreed so the haggling, buying and stacking started. The total for all the cargo they could get into the wagon came to $1,800, making he and Ryan's share $900 each.

Once Adkin counted out the gold and silver, he realized he had another big problem to solve before getting back on the trail.

All their profits, though separated into large saddle bags now, couldn't just be carried on horses all the way to Bent's Fort. Everyone knew Indian raiders and Comancheros hit every returning caravan they could because there was gold and more goods to steal.

Conrado suggested they take the money to Fort Union and have the quartermaster hold it until an Army-guarded caravan headed east and could carry the money to Bent's Fort.

That made sense to Adkin, knowing Fort Union was building up its forces with the recent arrival of the 3rd Cavalry and 37th Infantry.

"But that would be two days of worry," Adkin thought to himself. Then he laughed at himself as well. "What's two days when compared to arriving at Wagon Bed Springs and finding no water?"

On the fourth day, Adkin and Uribe were ready to move out. It took a few extra hours to round up the Army troops, as they had found the cantinas and senoritas a very attractive diversion from regular Army duties. Holmes and Rinehart and a couple of teamsters got caught out late the second night, too.

They also had a cook's wagon and an ambulance and two teams to take back. The commander at Fort Union had purchased them from the Aguirre brothers to be driven back to the fort.

Adkin had made sure he telegraphed Sanderson and Bent's Fort they were leaving Santa Fe June 7 – today.

Ray Dee popped his jip and slapped the reins on the yoked oxen hauling his double-wagon rig, the bullwhacker on the left side walking and cracking his bullwhip.

Adkin reached to his side and patted the saddlebag behind his saddle. His, Ryan's and Sanderson's profits, less new expenses for furs and hides, came to $11,000 in gold and silver. The money filled six saddle bags and were being carried by three horseback riders: Adkin, Uribe, and Ray Dee.

They were now headed back along the Santa Fe Trail, a place where Adkin was feeling was his true home. He couldn't quite put it into words, but he felt as if the trail and the Great Plains had put its brand on him, like several of the ranchers did with their cow herds and horses to identify them.

He loved these mountains between Santa Fe and Raton Pass, but is was in the Great Plains of Colorado and Kansas where he felt free – where a man could see forever at each hand of the clock on the horizon.

"Thank you Lord," Adkin whispered to himself.

•••

Late that first day, they had reached the Vado – or crossing – of the Pecos River southeast of Santa Fe. They decided to camp there on the north side of the river, where there was a small arroyo that had good grass and some timber.

Uribe suggested they hobble all the animals, and even set some picket stakes to tie down as many as possible.

"Señor Adkin, We are entering areas that can become very bad place for attacks by Comancheros and banditos," Uribe said.

Ray Dee agreed.

"It's a good idea," he said. "Comancheros like to ride into camps at night and shoot their guns to run off all the animals.

"Then we're sitting ducks if they're not satisfied with only the animals," Ray Dee added.

Adkin approved and they all got their orders to hobble every animal, including the oxen team and three teams of mules pulling the other three wagons of company goods. Adkin also wanted as many as possible to be inside the circle of all the wagons. The Sergeant leading the squad told his troops to forgo any tents and sleep with their clothes on and their rifle by their side – loaded. As many men as possible were ordered to sleep under the wagons.

Adkin's crew was ordered to do the same and be prepared for anything. They decided the look-out times, as the soldiers did likewise. That would put two men on watch each night.

Adkin quietly ordered Uribe and Ray Dee to place the saddlebags under their saddles that would be used for pillows.

Shortly after a meal of navy beans, bacon and sourdough, everyone decided to hit the bedrolls as the fire was allowed to die down to embers.

"At least we will have three or four nights of bright moon," Uribe said to Adkin as he laid down.

"If the clouds don't move in," Adkin responded.

About two hours later – around 10 p.m., Adkin was rocked awake by gunfire, thundering horse hooves and terrible screaming from men and beasts.

All the hands and soldiers were sitting upright, grabbing up their arms and firing in all directions as the Comancheros charged through the camp.

Adkin raised his pistol as a rider loomed into sight, and he shot but missed. Another came near the wagons to his right and this time, the rider twisted off his horse as the bullet hit him in his left side.

Within what seemed only about four or five minutes, the Comancheros were riding away, as the Sergeant yelled to his men to check the horses and mules.

Carl and Darrell were already checking their animals, and Ray Dee was yelling, "Is anybody hit? Is everyone okay?"

"Over here," a voice moaned.

Adkin recognized it. Uribe, too.

"Is that you, Sanpete," Uribe yelled.

"Yes, come quick," Sanpete cried out.

Adkin jumped over the body of the Comanchero as he followed Uribe into the moonlight away from the camp fire embers.

Other voices of soldiers were yelling out, "Okay over here," and "I'm good."

As Uribe bent down to look at Sanpete, the young man was sitting up with his legs stretched out, but he was holding his left leg at the knee.

Adkin lifted his torso as Uribe grabbed both legs – one was very limp – and they carried him near the fire pit. One of the men threw several logs into the embers. Sanpete never uttered a sound until they sat him down.

"I saw one of them swinging a knife and trying to cut the tie-downs on the horses and ran to stop him," Sanpete said. "Another one shot me with a rifle – he was very close."

Adkin held up a small piece of wood that had come aflame and held it close to Sanpete's leg. He had taken a bullet just below the left knee and it had shattered both bones. His foot and lower leg had fell askew when they put him down. There was very little skin or bone holding it together.

One of the soldiers quickly placed a cloth tourniquet with a piece of wood in the knot above Sanpete's knee.

"Go get the cot from the ambulance," the soldier ordered. "We need to get him to the ambulance quickly and clean this wound."

Everyone knew the injury could be deadly without help.

"There is a military surgeon back in Santa Fe," the Sergeant said. "We could send him back in the ambulance."

A soldier ran up to the Sergeant and reported an ox has been killed and one mule wounded, but she would have to be killed as well. The sergeant thanked him and turned back to Sanpete.

"This man needs medical attention Yates, more than we can do for him out here," he said.

"Señor, since they failed tonight to get our animals and lost one man, they will ambush us somewhere on the trail tomorrow," Uribe said. "My guess is there are around 20 of them. I saw a couple of Indians, too.

"I would guess they know of our gold and silver – there are many eyes and loose tongues in Santa Fe," he whispered in Adkin's ear.

The men looked to Adkin and the Sergeant for guidance.

"What if you and I take the gold to Fort Union right now?" Adkin said, motioning at Uribe. "It's about 40 miles, but I think we could make it by tomorrow noon."

"They won't try following us at night, and we have a full moon," he added.

"Sergeant, you and your men could go back to Santa Fe with Sanpete and get him to a surgeon," Adkin continued. "I think with this moon, you could get everything together and hit the trail fairly soon."

Uribe spoke up, "They won't know you're leaving, and when they come back at daylight, you will have at least 10 to 15 miles on them. Comancheros won't follow so close to Santa Fe and more soldiers."

"I think that's a good idea," the Sergeant said. "This man needs help bad. And we could wait until another train heads out – with more wagons – and guns."

•••

Ray Dee helped distribute the gold and silver he had in his saddle bags equally into Adkin's and Uribe's. Combined now, the two pairs of saddlebags weighed around 60 pounds each. Adkin decided to move his to Diablo's withers in front of his saddle horn. Uribe left his placed behind his saddle. They also had two fresh horses picked out to travel with them in case of an accident or tiredness.

Both stepped over to the ambulance to see Sanpete before they departed. But Sanpete, was already dazed. The soldier who was working the tourniquet and cleansing the wound said he gave Sanpete some laudanum.

They wished him well, but he would never remember it.

The rest of the caravan would wait in Santa Fe for a larger wagon train heading east. They didn't want to lose all their trade goods trying the trail on their own.

They shook hands with the Sergeant and told them to hurry. Then Adkin and Uribe swung into their saddles and headed southeast quietly and hoped to make Las Vegas in a couple of hours. The moonlight was very bright once away from camp.

"Don't worry Señor Adkin, I know this trail well," Uribe said.

Adkin wasn't too worried about traveling at night – not with a moon like this. But he was praying the Comancheros weren't camping somewhere further up the trail.

•••

As the eastern horizon started turning light gray, Adkin and Uribe could see Fort Union some two or three miles ahead. Adkin stroked Diablo's neck and whispered in his ear, "We made it old friend."

Guards opened the gate after hearing Adkin's identification in his English accent.

They went straight to the commandant's office and discovered he had just ordered breakfast and asked Adkin and Uribe if they would like something. They declined and told him about the attack. They desperately wanted to place their gold and silver in the fort's safe.

He ordered a soldier on the porch to take Adkin and Uribe to the quartermaster's office. They led their horses to another small building next to the stables and the soldier knocked on the door and announced he had men who required help.

After signing some papers with the quartermaster, he opened a large vault that had two doors and was nearly as tall as Adkin. He placed the saddle bags inside and closed it up.

Both men sighed as they looked at each other and shook their heads.

"Could you tell us where the telegraph ... oh, I see the poles," Adkin said.

"It's that attached room on the south end of the commander's quarters," the soldier said, pointing.

Adkin sent a telegraph to Conrado at the Aguierre Hotel and to the Sergeant stationed at the U.S. Army Depot in Santa Fe.

After dropping their horses at the stables, they quickly went to the mess hall and asked the cook for something to eat. Then they asked for a couple of cots in the barracks.

They slept deeply, even with all their clothes still on – and with their boots, too. Several soldiers passing by laughed at the sight, but nothing disturbed their sleep.

Adkin woke at 3 p.m. while he was dreaming about the sight of Sanpete's leg. He quickly stood, started to say something to wake Uribe but stayed silent. He grabbed his hat and went straight to the telegraph office.

"This came for you about 10 this morning, but I didn't want to wake you," the operator said. "It's all around the fort about what happened. Sounds like ya'll were lucky nobody got kilt."

Adkin snatched the telegram from him and read. It was from Conrado, who said the soldiers and Adkin's crew hadn't arrived by 9:30 and they had sent out a dozen armed riders down the trail to find them.

At about that time, the telegraph ticker started going off, and the operator quickly grabbed his book of paper and started scribbling. Adkin looked over his shoulder.

To: Adkin Yates. Stop.

Sanpete and others arrived at noon. Stop.

Sanpete carried to surgeon, surgeon unable to save Sanpete's leg. Removed at 2:30. Stop.

Surgeon just said at 2:50 Sanpete still alive. Stop.

More later. Stop.

C. Aguirre. Stop.

Adkin took the paper from the operator and thanked him softly. He turned and walked out the door reading the telegram over again, slowly.

It was hard for it to sink in, but deep down, Adkin knew it was most likely to happen after seeing the wound himself. Both bones totally shattered with only pieces of skin and tendons holding it on. But seeing it written out made him cringe. It was official: Sanpete had lost his leg saving some of their animals. He was Uribe's cousin. Adkin prayed he would survive.

Back in the barracks, Adkin shook Uribe gently until he sprung to a sitting position, asking, "What's happening?"

"Nothing Uribe, it's me, Adkin."

"Whew, guess I get a little jumpy," Uribe said.

Adkin told him about the telegrams and read them to him. Uribe was slow to comprehend at first, but then his eyes teared up and he lowered his head and held it between his hands.

"Pobrecito – mi primo," Uribe whispered. "He's only 22 but strong and not afraid to fight. We must pray he lives, Señor Adkin."

Adkin was suddenly overtaken by rage. Pure rage, and he didn't know what to do. This thieving, murdering band of Comancheros needed to pay for Sanpete.

Adkin remembered the words he heard Carson or Bent say one time, "Some people just need killing."

But what to do.

Then Adkin could hear his mother's voice, "Be patient, Adkin. Remember, patience is a virtue, and the ability to wait for something without getting angry or upset is a valuable quality in a person."

He felt calmer at the memory.

But Adkin made a pledge to himself if he found any of this band. He would calmly kill them where they stood.

•••

Before dusk after arriving at Fort Union, Adkin and Uribe received a telegram from Conrado. Sanpete had recovered consciousness and was doing well. The doctor said he should survive as long as no infection sets in.

But Sanpete wouldn't be able to be moved for a couple of weeks at best.

Conrado said another large caravan was leaving Santa Fe in three or four days, and it would have at least 50 troops with a howitzer. Ray Dee and the others were ready to travel under their protection.

Word of the first major attack of the season against Adkin and their train spread fast and had shifted military awareness into high gear.

Adkin was bothered having to wait another week for the caravan, but he and Uribe knew that was best. They had no business hitting the trail to La Junta, even with no gold on them. Their horses alone would mean death if they were spotted.

Adkin sent word to Conrado he would wait, but all his other men and teamsters need to make sure they're signed up with that next train, and to take care of the goods. He ask Conrado to take care of Sanpete, and he would pay all costs involved with this care. They would make arrangements to come for him or provide transportation at a later date.

Adkin then sent a telegram to La Junta in care of J.L. Sanderson when he arrived in there explaining they had been delayed by a Comanchero attack and Sanpete had lost a leg. He requested J.L. to telegraph him when he arrived in La Junta, and they could consolidate plans.

"Well Uribe, we have to sit and wait for five or six days before we can get back on the trail," Adkin said while they were leaving the little Western Union office.

"Si Señor Adkin," he said. "But a little rest won't kill us, si?"

•••

Fort Union was impressive in size, considering a full regiment was stationed there. The commander was a friendly man by the name of Colonel Job Garrison. But his friendliness wasn't spent on Indians, especially raiders.

"These murdering savages should be wiped off the face of the Earth," he would say, and often.

The day Adkin and Uribe had arrived, he sent out a detail squad of 25 cavalrymen almost immediately to search the trail south for 10 miles and encircle the whole southeast side from the fort.

Garrison barked the orders so every mounted man of the detail could hear.

"If you find any Indian raiders or Comancheros, arrest them and bring them to me," he said. "If they refuse, shoot the bastards dead and bring me all their possessions and animals."

Adkin wanted to go with the detail, but Garrison said it would be better he stay and rest.

"You're not in the right mental state to fight, Mister Yates," Garrison said. "You'll get your chances."

•••

About 48 hours after arriving at Fort Union, the camp came alive after an Indian scout raced into the fort describing an attack on a caravan just east of Watrous coming in on the Cimarron Dry Route of the Santa Fe Trail. Word was spreading fast that three teamsters had been killed and about 100 horses and mules stolen.

Garrison ordered three squads of 80 troopers mount up for combat and a howitzer hooked up to a wagon and team. Watrous was just 8 miles south of the fort, and he ordered his Captain to travel due east to Pilot Knobs, near Wagon Mound, another well-known landmark on the trail.

"Colonel, could Uribe and I go with your Captain?" Adkin asked. "It might be the band of Comancheros that attacked us, too."

"Sure Yates," Garrison said. "But you better by God follow the Captain's orders. This is a military outing. Understand?"

"Of course, Colonel. Thank you, sir," Adkin said, waving at Uribe on the porch. "Let's go partner. Saddle up."

Troopers riding double-wide at full gallop shouldn't take them but about three hours to reach the area of the landmarks of Pilot Knobs and Wagon Mound. Adkin was impressed the Captain was leading his detail at such a fast speed. The little howitzer was constantly bouncing a foot or two off the hard ground behind a wagon with the two-horse team.

•••

Once the shoe-looking mounds of Pilots Knob were within a couple of miles, the Captain raised his right arm and gave the order to walk the horses. Uribe and Adkin had been riding next to him with the trooper carrying their colors.

"Don't see any disturbed sand blowing from here, but we'll go slow on up ahead a few miles where Santa Clara Spring is," the Captain said. "That's a place troublemakers like to hang out between raids – lots of good water and grass."

They stayed in double file and skirted the west side of Pilots Knob. The Captain sent two scouts to the south and told them to stay on the east side of Wagon Mound.

"You see Comancheros or an Indian raiding party, you get your hides back to me as fast as lightning," he ordered the scouts. "We'll stay on the west side and ease in from the west at Clara Spring."

They spurred their mounts to full gallop and broke off to their right.

"There is a slight rise west of the spring and we'll stop and take a peek to see if any savages are in there," the Captain said. "By the way, we haven't been introduced – things hopping so fast.

"I'm Captain Don Parson, originally from Ohio," he said, holding out his hand.

Adkin reached over his saddle horn with his right hand to shake.

"Glad to have your acquaintance, Captain Parson," he said. "I'm Adkin Yates, and this is my partner, Uribe of Bent's Fort."

Parson tipped the brim of his hat toward Uribe. He seemed to have a distrust of Uribe's look. Granted Uribe looked to be a real hard case, very scruffy with a scar above his right eye where an arrow had creased his forehead. His mustache fairly bushy, but it was twisted down below the corners of his mouth. His beard was scrabbled, and he only shaved about once a month because it was so thin.

He had the dark blue, wide-brimmed Army hat with the gold braid hat band and knot in the front. But it had been shaped with the sides rolled up tight and pulled down at the front and back of the brim.

His shirt was bluish plaid with a frayed black leather vest over it, and neither had been washed in some time. His pants were drab light brown pantaloons with leather leggings up to his knees, like Adkin's but with more designs burned into the seams. They sat atop his burnished boots with large Mexican spurs on back that could probably kill a man if used just right.

Uribe also liked to wear his pistol with the gunbelt over his left shoulder and the gun holster hanging close to his right side and tied down to his belt. As far as Adkin was concerned, Uribe looked as mean as any mountain man he had seen, but Parson kept a narrow-eyed squint when he looked at Uribe.

When they reached the rise and no scouts were within sight, Parson raised his right arm for halt and turned to a Lieutenant to have him tell the men "quiet."

Parson then dismounted asked his Lieutenant to give him the eyeglass. He motioned for Adkin and Uribe to follow him on foot. They walked ahead about 50 yards and then Parson waved to get down on hands and knees.

They crawled about 20 yards and the wide, shallow arroyo before them came into full view. Parson laid down with his eyeglass in his hands and his elbows on the sand. Adkin could see some campfire smoke and a large herd of horses and mules on the north side of the grove of cottonwood and hackberry trees around the spring. Men that looked like Comancheros and numerous Indians were milling about.

"Well gentlemen, that's the thieving bastards we're looking for," Parson said. "There must be more than 200 horses pastured over there.

"They've had a busy season opening," he added. "Well, we're going to show them why the U.S. Army sent us out here."

As they eased back toward their horses, maintaining a low profile, the two scouts were racing up from the rear waving. They were excited when they reined in their mounts where the Captain's horse was.

"Captain Parson, The Comancheros and several Arapahoe are camped at the spring," the scout said. "They is probably 25 or 30 raiders there. And there are more horses and mules on the other side of the grove, probably 300 head."

"What is the best way from here to attack," Parson asked the scout.

He jumped from his pony, kneeled down and started drawing the area with his finger in the sand. He made a big X in the sand where the main camp was, two circles where all the animals were on the north side.

"Can we move about 30 troopers to the southeast side, over here," Parson asked pointing at the ground.

"Yes, but it will take about 30 minutes to get around there," the scout answered.

"Lieutenant, take Platoon A and follow the scouts to this position," Parson said using his finger to mark the spot, looking to the scout for agreement.

The scout nodded approval.

"Take the howitzer with you. We will head over to this area, which we can make before you get positioned," Parson said, looking to his pocket watch. "It's 2 p.m. now, check your watch.

"At 2:45 – that will give you time to get up to that flat, which is in range – you start pumping canister shells into that camp as fast as you can.

"When you see them scurrying around like rats, have your troopers charge," he continued. "Keep the howitzer going until right before you blast your own troops.

"When they have to run, it will be right into their stolen horses and that's going to create chaos," Parson said. "We'll be charging in from the north right at them. We'll worry about rounding up the animals later.

"Got that?

"Yes Sir, Captain," the Lieutenant said as he rose and trotted back into the troops yelling softly with his orders.

"Mount up men," Parson ordered, as the troopers rode off south with the little howitzer bouncing along.

"Keep it double file and quiet," Parson barked to another Lieutenant behind him. "Pass it back."

As they moved along, Adkin felt obligated to ask, "Don't suppose there's going to be an attempt to arrest them first?"

Parson turned his head at a tilt to Adkin with a dour look on his face. When he saw Adkin with a big smile, he finally smiled as well.

"Only the ones that are still alive will be arrested Mister Yates," Parson said, with a chuckle.

Parson realized what Adkin was asking: Could he and Uribe blast away at will? The Captain was anxious to see how this Englishman and his half-breed Indian would do in a real fight.

From Parson's answer, Adkin knew the Captain would let them blast away at will. It would be kill or be killed. Adkin felt a thrill shiver through his body.

It startled him in a way. He thought he should be afraid, but that was the furthest thing from his mind. He knew he might get to avenge his friend's horrible injury.

"This is for you Sanpete," Adkin thought to himself.

•••

Captain Parson halted his men behind a rise about a mile from the Comancheros' camp. Every now and then they could catch the sound of a horse's whinny.

They waited. Adkin and Uribe checked their pistols, made sure their rifles had cartridges and made sure additional shells could be grabbed as quickly as possible. All the troopers were doing likewise.

Adkin slid his long-bladed knife in and out of its sheath several times, ensuring it wasn't stuck tight from dampness.

Boom!

All the horses seemed to jump and start to shuffle. Parson kept his hand up in a halt order.

Another loud boom again, within a minute. They were doing a great job shooting, and loading with speed.

Boom.

Now they could hear the pounding of the earth from hundreds of animals. Those animals were headed right to them.

"Charge!" Parson yelled as loud as he could, even startling Adkin and Diablo a little. As they came over the rise at full speed, Adkin could see the horses spreading out left, right and straight for them. The Comancheros were running around, some mounting horses with only a blanket for a saddle.

"Those are probably the renegade Indians," Adkin thought to himself.

Parson's southern arm of cavalrymen were coming downhill toward the spring, and the little howitzer was still booming into the treeline at the spring. Adkin thought he actually saw a Comanchero fall to the ground while running.

As they neared the spring, Parson yelled "Fire" and shot his pistol toward the hoard of animals and men. Adkin had started the charge with his trusty Sharp's rifle held over his lap.

When he saw a bandit headed to their right, Adkin pulled Diablo to a dangerous stop and lifted the gun, in less than a few seconds, the big gun went off and the rider Adkin was aiming at fell off his horse backward.

Diablo got his spurs and was again charging through the dirt and dust. Lead was flying through the air everywhere. Uribe was reloading his pistol while at full gallop and quickly was firing. Adkin saw another Comanchero fall with Uribe's shot. Parson had his cutlass out, raised high above his head screaming "Charge."

They were now in the middle of the treelined spring area and dust was making it hard to see who was who. Adkin felt a bullet whiz by his head, it was a strange whirring sound, and Adkin thought it strangely exciting.

He felt a tug on his right leg. He looked down and a renegade was holding his stirrup and trying to stab his leg. The blade missed and sank into Diablo's lower flank just as Adkin placed the barrel of his pistol about a foot from the man's head and nearly blew it completely off when he pulled the trigger.

Adkin swung Diablo off to the right, and bounded off the big stud. He was trying to hold the reins, while Diablo continued dancing in a circle, crying out in pain. Adkin saw the wound, blood coming from it but not as much as he feared. He grabbed one of his leather tassels off his right arm and with his left hand, managed to stuff most of it into the hole, Diablo still prancing.

"As Adkin jumped back in the saddle, Diablo calmed down. It seemed to give the black steed comfort knowing Adkin was back in command. Adkin spurred the horse's left flank and yelled "Hee Yeah," and headed back to the west.

The gunfire was becoming less as Adkin and Diablo reached several hundred yards from the main fighting area. Adkin knew he had to stop the bleeding from his friend and companion.

He finally halted and bounced to the ground. He dug through this saddle bag and found a shirt. He started shredding it up and soon had a bandage made and used some twine to wrap around Diablo behind the saddle and secured the ripped up shirt in place.

Diablo was calm and back to his old self. One tough Indian pony, Adkin thought and smiled. Though he would have to have a closer look later, Diablo's wound didn't seem like it could kill him.

"I'll take care of you, boy," Adkin said while stroking his neck. He jumped back atop the horse and swung around back toward the spring. Things were quieter and the dust was settling.

As Adkin neared the central area, Captain Parson came riding over to him. Another single rifle shot rang out just north of them.

"You okay Mister Yates?" Parson asked.

"Yes Sir, and yourself?"

"Fine. Fine. Good day for killin' savages," Parson said, dust breaking in his facial lines as he smiled. "Your horse wounded?"

"Yessir. A renegade tried to stab my leg and missed," Adkin explained.

"Did you make that injun pay?"

"Yessir, one to the face."

"Good man," Parson said, smiling. "I saw that pull-up rifle shot you made in the charge. Damn good shooting for an Englishman."

"I've been shooting that rifle since I was a small child," Adkin said.

"Hard to believe you were ever small," Parson said, laughing.

Uribe came loping up. He, too, was smiling from ear-to-ear.

"We show them no good bandits who is Top Boss, si?" Uribe said.

Both Parson and Adkin answered, "Si" at the same time, eliciting laughter from all of them.

"I saw you fighting Uribe," Parson said. "You are a good shot, and I even saw you get pulled off your mount, and you took care of that heathen quickly with that blade of yours"

"Have to Capitan or he kill me," Uribe said. "Was glad my horse didn't run off. I don't like fighting in the dirt."

"Damn, you boys are a two-man killin' machine," Parson said. "I was wondering how you'd fare in a fight, but taking down four impresses the hell out of me. I'd be honored to have you ride with me any time."

"Thanks Captain," Adkin said.

Si, Capitan. Gracias," Uribe chimed in.

"Well men, let's get this cleaned up," Parson said, as another single shot rang out hundreds of yards away and a man yelled a blood-curdling scream.

As they walked their horses through the debris; a few bodies, scattered guns, arrows, bows, moccasins. Adkin grimaced at seeing a freshly scalped Comanchero, his old hat laying near his body.

"Our Ute and Paiute scouts like to collect those scalps," Parson said. "I think they'd rather have those than gold for their service."

Adkin looked to Uribe, and Uribe nodded his head in agreement.

Adkin could see horses strung out as far as the rise they hid behind before the charge. No telling how far and wide they are scattered, he thought.

One of Parson's Lieutenants came riding up reining his mount to a stop.

"Captain," he said while saluting. "We have 14 bandits dead and about that same wounded. A lot of them, maybe 20 or 25 seemed to have gotten away in all the dust. There's probably about 20 animals killed, too."

"What about our men, Lieutenant?" Parson asked.

"Only three wounded, Sir, none severely, they'll be okay."

"Great news Lieutenant," Parson said. "Get those stolen wagons gathered up with a detail and head to the fort as soon as possible. Hoof it through the night to get home. Don't dawdle."

"Yes Sir."

As he turned away and spurred his horse, Parson's other Lieutenant came in, saluting.

"I'm sending a detail with the wagons and all the stolen goods to the fort right away," Parson said. "We need to use the remaining troops to round up as many animals as they can before nightfall.

"We'll camp here for the night and, hopefully, find some more horses tomorrow and then get home," he added.

As they started setting camp, Parson said most of the outlaws that got away headed out into the desert area east of the trail.

"They know better than to move west near the fort," he said. "They'll gather whatever horses that scattered that way. Most of the animals will still be in this area along the creek and the spring because they're social animals and like to cling together."

Troopers were yelping and herding horses and mules into the low area where they had been before the Army raid. This time, the animals were being hobbled or long-lined between trees. Several ropes had been tied between cottonwoods to have makeshift corrals to place them together.

Adkin and Uribe removed the bandage on Diablo. Uribe rubbed some tobacco juice mixed with ground up yarrow flowers into the wound.

"It stops the bleeding, Señor," Uribe explained. "We will leave that paste there and let the clean air work on it."

As the sun started dipping below the horizon, the sky exploded with pinks, golds and orange colors, bouncing off clouds like butterflies floating through wildflowers.

Adkin still couldn't get over how much sky there was in the West. It seemed limitless and was painted something different every time one looked up and took in its magnificence.

Next month, he would turn 20 years old, he thought to himself, hardly believing the life he was now leading.

"And I still have my scalp," he whispered to himself. "Thank you Lord."

•••

Captain Parson was up early and yelling orders to check nearby for more stolen animals. The sky was suddenly full of ominous clouds in every direction.

Adkin went over to where he had tied off Diablo. He had visited him twice during the night, and the horse was doing well. Adkin now noticed a little ooze draining from Diablo's wound. He rubbed some fresh yarrow paste on the wound again.

"You men have one hour to get these animals ready to travel," Parson hollered to his men, who were scattering.

"How's that horse of yours, Mister Yates?" Parson asked. "We're moving out in one hour."

"He's fine Captain."

"Where did you find such a beautiful animal, son?" Parson asked.

"He was actually a gift from an Indian called Black Horse. He's Chief Satanta's medicine man," Adkin said. "They're Kiowas we met …"

"I know who the hell Satanta is, son," Parson interrupted Adkin. "How the hell did you come to meet him?"

"It's a long story, Captain," Adkin said. "I'll explain it later, I promise."

A light drizzle started falling just as they started moving out of the arroyo where Santa Clara Spring pushed clear cool water into the little creek that ran along the draw.

"Let's move it men," Parson barked loudly as at least a dozen of his troopers were now drovers moving probably a hundred head of horses and mules – mostly horses. Parson said there were probably 100 that were lost to the Comancheros.

"We'll take these to Fort Union and the stolen animals can be sent to Santa Fe with the next caravan going that way," Parson had said while they were breaking camp. "We'll let the owners fight over who's animal is who's."

Within an hour, rain was falling hard, and a north wind was blowing around 20 miles per hour. They had trouble keeping the herd moving west – they all wanted to turn their backs into the wind and go south. Parson had said this five-hour trip would probably now be a six-hour jaunt.

The rain kept washing the yarrow salve out of the wound on Diablo, and Adkin was worried.

"It's good to have so much rain clean his wound, Señor Adkin," Uribe told him. "I still have more yarrow paste for later."

Adkin knew the wound was not as deep as he had originally believed, and how it missed penetrating his stomach lining, Adkin couldn't guess. But he was worried about infection. That's what killed most everything and everybody out here in the West.

•••

It was still lightly raining when Fort Union came into sight. Troopers pushed the stolen animals into the corrals abutting the fort, and Adkin and Uribe headed to the fort's stables.

Adkin unsaddled Diablo and Uribe used up the last of his salve on the horse, urging Adkin not to worry.

"He's the biggest, strongest horse I ever know, Señor," Uribe said. "He will be like brand new mañana, I promise."

Captain Parson reported to Colonel Garrison on the raid; all the numbers and how the Barlow & Sanderson team did in the fight as well.

"They'd make damn good soldiers, Colonel," Parson said.

That evening, Adkin told Garrison and Parson the story how he got Diablo as a gift. Both officer's were duly impressed, and Adkin had been somewhat underwhelming in the total story. Uribe later said, "Why not tell them of the fight and how Ryan came along?"

Adkin just rolled his eyes and mumbled. He didn't see himself a hero.

Garrison informed them another southbound caravan was due in the next day headed for Santa Fe, and all the recovered animals were to be added to the train, with orders to detail 50 calvary to accompany them to Santa Fe.

Garrison then handed Adkin two telegrams. One noting Sanpete was doing good medically and even better mentally. Conrado said Sanpete had already ordered a wooden leg with a small carved foot he could put a moccasin on. Sanpete would have to stay another month or so.

The other telegram was from J.L., noting he was very sorry for Sanpete and the company would pay all medical and nursing costs.

He also said they were departing Colorado Springs June 12. They had been delayed at the new mines west of Denver. J. L. estimated they would be in La Junta in four days, maybe five.

Adkin looked at Uribe and told him J. L. and his crew were in Colorado Springs and will leave there tomorrow.

"Si, I know the town," Uribe said. "When the gold mines were found at Pike's Peak, the town was very wild and dangerous.

"They are only a few days from La Junta," he continued. "We can maybe meet them if we leave tomorrow."

Adkin asked the operator to send a message to Conrado in Santa Fe.

"When are the crew and wagons headed back?"

• • •

Colonel Garrison warned Adkin and Uribe trying to make it to La Junta own their own.

"This is the time for Injuns and Comancheros to attack everything they see on the trail," Garrison said. "I couldn't allow more than five or six troopers to escort you, and that would only be to Raton Pass."

"You probably don't know it, but the Army decided late last year that caravans couldn't proceed west on the Santa Fe Trail from Fort Larned unless they had at least 100 wagons together," Garrison added.

Just near sunset, the telegraph operator found Adkin and Uribe at the mess hall.

Adkin read the message and smiled at Uribe.

"Conrado said Ray Dee and the boys were leaving Santa Fe tomorrow as well, with a large freighters' train – more than 200 wagons – and 'mucho' soldiers," Adkin said, smiling. "Are you willing to try to get to La Junta from Raton Pass by ourselves?"

"Si, Señor," Uribe said, smiling. "All the banditos can do to us is kill us. No?"

"I prefer no, so let's talk with Garrison again and see if he will still allow some soldiers to go with us to Uncle Wootton's," Adkin said, as they headed off to the commander's quarters.

When Adkin told Garrison their plans and asked if he would still provide five or six cavalrymen to ride with them to Raton, Garrison's answer at first startled Adkin.

"Hell no," he growled. "I've changed my mind Yates. After talking with Captain Parson, you probably don't need anyone.

"But, I'll give you 20 troopers because I worry about them getting back alone if they have to."

• • •

Sanderson and his crew arrived at La Junta late June 16. J.L. went to the Western Union office and was told a telegram had come in the day before. It was from Adkin, who had said he and Uribe had departed Uncle Wootton's Ranch early June 15. Sanderson realized Adkin should arrive in La Junta tomorrow.

"Let's go ahead and camp here tonight," Sanderson told Ryan and his crew. "Adkin may arrive tomorrow. We'll wait until noon."

Sanderson's men took advantage of having some free time. Ryan went shopping and bought a strange top hat. It was treated wool, but had a four-inch brim, flat as a board, and the upper was stiff and rose about six-inches off the brim. It looked like a stove top. His men laughed and teased him, but he wore it proudly, smiling all through the teasing.

Dusty and Don Diego slept through most of the morning. Fransisco spent the best part of the time visiting with the Padre at the little church on the east side of town. Fransisco enjoyed reading the Bible and liked talking about scripture, which left out most of the crew.

J.L. was sending telegrams to just about everybody he knew it seemed. He was ordering more stage coaches, updating business plans with Barlow and informing Army commanders of stage coach station contracts they were establishing.

Stage coach lines had to register with the Army in order to receive approval for escorts by the calvary. Sanderson was informing officials all the way to Washington.

At noon, Sanderson stepped out on the ranch house porch and his men came straggling up from the boarding house.

"Where's Fransisco?" Sanderson asked.

"He's at the church," Ryan answered. "But he knows we're to meet at noon."

"What's with the hat?" Sanderson asked, smiling. The others started laughing, too.

"He wants to look like some of those Comancheros," Dusty said. "Next thing you know, he'll be wearing double gun belts criss-crossed off his shoulders."

"Hey, I've only seen a couple of bandits wearing this kind of hat, and some wear hats like your's, too," Ryan said.

"It's a top hat, J.L., and after a little wear, it will soften, and I'm going to put a slight tilt in it when that happens," Ryan explained. "It's dapper, don't you think?"

"Dapper? Don't you mean Dandy?" Dusty laughed.

"Okay. Okay. Let's start getting everything ready," Sanderson said. "I'm going to check the telegraph office in case there is any news. I don't know if there are any telegraph offices between here and Raton Pass."

"There wasn't any when we were through here a few months ago," Ryan said.

As Sanderson was walking out of the telegraph office, Ryan shouted, "Look. There," pointing to the south.

Two mounted horsemen leading two more horses, one with a small supply pack, were trotting through the mirage of the horizon, with dust rising up behind them.

"I'll bet that's Adkin and Uribe," Ryan exclaimed, smiling.

• • •

It was a happy reunion when Adkin and Uribe came riding up. Both their mounts had signs of fatigue, starting to sweat up in areas. Even Diablo looked tired to Ryan.

After all the hugs and slaps on the backs and laughter, Sanderson suggested they go in the cantina at the ranch house and have a refreshment.

"Refreshment hell, this calls for a whisky," Ryan hollered.

Adkin recalled the attack that cost Sanpete his leg, and how they got to fight the Comancheros that had been raiding the area around Watrous, where the Santa Fe Trail splits.

"But he's doing good, real good," Adkin added.

The two explained how they lost their Army escort at Uncle Woottoon's and rode the four horses hard for two days, switching saddles about every three hours or so. He mentioned Diablo's wound hadn't slowed the horse much at all, and it was nearly healed.

"We ride like bandits were chasing our tails," Uribe said, smiling.

The also explained Ray Dee and the gang are probably about four or five days behind them.

Sanderson told them they had better get back on the trail, that he wanted to get to Bent's Fort to exchange some money deals by way of the telegraph.

"We'll be at Bent's Fort long enough to catch up with Ray Dee and their wagons," Sanderson said. "We've got some fresh mounts if you want to let your horses cool down awhile and rest."

"Can we give them a good rub down and wait an hour?" Adkin asked. "And I want to sit on a bench awhile and drive a team, okay?"

"Sure," Sanderson said, patting Adkin on the shoulder. "Whatever you want, partner."

Sanderson was taken by Adkin's appearance. The young man looked worn yet experienced in the ways of the West. It pleased Sanderson his partner looked as if he had matured years in less than a year after he had hired Adkin.

The men all went out and rubbed down Adkin's and Uribe's animals. The horses almost spooked with so many hands and brushes all over their bodies. But it didn't take long, and one could see the horses were enjoying the attention.

Everybody went back in the cantina and talked about their recent experiences. Adkin reminded J.L. their gold and silver would be coming with Ray Dee and the others under military guard.

Sanderson reported his crew's activities in Colorado and the new silver mines being found and the financial possibilities.

"We know the trains will hurt our regular stage lines on the main trails in the years ahead, but it's going to open more possibilities running people and goods off these new train lines," Sanderson said. "That's where the money will be."

"People can take the train to Denver, but how do they get to the towns springing up near the mines outside Denver? Barlow & Sanderson, that's how," he added, smiling.

"I've also hired some men who were well recommended to build another headquarters branch at Junction City," Sanderson said. "We might well make that a new office. That's where the rails end now, and eventually, we have to offer service to California before long."

Adkin smiled. He enjoyed being around J.L., his mind was always working. Adkin had never thought about that. He kind of figured once the trains came west, it would kill the stage coach business.

Now he could see, it could double the business, because more and more people would be coming west on the trains. Then they would want to go to all the places where trains did not go.

Adkin just kept smiling to himself. He felt humbled and proud to be a part of J.L.'s company and his plans.

It was around 3 in the afternoon when they finally headed for Bent's Fort, which was only a full day's travel. So they would be spending one more night on the trail before getting to the comfort of the fort.

"It almost feels as if Bent's Fort is now my home," Adkin thought to himself.

Little did he know, Adkin would make the fort his home and headquarters for several more years.

They arrived at Bent's Fort June 19, 1867. Four days later, Ray Dee, Holmes and Long arrived with their company wagons – and everybody's gold and silver. It was like a rare family reunion. All the crew that Adkin had originally got to know in Leavenworth were together again.

They all talked about how life was treating them, their troubles, the good times mainly, and they all took in Uribe and the new hires, Fransisco and Don Diego, as if they were family, too, and especially Sanpete.

Uribe and Adkin detailed the horror of seeing his leg after the Comanchero attack. The crew clapped and cheered when Uribe detailed the counter-raid and revenge for Sanpete.

Adkin, J.L., Ryan and Ray Dee carried the bags to their bunk room, and Sanderson pulled out a tablet from his saddle bags.

They went over the profits and who's share was what.

Adkin had his work sheet with him, signed by both he and two Aguirre brothers.

Adkin's share was $2,700, the company's share was $5,400 and Ryan netted $4,900.

"That's great men," Sanderson said.

They then talked about who was interested in making other investments.

"Let me tell you right here and now, Barlow and I have no problem with you men having your side businesses – as long, and I mean this in every sense of the word – as long as it does not interfere with the company's business goals or profits," Sanderson said. "There are opportunities out here, and you three will be the front men for our western expansion. If you can make extra money on the side, that's fine, as long as your priorities are to the company and our goals and profits."

"In fact, Barlow and I are willing to help bankroll any side business you may want, as long as it helps the company's profits," Sanderson continued. "If your own interests can help the company, so much the better. We are willing to work with you."

"Think that over, and decide how you want your money handled," Sanderson added. "Ray Dee, I thank you for wanting to stay out here and offer your expertise to Adkin and Ryan. You, too, are welcome to propose any ideas that can make us money.

"The rest of us will be departing with the next eastbound caravan, which we're hearing may be in less than three days, so let me know your plans," he said. "I'll let you know what profits you two will have with your goods you purchased in Santa Fe after we get to Council Grove."

•••

Later that night, Adkin, Ryan and Ray Dee got together in the mess hall after it was cleaned and empty. Working with an oil lamp and a note pad, they discussed possible business plans.

"Why don't we build up our own freighting business," Ryan said. "The Santa Fe Trail will be busy as ever for the next four to six years – until the railroad arrives in Santa Fe anyway."

"But to be profitable, we need at least 40 to 50 wagons," Ray Dee said. "And I'm talking about those new Murphy wagons that can move, 8,000 to 10,000 pounds of goods.

"Those wagons would cost us at least $200 a wagon," he added.

Adkin was scribbling on the paper and looked up.

"What about you Rinehart? What are your plans?" Adkin asked. "Sanderson talked like you might only want to stay out here for a year."

"Well, that's what I said, because there was this little – well she's not little actually. But this Irish lass that works at the saloon was wanting to marry," Ray Dee said. "It's not that marriage scares me, it's that she's got a vicious side to her, know what I mean?

"But anyway, if we can make this work, I'll spend the rest of my life out here," he added. "I'm kind of taken by it to tell you the truth. It grows on you."

"I'm fine with that," Adkin said, "What about you, Ryan?"

He nodded agreement.

"Okay then, what do you think the profits would be on 8,000 pounds of goods?" Adkin asked.

"If we had to fill them, it could cost around $500 to $1,000. But, we could triple that in sales – and that's conservative," Ryan said.

"Okay, one wagon would costs us $200. Say we spent another $500 in goods," Adkin said. "If we sold those goods for $1,500, we'd have a profit of $800. That would be, in my opinion, per wagon every trip – at a minimum, and those new wagons could make at least two to three trips. Then we can sell the wagons for more than we originally paid for them.

"Imagine if we had 40 wagons, we'd earn at least $32,000 on the first trip," Adkin said, smiling.

"Yeah, but 40 wagons would cost $8,000 and 40 loads at just $500 a load would be $20,000 – that a $28,000 investment right up front," Ryan said.

"But Ryan, that would mean everything would be paid off on the first trip and with $4,000 in the bank," Ray Dee said.

"And then the second trip would be $500 to fill – $20,000 – but would sell for $60,000, or $40,000 in the bank," Adkin said. "And that doesn't include income from selling the wagons should we choose to and buying new ones."

"Holy cow," Ryan said.

Ray Dee fervently looked at Adkin and Ryan back and forth.

"Do you think J.L. would loan us $28,000 to get started?" Ray Dee asked.

"And we'd have to get another $20,000 to make the second trip," Ryan said. "It won't work without the second trip – that's everything."

"We also need to take into account the costs of teams of animals and teamsters and bullwhackers it would take," Adkin said, solemnly.

"Why don't we talk it over with J. L. and see what he thinks," Ray Dee said.

"But wait, do we three agree to be partners and want to even do this?" Ryan asked. "I mean, I'd love to do it and work with you two, but I want more details laid out."

"I agree, wholeheartedly," Ray Dee said.

"I gentlemen, would be pleased to be in a proper business with you two heathens," Adkin said in his most proper English accent.

They all laughed hard.

•••

Sanderson made an appointment with Commander Pierce the next morning to take possession of their gold and silver. Pierce handed over the bags and asked Sanderson to count it and sign a release.

"No need to count it Colonel, we have great trust in the U.S. Army," Sanderson said, laughing.

"Don't know if I do – at times," Pierce added, joining the laughter.

In a meeting later, Sanderson thought their business ideas were good, and he suggested to make it even better was to use Barlow & Sanderson Stagecoach Company to rent mules, or mostly oxen, teamsters and bullwhackers. The company could more easily expand its existing freighting business and knew where to hire additional personnel.

"You should calculate at paying about $150 a wagon for all those additional expenses per trip," Sanderson said. "Now about the investment costs.

"We, the company, could loan you your initial investment costs, but we'd need a more detailed plan listing the collateral and a contract for interest on the loan," Sanderson said. "We'll loan you the investment at 2 percent interest if you repay the total amount in six months. If not, it will be 4 percent for the next 12 months. We'll look at your second supply loan after we see how the initial loan works out.

"Of course, it will be in the contract the wagons and supplies are your responsibility. If they get stolen or burned to the ground, that's your responsibility, not the company's," Sanders continued. "We're not an insurance company.

"Why don't you list your plans and how you intend to operate your company, and I'll take it with me. Then I can work up a contract and send it to you for your approval, and we'll get started from there."

The men couldn't believe their ears. They were amazed – shaking hands, promising to make the company money as well as interest and to keep their company intertwined with Barlow & Sanderson.

"By the way, what are you going to call this company?" Sanderson asked.

They glanced back and forth at each other.

"We'll have to talk about that and let you know," Adkin said.

"And by the way, you three will also have to make an agreement how your company is set up," Sanderson added. "We'll need to have that as an attachment to the contract."

•••

The three got started working out their plans and how much they wanted to borrow, with a certain allowance for existing prices on 40 wagons, which is the amount they decided on.

"Do we need a contract between us, and who is president, and all that stuff?" Ray Dee asked.

"I'm good with a handshake from you men," Ryan said.

Adkin agreed, and Ray Dee said, "Fine with me, but what are we shaking on?"

"We divide everything equally between the three; expenses and profits, work and sweat included," Adkin said. "And if one wants out, he has to offer the sale of his 1/3rd share to the other two first."

They all shook hands and laughed, delighted with their opportunity.

The presented their written plan to Sanderson the next morning. He decided to telegraph Barlow with a few questions and said if he receives the right answers within the day, he could write a contract before departing Bent's Fort.

"That would save us all about two months with the mail service as it is," Sanderson said as they all started laughing because the fact was, Barlow & Sanderson had a large chunk of the money for that service coming in every month from the U.S. Government.

A few hours later, Sanderson told the crew he had the approval to write up an agreement right away, and he did so. By that next evening, he had the contract, and after detailing the clauses and sub-clauses, all four signed both copies Sanderson had produced.

The contract with the new freight hauling business was signed June 23, 1866, between Barlow & Sanderson and Yates, Ryan & Rinehart Freight Company. They had already decided to paint a large YR&R in yellow letters on each side of their new wagons.

All the plans were shared with the rest of the company crew, even including the new hires for duty in the West. Long and Holmes happily agreed to help them on the eastern end of the trail.

"We're leaving in the morning with the caravan, and the first thing I'll do is order 40 new Murphy wagons – the big haulers from their St. Louis manufacturing plant," Sanderson said. "Then I'll recommend trade goods – with your input, too, naturally – and start putting together 40 loads for Santa Fe.

"Hopefully, we can get it together by mid-August – if they can fill the wagon order fairly quick," Sanderson said. "Should be a lot of caravans travelling that time of year, too."

"We'll get your company lettering done on the wagons, too," Holmes said. "Those block letters like the Rock Island Railroad uses, too."

•••

The western crew now consisted of Adkin, Ryan, Rinehart, Uribe, Dusty, Don Diego, Fransisco and Sanpete. Sanderson had left orders for them to set up stagecoach stations throughout Colorado, as Sanderson was sending five more coaches to Bent's Fort as soon as he arrived back in Leavenworth, which he expected to do by late July.

Adkin had sent Ryan, Ray Dee and Uribe and Dusty to investigate areas west of Pueblo in southern Colorado within a week of Sanderson's departure.

Adkin had been busy establishing their western headquarters just outside of Bent's Fort. The Army had been very gracious in letting the company's crew stay there at the fort for a small stipend, but they were going to have to find their own place.

The fort was unique in that the Army had leased it for its use as well as built an adjoining Fort Lyon to the west. Adkin and his partners chose a site just northwest of the western side of Fort Lyon's walls. Up the side of the valley about a half mile from the river.

It was this decision that taught the three partners a two to one vote carried the decisions within the partnership. Ray Dee voted to build a headquarters southwest of the fort closer to the Arkansas River. His vote would have been disastrous, as it would later prove.

Adkin was responsible for building their new headquarters. The first thing they started on was a house/office with an adjoining bunk house and kitchen. As workers were concentrated on the wooden and adobe structures, Adkin led a team putting up a stockade with covered stables and a blacksmith shop. Adkin had assured his partners that blacksmith shops would help them keep their wagon investments in sound shape for longevity and condition when ready to sell them.

This would eventually be become a positive financial offshoot of the YR&R Freight Co. working with Barlow & Sanderson. They would build or purchase buildings for smittys along the trails to help maintain coaches, wagons and even railroaders in the coming years.

•••

On July 5, Adkin received word that Sanpete would be travelling with a freighter's wagon train the next day, and was expected to arrive in two weeks. Adkin was pleased, but he wasn't sure how Sanpete would fit in with the crew now. Uribe had told Adkin Sanpete turned 23 while recovering in Santa Fe.

Adkin was expecting more building supplies he had ordered through Sanderson, even though he and his partners had spent about $1,200 of their own money since starting the company headquarters. They had decided to ask Barlow & Sanderson to become one-quarter partners with them in the new headquarters.

That way, they all agreed, if either company wanted out, the other would have first chance to purchase the interests. Sanderson eagerly approved the deal, since having a blacksmith maintaining the wagons helps put money in their side of the freighting business, as well.

It was about this time the crew – and everybody in the Southwest – learned that Brigadier General Christopher "Kit" Carson and his wife, Josefa, had moved from Taos to Colorado to expand his ranching business, and he also was made Commander of Fort Garland.

Adkin waited to hear from Ryan to tell him the news about Carson, but he didn't see Ryan and his crew until around July 25. Apparently Ryan had just missed Carson, but ironically, they had temporarily set up a proposed stageline to Fort Garland from Walsenburg.

They both made a promise to themselves to go see Carson when time allowed.

An Englishman's Adventures on the Santa Fe Trail (1865-1889)

•••

On July 18, Sanpete arrived at Bent's Fort, and what a welcome he received. Even the Post Commander had a drum and fife crew play several songs for him when the wagon pulled up carrying the young man. He was smiling from ear-to-ear.

"Welcome friend," Adkin said as he reached up to help Sanpete get off the wagon bench.

"That's okay Mister Yates, I can do it," Sanpete said proudly, as he swung his wooden leg over the side and placed it on the front wheel of the wagon. He then pulled his good leg over and jumped to the ground landing mainly on this right foot and then standing up straight and reaching out to shake Adkin's hand.

His grin never faltered as he said, "So glad to be here again."

"We're so happy to see you, too," Adkin said. "Are you hungry?"

Sanpete said he was, and they headed to the mess hall. Sanpete walked with a slight limp, Adkin noticed, but barely perceptible. He's cheery attitude made Adkin's heart swell with pride for this small, yet gritty scout who almost got killed doing his duty when he didn't have to.

About a week later, Ryan and his crew returned from southern Colorado, and Uribe and his scouts – his family, so to speak – celebrated all night long. More than a dram of tequila and brandy was downed.

Ryan reported to Adkin they had heard more and more silver was being mined at Georgetown west of Denver. Ryan and Sanderson had been near there but never made it up to the town, which is nearly 9,000 feet of elevation. He suggested they set up lines through there as soon as possible.

Adkin agreed and he and Ryan assembled four others and made plans for a four-week trip.

The day after Ryan and his crew's return, Sanpete had told Uribe he still wanted to work for the company.

Uribe and Sanpete caught up with Adkin and told Adkin Sanpete's plan.

"Señor Adkin, Sanpete is not as good in the saddle with his wood leg and foot, but he's sure he can handle driving wagons or coaches – he wants your okay to still work for the company," Uribe said.

"I will work very hard Mister Yates," Sanpete pleaded.

"Of course you can still work for the company, Sanpete," Adkin said. "You can work wherever you feel comfortable."

With that, Ryan and Ray Dee started teaching Sanpete how to handle horse teams with a two-horse wagon at first, then he graduated to handling a four-horse team pulling a stagecoach.

Though Sanpete soon got the monicker of "Peg-Leg Pete," he accepted the name with pride. He also became one of the company's most dependable and best stagecoach teamsters in the West.

Peg-Leg Pete ended up driving stagecoaches for 20 years throughout northern New Mexico, western Kansas and all of Colorado.

Pete even had several shootouts with bandits and Indians. He could drop a bandit on horseback at two hundred yards with that old rifle of his. He became a well-known and beloved member of Barlow & Sanderson Overland Stagecoach Line.

He would eventually retire as the railroads took away more and more coach services. He built a nice home for he and his family in a new town established three miles up the Purgatoire River where it met the Arkansas, just a few miles from his ancestral home. The town was known as Boggsville, and two of its famous citizens would move into town in 1868 – Kit Carson and wife, Josefa and their children.

•••

The western crew, as they came to be known in the company, received four more new Concord coaches at the first of August. The new coaches had their rides improved with better axle springs.

Sanderson had telegraphed that traders and the Army were talking like caravans would be pushed across even through winter, unless blizzards were ongoing. The telegraph had changed everything.

More and more of the travellers were pioneers rather than freight traders. President Lincoln had signed the Homestead Act in 1862. Under the provisions, settlers could claim 160 acres of public land. They paid a small filing fee, and if they lived on the 160 acres for five continuous years, built a residence and grew crops or raised animals, they could then file for their deed for the property for free.

Not many moved west during the war years because all security troops were fighting each other in the Civil War. But in 1864, people were heading west as fast as they could. That year also proved to be one of the deadliest for people in caravans, too, because of constant Indian raids and attacks by Comancheros.

Adkin and his crew believed as the wagon trains kept coming, they most likely would not get much rest in the winter. Adkin understood it well: The West pulls at people's hearts and souls. They want freedom to determine their own way and personal liberty.

He was living proof how the West imbeds itself in a man – or a woman.

•••

Adkin was wanting to head into Colorado with Ryan and finalize some deals Ryan had found, but on Aug. 3, Sanderson telegraphed and said the 40 Murphy wagons of YR&R had been received in Leavenworth via railroad, ironically, and he was sure they could be loaded and ready to roll with a wagon caravan scheduled to depart Council Grove on August 15.

Sanderson had already hired crews of teamsters and bullwhackers. He had purchased oxen and the wagons would be double loads pulled by eight- to 10-yokes of oxen. All the goods were destined to Santa Fe, and the Aguirre brothers would be the designated sales agent. He dutifully noted the loan to YR&R had come to a total of $29,400.

"The pressure is on partner," Adkin said to Ryan, as Ray Dee stepped up.

"Our wagons will be headed this way August 15," Ryan said to Ray Dee. "And we're on the hook for $29,400, partner."

"How are we going to handle this?" Ray Dee asked. "Do you have a plan? God, that's a lot of money."

"We've been talking about it," Adkin said. "I need to see if we can place a smitty's shop somewhere around Fort Dodge. I'm hoping the Raths will let us put a blacksmith shop at their place at the Fort Hays Road. It's a perfect spot for wagon repairs before they get into Fort Dodge.

"We could go ahead and get that started, then ride back with our wagons to here," he added "Then you and Ryan could tag along with the loads to Santa Fe and make sure everything gets there in one piece."

"We need to deliver another Concord to Raton Pass anyway," Ryan said. "That route is getting busier and busier, and Uncle Wootton's road is good, but it's still tough on wagons, even Concords."

"We can take Peg-Leg Pete and Uribe, too," Ray Dee chimed in. "Y'all can keep getting the headquarters together."

The all agreed to the plan, and then got back to work on the stables.

•••

On August 16, most of the new headquarters had been completed. Additional fortification with adobe was still needed in the stables and corral areas. The main house had a large bunk house where up to a dozen men could sleep comfortably with straw mattresses on single cots. The adjoining mess hall and kitchen could also accommodate about two dozen.

Off the west side was the office with four desks, and it had its own entrance and small front porch.

A day earlier, the crew had received word their first shipment of wagons and goods had departed Leavenworth via train and would spend one day in Council Grove putting all the teams and wagons together. The wagon caravan would then depart Council Grove the next day, Aug. 17.

Adkin, Uribe and Dusty, gathered their travel supplies and decided to depart Aug. 16 with an extra string of six horses and catch a wagon train that passed through Bent's Fort the day before. The train had about 100 troops – infantry and calvary – travelling with it.

Adkin figured to make it to Fort Dodge in 10 to 12 days, while it would take their wagons about 15 to 17 days to reach Fort Dodge. That would give them time to find a location for a smitty's shop and to look for a good blacksmith in the area to operate it.

On August 27, Adkin and his men rode into Fort Dodge. One of the first soldiers Adkin saw was a tall, lanky Captain hastily walking toward them as they entered the fort.

"I'll be darned, you again," the Captain said.

"I see you're still wearing your scalp, too, Captain Phillips," Adkin said as he jumped out of his saddle. The two men grabbed shoulder, embracing and started laughing.

"I was hoping to see you again after that Clear Spring incident," Phillips said. "Are you going to be able to spend some time while you're here?"

"I sure am Captain, we'll be in the area for about a week or so," Adkin said. "Got some big business to tend to."

"Call me Sam, Yates. I feel like we've known each other a long time, yet it was only about a year ago we met," Phillips said. "I haven't been in a smooth-riding coach since I sat the bench with you on that Concord."

"If I remember right, you took some guff for getting that duty, too," Adkin said.

Phillips greeted Uribe and Dusty, whom he had met after the Clear Spring massacre. He invited the men to the mess hall for some grub.

Adkin explained their business with the company – to set up a blacksmith shop, and that they were going to see if Chris Rath would allow them to build it at his place on the Fort Hays Road. Phillips said he'd seen quite a few Barlow & Sanderson stages going back and forth through the area, especially from Fort Hays.

Phillips said they had two civilian smitty's at Fort Dodge, and he knew one very well.

"He's a good striker – a young man with no wife – and he does good work in a timely manner," Phillips said.

"That's kind of what we're looking for, and we have some carrots for the right man," Adkin said.

Phillips showed the men to the barracks and got them squared away with the quartermaster. Later that evening after supper, Adkin told Phillips about his own company. About the 40 wagons coming, his partners Ryan and Rinehart, and how they got the backing from Barlow & Sanderson.

"That's something I've been looking for Yates, a way to make a living out here," Phillips said. "I love it out here. I don't know how to explain it, but I want to remain out here the rest of my life."

"You don't have to explain it to me, Sam" Adkin said.

"You see, I've decided to resign from the Army before the end of the year. I joined the Union Army when I was 17, fighting for the North, and then re-enlisted in the new U.S. Army and came west.

"I know I've been treated well by the Army, made Captain faster than most I know, but I'm in love with a gal back home," Phillips said. "I just don't feel I can go through life without her. Do you know what I mean?"

"Not really, Sam. I haven't really found that yet, and I don't know if I ever will. But I respect your feelings, and I think that's wonderful. What's her name?"

"Mary Catherine Jarvis," Phillips said, with that far-away look in his eyes. "She's 17, and I've known her for years – her and her family. But it was when I saw her on my two-week Christmas leave that it really hit me.

"I've always felt close to her and liked her and all that," he continued. "But back there in Southern Ohio, I just wanted to pick her up and pack her right back out here with me. I told her all about the Plains; the sky, the sunsets, the millions of stars and meteors.

"We've written each other since and she says she loves me, too, and I plan on going back this Christmas and asking her to marry me," Phillips said. "But, I don't want her to be a military wife and living in forts where only a few women live.

"We have friends, actually one of her uncles, and two other families from Hocking County, Ohio – our area – that recently homesteaded some land in Indian Territory not far from the Kansas border – just south of here," Phillips said. "They call it some kind of lease with the Cherokee Tribe, who have the reservation there.

"I'm thinking of taking her there, if she marries me," he continued, with a chuckle. "I'll most likely try farming like the others, but I'll be looking for something more. I know how tough it is to farm out here."

They visited more about their lives, Adkin's adventures and how Sanpete lost a leg in an attack. Phillips related how they lost track of the Indians that stole the White women, the wagons at Clear Spring and ran for the Llano Estacado, where they disappeared.

"Have you seen the part of Llano Estacado called the Palo Duro Canyons?" Phillips asked. "They're in Texas."

"No I haven't."

"It's beautiful with all the ravines, canyons, the Prairie Dog Town Fork of the Salt Red River cutting through there, the cliffs a thousand-feet tall," Phillips said. "But it a scary place if you're chasing Indians. Deadly scary."

•••

The following days, the crew headed out to Rath's Ranch House east of Fort Dodge. Chris was there to meet them, said his brother Charles had been there only a week earlier but was back on the road with all his many businesses around the plains.

Chris didn't hesitate when asked if he would like to have a smitty's shop established at their ranch house. He had actually built an additional partition off his ranch house to handle the stagecoach business, which he said was making them all a lot of money.

They walked over to inspect the adobe building. It was full of tack; saddles, bridles, harnesses, feed bags – a large room actually.

"We could build a roof structure off this side and put in a forge and the anvil," Adkin said. "Keeping that smoke out of the building. We could winter proof it somewhat, too. You've got enough room for his tools, too. That's great."

"Now we just have to find a proper smitty," he added.

"There's a young bachelor in Fort Dodge, who we have used to iron some of our wagon axles," Chris said.

"We've heard of him already from Captain Phillips," Ryan interrupted. "Let's go have a talk with him. Can you go with us Chris?"

"Sure. Let me saddle a horse real quick."

They rode into the fort and headed to the stables. The young smitty's name was Irl Gaut.

They found Gaut pounding some horse shoes into shape for a large horse tied to the rail next to the shop. They introduced themselves, and Chris explained Barlow & Sanderson was wanting to put in a smitty's shop at the Raths' Ranch House and were looking for a partner. He told Gaut how Adkin had been raised by his blacksmith father and learned the craft well in England.

"We're looking for a partner, Mr. Gaut," Adkin started.

"Please, call me Irl."

"Okay Irl, we're willing to give you a part of the business that allows you to make more money if you build the business," Adkin said. "We want to offer you 49 percent of the shop's earnings, and we will pay for all the initial tools, the forge, and I'll build you an anvil like my father developed in England – it's very unique, with a horn on one end."

Gaut held out his hand immediately, smiling and thanking them for the opportunity. While shaking hands, Gaut said, "One question, who pays for tools that break or have to be replaced later?"

"You do," Adkin said.

"Okay, fine with me."

"Would you like to assist in the building design and how you would like it laid out?" Adkin asked.

"You betch ya," Gaut said. "Let me go tell Lieutenant Louderback he'll have to finish shoeing this here horse."

"No. No. Go ahead and keep your job until we can get one of those new fan-driven forges ordered," Adkin said. "Make a list of the tools you want, and we can order those, too. Don't forget anything. Bring me the list by tomorrow. I'll be around here somewhere."

With that, they made arrangements for building materials to put the forge next to the tack room at Rath's. Chris said there was a lumber mill near Fort Larned, and Adkin ordered planks and tin roofing materials via telegraph.

Adkin was in the Western Union office again the next day sending a telegraph to Sanderson ordering tools and a new forge for their new shop to be located at the Rath Ranch House on the Santa Fe Trail and junction of the Fort Hays Road.

Adkin could imagine Sanderson smiling and saying, "I can smell the money now."

Adkin would have to build a new anvil once back at his own blacksmith shop at headquarters. He decided he needed to build an inventory, because he sensed this business would not suffer the coming of the railroads. They needed smitty's and strikers as much as anyone, maybe more so. And the fort's blacksmiths wouldn't have jobs if the fort closed down – or were burnt down by Indians.

He could get good quality iron ingots from the Aguirre brothers in Santa Fe quicker than ordering them from Westport or Independence. He fired off a message to Conrado and ordered enough ingots to make at least four anvils.

•••

A few days after getting everything ordered for the new blacksmith's shop, their wagons arrived with the large caravan heading to Santa Fe. Long and Holmes were driving the first teams of oxen up to Fort Dodge.

They eagerly greeted Adkin and his crew.

"You might have to set up house out here, Carl, you're spending more time on the trail than at home," Ryan teased Long. Then pointed at Holmes and said, "Don't you ever work?"

"You don't think trying to keep these dullard slow pokes heading in the right direction every minute isn't work?" Darrell said, motioning to his oxen.

Adkin and the men couldn't get over how impressive those 40 wagons were, double-trained and with the large yellow letters, YR&R.

"Never thought I'd say a wagon is beautiful, but that's all I can say about those," Ryan said.

"I agree partner," Adkin said, with a huge smile.

"Any problems with any of the wagons?" Adkin asked Long.

"No sir, not a hitch," Long said. "And these are the biggest rollin' ships I've seen in awhile."

"Good news, and I hope it stays that way," Adkin said. "Because it feels as if they are carrying all our dreams and a million dollars – all at once."

"You worry too much, Yates," Ryan said. "Must be something English."

They all laughed, including Adkin, who added, "Maybe it's because we lost the Revolutionary War."

That got all them heaving with laughter.

The caravan decided to camp for the night just west of the fort along the river.

"Now we just have to get them all to Santa Fe," Adkin thought to himself when trying to go to sleep. He could still hear the gunshots and screams echoing through his head when they were attacked, and Sanpete would become Peg-Leg Pete.

On the morning of September 1, the caravan headed west with YR&R's wagons loaded with trade goods, and it was all valued at nearly $30,000 – a fortune to the men who dreamed it up. Adkin found himself praying a little more than usual each day.

•••

The caravan moved along slowly but steady, passing three eastbound wagon trains in the 12 days it took to reach Bent's Fort. It was quite a scene when a caravan of 300 wagons and all the accompanying animals, ambulances and chuckwagons passed another of similar size. Often, one would have to halt and squeeze up next to a hillock or the river in order for the other to pass by.

All the snorting and baying of animals, the dust, dogs barking, bullwhackers shouting and cracking whips – it was orderly chaos, and Adkin had a lot of respect for the wagon masters that orchestrated it all.

The hand off of the YR&R wagons went smooth, with Dusty, Fransisco and Adkin staying at headquarters, which they now called "our Bent's place." Ryan, Ray Dee, Uribe, Pete and Don Diego would continue to Santa Fe. Pete would be proudly handling a Concord.

Adkin prayed most the night. Maybe it is something being English, he said to himself about his worrying.

It would take his crew maybe four weeks to return with the money, gold and silver, and Adkin had decided to deliver a Concord to the station they had established at Walsenburg, southwest of La Junta, and that coach would run to Fort Garland.

Adkin was definitely going to go see his old friend Kit Carson.

•••

When Adkin approached the commander at Fort Lyons to seek a possible escort through southern Colorado, luck – or perfect timing – was on his side. He was told a company, or 200 troops, was being transferred to the 7th Calvary in Fort Kearney. One hundred from Fort Lyons and 100 from Fort Union.

They would be joining up at La Junta in three days. Adkin and Fransisco were welcome to travel with them as there were settlers going along, too. At least they would have an escort to La Junta.

Things got tense late on the first day out of Bent's Fort when about 100 Indians, mostly Cheyenne, stopped the caravan just past the Purgatoire River mouth.

Adkin happened to be close to the front and overheard some of the dialogue between an apparent Cheyenne Chief and an Army Scout. He made out some words, which surprised him. He found out later their language was an Algonquian language, with similarities to other tribes on the plains.

A Lieutenant reported back to a Captain, who sent the Lieutenant back to fetch several wagons.

They rolled up and soldiers started unloading bags of sugar, tobacco, quarters of salted beeves wrapped in cheesecloth and other supplies. The caravan sat there for nearly an hour while the Indians feasted and had their fill of nearly everything that had been laid out. They did carry away the flour and sugar bags with them.

Adkin figured there were probably about a hundred men who had cramps in their hands, as everybody in the caravan had a finger on some type of firearm the whole time.

Adkin learned after they got back to rolling along the Indians were from the Dakotas and heading south to look for buffalo and claimed they were starving.

"I promise you they were looking for more than food until they saw how many calvary was here," a young soldier told Adkin later.

When they arrived at La Junta, the army escort was on to Pueblo, and Adkin was now on his own to Walsenburg. The town was southwest of La Junta some 60 miles or so and the trail wasn't as sound as the Santa Fe Trail, nor as often used.

They stopped at Ablo Velasquez's station and asked him for advice to get to Walsenburg. Ablo was quick to offer four well-armed scouts to travel with them, for a small fee.

Though they had to spend one night on the lonely trail, no problems arose.

Once in Walsenburg. Fransisco introduced Adkin to Louis Petersen, their new station manager and who was excited to receive the new Concord.

Adkin relayed his plans to travel west to Fort Garland to see his friend, Commander Kit Carson. Petersen was impressed Adkin knew Carson, and in his Norwegian accent, kept saying, "Golly Gee. Golly Gee."

He told Adkin and Fransisco, if they could spend the night, he would have a few passengers for the first trip to Fort Garland.

"I've got passengers who have been waiting to make this trip for a couple of weeks, now," Petersen said.

They agreed to wait a night, and the next morning, about 9, Petersen had the coach ready – he was driving, had a shotgun rider on the bench with him and two men who actually looked like Comancheros on horseback and fully armed with rifles and pistols and long-bladed knives – plus the four guards Ablo had provided. Four men, passengers, were in the coach and three saddled horses were tied off the back of the coach.

Adkin thought his motley cortege looked more like marauders than businessmen. He smiled at the thought.

"We're ready if you are, Mister Yates," Petersen shouted.

Adkin was wondering – no worrying – if they would run into any trouble on this trail. It wasn't heavily used like the Santa Fe Trail, and he had never passed this way before. It was all new to him since they turned off at La Junta.

Fransisco had told him there were only two places that might provide cover for bandits waiting to ambush travellers. He assured him he would ride ahead at those places and check them out. One was known as La Veta Pass, as they were entering the upper Sangre de Cristo Range.

Petersen had told Adkin it was only 50 miles to Fort Garland, but he had a ranch house to spend the night and feed and rest the horses. Petersen had already made the arrangements once he had committed to the deal with Ryan the month earlier.

When they arrived at Fort Garland, Adkin announced his intentions.

"My name is Adkin Yates, and I wish to visit with General Carson," he shouted.

"And I am Louie Petersen with our first stagecoach passengers on the Barlow & Sanderson Line," Petersen added.

The gate swung open and they rode into the parade grounds. Adkin thought the buildings in the fort looked a little old, but he had been told it was established in 1858.

As Adkin, Dusty and Fransisco tied off their horses at the rail of the office, the door opened and loud boot sounds stomped out on the porch.

"Well, I'll be. If it isn't young Adkin Yates of England," Carson said.

"General …"

"Dammit man, you know I hate that. You better call me Kit or Carson or I'll have you thrown off these grounds," Carson said, laughing as he reached for Adkin's hand and shook it with both hands. Adkin put his other hand on Carson's shoulder and patted it strongly.

"Come on in here Yates, let me get a good look at you," Carson said as he motioned to the open office. Adkin introduced Dusty, Fransisco and Petersen who had affixed himself to Adkin's side after he jumped off the Concord and let his passengers out.

"Nice to meet you gentlemen," Carson said, nodding his head slightly. He said something to Dusty and Fransisco in Ute, and they smiled broadly. Adkin would find out later Carson had told them, "You ride with good man."

'Son, If I didn't know you are an English gentleman, I'd think you were a big, bruising mountain man," Carson said with chuckle.

"There is something out here in the West that does things to you, if you know what I mean, Kit," Adkin said.

"Hell man, don't I know it," Carson said, still laughing. "Been at it since I ran away from home at 15."

Carson had a servant bring in coffee and tea. He made a point to the servant to make "some of that tea that's from India."

"It's not from England, Yates, but I know you'll like it," Carson said.

They visited for about an hour, and Petersen got his new business into the conversation, which Carson congratulated him on, and praised him for teaming up with Barlow & Sanderson.

Carson also asked about J.L., and Adkin caught him up on J.L.'s movements and plans.

"He actually passed through Walsenburg about a month or so ago, but he didn't know you were here," Adkin said. "He, Tyler Ryan and Fransisco here were establishing stagecoach stations from here to Denver and out into the silver mines.

"Well, actually, we – my wife, Josefa, and the children, just moved here in early June," Carson said. "I wanted to expand my cattle business and found some great grazing south of here. Somehow, the Army thought I should also be the Commander of Fort Garland."

Carson finally said he had some papers he needed to read, and invited everyone to a home-cooked meal that evening. He had a soldier show them to the barracks and stabled their animals.

Petersen immediately went throughout and outside the fort, making his contacts for passenger service back to Walsenburg.

"And you can ride the newest Concord Coach all the way to Denver or to Santa Fe, New Mexico," he would shout his spiel.

That evening, they all met Carson's wife, Josefa.

"Gentlemen, this is my dear wife, Maria Josefa Jaramillo," Carson said proudly. "Most call her Josefa, but I call her Chipeta, which means little singing bird."

She bowed her head slightly, and said," Pleased to make your acquaintance, now I must help the servants with our supper."

She was a beautiful young woman with long black hair and dark eyes. It was obvious she was with child. Adkin thought she may be about five or six months pregnant.

Her Mexican accent and soft-spoken manners seemed the opposite of a gruff, uneducated man like Carson – who had trekked all over the Wild West fighting Indians and helping Indians for 40 years.

They had a big meal of beef steaks, beans and cornbread. Josefa had also served flour tortillas and showed then how to fill them with beans and roll them up to eat.

They learned Carson was totally dedicated to his "Chipeta" and their children. Josefa and Carson had five children together, but they had also taken in three orphaned Indian children through the years and had also adopted a Navajo boy. Only four of the youngest were living with them now.

"We're expecting another child in January," Carson said with a big grin.

After supper, Carson asked the men if sitting outside by the camp fire ring would be okay with them. He had a servant place chairs around the ring, keeping them upwind, as a light breeze was out of the southwest.

"I feel comfortable sitting by the evenin' fire when the weather is like this," Carson said. "Fall can be really nice at times."

Carson lit a cigar and two servants had whisky and glasses on trays for whoever wanted a drink. Carson didn't care for alcohol of any kind. Adkin refused a drink as well.

Carson asked the others if they knew the story behind Adkin's necklace? All did except Petersen.

"That was quite an incident," Carson said. "For a moment it looked like 3,000 Indians were going to kill every white man within 100 miles – and we'd be at the top of the list, right Yates?"

"Well, that was one time where youthful ignorance paid off," Adkin said. "I just did what was instinct."

"That kind of instinct is what keep men alive out here in this land, son," Carson said and then sat back looking to the stars.

Adkin thought Carson was looking tired or maybe it was his age, 56 or 57. He didn't look as vital and full of vigor as he did the year before at the Little Arkansas Treaty. Adkin thought he looked pale, but he didn't think of it much, maybe it was just the shine of the fire on Carson's face.

Adkin could imagine Carson had sat around camp fires for most of his wandering life. It was apparent Carson enjoyed it immensely.

At about 9, Josefa came out and bid goodnight to the men and disappeared into their home.

"She's the best thing that ever happened to me," Carson said wistfully. "I don't know what I'd do without her."

They discussed businesss and Adkin told Carson about their freighting business that was now underway.

"My guess is J.L. Sanderson is the best thing you ever ran into, huh Yates?" Carson asked with a smile.

"Amen," Adkin said, the glow of the fire exposing his smile, too.

Several times, they all sat there just staring into the flickering flames, nobody would say a word, just enjoying the cool Fall breeze with the wonderful fragrant smell of sage brush in the air.

Adkin felt a kindred spirit with Carson. They both shared that love of the West and the freedom it represented. He figured all sitting there felt the same way.

...

The next morning, Carson bid his farewells to the men and whispered into Adkin's ear, "Don't let any Comancheros or Injuns steal your wagons and goods. When in doubt, kill if you have to."

In later years, Adkin fully understood those words of wisdom, for Kit Carson had to kill whenever any Indians tried to stop him in his endeavors; whether trapping, guiding or with the Army, or leading the calvary into the Llano Estacado. And it proved to be a dichotomy for Carson who loved many Indians as well and loved them as peoples.

The return trip proved profitable for Petersen as he rounded up five paying passengers from the little village that was building up around the fort. One was an Army Lieutenant who was on a special leave and was going to help his mother and family after his father's death back in Indiana.

Adkin made it back to La Junta without any depredations by bandits or Indians. His worries were still centered around the 40 wagons headed to Santa Fe and the Aguirre brothers.

He stopped at the Western Union office in La Junta to see if any messages were being held there for him, but there was nothing. Hopefully, that was good news he thought to himself.

His visit with Carson was more memorable than he thought once he got back home. It was starting to dawn on him that Carson truly was the American frontiersman, trapper, soldier and guide – and one of the great heroes of the West. A living legend.

And, Kit was also a true friend. Adkin felt truly honored.

...

A day later, Adkin and his crew rode into sight of their headquarters and Fort Lyons – or what remained of Fort Lyons. They couldn't believe their eyes. Fort Lyons was nearly erased from the earth; walls torn down, debris stacked against what parts of buildings were remaining, some soldiers and people milling about picking up salvageable items and throwing them into wagons.

They spurred their mounts and rode up to some soldiers working through the rubbish.

"What in the world happened?" Adkin asked.

"Night before, the Arkansas turned into a killer," one man said. "It flooded out its banks like nobody's ever seen before.

"Y'all's place is okay. Lucky you built it on that butte up there," he added.

Adkin had heard tales about how these plains rivers could flood beyond belief. Now he knew why. He had seen great waters on the upper Cimarron on the Dry Route at Point of Rocks, but it was nothing like this.

The flooding had totally destroyed Fort Lyons. It had also killed two soldiers who were trying to save animals and two Indians who were camped outside the fort's walls.

"It came at us in the middle of the night," the soldier continued. "We never had a chance. Bet we've lost 100 horses and more other animals. Most of the folks are down at Bent' Fort."

Adkin could see Bent's Fort about a half a mile further east, and it looked fine.

"Bent's is okay, too," the soldier said. "When this fort was built as Fort Wise, old timers said it was too close to the river. They were right."

The crew rode up the butte a few hundred yards to their headquarters, and they could see the upper water line of the flood waters. They had reached within 50 feet of the front of their office and fence line for the stock yard.

"Ray Dee is going to be pleased he was out-voted on where to build our headquarters," Adkin thought to himself. Everything at their place was fine, but several local Indians were at the office pleading with their foreman, Mac MacIntosh.

Mac told Adkin they were needing food.

"Give them whatever you can Mac, including blankets," Adkin ordered. "We can re-supply from Bent's place or Fort Aubrey if we need to make a quick run."

As Adkin surveyed the scene from their front porch, he could see how the valley had changed., A grove of cypress below their place was gone, only a few stubs of stumps, remained. All the rest had been totally uprooted and swept away in the raging water.

He was thinking, "Where did all that water go? It's only been about 30 hours."

It would take a year, but the Army would re-build Fort Lyons 18 miles west of the old fort location – and a whole mile north of the Arkansas River.

Adkin and his crew were happy to stay put, only about three-quarters of a mile from Bent's Fort, which Adkin considered his western home anyway.

•••

About a week later, on Sept 16, 1866, Adkin received a telegram from Ryan and his crew that would change their lives forever. When Adkin finished reading the message, his knees felt weak and he nearly collapsed.

To Adkin Yates. Stop.

Arrived yesterday, no problems. Stop.

Aguirre brothers estimate total sales valued over $42,000. Stop.

Will be departing Sep. 18. Stop.

By 2-1 vote, decided to spend $10,000 on hides, skins, furs – and bundles of sheared wool – for return loads. Stop.

Congratulation partner. Stop.

Adkin slowly stumbled to his cot in the barracks and laid down. He kept reading the telegram over and over, as if his eyes had been playing tricks with his head.

Adkin began doing the math in his mind: More than $42,000. The loan was $29,400. The interest was $588. Rentals for men and animals were $150 per wagon ... or $6,000.

He jumped up and went into the office to grab a pen and paper. All that would total $35,988 owed to Barlow & Sanderson. Ryan and Ray Dee decided to invest $10,000 of the $42,000. That would leave $32,000 plus, but they should at least double that $10,000 in sales back in Westport.

So, if they pay Sanderson the $32,000 and earn $20,000 in fur sales, subtract $3,988 to finish off loan, that would leave total profit of a little more than $6,000 – and they would own 40 Murphy wagons outright.

Adkin had to lay the pen down, as his hands were shaking.

"Lord, thank you for your blessings," he said softly, remembering his father. "I will keep you close to my heart at all times."

Fransisco and Dusty walked into the office just as Adkin suddenly jumped straight out of his chair into the air and yelled, "We're going to be bloody rich."

When he turned and saw the faces on his crew, he felt a little embarrassed and said, "Sorry men, I just received very delightful news from Ryan and his crew."

"Great Boss," Dusty said smiling.

"When can we expect them back at headquarters?" Fransisco asked in his perfect English.

"About 15 or 16 days," Adkin answered.

Then it hit him: What if they get attacked and robbed – or killed – over the money?

"Blimey," he said to himself. "I've got to get over this worrying. It must be the money thing because I've not worried over much of anything since coming to the West."

That was it, he figured. He hadn't been in debt for even a pound, or a dollar, since leaving England. Debt is what he has no experience with. He didn't like it and made a vow that after one more load of trade goods, he would never borrow money again – if at all possible – he swore to himself.

"Let's get out in the stables, there's more work to finish up, and we have to prepare the forge area of the smitty's shop," Adkin said. "I've got iron ingots coming in next week from Santa Fe, and we'll get to work building some anvils."

Dusty and Fransisco looked at each other and frowned.

"It's not that bad," Adkin said, chuckling. "I'll show you how to do several things in blacksmithing if you want to learn."

"Sure Boss," Dusty said, now smiling with Fransisco.

•••

After Ryan and the crew arrived at Our Bent's, Adkin discovered the wagon train Ryan's men were travelling with were attacked a few days out of Uncle Wootton's place by a band of Indians, they thought they were Cheyenne or Arapahoe, but they were after a small herd of horses one of the freighters had purchased in Santa Fe. They lost about six or seven horses but no one was hurt or killed.

"Created quite a stir," Ray Dee said, laughing. "Especially since my butt was sitting above one of those lock-boxes full of gold and silver."

After all the math was finished – the sales total hit $43,230, YR&R would profit $7,242 if they receive $20,000 for their furs and skins. That would take time, but they notified Sanderson they were sending $30,000 to him on the next large, military-escorted Caravan. And they would pay off the loan totally with sales of their furs and skins.

Sanderson sent back word he'd glady loan them another $20,000 for more loads for a return trip. They agreed, but to use some of the Westport profits to reduce that $20,000 amount on the loan for the trade goods.

They agreed to also hold their wagons back long enough for Adkin to inspect and repair any that needed work. Long and Holmes volunteered, with Sanderson's approval, to stay with the wagons and then join the next caravan that was moving eastward.

It only took three days for Adkin to give his okay on the wagons; only two needed iron work on the axles and one had a wheel that he had to iron. Of course, all were greased and minor repairs made, like replacing pins on wagon tongues and hitches. They were like new.

They all realized these Murphy wagons were everything people were saying – tough and reliable.

Adkin was also impressed with the teams of oxen Sanderson had purchased. Long and Holmes said they were much more dependable than mules, easier to bed at night, but every now and then, they had to put leather booties on them to protect their hooves.

"We make fun of them plodders," Long said. "But they're the best animals God ever made to haul goods on the Santa Fe Trail."

Soon afterward, Long and Holmes joined another wagon train and departed with the 40 YR&R wagons. They both led the teams out with huge smiles as if they belonged to them alone.

About three weeks later, Sanderson sent them the final figures, and wanted their approval:

Payment on loan – $30,000

Fur sales – $24,500

Less final payment on first loan with rentals and interests – less $6,000 equals $18,500 in profits.

The YR&R crew decided to only spend that $18,500 on return trade goods – with no further loans for now. And they had $13,230 in reserves in the Bent's Fort vault.

Sanderson agreed, and wished them further success. He was also ordering more Concords. He would inform them of how many and when to expect them later.

•••

Sanderson sent word their 40 wagons were ready for a return trip, sought their input on proposed goods, which more and more iron tools were the number one requests, especially knives and band steel that arrowheads could be made from. But all iron tools were in demand. The classic and fancy cloths – and rolls of calico – were still viable goods as well.

Sanderson said he would have the loads together by the first of November. Weather would be the main concern, as there were plenty of people still wanting to put together wagon trains. The telegraph gave them a sense of security.

The YR&R crew was ecstatic about business and had delivered three Concords throughout Colorado, including Denver, which was growing like a prairie wildfire. The mines kept popping up or bigger and thicker veins of ores were being discovered in existing mines. They knew Colorado would need more Concords in the near future.

The blacksmith shop was always busy if Adkin was home. He showed many of the hands how to do basic smithing, but only Dusty seemed to be genuinely interested, and a good learner.

Adkin had sent an anvil to Rath's Ranch, with instructions for Chris Rath to put young Irl Gaut on the payroll as soon as he could quit his old job, as Gaut and Adkin had signed the partnership papers before Adkin departed Fort Dodge.

Within two more weeks, Adkin had made four more anvils, with plans to open more smitty shops throughout the stage line stops.

During most of September and October, the crew was disbursed delivering three more Concords throughout Colorado – two to the new Denver office.

Adkin had also set up three more blacksmith shops in southern Colorado, while he and Ryan made a gruelling jaunt to visit several mining towns. They were right in the heart of the Rocky Mountains. Adkin never would have believed the sights if he had not seen them himself.

Colorado was very impressive to Adkin and Ryan and proved the company's future was unlimited.

•••

Sanderson notified YR&R that its 40 wagons were leaving Westport by rail on October 30, 1866, and they should reach Bent's Fort office in four weeks or less.

Sanderson notified them the Union Pacific Eastern Division (UPED) Railroad had reached Junction City in June 1866. Caravans were now departing Junction City west along the Butterfield Overland Dispatch route to Fort Ellsworth; then southwest on a connecting road to Fort Zarah; where they resumed the main Santa Fe Trail.

Sanderson said very little wagon traffic was remaining east of Fort Zarah, but the railroad had reduced the actual wagon route to 699 miles. Freight was going to be in Santa Fe, New Mexico, quicker than ever.

The news created a buzz through headquarters as the YR&R crew realized their true fortunes would depend on this trip. It was all their own money invested in goods and wagons, and now their wagons were having less wear and tear.

In the meantime, several discussion were had about trying to consider stagecoach service on the Cimarron Route of the Santa Fe Trail, but the odds of running into water problems was too severe and dangerous. However, stagecoach route from Hays and Denver up to the Oregon trail were more attractive to Sanderson.

He also wanted to investigate a possible route all the way to California – other than the well-known California Trail. He had made the argument that plenty of wagons had used trails to get to the gold fields in the 1849 gold rush. Some had to travel the southern routes he insisted.

Adkin had talked with Ryan and Ray Dee about possibly putting a plan together to travel to California in early Spring of 1867.

•••

By mid-November, YR&R's profits netted the three partners nearly $45,000 – $44,876 to be exact after removing rental costs of teams and teamsters. When that money would reach Bent's Fort and placed in their account, they would have $58,107. YR&R was on the right path.

The decision was made by Adkin, Ryan and Rinehart the wagons, after additional repairs on their way back to Westport in December, they would sell them once they got back to Santa Fe.

They also took it upon themselves – with full approval of Sanderson – to contact Murphy in St. Louis and ordered 60 more wagons at $220 each. They notified Murphy they would wire the money from a Kansas City bank – all of it at $13,200 – and they were to be delivered in care of Barlow & Sanderson in the Westport branch office.

They did this as the old wagons reached Westport in early January before they were loaded with $25,000 worth of goods for the 40 wagons' final trip to Santa Fe.

Adkin had to cancel his trip to California, which most had realized would be difficult in January because of winter storms throughout the Rockies, but he and the crew received good news from Sanderson in February of 1867.

He said rumors in Washington were that Congress was going to establish an Indian Peace Commission because General William T. Sherman, commander of the Military Division of the Missouri, was wanting a new policy enacted to resolve the Indian problems in the west.

Sanderson said he had heard of several names that might be placed on this commission if it happens: Major General William S. Harney, who was now retired; Brigadier General Alfred H. Terry, commander of the Military Department of Dakotas; and Colonel Samuel F. Tappan, formerly of the First Colorado Volunteer Cavalry.

He said there might be another large peace treaty in an effort to finally put a stop to the constant raids on wagon trains, pioneers' homesteads and Army forts. If that happens, the Army will need large numbers of wagons and teams to haul goods to a treaty site.

He said he would keep them apprised of the situation as he found out more. The YR&R crew were happy to hear it because their new 60 Murphy wagons might be in their possession in time to haul goods for the Army.

Adkin was hoping he would get to see his friend General Harney again. He and Ryan both agreed Harney was one of a kind; a huge barrel-chested man who exuded power, respect – and fear.

"And can he cuss up a storm," Ryan said.

"He is intimidating, I give you that," Adkin responded.

Adkin and Ryan finally planned their westward trip, and took off in late February.

After three months, they returned to Colorado with expansion proposals for Sanderson to establish stagecoach service from Central Kansas to the Pacific Ocean.

It wasn't a southern route Sanderson had hoped for, but the men discovered all the travel was mostly to the Sutter's Mill area where gold was discovered in

1848. Numerous other gold mines were found, but most all were even further north of Sutter's Mill. That's where coach service could make the money.

Sanderson took over immediately, as was his style, and started with more orders of Concords, gathering teams of horses, hiring men. The UPED Railroad had announced it would be providing service to Fort Harker (near Fort Ellsworth) by June or July 1867, and Barlow and Sanderson was needing new property.

The company now had more than 200 employees and thousands of animals and all the tack those animals required to haul the hundreds of wagons and coaches it owned.

Sanderson told Adkin and the western crew he had found a spot in Junction City where they could move the official headquarters from Leavenworth to Junction City in the next few months.

Again, Sanderson's vision would pay off handsomely. By the end of 1867, the eastern newspapers were reporting, "The two entrepreneurs had established a route from Missouri to California over the Santa Fe Trail."

They also changed the name of the company to the Barlow and Sanderson Company, making it shorter but wealthier.

•••

While Adkin and Ryan were in California, the 60 large-capacity Murphys were delivered to the Westport warehouse March 15. Agreements had been made prior to the California trip to purchase more goods and make another Santa Fe run immediately upon delivery of the wagons – if Sanderson had no news of a peace treaty being planned.

As it was, Sanderson and Barlow had no more news other than Congress was still trying to formulate this new Indian Peace Commission. So, Sanderson's people oversaw purchasing and loading of goods for 60 wagons and they had departed Westport via rail on April 1, 1867. They had also painted the bright yellow YR&R on the sides of the wagons.

With the rail line reducing actual wagon train distance and time, Sanderson was saying the round trip to Santa Fe and back could be in the range of only 70 to 80 days.

•••

As the YR&R's new wagons made their maiden voyage to Santa Fe and back, Sanderson sent word the YR&R Freight Co. had netted $67,800. It could have been greater, but Barlow & Sanderson rental costs rose to $210 per wagon with the additional rail costs now included.

UPED then announced rail service would be extended to Hays City (near Fort Hays) in October of 1867. This would reduce the actual mileage wagons had to roll to 568 miles to Santa Fe, New Mexico. It was 75 miles (the feeder route) from Hays to Fort Dodge and 493 miles to Santa Fe on the actual Trail.

This practically ended most long distance Santa Fe Trail traffic east of Fort Dodge.

Events and activities were moving fast for everyone working for Barlow and Sanderson Co., as it was for the YR&R people as well. Both companies were expanding and making money.

•••

Near the end of July, Sanderson sent word that on July 20, 1867, Congress established the Indian Peace Commission to negotiate peace with Plains Indian tribes who were warring with the United States. Rumors were the commission was trying to set up a treaty sometime in August. He would keep them informed.

In the meantime, another shipment of goods were sent to Santa Fe by YR&R. With less wear and tear on their Murphys, Adkin and his partners were sure the wagons could make three or four round trips before having to sell them. That first 40 sold for more than twice what they cost, too.

When Sanderson told them about a possible peace treaty in late August or September, the YR&R crew decided to order 20 more wagons in early August and after delivery, to hold them just for that trip.

Sanderson had assured them Barlow and Sanderson's reputation would get them special treatment in providing wagons, coaches and ambulances for the treaty, and he would contract all of YR&R's wagons. And, of course, provide teamsters and animals – for a fee.

•••

In late July, Adkin and Ryan travelled to Rath's Ranch House to help Chris and their blacksmith partner, Irl Gaut, expand their smitty's shop. Business was so good, especially as rail traffic now came down from Hays City to Fort Dodge, they were needing two smittys and two anvils. Adkin had already shipped an anvil to Fort Dodge with a wagon freighter.

Adkin and Gaut hitched up a wagon team and went to Fort Dodge to pick up the anvil. While at the fort, a tall lanky man dressed like a banker walked up to them.

"You still eatin' dust on the Santa Fe Trail Yates?" a voice boomed.

Adkin turned around and saw his old friend.

"How are you Samuel Oscar Phillips?" Adkin asked as they embraced. "I see there is no uniform."

"I told you I was getting out so I could get married," Phillips said, grinning. "I got married January 22 in Hocking County, Ohio, and now we're here.

"Don't know if you heard, but the Army is preparing to rebuild Fort Dodge – with stone and eastern lumber – modern materials," he added laughing.

"Yes, Chris Rath told me that," Adkin said. "Forgive me Sam, this is Irl Gaut, he's a partner of ours who is a smitty out at Rath's Ranch House. Business is so good, we're hiring another blacksmith and expanding Gaut's shop."

"We know each other Mister Yates," Gaut interrupted.

"We sure do," Phillips said. "I was stationed here when he was hired as an Army contract smitty. Don't you remember? I suggested him."

"Why yes, come to think of it, I do," Adkin said. "Guess there's been so much going on, I can't keep up with everything that's going on in my own life."

"Sounds like you need to slow down and get yourself a good woman," Phillips said, smiling.

"Speaking of a good woman, where is your new wife?" Adkin asked.

"Mary Catherine is in the women's quarters right now. If you get time, I sure would like you to meet her," Phillips said. "I've told her a lot about you."

"Well, Tyler Ryan is with me, and if he's welcome, too, we could come in this evening for supper," Adkin said. "I know he'd like to see you and meet your new wife."

"That would be great," Phillips said. "And you're welcome, too, Gaut."

"Thanks, but I have a lot of work to do this evening," Gaut said. "Some other time, though. It's good to have you back in the area again, Captain … er I mean Mister Phillips."

"By the way, Sam, what are you doing here at Fort Dodge?" Adkin asked.

"I'm now a civilian construction contractor," Phillips said. "I agreed to come back and help oversee the reconstruction of the new fort. They had asked if I was interested before I resigned in December.

"That's great, Sam," Adkin said, "Glad to see it.

"What time this evening?" Adkin added. "Can't wait to visit and catch up."

Meet us at the officers' quarters at 8, okay?" Phillips said.

"Okay."

•••

Adkin and Ryan met Phillips and his wife for supper in the officer's mess that evening. Mary Catherine was a small dainty woman but Adkin could tell she was full of vinegar, as they say. She was not only spunky, but she had that attitude that she and Sam could do anything they wanted, and they would be successful.

When Adkin asked about Sam's previous plans to possibly move to western Indian Territory, it was Mary Catherine that spoke up.

"We do have family and friends there, but Sam has a wonderful opportunity to help the Army here, and we figure it is God's blessing he gets to assist those who gave him his career in service of his country," she said, smiling like the young woman she was.

"Well put, dear," Phillips said. "Believe it or not, she immediately saw the beauty of the Great Plains as I had tried to explain it."

"There is something out here that is mysterious; invoking fear as well as excitement – all at once," Mary Catherine belted out. "I realize now how Sam had some difficulty in describing it."

"Phillips, you found yourself a true partner," Ryan said. "And that's the most important thing out here."

"Well thank you Mister Ryan," she said.

"Please, Maam, call me Tyler," Ryan said, bowing his head a little to acknowledge this fiery woman.

Phillips indicated he would probably only be helping with the construction process at the new Fort Dodge until September or October, depending on weather.

"Once we, me and the engineer, finalize all the plans – the layouts of buildings, stables, barracks, etcetera – it will mostly be left to the carpenters and stone layers to complete things," Phillips said.

Phillips asked about YR&R Freight Company and how things were going. Adkin and Ryan gladly filled him in on their success thus far. And that they were going to order 20 more wagons in next month in August, hoping to hear a new peace treaty was going to happen in September.

They told Phillips about the new Indian Peace Commission, and that General Harney was a member.

"Ol' man Harney you say?" Phillips said, eyes wide and looking toward Mary Catherine. "Dear, you would love this man. Huge bear of a man – a little salty to put it politely – but robust and demanding respect like no one you've ever seen.

"Adkin, Ryan and I had the distinct pleasure to spend nearly two months with him for the Little Arkansas Treaty back in '65," he continued. "The man demands results and actions. I'd like to see him again.

"Do you think the treaty will be out here in Kansas again?" Phillips asked Adkin and Ryan.

"We're not sure where yet, but it will definitely be out here somewhere," Adin said. "This is where all the attacks are, and down into Texas and the Indian Territories."

He glanced at Mary Catherine and said, "Sorry Maam, don't mean to alarm you."

"That's okay. I'm well aware of the possibilities of Indian depredations out here," Mary Catherine said. "Sam and I can take care of ourselves."

What a woman, Adkin thought. Maybe naive, but refreshing and determined.

"General Sherman wants to protect the railroads' progress by any means – through peace or annihilation," Ryan added.

"Well, if you need another teamster and don't mind my wife travelling with us, give us a call – if I'm finished here at Fort Dodge – and I'll work for peanuts to see Harney and the sights of another Indian pow wow."

"It's a deal," Ryan said, and Adkin agreeing with a nod.

...

Adkin and Ryan returned to their place near Bent's Fort and were happily appraised that their latest YR&R trip netted them around $50,000 dollars, and that one wagon had broken an axle and was at Watrous being repaired so it could be sent back to Santa Fe to the Aguirres' place until the next YR&R trip.

In mid August, Sanderson sent word the Peace Commission met in St. Louis on August 6, 1867, and elected Nathaniel G. Taylor, Commissioner of Indian Affairs, as its president. Rumor is still that a peace treaty will meet sometime in September.

Adkin sent Sanderson a message to keep all their 59 wagons – and the 20 news ones due any day from Murphy – at Barlow and Sanderson's new Junction City headquarters just for the peace treaty, even if it meant waiting a couple of months.

Though the western crew stayed busy handling the growth of Colorado stagecoach business, everyone was awaiting news from the Indian Peace Commission.

Finally, in the first week of September, the commission announced a treaty about three weeks hence. Sanderson said everyone should proceed to make plans, which meant Adkin, Ryan and Ray Dee were to head to Fort Larned, where the Army was proclaiming would be the treaty site.

Sanderson confirmed all YR&R wagons had been accepted as freight haulers, as well as numerous coaches and ambulances from Barlow and Sanderson. Those wagons would depart from Junction City with the YR&R wagons, all to be loaded with supplies ordered by the U.S. Army. There were two other freighting companies involved as well.

Within five days, Sanderson sent telegrams to Fort Aubrey and Fort Dodge instructing the YR&R crew the treaty had been postponed and to await further instructions. Adkin and his men got the news when they arrived at Fort Dodge. They notified Sanderson where they were and waited.

And waited.

And waited.

They did get to visit with Sam and Mary Catherine again, though. Sam was still tied up with the reconstruction blueprints, so his travelling to the Peace Treaty was out for now.

News finally came that the Indian Peace Commission was going to gather at Fort Leavenworth the first few days of October and then travel by rail to Fort

Harker on the Smokey Hills River. Correspondents from nine newspapers were travelling with the commission to record the event, as well as other diplomats and special agents.

Sanderson confirmed all of the wagons had been filled with goods for the trip at three different sites, including all 79 of YR&R's wagons at Junction City.

The commission was joined there by an escort of 500 troops in dress uniform of the 7th U.S. Cavalry Regiment and Battery B of the 4th artillery, armed with two Gatling guns. They were under the command of Major Joel H. Elliott And, they were headed to Fort Larned.

Sanderson asked Adkin and his men to depart immediately for Fort Larned, and they did. They passed a 50-wagon caravan owned by the Army with an officer named Simpson as its train master. They were destined to Fort Larned from Fort Harker, where they had filled their wagons with gifts and ammunition, including Gatling Guns, Adkin would later find out at the treaty site.

Adkin and his crew arrived at Fort Larned, with the military train on their heels, on October 9, and hundreds of Indians were already camped around the fort.

The fort commander allowed Adkin and his men to stay within the fort. The commander told them several well-known chiefs were already there, including Little Raven of the Arapaho, Black Kettle of the Cheyenne and Satanta and Old Chief Satank of the Kiowa.

Adkin and Ryan looked at each other when Satanta's name was mentioned.

"Your old friend, yes?" Ray Dee asked.

"Well, don't know if friend is the right word," Ryan answered. "But we've met him and are wearing his gifts."

When Adkin asked the Commander if he knew where Satanta was camped, all he got was a blank stare and "No" for an answer.

The crew decided against just riding around the camps and asking wild Indians where Satanta was. They might be mistaken for assassins or troublemakers.

Just as Adkin and his men were starting to leave, a soldiers entered the doorway and announced that Jesse Chisholm wanted to speak with the Commander.

Adkin and Ryan were amazed to see the tall, white-haired Jesse walk through the door with giant strides to the Commander's desk.

"Mister Chisholm, I'd like you to meet representatives of Barlow and Sanderson Company ..."

"I know these men, Commander," Chisholm interjected. "How are you men – it's Yates and Ryan, isn't it?"

"Yes sir, Mister Chisholm," Adkin said, reaching out to shake Jesse's hand, and Ryan following suit.

"What brings you to Fort Larned" Chisholm asked.

"We're helping with freight wagons for the treaty here at Fort Larned." Ryan said.

"Great. I'm representing the Indians that are here, but I'm not sure this is going to happen – not here anyway," Chisholm said, turning to the fort Commander. "The chiefs are coming to see General Harney as soon as he arrives.

"They want to move the treaty site down to a traditional Kiowa spiritual site where Elm Creek empties into Medicine Lodge Creek."

Chisholm went on to explain that when working out the conditions to stage the Peace Treaty negotiations, Jesse had warned General Harney that a show of force on the part of the U.S. would be unacceptable to the Indians.

When confronted about producing a multitude of troops at the negotiations, Harney heartily explained to Chisholm that the troops were necessary because of the large numbers of news media, government personnel, foreign dignitaries and general spectators.

Harney had eventually offered to withdraw the troops if the Indians were afraid to continue the conference. Chisholm told the commander he would have a final talk with Harney when he arrived at Fort Larned,

•••

On the morning of October 11, the commission arrived with soldiers, a 2-mile long caravan of wagons of all kinds and with much pomp and circumstance. As soon as the commissioners arrived at the fort's office, the Commander told them several chiefs wanted to talk with them right away.

Adkin and his men were off to the side of all the officers and correspondents that hovered around the entrance to the office. They saw Harney, but he didn't notice them.

Within about 10 minutes, soldiers were escorting several chiefs into the office, the feathers on their war bonnets waving in a slight breeze above and behind their heads. They didn't see Satanta, but the crowd was so thick, he might have passed unseen. They did see a smiling Chisholm escorting the chiefs.

People were mumbling and quizzing each other about what was happening. One man said, he had heard the Indians were calling off the treaty. Another said they wanted to move the treaty. Adkin and his crew looked at each other.

"Amazing how word gets out like that," Adkin said.

They knew the man was correct – Chisholm had told them the day before. As the chiefs and Chisholm walked out and were escorted to the gate, Commission President Nathaniel G. Taylor, Commissioner of Indian Affairs, yelled out on the porch.

"Attention. Attention, folks," Taylor yelled in a boisterous voice. "We have agreed with a request of our red brethren to conduct these treaty negotiations at a traditional Indian ceremonial site on Medicine Lodge Creek. It's approximately 70 miles south of here.

"Negotiations will begin once we have established our camps there," he added. "We appreciate your patience and understanding."

With that, everybody started for their wagons, ambulances and horses. Fortunately, most of all the teamsters and drovers were still mounted and ready to roll.

Adkin, Ryan and Ray Dee headed for their horses and pack mules at the fort's stables. In three days, they would be where Medicine Lodge Creek joined Elm Creek.

They found their wagons, seeing the large yellow YR&R letters on them from a distance. But Ray Dee didn't recognize any of the teamsters who were driving them. They couldn't believe the size of this procession.

It consisted of a wagon train of about 200 wagons, 15 to 20 ambulances and about a dozen coaches. Plus all the troops in dress blues.

"Let's check out the coaches first," Adkin said.

As they approached a coach near the rear of a string of coaches, Adkin yelled at the driver and his shotgun guard, "Can you tell us where we may find General Harney?"

The guard raised his arm pointing forward and yelled, "He's in one of those front ambulances. Probably the very front one."

"Thanks," Adkin said, as they spurred their mounts and hurried forward at a gallop, pulling their fresh steeds behind them.

Adkin repeated his request as they reached the front ambulance. The driver, pointed behind him and said, "He's right here gentlemen.

"General Harney, these men are looking for you," he yelled back over his shoulder.

Harney's white-haired head with a big white beard popped out the side window and looked at the horseback men walking alongside his ambulance.

"What the hell do you men want?" he barked, apparently in his usual bad mood.

"General Harney, My name is Adkin Yates," Adkin said. "You may not remember me, but I was with you …"

"Hell yes, Yates. I remember you son. The Englishmen that helped us all keep our scalps at the Little Arkansas," Harney bellowed. "And that fellow there was with you if I remember right."

"Yes sir. Tyler Ryan here helped me considerably in that incident," Adkin said, as Ryan tipped the brim of his hat to Harney.

"I've got company with me, but when we camp tonight, come by and visit with me," Harney said.

"We'd be honored, sir," Adkin said as Harney waved and dropped the window sash back down.

•••

That evening, one large white canopy was erected near the commissioners' tents, and chairs were set up around a cook fire. Adkin, Ryan and Ray Dee made their way over and ask an aide to see General Harney. They were invited to have a seat as the aide scuttled off to find the General.

In short order, Harney and another man were walking toward them as they approached, Adkin and Ryan recognized General Sanborn was with Harney. They all stood and shook hands with the each other; Adkin introducing Rinehart.

"Well what are you young rascals up to?" Harney asked as they all sat down.

"Well General, We're representing Barlow and Sanderson, as well as we three are partners in the Yates, Ryan and Rinehart Freight Company," Adkin explained. "YR&R – you may have seen our wagons."

"Well I'll be damned," Harney chuckled. "J.L. has turned y'all into businessmen, has he?"

"Yes Sir," they all said.

They asked Harney and Sanborn what the commission was expecting.

"I guess Little Arkansas didn't work out as we all thought it would, did it?" Adkin asked.

"No, there were numerous problems after that treaty," Sanborn said. "And it was mainly our fault – not providing the supplies we said we would that winter."

"Those savages got hungry and went straight back to their old tricks – killing and stealing from God knows who," Harney said.

They asked Harney how negotiations with the Indians and Chisholm went?

"When discussing the amount of troops I brought along, Chisholm, the wise diplomat he is, emphasized the word 'fear,' and attributing it to us White men, when interpreting for Chief Ten Bears and Chief Satanta," Harney explained. "The Indians replied, 'Let the troops stay – but out of our way.'"

Harney then told them who was in the commission.

"We've been chosen from both military men and civilians" Harney started. "Generals Terry, Sanborn, Auger and me represent the military while Taylor upholds the interests of the Indian Bureau.

"General William T. Sherman had been assigned by the military to attend, but was called back to Washington by President Johnson. He was replaced by Auger," he continued. "Senator Henderson, of Missouri, represents Congress and Colonel Samuel F. Tappan stands for the nation at large."

Adkin asked if the U.S. was going to make similar offers of reservation lands for peace. Both Generals acknowledged that was the hope.

"But I'll tell you one thing, Sherman isn't going to fart around," Harney said. "The tribes better fall in line or he's going to war with them – all out war.

"I don't know if you know his reputation, but his march from Atlanta to the sea was one for the books. He destroyed everything in his sight. The man's ruthless and determined."

"And he has the full support of many in Washington – including President Grant," Sanborn added. "Sherman's not much on peace."

The Generals also let the freighters know it wasn't a secret concerning Sherman's thoughts. They assured the YR&R crew Sherman was telling everyone from Washington to Santa Fe his intentions.

The Generals said they were expecting at least the five major Plains tribes: The Comanches, Cheyenne, Arapahoe, the Kiowa and Kiowa Apache tribes.

Harney asked about Sanderson and was impressed the man had expanded into Colorado and everywhere down to Santa Fe – even providing coach service to California.

Adkin assured the Generals if they could be of any service whatsoever, to feel free to call upon them.

"By God we will," Harney said. "In fact, why don't you camp up here by us, and wherever we camp the next few weeks. I'll have our men provide you a spot. Would you mind if we provide the three of ya with a tent and cots?"

"No Sir," they all said over each other at once.

•••

As they walked back to gather their belongings and unhobble their horses, they noticed there were only a few tipi fires around the military camp. One of the soldiers told them most of the Indians that followed them out of Fort Larned had kept going.

"We've heard word is out about the Medicine Lodge Creek treaty and most of the Indians are ahead of us," he said. "They don't like the slow speed of a military caravan."

On the third day after departing Fort Larned, the countryside was turning very hilly, with red cedar trees in great abundance. The ravines and gullies were very deep in places with large tracts of red dirt that sloughed off during torrential rains. It was beautiful to Adkin, who had yet to see such land.

"There is a lot to like in Kansas," he thought to himself.

As they started into the Medicine Lodge Creek Valley, tipis started showing up everywhere. The wagon train and ambulances wound it's way to the junction of Elm Creek to establish camp. Men were already estimating more than 3,000 Indians were here.

Off to the east, hundreds of mounted warriors were forming a wedge pointed at the military train. Their faces and horses were painted with war paints and the Indians were in all their war paraphernalia. At once, this wedge started charging the train at full speed.

"What the hell?" Ryan asked looking shocked.

Then, as they neared, one line of warriors turned off to the left, encircling the soldiers. Then more off to the right, then again and again. Soon there were five distinct rings without hubs, and each spinning in the opposite direction as the rings tightened down a breakneck speed toward the soldiers.

All at once, they came to a complete stop at about a hundred yards out and whelped like happy pups, pumping their rifles or bows up and down.

The maneuver impressed most of the military wagon train, yet one could see a green soldier or a tinderfoot teamster here and there blinking and shaking uncontrollably – having never seen the giant spinning wheels-within-wheels formation before.

"I'll betch ya there's 300 lodges over there alone," a freighter said pointing off to the west. "And that's just Comanches – damn."

Once the military train started setting camp, Adkin and his crew rode over to the commissioners' area and a Lieutenant came running over and asked if they were with the Barlow and Sanderson Company. Once they confirmed who they were, he led them to a spot not more than 30 paces from the large canopy tent being set up. More than a dozen officer's tents were being dragged out of wagons just for the commissioners and officers alone.

Down by the creek confluence, soldiers and camp cooks were setting up cook's wagons and a feeding area with tables and stools to feed at least several hundred people. There was another mobile feeding station being set up west of the main camp.

These new cook's wagon, were now being officially called chuckwagons, after a Texas rancher introduced the concept a year earlier. This cattleman, Charles Goodnight, had modified the Studebaker wagon, a durable army-surplus wagon, to suit the needs of his cowboys driving cattle from Texas to sell in New Mexico.

He added a "chuck box" to the back of the wagon with drawers and shelves for storage space and a hinged lid to provide a flat preparation and feeding surface. He also attached a water barrel to the wagon and canvas was hung underneath to carry firewood.

•••

The next morning was October 11, 1867, and the treaty was preparing to begin about mid-morning. As chiefs started coming to the council circle, hundreds of Indians were following them. They finally saw Satanta and Black Horse, his medicine man and Mah-aht-Tay's father, though they didn't see her.

Comanche Chief Ten Bears was there, and so many chiefs they couldn't believe it. As they all assembled, they opened the council with the traditional smoking of the peace pipe. Once that ritual was completed, council members started literally scolding all the plains Indians.

Senator Henderson said these shameful violations of prior peace treaties "makes the hearts of our people very sad."

Other commission members said the government could no longer tolerate making war on Whites. They told the Indians what the Great Father wanted was to give the Indians their own lands away from White settlements and the Indians would be given tools and seeds and taught how to farm.

They said they would provide carpenters to teach them how to build houses and schools. They also said the Great Father would provide $25,000 for clothing and other necessities each year for 30 years.

But the catch was, the Indians had to cease all hostilities, live on the land provided and to promise not to interfere with railroads, White roads, forts or other White development.

Peace commissioner president Taylor then invited the Indians to speak out.

Ironically, Satanta was first to stand. He bent over and picked up a handful of the red sand and started rubbing it all over his hands as if he was sanitizing them. Then he went around the circle and shook hands with all in the council. Then he told the Whites – in his own way – he didn't think this council's offerings were worth much.

"This building homes for us is all nonsense," the translator spoke after Satanta began his speech. "We don't want you to build any for us. We would all die. Look at the Penatekas. Formerly they were powerful, but now they are weak and poor.

'I want all my land even from the Arkansas south to the Red River," he continued. "My country is small enough already. If you build us houses, the land will be smaller.

"Why do you insist on this? What good can come from it?" he added.

Penateka Chief Silver Brooch (Tosawa) spoke next for the Comanches. He had seen what happened to horse Indians living on the reservation. He spoke in a "calm and argumentative voice" condemning the plan outright.

"The Great Father sent a big chief down to us and promised medicines, houses and many other things," Tosawa said during his oration. "A great, great many years have gone by, but those things have never come."

The most stirring address of them all came from Ten Bears, the young Yamparika Chief who battled Kit Carson at Adobe Walls in the Texas Panhandle. He started his speech after donning wire-rimmed spectacles. His Comanche words were translated for the council as he spoke.

He first thanked everyone for being there, that it pleased his heart. He also claimed his people never drew a bow first, that it was the soldiers or whites that started their fights. He spoke of his experiences when his people were attacked by Carson at the headwaters of the Canadian River.

"Two years ago, I came upon this road following the buffalo, that my wives and children might have their cheeks plump and their bodies warm," he said. "But the soldiers fired upon us ... so it was up on the Canadian. Nor have we been made to cry once alone.

"The blue-dressed soldiers and the Utes came out from the night – and for campfires, they lit our lodges," Tosawa continued. "Instead of hunting game, they killed my braves, and the warriors of the tribe cut short their hair for the dead.

"So it was in Texas. They made sorrow in our camps, and we went out like the buffalo bulls when the cows are attacked," he said. "When we found them, we killed them, and their scalps hang in our lodges. The comanches are not weak and blind like the pups of a dog when seven sleeps old. They are strong and far-sighted like grown horses."

He went on to say he didn't like the idea of living on reservations and in houses. He said the things the council offers was not sweet like sugar but bitter like gourds.

"I do not want them," Tosawa continued. "I was born under the prairie, where the wind blew free and there was nothing to break the light of the sun. I was born where there were no enclosures and everything drew a free breath. I want to die there and not within walls.

"I know every stream and wood between the Rio Grande and the Arkansas," Tosawa continued. "I have hunted and lived over the country. I live like my fathers before me and like them, I lived happily."

He related a prior trip to Washington where he claimed the Great Father promised all the Comanche that the land was theirs and no one would interfere with them. He said his people would not give up the buffalo for sheep, and they would not live in houses.

He blamed the Tejanos, or Texans, for taking away a large part of their territory and that killed any chance of peace. And they would not live on reservations.

"Do not speak of it more," he said. "The Whites have the country which we loved, and we wish only to wander on the prairie til we die."

That pretty well summed up the Indians' attitudes, for they knew they weren't going to be allowed to wander anywhere. And they knew all this amounted to was a polite ultimatum.

•••

As the opening council broke up, with invitations for the chiefs to gather at mid-morning the following days and begin negotiations in ernest. The peace commission wanted to get signatures on treaties, regardless if those Indians signing didn't represent all the tribes' members.

As Satanta and Black Horse made their way through the crowd, Adkin and Ryan squeezed through Indians and soldiers to intercept Satanta.

"Chief Satanta, I am pleased to see you once again," Adkin said, as the big Kiowa Chief stopped and stared. "I am P'ahy-Ch'i, Adkin Yates of England.

Adkin placed his hand on his necklace and held it forward for Satanta and Black Horse to see.

"P'ahy-Ch'i," How are you my friend," Black Horse said smiling and reaching out and placing his hand on Adkin's shoulder.

"Yes, my moon-haired friend, Adkin Yates," Satanta finally grinned, recognizing Adkin.

Adkin pulled Ryan next to him.

"Remember Tyler Ryan, my friend who helped me and Mah-aht-Tay," Adkin said.

"Yes. Yes," Satanta said. "You come with us, yes?"

He and Black Horse started guiding them back to the Comanche camp which was several hundreds yards away.

"You still wear sign of Kiowa and Satanta around your neck?" Satanta asked as they made their way through the mass of Indians, who stared in awe that Satanta and Black Horse were laughing and smiling with two White men and repeatedly patting the Whites on their backs and shoulders.

"Yes, Satanta," I wear the sign everyday," Adkin said. "Ryan, too. We wear it because we are honored to be your friend."

Once they got to Satanta's tipi, which was larger than most, they were invited inside. Satanta also whispered in the ear of an Indian who ran off to another huge tipi nearby.

Adkin and Ryan were shown where to sit, and Satanta asked a woman for something and she skirted out the tipi rapidly.

Black Horse went over near the side and pulled a long-stemmed pipe from the furs. He sat down next to Satanta and held up the pipe with both hands while smiling broadly.

"We wish to smoke peace pipe with Yates and Ryan, a ritual we were not able to enjoy when we were at Little Arkansas, and you helped save my daughter from harm," Black Horse said, as he reached in the embers of the central fire place and pulled out a twig and lit the pipe.

He handed it to Satanta.

"Yes, we want to honor our friendship with you both," he said as he took a draw on the pipe. Adkin took it and said, "Thank you, we honor your friendship, too."

Adkin coughed a little on inhaling the bitter smoke, which brought smiles to the Indians. Ryan took a draw and smiled as he exhaled, not coughing. About that time, a large older man came through the tipi flap. Satanta and Black Horse stood immediately, and Adkin and Ryan followed suit. Adkin had seen this man, here and at the Little Arkansas Treaty.

His headdress proved he was a chief, and he wore a frown which looked as if it had been chiseled there years ago. Satanta spoke up.

"Satank, I wish you to meet Adkin Yates and Tyler Ryan," he said. "These are the White men who saved Mah-aht-Tay from harm at the Little Arkansas. You did not get to meet them then."

That's who he was. Satank, also known as Sitting Bear, the eldest and most respected Kiowa on the Great Plains. Even Satanta deferred to Satank's wishes – most of the time anyway.

Adkin had learned through James R. Mead and others that the chief system among tribes varied. There were no votes deciding upon leadership. It was through actions and decisions that brought forth chiefs and followers.

There were also differences on how Chiefs performed. Many chiefs were medicine men, too. They healed, saw visons which led their people from trouble or starvation. Or they settled disputes among the tribe.

There were also war chiefs. They were men who put together bands of friends and followers and led them on raids of stealing and killing of enemies. There was no age limit to becoming a war chief.

Satank, who was at least in his late 60s, had been an able warrior, and had become part of the Koitsenko (or Kaitsenko, Ko-eet-senko), the society of the bravest Kiowa warriors.

"An honor to meet you Chief Satank," Adkin said as he held out his hand. Still frowning, Satank actually took Adkin's hand and shook it for a longer than usual time. He did the same when meeting Ryan. He then motioned to all to sit down.

As they settled down again and started passing the pipe around again, three women came into the tipi carrying two steaming pots, and a basket and a large bundle of cotton cloth.

They placed the pots near the embers and laid out rolls of breads, berries, wild onions and when they unrolled the cotton cloth, there was a large piece of dark brown aged meat.

Black Horse, removing a knife from his waistband, reached over and sliced off a large piece of the meat and handed it to Adkin. He did the same for everyone else, saying, "Good buffalo meat." The women filled small gourds with a soup from the pots and handed one to everyone. Adkin didn't ask what was in it, but he was pleasantly surprised. It was very tasty.

They ate and Satanta asked about Diablo, a horse he had bred from a long line of powerful stallions and mares. Adkin had also learned the Comanches had established themselves as the finest horse breeders on the Great Plains. They had been at for more that 200 years.

He and everyone else also knew they were the best horse thieves on the Great Plains as well, according to them anyway.

Adkin and Ryan asked about Mah-aht-Tay. They were surprised when Black Horse said she was married – married a few months after returning to Southwest Kansas from the Little Arkansas Treaty. They looked at each other, thinking Mah-aht-Tay was only about 14 then.

"She was 16 when she married," Black Horse said as if reading their minds. "After Little Arkansas, I worried she may get spoiled so we found her a strong warrior to marry."

The discussion turned to the treaty negotiations. Satank's frown deepened, if that was possible. Black Horse just shook his head in a sad way. Satanta spoke up.

"The council will promise us many things, but we know they will not happen," he began, "We will disagree, but we will sign the papers. They know and we know, no good will come of it, and many will die rather than live on a small piece of the land in houses.

Adkin and Ryan couldn't help but agree.

"It seems many of these things were promised at the Little Arkansas Treaty," Adkin said. "Yet nothing happened."

"They are now offering less than two years ago," Satanta said.

After eating, the pipe was passed around again. Adkin quickly learned not to inhale. Satanta asked if they enjoyed the prairie dog stew? After much laughing, they all stood and shook hands and wished each other well.

"This council may last many moons, Yates," Satanta said. "We would like to welcome you to our lodge again before long. I would like to see Diablo, too."

"It would be a pleasure and our honor Chief Satanta," Adkin said as Ryan agreed.

•••

As they walked back, A young man dressed as a New Orleans dandy, in Adkin's opinion, halted them.

"Gentlemen, I would like to introduce myself. My name is Henry Morton Stanley, and I am a correspondent for the New York Herald," he said, with what sounded subtly like a Scottish accent. "I am here to cover the treaty and let all the people back east know what's happening on the frontiers' West.

"What's that got to do with us?" Ryan spoke up.

"Well, sirs, I noticed you were granted into Chief Satanta's tipi and you spent considerable time in there," Stanley said. "When I asked around, I was told a tale how you became friends with the Chief and his Medicine Man, Black Horse.

"I hear rumor you saved Black Horse's daughter from being ravaged by a white man," he added. "I would be very interested in your story and in publishing it in the Herald."

"There is no story, Sir," Adkin said as he started walking away.

"But Sir, our readers would be very interested in reading about your daring heroism and how it ingrained you into a friendship with the most deadly Indian on the frontier."

"As I said, Mister Stanley, There is no story to relate," Adkin said again, as he was walking faster now.

Stanley tried to stay up with the long-legged Englishman, and Ryan shouted, "You heard the man, there's no story friend."

They kept walking as Stanley halted and watched them disappear into the crowd.

As Adkin and Ryan approached the council circle, where a few chiefs were arguing with commissioners, they noticed two more mobile feeding stations had been set up. There were thousands of Indians throughout the hills and valley surrounding the campgrounds. Since it was getting dark, cooking fires were lighting up the hillsides.

"Yates, Ryan, get your asses over here," Harney yelled. "Where in the hell have you been? We've been looking for you for an hour."

"Sorry General, we've been visiting with Satank, Satanta and Black Horse," Adkin said.

"We had supper with them in Satanta's tipi," Ryan beamed.

"Well, good for you," Harney said, a little more relaxed. "We've got a problem which I think you can help us with."

"What's that General?" Adkin asked.

"Well, we've had to set up four feeding stations, but there's so many damn Indians here, we're already running low on supplies," he continued. "I've sent riders ahead to Fort Larned, and they should get there in two days to tell them we need more supplies immediately.

"Do you think you can send enough freight wagons to Larned in three days – three days back and bring those supplies?" Harney asked.

"Sure, General. How many wagons do you think you need?" Ryan answered.

"Well, the quartermaster has ordered 15,000 pounds of sugar, 6,000 pounds of coffee, 10,000 pounds of hard bread and 3,000 pounds of tobacco – we have enough other gifts, I hope," Harney said, noticing Adkin and Ryan were staring in awe. "Dammit men, there's between 5,000 and 10,000 Indians here."

"Sir, our new Murphys can carry at least 8,000 pounds a load," Adkin said, "We can send five wagons and should have it all back here in six days."

"Well, get those damn wagons headed out before daylight," Harney barked. "If you will."

"Ye sir," Adkin said, as he and Ryan headed off to their wagons and teamsters.

While arranging which wagons would leave, Simpson, the Lieutenant wagon master they had met on the trail approached Adkin and Ryan.

"If you need any teamsters, I have several that volunteered if you need them, Simpson said while a couple of young men were standing behind him.

"We'd be mighty pleased Mister to drive a couple of teams back for more supplies and get right back," this scrappy looking teen said.

"This here is Dixon, Mister Yates, Billy Dixon, and his friend, Frickie," Simpson said smiling. "They are on hire by the government and love any adventure they can find – but good men on the reins. And Billy here is the outfit's best shot – he's our meat hunter, too."

"Well. we have men ready to go, Lieutenant, but we sincerely thank you for the offer," Adkin said, while Dixon and Frickie looked suddenly sour.

"Well enough, Mister Yates," Simpson said as they turned away, Dixon and Frickie following with heads turned down.

"Thanks again men," Ryan said as they turned away.

•••

Six YR&R Freight wagons departed the Medicine Lodge Creek Treaty site just as the sky was turning gray on the horizon. Ray Dee volunteered to drive one of the wagons to oversee the loading goes well and return trip stays on time. They had decided bringing an extra wagon – just in case.

Negotiations started again about mid-morning on the second day, but not much was accomplished, according to talks with Harney late in the day.

That evening, Dixon and Frickie walked by their camp fire and asked if they could talk with Adkin and Ryan. They were invited to take a seat on a log by the fire ring.

"I noticed your accent was English, is that right?" Dixon asked Adkin.

"Quite right, my lad," Adkin said in his best English accent, while Ryan started lauging.

"Don't mind him boys, he just joshing with you," Ryan said. "He's been out here on the frontier for three years now – seeking adventure like y'all."

"That's what I like about the foreigners I've met out here – no offense," Dixon said. "They love the adventure as much as I do. I've worked with a German and Frenchy, a Frenchman. But I want to hunt and live out on the wild plains, not be a teamster the rest of my life.

And I will fight Indians if I have to," he added.

"How old are you, Billy?" Ryan asked.

"I'm 17, but I've been on my own since I was 14," Dixon said. "My folks died when I was 12 and I didn't particularly want to live with my Uncle in Missouri, so I headed to Fort Leavenworth and got a job.

"It's like this country is calling to me, luring me into danger and thrilling excitement all at once," Dixon continued. "I can't hardly put it into words."

"I know exactly how you feel and what you mean," Adkin said, smiling broadly at Dixon, who was only three years his younger. "Exactly."

They continued visiting for awhile, then Dixon and Frickie finally went back to their government camp area along the creek.

Dixon would come by every evening and visit about his dreams, and Adkin realized, this young man had lived a lot in a very short time. He reminded Adkin of himself. They became fast friends.

The treaty ground on and on, but on the seventh day, October 18, the five YR&R wagons arrived with fresh supplies and more and more Indians came out of their lodges for the free goods.

Adkin and Ryan took it upon themselves to ride over to Satanta's lodge and showed him Diablo. The big horse actually seemed to remember the Chief, and Satanta's grin never left his face. He asked Adkin if he could ride the stallion and when told yes, he sprang into the saddle in one hefty jump, never using the stirrups. He rode Diablo around his tipi several times, squealing and laughing like a child.

Commissioners reached a final agreement with the Comanche, Kiowa and Apache tribes on October 21. The Cheyenne decided to refuse the offers and went back into negotiations. The treaty signed by the Comanche, Kiowa and Apache tribes was, in effect, the same as the next treaty offers to the Cheyenne and Arapahoe tribes.

During signings, several Comanche branches were not represented. One branch was the Quahadis – they didn't sign and never did sign a treaty with the U.S. Government – ever.

After the signing, Adkin and Ryan approached Harney who was talking with Ten Bears, the Comanche Chief who represented the Yamparika branch. He had several young warriors surrounding him like guards.

Harney introduced Adkin and Ryan to Ten Bears and his men. One of them impressed Adkin, as he was almost as tall as Adkin and his arms were hugely muscled. His name was Quanah, one of the Quahadis, who Ten Bears described as a War Chief.

Adkin thought the young man was his own age or a little younger, but his English was very good, and he was very polite. He noted he had heard of Adkin from several Kiowa friends and stared at Adkin's necklace.

After they departed the council circle, Harney pulled Adkin off to the side.

"That Quanah is one to keep an eye on. He became a murdering war chief when he was only 17," Harney said. "He is the son of Cynthia Ann Parker, a White Texas girl who was kidnapped when she was 10 or 12 back in 1836, and she married an Indian Chief named Peta Nocona, who was later killed by soldiers. He was a wonton killer, too.

"She was known by everyone from here to New York for years, especially when they found her and re-captured her and her daughter, a sister to Quanah," Harney continued. "He and his younger brother escaped the soldiers during that raid, and now, he's an up and coming terror, in my opinion."

"How old is he now?" Adkin asked.

"He's probably only 18 or 19," Harney responded.

"Wow, unimaginable."

On October 28, the Cheyenne and Arapahoe came together to sign an agreement, nearly identical to the first treaty signed. But several details in the treaties had already been dismissed by the Indians before anyone left the valley.

When boiled down, according to the final arrangement, the Indians agreed to:

- Withdraw all opposition to the construction of the Pacific railroads.
- Relinquish their claims lying between the Platte and Arkansas.
- Withdraw to reservations set apart for them.

In return the Indians received the following concessions:

- A large reservation and an enormous amount of supplies. The Comanches, Kiowas and Apaches were assigned to a reserve north of the Red river. The Cheyennes and Arapahoes were allotted about three million acres in the Cherokee outlet in the Indian Territories of Oklahoma.
- The right to hunt south of the Arkansas river so long as the buffalo ranged there in such numbers as to justify the chase. No White settlements were to be allowed between the Arkansas River and the southern boundary of Kansas for a period of three years.

Most of the tribes were decentralized, and acceptance of the treaty was contingent upon ratification by three-quarters of the adult males of each of the tribes. This condition was part of the treaty.

In the end, the U.S. never obtained sufficient votes for such ratification, and thus the treaty was never made valid or legal. Conflict over treaty terms would continue for decades.

•••

On October 30, the military camp broke, while most signs of Indian lodges had already disappeared. Like the Little Arkansas Treaty, this one was a spectacle like no other to Adkin, Ryan and Ray Dee. When Harney said his goodbyes, his words would prove to be prophetic.

"This council will probably be the last great gathering of free Indians in the American West," Harney said.

Fortunately, they got to see Chisholm on the last day of treaty signings and said their goodbyes to the half-Cherokee frontiersman. He bid them farewell and good luck on their trading business. After all, Chisholm was a master tradesman most of his born days.

Little did they know then that Jesse Chisholm would be dead in less than five months. When Jesse's friends, James R. Mead and William Greiffenstein, along with others became aware of his death a few days afterward, they noted it with the help of a small keg of Kentucky's finest, honoring their friend with a fitting wake ending with a salute from their guns.

A stone marker was later placed at Jesse's grave that simply read:
Jesse Chisholm
Born 1805
Died March 4, 1868
No one left his home cold or hungry.

•••

Adkin and the YR&R crew decided to send their wagons back to Junction City by way of Fort Harker with the military wagon train, where they could load them on rail cars back to Barlow and Sanderson's new headquarters.

Before they could send the telegraph to Sanderson, he sent a message that the Union Pacific Eastern Division Railroad had just finished rails reaching Hays City at Fort Hays.

The YR&R crew then made the decision to put their wagons on the rails there instead of Fort Harker.

They also had to decide whether their older wagons could make one more trip to Santa Fe. Again, Ray Dee asked to oversee the return trip with the wagons to Junction City.

As Adkin and Ryan headed out, they travelled up Medicine Lodge Creek, a day behind Satanta and his Kiowa band. Satanta had told Adkin his tribe often wintered west of the headwaters of Medicine Lodge Creek.

They were told once they reached those headwaters, it was only about 15 to 20 miles northwest to the Arkansas River south of Rath's Ranch House. They should make Fort Dodge in three days.

•••

Once back in Fort Dodge, they telegraphed Sanderson and asked him and Ray Dee to thoroughly inspect the older wagons to ensure they could make one more trip to Santa Fe. They also asked him to put a list of goods together, according to what demand currently was, and costs estimates for YR&R. They also looked Sam Phillips up.

"Well gentlemen, I became unemployed October 30," Phillips said, smiling. "Not sure what we're goin' to do yet, but I wanted to give you first chance to utilize my services."

They all laughed.

"You know what? We could use a freight foreman," Adkin said. "What do you think Ryan – with Ray Dee off in Junction City for the next few months?"

"That would be fine with me, but what he means by foreman is part-time teamster, carpenter, repairman and animal wrangler," Ryan said, chuckling. "And it don't pay much – does it Adkin?"

"Oh, I figure we could pay $50 a month, but you'd be working for YR&R Freight Company," Adkin said. "There is a room at the stables that we could make habitable for a wife."

"Are you serious?" Phillips asked, bewildered. "You're not joshing me?"

Adkin looked directly at Ryan.

"Are we not serious?" Adkin asked him.

"We're very serious, Sam," Ryan said, looking back to Phillips, whose mouth was agape.

"Honestly, Sam, we've been talking about it for a few months. With us having to put Barlow and Sanderson first, it's taken away time we'd like to spend on our company," Adkin said. "We're spread out thin."

"Would you like to talk it over with Mary Catherine first and see what she thinks?" Ryan asked. "You would need to live at our new location next to Bent's Fort."

"We'd love to work for you, and trust me, Mary Catherine wants to stay out here. If I'm happy, she's happy," Phillips said excitedly. "I'm going to go tell her right now."

As he started away, he suddenly turned and asked, "When do we need to be ready?"

"Well, we could wait a couple of days for you to get your things gathered and find a wagon and team, things like that," Adkin said.

"We've got a wagon, a two-mule team and two saddle mares," Phillips beamed. "And everything we own will fit in that wagon."

"We can be ready by tomorrow morning – will that do?" he added.

"Sure. Sure," Adkin said, thoroughly enjoying Sam's excitement and enthusiasm. "Want to meet later for supper?"

"Let's share supper tomorrow evening while we're on the trail to adventure," Phillips blurted as he hurried away waving.

"Never seen a man so excited to get a job, especially an ex-U.S. Army Captain," Ryan said.

"Kind of reminds me of us, don't you think?" Adkin said.

They both laughed and slapped each other on the shoulder as they headed for the barracks.

• • •

The next evening, Adkin and Ryan discovered why having a woman cook was invaluable on the trail. She fried thick bacon slabs, then fried some potatoes in the bacon fat and had molasses to pour over all of it. And then there was Dutch oven bread and coffee.

"This is the sweetest, best tasting bread I've ever eaten in my whole life," Adkin said in a Scottish accent. "Me own mother couldn't outdo this."

"I've never tasted anything like it either," Ryan said. "Sam, if I can find a woman who can make bread like this, I might get married myself."

They laughed, and Mary Catherine took the compliments humbly.

"It's sourdough bread," she said, grinning. "I make sourdough biscuits as well. They're tasty, if I don't say so myself."

For the next three days, Mary Catherine proved to be a trooper. She never complained about anything, even when the mules threw their tantrums. She would snap that jerk line as powerful and loud as a man and yell at them.

Sam enjoyed riding his roan mare alongside Adkin and Ryan. The weather was cooling at nights, and they all knew winter storms were not far off. Sam told Adkin and Ryan he and Mary Catherine would make them proud they gave them the opportunity to stay out West on the Great Plains.

When they arrived at the new office and stables, the rest of the crew welcomed Sam and Mary Catherine with open arms. Uribe and Dusty already knew Sam, but were speechless meeting the beautiful Mary Catherine.

She wasn't. She shook everybody's hands like she was a politician working a crowd. She didn't blink when seeing YR&R's scouts, who didn't necessarily dress as businessmen.

"Wait til you eat the bread this woman can make," Ryan said to the crew.

They decided they had enough materials to put an addition on the back wall of the barracks and mess hall near the rear door for Sam and Mary Catherine.

Everyone worked from day break to dark to finish it in three weeks. Adkin figured that much construction work was due to the bread Mary Catherine was always making to treat the men. Every time they saw her pull out that Dutch oven, they started working double-time.

It was mostly adobe with log posts for roof beams with a small chimney above a heating and cooking stove. They actually put two windows in the outer walls and used wooden shutters for coverings, promising to order two glass window panes as soon as possible.

Once completed, it didn't take Mary Catherine long to sew window curtains, and she actually made her own small shelves by the stove area. She could use a hand saw with the best of them. And was adept with a hammer and nail.

Morale and disposition increased visibly around the place, and they all recognized it was because of Mary Catherine. Of course, Sam proved to be an asset as well. He could do about anything; he knew horses and mules. He was always helping grooming and feeding all the animals.

Things started slowing down about mid-November, and several hunting trips were planned. Sam always volunteered to help, and proved to be a true marksman with his fairly new designed Spencer rifle. It had a tubular magazine in the butt stock instead of under the barrel. The shooter had to manually cock the hammer after ejecting a spent cartridge and loading a new one with the lever.

In was at this time when Mary Catherine started asking what the men wanted for Thanksgiving dinner. All the men, with the exception of Sam, weren't really sure what she was talking about. Ryan said he had heard of it from some people he knew from New York who celebrated some kind of Thanksgiving Day.

"In 1863, President Abraham Lincoln issued a proclamation entreating all Americans to ask God to 'commend to his tender care all those who have become widows, orphans, mourners or sufferers in the lamentable civil strife' and to 'heal the wounds of the nation,'" Mary Catherine explained. "He scheduled Thanksgiving for the final Thursday in November.

"The traditions of the pilgrims were to eat venison and turkey," she continued. "We have some venison, but if you want roasted turkey, you'll have to provide me one – or two or three for this bunch."

Uribe knew where turkeys could be found in some ravines with large cottonwoods about an hour away. So he, Sam, Dusty and Don Diego took off turkey hunting. By evening, Adkin was getting uneasy. They should have been back by now, he thought to himself.

Suddenly, a saddled horse came running through the main gate. It was Don Diego's horse, and it had an arrow sticking out of its hindquarter. Most of the crew came running out from various places.

"Mount up men," Adkin yelled. "Grab all your guns, our men have been attacked."

Within a few minutes, six riders galloped away at full speed. The sun had just set, and Adkin was afraid tracking could become difficult in the dark. They knew where the others were going to look for turkeys, and it was along the Arkansas. That's the direction they headed.

They hadn't covered more than four miles when three horses were walking toward them in the gloom between sunset and total darkness. It was his men, and Adkin sighed in relief. Don Diego was riding double behind Uribe.

"Is anybody hurt?" Adkin asked.

"No, no, we're fine," Uribe said.

"Just a little shook up," Sam added.

They explained they had found some turkeys at their first spot, where a small creek entered the Arkansas. They managed to shoot one turkey, but decided to try another spot further west about a mile. While riding into the thickets there, they flushed more turkeys and dropped two more.

"But, with the first turkey, there must've been a dozen shots for that one turkey," Uribe said. "We figured a small band of Cheyenne probably heard the gunfire.

"By the time we were firing at turkeys at the second spot, they closed in on us and started shooting at us," he continued. "We got off our horses and took cover in the thickets and what little trees there were."

"I think we got a couple of them," Dusty said. "I saw Sam knock one off his pony there at the end. His friends came back and swooped him up."

"It didn't last that long," Sam said. "Once they hit Don Diego's horse, and he cut out for home, I think they figured he was headed for Bent's Fort. They didn't want to stick around if there was a chance soldiers were coming this way.

"They didn't want to die for just four horses and three turkeys," Uribe said, laughing.

Everybody laughed, mainly from relief of their previous anxiety.

"This is one Thanksgiving I'll never forget," Phillips said, chuckling. "We're lucky there was only about a dozen of them."

Their Thanksgiving proved a royal success with Mary Catherine roasting a couple of venison rump roasts and three turkeys over wood embers for several hours. She also had cooked up a pot of navy beans, boiled potatoes – and of course – plenty of her Dutch-oven bread, biscuits and jars of molasses.

She also led the men in prayer – after politely reminding the men to remove their hats.

"Dear Lord, thank you for this bountiful meal. Bless the deer and turkeys for sacrificing their lives for our benefit. Thank you, too, for keeping those bloodthirsty Cheyenne from killing our men – especially my husband, Samuel, if I may. And thank you for allowing us to share this wonderful place on your Great Plains. Amen," she said.

"What a woman," Adkin thought to himself. She's going to not only fit in, she's going to carve out her and Sam's place in this area. Adkin finally knew what a pioneering woman was. Mary Catherine was the epitome of one – and only 18.

By the next day, more good news; Don Diego's horse was on the mend. The arrow was only about an inch deep and after gently cutting it out, his wound looked very good. Uribe's yarrow flowers poultice was working its magic.

After Diablo's wound, Adkin asked Uribe to make up several jars of his yarrow paste for just such incidents. It not only stopped the bleeding, it healed the tissue at the wound.

•••

Christmas wasn't as pleasant as their Thanksgiving celebration. On December 10, they received a telegram from Uncle Dick Wootton who said the axle on his Concord coach had busted in two pieces. It was unrepairable – it would have to be replaced.

Fortunately, Sanderson had prepared for such a situation. He had shipped three extra axles to them earlier that Spring, as well as lynch pins used to attach wheels to the axles and extra skeins, the metal pieces covering each end of the axle and several drop tongues if needed.

It was decided Ryan, Sam, Fransisco and Peg-Leg Pete would take a wagon and haul a new axle to Uncle Dick, mainly because he said the only snow they had experienced at Raton Pass were dustings and no major accumulation had occurred, yet.

It would be chancy, but the men packed extra food supplies, clothes and blankets, a small wood stove and four extra horses. They also carried as much hay and oats as they could pack in the wagon. They all had experience in winter travel and knew what the risks were.

They rolled out of the yard with Pete yelling at his two mules, "Andale. Arriba."

The next evening, Adkin received a telegram from La Junta saying they had arrived there with no problems and were going on to Raton Pass.

Adkin's worry was there were no more Western Union services until they got to Uncle Dick's, and that was a four- to five-day trip. He was sure they had communicated with Wootton and received the go-ahead weather-wise. Now it was prayers.

No word came December 17, Adkin's estimation of their arrival at Raton Pass. He sent a telegram. He received an immediate response.

To Adkin Yates. Stop.

Snow storm hit during night. Stop.

No sign of crew yet. Stop.

Will telegraph upon arrival. Stop.

Uncle Wootton.

A certain dread came over Adkin, but he was hoping it would only delay them a short period.

He was wrong.

•••

Adkin received another message from Wootton two days later, informing him it was "still snowing" and no sign of crew.

This news finally set off real concerns within the men and Mary Catherine. The weather at their location was creating morning frosts on everything, yet it was not snowing. Adkin briefly though about taking another team to look for them, but the ominous dark blue skies off to the southwest brought him back to reality.

Sure enough, snow hit them the next afternoon, and then the wind came down from the Rockies with a vengeance. Snow began piling up and soon, snow drifts were nearly as high on the east side of each building as the roof.

Fortunately, the snow stopped the next day about noon, but the wind was relentless. The men took turns struggling to the stables to take care and feed the animals. The temperature was at 10 degrees and holding throughout the day. The next morning is was zero, and no rider could probably even get to them from the Western Union office at Bent's Fort.

All of them felt helpless.

The following day, Adkin and Uribe decided to saddle up and make their way to Bent's Fort. After all, it was only five miles.

It took them five hours, and there was no word from Uncle Dick or anyone. The Western Union operator said he was sure some lines were down – he couldn't get through to any other station in either direction.

This would require two repair teams with Army escorts going east and west to find the downed lines. With horrible drifts at every undulation of the ground, they would probably have to wait a few days before sending anyone out, and that is exactly what the Commander decided.

Adkin and Uribe were forced to spend the night and rest Diablo and Uribe's horse before setting out for home the next morning. When they arrived, they were greeted with exuberance as the rest of the crew feared harm had befallen them since they didn't return the same day.

Adkin passed along the news about the telegraph lines, and tried to ease Mary Catherine's fears and anxiety. Even as Adkin felt them just as much.

They prayed together aloud, but Mary Catherine never broke down or cried. Not in front of Adkin and the men anyway.

That same day, two scouts and two troopers from the new Fort Lyon site showed up at YR&R's stage station. It had taken them two days of hard travel to cover the 18 miles between them. They were headed to Bent's Fort for food supplies.

•••

On December 23, Uncle Dick telegraphed Adkin in care of the Western Union office at Bent's Fort. The messenger wasn't able to deliver it to Adkin until the following day.

To: Adkin Yates. Stop.
Rescue crew found your men Dec. 21 about 15 miles north. Stop.
All are alive. Stop.
Fransisco may loose some toes. Frostbite. Stop.
More details later. Stop.
Uncle Dick. Stop.

Mary Catherine said it was the greatest Christmas gift she had ever received knowing Sam and the others were alive.

"And poor Fransisco," Mary Catherine said. "May God bless and help him."

"Pete will be able to help him," Uribe said." He knows all too well what losing part of your own body does to a man. He knows how God steps in."

About four days later, Ryan telegraphed they planned on leaving Uncle Dick's Dec. 31, adding Wootton gave them a good price on another mule, and Fransisco only lost his little toe, and he was fine. Ryan noted they hoped to be home about January 8 or 9.

He added: Happy 1868!

•••

Within a week, most of the snow was gone around Bent's Fort and on January 8, Ryan, Sam, Fransisco and Peg-Leg Pete returned home. Fransisco still had a large bandage on his right foot, and the men helped him down so he could use his wooden walking crutches.

When Mary Catherine came running out, she almost knocked Sam to the ground – she flew through the air and landed right in the middle of his chest, making them both spin around in order to keep their balance.

It was fairly embarrassing to see her kissing his face all over. She finally sensed she was making a scene and started laughing while her face flushed bright red. Everybody was happy and pleased to be together again. Adkin realized this was now his second family.

All of them, especially Ryan, who he seemed to have known all his life. It amazed him how close he felt to these people in his life now.

They explained bad weather hit them just a day out from Raton Pass.

"At first, it started raining real hard and the temperature was dropping like a rock." Ryan said. "Then the wind hit, and we decided to find a small clearing by the trail with a lot of trees around.

"We were as wet as a beaver by the time we had the horses and mules unhitched and unsaddled," he continued. "Then the rain turned to ice pellets – hard blowing sleet. We put the animals on a string line rope tied between two trees – with hackamores.

"That's when the sleet turned to snow – big flakes flying sideways in the wind," Ryan said. "We managed to get out canvas tarps and tried making a lean-to, but the wind wouldn't have it. So we used the wagon as a tent center pole and hid under cover for probably 8 hours when the wind finally let us get out and start unloading supplies and the stove from the wagon.

"We actually put up two more tarps and staked down the corners," he continued. "Fortunately, we managed to get some rations out of the supply bags and had some jerky and hard cold biscuits to eat. We were also lucky we packed those bundles of dry wood for the stove.

"The trouble was Fransisco had been standing in rainwater when he was wrangling the animals and his moccasins froze before he knew it," Ryan continued. "We didn't realize it until he told us later his feet were hurting severely."

"I didn't know it was that bad," Fransisco said. "Once we started warming them up, we had to cut the deer skin off. It was my fault I didn't speak up sooner."

"By the next morning, the wind had slowed but it was snowing like the dickens," Ryan said. "That's when we discovered a mule had fell down during the night sometime and apparently, she wasn't able to get back up. She was frozen to the ground – dead – when we found her."

"Later in the day, we had to go out and try to find some more wood." Sam interjected. "We felt helpless because our wagon was totally buried, and we had to get through snow head-high to feed the animals.

"It was Ryan who found some more wood and dead pine branches under some blue pines," Sam continued. "He disappeared under the snow diggin' around with a hatchet like a pack rat."

They all laughed.

"How are you feeling now, Fransisco?" Adkin asked.

"I'm well and blessed to have these men looking after me," Fransisco answered. "Pete was telling Uncle Dick to cut off my whole leg, not just my toe. He was telling me he had an extra peg-leg he would rent me – for a small fee since we were good friends. Then he started calling me 'Missing Toe Sisco.'

"He got me laughing so hard, I didn't feel much pain when Uncle Dick cut that black ugly toe off – plus that bottle of tequila helped a little, too."

Again, everybody was laughing. Mary Catherine stood next to Sam as he sat in a chair while all the stories were being told. She never left his side, even keeping one arm wrapped around his shoulder. Adkin was glad to see her natural smile return to her face. She had been full of dread for days.

Ryan said they had actually cut about two feet of wood from the back of the wagon for firewood, too. He said if the wagon had not had the heavy Concord axle in it, it might have blown off the mountainside a couple of times. They did salvage the two metal skeins from the old broken axle, though.

They said the two Ute scouts Uncle Dick sent out to find them were pleasant sights. They not only had food, but coffee as well, since they had drank all of their's in about three days, and their water supply was short. They also helped dig out the wagon and had broke a lot of trail with their horses and two pack mules.

...

It took about two weeks for the Western Union workers and the Army to totally repair telegraph lines on both sides of Bent's Fort. They sent Sanderson a message saying the Santa Fe Trail was open again and ready for business – on the western end anyway. Sanderson relied no weather alerts were on the wires on the eastern end either. He reported the storm that trapped Ryan and his crew had swept across Kansas and was "... heading to New York City."

The YR&R wagons were inspected and only a few of the older ones required some repairs. Minor things, and Sanderson said they were ready to send another caravan to Santa Fe.

They made arrangements to purchase about $25,000 worth of trade goods, and Sanderson said he would find a suitable wagon train to join up with. He said the wagon route had been reduced to about 560 miles since the railroad had reached Fort Hays.

Now all the animals and wagons loaded with goods would be shipped via rail to Hays. Then it was only 75 miles to Fort Dodge and 493 miles to Santa Fe, New Mexico.

He reminded them the rail service fee had increased slightly as well. But with YR&R's 59 wagons and Barlow and Sanderson's 20, Sanderson said this trip should be their most profitable, yet.

Adkin, Ryan and Ray Dee also decided they would sell any older Murphys in Santa Fe and buy more later, after the final accounting. Ray Dee would be supervising the purchases of goods and getting everything shipped to Junction City and on to Fort Hays.

Sanderson also said the federal government was pressuring traders about selling guns and ammunition to Indians. He said he had been approached and had all their warehouses searched, even though he assured them he didn't trade in guns and armaments.

Sanderson said the sale of guns had been officially banned the year before, but the trader in competition in the stage business, David A. Butterfield, had sold the Indians tons of guns in 1867.

Butterfield had established the Butterfield Overland Despatch Stagecoach Line in 1865 across northern Kansas and to Denver.

Butterfield claimed he had approval from several top Indian Agents, including Colonel Bent, E. W. Wyncoop, and Colonel J. H. Leavenworth. Sanderson said he heard the Army is even threatening James Meade against selling arms to Indians.

Adkin and Ryan thought that was strange since the Army gave the Indians at Medicine Lodge Creek plenty of guns and ammunition.

The crew got word mid-February a large caravan had finally been organized, and that the Army was sending infantry and calvary troops with it, too. The 300-plus wagon train would be departing Junction City on March 1. They were estimating arriving in Santa Fe in five weeks.

Adkin and Ryan realized things were changing and fast.

•••

Shortly after they received word their shipment was on the rails for Fort Hays, Sam came to Adkin and Ryan with a proposal.

"Is there any way you men would entertain another business partner?" Phillips asked. "I have an inheritance that Mary Catherine and I have been saving to establish ourselves somewhere.

"Well, we've talked it over, and we want to stay out here in the west and raise a family," he continued. "I've got $5,000 we could invest in YR&R Freight. I know that's not enough to be a quarter partner, but we were wondering if that would be enough to be a 10-percent partner?

"Plus, Mary Catherine is carrying our first baby – she thinks it's due in late July," Phillips added with a huge grin.

Adkin and Ryan were momentarily in shock, but quickly congratulated Sam and slapped him on the back.

"Where's the cigars?" Ryan asked.

"Right here," Phillips said, pulling two out of his breast pocket.

Ryan reached into a desk drawer and pulled out a bottle and three tin cups.

"This calls for a toast," Ryan said, pouring a splash of brandy into the cups.

They all picked one up and clanged cups.

"Here's to Samuel Oscar Phillips and Mary Catherine's new baby," Adkin said. "May God bless him or her as He had blessed his parents."

"Here. Here," Ryan chimed in.

"Thanks friends," Phillips said, as they all took a sip.

After celebrating the news, Adkin urged them to take a chair.

"Now about this proposal of your's Sam," Adkin began. "Are you prepared to raise a baby out here – right here?"

"I know it sounds crazy, but baby's are born everywhere. Why not here?" Phillips said. "There's military surgeons at Bent's Fort and the new Fort Lyon. Gosh, there's people in Ohio that don't have any doctors as close as that and give birth with only midwives' help. Some do it all on their own."

"Why don't you give Ryan and me a little time to talk about it?" Adkin said. "And we have to ask Ray Dee his thoughts – is that okay?"

"Yes sir, I understand completely," Phillips said. "I just wanted to let you know how we felt."

"Thanks Sam."

•••

Within a week after March 4, word of the death of Jesse Chisholm swept across the country like a wildfire thanks to the telegraph. He died reportedly from food poisoning in the Oklahoma Territories not far from his home ranch.

The news was actually printed in newspapers from New York City to Washington to California. He was routinely called "a famed fur trader and Indian agent" of the West. To Adkin and Ryan – and so many others – he was a trusted friend.

It was told that Yamparika Chief Ten Bears laid his Medal of Peace he received from President Lincoln around Jesse's neck at his burial.

All the newspapers reported what was written on his headstone: "No one left his home cold or hungry."

•••

By late March, the caravan with YR&R's freight wagons passed through and arrived the second week of April in Santa Fe. Once again, the Aguirre brothers handled the sales, including most of the wagons. They were once more wallowing in cash and gold.

Conrado Aguirre said about 25 of the wagons were in very good shape, and YR&R asked they be loaded with skins, hides and sheep wool for a return trip.

Adkin and Ryan had discussed taking in Sam as a partner and all agreed he could have a 10 percent, and their ownership would drop to 30 percent each. Ryan proposed using Sam's cash and their burgeoning profits to buy 70 more big freighters. Murphy assured the men it would have 35 of the freight wagons in 30 days and in another 30, the balance of the order would be completed.

"I believe we can break up the wagon usage between here and Junction City," Ryan told Adkin and Ray Dee when Ray Dee was passing through. "We could use 20 to 30 wagons for freighting out here – there's plenty of demand with all these settlers moving out here."

They all agreed to ship building goods with 30 of their 95 wagons to their branch near Bent's Fort and use the others for Santa Fe trade. After all, it had made them hundreds of thousands of dollars in just two years.

Their wisdom prevailed as news that the railroad had ran tracks that reached the town of Phil Sheridan (soon renamed Sheridan) in June 1868. From there, westbound freight headed southwest over a wagon road to the new Fort Lyon, on the main Santa Fe Trail – just about 18 miles from YR&R's operations.

They then received word that the Cimarron Route was abandoned shortly after June, and most long distance Mountain Route traffic ceased east of Fort Lyon.

Adkin wasn't disturbed at news of closing the Dry Route – it had almost killed them.

Now the trail length from Sheridan to Santa Fe was only 428 miles: 120 miles (feeder route) from Sheridan to Fort Lyon and 308 miles (main route) from Fort Lyon to Santa Fe.

•••

It was shortly after Chisholm's death that the crew heard Kit Carson, who had been appointed Superintendent of Indian Affairs for the Colorado Territory, had moved to Boggsville. Carson had travelled to Washington D.C. by ambulance because of his worsening health.

Adkin and Ryan had made a promise when he got back to Boggsville, where Uribe's family now lived, they would pay him a visit.

Word came that Carson was coming home, but on April 13, Josefa, gave birth to their seventh child two days after he arrived home. Two weeks later, before Adkin and Ryan could see him, Josefa died of complications from the birth.

They heard rumors that Carson was devastated and heartbroken and that he had departed Boggsville. While trying to find out where he was, word came Carson had died at new Fort Lyons on May 23 from a ruptured abdominal aneurism.

Adkin, Ryan, Sam and Uribe went to Boggsville for Carson's burial. It was a sad and moving moment in Adkin's life, as he regretted not seeing Carson prior to his death, and Carson had been so close to Adkin.

•••

Sam signed a partnership agreement with the three YR&R partners in May, and was instantly involved with finding out where young towns or trading posts were being established in the western area, including contacting Mary Catherine's Uncle in the Indian Territories of Oklahoma.

Zebulon Jarvis was a brother to Joel Jarvis, Mary Catherine's father, and Zeb had signed a deal with the Arapahoes to lease land in Blaine County in the Indian Territories of Oklahoma through the Indian agent there, Jesse Chisholm. Zeb had established a small ranch house and trading post there, and he and his two sons farmed a little and helped Zeb.

Sam sent word they were looking to help provide eastern goods to settlers and trading posts from their operations locations in Eastern Colorado or from Fort Dodge.

In June, word spread some 400 Indians of the Cheyenne under Chief Tall Bull had raided Council Grove and the nearby Kaw Reservation Indians on their way north to hunt the buffalo. They had eastern Kansas in an all-out panic and fear of Indian raids.

Tall Bull didn't sign the Medicine Lodge Creek Treaty, which, unfortunately, did not bring peace to the frontier as had hoped.

They had yet to hear back from Zeb Jarvis when Mary Catherine gave birth to her and Sam's first son on July 30, 1868. It was the same day Adkin turned 22.

The couple named the boy James Adam Phillips. They chose Adam because they knew Adkin was Scottish for Adam. Adkin teared up when notified why the boy was named James Adam Phillips.

Sanderson had informed the western crew all the raids by Indians had practically nullified credibility of the Indian Peace Commission and the Indian Bureau.

He said word was the military was going to take over all security matters west of the Mississippi by General Sherman, who relegated the quest to General Philip Sheridan who would be in charge of a "winter campaign" against warring tribes in Kansas, Oklahoma and Texas.

Sanderson wasn't sure what that "winter campaign" involved, but he said he would inform them when he found out anything.

•••

Through Sanderson, word of mouth and military reports, as a result of the Kaw Reservation attack and the surrounding attacks on settlers who had their stock stolen or killed, General Sheridan had issued an order to supply Kansas Governor Samuel J. Crawford 15,000 rounds of ammunition to be distributed among the frontier settlers along the Santa Fe Trail.

Sheridan had also dispatched cavalry from Forts Harker and Riley to the Council Grove vicinity for protection against raids. He ordered two companies of calvary – in cooperation with the troops at Fort Harker – to patrol the frontier border from Fort Harker south to Wichita.

Crawford appealed to the President that summer and requested the military remove all Indians from Kansas. Sheridan was re-enforcing areas of vulnerability with more troops, and he promised Crawford he would force all Indians back onto their reservations in Kansas.

•••

During the second week of August, the crew learned that around 200 Cheyennes were on the warpath under the command of the Dog Soldier Chief,

Red Nose, and The-Man-Who-Breaks-The-Marrow-Bones, a prominent member of Black Kettle's band.

The raiders began on the Smoky Hill Valley and Kansas Pacific railroad and swept northward to the Saline River and onto the Solomon and Republican River Valleys. In just a few days they had killed at least a dozen settlers, raped several women, some of whom were taken hostage, burned and ransacked houses, stolen stock, driven hundreds of settlers from the region and paralyzed the citizens of northern Kansas with fright.

Then in late August, Sanderson told Adkin and the men that Governor Crawford's complaints to the President had evidently produced results. Sanderson said Barlow told him the War Department had been given a free hand to do whatever was necessary to end the Indian Wars.

The Indians in September resumed their raids in earnest, and Adkin and the others were nearly involved directly. The Comanches and Kiowas raided Fort Dodge on September 3, killing four soldiers and wounding 17 before being driven off.

They received word that a Mexican wagon train was attacked on the Santa Fe Trail near Fort Dodge by Cheyennes and Arapahoes. They learned it was a caravan organized by the Aguirre brothers.

Sixteen of the Mexicans were reported killed and scalped, and fortunately, none of the brothers were travelling with the wagon train.

News came that on September 7, Sheridan had ordered troops to invade the region south of the Arkansas River to make war on the families and run off the stock of the Cheyennes and their allies.

•••

Though the freighting businesses were nervous, trade along the Santa Fe Trail stayed brisk. But the wagon masters and caravan operators were reluctant to make the trip, especially after news carried up and down the Santa Fe Trail like wildfire that a woman, Clara Blinn, and her 2-year-old son had been taken hostage just a few miles west of the New Fort Lyon on Colorado Territory.

It appears several men organized a wagon train of eight wagons, 100 cattle, 10 men and Clara and her son, Willie, who were moving back to Fort Dodge to be nearer to family.

They had departed Bogg's Ranch in Colorado Territory on October 5 or 6. On the 7th, they were attacked by about 100 Indians, who stole four wagons of goods and the woman and boy.

But the Indians grew to about 200 and kept attacking the remaining traders in the wagon train. The fighting continued until Oct, 12 when the Indians rode off to the southwest.

Witnesses claimed the Indians were mostly Cheyenne and Arapahoes, but one man claimed he saw Satanta among the attackers. Adkin had trouble believing Satanta would do that, but he did have the reputation of killing at least 40 White men.

After that news, wagonsmasters and traders were apprehensive about departing on the trail until they had at least around 300 wagons and plenty of arms and ammunition for everyone involved. And word from the Army was it would provide calvary between certain Forts and locations.

It worked most of the time, the exception being the attack near Fort Dodge while the wagon train was returning to Santa Fe.

"You know we saw those people a month earlier when they came through," Ryan said.

"I think we might know some of those who got killed," Uribe added.

"All this was predictable," Adkin said. "Everyone – the Chiefs, the peace commissioners, everyone – knew the Medicine Lodge Creek Treaty was a farce. The Indians aren't made for living on farms."

"That is a fact," Phillips added. "Anyone who has been around Indians even a month knows that. And what's bad, the U.S. government has given them all kinds of arms and ammunition the last few years."

"I'm not a medicine man, but I think this summer has been a bad omen for peace," Ryan added. "It will probably only get worse."

"We have to all be very careful – and every day," Adkin added. "We need to double our guards."

•••

The YR&R crew got word when their final wagon order was completed, but they decided to take some time to see what was happening with the new war on Indians. Sanderson assured them something was being planned.

Sanderson sent a telegram reporting Sheridan had approved a proposal by Governor Crawford to organize a battalion of citizen militiamen and approved arming them and providing 60 day's of rations.

Sanderson said this militia would guard the settlements from the Republican River to the Arkansas. He also told Adkin the Army was issuing bids for maybe up to 200 wagons to help in preparations to supply this frontier militia.

YR&R Freight immediately put in a bid for 100 wagons, even though the company only owned 95. Sanderson said he would provide the other five wagons if they got the bid. He admitted Barlow and Sanderson Company only had about 20 wagons at Junction City, the others out on the Santa Fe Trail.

Two days after bidding, they received word they were picked to provide 50 wagons for the job. Sanderson started immediately gathering supplies. There were going to be 500 new Spencer carbines from Fort Leavenworth, plus all the other supplies for several locations the militia would patrol from.

The headquarters for arms, supplies – and enlistments – were assembling at Saliva. One company each was to be stationed in: Lake Sibley, Solomon Valley, Saliva, Marion Centre, and Topeka. Wagons of supplies were ready by September 28, and they headed out to their respective locations.

Crawford had promised Sheridan he would supply able and honorable men for the militia, and he raised 1,300 volunteers in three weeks. They were to be called the 19th Kansas Volunteer Cavalry for service under General George Armstrong Custer.

Phillips notified the YR&R crew he had received a long letter from Zeb Jarvis in the Indian Territories. Zeb's information was enlightening and encouraging for business in that country.

Zeb informed Sam he was actually in business with Jesse Chisholm and James R. Mead up on the Little Arkansas River. It was those two who actually set Zeb up in the trading business. He said he is still working with Jesse's family since his death in March.

When Adkin and Ryan told Sam of their friendship with Chisholm and Mead, they all decided at some future date, they would need to visit with Mead and Zeb to see if there were possible business dealing they could participate in with their freight hauling – or even stagecoach service.

Word reached Sanderson in October that Sheridan wanted more sites established south of the Cimarron River to provide war supplies so he could win this "winter campaign." Rumor was General Alfred Sully had told Sheridan about a site in western Oklahoma that would make a good place to re-supply and create a protected supply road from Fort Dodge south into the Indian Territories.

This new place was quickly spreading by rumor to being called Camp Supply, though many were not sure where the site was located by Sully.

Sanderson told Adkin and the crew he had been told supplies were being shipped to Fort Dodge for a special mission to construct this new Camp Supply. He informed the crew he had put teamsters and teams of mules on the remaining 45 wagons belonging to YR&R Freight and sent them out of Junction City to Fort Dodge.

Sanderson said this foray into the Indian Territories could be an opportunity to investigate whether off-trail stagecoach service was viable, and if not now, maybe in the near future.

Adkin telegraphed Fort Dodge and informed Commander Elliot he could provide an additional 45 wagons to the Army, and was told they would be put in service. Adkin was also told part of the 19th Kansas Volunteer Calvary would also be involved in the plans.

Adkin, Ryan, Uribe and Sam, despite protestations from Adkin about Sam leaving his newborn son, departed for Fort Dodge November 6 on horseback with each leading a pack mule.

"Sanderson said our 45 wagons should already be at Fort Dodge and probably loaded," Adkin told his men. "This will also give us a chance to see if stagecoach service down into Oklahoma is a possibility, too."

When they arrived at Fort Dodge three days later, their YR&R wagons were still being loaded, mostly with building supplies. There were wagons all around the fort fully loaded with another line of empties, as were some of their's, awaiting loading.

After making contact with officers and the Army wagon master, Adkin and his men were told they would be departing Fort Dodge at daybreak on November 12 and meeting up with two additional columns of U.S. Army cavalry and infantry troops from forts Bascom in New Mexico and Fort Lyon in Colorado, along with Major Elliot's company from Fort Dodge.

Elliot told Adkin and his crew his company was ordered to converge on the Indian Territory and strike the Southern Cheyenne and the Southern Arapaho. The main force would be the Seventh Cavalry led by Lieutenant Colonel George A. Custer.

Custer's troops were coming down from Fort Hays to Fort harker and were to rendezvous with the Nineteenth Kansas Volunteer Cavalry, which was advancing from Topeka under command of Colonel Samuel Crawford, at the newly established Camp Supply in the Indian Territory.

They learned Governor Crawford had resigned his governorship on November 4 in order to take command of his Kansas Volunteers.

Adkin and some 200 other wagons reached Mulberry Creek just south of Fort Dodge, within the hour, the other troops were rolling in to join the expedition south.

"Golly, there must be at least 350 wagons here," Ryan said. "This is more than just establishing a supply point."

"I believe you are quite right," Adkin replied, with a chuckle.

Adkin and Sam volunteered to drive a team and a wagon, while Ryan and Uribe rode horseback. Their steeds and mules were lashed behind their wagons in the caravan, which spread out for nearly a mile.

That evening, Adkin and Ryan asked the aides at the officers' tents if they could talk with the joint commander, General Sully. In short order, they were led into a large tent with several men surrounding a table with a map on it. General Sully spoke up.

"Welcome gentlemen, I'm General Sully," he said, reaching out his hand. "And you must be Adkin Yates and Tyler Ryan – I've heard of you both – with Barlow and Sanderson Stagecoach Company."

Adkin shook his hand and nodded to Ryan. "This is Tyler Ryan, General. We, too have heard of you."

"I'd like you to meet Colonel George Custer, commander of the 7th U.S. Calvary," Sully said. "And these men are our scouts. You know Commander Major Elliot."

Everyone shook hands and greeted the others.

Adkin and Ryan couldn't help but notice Custer wore a buckskin shirt with leather thongs along the sleeves and a broad-brimmed beaver-skin hat, even though he was a Colonel in the U.S. Army.

Custer's face was thin and chisled with high cheek bones and a long straight nose sitting atop a bushy blond mustachio. And his curly blond hair ran down past his collar.

"What can we do for you, Mister Yates?" the General asked.

"Sir, we're here to actually ask you, 'What can we do to assist you on this expedition?'" Adkin said. "We are totally at your disposal.

"You may not be aware, but Ryan and I are also co-owners of YR&R Freight Company – you may have seen our insignias on several supply wagons," Adkin continued. "I have men, including Indian Scouts, teamsters and wranglers if we can be of service – other than just hauling supplies."

"Well that's great Mister Yates," Sully said. "Let us show you where we're headed and share some of our plans."

They motioned Adkin and Ryan to gather around the maps on the table. Sully pointed to a spot in Indian Territory just east of the Texas Panhandle.

"We're going to establish a supply camp here, where Wolf Creek joins the North Canadian," Sully said. "It's the first of many supply sites we'll be establishing down into Texas.

"If you know the country, and of any difficult places, please let us know," Sully said.

"We have not travelled south of the headwaters of Medicine Lodge Creek," Adkin said. "But our head scout knows the country south of the Cimarron and the Canadian.

"We will ask him and let you know," Adkin added.

"Do you know if this area immediately south of here offers any chances of warring Indians?" Custer asked. "We will be a slow-moving caravan with 400 wagons and infantry."

"No sir, we have not heard of any Indian depredations – recently, anyway," Adkin replied. "We hear most of them are setting up the winter camps."

"Well, gentlemen, if we are attacked, can your men handle fighting?" Custer asked.

"Yes sir," Ryan answered. "Most of our men have a lot of experience fighting out here. You just tell us what you want, and it will be done, Colonel."

"That's great," Sully said. "We'll be heading out at daylight, and hopefully, we'll have a peaceful trip."

Sully invited Adkin and Ryan to dine with them.

"Maybe next time, General," Adkin said. "But we need to gather our men and make sure they are prepared – if you don't mind."

With that, they returned to their camp and discussed what they had learned from Sully and his officers with the men.

"That country should be fairly easy to travel, even with all the infantry and wagons," Uribe said. "The main crossings will be Calvary Creek, Bear Creek and the Beaver River."

As each day passed, Adkin noticed more and more infantry troops were hitching rides in the wagons instead of walking.

Custer also noticed, as he later wrote in his report of the trip: "In the afternoon there would be little evidence perceptible to the eye that infantry formed any portion of the expedition, save here and there the butt of a musket or point of a bayonet peeping out from under the canvas wagon-covers."

Uribe had been correct: The country was favorable for a large caravan. Often they could form four parallel columns of wagons in close formation to make time and provide security.

They arrived November 18, and Sully announced the site where Camp Supply would be constructed. He also pronounced they had completed a new road, naming it the Military Road from Fort Dodge.

Men and soldiers immediately started unloading wagons with engineers marking off different dimensions for the walls of the camp, and word was redoubts would totally enclose the camp.

Rumors were also spreading throughout camp thousands of Indians were wintering south of Camp Supply below the Canadian River and down to the Washita River. Scouts had reported seeing hundreds of lodges spread along 20 to 30 miles of the Washita.

People were also wondering where Crawford and the 19th Kansas Militia was, too. They had been expected to arrive at Wolf Creek before Sully and his troops. They had departed Topeka November 5.

Adkin worried as well, as there were more YR&R Freight wagons in that train. He wasn't sure how many Crawford was using for his caravan, because other wagons were spread out to some other sites of the Volunteers with the 19th.

On the other hand, the crew had all agreed the new military road would handle stagecoach service with the elegant Concords. The only trouble, the trail offered no places with established stables or ranch houses. Those would come in time, Adkin thought to himself.

•••

A mounted soldier rode into the YR&R camp area the morning of November 20, telling Adkin he was requested to come talk with General Sully immediately. Adkin motioned to Ryan he wanted him to come along.

Once inside the officers' tent, Sully looked exasperated.

"Mister Yates, Mister Ryan, I need your help right away," Sully began. "Are your wagons completely unloaded yet?"

"I think there's only two or three over on the east side that still have a few building supplies in them, at least as of last night," Ryan said. "But several of our men were headed over there before your rider came to tell us you wanted to see us."

"Well, we still don't know where the 19th Kansas Militia is. They have supplies, but we need more right away if we're going to get this place built and secured," Sully continued. "Could you round up every empty wagon you have and get them back to Fort Dodge for more supplies?"

"We'll have them ready to roll within the hour, General," Adkin said.

"Well, get going men, Lieutenant Dory will accompany your teams," Sully said. "He has the list of goods we need, and several other freighters will be following you out."

Adkin and Ryan set about locating their crews; teamsters and wranglers. Ryan decided he would ramrod their 45 wagons, and Sam would help him. Adkin would stay, but encouraged Sam to at least telegraph Mary Catherine when he got to Fort Dodge and let her know he would be on the expedition a few more weeks than expected.

By 9 that morning, YR&R wagons were rolling out of Camp Supply with additional wagons filing in behind them. Sully later confirmed to Adkin he sent back 250 empty wagons for more supplies.

On the afternoon of November 22, a bitterly cold snow storm hit the area. The snow was fairly deep, and everyone was worried for two reasons. One was they still didn't know where Colonel Crawford and his militia were, and two, they were hoping the empty wagons headed for Fort Dodge were not stranded or delayed.

Adkin noticed loud voices and men shouting orders outside his tent on the following morning and looked out on the camp grounds to see calvary troops mounting – and a lot of them. There were also about 15 supply wagons with teams. In short order, they were being led out of camp by Colonel Custer, the troops riding double-line.

Sully later told Adkin he wasn't at liberty to tell Adkin where Custer was headed or what he was doing.

"All I can say, Mister Yates, is Custer – as well as me – are following orders of General Sheridan," Sully said. "Those orders include seeking out warring Indians and ordering them to move to peaceful forts or surrender."

"I understand, General," Adkin said. "I didn't intend to be so nosy, it just surprised me so many would brave this snow and cold to venture out."

Adkin found himself hurrying back to his tent where Uribe was stoking the fire in the little cooking stove they had brought along. Both men knew that particular item of baggage was essential during winter on the Great Plains.

"I'm getting back in my cot. It's cold out there," Adkin said, as he started telling Uribe what little information he got out of Sully.

"That Custer is looking for Indians to kill," Uribe said. "He loves fighting and killing. I can see it in his eyes."

•••

It wasn't until November 28 that the 19th Kansas Militia led by Colonel Crawford arrived at Camp Supply, and Adkin thought they looked as if they had been in a losing battle. They were dressed poorly, many with rags wrapped around their feet, worn coats and pants – and looking bent-over weary. Numerous wagons were tied together, making it difficult on the mules, especially in snow.

He quickly noticed some wagons with YR&R painted on their sides. He ran over to the lead team and introduced himself to a teamster named Tom Marcellus, a large man whose hand actually engulfed Adkin's.

"Nice to meet you Mister Yates, I've heard much about you," Marcellus said.

"Mister Marcellus, do you know how many of our wagons are in this train," Adkin asked. "And is Ray Dee Rinehart with you?"

"There are 35 wagons, one chuckwagon and 50 men at your service," Marcellus answered. "And no, Ray Dee is not with us, but he made me foreman of our crew. The train is under Lieutenant Simpson, the Army wagon master from Fort Harker.

"And please call me Tom, if you don't mind," he added.

"Why no, Tom," Adkin said smiling. "You go ahead and follow the wagon master and I'll catch up with you later and take you to our camp."

Adkin and Uribe knew there had to be problems since it took them 14 days to get from Topeka to Camp Supply.

"They must have got lost or the storm last week hurt them badly," Uribe said.

"I agree," Adkin said. "After they all get settled, let's go meet the former governor – what do you say?"

"You go. I don't like politicians much," Uribe said, shaking his head side to side.

"But he resigned – he's a Colonel of a battalion now," Adkin said.

"Once a two-tongued rascal, always a two-tongued rascal," Uribe said, chuckling. "No bueno por mio."

Adkin and Uribe caught up with Tom and the other men as the wagons had been parked at various locations around the camp's perimeter as well as inside.

Tom said one of their wagons, as well as the chuckwagon, needed to be driven to the YR&R camp grounds, as the wagon had most all their personal supplies.

Tom also explained Ray Dee had led the other wagons to sites established in eastern Kansas by General Sheridan for the some of the Volunteers of the 19th to be stationed.

They were shown the camp area, and Adkin asked Uribe to handle their needs, as he wanted to meet Colonel Crawford.

He walked through the crowded grounds and made his way to the officer's tents. Crawford's men were setting up their tents and making an addition to the temporary corral with rope and willow limbs. And they were cussing.

Sully was outside his tent talking with another officer. Adkin recognized the spread eagle insignia below his epaulets and knew he was a Colonel.

"Mister Yates, I'm glad you came by," Sully said. "I have someone I want you to meet.

"Colonel Crawford, this is Adkin Yates, a representative of Barlow and Sanderson Company and a co-owner of YR&R Freight Company," Sully said. "Mister Yates, this is Colonel Samuel J. Crawford, former Governor of the great State of Kansas."

"Pleased to meet you Yates," Crawford said as he shook hands with Adkin.

"An honor to meet you Colonel Crawford," Adkin replied.

"Let's go inside, it's getting cold," Sully said as he opened the tent flaps.

Once inside, the men sat down on chairs circled around a large pot-bellied stove. Seven or eight cots and bedding were stacked against two walls.

Crawford had a striking bearing. When he removed his hat, his baldness was immediate. But, it only travelled back to the middle of his head. Then long curly hair encircled his ears and nearly to his collar. His eyes were deep-set and his cheeks sunken. He wore a mustache and a chin beard that came down over his top coat buttons of his uniform.

"The Colonel was just telling me they encountered numerous hardships on the trail here," Sully said.

"I hope the hardships were not too costly or harmful," Adkin said. "How many volunteers accompany you, Colonel?"

"We number 1,300 men, plus 50 officers, 1,150 horses and 100 mules," Crawford said with pride. "Well actually, we have fewer animals now – we had to eat a few that died from exhaustion or starvation.

"It's been a difficult journey, but we're here and ready to serve General Sully and the 7th Calvary – when it returns," Crawford said with a bit of hurt in his voice that inferred he didn't like it that Custer went on without waiting for him and his men.

About that time, several officers arrived at the tent and announced themselves. The tent flaps opened when Sully shouted, "Let them enter."

In walked four soldiers, looking like standard U.S. Army. All at once, Adkin recognized one of them. It was J.M. Hadley, who was a Lieutenant when he was accompanying General Harney to the Little Arkansas River Peace Treaty. He was now wearing Captain's bars.

It was Hadley that stepped forward and identified himself. He asked Sully if they could use the south side of the camp to erect a larger corral for their animals. They would be closer to their camp tents and the temporary rope corrals were not effective. He also wanted to encircle numerous wagons to assist the enclosure.

Sully gave his approval, and turned to Crawford and asked for further introductions. As Crawford introduced all four men, he introduced General Sully and Adkin.

Once finished, Hadley spoke up.

"It's very good to see you again, Yates," Hadley said, smiling. "My daring friend from England."

Adkin stepped forward and gave Hadley an embrace.

"It is very good indeed to see you once again Hadley," Adkin said. "I mean Captain Hadley."

They both laughed and shook each others shoulders.

"General, Colonel, I travelled from Fort Leavenworth to the Little Arkansas Treaty with this man back in '65 when I was an aide to General Harney before he retired from active duty.

"I was witness to Kiowa Chief Satanta giving him that necklace he wears," Hadley said. "He showed true bravery in protecting Medicine Man Black Horse's daughter from savagery by a white man."

"That's enough Captain," Adkin said. "Let's not drag up the past."

"Come to think of it, I remember hearing something about that," Crawford said. "It was Jesse Leavenworth who mentioned it."

"Yes sir," Hadley said. "Mr. Leavenworth was representing the Kiowa, Cheyenne and another tribe, I don't remember. But he witnessed Satanta's gift – as well as Black Horse's gift. A big black stallion."

"Do you still have that beast, Yates?" Hadley turned and asked Adkin.

"I sure do," Adkin said. "He's still the best horse I've yet to see."

"Well, you men get to work, and let's get this place built," Sully said. "And you two can catch up later."

They said their goodbyes to Crawford and Sully and departed.

Once outside, Adkin invited Hadley to eat supper with he and Uribe and some of his men. Hadley agreed, and Adkin told him where his tent was.

"We've actually put up a sign in front," Adkin said, chuckling. "It reads 'YR&R Freight' in yellow letters."

•••

That evening, Hadley came over, met Uribe and Tom, and they shared some fresh venison Uribe shot a few days earlier, along with some hard biscuits. Uribe tried watching how Mary Catherine made bread and biscuits, but he just didn't have the knack to produce the same quality.

The other YR&R crew were gathering around their chuckwagon, as Uribe had turned over the remaining deer meat to their cook.

Hadley asked what happened to Tyler Ryan. Adkin informed him about he and Ryan's business adventures establishing stage stations along the Santa Fe Trail, and including starting their own freight business.

Adkin then asked what kind of problems had he and the 19th militia ran into.

"Marcellus here can tell you, things started well after leaving Topeka," Hadley started. "The trails were good, not much grass though for the animals. We departed Topeka with animal forage for seven days and only nine days of rations – and that was for 1,350 men and almost 1,200 horses.

"On November 9, guess who we ran into while camped at the South Fork of the Cottonwood?" Hadley asked. "It was James Mead and some of his men. He came over and met with us in Colonel Crawford's tent. He was wanting to know where we were headed, but Crawford wouldn't tell him exactly.

"The Colonel just hinted how did we get to south of the Canadian. Mead said it was difficult country down that way and wanted to meet our guides," he continued. "We brought in Jack Stillwell and Bill 'Apache' Simmons – our guides.

"Mead wasn't impressed and asked Jack and Bill a few questions," Hadley said. "Then right there, and in front of the guides, Mead says, 'These men, who I have never seen before, know nothing of that part of the country – or I would have seen them before.'

"I have a couple of scouts with me that know that country well," Mead told him. "I can furnish them to you."

"Well that singed the Colonel's feathers, and he was mad. He cussed out Mead – and they've known each other for several years – and told Mead, 'By God, General Sherman had provided these guides, and they were going to take them through – and he had no God damn authority or money to hire some other sons of bitches.'

"Mead told him fine, and good luck and walked out of the tent," Hadley said. "And that's when our luck turned. We should have listened to Jim, You and I both know that man never leads someone into trouble."

"We didn't know that then," Marcellus said. "But there were days we weren't sure where we were going. Now it makes sense."

"I can't believe Crawford would treat Mead that way," Adkin said. "Mead is a Kansas legend, and he's travelled, hunted and traded in every spot in the state since 1859."

"I think it was because Jim just openly cast aspersions on our guides, and it insulted the Colonel's pride," Hadley said. "I know Jim would not intentionally hurt anyone's feelings – he was just being his honest, blunt self. You know Jim.

"Anyway, the next night, we camped in the woods north of El Dorado on Walnut Creek. That's where Cox and his crew – they're contract freighters – met up with us and his wagons," Hadley continued. "We were camped on the west bank of the Whitewater on the 11th. Then we passed by Jim's place. He wasn't there, but his foreman sold us some supplies and a rick of hay.

"We made that new Camp Beecher by noon the next day – it's near the junction of the Big Arkansas and the Little Arkansas. You know, just a little south of where we had the big pow wow in '65," he said. "All this time we had been travelling through muddy and rough roads. It was slow going. We only made seven miles further before camping with the Caddos at Cowskin Grove.

"We got on down to the Ninnescah, about 18 miles and camped," Hadley continued. "Then got in 25 miles the next day to the Chikaskia. Then all hell broke loose. We couldn't find suitable trails, did some back-tracking. It was a mess.

"We made it to several miles above the mouth of Medicine Lodge creek," he said. "And a spooked mule caused an all-out stampede of nearly every animal we had. Mules and wagons were going off in every direction. We lost mules – had to kill a bunch – and wagons too torn up to pull. That caused several more days of delay.

"Then we got hit by a terrible snow storm on the 22nd – y'all probably got some of it, too," he continued. "That nearly destroyed our expedition right there. We were out of hay and mules and horses started dying – we ate them to stay alive ourselves.

"It was a hell of a trip, and we know now we should have heeded Jim Mead's suggestions," Hadley added.

"See, Señor? I toll you a good scout will save your life," Uribe said, smiling at Adkin.

"Si Uribe, I agree," Adkin added, and they all laughed together.

Hadley asked if they knew where Colonel Custer went? Adkin told him what Sully had said, and Hadley understood.

"That's what we had to tell Jim Mead when we saw him," Hadley said. "I don't know all the details myself, and what I do know, I'm supposed to keep it close to the vest."

After Hadley said his good nights, he left for his tent. Tom was impressed with Captain Hadley.

"You know, I didn't have a lot of discussions with the Captain, but I felt like he was a decent man the way he treated us teamsters," Marcellus said. "His open honesty this evening – that we were lost as a rabid dog on the trail – says a lot about his character – in my opinion anyway."

"He's a real fine man," Adkin said. "I travelled with him for nearly two months while he was an aide to General Harney – and only a Lieutenant then."

Tom bid farewell and thanked them for the meal.

"Want to make sure my men are comfortable and warm," Marcellus said grinning. "They've been through hell and high snow."

"Good night Tom," Adkin said.

Uribe spoke up and said there must be some big secret plan to attack Indians.

"Or something else big, Señor," he said. "The soldiers never fight in the winter before, Nobody fights – it's winter and time to get plenty sleep and stay warm."

"I agree," Adkin said. "Let's get some sleep – Ryan and Sam should be on their way back by now."

Adkin laid in his bed thinking it was a hardship when the telegraph couldn't be utilized for communication. He was hoping Ryan and Sam weren't having any problems. He was also hoping the Army's orders included bringing more rations.

The hard cold and deep snow had forced about 100 Indians, mostly beleaguered older Cheyennes who had probably been semi-abandoned by the major bands, to seek safety of the Army.

Adkin had heard Sully was sending out scouts to tell any Indian lodges in the area, they could receive food and supplies if they surrendered their arms and came to Camp Supply.

At this rate, Adkin surmised, it wouldn't be long until Camp Supply would be besieged by cold, hungry Indians – and tipi lodges everywhere.

•••

As the camp was awakening the next morning at Camp Supply, little did anyone know but that day, November 29, 1868, would be recorded in the history of the "winter campaign," as Colonel Custer and the 7th Calvary attacked Black Kettle's Cheyenne band on the upper Washita River.

Custer would later be accused of slaughter by some and a hero by others. He would also face derision for leaving Major Elliot behind, bever looking for them at all.

It was also the day Billy Dixon walked up and pumped Adkin's hand like a water well handle.

"Great to see you Mister Yates," Dixon said. "Remember me? At Medicine Lodge Creek Treaty?"

Of course, Billy – and call me Adkin, please," Adkin said smiling. He really liked this young man. He could see his grit and determination. "Awful good to see you here.

"I thought about you when I heard freighters joined the train – wondering if you were still breaking mules."

"Yes sir, still pulling freight and enjoying the Plains, like it was another world of total fascination," Dixon said, grinning from ear to ear.

Me and a friend were hired by a man named Cox in Leavenworth," Dixon said. "He had just received 600 mules from Missouri and landed this contract, too.

"He told us those mules were well broken, but they turned out to all be shave-tails; as wild as you could imagine," he continued. "It was all we could do to get them to Fort Hays to take on freight.

Adkin could tell Dixon had put on weight, not necessarily taller, but fuller, like a bull dog. His grip was strong and earnest, something Adkin valued.

Adkin pointed over to where the YR&R Freight sign was and invited Billy to come over for supper at dark.

"I'll be there, Mist... or Adkin. You can count on it."

•••

On the afternoon of December 1, the 250 wagons from Fort Dodge arrived amid much fanfare. By the looks of the eager unloading, supplies of all kinds would quickly be used or consumed. The quartermaster, under orders from Sully, started immediately passing out food to some 150 Indians who were lining up – some even offering to help work for food and blankets.

It was quite a scene with all the hungry Indians and infantry soldiers and carpenters working like a finely orchestrated ant hill.

"Why can't Whites and Indians work like this everywhere?" Adkin asked himself.

"Because the Indians are losing their way of life," he answered himself.

Ryan and Sam reported the trip went well, with no major problems. And, Sam said he had telegraphed Mary Catherine his well wishes for his family and said it may be late December before he could make it home.

Custer and his calvary, including his supply wagons rolled back into Camp Supply a day later on December 2, just as Adkin and the YR&R crew were preparing to decide whether to head back to Junction City or home.

General Sully called all the freighters together to ask for additional help.

"Men, I need at least another 180 loads of supplies from Fort Dodge as soon as possible," Sully yelled at the men. "As you can see, there are now almost 1,000 Indians needing food and supplies.

"Can I count on you?" he added. "You'll be well compensated."

Adkin immediately raised his arm, "You can count on 80 wagons with YR&R Freight Company, sir," he shouted out.

Cox started yelling he would provide additional wagons. Within a minute or so, Sully had 180 empty wagons.

"Well, hitch your teams and start lining up over there by the creek," Sully shouted. "Lieutenant Dory will again accompany your teams with my orders. Please treat him as well as you did last trip."

Uribe volunteered to drive a team and wagon on the return trip. Ryan was beginning to say he would go, too, but Adkin interrupted him.

"Ryan, I don't mind if you go, but I'd like to have Sam go along as well," Adkin said. "Sam, I would like you to go and then hitch a ride on the next wagon train to go home and spend a couple of weeks with your family."

"But Adkin, I can still bring the loads back here," Phillips argued. "Mary Catherine is fine. She's a good tough woman."

"We all know that Sam, but I think it's important for you to spend some time with her and Adam," Adkin said. "And, we've been talking to some of the officers and they are sure more supplies will be ordered in the coming weeks and months.

"I suggest you spend 10 days to two weeks at home, then telegraph Fort Dodge and find out if they know when the next loads are expected to come back through to Camp Supply," Adkin said. "I'm predicting the next orders from Sully will be around Christmas time.

"You can then get back to Fort Dodge and help bring down our wagons," Adkin added. "How does that sound?"

"That makes great sense to me," Ryan spoke up.

"Sure Sam, you go see the Missus and that boy," Uribe said. "He need to know his Pa Pa."

Sam relented and said he would go home for awhile, after all he said he was still hoping to go see Zeb Jarvis.

"Okay, you men, I'll go, but I'll be back in about three weeks or so," Phillips said. "And Adkin, we might have to go try and find Zeb. It shouldn't be hard to find him. Might be some business for freighting down there."

"We'll see Sam, but let's get these wagons hitched and get back up for some loads at Fort Dodge," Adkin said.

As the men spread out to go to wagons and get the teams, Adkin pulled Ryan to the side.

"Since all of you are going, I'd like that foreman of Ray Dee's to stay here and help me with our extra animals and wranglers. His name is Tom Marcellus."

"No problem, I'll go find him right now," Ryan said.

"Wait, here is a promissory note signed by General Sully for our freighting charges up to now," Adkin said, handing him a leather pouch. "I worked with the quartermaster last night. We're receiving $50 a day, going and coming for freight, and that's per wagon. We're paying Sanderson $10 a day for the teamsters and wranglers.

"So when you get this note to the Fort Dodge quartermaster, have him telegraph 20 percent to Barlow and Sanderson Company in Junction City and the balance to us at Bent's Fort," Adkin said. "The note is for $11,925, so send $2,385 to Sanderson – there's an instruction sheet in here that has it all written out for you."

"Holy cow, I knew we were making money, but I had no idea it was this much," Ryan said.

"By the looks of it and how many bands of Indians that are showing up, it's going to be like a gold mine around here just bringing in supplies for several months at least," Adkin said, smiling.

"I believe your right, unless all these bands coming in take up arms and ravage Camp Supply," Ryan said.

"That's why we're invaluable to Sully," Adkin said. "As long as he has plenty supplies and food – and ammunition – he can keep the peace around here. It's what Colonel Custer is up to that unsettles me.

"He just rolled in and talk is he slaughtered more than 300 Indians while he was out, including women and children," Adkin said. "I'll find out more while you're away. That might influence our plans at a later date."

"Alright, Adkin, we'll be out of here in 30 minutes, but you keep your eyes and ears open," Ryan said, with a wink and a crooked smile. "If it looks bad, hightail it out of here and head to Fort Dodge as fast as Diablo can carry you, you hear?"

"I fully understand my good man," Adkin said in his full-blown English accent.

•••

After all the freighters had departed for Fort Dodge, the rumor mill started grinding away throughout the camp about what Custer had done on the Washita River.

After supping with Tom and a few of the men, Adkin wandered over toward the officer's tents. Several men were walking back to the tents from the chuckwagon nearby. Adkin then saw Hadley heading to the chuckwagon with his tin plate and cup.

"Hey Hadley, you have a minute?" Adkin asked.

"Sure, walk with me while I return my supper plate to Cookie," Hadley said. "What's on your mind?"

"Well, the camp is buzzing like a bee hive about Custer's exploits on the Washita River," Adkin said. "Just being nosey I guess, but was interested in finding some facts rather than just rumors."

"Here you go Cookie. It was a great stew and great cornmeal," Hadley said to the chuckwagon cook. "Could I have a refill on some of that coffee?

"Would you like a cup, Yates?" he turned to Adkin.

"Why yes, thank you," Adkin replied. "Could we have another tin Cookie? I'll bring it back in awhile," Hadley said as they walked away. "Let's go over by the fire. I'm having trouble staying warm in this damn place," Hadley said.

"Do you know if it's true Custer killed women and children?" Adkin asked as they stood with their backs to a large bonfire. Other soldiers were huddled together nearby also warming themselves before retiring to their tents, but they were out of earshot.

"Well, let me just tell you what I know, Yates," Hadley said with a sigh. "Some of it is rumor, too, I suspect because I wasn't there. But I did talk to several men who were on the excursion.

"Apparently they were headed south to the Canadian and the Antelope Hills when some of Major Elliot's scouts reported they had spotted a camp of Cheyenne on the Washita just south of the Antelope Hills," Hadley said. "Custer regrouped and took off for them with his supply wagons left behind him. On the night of the 27th, he stopped on a ridge behind a Cheyenne camp with about 250 people, according to the Osage scouts. He planned on a four-tonged attack, with Elliot leading two companies around the east and coming up behind the Indians on the southeast.

"It was Black Kettle's people and Custer decided to attack at dawn on the 28th," Hadley continued. "I was told an Indian fired a shot when he saw Custer's men coming to warn his people. Then the fighting started, and it only took about 10 minutes to totally overrun the village.

"They were still fighting until about 3 in the afternoon when they discovered more Indians were coming to help Black Kettle from downriver around the bend," he continued. "They were Arapahoes – their Chief Little Raven, more Cheyenne, and Kiowa Chief Satanta. Anyway, Elliot saw some of the Indians trying to escape and heading east, and he and a couple of dozen men went after them.

"Well, nobody knows what happened to Elliot and his men – they're still missing," Hadley added. "Custer didn't send anyone to look for them because hundreds of Indians were coming from the east.

"Custer meanwhile skedaddled since estimates were more than a thousand Indians were camped downstream along the Washita," Hadley said. "He was told Elliot couldn't be found but left anyway. Black Kettle was killed for sure, and Custer claimed he killed a little over a hundred warriors. Plus he captured fifty-some women and children and brought them back."

"Black Kettle was actually killed?" Adkin asked. "I met him at the Medicine Lodge Creek Treaty."

"Yep, Black Kettle is dead – and Major Elliot and the men that went with him are missing, too," Hadley said. "Custer is in hot water. You see, the talk is Black Kettle just camped there a few days ago because he and his people were asking for security and food at Fort Cobb just a week before.

"Black Kettle actually signed a peace document with General William B. Hazen on November 20, and decided to move his people to the Washita where there were literally thousands of other wintering Indians. He figured he'd be safer there. Was he ever wrong.

"I know General Hazen, too," Adkin said. "He's a good man."

"Well, the men I talked to said they saw squaws and kids get shot or hit with clubs or speared, but they claim it was the Osage scouts doing that. They said the Osage took a lot of scalps, too – and mutilated bodies," he continued. "You can be sure there will be a military enquiry on this.

"Can't believe he would allow that, especially since he had been on suspension just a few months ago after being found guilty of leaving his post without leave in a court-martial.

I think the real problems for Custer will be leaving Elliot and his men," Hadley said. "Custer seems to think he'll ride in any time now, but others who saw the Indians down river said Elliot wouldn't stand a chance against them with only a couple of dozen troops.

"I've already heard some officers departed to catch up with the wagon train to Fort Dodge to file official reports, which Custer will have to do, also," he added.

"That's about all I know or have heard," Hadley said, as he finished his coffee.

"I guess I just didn't think this was what the 'winter campaign' was about," Adkin said.

"Well, you didn't hear it from me, but we're going after the southern Cheyenne and the Arapahoe for past depredations – with orders to kill 'em or force 'em into reservations," Hadley said. "I need to get in my tent and my warm cot, Yates."

"Wait, what are they going to do with the women and children they captured?" Adkin asked.

"All I know is they were put in the large tent over by the stables they're building," Hadley said. "With a bunch of armed guards.

"Most likely they took them to use as barter for White women and children that have been taken in raids against settlers," he said.

"Thanks Hadley and good night,' Adkin said. "Give me your cup, and I'll take it over to Cookie."

"Good night Yates"

•••

The next day, the buzz around Camp Supply was still at full steam. Everybody was talking about Custer's foray to the Washita. Arguments abounded whether he was a murderer or a hero. And there was the mystery surrounding where Elliot was.

Adkin had trouble now even thinking Custer was some kind of valiant warrior when he could let his men – or even his scouts – kill helpless children or women. Adkin's heritage of being a warrior had long and deep traditions that never included children intentionally being killed in battle.

The other anxiety growing through the camp was whether those thousands of Indians only a few days ride away, might take revenge on Camp Supply. Adkin had hear Sully was allaying those fears saying the number of troops; calvary and infantry could withstand any attack.

He may be right, Adkin thought, because the walls and buildings were taking place. In fact, the officer's quarters and barracks were going up faster than Adkin thought possible, especially with the snow and cold. But the engineers had men working from sun up to sun down. Many said it was the only way to stay warm enough to survive.

Of course, Adkin had to admit to himself the General was working with 650 loads of supplies since November 12, almost a month to the day. And another 180 wagons were on the trail now.

•••

A couple of days later, rumors were spreading some of the troops that were responsible for guarding the captured women and children were having their way with some of the squaws. Adkin quickly tracked down Hadley and asked him about it.

"Is it true some of the guards are raping the Indian women?" Adkin asked with a tinge of anger in his voice.

"Easy friend, that's just rumors, and Sully has assigned a Lieutenant to investigate and warn them that any soldier mistreating the prisoners will be court-martialed," Hadley explained. "Please Yates, don't believe some of this talk we're all murderers. We have some of the finest officers in the West out here."

"I'm sorry Hadley. You're right. Guess I'm turning into an old woman listening to all the rabble," Adkin said. "I'm sure you officers have it under control."

•••

On the day Ryan, Uribe and Sam should have arrived in Fort Dodge, Adkin noticed a chuckwagon had been pulled up to the side of the prisoners' tent for their noon meal.

He walked over and watched as the guards led the women and children to the back of the tent to the chuckwagon. The guards, all of whom carried carbines, kept them in something of a single file, but children were wanting to hold onto their mother's dresses and smocks.

Adkin noticed one guard standing at the chuckwagon kept shouting orders.

"Keep moving you filthy dogs," He yelled. "Move along, this isn't a pow wow." The guard even pushed some of the women – and even a child – with the butt of his rifle. Adkin moved closer.

"You, get moving or you don't eat," he shouted at a woman who was crouched over, holding her stomach and moaning in pain.

"Move you ignorant squaw."

Then he punched her violently in the side of her mid-drift with the butt of his carbine. When she straightened up and yelled in agony, Adkin could see she was pregnant. Adkin was bolting toward the chuckwagon by the time she fell on the frozen ground screaming. The guard kicked her in the back as she lay curled up and crying out in pain.

As Adkin crashed into the guard as he twirled around while trying to shoulder his rifle. Adkin grabbed both his arms and slammed him up against the rear wheel of the chuckwagon. The man's back cracked as he hit the spokes and Adkin slammed a right fist between his eyes, just at the top his nose.

Blood immediately spewed everywhere as the man collapsed to his side as soon as Adkin released his other arm. Adkin, the cook, the woman on the ground and several other women had blood specks which had been sprayed all over them.

"Hold it right there, Mister," a booming voice came from behind Adkin. He turned to see two guards aiming their rifles right at him. "You're going to have to go with us, Mister. What's your name?"

"My name if Adkin Yates, and this man was beating this pregnant woman with his rifle," Adkin said. "And he kicked her after he knocked her down."

"Adkin. Adkin Yates," the woman on the ground faintly moaned in English. "It is me, Mah-aht-Tay. Mah-aht-Tay."

"Is that you, Páhy-Chi," she groaned as she passed out, and her eyes closed.

Adkin fell to his knees next to her side and rolled her over slightly, removing the head blanket from her face.

"Mah-aht-Tay – Matty," he bellowed, as tears started forming in his eyes. It was the little beautiful daughter of Black Horse laying there in the snow. He noticed blood starting to pool by her hips through her woolen smock.

"This woman needs a doctor," Adkin yelled at the guards pointing their guns at him. More guards and soldiers had gathered. "Please help me get her to the Post Surgeon."

He rolled her on her back and gently lifted her in both arms as he stood and kicked the leg of the fallen guard over so he could stand upright.

"I said stop, Yates, or I'll shoot," the guard said.

"Then you'll have to shoot me because I intend to help this girl," Adkin said as he strode forward. "Now where is the Post Surgeon's office?"

Everybody parted to make a path for the burly young man, and a soldier said, "Right this way, Yates."

When they arrived, the lead soldier opened the tent flaps for Adkin and the girl. The Surgeon quickly pointed to a cot by the wood stove and told Adkin to place her there.

"She's with child, doctor, and she was hit in the stomach with a rifle butt – hard, too," Adkin said. "She was beaten by a guard who will probably be carried in here any moment."

The Surgeon started rushing people out of the tent and yelled to his aide, a short, wiry man who had deep concern on his face. Sure enough, four soldiers carried in the guard Adkin had hit. The doc pointed at another cot.

"Lay him there," he ordered.

The guard's face was already turning a blueish black and his purple nose laid off to the side of his face. The blood was all over the front of his uniform, and it was starting to blacken from the cold. He was still unconscious.

"Yates. You're still going to have to come with me and see our Commander, Colonel Custer," the guard said, still semi-aiming his weapon at Adkin.

"Yes Private. I understand," Adkin said as he looked back to the Surgeon. "Please take good care of her, Doctor. I know her and her father. He is Black Horse, Medicine Man to Kiowa Chief Satanta. They are not far away."

The Surgeon had a look of worry, but he nodded his head in agreement. Adkin walked out the tent, ducking as he went through the flaps.

•••

"Colonel Custer, this man Yates has physically attacked Sergeant Martinez while the Indian women were getting their meals at the chuckwagon," the guard said. "Yates hit Martinez so hard, he's still out. His face is a mess and it looks like his nose is broken for sure.

"He's in the Post Surgeon's tent getting the doc's help," he added.

"What's this about Yates?" Custer stood and asked. "I remember meeting you. Why would you strike a military guard?"

"Well, Colonel Custer, I just happened to walk by when the women and children were being fed at the chuckwagon," Adkin began. "This guard, Martinez I guess, was yelling some obscenities at the women, and one was approaching holding her stomach and moaning. She apparently wasn't walking as fast as Martinez wanted her to do, so he struck her – he slammed his rifle butt in her midsection. As she fell to the ground, I could see she was with child, and he kicked her while she was down.

"I guess I lost my better judgement for a moment and rushed over and grabbed Martinez and slugged him once above his nose," Adkin continued.

"When I identified myself to the other guards, the woman on the ground knew me – and I recognized her just before she passed out.

"She is the daughter of Black Horse, a close confidant of Kiowa Chief Satanta," he continued. "I actually saved this girl from being molested when she was 16 at the Little Arkansas River Peace treaty in '65.

"Her name is Mah-aht-Tay, sir, and she looks to be in pretty bad shape – she was passing blood from somewhere," he added and then stood silent.

After a few moments, Custer grasped his hands behind his back and started taking steps back and forth.

"Well Yates, even if what you say is true, I won't tolerate any man molesting my men," Custer said. "Are there any witnesses that can verify your story?"

"Yes, there must have been 15 to 20 women and children who saw Martinez strike her," Adkin said.

"Any guards see it?" Custer asked.

"I don't know. There was another guard at the corner of the tent as they came around to the chuckwagon," Adkin said.

"Well, Yates. I'm placing you under arrest for assaulting one of my men. Since we have no brig yet, you will be bound and placed in a two-man tent under guard until we can try you," Custer said as he stopped pacing and looked Adkin right in the eyes. "And if I was you, I would be praying Sergeant Martinez makes it through okay.

"Take him away, and set up his tent brig next to the womens' quarters with orders for the guards to keep an eye on him," Custer added. "Place legs irons on him as well."

Adkin wanted to scream at Custer that Martinez had it coming, but he knew an egotist like Custer would just get meaner, not more understanding. But it deeply disturbed Adkin that Custer would think him a liar.

•••

Several soldiers started erecting a two-man tent while two others were hammering the pins in the legs irons as Adkin stood there in the cold. Several more soldiers pushed a two-wheel cart up to the tent and began throwing blankets and several buffalo robes inside on the snow. They also placed a large clay water jug in there, presumedly for when nature calls, Adkin suspected.

"Does not a prisoner receive a stove? Or a cot?" Adkin asked, as the soldiers pushed him inside.

"If the Colonel wanted you to have a stove or a cot, he would have said so," one of them hissed. "That's why he put you in an overnight pup tent."

"Stay warm Indian lover," another said with a smirk.

"I have a right to talk to my foreman," Adkin said. "His name is Tom Marcellus, and he's at the YR&R Freight camp.

"Tell Custer I have a right to talk with my foreman," he added as they tied the flaps together and walked away.

Adkin could hear several soldiers outside talking about where they would post guards. He looked around and decided the first priority was to use his boots to kick and push as much snow as possible to the outer sides.

He did this for about 30 minutes and was tiring quickly. He had to stoop over even in the middle of the tent. And he had to bend over more as he reached the sides.

He then pulled one of the buffalo robes into the middle to make a padding. It smelled terribly.

"Sure wasn't cleaned and cured by an Indian," he mumbled to himself.

He laid down and started pulling the blankets over him. There were only four, but they were good woolen Army blankets. He then pulled the other buffalo hide over the blankets and laid his head back, staring at the white canvas ceiling.

"What have you gotten yourself into this time, Yates," he thought to himself. "Slugging that Martinez isn't the problem. The problem is that he was one of Custer's men. And I can see Custer is not a balanced man"

Near sunset, he heard soldiers untying the flaps.

"Here's your supper and some water," one said. "Don't waste it 'cause you won't get anything until tomorrow."

He rolled the blankets and robe back and crawled over to the door. The wood bowl had some watered-down white navy beans, and that was it. There was a spoon but no meat, onions, potatoes – or salt – nothing but beans.

His water only filled half an Army canteen. He would have to sleep with it under the covers to keep it from freezing during the night.

And it proved to be a cold night. The hard frozen ground creeped through the bottom hide and kept him trying to stay in one position as to not roll over onto another frozen spot. At daylight, he drank most of his remaining water and relieved himself in the clay jug.

He waited and waited, and realized he wasn't going to be eating a fancy breakfast. In fact, it wasn't until about noon that he was given another bowl of navy beans and they poured water into his canteen about half way again.

"Hey, I have a right to speak with my foremen," Adkin protested. "Why hasn't he come to see me? Have you told him I want to speak with him?"

'Relax Indian lover. Colonel Custer is running the show now," One soldier said as they were re-tying the flaps. "And, you're lucky. Sergeant Martinez didn't die last night, and he's talking. He said you're a liar, Yates."

•••

About an hour later, Adkin heard some scuffling and cursing outside. He sat upright.

"Here is a note from Custer," A voice yelled. "Let me go or you'll have two of us in that tent, because I'm getting ready to break every bone in your face, too.

"Let me see him, my name is Tom Marcellus, and Custer said I can talk with him," Marcellus said. "Read the note Blue Boy."

The flaps opened and Tom stooped over to enter.

"How you doing Boss?" he asked as he kneeled on one knee. "I didn't find out where you were until earlier today. We didn't know what to think when you didn't come to camp last night.

"We looked everywhere, and all the soldiers were mum – not a word," Marcellus continued. "Then Hadley came by and whispered what happened. I tried to come over, but they said only Custer could approve any visitors.

"So, I went to see him, and he's an asshole," he continued. "Said he was going to throw you in a military brig for years. I argued and said whatever happened, you wouldn't lie about it, but he said no Indian women spoke up yesterday evening when asked what they saw.

"They're not backing you, Boss," Marcellus said. "What are we going to do?"

"See if General Sully will talk with you," Adkin said, sitting atop his bedding. "Ask the General if he will come see me personally, so I can plead my case. Tell him I'll be happy to be placed under arrest at my tent, and I give my word I won't try to escape – my word."

"Okay Boss, I'll see what I can do," Marcellus said. "These damn Bluecoats are starting to aggravate me to the hilt. They're calling you an Indian lover, and that you love this girl and you were jealous of the guard – all kinds of bullshit."

"They're Custer's offspring, and what I've heard and now seen, they're a bunch of ruffians and cowards," Adkin said. "Go now, see what Sully says, and keep that note giving you visitation rights, eh?

"Also, please go by the Post Surgeon's tent and check on Mah-aht-Tay, Black Horse's daughter," Adkin said, with a worried frown on his face. "She looked to be bleeding fairly bad."

Marcellus never came back that day. Once again, Adkin got watery beans and a little water for his evening meal. This time though, they had a small piece of bread that had been broken off a full loaf. It was tasty, but it was another miserable night.

Adkin kept remembering other nights on the trail that weren't too comfortable, either, but they made it through those. He couldn't decide if freezing weather was worse or 110 degrees when they went to bed near Wagon Bed Springs.

He also thought about what kind of man rises to the rank of Brevet General in the American War, and then becomes an Army officer and goes AWOL and is court-martialed, then comes back a Colonel. Then he immediately heads out of camp to attack a Chief whose band had just signed a peace agreement.

And then he proceeds to let women and children be slaughtered under his command. He also captures women and children to use for barter, but allows his men to rape and abuse the women while being held as hostages.

He remembered what his mother had always preached to him; "It's a sin to hate another person – never hate, Adkin." But Custer was making him re-evaluate that premise. Maybe is wasn't hate.

Maybe it's sheer contempt for an officer who would force him to sleep in smelly buffalo hides, only feed him two meals a day – and threaten to imprison him for defending a helpless pregnant Indian woman.

"Quit feeling sorry for yourself, Yates," he said to himself. "You're stronger than that madman, and God watches over those who live by the book.

"If men strive, and hurt a woman with child, so that there is a miscarriage, and yet no mischief follows: he shall be surely punished, according as the woman's husband will lay upon him; and he shall pay as the judges determine."

Strangely, he could remember that verse, but how, he didn't know. But it also made him ponder, who and where is her husband?

•••

An hour or so after sunrise, Adkin heard voices approaching his tent.

"Bring him out of there this moment," Adkin recognized it was Sully. "And remove his irons, immediately."

Adkin found himself being pulled to an upright position, feeling a little weak-legged, he staggered to the entrance. His hand irons and leg chains didn't help.

"Good morning, General Sully," Adkin blurted. "I'm happy to see you. I have much to explain and hope you will allow me some time to do so."

"Get these irons off him now," Sully shouted as several soldiers were kneeling and chiseling off the pins on his leg irons. Two more were using a key to unlock his wrist irons.

"Bring him along," Sully ordered.

Tom pulled himself under one of Adkin's arms to help support him in walking. Another private helped under the other arm.

They steadied him to the officer's tent and placed him in a chair next to the stove.

"Get him some coffee," Sully commanded several aides. Tom waited outside. While the aides hurried from the tent, Adkin noticed someone pacing near the rear tent wall. It was Custer.

"Now Yates. I want you to tell me what happened that caused this commotion that's rampaging through this camp like mutiny," Sully said. "Everybody is taking sides and wanting to go to war over this.

"What caused this?" Sully asked, as he sat down next to Adkin.

Adkin went over his story as he had told Custer. He reiterated he had no idea the abused woman was a friend and the daughter of Kiowa Chief Black Horse. He admitted, since his temper cooled down, he acted irrationally by hitting Martinez.

"I am sorry. I responded impulsively," Adkin said. "I just lost control when I realized she was with child and had been hit in the midsection with a rifle butt."

"There you have it, General," Custer spoke up. "He admits he lost control, and he nearly killed Sergeant Antonio Martinez for false reasons."

Adkin looked up at Custer.

"What do you mean false reasons, Colonel?" Adkin asked spitting out Colonel in a sarcastic tone. Sully raised his palm to Adkin.

"Well, no Indian women came forward when asked what they witnessed, and the cook claimed he saw nothing," Custer said. "Plus the Sergeant claimed the woman fell down, that she was probably going into labor or something, He claims you attacked him from behind like a coward."

"That's a lie," Adkin said. "He hit her – no – he slammed his rifle butt into her stomach," Adkin said. "And then kicked her while she was on the ground.

"It is he, Colonel, who is the coward. A damned bloody coward," Adkin growled as he stood up to his full height.

"Okay, okay, gentlemen," Sully waved his hands. "Let's settle down. This is going to have to be resolved, and I propose a military tribunal. General Sheridan is headed this way.

"We need three major officers to hear this case, and unfortunately, Colonel Crawford can't sit on the tribunal as a volunteer commander," Sully said. "In the meantime, I want Yates to wait for the hearing in the comfort of his own tent.

"Yates, you will stay in your tent until such time as we conduct the hearing," he continued. "I don't want you wandering around camp or even feeding your animals. Do you understand – and give me your word?"

"Yes, General, I give you my word, and I thank you for your compassion," Adkin said.

"And as for you Colonel, I will not have officers under my command arresting civilians and not informing me until two days later," Sully said. "Do you understand?"

"Yes General," Custer said while giving Adkin a less than friendly glare.

"As they walked out of the tent, Sully stopped Adkin as Tom walked up.

"I'm sorry that you had to endure two nights sleeping on the ground, Yates," he said. "Hopefully, you can find some witnesses who can assist in your defense. Striking a Sergeant, especially that hard, does have consequences."

"I understand, General," Adkin said as he headed to the YR&R camp.

•••

Before they reached camp, Adkin asked Tom if he had talked with the Post Surgeon.

"I did, Boss, and the doc said she's still going in and out of consciousness," Marcellus said. "She lost the baby, Boss. The poor little guy was dead when he came out.

"Doc says she's lost a lot of blood. He's pretty worried about her making it," he added.

"Bloody hell," Adkin said, forgetting his aversion to cussing.

Many of the soldiers, including the militiamen, stared at Adkin as they headed toward their camp. Only one voice was heard saying, "He's going to pay for attacking a trooper without cause." Tom turned and gave the man a hard stare.

Adkin was grateful to be back in his own tent. Tom helped by fetching him a fine breakfast of bacon slabs, fried potatoes and a whole loaf of bread and a tin of molasses where he dipped his bread and bacon.

"This is a royal meal, Tom. Thank you," Adkin said as he wolfed down the food.

The following morning, the camp was again in a stir. Scouts had arrived informing General Sully that a party of abut 100 Indians were approaching under a white flag. They were being led by Arapahoe Chief Little Raven and Kiowa Chief Satanta and several Comanche Chiefs. They wanted to deal for their women and children.

Adkin peered from his tent as the Indians rode in, nearly each one with a rifle barrel in the air. They halted at Sully's tent and he invited them in. It looked like about six Chiefs entered with Sully.

A few minutes later, Satanta and another Indian left with two soldiers. It looked as if they were headed to the Post Surgeon's tent. A little later, Satanta was striding in his stocky way toward the prisoners' tent. Adkin couldn't see much, but he later noticed Satanta coming back to Sully's tent.

When they all exited the tent, the Chiefs waved their arms and a several wagons came up from behind with three white women and two white boys in the lead wagon. They were bundled in rags and looked weary.

As they got out of the wagon, soldiers were leading all the women and children that had been imprisoned up to Sully's tent. They were quickly grabbed up by Indians and put in the wagons and on the backs of horses, and just walking away crying.

The exchange had been made, but Adkin couldn't see if they had went to the Surgeon's tent to get Mah-aht-Tay or not. He would learn a few hours later she was placed in the wagon via a gurney with some of the other women and hauled off – still ill, in the Surgeon's opinion.

The re-supply wagon train finally arrived and Adkin and Tom had to update what was happening with Adkin to Ryan, Sam, Uribe and Ray Dee, who had made his way back to Fort Dodge after hearing about the loads that were travelling down to Camp Supply.

Fortunately for Adkin, he was called to Sully's tent within about two hours of Sheridan's arrival.

Sully had set up a table where he, Custer and Sheridan sat behind it and with one chair facing the tribunal. Adkin was put under oath, and he was asked to repeat his account of what happened prior to him attacking Sergeant Martinez.

It was the same story as before, and then Adkin was asked to stand aside and Martinez was sworn in to tell his story.

He kept to his account of the squaw falling down, and the doctor could prove it because he said the woman's child was born dead. He didn't have anything to do with it.

At that point, Sully halted the proceedings and asked Martinez to stand.

"Sergeant Martinez, I'm placing you under arrest for assaulting a female prisoner and causing the death of her child," Sully said. "You will be held until we can court-martial you at a later date. I just wanted to hear what you had to say. You lied, Sergeant Martinez."

Martinez started muttering, "I don't do nawthing," and Sully continued.

"First, the Post Surgeon has supplied a written affidavit that the woman's child was about a month shy of being full term," Sully began. "Second, she had a bad bruise to her left side just below her ribs, and another severe bruise on her spine, just above her hips in her back.

"Also, Kiowa Chief Satanta talked with the women prisoners and claimed more than 10 saw the incident, but were afraid they would be beaten if they spoke up," Sully said. "An interpreter witnessed this, and we have no reason to believe Satanta would share such a story when he had no knowledge of what happened – other than his Medicine Man's daughter is seriously injured.

"General Sheridan's adjutant has openly shared his support of and belief in Adkin Yates, having known the man for several years," Sully continued. "Yates, you are free of any charges whatsoever, and please accept our apologies."

Adkin was thrilled, but Custer sat there stone-faced uttering not a word.

•••

The pressing concern for Adkin was that Mah-aht-Tay could die without medical support from an Army Surgeon. He would start making plans to find Satanta and his band.

Meanwhile, Camp Supply was taking shape. The officer's quarters were completed, as well as the barracks and stables. Word was Martinez was being held in the stables, as the brig hadn't been built yet.

Sully had order another 200 wagons off to Fort Dodge for more supplies, and the crew was hoping Sam made his way back to Dodge to join up with them again.

Most of the military was making plans to chase Indians, including Custer and Sheridan and Crawford, actually departing the day after the tribunal. They departed Camp Supply on December 11.

Word was when the combined forces advanced again on the Washita Battle area, the remaining Indians took flight. Uribe reported to Adkin he heard scouts saying the Kiowas and Comanches fled to the Wichita Mountains, while the Cheyenne and Arapahoes went even further south.

"That's the way we need to head then, the Wichita Mountains," Adkin said. "The wagon train should be here in a few days. If Sam is along, I want to take him and two others to find Satanta, and we can also make a trip to Sam's family in the Indian Territories. This Zeb Jarvis is Mary Catherine's uncle, and he is friends with Mead. Chisholm helped him, also."

"I'd like to string along, Boss. If that's alright with you," Marcellus said.

"Sure Tom, that's fine," Adkin responded.

The day Sam and the rest of the crew arrived from Fort Dodge, soldiers in a wagon rolled into camp with the body of Sergeant Antonio Martinez. His guards had discovered he was missing that morning.

Somehow, Martinez had been whisked away in the night from his room at the stables. No soldiers heard or saw a thing, which was troublesome since Indians would have to cross nearly a hundred yards of open ground from the timber line to get to him.

Martinez was found about a quarter of a mile from the eastern wall near Wolf Creek. He had more than 30 arrows in his body, he was scalped and his testicles had been cut off and were stuck in his mouth. He was also missing both hands and both feet, boots and all. His eyes had been gouged out and his wrist and legs irons were left at the site, covered in blood.

Everybody remaining in camp was suddenly very nervous, especially considering Indians could infiltrate their camp unnoticed and remove someone without a sound.

Sergeant C. Antonio Martinez was the first to be buried at the new Camp Supply cemetery. He was 22.

•••

General Sully was again putting together plans for another supply run to Fort Dodge, and the crew decided Ray Dee would ramrod the wagons back and telegraph headquarters for more help. Many of the original teamsters were wanting to go home for awhile and get some rest and see family. Adkin couldn't blame them, and he was sure as soon as they got to Fort Dodge, they would head home.

Ray Dee said he would also telegraph the YR&R crew still at Bent's Fort to see what they needed. Adkin had left them with plenty of money and told them to contact Sanderson with their needs while he was away where Western Union had yet to lay in lines.

Adkin, Ryan, Sam, Uribe and Tom made plans to use one of the freight wagons and a team of two mules and another five head of fresh saddle horses to head for Fort Cobb to see if General Hazen knew where Satanta was.

They would travel with no military backup, and it could get dangerous. They made sure they had all the ammunition and arms they could carry.

But before they could leave, bad news hit Camp Supply, again. Custer and Sheridan had found Major Elliot and 17 of his men's mutilated bodies a few miles east of Black Kettle's burned out camp.

They had also found the bodies of a White woman named Blinn and her young son. They had been captured months earlier by Indians on the Santa Fe Trail near Fort Lyon.

Rumors were that a witness of her capture identified Chief Satanta as a leader of the band that attacked them on the Trail.

When Sheridan saw the bodies of the Blinn woman and her son, he immediately sent out an arrest order for Satanta, believing Satanta had killed her before trading for the Squaws and children Custer had taken hostage.

•••

Adkin and his crew departed Camp Supply December 18, while Custer and Sheridan were still chasing bands throughout western Oklahoma. Rumor had it Sheridan's troops had caught the Kiowas near Fort Cobb two days earlier and were preparing to annihilate the village when Fort Cobb's General Hazen sent a written message to the force that the Kiowas had surrendered to him and should not be attacked.

Adkin smiled when hearing the news, as he knew it would anger Custer not being able to kill more Indians. But rumor was Satanta was not there.

Adkin was sure General Hazen would know where to find Satanta, so they would travel the same route the military took, right down the Washita River. Adkin had promised himself he would stand at the sight where Black Kettle died and pay homage.

After crossing the Canadian, which was no problem as it was low and mostly frozen, they reached the Washita. Following it downstream, they were headed southeast and then encountered a large bend turning back to the north.

As they stayed on the west side of the river, they started gaining high ground from the hills off to their left. They were noticing the river was making another large bend back east and then south again – like a huge horseshoe.

That's when Uribe shouted, "Look, across the river."

There were the remains of Black Kettle's camp. They quickly headed south and crossed the Washita.

All around them were burned out tipis, travois and lodge poles, some burned remains of hides, blankets and robes, ragged clothing in places. Everything was levelled.

One could see where the tipi camp fires were located in the middle of the lodges. Adkin had a hard time trying to understand the panic they felt when Custer's troops came in from all directions and hit them at dawn while most were in their blankets trying to stay warm.

Off to the south of the camp, lay hundreds of carcasses and bones of ponies Custer's men had killed. Crows and magpies still were picking from the bones. They later learned Custer had order his troops to shoot more than 900 horses because he was in a hurry not to get trapped by the 1,000 Indians coming to help Black Kettle.

Adkin and his crew slowly walked through the camp, their horses softly stepping over debris everywhere. Tom was having problems maneuvering the wagon through the rubble.

A light snow had dusted the area since the attack, yet there was plenty of evidence of a complete slaughter.

"Let's see if we can make more miles before dark," Adkin said, breaking the silence.

"Si Señor, I don't want to camp in this place," Uribe said with dread in his voice.

A few miles east, there was another scene of a previous fight. There were arrows, some broken spears and the bones of mules or horses – the wolves and coyotes having cleaned most of them.

"This is probably where Major Elliot's men got caught by the Indians that were coming upriver when they heard Custer's fire," Ryan said. "I heard Elliot had swung around to the east to attack."

"They say 17 soldiers got killed here," Uribe said. "I no want to camp here either."

"No, let's move on a few more miles," Adkin said.

They followed the trail along the Washita on further south until it had leveled out eastward again. They could see many horses and some wagons had moved through the area in the last few weeks.

Adkin made mental notes whether this part of the trail to Fort Cobb could sustain comfortable stagecoach service. He later discovered Ryan had been doing the same thing. They agreed it was possible, but maybe there was a better trail to be found from Camp Supply to Fort Cobb.

•••

On the second day out of the Washita Battle area, they arrived at Fort Cobb. The fort was surrounded by lodges and hundreds of Indians. Uribe said they were mostly Cheyenne. They announced themselves at the fort and asked to meet with General Hazen.

General William Babcock Hazen had found himself in the middle of a battle between the military and the Indian Bureau, and he was actually appointed by both branches of government to his position at Fort Cobb. Adkin hadn't appreciated his conflicting orders until they sat down to talk. Adkin brought up the Custer attack.

"As the commander of the military's Southern Indian District, I warned Black Kettle on November 20, that the military was pursuing the Cheyenne and the Arapaho," Hazen said. "Black Kettle was here at Fort Cobb seeking protection and supplies for his band.

"Ironically, I told him he couldn't stay here, so he planned to move his village to the larger Cheyenne encampments up on the Washita," He continued. "He and his band had been attacked at Sand Creek in Colorado in 1864, and he hoped to find safety in numbers.

"I even gave him a letter of protection, and he signed an agreement he would not make war this winter," Hazen added. "That damn Custer just wanted to kill, and by God, nothing was going to stop him. He could have easily entered that camp and asked them to surrender, and Black Kettle would have shown him my letter.

"Custer was very lucky because thousands of Indians were camped further down the Washita, and they got some of Elliot's men," he continued. "If that Satanta had caught him, Custer's scalp would be hanging in Satanta's lodge today."

"That's who I want to discuss with you, General," Adkin started. "I'm wanting to find Satanta's camp so I can talk to him."

"Talk to him? Talk to Satanta?" Hazen asked, with confusion on his face.

Adkin related what happened at Camp Supply, explaining the freighting business they were doing with the Army, and how Custer captured a bunch of women and children for trade.

Adkin explained the pregnant girl, his connection with her and Black Horse and Satanta.

"My horse is a stallion Black Horse gave me, and this necklace was given as a gift from Satanta himself, to offer me protection among his people," Adkin said, holding up the necklace for Hazen to examine.

"I renewed my friendship with him at the Medicine Lodge Creek Peace Treaty last year," Adkin added.

"Well, that's quite a tale, and one that nobody could make up," Hazen said, chuckling. "If you go due southwest of here, in about 20 miles you'll reach the foothills of the Wichita Mountains. They're not really mountains like most people think – the highest peak is only about 2,400 feet elevation – but when you get there, someone will contact you.

"By that, I mean Indians will be at lookouts to watch for anyone nearing their villages," Hazen continued. "You need to carry a white flag – high in the air – and then tell whoever stops you what you need and who you are.

"I don't know exactly where he's located but he's in those hills for sure," he said. "I know that from my scouts who reported that after Custer and the 19th headed further south looking for him and the other tribes, Satanta circled back into the hills.

"As far as I know, Custer is chasing the Cheyenne and Arapahoe now," Hazen added.

Adkin thanked Hazen and asked if they might camp there overnight and leave early the next day. He also said they would be coming back through on their return journey.

•••

The crew had the team hitched and mounts saddled and silently rode out of Fort Cobb before the sun had peeked over the horizon. They checked their compass and headed southwest. By noon, they could see the so-called mountains on the horizon. As they got closer, the timber seemed to grow thicker in places.

"I think we should get out the flag, don't you?" Uribe asked Adkin.

"Yes, I think you're right," Adkin said.

"I was thinking that about two miles back, Boss," Tom said from the wagon. He and Sam had been taking turns handling the mules.

As they approached a small canyon-like area where rainwater had etched out a small ravine, they heard a voice.

"Haaa-alt," someone yelled.

"Alto," the voice yelled again.

Then two mounted ponies came out of the ravine with Indians on their backs and faced the crew from about 50 yards.

"Oye, hablo Español," Uribe said.

"Si," one of them said.

Uribe went ahead in Spanish and told them they wanted – "a hablo con jeffe Satanta."

He then asked, "Es posible?"

Then Adkin heard his name and Tyler Ryan's, too.

"Bueno, bueno," one said raising his arm and waving. "I also hablo English, y Adkin Yates muy welcome – bienvenidos amigo."

Adkin and the others understood that. The Indians loped down to them and said, "You come with us. Páhy-Chi always welcome in Kiowa lodges. We know you."

•••

The trek to the Kiowa lodges was indeed difficult, the small trail barely accommodated a wagon, and then the trail went through dry rock stream beds and made numerous switchbacks.

About 30 minutes after meeting the lookouts, they were entering a large grassy hollow edged in timber. There must have been at least 100 tipis, smoke venting from every one.

On the upper side of the clearing, there were five larger tipis or lodges. These belonged to important Chiefs. They rode up to one with blue-painted, triangle bottoms on the hides and a blue stripe about head-high. This was Satanta's, Adkin and Ryan had been in it before – or at least one painted identically.

They dismounted as the lead lookout was talking through the flap. He then motioned Adkin and Ryan to enter – motioning to the others to stay back. As their eyes adjusted to the dark smokey interior, Satanta said, "Hachó Yates, welcome to my lodge."

"Hachó Chief Satanta," Adkin said. He learned the last time they met Satanta, that hachó meant something akin to "how's it going?" for there was no word in Kiowa that was strictly hello.

Satanta reached out and embraced Adkin and did the same to Ryan. He asked them to sit by the cooking fire.

"My friends, you come to our winter grounds to see me?" he asked. "I hope you not doing work for the Bluecoats. Many soldiers in our winter territories killing and ravaging our lodges.

"And this was promised to be our 'reservation' where we would be safe and provided food for our cold hungry squaws and children," Satanta added.

"Colonel Custer, the Yellow Hair, raided the Cheyenne and killed Black Kettle," he said.

"I know that Black Kettle was killed," Adkin said. "That is the start of my story I must tell you."

Satanta was all ears while Adkin related the aftermath of the Washita Battle and Custer bringing back hostages – the women and children. He explained he and his crew were at Camp Supply from the first wagons arriving at Wolf Creek.

He then began telling Satanta about the woman he saw being abused by a soldier guard.

"Wait," Satanta interrupted, holding up his palm.

He looked startled and stood up immediately. He went to the entryway and stepped outside. Adkin looked at Ryan and gave him a quizzical look. They heard Satanta and several other voices chattering away.

"We've got to learn more Indian languages, Ryan, if we are to survive this country," Adkin whispered.

Satanta stepped back in and closed the large buffalo hide flap.

"Please tell me more, Yates," Satanta said as he sat back down.

Adkin explained how he stepped in after the woman had been kicked and busted the man in his face.

"When I told the soldier who arrested me my name, the woman on the ground called to me," Adkin said. "When I looked further, it was Mah-aht-Tay, and she was badly injured.

"I carried her to the medical tent where the doctor took her into his care," Adkin continued. "But I was arrested and was unable to see her again. I saw from a distance when you came to trade for her and the others.

"I have been very troubled not knowing how she is or even if she lived," he said, almost tearing up saying it out loud. "She has become special to me because of the way our paths have crossed."

A voice at the entrance called out, "Hachó Satanta," and Satanta said, "Come."

The flap opened and in stepped Black Horse. Adkin could never forget that chiseled face and crooked smile. His short feathered head bonnet was also one of the most decorated Adkin had ever seen anywhere.

"Hello my friend, Adkin Yates," Black Horse said grinning.

Someone was following him into the lodge. It was a woman by stature, and when she pulled the blanket off her head, Adkin saw that big beautiful smile of Mah-aht-Tay. He jumped to his feet, as did Ryan and Satanta.

"Mah-aht-Tay," he said as he stepped near her, unsure if he should even touch her. They stood there momentarily without speaking. Her teeth were perfectly white and her big doe eyes were shining.

"You are well?" Adkin asked her, then looking to Black Horse. "Is she well?"

"Yes, I am well now," Mah-aht-tay said softly. "You come to save my life again Adkin Yates. I am happy you come here."

Satanta motioned for everyone to sit and immediately picked up his pipe and lit it. It was passed around to all the men.

Then they started chatting. Satanta spoke the most English, but Adkin was surprised how much English Mah-aht-Tay and her father spoke, as well.

Satanta explained Mah-aht-Tay had married soon after the Little Arkansas Peace Treaty three full seasons earlier to a Cheyenne warrior named Little Robe, son of peacemaker Chief Wolf Robe. Little Robe was married before but his wife died from fever, and he had been without a woman for a year.

Black Horse was good friends with Black Kettle. Black Horse arranged the marriage and she moved to Black Kettle's band.

"Little Robe was killed by Custer that day they took Mah-aht-tay," Satanta said. "She had troubles to have children, but finally was with child when the soldier killed her unborn son just one moon from life."

"Yes, I know," Adkin said barely audible. "My heart breaks for her agony and pain."

There was total silence for a minute or so.

Suddenly, Black Horse stood and asked the others to rise. He then took Mah-aht-Tay's hand and put it in Adkin's hand and clasped them together with both his hands. He looked to the sky, closed his eyes and said something in Kiowa, then wailed loudly several times and swayed back and forth.

He then looked to Adkin and said, "My daughter is now your woman, Adkin Yates. I am pleased as the young pony in the tall spring grass.

Adkin's eyes started to glaze over, and he mumbled, "What did you say?"

Satanta spoke up.

"Adkin Yates, the sun, the moon and the stars have spoken to Black Horse and Mah-aht-Tay that you are the one for this woman," Satanta said. "She owes you her life – now twice the spirits have brought you together. Black Horse is giving you his daughter.

"It is forever, in the eyes and hearts of both her and her father," he said solemnly.

"What? What are you saying?" Adkin said.

"You are now married, Adkin," Ryan said smiling. "She is your new bride, and it's from now on."

"Married?" he asked looking around at each of them. "Married? I didn't ask to be married. I didn't say that did I Ryan?"

"This woman will treat you well Yates," Satanta said. "She is hard worker, beautiful as a fawn, and she is still young and may be able to bear you many children."

"But Chief Satanta, Chief Black Horse ..."

"I think you should shut up, Adkin, and don't say another word – if you're smart," Ryan interrupted.

Black Horse said he would gather her belongings, and actually bear hugged Adkin with both arms.

"We must now smoke the pipe again," Black Horse said as he motioned for all to sit, except Mah-aht-Tay. She turned to Adkin and smiled.

"When I was harmed, I remember you called me Mat-ti," she said shyly. "I like that name Adkin Yates, thank you. You call me Mat-ti, si?"

She pulled the blanket over her head and scurried out of the tipi giggling.

Satanta lit the pipe and handed it to Black Horse, who said the spirits of life had blessed he, his daughter and the Kiowa People. He took a puff, wailed to the heavens again and handed it to Adkin.

Adkin just sat there, still in a daze.

"Take the pipe, Adkin," Ryan said, grinning more and more by the minute.

"We are proud you will now truly be in the Kiowa family," Satanta said. "Tonight we celebrate you taking Mah-aht-Tay as your woman."

Ryan was having difficulty in not laughing out loud.

•••

Satanta led the group out of his tipi and barked some orders to several of the women and men surrounding his lodge and Adkin's men. Adkin later remembered looking at Tom and seeing the huge man trembling from fear with all the Indians around him holding the bridles of the mules.

Satanta then raised his arms and shouted at the top of his lungs in Kiowa. Adkin heard Black Horse and then his name and then Mah-aht-Tay's names interspersed in the announcement.

Suddenly, all the Indians started yelping and wailing and jumping up and down, stomping their feet, even waving their arms back and forth. The mules nearly jumped over the tipi when it started.

Ryan stepped up on the wagon's foot rail and held up his arms.

"Men, I want to announce this in English, as well," Ryan said above the Indians, who hushed a little. "Our partner and friend, Adkin Yates is now married to Black Horse's daughter, Mah-aht-Tay."

After the Indians realized Ryan was finished, they went back to yelping, and several rhythmic drum beats were beginning.

Several Indians came up to Ryan and Adkin, who still looked like a statue, and as white, were led by the hand away from Satanta's tipi. Others led the mules and motioned for the men in Adkin's crew.

They were led to another tipi nearby, which was being cleared out by several women. They were removing some personal items and clothing. The men were led in and told this was their lodge for the night.

"Adkin, what is happening – you're married?" Sam asked.

"Señor, what are you doing?" Uribe spoke up.

Ryan stepped forward and raised his palm as to signal 'stop.'

"Gentlemen, Black Horse gave his daughter to Adkin because this is the second time Adkin has protected her from further harm," Ryan said. "The girl's husband was killed in the Washita Battle a few weeks ago, and Black Horse and Chief Satanta feel like this is fate and so they married the girl to Adkin."

"This can't be happening. This is, is, is all a dream," Adkin stuttered. "I can't marry now. I can't marry anyone now."

"Sit over here Adkin," Ryan said.

They all gathered around Adkin offering encouragement.

"Señor, she is a lovely girl – muy bonita," Uribe said. "I saw her leaving Satanta's lodge."

"Gosh. Maybe it's a blessing, Boss," Marcellus said. "At least you have someone to share your life with."

"Let's go outside for awhile, men," Ryan said. "Let it sink in and give him some time. He's still in shock."

As they filed out of the tipi, Sam kneeled next to Adkin.

"Tom's right, Adkin, it may be a blessing," Phillips said. "I realize you never wanted to marry until you found the right woman, but you don't have to take this woman as a wife if you prefer not to, if you know what I mean. She can help you as a partner – as someone to manage your household – even though you don't really have one yet.

"But I promise you this; Mary Catherine and I will help you with making Mah-aht-Tay a part of our lives – all our lives."

Sam stood, and he, too, walked out of the tipi, leaving Adkin by himself and his thoughts to sit in the dim light of the cook fire.

•••

Sitting alone, Adkin started absorbing what had happened. His "why" was beginning to make sense.

He had helped a small girl three years ago. Helped her again when she was at Camp Supply – Black Horse was overwhelmed with gratitude, that's all. Satanta's involved because he is Black Horse's great friend, that's all.

The girl had really suffered this last time – her husband, the father of her baby – had been killed, she was taken prisoner, and then she loses her son and nearly her own life. That's a lot of pain, misery and sorrow in only a few weeks.

He felt badly for her, as most Christian's would. He showed that concern for her, and her father and Satanta were witnesses to those feelings. But Adkin didn't have marriage feelings – he didn't love Mah-aht-Tay like that.

"What was he going to do? He slowly realized he couldn't walk out in front of the Kiowa Chief and his Medicine Man and all their tribe and say, 'No, I don't want to marry this woman.'

"How stupid, Yates," he thought to himself.

He definitely felt for this girl – or woman now. She was sweet and pretty, and he did sincerely care if she was treated well.

"Maybe if I give her a home to take care of, some animals, make her life better by living in the 'White' world – she would be happy and not have to live the hard life of an Indian squaw," he said to himself.

"I know, I will take her in like she was a little sister – look after her, make her life easier," he suggested to himself. "That's it – like adopting the child of a neighbor couple who had died of some reasons – leaving an orphan."

And he thought about what Sam had said, that he and Mary Catherine would help integrate her into their freighting family. That made sense. Mary Catherine would be a great influence on her, and Mah-aht-Tay could help with Mary Catherine's new baby.

"That's how I'm going to have to handle this for now. I can't insult my Kiowa friends – and it's not like they are just a couple of average warriors," he said to himself. "I have adopted her, even though they believe it's marriage."

Adkin stood, smiled to himself and opened the tipi flap and stepped outside. Indians and his men all started celebrating again, Indians yelping and his crew clapping hands, saying, "Congratulations."

Adkin grinned uneasily.

•••

That night, there was great energy throughout the Kiowa village, Adkin and his men sat in a large half circle on buffalo robes with Satanta in the middle, Black Horse to his right, Mah-aht-Tay to his right, Adkin next to her, and then Ryan and the crew sitting to Ryan's right. On Satanta's left sat other Chiefs and notables of the band. Each had a Chief's headdress of various sizes and decorations.

A large fire pit sat out to the side and several quarters of buffalo were on a long iron rods slowly being turned while the meat roasted. The Indians loved their meats roasted in this fashion.

A vinegary alcoholic drink was being passed around and several bottles of brandy and whisky, most likely proffered from traders or thievery from freighters. Adkin found himself imbibing a little more than he usually did.

It was late when most were ready to retire. As Adkin rose with the others, Satanta said there was a special lodge for he and Mah-aht-Tay and pointed to a small tipi that had been erected off to the side of Satanta's lodge.

Adkin hadn't imagined this.

"That's okay, she can stay with her father tonight," Adkin blurted.

Both Black Horse and Satanta gave Adkin a leering frown, and just as he noticed Mah-aht-Tay drop her head and facing downward like she wanted to crawl into a hole, Ryan elbowed Adkin hard.

"Oh, yes. I see, I see," Adkin said to the Chiefs. "Let me gather my things …"

"We've already given them your bedroll and clothes bag, Adkin," Ryan said, elbowing Adkin again.

"Yes, yes … okay," Adkin slurred, and slowly reached out his hand to Mah-aht-Tay.

She saw his hand and looked up into his face and smiled. She placed her hand in his, and he led her toward the tipi, looking back several times at his crew.

•••

The following morning, everyone was enjoying the bright daylight leisurely, moving slowly around the camp. When Adkin and Mah-aht-Tay came out of the special tipi. Ryan came over and greeted them.

"Good morning Missus Yates," Ryan said as he touched the brim of his hat.

"Hello Ryan," she said softly.

"You can call her Matty, Ryan" Adkin said sternly. "We don't have to use that Missus Yates stuff, okay?"

"I like be called Mat-ti," Mah-aht-Tay said, grinning from ear-to-ear.

The others were milling around the wagon, packing their belongings and supplies.

"If we're going to go find Zeb, we might want to get on the trail," Phillips said. "He included a crude map to his place in Blaine County. It looks like it might be four or five days north of here."

"Yes, you're right Sam, we need to get going," Adkin said. "Things are moving kind of slow around here. You'd think it was a nice spring day without a care in the world."

"I heard some of the Indians kept celebrating and dancing and – of course, drinking until just a hour or so ago," Ryan said.

"Si, I was with them until about four," Uribe said sheepishly. "Make many new Kiowa friends, now that Adkin is a real Kiowa."

"Okay, that's enough," Adkin said. "Let's get Matty's belongings loaded, and we'll hit the trail."

Satanta and Black Horse walked up as they were loading Matty's belongings, mainly hides, robes and jewelry. She had two boxes of beads, animal teeth, feathers and necklaces.

"Looks like you'll have to keep her in baubles, Boss," Tom said as he walked by with a large box of beads.

"Where you go now, Adkin Yates?" Satanta said. Adkin sensed he was still weary Adkin might tell the Bluecoats where he was camped.

"We are going back through Fort Cobb and then to Blaine County to find Sam's relative – the uncle of his wife – Zeb Jarvis," Adkin said, hoping to allay Satanta's fears. "We want to see if we can do freighting with Zeb, as we have 90 wagons now."

"We know Jarvis," Satanta said calmly. "He good friend of Mead and Chisholm, before he die."

"Yes, that's him," Adkin said, as Sam hurried over. "Can you tell us where to find Zeb?"

"His ranch is south of the Cimarron and twice that north of the Canadian," Satanta said. "He is very fair with the Kiowa, give us more for our skins and furs."

Sam pulled his map out of his shirt pocket and unfolded it. He showed it to Satanta and pointed to an "X."

"Yes, that is close," Satanta said. He moved his finger slightly left of the "X" and said, "There is a small creek that turns north, follow it for three or four miles, and his place is in a beautiful clearing, the creek runs by it to the Cimarron.

"But there will be no water in it now," Satanta added. "Jarvis has the sign of the Arapahoe and the Kiowa on his trading post — many Arapahoe winter in that area, too. Mah-aht-Tay can speak with them if they make trouble for you."

"Thanks, Chief," Phillips said, hurrying back to the wagon.

"Chief, can I ask you something very personal? You don't have to answer me, because I respect you for how you treat me and Ryan," Adkin asked, as he moved to Satanta's side where no one else could hear him.

"What troubles you Adkin Yates?" Satanta said.

"Were you responsible for taking a white woman, Clara Blinn, and her 2-year-old son from near Fort Lyon back in early October?" Adkin asked.

"No, Adkin Yates, I did not take that woman and her son – I was not even there," Satanta said.

"Thank you, Satanta, you have lightened my heart," Adkin said, and stepped back and smiled.

"I was also not camped along the Washita when Custer killed Black Kettle," Satanta continued. "Mah-aht-Tay was there with her husband's tribe, but my people were camped here. When I hear Mah-aht-Tay was captured by Custer, we go to Camp Supply to help free her."

Adkin stood there, not sure what to say. He knew Custer and Sheridan were telling everyone that Satanta was at Washita and killed the Blinn woman and her son before fleeing.

"I hope your travels will be safe, Adkin Yates," Satanta said, patting Adkin on the back shoulder.

"Thank you Satanta, Great Chief of the Kiowa People," Adkin said, then turning to Black Horse. "And thank you Black Horse, great Medicine Man of the Kiowa People.

"I give you my word I will take good care of Mah-aht-Tay, and no harm will come to her while I am with her," Adkin said.

Black Horse again hugged Adkin like a long-lost brother, yet the top of his head only reached Adkin's chin.

As they rode out, Kiowa lined the trail north and all waved and shouted things to Mah-aht-Tay and the crew. Adkin felt pride, in a way, that he and his crew would at least be safe among the Kiowa.

•••

That evening, they rolled into Fort Cobb again, and spoke with General Hazen, who stared mightily when Matty walked in with he and Ryan.

"General Hazen, I would like you to meet Matty … um, ah … Matty … my new wife – she's Kiowa," Adkin mumbled. "Matty, this is General William Hazen. Big Medicine here at Fort Cobb."

Matty bowed her head and smiled.

"Hello," she said.

"Well y'all just have a seat and I'll rustle us up some coffee," Hazen said, turning to shout some orders to aides.

"Well young man, you're writing a fast and odd story while travelling this here western frontier," Hazen said. "Was that why you were looking for Satanta – to marry this girl?"

"No sir, I just wanted to know she was alive and safe, but her father and Satanta mistook my feelings, and her father married us on the spot while I was just standing there," Adkin said, knowing Matty didn't understand all his words.

The General burst out laughing, but caught himself after seeing Adkin's frown. But then Adkin and Ryan started laughing, too, thinking about how crazy that sounded. They all were laughing and chuckling, and Matty sat there and smiled while looking at all these men.

"Unbelievable, I know, but it's true, General," Adkin said.

Coffee was served and the men began talking business. Adkin told Hazen where they were going, and the General knew of Jarvis, though he never met him personally.

"He was working for Chisholm before Jesse died," Hazen said.

"Well, we're interested in finding out if there is enough freighting business to put wagons and teams at Jarvis' place," Ryan said. 'We've done a lot of work for the Army since we started the business, and Camp Supply will probably not need as many provisions as it turns to spring."

"I'll tell you something, but you didn't hear me say it – even though nobody has told me not to say it – but we're getting ready to build another supply camp down in the area you just came from," Hazen said. "They're establishing a place Sheridan is calling Camp Wichita. It's just about 10 miles east of where y'all went.

"There's a place there called Medicine Bluff, and that's where Sheridan wants another supply base so he can prosecute the tribes," Hazen continued. "You know Sheridan has hooked up with Custer and the 19th now, and he's even going down into Texas chasing what he calls 'hostiles,' which is any Indian they find."

'The way Sheridan talked, they will start the camp in early January," Hazen added. "Have your people contact Leavenworth or reach out to General Sherman. I wouldn't, he's an ass, too. But check it out."

"Thanks General, we surely will," Adkin said.

Adkin asked Hazen about stagecoach service in the area.

"General, do you think stagecoach travel is or will be a desirable service in this part of the Territories?" Adkin asked.

"Well hell yes, Mister Yates," Hazen said. "Now that we have Camp Supply and the army is wanting to establish another camp south of here, it begs for settlers to open this country up."

"Well, We're looking into that as well as the freighting business," Adkin said.

"There's one other thing," Hazen bent forward and looked serious. "We just got news that soldiers sifting through the Washita Battle area – probably just a few days after you passed through there – found the body of a white woman.

"You may have heard of her, Clara Blinn?" He continued. "Well they found her and her son's bodies hidden under a brush pile aways down the Washita.

"Word is out that Sheridan has issued an arrest warrant for Chief Satanta because Sheridan believes Satanta was the one that took her captive in the first place," Hazen said. "I wouldn't be surprised if the 7th and the 19th circle back and comb those hills in the Wichita Mountains looking for Satanta."

Adkin just sat there for a moment, and then finally realized he needed to say something.

"You're right General, That's what I would do, too," Adkin said. "Sheridan is definitely chasing down every bad Indian out there.

"Well General, we probably better get moving," Adkin said as he stood.

"Would ya'll care to sup with me this evening?" Hazen asked. "Even the … Missus?"

"Maybe next time General. If you don't mind, we'd like to get with your quartermaster and purchase some supplies for our trip tomorrow," Adkin said. "And I know it's getting late, and we don't want to interfere with his evening meal."

"Why sure, I understand. I'll have my aide take you over there right now," Hazen said. "Good luck to you and your men.

"What a unique story," Hazen mumbled as they all walked out the door. "But she is a pretty little thing."

•••

Once outside, Adkin pulled Uribe to the side. He whispered what Hazen had told him about the White Woman and her son being found dead – and how Sheridan was looking for Satanta with a warrant for his arrest.

"I want you to take a fresh horse with you, and ride back to Satanta's lodges and tell him Sheridan and Custer are going to look for him there," Adkin said. "Tell him Sheridan wants him because Sheridan believes Satanta took the woman and her son captive back in October."

"Maybe he did, Señor," Uribe interrupted.

"I know he did not, Uribe," Adkin said sternly. "Trust me. I want you to warn Satanta Sheridan is after him. I would go myself, but I don't think I could find the crew up the trail to Jarvis' ranch.

"Besides, I think you have a better chance of surviving this country than a big 'ol white man," he added, grinning.

"Si Señor, I will go like the wind," Uribe said, feeling important that Adkin would ask him such a favor. "I can make the trip to Satanta's in probably 5 to 6 hours.

"I will find you in the second day of your travels," Uribe added.

As he pulled a horse from the crew's string of horses behind the wagon, Ryan walked over.

"What's going on?" he asked Adkin.

"When Hazen said 'I wouldn't be surprised if the 7th and the 19th circle back and comb those hills,' it was code for Hazen has already sent word to Sheridan where Satanta is camped," Adkin said. "Don't you see, Hazen had to do that when Sheridan told him he had an arrest warrant for Satanta, and Sheridan wanted to know where Satanta was. Hazen couldn't afford to lie to Sheridan.

"I'm sending Uribe back to warn Satanta" Adkin said. "I'm sorry for not talking it over with you first. I would go myself, but I'd end up lost and alone in the Indian Territories.

"He's putting his supply packs together if you think it's a bad idea – we can stop him," Adkin added.

"No. No, I think you're right," Ryan said. "I would like to do it, too, but I'm like you – I don't know where to go exactly. It's not like we're following one river all the way, we've got to cross several."

"And we're both White Men," Adkin said.

They turned around to see Uribe mount up. He reined his horse toward them.

"I will go out and tell the guard at the gate I'm scouting ahead – then go north until I'm out of sight," Uribe leaned over and whispered. "I will then circle back and be at Satanta's before the sun rises."

And he was off.

Adkin then saw Hazen's aide coming. He would take them to the supply warehouse. Adkin made a mental note to make sure he bought plenty of tobacco for Uribe for when he returns on the trail north.

While they were setting up their tent and stove, Sam asked where Uribe was. Adkin and Ryan said he was going to scout the trail north.

"Don't worry, he'll find us," Ryan said, knowing he and Adkin had to keep the truth – for now anyway – from the crew lest they get in trouble for abetting Satanta. They knew Sheridan would throw anybody assisting Satanta in the brig at Leavenworth for a long, long time.

Adkin discovered a problem that night concerning having a new wife – where does she sleep? After setting their tent, Adkin helped Matty bring her bedroll of buffalo robes and her clothes bag into the tent and placed them near the corner he usually slept in.

He tried to tell her she would be safe, and that when travelling they often were all forced to sleep in the big Army tent together with the stove. None of the crew said a word as he was explaining she would sleep next to him, but the men were glancing back and forth trying not to laugh.

Matty seemed to understand and started helping carry in firewood from the wagon, and she held out her arms when Tom and Sam were unloading some bags of food and essentials, gladly carrying them into the tent.

After eating a small cold meal, everyone nestled into their bedrolls with Matty laying inside of Adkin nearer the stove. When the lantern was turned off, the men started saying, "Goodnight Matty," Once finished, there was a moment of silence, then Matty said, "Hello," believing that English word was a warm word of acceptance.

All the men had a silent smile on their faces, including Adkin.

•••

Adkin woke the crew about 6, nearly two hours before sunrise, urging them to hasten and get their gear together so they could hit the trail. Once all saddled up, sitting Matty on the wagon seat, and with Tom taking first shift in driving the wagon, they headed for the gate.

As they spoke with the two guards on duty at the gate, Adkin leaned out of his saddle and handed one of them a piece of folded paper.

"Would you see to it that General Hazen gets this after he wakes up," Adkin asked. "We wanted to let him know how much we appreciate his hospitality."

"Yes sir. Y'all be careful out there," the soldier said, making Adkin believe a lot of the forts were being manned by Confederate southerners hearing their accents.

"Better than going to prison, I guess," Adkin thought to himself.

Once they got out of earshot of any soldiers, Adkin told the crew about rumors, from an Army General, that another supply post was going up south of Fort Cobb to help Sheridan prosecute his winter campaign against certain tribes.

Sam got excited saying his uncle-in-law could be of great assistance if that were true. The others agreed wholeheartedly.

"We could work it two ways," Ryan said. "If freight wagons had to take supplies directly from Fort Dodge to this new camp, it would be shorter going by way of Jarvis' Ranch, maybe.

"Or if we had to, we can carry some freight from Dodge to Camp Supply, and then the rest to the new camp," Ryan continued. "Jarvis would give us a central point to control a lot of wagons for traffic going either way. And it might be an ideal place to offer stagecoach service on these branches off the Santa Fe Trail – away from the rail lines."

"The important thing will probably be how much manpower Jarvis can supply." Adkin said. "Rounding up reliable teamsters and wranglers will be key to the business."

"And we have to have animals," he added.

"More and more people are coming westward," Sam said. "I'd guess Jarvis has contacts throughout a wide area – especially if he was doing business with Chisholm and Mead."

"That's true," Ryan added.

•••

They made it to the Canadian River that first evening, but had to do a little looking until they found a place to cross. The crossing had been used by others, which was a good sign. The Canadian here was wide, maybe more than a quarter of a mile, and it was covered by ice everywhere. The worst danger was horses or mules breaking through and getting spooked if they didn't touch bottom right away.

"Let's go ahead two-by-two with the horses, and Tom, you wait to see how it goes," Ryan said.

Tom had taken the reins of the mules a few hours earlier, and he had more experience with teams and wagons than Sam did anyway.

Adkin went to the wagon and asked Matty to ride behind him on Diablo. After some additional hand signals, She stood, grabbed her blanket and slipped on the horse's back behind Adkin.

Then he and Ryan started out first, slowly tracking straight to the other side. There was enough snow over most of the ice to keep it from being too slippery, but there was some creaking and cracking sounds.

When they reached the other side, they turned and yelled for Sam to ride his mount and to bring one of the other horses across on a lead. Sam managed to stay in the same tracks and was also successful getting to the north bank.

Adkin had Matty slip off Diablo near several large walnut trees near the bank.

"Well, we have two more horses and a two-mule team and wagon to get across," Adkin said, as he reined Diablo back to the south bank with Ryan following. Sam tied the fresh horse up by Matty and stayed in the saddle with a lariat ready if something happened.

Tom was told to follow the tracks as best he could, and Adkin and Ryan would each lead another horse a good distance behind the wagon.

After making about two thirds of the way across, the ice started cracking louder than they had heard with just the horses.

Then there was a loud crack, sounding like a rifle shot, and the left back wheel of the wagon had fallen through the ice.

The mules cried out, and stomped while Tom was yelling "Whoa, whoa," and using the reins to halt their attempts to go forward.

"Get your lariat and hook it to the wagon," Adkin shouted to Ryan as he jumped off Diablo and hustled over to the wagon. He was trying to lift up the back corner as Ryan tied off a rope and got back on his mount.

"Okay, pull," Adkin yelled. 'Tom whip them on."

As Adkin was groaning with his attempt to lift the wheel higher, he crashed through the ice and nearly disappeared, only his head was above the river and his arms started thrashing for something to hold onto.

Tom, jumped from the bench and ran to the back.

"Grab the wagon," he shouted, as he reached for Adkin.

He grabbed Adkin's left arm and Adkin had reached up and secured a hold on the back of the wagon with his other hand.

Together they strained and pulled Adkin toward the side and forward. Finally, Adkin was able to get his knees on the surface of the ice and snow.

"Whew, there's a running river under that ice," Adkin sputtered, still spitting out water and ice.

"Let's get you to Diablo and to the bank," Tom said as Ryan came up to help.

They got Adkin to the north side and Sam laid his bedroll blankets down and told Adkin to get out of those wet leathers he was wearing or he might end up like Peg-Leg Pete – or worse. Matty was helping spread out the bedding and assisting Adkin in removing his clothes.

As Adkin was fumbling with his leather leggings, Ryan told Sam to leave Adkin for a moment.

"We have to tie at least five horses to that wagon, and we need to do it quick," Ryan said. "Spread the lengths out so they're not side by side."

Within a few minutes, Ryan was yelling, "Yee haw," and telling to Tom to whip those mules. Just as they really got all the animals in sync, the wagon popped up like it was on a spring and the mules almost fell down as they skittered across the ice.

Once on the bank, Ryan and Sam ran over to Adkin. Matty had left Adkin's long-john bottoms on, and he was shaking under the blankets. His Buffalo coat, his buckskin jacket and pants, along with his leggings were laying in the snow already frozen as hard as rocks.

"Where are your boots?" Ryan asked nervously.

Adkin was turning blue and quivering so hard he couldn't answer audibly. Matty was massaging his cheeks with both hands

"He's still wearing them," Sam said, turning to Tom. "Tom, get that …"

"I got it Sam," Tom said as he heaved the stove out of the wagon and started toward them. Ryan took off and grabbed some of their firewood from the wagon and followed quickly back to Adkin.

After getting a fire going, they moved Adkin around so his feet were sticking out from beneath the blankets by the stove. They added more blankets and a buffalo robe on top of him.

Matty shoved her way close to Adkin. She then took one arm at a time and massaged it up and down trying to keep blood in his hands and fingers. After a few minutes with one arm, she would put it back under the bedding and pull out the other and repeat the process.

Sam then started massaging Adkins legs through the blankets and robe, mimicking Matty.

Adkin was still shaking hard, and yet to say anything, but he was conscious and aware what was going on, even though he was blue. Ryan was thinking a lesser man might not have had that kind of strength and would've passed out. That can be deadly because then one loses the power to fight.

It probably took about 30 minutes from when they lit the stove that Adkin said something.

"My feet hurt, but that's a good sign, si?" he said with a wry smile.

They had removed his boots once the leather had thawed and warmed up.

"Yes that's a good sign, you crazy Englishman," Ryan said tersely. "Was you trying to kill yourself?"

"I'm too spontaneous, as my mother always put it," Adkin said with a weak grin.

"If Tom hadn't got a grip on you, you might have been down river about five miles by now – under the ice," Ryan said.

Sam could sense Ryan's love for his friend. His fear of Adkin dying scared him, and Ryan was now getting angry. It was a very common thing that men turn their fear into anger. Sam had learned that during the war and after becoming a leader in the Army.

Tom had stayed busy clearing an area for their tent and then erecting it.

"We can move the Boss in here with the stove, as soon as you're ready," Tom said.

Two of them used two poles to heft the stove and move it into the tent. Three of them then lifted Adkin, blankets and all and carried him into the tent.

"Damn, you're almost heavier than me," Tom said laughing.

They finished putting all their bedrolls and belongings inside, where the temperature was already warming up – for everyone.

"I plum forgot, are the animals okay?" Ryan asked.

"I hobbled all of them and tossed them a little hay," Tom said beaming. "Y'all were busy saving Boss here. I had to do something."

They all laughed except for Adkin – he had fallen asleep. Matty had a look of sadness and worry on her face.

Adkin moaned in pain sometime during the night, and only Ryan heard it. He started to rise but saw Matty in the dim light of the stove's embers lift Adkin's bedding and crawl in next to him and pull her buffalo robe on top of them.

Ryan's worries about his friend suddenly eased. He realized Adkin had another person to help take care of the man Ryan had learned to love like a brother.

•••

When Matty pulled the robe back far enough to show her head out of the pile of buffalo hides and wolf furs in the morning, Tom was squatting next to the stove making coffee. He smiled at Matty.

"Good morning, Matty," Tom said, remembering Adkin's order to drop that Missus Yates stuff.

"Hello," she responded smiling.

As she crawled out from under the bedding fully clothed, Adkin woke up and moaned, "Oh goodness, I hurt all over."

"That ice water will take it out of ya, Boss," Tom said. The others were awakening and Tom told them the coffee was nearly ready.

Matty, who was still fully dressed, was up and digging through the food bags. She pulled out the cheese-cloth wrapped side of bacon and venison jerky and a jar of molasses. She moved over next to Tom and placed a skillet on the stove top and started carving off chunks of bacon with a knife.

Tom started filling cups with coffee and handing them to those who weren't busy rolling up their bedding and robes. He gave Matty plenty of room. This was the first morning for a real breakfast, and she took to it like an otter takes to water.

Adkin rolled over on his side and asked Tom for a cup. He took a couple of sips and laid it down next to him and fell back in his bedding.

"Ryan, could you do me a favor?" Adkin asked.

"Sure."

"Would you check my feet and tell me what they look like," Adkin said. "And I want the truth – the color of my toes, everything."

"Sure," Ryan said, as he went over to start pulling up the bedding from Adkin's feet.

Matty stopped what she was doing and looked to see what Ryan was up to.

Once Adkin's bare feet were exposed, Matty leaned over to get a good view, as did everybody.

"Well, your toes are a little bruised looking, but they're not black," Ryan reported.

"Are they purple?" Adkin asked. "No, Adkin, they're not purple," Ryan said. "And your feet look pretty good, too. Not much discoloration at all. Can you wiggle your toes?"

Everyone watched and a moment passed before Adkin's toes started moving a little, but they were all moving.

The men looked around to see Matty smiling from ear-to-ear. She went back to cooking the bacon. The crew started laughing and telling Adkin he wouldn't be joining the Peg-Leg Pete club, yet.

Adkin grinned.

"I don't think I've ever smelled better bacon in my life," he added, as Ryan covered his feet.

"That's because your Missus is cooking today, Boss," Tom said chuckling.

Adkin stayed under covers while eating, and they all agreed he should stay warm and rest.

"It won't hurt us taking a day off," Ryan said. "And we can wait for Uribe to return."

Sam and Tom went out and took care of the animals, and Matty cleaned up the breakfast utensils with a small bowl of water from thawed snow she went out and collected. Ryan was amazed at what she could do with one small cup of water. Lessons from a Plains Indian, he thought to himself.

The men found some dead downfall and cut some more firewood. Finding small limbs for their heating and cooking stove was vital. They had some, but one could never have enough. Adkin's accident proved that. They used double what they normally would have for a night on the trail.

Matty hovered around Adkin all day. She would massage his arms about every four hours and rub his feet gently using some lard-like balm that none of them could identify. But Adkin said it felt cool – and very soothing – on his feet.

She would tuck all his blankets, furs and robes tightly around him, and ask him if he wanted food or drink. She would use her hands, like her first two fingers pressed with her thumb and poking it in her mouth for food and cupping her palm and bringing it to her lips for drinking.

The men noticed all of this without words, at least in front of her, and were finding themselves happy Adkin had this woman. She was full of vigor, hard work and she cared about their friend more than they realized. Plus, she was cute as a kitten.

"If Adkin was forced into this marriage, I don't think he could've done better," Tom said to Ryan while they were outside cutting firewood. "The little gal really cares for him, you can see it."

"I'm beginning to think so myself, Tom," Ryan said.

•••

When the crew was preparing for an early evening meal and tending to their animals, Uribe rode up on the south bank of the Canadian, and yelled greetings across the river. It echoed down the shallow valley.

"Amigos, Uribe has arrived to the party," he shouted.

As he crossed the ice, he swerved wide of where the wagon and Adkin had broken through and reached their camp on the north bank.

Everyone was outside except for Adkin, and that was Uribe's first question. "Where is Adkin?" he asked.

At that time, the tent flap opened and Adkin stepped out. He was dressed except without his leggings and only moccasins.

He halted immediately and swayed a bit. Matty scurried over to him and wrapped an arm around his waist. He placed his arm across her shoulders to help keep his balance.

"What happened?" Uribe said urgently.

Ryan and the crew began telling Uribe why there was a hole in the river about 100 yards from the north bank. Uribe walked up to Adkin and Matty and whispered in Adkin's ear.

"Señor, your message was generously received and appreciated mucho," Uribe said, reaching for Adkin's hand and placing a small leather bag in it with something large and heavy in it. Adkin looked down and opened the bag. There sat a large rugged nugget of gold the size of a hen's egg.

"He told me, 'May the spirits watch over you and Matty," and that if you ever need anything or any help, send for him right away," Uribe said, smiling. He stepped back and grabbed Adkin's shoulder.

"It's good you are alive my friend," Uribe said so all could hear. "Few ever live if they are swept under the ice in such a big river."

Uribe turned to Matty.

"You take good care of our friend, si?" he said.

Matty shook her head in agreement and said, "Si. Hello."

Uribe hadn't realized how small she was until seeing her there with her arm around Adkin's waist. Well around to his side, but not all the way around. Her head only came to his armpits, which made Adkin look like a giant.

"Next to her, you look larger than Big Tom," Uribe said, and everyone laughed. "And I know that's not possible."

They all started jabbering like a bunch of hens; about the ice, about the trail; and about where Uribe had been.

"Why did you come in from the south to the Canadian when you were supposed to be scouting north for us?" Sam asked.

Uribe and Ryan turned to see what Adkin was going to say.

'Men, what I'm about to tell you could possibly place you in danger, even prison," Adkin began, still leaning against Matty. "I sent Uribe on a secret mission, and if you prefer to stay out of it, I don't blame you – you can walk over to the trees, and I'll fill you in what Uribe has done, on my request.

Tom and Sam glanced back and forth but neither walked away.

"We're with you, Boss," Tom said, with Sam saying the same.

Adkin went over why he asked Uribe to ride back to Satanta and tell them what they had learned from General Hazen. Adkin also said he had personally asked Satanta about the White Woman's capture, and Satanta said he didn't take her.

"I believe him, men," Adkin said. "If he had captured the woman and her son, he would brag about it. That's how Satanta is. He's arrogant and is not scared of any man, White or Indian."

"I agree with what you did," Sam said. "And it pleases me to know Custer couldn't kill him or arrest him. Custer would like nothing more than to add Satanta's scalp to his belt. That Custer should be sent back up to Fort Hays where he belongs."

"Yeah, Boss. I don't care about that," Tom spoke up. "And I don't mind saying if Satanta is your friend, he's my friend, too."

"Well, I had told Ryan, and I wanted to tell you all right away, but I didn't want to put you in harm's way if anything bad happened," Adkin said.

"And it's a secret we should never divulge lest we all go to jail," Adkin added.

Everybody went back to talking; Sam asking Uribe how much further did they have to get to Jarvis' place; Tom wanting to know if Uribe had encountered any warring Indians; And Ryan finally asking Uribe if he was hungry.

"Si señor, Uribe always hungry," he said, grinning.

Adkin turned with Matty and stepped back into the tent, complaining his feet were getting cold again. Matty helped him lay back in his bedroll like Adkin was a small child. Adkin slipped the gold nugget into his leather pouch he carried his compass in. He would have to decide what to do with this extravagant gift.

When Ryan came in, he had two pots and a skillet. Tom was carrying another food sack. Matty jumped up and went over and tried to take the implements from Ryan. He held on to them and snatched them away from her. Ryan gave her a look Adkin didn't really appreciate.

As Ryan started placing them next to the stove, Matty shied away and went back to sitting on the robes at Adkin's side. Adkin saw something that he intended to put a stop to right away – like he did with the "Missus Yates" talk.

"Ryan, Matty just wants to fit in, and it's been her work as a Kiowa woman to make the food for all the men," Adkin said. "Roasting meat is absolutely the only thing a Kiowa man would be caught doing. All the rest is woman's work – ever since girls are big enough to walk."

Ryan looked at Adkin a minute, like he was absorbing what Adkin had just said. He then smiled.

Ryan picked up the food sack Tom had laid by the stove, and held it out to Matty. She sat there, and Ryan took a step toward her.

"Here Matty, would you help make supper for us?" Ryan said, using his fingers and thumb together like she did putting them in his mouth.

She sprung forward like a Great Plains Jack Rabbit and grabbed the food sack. Ryan looked at Adkin and smiled.

"Thank you friend," Adkin said.

This wasn't lost on the others. They smiled and laughed a little, but not too loud to disturb Matty who was concentrating on getting things out to eat. She would turn to Adkin and Ryan and hold some Buffalo meat out for approval. She did the same for the potatoes.

"This will work fine having a good woman cooking for us," Uribe said. "I don't mind."

"Well, we may have to show her certain things we want like salt or how we like bacon fried," Adkin said. "But she will learn, I'm sure."

"Once we get her under Mary Catherine's wing, she'll be a hell of a cook," Sam said. Everyone agreed and laughed.

"I miss Maria Catrina's bread," Uribe moaned, and everyone broke out giggling again.

•••

As they were breaking camp the next morning, Adkin noticed Matty sneaked off into the brush, most likely to answer nature's call. She had eased out of the tent as well during the night by herself. Adkin's concern was she might come to harm – from either humans or animals – and he had promised her father she would be safe with him.

He was going to have to ponder this dilemma and how to solve it.

Uribe announced good news after consulting the map Sam had from Jarvis.

"We should cross the North Canadian in about 10 miles, and then we will travel through the area Cheyenne warrior Roman Nose and his band wintered until he was killed several months ago up on the Republican River," Uribe said. "Then Jarvis Ranch would be only seven or eight miles more."

"We should be there by evening at least," he added.

Crossing the North Canadian was quick and easy, which pleased Adkin and allayed his fears of crossing an icy river again.

They rode on through the area Uribe said was once where Roman Nose wintered. It was a beautiful valley just east of the North Canadian and the clearing was perfectly circular. They could see where tipi fire rings had been built before, though it didn't look as if any Indians had camped there so far this winter.

A few miles further, Uribe pointed to a small ravine, and asked Sam to check the map again. They decided it was possible the one Satanta pointed out, so they headed off northeast. Within a couple of miles, the ravine opened into a large hollow with several buildings, a corral and stables were sitting upon a snowy scene with smoke coming from two of the three buildings.

"That's got to be it," Sam said, and they all headed toward the ranch.

Within a 100 yards, an older man with a rifle ran to the front gate.

"Could I ask who you folks be," he shouted out.

"My name is Sam Phillips," Phillips yelled back, standing up in the wagon. "My wife is Mary Catherine Jarvis Phillips, Zeb Jarvis' niece."

"These men are my associates," he added.

"Well then, get on in here and we can warm you up," the man said lowering his gun. "My name just happens to be Zeb Jarvis."

As they approached the gate, the log one had to ride under over the two posts had the sign of the Kiowa and the Arapahoe burned in like brands.

Sam bounded out of the wagon and reached for Zeb's hand, but Jarvis gave Sam a bear hug.

"I'm so glad to see you nephew," Jarvis said. "How is that sweet little Niece of mine doing?"

"She's just fine, Uncle Zeb, and so is our newborn son, James Adam Phillips."

Jarvis' eyes ballooned in surprise.

"You don't say – that's wonderful lad. Y'all tie off your animals and let's all get inside," Jarvis said.

Once indoors, one could see Jarvis was doing fairly well for himself. He owned several items that had been shipped from New York or Pennsylvania.

Coming out of another room was a squat, sturdy woman with a full apron on with flour on it.

"Gentlemen, Sam, this is your Aunt Elizabeth, though she prefers Beth or Missus Jarvis," Jarvis said. "Momma, I don't know everybody yet, but this here is Sam Phillips, Mary Catherine's husband.

"And Sam said Mary Catherine have a new baby boy – born July 30," he added.

Beth came over and hugged Sam and kissed him on his cheek.

"I knew you when you was only 2 or 3 and your parents lived in Ohio where we were raised," Beth said. "We moved to Missouri when Mary Catherine was only about 6 or 7 herself.

"My, my, listen to me chatter away," Beth said. "Who are all these folks?"

Sam started with Adkin and his new bride, Matty.

"I'll explain more later about how Adkin and Matty met – it's quite a story in itself," Phillips said, then introducing Ryan, Uribe and Tom.

Beth walked over to Matty and took her hand.

"Welcome to our home Matty. I'm very pleased to meet you, my dear," Beth said.

"Hello," Matty said with a genuine smile.

Beth had everyone take a seat and hurried off to the other room, which must've been a separate kitchen, because a large stone fire place with burning logs was on the north wall of the log ranch house.

Sam kept explaining how all the men came to work together, and some off their most recent adventures, like Adkin nearly meeting his demise in the Canadian.

Suddenly, Sam remembered Zeb and Beth had two grown sons.

"Where are your boys, Uncle Zeb?" Phillips asked. "Darwin and Doyle, I believe."

"Well, they're not really boys any more," Jarvis said. "Darwin is 25, and Doyle is 23, and they should be back home by tomorrow or the next day. They're picking up four wagon loads of supplies at Mead's Ranch in Kansas.

"They're travelling with our four ranch hands for security reasons – what with the Cheyennes on the war path," he continued. "That's why I'm guarding the house here. It's just me and Momma."

Sam went into how he, Adkin and Ryan knew Mead and had spent considerable time with Mead when they all attended the Little Arkansas River Peace Treaty.

"You don't say?" Jarvis perked up. "There's a chance Jim might come back with the boys. He said he wanted to straighten out the books with us, since Mister Chisholm died back in March."

Adkin spoke up and explained he knew Chisholm as well. Had met him first at Fort Dodge shortly after the fort was established in 1865. Adkin asked how Jarvis, Chisholm and Mead were all tied together.

"Well, when we first came out here, back in '61, wasn't it Momma? Yes, '61," Jarvis began. "We followed two couples – we lived in Missouri then – who had contacts with Chisholm, through the Indians.

"After we got here, we met up with Chisholm – his original ranch is only about three day's ride southeast of here – and he said we could help him in his trading business, delivering goods and picking up goods, horses, mules, cattle – you name it," Jarvis continued. "Well, one family hated it out here, and they went back to Missouri. The other family, the husband died of pneumonia and his wife went all the way back to Ohio.

"That left us here, and Chisholm treated us well, and that's how we met Jim Mead," he said. "We delivered a wagon load of buffalo hides to Jim back in '63 or '64. It was up at the junction of the Little Arkansas with the big Arkansas – Chisholm actually had built a corral up there, it's pretty.

"It was about that time the boys came back from serving in the Union Army," he said. "That really helped, having more hands we didn't have to hire.

"Anyway, Jim gave us some chances to get involved with buying and trading some goods with the Indians and settlers, and we earned a percentage," Jarvis said. "Like we did with Chisholm. We actually have some money, not a lot, but money owed us from Chisholm's trading profits.

"We mentioned it to Jim when he was down here right after Chisholm's burial, and he said he would take care of any of Chisholm's debts. They had been trading and dealing with each other for years," Jarvis said. "He might show up with Darwin and Doyle – it's the slow season."

"It would warm my heart, and Ryan's, to see Jim again," Adkin said.
"Amen, a really good man," Ryan chimed in.

•••

Beth came out with a tray of clay mugs and a pot of coffee and served everyone – Matty first, of course. Matty looked at Adkin and he nodded approval and she then took the cup with both hands and sipped. She turned to Adkin and smiled, with those snow-white teeth gleaming.

They talked more about the trading business and asked Jarvis if he might be interested in establishing an YR&R Freight station for work going on at the new Camp Wichita down near Medicine Bluff. They explained how profitable the business had been – and still is – at Camp Supply, which Jarvis had heard about being built.

Adkin also brought up the possibility of establishing stagecoach service in the Territories, as he and Ryan also represented Barlow and Sanderson stagecoach company.

"I'm sure we would be interested in either or both,' Jarvis said. "But I need to discuss it with my boys, before I commit to any details. We've kind of spoke about it after receiving Sam's letter."

"Oh, we understand that," Ryan spoke up. "We'll put some numbers together and a proposed plan, and we'll talk it over when your sons get home."

Jarvis showed the crew to the warehouse, which housed a bunkhouse as well. There were plenty of cots, some even stacked in the corner – and a big pot-bellied stove. The crew started unloading their things, and Jarvis invited them to eat at 7 p.m.

Beth made a big meal that evening, and Jarvis passed around some cigars afterward. Uribe asked if he could smoke the small pipe he carried everywhere.

After discussions about the Indian attacks that summer and fall, they finally rose to leave for the bunkhouse.

"Mister Yates, would you mind if I invited Matty to stay in our extra room tonight?" Beth asked. "She would be much more comfortable in a feather bed."

Adkin turned to Matty and asked her in English and then used his hands, palms together against his face showing sleeping and pointing to the room.

"Here, show her the room," Beth said.

"Adkin took her into the room and sat on the bed. He reached up and took her arm and encouraged her to sit next to him.

When she sat down, her eyes widened and she jumped back up, slowly shaking her head no.

"I guess she's never seen a feather bed before Missus Jarvis," Adkin said, smiling. "Maybe next time."

They all went out to the bunkhouse, and Adkin laid Matty's bedroll and clothes bag on the cot next to his. She still was confused about what a cot was. She kneeled and looked under it and turned to Adkin.

Adkin started laying his bedroll out and stretching the blankets across the cot. She smiled and followed suit. After taking his boots off and removing his leggings, Adkin laid down of the cot and pulled the bankets up for cover.

Matty smiled and did the same. While lying there, she turned her head over and looked underneath the cot. She rolled back and grinned at Adkin like she had just discovered something very important.

"The others watched with smiles and muted giggles while shaking their heads.

"Poor thing, she's now living in a whole different world," Sam whispered. "Wonder if Aunt Jarvis would let me sleep on that feather bed?"

...

The following morning, while the men were being given a tour of the ranch by Jarvis, Beth had convinced Matty to help her in the kitchen. Again, Matty was in awe of such a room. It had a larder, several cupboards, things Matty had no idea what they were called. Beth was slow and deliberate and showed Matty all the things in her kitchen.

Matty was enthralled about how many skillets, pots and baking pans were hanging next to the stove and stacked on a counter. And Matty walked around the stove several times. It was huge.

"It's called a Dwyer Stove, my dear, shipped in this summer from Detroit," Beth said, just to make small talk. She was certain Matty had no idea of what she was saying.

Beth chuckled to herself, wanting to tell Matty she had cooked for up to 100 Indians before, which used up every item of food they had at the ranch, but it saved them from death. Beth was always cooking for lots of ranch hands or Indians stopping by because they were hungry.

Beth reached into the vegetable bin and grabbed some potatoes. She laid them on a cutting board on the counter next to the stove and handed Matty a knife. She pointed to the potatoes. Matty smiled and started cutting them in half.

Beth took the knife, and quartered them, and quartered them again, and handed Matty the knife.

Matty did the next one in the same amount of pieces Beth had done. Beth put a large wooden bowl next to the potatoes, and she put the cut pieces in the bowl. Matty mimicked her again and put the potatoes in the bowl, smiling the whole time.

Beth placed two skillets on two of the four burners the stove had. After Matty had cut up the spuds and placed them in a bowl, Beth took them over to a sink drain and poured some water on them and rinsed them off. She dried them off with a hand towel then took them and placed them in the skillet and put in a big blob of lard. It started melting and Matty was in awe of this stove.

There were two baking ovens and that's where Beth placed the biscuits, after pulling a lever on a flour bin above the counter, and then using yeast, milk, lard and some sugar. Beth also had Matty slice up bacon, much thinner than Matty had learned with her people.

That was placed on another burner plate, and Beth opened one fire-pit door and placed a few more chunks of wood on the hot embers. The smell of bacon, potatoes and biscuits was too much for Matty.

She stepped back and just stared and sniffed. All this cooking at one time – together. Matty was learning quick what Whites were capable of. It scared her in a way, but she was amazed.

•••

Jarvis showed the crew the size of his corral and stables. He was proud of it.

"Back in '65, this corral was used by Chisholm to go out and gather several hundred head of cattle," Jarvis said. "He had received an order from the Army for around 500 head of beeves for the forts along the Santa Fe Trail up in Kansas. Mr. Chisholm kept them here until he had enough to meet the order and then herded them off to Kansas."

"I believe he delivered 200 of them to Fort Dodge," Adkin said. "That's where we met Mr. Chisholm."

"We even ate some of those same cattle," Ryan said, laughing.

Jarvis turned quiet.

"It was a sad day when Chisholm died last March," he said. "He died about 40 miles southeast of here down on the North Canadian.

Jarvis then took them to the other outbuilding. This was the trading post. The shelves seemed sparse, with only a few items remaining in stock. Jarvis noticed their observations.

"As you can see, this is why my sons had to make a trip north," Jarvis said. "We're nearly out of everything. We had about 50 Cheyenne come through here last month, and they nearly cleaned us out of all our food-stuffs, like flour, sugar and tobacco.

"And we can't keep ammunition on the shelves at all," he continued. "The Indians will give you their best furs and hides for powder and bullets in the popular calibers – even old lead balls, especially in .44 caliber.

"Knives, hatchets, axes are the same thing," Jarvis said. "I could probably trade one wagon of those for four wagons of furs – and in a week after word got out I had them."

"Hopefully, if we secure an Army contract for the new fort, it will open up another avenue for income, Uncle Zeb," Sam said.

"That was my thoughts as well, Sam," Jarvis said, chuckling. "Trading with the Indians has always been like walking on thin ice, and thankfully, we've had great lessons in making a living like this from Mister Chisholm. And we're getting a few more families moving out here trying to start farms."

As they walked out of the trading post, four quick shots rang out down in the ravine – definitely from a repeating rifle.

"That's my sons, gentlemen," Jarvis said. "That's our own code letting us know it's them."

They turned back walking toward the front gate. As soon as they reached it, two mounted riders cam into view. One waved.

Behind them were teams of mules – eight-mule teams pulling two wagons each. The there was six riders, one dressed like an Indian scout. As they neared, Jarvis suddenly shouted.

"Well goodness gracious, if it isn't Mister James Mead," he yelled while raising an arm. "Welcome back to Oklahoma, Jim."

"It's good to see you, too, Zeb," Mead shouted back.

As his horse neared, Mead frowned and started realizing he knew some of these men standing with Jarvis.

"I'll be, is that Adkin Yates and Tyler Ryan standing there like ghosts of the Plains?" Mead asked, as he stopped and started dismounting.

"I see you are still wearing your scalp, Jim Mead," Adkin said, laughing as he embraced Mead by his shoulders.

"Same to you Yates, and your scalp is getting more attractive with all those golden locks," Mead said, laughing. "And look at you Mister Ryan, you two look like true frontiersmen, and that's a compliment from an old frontiersman that's beginning to look more and more like a politician."

Mead greeted Jarvis with a handshake and pats on the back, Jarvis hugged his sons and introduced them and the ranch hands to everyone. Adkin introduced his crew to all, and Mead named his three men who rode with him. They then headed to the post to unhitch the wagons near the front door, then led the teams and horses to the stables.

Sam then walked up to Mead.

"Mister Mead, you may not remember me, but I sat with you quite a bit on the Concord when we travelled to the Little Arkansas Treaty, and …"

"Of course I remember, you Lieutenant Phillips," Mead said. "Why yes, I thought that name sounded familiar. So you're no longer in the Army?"

"No sir, I resigned in December of '66 so I could get married – and settle into civilian life," Phillips said. "I now work for YR&R Freight – with Adkin and Ryan."

"Well good for you," Mead said.

Meanwhile, all the men were visiting and talking amongst themselves, explaining who and where they were and came from.

"So what brings you down into the Territories, Adkin?" Mead asked. "The last I heard was you men were toiling away establishing stage stations along the Santa Fe Trail – and doing it quite successfully."

"It's a long story, Jim, and it's all happened in a short time," Adkin said.

"Do you remember the little Indian girl, Mah-aht-Tay, the daughter of Black Horse? Back in '65?" he asked.

"Of course I do, I have recounted that story to many of my acquaintances over the last three years," Mead said.

"Well, she is now my wife," Adkin said. "Her father married us four days ago – Satanta was a witness."

"Holy cow, that's unbelievable, Adkin," Mead said. "Is that really true? What ... how did that happen?"

"Again, I'll explain it later," Adkin said. "I can't believe it myself, but it's true. We're married, and she's up at the house with Missus Jarvis right now."

"You mention Satanta was a witness," Mead said. "You must have seen him right before Colonel Custer arrested him in the Wichita Mountains for murder."

Adkin looked around at his men.

"That's where we ran into him," Adkin said with a quizzical look on his face.

"Funny thing was, The Quakers in the Indian office ordered Satanta and Lone Wolf, his top war chief, to be released three days later," Mead said. "I heard it directly from a scout who had been at Camp Supply and saw it."

Adkin was thinking Satanta was probably arrested just hours after being warned by Uribe. Apparently, Uribe never encountered Custer's troops – the troops had to come into those mountains from the south or west.

Just then, Jarvis held up both arms.

"Gentlemen, could I have your attention?" he said. "I'll go tell Momma there will be 10 more for breakfast, if you will help start unloading these wagons."

Several cheers went up, and Jarvis started off to the ranch house.

•••

Once Beth received news her sons were home, and breakfast would include 10 more men, she dove into the problem head-first. She handed Matty twice the potatoes that were already frying, and another large slab of salt-cured bacon to start carving on.

Matty saw Beth show her both hands with fingers extended saying "diez mas hombres," hoping like many Indians, Matty would understand some Spanish. Matty did, and started hurrying about the chores Beth gave her.

While Beth started on more biscuit dough, Matty had the potatoes cut, exactly as shown, and had started on the bacon. Beth showed Matty to use the same large skillet they had fried everything in before.

Both women were working together at a speed Beth had done many times in her life since moving to the Indian Territories. Beth was impressed how fast Matty learned.

Within 30 minutes after Jarvis told the women 10 more would be eating, Beth was ringing the dinner bell, shouting "Come and get it."

"That's Momma for ya," Jarvis said smiling. "That woman never fails to amaze me.

"Okay, men, let's go get some chow – we can finish this afterward," he added.

When they entered the dining room, with a long split-log table that would probably sit 20 if needed, Adkin introduced Matty to Mead, and asked him to please call her Matty. The others grinned, they knew the rules already. "No Missus Yates."

Jim was gracious, shaking her hand and saying something in Kiowa. Matty smiled and bowed slightly. Then Mead hugged Beth, since they had been friends for seven years.

While eating, Adkin told Mead about the new camp the Army was talking about building down below Fort Cobb, and Mead said he had heard it also, from a military group of calvary roaming central Kansas below the Santa Fe Trail looking for warring Indians.

"That's the new official wording for killing at will," Mead said. "They say, 'Seeking warring Indians.' But yes, they are saying a new Camp Wichita will be established after the new year."

"We've got to get to Fort Dodge before they give all the bids away on the freighting," Adkin said, looking panicked now. "Do you know how long it takes to get from here to say Camp Supply?"

"I sure do, I know this country well and have travelled it for years," Mead said. "It's less than a day to get to the North Canadian, and then you just follow it upstream for four or five days. How many wagons are you travelling with?"

"Just one, and four of us ... I mean five of us now on horseback, with Matty," Adkin said.

"Well today is December 19, and I would be more than glad to guide you through to the North Canadian," Mead said. "How many days is it from Camp Supply to Fort Dodge?"

"It's six days, but with only one wagon, I think we could make it in five," Adkin said. "That would be about 10 days, so we could get there by December 30 or 31. That should be in time, I hope."

"Well, let's discuss it more this evening after we help Jarvis with his chores," Mead said. "I would also like to sit with you and Jarvis to talk business."

"That would be great, exactly what I had in mind – picking your brain, so to speak," Adkin said chuckling.

Adkin noticed Matty kept an eye on him, and smiled when he caught her glancing his way. Beth was still bustling around adding some more fried bacon to the table platter.

"Mister Yates, your Matty is one of the brightest young women I have met in quite some time," Beth said as she passed behind Adkin and Mead at the table. "She's a jewel, a real jewel."

"Thank you Missus Jarvis," Adkin responded. He looked to Matty, and she was all smiles.

"It's a lovely smile at that," Adkin thought to himself. "And that's what's important, keeping her happy – and safe."

Adkin suddenly remembered Mead talking Kiowa to Matty when he met her.

"Say Jim, what did you say to Matty when you met her – you know in Kiowa?" Adkin asked.

"I told her she had been chosen by the spirits to take care of you – and she agreed," Mead said smiling. "Do you believe in fate, Adkin? I do."

The men later finished unloading all the trade goods the Jarvis boys had hauled from Mead's Ranch as well as several other spots along the trail. Several of the men, including Mead, Adkin, Ryan and Jarvis, sat in chairs on the porch talking.

"You know, I ran into Sam Crawford up on the South Fork of the Cottonwood the first week of November," Mead said. "He was leading his new command, the 19th Kansas Volunteers to the Camp Supply site.

"I told him he couldn't get through that country with the scouts he had then, but he cussed me to hades and back," he continued. "I couldn't take that from him. I had to walk out of his tent before I was tempted to break his nose right there in front of his officers.

"I've known Sam since before he became governor," Mead said. "He worked with me when I filed a 160-acre claim this summer down on that spot at the junction of the Little Arkansas and the Big Arkansas – the spot I got from Chisholm. Do you remember it?"

"I sure do, its a beautiful place," Adkin said, with Ryan nodding his knowledge of the site.

"Well, some of my friends and I are surveying a town platt there, laying out lots," Mead said. "We're going to start us a town, and we're going to call it Wichita, Kansas.

"And the big news just occurred after I saw Sam ... hey Zeb, I've been waiting to tell you this, too," Mead said, smiling like a cat that was playing with a live mouse. "I was elected as the Kansas State Republican Senator from the 15th District of Kansas.

"What do you think about that?" he asked grinning

"So that's what you meant by saying you're now dressing like a politician, eh?" Jarvis said laughing. Several laughed.

"Congratulations Jim," Ryan said. "I think you can do good. You know and like the Indians, but you're not a rosewater dreamer."

All laughed then.

"Would anyone like a taste of whiskey before dinner?" Jarvis asked. Most raised their hands.

Before dinner preparations, Beth pulled Adkin to the side and told him how Matty took to all her instructions and how much she helped, especially after the arrival of the others.

"She's special, Mister Yates," Beth said. "She learned everything I showed her the first time, then did it over again without ever pausing for a moment.

"I just wanted to tell you. I know you probably already know it, but I think she's a very special little gal," Beth said.

"Thank you very much," Adkin said, as Beth said she needed to get in the kitchen and that she was glad Matty was helping.

Adkin looked up to see Matty standing at the kitchen door, staring and smiling at him.

Adkin felt a little strange. He had never had someone hover over him like that since he was a small boy in Olney. His mother watched him like a hawk for several years when he was young, but sometime there when he was about 10 or 11, she seemed to untie the apron strings.

"Maybe it has something about being a woman," he thought to himself. "Now I'm thinking of her as a woman when she's a little girl. But she can't be a little girl at 19 or 20 years old. She's even been married."

After a few drinks, Several of the hands started politely arguing about who had the fastest horse. Uribe, of course, talked the best game.

"This horse I have, he can beat any Indian pony – rest only five minutes and outrun another fresh Indian pony," he bragged.

The others were laughing.

Darwin, Jarvis' eldest, said his horse ran down a whitetail deer in less than a mile. After several claims started getting more ridiculous, it seemed everyone was then trying to tell the biggest whopper, like they forgot about horse racing.

Beth walked out on the porch and told them supper was ready. After the porch crowd entered the house, she rang the triangle dinner bell and screamed her usual entreaty.

"Come and get it," to the others that had wandered away from the house.

•••

After eating, Adkin, Ryan, Sam, Jarvis as well as his two sons and Mead all sat down in the living room to discusss the freighting business and the possibilities of offering stagecoach service.

Adkin and Ryan proposed using Jarvis' trading post as a way station and repair shop for up to 30 wagons for freighting. They offered Jarvis two options: 50 percent of the income if he provided the teamsters and teams, or 40 percent if YR&R Freight had to supply the men and teams.

After some discussion, Mead spoke up and made Jarvis an offer.

"What if I provide all the men, teams and the equipment for a repair shop, including a blacksmith's tools, would you pay me 25 percent?" He asked. "And that would mean you could take YR&R's offer at 50 percent.

"That would earn you 25 percent of the loads and all you have to do is take care of the teams with forage and care," Mead continued. "Of course you would have to bunk and feed the men from time to time.

"How many loads has YR&R been involved with assisting Camp Supply's construction, Adkin?" Mead asked.

"Well, let's see," Adkin began. "We were part of the first 350 wagons down from Fort Dodge, we had 35 wagons come with the 19th Kansas Militia, Sully ordered another 250 wagons on the second re-supply and 180 wagons before we went looking for Satanta, and Sully was looking to order more supplies by year's end.

"We may have missed out on that trip, unless Ray Dee, our other partner, got a bid in," Adkin said. "The business is brisk since we've never seen this kind of 'winter campaign' against the Indians before. We expect the same for this new Camp Wichita.

"Now remember, we only have 95 wagons currently, but we have a ready-market for used wagons in Santa Fe," Adkin continued. "And we will buy new ones when needed and, hopefully, expand our overall wagon numbers."

Jarvis asked his sons what they thought, and they both said it would be like getting 25 percent for little or nothing.

"Gee Father, We would be getting paid good wages for basically feeding horses and men," Doyle said. "And you know our plans for planting forage is working real good now. We can just plant some more hay or oats, and we'll be in good shape."

Jarvis looked to Darwin, and he nodded in agreement.

"Well, that's good enough for me," Jarvis said. "And Jim, if you're willing to take care of the men and animals, we'd enjoy being in business with you, too.

"I'm in," Mead said, looking to Adkin and Ryan. "Will that work for YR&R?"

"Yes sir, it would be most agreeable with us. Right Ryan?" Adkin said, standing up and reaching for Jarvis' hand to shake.

"Let's discuss stagecoach service," Adkin said. "Do you think there is a demand for service from Fort Dodge – or other places along the Santa Fe Trail to here and on down to the Camps Cobb and Wichita?"

"I believe there is, Adkin," Mead said. "Stagecoaches could leave Fort Dodge, travel to Camp Supply, then down to Fort Cobb and Camp Wichita, others could come from Fort Larned down to here, and then to Supply, Cobb or Wichita."

"That's true," Jarvis said.

"What if Barlow and Sanderson offered you both the same deal on stagecoach service: We pay Jarvis 50 percent, provide at least two coaches and you two provide men, drivers, and the animals," Adkin asked.

"I'm in on that, too," Mead said, with Jarvis and his boys also quickly approving the offer.

Everybody laughed, shook hands, and Adkin asked Jarvis to sign two agreements, with Mead as witness. Adkin asked for a few more pieces of paper from Jarvis for the Barlow and Sanderson offer.

Darwin went to the bookshelf and pulled out two bottles of liquor and started pulling out glasses, as well.

Jarvis called out to Beth, and she and Matty came out from the kitchen with two large pies in each woman's hands. Adkin thought Matty looked cute, and small, in one of Beth's cooking aprons. She had a spot of flour on her cheek.

Doyle went out on the porch and yelled at the others.

"Fresh pies being served – and a taste of whiskey, too." Soon boots could be heard pounding across the wooden porch.

After celebrating and explaining the deal to everyone, Adkin told his crew to make preparations to head out the next morning, and Mead did likewise with his men. Ryan told Jarvis his crew would need some more supplies for the 10-day trip to Fort Dodge.

Jarvis instructed his boys to go with Ryan and find what he needed and get it loaded now. That way they wouldn't have to take time in the morning to get it done.

"That would be great," Ryan said. "We like to head out before sunrise. Is that fine with you Senator Jim?"

"You won't be waiting on us, son," Mead said, laughing.

•••

Once on the trail and the sun above the horizon, Adkin asked Mead if he could lay out the best trail for stagecoaches from Camp Supply to Fort Cobb, as they had travelled down through the Washita Battle sites.

"There has to be a better trail than what we travelled," Adkin said. "Especially for a stagecoach."

"No problem, and this trail we're on now can be the cut-off for those wanting to go east off the Canadian River to Jarvis' Ranch House," Mead said. "Looks like you boys and J.L. figured out how to stay in business once the railroads get to all the places on the Santa Fe Trail."

"Yes, Sanderson figured that out more than two years ago. That's when we started setting stagecoach routes all over Colorado," Adkin said. "Hey, that reminds me, I forgot to tell you where I last saw Colonel Kit Carson.

"It was at Fort Garland in Colorado. We were establishing stagecoach routes and Fort Garland was at the end of one of the routes," Adkin said. "His health forced him to resign back in March, I think.

"He actually moved to Boggsville – only about 25 miles from our Colorado branch office," Adkin continued. "But he made a trip to Washington, and didn't get back until two days before his wife gave birth to their seventh child – and she died two weeks later.

"We heard he departed Boggsville, but we weren't sure where he was – that's until we heard he died at New Fort Lyons.

"That was only 18 miles from us, and it hurts not knowing that he was there and not being able to see him before he died," Adkin said.

"Yes, I understand," Mead said. "He was a special and unique man – a true frontiersman, someone I admired as a youth and who gave me inspiration when I came out here 1859.

"It's been a bad year what with the death of Carson and then followed a month later with Chisholm. I just missed seeing him about a week before he died. I was actually going to see him with $3,000 worth of goods he wanted," Meade continued. "Makes a man feel old, but I wouldn't trade my time on the Great Plains for anything in the world.

"I really didn't start living until I rolled into Fort Leavenworth as a youngster," he added.

"I know exactly how you feel, Jim," Adkin said. "I've only been out here for about 2-and-a-half years, and it gets in your blood so quickly and thoroughly, it's hard to explain."

•••

Adkin had been pulling his writing pad from his saddle bags every few miles, marking landmarks, such as huge pines or elms, where small creeks crossed the trail, or cliffs and bluffs they encountered and which way they traversed them. He would hand it to Mead, every now and then, and Mead would give his approval.

"You should've been a surveyor and map maker, Yates," he said.

"You're quite good at this."

It was shortly after noon when they topped a rise and could spot the North Canadian just a mile away. The gentle slope to the river was treeless pasture land, and it was a direct line to the water. An easy road for a Concord.

"This is where I turn back north, Yates," Mead said. "Mark this clearing from two points down the slope. Stop halfway and write down your landmarks back here to the treeline, and then do it again when you reach the river.

"If I was you, I'd stay along the north bank of the river all the way to Camp Supply," he continued. "You'll see the big bends and you can cross to them directly to take some time off your travels.

"God speed, and good luck," Mead added. "Look me up when you're out my way."

"I want to thank you Jim, and it was great being able to visit with you again," Adkin said, as Ryan and the others rode over to Adkin and Mead. "Let's hope our venture in freighting and the stagecoach business will be very profitable."

"We'll make it profitable, Yates," Mead said, reaching out to shake Adkin's hand.

Mead said his farewells to the others, shook hands then signaled his men, and they reined their mounts and headed north.

"Be sure and hang on to your scalps, my friends," he yelled over his shoulder, laughing.

"Well men – and Matty – we follow the river upstream to Camp Supply," Adkin said. "Hopefully, we make it in four days."

•••

Matty did most of the cooking that first night along the North Canadian. Ryan and Tom helped her by carrying the bags and utensils into the tent.

After eating, Matty indicated she was going outside, and being dead winter, the sun was already down and darkness had set in.

Adkin followed her out the tent, and she stopped, shooing him away, indicating he go back. Adkin pulled his knife out of it's sheath and held it out for her. She smiled, understanding he wanted her to be able to protect herself.

She bent over, pulled her buckskin dress up to her knee and pulled a leather sheath out from the top of her knee-high deerskin moccasins. She slid a 6-inch narrow-bladed knife from the sheath and held it before Adkin's surprised face.

She laughed as she put it back in her high-top moccasin and ran into the bushes. He shook his head as he slowly turned and walked back into the tent.

"She's carrying her own knife," Adkin said, not realizing he was speaking out loud.

"Of course, Señor, every Indian – man, woman, child, carries a knife," Uribe said, chuckling. "Even old Indian grandma, she have a knife."

They all laughed.

•••

An Englishman's Adventures on the Santa Fe Trail (1865-1889)

On December 23, they rode into Camp Supply. Amazingly, Ray Dee had arrived the evening before from Fort Hays through Fort Dodge, ramrodding 50 wagons of supplies to Camp Supply. It was like a family reunion. Even some of the soldiers not out hunting Indians were glad to see the crew. General Sully especially.

"Where have you been for three weeks, Mister Yates?" Sully asked. "As you probably noticed riding in, we have become the feeding station this winter for about every peaceful Indian within 100 miles."

"Well, we were scouting possible future stagecoach routes, and I ran across Chief Satanta down near Fort Cobb," Adkin said. "Next thing I know, Black Horse married his daughter off to me because I have helped her twice while she was in danger.

"General Sully, I'd like to introduce you to Matty," he added.

"Nice to meet you, Matty," Sully said, eyes wide opened. "Did you know Sheridan, Custer and Crawford are looking for Satanta?"

"Yes sir, when we passed back through Fort Cobb, General Hazen informed us the Army was looking for Satanta, and several others. We told him Satanta was in the Wichita Mountains just outside of Fort Cobb," Adkin said. "I wouldn't be surprised if they haven't captured or killed Satanta by now."

"I guess the Cheyenne and the Arapahoes had killed the missing White Woman and her son at the Washita Battle – that's what Hazen told us," Adkin added.

"Well, there is no positive proof as yet who killed that woman and her boy, but you're lucky you didn't get caught up in any of that," Sully said. "It hasn't been pleasant."

"We have established a stagecoach station at Zeb Jarvis' Ranch House in Blaine County, Oklahoma, and we ran into his partner, James R. Mead of Kansas," Adkin said. "Mead mentioned the Army may be contemplating establishing another supply camp below Fort Cobb along the Medicine Bluffs."

"You hear correctly, Mister Yates, and I believe you can be of help," Sully said. "How many wagons can you come up with at Fort Hays or Dodge by … say … January 2nd or 3rd?"

"What about that, Ray Dee?" Adkin asked.

"Well, we have 50 here, 30 at Fort Dodge and 15 at Junction City," Ray Dee said. "But we have no way to ask Sanderson to send us those wagons until we get back to Fort Dodge."

"I'm sending an urgent message to Fort Dodge within the next hour by way of a special courier on horseback. He'll be there in three days," Sully said. "We can have Fort Dodge telegraph Junction City for you."

"Well then General, we could have 95 wagons assembled by the dates you asked about," Adkin said, grinning.

"Good deal," Sully said. "Are you going to Fort Dodge, too?"

"Yes sir, I want to have all our men handling this job, and we actually have to put in an order to St. Louis to purchase more wagons – and a couple of Concord coaches," Adkin said, laughing.

"Actually, we should depart as soon as possible to get everything together," he continued, turning to Ray Dee. "When will the wagons you brought in be ready to roll out?"

"They're ready. We unloaded most last evening and the remainders early this morning," Ray Dee said. "We just need to give them an inspection, maybe some grease, but they can be ready within the hour.

"Okay, gentlemen, let's get moving, and General, we sincerely thank you for allowing us to provide service to the U.S. Army," Adkin said. "It's a great honor, sir."

"Good deal," Sully said. "Thank you, and you'll probably be part of another 300- to 400-wagon caravan."

"So be careful out there," Sully added. "The Cheyenne have made it clear they are on the war path."

...

Matty was preparing the evening meal that first night out of Camp Supply, when Uribe walked up and said something in an Indian language. She replied and he laughed. Then he said something again, and she answered like she was talking with one of her Indian friends.

Adkin walked up and she smiled at him.

"Hello Adkin," Matty said, plain as day.

"She's learning English quicker than I thought she would," Adkin said to Uribe.

"I learn English so I can live in White Man's world," she said, smiling.

Uribe started laughing.

"English is just a beginning, Señor," Uribe said. "She knows every dialect of Indian languages I know – that's seven. And she knows sign language."

"Spanish, Kiowa, Comanche, Cheyenne, Arapahoe, Osage and Ute," he added. "She probably knows more.

"Apache," Matty said.

"See, I'm telling you Señor, this woman knows everything, just about," Uribe said, walking away. "Caramba."

"Matty, you teach me to speak Kiowa?" Adkin asked using what little sign he knew.

"Yes, Adkin," she answered with a grin.

From that day on while travelling to Fort Dodge, Adkin spent more and more time with Matty. He would try using his hands in asking about things – pointing and asking "how to say" this or that. She was patient with Adkin's mispronunciations. And his accent.

Adkin could speak a little Scottish and Irish. That was from being raised in Olney and spending time with his Scot mother, plus travellers coming through the Bull Inn.

But there were sounds in Kiowa – and many Algonquian languages – that were gutteral, from deep down the throat. But Adkin kept learning, and Matty was learning more English as well.

Christmas Day came along, but for travellers on the trail to Fort Dodge in the middle of winter, there was not much Christmas celebration per say. Adkin did ask for everyone to pause as he gave thanks to God Almighty before their evening meal and asked for God to protect them.

On the afternoon of December 28, they arrived at Fort Dodge. Adkin and the crew who had been with him lately, couldn't believe how much the fort had grown – in size, soldiers and activity. It was bustling to say the least.

Ray Dee led Adkin and Ryan to the quartermaster he had been working with on the last two loads to Camp Supply. They gave the quartermaster the leather pouch with General Sully's requests and his orders to use 95 wagons from YR&R Freight Company for loads to Camp Wichita in southern Oklahoma.

Adkin and Ryan then strode over to the Western Union office and started sending messages to Sanderson.

They started with the order for two more Concords and informed Sanderson of the coach station to be set up at Jarvis' Ranch House. They listed the details of the place, the partnership Jarvis will have on his own with James Mead, and the enthusiasm of Jarvis and Mead.

They then sent another telegraph to J. Murphy in St. Louis ordering 25 more freight wagons to be delivered to Fort Dodge in care of YR&R Freight. They asked for a detailed invoice and assured Murphy they would wire payment once the invoice was received.

Adkin realized they should inform Sanderson of their expansion plans with YR&R receiving more hauling contracts for this new Camp Wichita. So another telegraph was fired off to Sanderson.

Since it was late in the day, they didn't expect to hear from Sanderson until the next day. They decided to ask the fort's co-commander if there were any visitors' rooms available in the fort.

"Let's celebrate tonight with a warm room and a roof over our heads," Adkin had shouted, and laughing.

Since Elliot had been killed fighting with Custer, they were unsure who to ask. Ray Dee said he was only working with the quartermaster – he didn't know either.

After asking around, they discovered a Colonel Brooks Lyles was in command. They went and met him and asked about the rooms. He seemed genial and said they could provide two rooms, at a "reasonable cost" he added.

They didn't mind, it was like a celebration being back among so many people – back in civilization. They wanted to splurge.

"Well there's six men, and then my wife," Adkin said. "So we'll need seven cots, five in one room and two in the other. All our teamsters and wranglers will stay in their tents with the wagons."

"I'll have my aide, Sergeant Hulse, set you up," Lyles said.

He walked to the door, and called out to the Sergeant. He also noticed Tom and Matty sitting in the wagon directly in front, with four others on horseback.

"Excuse me Mister Yates, is that your rig out front … er with the Indian woman in it?" Lyles asked.

"Yes sir, that's my wife and those are my men who will be staying in the other room," Adkin said. "Is something wrong?"

"I'm afraid there is, Mister Yates," Lyles started. "We can't allow an Indian to stay in the visitor's rooms, it's never been done. In fact, it's never been asked or therefore allowed, that I'm aware of.

"I'm afraid it would affect morale of our troops who are under direct orders from General Sheridan to force all Indians in this whole area onto their reservations 'or else,'" he added. "As temporary commander, I couldn't allow it. I might get in trouble."

"Colonel," Adkin said in a loud angry voice. "That's my wife, Indian or not …"

"Adkin. Adkin, hold it down," Ryan interrupted. "Anger won't help old friend.

"Colonel Lyles, this woman is from royalty among the Kiowa Nation – like a princess," Ryan said in a gentle voice. "She's the daughter of Black Horse, a famous Kiowa Medicine Man – Chief Satanta's Medicine Man to be exact …

Before Ryan could continued, Lyles' eyes widened and he shouted. "That's even worse. Do you know what would happened if these troops heard we were putting up Satanta's Medicine Man's daughter in our visitor's rooms?

"No, I'm sorry, it's out of the question," he stopped as Adkin took two large steps toward the Colonel with his hands by his side with curled up in fists. Ryan grabbed his arm and stopped him from getting near Lyles.

"No Adkin. Come on, we can celebrate on our own," Ryan said. "We don't need to stay under a roof to celebrate tonight.

"Let's go find us place on the river and eat a big meal, drink some rum and forget about this place," Ryan added, pulling Adkin away.

Adkin gave the Colonel a look Ryan had seen a few times before, and those who got that look either got their faces broke up or died.

Adkin finally broke his glare at Lyles and turned and walked out. Ryan told the crew there were no rooms available that night, but they would celebrate at their camp.

"Come, I know a pretty little spot down by the river bank," Ryan said, as he swung into his saddle.

Matty could tell, as well as the others, something was bothering Adkin. He looked really steamed and angry – his face was flushed red – but he said nothing as he mounted Diablo and reined him away from Lyles' office.

•••

As they worked their way down to the Big Arkansas from the fort, crowds and shanties were everywhere. There were Indians, trappers, a few buffalo hunters and wagons and teams tied up to them. Tents and square wooden huts that could only sleep maybe two men.

"Is this a sign of progress?" Ryan asked Adkin. "Next thing you know, there'll be a town here."

"Well, where you find hundreds of wagons of supplies going south, someone is making money, and they need teamsters, wranglers and tradesmen," Adkin said.

"And you will find whisky and women to keep all these men happy," Uribe said, smiling.

Ryan spotted the place he had remembered, a spot where several small willows used to stand. Now it was covered with wood and canvas shanties and men sitting around smoking, playing cards and passing bottles around – and no sign of the willows.

"We'll have to go a little further west to find us a camp," Ryan said.

They finally found a spot and moved an additional couple of hundred yards to have some privacy. While putting up the tent, Uribe kept talking about seeing some women scantly clothed at one of the tents in the crowd.

"Ayee, one of those womans winked her eyes at me, I think," he said.

"You better be careful with those women, Uribe," Ryan said.

Ray Dee interrupted, "They will take your money and might even kill you for only a small amount of gold dust."

"If I know you, Ray Dee, you've already reconnoitered some of these hovels," Ryan said laughing. "I remember some incidents in Leavenworth ..."

"Nobody goes wandering around exploring until we at least have our evening meal," Adkin interrupted, while Tom was wrestling the heavy stove into the tent by himself.

Adkin was hoping Matty wasn't understanding all this talk of wild women, but she had to know how life around some forts was. There were hangers-on looking for work and loose women looking for hangers-on with money.

Adkin still was upset about how Colonel Lyles turned them down. But he was glad Ryan dragged him out of there before Adkin's instincts overcame his better judgement.

Adkin was understanding this was something he would have to deal with and stay composed. Look at his heroes on the frontier: Carson, Bent, Chisholm – all had been married to Indians, some had several Indian wives.

He would have to deal with bias and prejudice. He would be called an Indian lover, and other derogatory names, but he knew better, and his friends knew better.

"Indian lover, heh!" he said to himself. "I've seen first-hand how savage Indians can be – their mutilations, and their torture before killing. But I also know that killing is in their soul – all they have known for hundreds of years is hunting, having families and killing their enemies and taking slaves."

"We didn't tell the Western Union man where we would be camping," Ray Dee said. "You might want to get over there first thing in the morning to see if Sanderson has wired back."

"I will, I'll be there when he opens," Adkin said.

After a meal of salted buffalo meat, fresh from Jarvis' store, Uribe, Tom and Ray Dee decided to go "exploring." Ray Dee looked at Adkin and Ryan and held out both arms with his palms up and hunched his shoulders up.

"Well, somebody should go with them and keep them from trouble," Ray Dee said, smiling.

"You guys, better be on your best behavior," Ryan said. "We don't need any problems – we'd hate to leave you in the brig."

"Don't stay out too late," Adkin said, adding, "Please?"

•••

Adkin was up and out of their tent as the sky started turning gray. He hustled to the Western Union office next to Colonel Lyles' quarters, hoping he didn't run into the spineless Colonel.

He ran up the four steps to the porch and tried the office door, but it was locked. Fortunately, there were two chairs on each side of the door. He took a seat.

He was hoping to hear good news from Sanderson: One, they would get two Concords in a decent time; and two, their other wagons could be put on a train and make it to Fort Dodge within a week; and three, Murphy will be able to fill their wagon order within a reasonable time.

Then he began thinking about the boys out drinking last night. They were fairly rowdy when they got back to the tent – Uribe being the loudest, but Tom seeming the drunkest.

"Maybe that's just Tom," Adkin thought to himself. "Tom is quiet even when not drinking," and Adkin had not seen any of his crew drink too much.

Their boisterous laughing woke them all, and Matty just giggled at their antics. Adkin imagined she had seen plenty of her brethren drunk before. "Our crew probably seem like children compared to a bunch of drunk Indians," Adkin thought, grinning to himself.

The clerk soon arrived to unlock the door to the office.

"Mister Yates, I received two telegrams for you late yesterday evening, but was unable to try and find you," the clerk said. "I'm pleased to see you – save my boy from having to run you down."

Adkin read through the first one: Murphy would have the 25 wagons delivered to Fort Dodge in five to seven days – they had them in inventory ready to go. The invoice was for $6,000.

The other telegraph was from J.L. and he and the Concords, as well as YR&R's additional wagons would be departing Junction City tomorrow, December 30, needing only the time to round up the men and a few supplies.

"Looking forward to seeing you, partner," J.L. had said in his telegraph.

"This is great, J.L. is coming, too," Adkin shouted out. He slapped the clerk on the back, nearly knocking him off his feet and hurried to the door.

"Who the hell is J.L.?" the clerk mumbled.

•••

Adkin had stopped by the quartermaster's office and filled out the paperwork to have $6,000 transferred from the YR&R account at Bent's Fort to J. Murphy Co. in St. Louis, Missouri, before heading back to their camp.

"I need some tea, Matty," Adkin shouted as he slid out of the saddle at their camp. He could see smoke wafting from the tent stove pipe, and knew someone was awake.

When he opened the tent flap, Matty turned around to face him with a tin cup of tea, holding it out to him with both hands – and that ever-present smile. He smiled back at her with genuine happiness.

"Maybe it was because of the good news he carried in the form of telegrams, he thought, or maybe this beautiful little Kiowa woman was so darn sweet."

Then it hit him, she either understood what he yelled from outside or she was ahead of him, knowing already what he liked and would want. It puzzled him briefly.

"Hey you lazy dogs, get out of those bedrolls," Adkin yelled, taking the tea from Matty with a slight bow of his head. "Thank you Matty.

"Within the week, we should have our Concords, our additional wagons from Junction City and our new Murphys from St. Louis," Adkin said amid groans and a moaning of, "quit yelling" coming from under buffalo hides somewhere.

"And to top it off, J.L. is coming out with the Junction City wagons," he added, laughing. "Come on, wake up. We have plans to make and things to do."

"Oh, mi Caballo," Uribe whined. "Those womans make me drink mucho."

"I don't want to hear any crying, you men were warned about exploring amongst this crowd here," Adkin said.

As Ryan stood, Matty handed him a cup and poured coffee in it for him.

As the others were pulling back hides and furs, Matty started frying bacon in a skillet. She was cooking two small corn-bread-like pancakes in another skillet. The coffee pot and the two skillets were precariously perched on the stove top, no space to spare.

"We'll have everything in a week – ready to go?" Ryan asked.

"Well, we'll have to make sure we have the teamsters and everybody needed to haul goods," Adkin said. "And we have to coordinate with the Army on supplies and such. But all our wagons will be here, and we have to make sure they're all in good enough shape to make that trip all the way down to Camp Wichita."

...

Adkin and Ryan went to see Colonel Lyles to tell him YR&R Freight would be able to amass up to 120 wagons for service, even though his orders from General Sully called for 95.

"I don't see a problem with that, Mister Yates and Mister Ryan," Lyles said. "I'd be happy on behalf of the U.S. Army to approve your offer of providing us with more wagons.

"And, word on the grapevine is General Sully will soon be reassigned back east," Lyles added.

Lyles then pulled out some papers listing various supplies for the new camp. Most were building supplies, but there were also food stuffs, such as sugar, flour, coffee and rice. He told them to coordinate loading the wagons with the quartermaster and where to keep and store wagons loaded early, prior to departure.

Both men thanked the Colonel and headed to the quartermaster's office.

"I think the Colonel is trying to reach out to you, Adkin," Ryan said. "I think he feels bad about Matty, but he's scared of getting in trouble."

"You're right, and I've realized I will have to deal with an Indian wife and all the baggage other people have with that," Adkin said, smiling. "If Kit, Bent and Chisholm can live with it, so can I."

Ryan smiled and slapped Adkin on the shoulder.

They reported to the quartermaster, and said they would start sending wagons over to his wagon master for loading as soon as the wagons passed inspections.

Apparently, the Army had built temporary fencing behind the fort to store loaded wagons and "keep them safe from pilfering and theft – by Indians or rabble," as the quartermaster put it.

"Make sure they are tarped down well after they are loaded," he added.

Adkin asked permission to use the fort's blacksmith shop if needed for wagon repairs. It was approved, and he said he would send a note to the smitty that YR&R Freight would have shop privileges – when not busy.

Back at camp, everyone was ordered to get with all the teamsters and wranglers to start a methodic inspection of the wagons they had at the fort currently. Once they were approved, they were to be marked.

Wagons needing repairs or replacement parts were to be separated and then inspected by either Ray Dee, Ryan or Adkin. They would then be taken to the blacksmith shop.

Everyone started saddling up, and hitched the mules to their supply wagon. As they prepared to go to the teamsters camp, back a few miles west, Adkin noticed Matty was standing there all alone by the tent. And she wasn't smiling. Tom had already started off in the wagon.

"Come Matty," Adkin said, holding out his left hand.

She ran to Diablo, and as she grabbed Adkin's arm, he removed his boot from the stirrup. But she didn't use the stirrup; she sprung like an antelope and landed behind him on Diablo's haunches.

"She was light as a feather, or could jump as high as a deer," he thought.

"Matty ready," she said as she reached both arms around him and squeezed tightly with the side of her face pressed against his back. Adkin couldn't help but smile himself, and though he didn't look back, he knew Matty was smiling, too.

"Well, now that we're all ready, let's go," Ryan said. "We got work to do."

•••

They met with the men, and several couldn't take their eyes off Matty as soon as Adkin had swung his right leg over the saddle horn, dropped to the ground and turned to catch Matty as she slid to the ground. Adkin knew this was another "thing" he was going to have to deal with. A beautiful Kiowa wife.

Many of the men shouted out Tom's name, as Tom had been one of them on several caravans. Tom looked a little embarrassed at the attention and friendliness he was receiving from the men.

"It's great to see all you yahoos again," he yelled, while the men chuckled with him. Tom introduced Adkin, Ryan and the rest of the YR&R crew, including "Adkin's wife, Matty – a Kiowa princess," as Tom put it. They all knew Ray Dee, as he had hired some of the men himself.

Adkin told the men what they needed to do, and that was bring up any repairs or replacements their wagons needed. He told them they were going to be on a journey of probably 200 miles over areas that had only Indian and trappers' trails.

"As we clear a wagon for duty, let's line them up over here, all you men can help with that," Adkin said. "Once we get about 15 or 20, we'll notify the Army wagon master and then hitch up your teams and take them to the Army depot inside the fort.

"Oh, I almost forgot: J.L. Sanderson is arriving within the week with 25 more new wagons, with teams and teamsters – plus two Concords that will be delivered along the way south," Adkin shouted.

They appointed an area for wagons that needed attention, and started recording the problems reported by their drivers or wranglers.

Work was progressing on the wagons, and fortunately, only a few had been in what Adkin would call "poor shape." After two days of sorting the wagons, the New Year – 1869 – reared its head, and there was quite a night of celebration. All the people in the surrounding shanty-town hit the liquor fairly hard, as there was gunfire going off most of the night, even into the wee hours.

Luckily, nobody was found dead the next day, but about a dozen had been thrown in the fort's brig for fighting and assault. The only law was Army troopers making the rounds outside the fort trying to keep the peace.

Adkin had to work in the blacksmith shop several days, ironing axles with new iron sheeting and making tongue loops and hitches here and there. Several wheels had to be re-banded as well.

When Adkin went to the fort, he asked someone to stay with Matty while he worked. Uribe, Tom and Sam often volunteered. And Adkin would have to hear their relentless bragging about what a decent, kind, and caring woman Matty was. It was like they were trying to convince him he got a good deal in a one-sided horse trade.

Adkin would smile as the volunteer rattled off her accomplishments for the day, from sewing to washing clothes with water they would carry from the river, and of course, her cooking.

The only complaint he heard was "Sometimes her cornbread cakes were a little chewy."

Adkin had to laugh out loud.

"I have to tell her someway that those are not fit for men – White Men anyway," he said, while the men laughed. "But I appreciate you being kind to her and not hurting her feelings."

While the flattery of Matty was nice, Adkin had been feeling closer and closer to her as well. The way she handed him something and touched the back of his hand, And he loved to have her pressed up against him on Diablo; she rode as if she was just another muscle of the huge steed – flowing in unison and at total ease.

Adkin was realizing Matty was a special woman. He was beginning to believe he was the lucky one. Yet it made him feel uneasy to think about her in a romantic way.

"That's too far off right now," he would tell himself.

•••

On January 3, 1870, another small wagon train pulled into the Fort Dodge grounds. J.L. Sanderson was naturally driving the lead Concord, followed by another brand new coach and 25 new Murphy wagons with the yellow YR&R Freight Co. painted on their sides.

Adkin, his crew and Matty, met them as they pulled into the fort's gates. Lyles was there, too, having soldiers directing the wagons to the warehouses for loading. He welcomed Sanderson and told Sanderson and the YR&R crew they would have to be ready to roll in three days to Camp Wichita.

Sanderson got permission to place the two Concords under the fort's security.

Then the greetings began between old and new friends. Sanderson was amused how much Adkin had changed into a mountain man, and he teased Ryan how Ryan had aged.

"I believe I see some white hairs slipping in there on your head," Sanderson said.

"You would be white-haired, too, having to deal with this bunch," Ryan responded laughing.

"And this has to be Matty. How are you dear?" Sanderson said, as he reached out his hand.

Matty shrunk a little and looked at Adkin.

"This is the friend I told you about, Mister Sanderson," He said, as she then reached out and took Sanderson's hand.

"Hello Meester Sand-or sun," she said, softly.

"Adkin, you have to be the luckiest Englishman that ever reached our shores," Sanderson said, after releasing Matty's hand. "She is the loveliest thing I have ever seen on this frontier."

Adkin nodded, and a few "amens" were heard, and everybody started chattering away.

Ryan convinced everyone to leave the grounds and go to their camp down by the river. Somebody mentioned there was a shanty cantina just south of the fort. Several recommended they stop for a drink.

"Matty and I will pass," Adkin said. "But you gentlemen go ahead."

Sanderson saw the look Adkin had on his face and realized Adkin wouldn't expose his Indian wife to something like that.

"I'll pass, too, for now," Sanderson said. "I need to talk with some of you boys – and the sooner the better."

The stakeholders of Barlow and Sanderson knew who they were, but after a few moments of indecision, Ray Dee spoke up.

"We have tequila, rum and brandy at camp. Besides, that cantina is expensive, and I know," he said, with everyone laughing with him.

All decided to go to the camp and celebrate.

•••

That evening at the campsite, merriment prevailed with old stories making the rounds, even back before Adkin joined the Barlow and Sanderson team in the late summer of 1865. Most of the old-timers remembered a particular saloon girl Ray Dee nearly got entrapped by in Leavenworth.

"Thank God, J.L. let me come out west with him that fall and stay awhile, lest I'd be stuck washing dishes in an apron with lil' ones screaming around me," Ray Dee said, laughing.

Talks covered the winter campaign by the Army, and Sanderson said Barlow was having a front row seat in watching the battle between the Army and the Office of Indian Affairs. Sanderson said Sherman and Sheridan were winning for now.

"You're right," Ryan said. "We heard most all the Cheyennes in the area, and a few others, moved to their reservations after the Washita Battle."

"Well, Barlow has heard the Army will probably build more camps or forts further south and even into the Texas Panhandle," Sanderson said. "That will only help our businesses what with opening new areas for settlement."

"And more areas where settlers can be massacred," Adkin added.

Though Sanderson brought along a cook wagon with him, Matty still prepared meals for the tent residents, which included Ryan, Ray Dee, Uribe, Sam, Tom and now J.L.

"She's cooks very well," Sanderson said as she was down at the river fetching some water – with Big Tom right by her side. "And she is very attractive, Adkin. Are you planning on children?"

"Oh no, J.L. It's not like that," Adkin said. "It's more like I'm her protector – her big brother."

"Well if I had a sister that looked like that...," Ryan started.

Adkin shot him a glare.

"Okay. Okay, I'm just sayin'" Ryan said, starting to chuckle with the others. Adkin finally started smiling as well realizing he was showing that defensiveness again.

Sanderson asked what plans the YR&R group had?

Adkin told him the details of the Camp Wichita hauling, and how they were going to use Mead's services as well as Jarvis' family and location.

"That should keep us busy for the next six to eight months – not only with Camp Wichita but with Camp Supply as well," Adkin said. "We haven't planned much after that, what with the Santa Fe trade becoming less and less. But we will have to take another load down there to sell some older wagons at top prices."

"We hear the railroad will be into eastern Colorado within a year," Sanderson said. "We have to expand coach service."

That's when Sanderson explained he was going on with two wagons of supplies and a dozen armed men all the way to California.

"We're determined to offer coach service from Kansas City to California," he said. "And by God, I'm going to do it."

•••

The following day, Sanderson asked Adkin and Ryan if he could settle their accounts over the last four of five months.

"We're getting behind, and I don't want anything to come between our two companies – which I still believe is an asset to us both," he said. "We've got to balance the books with the teams, teamsters and hands. I've been paying their wages, but I need to recoup that outstanding money."

"Sure J.L., we understand that," Adkin said. "And we need to get this all squared away, too."

After some more discussion, Adkin had an idea.

"Why don't I, Ryan and Sam travel with you to our place near Bent's Fort, and we can sit down with all the books there, as much of it is there already through our transfers of cash and gold," Adkin said. "The rest of the crew can go south to Camp Wichita."

"I've got a better plan," Ryan spoke up. "Why don't I go south with the boys, and you and Sam handle the books.

"You know that stuff gives me a headache," he added with a chuckle. "Sam is much better at that stuff than me."

They all agreed to that.

Sam was told he was going home for awhile, which didn't break his heart, and Adkin told Matty they were moving on to "his home" in Colorado. Surprisingly, she acted as if she knew what he was talking about.

Her English was coming along quite well, Adkin thought, and she had taught him numerous ways to say and sign things in Kiowa – and Spanish. She and Uribe almost entirely communicated in Spanish nowadays. And Uribe loved it. He called her his pretty little Señora.

The following day, Lyles sent a message to Adkin saying the wagons were loaded and would be heading out the next day. He included a courier had delivered orders from General Sheridan that his troops would be staking out the camp's perimeters any day.

So on the morning of January 7, two Concords belonging to Barlow and Sanderson, 95 wagons of YR&R Freight with full teams of mules and about three dozen extras horses and mules headed south to Camp Supply and onward.

Uribe had asked to travel with Adkin and Matty, and he, Adkin, Matty, Sam and Sanderson waved goodbye to the others. Once out of sight, they cracked the whips and reined their horses northwest along the Santa Fe Trail. Adkin smiled to himself as they left Fort Dodge behind them, comforted by being back on the trail he so loved.

...

In the late afternoon of January 19, Adkin and his crew rolled past Bent's Fort and into the Freighter's Camp, as it had become to be known. All the gang was there, and Mary Catherine came running out with little Adam clutched to her breast.

Sam seemed to leap 10 feet out of the wagon seat and then run and greet her and his son. Don Diego, Dusty and Fransisco came hustling out of the main office with Peg-Leg Pete hopping along on his crutch behind them waving.

"Adkin couldn't believe how much he had missed his friends. And they swarmed around Diablo until he finally dismounted, and Dusty grabbed the reins. A few moments of revelry gave way to silence as Adkin reached over to Matty, still sitting in her saddle, and she slid off into his arms.

"Men, and Mary Catherine, I want you to meet a new member of our family," Adkin said smiling from ear to ear. "This is Matty, our Kiowa Princess. Please make her feel at home."

Mary Catherine stepped over immediately, and reached out her hand.

"Welcome to your new home, Matty," she said.

Matty reached out and said, "Hello, please to meet you. Hello."

Mary Catherine showed Adam to Matty, and Matty reached for the boy, halting briefly until Mary catherine nodded her assent.

Matty held him out at arm's length, grinning at him until he started smiling back at Matty. She then hugged him close with her cheek against his. Adkin and the others could see it was love at first sight.

"Hey Boss," Sanpete said. "We have a surprise for you and the Missus …

"Matty, Peg-Leg. Matty," Adkin interrupted, but smiling.

"Well yes, Matty. Anyway, look over there," he said pointing just west of the stables.

There against the outer fence was a small adobe, partly sod and lumber building with a rock chimney, and smoke was wafting from it.

"There are a few things left to do inside, but it's ready to use now," Sanpete said.

"It's your new home – just to get you started and to have your own privacy," Don Diego added.

Adkin just stood there a moment with no comment. Then he started smiling and turned to his friends.

"Thank you men, That is very considerate," Adkin said, taking Matty by the shoulder and pointing her toward the building. He said something in Kiowa, used some sign and Uribe heard him finish with "su nueva casa."

Matty's eyes lit up and she glanced back and forth to everybody and then tears welled up in her eyes. She buried her face in Adkin's shoulder and mumbled "Gracious, Gracious."

"Here. Here," he said. "Let's go look at your new home."

The guys were grabbing personal bags and bedrolls from the wagons and headed to the bunkhouse and Matty's new home. Sam and Mary Catherine walked with Adkin and Matty, Sam not letting go of Adam. The boy was nearly five months old and his hair and eyes were already starting to look like Sam's – thick and dark.

As they entered, Don Diego spoke up.

"We haven't finished the cook's area yet, still need a table and shelves," he said. "But the bed's ready – we all helped to gather all the feathers we could find at Bent's Fort chicken coup.

"There some chickens over there that are probably running around naked," he chuckled with the others laughing, too.

Matty was in awe. There was a large cook stove on the west side of the room, which was probably 20 feet by 15 feet overall. The bed with two clothes boxes, and a chair were on the east end near the small stone fireplace and a basket of chopped wood.

A lumber-hewn table with five chairs was in the middle with a rocker and an oval buffalo rug covering the plank boards which covered the ground throughout the whole house.

Matty again buried her head in Adkin's shoulder, crying softly.

"Why don't we give her some time, folks," Adkin said. "She's a little overwhelmed right now."

"Sure, you're right Adkin," Mary Catherine said. "We'll all get together at say, 7, for supper at the bunkhouse? Is that okay with everybody?"

Several shouts of "yes" and "sounds good" were heard as everybody cleared out of the new little house, and Adkin held Matty tight.

•••

Matty finally stopped crying after all had gone, and she slowly started exploring every nook and cranny. Moving a chair here and there. Adkin encouraged her to unload her bag of belongings into a large clothes box – or wooden trunk – in the bedroom area.

That's when he realized there was only one bed, and that created a problem he hadn't thought about – he wasn't sure they should sleep together. They had their separate bedrolls on the trail and nothing was strange about it, what with all the men and such.

He'd worry about that later. They would need to freshen up for supper. The guys had even thought that through. There was a small keg of water sitting next to the fireplace with a small table and large wooden wash bowl next to it.

He ladled some water into the bowl and splashed water in his face several times, forgetting to have a towel at hand. Matty had reached down in the shelves of the table and grabbed one of the folded face cloths and handed it to him.

"Thank you Matty," he said as he dried his face.

"Thank you Páhy-Chi," she said with a big smile, using his Kiowa name that Satanta had given him. It meant Moon Hair, and Adkin's locks were still golden and curly.

"First thing tomorrow, we're going to have hot baths, Matty," he said smiling, knowing she didn't probably understand what hot bath meant. Mary Catherine will show her, he thought.

When Adkin and Matty arrived at the bunkhouse, Matty seemed a little concerned all the meal had nearly been completed by Mary Catherine and two Mexican women helping her. Adkin assured Matty this was only because it was a celebration of everyone coming together and that Matty would get to cook plenty for this wild bunch in the coming months.

Supper-table talk centered around the need to offer more coach service on the western end of the Santa Fe Trail.

"In fact, we could keep a dozen or two freight wagons busy, too," Fransisco said, with the home crew agreeing.

Sanderson looked at them and asked how many more Concords could they keep busy.

"And I mean busy, we can't afford Concords sitting at stations for a week here or a week there," Sanderson said.

"We could keep two more, possibly three very busy," Peg-Leg said. "I'm driving regular between here and Pueblo – every day it seems. Colorado is exploding with settlers since the rails have reached Sheridan, Colorado."

"It's only 120 miles to the new Fort Lyons over here from Sheridan," Fransisco said. "We could run that line until the rails reach Kit Carson, which they say will happen this summer."

"How about I order three more coaches?" Sanderson asked them all. "What do you say?"

"I say yes, and I think we need to order more freight wagons, Adkin," Sam spoke up. "What say you?"

"I agree," Adkin said. "But let's finish up balancing the books in the morning between the two companies and see where we stand, financially, that is, before we order more freighters."

"That's a deal," Sam said, with the others nodding in agreement.

When Adkin and Matty reached their new home, Adkin was faced with the sleeping arrangements. He started to pull out his bedroll, but Matty beat him to it – she pulled hers out and unfolded the big buffalo rug and several furs next to the feather bed.

She smiled and told Adkin, "I Kiowa, not good to sleep in that," pointing at the bed. He laughed and that eased his mind. He would teach her later the comforts of a feather bed that kept one elevated off the cold wooden floor.

•••

Matty was happy as a June bug in May when Mary Catherine and the Mexican women let her help at breakfast the next morning. Matty had no problems communicating with the Mexicans. In fact she learned one woman was half Arapahoe. Matty was pleased to tell her that her old Kiowa friend Chief Satanta's mother was an Arapahoe, too.

The men had their books out, cross-checking the logs to see they were entered. They found some recent receipts for goods and supplies within the last few months that had not been entered, yet the loose receipts were at least stuck in the pages.

Sanderson presented a bill for services since the last payment he had transferred to him, and they checked that.

"J.L., you forgot the wagons that travelled with General Crawford's militia before they joined up with Crawford at Fort Larned," Adkin said grinning. "Are those services free?"

"By golly, your right, and no, they are not free," he answered laughing.

They got back to tallying the miles, 15 wagons, etcetera and added those to the overall invoice.

The YR&R crew looked at their balance sheets and realized they were looking good, but it would be another month or so to receive payments for this round of hauling to the new Camp Wichita. They figured that would put more than $16,000 gross in the books.

"When they looked at their total cash holdings, it came to a little more than $52,000, including estimated income from the present hauling into the Oklahoma Territories – less the payment they needed to transfer to Barlow and Sanderson Company.

Sam brought up another $1,300 that Mary Catherine had recorded from stage station operators that had sent payments due Barlow and Sanderson directly to the YR&R office either because they didn't get along with fort commanders or because it was easier sending via a wagon train or a military caravan.

"Sanderson was pleasantly surprised, because most all income from stage operators was usually wired directly to headquarters in Junction City.

YR&R's equipment collectively now included 95 freighters, two ambulances and three cook wagons – plus their buildings at the Home Office.

"I'd say you men are doing quite well," Sanderson said. "And you have made us a pile of profits as well.

"I say if it ain't broke, don't fix it," he added with a laugh.

Sam suggested they go ahead and order 25 more freight wagons just for use on the western end of the trail. But Adkin reminded him that probably 25 to 45 wagons may be on their last legs.

"We'll have to separate those wagons out when they get back to Fort Dodge and then see if we can gather some freight and take them on to Santa Fe and sell them through the Aguierre brothers," Adkin said. "They will need to be replaced if the Army gives us another big contract."

"Well, one thing about it is we can make those decisions faster now that we're back on the telegraph lines," Sam said. "Why don't we go ahead and order wagons for out here right now. Then we can decide what we need to replace when the gang gets back to Fort Dodge."

"Agreed," Adkin said. "I'll leave messages for Ryan and Ray Dee, too. We need their thoughts."

"Speaking of the Aguierre brothers," Sanderson interrupted. "I'll need to get it touch and let them know my plans on going to California. I plan on hitting the Gila Trail out of Santa Fe and taking it all the way to southern California."

"I'm sure they'll have anything you need, J.L., including scouts," Adkin said. "We can go over to the Western Union office this afternoon and light up those telegraph lines."

Once all the business was settled, Adkin got with Mary Catherine and told her about his thoughts on showing Matty how to take a hot bath. She was surprised at first, and then winked and said, "Don't worry, I'll take care of her."

"She'll be scared I'm sure," Adkin said. "She's used to bathing with about a bowl full of heated water – and out in the bushes in the snow."

"We women know a few things Mister Yates," she answered, grinning as she hurried off to the bunkhouse where the women were finishing cleaning up.

Adkin got up from the office table they had been working at and stepped outside on the porch. It was a cool morning with a bright blue sky and not a cloud in sight. One could catch glimpses of the snow-capped Rocky Mountains on the western Horizon.

Everything around them seemed flat and forever in each direction. They could see smoke trails from Bent's Fort to the east of them, but the horizon looked stark with patches of snow collected on the south sides of small ravines and around some sage and yucca plants.

But Adkin knew it was not flat – not flat at all. There could be 200 Indian raiders on horseback less than a mile from them and they wouldn't be seen in the undulating fields of grasses and pasture land. That was something that amazed him from his first foray into the western frontier – it is not flat, regardless of the illusion.

"It's got a beauty all of its own, doesn't it?" Sam said as he stepped out beside Adkin. "There's nothing like the Great Plains of western Kansas and eastern Colorado."

"Maybe that's why it has been the central point of so many Indians the last two or three centuries," Adkin said. "It looks empty, but when the buffalo come up from Texas looking for fresh grazing in the spring, this area becomes a garden of living things – resources for thousands of peoples who live the nomad life.

"I feel like those days are slipping from the history of America, Sam," he said. "And I don't know if that's good or bad."

"I know what you mean friend," he said, patting Adkin's shoulder.

"Oh, and by the way, we're expecting another baby next fall," Sam said, as Adkin laughed and congratulated him.

•••

When the men got back from Bent's Fort and sending telegrams, Adkin found Matty at Mary Catherine's place. She had on an elk skin dress with beads and elk's teeth interwoven in half-moon patterns around her neck. Her hair was braided on each side and she had small red feathers from Cardinals above each ear.

Her moccasins were beaded and came up half way on her calves. The bead work was amazing, and he had never seen any of this before. He wondered where she kept it in her smallish clothes bag.

Mary Catherine smiled and asked Adkin what he thought of his Matty after her first "hot bath?"

"And I talked her into allowing me to rub a little lilac perfume on her neck, just for you," Mary Catherine said.

Adkin took Matty by the hand and walked slowly around her, then bent over and sniffed her neck. He stood back and smiled.

"Usted es muy hermosa," he said, meaning she looked beautiful.

She smiled while flushing from embarrassment with all the attention.

"Now you men get to work finishing Matty's house and leave us women to do our chores," Mary Catherine said, as she handed Adam to Matty.

"Sam, that boy is going to be handled and pawed more by Matty than you at this rate," Adkin said.

"I know, but I can live with that," he answered.

With the railroad now stopping at Fort Harker or at Sheridan, Colorado, Sanderson estimated the Concords would arrive in about a week to 10 days. He explained the Concord, New Hampshire company was now assembling and distributing coaches and wagons out of Westport. He said Murphy, Studebaker and several other wagon wheelwrights were doing the same.

"You should have everything you ordered about the same time," Sanderson said. "I knew it was coming, but it still amazes me how fast times are changing."

He added as soon as he heard from the Aguierre brothers, he would be hitting the Santa Fe Trail and proceeding with his California plans. Adkin had asked if Sanderson would like him to accompany J.L., but he waved it off.

"I've been planning this a long time, ever since Butterfield opened a mail service route out there in '60 or '61," Sanderson said. "We need ya'll here to keep expanding coach service to all these outlying areas. You wait and see, settlers will start establishing little towns all over the place. It's just getting started."

•••

Sanderson and his crew departed for Santa Fe on January 11. A large caravan was heading that way and Sanderson appreciated the timing. He had planned on leaving the day before, but scouts had arrived with the news a wagon train was coming through.

In fact, it was supposed to gather up nearly 100 more wagons at the New Fort Lyon from travellers using the rails to get to Sheridan before unloading their wagons for the overland trail to Santa Fe.

Things were moving along with the completion of Adkin and Matty's house. She finally insisted to Adkin she needed some supplies at Bent's Fort. He took her to the commissary – which was probably the largest west of Fort Leavenworth – and she bought several sheep skins, deer skins and furs.

Then to his amazement, she picked out about a dozen small bags of various sized and colored beads. He immediately, and wrongly, thought it was for jewelry. She proved him wrong.

Her first project was a pair of small moccasins, detailed with beads and a small turtle in the center of each one, surrounded by swirls of beads. Though the boy was three to five months from walking, Matty wanted him to have the brightest and most creative shoes in the compound.

Adkin thought they were exquisite. She made Mary Catherine a deer-skin mid-calf dress, again with beaded patterns and a leather sash at the waist. It was also remarkable, and Mary Catherine looked royal as an Indian Princess herself.

Matty only made one outfit for herself, and it was a nice sheepskin wrap-around, long-sleeved dress with beads and sheep's wool around the hood and cuffs. She also made matching high-top moccasins that laced up with leather thongs.

All the rest she got at the fort was used on baby Adam. He had new full-length shirts that could be tied together under his feet and keep him swaddled from the neck down. She made him a small parka with beads and several snug leather hats with ear muffs that tied together under his chin.

Adkin realized, he would be shopping at the fort more often, but he was proud of her love for others and her talents with leather, beads and furs.

They received the coaches and Adkin went on several trips into southwestern Colorado with Sanpete, Uribe and Dusty. They established several more routes

When Ryan and the Camp Wichita gang got back to Fort Dodge, Ryan telegraphed Adkin the Army was wanting to use at least another 75 wagons from

YR&R for more loads of goods. The camp was now officially being called Fort Sill.

Adkin asked Ryan and Ray Dee to inspect the wagons and pull out the ones that should be sold in Santa Fe. They determined about 40 should be sold, and that would only leave 55 remaining to work the Fort Sill contract.

Adkin had Ryan contact Murphy or Studebaker to see how fast they could deliver 40 more wagons to Fort Dodge, and gave Ryan approval to purchase them if they met the Army's deadlines for the return trip to Fort Sill.

The next morning, Ryan notified Adkin he had 40 new freight wagons on order and sent Adkin the invoice number for payment.

Ryan's concern was getting the 40 wagons to Santa Fe. He was going to use nearly every teamster he currently had to make the return to Fort Sill.

Adkin was sure Ryan could hire enough men in Fort Dodge to drive them to Bent's Fort if not all the way to Santa Fe. There was plenty of people for hire at Bent's Fort and New Fort Lyon.

Ryan's best news was he was transferring Army money to YR&R Freight in the amount of $14,500.

Within two weeks, Ryan had led the 40 wagons for sale back to the Home Office. About half the drivers hired in Fort Dodge agreed to go onto Santa Fe. Then they hired more men at Bent's Fort. Some looked like Comancheros, but they figured all they were needed for was driving teams with mostly empty wagons.

Adkin and Sam were able to secure some orders from the Aguierre brothers and a few other traders they knew in Santa Fe. They ended up purchasing enough goods at Bent's Fort to fill about a dozen of the wagons.

The Aguierre brothers had already agreed to buy all 40 wagons at $400 each, if Adkin and Ryan confirmed they were in "decent" shape. They went over all of them, repaired about 20 of them with ironing wheels and axles and several other things like tongues and harnesses, etcetera. Greased them all up and refreshed a few with new wood planks.

Adkin and Ryan gave Fransisco and Sanpete authority to take the wagons to Santa Fe and transact the deal. They waited for the next caravan and took of mid-February.

Then they got word of bad news concerning their old friend James R. Mead. One of Jarvis' sons telegraphed them the sad news.

Jim's wife, Agnes, gave birth to a son, J. William Mead on March 29, at their ranch in Towanda, but Agnes died 18 days later. Jarvis' boy said word was Jim was terribly depressed.

Adkin and Ryan mailed a letter of condolence to Jim at his home in Towanda, not knowing how long it would take to reach Jim.

•••

As spring was awakening the landscape in mid-May, two Kiowa warriors rode into the Freighters Ranch, as they called it. They had tracked Adkin and Mah-aht-Tay through Fort Dodge. They had been looking for Mah-aht-Tay for six days of hard riding.

When they rode over to Matty's house, she ran out to greet them, Adkin walking behind her.

"After speaking just a few words, Matty turned to Adkin.

"Black Horse very ill," she said in English as tears welled in her eyes. "I must go to him."

"I will go, too," Adkin said as Uribe and some of the men came over to see what was happening. Adkin told them Matty's father was sick, and they would have to hurry and go to him.

Uribe immediately said he was going. Dusty and Fransisco said they would go, too.

"Come mi caballeros, lets load a wagon with a few weeks of supplies and a tent and stove," Uribe ordered as men ran off toward the stables.

Matty told the warriors, one of whom she called Do-hah-Tay, to wait, they would load supplies and follow them.

Within about 30 minutes, a wagon was loaded with food stuffs and lodging supplies and a team of mules were hitched up. Dusty and Uribe had saddled Diablo and another mare Matty liked and put four more horses on a tag line tied off the back of the wagon.

As Adkin threw his and Matty's bed rolls and clothes bags into the wagon, he asked Matty to find out where they were headed. Ryan was there and wanted to know where to look if trouble arose.

She said some Kiowa words, and turned to Adkin and Ryan.

"It's along the Cimarron River where Kansas meets the Indian Territories," she said. "It's a traditional camp where we stay until the buffalo move up into Texas – a small creek enters the Cimarron there."

"I think I know where she is speaking of," Uribe said. "It is a little southwest of Fort Dodge about 80 miles."

Once all mounted and ready to roll, Adkin ask Ryan and Sam to take care of things.

"We will try to get word to you from Fort Dodge in a week or two," Adkin said. "Don't worry, we have a Kiowa Princess with us."

"You're the one who should worry, you're the only White Man in this bunch – and that mane of yours would make a beautiful scalp," Ryan said with a chuckle.

He stepped over to Matty who was in her saddle.

"I hope the spirits watch over Black Horse," Ryan said. "Tell him I wish my Kiowa friend well."

She nodded an understanding and they then turned toward Bent's Fort, where Matty said they would cross the Arkansas and then turn southeast in a direct line to the Cimarron, bypassing Fort Dodge.

They crossed the old Aubrey Cutoff Trail and headed to Lower Spring on the deserted Dry Route of the Santa Fe Trail. They then followed the Cimarron to the bluff above about 200 lodges sitting along the Cimarron River and between a little creek Uribe said was called Crooked Creek by local traders in that area. He said the creek was fed by numerous natural water springs gurgling to the surface.

They had been on the trail for six days.

After the dry barren areas around Lower Spring, this small valley was rich in green plant life, and quite beautiful to Adkin. It surprised him how the valley just appeared out of nowhere, and tall Cottonwoods, Elms and Hackberries abounded in these lush grasslands. Even wildflowers were blooming everywhere. Willows and tall reeds lined much of the north bank of the Cimarron here.

After experienceing some of that Dry Route between Aubrey Cutoff and Lower Spring, this was as different as night and day compared to the dry, desert-like sand hills of sage brush and yucca plants they had crossed. This was like a little Eden, Adkin thought.

As they slowly rode into the village, people were greeting Matty – old friends and family. She was beaming but her brow still showed concern for her father, Black Horse. His tipi would be amongst the seven or eight tall ones near the creek's confluence with the Cimarron.

Matty knew the markings on his lodge and pointed where to stop. She jumped from her horse and ran inside the tipi, with several friends and family following her in.

Adkin and the others on horseback dismounted and tied their horses to the wagon. Fransisco had been driving the team and had set the wagon brake securely.

After what seemed like about 15 minutes, Matty wobbled out of the tipi flap with both hands to her face, She was crying and Adkin caught her as she collapsed in his arms.

"He die this morning, Adkin," she wept. "His spirit has passed on the wind."

He held her close as she cried, and he didn't know what to say. Father and daughter had been so close, Adkin's heart hurt for her. She had lived a hard 20 years, and losing her father had to be the ultimate after losing her baby at Camp Supply.

Nobody spoke, their heads turned down looking at the ground, when Satanta stepped out of the lodge. When he stood up, his full scarred, barrel-chest expanded and his 6-feet-plus form seemed larger than life. His eyes looked red and swollen, as if he had shed tears himself.

He let out several blood-curdling yelps and started chanting song-like words.

After a couple of minutes, he stood tall and raised both arms and placed his palms upward to the sky. All the Indians in sight did likewise, and all started chanting in a low voice, as to not wake the dead it seemed to Adkin.

He then stepped toward Adkin and shook his arm in the Indian way, and placed his other hand on Adkin's shoulder.

"I am pleased you bring Mah-aht-Tay to see her father," Satanta said. "He love her very much."

He then turned and walked over to his tipi a few paces away with several women following him. He disappeared without saying another word. Adkin could sense he was terribly sad losing his Medicine Man.

Matty had told Adkin about the special lance and war shields Black Horse made for Satanta. The shield was made of two separate buffalo hides dried and hardened in fire and then stitched together with pages from White Men's books tamped in between the shields to make one powerful protection. Matty claimed it had stopped bullets from soldiers' guns.

Do-hah-Tay approached Matty and said something to her. Adkin understood something about a lodge to eat and sleep. She nodded and she pulled on Adkin to follow the warrior to another tipi that was partly cleared out for visitors.

Fransisco and the men staked the wagon down and hobbled the mules and horses. They took a lot of supplies into the tipi.

"We can use everything but the tent and stove," Uribe told the others. "It's my guess Señor, but this may take a week. There will be mucho visitors and mucho celebrations of his life."

•••

After settling in their tipi, several women came and took Matty away with them. She told Adkin she would be back.

"These are my family," she said when leaving.

Adkin and the guys got their belongings situated. It was amazingly large when everyone got spread around the walls of the lodge. And heat from the center cooking/heating embers kept it comfortable everywhere.

That evening, Adkin, Ryan and Matty were invited to Satanta's lodge for a meal and stories of Black Horse. Every now and then, Matty would started weeping quietly as Satanta told how brave Black Horse was, and about his prowess as a Medicine Man.

"He can heal man, woman, child and any animal we know," Satanta said. "And I am happy he passed much healing magic to you, Mah-aht-Tay."

When they walked back to their lodge, Matty told Adkin a part of her spirit was gone since she never got to say farewell to her father. Adkin held her close as she cried and cried before going into their tipi.

The following morning, her female family members helped her slash and cut off most her hair as a sign of her mourning. Adkin was bothered by the tradition. He loved the shine of her black hair, especially when she rarely undid the braids and let it hang down around her shoulders. He thought she now looked like a coyote with mange.

"It will quickly grow out in time," Adkin thought to himself.

The next three days, Chiefs from around the Plains came to pay respects to Black Horse and the Kiowas. There was much drinking of all kinds of alcohol that traders had given the Indians. Some were also eating peyote, a hallucinogen, to visit Black Horse and his spirit.

His body had been wrapped in woven blankets with fancy designs and fringes and laid out in his tipi for people to see and talk to him in private. Matty told Adkin he would be buried at a secret location after the mourning period and all his belongings burned and buried as well.

On the fourth day, Matty wanted to saddle their horses and visit a place she had known since a small girl. She called it the Creek Garden. They saddled up and Adkin followed her as she turned west, riding away from Crooked Creek and it's crystal clear waters.

They rode about 7 or 8 miles, where a small little creek flowed down from the north into the Cimarron. As they climbed a small knoll to the north, the little stream had carved a 20-feet high cliff in the sandstone and earth.

In the back, where Matty slid off her horse, there was an old stone edged fire pit where Indians had probably stayed or stopped during their nomadic travels for protection and a place to build a fire without the usual challenges of high winds on the surrounding plains of tall grasses.

Where the spring creek met the Cimarron, there were willows, small Elms, hackberries and various other trees, not many, but clumped together along about 100 feet of the creek. The fire pit was somewhat higher and when Adkin dismounted and eyed the creek at this bend, it was truly beautiful, with the undulating grassy plains on the horizon as far as the eye could see. And the Cimarron Valley south of them from horizon to horizon.

But this small spot was full of plants, sandhill plumb bushes, flowers and tall buffalo and blue-stem grasses. To Adkin, it looked somewhat like spots on the Buckinghamshire pasture lands in England. It was refreshing to stand in this small oasis on the Great Plains.

Matty grabbed a sheepskin she had in her saddle bags and laid it out to sit on. Adkin sat beside her as she just stared at all before them, not saying anything. After a few moments, she started talking about Black Horse.

She told Adkin how he taught her to gather many healing flowers and roots right here when she was maybe three or four seasons old. She pointed out a strange looking small tree in the group that had weird bends in its lower branches, and it was only about 15-feet tall overall.

She said it was a Black Gum tree, and its bark was healing, and the tree is very rare in western Kansas. She pointed out the Yarrow flowers, which Adkin was familiar with. It had stopped the bleeding in Diablo's wound when a Comanchero stabbed the horse after missing Adkin's leg.

As she talked more, her voice cracked and she started weeping again. Adkin pulled her close and rubbed her cheek, wiping away the tears as she rested her head on his shoulder. He didn't speak. He knew there was nothing he could say to alleviate her pain – to lessen her grief.

Finally, she started breathing regularly, and when she raised her face to look into Adkin's eyes. She kissed him gently on the mouth, then kissed his cheeks, his nose, his eyelids, his chin – all softly as a butterfly landing on his face at different places.

He backed his face away to look into her eyes. They were sad with a look of longing for something kind and peaceful. He then kissed her with a feeling of love for her he had never imagined.

They were like two children slowly touching and kissing, exploring the feelings and physical touch of each other laying together on the sheep skin with deep fragrant grass all about them and the soft ripple of the creek and songbirds making their magic music.

Within a few minutes, they had both slowly undressed each other in the bright morning sun and became husband and wife in the eyes of God.

Adkin knew this was the woman for him. He also knew he had been ignoring all the signs, partly out of fear of acknowledging them, and partly because he wasn't paying attention when he should have been.

The relief of realizing Matty was the answer to the years of his determination to stay chaste until he was in love, was wondrous to him. The love he had for her suddenly erupted from his heart and soul in ways that scared him. He silently gave thanks to God.

"I love you. Matty," he whispered in her ear as they laid together. "I promise I will always love and protect you"

She nodded, a smile on her lips and in her eyes.

"I love you first time I see you when you save me," Matty said. "I never think I see you again in this life."

"The spirits bring us together – it is fate, I believe," she added.

They laid there under a warm spring sun with the bountiful life of the Great Plains surrounding them. She told him this place was always very special to her, and now it is their special place forever.

"This is where we have our spirit lodge – in our hearts," Matty said.

•••

They arrived back at the village in late afternoon, and the camp was abuzz with rumors soldiers had been spotted southwest of them along the Canadian River.

"They are saying the calvary are a couple of days from here, Señor," Uribe said to Adkin as he dismounted and helped Matty. She had a leather satchel of materials she had collected at their spot – medicinal flowers, stems, roots and even slivers of tree bark she scraped off the Black Gum tree.

Satanta walked over to their tipi and told them his people would have to move from the Cimarron.

"We will bury Black Horse in the next hour," Satanta said, looking at Matty. "And then make ready to move out at daybreak tomorrow."

"I don't like soldiers when they arrest me or my people," he continued. "We will have to seek safety in Texas, but it's best you not know where we go."

"We understand Great Chief," Adkin said.

"Satanta turned to Matty and said some things in Kiowa. When she smiled and hugged the big man, he spoke in English.

"You look happy Mah-aht-Tay," he said. "I wish you peace and long life – you are like daughter to me."

She smiled and said, "I am happy."

"I know you will treat her well Adkin Yates," Satanta said. "I wish you peace and long life, too. And your men."

The two men embraced with their arms interlocked, and with that, he turned and shouted orders to some warriors near his lodge.

"They will now bury my father in secret place. Only two men will know, and they can never tell another person in this life," Matty explained to Adkin and the others.

"Well, we need to hustle up and load up the wagon and leave for home in the morning – don't you think, Señor?" Uribe said.

"Yes, you're right," Adkin said. "In fact, is there any reason we can't leave in an hour or so and travel at least a few hours before striking camp?" Adkin asked.

Everybody looked at each other, and Dusty said, "We can be ready in about 20 minutes, Boss. Right men?"

All agreed and started grabbing belongings from their guest tipi. Fransisco and Dusty untied the mules and started putting on their harnesses so they could be hitched to the wagon.

Matty was putting her things in her boxes and bags. She snuck a look at Adkin when she could and if she caught his eye, she smiled at him as if they shared a secret. He loved it and smiled back.

As they worked loading the wagon, Do-hah-Tay and three other Kiowa warriors on horseback rode up to them. He said some words to Matty, and she told Adkin and the men that Satanta had ordered Do-hah-tay and his men to travel with them back to Freighters Ranch in Colorado.

Adkin didn't think it necessary, but he wasn't going to disobey an order from Satanta. And extra security wasn't a bad thing, either.

•••

The crew made it about 15 miles up the Cimarron before setting camp for the evening. Since it was dark, they passed on setting their tent and only made a small fire. All of them simply laid out their bedrolls, and it was especially warm for a mid-May night.

It would be the first time sleeping next to Matty thinking of how they consummated their marriage for Adkin. He was sure the crew noticed how much they smiled and laughed together after departing Crooked Creek.

"But, they better get used to it, because we are now joined in love," Adkin thought to himself as he drifted off to sleep. Matty, too, fell asleep with a grin on her face.

They made it to Freighters' Ranch in six days without incident or any problems. And everybody had noticed the difference in the relationship between Adkin and Matty. Uribe couldn't help himself when they got back. He told every ear there about the change, and the whole crew understood and were happy for the couple.

In fact, Adkin introduced Matty to a wagon master leading a train to Santa Fe as, "My wife, Missus Matty Yates." That mention of Missus Yates was confirmation to the gossip hens that something special had happened on the trip to her father's funeral celebration.

Little did the crew know though that Matty had discontinued her desire to sleep next to the feather bed in their new home. She gladly relented when Adkin asked her to sleep in the bed with him. At first, she was amazed at the softness.

"It reminds me when we lay together in the soft, tall grass at out spiritual lodge in Kansas," she said as they snuggled under the soft furs – her skin warm and soft next to him.

•••

They learned in May that William Bent had died in Westport on May 19, almost a year after Kit Carson's death. They estimated his wealth in assets and property to be worth up to $200,000.

Unfortunately, he had divorced his wife and had made no arrangements for a will. Nobody could figure out where all the money went, but it wasn't passed on to any of his sons or heirs.

Again, those in the crew who knew Bent, all had their names attached to the condolence message sent to the address of his home in Westport. Matty even asked to have her blessings sent, as she had known Bent since she was a small child.

•••

The crew learned Union Pacific had been renamed Kansas Pacific Railroad and had rails into Kit Carson, Colorado, now. But Sheridan, Colorado, was still closer to them as it was nearly due north of their ranch.

All 40 wagons for sale made it to Santa Fe, and the Aguierre brothers purchased them all. Ray Dee had led the crew and was coming back with a new herd of horses he bought with some of the proceeds. He had to wait four days to find a caravan to join.

As summer set in, the days got hotter and drier in eastern Colorado. A few dust storms had already hit the area by early June.

In July, Sanderson sent word they had bought out the Denver and Santa Fe Stage Line and renamed it the Southern Overland Mail and Express in July. Sanderson said it was all done by telegrams and Barlow's talks with the bankers and owners.

They received word from Sanderson that Jim Mead's son, J. William – the new son that Agnes Mead died from delivery problems – had been sent back east and died August 10. Again, the crew sent a letter of condolence to Jim via the postal service.

Western Union was making headway in running lines into the areas branching off the Santa Fe Trail, just as everyone forecasted. They heard it wouldn't be long and telegraph lines would be reaching places in central and southern Kansas and even down to forts or supply camps in the Indian Territories.

The YR&R crew was having success in signing hauling contracts, especially in southern Colorado. There were also mines being established across the Rockies into western Colorado. There were harrowing trails, but loads were well paid.

Peg-Leg Pete had worked his way into being the camp's unofficial wagon master, as he helped with the logistics of stagecoach routes and freighting wagons. He seldom drove wheeled vehicles any more, and that was fine with the co-owners. Sanpete had shown a real leadership quality. Much like Ray Dee, too.

On one of their shopping trips to Bent's Fort, Adkin bought himself a new Henry Repeating Arms lever action rifle. It shot a .44 caliber brass shell with a 250 grain bullet.

He still had his father's trusty Sharp's rifle, but this new lever action could fire 17 rounds in a matter of seconds. It held 16 in the magazine with one in the chamber. In fact, some of the Civil War soldiers called it a Henry 16 or Henry 17.

Akin really enjoyed the rifle. He and some of the crew would practice behind the ranch, and Adkin became quite good with it. He could hit a gallon lard can and keep it moving for yards with shot after shot. He proudly carried it in a new thong-fringed leather rifle scabbard on his saddle. It was much easier to pull out than the old long Sharp's.

Several buffalo herds had moved by that early summer, and the crew had harvested several. Buffalo meat became a consistent staple, but no one complained.

Between Matty and Mary Catherine, they ate like kings. Both women had different recipes and shared them in several differing ways.

Matty also taught Mary Catherine how to scrape, clean and salt-cure buffalo hides. Matty asked Adkin to kill more so she could make everybody a hide robe they could use in summer as bedding or in winter for warmth. By mid-summer, between YR&R and Barlow and Sanderson, there were about 20 people working at the ranch.

Adkin didn't think they could handle that much meat, but Matty said they would share it with families at Bent's Fort. So, the next herd that moved through, the crew shot 15 buffalo. But they ended up giving two away to a Cheyenne hunting party that was following the herd and were initially upset seeing the YR&R crew out hunting what they perceived was their herd.

Raiding Indians were still in the news, too. Indians were unable to get the food stuffs promised them at the reservations in the Territories, so they went back to their traditional ways: Hunting the buffalo herds, raiding settlers and wagon trains and stealing horses and mules.

Other developments included that after the establishment of Camp Wichita, Sheridan renamed it Fort Sill. Then a few months later, President Ulysses Grant approved a peace policy placing responsibility for the Southwest tribes under Quaker Indian agents, with the first Quaker agent assigned to the Kiowa and Comanche agency was Lawrie Tatum.

Tatum made sure that Fort Sill soldiers were restricted from taking punitive actions against the Indians who had supposedly surrendered and stayed at Fort Sill. The Indians interpreted this as a sign of weakness, so they resumed raiding the Texas Frontier and then came running back to the sanctuary of Fort Sill.

Indians were devastating West Texas, and many settlers were moving back east of Fort Worth, as raiders, mostly Comanches, Kiowa, Arapahoes and Apaches, were ransacking every ranch or farm west of a line from Fort Worth south to the Rio Grande River.

With these stories, the crew learned a new expression that came out of West Texas: Comanche Moon was now what they called a full moon. That was because Comanches loved raiding settlers during the night, especially on a full moon. Rumors were what few settlers remained on the Frontier, they would stay up all night protecting their property during Comanche Moons.

Texas was hiring more and more Rangers to help fight the Indians and constantly complaining to Washington for additional help.

Sheridan's massive winter campaign involved six cavalry regiments accompanied by Frontier scouts such as Buffalo Bill Cody, Wild Bill Hickok, Ben Clark and Jack Stilwell, who got the 19th Kansas Militia lost when it was trying to find Camp Supply, now renamed Fort Supply.

Troops camped at the location of the new fort included the 7th Cavalry under Custer's command, the 19th Kansas Volunteers and the 10th Cavalry, a

An Englishman's Adventures on the Santa Fe Trail (1865-1889)

distinguished group of black "Buffalo Soldiers" who constructed many of the stone buildings surrounding the post quadrangle.

YR&R Freight wagons worked the Fort Supply to Fort Sill roads carrying Army supplies until the winter of 1869-70.

On September 5, 1969, Mary Catherine had given birth to a girl, who they named Anna. Now little James Adam Phillips had a sibling. Sam was petrified having a girl, but he soon fell hard for the little lass, just as all his friends knew he would.

...

In April 1870, Ryan called a meeting with the other share holders: Adkin, Ray Dee and Sam. He proposed they rethink their location for Freighters' Ranch, especially since Carl Long and Darrell Holmes decided they wanted to work with Sanderson in Junction City.

"A few weeks ago, we delivered building materials – six wagon loads – to a new little settlement just a few miles north of Boggsville and along the south side of the Arkansas," Ryan began. "The families there built a small bridge over the river in February, and now all the Santa Fe Trail traffic crosses there and follows the south side of the river and merges with the old trail.

"We know it will be likely less than a year or so that a railroad will be coming this way – probably the Atchison-Topeka and the Santa Fe – and when it comes, it will surely cross the river near this new little town," he continued. "They're calling it Las Animas City, and it is already competing with a bunch of Boggsville's businesses.

"I'm proposing we move our headquarters – both Barlow and Sanderson Company and YR&R Freight to just outside this new town. It would be ideal for a railroad center, and we could utilize the location much better than here for freighting and stage services," he added. "What do you think?"

"I think we should ride over there and check out the location, since I haven't seen it yet," Ray Dee said.

"I think you're right, Ray Dee. What say you Sam?" Adkin asked.

"I'm in," he responded with a chuckle.

The next day, on horseback, they rode the 18 miles to Fort Lyon, and then the 7 miles to Las Animas City. It was just a hop, skip and a jump west of the confluence with the Purgatoire River. Adkin remembered Uribe had family that lived on the Purgatoire further south in a small village that had been there for decades.

They crossed the bridge that evening and found a trading post. They discovered its owner was Agapito Rivali, and he had a room and could provide four cots. They took him up on his offer and spent the night.

The following morning, Adkin wanted to ride to Boggsville, only about three miles south, and pay homage to Kit Carson's grave. They all agreed. The gardener where he was buried told them he had heard Carson's family were preparing to come and move his body to Taos, New Mexico, Carson's and Josefa's real home.

The garden of the home where they were buried belonged to L.A. Allen, a lawman. Adkin and his crew had heard of him, but the gardener said Allen was away at the time.

After paying their respects to Carson's and his wife, Josefa's, graves, they rode back into Las Animas City. After asking around, they discovered a man named John W. Prowers owned the land on the southwest and west side of the village.

They rode out there and found a sheep herder handling several hundred head of the wooly animals. He was Mexican and told them Prowers was rounding up more strays along a creek one mile west.

Within a short time, they found him and hailed him down. After some discussion, they discovered he had joined up with Thomas Boggs in 1867 – a man who had worked for the Bents since about 1843. Prowers had been a teamster who had worked for William Bent, himself, and as the Sutler at Old Fort Lyon.

They told him of their personal connection with William Bent and their friendship. He was delighted and told them he did have land for sale – right where they were standing. He said he could sell them up to 100 acres if they needed it.

"I don't mind selling off some of this," Prowers said. "Most of my investments are in Boggsville. We think this area will become a great railroad center in the next few years."

They asked him to show them the property along the north closer to Las Animas City and the new Santa Fe Trail cut everyone was now using. By chance, the small creek he was working zig-zagged northeast all the way to the Arkansas.

After looking it over, Adkin thought about 40 acres – with the west being the creek, the Arkansas River on the north and Las Animas City about a mile east, would be an ideal spot.

Prowers pointed out that would include the Santa Fe Trail road, and he suggested that would increase the property's value.

"How much," Ryan asked.

"I'd have to have $30 an acre," Prowers said.

"That is high considering there are only trees along the Arkansas and over there where the creek flows into the river," Adkin said. "What do you all think?"

Sam believed not having to remove any tree stumps was good news if they relocated there. Ray Dee agreed.

"We could take down much of our present camp and move it here in wagons, Adkin," Ryan said. "I just wonder if the railroad will go south of through Boggsville, like Mr. Prowers here says."

"That's still only 3 or 4 miles to a railhead," Adkin said.

"I tell you gentlemen what I can do. Any friends of Colonel Bent – bless his poor departed soul – are friends of mine," Prowers interrupted. "I'll survey off 50 acres, with a half-mile of river front for $25 an acre."

The crew excused themselves and walked several yards away to talk. After going over the positives, such as having room to grow or selling off unneeded land, and the wagon trains crossing their land and the possibility of a railroad close by in the future, Adkin asked what were the negatives.

"We have to work tearing down our place timber by timber, sod brick by sod brick and packing it all over here, plus we'll have to buy more building supplies," Ray Dee said, with Sam agreeing.

"Well, we're in the hauling business – we got our own wagons – and it's only a one-day trip over here," Ryan said.

"And what if the railroad doesn't go through Boggsville and instead comes right through this very spot?" Adkin asked with a big smile.

"Let's do it," Adkin said after a short moment of quiet.

They all laughed, slapped each other on the backs and headed toward Prowers.

"Fifty acres it is Mister Prowers," Adkin said. "And with great appreciation for your kind and generous offer."

One immediate advantage was this new little village already had a Western Union office since the Santa Fe Trail traffic had started using the bridge and crossing the Arkansas right there. They immediately had $1,250 wired from their account at Bent's Fort to Prowers' account in Trinidad, Colorado, where Prowers had an interest in a coal mine there.

When they arrived back at their ranch, Adkin told Matty they were all moving to a new ranch. She thought about it for a moment and frowned. She was disappointed she would lose her feather bed. Adkin assured her, he would take the bed with them and he would build her a much bigger lodge with maybe three or four rooms.

She didn't quite understand the concept of rooms, but she was pleased she wasn't leaving her feather bed behind. Adkin couldn't help but laugh inside. It made him happy seeing her take such joy in even the littlest things. She was teaching him how to appreciate those little things, and it made him glow with pride.

•••

It took the crew a little more than three months to move their frontier headquarters to Las Animas. This was done while maintaining existing stagecoach and freighting business.

During that time, young Adam Phillips came down with a severe fever and then respiratory problems. Mary Catherine was sure it was because she allowed

Adam to make a freight load to Las Animas with Sam and the men. The boy had probably breathed too much dust, thus the bronchial problems.

It was Matty who jumped into the kitchen and started making salves and liquids to use in soups from her assortment of healing plants. Mary Catherine had some of her family's cures on hand, too. Within a week, Adam was breathing much better and was without fever.

It was a few days before Adkin's 22nd birthday that the last of everything wanted or needed from the old ranch rolled into their new location at Las Animas City. It was as though they had moved to a metropolitan area, Las Animas City was growing, had several trading posts and merchants and a doctor, and there were plenty of amenities in Boggsville as well – only about four miles away.

•••

A few weeks later, in mid-August, they were visited by their old friend Charles Rath. He and a small band of men, rode into their new ranch with six pack mules and six backup horses, as well as the six they were riding. He was travelling with a man named Charles Goodnight.

Adkin also immediately noticed one of their group was a wily looking Black man. Adkin had seen plenty of Blacks after arriving in America, but they usually worked together with each other. It was somewhat curious this black man was constantly at Goodnight's side. He dressed much like a scout, but he wore chaps.

After introductions, especially with Adkin's new wife, the groups settled down to a meal in the new mess hall in the bunk house. Adkin met the Black Man. His name was Bose Ikard.

Goodnight briefly explained Bose was a former slave and had honed his cowboy skills on numerous cattle drives with Goodnight.

That evening, discussions would lead Adkin and Ryan into another of their great adventures.

Rath explained he was travelling with Goodnight because the man knew the Texas Panhandle and West Texas as well as any White Man.

"You know I've made a living providing goods and fresh meat to the Army while it's building rails or forts out here on the frontier," Rath said. "Well, Charles here is a cattleman that knows how to get beeves to market in New Mexico and Colorado. Plus he's a former Texas Ranger.

'During his travels, he believes a man could get rich providing buffalo meat or, more importantly, beef to the Army and the hides to eastern markets," Rath continued. "I want to investigate those possibilities.

"In fact, I'm risking my new marriage on it," Rath added laughing. "I got married back in Ohio on April 26. Charles is even braver than me. He just married three weeks ago."

"That's right, July 26 was my wedding day," Goodnight said, chuckling. "But my Molly knows business is business. Plus, I need to make this trip before winter sets in."

The two explained how Goodnight and his former partner Oliver Loving had blazed a cattle trail from Fort Belknap, Texas, 500 miles west to Fort Sumner, New Mexico, which became known as the Goodnight-Loving Trail.

"What about the Indians in the Llano Estacado of west Texas?" Ryan asked.

"Well, they can be troublesome, but I've learned how to get along with them," Goodnight said. As long as you don't try to mislead them or make fools of them, it usually works out."

Rath told them how Goodnight's former partner, Loving, got killed on their third cattle drive to New Mexico by a band of Comanches.

"Oliver got attacked by about 500 Comanches on the upper Pecos River," Rath started. "He got wounded in the leg with an arrow but made it to Fort Sumner in New Mexico. Gangrene set in, but they were unable to remove it, and he died.

"Charles kept a promise to Oliver to bury him in Weatherford, Texas, and carried his body from Fort Sumner back home," Rath said.

"He was a close and trusted friend," Goodnight said. "I still miss him very much. And that is why I continue to establish new cattle routes to market, especially up into Colorado.

"And I'm always looking for more opportunities to establish cattle ranches – the sky is the limit out here," he added.

Adkin and the crew immediately thought about the possibilities of moving buffalo hides, meat and establishing new stagecoach routes. The mumbling and discussions were heard all around the table.

Adkin asked them if his companies' services would make sense in the middle of the Indians's last frontier.

"Not many White Men have ever succeeded in those areas that I'm aware of," Adkin said. "Even William Bent and his brother failed at building a trading post back there in the mid-'40s at Adobe Walls."

"There are always risks," Goodnight spoke up. "I've been taking them since my family moved to Waco, Texas, when I was 10.

"But let me tell you this," he continued. "On our first cattle drive to Fort Sumner, we lost more than 400 head, mainly to thirst from searing heat and drownings at river crossings. But the 1,600 cattle that survived the trip brought good prices. When I headed back to Texas, my pack mule carried $12,000 in gold."

"That's good enough for me," Ryan said. "We have to check this out, Adkin."

"I agree," Adkin said. "Would you gentlemen allow us to go with you on this excursion?"

"They looked at each other, then Goodnight responded.

"Only a few, if you don't mind," he said. "We need to travel light and fast, no wagons just supply mules and an extra mount when needed."

"If I could make a suggestion, Adkin," Rath interrupted. "You and Ryan have been made honorary members of the Kiowas, your gifts from Satanta are evident. Should sensitive encounters with hostile natives confront us, that may help."

Adkin looked to Uribe.

"Uribe, we may need your knowledge of scouting, would you want to make this trip into the great unknown?" he asked.

"Si Señor. I would love to travel El Llano Estacado with you and Señor Ryan," he said, grinning from ear to ear.

"Could you manage three of us, Mister Goodnight?" Adkin asked.

"Please call me Charles," Goodnight said, holding his hand out as if sealing an agreement.

"What do we call you Charles?" Ryan looked to Rath.

"Call me Charley, cause I'm the youngest – I was born in August of 1836," he said. "Sir Charles was born in March, thus 5-months older, so he gets that moniker, and I'm just a Charley."

They all laughed.

•••

Matty wasn't at all disturbed Adkin would be taking a trip which would take him away for maybe six weeks. Adkin was upset for a moment, then realized Indian women were used to their warriors being gone long periods, especially if they were successful in stealing hundreds of horses or running down buffalo herds over miles of plains.

Matty was eager to help Mary Catherine with the children. She had already started making gifts for the little girl, Anna. It amazed Adkin the name they had chosen. He had never told them his mother's name was Anna.

Mary Catherine was just happy Sam wasn't being dragged into this great unknown and dangerous Indian territory, but some of the men wanted badly to go along. Adkin and Ryan told them why they couldn't, but to be ready if they received a telegraph from them needing help.

They told the crew they were heading north to Kit Carson, Colorado, to investigate how the railroad was progressing: The Kansas Pacific had established its railhead in Kit Carson. Charles had said he wanted to snoop around and see if they could find out any future plans of the railroad people, as he was interested in finding a cattle trail that could reach into Colorado from Fort Sumner in New Mexico.

Once they checked out that area and felt out the market for beeves on the hoof and buffalo meat or hides, they would then head down to Pueblo and pick up the Santa Fe Trail again all the way to just east of Santa Fe, New Mexico.

Charles knew the Pecos River ran through that area, and that was the river he and Loving followed up to break trail for their first cattle drive to Fort Sumner from south Texas.

With about two weeks worth of supplies and much more in ammunition, the nine riders departed Las Animas City August 18, 1870, plodding over the wooden bridge spanning the Arkansas headed for Kit Carson – about a two-and-a-half day ride.

It was on their first night at camp that Charley brought up the fact Goodnight had been a Texas Ranger when he helped capture Cynthia Ann Parker, a White Woman who had been carried away by Comanches in 1836 when she was only about 12.

"Charles was in the raid in 1860 that found her and her daughter," Rath said. "The soldiers also killed her husband, Chief Peta Nocona.

"Tell them about it, Charles," Rath urged.

"Well, I haven't talked about that for quite awhile," Goodnight sighed. "Those were bloody days for sure and horrible memories.

"I guess I need to start with how I first saw what Nocona's savages could do," he started. "I lived in Parker County, Texas, just outside the little town of Weatherford. Nocona and his band had been raiding settlers all around that area, and in late November, they hit Parker County close to Weatherford.

"First, they raided a friend's place – John Brown," Goodnight continued. "They stabbed him with lances through every body part they could find – killed him – cut off his own nose and stole his horses. Then they rode west to Stagg Prairie, near the Parker County line and attacked Ezra Sherman and his family.

"This poor fella, Ezra, didn't even own a gun – a real greenhorn. He had moved his wife, Martha, and three young'uns out there," he continued. "Martha later said 17 warriors came upon their house and asked for something to eat, which they got fed.

"Then the Indians said for them to leave – and it was pourin' down rain – so they left runnin' to a nearby farm. Their 7-year-old got away and hid, but the others were run down by the savages. They dragged Martha back to near the house – now mind you, she was nine months pregnant, too – and a bunch of them ravaged her, and then they shot several arrows into her stomach.

"But what was really sick, they scalped her – but they started below her ears and then peeled off the entire top of her head," Goodnight said. "And to beat it all, she lived – she had dragged herself back to the cabin, and that's where she was later found by Ezra.

"Of course she had a still-born, but she lived for four more days before passing, but she was able to tell her story," he continued. "Poor woman.

"Her son made it to the neighbor who rode to town and told us what happened. Several of us rode out immediately. I talked with her, and she was a fearful sight."

Goodnight stopped talking and was looking down at his feet as he sat there, the glow of flames flickering off his face and a tear slowly rolling down his cheek.

Adkin and the men glanced at each other horrified, feeling the pain Goodnight was expressing. Then he spoke again without looking up.

"In those three days, November 26, 27 and 28, Nocona's band of Comanches killed 23 people just in that immediate area," Goodnight said. "A few days after Martha died, there were 100 deserted farms in the area – everyone was headed back east, away from the Frontier.

"After riding out to see Ezra and Martha, I decided to try and form a posse, riding around that night like a mad man – and I was mad," he continued. "I found eight men who said they'd ride with me and trail the raiders. We met the next morning at Isaac Lynn's place – his daughter and her husband had recently been killed by Comanches.

"So we took off – still raining to beat hell – tracking Nocona's band, which was easy because they were travelling with about 150 head of stolen horses," Goodnight said. "We tracked them for at least 120 miles – forever raining – and we were cold, wet, hungry, no real bedding. But we finally spotted their camp with what looked like 100 lodges – it was near Mule Creek, where it flows into the Pease River.

"We knew there were too many for us to attack, so we headed back to Weatherford to put together a force," he continued. "We worked with the Rangers and the Army and by December 13, we all met at Fort Belknap. We had 40 Texas Rangers, 21 soldiers from Fort Cooper and 70 volunteers. I was going to scout and lead them to the village.

"The commander of our force was Sul Ross – he was only 23 at the time, and hell, I was just 24. Sul later became Governor of Texas."

"We met Ross after he became commander of the Kansas 19th Volunteers when they arrived at Camp Supply," Adkin said. "Sorry, go ahead."

"Anyway, we headed northwest in bitter cold – the nights were frosty and there wasn't much wood at all along the trail," Goodnight continued. "We had rain, heavy fog and thunderstorms – not a comfortable venture.

"Then on December 19, we came upon the village, but there weren't the 500 Indians I thought there were, but we attacked anyway," Goodnight continued. "Oh, I forgot – the day before, we found a little girl's belt in a pillow slip and Martha's Bible. Can you imagine?

"I knew the Indians liked to steal every book they found because they would stuff paper down between the two buffalo hides they used to make war shields," he said. "But where was I?

"Oh yeah, we only saw women and children packing mules and horses with buffalo meat, hides and tipi poles, so Ross sent some troops around the back in case they tried fleeing," he continued. "We went after them – probably only about two dozen Indians with some old men and the women.

"We Rangers spared most of the women, but the troopers killed everyone they encountered – shot them down where they stood," he said. "Ross and his Mexican manservant saw several people fleeing on horseback. One stopped and showed her breasts, and she had a child with her. One of the troopers captured her.

"About a mile out, they caught the painted warrior – he was naked to his waist – with someone behind him on the horse. Ross shot the back one, and she pulled the warrior off the horse," Goodnight said. "The savage shot an arrow into Ross' horse, but he got off a shot that hit the Indian in his elbow, breaking his arm. Ross said the man got off many arrows in a very short time before he shot him in the arm.

"Ross then shot him through the body twice, but it didn't kill him. He started wailing a wild song and Ross had his Mexican put him out of his misery with a load of buckshot," he said. "Come to find out, witnesses confirmed it was Chief Peta Nocona, the savage killer of west Texas – and Martha Sherman and her unborn child.

"Then we realized the captured woman with her child was blue-eyed and a white woman – she was just covered in buffalo blood and grease fat. It had to be that Cynthia Ann Parker who had been captured by Nocona years earlier," he continued. "We also discovered two young boys got away, and we found out they were the children of Parker and Nocona – the oldest one turned out to be Chief Quanah Parker, now of the Quahadi Comanches – he was only about 12 or 13 then.

"I gathered 10 of my scouts and we pursued the two riders for miles," Goodnight continued. "We crossed the western plains somewhere between 75 to 100 miles until we reached a large canyon on the Llano Estacado. There they rode down into a large Indian village, and we could see they created a big commotion, so we headed back to Mule Creek and home.

"I know now the two were Quanah and his little brother, Peanuts – Peanuts was about 10 then," he added. "For children, they could really ride – and they followed the trail left by the others who had departed the Mule Creek site a few days before – even riding all through the night."

"We stood right next to Quanah at the Medicine Lodge Creek Treaty in '67," Ryan said. "He's a big imposing Indian, and we were told he was one to keep an eye on."

"The apple didn't fall far from the tree there," Rath said. "He's a murdering raider today – all over west Texas, the Panhandle and western Oklahoma – just like his pappy."

"What happened to the woman and her child?" Adkin asked.

"We took her back to Fort Belknap, and they sent her on to Fort Cooper," Goodnight responded. "Eventually they got her back to her kin, but she never was right again – always tried escaping, never spoke English again.

Her little girl was named Prairie Flower. I heard the girl died in '64. Last I know, Cynthia Ann is living with kin around Fort Worth I think."

Goodnight looked weary and sad. He poured out his coffee grounds and told the men he was going to get some sleep. He walked a short distance and started unrolling his blankets and hides.

The rest of the men did the same, and all ended up circling the embers in the fire pit. Uribe threw a couple of fresh logs on to get it flaring – just enough light to keep the wolves at bay.

•••

Once in Kit Carson, Colorado, Rath said he was unimpressed with the small tent city and wooden shanties, declaring he didn't think a general store or market had much of a chance there.

Uribe showed them where Sanderson and Barlow's stage station was. It was one of only about five actual buildings, and most of it was stables and forage storage for the horses. A man named Jorge Cassita came out to meet them. Adkin, Ryan and Uribe greeted him and went into his small office attached to the stables.

Goodnight and Rath's men stayed at the station to feed their horses some fresh oats. The two businessmen rode on through town to speak with townsmen and railroad people.

About 6 p.m., and they only arrived in Kit Carson at noon, they both came back to the station.

"This is not where the action is going to happen," Goodnight said, with Rath nodding his head in agreement. "The railroad people we found said plans are underway to take the rails to Colorado City.

"They said William Jackson Palmer, the old Civil War General who is their Colorado Territory surveyor, already has laid out a route just east of Pikes Peak along Fountain Creek," he continued. "Looks like the Kansas Pacific Railway will be headed to Denver.

"Another problem is there are no railhead corrals here, and that takes a lot of money to construct," Goodnight said. "And I don't think shipping cattle from here back east would be that profitable. I think the better profit would be to drive cattle to Colorado City or all the way to Denver – the miners will pay top dollar for fresh beeves."

"And those reasons are why I don't feel comfortable with establishing my own clearing house here for buffalo hides or meat," Rath said. "I agree with Charles that the markets for what I want to do is further up – or down – the line."

"Well, we're already providing stage service in the area, but Jorge thinks business will improve – profit wise – as more and more settlers are arriving on the railroad and needing transportation," Adkin explained to Goodnight and Rath.

"We're doing better, too, at carrying gold and silver in the stagecoach boots for the miners."

"In fact, that's Jorge's biggest worry – hiring more armed security guards to ride atop," Ryan added. "He's been robbed once and fought off three other attempts in the last five months. Nobody killed yet, thank goodness, but bandits are figuring out who is hauling gold and silver."

Goodnight laughed when he saw Jorge had a chuckwagon in his yard.

"It's not bad, some additions I approve of, like extra tarps rolled up and lashed to the chuck box," Goodnight said to Rath.

Rath laughed, too, explaining to the others it was Goodnight who created the "chuckwagon" back in '66 on his first cattled drive to Fort Sumner for his cowboys.

"No joshin?" Ryan asked. "We saw a couple of those at the Medicine Lodge Creek Peace Treaty in '67. Impressive."

At supper, cooked by Jorge's wife and several other women, the men all decided they had seen enough of Kit Carson and agreed to head west in the morning and check out Colorado City. One good thing about their current location was they would get to sleep with a roof overhead, even though the stench of the stables was ever present.

•••

It was a long, hard three days to get to Colorado City. Rains on their first night out of Kit Carson has swollen Horse Creek, and it took them nearly two hours to find a place the animals could swim the current and not drift too far downstream.

They arrived in Colorado City near sunset on August 23. Again, Barlow and Sanderson had a place to stay at one of their stagecoach stations. It was ran by one of the Velasquez' cousins, Franco.

During their supper, Franco gave them some names of businessmen he knew. He also said rumors were the Kansas Pacific would be reaching Colorado City by the spring of 1871.

The next morning, Adkin and Ryan consulted with Franco on how to improve profits, which were currently suitable.

"Get rid of the Overland Stage Company," was Franco's answer. "But with people coming in from back east, there's plenty of business for everybody in reality."

Goodnight was much more impressed with the size and feel of Colorado City. And Rath believed once the railhead reached there, he could sell railcars full of buffalo meat – salted and fresh – to the Army forts heading back east.

After all, Rath had made a good living by serving the Army. He had a knack with commanders and usually came out of bidding wars as the winner.

His reputation for providing what he said he could – his honesty – carried a lot of weight.

Though he was living with his new wife back in Topeka, Rath had secured several military contracts for buffalo meat. That was his primary concern travelling with Goodnight – to find ways to fill and keep those orders, hopefully from the Texas Panhandle or southeast Colorado.

Both men considered Colorado City to be an ideal place to either ship product east or to sell cattle from the Panhandle or West Texas. They all shared information and ideas that night at their evening meal and agreed to head out the next morning. They would be going south.

Adkin enjoyed listening to Goodnight and Rath. Both men had an eye for business, and he instantly saw why they were successful. They were realists and treated everybody with respect, and they were up front about what their intentions were – to make money and make money for those who assisted them. In a word, they were sincere.

Those attributes fit in with Adkin's,' the ones he had learned from his father in Olney. But he felt empowered hearing it from true frontiersman who had literally scratched and clawed success out of this rugged and dangerous country. Next stop – The Pueblo.

They rode hard to Pueblo and made the 35 miles in one day. They spent the night with Barlow and Sanderson station manager Mello Velasquez. His brother, Ablo, was the station master in La Junta.

Mello had good business reports for Adkin and Ryan, but the men hit their bedrolls early in order to get a very early start for Uncle Dick Wootton's ranch in Raton Pass. They were going to try and make the 95 miles in two days.

As the men prepared for sleep, Mello and two of his men repacked several of the travellers' mules with fresh supplies of sugar, flour and yeast, coffee, molasses and about five pounds of Mello's cured venison jerky, a meat Adkin had developed a real fondness for. He realized smoked and dry-heated meats were his favorites.

•••

On the evening of August 30, they rode into Uncle Dick Wootton's ranch at Raton Pass. It had been several years for Adkin to see Wootton. He had another new wife – Adkin wasn't sure which number she was – and about five or six children running the grounds.

Wootton had added onto his main house, and it had a front veranda now of about 40 feet. Quite impressive, and Adkin knew it was that toll road that was making Wootton plenty of money, even at 25-cents a horse.

Wootton claimed he would be in business for many more years.

"Ain't no railroad comin' up here anytime soon," he said. "But, if you're wanting to drive a herd of beeves through here, Mr. Goodnight, I'll make you a fair and decent price."

"What if I was to drive 2,000 head through here?" Goodnight asked. "Could your toll road handle that?"

Wootton scratched his chin, thinking and calculating.

"How about a nickle a head?" Wootton proffered. "That would be $300, and it will probably take all day, 'cause the road isn't too wide in some areas. And I'd have to halt other traffic for the duration."

"Would you take 3-cents a head?" Goodnight offered. "You can earn additional money off the others having to wait for us by selling them extra food and refreshments."

"That's okay with me," Wootton said, as Goodnight and he shook hands. "Well, let's celebrate."

Wootton broke out a bottle of brandy, and everybody had a shot. Adkin even partook, as youngsters ran all over the house squealing and yelling.

The men departed at daybreak August 31, Goodnight stopping every few miles taking notes on his tablet and placing it back into his satchel he had tied to his saddle bag.

"Meticulous," Adkin thought to himself. "And very smart to keep information written down for later research."

As they reached the village of Willow Springs below the toll road, they stopped to water their animals.

"I think I may have to renegotiate my agreement with Wootton," Goodnight said. "With all those narrow places – now the road is great, level, all that – but I'm afraid we won't be able to watch every beeve and some are going to get rambunctious and fall off the trail."

"We're going to loose some beeves, I can tell you that," he continued. "And, Wootton and his Utes will be able to use ropes and whatnot to drag them up and have fresh beef to eat or sale."

"I was wondering about that, too," Rath said. "There are some deadly drop offs along there. But I'm sure Uncle Dick will work with you – he's onery but fair."

They all laughed. Adkin found the jerky on the pack mule and passed around the bag, taking three pieces about a foot long each for himself. They all filled their canteens as well.

They waited for Goodnight to take his notes – writing down where he could see safe passage for a huge herd of Texas cattle – and then mounted up and spurred their horses south along the Santa Fe Trail.

Adkin always felt a thrill knowing he was riding the famous trail he had fallen in love with as a teenager in England. He loved it even more knowing Diablo and he were riding through its history.

•••

Three days later, they were approaching Watrous where the old abandoned Dry Route of the Santa Fe Trail took off northeast. Goodnight and Rath had said they would probably turn off the Santa Fe Trail at Las Vegas, New Mexico, where Gallinas Creek swept southeast and joined the Pecos River 20-plus miles downstream.

Adkin and Ryan asked them if they could wait for them while they went on to Santa Fe and took care of some business with the Aguirre Brothers.

"We should not hold you up for but three or four days," Adkin said. "We'll make haste."

Once in Watrous, Rath informed Adkin and Ryan they, too, would like to visit with the Aguirre brothers, as they were longtime traders in the area and may have some advice about possible cattle trails of buffalo herds and markets.

They all stopped in Las Vegas just long enough for Adkin to send a telegram to the brothers telling them they would arrive in Santa Fe the next morning – probably around 10.

As they rode into Santa Fe, Adkin could hardly believe how much the town had grown, and the Aguirre's place had also been expanded. Another wing of rooms had been added on the south side of the main hotel and stables. Their corral was teeming with animals; oxen, mules and horses – even some burros.

When they rode up and were tying off their animals, Conrado came running out on the porch, his arms wide open.

"Bienvenidos mis amigos," he yelled as he approached Adkin, placing him in a bear-hug, but not quite strong enough to lift Adkin off the ground. He hugged Ryan and Uribe as well.

"Where have you been my friends?" Conrado asked. "You have not been to visit us in several years. We only talk through the telegrams – no bueno."

"We are sorry not to have come to see you sooner, Conrado, but we have been very busy," Adkin said.

"Many adventures, si?" Conrado asked, knowing Adkin believed life on the Frontier was one adventure after another.

"Si, Conrado, mucho adventures."

Conrado met Goodnight and Rath, saying he had heard of the great Texas cattleman Goodnight.

He claimed he had heard Rath's name as well, but as a freighter, trader and stagecoach man.

"That's close enough for me," Rath said, chuckling.

Conrado herded everybody up and commanded they enter the front of the hotel, leading them to the bar area.

While ordering drinks of those requesting, Conrado turned to Adkin, Ryan and Uribe with a solemn face.

"My brother Epifanio was killed a few months ago by Indians," he said, shaking his head. "After all the years of fighting Indians, Comancheros and bandits, he finally died at the hands of people he would help, if only they asked."

"Sorry to hear that, Conrado," Adkin said.

After several uncomfortable minutes, they then turned to business, and Goodnight was thrilled to learn how much Conrado knew of the country Goodnight was interested in. He even pulled out a map and showed Goodnight a well-travelled trail along the Pecos River to Fort Sumner.

The headwaters of the Pecos was actually a small stream crossing below Santa Fe, but if travelling from north to south or vice versa, following Gallinas Creek reduced the mileage by about 20 miles, according to Conrado.

"Here, you take this map," Conrado said. "I have several of all of New Mexico down into Old Mexico."

Conrado explained he was only in Santa Fe to clear up some business after his brother had passed. He told them he was actually currently living in Nogales, Sonora, Mexico.

He was blunt with Rath when it came to hunting buffalo in southeastern New Mexico.

"If it isn't the Comanches and Kiowas, it's the Apaches that will kill Whites in that country," Conrado said. "There is very little safety from Fort Sumner to Fort Belknap in Texas."

"That's for sure," Goodnight said.

Adkin asked if they could go over the books with Sanderson and Barlow services, as he had brought along some notes on outstanding invoices. Adkin said he wasn't sure if their books were correct or not.

Conrado asked to be excused to take Adkin and Ryan to his office. He also ordered his bartender to make sure all the men got something to eat.

Once they all went over services rendered or equipment delivered, Conrado discovered his Santa Fe manager had overlooked several months of stagecoach service, as well as freighting services and the sale of several wagons.

The total came to nearly $800.

"I am very embarrassed by this," Conrado said. "It seems my people here are not as fastidious as I ... and I will address that with them."

"Don't worry about it, Conrado," Adkin said. "With all the business ventures you have, it's understandable he overlooked a few details."

"We were sure that was what it was. Please amigo, don't be hard on whoever this happened to," Ryan said.

Conrado was saddened, saying he would wire the money right away.

Adkin slapped Conrado on the back.

"Now let's go have a nice meal and talk about the good things we have shared and how blessed we are," he said.

"Si amigo," Conrado said, as a slight smile crept onto his face.

Conrado was able to tell Goodnight and Rath very important issues concerning the area they were headed to. Adkin soaked it all in, as he and Ryan had never rode any further south than Santa Fe – or Las Vegas.

Of course, stage service south was taboo, as the Aguirre brothers had opened up all the trails south to Mexico themselves, before Adkin and Ryan ever came that way.

With Conrado's detailed information, he convinced Goodnight and Rath they didn't need to go back to Las Vegas and travel the Gallinas Creek.

"Just follow the trail to Las Vegas, about 20 miles out – and take the Pecos crossing southeast. You will then come to where Gallinas Creek flows into the Pecos. It is a well trodden trail, you will see Señors," Conrado explained.

After discussing business and dealing with maps, it was late afternoon, and Conrado convinced the men to spend the night and share a late supper that evening. It also gave them time to re-supply their pack mules.

•••

As the men rode out of Santa Fe on the dawn of September 4, the cool breeze coming off the mountains were perfect, probably in the high 60s and Adkin loved the smell of cactus and sage around them. The soft sand muffled the animals' hooves, and the rising sun put a golden glaze on the mountain tops off to the west.

"Off on another exciting adventure," Adkin thought to himself, a smile sneaking across his face.

They reached the Pecos crossing at midday, and headed southeast, hoping to reach the confluence of Gallinas Creek by dark. They were making good time, but Goodnight kept reminding them the more miles from Santa Fe, the more dangerous it became, as Indians and Comancheros were rampant the further south they travelled.

Adkin understood Goodnight's apprehension, as his partner, Loving, had ben shot with arrows south of Fort Sumner – which was only about two days ahead – and made it back to the fort for treatment, but died of gangrene.

As planned, they camped at the Gallinas Creek – Pecos River junction. It was a heavily travelled area, and many old or fresh camp sites could be seen within several hundred yards in any direction.

Adkin and Ryan were worried how many were used by hostiles and which were White Men, They decided few if any were sites where Whites had camped. They were starting to feel uneasy, and Uribe didn't help.

"Are all your guns loaded, Señors?" Uribe asked. "If Indians come, we have no time to load up."

"Yes, we're ready Uribe," Adkin said, thinking about his new carbine – 17 bullets, his Remington coach gun – both barrels with double-ought buckshot, and his revolver – six shots with two extra cylinders – and his Bowie Knife.

"If they can get to me through all that, I deserve to lose my hair," he thought to himself, but he stifled his chuckle. It wasn't really funny.

All the men were heavily armed. Adkin had found out early in their adventure that only one man was travelling with Rath, and the three others were tough cattlemen of Goodnight's. They had all been drovers and they looked like White Comancheros to Adkin – rough, quiet loners but with large knotted hands from throwing lariats and handling reins for 12 hours a day.

Goodnight carried his revolver on his left hip, with a crosshand holster. He grabbed the pistol with his right hand off his left side. He has said it came easy for him to learn that way. He also carried the new Henry 17, as did Rath and Ryan.

Uribe and the others carried models of the Spencer carbine in .56-56 Spencer cartridges. The bullets were harder to find, but they could knock down a bull buffalo at 500 yards.

Uribe had also started carrying two pistols when travelling, one on each hip. He also liked to carry two ammunition belts criss-crossed over his shoulders. One was for rifle bullets, the other for Colt cartridges for his pistols.

Adkin had noticed both Goodnight and Rath had extra Henrys wrapped in scabbards on their pack mules. In all, Adkin figured they had the firepower of a platoon of 20 troopers, at least. He also knew most of the supplies – and weight – on the mules were ammunition. That eased his concerns considerably when he started worrying about Indian attacks.

As they camped that night, Rath and Goodnight said they may change their original plans of going all the way to the Eddy-Bissell Cattle ranch owned by Charles Eddy in far southeast New Mexico. That is where Goodnight and Loving drove cattle to from Weatherford, Texas.

"I was thinking of cutting due east at Fort Sumner and checking out the far West Texas Panhandle to the Llano Estacado canyons on its eastern edge," Goodnight said. "I have heard the Indians have made a hidden trail through the canyons from east to west and they have driven their animals through there for years."

"Supposedly, no White Man has found this mysterious trail – or trails," Rath said. "Old Texas Rangers claim when they chase bands of Indians who have stolen hundreds of horses, they lose them in those canyons. It's as if they just disappear.

"They claim there has to be a trail through there somewhere," he added. "If we could find it, it would open up Texas to the west side of the Llano Estacado – those canyons and outcroppings are 200 miles long – north to south.

"What do you think?" Rath asked Adkin, Ryan and Uribe.

Adkin spoke up first.

"I personally would love to scour that area," Adkin said. "Not necessarily for business, but more of curiosity."

"Curiosity killed the cat," Ryan said, as Uribe sat there and shrugged his shoulders.

"If we went that way, it would reduce our travelling time considerably in reaching Jarvis' Ranch, which we wanted to check on anyway," Adkin said.

"True. I don't see why not," Ryan said. "What about you, Uribe?"

"Me? I don't see why not, either – other than Comanches, Southern Cheyenne, Arapahoes, Kiowa and Apaches?" Uribe said, but with a big smile on his face.

They all laughed, but Adkin knew Uribe wasn't afraid of a fight – any fight.

•••

A day-and-a-half out from Fort Sumner, Goodnight pointed out the escarpment on the eastern horizon was the western edge of the Llano Estacado, which Goodnight said he had heard it was 150 miles across.

He noted a famous report by Army Captain Randolph Marcy, who led an expedition to the headwaters of the Canadian and other areas back in 1852, called the Llano Estacado a high plains, level, without shrubs or trees as far as the eye could see.

Marcy also said animals shunned the area because a lack of water and even Indians fear crossing it except at a few places.

"That's what I want to find," Goodnight said. "A place we could move cattle across it without killing all of them of thirst."

Rath chimed in that even the old spaniard Coronado had travelled the area back in 1500s and reported to the King of Spain the area was so vast, that he couldn't find its limit anywhere, and it had no land marks – like he had been swallowed up by the sea.

"The explorer Coronado was the one who named it Llano Estacado – it's Spanish for palisaded plain," Rath said. "He said something like, '… there was no stones, nor rising grounds, nor a tree, nor a shrub, nor anything to go by.'"

"Something like that," Rath added with a chuckle. "I have a book back in Topeka that has the exact letter he wrote. Sounds like it even scared the old gold hunting explorer – ha."

They spent the night at a settlement called Aqua Negra Chiquita – little black water. It was on the map Conrado had given them. He had explained it was a watering hole about 40 miles northwest of Fort Sumner. They were sure they could cover that distance the next day.

•••

They rode into Fort Sumner in the late afternoon of September 7. Goodnight explained the encampment outside the fort's walls.

An Englishman's Adventures on the Santa Fe Trail (1865-1889)

"This area is called the Bosque Redondo," he said. "It was built back in '64 or '65, I believe. It's where the Army placed the 8,000 or so Navajos and Mescaleros that Colonel Kit Carson captured and confined here.

"The water from the Pecos and lack of food created massive problems afterward – it was a total mess," Goodnight added, saying nothing else.

Goodnight was welcomed by the fort's gate guards immediately, and they all entered. Adkin could tell this wasn't an ordinary fort. As they dismounted, Goodnight explained the scene.

The Army abandoned the fort last year," he said. "The remnants of scouts and mercenaries, if you will, have taken the fort over and now use it as a trading post and to help maintain a safe place for those who need a haven from raiding Indians or Comancheros.

"Some of these men look like Comancheros," Rath said, pointing out exactly what the others were thinking.

"They may be – I'd recommend keeping your eyes open and your head on a swivel while we're here," Goodnight said. "We'll only be here for the night, and we'll depart early.

Goodnight motioned for everybody to wait while he went into the old commander's office. Adkin and his men tied off their horses, eyeing the situation in every direction. Goodnight soon reappeared and asked Adkin, Ryan and Rath to enter the office.

Inside, they were introduced to a huge man Goodnight called General Alfonso Andrade, wearing criss-crossing ammo belts like Uribe wore. He had a big bushy mustache which drooped down at the edges of his mouth about 5-inches. He was wearing the bluecoat of an Army Captain, and a big sombrero hung on a peg by the door.

"Bienvenidos, amigos," he belted out as he shook hands with everybody, and encouraged them to take a seat. "How can Andrade assist you gentlemen?"

Goodnight explained he was very familiar with the trail he and Loving broke down the Pecos River to Horsehead Crossing and on to central Texas, but that they wanted to travel east and seek the possibility of cattle trails across the Llano Estacado. Andrade acknowledged he had heard good things of Goodnight and Loving. But Goodnight's plans didn't impress him.

"Ha, cattle trails across the desert," Andrade laughed. "That is loco, Señor. They will all die eating only sand."

"That's for sure, but we are only looking," Goodnight said. "But I have heard stories of Indians bringing horses here to sell – hundreds. Isn't that true?"

Andrade admitted he had seen that several times in the last few years, but he explained he always believed they came up the Pecos, not from the east.

"But it may be possible they crossed a short distance south of here and then came north to the fort?" Goodnight countered.

"Es po-si-blay" Andrade said.

Goodnight asked if Andrade knew of a watering hole named Portales.

Andrade said he knew such a place. He said it was about 55 miles southeast of them.

"There are great slabs of flat rocks where wells from the Llano come out," Andrade said. "There is a small village there and a priest has made a small adobe church for his people and some Indians."

His details matched the map Conrado had given Goodnight, though Goodnight didn't show the map to Andrade. Goodnight asked no further questions.

With that, the general offered refreshments, but the men asked if they could purchase some supplies first, then they would join him for a drink.

They went outside, and Goodnight led them to the old depot, where they loaded up on supplies, especially extra water bags for each animal. Goodnight explained they could fill them just before riding up the escarpment and hitting the High Plains.

"There is a place we're headed next where there is supposed to be very good water – with artesian springs coming from the bedrock of the escarpment of the Llano," Goodnight said.

Back at the office, Andrade was generous and had several kinds of alcohol available. Goodnight let word pass around not to indulge too much, as he didn't want anybody sleeping through a fight if it came upon them in the night. Luckily, Andrade also fed them well at supper, and a big meal would help negate some of the liquor.

•••

A little before daybreak the next morning, the nine men with their mules and horses rode out of Fort Sumner without fanfare. As they left the buildings and shanty's of the town built up around the old fort, Goodnight mentioned there were no people on the street interested in checking which way they were headed.

There was only an old Mexican man herding his burro pulling a cart full of hay on the streets that morning on the edge of town – the sun had yet to strike the horizon. All was quiet.

Strangely, the old man hallooed them, and said he had a message of importance. Once they gathered around him, he said Andrade was not the leader of the fort. He said the fort was owned by the cattle baron named Lucien B. Maxwell, and that Maxwell was away on business.

"He and his men are in Santa Fe buying goods and lumber to rebuild the fort," the old man said.

Goodnight and Rath knew Maxwell.

"Señor Maxwell is going to bring his family here to live," the old man said. "Andrade is an imposter. He has already killed the two men Señor Maxwell left behind to watch over the fort that he buy from the Army."

They thanked the man and Rath tossed him a silver coin, as he turned his burro back toward town.

"Maxwell owns the famous old Maxwell Ranch, the largest ranch in the West," Goodnight said. "In fact, some of the areas we travelled through around Las Vegas is part of his domain.

"People say he owns 1.7 million acres in New Mexico and Colorado," he added.

All this now made sense to the crew; Andrade peppering them with questions, the ruffians in the courtyard.

Adkin was sure the empty streets were meant to make them feel they were safe. He and several others of the group had discussed the men inside the fort – apparently working for Andrade. They were rough hewn men.

Adkin mentioned he felt Andrade's helpfulness and generosity seemed far from genuine.

"It was if the man was fishing for more information," Adkin said.

Andrade had asked if they had been on a cattle drive and if they had sold beeves and where. He acted as if he didn't believe they were only exploring business opportunities.

Ryan said he didn't trust the man. They all agreed.

They rode southeast, and once they got about five miles out, Goodnight stopped and told the others exactly where they were going.

"According to the map, this Portales settlement is where we climb onto the Llano Estacado," he said. "There is supposed to be good water there, and I think we should all fill up with all the water we and the mules can carry, because it will be about 25 miles to the next water, and Conrado wasn't sure how good the water is there.

"Let's make the best of it today, because we'll most likely have to camp at nightfall," Goodnight added. "We won't reach Portales until tomorrow."

Later, as evening crept closer, Uribe rode up to Adkin and talked softly.

"Señor Adkin, what do you think if I ride back behind and see if anyone from the fort is following us?" Uribe asked. "I have a bad feeling."

Adkin motioned for him to come with him and catch up beside Goodnight and Rath. He told the two men what Uribe wanted to do. One of Goodnight's men was scouting ahead, probably 10 to 15 miles, but Goodnight and Rath said they had been thinking similar thoughts.

"That's a great idea – we were just talking about that," Goodnight said. "We've been thinking Andrade has something up his sleeve.

"Do you want one of our men to accompany you, Uribe?" Rath asked.

"No. No, Señor, it is best if I am alone, no dust, I can be quiet," he said. "If I come into trouble, I will shoot my rifle three times. If not, I will follow your trail to camp.

"I will catch you by sunset," Uribe added.

•••

Once they established a camp site, Rath reminded Adkin how much money they made in northeastern New Mexico the previous two years.

"I was surprised we were able to hang on to so much of the military freight for Fort Bascom up on the Canadian here in New Mexico," Rath said. "I didn't think we could compete with the Santa Fe traders as well as we did."

"It was your connections with the military there at Fort Dodge that helped," Adkin said. "Plus, you were more successful at accumulating tons of supplies there than they could down here."

"Well, it was my friendship with the Fort Dodge sutler, Bob Wright – a former Barlow and Sanderson employee," Rath said chuckling.

"Yes, I remember meeting Bob at Fort Dodge – nice guy," Adkin said.

"I knew him briefly before he quit working for us in Leavenworth," Ryan spoke up. "He was a tough guy – never took gruff from anyone, and J.L. thought a lot of him – hated to see him go."

"He's not working as the sutler anymore either," Rath said. "And I'm now hearing the Army is going to decommission Fort Bascom by the end of the year."

"That's what we're hearing, too," Adkin said. "We haven't had a shipment to Fort Bascom in nearly a year."

As the sun neared the horizon, Adkin was worried about Uribe. He kept looking back, as did Ryan and Goodnight, but there was no dust trail of a horse being ridden fast across he hard-packed sand and clay.

Goodnight asked if a small hollow ahead would make for a good camp. They were in a shallow canyon with a dry gully, but Adkin saw a place further ahead that had two sets of trees – small but thick red cedars and some kind of pine.

"Let's get into those trees, it may be safer," Adkin said.

They agreed and Goodnight suggested they hobble all the animals. At that time, they could see a single rider creating a dust trail behind him. It was Uribe just loping along.

As he reined his sweat covered mount to a stop, he jumped from his saddle.

"We have company coming, Señors," he said, somewhat winded. "There are about 14 to 16 armed Comancheros, and guess who is leading them?

"Si, ees Andrade himself," he continued. "They are about three hours behind on our trail."

It was already 8 p.m. when Uribe rode up. They all knew they had time to plan and set up.

"Well, we surely won't set any tarps up," Goodnight said. "And we'll need to cross-hobble the animals."

"I'll bet that murdering bastard thinks we have a lot of gold on us," he added.

"I've got an idea," Ryan said.

They all listened and agreed to an overall defense. Ryan had suggested they build a camp fire and then place all their bedrolls around it.

"But we hide among the trees here and wait for them to attack the empty bedrolls," he said.

They agreed to build the fire big and bright, as though they were not expecting any trouble. They would cluster the bedrolls closely together, so it looked as if eight or nine were there sleeping. The Comancheros would know at least one man should be on lookout, but if they can't find him, they would attack anyway.

"We can cut some branches from the cedars and help hide – the trees are more sparse than I'd like," Adkin said.

Uribe suggested they go ahead and put up a tarp A-frame shelter and keep four bedrolls stashed in the mules' packs, keeping them with the animals about sixty or seventy yards away.

"If we put the tarp over there," Uribe said, pointing to a large cedar. "I can hide behind in the tree and throw a stick of dynamite in the shelter when they run in there to shoot you."

He was pointing toward Adkin, Ryan, Goodnight and Rath when he said "shoot you."

Luckily, they had purchased several sticks of dynamite from Conrado at his urging – and he mentioned it for such an incident as they were now facing

"When they attack, they will know if only five bedrolls are around the fire – there will be the four leaders under the tarp – with the gold," Uribe continued. "They will send at least four or five men into the tarp exactly when they start shooting the bedrolls."

"It makes very good sense," Goodnight said. "But you're facing real danger if you're seen before they enter the tarp, Uribe."

"They no see Uribe, Señor, until they on their trip to see the devil," he said, laughing.

They all got to work hobbling the front two legs of the animals, then running a rope connecting the hobble to one back leg of the animal. They situated them in a small clump of bushes about 70 yards away. They knew a stick of dynamite would spook them, but they would be unable to stampede.

They stacked their mule supply racks off to the side out of harm's way and covered them with boughs cut off some of he cedars.

Adkin and the men took several cedar limbs and downed sticks and brush to create hiding spots on three sides of the tarp and fire pit. They set them at about 30 to 50 yards away from the center of the camp with the five bedrolls.

They left open a clearing straight into the camp from the north, exactly the way they entered the area.

As they got the fire roaring, they gathered to make sure everyone was on the same plan. They would wait for Andrade and his men to attack – they figured he would wait until at least midnight to ensure nobody was up. He wouldn't even be at their site until about 11. They got into their positions.

As Adkin looked into the camp from his hiding place, it looked just as if five men were already asleep – it looked very normal. He looked to Ryan off to his left and gave him a thumbs-up. Ryan returned the sign. Everybody was in place. Now is was just waiting.

•••

Adkin was starting to get a leg cramp from squatting and sat back on his butt to extend his legs. A quick look at his pocket watch showed it was 2 a.m., and no sign of Andrade. He was praying none of the men had fallen asleep or been discovered by Andrade or his men.

The fire had burned down, but there was still a good orange glow from the embers, and the moon was nearly full. There was enough light for shooting, and he was grateful for that.

Suddenly, just as he was getting comfortable in his new position, gunfire erupted simultaneously with yelps and horse hooves thundering in. Dirt from bullets were surrounding the bedrolls and six men rode directly up to the front of the tarp shelter and flew off their horses running into the tarp and shooting pistols and rifles.

In that second, a huge blast of fire, dirt and shredded humans filled the air. Adkin found himself blinking at the brightness of the blast, but then saw a horse-mounted Comanchero nearly atop him, and he shot the man in the upper back with his pistol as he passed by within three feet.

By the way the Comanchero's head fell sideways before he slid off his bucking horse, Adkin guessed he had hit him in the spine just below his neck

Comancheros were falling everywhere as horses whinnied and kicked up dust. Shots were coming in on the horsemen as they had ridden completely into the trap. They were falling from their horses, some screaming, and one pulled his horse down and over him – killing him instantly.

Adkin noticed one rider at the rear of the attack had spun his horse around several times as he was trying to shoot his pistol into the camping area in general. It was Andrade, naturally being the coward and letting his men lead the charge into camp while he hung back.

Adkin raised his Henry, but a blast from his left whizzed by his head and slammed into Andrade's chest. It knocked him off his mount, and as he tied to stand, Adkin let go with the Henry, dropping Andrade with another shot to his chest.

As he hit the ground, his death grip on his pistol fired off one final round into the night sky.

Suddenly, all was quiet again, but then they heard the sound of a horse thundering away back to the north. It was either a stampeding horse of Andrade's men or a Comanchero was skedaddling back to Fort Sumner.

Then they heard, "Yaaa ... Andale. Andale," signifying it was one that got away.

Goodnight and Rath came into the camp center as others were making their way out of their hiding places. Adkin and Ryan started in also.

"Was that you who knocked Andrade off his horse?" Adkin asked Ryan.

"Yep, I saw him back there watching as his men were being cut down.

"You almost hit me, your bullet zinged right by," Adkin said.

"Well it didn't hit you, right?" Ryan asked chuckling.

"Anyone hurt," Goodnight hollered. Nobody said a word. After a moment, a sound came from behind the large cedar that had been torn into by the dynamite.

"I was wounded by a band of yucca plants," Uribe shouted, chuckling as he hobbled into the camp.

"I was running like a rabbit after throwing the dynamite, and a band of yuccas attacked me – I'm bleeding I tell you," he said looking down at small blood stains seeping through his pants on his left leg below his knee.

Everyone started laughing. It was funny that the only harm inflicted was by yuccas and not Comanchero gunfire.

"I'm pleased the yuccas were not any closer to the tarp, or you may have been in pieces like some of these bandits," Goodnight said.

They found six saddled horses in the area, surmising the others took off for home, wherever that was. They gathered them up to take along on their trip.

On Andrade's body, they found he had two gold pieces, which they took, along with his gun belts and two pistols and his rifle. Uribe insisted Andrade should be buried with his boots.

After gathering up the killed men – and some pieces of human heads, torsos and limbs, they calculated that 14 were dead, and possibly one got away. Goodnight insisted they try to get an hour of sleep and then they must bury the Comancheros.

"It's our Christian duty men," Goodnight said. "I know it's tough giving any of these murderers any respect, but we must. If you can't, that's okay, but we're going to bury them."

He was pointing at Rath and his men. After a fitful nap, Adkin was ready to help dig the small ditch in the dry gulch. Everybody helped and soon all the men and pieces were covered by dirt and sand.

Goodnight had even drawn lettering on a large flat stone's side and placed it on-edge at the grave.

"Here lies Comanchero Alfonso Andrade and 14 of his men – Sep. 9, 1870, killed by innocents they had attacked."

Goodnight had written it with one of his markers.

As he stood up and backed away, Goodnight said, "We are pretty sure these men were not blessed by the Lord, but perhaps they can find that when they meet him personally."

Nobody else said a word, but Uribe made the sign of the cross as he knelt next to their grave.

Thay had collected a load of rifles, pistols, knives and ammunition. It would put a few more pounds on their pack animals, but worth the effort.

It was around noon when they left the camp, which Uribe named the "Comanchero Death Camp." As they hit the trail to Portales, Uribe pointed out what Adkin had been thinking.

"When the next big rain comes, their bones will be scattered across the plains," Uribe said, shaking his head, almost sadly.

Adkin agreed because they were buried in a dry gulch that had been cut out of the prairie by heavy rains – however rare those rains were.

Uribe mentioned several of he men looked to be Mescaleros and Chiricahua – bands associated with the southern Apaches.

"You know boss, my ears are still ringing," Uribe said, smiling as they rode along with their memories of the "Comanchero Death Camp."

•••

They made it to Portales in early evening. There were a few sod and adobe huts or houses and one nice, little adobe Church with a bell steeple. Several children ran along the riders shouting and laughing. They were asking for "Comidas" and "Azucar" with their hands out.

A short distance behind the church, Adkin noticed a large flat slab of stone where water was gently flowing over its edge at numerous places and being collected in a small clear pools below. There were also seeps in the caliche rock cliffs above the slab. Several women were at the pool filling buckets and water bags made of goat hides.

As they dismounted, a priest walked out of the church and sauntered up to them in his brown, hooded robe.

"Bienvenidos. My name is Father Cordova," he said. "Welcome to Portales."

Goodnight extended his hand.

"A pleasure to meet you Father," he said. "If possible, we would like to fill out water bags as we are headed to the Llano Estacado."

"But Señor, you are already on the Llano, this is just a low cut on its western edge called the Blackwater Draw. The Blackwater River is about 30 miles northeast of here," the priest said. "But it does get even more flat past that ridge of cliffs above.

"We do not own the water – it is God's gift – and to all men and all wildlife," Cordova said. "Por favor, help yourself."

As the men started gathering water in all their bags, Goodnight asked Cordova if any of his people travelled to Fort Sumner often. The priest said several of his flock made runs to the fort for supplies for their commune.

Goodnight explained he and his men had been attacked by an outlaw called Andrade, and Andrade had been killed. The priest immediately knew the name.

"Andrade is a bad one, Señor," Cordova said, while making the sign of the cross. "Good riddance – with God's permission – he has killed some of my flock. He once rode with Geronimo's band of savages."

Goodnight explained he wanted to write a message to Mister Lucien Maxwell, the owner of the fort where they met Andrade. The priest said he would see it got to Maxwell on their next trip for supplies.

Goodnight scribbled out a message relating how Andrade pretended to be the leader of the fort, and how he followed and attacked their camp. He told Maxwell how they hid and ambushed the raiders and killed 14, plus Andrade, and buried them in the gulch. Goodnight drew a crude map showing where the gulch was.

He ended the message that if any legal inquiries were conducted, he could be reached at this address in Weatherford, Texas.

Goodnight folded the letter up and tied red ribbon around it enclosing all four sides as if it were a gift. He gave it to the priest and thanked him for taking care of it and getting it to Maxwell.

Within an hour, all the water bags were filled and loaded on the mules, and they were ready to depart. Father Cordova confirmed the direction to Blackwater River, calling it a creek, and said sometimes the water, when low, wasn't fit for man, but animals could drink it in small amounts.

They headed out with about seven hours of daylight remaining on September 9. The strangest day of their journey by far.

•••

Once they made the climb out of the little valley and over the caliche cliffs, the land turned literally into a table top of vast grasslands – as far as the eye could see. It was just as General Marcy had written – no stump, tree or ground swell interrupted the horizon to the north, east and south. It almost hurt one's eyes in trying to discern distance and perception. The heat from the Plains was already producing mirages on the horizon.

"Remarkable," Adkin thought to himself. "How did Indians know how and where to navigate this land? He was glad Goodnight was a natural explorer, and had covered most of the Frontier. Goodnight's trail mapping would come in handy, and make him even wealthier in later years. Adkin wondered what Goodnight was writing because Rath had said he wasn't sure Goodnight could even read or write, according to rumors. Maybe he was drawing creeks and buttes, who knows, but he was always scribbling something in that notebook.

"Well men, we should be in Texas now, according to my calculations," Goodnight said. "It's going to look like this for many miles I'm afraid – at least until we reach the caprock areas on the other side of the Llano."

Once evening neared, Adkin was wondering where in the world would they find any natural shelter to camp for the night. It seemed they were travelling out of a lower place on the Plains and heading so slightly higher going northeast. But when he asked Ryan about that theory, Ryan said he couldn't tell.

"I can't see anything, and I don't know shit, Adkin," Ryan said. "It's too much to waste time on frettin' about."

Adkin was thinking it was a wonderful place to run stagecoaches across – no real bumps, straight as one could imagine. There was just one major problem – no towns or villages or mines or railroads – take your pick.

Suddenly off to the east, a black looking cloud seemed to be covering the ground out of a shallow funnel on the plains and expanding as it swarmed southward.

"Buffalo," Rath shouted. "Look at that, there's thousands of buffalo."

He was excited, and it was wonderous to Adkin. He had seen several buffalo herds in Kansas, but this one was twice or three times bigger than anything he had ever seen. They kept coming out of nowhere and filling the grasslands with hundreds and hundreds of buffalo.

Goodnight held up his hand and yelled "Halt, men."

"Everyone dismount and try to get your animals down," he shouted. "Those are Indians coming up behind the herd. They're stampeding them in a hunt."

Men were forcing their horses down, but several of the mules refused to lay down. They were all hoping they were far enough away to not be seen.

As the rumbling sound reached them, it was as if several trains were coming down the tracks together. The rumbling was perceptible in the ground underneath them. They were at least two to three miles away, and heading on southward or even southeast. That was good news.

The bad news would be if they were spotted and the Indians would be more interested in them than buffalo. The men finally got the last two mules to lay down, and everybody peeked over their mounts to watch the buffalo hunt.

Goodnight finally broke their silence.

"I'll bet there is a gulch or shallow swale ahead of them where the buffalo will be met with the rest of the hunters and they'll slaughter all they need," he said. "I don't see any dead buffalo on the ground yet – or any Indians shooting arrows and no gun shots either."

It took another 20 minutes for the herd and the Indians – they estimate there were about 20 Indians – to disappear on the horizon. That's when Adkin realized this plateau was similar – in a smaller scale – than some pasture land in Kansas and eastern Colorado: It's not as flat as it seems and looks.

As they all stood and got the animals back on their feet, a couple of mules' pack-boards had to be re-tied as they had shifted in the melee. Bose Ikard, Goodnight's right-hand man was very efficient when it came to pack boards. It took real talent to get them balanced and tied down. Ikard could do it faster than any man Adkin had seen.

"There's no proof they didn't see us," Goodnight said. "They may have but the buffalo were more important – now anyway.

"There's a possibility they may come looking for us later tonight," he continued. "I think it's best we make haste and see how far we can get before stopping for the night.

"And, there's not going to be a fire tonight for sure. We sleep on the ground with two-man watches – okay?" Goodnight added.

The men spurred their mounts and tugged on the pack mules' tow ropes. They had a few hours before dark, and they all started into a slow trot.

•••

The men spent another fitful night on the plains, but the Indian hunting party had apparently not seen them. They determined it was probably about another 10 miles to intersect Blackwater Creek.

As they plodded along, several of the men, including Adkin, were close to falling asleep in the saddle. They all had been awake for nearly 40 to 45 hours out of the last 50. And they had faced an attack by 16 Comancheros and then tried sleeping on hardpan on the open plains in a very shallow hollow and wind around 20 miles per hour.

Adkin was also seeing castles among mountains on the horizon as the morning heated up. He knew they were desert hallucinations, but they looked so real at times.

Adkin kept catching himself allowing his eyes to close, then blinking several times, he suddenly saw a low line of small bushes and a few stunted mesquite trees zig-zagging across the plains before them. More illusions he thought to himself.

"Ees the Blackwater, si?" Uribe yelled.

"Great," Adkin thought to himself. "It's not a mirage."

Once they reached the tiny stream, it was barely flowing, and it had several pools that created water depths of maybe three feet. Goodnight was first to jump out of his saddle and kneel next to a still-looking pool. He cupped his hand and tasted it.

"It close, men – lots of acidity," he said, taking another sip with his hand. "I think it's fine for the animals, but maybe we should only drink a little, and follow it with some good water we're packing."

"How much further is the next water supposed to be, Charles?" Rath asked.

Goodnight walked back and took out his map from his saddlebags and unfolded it.

"Well, we're supposed to follow this creek east for about 15 miles, then turn northeast," he said. "Then it's open ground for about another 20 miles to an unnamed creek – then keeping the same heading, about 20 miles to Tule Creek, which has good water."

The men sighed with relief and agreed to drink Blackwater and fresh water at 50-50 percentages as they followed it down-river.

Adkin made a suggestion.

"What do you men think if we tried catching up on some sleep right here?" he asked no one in particular. "We could really use the rest – our animals, too. I don't know about the rest of you, but I'm about to fall out of my saddle."

"I think that's a great idea Goodnight said. "We can be hidden down here in the brush, and nobody would know we're sleeping here in the middle of the day."

"Let's find the best place along here to keep the animals hidden, as well," Rath said, while several of the men exhaled with moans of, "Thank you God."

•••

Uribe woke everyone at 3 p.m., and Rath said he hadn't seen anyone while taking his watch. He looked okay, but Adkin and the others knew he'd sleep a hard sleep later tonight. Goodnight suggested they ride the 10 miles or so to where Blackwater turned due south – their departing spot for the next water northeast of them.

Rath did say he saw another buffalo herd, much smaller – just a couple of hundred of them – move along grazing to their east again.

"If a man could assemble a team of hunters and skinners and come out here, they could fill as many wagons as they could manage in a couple of days," Rath said, with a smile as if he had just made a bundle of money.

Several of the men laughed, knowing it would be nearly impossible to get anything to a market from "here."

"I think, we're in the middle of Hell, Señor Rath, and I don't see any railroad tracks yet," Uribe spoke up, causing more and louder laughter. Even Rath busted out chuckling.

An Englishman's Adventures on the Santa Fe Trail (1865-1889)

"I think you're exactly right, Uribe," Rath said.

Within a couple of hours, the creek took a sharp turn south, and they could see it meandered south for as far as they could see. They decided to seek a camp hidden by brush and what mesquites were available.

Once they agreed on a site, they again hobbled their animals, and laid out their bedrolls. They also believed it was best to not set up a tarpaulin A-frame and absolutely no fire. That meant another meal of jerky, dried buffalo meat and raw potatoes.

Adkin agreed to take the 4 to 6 a.m. watch, and would be awakened by one of Goodnight's men. Adkin quickly fell asleep on his bedroll, as the air was still warm. They all had noticed it might reach 75 during the day, but it dropped to the chilly low 40s in the early morning hours.

Adkin was woke at 4, and he grabbed his rifle, buckled on his gun belt and went over to the southern edge of their little grove of brush and trees. The creek was slowly gurgling to their west. He suddenly heard a wolf calling downstream. Then several more joined in.

"What in the world is a large wolf pack doing out here on the plains," he asked himself, then realizing in the next moment, "Buffalo and their calves."

Adkin's amazement of how much wildlife lived on the Llano Estacado would continue the longer they travelled it's grassy and sandy plains.

At 6, with the sky turning a soft gray in the east and an easy southwesterly breeze, he shook everyone awake to get a start on a new day. Adkin was glad they had totally refreshed after such chaos for 50-some hours.

By 6:30 a.m. on September 10, they were headed northeast from Blackwater Creek and into the vast empty horizon – a stark looking vista that promised nothing – nothing but the unknown and danger.

•••

Sure enough, using Conrado's map and Goodnight's sense of navigation, their 35-degree heading brought them to a clear unnamed creek with good water. It was about 20 miles or less from Blackwater. They would learn later, the waterway was called Running Water Creek to some, and it joined the White River in the central Texas Panhandle.

While they refreshed their animals and allowed them to feed for about an hour, they decided to eat a warm meal for a change.

The smell of frying bacon and hot coffee was enough to get the men foaming at the mouth for hot food. They also fried some sliced potatoes and made a watery gravy with the drippings and flour.

Charley also pinched off large pieces of hard bread from loaves they had purchased at Fort Sumner and laid them out.

The men snatched them up as fast as Rath could place them in a wooden bowl. Adkin was thinking he hadn't tasted anything so good in years. The others were like children who hadn't been fed in days.

Goodnight started laughing in the silence where the only sounds were slurping, chewing and oohing and aahing.

"Charley, these men think you're about the best cook on the Frontier right about now," Goodnight said, laughing.

"He is, Señor," Uribe stopped chewing long enough to say. "He is numero uno."

"This is great Charley," Adkin said. "We needed this."

"Amen. Amen," Ryan said with several others just mumbling while they attacked the food. Within about 10 minutes, there wasn't a crumb or piece of food remaining in any bowl or skillet.

They all sat back – even laid back on the ground. They were content. Adkin started chuckling at the sight, then Ryan, too. Soon everybody was laughing and pointing at each other.

"Look at Uribe – he's so full he can't sit up," one of the men said.

"What about you?" Uribe said laughing.

Everyone guffawed and hooted until they hurt even more than their stuffed bellies did.

"Enjoy while you can," Goodnight said. "There's no telling when we can do this again."

"Charles, you're a killjoy," Rath said laughing. "But you're probably right."

•••

After gathering the animals, loading the packs on the mules, hooking up the extra horses and saddling their mounts, Goodnight pointed northeast.

"We're headed 45 degrees that-a-way to the Tule River," he said, his arm suspended. "When we reach that, we'll decide how to best to find the upper Palo Duro Canyon and the Canadian."

Off they rode, the landscape looking the same – seemingly endless and dull. The grasses turning yellow – soon to be waving gold. But Adkin noticed the field mice – especially the kangaroo rats. They even saw some side-winders, rattle snakes and a few hog-nose vipers.

The men said the vipers weren't poisonous, but they looked ferocious to Adkin. He had heard of the hog-nose but never had seen one.

Diablo thought like Adkin, especially when one popped his head up about a foot off the ground, flared his viper-like head and hissed with that tongue flickering.

Diablo stomped and whinnied loudly as he backed up from the snake. If it aggravated Diablo, it aggravated Adkin, too. He loved his big black stallion, they thought alike.

An Englishman's Adventures on the Santa Fe Trail (1865-1889)

They saw more buffalo, and – thankfully – no Indians. Rath was sure his next fortune would lie in buffalo hides and meat.

"I've got to put some teams together to hunt this Texas Panhandle," Rath said, smiling like a cat stalking a mouse.

They also encountered lots of antelopes – as some people called them. Some also called them Pronghorn Antelopes. Ryan said they were actually goats native to the West. Regardless, they were everywhere.

Adkin had hunted and eaten them, but he had never seen so many. He actually loved Antelope meat – dried or freshly roasted, like the Kiowa cooked them.

They had noticed lots of animal tracks across the plains, too. There were even horse tracks among buffalo trails. Everyone was sure they were Indian pony tracks they were finding. There was no sign of an iron horse shoe.

Adkin was actually amazed at several areas where hundreds of animals made their own small roadways coming and going. Goodnight kept quietly making notes in his tablet.

By late evening, they had reached the Tule, meaning they had made about 50 miles – and had a hot meal – for that day. They were happy and pleased at their success, until Goodnight spoke.

"Men, I don't feel like it's safe to have a fire here," he said. "We've seen plenty of horse tracks, and I'll bet they're not White hunters out this far west."

"I'm just speaking my mind – what do y'all think?" he added.

"I'm with Charles," Adkin spoke up. "There's Indians and buffalo around here, and I'm sure those horse tracks are not Whites either."

There were several mumbles, but they agreed to camp without fire – or another hot meal for the night. During the night, one of Goodnight's men shouted for everyone to wake up. He was hysterical.

They're everywhere," he said. "Maybe it's Indians."

As Adkin's head cleared from sleep, he heard the rumbling. He could feel it, too.

"It's buffalo – they're stampeding," Rath yelled as several of the huge animals came within sight to the west of their camp.

"Get behind the mesquite bushes," he added, as everyone was scrambling for some kind of cover. Adkin slid behind a small mesquite with his rifle in his hand.

Several of the animals came directly through the camp, knocking bedrolls and saddles around. Fortunately, their animals were hobbled in a cove behind their camp.

As their rumbling slowed, there were no more buffalo close by. Their hooves were pounding away to the west. As men came out of hiding, everyone took stock of where their bedroll was – or if their saddles had been damaged. A ruined saddle meant riding bareback – a painful proposition for a saddle tramp.

After an accounting, no real damage had been done, even though there was a missing buffalo skin.

"De buffalo wanted a hide from his old amigo, so he took it with him," Uribe joked. "He's taking it to buffalo heaven."

Everyone started laughing again. Adkin knew it was predictable – when men face extreme danger and survive, laughing is the best medicine to rid oneself of the anxiety and fear.

When the watch guard told them he had heard wolves nearby, they surmised wolves must have attacked a calf or a crippled buffalo, and that disturbance eventually led to a night-time stampede.

Since it was nearly 5 in the morning, they decided trying to sleep an hour or so was futile. Goodnight suggested they prepare everything for a hot breakfast, and once there was enough daylight to keep a glaring fire from being seen, they would cook.

"But let's keep the fire as small as possible, okay?" he said.

•••

At daybreak, not finding a wolf-killed buffalo carcass anywhere nearby, they headed north after filling all the water carriers.

"It may take us 60 miles before we see water again," Goodnight said. "Let's go on water rations for us men, and we'll see how the animals are doing each stop before watering.

"We will head nearly due north until we find the Prairie Dog Town Fork of the Red River, which originally created the Palo Duro Canyon," he continued. "I have travelled up the Palo Duro Canyon from the east, except for about the last 20 miles in my estimation.

"Hundreds of bands and tribes winter in that canyon, but it's still September, so it may be a little safer."

Off they rode with the sun creeping up over the horizon, painting all the grasses with a golden hue – it was beautiful but stark. Adkin could see why few Whites had travelled this country. It was deadly in so many ways, but settlement of the West was coming, no matter who or what was in the way.

Though Adkin had problems visualizing it, Goodnight and Rath were sure the area would one day be full of cattle ranches. But Rath, was sure the buffalo would need to be thinned first, and he envisioned a fortune in that endeavor.

In fact, by midday, they saw another large buffalo herd meandering off to their west, no Indians trailing them. More good news.

It was September 12, and they figured it would be two hard days getting to the Prairie Dog Town Fork of the Red River. What was worrisome at the moment was the day had heated up to about 75 degrees, it was enough to create those heat mirages on the horizon.

Instead of castles and mountains, Adkin was seeing hordes of attacking Indians with dust rising high into the air. He shook his head, knowing his own mind was creating such nonsense.

He decided not to look at it, and instead study the small creatures that would appear out of nowhere and scurry away into the desert surroundings. Lizards, scorpions, small snakes, mice and huge black beetles slogging through the sand.

And birds. Adkin discovered all types of birds flew by from time to time. Small sparrow-like ones plus wrens of different types. These were birds that apparently nested in sage brush or yuccas or the stunted mesquite that had mysteriously taken root in some places.

And of course, they often saw the large vultures circling off on the horizon. God's ultimate cleaners of the land. They also saw flycatchers and the roadrunners – a remarkable bird that seemed to never fly. He would just run off as fast as anything Adkin had ever seen.

When they stopped for camp, their animals were very thirsty, and the men knew they would have to drink as little as possible. With warm temperatures, each animal could easily drink 5 gallons a day, and they had about 30 animals. The water was going to be tight the next 24 hours. And they all knew if they were spotted by Indian's, that number of animals was a big target of trouble.

"Y'all know, if we're attacked, we're going to have to leave our spare horses immediately and hope that will satisfy them," Goodnight had said numerous times. "Then we'll just need to prioritize at the moment. Let's just hope it doesn't come to that."

•••

The next day wasn't as hot, but water was low by noon when they stopped to eat. They felt sure they would reach the Prairie Dog Town Fork by nightfall, and the men only received one cup of water at noon. That had supplemented their one cup at daybreak earlier.

Sure enough, at around 6 that evening, they approached a small ravine probably only a 100 yards wide and 10- to 20-feet deep. It had scrub trees, willows and a few cottonwoods and mesquite – and the Prairie Dog Town Fork of the Red River. It was clear cool water, and the stream was narrow and shallow at this spot. Every man was laying down next to an animal or two – all of them sucking up their fill of the sweet water.

Adkin laughed to himself when he realized the men were slurping as loud as the mules and horses. They had crossed two other ravines, but they had been dry, probably never having much water until heavy rains on the Plains.

After filling up on water, Goodnight wanted to travel the stream east until finding it's caprock where he knew a big canyon spread out across the eastern side of the Llano Estacado. He had seen it from the east looking westward, and this small ravine did not compare to what he had seen.

They followed the ravine on the northern side of the Prairie Dog Town Fork. The ravine's width was expanding wider and wider in short order. Finally, after about 10 miles, they could see the canyon before them. The width was now about half a mile if not more in places, the little stream was falling in and out of sight down through the rocks and bushes.

They held up their mounts when they reached a cliff that dropped off before them at least 1,000 feet straight downward into the canyon. It was a valley of canyons like nothing Adkin had ever seen. It had been cut through the caprock edge of the Llano through eons of time, water and erosion.

They sat in their saddles, no one said a word, as they were all breathless. What a canyon – zig-zagging off to the southeast as far as the eye could see. The little stream had turned into more of a river, but it was hard to see throughout the valley.

They sat in silence for at least three or four minutes until Uribe spoke up.

"There are lodges down the valley," he said, pointing to the canyon's far south side. "It looks to be maybe 10 miles away – see the smoke?"

Sure enough, one could make out small splotches of white tipis and smoke wafting up from most of them. They were hidden by a jutting cliff, but clearly visible when one strained to see. Goodnight pulled his spotting scope from his saddlebag and looked hard and long.

"I can't make out the decorations, but my guess is they are Comanches or Kiowa," Goodnight said. "I've heard some of the bands move in early to get the best areas for winter. Of course, the Comanch love the upper Canadian, too. And that's where we're headed next."

"I don't believe they could see us, even with their watchouts down there," Rath said. "But what a canyon and valley. This looks like Eden to an old dusty freighter."

"You got that right," Goodnight said. "This area would make a great cattle range – with water in the canyon and buffalo grass as far as the eye can see on top."

Goodnight's visions were prophetic, as years later, he would start one of the biggest cattle ranches in the Texas Panhandle right near this exact spot at Palo Duro Canyon.

"We best back up and head north," Goodnight said. "I think we can make the Canadian River by tomorrow night."

•••

That evening, they were again spending the night on the High Plains – meaning no fire and cold jerky and bread and molasses for supper. Goodnight starting discussing his plans, asking the same of the others.

"I think once we explore the upper Canadian River Canyon – and old Adobe Walls – I'll head back to my bride," Goodnight said, inferring he wanted to head to Weatherford, Texas. A long trip, still, but he had three men who had proven tough trail hands and good fighters.

Adkin looked at Ryan and Uribe and said they still wanted to check on Zeb Jarvis' and James Mead's operations at Jarvis' place southeast of Fort Supply. Both men shook their heads in agreement once Adkin had detailed their plans. That left Rath to see where he was headed.

"Well, I don't need to go to central Texas," he sighed. "And I don't want to go into the middle of the Indian Territories, either.

"My best bet is to hightail it to Fort Dodge, which means we'll travel with you men, Adkin, to Camp Supply," Rath said. "I think the Military Road is safe enough today that me and Sol can get to Dodge in five days from there."

Sol Hart was the man riding with Rath. He had been one of their freighters and stage drivers on the Dodge to Fort Hays Road. Rath had mentioned earlier in their trip that Sol had fought his way out of numerous scrapes between Indians and bandits.

Adkin knew if Sol rode shotgun with Rath, he would be a fine man indeed. Charley and his brother Chris, had made a lot of money for Barlow and Sanderson, as well as profits for YR&R, too. Rath's true love seemed to be freighting and establishing trading posts.

"We'd enjoy your company, Charley – Sol," Ryan said, laughing.

"And travelling with y'all might save our scalps," Rath said in reply, also chuckling.

•••

On the evening of September 16, they approached the valley made by the Canadian River through the eons. Adkin admired this river and its importance to people living on the frontier. It was used by peoples native to the area for centuries, and now Americans and peoples from all over the world used it as well.

He knew it flowed through all of Oklahoma to the State of Arkansas. It was surely one of the top four or five rivers on the Western Frontier to Colorado.

Again, the canyon opened up before them – not as severe or deep as Palo Duro, but awfully amazing as well. These sights after crossing the Llano Estacado were awesome, something Adkin had no words for.

He remembered someone telling him, "You can't explain the caprock canyons coming off the Llano Estacado – you have to see them to really feel them."

How true, Adkin thought to himself. Even Matty had tried to tell him of their beauty, but between languages and understanding, it's beyond words.

Adkin sat there in his saddle – as all of the men did – and took in the vastness of the landscape. It was a place not many White Men had seen, let alone travelled.

"Down that river about 10 miles, I'm guessing – is where Bent's old trading post, Adobe Walls, is," Goodnight said. That's where Kit Carson had a famous fight with Comanches and Kiowas back in '64.

"We got to hear about it from the horse's mouth," Ryan interrupted. "Carson told us everything about it and how he came close to being scalped and killed. He didn't consider it much of a victory."

"He told us he got his butt kicked and chased up this canyon for four days – not knowing if they were going to live or not," Adkin added.

"I believe that. I've heard similar rumors through the years from some who say they were there," Goodnight said. "This is where we have to keep an eye out for Indians – especially Comanches."

"Like we haven't been doing that for the last two weeks, Señor?" Uribe asked, laughing. "I tink I have grown eyes in the back of mi cabeza, and mi cabeza can now spin like an owl's."

Everybody agreed while laughing. Uribe definitely had a way with words, and they all felt the same way.

They eased their way down what looked to be a game trail toward the river. It wasn't too steep, and they found a place well hidden among trees and brush to set camp. It was back behind the view down the main canyon, and they all agreed it should be safe to build a small cooking fire at least.

The temperature was falling with a north breeze coming across the Llano and swooping down the valley walls. They couldn't see the darkening clouds off to the north racing down upon them.

Shortly after eating some fried bacon and buffalo meat with potatoes and coffee, Rath mentioned he hoped a norther' wasn't building up.

"It's about that time of year when those storms develop in the north country or off the Rockies and funnel down across these plains," Rath said, while looking upward. "That's the bad thing about being down here and not being able to see the horizon."

About that time, streaks of lightning flashed across the darkening sky, fingers of electricity zig-zagging everywhere as a huge explosion occurred about a hundred yards down-river. Several of the men saw it explode when the huge bolt hit a tall Cottonwood. The tree blew apart as if it were hit by a cannon shell. What was remaining was afire, flashing in the winds that were increasing rapidly.

Rain drops started pelting them. Large ones the size of a silver coins and widely separated, but they hurt when they hit as they were flying diagonally.

"Make sure the rest of the animals are hobbled – quickly," Goodnight said, thanking God most had already been hobbled before eating. "And grab those supply packs – we need two tarpaulins."

"I know there's a tarp and rope by that white-spotted mule's pack over there," Rath said, as everyone scattered finding supplies such as bedrolls, saddles, poles, ropes, stakes, mallets and rifles and ammunition.

More lightning and cracking of thunder filled the sky and the canyon. The wind was blowing about 35 miles an hour, and it took six men to hold the four corners and two sides as they pounded in stakes on the north side. Three poles were quickly held in place – one on each end and one in the middle as the tarpaulin whipped in the wind, pulling men to the ground every now and then.

They then fought the wind to set the other tarpaulin on the first one's end.

They finally had an A-frame set that measured about 20 feet in length with open ends – if it would stay together. That seemed to help keep the wind flowing through as men put in more stakes and ropes – some tied to several small trees and bushes nearby. Others were gathering their goods and throwing them under the tarpaulin.

"Then the hail stones began screaming through the air with thuds as they pounded everything in their way. The men were diving for cover under the uneasy shelter. Adkin knew what hail could do – he still had a slight scar from years ago. Thankfully, these hailstones were only the size of acorns. But they could still be very dangerous. The men were worried about the animals.

Adkin and Ryan tried to lean out the southern end to see where the animals were. They noticed several were actually huddled up among the bushes, packed together like sheep. Ryan got walloped by some stones and stepped back under the tarp, but tripped over a saddle and hit the ground hard.

"Damn, that hurt," Ryan finally said, while Uribe and others started laughing, realizing he was unhurt, just humiliated.

As quickly as the hail began, the heavy rain started. It was so dense, they couldn't see more than 20 feet out either end of their shelter. Three men were still holding rope ends and poles. Uribe was pounding another stake for a rope which could be tied to the center pole. It now had six ropes from it staked to the ground. It was still moving back and forth from the wind tearing at the tarpaulin.

As everybody was trying to secure equipment, saddles and bedrolls, Adkin spoke up.

"If this continues, we may have to move to higher ground," he said. "By my estimate, we're only about 10-feet above the river's level when this started."

"I know, we'll have to keep an eye on things," Goodnight said.

The rain let up some, but it was still falling substantially. Adkin kept peeking out the north end of the shelter, as it was closest to the Canadian River.

He had heard the horror stories of how the Canadian and the Cimarron could turn into killer rivers within hours of big rains upstream. In fact, traders and military men claimed four rivers could kill you or your entire caravan in this country – the Arkansas, the Cimarron, and the North Canadian and the Canadian. Within a few years, the North Canadian would be named the Beaver River through the Indian lands to Camp Supply.

And all claimed title to killer rivers when flooding.

Probably a half-hour later, the rain became a light drizzle and the wind nearly stopped altogether. They could still see and hear lightning and thunder as the storm charged off into the southern darkness.

Adkin, Sol and Ryan went and inspected the animals. No injuries or blood was spotted, but they were fairly jumpy when the men started running their hands over their skins, feeling for knots or abrasions. They soon relaxed, though.

The men decided to see if they could rustle up enough materials to build a fire at the end of the shelter – not only for a warmth, but to dry some of their belongings. They were sure no Indians would be out in this unruly night and could see a fire where they were located.

•••

Adkin volunteered to take first watch around 9 p.m. He wanted to keep an eye on the river. The first thing he did after grabbing his Henry and a blanket, was to stick a small branch into the mud at the river's edge. Its top was about 2-feet above the water.

He would walk around camp, quietly stopping at intervals, to listen for danger or the calling of wolves, which he didn't hear early. It was around 11 when he heard the first wolves downstream. He then checked the branch again, and water had only came up about 6 inches.

He was relieved as he went and woke Uribe, telling him where the branch was and warning Uribe to keep checking it every 30 minutes or so. Uribe pulled his wool coat on and rubbed sleep from his eyes.

"Bueno, Boss," he said as he walked toward the river.

Adkin settled into his bedroll and drifted off to sleep as wolves were singing their lonesome howls at the silver moon.

•••

After a hot breakfast, they crossed the river and followed its meanderings northeasterly. Goodnight estimated Adobe Walls ruins were about 60 to 70 miles ahead. Though Rath had yet to travel to Adobe Walls, he knew the headwaters of the Wolf north of there and had gone south to the Canadian River but was forced to go east to the Antelope Hills in Indian Territory.

During the day, the valley got wider and wider and seemingly shallower. The Canadian River itself got wider and stronger. They figured it was from the storm the night before.

They spent the night further away from water – on higher ground than usual. They had also seen signs of a horse herd being moved from north to south – maybe around 50 or more head. It trailed along the north side of the river for a couple of hundred yards then crossed at a shallow, rocky section of the Canadian. The tracks then went due south again.

"Ees probably an Indian raiding party moving stolen horses to their winter grounds," Uribe said.

"I would guess they belong to the band we saw in the Palo Duro Canyon," Goodnight said.

They decided once again to not build a camp fire, thinking it could be spotted from anyone riding the valley rims on either side.

"I would rather eat jerky than bring down a bunch of Comanches right now," Ryan said as they hobbled their animals near camp.

The temperature was dropping, the storm probably leading colder air down from the Rockies. The men had plenty of blankets, and more importantly, buffalo hides and animal skins to warm them.

As Adkin lay there, snuggling into his hides, he scanned the wide open sky. Not one cloud blurred or hid any stars in the night sky. And it was full of billions of stars. Every now and then, one streaked across the heavens with a trail of flame and white light.

Adkin said his usual prayer to himself, "I promise, Lord, I will keep you close in my heart." He was also thinking of Matty and how much he really missed her. It surprised him in a way to feel so much for her. He smiled to himself as he drifted off into slumber.

Once it was bright enough in the morning, they built a small fire and ate a hot meal before loading up and heading down the river again. They were hoping to make Adobe Walls, but Goodnight was still assuring everyone he was just guessing.

They stopped at noon to water the animals and take a rest. The area was still bleak in a way. It had rock and flint cliffs as it climbed out of the valley – really no heavy vegetation. But along the waterway, there were patches of beautiful stunted trees and brush – even some water reeds in places and water lilies, their blooms lost to fall weather.

"By my estimate, we've travelled around 50 miles since departing the Llano into this canyon," Goodnight said. "We should find Adobe Walls sometime today."

After an hour of relaxation, and a brief nap by some of the men, they remounted and took off – still heading northeast following the Canadian.

It was around 4 p.m., when they noticed smoke tailing off into the sky from a place about a half a mile up from the river on the northern side of the valley. They halted, and Goodnight took out his scope.

"Well, looks like we found Adobe Walls," he said. "There's old adobe looking walls or ruins and several remains of some stone walls – most torn down. There's also a tent, several horses and a freight wagon.

"The trouble, as I see it, is who is causing that smoke that's pouring out of the tent?" Goodnight asked. "Indians or Whites?"

"Ees got to be gringos," Uribe said, chuckling, "Indians don't use fireplaces – for cooking or warming – or tents, except tipis."

"I think Uribe's right," Adkin added. "Only Whites would be that stupid out here in Indian country."

Several laughed but agreed.

"I say Adkin and I ride up and announce ourselves while ya'll stay hidden," Ryan said. "If it's Indians in there, we have a chance of parlaying with them, since Adkin wears Satanta's sign, and I have a sign of the Kiowa, too."

Rath spoke up, "One thing about it is, there can't be but four or five there at best right now if it's Indians. There's just a few horses, unless the others are out raiding."

"I like Ryan's plan," Goodnight said. "We stay hidden back here and wait til we get some sign of trouble – or a sign it's safe."

"Let's do it, Ryan," Adkin said. "We'll take an extra horse for each of us and one pack mule, as if we were travelling by ourselves."

Good idea," Goodnight said, as Ryan and Adkin each tied off a horse with a mule loaded with supplies to tag along.

"Good luck, Señors," Uribe said. "We will have your backs, just let us know – start shooting like Hell, and we'll come in."

"Fire off two pistol shots if it's safe – the Indians already know there's someone in that area – all that smoke. Then we'll return the shots," Goodnight said. "Be careful, and remember, don't turn your back on anyone – White or Injun."

•••

Within a few hundred yards of the adobe ruins, a shout startled them and their animals.

"Who goes there?" a voice yelled from off to their left and up 20 or 30 feet above them. "What's your name and what's your business?"

Adkin noticed a rifle barrel was now sticking out the tent flap, too, nodding his head to Adkin, who then saw it as well.

"My name is Adkin Yates," he said. "And this is my partner, Tyler Ryan. We work for Barlow and Sanderson Company – stagecoach business."

"Don't touch those guns," the voice in the rocks bellowed, while the tent flap slowly swung open. As a rifle came into view, a large man stepped out on the ground, his spurs jingling in the stillness.

"Yates and Ryan, is it?" the man barked. "Would yee also be a part of YR&R Freight?"

"Co-owners, as a matter of fact, Sir," Adkin said, feeling immediate relief.

"Well neighbors, get off those horses and come have some good, hot coffee – well hot anyway," he said. "My name is L.A. Allen, Sheriff of Southeastern Colorado. I believe I saw your names in the book when you visited Kit Carson's grave a few years back.

"That was my house where Colonel Carson and Josefa were buried then, gentlemen. I was away during that time and didn't get to meet you," Allen said as Adkin and Ryan walked over and shook hands with Allen. "You may have heard, my friend, W.K. Irwin, and I moved the Carsons later to Taos where they lay today."

"Well, we're sure glad to meet you Sheriff, especially out here," Adkin said with his voice full of relief. "If you don't mind, we have seven other friends with us who are waiting up there to see if we got shot up first."

"Well Hell yes, signal them everything is okay," Allen said.

Ryan walked over closer to the river below and shot his pistol twice. A few seconds later, two shots echoed down the canyon from the others.

"Who you travelling with, if you don't mind me asking?" Allen said. "It's the Sheriff in me – I'm nosey and always looking for outlaws."

"Don't think you'll find any with our crowd, Sheriff," Adkin said. "Charley Rath and his man, Sol Hart, is with us and we have Charles Goodnight and his three …"

"Goodnight, you say?" Allen interrupted with a huge smile. "Texas Ranger Charles Goodnight?"

"Why yes, but I think those Ranger days are behind him," Adkin said. "He's now a cattleman."

"Well, I'll be damned," Allen said shaking his head. "I haven't seen Charles since the good residents of Pueblo took that outlaw William "Cyrus" Coe from a military jail and hanged him high on Santa Fe Avenue in 1868.

"Charles and a few us chased those Coe gang outlaws all over the country in those years after the war," Allen said, looking as if he remembered those years fondly.

"Look, here they come," Ryan said. "I'm sure he will be pleased to know its you here at Adobe Walls. We've seen signs of Indians for the last two days since coming up from the Palo Duro Canyon."

"What the Hell y'all doing down that way?" Allen asked.

"It's a long story Sheriff, we'll let Rath and Goodnight explain," Adkin said laughing, as three men came out of the tent and the watch man in the rocks above made it to the group.

•••

As Adkin's gang pulled up on their reins, Goodnight's eyes opened wide.

"Is that you, you old varmint?" he boomed. "L.A. Allen, the only man in the West who thought he could clean up No-Man's Land – and pert-neart did."

As Goodnight jumped from his saddle, Allen walked over and they embraced, Allen picking Goodnight completely off the ground. Allen was well over 6 feet, and carried about 220 pounds, slightly larger a man than Goodnight.

"Pleased as Hell to see you again Ranger," Allen said. "Mighty pleased."

Goodnight then started introducing Rath, his men, and Goodnight's hands. Allen started introducing his four men.

But before he could get started, Ryan said, "Don't I know you – say from Camp Supply?"

"Why yes, that's it. I'm George Brown, was with the 7th Calvary as a scout and a freighter," the man said. "Some now call me Hoo Doo Brown."

He shook Ryan's hand.

Then Allen introduced a man named George Reighard, a Dave Mather and they said the man in the rocks was Henry L. Sitler.

"These men are helping me look for some remnants of the old Coe gang, Charles," Allen said, looking to Goodnight. "I'm trying to run down 'Esquire' Smith and Ira Schofield, he's only about 23 years old. Those two are wanted for murder in Trinidad, and word is they're hiding out down here somewhere.

"You're the old trail boss, want to get in on the action?" he added.

"I'm afraid not, Sheriff. We're looking for business opportunities so we can make some money if the Army can ever provide safety our here south of the Arkansas.

"Well, we had a visitor drop by just this morning; a Comanche War Chief named Quanah Parker," Allen said. "Ever heard of him?"

"Hell yes, he's a bad one, I hear," Goodnight said. "I was with the group that re-captured his mother, Cynthia Ann Parker and killed his father, Peta Nocona.

"I hope he doesn't find out I'm here," Goodnight added, looking worried.

"That's right, I remember that now that you mention it. Well, he and three of his warriors came in carrying the white flag," Allen continued. "He asked us what we were doing here, and we told him we were on the trail of some bandits wanted in Kansas – he didn't know them.

"But he told us to leave their buffalo alone – he saw our wagon and, I guess, thought we were buffalo hunters," Allen said. "I told him we weren't hunting buffalo, only banditos – that it was a supply wagon. Guess we didn't have enough horses for him to fight us.

"He suggested we not stay long in this country, as other Comanche bands are coming for winter and not as understanding as he is," Allen added. "So, we're planning on leaving tomorrow morning – almost left a couple of hours ago."

"I understand. We'll be going with you," Goodnight said, as Allen then shouted for his men to help take care of the animals and water them. The others were invited into the old adobe building, what was remaining.

"It's been upgraded this last year by buffalo hunters that sneak in here, get a load or two of hides and skedaddle before they get scalped." Allen said. "I hear it's very lucrative. This man Otero, in La Junta I believe, is paying top dollar for buffalo hides."

Rath made a mental note of the man's name.

After getting all the animals taken care of and everybody chatting like old hens about where they're from, what do they do and where do they live and work, they made plans for a combined feast.

Adkin was so relieved to find a White lawman and posse, he felt like there wasn't a worry in the world. They had a total of 14 men who could handle guns and fighting. He sighed heavily to himself.

•••

After eating, the stories started, especially when Allen brought up the old days of chasing the Coe Gang with Goodnight.

"He was a smooth-talking marauder for sure," Allen said. "But after stealing every mule he could find and robbing all those Santa Fe Trail caravans, he got into the killing."

"Some people got to calling Coe the Prairie Robin Hood, and that really irked me," Goodnight said. "He had been captured before but got away."

"Well thing got serious when I was made Captain of the Rangers of Southeast Colorado," Allen continued. "We got word Coe was holed up at an adobe hut in Union County, New Mexico.

"We got hooked up with Goodnight here and some of his Texas Rangers and swept in on the gang in May of '68," Allen said. "We actually caught them off-guard and took the 11 outlaws out to a nearby Cottonwood tree and hanged them.

"We found out Coe was about 15 miles away and snuck up on him and captured him, too," Allen said.

"I had been chasing him for a couple of years," Goodnight said. "And I actually passed him on the road on a visit to the ranch of Madison "Old Mad" Emory in New Mexico. We didn't know what each other looked like.

"Emory told me later on down the road who it was, and he was out to kill me. I about had a kitten," Goodnight continued. "That was in late '67, and it was at Emory's when it all came together."

"Yep, we got Coe chained up and strapped across a horse and hauled his ass to Pueblo – there was a big reward for him," Allen said. "We were preparing for a high-falutin' public hangin', but fate changed the program.

"It turned into a big party of prisoners, and all the Coe Gang was invited," Allen continued, chuckling. "The day before we got to Pueblo, 14 or 16 other members of the gang were brought to Pueblo from Fort Lyon by Captain Matthew Berry and Captain Lee Gillette of the 7th.

"Plus, eight more of the gang were brought in from the jail in Trinidad," he added. "They all filled the court while officers of a grand jury from Fort Lyon testified against them.

"You should've seen it, these rustlers thought it was all a joke, acting cocky and all," Allen said. "They were bound over for trial for a later date."

"Meanwhile, Coe was being jailed under the watch of Sergeant Luke Cahill who's superior was Major James Casey," Goodnight said. "Cahill was given strict orders that no one was to be allowed within 100 yards of the place.

"Then about a week later, I was staying at the Pueblo Drovers' Hotel, and Sheriff Price showed up at midnight in a buggy at the jail, and demanded that Coe be turned over to him so Coe could be moved to a safer place," Goodnight continued. "Of course, since Cahill had no orders from General Penrose, he wouldn't hand over Coe."

"That's when things got interesting," Allen interrupted. "Ol' Sheriff Price was back a little after midnight with General Penrose with him. Penrose ordered Cahill to turn Coe over to Price, saying he was sick and tired of this outlaw, or something to that affect.

"So Price went in, woke Coe up and brought him out in shackles and put him in the wagon with Price," Allen said. "They didn't make it down the street very far 'til a group of vigilantes stopped Price near a Cottonwood tree not far from the Fountain River.

"They put a noose around Coe's neck and drove that wagon out from under him," Allen added. "Coe squirmed and twisted for a whole 10 minutes before he died."

"I went down again early the next morning, scared he wasn't really dead," Goodnight said. "But he was surely dead, as the branch had weakened, and his knees were touching the ground, and his neck was still tight in the noose."

Everybody just sat there, not saying a word – contemplating what it must feel like to be hanged. Several had seen hangings, but everyone feared it almost as bad as being scalped alive.

"Whew, that's quite a story," Adkin broke the silence. "We had heard of Coe. If I remember, he was a stonemason once at Old Fort Lyon. During some of these robberies, we were down at the Medicine Lodge Creek Treaty – so we missed some of that turbulence.

"I think we should try and get a good sleep," Allen spoke up. "That warning from Quanah was for real. I'm just hoping none of his spies saw y'all ride in with all those horses and mules."

"You're right, Sheriff. I believe Comanches love stealing horses more than anything," Goodnight said. "And I mean anything."

"I've been thinking, if we get in a hurry in the morning, we can't climb out of this canyon just anywhere with a wagon," Allen said. "We best get our supplies out of it, lash them to some horses and leave that wagon for Quanah – a parting gift so to speak."

Several laughed, but two of Allen's posse went outside to unload what supplies they had in the wagon.

"That old wagon is worn out anyway," Reighard said. "Plus, I don't want to try and drive it up the side of one of these cliffs."

Everyone started preparing for an early departure, making sure packs were ready for the mules, and they inspected their personal supplies. Allen suggested they sleep fully dressed and ready to ride if any attack comes in the night.

Uribe and Reighard volunteered for the first watch, deciding to take opposite ends of the camp to start, and rotating every 20 minutes around camp.

The men slept with as little bedding as possible, keeping the big buffalo hides in the packs. Slowly, they drifted off, but Adkin was worried about the possible dangers ahead. That's what kept them alive – not taking safety for granted.

•••

As the sky was just turning, everyone was jostled out of sleep and set about ensuring all the packs were tied onto the mules, horses saddled and within 15 minutes, they were mounting their horses and moving eastward along the river. The trail was obvious and had been made by Indians that used the area for decades if not centuries.

As the sun crested the canyon walls and light fell into the valley, Uribe shouted, "Look, a signal," as he pointed back to their right and toward the southern wall of the canyon. Adkin saw it just briefly. But several of the men said they saw it, too.

"A glint of sunlight flashed at them several times from the rocks near the canyon's top.

"They're using a mirror to tell someone we're moving out," Allen said.

"Or a signal to attack us," Goodnight said. "We've got to make it to a place where we can get out of this valley."

"Let's go men, double time," Allen shouted. "Be watching ahead for any ambush spots."

Everybody spurred their mounts a pulled the tow ropes taut as they galloped down the side of the Canadian. Fortunately, the trail was packed sand and there were very few rocks. Uribe and Ryan moved toward the back of their small caravan, which was moving in single file because of the trail.

"I saw the signal again," Uribe shouted, barely audible to Adkin, who was about four horse lengths behind Allen and Goodnight.

"Uribe said they're still signalling," Adkin bellowed loudly for those in front to hear. Goodnight waved in understanding.

One of Goodnight's men was sent ahead and was only seen for short stretches as he was about 300 yards ahead, moving in and out of sight along the river's bank.

Suddenly, he turned his horse to the left and started climbing upward toward the ridge. As he darted around rocks and small outcroppings, he was waving to follow him up the draw.

Allen and Goodnight started waving, too, when they reached the turnoff. Allen pulled up is mount as Goodnight started his climb.

"Keep moving men," Allen shouted as the riders and two animals were passing by and heading up the trail. "Come on, keep these animals moving."

Once most of the men and animals had turned, Allen kicked his horse into a trot as he, too, climbed the ridge.

It took about 10 minutes, and Adkin could see the scout had reached the ridge's edge ahead and was waving and yelling for the others to hurry.

"Comanches. Comanches," Adkin heard him shout as he pointed back behind them. Adkin slowed a little and looked back down the valley. He could see a cloud of dust and about a dozen or so Indians on their ponies, yelping and whipping their mounts along the trail. They were about a mile behind them but moving fast.

As Goodnight topped the ridge, he spotted the Comanches and kept waving the men through and onto the plains. He turned back to the north and saw an outcropping of large boulders about 100 yards away. He yelled at the men to stop on the other side of the outcrop.

As the rear of their group crested the ridge, Goodnight, Allen and Adkin stopped everybody, telling them to stay behind the rocks,

They started telling certain men to get down from their horses and take cover in the rocks.

"We're going to blast the bastards," Allen said. "They'll be cocky – thinking their ponies can easily run us down on the plains. You men hold the reins of the animals and stay in your saddles.

"As soon as they crest the ridge and head this way, you wait for my orders to fire," Allen continued. "Got that, men?"

Everybody nodded in agreement. Adkin, Ryan and Uribe had their rifles out, as well as Goodnight, Rath, Hart and Allen and Reighard with his old buffalo gun.

"There only looked to be 20 or less, men," Allen yelled. "After they turn back and drop below the ridge line, we're going to mount up and get the hell out of here."

Just as he finished his orders, the first of the Comanches crested the ridge and looked confused momentarily. They slowed their ponies as the remaining warriors came on top. They didn't see anything – no dust, no Whites, no horses.

They were about 60 yards out when it looked as if they had figured out something was wrong, and they pointed directly at the large rock outcropping, saying something.

"Fire," came the order from Allen, and at least eight rifles let loose a cannonade of deadly lead. Most had repeating rifles and a second round of fire hit the Comanches, as they were turning back to the ridge, yelping.

Several fell on the first volley, and they were retreating to the ridge when the second volley hit them. Two more fell from their ponies. A few more shots went off into the valley sky as the last of them disappeared from sight.

"Mount up and move out," Allen shouted. "Now!"

The shooters grabbed their reins and jumped into their saddles and turned due north, galloping as fast as the mules would allow. Adkin kept looking back, fearing they would attack again, but there was no Comanche in sight.

After galloping for five or six miles, Allen and Goodnight gave orders to slow to a trot, hoping the animals could hold that pace for a few more miles. Rath sent Hart ahead to scout

"Keep an eye out for a place to hole up and force another ambush if we need to," Allen shouted at Hart as he rode off.

Allen sent word back to watch the animals and pull up if one looks injured, whether inside or on their exteriors. Adkin kept an eye on those trailing. Everything looked okay for the time being. He knew they would have to stop and walk soon in order to not harm the horses.

Adkin checked Diablo, looking at his legs to see if he had damaged anything going through the rocks and scrub brush. Diablo looked fine, He had a small amount of sweat foam around his saddle cinches and his bridle, but that was it.

What a horse, Adkin thought to himself – again. Diablo was nearly seven years old now and had proved to be one of the best steeds on the Frontier as far as Adkin was concerned.

Allen finally told the crew to slow to a walk and let the animals cool down. They had made about 10 miles from the outcroppings and no Comanches were in sight.

"They didn't have enough warriors to try again," Goodnight said. "That's one thing about Indians: If they don't have superior advantages, they'll cut and run in a heartbeat."

"That's fine with me, Charles," Rath said, grinning.

"Me, too, Charley."

"But I'll wager a gold piece, Quanah won't be as pleasant the next time we meet," Allen interjected. "And I don't plan on crossing paths with him again."

•••

They walked the animals for several more miles until they saw a dry ravine with numerous mesquite and plum bushes,

"Let's get down in there and rest these animals," Allen said. "We'll keep a lookout up here to watch the plains behind us, even though I think we're through with that bunch. They're not going to leave their spot on the Canadian to chase only 40 horses and mules. Plus, they've got to gather up their wounded and dead."

Once they got settled in and removed packs and saddles, the men took water bags and several bowls around watering animals. It was painstaking but had to be done.

"They can get their fill in about 10 more miles when we reach Wolf Creek," Allen said. "We never talked about where you fellas are headed."

"Well, we were going to follow the Canadian to Blaine County Oklahoma," Adkin said. "We have a business partner there we were going to drop in on and see how it's going."

"The danger in that is going through the Antelope Hills – a notorious place for Indians," Allen said. "The Canadian flows right through there."

"Maybe we should follow Wolf Creek to Fort Supply, then go to see Zeb from there," Adkin said, looking to his men. "It would add a couple of days, but it might be safer."

"I'm headed to Dodge City Sheriff, where you going next?" Rath said.

"I'm cutting right up to Dodge City directly – hitting the Kiowa Creek, the Beaver then crossing the Cimarron," Allen said.

"You're not going to Supply?" Rath asked.

"No, this route we stumbled on chasing some of the old Coe gang," Allen said. "It's a nice trail and cuts days off by avoiding Fort Supply.

"Would you mind if we travel with you to Dodge, then?" Rath asked.

"Not at all, Charley," Allen said. "What about you Charles?"

"I think we'll go with Adkin and go the long way around to get back to Texas," Goodnight said. "I don't particularly want to travel straight down the western side of the Indian Territories."

Once that was settled, Adkin was curious as to where Allen crossed the Cimarron River, as he and Matty's special place was along there somewhere.

"Excuse me Sheriff, I heard you mention you cross the Cimarron on your way back to Fort Dodge," Adkin said. "My wife and I found a very special place on the Cimarron just a few miles west of where Crooked Creek empties into the Cimarron.

"Do you cross anywhere near there?" Adkin added.

"Why yes, Adkin," Allen said. "We follow Kiowa Creek to the Cimarron and go almost due north to Dodge. That crossing is only about 10 miles east of Crooked Creek."

"My wife and I want to build a place there when we can," Adkin said. "A place to get away from everything and just enjoy each other and mother nature.

"She's Kiowa, by the way, and the place was somewhere she's known since being a little girl," Adkin added.

"I'll be damned," Allen said. "Kiowa you say? I know that place – the Kiowa have used it as a watering hole for eons, I reckon. Several years ago, I saw at least 100 tipis in that area – stretched out for about half a mile along the Cimarron.

"I've been all over the Neutral Strip for the last five years chasing outlaws," Allen continued. "How did you end up marrying a Kiowa woman? If you don't mind me asking." Allen said.

"It's a long story, I assure you," Adkin said, chuckling.

"Well, I noticed that neck piece you wear, and Ryan's – are those long stories, too.

"Yes sir," Adkin said. "I promise to tell you later."

"She's a Kiowa Princess, Señor," Uribe interrupted. "She is the daughter of Black Horse, Chief Satanta's Medicine Man – though Black Horse ees dead now.

"Her name ees Mah-aht-tay, But we call her Matty," Uribe added.

"Fascinating," Allen said, with a surprised look on his face. "Well, you two have picked out a beautiful place to build a house. When you're in that area, it's hard to realize you're in western Kansas or Oklahoma."

"Yes sir, that's how we feel about it," Adkin said. "Wish we could go with you, but we'll check it out on our return trip home."

"Well, I tell you one thing, Adkin Yates, when you get back to Las Animas City, I order you and your wife, Matty, to come to dinner at our place in Boggsville," Allen said with a big grin. "Do you understand?"

"And you can tell me the stories about Matty," he added.

"Yes sir, we'll be there," Adkin said. "I promise."

After two hours, they decided to head for Wolf Creek. Allen had said it was only about 10 miles. The animals were still a little tired, but they all got to moving normally once saddled up and the packs lashed down. It was only 2 in the afternoon.

Adkin could see the landscape was changing back to what he knew of the normal Great Plains. There were rolling pasture lands with much more sage and yucca, Devil's claws and the usual tall rye grass and Russian Thistle here and there.

Coming up over a small rolling mound, they came upon a swale that looked as if rainwater had accumulated in it during heavy rains. Sure enough, about 100 yards further was Wolf Creek snaking off to the east.

They stopped at the creek and gave their animals their heads. Naturally, they filled their gullets as quickly as possible. They had actually had enough and quit drinking before the men could fill all their water bags.

"Well, men, here's where we part," Allen said. "I appreciate all of you and your efforts to save our scalps back there – and to think, that was only about 10 hours ago."

"It seems longer than that," Rath said.

"Adkin, Ryan and Uribe, it's been a pleasure riding with you and getting to meet you," Allen said, while walking over to shake each one's hand. "We're neighbors now, and feel free to drop in any time. I honestly think I'm going to be around home a lot more now, there's only about two or three of Coe's men left out here, and if they're smart, they'll keep going until they're a long ways away from my noose."

"And Charles, you old Ranger. I look forward to hearing from you – you got my address now – as I know you'll be successful," Allen said. "You're as dogged as they come when you want something."

"I'll be in touch Sheriff, promise," Goodnight said. "And I may be back this way next summer – definitely some areas out here in the Panhandles that have great grasslands for cattle herds."

"That's for sure, as long as Injuns don't kill off your cowhands," Allen said, laughing.

"We're heading on – it's only 10 or 12 more miles to Kiowa Creek," Allen continued. "That's where we'll probably camp for the night."

Everybody said their farewells with promises to drop in on them if they were in the area.

"Well, let's head out men, daylight's burnin'," Allen said, as they spurred their horses and kept on a northerly heading.

"Señor Sheriff, can I have that wagon at Adobe Walls if it's still there when I go back?" Uribe asked, laughing.

"Son, it's your's, but if you're smart, you won't head back that way for quite awhile," Allen said as he waved.

As they rode off, Goodnight spoke up.

"What you say, men, that we spend the rest of the day right here?" he asked. "I don't believe any of the Canadian Comanche bands will be around here.

"There's a cozy looking spot right over there," Ryan said, pointing to a small grove around 200 yards downstream. "Just enough trees and brush to hide us and the animals."

"I agree wholeheartedly," Adkin said, while the others moaned approval like weary scrub maids.

Once they settled in, it was obvious everybody was needing a good rest and another hot meal. Goodnight mentioned he was not aware L.A. Allen lived in Boggsville.

"And we went right through there," Goodnight said. "For some reason, I thought he lived in La Junta or Pueblo – or, I heard once he was in Trinidad.

"Anyway, he's quite the lawman," he continued. "There is no place he won't go to track down an outlaw. People were always warning him to stay out of No Man's Land, and he'd say, 'Hell isn't too far to go to hang a killer.'"

"Did you know he was raised as a boy by Kit Carson?" Goodnight said. "He doesn't talk much about it – he called Carson Chris, Kit's real name, Christopher Carson.

He lived with Carson and Carson taught the boy scouting, freighting, shooting – all that frontiersman stuff Carson knew," Goodnight said. "And that's all Carson knew – he wasn't really an educated man – book learnin' anyway. But what a fella. He could speak almost as many Indian languages as old man Bent"

"I know what you mean, we rode with him for weeks from the Medicine Lodge Treaty grounds," Adkin said. "And with Bent, he was a good friend to us."

"I heard Rath talking with those Dodge men, looks like he's got them interested in hunting buffalo next year for him," Goodnight said. "Tough way to make a dollar, but, Rath can turn a dollar into $100 before you can blink. He's a real trader and merchant – and he has never forgot the freighting business – what got him to where he is today.

"I admire that," Goodnight added, as he leaned back against his saddle and sipped his coffee.

"What have you found during this trip, Charles?" Adkin asked.

"Well, it's possible to drive cattle from central Texas all the way to Denver, in my opinion," Goodnight said. "And there are some very good places to establish cattle operations – from southeast Colorado to the expanse of the Llano, if the Army can settle the Indian problems.

"I don't know if some of those tribes will ever settle down on a reservation," he continued. "That means a lot of deaths, I'm sorry to say."

"What have you learned, Adkin?" Goodnight asked.

"It's tied to your hopes – that the Texas Panhandle can be safe," Adkin said. "The country is made for comfortable stagecoach service – just look at it. I believe if it's safe, settlers will flood this country like ants – and that means freighting, too. And little communities growing, needing supplies and stages to get here and there."

"You're correct, Sir," Goodnight said. "And I'm betting it will happen – in fact I KNOW it will happen – it's just WHEN will it happen?"

"I totally agree, Sir," Adkin sighed.

"Want some bacon tonight, Boss?" Uribe asked.

"Sure, but keep in mind we're probably three days out from Fort Supply," Adkin said. "Don't cook all of it tonight."

•••

The next morning was September 22, and was one of the most pleasant mornings Adkin could remember. There was a slight whisper of a southwest breeze that carried a little warmth with it. The birds were chirping and singing like it was spring.

Adkin could hear the soft rippling of the water gently flowing down Wolf Creek. It reminded Adkin that fresh-roasted fish was a favorite of his, too. But, fishing gear wasn't suitable for this excursion.

But, he also knew Uribe could make a rudimentary spear for lancing fish, and he was good at it. Adkin made a mental note to ask Uribe to fish if they found a shallow clear pool on Wolf Creek. He felt very safe for some unknown reason, maybe because he was close to country he had travelled before.

They had been gone from Las Animas City – and his Matty – for a month and two days. With what was ahead of them, he probably wouldn't get home for another 18 to 20 days.

"A long time," Adkin thought to himself. "But not as long as poor Charles, he has to go way down into Texas – probably 250 more miles, whew."

Sure enough, they came upon a beautifully clear water pool on Wolf Creek late that day, and Adkin had asked Uribe earlier to search for a fishing lance while they travelled. He had cut one from a black willow, and when they came upon the pool, Uribe looked to Adkin who gave him the nod.

"We'll camp here if it's okay with you, Charles," Adkin said. "And if it goes well, we'll fry some fish up tonight – right Uribe?"

"Si Boss, I will fix my lance right away,"" Uribe said.

While the others started unloading packs, saddles and hobbling animals in the bluegrass in the grove around the pond, Uribe had already used his knife and carved the barbed end of the willow.

As they started to gather firewood, Uribe was already wading through the waters like a white heron, quietly and one small step at a time. Within about five minutes, the were startled when Uribe let out a yelp.

"Arriba…Arriba, I have one," he shouted as he held up his spear with a fish on the end. "Ees el pescado de gato – a catfish Señors."

He walked over to the bank and tossed the fish toward the main camp.

"Don't let this get away, heh, heh," he said as he turned back to work. "I will get some more."

One of Goodnight's men grabbed the fish and skinned it, gutted it, rinsed it off and laid it in a skillet near the fire pit. He threw a small hand towel over it to keep dust or insects from alighting on the fish.

While everyone was talking about past events on the trip or what they were going to do in the near future, Uribe managed to spear four more catfish. Once those were cleaned, the cook – Goodnight's man, Ikard – cut them in half lengthwise, dusted them in flour and salt and fried them in hot lard.

An Englishman's Adventures on the Santa Fe Trail (1865-1889)

Everyone got a fair share, and with hot coffee and bread, the meal was a success. Adkin loved it because it reminded him of Captain Carbeauneau and New Orleans, where fish was cooked that way and every other way one could imagine. Only missing ingredient was the spicy creole seasonings.

"That was a great change of menu," Goodnight said. "We may have to appoint Uribe our Fishing Captain."

Uribe laughed, saying if he had to do that much, he would need a better spear, one with a point hardened in fire and made of oak or ash.

• • •

They arrived at Fort Supply late in the evening on September 23. Adkin was amazed at its growth: It had almost doubled its original size, and a small community had grown up around it. There were tents, wood plank shanties and Indian tipis everywhere.

And the people – mingling around were teamsters and bullwhackers; Indians, with squaws and children; negroes, some wearing Army uniforms; Mexicans and men looking like dangerous Comancheros.

"Has it only been a little less than two years for it to turn into this" Adkin asked out loud, as they walked their animals through the maze of people and dwellings.

"When they got to the fort's gate, Goodnight announced them, using the names of the stagecoach company and YR&R Freight Company, too. The gate opened and they were instructed to go to the Post Adjutant's office and state their business to Lieutenant E.A. Belger.

This they did, with Adkin, Ryan and Goodnight going in to talk with Belger, a likeable man who had been there nearly two years. He agreed to sell them supplies, Goodnight needing the most. He had heard of Goodnight, and agreed he has used YR&R Freight a lot over the time he had been there, but not as much in the last year.

"We're heading into the Territories down the North Canadian – to Blaine County and Zeb Jarvis' Ranch House to be specific," Adkin said. "He's our agent in this country."

"I know Jarvis and his boys," Belger said. "Is his funeral what brings you down here?"

"Who's funeral?" Adkin spit it out in astonishment.

"Why Zeb's. He died about 12 or 15 days ago," Belger said. "They said it was his heart. They say after his wife, Beth, died last month, he stopped eating, wouldn't do any of his chores and just sat around mumbling."

"Oh My Lord, this is the first we have heard of any of this," Adkin said, as he took a seat on a chair near Belger's desk and put his face in his hands. "We've been on the trail since August 18th."

"I'm sorry to break the news to you. I just figured you knew," Belger said. "I'm not sure if they've buried him or not, but they probably have.

"If you're travelling that way, fortunately, Indian depredations have been very few in that area," he continued. "But I'm sorry for your loss. Zeb was quite a fella."

Adkin just sat there. He wasn't that emotional about Zeb's passing, he just felt so bad for Sam and Mary Catherine. She has lost her Aunt Elizabeth and Uncle Zebulon. This also puts their business operations into question.

Goodnight broke the silence.

"Any Indian troubles south of there – down toward Fort Sill?" he asked the Lieutenant.

"Sir, there's always something going on down there," Belger said. "There are so many bands of Indians that love wintering in the Wichita Mountains – and they're thick between the Salt Fork of the Red and the Red River.

"But, there is a military caravan heading to Fort Sill with troops and building supplies as we speak," Belger said, with a big grin on is face. Even Adkin looked up, this would help Goodnight significantly.

"In fact, they're supposed to be in here in two days," he continued. "We've heard there's going to be more than 200 wagons and 1,000 troops and calvary."

Goodnight looked at Adkin and smiled.

"The good Lord couldn't have blessed me at a better time," Goodnight said.

"That's great news for you and your boys, Charles," Adkin said.

"And I wouldn't be surprised if some of your freight wagons were in that caravan, Mister Yates," Belger said. "Y'all are welcome to stay here until they arrive."

"I'll take you up on that Lieutenant – I have four men with me – if you don't mind," Goodnight said.

"No problem," Belger said.

"What do you think, Ryan?" Adkin asked his partner. "I'm feeling like we need to get to Zeb's place as soon as possible."

"I agree, his boys got to be in a bind right now," Ryan said. "We've got to see what we can do – if there's anything we can do.

"Let's supply up and leave early tomorrow," he added.

"Yes, that's probably best," Adkin said. "If our boys are hauling freight, Ray Dee or Tom Marcellus, or one of them is handling things – they don't need us. We need to get to Zeb's."

•••

Within two trouble-free days – with the exception of 30 to 40 mph winds the first day and eating a lot of sand and dirt, they pulled into Zeb's Ranch House – a total of 85 miles, and nobody was at the gate. It was around 7 p.m. and the sun had just dipped below the horizon.

"This doesn't feel right," Adkin said. "Uribe, you go around back. Let us know if you see anything."

Adkin and Ryan slowly dismounted and tied their horses to the rail at the front of the porch. Suddenly, the front door flew open. Adkin and Ryan immediately had their pistols out of their holsters.

"Whoa, don't shoot, boys. It's me, Sam," Phillips said. "Easy."

"Damn it, Sam, you could've got killed coming out like that," Ryan said, somewhat irritated he almost shot his friend. "We weren't sure what was going on with no one watching the road in."

"Sorry about that, but things are a mess around here," Phillips said. "Both Beth and ..."

"We know, Sam," Adkin interrupted. "We heard it at Fort Supply two days ago. We've been riding hard to get here to see if we can help."

Uribe then came around and saw them standing on the porch.

"Sam, ees not good to have no guard out front," he said, chuckling. "But ees good to see you, amigo."

About that time, Mary Catherine walked out on the porch, with baby Anna in her arms. Adkin had to think for a moment, guessing Anna was near 12 months old.

"Oh Adkin, men, it's wonderful to see you," she said, almost tearing up. "We're facing hard times here, and we need strong friends right now."

"Mary Catherine, I am so sorry to hear of your misfortune," Adkin stuttered, never imagining she would be here – and with Sam and the baby.

He was even more astonished as Darwin Jarvis walked out with little Adam following his footsteps. Adam was a toddler now, 2 years old, and hopping around pretty good.

"Hello, men. It's a blessing you are here," Darwin said, as Uribe tied off his horse. "But why don't we all come in the house, it's getting too cool out here for these babies to be out."

They all crowded into the living room of the big ranch house. Jarvis and Beth were so proud of their home and business they had carved out of the Indian Territories. It was something to be proud of, too, Adkin thought. Most White Settlers never lived long enough to build big log homes.

As everybody hugged and shared their greetings, Mary Catherine, whispered in Adkin's ear as she hugged him.

"I'm so glad you're here. Adkin. Sam is tormenting himself on what we're going to have to do," she said. "Please help him be strong, and assure him he's doing the right thing."

Adkin wasn't sure what she was referring to, yet, but he would do anything for this family. He considered them his family as well. But something was amiss if all the Phillips' were here. As she stepped back, it was if she was reading Adkin's mind.

"Matty is well and okay, Adkin. She is being watched by the men, and Dusty has a new wife, Margarite, and she and Matty are the best of friends already," Mary Catherine said. "Margarite is part Ute, so they can jabber in several different languages.

"But she does miss you terribly, Adkin," she added.

"I miss her, too," he said without thinking.

Mary Catherine fetched some leftovers from supper, and while the travellers were snacking, Sam started.

"We didn't know how to contact you when Beth died," Phillips said. "We got a telegram saying she died August 20, it came a few days after y'all left Las Animas. Then 12 days ago, we got news Zeb died, and Doyle had a breakdown and left for home – Perry County, Ohio, home.

"I had to make a snap decision. Adkin," he continued. "I felt obligated – to our family and our businesses to come here and do whatever it takes.

"I know that's not how you treat your partners – well Ray Dee knew – and I apologize for just up and leaving Las Animas City," Phillips said. "But me, Mary Catherine and Darwin are going to take this over and keep a successful business going – God willing."

"You don't have to apologize to us, Sam," Adkin said, nodding to Ryan and Uribe. "We're behind you a hundred percent – whatever you decide."

"I would have done the same thing, Sam," Ryan said.

Sam put his face in his hands and started weeping, his shoulders heaving as he sat there. Mary Catherine walked over to him and put her arm around his shoulder and she kissed him on top of his head. As she stood upright, she looked at Adkin and mouthed "Thank you" without making a sound.

So that was what she had been talking about: Sam was worried his decision to move into Zeb's business might displease him and Ryan. That was what was tormenting him.

"We'll help y'all get on your feet – anything you need," Ryan barked out. "You just name it."

"Really Sam, do you think you need anything right now?" Adkin asked.

Darwin spoke up, "We're actually in better shape than Sam thinks, Adkin. I've telegraphed a lawyer in Topeka, and he's making arrangements to make us – and Doyle, though he doesn't know it – legal owners of this Ranch House.

"The local Indian Agent is helping get our names on the lease with the Indians to ensure we can still do business here in the Cherokee Strip," he added, as Sam finally looked up and wiped the tears off his cheeks.

"Right now, it's just getting all the papers changed and signed," Phillips said. "We have everything we need – supplies, wagons, animals. James Mead has already assured us he'll help – he's the one that found us a trustworthy lawyer.

"He promised, 'Y'all won't miss a beat with me,'" Phillips continued. "He's having his papers drawn up with us, too, as his new partners here, so that's a big part of us continuing. Only way you could do much is if you was a lawyer," Phillips said with a slight chuckle.

"How about the Honorable Uribe Mendosa?" Uribe asked while grinning big. "I can write my name, and I sign anything you need."

They all laughed, lightening the mood considerably.

Then Darwin asked where they had been, and wanted to know more about the Llano Estacado. Ryan and Uribe started jabbering, Mary Catherine was fussing with the children, and everybody was curious how their lives were going and what was happening back in Las Animas City.

Adkin walked over to Sam and embraced him.

"Sam, don't you ever think that I could be disappointed in anything you choose to do to help your family, okay?" Adkin said. "I'll always have your back, no matter what."

"Thanks, Adkin," he said. "You and Ryan were the ones that gave me a chance to make a living out here. You know, when Mary Catherine and I got married, we originally thought we would come right here and see if we could make it with Zeb and Beth.

"But you gave me a job and allowed me to make a living – build up a little nest egg – and look where fate has now brought us," Phillips said. "Right here to Blaine County, Oklahoma, in the Indian Territories. Everything we own is still in our wagon in the barn – we just got here yesterday ourselves."

"Well, one thing, we'll still be working together – we never considered you just working for me or Ryan or Ray Dee," Adkin said. "It was never like that with us. You're still a partner with YR&R as long as you want. But now, you're a partner with Darwin as well as with James Mead – and the stagecoach business, too.

"As far as I see it, you have great opportunities ahead – long as you keep your scalp," Adkin added, laughing.

"You got that right," Phillips said as he shook Adkin's hand again.

• • •

The next morning, Mary Catherine was running the big kitchen, cooking for about a dozen men and two Mexican women, including Jarvis' four hands that worked the ranch and additional chores.

"You know, it almost brings me to tears to see Mary Catherine in there arranging everything – it's like momma used to do for so many years," Darwin said. "I really miss them both."

"God works in mysterious ways, Darwin," Adkin said. "Maybe He's testing you to see if you can honor your father and mother – that's all that is important to Him. If you can see it that way, I honestly believe your life can move forward, and you'll be happy and blessed."

"Thanks, Adkin."

Uribe decided they were going to need some more supplies. He wanted fresh eggs, cornmeal and crackers. Darwin teased Sam.

"Well, you've made your first sale from Jarvis' Trading Post, Sam, and you've been here less that 48 hours," Darwin said, chuckling.

"Well. God wants us to keep Zeb's dream alive, and that's what we're going to do," he said. Mary Catherine walked over and kissed Sam on the cheek and returned to the kitchen.

One of the Mexican women was carrying around little Anna in a sling across her bosom. Adam was everywhere. He was far from shy and would walk up to anyone once – twice if that someone had lifted him up and showed him affection.

He seemed to have an affinity for Adkin. Maybe it was Adkin's long curly locks that hung down into his collar. Adam always like pulling them and laughing. Adam also like tugging at Adkin's Kiowa necklace with beaver teeth.

Of course, Adkin gave the boy all the attention he could stand. He'd throw him up in the air and lightly rub his mustache and scraggly beard on the boy's belly and tickle him.

Adam would run off to someone else and play around the house, but it wasn't long and he'd be back at Adkin's knees wanting to get in the rocker with Adkin. Or ask to "Whoopee?" – what Adkin said when he tossed Adam in the air.

Little Anna wasn't yet as rambunctious as Adam, but Adkin felt given time, she'd be like Adam and her mother – busy, busy, busy. Anna had just turned 1 a few days earlier.

Sam had explained that Doyle had left three days after Zeb's death. Darwin told Sam his younger brother had been terribly sad after losing their mother, Beth. Then Doyle just had a major breakdown the day Zeb died, he just laid across Beth's grave and cried.

"Darwin said he stayed out there for two nights," Sam told Adkin. "Darwin finally got him to the house and the next morning, Doyle had a wagon loaded with a two-mule team hitched up, two saddle horses tied on the back of the wagon, and told Darwin, 'I'm leaving this cursed country for good, I'm going back to civilization.'"

Sam said Doyle pointed a rifle at him when Darwin tried to talk him out of leaving. He didn't want to even stay for Zeb's burial.

"Darwin said he 'saw the devil in his brother's eyes,' and let him go," Sam said. "Poor man. Darwin said Doyle never liked leaving Ohio, since he was around

13 or 14 when they came out west. Darwin said Doyle was just a broken man, and it was God's work taking him to Ohio."

"Well, you and Mary Catherine have your work ahead of you, Sam" Adkin said. "I realize you know that, but again, you get word to us if you need anything. Let's make this work partner."

"Thanks Adkin, that means the world to us," Phillips said. "Oh, by the way, it's been so hectic – but Mary Catherine is expecting again.

"She thinks it will come in late January of '71," he added with a big grin.

"Well, Sam, you have a beautiful place here to raise a mess of kids – and a business to help pay for a mess of kids," Adkin said. "That's wonderful."

Adkin explained he, Ryan and Uribe would be leaving the next morning, September 26. They would be going back to Fort Dodge, and then on to Colorado.

"The good news is you can catch the rails north of Dodge and get all the way to Kit Carson in two days," Phillips said. "They'll load any animals you got and wagons, too. You can make it back to Las Animas City in six to seven days now. It's the future alright. But, like you say, we can give settlers service to travel off those iron tracks and go north or south across the High Plains."

That night after supper, Mary Catherine caught Adkin staring at stars on the moonlit porch.

"I want to thank you Adkin Yates," she began. "When my new husband told me he wanted to go west, I was as thrilled as him. Then we ran into you and Ryan, and his dream of moving to Oklahoma changed. He wanted to work for you two.

"I wasn't too thrilled at first, but after knowing y'all a short while, you were both everything Sam said you were – after your trip together to the Little Arkansas River Treaty, you saving that Indian girl, as he told it. Then meeting Matty and getting to know how sweet and good she is. It was fate indeed you two were to marry and share your lives together.

"Well, fate has intervened in our family, and Sam knew what we had to do, but it broke his heart to make that decision without telling you and Ryan or getting your input," Mary Catherine said. "That's how much he thinks of y'all. I'm so happy you supported him the way you did – in front of everybody, It soothes my heart in these troubling times …"

Then she started softly crying and Adkin put an arm around her shoulders looking to the sky. Sam walked out on the porch.

"Is everything okay?" he asked. "Mary Catherine, are you crying? Honey …"

"She's okay, Sam," Adkin interrupted. "She was saying she was going to miss us, and especially Matty."

"That's right, Sam," she said, drying her eyes with a frilly hankerchief. "We'll both miss the Yates family – and our freighting family, too."

Sam put his arm around her and pulled her close.

"I don't want you to be sad Mary Catherine," he said. "Let's look back and remember the wonderful things we all shared. Okay?"

"Yes dear," she said as she laid her head on Sam's shoulder, and they all gazed into the starlit night.

•••

As everybody was stirring the next morning, Ryan asked if anyone had seen Adkin – that his gear was gone.

"He's out at the family plot saying his goodbyes to Zeb and Beth," Sam said. "He didn't want any company, and he's already got Diablo ready to ride."

There was bustle everywhere, but Mary Catherine assured everyone breakfast was almost ready.

"You're not leaving this ranch without a good breakfast," She yelled from the kitchen. "Anyone trying to ride out of here without eating, might get shot."

Uribe was in the living room playing with young Adam, who was not sitting still for too long.

They all gathered around the long table and Sam offered a short prayer. Mary Catherine had it all out: Bacon, venison steaks, gravy, fried potatoes, fried eggs – as many as wanted or asked for, hot coffee and English Tea, her fresh bread with churned butter and molasses – and her famous biscuits.

"I may cry knowing I'm not going to have these biscuits again, Maria Caterina," Uribe moaned like a child. "No bueno, no bueno."

"Oh Uribe, pobrecito, you have been away from home too long," Mary Catherine said, laughing. "Matty has learned my secrets and can bake sourdough biscuits as good as mine every time."

"Oh Señora, that is a blessing from God," Uribe said, chuckling. "Gracias. Gracias."

Laughter went around the table.

After eating, the men were checking the tethers and tie-downs on the pack mules, they checked saddle cinches and made sure water bags were full and easily available.

"Guess we better hit the road, Sam, light's a burning," Ryan said from his saddle. "Goodbye Mary Catherine, and God Bless you and yours."

Adkin embraced Sam and hugged Mary Catherine, who was holding Anna. He picked up little Adam and told him "bye-bye." The boy just squirmed, wanting to get back on the ground. Adkin pulled himself up onto Diablo.

"Take care of our family, Sam, and you just yell if you need anything – we'll come running," Adkin said, as he reined his big black stallion toward the road.

"Thanks," Phillips said, waving. "Be careful, and we'll see you soon, I hope."

It was the morning of September 26, and Adkin's thoughts turned to Matty. He was counting the days – maybe eight – until he could see her lovely face and her beautiful smile.

...

When they arrived in Fort Supply, Belger told them the Fort Sill caravan departed two days before, and Goodnight and his men were happy to see such a train of wagons and troopers to travel with for several hundred miles.

He also informed them YR&R had about 30 wagons in the caravan, and its wagon master was Tom Marcellus.

"He's a damn big man," Belger said to Adkin.

Adkin told Belger they couldn't stay long, they just wanted to fill a couple of water bags.

Within an hour of arriving, they were back on the trail to Fort Dodge. Belger had told them there was a new trail cut just a little east of the old one.

"It saves about 20 miles off the old original trail," he said. "You'll see where all the traffic goes now, you can't miss it – good luck."

They rode into Fort Dodge on October 2, and they were all three astonished. A community – or town – was growing up around west and south of the fort. As they crossed a small bridge built at the old crossing at Mulberry Creek, there was a board shanty on the north side of the bridge. Adkin read a sign with big letters: A.H. Dugan, then another smaller underneath noting "Whiskey Here, when available"

They rode in a little further and shanties, a few storefronts and tents – all kinds of tents looking like bordellos as a few women were standing at the tent flap openings.

"Adkin Yates, is that you?" a voice from the crowd bellowed. "Over here. Ryan, Uribe, ya'll come over here."

Adkin looked over and standing by a horse rail was a man waving, "It's me, Hoo Doo Brown."

They turned their horses to where Hoo Doo was yelling and stopped at the rail.

"I see ya'll still have your hair," Brown said. "Must have been an easy time in the Territories."

"How are you Hoo Doo?" Adkin asked, while Ryan and Uribe were smiling.

"I'm great Yates, and how are you trail busters doing?"

Ryan spoke up.

"I enjoyed The Territories a hell of a lot better than the Llano Estacado," he said, "That's for sure."

"I love all de lands," Uribe said, grinning. "Uribe fears nothing – as everybody knows."

They all laughed. Brown invited them to come into the shanty behind him for a drink.

"They got cool beer in this place," Brown said. "It's homemade, but he does a good job."

They tied off their horses and the mules. Ryan gave an Indian boy a dollar coin and told him to watch the horses.

"Don't let anyone touch these animals, or I'll hunt you down and tan your hide," Ryan said. "Okay?"

The boy was ecstatic and smiled while bobbing his head up and down. That dollar would feed his family for many days.

"I will do good, Mister," he said.

Inside the shanty, which was made with that new plywood that was developed at the end of the war. It looked nice, but a strong wind could take it down in a heartbeat.

They sat at a wooden table with small three-legged stools. The floor was packed dirt, and it looked as most of the patrons never hit the brass spittoons that were spread around the place. There were two windows per side and a long log slab that served as a bar.

Brown had ordered four beers and an older woman brought them to their table, Brown paid her with some coins. She was happy and smiled, showing she was missing several teeth.

"So how was your trip to Oklahoma?" Brown asked.

Adkin told him about the deaths of their agent and his wife, the turmoil created, and how Sam and his family took over the operations.

Brown just shook his head.

"You never know when the good Lord will come down and just snatch you up," he said.

When asked, Brown said he had some good talks with Rath and was actually looking to help Rath set up a buffalo hunting business. Brown had been scouting east of Dodge, and said there were still thousands of buffalo around Dodge.

"I know Charley has his heart set on hunting the Llano, but my God, if we can get our quotas around here, it would be a lot safer."

"Knowing Charley, he'll do what's best for everyone," Ryan said.

Brown said Charley was trying to square away some Army contracts for meat, then find ways to also get good money for the hides. He indicated another man they met on the upper Canadian River, George Reighard, was helping him scout.

"We're just hoping Sheridan gets things taken care of out here now that he's replaced General Sherman," Brown said. "I think he will.

"Have you ever met the man?" Brown asked.

"We saw him briefly at Camp Supply back in '68," Adkin said.

"Well, I've met and talked with him. He not only looks like a mean bastard, he is one," Brown said. "He hates Injuns enough to take it to them, I'll tell you that."

They also found out Henry L. Sitler was in the Dodge area. He had also been riding with Sheriff Allen up the Canadian when they all met.

"Most call him H.L. or just Sitler," Brown said. "Last I heard, he's interested in seeing if he can start a cattle herd up north of here. He's a good man – steady and tougher than he looks."

"Well, Hoo Doo, what's the quickest route to Las Animas City, Colorado?" Adkin asked.

"Las Animas?"

"Or Fort Lyons?"

"Oh, yeah. Well it's three days to Hays City to catch the railroad, but then it's only two days to Sheridan, Colorado, and then a day down to Fort Lyons," Brown said, using his fingers. "Six days at best."

"I think we can make it in six days along the Santa Fe Trail, Adkin, with just horses," Ryan said. "Is there a market here for pack mules, Hoo Doo?"

"There's a market here for anything," he answered. "Sure, you'll get a good price for mules here with pack boards."

"I think you're right, Ryan," Adkin said. What do you think Uribe?"

"Without mules, we can make 30 miles a day at least," Uribe said. "Six days or less."

"There's a few places to take on supplies along the trail now, too," Brown said.

"We can pack what we need on our horses," Adkin said. "Well, Hoo Doo, could you help us sell three mules? And find a safe place to sleep tonight?"

"No problem, Yates. Let's get out of here," Brown said.

"While you sell the mules, I'm going to send a telegraph telling them to expect us in six days from tomorrow," Adkin said.

"Hey, there's a new Western Union office right down the street, now," Brown said. "You don't have to go down to the fort."

At the horse rail, the young Indian boy was walking around the animals with a switch, waving off flies. He was also shouting at people that got too close to them. He looked relieved to give up his watch over the small herd.

•••

Brown was right about the mules. The owner of a blacksmith shop, which also stabled and sold animals paid $100 each for the mules and pack boards. That was good fortune, considering they thought the mules may be worth $40.

They had to go through their packs and save what they could. Uribe filled his saddle bags and used some burlap bags to hang on his extra horse.

"I'm not giving away nada," he said.

Adkin came riding up and was pleased to hear the selling price. Brown said they needed to head back to the building with Dugan's on it by the bridge at Mulberry Creek.

"He's got some sleeping rooms with cots and old beds, plus he has stables where we can keep your horses," Brown said. "I've got a place, but it's with an old widow who rents out two rooms – and they're both taken."

Brown went inside with them and introduced them to Dugan, a rough looking man but with a pleasant smile and demeanor. Brown told him to treat his friends with great respect, that they were friends of Chief Satanta.

Dugan looked impressed.

"I'll come by early, and say my goodbyes," Brown said. "Your best bet is to eat breakfast later on the trail. There's not much around here for that – unless you're at a boarding house."

Brown took off and the three were shown to a room with a plank-board floor and about six places to sleep – four cots and what looked like two beds made for children. They threw their bedrolls on the cots and went out to put their animals in the stable.

Dugan actually had a kitchen area with stove and a table. He fed them soupy beans with chopped onions and buffalo chunks in it. With bread from an old loaf, it was actually very tasty and filling.

Adkin awoke early, and called to the others. As they stirred, Adkin walked to a curtain and pulled it back to see out the window. The sky was just beginning to lighten in the east.

It was October 3, and Adkin was thinking it would only be six more days until he could see Matty. He was startled that she had become so embedded in his thoughts – and his heart.

"Maybe it's time I settled down some," he thought to himself. "My thoughts keep going back to our special place on the Cimarron River. Maybe we could live there but how? It's only a two-day's ride south of here in Dodge. Oh well, it's impossible to think about just he and Matty living in paradise with no problems in the world. But what's wrong with dreaming?"

As they stepped outside to go into Dugan's stable, Brown rode up. He was wearing a nice wool coat with the skin-side out and the wool against his body.

"A little cool this morning, but I see y'all are up and ready to ride," he said. "I'll ride with you for a bit."

They rode west along a street which was actually the Santa Fe Trail before there was even a fort here in the area. The Arkansas River was on their left, and Adkin tried visualizing how it looked when Becknell first traveled through here in the 1820s.

"I wanted to tell you Hoo Doo, if things don't come together with Charley Rath, telegraph us in Las Animas City, we've got room for good hands," Adkin said. "We actually lost a good hand just recently. He's the man that moved to the Territories to take over that agency."

"Well, I've freighted all over the place, and I don't mind it. But I'm just hoping something comes out of this buffalo hunting trade," Brown said. "I truthfully believe it could make us a lot of money."

"Oh, I agree," Adkin said. "And I hope you and Charley can put it all together. But, I'm just saying, if it falls apart, you're welcome to come out and see our operation."

"I really appreciate that, and I'll keep it in mind," Brown said. He pulled up on his reins and the others stopped as well.

"I better get back into town," he said. "It was a pleasure to see y'all again, and I'll try to stay in touch."

He leaned out of his saddle to shake hands with them and waved as he headed back east.

"Say hello to Charley for us when you see him," Adkin said.

•••

They had passed three eastbound caravans in five days, and only the last one had encountered trouble. It was a small train of 40 wagons and about 200 mules, which would make a handsome income if they could get them to Westport. Seems about two dozen Arapahoes had attacked them east of Old Fort Bent the day before.

The wagon master said what saved them was a detail of calvary was travelling west from Bent's new fort.

"We were just circling up the wagons, bullets and arrows flying everywhere, when the soldiers came up over a rise," the man explained. "They looked like a company coming over the hill, and the Injuns lit out fast. But, it was funny, there were only about 15 troopers in all."

Adkin assured them they hadn't seen any troubles, but made a suggestion to halt in Dodge and wait for a larger train to hook up with. The wagon master agreed, saying they had wanted to make good time, but keeping their animals and scalps had become the new priority.

They all laughed.

It was getting late, and Adkin estimated they were approaching Bent's Fort within a couple of hours.

"What do you think about riding on into the night?" Adkin asked Ryan and Uribe.

"Not if there is a possibility of a band of Arapahoes looking to raid those on the trail," Ryan said.

"Maybe better, Boss, we stay the night in Bent's Fort," Uribe said. "Then if we leave early next day, we ride hard and get home tomorrow night – with our scalps."

Adkin started chuckling.

"You're both right, I don't know what I was thinking," Adkin said.

"It was Matty, Señor," Uribe said giggling. "You thinking of your Kiowa Princess – I think. Si?"

Adkin laughed even harder, knowing Uribe was absolutely correct. Ryan was laughing hard as well.

...

They rode into Las Animas City in the evening of October 9, 1870. And as they crossed the bridge over the Arkansas River, Adkin caught sight of the YR&R Freight yard, its office and barracks and stables behind the office. There was smoke coming up behind the west end of the bunkhouse. Adkin figured they must be burning garbage, since there were no signs of emergency.

When they rode through the front gate, Adkin sensed a tenseness he had never really felt arriving at home, wherever home had been. He knew it was seeing Matty, he missed her so.

Then he saw several people come running toward them as they reined up to the horse rails. Dusty and Fransisco came up to them, along with hired hands and freighters – welcoming them home. Ray Dee and Peg-Leg Pete stood on the porch.

Everyone was talking as Adkin rolled out of his saddle. As soon as he touched the ground, someone jumped right in the middle of his back. It nearly knocked him down, and several started laughing and pointing. As he turned, Matty let go of him and dropped in front of him.

He looked down in her eyes, and she was breathing hard and smiling, but still had yet to speak a word.

"I am happy for you to be back home, my husband," she said with her accent, apparent that she had practiced this for sometime.

"I am very, very happy to see you, my wife," Adkin said as he grabbed her with both hands under her arms and lifted her to his face and kissed her with all he had, right there in front of the world to see. She wrapped her arms around the big man's neck and kissed him back, almost knocking his hat off.

"Hey, save some of that for later," Ray Dee said, with everyone laughing.

Adkin let her down and put his arm around her shoulders as he led her up the steps to the porch. He embraced Ray Dee and Sanpete as the others came up on the porch. Everyone went inside and talked and talked. When Adkin wasn't embracing someone or shaking hands, he had his arm around Matty. He kept constantly smiling at her and whispering in her ear.

Matty was beaming, enjoying every moment of their greeting. Matty then snagged Margarite's arm as she passed by when talking with someone and pulled her into Adkin's view.

"Adkin, this my friend, Margarite. She is new bride to Dusty," Matty said. "She my very good friend."

Adkin shook Margarite's hand and told her he was happy to meet her, and if she was a friend of Matty's, she was also friend of his.

Margarite was a pretty woman, small like Matty but heavier, and she wore her hair down, all of it combed straight down with only a headband. Margarite's hair was as dark as her eyes, and it hung down to her bottom. It was starkly different than the way Matty wore her's in two braids.

Adkin was impressed, Margarite could speak good English. Adkin also realized Matty had very much improved her English during his absence, as well.

He kept looking at her, his love showing everybody there how much he cared for this beautiful petite woman.

"She truly is my little Kiowa Princess," he thought to himself. He felt a constant urge to just hold her and hug her close.

"Hey people, let's get our friends settled," Ray Dee shouted. "Get these horses stabled and rubbed down, fed and their gear stashed in their quarters.

"I would ask you women to prepare your special supper and be ready to serve us peons in about one hour, okay?" he added.

Adkin started to turn to help with unsaddling Diablo, but stopped after one step. He turned back to Matty.

"They know how to unsaddle a horse," he said. "I will stay right here."

Matty stood on her tiptoes and kissed Adkin again, softly and longingly.

"Me, Margarite go to finish big meal for you, Ryan and Uribe," she said. "We plan for many days."

He reluctantly let go of her hand as she and Margarite turned toward the kitchen.

"I didn't realize just how much I missed her," Adkin said as Ray Dee stepped up next to him.

"She's a wonderful woman, Adkin," Ray Dee said. "She has been nothing but helpful, and she can outwork most of the men here. She even likes to chop firewood.

"I have to keep telling her we'll do whatever chore she wants done, but she insists on doing just about anything she needs," he continued. "Wait until you see the meal she planned – well we suggested a few things, but her and Margarite and the other two women have taken over.

"She's been as lively as a rabbit being chased by a fox since we got your telegraph," Ray Dee said. "Never seen a woman so happy to see her man – amazing."

"You're a lucky son-of-a-gun, Adkin, but I think you know that," he added, grinning.

Adkin explained what happened in Oklahoma and how Sam had been uneasy about moving down there.

"He was very unhappy leaving here, but he knew he had to," Ray Dee said. "I told him you wouldn't care if that's what he and his wife decided to do."

"Ironically, if we were here, that's probably what we would have asked him to do, since that service down there is making money," Adkin said. "But I think things worked out for the best. They'll do good down there.

"Did he tell you Mary Catherine is expecting again?" Adkin asked.

"No. Really? Guess they're going to raise all the freighters they're goin' need, huh?" Ray Dee said, laughing.

•••

Adkin gathered some clean clothes and had said he was going to take a hot bath, over Uribe's claims he asked first.

"Don't worry Uribe, I won't take long," Adkin said. "You and the men just get your water hot while I'm bathing."

After Adkin had dressed in clean buckskins he had left behind, Ray Dee led him outside and around the end of the bunkhouse where Adkin had first noticed the smoke when they rode into the yard.

"Look at this, Ray Dee said, pointing. "Matty's plan for a welcome home meal."

There was a large circle of embers and two metal spits straddling the coals. One spit was a hindquarter of a beeve, and a whole hog was on the other spit. An Indian woman, wearing a cooking apron that looked familiar slowly rolling the hog.

She beamed a big smile at the men and stood more upright, proud to be roasting meat for the big meal. At that moment, Matty came up to them hurriedly.

"I want you to have big meal," she said as she wrapped her arm around Adkin's waist. She then said something to the woman in Indian, and the woman went over to the beeve and started turning it slowly.

"Her name is Moh-bay, she is Arapahoe," Matty said.

Adkin nodded to her and said, "Hello Moh-Bay."

"She wear apron Mary Kat-er-rind give her," Matty said. "She very proud to own."

"How is Mary Kat-er-rind?" Matty asked. "And Adam and Anna – are they well?"

Adkin told her they were all doing fine under the circumstances of losing two family members in a short time. Matty looked down at the ground, knowing full well about losing someone close.

"She not too sad?" she asked.

Adkin assured her Mary Catherine was fine, and told her Mary Catherine was going to have another baby in four full moons. Matty was very excited.

"One day, we go see her and Mister Sam and babies, yes?" she asked Adkin.

"Yes Matty, some day, I promise"

They walked back to the bunkhouse where everybody was gathering. Ray Dee told Adkin they now employ six permanent hands at the yard, and had at least that many available part-time to run freight jobs.

"Three of these women who help Matty and Margarite are wives of the hands working here," Ray Dee said. "They're good people. Several were here when y'all left back in August. Of course, there's a few children, too. You know, it's family."

"I thought several looked familiar," Adkin said. "I really need to take more time and get to know everybody here. I want them to know I appreciate them helping us, and that I care about that – and their lives. That they are family, too.

"Life is short, Ray Dee – and shorter for others, if you know what I mean," Adkin added.

The hum of conversation stopped as three men entered the west door, each carrying a large wooden tray of meat in huge chunks. An awe came over the crowd.

They laid the meat trays down spaced evenly down the 20-foot table, as the women started coming out fo the kitchen carrying bowls, trays and platters of other foods.

They were laying them out with eating utensils rolled up in cloth towels before each chair. Adkin was remembering the fancy hotel in St. Louis where he and J.L. Sanderson stayed back in 1865.

There were boiled potatoes, carrots, turnips and onions, roasted ears of corn and slices of squash. There were several platters of biscuits and some loaves of fresh bread where one could cut off any size they wanted.

Adkin caught Uribe's eye after Uribe saw the platters of biscuits. He winked at Adkin and smiled big, licking his lips.

There was homemade butter all along the table, as well bowls of honey and molasses. There were also bowls of raw salt and small jugs of a Mexican sauce that was quite spicy and hot. There was a small pot of blood gravy with a gourd ladle.

"Where did this all come from?" Adkin whispered to Ray Dee.

"From our stores, where else," he said. "The women started filling our cool storage well with vegetables as late as two or three weeks ago.

"Our garden was very fruitful this fall, thanks to the women, and a few of the guys, too," he continued. "We should have vegetables through the entire winter."

"You have done well, Ray Dee, and no one appreciates it more than me," Adkin said. "Thank you friend."

"It's teamwork, Adkin, just like you and J.L. always preached to us – it works, partner," Ray Dee said, patting Adkin on the shoulder.

Matty carried in several trays and platters, smiling at Adkin the whole time. She made sure the children, sitting a small table off to the back were fed. There were five of them, looking to be between 3 or 4 and up to 11 or 12.

Finally Matty sat down next to Adkin once everything had been placed on the table and everyone was ready to eat.

Adkin stood.

"Men, ladies, friends, I want to thank you for everything," he said slowly. "I would like to pray.

"Lord, thank you for this food, bless the hands that planted it, grew it, harvested it, stored it and cooked it – your bounty. Please help us all to know Your love for us, and as my father always said, 'Keep God close in your heart,' Amen."

There were several "Amens" as well as everyone starting to pass the platters and reaching for foods. Adkin took some pork, a rarity for him, and a piece of roasted beef. Matty just kept staring at him. Adkin began to think her smile had been frozen on her face. It made him swell with pride.

Near the end of the meal, Adkin stood again and told everyone of their meeting with Sam and Mary Catherine, how they were going to take over operations of Jarvis' Ranch with Mary Catherine's cousin, Darwin Jarvis. He assured their friends, the Phillips family were of strong stock and would do very well.

He reaffirmed the freighting and stagecoach business would continue to grow, even with the railroads coming. Explaining how travellers and settlers would want to expand their wandering off the railways and build communities and towns further and further away from the rails.

He told them the Barlow and Sanderson Company, as well as YR&R Freight would be successful as long as they all worked as a team, turning to Ray Dee and winking.

"I consider all of you a part of my family, and I'm very fortunate and proud to call you my family – thank you," he said and then sat down.

The freighting family all applauded Adkin's little speech, some whooping it up. Ray Dee stood and held up his arms.

"Ladies and gentlemen, I have a surprise of my own," he said. "Dusty, please come in."

They looked back toward the kitchen area as five of the men came in with trays full of bottles and cups. They started placing them along the table.

There was brandy, rum, whiskey, a few bottles of wine and jugs of beer. Ray Dee looked at Adkin and shrugged his shoulders. Adkin smiled and clapped his hands, signaling his absolute approval.

•••

Afterward, several of the men gathered in the front office, some smoked a cigar, Uribe and his Ute friends had their pipes and tobacco pouches out. Ryan was still clutching a bottle of brandy he took from the bunkhouse.

"I counted 23 adults and five children this evening Ray Dee," Adkin said. "We've got quite an impressive family here. I've observed my participation here is not what has made this operation a success."

Several of the men gathered around Adkin as he spoke. They noticed he had a concerned tone as he spoke.

"I've been thinking, I may take some time off and get away for awhile," he said, as several grumbled disapproval. "Here me out, please. I've been thinking about this for several weeks now, It's not just something that hit me out of the blue.

"I'm thinking about taking Matty to our special place on the Cimarron River – a couple of you know where I'm talking about – and build us a little house overlooking the river. It would be a place we could retire to later.

"I just feel it is the right time to do this," he continued. "We would leave in the early spring and return back here – say around this time next year, before winter sets in.

"I can help as much as possible the next six months here and do whatever is necessary to keep our operation going forward," Adkin said. "But I see now you men are the heart of YR&R and our partnership with J.L. I have not talked to him about this, yet. But I want your blessing before I go any further.

"Goodness, I haven't even talked with Matty about this either," he added, chuckling.

Nobody said anything right away. It was quiet for nearly a whole minute with everyone gathering their thoughts. Finally, Ryan spoke.

"Men, Adkin Yates walked into our yard in Leavenworth five years ago with J.L. Sanderson, who had hired him in St. Louis – J.L. saw him knock an obstinate steamboat mechanic into the river when they docked there," Ryan began, smiling. "At first, I was fearful this youngster was infringing on my supervisor position – and I wasn't immediately his biggest supporter."

Ray Dee laughed, remembering how Ryan was jealous of Adkin's and J.L.'s friendship.

"But after working with him, making our trek to the Little Arkansas Peace Treaty – him protecting the woman who would become his wife – he has earned my utmost respect as a human being, and a man," Ryan said. "When you are with

Adkin Yates, this big strapping Englishman, he has your back, and you willingly, no happily, will cover his back.

"If he wants to take his bride and build her a home, I think we should support him in every aspect of that endeavor," Ryan said, looking about to every man there.

"What do you say, men?"

Everyone started clapping and shouting their approvals. It was so loud, the women heard it in the bunkhouse kitchen where they were finishing their cleanup of the feast. It was the first thing Matty asked Adkin about when he entered their private quarters near the bunkhouse.

"Why the men shout and laugh, act crazy?" Matty said, cupping her hand by her ear. "We hear from kitchen."

"My friends and partners will allow me to take maybe eight moons to rest and not work with freighting and stagecoaches," he said, grinning. "Starting in the spring when flowers start to bud and the green grass breaks through the ground."

Matty frowned, looking unsure of what he was saying – or its true meaning.

"I want to take you to our spiritual place on the Cimarron – where you went many times with your father when you were very young," Adkin said. "Where we became man and wife, near Crooked Creek."

"I know the place, well," she said. "It is often in my dreams."

"Well, when the cold winds and snows are gone, we will go there together and build our own lodge," Adkin said.

"Go together? Build a White Man's lodge?"

"Yes Matty," he said. "We will go together and build a house."

"Oh Adkin, this like a dream," Matty said as she wrapped her hands behind his neck. "Can this be true?"

"Yes, my love," he said as he kissed her and lifted her off her feet. He was still kissing her as he turned toward their feather bed, and then laid her down and turned to darken the two oil lamps which had lit the room.

•••

At daybreak, Matty was whispering in his ear, asking for him to tell her again when they would go and where and what they would do. She insisted she had a dream and the spirits told her lies. Adkin laughed and went over all the plans again.

She was smiling and kissing his cheek over and over. Then she stopped and a frown came over her face.

"We not go soon?" she asked.

"No Matty, we cannot build a house during winter time," he said. "We will have to take wagons of wood and supplies from Fort Dodge to build the house.

"We need dry roads. And men can't work out in the cold or snow every day." Adkin continued. "We have to wait until Spring – maybe March."

He knew she didn't understand months just yet, though she had heard them before. He made a note to himself to teach her what each month was and how it was, weather wise, that month. Her only reference now was one full moon to the next one was a month – maybe six full moons.

After they dressed, they were off to the bunkhouse, Matty nearly pulling Adkin's arm off making him hurry.

"We have to cook for everyone," she explained.

Once inside the mess hall, it was already warm, as some of the women had come in and started a fire in the pot-bellied stove on the east end, while the cooking stove was heating up in the kitchen on the west end.

It hit Adkin just how much work Matty was doing while he was traipsing around the country. She was overseeing three meals a day for up to about 20 people.

"My God," he thought to himself. "I've forced her into slavery. And Ray Dee said she also cuts firewood and helps with the animals. When does she have the time? This will have to stop."

After eating a fine breakfast, Ray Dee, Ryan and Adkin met in the office to go over the books. Adkin wanted to get a handle on what business was ongoing and where were the priorities. He wanted to be up to speed on all the operations before he telegraphed Sanderson about his plans for the spring of '71.

A little before breaking for lunch, Adkin brought up Matty's role in the operations.

"I know we all have chores and jobs to handle – teamwork and all – but it seems to me I have put Matty into a position where she works from sunup to dark," he started. "I feel like I've put her in slavery, and truthfully, I don't feel good about it."

"I don't like it either, Adkin," Ray Dee said. "But every time I try to relieve her of any of her duties, she gets upset and says that's her job. I'm serious."

Ryan laughed and shook his head.

"Sounds like it's up to you to try and stop her from doing so much work … Boss," he said, emphasizing Boss as if Adkin couldn't boss her around either. Ray Dee laughed, too.

"You're right. I'll talk with her," Adkin said, trying to put on a bold face.

After breakfast, Ryan noticed Adkin took Matty off to the side in the kitchen pantry. He whispered to Ray Dee that Adkin was probably telling Matty she wasn't going to have to work as much anymore.

"Wanna wager what will happen?" Ryan asked.

"No, we'd both be betting he fails," Ray Dee said, chuckling.

After about 10 minutes, Adkin came out and walked over to Ray Dee and Ryan.

"I have come to believe Matty is quite happy indeed with her daily endeavors in which she has voluntarily sought to engage in," Adkin said with a proper British accent.

Then they all started laughing and hooting it up.

"I told you, Adkin," Ray Dee said, laughing harder and harder. A few others in the bunkhouse mess hall were staring at the three men laughing like school children.

Ryan was holding his gut and bent over. Ray Dee kept slapping Ryan on the back, trying to keep him breathing. Adkin's face was red as a beet, but he kept howling and slapping his knees.

"Guess she's not going to spend much time in a rocker, eh?" Ryan gasped, which brought out another round of hoots between the three.

"Guess not," Adkin coughed out while wheezing between howls.

•••

The three made it to the office and once again delved into the businesses. Adkin and Ryan said they knew YR&R had 30 wagons working the Fort Sill route south of Fort Supply.

"It's actually 40, Lieutenant Belger got it wrong," Ray Dee said. "Tom is ramrodding that train. And we have 30 wagons hauling supplies to miners in southern Colorado, west of Fort Garland, where Colonel Carson was commander for a short time. Don Diego is handling that job.

"We also have 15 wagons in Junction City at Barlow and Sanderson's yard," he continued. "And we've got five here, and they're in rough shape. Each one could use some repairs.

"One good thing is J.L. sent four new Concords out on the train to Sheridan," Ray Dee said. "We sent one to Denver, two to La Junta and one to Uncle Dick Wootton at Raton Pass."

Adkin asked how much used wagons were selling for in Santa Fe. Ray Dee said they were still getting good prices, not two or three times as much as they used to, but they could get about $250 to $300 for a decent used wagon.

Ray Dee was to work up a report on how many wagons needed repairs, how many needed to be sold off, and how many to buy to keep the fleet up around 90 to 100 wagons.

He said he could have that information in a couple of days. Ray Dee wanted to send some telegrams, east and west. In the meantime, Adkin said he would work on the five wagons they had in the yard.

"Dusty got Fransisco interested in blacksmithing, and he has taken a liking to it. But he's only good with the little things, like making horse shoes, things like that," Ray Dee said. "He doesn't know enough to re-iron an axle or a wheel, but he could be taught."

"I'll be glad to help," Adkin said, as he headed for the blacksmith shop by the stables.

While Adkin made a list of what the old wagons needed, he kept thinking about how he was going to tell Sanderson he'd be taking an eight-month leave of absence. He was going to have to sit down in the evening after supper and make out his telegraph so he could get it sent tomorrow.

"The sooner the better," Adkin thought to himself.

Once Adkin got to his quarters after supper, he sat down at the table. Matty was still in the kitchen cleaning and preparing for tomorrow's breakfast. She just never stopped. Adkin blamed himself in a way, being away from her for so long, she didn't have anything to do but work.

As he sat there contemplating what to say to Sanderson, he decided to keep it short and to the point.

"To: J.L. Sanderson, Junction City Kansas – Stop.

I am wanting to take leave of absence – unpaid of course, in March of 1871 to go to Cimarron River and build a retirement house for Matty. But I'm not planning on retirement. We will come back to work around Oct. 1. – Stop

From: Adkin Yates – Stop

That ought to do it. He folded it and left it on the table. He decided to undress and get into his sleeping wear, long johns, and laid down, staring at the beams in the roof.

He started thinking how his experience of seeing Indian villages and how the women took care of everything. They cleaned and skinned – expertly skinned – every critter that was brought to them. They could tan any hide in the world, too. Probably could make a shirt out of mouse skins if they had to.

He had seen women covered in blood and fat, smelling of rot from yards away, cleaning the lodge, and when the tipis had to come down or put up, it was the women. The poles each weighed probably 40 pounds or better.

The women built all the travois they needed to travel, fed and took care of all the other animals, except the horses – that was the only chore Adkin could think of that men did. The women also bore the children and raised them, taught all the young girls to do everything they did, sew parkas, coats, blankets, deer-skin dresses, how to bead for decorations and rituals.

"Wow," Adkin thought. "Matty may think the work here is like taking holiday compared to her old world. All I know, if she is truly happy, I won't stop her, though I don't know if I really could. And I don't want to know."

He was about to doze off when he was awaken by Matty as she slipped under the buffalo hides covering the bed. Adkin reached over and felt her silky soft skin – she was totally naked, and he pulled her close and kissed her.

•••

The Western Union office opened at 9 the next morning, and Adkin was there. He sent his message to Sanderson and then sent one to his bank in Westport, and to their YR&R accountant in Junction City. He wanted to find out where he stood financially. When he had more communication with Sanderson, he would ask J.L. to inform him of his stock value.

It was sensitive information, and Only Sanderson and Adkin knew of it. Adkin had been given a percentage of profits bonus clause shortly after he bought his first 100 shares. Adkin didn't like keeping it from the others, but believed Sanderson had something secret between them all, just to make them feel special. Sanderson was like that.

The clause gave Adkin a 10 percent bonus on all net profits – after expenses – and he could re-invest those bonuses in additional shares, to be distributed annually, if the company was profitable. Adkin had given Sanderson his request to have it all re-invested that first year, and every year since.

By agreement, Sanderson asked Adkin to never mention it, if at all possible, within a telegraph. They had discussed it, and Sanderson had given Adkin a legal contract after that first year, which Adkin had hidden in his Bible.

Adkin decided he would just telegraph Sanderson that he would like a letter totalling his financial investments in the Kansas City First National Bank in Westport. Sanderson would know, and put it in a sealed letter and have it posted to Adkin, alone.

Luckily, the Western Union boy rode up into the yard on his bicycle the next day and gave Adkin a "telegram for Mister Yates from a Mister Sanderson."

After reading it, he had the boy wait while he went into the office and wrote out a reply. It was a request for the investment totals on the Kansas City Bank. He gave it to the boy and told him to have the clerk send it right away. He gave the boy a coin for his service.

Then he smiled, and held up the telegraph and shouted to Peg-Leg Pete, who had been sitting on the porch.

"Hey Sanpete, our old friend J.L. Sanderson is coming to visit us, be here around October 20," Adkin said.

News spread fast and everyone was excited. J.L. was popular with the men and the women or wives. He treated everyone as a friend, totally believing you get treated by how you treat others. He would support you if you were genuine, but you didn't want him as an enemy.

Adkin had seen him in a fight with fisticuffs, and he more than held his own. Adkin smiled at the memory of fighting the German mechanic and his friends in St. Louie. The Germans got pounded.

Most of the operations kept rolling along smoothly. Peg-Leg showed he was a real logistics man. He could remember every agreement, shipment, who ordered what and how much.

Adkin never saw him write anything down, but one evening, Adkin went to the office late to fetch something, and Peg-Leg was writing in a big hard-covered log book all the day's work and movements of freighting wagons, stagecoaches, mule teams, everything.

"That's great, Sanpete. I was wondering how you operated," Adkin said, after sneaking up behind and reading the book over his shoulder. Sanpete jumped from being startled.

"Why do you wait until late to record everything?" Adkin asked.

"Because if you stop every minute to write down your work, you never get any work done," Sanpete answered matter-of-factly.

"I guess you're right," Adkin said, gently patting Sanpete on the back. "I just want you to know how much we appreciate all your hard work. I am very, very proud we hired you – you are a good man, Sanpete."

"Why thank you, Boss" he said. "This job is my life, and I am not going to waste one minute of life, if you understand me."

"Indeed I do, keep up the great work," Adkin said as he turned away. "Good night, Sanpete."

"Night, Boss."

How can one appraise how much a man does for another and the business when he gives up a leg in the duty of his job – and keeps smiling and keeps living life to its fullest – ignoring the term cripple? Adkin was proud of his family, indeed.

•••

Word quickly spread Sanderson was coming to Las Animas City, and everyone was paying a little more attention to tidiness and wanting to present the grounds appropriately – nice and clean.

One day, Thomas Boggs dropped in to meet Adkin and Ryan, as he had met the rest of the men operating the companies while Adkin and Ryan were crossing the Llano Estacado with Goodnight and Rath.

Boggs was a slight man, looking like a banker rather than the Indian trader Adkin knew of him. He was very kind, and his relationship with William Bent and Colonel Carson intrigued Adkin, as both those men were heroes to Adkin and many other Americans that never even stepped foot in the West. He was very kind to Matty and complimented her dress beading.

Boggs invited them to supper in a couple of days, he also asked Adkin and Ryan to bring their partners, wives or friends.

"We can seat 10 more if you like," Boggs said.

"It will only be four of us Mister Boggs; myself, Matty, Ryan here and Ray Dee Rinehart," Adkin said.

"Very well, we'll see you Friday evening then, say around 8?" he said. "My house is two down from Prowers, you can miss it, there's a post box with our name on it by the road."

"We look forward to seeing you then, and thank you," Adkin said, as Boggs stepped up into his one-horse buggy and turned for the main gate.

About that time Ray Dee walked over from the stables.

"Was that Tom Boggs," he asked.

"Yes sir, and he's invited us – including you – to supper Friday night at his home, with his wife," Ryan said. "So you better start bathing now, you old pole cat,"

They laughed as Ray Dee, said he'd save some water – and soap – for Ryan.

"You know, I'm not sure, but I think I heard he's the mayor or something of Bent County," Ray Dee said. "I guess while we were moving here and building this place, they made this area Bent County and Boggsville is the county seat.

"Then, of course, y'all took off for lands unknown," he continued. "Tom is pretty much a big shot in these parts – he's well known and respected.

"Wonder why he wants to mingle with saddle tramps like y'all," he said, laughing as he ran into the office to escape a punch in the arm from Ryan.

• • •

The evening of the supper at Boggs, Matty came out of the bedroom wearing her long deerskin dress with all the bands of elk teeth across the front, her wedding dress so to speak. She had made it all herself, and she was very proud of it.

She had also wrapped beautiful strips of mink fur around and down her braids, with small leather thongs tied about every four inches to keep the mink in place.

"You look beautiful, Matty," Adkin said as he walked up to her and put his hands on her shoulders. "As beautiful as all the flowers at our spiritual place."

He bent down and kissed her softly.

"You look beautiful, too, Páhy-Chi," she said.

Ray Dee drove them to the Boggs' house in the YR&R ambulance they kept for special events.

Once inside, Boggs introduced his wife, Rumalda. As Boggs asked the men to sit, Rumalda took Matty with her to another room, asking her in Kiowa, Adkin found out later, if she had lived long in Las Animas City.

Boggs asked if anyone cared for a brandy or a smoke, he had a large cedar box of cigars. When Ryan said he'd like a brandy, Mister Boggs, Boggs insisted they call him Tom.

"Your wife is very beautiful, Tom, and her name is very unique," Adkin said. "I've never encountered that, Rumalda. It flows off the tongue."

"She's a very unique woman, too – I am blessed," Boggs said. "I had been working for the Bent brothers and Ceran St. Vrain when I came out here, and then I met Rumalda down in Taos. Her full name is Ramalda Luna Bent.

"She was the stepdaughter of Charles Bent, and I fell in love with her at first sight. She was tall, dark hair and olive skin," Boggs continued. "I asked Charles about marrying her, and he wasn't too sure at first. He told me she was only 14, which made me stutter, to tell you the truth. She looked 18 or older.

"But I told Charles I was in love, and I didn't want to take a chance of losing her to another – hell I was only 22 at the time myself. Well, he wanted to talk to her, and I guess she jumped up around his neck and had been dreaming of the same thing – to be my wife.

"And like they say, the rest is history. We've been married 24 years now," he added.

"That's very romantic, indeed," Adkin said.

Boggs asked how Adkin met Matty, and Adkin told an abbreviated version after the incident at the Little Arkansas Treaty. That's when Ryan interrupted and said Adkin left out the part about being arrested by the Army after knocking the teeth out of an officer that killed Matty's child with a rifle butt at Fort Supply. Even though Adkin didn't know it was Matty being beaten at first.

Ryan went on to tell how they followed Matty into the Wichita Mountains and found her and her father, Black Horse, and Satanta.

"Black Horse suddenly made Adkin and Matty stand up, he took their hands – one on each side – and started yelping to the heavens and, bam, they was married," he added.

"Not quite as romantic as your story, Tom," Adkin said sheepishly. "But I love her all the same."

"Fascinating, sounds like something out of one of those dime novels from back east," Boggs said, chuckling.

"Let's go spend some time with the women and then eat, okay?" he added.

"Sounds good," Ray Dee said.

During supper, Ryan told how Adkin had come to be hired by J.L. Sanderson, and what they had been doing for five years. Ray Dee told of how he remembered the day Adkin walked into the Leavenworth yard with a big-brimmed straw hat, looking like a farmer from Pennsylvania Quaker Country.

They had a deluxe meal of roasted squab – a small chicken for each person, broiled fish fillets from the Arkansas' waters and fried pork chops. There were also all sorts of vegetables to choose from.

Adkin couldn't believe how wonderful everything was, and not a single piece of red meat anywhere. He knew whatever Boggs did, it must pay well.

'Pardon my ignorance, but I have spent very little time in Las Animas City since we moved here – I've been out of the country for nearly eight weeks – but are you the Mayor of Boggsville?" Adkin asked.

"No," he said, laughing. "I am the Sheriff though. Sheriff of Bent County."

"Oh, Sheriff is it?" Adkin said with eyebrows raised high. "My apologies, we weren't aware."

"That's no problem. Adkin. I've already heard a lot about you from another Sheriff – a friend of mine – L.A. Allen," Boggs said. "He speaks well of you and your men."

"I'm glad of that," Adkin said, smiling now. "That's one man I have no plans of angering or getting on his bad side."

They all laughed heartily.

"Is Sheriff Allen back home yet?" Adkin asked. "And are you both Sheriffs of Bent County?"

"No and no. He's Sheriff of Southeast Colorado, and he's off somewhere – probably hanging someone right now."

Laughter spread around the table again.

Matty said little during the meal, she was seated between Adkin and Ramalda, but Ramalda asked her questions in Kiowa many times. Matty would respond in Kiowa and then look at Adkin, smiling and looking very happy.

She told Adkin she really liked the chicken cooked like that and was going to buy more chickens than just the layers they now had at the yard. Adkin would have to talk with her later. It would take a lot of young chickens to feed 20 people at the yard.

Boggs offered after-dinner brandy, but it was getting late, and the crew had very full bellies. They thanked Tom and Ramalda for their hospitality and promised to have them out to the yard for a meal.

"Maybe when Sheriff Allen gets home, we can all get together," Adkin shouted as they rode away.

•••

A few days later, Adkin received a large envelope by posted mail. It was a long letter from James R. Mead. Adkin laughed to himself, since Since Barlow and Sanderson had most of the U.S. mail contracts in these parts.

Jim informed them he had mailed official papers to Darwin Jarvis confirming his new contract with Jim to provide teamsters and animals for the freighting business. He sent his condolences about Zeb and Beth's deaths.

He said he sold his ranch at Towanda, but kept the trading post and post office there, that he hired a man named Tim Peet to run it. Jim now lives in a frame house in his Wichita, the place he staked out in 1868. He said he's laying out a town there and has given up some of his land to build an Episcopal Church.

He was appointed Chairman of the Kansas House-Senate Joint Ways and Means Committee. He was also appointed United States Deputy Marshall of Sedgwick, Butler, Sumner and Cowley counties.

"The man is rich in ideas and one unique individual," Adkin said as he was reading the letter to Ryan and Ray Dee. "Wouldn't surprise me if he became Governor of Kansas someday – if he'd want it."

He said he's looking to put together a railroad company to handle transportation in central Kansas.

"Mead wishes us well, and says we should be able to make healthy profits with Sam at Jarvis' place, as the whole of that country is opening up for settlement," Adkin said. "If he gets out this way, he says he'll stop by."

"He closes with 'Be sure to hold onto your scalps.'" he added.

They chuckled.

"To think everything he has started with a man, a rifle, a love of hunting and a gift of survival among wild Indians," Ryan said. "He's really something."

The men had everything clean and shiny by the 19th, expecting Sanderson the next day. He had telegraphed saying he was on schedule to arrive the afternoon of October 20, and he was bringing five more new Concords.

"Guess we're making plenty of dinero, Boss,' Uribe said. "If we can buy these Concords and ship them all around."

"I love it," Peg-Leg Pete said. "I want to deliver one of them for sure. I haven't been in a coach seat for some time, and I'm restless to get out of this office."

"Plus, those Concords are the finest riding wagons ever made by man," he added, with a huge grin.

"What if J.L. wants you to take one to California?" Ray Dee asked. "You fine with that?"

"I'd have to think about that," Peg-Leg said, frowning.

The men started laughing.

"Because I don't know if this place could keep operating with me gone a couple of months." he added.

Several hoots went out from the men around.

•••

The next day, someone near the front gate started shouting, "They're here. They're here," and pointing toward the bridge.

Adkin and Ryan stepped out onto the porch, while Ray Dee and Uribe and others started for the office from various spots in the back of the yard.

It was quite a sight, six brand new Concord Stagecoaches each being pulled by beautiful four-horse teams, and two freight wagons behind them and a small herd of about 30 horses and a few mules. There were also six wranglers saddled up moving the horses along.

The front stage came to a halt right in front of the office, with the others rolling to a stop, too.

"Got any room here to park these babies?" Sanderson barked from the driver's seat, with a huge smile on his face.

"We sure do," Adkin yelled back.

"Just leave them right there, and we'll see to it they get some good care," Ryan hollered.

Sanderson hit the ground about the time Adkin reached him. They embraced. Then Ryan and the others did the same. Questions were flying around.

"How was the trip?"

"Any problems?"

"Are y'all thirsty?"

That got Sanderson's attention.

"Hell yes we're thirsty," he said, laughing.

"Well come on in, J.L.," Adkin said. "Uribe, get the boys to park these coaches and wagons at the stables, then have all J.L.'s men gather in the mess hall after taking care of all the animals, there's plenty room in the corral."

"Come on in here," Ryan said, putting his arm around Sanderson's shoulder. "You know for a 70-year-old man, you can still drive a coach fairly well."

"Listen here, Tyler Ryan, I'm not putting up with any guff from a youngster like you," Sanderson said, as they all laughed. "Besides, I just turned 50 last July. I'll have you know I can still put my fist through a solid plank board."

Once inside, the office, Matty and Margarite were there with a tray of glass goblets and several crystal bottles of liquor.

Sanderson walked over to Matty, and said, "Hello, Matty, good to see you again."

He had his hand out, but she smiled and hugged his neck. As she released him, she said, "Good to see you Meester Sanderson, mighty good," in perfect English.

She then introduced Margarite, and Sanderson asked for a shot of brandy, which Matty poured. Ryan asked for the same, Adkin asked for a shot of rum, which surprised them. It was only 2 in the afternoon, and Adkin, if he did have liquor, usually had it in the evenings or late.

"It is really good to see you my friend," Adkin said. "It's like putting a real face on the telegrams and letters."

"I know what you mean," Sanderson said. "I'm glad I caught you all here – of course, without Sam and Mary Catherine. You men have meant everything to our success out here, and it just keeps getting better.

"I've got good news for ya'll about how we're growing, where we're going – all kinds of things" he added.

"Well, let's wait until we get everybody together in the mess hall over at the bunkhouse, if you don't mind," Adkin interrupted. "We want to welcome you formally."

"By all means," Sanderson said, as his slugged down the remainder of his brandy. Matty walked toward him, but he waved her off.

"I'll wait to have another, Matty, when we gather all the men, okay?" he said, as she smiled and turned away.

He told them they had encountered no problems with Indians, or any other brigands during the trip. Of course, they had everything shipped by rail from Junction City to Kit Carson, and then it was just two days of fast travel to Las Animas City.

"You men have built a wonderful place here, we're proud to be a part of it," Sanderson continued. "I'd like a full tour later – it looks great, what I've seen so far."

"We're proud of it," Ray Dee said. "Ryan and Adkin hadn't spent much time here lately, been galavantin' around with Charley Rath and Charles Goodnight."

"That's a pair to draw to," Sanderson said. "Good men, and they know this country as well as any. They'll help get this country settled and growing, mark my words."

"I wouldn't wager against either of them, right Adkin?" Ryan said.

"Not ever."

Uribe came through the front door panting.

"We have everybody assembled, Señors, and all the animals are bueno," Uribe said with is usual toothy grin. Matty and Margarite immediately scooted out the back door headed to the mess hall.

"Well, let's go talk with the men, shall we?" Sanderson said.

Once they walked into the mess hall, Sanderson introduced Adkin Yates, Tyler Ryan and Ray Dee Rinehart to all his men and introduced his numerous teamsters and wranglers to everybody assembled – naming them off one-by-one.

"Ladies and gentlemen, these three men," he said pointing at Adkin, Ryan and Ray Dee. "Were part of our original team at Leavenworth back in '65 when we decided to head west with our services. Barlow and Sanderson Company owes them a great deal of gratitude for securing most of our routes out here – often facing death at every turn.

"I want all of you to introduce yourselves to their crew here in Las Animas, and get to know them," he continued. "Do you know why? Because they are part of your family, and you are a part of their family."

There was a short silence after Sanderson stopped talking. Then men started turning side to side, seeking strangers and shaking their hands. The murmuring spread around the big room.

Adkin, caught Matty's eye where she stood at the kitchen entrance. He waved to her, swinging his arm in a way to bring on the drinks. She turned and started talking with the others.

Here they came, seven Mexican women, two Indian women and Margarite and Matty – each carrying a tray with cups and bottles of liquor and beer. Placing them on the long table and side tables.

"Men," Adkin yelled. "Men, please. May I have your attention. Please help yourselves to refreshments. We would like to propose a toast."

The buzz in the air got louder as bottles were being passed around and cups were being filled. It didn't take long until everybody had a cup of something in their hand.

Adkin noticed Matty was back on watch at the kitchen door. He smiled and winked at her. She smiled back and made a small gesture with her hand. This had been rehearsed for days, and she was excited to help put it together.

"I want to toast a man who had a vision. A man who then put his vision into plans and action," Adkin said loudly. "A man who was responsible for making Barlow and Sanderson Company a successful operation throughout this Frontier.

"I honor him as a friend – as most of you do – and I toast him – Mister Jared L. Sanderson – the Stagecoach King of the West."

Many said, "Here. Here," and everybody turned their cups up and slammed down the contents. Then a big roar went off in the room with hoorays and howls of adoration.

Sanderson looked to his three explorers and saluted them with a raised cup, and then downed his shot of brandy.

After the clapping and salutations, Sanderson held up both arms, as Matty crept up to his side and refilled his cup with brandy. He quickly gave her a nod and smiled.

"Men – and ladies of our family, too – I have some news I think you'll find inspiring and make you feel hopeful of your involvement with Barlow and Sanderson," he began. "First, we will be opening up routes in northern Colorado, Wyoming and Nebraska by early 1871."

Several interrupted his speech with clapping and hooting.

"Okay, okay. Let me continue," he said. "The six Concords we rolled up in will be dispersed as follows: Two in northern New Mexico, one at Fort Garland, one in Leadville, and two for the Denver area. Most of these will be providing supplies to miners and, of course, end-of-the-line customers wanting to get into the hinterlands."

Again clapping and murmuring.

"We have also shipped three more Concords with horses via rail to Cheyenne, Wyoming," he said. "The railroad got to Cheyenne a few years back, and we envision great growth out of that area. "We'll pick them up after we make our way to Denver.

"Plus, we are doing well in California, and have expansion plans out there for 1872 or '73." depending," he added with a chuckle. "But now, I want to let y'all know how much we have expanded, and I think the numbers will be a surprise to most of you.

"Two weeks ago, we bought out the Denver and Santa Fe Stage Line and renamed it the Southern Overland Mail and Express," he said, while several murmurs were heard. "And we're in the process of moving our headquarters to Denver."

Several started clapping, but J.L. continued.

"So, as of July 31, 1870, there are 350 men, and some fine women, working for Barlow and Sanderson nationwide," Sanderson said, and again, he was interrupted by applause. "Wait a minute, I have more."

"We, as a company have 289 stagecoaches now in service or on order, and 98 percent are Concords, the finest made, and we own around 2,400 horses – and some of the finest horseflesh around, too," he continued. "And, for 1869, we brought in a total gross sum of $380,000 in goods and services, including from our 65 national mail contracts."

All the men went wild, clapping and hollering. Adkin was afraid someone might start shooting holes through the roof with their pistols. Sanderson held up both arms again, quieting them.

"Men. Men. The good news is we're projecting a gross revenue of $500,000 for this year – we're well on our way," he said. "And, and, with our current expansion plans for the next three years, we're planning on doubling that – we're shooting for an annual revenue of $1 million by the end of 1873."

Another roar tore through the mess hall and bunkhouse. Even Adkin was shouting and clapping. He looked at Ryan and Ray Dee and just shook his head in disbelief. Adkin knew the company was doing well, but he and the others had no idea it was growing like this.

"Men, I want you to know how much we appreciate everyone's efforts," Sanderson said. "So now, how about another drink? And get to know everybody in your family that works out of this location – that's an order. Okay?"

There were no objections, especially having another drink. Matty and the women carried some bottles around the tables, looking for any that were empty. They placed a couple bottles down nearly empty.

Then Adkin took to the soapbox.

"Men, could I have your attention for just a moment?" he shouted above the chit-chat. "We will be serving supper a little early this evening – due to all the travelling that is still needed and early departures tomorrow morning.

"So, please meet back here at 6, and don't drink too much – there's a lot of work ahead of all of us," he said, laughing and knowing it meant nothing to these men. "We're going to show J.L. our new yard here in Las Animas City, and anyone else that wants to tour with us is welcome."

As they gathered, Ryan led them out the west end and down the steps.

493

"What do you want to see first, J.L.?" Ryan asked.

"All of it, but let's see the stables and the corral first – you know me, I'm an animal man, they're are our bread and butter so to speak."

They showed Sanderson the stables, a long row that could easily hold 30 head, and the attached tack room was large, with all kinds of equipment, including the $100-harnesses for a four- to eight-horse stagecoach team.

The corrals were behind the stables, with gates on three sides, making for easy movement of herds. There were also two large feed bins, one on each side, and the horses they had brought in were mouthing wads of fresh forage.

That's when Sanderson saw several men turning a large beef quarter on the roasting spit behind the kitchen.

"That's one way to cook for a crowd," he said, chuckling.

On the back side of the stable, between the corral and feed barn where forage and grain was stored sat the blacksmith shop, featuring one of Adkin's revolutionary two ended anvils.

Sanderson rubbed his hands along the anvil and looked to Adkin.

"Reminds me when I was a youngster in Vermont growing up," he said, smiling. "What about you, Yates?"

"Yes sir. My father was pounding on one as long as I can remember," Adkin said.

They had to walk back to the east side of the mess hall, where the bunkhouse and dormitory rooms were housed. There were enough rooms and cots, with complete sets of blankets, to sleep 30 men, though they were not needed, as yet.

Sanderson was impressed.

"Now I know where all those spending requests were going," he laughed. "You men now, if you need more help, hire them. But make sure you hire men that will be an asset, not a liability.

"And I know you do that, it's just a reminder," he added chuckling.

They then walked back to the office. Sanderson said he would like to meet individually with each one in private.

"How about I start with Adkin, first, if that's okay with y'all?" Sanderson said to Ryan and Ray Dee.

"Sure, Boss," Ray Dee said. "We'll be in the mess hall."

"I'll have Adkin send for Ryan when we're through here," he said. "And then you, Ray Dee."

Once their boot steps walked off the porch, Sanderson asked Adkin to detail his desire to build a house for Matty. Adkin told him about the place, that it was where Satanta's band often stayed in the early spring before the buffalo started migrating north.

"I was wanting to take a seven- to eight-month leave of absence – and without salary, of course – to build it and spend the summer in it with Matty," Adkin said.

An Englishman's Adventures on the Santa Fe Trail (1865-1889)

"Adkin, I don't care about the salary part. I just wanted to hear your reasoning, and I'm worried if you will be safe – just the two of you on the Cimarron all by yourselves?" Sanderson said.

"I feel good about it," Adkin said. "I'm Kiowa family now, and Satanta carries a lot of weight with all the other bands in that area, even with the Comanches. I don't think they will bother us. We plan on painting the sign of the Kiowa on our front door."

'Well, that's all I had," Sanderson said. "Oh, sorry, one other question about this. Do you feel the others can handle things while you're gone? You know, spending, handling the men, all the management decisions?"

"That's why I thought about this," Adkin said. "Ryan and I were on that trek with Rath and Goodnight for eight weeks, and they didn't miss a step here. That squat little German may be half crazy at times, but Ray Dee can manage, and Peg-Leg Pete is a mastermind of organization.

"Do you know he writes down everything that happens each and every day – but he waits til before bed to write it all down?" Adkin said, laughing. "They can handle it, J.L., and I'm very proud of that.

"Plus, we'll come back in the fall, and I can help ensure all the new routes are running smooth," Adkin said. "You know me, I love to travel – just like you."

"Well, you have my permission to take leave, but I'll keep you on the payroll if you don't mind," Sanderson said, laughing. "I wouldn't want you to think you were free to take another offer if you get one out there – and who knows.

"Now, about your financial situation with the company," he said. "You've been using most your salary to invest – and your gains on stock are being re-invested as well.

"I think you may be interested to know you have $41,950 available as of October 1 this year," he said with a crafty smile. "You're a wealthy young man, Adkin Yates. And I have a suggestion on how to purchase the materials for a new house."

Adkin just sat there a moment, and slowly let out a soft sigh.

"That's a lot of money J.L.," he said, doing some mental math, what with his share of YR&R Freight sitting at about $30,000 as of last week. He grinned at Sanderson, realizing he was somewhat of a wealthy man.

"You're full of great news today, J.L. What is your suggestion?

"Well, how much are you planning on spending," Sanderson asked.

"I'm not sure what it will cost, but I was thinking $2,000 would cover everything," he said, explaining all the materials will have to come from Fort Dodge or sent into Dodge. It's not going to be fancy.

"I was planning on asking some friends in Dodge to help and haul it down and help us build it," Adkin said. "It could cost more, or less. I'm not sure."

Sanderson interjected, "Just pull out $1,500 from our account, and we'll send it immediately. I'll send the telegrams with orders. Then if you need more, you or a friend just has to telegraph our headquarters again for more – whatever you need will be wired to Fort Dodge.

"Now here's what I offer," he continued. "We'll write it up as a loan, and the interest your earning on the stock and re-investment income that's also coming in will then cover the loan amount. Then it goes back into you buying more stock."

"That's great, J.L., where do I sign?"

"Just shake my hand Adkin, that's always been good enough for me," Sanderson said as the two shook hands. "I'll send the orders first thing in the morning before we head out."

"I hope nothing but the best for you and Matty," Sanderson added. "Now go fetch Ryan for me, okay?"

'Thank you J.L.," Adkin said as he went out the door.

As he was walking to the mess hall, Adkin's earlier feelings about how Sanderson dealt with his partners was all on an individual basis.

"What a man," Adkin thought to himself, as he openly smiled. "God blessed me that day in St. Louis when I left the boat after knocking that German mechanic over the rail and into the Mississippi."

•••

When everybody gathered back at the mess hall – where several seemed to have stayed the entire afternoon to Adkin – the women were laying out plates and utensils. They were also putting out clay ewers of water.

Matty saw Adkin come in and waved and smiled. He smiled but headed straight to her. She looked surprised as he stopped right in front of her. He bent over and kissed her and wrapped his arms around her. It was brief, but Matty was beaming.

"Guess he wants some of those yahoos to know Matty is his woman," Sanderson said, laughing. "That pretty well lets everybody know – even those who aren't here yet."

Once it seemed all had gathered, Sanderson once again, thanked everyone, and said despite their overall success, it wasn't a guarantee for future growth unless every single person did their job, and backed up every man in the company when needed.

The applause was still loud. Adkin was impressed how Sanderson could build self-esteem in people. Sanderson was indeed a superb businessman.

Adkin waved to the women to bring in the meal, and four men entered first with huge trays and platters of roasted beef. The men oohed and aahed as the women were right behind with vegetables of all kinds. Adkin was worried if their vegetable bin would make it through the winter.

Ryan and Ray Dee seemed happy and were constantly laughing and teasing everybody. Adkin figured they had received good news from Sanderson of newfound wealth as well. He was happy for them, they deserved it.

As the sky was brightening the next morning, Sanderson asked Adkin to take him to the Western Union Office, which was only about a mile way. Sanderson jumped on one of the saddled horses at the rail.

"That's okay, you horse thief," Ryan shouted. "Just as long as you bring him back, we won't send out a posse."

Sanderson waved as he took off with Adkin on Diablo.

They arrived just as the clerk was keying the lock on the office door, and he laughed.

"Must have a message burning a hole in your pocket," he said, as the door swung open.

Sanderson handed him a sheet of paper, and ask what was the cost. The clerk said it was pretty long, and after several minutes he spoke up and Sanderson shook a few coins out of a leather pouch and thanked the man.

"Please get it off as soon as you can warm that thing up," Sanderson said, giggling. "And don't worry or wait for a reply, it's not coming."

Back at the yard, Sanderson crawled up on the driver's seat of the front Concord. He looked back at Peg-Leg Pete.

"Are you ready Sanpete? he hollered. "You haven't forgotten how to handle a team, have you?"

"I can handle any team on the Frontier, Boss," Sanpete barked back. "You just don't lollygag around or you might get run over."

Everybody laughed, Sanderson waved to those on the porch, including Matty and Margarite. Adkin told Peg-Leg to be careful and to come back.

"Don't let J.L. talk you into gong into the badlands through Wyoming," Adkin yelled.

Peg-Leg had asked them after the meal to take one of the Concords to Leadville. He had heard Leadville was located in one of the most beautiful mountain ranges in Colorado. He wanted to see it.

But Sanpete's desire would require at least three other men and horses to tag along so they could make it back in some small force of security. Fortunately, Don Diego and Fransisco and another teamster volunteered for the adventure.

The journey should only require them to be gone about four to five weeks. Sanderson had teased Peg-Leg that there was no bonus pay to drive a Concord.

"Boss, I'll pay you. How much you need?" Sanpete said, which busted up Sanderson, who just shook his head.

"We might need to get him out on the trail a few more times during the year. What do you think?" Ryan said to Adkin and Ray Dee, who both agreed.

497

That evening, Adkin thanked Matty for all her efforts and leadership for handling the kitchen staff and men helping with roasting the meat and managing the fire pit.

"I good chef?" Matty asked Adkin as they lay between the soft furs in their feather bed. "I like the word chef – Margarite tell me what it mean."

"No, you are Great Chief," Adkin said, making the sign of chief: Holding his right hand at his side pointing upwards, and raising his hand in gradual circle as high as the top of his head, then arching toward his front and downward.

"Okay, Great Chief," she said giggling. Then she kissed her man, and he kissed her back feeling the warmth of true love in his heart.

...

The next morning, Adkin told Matty what he wanted to do at their spiritual place on the Cimarron. He took a piece of paper and a pen and started drawing what he envisioned.

"I want to build a rock fireplace, back here where the old fire pit has been for years," he said, making a circle near the back of the cliff, which is mostly protected from the winds. The cliffs come together at the back at nearly 15 feet or so and at about a 45 degree angle. Each cliff falls off in height to the ground within about 20 yards or so.

He explained they would use rocks to build the fireplace and flue. He then drew out that end of the house as a triangle, where they would use planks to come out from the fireplace and then they would push and shovel earth between the cliffs and wood. That would come out where the width of the house would be 30-feet wide.

From there they would come straight out another 30 feet, with a 15-feet bedroom corner walled off for privacy coming off the front wall, near the front door and entryway. The other space would include a pot-bellied stove that could also be used for cooking, as well as the fireplace area.

Then a living area around the stove and into the kitchen and food pantry areas. Matty just sat there, not saying a word. Her eyes would dart back and forth, as he drew. She looked concerned.

"Is something wrong, Matty, something you don't like or want?" he asked.

"She looked up and started smiling.

"No, my husband," She said with smiling eyes. But this is all for me and you?"

"Yes, my wife, just for you and me," he answered.

"We live there forever?" she asked.

"No, not yet," he said, knowing this was going to be complicated to explain.

"We will stay maybe eight moons – months," he said. "And then we come back here to Las Animas for winter."

"Oh, that okay. I would miss my friends here and my job. Good to come back and be with them."

He just chuckled to himself – her "job" that she loved to say after hearing Adkin and Ryan talking about her chores. It worried Adkin because he thought she worked too much. She had heard Adkin say, "That's not her job." Then later, she told him in no uncertain terms that the chores and her involvement was her "job."

Adkin was at first surprised she wouldn't be staying in the new house forever, but then he remembered she had been raised in a nomadic lifestyle where, there was never a "forever" place – except the Kiowa lived under the open skies "forever."

With plans sketched out, Adkin began calculating needed board footage, a door, four windows, stove, table, chairs – then he realized he was not a stonemason. How much rock would be needed to build the fireplace 15-feet tall.

He decided once he determined its size with a base big enough to have cooking grills and pot holders that swing in and out over the embers, the flue size, squared and its height, he could telegraph Hoo Doo Brown and ask for his advice.

That reminded him he would need to contact Hoo Doo to see if he would help organize this project from the Fort Dodge location. Adkin decided to telegraph him the next day to see if Hoo Doo would be available and would like to participate.

He could then proceed with calculations on rock, mortar, boards, roofing and all the other things that came to mind. He was finding out, the more he thought about it, the more details came up. He was constantly writing down items that would be needed, leaving bits of paper all over, which Ryan, Ray Dee and Matty would gather up and return to Adkin.

Adkin's first message to Brown was answered the following day. Hoo Doo said he would consider it an honor to help Adkin and his wife. He said he also talked with George Reighard, Henry L. Sitler and Charley Bassett – and they would help with the build, too.

Brown said Bassett was a man of all trades, and was a pretty fair rock mason. Sitler, according to Brown, was a good carpenter and design engineer. He also assured Adkin if any other business called one or more men away from the project, he could find more help.

He also said Bassett mentioned he had seen two possible places for limestone and flint slate. One was along a small artesian well on upper Crooked Creek. The other was further east along the Cimarron where Bluff Creek enters the Cimarron.

"Hoo Doo assures us we can find enough rock to build our fireplace," Adkin mentioned to Matty, who suddenly took an interest.

"Yes, there are rock cliffs near Bluff Creek – we find mucho, mucho rocks there," she said smiling, not realizing she threw some of her Spanish into her sentence.

...

Plans for the Cimarron House, as it came to be known by the crew at the yard, we're going along well. Brown had told Adkin he had found a source of good and cheap wood near Fort Zarah, which had been abandoned by the Army in '69.

Brown reported to Adkin there was a buffalo hunter that lived west of Fort Zarah who would mill wood on order at a very reasonable price, but he didn't carry much inventory. Brown said his name was Weldon Campbell, a former Lieutenant with the New Mexico Volunteers of the U.S. Army. And he owned a small sawmill.

Adkin thought the name familiar and asked Ryan about it. Ryan thought a moment, and then his eyes flew open.

"Lieutenant Weldon Campbell worked for Captain Pettis with the military escort protecting the telegraph linemen east of Bent's Fort," Ryan said. "Remember, we were travelling with Bent and Colonel Carson when we rode up on all those workers and the Army escort?"

"That's right, he came out to meet us – Carson and Bent knew him, too," Adkin said. "Well, apparently, he's got a small sawmill on the Arkansas River at the Great Bend in the river."

"I'll only say one thing," Ryan began. "If he served under Pettis and was friends with Carson and Bent – you can't go wrong doing business with him."

"That's the truth," Adkin said while grinning.

He decided to get word to Brown, since it was mid-November, and have Hoo Doo tell Campbell Adkin would be wanting to order enough board-feet to build a 30-foot by 40-foot house with two-and-a-half rooms within. And with a gabled roof and ceiling timbers, which could be procured at the site.

Adkin figured with the back area of the house an actual triangle, he would have more than enough lumber to do what he envisioned.

And the walls were to be at least 8-feet high, as Adkin always had trouble with buildings, houses and soddys with 6-feet ceilings. He wasn't going to be bending over in his own house.

Adkin instructed Brown he wanted Campbell to know who was ordering the wood, and that: "Adkin was with Colonels Carson and Bent when Campbell was a Lieutenant with Captain Pettis when the Army was escorting Western Union workers on the telegraph line east of Bent's Fort."

Adkin also said he would send a downpayment on February 1, 1871, to have all the lumber cut and ready to haul off around March 30, if Campbell needed finances to help get the timber gathered and milled.

Brown agreed to contact Campbell and send the message, adding he thought Adkin was a little too generous – fearing this man may run off with the downpayment, as the Great Bend area was mainly just a small village full of buffalo hunters that lived near the fort there.

Adkin couldn't help but laugh at Brown's worries, after all, he was scouting buffalo herds for he and others to hunt for Charley Rath. Adkin told Ryan maybe buffalo hunters were a better breed of men in Fort Dodge than at Great Bend. They both howled with laughter.

"But I would wager they both smell the same," Ryan said, eliciting even more laughter.

Within a couple of weeks, Brown telegraphed Adkin saying Campbell didn't require a downpayment or a deposit. He would have the board-feet, framing boards, roof rafters, etc., ready by March 30.

And to Brown's amazement, Campbell wanted to know if it was possible he could come down with the loads and help build Adkin and Matty's new house?

"With Campbell's cost estimates and Brown's estimates, Adkin realized he was over budget and not one piece of wood was at the location, yet. He knew he was gong to have to have Sanderson send at least $3,000 to Fort Dodge come March.

•••

Not much happened during the winter of 1870-'71 – good or bad. There was only two real snow storms, but they were not major blizzards that killed stock and wildlife, like elk, antelope or deer.

Sanpete and Don Diego and Fransisco returned from Leadville. Seems Peg-Leg was accosted by a dance hall woman named Frenchy – that's how he put it, anyway.

Don Diego and Fransisco said the woman fell in love with Sanpete because he could still dance well with a peg-leg.

They all laughed while Sanpete turned red with embarrassment.

"What can I say? Some women find me adorable, that's what Frenchy says."

They were hooting and howling now, repeating "Adorable?" and "I love you Frenchy."

"I had a good time. Thank you for letting me go to Leadville," Sanpete said, smiling from ear-to-ear. "It is a beautiful place."

"And a beautiful Frenchy, eh?" Don Diego said, still laughing.

•••

The stagecoach and freighting slowed down to nearly nothing that winter, like most winters. Settlers didn't want to travel in small numbers along the Santa Fe Trail, especially without military escorts.

No major Indian depredations were reported either, which made everyone feel safer. Of course, being on the edge of Las Animas City and Boggsvile four miles south, gave Adkin a lot more sense of security than when they were between Fort Lyon and Bent's Fort.

Margarite announced she and Dusty were going to have a baby in July. Two other wives of the hands were pregnant, too. Adkin felt like their yard had turned into its own little city. He was glad Las Animas had a school and a church, lest he and the other partners would have to build them to handle just their business family.

Matty continued to find time for her bead work and sewing. She had talked several of the men who ran trap lines west along the Arkansas to sell her otter, beaver, marten and mink skins, that she cured to perfection. She used them as linings, or ruff around collars on hoods even vests for ladies and men.

Adkin realized this woman could do anything she put her mind to. Then he'd laugh at himself, remembering most of the great men he knew or had met on the Frontier had Indian wives.

"That's because those men were smart," he liked to think to himself. He believed his Matty was the mot remarkable woman he could have ever met.

It was along those thoughts that Adkin had decided that winter, to write down everything he could remember about what his life had been like from the day he departed England on The Euterpe. He had some diary notes hidden somewhere, but he wanted a more detailed daily diary whenever possible.

He also wanted something for his family back in England to know, for he seldom wrote home any more, and that bothered him.

It was a battle at times trying to remember some of his true feelings he experienced in his travels – like when he was sitting on a bench in Jackson Square in New Orleans, having just celebrated his 19th birthday and enjoying the morning sun on a sky-blue day and finding out his steamer to St. Louis had come into port.

He found himself writing a lot after supper and sometimes he sensed it bothered Matty, as she was always wanting his attention when either he was working or busy with projects. He realized she didn't think writing was a project at all.

So he tried to keep his scribbling hidden from her when he could, like when she was sewing or tanning hides. As he wrote, he decided once he got to the current winter, he was going to be like Goodnight, a man who recorded every day's business and memories. Peg-Leg Pete was an inspiration, too.

By the end of January, he had filled two hard-cover log books of his memoirs, and he kept them on the top shelf of their tiny kitchen, far above Matty's reach, though he knew she couldn't read, just to keep them out of anyone's accidental view. He had also found some notes stashed away in an old trunk of his belongings that they had brought from the old yard. He edited them and added them to his collections of thoughts.

In late February, Adkin fired off telegrams to Hoo Doo Brown and Sanderson's office requesting the money be wired to his name at Fort Dodge on March 10, the day he and Matty planned on departing for Dodge themselves.

When Uribe found out the exact date Adkin and Matty would be leaving, he approached Adkin and Ryan together at the office.

"Señors, I have grande problema to discuss with you," Uribe said, looking sad. "When Adkin and Miss Matty leave, I will have no more sourdough biscuits or bread. What am I to do? I may not be able to live without Miss Matty's biscuits and bread."

Ryan had a startled frown on his face, as if he was pondering if Uribe was sane or what. Adkin couldn't keep a straight face. He immediately burst out laughing.

"But Señors, you don't want me to die, no?" Uribe said.

Then Ryan caught on and started laughing as well.

"Oh, Uribe," Adkin said, while catching his breath. "Why can't you just say, 'Can I go with you to help build your new house?'"

Ryan was howling now, wheezing almost.

"I don't want your death on my hands, Uribe," Ryan finally said, between coughs. "You best go with Señor Adkin and Miss Matty. Don't you agree Adkin?"

"By all means," Adkin said. "We're leaving on March 10, Uribe, so be ready."

"I know, Señor, and I'm already packed," he said grinning like a cat that had cached its dead mouse. He quickly turned and walked out the door while Adkin and Ryan were still laughing.

On March 9, Adkin received a telegram from the young quartermaster, a Lieutenant Hamm, who had received word Adkin and Matty would be travelling through Bent's Fort on the evening of March 10, and he asked Adkin if it was okay if he could send 10 calvary troopers to escort Adkin to Fort Dodge?

"He said word had travelled along the Santa Fe Trail about our new house, and he wants to escort us to Dodge," Adkin told the guys in the office. "I can't believe how gossip gets carried all across this country. Wouldn't surprise me if it was published in the Kansas Weekly Herald newspaper in Leavenworth."

The men started laughing, asking Adkin why he was surprised?

"You told every blabbermouth in the country from here to Dodge to Great Bend to Junction City," Ray Dee said. "What do you expect?"

Once Adkin started chuckling at himself, he decided is was a very kind and generous offer. He really did appreciate it, especially considering Matty would be with him. He wouldn't be able to live with himself if something harmful happened to her.

He sent a telegram to Lieutenant Hamm the morning of the 10th saying they would be there that night and thanked him for – and accepted – his generous offer.

∙∙∙

The trip to Bent's Fort was uneventful. Uribe rode horseback with two other hands from the yard, while Adkin and Matty rode in a freight wagon mostly full of extra tools, clothing and Matty's things, which included her large box of beads and sewing supplies.

The two other men would return to Las Animas City after the Army put on an escort at Bent's Fort.

Diablo and a roan mare Matty called Tóngúl, which was Kiowa for Swift Red Hawk, were tethered to the back of the wagon. Tóngúl had a long red tail and mane, and the horse was very fast. Matty loved the mare, and it was a gift from the Prowers family in Boggsville – actually from Amache Prowers.

Both horses were saddled, and Matty's travelling buckskin dress had front and back slits which would allow her to mount Tóngúl very quickly. A string of three other horses were being towed also – for the trip south out of Fort Dodge.

Campbell had estimated back in February it would take six wagons to haul his milled materials south. Adkin had left word for Tom Marcellus at Fort Dodge, to hold back six wagons for the building materials, and to line up teams and teamsters to go get the wood March 10 in Great Bend.

It took about wo weeks for Tom to return a telegram that he had it covered. They had actually just finished their last Army order, and he would personally pick up the wood. They were scheduled to get back to Dodge by March 15.

Hoo Doo Brown was waiting for them when they pulled into Fort Dodge on March 15, He was accompanied by Sitler, Reighard and Basset.

As Adkin jumped off the wagon, he was warmly greeted by the Dodge men. He then went around and helped Matty down and introduced them to her. They each took off their hats, and shook her hand. Adkin could tell she was in awe. She was thinking it was because her husband was like a chief among White Men – he was treated very well by all she had met while with Adkin.

Hoo Doo led them to an office that Sitler had established. Sitler was convinced the little community cropping up west of Fort Dodge would one day be a city, if he had anything to do with it. Brown said Sitler was building a nice frame house just west of the community of Dodge, as some were already calling it.

After a few drinks and some cold food, a man came running in yelling for Mister Brown. He said a big man with seven wagons of building materials was looking for Brown.

"That's your man, Marcellus, I would wager," Brown said to Adkin. "I met with him several times before he took off for Great Bend. He's a mountain of a man."

They went outside and could see Tom about 200 yards down the roadway. Both Brown and Adkin ran out in the middle and started waving their arms and yelling, "Tom" and "Marcellus" almost simultaneous.

He saw them and snapped the reins on his team. He pulled up and yelled his greetings as he jumped from the wagon. After nearly breaking Adkin's ribs, he walked immediately to Matty and shook her hand.

"It makes my heart feel good to see you again, Missus Yates," he said, with his hat in his other huge paw. She reached out her hand.

"So good to see you, Meester Tom," she said, just beaming. She looked like a small doe shaking hands with a bent over grizzly bear.

As Tom met with Uribe, and shook hands with the Dodge men, including Bassett, whom he had yet to meet, Weldon Campbell walked up to Adkin.

"Mister Yates, I'm ..."

"Lieutenant Campbell," Adkin interrupted, as he grabbed Campbell's hand. "My it's good to see you again – it's been a few years – are you faring well?"

"Yes sir, I am," Campbell said. "I couldn't believe it when I got word from Mister Brown you were wanting to have me mill lumber for you."

"Well, when we heard your name, it was like a blessing that we could re-connect with you," Adkin said, as he turned Campbell to Matty. "And please, Weldon, call me Adkin."

He introduced Matty and told her this was the man who cut every board they would use in their new home. She was tickled and started asking Campbell questions, like wanting to know if he was still planning to "help put the lodge together?"

After all the introductions, they all squeezed into Sitler's office again. Tom explained he took seven wagons to Great Bend, since he had extras, and he was glad he did.

"Weldon here is a very talented man," Marcellus said. "Wait until you see his work, and the fact it came from a small rough-cut mill with a steam engine spinning those belts. He brought a lot of his tools, too."

"I can't wait," Adkin said. "Hoo Doo, what's next?"

"Well, we've got three more wagons lined up from Tom that Bassett is going to use to haul rock," Brown said. "He's going to head off to Bluff Creek with his men – and some of your hands that Tom's been working with – and load up flint shale and bring it upstream to your place.

"We'll go straight on down and by the time we unload the lumber, establish a camp and corral, Bassett should show up with the rock," Brown said. "Sitler here is convinced we should build the fireplace and chimney first, then we can construct the house, as y'all want it, anchored to it."

"I agree wholeheartedly," Adkin said. "Now we just need to get a good meal in us and a good night's sleep."

Brown and Reighard had lined up a meal in the back of a "hotel" that had somewhat of a questionable reputation, but the food was good.

Sleeping accommodations were in two different places, but Adkin and Matty chose to sleep in their wagon, which they covered with a tarp, and it contained plenty of soft furs and buffalo hides.

•••

At daybreak, March 16, they all headed south across the bridge over the Arkansas River heading to Mulberry Creek. After the crossing, Bassett and his crew turned southeast along the Arkansas before heading south to intersect Bluff Creek.

Adkin and Brown and their crews headed southwest. They would hit Crooked Creek in about 15 miles and follow it until it dumped into the Cimarron. Then it was back upstream about six to eight miles to Adkin and Matty's site.

Adkin was impressed with Brown's arrangements. There were 10 wagons, two were Brown's supplies and tents for the camp. There were three pack mules, mainly loaded down with food and drink, according to Brown who winked when he said, "Drink."

There were 15 men – armed men, Adkin noticed – and about 20-plus horses. This didn't include Bassett and his crew of three wagons, a pack mule and six men and horses.

If the weather held steady, they may be able to build this house in a month with this many people, thought Adkin. And warm southwesterly winds were helping their plans.

They should reach the site early on their third day, and Adkin was starting to get really excited. It had been fun planning and organizing everything for months, but now that he was only a few days from their special place – the Cimarron House," he was thrilled.

That first night, Matty was helped by Brown and Tom in preparing food for everyone. It wasn't fancy, but they got some hot food in them – soup thickened with flour, with buffalo meat, potatoes and onions in it.

The men talked, getting to know each other better and re-acquainting old friendships. Campbell was excited meeting the Dodge men and discovering they, too, were planning on cashing in on buffalo hunting.

Campbell was able to tell them about his scouting for the herds up in the Great Bend area of the Arkansas River, while the Dodge men told him about the Texas Panhandle and the Llano Estacado.

He was fascinated with their stories of a land he had yet been able to explore, just as Adkin had been last fall. He had also heard tales from Pettis when Pettis fought with Colonel Carson at Adobe Walls.

"Of course, you know, Adkin, this place you're building is going to be used by every outlaw or settler or band of Indians that comes along," Brown said. "If you're not here in the winter, it's open house."

"I know Hoo Doo, and we're prepared for that," Adkin said. "And we know the law of the Frontier – my place is your place. We hope people will take care of it because it will be a haven for getting out of the snow and ice, or to hole up for long enough to get well if they're injured.

"The only thing we're going to do is paint two signs on the front porch," he continued. "One will be the sign of the Kiowa, and the other will be the sign of the Comanche – with 'welcome' on each. Matty has already drawn them for me, and she will paint them on our place.

"We also plan on leaving a book – for those who can read English – welcoming settlers or soldiers, anyone travelling, to our shelter – and who we are – and ask them to sign the book and tell us a little about themselves," Adkin said. "We plan on telling them they're welcome to everything, and if possible, to replace what they use at a later date – when they can.

"That's the way of the Frontier, and we plan to live by that," he added, with a smile.

"You're right, and it looks like you and Matty know exactly what you're doing," Brown said. "And I have great respect for that, Adkin Yates – great respect."

•••

On March 18, a little before noon, Adkin and Matty recognized where they were, and Matty kicked Tóngúl into a lope. She had told Adkin that morning she wanted to ride Tóngúl since it was only a few miles to their spiritual place.

As she took off, her braids flew up behind her small head and she waved Adkin onward, grinning and giggling. Within about a half mile, they reined up where the little creek had etched its way from the bluffed ravine and down into the Cimarron River.

The grasses were greening – the blue stem already a bright blueish green – and a few wildflowers were budding – and many of the trees were already sprouting tiny new leaves.

Both slid off their mounts and Adkin put his arm around Matty as they took in the landscape.

"Oh my husband, I am very happy we are here again," Matty said, as she turned and stood up on her toes and kissed him on the cheek. He turned and kissed her and picked her up in his arms.

"And I will know my father's spirit lives in this valley near me," she said.

"This will forever be our spiritual place, Mah-aht-tay," he said as he put her back on the ground.

They turned when they heard the men shouting at their teams as they came rolling upon the site.

"I'll be damned," Brown said. "I've been all over this country, and I never came across this place. It is absolutely beautiful. It is very fitting for you, Adkin – and your Matty."

As men were dismounting or unloading from the wagons, they were in awe of this break in the seemingly table-top landscape dropping into this wide, but shallow valley. How it just sank into the triangular ravine with trees and brush up and down the river and up the small creek bed.

Sitler also said he had travelled the area and never knew of this particular place. The others echoed their surprise. Adkin and Matty walked up into the ravine by the bluff where the Kiowa had camped for years.

"The elders' fire pit is still here," Matty said, remembering her childhood days with her father and mother. The old ashess were still surrounded by even older stones, that had probably been laid there a century before and used by the travellers over time, regardless of culture or race.

"That is where we will build a big rock fireplace, and the Kiowa are still welcome to come in winter and warm themselves from the cold, brutal winds," Adkin said.

Matty just smiled and put her arms around his waist and squeezed hard.

"This is quite the place, Yates," Sitler said. "I couldn't quite visualize what your plans were when you told us, but it makes sense now, seeing how the bluffs drop right off into this ravine and the little creek over there."

"I can see it, too," Campbell said. "I didn't understand the triangle part, but it's perfect for this site."

Campbell and Sitler started deciding where to start unloading lumber. Campbell suggested it would be more efficient if they made two piles, one on each side of the build – one for framing and siding, the other for windows, porch and roofing.

It wasn't long that men were unloading planks, and assorted lumber, Campbell supervising which went where. He walked off 20 paces off each angle from the old fire pit and drove stakes in the ground and tied off small strips of ribbons.

As evening neared, they stopped with the lumber and tools and set up two large tents down near the Cimarron in deep blue-stem grass. The tents were affixed to each other to make a large enclosure.

Tom helped with the small heating and cooking stove. He was the only one who could wrap his arms around it and heft it easily upon his chest and carry it like a baby to the tent.

As they began making plans for supper, they were still looking for Bassett and his wagons. Brown said it may have taken longer than half a day to load up enough flint rock to fill the wagons.

That evening, they ate well and made detailed plans for construction, Campbell and Sitler studied Adkin's drawings and plans for the house, each discussing the best means for accomplishing Adkin's goals.

The first thing they agreed on was the living area needed to be adjacent to the fireplace in the rear triangle, then make the hallway area, which would be wide, the kitchen and dining area with the entryway off the side of a big bedroom.

"If we do it like this, it will give more room for extra visitors to place bedrolls here around the pot-bellied cooking stove," Campbell said.

"And it would even allow room for bedrolls off the entryway room – close to heat in the winter," Sitler said. "We could build a woodbox right here by the stove for easy stoking during the night."

"I agree – good ideas," Adkin said. "We'll stake off the exact exterior and interior sections tomorrow."

•••

That night after their meal, the wind picked up out of the north, and the men worried if the tents were going to stay upright. The temperature dropped very quick and dramatically. Adkin was worried, but he finally drifted off to sleep about 2 in the morning – the wind still howling.

When he awoke, only Reighard was up, and he was standing at the tent flaps, peeking through a small opening he had made. Adkin was initially glad the wind wasn't beating the sides of the tent, but there was a distinct chill in the air.

"Ya might wanna look at this, Adkin," Reighard said. "Might hamper Bassett's arrival some."

Adkin threw two pieces of wood into the stove and shuffled over to the tent flap. He opened the slit wider and and mumbled.

"Holy cow, wouldn't you know it," he sighed. "One more assault from Old Man Winter."

There was about 2-feet of snow covering the ground and everything else. On the south side of things were drifts as high as whatever it drifted around. Adkin could see a couple of wagons from his vantage point, and snow on the downwind side was as high as the wagons.

"I'll check the livestock," Reighard said with a crooked smile. "Might wanna wake everybody – we got some chores to do."

Several heard Adkin and Reighard talking and started waking and moving around under blankets and furs.

"We might want to get started men, Old Man Winter dropped a couple of feet of snow on us last night," Adkin said loudly.

"Snow?" Uribe said. "That's not right. What did we do wrong to anger mis Dios? Ay caramba."

People were grumbling, some asking where their clothes bag was.

"I need some more clothes," someone growled.

"Where's my boots?" another asked. "I knew I should have kept them on."

"Anyone making coffee?" came from under a buffalo hide.

Matty crawled out from under her and Adkin's robes and furs. Her eyes smiled at Adkin when she found him standing by the door. Her grin showed her flashing white teeth, and Adkin's heart skipped a beat just seeing her looking so young and alert with those large doe-sized eyes.

She grabbed a blanket from the pile and wrapped it around her shoulders. She immediately went to the stove where a water bag lay next to it and filled the coffee pot and a small pan with water. She placed both on the stove and added a couple of more pieces of wood, quickly snapping the fire box door closed.

She rummaged through the food box and found the coffee grounds and added them to the top seave and put it in the coffee pot. Then she started pulling out tin cups and a jug of molasses – her favorite additive to coffee. She also found the cigar box full of tea bags for Adkin. She put two of the small tea bags into the small pan of water heating up.

As men got bundled up, they headed out, some cussing, and they started helping Reigard with the livestock. They had been penned with lariats in the trees by the river, surrounded on two sides by sand plum bushes. The bushes' natural thorns protected the animals from most predators.

When Adkin got over to them, he noticed they had cleared the area fairly well by just constantly moving around, staying warm.

"We need to shovel and sweep the lumber piles," Adkin said, as Campbell walked up.

"I wish a hadn't rolled up the tarps I had over the lumber for hauling," Campbell said. "I had no idea."

"Don't worry, we'll get the snow cleared off. It's not that wet a snow," Adkin said, looking to the sky. "Look how clear it is, and it seems to be warming already."

"This strange snow storm is going to hold up Bassett," Brown said as he walked up. "Maybe we should send some men downstream and see if they can find them."

"That's a good idea, can you round up three or four men to saddle up and go looking for Bassett?" Adkin asked. "Tell them to take it easy on the horses, don't push them too hard."

"Got it," Brown said as he went looking for men fully dressed and up and out.

Tom walked up to Adkin shaking his head.

"You know, I met this old timer in Great Bend who came out here in the 1850s, travelling the Santa Fe Trail as a bullwhacker and teamster for years," Marcellus said. "When I told him where we were going with the lumber, he said don't be surprised if a March blizzard hits us.

"Seriously, he said every third to fifth year, just when everybody thinks spring is in the air, a March blizzard hits the Great Plains," he continued. "Dang it if he wasn't right."

...

The men cleared most of the snow off the two piles of building supplies, but Campbell suggested they not cover the wood with tarps.

"It'll be better if we let the sunlight and air dry it all out," he said. "Let's stack the lumber on the tarps, keep it off the mud."

Most of the work centered around the lumber supplies for the entire morning. A team was hitched to move a couple of wagons out of the way, and the men made several mentions it was getting warmer by the hour. Several shed their outer coats and put them back in the tents.

After a quick meal of cold jerky, dried buffalo, molasses and bread and coffee, one of the men who had took out shortly after daybreak looking for Bassett came riding back into camp along the same tracks he and three others made leaving.

"Bassett and his men are just about an hour away," he yelled as he walked up to Brown and Adkin. "They got caught in the winds yesterday evening and ended up camping about 10 miles downstream.

"They were as surprised as us this morning, but had made it about five miles when we found them," he continued. "Everybody is okay, and their teams are in good shape."

"Great. Thanks Dave," Brown said. "Get down and go get yourself some hot coffee. Matty has some food, too."

"Well, good news they're okay, and it sounds like we'll be getting our rock today," Adkin said.

"Yeah, but it's going to be a real muddy mess by tonight with this crazy weather," Brown said. "It's melting this snow faster than a spring rain disappears into a dry gulch.

"Trouble is this won't disappear, it will turn to mud," Brown added, chuckling. "Oink, oink."

"Well, we can stomp out the exterior dimensions and unload rock the rest of the day, and see where we are in the morning.

Around 3 in the afternoon, Bassett and his three wagons and men came into view along the north bank of the river. It proved lucky because most of the drifting was on the south side created by the north winds.

After greetings and discussing where to unload the rock, Campbell suggested they use more cover tarps be laid on the ground with the rocks then stacked on the tarps to keep them from sinking into the mud that was already forming in low spots.

While people were stirring around camp, Matty snuck up behind Adkin and slid her arms around his waist.

"Hello husband," she said softly. "I wish to show you something – a good omen from the snow."

He turned as she led him by the hand to where one of the wagons had been during the storm, but had been moved.

"See … the seeds of the plants and flowers are not dead," she said pointing at some plants that had been bent down to the ground.

He frowned, not knowing what she meant.

"Seeds not dead?" he asked.

"Yes, look," she said, reaching down and pulling out several plants with her hands. She pointed to the buds.

"See, not dead,"

"Oh, I see now, the seeds – Whites call them buds, where a leaf or flowers come out," he said, smiling and realizing she had feared the snow may have damaged the flora of the area. He gave her a hug.

"I see, our place will be beautiful again," he said. "It's not dead."

"The snow will make more flowers and grass," she said, hugging the big man with all her heart.

•••

After unloading rock, most of it flint and slate, Campbell estimated it may not be enough to build a 15-feet chimney off a 6-feet wide by 5-feet tall and 4-feet deep fireplace.

"But, If not, I noticed when we arrived, there is a lot of limestone rock along the top of the cliffs," Campbell said. "I'm sure we can supplement whatever we need from that.

"There's limestone outcroppings under that snow?" Bassett asked Adkin and Campbell.

"Yes, the tops of these cliffs are all limestone," Campbell said.

"That's the best news I've heard this trip," Bassett said. "If those cliffs are limestone outcroppings, then I'll wager there is plenty of crushed limestone along the walls of that creek bed under the snow over there."

"I would imagine," Adkin said.

"Well, we will use that limestone – I brought a hand-cranked rock crusher – and add some clay from the river bank, and we'll have some of the best mortar available anywhere," Bassett said. "I'll bet there's some gypsum in that sediment, too, and that makes it even better. This is great news."

•••

Matty made a large calderon of soup with chunks of buffalo and made her biscuits in a Dutch oven, much to the delight of the men – especially Uribe, who tried to bribe her to make him extra biscuits.

"I will bring you many furs and hides when I can," he pleaded, with her laughing but promising she would make him extras. But he could tell no one else. Of course, she immediately told Adkin when Uribe wasn't watching – and she was giggling the whole time.

Sitting around the stove, Adkin got to know a little more about the men who surrounded he and Matty.

Dave Mather was the one who returned to camp with news Bassett was okay and would arrive soon. Mather said he'd been wanting to talk with Adkin because of Adkin's English accent.

"I come from a family of seafaring kin in Massachusetts," Mather said. "And my ancestors were rugged English sailors of the Seven Seas. I've heard so many adventures from my family."

He asked Adkin if Adkin had ever heard of any sailors named Mathers in England. Adkin had to say no, explaining his families were Midlanders from central England – farmers, coachmen and blacksmiths.

Mather seemed to lose interest in further conversation and left to check on the livestock with Tom and Reighard.

"Dave's a good man – good with a rifle and a pistol, too – just a little quiet, though," Brown said. "I think he really wants to be a lawman, but I know he's proud to be from English stock. He's signed on to hunt buffalo with us when we get word from Charley Rath that he has the contracts in hand for meat for the Army."

Sitler had an interesting background, according to Brown.

"Sitler is originally from Pennsylvania, and he fought for the North. But he got captured and spent about six months in a Rebel prison before he was turned out," Brown said. "Then he spent time in the Solomon Valley near Salina, where he tried some farming but ended up hunting buffalo and other wild game.

"That brought him to Fort Dodge two years ago, and now he mostly hauls freight for a living," Brown continued. "He lives in a soddy in Dodge down by the river but is planning on a frame house west of town. He's wanting to get in on this buffalo hunting, too."

Adkin and Ryan had met George Reighard at Camp Supply. He was a freighter and continued working the Military Road supplying the camp for one of YR&R Freight's competitors, Lee & Reynolds.

Adkin never really considered the term "competitors" because the Army was hiring every wagon it could find, and they often worked together with other freighters and numerous teamsters, and wagon masters frequently worked back and forth with freighters. It was more like family than competitors.

Reighard ended up even doing some scouting for the Army with "Wild Bill" Hickock and Jack Stilwell, who got the 19th Kansas Volunteers lost on their initial trip to Camp Supply.

"He has that old Sharp's rifle and can knock down a buffalo bull at 700 to 800 yards every time," Brown said.

...

The next day, the snow was mostly melted and mud was now the new enemy, but the men managed to stake off and string the exterior dimensions. Bassett and his men started retrieving fine limestone gravel from the ravine, clay and sand from the bank of the Cimarron and begin mixing mortar.

With the third day, Basset had the base foundation of the fireplace, and Matty was excited.

"It is so big," she said, smiling and holding her hands together. "It will allow me to make big meals for our friends."

Corner posts and wall support posts were put in, and all hands then devoted time to the fireplace and chimney. Rock was placed, mortar mixed, and Bassett was atop finding decent-sized limestone rocks to fill places within the slate – it was much easier to use an axe or hatchet and shape the limestone.

On the forth day, Uribe came off the south cliff shouting, "Elk, elk, just over there."

In just a few moments, Uribe and Reighard were mounted and riding off upstream along the river. Adkin watched them turn right and head up the slope of the valley until they were out of sight. Within about five minutes, three shots were heard. Adkin knew there was only one shot from the Sharp's and the other two were Uribe's Spencer.

A couple of men working on the outcroppings were first to see Uribe and Reighard.

"Here they come," one of them shouted, pointing west.

"They're dragging two elks," the other yelled. A cheer went up through the workers, and they stopped and came down lower to see the hunters smiling and waving, while dragging two large elk behind them – one with huge antlers.

Adkin was very happy. He had found elk to be his most favored meat. Though he loved buffalo and antelope, elk had less fat than the others and he preferred it like his favorite way to prepare antelope – roasted over open flames, charred on the outside and only slightly cooked on the inside.

With the chimney at about 6-feet tall, the men had a big meal of elk that night – and the next week as well – and Matty had two elk hides and two sets of valuable elk teeth she could use on her clothing – and she had a set of antlers.

"You might get mucho extra biscuits, Uribe," she whispered in his ear that first night. He winked and grinned at Adkin sitting on the other side of Matty.

•••

The chimney was finally finished and standing like a lone sentinel of the valley. It was completed in six days, and everybody was delighted and slapping each other on the back.

"I have to say Mister Bassett, your work is exemplary, well done," Adkin said as he held out his hand.

"Don't know that word exactly, but you look pleased," Bassett said as he shook Adkin's hand, while others laughed.

"Now we can started building the walls off the chimney and get this triangle knocked out in a few days," Sitler said. "We will push and dirt and gravel from the cliffs behind the walls. The back will be as solid as a soddy, with a chimney sticking out."

About that time, One of the men down at the river tending the livestock, yelled, "Indians," while pointing upstream along the ridge.

As Indians on horseback started filling the horizon east of them, more started lining up on the butte west of them.

"There's got to be about 200 of them, Señor," Uribe said as he pulled his rifle out. "They look to be Comanches."

"Hold it men," Brown said, as others were scurrying to get their rifles out or buckle up their pistol holsters. "Take it easy, we can't win a shooting fight."

"What do you suggest Mister Yates?" Brown asked with real concern in his voice. "This is your picnic."

Matty came running up to Adkin and held his arm.

"They are Comanche, my husband, I may know some of their Chiefs," she said. "We should ride up to speak with them."

"Saddle up Diablo and Tóngúl, Uribe, please?" Adkin said. "Someone get me a white cloth to attach to a limb."

Several started moving about finding and tying a white rag to a piece of branch. Uribe quickly pulled the two horses up to Adkin and Matty. Adkin helped her onto Tóngúl, and he stepped into the stirrup and swung himself onto Diablo.

Together, they headed downstream to the closest rise out of the valley. Adkin was holding the flag up with his left hand and his right hand held high in front of him holding the reins. He didn't want them thinking he had a gun in his hand or even near his pistol.

There were several Indians moving parallel with them above, and as they reached the top of the ridge, the ponies parted and Chief Ten Bears rode up to greet them.

Adkin recognized him immediately – the white-haired, well-spoken War Chief of the Yamparika Comanches.

Matty glanced at Adkin, whispering, "Ten Bears," as Adkin nodded his understanding. Adkin help up his hand.

"Great Chief Ten Bears," he said firmly. "I am Adkin Yates, and this is my wife, Mah-aht-Tay, daughter of Great Medicine Man Black Horse of the Kiowa. We greet you with friendship."

Ten Bears cocked his head, momentarily, and looked at his Medicine Man next to him, who grunted something short. He then looked back to Adkin and Matty.

"I know you Adkin Yates," he said. "You saved this woman when she a girl at Little Arkansas Peace Pow Wow, yes?"

"Yes, Ten Bears," Adkin said. "I remember you, too. And at the Medicine Lodge Creek Treaty, too."

"You wear the sign of friendship of Chief Satanta," Ten Bears said. "I remember Satanta giving you that sign. I remember Black Horse giving you the horse you ride.

"I remember you, too, Mah-aht-Tay. You have grown into a beautiful woman," he added. "I am glad to see it is you with these Whites."

Adkin's thoughts jumped back several years when he, Uribe and Dusty found the dead at Cedar Springs on the Dry Route of the Santa Fe Trail. It was a ghastly sight.

"We are moving across to the Northern Llano Estacado to follow the buffalo," Ten Bears said, interrupting Adkin's thoughts. "What is your business here Adkin Yates?"

"See that rock chimney?"

Matty interrupted softly with an Indian word, probably explaining chimney.

"I build a White Man lodge for me and Mah-aht-Tay to spend winter seasons in. It is a special place for her and her family – the Kiowa stay in this area many years."

"Yes, I see. I remember the Kiowa stay here for winter seasons for many, many years, like we stay on Northern Canadian River before the peace treaties," he said. "Now we wander between reservation and all of Llano Estacado, which the Great White Father gave to Ten Bears many years ago. Now he takes it back and wants us to live in Oklahoma reservation.

"But, we cannot live like farmers, so we follow the buffalo, which my father and his father did," Ten Bears said. "I like that you build lodge for your woman, that is good."

"We would be honored if you would come down and have some fresh roasted elk with us Ten Bears," Adkin said.

"We must move on, there are many soldiers on the Canadian south of us looking for Indians who want to live on the Plains," he said. "But maybe I rest in your lodge next winter when we return, yes?"

"Yes, we would be proud to have Ten Bears stay in our lodge – anytime," Adkin said. "You are always welcome, and we will paint the signs of the Kiowa and the Comanche on our lodge for all to see."

"Thank you Adkin Yates," Ten Bears said. "Go in peace as a friend of Ten Bears, and I wish you well with your woman and your summer lodge.

"Here is a gift of our friendship so all know we are friends," Ten Bears said as he took off a leather wrist band that was beaded and had one small cardinal feather hanging from it.

Adkin was caught off guard, he hadn't remembered to always carry a gift for friends – especially Indian friends.

Adkin undid his belt buckle and slid the sheath holding his Bowie Knife from the belt. He handed it to Ten Bears.

"This is for my friend the Great Chief Ten Bears," Adkin said. "I hope it serves you well."

Ten Bears smiled – a really big smile, and Adkin knew the man appreciated it very much, even without a word spoken.

With a simple raised hand gesture, Ten Bears kicked his pony in the flanks, and he led his clan around Adkin and Matty as Adkin waved, more for his crew than a gesture to Ten Bears.

The warriors continued en masse crowding around and down into the valley, crossing the Cimarron about 300 yards downstream of Adkin's crew. They just stood there, with Uribe waving back at Adkin, who could see Uribe's toothy grin, even from the ridge.

Then the horses and mules with travoises came down, being led by the women and children. They were carrying the tipi poles and skins and buffalo meat in various stages of preparation. It took them nearly 30 minutes for the band to get down and across the river. Adkin figured it was closer to 400 Indians in total.

Matty spoke soft words to many of the women as they passed by with curious stares. Most smiled back at Matty after she spoke, and some even mumbled in return.

•••

Finally, Adkin and Matty brought up the rear and rode back to the home site where everybody started clapping and breathing easier.

"You did great Adkin," Brown said. "We was a little worried there for a bit."

"Fortunately, it was Ten Bears, someone I had seen twice before at peace treaties," Adkin said, as he dismounted Diablo and helped Matty down. "He remembered me and Matty. He wished us well with our new lodge."

Several men laughed, and Uribe made the point is was going to be more than just a lodge.

"Ten Bears say he may stay here next winter," Matty said proudly.

"Old Ten Bears is famous back east," Reighard said. "He's even visited the President of these here United States in Washington."

"I remember hearing his speech at Medicine Lodge Creek was printed in eastern newspapers," Brown said.

"I was fortunate to hear it in person, and he proved to many all Indians are not ignorant," Adkin said. "Ten Bears was quite eloquent in his pleading to the Indian Peace Commission.

"But, as I saw from the treaty in '65, not much ever really happens," Adkin added, with a frown.

"But, he now owns my old Bowie Knife I've been carrying for five years," Adkin continued. "That will teach me to always have an emergency gift for War Chiefs."

Everybody laughed as he squeezed his hand through the leather wrist band Ten Bears had given him. He held it up to show the men.

"You're goin' end up clothed from head to toe with Injun trinkets if you don't watch it," Marcellus said.

When Adkin was later alone with Matty, he asked what she had said to the Comanche women.

"I say I wish them safe travels and hope their babies are safe. That I hope the spirits watch over their families," she said.

Adkin hugged her and kissed her on her forehead.

"May the spirits forever watch over my Matty," he said, smiling at his Kiowa Princess.

The men went back to work with added zeal. Adkin wondered if it was relief they hadn't been attacked by Indians, which would have surely meant death – or they wanted to finish as quickly as possible, realizing Indians were all over this country, now that spring was in the air.

The reason for zeal was soon explained.

"The boys want to get back to Dodge as soon as possible after that scare," Brown said as he walked by Adkin. "We may have this place up in a few weeks at this new pace."

•••

Brown was correct, the men were finishing the roofing with red cedar shingles on April 15, and plans and preparations for the return to Dodge were completed. Adkin wrote out two telegrams for Brown to send to Sanderson and Company when he got back to Dodge.

One was for a money request of $800 made out to Brown. Two hundred dollars was for Bassett's extra work of gathering rock and mortar materials – the fireplace and chimney took more than the three wagons of rock Bassett had collected on Bluff Creek.

"I want $100 extra to go to Campbell for his trip here to oversee the work – he volunteered. He's working up the invoice for the lumber, which I'll settle later. I want you to divide up the rest between you and your men, Hoo Doo," Adkin said in front of everyone.

"But Adkin, you've already paid us up front," Brown said. "And we accepted it because it was fair – we knew what we were getting into."

"Well, let's just call it extra 'scare pay' – because when I saw all those Comanches lined up along the valley ridge a half mile on each side, I was scared as any of you," he said laughing. The men guffawed as well.

The other telegram was to Ryan and Ray Dee telling them they had finished and would leave on October 1 and be back around October 9 or 10.

"Matty and I want to thank each one of you, and words can't describe what it means to us that you helped with our dream," Adkin said. "Please drop in any summer – or use it in the winter – you are all welcome."

People started shaking hands and Matty was nearly finished with their last evening meal together. When Adkin spoke with Campbell, he asked him a question out of earshot of the others.

"Hey Campbell, I was wondering if you would like to come to work with us at YR&R Freight Company?" he asked. "I know you're set up with your mill in Great Bend, but we need a man with your sensibilities – someone who is dependable and trustworthy."

"First off, I've told you, just call me Weldon," he said, chuckling. "That mill is all that keeps me in Great Bend. And most of the buffalo in that area are wiped out. Are there any trees around your place in Colorado?"

"Not enough, I'm afraid," Adkin said. "But if you could sell it or lease it out, I'd pay you $60 a month, feed you and put a nice roof over your head.

"And a chance to earn more with incentives – and there's a lot of buffalo out that way," Adkin added. "Plus it's steady and lots of travel."

"I tell you what, let me think on it, if that's acceptable?" Campbell said. "When are you going back to Las Animas City?"

"We'll probably leave here around October 1, and it'll take us about eight or nine days to get back," he answered.

"I'll let you know something before you leave here, okay? Campbell said.

Adkin offered his hand and they shook. "That's good enough for me."

Adkin was hoping to replace Sam Phillips with someone who could handle leadership and make solid decisions, and he felt Campbell was that kind of man. But waiting that long may not work out, Adkin thought to himself.

•••

Before sunrise on the morning of April 16, all the Dodge men – and Campbell – departed. Going with them was Uribe and Tom, who seemed upset that Adkin and Matty were foolish enough to stay at this new house all by themselves.

"I know it's none of my business, but I think you're asking for trouble being alone," Marcellus had told Adkin while alone together. "I would be glad to stay and help – you know hunt and gather, take care of the horses, provide some more guns."

"Thanks, Tom. That's very decent of you, and I really appreciate it," Adkin said. "But this is something Matty and I have planned for some time. We know what could happen, but we believe we're prepared to deal with any hostiles in our own ways.

"I hope you understand, and we'll see you in the fall," he added.

Tom handed Adkin another big-bladed knife in a sheath, saying Adkin could return it when he got back to Las Animas.

Uribe stood in front of Adkin and Matty, looking as if he was going to weep. He then hugged Adkin and said, "Adios, mi amigo."

He then turned to Matty and held out his hand. She bent forward and hugged him, and spoke before he could open his mouth.

"Adios, mi amigo," she said. "Y vaya con dios. Hasta la vista, Uribe."

He turned without saying more, which was unlike Uribe, and got on his horse. Adkin figured he was taking this separation pretty hard. It warmed his heart knowing Uribe cared that much. And Adkin cared as much for Uribe, for Uribe was one of the first two men he and Ryan hired to work full-time for Barlow and Sanderson – Uribe and Dusty.

Adkin reminded Brown he and Matty would probably be coming to Dodge about every 30 to 50 days to buy supplies they couldn't hunt or pick off the land. Brown assured Adkin that Dodge was booming and supplies were not a problem.

"They may cost more than normal, but anything you want can usually be found in Dodge," Brown said, chuckling

As they all rode off waving, Adkin and Matty looked at each other and then around their place. They had no mules or beeves; one wagon with a two-horse team with harnesses and reins; only enough saddles and tack for two of the four horses they had. Also Adkin's two rifles; the old Sharps and the new Henry; plus the Remington coach shotgun and two Colt pistols. And a large wooden case of ammunition that Matty had no chance of lifting alone.

They walked back into their home and closed the door.

"It's so early, I was thinking we might want to go back to bed – how about it?" Adkin asked.

Matty took his arm and quickly dragged him to the bedroom and slammed the door behind them.

•••

Adkin spent the first few weeks chopping down some sycamores from the river bank and using remnants of the lumber he had left over from the house build to construct a roofed, three-sided stable to afford security for their horses during rain or direct sunlight during a hot summer that was surely on the way.

Matty had stretched two coyote hides over a ring of a willow limb she had formed in almost prefect circles. Both skins had been tempered and dried almost to the hardness of wood. She began painting the signs of the Kiowa and the Comanche.

The Kiowa sign was the simplest, with a black outer edge of the ring and the left half green from top to bottom and then equal in size, the right side was painted yellow. She then painted the silhouette of a black buffalo head in the center with an arrow-head "V" below its chin.

The Comanche sign had an outer red ring lined inside with a thin blue line. Then off-centered to the left was a blue field in a double, backward "S" on its right side, with the remaining right field painted yellow. She then painted a black stick horse with a rider holding a lance and a war shield.

Adkin nailed them both to the front porch posts that held up the porch roofing.

Matty also spent hours roaming nearby fields selecting grasses, plant roots or bulbs she knew would be useful in food or for medicinal purposes. She also reminded Adkin he would need to locate the seeds they had packed and brought with them to plant a garden.

Matty had learned to use a shovel at her previous homes, which made breaking the soil much easier than the old hatchet she used in her tribal life.

Adkin went out afoot several times to kill some game, as deer were plentiful along the Cimarron, and he also bagged a couple of turkeys on one occasion. He enjoyed the fact he could walk out his door and harvest meat.

Matty made it her job to use a horse to drag up deadfall from the river and then use the axe to chop firewood, where she stored it off the side of their front door. Adkin had made a wooden rain cover above the woodpile.

He finally had to tell Matty she need not cut any more wood.

"We've got enough for an entire winter, but we will not be here all winter," he said.

"But our friends – or new friends who come along – may need it," she said, smiling.

The days got longer, the sun warmer and their love more blissful. Adkin could not ever remember being so contented with life. He made sure he kept his notebook current, hoping one day they may have a child to bequeath it to.

Adkin also remembered the Fort Supply doctor testifying at his trial that the abuse Matty received at the hands of Martinez may have destroyed her ability to have more children. Though he knew that was possible, he believed his faith in God could offer the chance she could have another baby, too.

"It's in God's hands," he would say to himself when he thought about it. Ironically, she never mentioned a word about children, and Adkin thought maybe she had a feeling it could not happen, either.

•••

Adkin finished building a small corral with limbs and posts cut from timber he found further down the river, almost to Crooked Creek. He made sure the corral would hold about 20 head of livestock if needed. Having the roofed stable worked out well – they had a brief hail storm and rain about three weeks after the men had returned to Dodge.

Matty got the garden planted with seeds for corn, green onions, potatoes, turnip greens, summer squash, watermelons and pumpkins. Matty assured Adkin she would handle watering duties by keeping a water barrel full that she could pail out enough water to keep the small garden alive.

Adkin also devised a fish spear, similar to how Uribe constructed his, and managed to snag a few. After careful study, and without Adkin's knowledge, Matty made herself a bow from a black willow branch and several arrows from hackberry branches. She chiseled her own arrowheads from the nearby quartz outcroppings in the sandstone.

She then snuck down to the river and waded the shallows and killed two fish in short order and took them up to Adkin, who was checking the shoes on the horses.

"I will gladly show my husband how to shoot my poorly made bow for the pescados – the fish," she said with a wry smile.

"Maybe I should let my wife be the Fish Chief," Adkin said. "Then I can sleep in the shade on the cool grass."

They both laughed, but the following day, Adkin was asking Matty to help him select the right limb to try and make a strong bow for him to learn to use.

By the time fledglings were leaving the nest and most every wildflower had burst free, Adkin decided it was time to refresh their supplies, like salt, sugar, flour – the things they needed. Plus, he was looking to get back in the saddle again.

He hadn't realized how much he enjoyed working with stagecoach stations, ordering, delivering parts and making repairs. And he liked being on the trail to somewhere. Matty saw it, too.

She naturally understood, for she, too, was a nomad and enjoyed travelling. And with Adkin, she didn't have to work nearly as much as she did when living with her bands.

It was on May 30, 1871, they hitched the team up to their wagon, tied Diablo and Tóngúl to the back and departed their new home for Dodge City.

An Englishman's Adventures on the Santa Fe Trail (1865-1889)

...

When they crossed the bridge entering Dodge, it was apparent to Adkin Dodge was filling up. It would soon be a real town, he thought to himself. George M. Hoover's whisky bar even looked improved, though it was only a structure of sod and boards.

As they drove up to a stop in front of Hoover's, three men stepped out the front.

"Well, I'll be damned, if it isn't Mister and Missus Adkin Yates," Reighard yelled. "How are you Adkin, Miss Matty?"

Adkin jumped off the wagon, while Matty sat still. She waved.

"Hello Meester Reighard," she said softly.

Reighard reached his hand out as Adkin grabbed it and they shook hands.

"Hello George, We're doing well," Adkin said. "How about you?"

"Great," he said smiling. "Guess who is inside talking with the men?"

"Charley Rath just got into town yesterday, and he's organizin' a buffalo hide company – sorta, anyways," he added.

They went in as Adkin waved to Matty to wait.

"I'll just be a minute, Matty."

He entered with Reighard and wasn't inside but a short time when Rath came hurrying out the door and made a bee-line to Matty.

"How are you Miss Matty?" Rath asked, shaking her hand. "You look beautiful. I guess country living on the Cimarron is doing you both good. Adkin looks healthy, too."

"We like very much our new special place," she said demurely.

Adkin had walked out behind Rath with several other men. Along with Reighard, Matty recognized Bassett and Hoo Doo Brown, who also shook hands with Matty and tipped his hat like the others.

"You're just in time," Rath said. "We're gathering to go out to H.L. Sitler's place he's building west of town. You need to come with us, as we've set up camp out there to meet with those who may be interested in buffalo hunting. There's a few other men out there, too."

"Do we have time to go to the fort and send a few telegrams?" Adkin asked.

"Hell yes," Rath barked. "Sorry Miss Matty. We'll wait for you to get back here, and we'll all go to Sitler's together."

Adkin crawled back onto the bench and snapped the reins on the backs of his team and they headed east. It was about a mile to the fort, but Adkin wanted to get off a telegraph to Ryan and Sanderson.

He informed Ryan and Ray Dee he had made an offer of employment to Weldon Campbell, who Ryan knew. But Campbell hadn't responded yet. Adkin said if he did hire him, he would send Campbell to Las Animas City right away.

He also sent a message to J.L. Sanderson to Denver and Junction City, in care of Barlow and Sanderson. Adkin wasn't sure where J.L. was, but he would eventually get the message.

Adkin informed him the house was built, and he would be back at Fort Dodge in 30 to 45 days, if he wanted to leave a message. And he told Sanderson he would be back at Las Animas the first week of October.

When he and Matty rolled back to Hoover's the others were waiting. There were six men, and they all followed Rath and the wagon westward along the banks of the Big Arkansas. Adkin had an affinity for the river. Its waters were the heartstring of the Santa Fe Trail in the West, and he loved watching it roll along.

About five miles out, there was a large hill on the north side, and Adkin could see a building, men, horses and wagons with teams and a couple of large tents.

"That's Sitler's place," Rath said. "He got started on it as soon as he got back from your place. Guess you gave him the inspiration to build out here.

"He's got some beeves grazing around and plans on becoming a money-makin' rancher," Rath added with a chuckle, like it couldn't be done.

Sitler was the first to walk up to them as they approached. When he saw Adkin and Matty, he took off his hat and slightly bowed to Matty.

"Welcome Missus Yates to my humble abode," he said smiling. "It not as fine as your home, but it's big."

Adkin noticed it was large and made mostly of wood planks. He couldn't see, but he guessed it had three or four rooms, or more, at that size.

Sitler then turned to Adkin and shook his hand.

"Great to see you, Adkin. I hope all is well," he said. "Haven't had any trouble with hostiles, I hope."

"Nope. Haven't seen anyone since Ten Bears rode through," Adkin said as he took off his hat. "Still got my hair"

They all laughed and Sitler invited everyone inside, as his three men gathered around shaking hands and greeting the others. They all seemed to know one another.

Sitler first introduced a man named Robert M. Wright. He was a tall, lean man with not much of a chin, but he had piercing eyes and a wry smile under a bushy mustache. Adkin thought he had heard his name before but he couldn't immediately remember.

He removed his hat and shook Matty's hand first, saying he was pleased to meet Missus Yates. She nodded a "Hello," looking shier than normal. He then turned to Adkin.

"How's Tyler doing Mister Yates?" he asked, catching Adkin a little off balance as they were shaking hands. "He's an old friend, and I hear he's still working for J.L. and started his own freighting business with you."

An Englishman's Adventures on the Santa Fe Trail (1865-1889)

It then dawned on Adkin that Wright had once worked for Barlow and Sanderson before Adkin had arrived in 1865.

"Nice to meet you Wright, I now remember hearing Ryan say you had worked at the Leavenworth headquarters," Adkin said, smiling. "He speaks highly of you."

"I appreciate that," Wright said. "When I reached Barlow and Sanderson, it was Tyler Ryan who helped me get my feet on the ground and encouraged me.

"During those three years in the early 1860s, I ended up crossing the Great Plains several times in wagons and, finally – with Tyler's approval – twice across driving stagecoaches," he added with a chuckle. "Tyler was a task-master but the fairest man I had met up til then."

"He's mellowed some," Adkin said, laughing. "Time – and dodging Indians and Comancheros – makes a man a little less concerned with the little things."

"You were also the Sutler at Fort Dodge at one time if I remember correctly," Adkin said.

"Yes, I ended up in that hell-hole right when the first wagons of lumber and building supplies arrived – I was with them. But I had to live in a mud hole in the river bank for five months," Wright said, laughing.

"We just missed meeting you during that time," Adkin said. "We were establishing stage stations along the Santa Fe Trail in '65."

"Hey, you two can catch up on old times later, I want you to meet these other men," Rath interrupted.

He introduced James H. "Dog" Kelley and A. J. Anthony. All the men, according to Rath, were going to form a buffalo hunting outfit. Their plans called for three shooters and the other six skinning. They would also take four wagons and teams out with them to bring back the hides and meat.

"I landed a contract to provide meat to the Army for all the forts along here and even into New Mexico," Rath said. "We're going to haul most of the hides to the railhead at Fort Hays for markets back east. The meat will be distributed along the Santa Fe Trail forts after it's salted and dried."

"Well, I wish you men all the best, and hope the Indians don't disturb you too much," Adkin said with a smile.

"Now Adkin, don't throw salt on the cake," Rath said, laughing. "Several of these men are able scouts, it's after we kill the buffs and start skinning is when we have to be alert."

"Well, you know Ten Bears is out on the upper Canadian River hunting them, too," Adkin said. "I think it might be wise to stay away from that area."

"Don't worry," Reighard said. "We've found plenty buffalo just northeast of Dodge about 50 miles – a large herd of probably 1,000 animals were out there two days ago."

"My source in the military also tells me they are sending a large troop of calvary onto the Llano Estacado this summer to round up tribes and herd them back to the Oklahoma reservations," Rath said. "The Army appointed Colonel Ranald Mackenzie Commander of the Fourth United States Cavalry at Fort Concho in February."

"And a month later, Mackenzie moved his headquarters to Fort Richardson," Rath added.

"Like I said, good luck," Adkin said. "And good luck to whoever this Mackenzie is, too."

"Hey, I almost for got to tell you, General Sherman personally arrested your old friend, Satanta, with old Satank and Big Tree on the Commandant's porch at Fort Sill just last week and charged them with murder – word is they were arrested May 27. Sherman is goin' to ship 'em down to Fort Richardson, where Mackenzie is, to put them on trial."

Adkin couldn't believe it.

"Are you sure, Charley?" Adkin said. "Satanta?"

"That's from the Army folks at Fort Dodge," Rath said. "Word is burning up the wires about it. Seems Sherman was travelling down to Fort Sill to check on some complaints from the Indians, and he almost got killed himself.

"Story is about a hundred Kiowas, Comanches, Kiowa-Apaches, Arapahoes, and Cheyennes from the Fort Sill Reservation crossed the Red River into Texas in mid-May, upset with their reservation life, I guess," Rath continued. "The Injuns saw Sherman's group but didn't attack. Instead they caught a small wagon train belonging to freighter Henry Warren. You remember him don't you?"

"Yes, I met him in Santa Fe a few years ago," Adkin said, almost numb from this news.

"Well, the Injuns killed the wagon master and six other teamsters," Rath said. "They allowed three teamsters to skedaddle – then the Injuns all hightailed it back to the reservation.

"Sherman was peeved, to say the least, so he caught up with Satanta and them at Fort Sill and threw them in the brig," he said. "Word is a trial is set for next month.

"They're calling it the 'Warren wagon train raid,'" Rath added. "It happened east of Salt Creek and about 20 miles west of Fort Richardson."

Adkin was stunned. He knew Satanta must have had sound reasons, but Adkin couldn't imagine why they would attack a wagon train and not Sherman himself – especially if Sherman was the point of their problems with the Army.

It just didn't make sense.

He looked at Matty, and she looked confused, not apprehending all the news. He wasn't looking forward to telling her the truth.

•••

Sitler said his men were going to cook up supper, and invited Adkin and Matty to stay in his place for the night. Though the house was not quite completed, he had a room with a bed in it where he had been sleeping during construction.

"Please stay, I'll bunk with the men in the tents," Sitler said. "It's nice weather to be outside anyway."

They accepted and Adkin fetched Matty's trunk from the wagon, while she grabbed a couple of furs.

During the meal, the men gabbed and gabbed. Some about the wealth they were predicting to earn. Some purely gossip about who was going to marry who. Adkin found out Wright already had five children through a couple of marriages. Wright didn't go into details, and Adkin didn't ask. He figured his wife and children must be staying with family or friends until the house is completed.

Matty could barely eat, she was peppered with questions about the new house, the river, what kind of trees and plants. She was proud to tell them about "her" rare Black Gum Tree, her garden and the numerous natural medicinal plants, too. The men who had not met Matty on the Cimarron were totally enthralled with her – the same as the ones who knew her.

"As always," Adkin thought to himself.

Rath and Wright told Adkin to go see Major E. B. Kirk, the quartermaster at Fort Dodge, for their supplies.

"Hell, I'll go with you," Wright said. "The Major is a good friend of mine – if you don't mind?"

"Why no. Maybe you can convince him to give me some good prices," Adkin said with a chuckle.

"Don't hold your breath, he's 110 percent Army," Wright said laughing, too.

•••

Major Kirk did indeed offer Adkin good prices on all the food and supplies Adkin and Matty needed – even a lower price on a box of nails, and a bale of wire and rope.

"Any friend of Bob's is a friend of mine, Mister Yates," Kirk said. "Plus, anyone brave enough to build a house where you did deserves respect."

Kirk questioned Adkin why he built a place near the Cimarron – Crooked Creek confluence. Adkin explained he was married to the Kiowa daughter of Black Horse, who was a friend of Satanta's and the Comanche Chief Ten Bears. Adkin showed Kirk his gifts he wore.

"Oh, I see," Kirk said with eyes wide open. "You just might be able to make it then. That's good company to know if hostiles come upon y'all."

Kirk and several soldiers helped load Adkin's wagon, and Adkin gave him currency he had brought along from Las Animas. People on the Great Plains were just getting comfortable using paper money, though it was commonplace back east, according to travellers.

"Has any of the boys told you we're going to build a real town here along the Arkansas?" Kirk asked. "We're working on a plat that will lay out all the lots."

"Really?" Adkin asked. "No one said anything about it."

"It's more talk than anything right now," Wright said. "But, Sitler is working on a plat. He wants it to be centered out near his place, naturally."

"That's because he's checked out where the border of the military reservation is, Bob. You know that," Kirk said. "It can't be surveyed on military property."

"Yeah, that's true," Wright said.

"I tell you Mister Yates, by this time next summer, we're going be building a town," Kirk said. "We're going to sell lots for $10 a piece, and if I was you, I'd get in on it when you can."

"Get him, turning into a land agent already," Wright teased Kirk with a laugh.

"Mark my words," Kirk said smiling.

Adkin promised he would consider investing in Dodge when it happened, and more importantly, he would be coming back to see the Major in about 40 days for more supplies.

"By the way, Have you heard any news from Fort Sill about the Warren wagon train raid – has Chief Satanta and Satank gone on trial?" Adkin asked.

"No, I only know they're being held in the brig at Fort Sill, but they're going to move them down to Fort Richardson pretty soon," Kirk answered.

After farewells and hand shakes, Adkin and Wright headed out to Sitler's place.

"Nice to meet you, Yates," Kirk shouted. "See you later, and if you have time, bring the Missus, I'd like to meet her as well."

"A very pleasant fellow," Adkin said.

"He's a very decent man, and tougher than nails," Wright said. "Nobody realizes how mean he can get in a fight – saw it myself when we were attacked by Cheyenne in a military train outside Pueblo. I was freighting with them.

"When we circled up, arrows and bullets were flying everywhere," he continued. "He stood out there in the middle directing firing lines, where to spread out the ammunition boxes. One Indian jumped through on horseback, and Kirk grabbed him off that pony so fast, that Injun didn't even have a chance to get up and fight.

"Kirk grabbed the Cheyenne's own hatchet and split his head open so fast, he died with his mouth wide open like he was yellin' at the top of his lungs," Wright said. "Kirk went right back to giving orders and firing his pistol between wagons.

"He never did hide behind anything in the 30 minutes it took for them to decide we weren't going to give up," he added. "We had a couple of wounded, but they lost eight, including the one Kirk thumped with that hatchet. Split him open like a melon.

"It was a sight," Wright added.

Adkin was amazed once again. It seem to be a fact that every person who had decided to make their life on the Great Plains could be a hard case. That realization one may have to take dangerous and deadly actions to survive is exactly why they did survive.

It's emotionally crushing to kill another human, but Adkin realized there was often no other choice in the West. It was truly kill or be killed at times. Kirk was just another "very decent man" who has had to kill to survive living the lifestyle he has chosen.

Adkin stopped by the telegraph office and discovered he had two replies. Ryan said things were going well in Las Animas and he and Ray Dee had hired two men that were experienced in the stage business and freighting. Their names were John Braden and William Hepburn Russell.

Ryan said they could still use good help if Adkin could hire the Campbell man. He also confirmed he wired $3,000 to the Sutler at Fort Dodge. Adkin suddenly realized Major Kirk and the Sutler had yet to receive the money. It would probably come in that day.

Sanderson responded he was glad to hear from Adkin and said they could use him as soon as Adkin could get back. The Colorado and California routes were "growing faster than a prairie fire."

•••

At Sitler's, the camp was buzzing with excitement to get the buffalo hunt under way. Plans called for them to take off that evening so they could make about 15 miles along the Santa fe Trail, where they could spend the night at Chris Rath's Trading Post on the Hays cutoff.

They then planned on heading due north to Buckner Creek and follow it northeast until it dumped into the Pawnee River. That's the general area their scouting found the large herd they would hunt.

Adkin was glad to see Matty when he returned. She seemed as excited as the hunters. They had kept her busy with tales of hunting and fighting Comancheros in New Mexico and West Texas. Adkin even had a tinge of wishing he could go on the buffalo hunt.

But it was back to their special place, where the greenery was wonderful, even the white blossoms of the Dog Woods brightened the whole area around their spot on the Cimarron.

As everybody was making preparations to leave, the hunters all paid their respects to Adkin and Matty – mainly Matty, Adkin noticed. She seemed to be blossoming herself the more she was around Whites – especially goodhearted, mannerly men.

Sitler came over with what looked like a bean sack and threw it in Adkin's wagon.

"It's some salt-dried antelope – almost jerked," Sitler said. "Should last you a few weeks. I heard you liked antelope, and we' got 'em by the hundreds up north."

"Thank you very much Mister Sitler," Adkin said, tipping his hat. Matty said, "Thank you," also.

"Hey, Major Kirk said you men are going to draw up a plat with township plots for sale next summer," Adkin said. "Any truth to that?"

"Why yes indeed," Sitler said. "That's our hopes. We know a man with the Santa Fe Railroad who expects the railroad to lay track through here in about a year. We want to be a stop where eastern buyers can pick up buffalo hides and meat and whatever else we can provide."

"You know, if you get it going and at the price Kirk told me per lot, sign me up for 50 of those lots – if it is $500 as Kirk says," Adkin said with a wink. "I believe this place has the right kind of men to make it happen, Mister Sitler."

'Well thanks Mister Yates," Sitler said laughing. "When we get everything arranged and surveyed, we'll let you know, and I promise that $10 a lot price will be good for you, too. Fifty lots it is."

With that, Adkin slapped the reins and turned the wagon east to get to the Arkansas River bridge and cross at Hoover's Whiskey Bar. In two-and-a-half days, they would be back in their little Eden.

While rolling out of Dodge, Adkin brought up Satanta and his jailing. She started crying immediately, asking Adkin what could they do? He tried to comfort her and said Satanta would have to face charges if it was true. If it wasn't, he would be set free. It was the American way.

•••

As they topped the small knoll just a couple of miles upstream of the Crooked Creek confluence with the Cimarron, Adkin and Matty could see smoke on the horizon. They both looked at each other with dread. They knew it had to be their place.

"Adkin immediately jumped off the wagon seat and ran back to Diablo and untied his tether.

"Matty, take the wagon and try to get down there in the willows and brush behind us," Adkin barked as he pointed to the river. "Take this Henry, and shoot to kill."

Adkin handed her the gun as he sat upon Diablo by her side of the wagon.

"Stay hidden until I return," he said. "If I don't get back by dark, take the team and wagon to Dodge, they can help you there."

He leaned over and kissed her lightly and then kicked Diablo in the flanks and sped off to the west and the smoke.

An Englishman's Adventures on the Santa Fe Trail (1865-1889)

As he rounded the bend to see the ravine their house was in, he finally took a deep breath. The smoke was only coming from the chimney, and he got a whiff of buffalo meat roasting. And there was smoke filling the sky in the small bend in every direction up and down the river.

It was coming from tipis.

As he mentally counted the lodges, he could see there must be 50 or more tipis within a half mile of the house. He also noticed the painted decorations on them looked to be Comanche. Just then four warriors were riding hard right at him yelping with excitement.

Adkin threw up both hands with palms outward, signing he was no harm. They shouted a few Comanche words at him, but he shook his head in no understanding.

"I speak English," he said. "Do you have Chief who speaks English?"

They looked back and forth at each other briefly, and then one motioned for Adkin to come with them. He followed them to a very large tipi, which Adkin knew reflected the status of a Chief. It was set up within 20-feet of the front porch of their house.

Just then a tall, muscular Indian walked out the tipi flap. As he stood erect, naked to his waist and deer-skin breeches, Adkin saw his arms were the size of firewood. His hair was braided on both sides and covered with mink fur. He wore only two long, upright eagle feathers on the back of his head.

He then recognized the handsome face of an Indian he saw briefly at the peace treaty. It was Chief Quanah Parker – the half breed leader of a very violent band of he Comanches.

"What is your name?" Quanah asked crossing his large forearms.

"My name is Adkin Yates, and I know you are the Great Chief Quanah Parker. I have seen you at the peace treaty with the Indian Commission.

"This house is my home," Adkin continued. "You are welcome, as you see, we have put up the sign of the Comanche to welcome them to shelter and food."

"I see the sign. I also see sign of Kiowa," Quanah said. "Why you welcome Comanche and Kiowa to your home?"

Adkin couldn't believe this man was speaking English so well.

"My wife is Kiowa," Adkin said, trying to stand as erect as Quanah. "She is the daughter of Satanta's Great Medicine Man Black Horse, who died last year and is buried somewhere nearby.

"Her Kiowa name is Mah-aht-Tay," he added. "I call her Matty."

"I see your sign of friendship with Satanta," Quanah pointed to Adkin's neck. "What is that on your arm?"

Adkin held out his right arm and rolled his wrist around several times.

"This is sign of friendship from Great Comanche Chief Ten Bears," Adkin said. "He passed this way four moons ago on his way to upper Canadian River with his band."

Quanah stood there a moment without speaking. He finally let his arms fall by his side, seeming to relax.

"Where is this woman of your's called Mat-tee," he asked.

"She is with our wagon of supplies back about two miles on the Cimarron," Adkin said. "We were afraid someone was burning our new home, and I asked her to hide."

"I am making roast buffalo for my family in your welcome house," Quanah said. "You should get your woman and eat with us, Adkin Yates."

He turned and dipped under the tipi flap and left Adkin standing there. Without a word, Adkin reined Diablo around and started loping back down the valley with the four warriors following a few yards behind him.

•••

Adkin walked their team and wagon right up to the front of Quanah's main tent. He set the brake, tied the reins off on the brake handle, slowly walked around to the other side and helped Matty down from the wagon. Two women bowed and opened the tipi flaps.

As they entered, it took a moment for their eyes to adjust to the dimness of the lodge.

"Please, sit," Adkin heard a voice, knowing it was Quanah's They hesitated briefly and Matty sat first, pulling on Adkin's arm to sit beside her.

Adkin's sight was finally registering everything, and Quanah sat across from them with a small bed of coals between them in the tipi's fire pit.

"So this is your woman, Adkin Yates?" he asked.

"Yes Great Chief Quanah, this is Matty, my wife," Adkin responded.

Quanah examined Matty for a moment and said something in Comanche, Adkin thought.

"She responded in Indian language and then said softly in English, "I am honored to meet the great Quahadi Chief Quanah Parker."

She bowed her head, knowing it was rare an Indian even allowed a squaw to speak, let alone asked a question.

Quanah turned his attention back to Adkin.

"I have heard your name Adkin Yates," he said. "Are you part of the Barlow Sanderson stageline?"

"That is correct," Adkin said. "I came from England in the summer of 1865 and went to work for Sanderson, because I am a master blacksmith."

This caught Quanah off guard and he gave a quizzical look to a man standing with the two women off to his left. The man said something, and Quanah raised his head and mumbled, "Oh, yes."

"Can you put iron moccasins on my horses' feet?" he asked.

"Yes, I just happened to purchase more iron shoes when I was at Fort Dodge," Adkin said with a smile. "They are in the wagon outside."

Quanah smiled, then turned to Matty again.

"I knew your father, Black Horse, when I was young," he said. "I met him at Palo Duro shortly after my father died. I am sorry to not be able to come to honor his death."

Matty simply bowed. She hadn't been asked a question, so she didn't push her luck by speaking again. She also knew of Quanah's reputation for brutality.

He and his Quahadis had been ravaging Texan settlers west of Weatherford, Texas, down to Mexico for the last few years. All knew the Quahadis had never signed any treaty, and they murdered and plundered at will.

"Your lodge is very solid – good cooking fire pit," Quanah said to Adkin. "But the sleeping stand is strange."

Matty let a slight giggle escape her lips before she could get her hand across her mouth. Quanah asked her something in Indian.

She was surprised again.

"Yes, Great Chief, I sleep there. It is called a feather bed," she said. "It was strange to me, too, at first. I had to try many times, and then it was very good."

"I prefer my robes and furs," Quanah said flatly, turning to Adkin. "Ten Bears was on way to Llano Estacado, si? To hunt buffalo?" Quanah asked.

"Yes, to follow the buffalo," Adkin said.

"Ten Bears faces trouble with soldiers for leaving reservation lands," Quanah said matter of factly, and shaking his head. "But I told him reservation life not life for Comanches. I will die first – not live on reservations.

"We will be going to the Llano as well – soon," he said. "First, we eat."

Quanah waved at the two women and the man, and they scurried out the tipi. Quanah then picked up his pipe and lit it. After blowing the smoke straight upward, he made some singing sounds and then handed the pipe to Adkin.

The smoke initially hurt Adkin's throat as he accidently inhaled a little – it didn't taste like tobacco. As he caught his breath, he looked at Matty. She gave him a look like, "Don't hand that pipe to me – squaws never smoke with men." Adkin handed the pipe back to Quanah. But he felt light-headed for a bit.

He would find out later from Matty, that she had heard Quanah preferred to smoke peyote, made from cactus.

∴

As they waited for the food, Quanah started discussing how the Whites were killing off buffalo more and more, which made him sad and angry. He also wanted to know about England – where was it, what kind of people lived there.

Those discussions went on into the meal, which was delivered on wooden trays. It was only roasted buffalo and fresh wild onions – and a pile of sugar. Adkin assumed it was Quanah's favorite, because he constantly dipped his onion into the sugar and then bit off the end.

"Are there any Comanches or Kiowas in this England – any tribes?" Quanah asked while gnawing at a large piece of blackened meat.

"We have dark-skin people from tribes of Africa and Caribbean Islands that live in England," Adkin said. "Those are other countries."

"Do they have many horses?" Quanah asked.

"No. Most people in England only have a few horses, except people like my father who has stagecoaches for travellers," Adkin said. "We had many horses, but not like the Comanches. We had only about 20 horses."

"You were very poor. That is bad, I am sorry for you, Adkin Yates," Quanah said, showing real empathy.

"Yes poor, but very happy family," Adkin said.

Quanah went on and on about how many Whites were filling his country, taking land that belonged to them. He gave the example how the Great White Father in Washington had signed papers to give Ten Bears all of the Texas Llano Estacado.

"Then he take it away from Ten Bears," Quanah said. "Words from Washington no good."

Quanah wanted to know how he and Matty met, so Adkin had to go into the whole story of how he intervened twice to help her, and how they were married in the Wichita Mountains.

Then Quanah talked for a long time of his love of the Wichita Mountains. He said he preferred Blanco Canyon below the Palo Duro.

"It is where the Quahadis raised me and my little brother," he said wistfully.

He never did mention his mother, and Adkin was wary of asking. Even though Goodnight thought it was Quanah Parker and his brother who escaped the Pease River fight where Peta Nocona was killed, Goodnight could not swear in court it was Quanah.

He didn't know what Quanah even looked like. Only a few Whites had even seen Quanah, and Adkin, Ryan and Rath did see him at the Medicine Lodge Peace Treaty. So they were told.

It was then Adkin told Quanah the news he had heard in Dodge about Satanta, old Satank and Big Tree getting arrested by Sherman – and about the Warren Raid.

"If they were to be captured, they should have at least killed Sherman," Quanah said. "Bad, very bad."

He didn't say more, just went into a thoughtful stare.

It was about 8 o'clock, and Quanah suggested Adkin and Matty might want to sleep in their strange bed.

Adkin explained he needed to put away his team and horses and to feed and water them. Quanah immediately called in a warrior and gave him instructions to give Adkin help with the animals.

Adkin thanked him, and he and Matty rose to leave.

"You put iron shoes on my horse tomorrow, Adkin Yates? Yes?" Quanah asked with a smile.

"Yes, Great Chief, tomorrow."

They slipped out the tipi and turned and got back on their wagon. They were followed by several men to the corral and helped throw out hay and carried water pails from the nearby river and poured it into their troughs.

As they walked back to their house, children and women were humming with soft words and giggles. Matty made several hand signs showing peace, always with a warm grin.

As they entered their home, Adkin wasn't sure what they would find, but things looked fairly good. There were a few items out of place, like they had been inspected and thrown around randomly.

Matty showed him the sugar and coffee bins and they were empty, and most of the flour was gone. But, remarkably, their pots, pans and utensils were intact. There was a mess around the cooking pit in the fireplace, but Matty said she would clean it tomorrow while Adkin shod Quanah's horse.

"I told you the feather bed was strange for Indian," Matty said, chuckling. "It is funny fearless War Chief think same."

"That was funny, indeed. But I'm glad he didn't like it or we might be sleeping on the ground tonight," Adkin said, smiling.

•••

The entire camp came alive shortly before sunrise, and it woke Adkin and Matty. They could hear dogs barking, children playing and women shouting orders at them while they prepared morning meals.

Adkin dressed quickly and walked outside and down to the wagon. He removed its tarp over the supplies, and several people kept their eyes on him without a word. He dug around and pulled out a heavy bag and it clanked as he dropped it and knelt down.

He reached in a pulled out four horse shoes and held them up for all to see. Several of the men laughed and yelped their approval, apparently knowing just what they were. Adkin took them over to a wooden box under the end eave of the stable and pulled out some iron tools, including a large hammer and some tongs.

Next to the boy was a stand made from a large log but only about three-feet tall. On top was an iron anvil. A fire pit was on the end, where nearly half of it was outside the eave of the stable's roof. Adkin tossed some small limbs on the pile and poured some oil on them and lit it with a match.

If one didn't know better, it looked as if the fire pit was to warm the horses in cold weather. But in reality, it was a poor-man's version of a smitty's shop. Adkin knew he would need to do iron work on various equipment to live the summer on the Cimarron.

He laid the shoes and tools upon the box lid and walked back up to Quanah's tipi. A squaw ran into the lodge as Adkin approached. Shortly after, Quanah stepped out and stood still.

"Great Chief, I am here to put iron shoes on your horse," Adkin said with a smile, feeling a lot more comfortable with Quanah than during his first encounter. "Is your horse near?"

Quanah barked at a warrior standing close, and he ran around the back of the tipis toward the small creek off the side of the main ravine. In a few moments, he returned leading a huge black stallion that looked to be an identical twin to Diablo.

"This is my horse," Quanah said. "His name is Buffalo Hump, but I don't know if he will like you when you try to put iron shoes on him. His spirit is like the wind, strong and ever present."

Adkin slowly walked up to the warrior who held the lead lariat which was attached to a rope, hackamore-style bridle. Adkin put his hand on the rope, but the warrior looked at Quanah before he got the nod to release his grip and allow Adkin to hold the horse.

Adkin walked closer to Buffalo Hump, looking straight into his eyes. As he reached out his other arm, the horse neighed and snapped his head up and down a few times and stomped a front leg.

"Don't worry, boy," Adkin said softly. "I will be your friend."

He reached out and ran his hand down the side of Buffalo Hump's neck several times. He then reached up and straightened the mane between his ears, and running his hand down the steed's face.

After some petting and whispering words into Buffalo Hump's ear, Adkin turned slowly toward the stable and the horse followed him very peacefully. Quanah smiled at his people and fell in behind Adkin and Buffalo Hump.

When they reached the corral and stable, the other horses inside the corral all noticed when Buffalo Hump walked up into their vision. Especially Diablo. He snorted several times and actually started walking toward where Adkin, Buffalo Hump and Quanah stood.

"Your horse may not like Buffalo Hump – he looks angry," Quanah said smiling. "What is his name?"

"He is Diablo, a gift from Black Horse himself," Adkin said. "He is now about 6 whole seasons old. Very strong and proud horse."

"He is beautiful horse – I can see the Kiowa in him," Quanah said, chuckling. "I hope he knows Comanche is friend of the Kiowa."

Adkin wasn't sure judged by the way Diablo was carrying his head down as he approached. When he reached the fence line, he stood erect, only twitching to shoo flies away. Buffalo Hump finally leaned his head out and Diablo did likewise. Adkin kept a tight grip on the lariat, but allowed Buffalo Hump to lean forward over the fence post.

The horses smelled each other, tossed their heads around almost simultaneously, snorting a little, and then Diablo turned and sauntered back to the other horses who were already standing in the tree shade, nibbling on the green grass.

"It is an omen, Adkin Yates," Quanah said, sounding very serious. "If two wild stallions can get along, maybe you and I can do the same."

"I would almost believe they could be blood brothers," he added smiling again, hoping Quanah understood the inference.

"Only men can decide if they live together or die together," Adkin continued. "Paper treaties mean nothing when compared to how men agree to live together."

"You are wise – for a White Man," Quanah said sincerely.

"I have heard the name of Buffalo Hump before but cannot remember where or what it means," Adkin said as he stoked the fire pit.

"It is the name of a brave War Chief called Buffalo Hump – a Penateka Comanche," Quanah said. "He was a visionary and tried to push the Tejanos into the sea in south Texas. He made it to the big gulf and returned with thousands of horses and mules. He killed many Tejanos.

"I was born into the Penateka band, but it was the Quahadis who took in me and my brother after our father died," he continued. "But all bands of the Comanches hate the Tejanos. They take our land, kill our buffalo, and fight every Indian they see."

There it was again, Quanah refused to even mention "mother," so Adkin dropped the thought of asking him about her. He went to rubbing Buffalo Hump's legs, getting the animal comfortable with this touch.

Finally, he took the shoe from Quanah, who had been examining it while they talked, and lifted Buffalo Hump's back leg and straddled it. The horse remained calm, and Adkin held the shoe to the bottom of the hoof.

He was immediately thankful Buffalo Hump was such a large horse because Adkin's extra shoes were a large size compared to most of the Comanche ponies Adkin had seen. It was a lot of work to downsize a shoe rather than just shape it to the hoof.

He let the leg back down.

"This only needs to be fitted with a few strikes of the hammer," he said, smiling at Quanah.

He threw it into the fire pit embers and used a goat skin air pump to blow into the fire, swirling some embers around in the air. He asked Quanah where he usually wintered. Quanah thought about it for a long moment.

"If we are to be friends, I think it unwise to talk of where I will stop or where I go," Quanah said. "It may cause trouble between us."

"I'm sorry Great Chief," Adkin said quickly. "I understand, and I agree. It is not my business. I am sorry."

Adkin pulled the shoe out of the fire and grabbed a hammer and beat on the sides several times. Then dipped the shoe in a pail of water where it hissed and bubbled. He then lifted the stallion's same leg and held it to the hoof. He grabbed a small nail and hammered it through the shoe and through the hoof's edge. He did this all around the shoe.

Then he reached for scissors that could clip the points off the nail. He grabbed a metal file and started filing away the remaining metal tips where they stuck out of the hoof, rounding the edges off for a complete smooth and flush fit. He put Buffalo Hump's foot down and stood upright.

"There you go big boy. One new shoe and three to go," Adkin said as he continued to stroke the big horse's neck and shoulders. Quanah could tell Adkin had a way with horses.

Buffalo Hump picked the foot up several times, but then went back to standing still and looking undisturbed. The Indians standing around watching softly clapped and laughed, seeming happy things were going well.

They knew – as well as Adkin knew – if Adkin injured Buffalo Hump, Quanah would probably kill Adkin on the spot.

As Adkin smiled, he realized he and Quanah were nearly the same height and the same age. He decided to not ask Quanah his age, as many Indians were unaware of what age really meant. It was life experience that ruled tribal rank and success. It was simply, young is young and old is old.

Adkin finished sizing and nailing on the other shoes, and Quanah looked happy.

"The soldiers will think a White Man rides with us when we travel our lands," he said, laughing. "And those rabid dogs, the Tonks, who scout for them will not know what is going on."

•••

When Adkin and Quanah turned toward the house and Quanah's tipi, they saw Matty playing with several squaws and many children. They were hitting a hoop made of bended reeds tied together, hitting it with a small stick, trying to keep it rolling around to each other.

The giggling and shrill laughter stopped as Quanah approached. He waved his hands and shouted something in Comanche. The game then started again and laughter rang out. Adkin realized Quanah gave them approval to continue their fun.

Adkin just stood there a moment soaking in the scene as a warrior took Buffalo Hump back to his rope corral. Quanah sat down on some buffalo robes as the sun felt warm. He motioned for Adkin to sit as well, which he did.

"Your woman likes children, yes?" Quanah asked. "Will you two have children, too?"

"I would like very much, but she may not be able to have children," Adkin said. "She was injured by the soldier at Fort Supply, which killed her baby inside of her."

"I see," Quanah said, not saying anything more. He leaned back and lifted his eyes to the sky. He then shut them and seemed to simply enjoy the sun on his face. Adkin was thinking, "here we are around June 6 or 7, he hadn't checked his calendar, and Comanche Chief Quanah Parker was sitting in his yard, soaking up the sun."

"No one would ever guess this could happen," he said to himself. "Not even me."

"Has your buffalo hunting been good so far this summer?" Adkin asked.

"Not like years past," Quanah answered. "Most of the buffalo that wintered in the south to Mexico do not come down that far anymore. They are stopping northward of their old ranges."

Quanah then brought up the increase of White buffalo hunters.

"These men hunt buffalo just to kill them and take their hides," Quanah said. "They are not soldiers, only buffalo killers. And we know they will become a mighty enemy – soon. And we will kill them when we find them."

The buffalo was everything to the Comanches, according to Quanah.

"We love the meat – roasted or boiled in copper pots," he said. "We dry the meat in thin strips so we can travel far distances and even use it through the winter. White Men don't know how important buffalo is to our people.

"We eat the kidneys and the stomach," Quanah continued, patting his belly. "When we kill a female buffalo, we mix her milk with warm blood to drink. The children come running to a kill wanting the liver and gallbladder – they squeeze the salt liquids from the gallbladder onto the liver and eat it immediately.

"One of our most treasured foods from buffalo is if we kill a young calf who still drinks from its mother, we drink the young one's curdled milk from its stomach," he said. "Whites take nothing but the skins, leaving all the needed food and drink our people need to live in Comancheria."

There was a term Adkin hadn't heard in awhile: Comancheria. He had forgotten the Comanches were one of the most dominant tribes from the Platte

River in the north to Santa Fe, New Mexico, in the west, all of Texas to its eastern border and then to the gulf and south into northern Old Mexico. Adkin didn't know how to respond when Quanah stopped talking and just stared into the sky.

"I wish you well and success for good hunting," Adkin said, finally.

"We will move tomorrow to better hunting grounds," Quanah said. "I have rested too long, but your lodge was a welcome sight, and the area is very special. I see why you make lodge here."

At that moment, a willow loop rolled right into Quanah's legs and fell over. Matty ran up and stopped as Quanah reached for the loop. He handed it to Matty.

"The loop is like the circle of life, the seasons coming and going for eternity," he said. "You enjoy life, yes, Mat-tee?"

She was shocked again to be asked something by a Chief in front of everyone.

"Yes Great Chief. I like life – life with my husband," she said breathlessly.

"Please sit," he said as she rolled the loop to the children standing around with their eyes and mouths agape.

Matty sat down on the other side of Adkin and bowed her head to Quanah.

"What is your favorite thing to do here in this special place," Quanah asked, leaving her even more astounded.

She sat there not knowing just what to say. She loved the wildlife, her garden, the little creek bubbling down to the Cimarron – and she loved the Cimarron, having grown up for many seasons along it banks. She loved her new house. Then it hit her.

"I like to shoot the pescados – fish – with my own bow and arrows," she said, smiling cautiously, hoping it didn't sound too silly.

"I can kill more fish than my husband," she added, giggling and looking to Adkin.

"She tells the truth Great Chief," Adkin said starting to laugh. "I am not good with her bow, but I am going to try and make a bow for me and learn from her how to shoot better."

By the time Adkin got all that out, Quanah was starting to laugh, too.

"It is good you can say your woman is better shooter than you," he said, really laughing now.

They all laughed, and his people watching them were chuckling, too, even though most all had no idea what was being said.

Quanah suddenly waved to a warrior nearby. Between laughs, he spoke to him in Comanche. Matty didn't hear him, and she gave Adkin a quizzical look.

"You and your woman have been kind to me and my people," Quanah said. "I want you to have special gift of our friendship."

"That is not needed Great Chief," Adkin said. "Our friendship does not need gifts. Sharing buffalo meat, laughter and good talk is enough."

Quanah waved his hand as if signalling Adkin to be quiet. Suddenly the warrior he had spoken with came back carrying a long bow with two eagle feathers tied on each end. The whittled hand grip was wrapped in a fine leather thong over the entire area where it was made to be gripped. There was also a decorated leather quiver with about 30 arrows in it.

Quanah took the bow and pulled out his knife and started whittling on the wood above the grip. He didn't take long before he handed it to Adkin.

"Take this Adkin Yates, and have your woman help you learn to shoot pescados," Quanah said, starting to chuckle again. But his smile was warm to Adkin. He felt there was maybe something special about this fearless but deadly Chief.

Adkin looked at what Quanah had etched into the wood. There were two initials; a "K" and a "P" following the "K." Adkin took it to mean Quanah Parker, and the Chief confirmed it when Adkin gave him a glance of inquiry.

"The K is for Kwih-nai, which is my name, meaning fragrance like smell of flower," Quanah said. "But everybody call me Quanah.

"It is my bow – from Quanah Parker, to my friend Adkin Yates – and his wife Mat-tee, who is a better fish killer for now," he said grinning.

Adkin was touched by his kindness and his sense of humor. He now realized how James Mead could describe Satanta in glowing terms at times. Of course, Adkin had made friends with Satanta, as well, and understood the good side of the man – just like Quanah.

This time, Adkin was ready for exchanging gifts. He whispered in Matty's ear and she bolted from her buffalo skin, slowing enough to bow to Quanah as she hurried away. While Matty was gone, Quanah was telling Adkin if there were more time, he would show Adkin how to arrow pescados.

"You must aim lower than your eyes tell you," he said.

As soon as Matty entered the lodge again, she handed Adkin a white bag which was tied at the top with a leather thong.

"I wish to give my friend Great Chief Quanah this gift," Adkin said, handing the bag to Quanah. "It is from the green fields of the country of Kentucky in the east."

Quanah opened the bag, which was about the size of a small feed bag for a horse. The big Indian looked back up to Adkin and smiled.

"This is the famous Kentucky tobacco?" he asked, putting his face deeper into the bag and smelling the rich tobacco.

"Yes."

"We must smoke," he said, reaching for his decorated pipe.

He loaded the bowl and took a piece of straw and lit it in the coals of his lodge fire pit and touched it to the tobacco. He again did his little ritual of looking to the sky and singing softly, then handing the pipe to Adkin, who only took a short draw.

Quanah smiled and took another puff, savoring the tobacco taste. He handed it back to Adkin, but Adkin politely refused saying he wanted Quanah to not waste the tobacco on him, it was for Quanah.

Quanah seemed grateful and shook Adkin's hand like White men do, though Quanah pumped his hand several more times than usual.

That evening, Matty served some of the antelope Sitler had given them in Dodge. She stewed it adding onions and potatoes. Quanah approved and ate two bowls with some bread.

"I thank you for showing me how to put iron shoes on horses," Quanah said. "I will show others, and we someday will get the tools to do many of our ponies."

Adkin was stunned. At first he was thinking, "This man couldn't have learned enough to think he could actually shoe a horse." But then Adkin realized Quanah was an exceptional person. He apparently has learned good English – maybe from White captives or Comancheros or Mexicans – regardless, it was apparent Quanah was a fast learner.

After studying the matter a few moments, Adkin chuckled to himself, coming to the conclusion that Quanah just might be able to shoe a horse after watching Adkin do it one time.

"You will make the Tonkawa scouts crazy – loco," Adkin said, laughing. Quanah laughed along nodding his head.

•••

The next morning, all the tipis were down, rolled up and placed with their poles on travoises, ready for travel. Women were rounding up children – all the toddlers had been wrapped and placed in the various cradleboards and baskets.

Warriors had managed to move their horse herd east about 300 yards and were starting them across the Cimarron in the exact place Ten Bears had crossed. Adkin felt they were headed to the Llano Estacado as well and to either Palo Duro Canyon or Blanco Canyon. But he would tell no one what little he did know.

Adkin and Matty were standing outside the porch watching the living mass of humans, animals and barking dogs begin to move out in coordinated chaos. Matty was smiling, possibly remembering all the times she experienced the same kind of nomadic life.

Just then, Quanah rode up on Buffalo Hump, who whinnied and stomped like the big stallion he was. Adkin reached out and stroked the horse's face and neck.

"Not many men – White or Indian – can do that," Quanah said, smiling. "I wish you well Adkin Yates. And I wish you happy life Mat-tee."

"Thank you great Chief Quanah Parker," Adkin said, raising his right hand up with the palm facing Quanah. "You and your people are always welcome to stay in our lodge."

"Vaya con Dios, Jefe Quanah," Matty said softly. "Go in peace."

Quanah smiled and reined Buffalo Hump around and kicked him with the heels of his moccasins. The big horse leapt forward and started loping toward the chain of Indians and animals moving east to cross the Cimarron.

It was June 8, 1871, and Adkin knew the last few days would never be forgotten. A smile crept across his face, and Matty knew Adkin was happy.

•••

The visit with Quanah and his band, which Adkin estimated at about 300 total people, was pleasant, and it wasn't until the second morning after their departure that Adkin discovered Quanah had signed the guest book on the stand next to the door. Adkin had asked visitors to sign their name and their current home.

Adkin noticed when he opened it, the very first line had large letters: "KP" for Kwih-nai Parker, which Adkin wrote in parenthesis with a dash adding "Quanah Parker." Adkin smiled and closed the book.

But Adkin couldn't help but worry about Satanta. Though he kept busy around the house, he thought about him more and more. And Matty seemed to be worried as well, though she didn't talk about it either since leaving Dodge.

One evening after eating, Matty asked Adkin if there was anything they could do to help Satanta. He smiled at her, knowing she was upset, too.

"I've been trying to think of something, but I can't see where we could be of help in any way," he said. "If we travelled to Fort Sill or Fort Richardson, what could we say on his behalf?

"Apparently, he and others left the reservations and went into Texas. He knew if they crossed the Red River whey could get into trouble," Adkin said. "Sherman must have proof Satanta's band of Kiowa was at the raid."

"That is what I fear, he has words from others who saw him there," Matty said, looking down at their table top with her hands on her lap. "What can they do to him?"

"I'm not sure," Adkin said, knowing full well if he and the others are convicted by a White jury, they could be sentenced to death.

"We will find out when we return to Dodge in about one full moon," he added. "These things take a long time – not much can happen to him in that time."

They went about their tasks, and trying to enjoy their solitude and the beauty of their area. It was actually easy, and Adkin found himself realizing the house was in an area that truly could be called "Eden."

He would walk out and sit on the small porch shortly before sunrise and sip his tea. Down below, the wild turkeys were gobbling as they drifted down from their perches in the large Cottonwoods. It was the toms gathering to roam the river banks while the hens were collecting their chicks from their ground nests to look for food.

Whitetail does were working along the river with their fawns, dancing every now and then – standing on their hind legs and pawing at each other or nibbling leaves from tree limbs overhead. The fawns were learning the game, too. It always brought a smile to Adkin's face.

Adkin was also quick to offer to try and kill some fish with his new bow. He was sure with excellent equipment, he could succeed.

"Have some fun" Matty teased with a big grin. "If you want to eat fish, I will help later."

"Hey, don't be so hard on your husband," Adkin said, chuckling while he grabbed the beautiful longbow from Quanah. He had briefly wondered what that equipment would be worth in Westport. But he knew he would never let it go to anyone at any price.

Adkin took Quanah's suggestion to shoot low at fish, and after about half a dozen attempts, Adkin finally speared a large carp sitting in only 12-inches of water by the reeds. He ran back up to the house, yelling for Matty and waving his arrowed fish above is head.

"You look like young warrior who just killed his first animal," Matty said, laughing, which then triggered Adkin's funny-bone and he started laughing loudly, as well.

•••

The days seemed longer and more wonderful as Adkin and Matty just enjoyed the summer and their new lodge. Adkin was getting better and better with Quanah's bow, but he broke one of the arrows hitting some rocks under water. Matty tried to mend it, but it wasn't the same. Adkin retired it to a place on the wall above the kitchen table. He said he would thank God – and Quanah – every time they ate fish.

Matty told Adkin if he could kill a few deer, say two or three, she would make him some new leggings. He had bought his in Santa Fe and worn them for several years. She said she would make better ones with decorative beading to represent a great Chief.

He laughed but went deer hunting just the same, as there were plenty of deer east of their home where Crooked Creek came into the valley. He decided to kill one a week, to give Matty her time to prepare the hide, the meat, bones, etcetera. She also scraped all the velvet off the bucks' antlers to make a medicinal ointment to rub on open wounds to help them heal.

An Englishman's Adventures on the Santa Fe Trail (1865-1889)

The month went by with no interruptions by any other living humans. In a way, Adkin couldn't believe how much he actually enjoyed the solitude. But then he found himself wanting to know what was happening in the real world around them.

"It is no good to wonder what things are happening when you cannot change them if you want," Matty would tell him, as much for herself as his, as she was constantly worried what was happening to Satanta.

In the first week of July, Adkin started telling Matty to help him make a list of what supplies they would need in Dodge.

"I think we should leave on July 25 for Fort Dodge," Adkin said. "Our supplies of sugar, flour and salt will be okay til then."

"Did I say I want more molasses this trip?" Matty asked. "It is Mary Catherine's fault I love to eat those biscuits with much molasses."

Adkin chuckled and nodded affirmatively, then he wondered how Sam, Mary Catherine and the children were faring in Blaine County, Oklahoma. It was a beautiful place to live – at Zeb's old ranch – but it was square in the middle of all kinds of tribes that didn't necessarily get along.

"Knowing Mary Catherine, she's tamed every Indian within miles with her Biblical sternness and her love of people," Adkin thought to himself with a smile.

On the day before departing, Matty reminded Adkin she needed another large steel sewing needle.

"The one Mary Catherine gave me broke this morning while I was sewing your leggings," Matty said.

"You can make another with the bone of the deer – like the old days," Adkin teased her and smiling.

"I not live in the old days any more," she barked back. "That is your fault my husband."

...

They crossed the bridge over the Arkansas on July 18 and immediately realized Hoover's Whisky Bar had upgraded even more. Gone were the side tarp walls on the back side structure – replaced by wooden planked walls. Adkin didn't stop but reined his wagon team to the east for Fort Dodge and the telegraph office.

As they entered Fort Dodge, Adkin told the guards he needed to see Quartermaster Major E. B. Kirk. The guard pointed to the warehouse, and Adkin turned his team that way.

When Adkin halted their team and jumped from the seat, Bob Wright walked out the door.

"Adkin Yates – and Missus Yates – how are you faring my friends," Wright shouted. "It is good to see you again."

"Good to see you Mister Wright," Adkin said, while Matty smiled and nodded but said nothing. "When are you going to start selling those city plots?"

"The Good Lord must have talked to you in a dream," Wright said. "I was just discussing our survey with Major Kirk.

"Sir, I am happy to report we are in the process of selling plots as of yesterday," Wright added.

"Well, if you can wait until I deposit my order with the Major, Matty and I would like to see the survey and choose some lots," Adkin said, smiling at Matty.

"Well, if it isn't the Yates family," a voice boomed from the doorway as Major Kirk stepped out onto the porch.

"Welcome back to Fort Dodge. I heard Bob here talking with someone about the town survey. Your timing couldn't have been better, Mister Yates."

The men all shook hands and Kirk invited Adkin into his office. Wright helped Matty get down from the wagon and followed them into the building.

Adkin went over the list of supplies with Kirk, who assured he and Matty the supplies would be no problem. Kirk asked them all to sit down at a table and waved Wright over.

"First, have you heard anything about Satanta?" Adkin asked Kirk.

"No, other than he's going to be tried for murder, but that's not happened yet, as far as I know.

"Oh, but we did hear Old Chief Satank jumped a guard at Fort Sill and Satank was killed," Kirk added, but then looked to Wright, not saying any more.

"Bob, you need to show Yates our township survey, and tell him what Rath's men told us," Kirk said, changing the subject.

Wright laid his leather satchel down and opened it. He slid out several papers and unfolded one. It was a township survey which started on the west side of the military property line established by the federal government.

"Now this is nearly five miles from where we're sitting right now," Wright said. "Actually right where you crossed the bridge over the Arkansas. This out here is where Sitler has purchased lots over this ridge north of the river. This 'S' is where he's building."

Wright went on to show all the lots that were platted with the bridge being the main center street going north from the river. But Adkin noticed it was labeled Second Street. Wright pointed to several blocks he purchased along the river.

"A couple of Rath's men were looking for buffalo herds last week about 100 miles east of here just southwest of the Arkansas when they came upon a surveying party," Wright continued. "They were with the Atchison, Topeka and Santa Fe Railroad, mind you. They said they had travelled west from the Emporia area, where tracks were being laid up to just about 20 miles east of the Little Arkansas River.

"We're pretty sure they're going to follow most of the Santa Fe Trail to here," he said. "And we think they'll lay track along this north ridge – they wouldn't want a flood to destroy tracks right along the river.

"So all these lots, we have 600 total, are what we have to sell to raise the $6,000 needed to certify a township under the Dodge City Town Company," Wright said.

"Those lots with initials were sold yesterday, Yates," Kirk interrupted.

Wright pointed out where many sites were taken. Most of the lots along the eastern edge closest to the Army property were already taken, as well as those right along the north bank of the Arkansas. And then Adkin noticed the northwest quadrant wasn't spoken for. He pointed at a spot right along the ridge of the small valley and ran his finger northward.

"Is it possible for me to purchase these lots, say five lots wide and 10 high right off the side of the bridge street?" Adkin asked, as Kirk and Wright glanced at each other with broad smiles. The south lots were right along the north ridge overlooking the river.

"Why it certainly is," Wright said, as Kirk slapped Adkin on the back, nearly rocking Adkin from his chair.

The lots Adkin chose were along Walnut on the south and between Second Avenue on the east, Fourth on the west and Vine on the north – what eventually would be in downtown Dodge City in the coming years. It would prove to be one of Adkin's additional financially successful decisions of his young life.

"If you'll grab me a cash transfer certificate, Major, I'll fill out the $500 note right now," Adkin said. "It will be transferred from my account in Junction City as soon as they receive the telegram."

"Great – this is great, Yates," Wright said. "You just wait, by this time next year, we'll be seeing the railroad come through here, and it will change this part of Kansas forever."

...

There were several telegraphs and a posted letter waiting for Adkin at the Western Union Office. One of the telegrams was from James Mead, and it had come in only one week before.

Mead was excited to let Adkin and his crew know that the Santa Fe Railroad had laid tracks into Emporia during the fourth of July weekend with great fanfare. Mead said rumor was the rails would reach Fort Dodge the following summer once additional grant money was approved by the U.S. Senate.

Adkin told Matty what Mead had said in the telegram, explaining if the railroad came through Dodge, their investments in the lots would pay off handsomely. She smiled, though not really understanding.

Another wire was from Ryan and Ray Dee. Business was brisk in Colorado with stage lines, but J.L. was set on expanding service into California and points between. Ray Dee was going to supervise a wagon train from Kit Carson, Colorado, where eight Concords were to be delivered by way of rail. J.L. and Ray Dee were scheduled to leave the last week of July.

"Everything is in order" – Stop.
"Enjoy your summer" – Stop
T. Ryan. – Stop.

Adkin smiled and explained what info was in the message. He felt a pang of envy, having wanted to go to California just to see all the wonders he had heard about. But he also wanted to cross the Rocky Mountains just for the experience.

"Oh well, some other time, perhaps," he thought to himself.

He wrote out a message to Ryan and Ray Dee, telling them "all was in order," and they would be back to Las Animas a little after October 1, as planned.

The letter was from Sam and Mary Catherine. It was her handwriting, and she was excited. She had given birth to another girl – named her Rosa after the woman who helped Mary Catherine with the pregnancy and birth.

She reported all were doing very well and had expanded the Jarvis Ranch House grounds. Sam and Darwin had successfully planted forage crops of oats and barley. This will aid in feeding all the stock, she explained.

She said James Allen and little Anna were growing like weeds but all were in good health. She said James Mead had visited in April, but he was busy with building a town on the old land he filed on between the Arkansas and Little Arkansas Rivers – land he had traded Jesse Chisholm for years ago.

She reported business was good freighting between Emporia and Fort Supply, as well as from Fort Gibson to Fort Supply and Fort Sill.

She invited them to visit whenever possible, that they missed the freighting crews. And Mary Catherine asked Adkin to tell Matty she especially missed her – like a sister. A tear leaked from Matty's eye when Adkin told her.

"Maybe one day we go see Mary Catherine and her babies, si?" Matty asked softly.

"Yes, Matty. We will," he said.

There was also a telegram from Weldon Campbell in Great Bend. He had joined Rath's buffalo hunters and was scouting for herds south of Great Bend. He said they were planning on several summer hunts and hoping to load the hides for market at the new railhead in Emporia.

He wanted Adkin to know he would make up his mind about working for Adkin by summer's end and after the buffalo hunts. Adkin realized Campbell would make plenty of fast money hunting and would likely prefer that over running wagon trains and handling stock and all the other necessities of freighting. But, he would wait and see.

...

An Englishman's Adventures on the Santa Fe Trail (1865-1889)

Adkin and Matty told the soldiers loading their wagon with their supplies they would return in a couple of hours. They mounted Diablo and Tóngúl and rode off west to see Sitler.

Sitler's place was near completion, but there were only a few men around. As Adkin and Matty tied off their horses in front of Sitler's, he stepped out on the porch.

"Great to see you two," he said with his arms stretched out. "How are you doing living in the Cimarron House? Any Indian problems?"

"Well, Chief Quanah Parker stopped by for about three days for a visit," Adkin said as they walked up on the porch where Adkin shook hands with Sitler and Matty gave him a quick hug.

"Quanah?" he looked shocked. "Are you jesting me?"

"No, he liked the Cimarron House and rested a few days preparing for their buffalo hunts on the Llano Estacado," Adkin said, teasingly.

Sitler invited them inside as Adkin filled him in on Quanah's visit and how the deadly Chief took a liking to he and Matty.

"Of course, it didn't hurt when he saw the gifts I had received from Satanta and Ten Bears," Adkin said. "He even gave me his hunting bow and dozens of arrows as a gift."

"I'll be danged. For an Englishman, you seem to have been born with a horse shoe up your … ah, well you know what I mean," Sitler said looking to Matty.

He asked a Mexican woman to bring glasses of fresh water for them and began talking about the township plans. Adkin informed him of the lots he bought and Sitler was very excited for Adkin.

"I looked at some of those myself, but I wanted this area out here in case the town gets big. I'll still be out here overlooking my cattle.

"You'll do well with that investment, even if you don't build there," Sitler added.

Rath and the others had travelled east after hearing of the buffalo south and west of the Great Bend in the Arkansas River.

"They've got six wagons and are hoping to sell the hides at Emporia," Sitler said. "I hope all goes well. I've already contacted a buyer in Westport who says he'll purchase the hides if they can get them to Emporia.

"I've got an interest in the hunting party and might make some profit," he leaned over to Adkin and whispered and then smiled at Matty.

Adkin asked Sitler if he had heard any more about Satanta, besides the news that Satank was killed.

"Not a word," Sitler said. "But word is he's been moved to Fort Richardson in Texas for trial. That's all I know."

Sitler told Adkin Rath had word from Goodnight that he and another rancher named John Chisum were going to blaze a cattle trail from New Mexico to Colorado and eventually to Wyoming.

"I don't doubt that Charles will meet a profitable end with that endeavor," Adkin said with a chuckle. "I travelled with him down through New Mexico and know the route he has selected. He kept copious notes along the trail."

After visiting with Sitler and catching up on the local rumors and what was happening in the area, Adkin and Matty bid farewell to Sitler and headed back to Fort Dodge.

They went directly to the supply depot, signed the papers and drove the wagon over to Kirk's office. They went over the invoice and, again, Adkin signed the bill of laden to be telegraphed to his bank in Junction City. Adkin wanted to leave so as to make it to the camp grounds south of Mulberry Creek, which were widely used by locals in the area.

As they were crossing the bridge over the Big Arkansas, Adkin brought up Sam and Mary Catherine.

"I've been thinking all day about going to see Sam and Mary Catherine and the children," Adkin said to Matty. "I have a thought, and I want your opinion."

He asked her if she would mind leaving the Cimarron House early in order to travel to Blaine County to see the Phillips' and the operation.

"We have enough supplies to last until about the second week of September," he said. "What if we leave for Oklahoma that first week of September? That would give us three weeks to get back to Las Animas – or about seven days with Sam and Mary Catherine."

"Oh yes, Adkin, That would make me very happy," She said, jumping over and grabbing him around the neck, nearly choking him with her eagerness. "Yes, yes, yes. Can we go for sure?"

"Yes Matty. Easy or you'll break my neck," he said with both of them bursting into laughter.

•••

A few hours later, they came upon Mulberry Creek and Adkin pulled up the team and stopped the wagon. There were several tents and a cooking fire already ablaze. Crowded around the camp were six wagons along with at least a dozen mules and that many horses. It was nearly sunset, meaning they had about 30 minutes of dusk remaining before dark.

Adkin took out his telescope and checked out the camping area. He told Matty it looked like either freighters or White hunters.

"There's maybe six or seven that I can see," Adkin said. "I think it will be safe, but don't sit too close in case I have to draw my pistol."

He reached back and slid his Henry next to his left leg where it could easily be reached. They rode up to the creek and slowly started crossing it, which caught the attention of the men in their camp. Adkin hollered as they crossed.

"Hey there, My name is Adkin Yates," he shouted. "Is it okay if me and my wife come into your camp?"

"Sure, come on in Mister Yates," a voice bellowed back.

As they pulled up, Adkin eyed the men in sight, carefully looking to see if any threatening faces were visible. They all looked very young with the exception of a couple.

"How are you Mister Yates? – Missus Yates?" One of the men stepped forward. "Remember me …"

"Well, hello Mister Bassett," Adkin said with a big grin

"Hello Charley," Matty said, smiling, too.

Adkin jumped from the wagon and embraced Bassett, as Matty was climbing down.

"It's good to see you my friend," Adkin said.

"Likewise," Bassett said, while shaking hands with Matty. "Y'all been to Fort Dodge to re-supply?"

"Yes indeed," Adkin said. "And what are you doing out here and not in Dodge?"

"Don't want these young men gettin' liquored up," Bassett said. "We've got some huntin' to do."

Bassett then introduced Adkin and Matty to his hunters; brothers Ed and William "Bill" Masterson, Billy Dixon, Tom Nixon, "Prairie Dog" Dave Morrow and Wyatt S. Earp.

Bassett explained he ran into the Mastersons and Earp on the upper Salt Fork of the Arkansas south of Medicine Lodge Creek hunting buffalo.

"They were managing about 20 head a week, but I convinced them we could double that, or better, by teaming up with us," Bassett said. "They're all good kids and eager."

Everybody shook hands and the younger ones were captivated by Matty. Bassett had introduced her as a Kiowa Princess, and their eyes widened like she was actually some kind of queen. They were all acutely mannered, removing hats, bowing and stuttering.

Adkin couldn't help but laugh to himself. They seemed very young, yet he was only 24 himself. He did discover during the evening that five of them were relatively new to the open West and the Great Plains.

Earp being a Missouri man who had lived briefly in California as a freighter. The Masterson's were impressive for being 18 and 19, Ed being the elder. But Bill, or Bat, as they were calling him, was about 6-feet-3, nearly as tall as Adkin and looked very wiry and strong for 18. They had met Dixon when he was a freighter working the Military Road to Camp Supply. They knew him to be a good hard worker. He and Nixon seemed to look a little more like seasoned buffalo hunters.

"Prairie Dog" – definitely older – had fought with the Union in California, and ended up in Hays City. He claimed to know Charley and Chris Rath, Adkin's business partners as he explained.

"The boys here have some buffalo sighted southeast of here along the Salt Fork of the Arkansas and that's where we're headed," Bassett said. "We re-supplied yesterday – just missed you somehow."

Adkin told the men how Bassett had helped he and Matty build their dream home – the Cimarron House – and bragged up Bassett as much as possible. Bassett blushed a little, but said he was honored to be a part of the house raising.

"You know Rath and some of his hunters are working the Arkansas south of the Great Bend, don't you," Adkin asked Bassett.

"Yep, we agreed to help each other as much as possible," Bassett said. "There's no competition there – because there's a lot of buffalo out here."

"We're just going to hunt til hard winter sets in and hope we make enough to live on for a few months til Spring," Bassett said.

Adkin told them about Sam Phillips and Darwin Jarvis running freight out of Blaine County Oklahoma. He also told them where their Ranch House was located.

"If you boys have freighting experience, Sam might be able to give you work through the winter, if there's enough freight moving," Adkin said. "They are my partners and very fair men."

"Thanks for the information Mister Yates, That may come in handy when the snow starts blowing," Earp said.

"You can call me Adkin – all of you can if you prefer," Adkin said.

"Thanks Adkin," Ed and Bill answered together.

"Now let's cook up some bacon and eat," Bassett said, as Matty asked if she could help with the meal.

"No Little Lady, you just take a seat and rest yourself," Bassett said, smiling. "It's my turn to cook for you after all those wonderful meals you cooked for us at the Cimarron House."

During the meal, Bassett asked how things were progressing at their new home. Adkin told him about the corral and stables he had just about finished. Adkin then brought up Quanah's visit, and suddenly, all the men were paying rapt attention to what Adkin was saying.

They could hardly believe Adkin and Matty made friends with Quanah. They almost feinted when Adkin told them about the long bow and arrows.

"That Comanche is developing a reputation for cold-blooded murder as bad as his father's was," Prairie Dog said. Adkin realized he was older if he knew about Peta Nocona, Quanah's father.

"He doesn't seem to take to the White Man's ways," Adkin said. "He's convinced we're all a pack of liars and killers. But, I guess that's all he's really seen – from his point of view."

"Which way did he go?" Earp asked. "He's not out this way is he?"

"No, he and his band headed west to the Llano Estacado for buffalo," Adkin said, while he noticed Earp actually sighed. "There's about 300 of them but only about 100 warriors, I'd guess."

"Damn, I've seen what 100 Comanches can do," Bassett said. "It ain't pretty."

"Amen," Prairie Dog said.

"Hey Adkin, we were going to ride along Crooked creek to the Cimarron – mind if we ride with you and Matty?" Bassett asked.

"No, not at all," Adkin said. "We'd enjoy the company."

They chatted into the night talking about freighting, the Indian campaign Sherman and Sheridan were pushing – and the railroads. Seemed all were sure the rails would bring civilization and law and order to the Great Plains.

When Matty went to the wagon to get their bed rolls ready, Adkin excused himself and left the men talking around the fire. Adkin put out some oats for the animals and made sure the horses were hobbled. He took no chances even if Fort Dodge was less than two hours away.

It was a warm evening, and Adkin and Matty only covered with an old gray Army blanket while they lay upon soft buffalo robes and beaver pelts. As Matty straightened the buffalo hide under her, she spoke softly.

"That reminds me, I will need for you to kill me a buffalo several weeks before we go to see Mary Catherine," she whispered. "I have to make pemmican with the rest of our jerky for the winter – and to give some to Mary Catherine and her babies."

"I will my Princess," Adkin said as he kissed her cheek, understanding Matty was really excited to go see the Phillips clan.

•••

Adkin awoke as Bassett and Prairie Dog were starting the coffee pot and woke Matty. He helped her get out of the wagon, and waved to the men around the embers. The two walked down along the creek and Matty went into the bushes using a small pail of water to freshen up.

Adkin stood guard and searched the sky for signs of weather. It wasn't uncommon for summer squalls to kick up and form cyclones. It looked to be a good day for travel with only a soft, sage-scented breeze out of the southwest.

Once in camp, Adkin and Matty had a cup of coffee with the men, while they were discussing the trail from the Cimarron to the Salt Fork of the Arkansas.

Adkin was impressed by the men Bassett had put together, But he knew he shouldn't be surprised – look at how Bassett and the men helped build the Cimarron House. Good men all. Adkin also felt Matty had a proper influence on most men, whether they were good or bad. Little did Adkin know then that several of those men would become long-time friends of his.

Once everyone was mounted or in the wagon seats, they headed south-southwest to cross Crooked Creek. It was a well-worn trail nowadays. In 2-and-a-half days, Adkin and Matty would be back at their summer home. Adkin felt a sense of peace just thinking about it. Matty was smiling from ear-to-ear.

As they topped a slight rise about a half a mile above Crooked Creek, they could see a mounted horsemen riding toward them up the trail. Adkin reined his team to a stop while Bassett stopped next to him on his horse. The others followed by stopping the wagons and steeds.

"Looks to be a dozen riders – maybe Comancheros," Dog said. "I don't recognize anyone. You men know any of those riders?"

Several "no's were heard. Adkin kept his eyes on them, trying to decipher if he had ever seen any of the men now riding right up to them. Adkin elbowed Matty slightly so she would move away from his Colt on his right side. Adkin disliked seeing riders out here on the plains with no wagons. They were neither freighters nor traders for sure.

"Bueno Señors – y Señorita," the head rider said, tipping his sombrero slightly toward Matty. "How are you fine people doing this wonderful morning?"

Bassett had his rifle slung over his saddle horn, and the others, except for Prairie Dog, were sitting on wagon benches not saying a word. Billy Dixon was trying to ease his rifle onto his lap.

"We are doing fine Señor," Adkin said. "We are headed to Crooked Creek to visit friends."

Adkin glanced quickly at Bassett who shook his head sideways slightly, letting Adkin know he didn't trust these men. They were a mix of Mexicans and Indians – rough looking Comancheros for sure.

"What are you hauling in those wagons," the head one asked, while twisting his long, black mustache. As he did that several of his men eased their mounts off to his flanks while several of them held rifles up, the butts resting on their thighs. "Are you traders helping your friends on Crooked Creek?"

"No, we're buffalo hunters," Bassett barked loudly with anger in his voice.

"Oh, buffalo hunters," the man said smiling. "That means you have mucho supplies, si?"

Before Bassett could answer, the man pulled a pistol from his waistband and shot at Bassett but missed him.

Adkin reacted in a split second, pulling his Colt and shooting the head man right in his chest, knocking him out of his saddle. But before the man hit the ground, Adkin had put another bullet through the face of the Comanchero next to him while he was levelling his rifle. The back of his head exploded.

Several Comancheros by then started shooting while Bassett and his men started firing, too. But within seconds the Comancheros realized their leader and right-hand man had been instantly killed. Only about a dozen shots were fired by them as they turned to flee.

Bassett dropped another one off his horse as he turned away – shot square in his back and exiting the left side of his chest. Prairie Dog wounded another who managed to stay in his saddle as they headed west in a cloud of dust with three unmounted horses following the others.

It was all over in about 15 or 20 seconds, and Adkin was sliding his Colt back into his holster, then hugging Matty – making sure she was not hit.

"Is everyone okay?" Bassett shouted.

All reported they were fine, though they were trying to settle the animals which were still snorting and pawing the ground at all the ruckus.

"I didn't even get off a shot," Earp said. "But I did hear a bullet zip right by my head – never heard that before."

"Dang, I never saw a man before who was quick as a thought with a pistol," Earp continued. "I've heard of it, but dang, that was fast and deadly."

"Whew, that's too much excitement for this early in the trip," Ed Masterson said, with his younger brother shaking his head in agreement.

Tom was reloading his pistol and Billy said he didn't know why he tried to grab his old Sharp's buffalo gun first.

"That could've got me killed," he said, half chuckling while several others laughed, too.

"I've never seen a man sitting still on a wagon bench pull and fire that fast – and that accurate," Bassett said to Adkin. "Do you practice that?"

Adkin slowly looked at Bassett.

"No, I've never had to pull on a man like that before," Adkin said softly.

Bassett just shook his head and said nothing more.

Several of the men got off their wagons and checked their animals, making sure they or nothing of value was hit. There was one water barrel that was hit, but the hole was near the top and not much water was wasted.

"Well, I guess we should bury these bastards you reckon?" Bassett said, looking at the three dead Comancheros. "I doubt the others will come back for 'em."

"I don't know," Prairie Dog said. "They may try to catch up with us after dark and seek revenge. Maybe we should leave them to the vultures and make haste."

"I'll bury them" Adkin spoke out. He got down from his wagon and walked to the back and pulled out a spade. "Even vermin are God's creatures."

Without a word, the others fetched their shovels and started helping Adkin dig a narrow ditch that would hold three bodies – deep enough to keep them from coyotes. They removed their weapons before dragging them into the grave. They quickly covered them and patted down the loose dirt with the spades.

Adkin took off his hat and mumbled a few words that no one could make out. He put his hat back on and walked to his wagon. Without a word, he slapped the reins on his team and headed onward toward Crooked Creek. The others followed, still amazed at what they had seen.

"People ain't goin' believe this when I tell 'em," Billy said to Prairie Dog as he rode next to Billy's wagon. "Killin' two Comancheros in two seconds from a wagon bench – with a Colt pistol."

About two hours later, Adkin signaled to Bassett by pointing at a camp site along Crooked Creek.

"We've stayed here before several times," Adkin said. "There's good grass for the animals and only two sides that anyone can sneak up on you."

They camped, and Matty was glad Adkin asked her to cook for everyone. He assured Bassett and his men it was their turn to provide the evening meal. Matty outdid herself, even making her famous biscuits in her old Dutch oven. Adkin didn't say much while she worked away.

"I don't particularly like killing men," Adkin said to Bassett as Bassett sat down beside him on a cottonwood log. "But, back in '67, I was riding with William Bent when we came upon some Kwaharu Comanches. He had to kill one, and he didn't hesitate. He warned me about hesitating – that it would get you killed.

"I've never forgot that, and it has saved me several times, but I have never had to drawn down on anyone like that," he added.

"I understand, Adkin," Bassett said. "That's the law of the West. It's kill or be killed. I just wanted to thank you for saving my life. He might've hit me with another shot, but you stopped him from getting it off.

"Thanks," he added while reaching out to shake Adkin's hand. Adkin took it, and they both shook hard. Bassett started smiling, and Adkin finally started grinning back at him.

"The meal is ready," Matty shouted, beaming as the men came hustling up to the cook fire.

...

After eating, several of the men asked Adkin how he got so accurate with his Colts. Adkin assured them it was simple practice, which Adkin tried to do very often – a habit he had developed after buying his first pistol.

"Tyler Ryan and I have shot thousands of rounds practicing," Adkin said. "He's better than me at times, too."

As Matty was cleaning up and putting away her kitchen utensils, Bassett told Adkin they would ride with them to the Cimarron and then turn due east to intercept the Salt Fork.

"We could follow the Cimarron all the way, but it meanders so much, it takes two days more going that way," Bassett said. "If we stay due east, we can cut off 30 or 40 miles getting where we need to get."

"You're more than welcome to come over to the Cimarron House for a night," Adkin said. "It's only 8 miles west."

"That would be nice, but we need to get up there and start killin' buffalo," Bassett said. "We're hoping to move the herds northward where Rath and his hunting party can intercept them.

"We can make a lot of money, but we have to get to shootin' and skinnin' for that to happen," he added laughing. "Do you think it will be safe at your place?"

"We'll be able to know if anyone has been there," Adkin said. "We're careful, really."

"I'm sure, it's just natural to worry about friends," Bassett said, chuckling.

The next day was again bright and sunny with a slight southwest wind. They continued down Crooked Creek, and it was about two hours before sunset when they saw the creek dumping into the Cimarron. The Cimarron valley wasn't deep but it was wide along this stretch, and trees and plant life were abundant.

"Like I told you before, Adkin, this little area of the Cimarron is beautiful," Bassett said. "It's a fitting place for you and Matty, but I predict when settlers find this spot, you're going to have plenty of neighbors. And that railroad is going to bring them, mark my words."

Adkin laughed and said he wasn't going to argue the point.

"You know, I'm not sure if our place is in Kansas or the Indian Territories, yet," Adkin said smiling. "And I don't even want to hire surveyors because they'll tell others about it."

"Well, if I was you, I would go ahead and mark off what you think 260 acres is with posts and some rocks and put your name and date on them so you can file someday – or make a deal with some tribe," Bassett said.

"That's a good idea Charley. Think I will do that, just in case."

"And for your information, I've heard from Army people at Fort Dodge that Crooked Creek enters the Cimarron three miles into the Territories. So you might take that for what it's worth.

"Well, we better get moving – we have a few hours to make some distance yet," Bassett added, reaching out to shake Adkin's hand.

Seeing this, Bassett's men started getting off their wagons and walking over. Prairie Dog reined his mount their way also. Every man reached up to shake Adkin's hand, several thanking him for his shooting skills.

"I'll never forget your warning about hesitating – that it could get you killed," Earp said, smiling.

Adkin looked to Bassett, who smiled and hunched his shoulders up. He knew Adkin knew who told Earp and the others what Adkin had said. Adkin just smiled at Bassett.

Once everybody was back in their places, Bassett and his crew turned east along the north side of the Cimarron, as there was another crossing a few miles east where the Military Road to Fort Supply crossed.

Adkin turned their horse team west, home was only a few miles away. It was July 23, 1871.

•••

Adkin didn't even mention to Matty he turned 25 on July 30. In fact, he didn't remember it until late that day when writing in his diary, and he confirmed the date.

They enjoyed the lazy days of summer, but seldom a day passed without doing chores, hunting or Matty collecting plant life of all types. She reminded him mid-August, she wanted a fresh buffalo kill, if possible.

Adkin and Diablo started searches around the immediate area, but it wasn't until the fourth day, and Adkin was about 10 miles west of the house when he came across about 200 herd of buffalo. A small herd but one which apparently had spent the summer in the area along the Cimarron.

By the time he shot it, it was too late to fetch the wagon and get back. So he left it gutted so it would cool inside and then covered it with tree limbs to try and keep the crows and vultures from seeing it. He did make it home that night, and then departed two hours before sunrise so he could get to it quickly.

To his surprise, no major damage was done to the animal by scavengers, and Adkin was able to quarter it and hoist the pieces into the wagon. The head was all he could manage. He was sure it weighed 100 pounds.

Matty was exhilarated. She immediately started cutting away fat and boiling it down to a thick, milky liquid. She had already pounded several types of jerky into powder and had that collected in bags.

Once she set out her tins, she melted the fat in her copper cooking pot, and then poured in the powdered jerky and once mixed thoroughly, she would start adding wild berries; strawberries, blue berries, mulberries and unpitted wild sandhill plumbs and about a pound of sugar.

When that was all combined, she would spoon the mixture into the tins and set them out to cool and semi-dry. She then placed small pieces of waxed paper Adkin had bought her for lids and tied them off with small strings.

Once she had about 40 tins, she turned her attention to finishing off the buffalo hide while drying fresh meat for smoking and turning into fresh jerky.

When the hide had been completely scraped of any meat or fat, she took the brains and stirred them with a knife til she had a gelatinous mixture to start spreading it over the entire skin and rubbing it in.

Adkin couldn't believe how hard she worked for a couple of weeks on that single buffalo. Whenever he caught her eye, she was smiling as if she were in heaven. But then he would think, as a Kiowa squaw, she and the other women did this daily through the summer and late fall months every year – in addition to all their other chores.

He would just shake his head in amazement – thanking God He had brought this woman into his life. He often though about his parents and how they would accept Matty. He was sure they would love her as much as he did.

Matty also finished Adkin's new leggings. They had leather fringe down the entire sides with beads on many of the leather thongs below the knee to the foot. The tops came up to a few inches above his knees. He loved them and started wearing them immediately. Though his other ones were a little scruffy, he folded them and stored them for back ups if needed.

As they reached the last week of August, Adkin didn't have to remind Matty they would need to start planning and preparing to leave the house and head to Blaine County, Oklahoma.

Again she was excited, and she reminded Adkin they needed to find out what had happened to Satanta. Adkin knew they wouldn't be able to do that until they reached Fort Supply, which may take four or five days.

•••

Adkin and Matty departed September 1, 1871, along the route Bassett and his men took to reach the Salt Fork of the Arkansas – they headed due east instead of following the Cimarron arching back upward. They would turn south once they came across the Military Road and go to Fort Supply.

From Supply, it was 85 miles to Blaine County and Jarvis' Ranch. Adkin was trying to remember who his contact at Fort Supply was. Suddenly, he remembered it was General Alfred Sully who had helped in his release from custody after breaking Sergeant Martinez's face.

Though Sully was a Brigadier General in the war, he had reverted back to Major in the U.S. Army. But Adkin thought he had heard Sully moved on out west, either California or Oregon. He'd soon find out who was in command at Fort Supply now.

The three days it took to reach the Military Road was uneventful, and Adkin guessed it was only about 20 miles due south to reach Fort Supply.

"If we leave before sunrise tomorrow, we should be at Fort Supply by sunset," he told Matty, while she prepared to skillet fry some smoked buffalo meat.

•••

As they rolled into Fort Supply, Adkin couldn't imagine the changes. The two bastions were taller at the opposing corners of the stockade, and off the two other corners were stables and corrals for animals. Surrounding the outer walls were numerous large Army tents set up for troops.

As the guard allowed them entrance to the huge front gate, Adkin saw that all three walls had barracks, a smitty's shop, dining hall and officers's quarters. It was quite a difference than the last time he was there. Troop tents were everywhere, too.

He looked at Matty, and she wasn't smiling. He realized she didn't have fond memories of this place. She had been kidnapped while she was a pregnant widow, brought here and then brutally beaten, which ended up killing her unborn child. She was lucky to be alive.

Adkin put his arm around her and pulled her close while he held the team's reins in his other hand. He smiled at her.

"We'll only stay the night and get out of here early tomorrow morning," he said.

"I don't even remember leaving here in Satanta's wagon," she said. "I came awake on the trail and saw it was my people and Satanta carrying me away.

"It was Satanta who told me it was you who stopped the soldier from killing me, too. I didn't remember it was you for several days" she said. "That is when I knew the spirits wanted us to be together."

He kissed her on her cheek, and she smiled.

Adkin pulled their team up at the commandant's office. He got down and walked around to help Matty off the wagon. Together they walked up the steps to the porch and asked the aides at the door to see the commander.

"Trooper, my name is Adkin Yates and this is my wife, Matty," Adkin said. "May I ask who is the Commander, and is it possible we could talk to him?"

"Mister Yates, the fort's Commander is Major Rustin Watt, and I will see if he is available to accept visitors," the trooper said, turning and opening the door and stepping inside.

He was back in only a few moments, holding the door open and standing aside.

"Please come in Mister and Missus Yates, the Major would like to see you right away," he said as Adkin and Matty stepped by and entered the office.

"Mister Yates – and Missus Yates – what a pleasure to meet you. I'm Major Watt, and your reputation proceeds you," Watt said. "Please, have a seat. Do you care for some coffee or a drink?"

"No, Major, thank you though," Adkin said while shaking Watt's hand. "This is my wife, Matty."

"Yes, yes, I know your name, too," Watt said, reaching out to shake Matty's hand. "Both of you have become a local legend of bravery and love. Many people know of your troubles here and the ending of love and marriage.

"The lore is carried on through the hearts of romantics and gentlemen of honor," he added, while beaming at Adkin and Matty. "I hope you will sup with me this evening."

Watt assured them he was going to have his meal within the hour, and they both could refresh with bowls of hot water and fresh towels near the back room of the office.

They agreed and took turns washing their faces and drying off. Matty straightened one of her braids and re-tied the bottom knot with her bright yellow ribbon. She had accumulated braid ribbons of every color known to man, it seemed to Adkin.

Prior to the meal, Watt was very inquisitive about the story he had heard about the two. He had heard Adkin had saved her from a teamster back in '65, then saved her again from a soldier in '68 here at Camp Supply.

"Then you followed her south to catch up with her and marry her?" Watt asked, eagerly.

"Well, I was really concerned about whether she lived or was terribly injured at first," Adkin said. "But when I saw her – and she was okay, it pleased me immensely."

"Then her father married us in his tipi, and it was the most wonderful thing to ever happen to me," he added, smiling at Matty. He couldn't tell Watt he was a nervous wreck for many months before realizing he was falling in love with her.

"Gosh, that's so romantic – and proof love is mightier than the misdeeds of unholy men," Watt said. "I am so honored you have stopped at Fort Supply."

Adkin had mentioned earlier they were off to see close friends and business partners in the Indian Territories. Then he brought up Satanta.

"Have you heard any news about Kiowa Chief Satanta?" Adkin asked. "We heard he had been arrested for the Warren Wagon Train Massacre. He was best man at our wedding. Matty's father was his Medicine Man, Black Horse, who has since passed away."

"Yes. Yes. Satanta. Last news I received was he was at Fort Sill when Chief Satank tried to escape and got killed," Watt said.

"Yes we heard about that," Adkin said.

"Well, Sherman had Satanta and Chief Big Tree taken to Fort Richardson for trial. They were tried separately, and I believe it was the day after the Fourth of July that Satanta was found guilty, and the next day, Big Tree was found guilty, too.

"Sherman ordered them to be hung," he continued. "It really shocked a lot of people, because Indians have never been tried in a U.S. civil court before."

Matty had brought her palms up to her cheeks, looking scared.

"Anyway, word is Indian Agent Tatum, a Quaker, and Judge Charles Soward, who presided over the trial, are arguing the two should not be hanged, and are trying to get their sentences reduced to life imprisonment.

"I have no idea what's happened since. For all I know, they may have been hanged by now," he added, as Matty made a painful moan under her breath. "I'm sorry Missus Yates, I shouldn't have said that. I do know there is no news of he and Big Tree being hung, yet."

"Thank you Major, that's good news in a way. I'm sure if they had been hung, the news would sweep the Great Plains like a cyclone," Adkin said. "I'm sure he is still alive Matty."

After supper, Watt showed Adkin and Matty a guest room on the south end of the office meant for visiting officers and pleaded they stay there for the night. Adkin accepted, and he and Matty went out and gathered their clothes bags and a couple of furs that Matty always like having around her for sleeping.

Adkin also checked Diablo and Tóngúl and made sure the tarp was secured on the wagon.

Watt ordered the two guards to take their animals to the stables, unhitch the team, unsaddle the horses and feed them and put them up for the night.

Early the next morning, Adkin made his way to the bathing room and washed his face again. As he was going back to Matty, Watt came out of his bedroom.

"I wanted to make sure I didn't miss you this morning, Mister Yates," Watt said. "I knew you wanted to get an early start. I'll get the men to retrieve your wagon and animals – they shouldn't take long at all."

"Thank you Major Watt, you've been very kind, and I appreciate that," Adkin said. "Matty grew up with Satanta, and he's like her father now that her father has died. She's very concerned, but ready for whatever happens."

"I understand," Watt said. "I hope she doesn't have to deal with that – bless her heart."

"Thanks, we'll be ready soon," Adkin said.

Watt asked them if they would like some coffee, but they refused, Adkin saying they liked to stop for a mid-morning meal.

After shaking hands, Watt led them out the front, and their wagon and horses were there ready to roll.

"Thanks again, Major," Adkin said, with Matty echoing the same thanks.

"You two be careful out there – and stop by any time," Watt said as he waved.

•••

The trail to Blaine County seemed to be well travelled. Adkin remembered how they had blazed a trail from Jarvis' to Fort Supply years earlier, but it looks like others have since used it as well. It would take them at least four-and-a-half days to get there.

The trip to Jarvis' Ranch was uneventful, with the exception of Adkin and Matty meeting six Cherokee warriors scouting for buffalo. Matty was able to make sign with them and some talk. The warriors had only been on the trail for about five hours, wanting to reach the Panhandle sooner.

At first, Adkin noticed they had their eyes on their team and horses tied on the back of the wagon. But when Adkin spoke up with the Peace sign of raised arm, they saw his bracelet and the necklace. There was some quick talk between them and then Matty spoke up, telling them they were friends – friends of Satanta, Ten Bears and Quanah.

After all that, they told her where they were headed, and when Adkin got off the wagon to fetch something from the back, they looked intimidated watching the huge White Man dressed in leather with long hair pull something out of the wagon.

He came around from the back carrying a small bag. Matty recognized it immediately. Adkin liked to carry his gift of tobacco in these small bags, and Adkin handed it to the lead warrior.

"Please take this tobacco as a token of our friendship," Adkin said in English.

The Cherokee looked as if he might have understood something of what Adkin said, then Matty signed it to the Indians. They all smiled and immediately rode off with a few yelps, but smiling broadly.

"I think they afraid of you Great White Chief," Matty said playfully.

On September 10, Adkin slapped the reins on their team and headed down the ridge into the flats of the valley that Jarvis' Ranch House was snuggled in.

When they got within sight of the front gate, Adkin realized they had replaced the old one with huge poles and a wooden sign above the road with several signs of Indian tribes. Adkin recognized the Kiowa and the Comanche, but there were at least five more.

A farm hand was running toward them from a horse-drawn plow about 200 yards away. He was carrying a rifle and started yelling, "We got visitors. We got visitors," as loud as he could.

By the time he reached Adkin and Matty, several people were on the porch and two more men were hustling over from the stables, also carrying long guns.

"We are friends, young man," Adkin said to the man who ran from the plow. "My name is Adkin Yates, and this is my wife, Matty."

"Did you say Yates?" he asked. "Yes, Adkin Yates, good friends of Sam and Mary Catherine – and Darwin Jarvis," Adkin added.

"Welcome, welcome Mister Yates," he said, then turning to the main house he hollered. "It's the Yates – Adkin and Matty Yates."

Adkin hit the reins again and headed to the front porch. He saw Mary Catherine as she handed a baby over to an Indian woman and started down the steps off the porch.

She was waving both arms over her head and yelling "Adkin, Matty – oh my Goodness – it's Adkin and Matty."

Darwin and Sam were coming over from the stables, as well as about six or seven other men and a couple of women. Adkin thought it looked like a small town of people and buildings – more outbuildings than when he last saw the place.

Matty jumped from the wagon and nearly fell down when she hit ground and immediately hugged Mary Catherine. They were screeching like a couple of hens fighting over a grasshopper.

As Adkin tied off the reins, Sam and Darwin reached him and he embraced both men.

"So good to see you, Adkin," Sam said, Darwin agreeing and slapping Adkin on the back.

"It's great to see you, too, Sam and Darwin. How are you doing out here in Oklahoma?" Adkin said.

The women finally quit jumping up and down, and Mary Catherine made her way around to the men. She jumped up and wrapped her arms around Adkin, kissing him on the cheek.

"If it isn't my favorite Englishman – How are you Adkin Yates?" she asked as he sat her back on the ground.

"I am fine, Miss Mary Catherine, I am happy to see you are well," he said, laughing.

Two children were on the porch, the oldest was dark headed and wiry, just like Sam.

"Is that James Adam?" he asked loud enough for the boy to hear.

"It sure is," Sam said. "Come over here Adam and say hello to Uncle Adkin – do you remember him?"

"Kind of," the boy said as he came down the steps and shook hands with Adkin, who told Adam he was only this big last time he saw him – holding his hand about knee level.

"The little girl is Anna, yes?" Adkin asked. She was standing on the porch hanging on to the Indian woman's skirt next to her on the porch. Her hair was a lighter brown and curly to the shoulders.

Matty went up on the porch about the time Mary Catherine did, and then it was the women fussing over all the children, including the baby.

Sam was introducing some of the hands; a couple of teamsters, and three were helping with the farming of forage crops. Sam said Darwin's idea of growing forage for winter was a big success in its first year, saving them considerable feed costs.

Everybody finally made their way through the door and into the main house. Adkin realized Mary Catherine had remodeled the interior as she saw fit. It was part English Colonial with wall tapestries yet full of western art and artifacts.

Adkin took a seat in the living room and felt completely comfortable and relaxed seeing his old friend Sam and how his family had grown since the days they rode the bench on a Concord carrying Army big shots to the Little Arkansas Peace Treaty.

"It was six years ago that we met, remember Sam?" Adkin said with a sense of nostalgia.

"I sure do, Adkin," Sam said. "It seems at times to be 16 years and at other times, just yesterday."

•••

While the women were preparing supper, Sam and Darwin filled Adkin in on the business. It was good, and they were, obviously, proud to be making profits every month.

"You just missed Jim Mead," Sam said. "He's back in Wichita – you know they filed their township papers about this time last year. Yes, in August I believe. Jim's really excited, he owns about every property along main street, and it's growing."

"Jim deserves it, his success is hard-earned," Adkin said.

Sam explained that Mead had informed them all the paperwork confirming the Jarvis Ranch lease with the Cherokee Tribe and their Indian Agent was in proper order. And they were guaranteed a peaceful existence.

"As much as a piece of paper can guarantee anything," Sam said, knowing all too well how paper treaties have been dealt with by both sides of the agreements.

Darwin explained they had built two more outbuildings: One to store forage and to make their own silage, and another for farming equipment, repairs and storage. He said if things go well, they might be able to trade or sell some of their extra forage.

They asked about the new Cimarron House, and Adkin explained its construction, and some of the visitors already. He also brought up Satanta and his trial.

"Yes, we heard about that.

Sam said. "It's too bad, but the Indians don't realize what this reservation program actually entails – especially when you have Sherman wanting to kill each one of them."

"But they do understand attacking an unarmed wagon train and killing innocents," Adkin said.

Sam said Jim reported the railroad would reach either Wichita or Newton next summer and go even further west, maybe even to Fort Dodge. Adkin also assured them the rails would reach Fort Dodge, too, according to his own sources in Fort Dodge.

"And they're starting a town soon," Adkin said. "I've bought 50 lots along the ridge west of Fort Dodge myself – above the river bottom."

"Well, good for you," Sam said, with Darwin agreeing to the sentiment.

Adkin asked if they had heard any news from the Las Animas Ranch, and Sam said Dusty and his wife had a baby, according to what Jim had heard. And that Ryan was seeing an Indian woman, who was maybe half Mexican, too.

"Jim wasn't sure, but he's involved with a woman for sure," Sam said. "It's about time for him to settle down, don't you think?"

"I'm not sure about that, but then I've never really thought much about it," Adkin said. "I just hope he's happy."

"Speaking of settling down, how many children must you have to be considered 'settled down?'" Adkin asked with a chuckle.

"Well, we're both from big families, and we believe it's God's will if children are the result of love," Sam said. "It's a true blessing that I can't even put into words."

Sam got quiet. He knew Adkin wanted children, too, but Matty might not ever be able to have them. Sam changed the subject.

"What is J.L. planning to expand Barlow and Sanderson coach service?" Sam asked.

"Well, last I knew, he was headed to California, laying out routes," Adkin said. "Ray Dee is with him. I think they're coming back to Las Animas before winter sets in."

"Winter can set in quick in those mountain ranges," Sam said.

During supper, Matty told Adkin how happy she was to be cooking with Mary Catherine in that big kitchen Beth Jarvis had designed and laid out.

"Mary Catherine has put some of her things in there to make it feel more like her special cooking room," Matty whispered to Adkin later.

Sam talked about their ranch family – five full-time hands between farming and wrangling the animals; three women (two Mexicans and one Cheyenne, who came along with the men); and nearly a dozen part-time teamsters who lived down the valley near the Cimarron River.

Sam explained the crew was eating in the staff house, which resembled a barracks now, complete with a kitchen and dining room with a long table.

"There's actually all kinds of settlers trying to put down stakes in the area, but they are subject to the whims of the Indian Agent when it comes to making permanent plans," Darwin said at supper. "If the government ever decides how to divide up this country, I think we'll see real positive growth."

After the meal, Adkin and Matty gave the children lots of attention. Adkin grabbed Adam and hefted the child up to eye level.

"I used to take you like this, and then throw you to the sky – like this," Adkin said as he tossed the nearly 5-year-old into the air and caught him.

As he set him back on the floor, Adam said, "I do remember that, Uncle Adkin, but I'm too big for that now."

They all laughed, Sam saying, "See how fast they grow up. He now thinks he's an adult."

Matty kept a tight grip on baby Rosa, and no one could catch little Anna, who was 3 now and never stayed in one spot for more than three seconds, if that.

Adkin and Matty stayed for three days and nights, and made plans to depart the fourth morning. Adkin could hardly believe how successful Sam and Darwin were operating the business. But he knew from the first day he met Sam, the young soldier who had been wounded at the end of the Civil War, was a special person. One who wasn't embittered by war and eternally grateful God was in his life.

The next day, Adkin was digging around in his wagon when he saw the bow Chief Quanah gave him. He showed it to Sam who was standing there waiting.

"Remember I told you Quanah stopped by our Cimarron House?" Adkin asked. "I forgot to tell you he gave me his bow because he couldn't stop laughing when I told him Matty was the fish killer in our family with a bow. He told me to practice."

"You mean he just gave you his bow, a quiver and all those arrows – look at that quiver, all the decorations," Sam said. "Why do all these Chiefs just hand you gifts?

"I think it's the English accent," Sam continued, laughing. "Maybe I should try that accent with the next Indians I meet that I don't know."

"I think you should just keep that black curly hair of yours cropped short the way you do," Adkin said, laughing with Sam. "No Indian would want that scalp hanging in their lodge."

Sam told Mary Catherine about the bow, but she said Matty had already related the whole story to her.

"How Quanah thought it was so funny that Matty was a better shot than Adkin with a bow," Mary Catherine said, chuckling.

On the morning they were leaving, Matty and Mary Catherine cried, more happily than that of misery.

"We're hearing rumors a north-south rail line is eventually coming our way," Sam said. "If it does, we'll telegraph you at Las Animas, cause the railroad always brings the telegraph lines, as well."

"You do that," Adkin said as he turned their team around toward the front gate. "God bless you all."

"Bye, God bless you, too," Mary Catherine shouted. "Please be careful."

By the time they rolled under the large front gate, Matty had her head on Adkin's shoulder softly crying.

"I will miss them mucho," Matty said between sniffles.

"They are wonderful people," Adkin said.

•••

Adkin decided they would travel due north and intercept the Cimarron River. Sam had told him a well-used trail followed the Cimarron all the way to the Military Road north of Fort Supply. The trail would save nearly two days travel to Fort Dodge and the Santa Fe Trail.

Sure enough, they made it to Fort Dodge in seven days. It would be about seven or eight days to Las Animas City. When Adkin crossed the bridge at the Arkansas River, things were bustling. It looked as if 20 new shanties or tin buildings had sprouted up along the main street up to the ridge, where Adkin and Matty now owned land.

"Hey Yates – Adkin Yates," a voice boomed from the people mingling along a board walkway on their right. Adkin turned and recognized Henry Sitler.

"Sitler," Adkin yelled and stopped his team. He backed the horses up a few yards as Sitler came running up next to Matty and shook her hand.

"How are you Missus Yates," he asked as he tipped his bowler derby.

"Fine."

"Civilization is progressing Yates. Ever since we drew up a town plat, people are starting to believe we can create a prosperous city out here in the desert," Sitler said laughing.

"Have you some time for me to show you something?" Sitler asked. "It will just take a few minutes."

"Sure, what is it?" Adkin asked.

"Let me get my horse," Sitler said as he went back to a horse rail and jumped up on his mount and turned it back to Adkin's wagon. "Just follow me up the hill."

Sitler spurred his horse and headed north up the main road, where Adkin's lots were located on the ridge. Within a few minutes, Sitler had stopped at the top of the hill and whirled his horse around. Adkin pulled up the wagon next to him.

"Look at this Yates," Sitler said, waving his arm from side to side. "Back to the east and then all the way west – look at progress."

"You can stand here on this hill and there is traffic as far as you can see, 24-hours a day, seven days a week on the Santa Fe Trail," Sitler said.

Adkin was seeing exactly what Sitler was saying. There were wagon trains, caravans as far as the eye could see. Some were on the horizon, while others were just a few miles behind the others. He looked at Matty.

"And we own these lots right back here," Adkin said waving his arm back to his right and northward.

"Me and Bob Wright have already had inquiries into who owns those lots, Yates," Sitler said. "We told them it was you, and they want us to ask if you're ready to sell any, yet."

"Really?" Adkin asked in amazement.

"You could probably make double on what you paid for them today, if you was a wantin' to sell them," he answered.

Adkin looked at the entire scene, from east to west and south through the Arkansas Valley. He could actually envision a town now. It was forming right before their eyes.

"What would you think about having another home here – right there – overlooking this new town?" Adkin asked Matty.

She kind of shrugged her shoulders, not looking emotionally excited at all.

"Well, just something to think about," Adkin said, then looking back to Sitler. "This is a fine place to have a house, though. Nice vista."

"It sure is, and it would be a great investment once the railroad gets here," Sitler said.

Adkin was thinking the same thing. It would also be a great place to have a freighting business and additional coach service. Right now, Chris Rath and Charley Rath had the service north to Hays City, but once the railroad gets to Dodge, people will be wanting to head south to spread out and settle.

Adkin decided he would talk this over with Ryan and Ray Dee – and of course, J.L. Sanderson.

Sitler updated Adkin on Rath's and Bassett's hunting parties, although no hides or meat had reached Dodge, yet. He also said Major Kirk was planning on resigning from the military in the summer of '72.

"He wants to be helpful in founding a town," Sitler said.

Finally, Adkin told Sitler he needed to get to the Western Union office to use their telegraph. He thanked Sitler for showing them the vista from their property, and how the Santa Fe Trail was as busy as ever.

"It will be easy for y'all to hook up with a train headed to Las Animas," Sitler said. "You won't have to travel alone."

With that, Adkin turned the team southward to reach the road to Fort Dodge.

He went directly to the telegraph office and sent a message to Ryan, informing him they should be home in seven or eight days. They would spend the night at Fort Dodge, so any responding message should be sent by 9 a.m. tomorrow, if received in time in Las Animas.

They then went to see Major Kirk and ask for a room for the night. Kirk was excited to see them, and he repeated what Sitler had said about people already asking about lots atop the ridge.

Adkin gave Kirk a brief update on what and where they had been doing and travelling. They then asked about the room.

Kirk could see they were tired and made arrangements for troopers to take care of their wagon and the animals. He also helped Adkin carry he and Matty's belongings to a room at the barracks just for guests.

•••

Adkin checked the telegraph office at 8, but there was no message for him, so he turned the rig westward to go into Dodge and wait to see if there was a caravan expected to be leaving soon. They had said their farewells to Kirk the evening before.

As it was, there was a wagon train just preparing to depart Dodge. One of the settlers near the back told Adkin the wagon master was a Mister H. W. Jones, an older man who had travelled the Santa Fe Trail for years. The man pointed out Jones who was up front of at least 100 wagons riding a big cream-colored buckskin with a black mane and black feet.

Adkin worked his wagon up quickly.

"Mister Jones, Mister Jones," Adkin yelled, and Jones caught his name and looked back at Adkin waving.

Jones rode back a few yards and pulled up beside Adkin, who introduced himself and explained they were heading to Las Animas City and wanted permission to ride with Jones and his caravan.

"What kind of business you in Mister Yates," Jones asked, knowing well how thieves planted spies on trains to see what valuables were there for the taking.

"I'm a part owner of Barlow and Sanderson Company and co-owner of YR&R Freight Company, Sir," Adkin said.

"Well, nice to meet you Mister Yates, I know both those businesses, and I know Tyler Ryan, too," Jones said. "Welcome to our caravan – just fall in where you can, we're heading out now."

Jones turned his buckskin back toward the front before Adkin could thank him and kicked up dust as he raced to the front of the caravan yelling, "Let's go folks."

Adkin eased his wagon in one of the lines, as it was being formed in two parallel lines to move out. The trail in these parts was very wide and offered that safety of bunching up the wagons closer in case of attack.

"Once out on the plains, Jones might even order us to form four, five or six lines abreast," Adkin thought to himself.

He smiled at Matty. It was September 22, 1871.

"We will be in Las Animas in seven or eight days," he said. Matty smiled bleakly. Adkin knew it would take her friends at Las Animas to shake her out of her sadness of leaving Mary Catherine and her family.

•••

No real problems arose on the trail, other than a few wives of White settlers who didn't seem to think much of Matty – or more importantly, an Indian Squaw married to a White Man.

"They would learn tolerance of everyone out on the prairies in time – if they survived," Adkin thought to himself.

Adkin assured Matty some of those women had never known real Indians so they were actually scared of her, and that is why they scowled at her.

"If you were to bark loudly at one like a dog, she would probably wet herself," Adkin said, and Matty giggled.

They did meet other families that were looking for that dream of owning land and having to report to no one except their families. Adkin admired that desire to set off on adventure, but he also now knew it comes with some deep sorrow at times reaching for that freedom and independence.

And plenty of danger.

After meeting some of the settlers, Adkin often wondered how they would adapt to the West, or which ones were likely to end up returning to "civilization" back east? He didn't hold out much hope for the ones who scorned him and his "Indian Squaw."

One day, Adkin volunteered to hunt meat with six others. He enjoyed saddling up Diablo and hitting the prairie swales. Though he didn't get a chance to shoot, he had a jolly time helping skin a couple of antelopes with his hunting crew.

When he got back to Matty, plugging along in the wagon, Adkin asked if she was okay?

She explained a White woman rode up to her earlier on horseback.

"She was riding side-ways, and ask me if it was true that Indian squaws seldom washed themselves," Matty said, with a twinkle in her eyes. "I told her that was true.

"She then asked, 'What does your man think of that?' I said, 'He thinks washing twice a year is too much washing,'" Matty said, starting to ease into a smile.

"When her eyes got real big, I barked at her, went, 'Arrrff. Arrrff,' and I think you were right," Matty added, starting to laugh now. "She rode away fast."

Adkin guffawed, and then started to howl like a wolf. Several of the wagons nearby could hear him and just looked on nonplussed. Adkin was sure that particular White Woman and her friends would not bother Matty ever again.

They laughed and laughed.

•••

They got to see old friends at Bent's Fort on September 29 and enjoyed visiting and catching up.

"Well my beautiful wife, we will be in Las Animas this afternoon," Adkin said as he popped the reins on their team. He pulled in behind other wagons that were moving westward after purchasing a few supplies at the fort – mainly more beads.

"I tried to give Jones some money for allowing us to ride in his caravan," Adkin said. "But he said it was his pleasure to have us, and someday I could repay the favor.

"I told him we would be pulling away at Las Animas, and he said they would not stop right there, he wants to make La Junta for camp," Adkin added. "He's a nice man."

Matty agreed.

•••

When they topped the low knoll just east of Las Animas City, they could see the town. It was woven throughout the trees that grew along the Arkansas and where the Purgatoire River merged with the major artery of the West.

Adkin and Matty looked at each other with huge smiles.

"Didn't realized I missed this bunch so much," Adkin said thinking of his partners and friends."

"I feel same way,' Matty said.

Adkin moved his team out of line and set them into a trot to reach wagon master H. W. Jones at the head of the caravan.

"Mister Jones," Adkin hollered.

"This is where we're dropping out. I want to thank you again for your hospitality."

The gray-haired Jones smiled which wrinkled his weathered face even more and tipped his hat.

"Good luck to you two, and God bless."

Matty waved as Adkin turned the team down the west road. He could see the headquarters and immediately realized the men had rail-fenced the entire property with long, small limbs or trees.

When they rode through the large covered gate, some of the hands nearby started shouting, "It's Adkin and Matty!" Others yelling, "The Yates are back!"

By the time they travelled the long roadway up to the main office, they were surrounded by people, even many of the women came out on the porch.

Uribe was the first to run up and grab the harness on the team.

"Bienvenidos mis amigos," he said beaming.

"Great to see you, too, Uribe," Adkin said as he was climbing down off the wagon. "I see you still have your hair."

They hugged while someone was helping Matty down. Several of the women surrounded her and were hugging and kissing her cheeks. One was actually weeping happy tears.

"Well you old, wild Englishman, didn't know if you'd ever come back from the Cimarron House," Ryan said, standing on the porch with his fists resting on each hip.

Ray Dee was next to him grinning, while Peg-Leg Pete took off his hat and gave a loud Indian whoop. Dusty had an arm around his wife, and she was holding a baby swathed in a red calico covering.

"Where's Don Diego and Francisco," Adkin asked as he reached the porch and everyone gathered around to slap him on the back?

"Somebody has to work," Ryan said. "They're delivering a few more stages throughout Colorado and up into Wyoming. They and our new hand, Weldon Campbell, took off two weeks ago. Won't be back for two or three more weeks."

"Did you say Campbell?" Adkin asked in disbelief.

"Yes, Campbell," Ryan said. "He told me all about his adventures with you and Matty. Said you offered him a job. I didn't have any way of contacting you, so I hired him – mainly because I believed every word he told me."

"Well, I'll be," Adkin said. "I did ask him to work with us, which I telegraphed you about. He thought it may take longer to make a decision – had to take care of his business in Great Bend."

"Well, he decided to bring his business here," Ryan said. "We're now in the saw mill business, too. Took four wagon loads to get all his stuff here.

"It's over in that building," Ryan said pointing to the southwest corner of he property. "See all this new fencing? "Weldon Campbell's work."

It didn't take long for Matty to pull Dusty's baby into her own arms and start gently petting its face. The chatter was getting so loud, Ryan finally shouted.

"Everyone, let's meet in one hour in the dining hall, Okay?"

Some of them started drifting away from the office in different directions to finish chores or prepare for supper, which the men had already planned since receiving the telegram they were coming. It was going to be roasted buffalo and all the trimmings.

"All the talk and questions had Adkin almost dizzy by the time Ryan spoke up and said they should get to their house.

"I'm sure your wagon is there and most of it unloaded in your house by now," Ryan said. "If you need something removed, let us know later. Y'all go get ready for a fine supper."

They walked the short distance to their little dwelling west of the stables and barracks. A small swarm of men were carrying pelts and furs and other sundries into their house. Several of the men Adkin didn't recognize.

Once inside and after the men had rolled off with the animals, Adkin took Matty in his arms and kissed her forehead.

"I love you, my little Kiowa Princess."

"She rose on her toes and pulled him down to kiss him on the lips.

"I love you, my husband."

•••

After a filling supper and all the visiting, Ryan suggested to Adkin that he and Matty retire early so they could rest up after their long trip from Sam's place.

"We can catch up on all the business in the morning," Ryan said, with Uribe speaking up.

"Si Señor, we will put you to work mañana – if you remember how to work," Uribe said with a wink.

"I think we'll take you up on that," Adkin said, standing and offering his hand to Matty who stood and circled his waist with her arm.

When they reached their little house, Matty laughed.

"I am actually looking forward to sleeping in our feather bed," she said. "See, you have turned me into a spoiled woman who acts like an old soft White Woman."

"You are no White Woman," Adkin said as he grabbed her and kissed her.

•••

Adkin and Matty took their usual place at the long breakfast table the next morning – after Matty had spent about 15 minutes making sure everything in the kitchen was going well. She felt as though it was still her kitchen, even though it was running well without her supervision.

Adkin smiled as he looked past her empty chair to Ryan.

"She's overseeing the staff to make sure nobody dies of starvation," he said with a chuckle. "Funny, you don't look malnourished."

Ryan laughed as Matty came out of the kitchen and made her way to the table. Staff followed her carrying trays of scrambled eggs covered with goat cheese and bowls of salsa for those who liked them a little spicier.

There were trays of meats; bacon, broiled buffalo and antelope strips and pieces of roasted chicken. One tray sat in the middle had vegetables; fresh sliced tomatoes, several kinds of grilled squash and bunches of raw wild onions. Another tray being passed around was broiled potato slices covered with large Spanish onions that were sauteed in butter.

Two women came out with a large clay pitcher in each hand full of hot coffee. One woman hurried to Adkin and sat out his cup and a bowl of tea leaves and a pitcher of steaming water. Matty smiled and nodded to the woman who shuffled away smiling.

"It has been awhile since you had your favorite English tea, my husband," Matty said grinning at Adkin.

"Thank you Princess," Adkin said.

"Princess?" Ryan asked with a curious tone.

"I have developed the habit of calling her my Kiowa Princess," Adkin said proudly.

"Well I agree wholeheartedly with that," Ryan said with a hoot. "I can't wait until you meet my Princess – she'll be coming over for dinner tonight. We've planned a big fiesta for your homecoming. Even old Sheriff L. A. Allen is dropping by."

"Sounds like a fine time," Adkin said, nodding his head. "I've heard you had met a woman in which you have been wooing in public."

"I plan on making her my bride if she will have me ... and her aunt and uncle approve," Ryan said, with a mischievous grin. "They will be escorting her to the party tonight, and I plan on asking them for her hand."

"Never thought I'd see the day," Adkin said. "But, I realize I've been so focused on my life with Matty, I haven't considered your happiness. I'm sorry for that."

"But I'm very happy for you, partner. Very happy," he added.

"Me happy, too, Tyler Ryan," Matty said smiling. "It is good you find a Princess for you."

After finishing breakfast, Matty whispered in Adkin's ear and then scurried off to the kitchen.

"Let's get to the office, and I'll get you caught up on what the businesses are doing," Ryan said.

"Let's go," Adkin said.

As they got to the office, a young boy who barely fit in his saddle came racing up to the horse rails, slid to a stop and hit the ground as his mount caught its balance.

"Message for Mister Ryan and a message for a Mister Yates," the boy said. "Don't know who that is Mister Ryan, but that's what I was told, and I've heard stories about this Yates fella – Indian fighter and all."

"Well, Donnie, this is Mister Yates right here," Ryan said as Adkin reached out his hand to shake the boy's hand. "He just arrived yesterday."

"Nice to meet you Mister ... Donnie," Adkin said.

"Donnie Boggs at your service, sir," Donnie said as he shook hands with Adkin, then grabbing one of the telegrams out of his left hand, he gave it to Adkin. Then he moved toward Ryan.

"This one is for you, Mister Ryan."

"Thanks Donnie," Ryan said. "You and your family planning to come over tonight for the fiesta?"

"Yes sir, we sure are," Donnie answered, then turned back to Adkin. "Excuse me Mister Yates, but it true you're married to a Kiowa Princess and you fought Indians all along the Santa Fe Trail?"

"Well, part of that is true but some of the other may be stretching the truth a little," Adkin said. "I'll explain what I mean later this evening, if that's okay with you."

"That's fine with me, Mister Yates. Gosh, I can't wait to tell the guys," Donnie said with a huge grin. As he started to reach for his horse's reins hanging over the rail, Adkin spoke up.

"Mister Boggs, I would like for you to have this for taking the time to deliver these messages to us," Adkin said as he flipped a half-dime coin to Donnie.

"Why thank you, sir," he said as he caught the coin and studied it. "Wow thanks. This is one of the new 1870-S coins. I've only seen one before, but it wasn't mine."

He jumped up grabbing the saddle horn and pulled himself up and into the saddle as quick as a squirrel, never once putting a foot in the stirrups, which hung loose about a foot below his tiny boots.

"See ya tonight," he said as he slapped the reins on his mount's flank and kicked with his stunted legs and waving with his loose hand.

"That's Thomas Boggs's grandson," Ryan said. "He's a real pistol, works for Western Union as a 'U.S. Telegraph Deliveryman,' as he likes to put it.

"He seems to be very bright and well mannered," Adkin said. "But he seems a bit small for the job."

"Hell, he's small because he's only 6 years old," Ryan said, laughing. "He don't know that though, he thinks he's about 16."

They both laughed as they made their way up the steps and into the office.

"Mine's from Don Diego," Ryan said as he held the telegram. "They left Fort Collins yesterday, so they're on schedule – should be two weeks to get back.

"We heard from a local businessman there, Joseph Mason is his name, that a colony of farmers are gathering back east and planning on relocating to Fort Collins next year in the spring," Ryan said smiling. "They're talking hundreds of settlers – they'll need freighting and coach services."

"This is from J.L.," Adkin said. "He says he is going to northern California and wants to know if I want to go and help him set up the stage stations out there.

"Damn, he knows I've always wanted to see California, but we just got back, and I don't know if I should leave Matty so quick," Adkin said, sitting down in a chair with a sigh. "He wants to leave as soon as I can get there – they have to cross the Rockies before mid-October."

Adkin sat there taking his hat off and rubbing his forehead back and forth. To Ryan, the expression on Adkin's face looked like he just got news someone close had died.

"Why don't you simply ask Matty, and see how she feels about it," Ryan said.

"You're right, I've got to talk to her right now," Adkin said as he stood up erect and pulled his hat on tight. He didn't look back or say a word as he stomped out onto the porch and down the steps.

...

It wasn't 10 minutes later that Ryan heard heavy footfalls on the porch and the front door swung open.

"She told me to go – and then turned to the women and started jabbering with them," Adkin said as he stood in the doorway. "She didn't even think about it more than a second."

"Well why don't you close the door, and tell me all about it," Ryan said, as if he was talking to Donnie Boggs.

Adkin came over to a chair and sat down.

"She said, 'You always say you like to see this California village. You go and stay safe for me,'" Adkin said looking bewildered.

"That was it, she turned around and went over to the women and they all started babbling and giggling," he added.

"You sound like she hurt your feelings or something," Ryan said while trying to keep from bursting out laughing. "Are your wittle feelings hurt, Mister Yates?"

At that, Ryan lost control and cracked up totally, laughing loudly and bent over and slapped his thighs.

Adkin looked up, startled at first, then a big smile broke across his face and he, too, started howling with laughter. Both men were laughing so hard they didn't hear Uribe come through the front door.

"What ees de joke?" he asked.

They both halted briefly while turning around to see Uribe, then broke up with laughter again. Uribe couldn't help himself, he started laughing at their antics, too. Soon all were laughing. Adkin slowly stood and coughed a few times, clearing his throat.

"I know it's early, but I need a brandy," he said, giggling still.

"I'll have one, too," Ryan said, looking to Uribe.

"Si, I love brandy any time, mis amigos," Uribe said. "Maybe you tell me what so funny?"

"Matty told Adkin here that it was okay for him to go to California with Sanderson," Ryan said.

"Dats not so funny to me," Uribe said.

577

"Adkin was sitting here trying to feel sorry for himself that maybe she didn't care enough about him," Ryan continued. "He looked like Diablo had died. You had to see it – it was hilarious, and I teased him and started laughing, and he broke down – seeing how stupid he sounded."

"I guess so, Uribe said. "Anyway, laughing ees muy bueno for everyone."

"Yes, Uribe, you are correct," Adkin said as he was catching his breath, and Ryan was filling Adkin's mug from a small crystal decanter.

"So, Señor Adkin, Uribe goes with you to California, si?" Uribe asked while smiling. "You need me for protection and to keep you laughing."

"Si, Uribe. You are going with me – if Ryan says it's okay."

"It's fine with me," Ryan said as he handed Uribe a mug of brandy. When Ryan had poured his brandy, he held it up and said, "A toast. To Adkin and Uribe – may you have a safe trip to California with laughter all the way."

They all chuckled as they held their mugs aloft, and then threw down the shots of the strong liquor.

•••

As everybody around the ranch busied themselves with arranging the fiesta, Ryan took Adkin into the Smitty's shop next to the roasting buffalo quarter on a spit.

"I wanted to let you know about Kanaka, the woman I hope to marry," Ryan started. "She is Cheyenne – her name means gold – and her mother was a sister of Amache Ochinee Prowers, you know, John Prowers' wife – the big sod and plank house right when you ride into Boggsville?

"Oh yes, I've met Amache, last winter at Sheriff Allen's dinner party," Adkin said. "Charming woman."

"Well Amache and Kanaka's mothers were sisters. Their father was Cheyenne Peace Chief Ochinee – Lone Bear – who was murdered in 1864 in the Sand Creek Massacre," Ryan continued. "Their mothers also died in that massacre at the hands of Chivington. Kanaka was only 10 and only survived because one of the women dragged her and four other children into a small sand cave along the river bank and covered the entrance with dirt, rocks and brush.

"Kanaka still remembers the soldiers looking for and finding women and children hiding by the river and hearing the shots when they were killed," he said. "When they came out of hiding the next day, they found the slaughter, babies cut open and everyone scalped and mutilated.

"John told me she still has bad dreams now and then, and it's been 7 years – she's close to 18, but she has experienced a lot of life and is a true survivor.

"I know, it sounds ridiculous for a 37-year-old Missourian to be marrying an 18-year-old Cheyenne woman," Ryan said. "But John married Amache when she was only 16, back in 1860. In fact, had she not married John, she would have been at Sand Creek where most of her family was mutilated.

"Plus, I fell in love with her the moment I saw her at the Western Union office," Ryan said with a big grin. "That was one week after you and Matty left to go build your Cimarron House – March 16th. We were both there to send telegrams out. She lives with John and Amache."

"A few days later, I ran into John and asked him if it was possible I could formerly call on Kanaka – that my intentions were honorable – and I would like to get to know her better," he continued. "He thought about it a moment, rubbed his chin, then looked me in the eyes, smiled and said, 'I think I can arrange that, but I'll have to discuss it with my wife, you understand.' I said great.

"So about a week later, a runner rode out with a note that I was invited to dinner with John, his wife and Kanaka the following evening," Ryan said with a sparkle in his eye. "Adkin, this ol' teamster was like a kid eyeing all those jars of candies at the General Store. I can't explain it."

"Don't try old friend," Adkin said, patting Ryan on the shoulder. "I know exactly how you feel. I'm very happy for you, and I can't wait to meet her. How are you going to ask John and Amache with all the people around tonight?"

"I've discussed it with John – but don't tell a soul," Ryan whispered while looking around the shop. "If Amache found out he was helping me, she may take it the wrong way, according to what John said.

"I'm going to offer them a business deal and ask the three of them to go to the office and once there, I'm going to ask John and Amache for her hand – if she will have me," Ryan said. "Tell you the truth, I'm a nervous wreck and half scared that something may go wrong. This is worse than staring down a bunch of blood-thirsty Comanches."

"Forget that, everything will work out fine, I'm sure," Adkin said.

"Oh, I forgot. I really am going to offer an investment in the purchase of some more cattle – and Amache is an equal partner with John in their businesses," Ryan said. "Im going to invest $5,000 in a large herd of these new Hereford cattle with the Prowers – they have the land and the cow punchers.

"Did you know these cattle originated in Herefordshire, in the West Midlands of England?" Ryan asked.

"No, that's amazing," Adkin said.

"Then I'm changing the subject and asking for Kanaka's hand," Ryan added.

"Should be quite a fiesta tonight," Adkin said. "I better go get cleaned up."

• • •

More than 20 wheeled vehicles and 50 people came through the front gate, including L.A. Allen and his wife and a few of his hands that had worked for

YR&R Freight, Thomas Boggs and his bunch – including little Donnie sitting high in the saddle of his big bay horse, friends of Kit Carson's they had met when buying the property and moving in, and of course, John and Amache Prowers and their 9-year-old daughter, Mary – and Kanaka.

When Kanaka was helped off the buckboard by Ryan, Adkin was struck by her height. She was at least 5-feet, 9- or 10-inches, and her facial features, once the Spanish-style veil was removed, was pure beauty. Adkin had never seen such a beautiful Indian – other than Matty – in his experiences in America.

"Wow," he said to himself. "I can see how Ryan fell at first sight. She looks more like being in her early or mid-20s than a 17-year-old girl."

After introductions, everybody was gathering in the dining hall at the barracks. Men and women were still tending the side of roasted buffalo over the embers, but women had started laying out trays of drinks on the tables; pails of beer with mugs, cool water and glasses of buttermilk. They were also taking orders from the male guests for anything stronger.

Adkin and Matty were taken aback when Amache ordered a tequila with a slice of lime, which was grown in her hot house.

"She's partial to having a few of those when she's nervous," Prowers whispered to Ryan, who was sitting next to him with Amache on the other side with Kanaka to her side.

Prowers asked Adkin how his summer went and was filled in on he and Matty's adventures and visitors. They talked about trains; where and when they were coming.

"Trains are a double-edged sword," Boggs said. "They bring much needed goods for cheap prices and such, but they also bring more and more settlers who seem to think they can just grab any land they take a hankerin' for."

"I know what you mean, Tom," John spoke up. "We had to run off squatters down on the Purgatoire – just south of the old Indian village that had been abandoned some years before Amache and I moved here in '67."

Adkin and Ryan knew about that old Indian village – it was where Uribe and his family had lived years ago. Prowers had purchased as much of the land in the area as he could after arriving in Boggsville – along with his friends Thomas Boggs and Kit Carson.

"Looks like we're close to increasing our holdings," Prowers continued. "The government is finalizing a land grant for reparations to Amache for the massacre of her family at Sand Creek."

"They took that coyote Chivington to the courts and found him guilty, but they never did a thing to him," Amache said. "He's still walking free. He should hang."

"We know dear," Prowers said putting his arm around Amache's shoulder. "Let's not ruin the evening talking about that mongrel. God will take care of him. Anyway, it looks like it's going to be a sizable land grant."

"That reminds me, John," Ryan said. "After supper, I would like to show you and Amache – and Kanaka – an investment deal I'm working on, and I think you may want to help me."

John agreed, even Amache nodding her head as she sipped her tequila. Kanaka smiled demurely, still unaware Ryan was going to ask for her hand. Ryan winked at Adkin. Amache asked Matty if she would look after little Mary when they went to the office.

Matty noticed the wink and Ryan's sly smile, and ask Adkin what was going on. Adkin whispered it was something special and a surprise that would come out later in the evening.

Matty smiled. She had a look on her face that Adkin had seen before. Matty suspected something big. It didn't surprise Adkin, he knew his Kiowa Princess had innate powers of understanding people.

She had connected with Kanaka immediately. Both young women who had hard Indian upbringings and had seen plenty of fighting and death. It instilled a love of life in them that many other women – or even some men – never truly understood.

Adkin knew it and had realized soon after marrying Matty why Bent, Carson, Prowers and many other trappers and traders often fell in love with Indian women. They were indeed special.

Adkin was impressed how well Kanaka's English was. Her accent did have a small Spanish tilt, but not as bad as Uribe's. She was well voiced and seemed to take in every word everybody was saying. Adkin found out later from Matty that Kanaka spoke English, French, German, Spanish and seven or eight Indian languages.

After a grand meal with all the trimmings, Ryan asked John and the women to go to the office and look at his investment plans. This time, Adkin winked at Ryan when he caught his eye as they were leaving he table.

'Tell me," Matty said as they walked out of the barracks.

"Okay. Okay," Adkin grinned. "Ryan is going to ask for Kanaka's hand in marriage."

"I knew it," Matty exclaimed loudly.

"Shush. Keep it down," Adkin said. "We'll know soon what happens. When they come back, just look at Ryan's face – it will tell us what happened."

"If Kanaka has any say, they will marry," Matty said. "She told me Ryan is her dream man. She loves him mucho, mucho."

Matty could hardly control herself. She was giggling and talking to everybody. Her spirits were high, and Adkin had to admit to himself, his spirits were soaring right along with hers. He had a huge grin on his face as he visited with his friends.

...

Only a handful of guests had departed when Ryan and the Prowers returned to the barracks. Everyone was enjoying the free alcohol and visiting with friends, and to Adkin, this fiesta looked like it would go well into the early morning hours. He smiled to himself. It was fun, but tomorrow he would have to start arranging his affairs and preparing to head to Denver.

Matty was waving at him and grinning from ear to ear. She pointed to the west doorway where Ryan was entering. Ryan had a smile that said it all. When they reached the end of the table, Ryan stood on a chair and yelled to the guests.

"Ladies and gentlemen, would you please gather round, we would like to share some important information with you, our dear friends and neighbors," Ryan said, then looking to John Prowers. "Mister John Prowers has an announcement he would like to make."

Matty and Mary had made their way over to Adkin, and Matty was gripping his hand tightly with Mary in the other hand. He had to admit his heartbeat was fluttering as much as hers.

Prowers stepped forward as Ryan got down off the chair.

"Friends, Tyler Ryan has agreed to invest with the Prowers Ranch in the accumulation of a couple of hundred head of Hereford yearlings before winter sets in and 200 more Hereford calves next spring," Prowers said.

Many of the guests clapped and whooped it up. Some knew this would bring more employment to the area and extra jobs for them, as well.

"And now, here, here. My dear wife, Amy, has an announcement, too," Prowers said.

"Ladies, gentlemen, mis amigos, it is with great delight I announce the engagement of my beautiful niece, Kanaka Prowers to Mister Tyler Ryan," Amache said, looking at the couple who were standing close to each other and smiling.

The crowd went wild, with hoots and shouts of approval and clapping.

"The wedding," Amache yelled over the crowd with both arms in the air calling for quiet. "The wedding has been set for March 1 next spring, and everybody is invited to this wonderful wedding."

The guests got loud again as Adkin, Matty and Mary approached Ryan and Kanaka, and Adkin shook Ryan's hand and John's. Matty hugged Kanaka and Amache and spoke in Cheyenne. Adkin thought she was saying they were very happy for the couple.

Several people started milling out the east doors, but they were not leaving. Adkin checked outside after visiting with the Prowers and noticed lots of folks were standing around the cooking pit which had been stoked with news logs and was blazing mightily. Several had brought chairs from the dining hall to sit on around the bonfire.

"It's going to be a long night," Adkin thought to himself with a grin.

•••

Adkin awoke early, despite not getting to bed until after midnight. He noticed several caballeros sleeping in bedrolls near the white embers of the cooking fire pit on his way to the office. One was just laying there fully dressed, boots and all but no covers. When he walked in the office, Ryan was already at his desk.

"How you doin' partner?" Ryan asked, beaming. "What a night, eh?"

"Congratulations again, you've found a good, decent woman," Adkin said. "I'm glad you picked March 1. I'll probably be away for four months at least."

"That's why I suggested it," Ryan said. "I couldn't get married without my best man. Besides, I think Amache was relieved it wasn't going to happen right away. I think she'll plan a humdinger of a wedding."

"I would imagine, that's her only surviving family, as far as I know."

"When you planning to leave?" Ryan asked.

"Probably day after tomorrow, that will be October 2, and I should be able to hook up with J.L. in about a week or so," Adkin said. "I better get to the telegraph office and confirm to J.L. I'm coming."

"Be sure to tell him about the wedding," Ryan said, laughing. "Oh, and tell him Uribe is coming with you, too."

"Will do," Adkin said. "I better get Diablo saddled up and head to town now. I'll have breakfast when I get back."

As he was walking to the stables, Matty came out of their house and hurried to intercept him.

"Are you going to town?" she asked. "Probably have to tell Mister Sanderson of your plans, si?"

"Yes, I'm going to telegraph him – and tell him about Ryan's engagement, too," Adkin said.

"When will you go?"

"Day after tomorrow. We have to pass over the Rocky Mountains before late October to be safe."

She reached up around his neck and pulled his face close to her's. After softly caressing his cheeks with both hands, she cupped his face in her palms and kissed him on the mouth right there – essentially in the middle of the yard – where anybody could see.

"I will miss you, my husband. Very, very much," she said as she quickly turned and bounced off for the barracks. "I will have your meal ready when you get back."

Suddenly, he felt better about the California trip. She does care, and he knew it deep down.

"What a woman," he thought.

...

By the evening of Oct. 1, 1872, Adkin and Uribe had assembled their small caravan to head off to Denver in order to join J.L. Sanderson and his train to go to northern California to establish more stagecoach stations and auxillary routes.

Five additional riders were going as far as Denver, one driving a rebuilt Concord for a station near Denver. Sanderson had stopped shipping newly purchased stages to Las Animas City since the rail service had arrived in Denver.

That's where all the new Concords and freight wagons were headed. Business was booming in Colorado and Wyoming, and now Adkin would assist in pushing into California to expand the original line Sanderson had established the year before.

That last night snuggling next to Matty, who had slipped into sleep after tearing up when she said she would be half a person until Adkin returned. Adkin laid there thinking of what she said.

"I'm going to try to never leave her side again after this trip," he said to himself. "I'll take her with me because she, too, makes me whole."

He closed his eyes and drifted off into slumber.

There was a sense of excitement as Adkin and Matty walked over to the stables an hour before sunrise. The men would stop for a meal after three or four hours on the trail, a tradition many caravaners observed.

"Diablo is ready to go," Uribe said. "I have lashed your bedroll to the saddle, the roll you gave me last night, Señor Adkin."

Adkin handed him a small bag and asked him to tie it to the saddle horn.

"I can't forget my lovely tea leaves," he said in his best proper English accent. Uribe chuckled along with Matty.

Ryan approached and handed a leather satchel to Adkin.

"Please see that J.L. gets these papers, Adkin. "They're originals of numerous stageline contracts and some papers concerning loans to some of our various operators."

"No problem," Adkin said as he turned to stash them in his saddle bags.

He turned to Matty, and nearly got emotional right there. She was trying her best not to cry in front of all the men and women gathered to see the caravan off.

He remembered his promise he made to himself last night and told her he'd be back before she could imagine. She tip-toed and kissed him without shame.

"Be safe my husband, and telegraph when you can," she said, smiling.

Adkin hefted himself into Diablo's saddle and hollered to the group.

"Let's head 'em up the trail, men," he shouted while waving his arm forward with his hat in his hand. The train moved out with the Concord and a six-mule team on a supply wagon and four riders on horseback with a small herd of about a dozen horses following.

Adkin turned back and waved to Matty when they reached the gate. She waved and smiled.

•••

Time seemed to slowly crawl for Matty those first 10 days until they received a message the men were safely in Denver and there were no hardships or problems. They would be joining Sanderson's train of five Concords and five freight wagons with a herd of mules and horses.

They were scheduled to depart Denver Oct. 14 travelling north to Cheyenne, Wyoming, where they would load all the wagons, animals and men onto the Union Pacific Railroad, which had been completed in 1869. They would then take the rails all the way over the Rocky Mountain range and eventually into Sacramento, California.

As Ryan read the telegram, he then said, "Adkin said to tell his Matty that he loves her very much." He looked to Matty who placed her hands over her face and slowly turned away, softly crying.

"Are you okay, Matty," Ryan asked.

"Yes, I am very happy," she sniffled as she walked out the door past little Donnie, who was waiting for his stipend. Matty's hands were still covering her face.

Ryan didn't expect to hear from them again until they reached Cheyenne right before catching the train to California. Once riding the rails, there were Western Union offices all along most of the stops on the Overland Route Railroad line.

•••

A few days after hearing from Adkin and Uribe, a company of troopers and calvary from Fort Dodge stopped by the headquarters asking Ryan's help in fixing a couple of wagons and a howitzer axle.

Several of the soldiers told Ryan the founders of Dodge had tried to name their small city Buffalo City, but they discovered another town was using that moniker, so they named the new town Dodge City.

They also said since Texas cattlemen found out the rail head was finished to Dodge City last month, a large herd from the northern Llano Estacado had arrived just last week and the town was already full of drunk cowboys and tent bordellos.

"I counted three wagons of women of ill repute come into town the night before we left for Santa Fe," one soldier said, laughing. "I hope to get back there next month after my duty assignment."

He also noted since the Atchison, Topeka and Santa Fe Railroad arrived in Dodge, a town was waiting.

"Already, south of the tracks, they've built frame buildings and tents, housing, two grocery stores and two general merchandise stores, a dance hall, a restaurant, a barber shop, a blacksmith shop – even a saloon next to Sitler's original sod house," the soldier said. "Dodge City is already setting a record for growth."

There was a stir around camp the evening of November 3, and Matty heard someone mention Chief Satanta's name. She immediately ran to the office to see Ryan.

"Hello Matty," he said as she hurried through the door. "I was just getting ready to send for you.

"I've got a telegram saying Texas Governor Edmund Davis has commuted Satanta's and Big Tree's death sentences yesterday. They are to serve life imprisonment in Huntsville, Texas."

She had a puzzled blank look on her face.

"They are not going to be hung," Ryan added, as Matty's face lit up with understanding. She then broke down and sat in a chair by his desk and held her face in her hands.

"Oh thank you Great Spirit," Matty said as tears ran down her cheeks.

Ryan knew how important Satanta had been in her life, and now that her father had died, she held Satanta even closer in her heart. She finally stood and wiped away the tears on her cheeks.

She stretched upright and held herself erect as a tall pine.

"The Great Kiowa Chief Satanta lives still," she said smiling. "He still lives among us and in our hearts."

She turned toward the door and stopped before opening it.

"Thank you Mister Ryan, you are a good man, and Kanaka is lucky to marry you," she said as she walked out.

Ryan was thinking, "All I did was read a telegram. Glad it wasn't news of Satanta's hanging."

Ryan called Donnie into the office and handed him a message to send to Mister Yates in Sacramento, California. Ryan figured Adkin and J.L. would reach Sacramento in three weeks or less, and he knew Adkin had a true fondness for Satanta, as well.

•••

On November 14, 1872, Ryan got word the California team had reached Sacramento, and all was well. The only problem was several of the men had motion sickness for several days out of Cheyenne, having never ridden on a train. But they made it over the mountains without any incidents of heavy snowfall.

Adkin reported they would spend the next two to three months expanding stage services and some freighting business from Sanderson's original Kansas to San Fransisco route. They were somewhat behind Butterfield and Wells Fargo, but J.L. was determined there was going to be enough business for all – California was booming.

Again, Adkin sent words just for Matty. "Tell her I miss her like a butterfly misses a soft spring breeze." Ryan was impressed that Adkin showed such a poetic side, and again, Matty shed some tears of happiness.

Ryan was getting a little worried that Matty had taken to riding Tóngúl almost daily over to the Prowers to visit or spend the entire day with Kanaka and Amache. She loved spending time with the women, but Ryan feared her riding alone, even though it was only about four miles away.

From time to time, Weldon Campbell would escort her, and then he would visit with several of the farmers and engineers who were constructing Las Animas' and Boggsville's irrigation canals. The area was becoming popular – and somewhat famous – for its crops of vegetables and even some fruit orchards produced with irrigation.

Campbell had hustled up some business for his lumber mill by helping with supplies to aid in diverting waters from various canals. He was becoming adept in building control doors and water diverters. He was also learning from Fransisco about blacksmith work and making hinges and turnstiles.

There was also news about the Indian Campaign. It spread that Colonel Ranald Mackenzie had assumed command of the Fourth United States Cavalry at Fort Concho in 1871, and had moved its headquarters to Fort Richardson.

He had began a series of expeditions into the uncharted Panhandle and Llano Estacado in an effort to drive renegade Indians back onto their reservations.

In October of '71, his troops skirmished with a band of Comanches in Blanco Canyon, where he was wounded. When Matty heard of this, she wondered if Chief Quanah was involved, for that's where he was headed after his stay with she and Adkin at their dream house.

The big news was Mackenzie had defeated another Comanche band on September 29, 1872, near the Big Springs, which would later become the site of Lefors, Texas.

•••

By Christmas, Matty's trips to the Prowers had become more and more fewer, and Ryan ask Matty about it.

"There are no problems. I love Kanaka – she is like a sister," Matty said. "And Amache is wonderful, such strength in a young woman. But they work all the time now on the wedding.

"I know nothing about it and don't like it," she continued. "Standing in Satanta's tipi with Adkin and my father was perfect marriage. They talk too much about music, clothes and eating.

"It's not for me. We will have more fun when you finally get married," she added, smiling. "And when you have all those papooses to take care of."

"What?" Ryan choked out. "How many … ah … papooses does Kanaka want?"

"Many, many," Matty said laughing as she turned toward the barracks, leaving Ryan standing there with eyes bulging and gasping for air.

On December 28, they received news the Santa Fe Railroad had reached the Kansas-Colorado border, ahead of its scheduled March 3, 1873, deadline – two days after Ryan and Kanaka's planned wedding.

Ryan figured many of his friends in Dodge City may be able to attend his wedding if they could get to the end of the line near the Old Granada site in just two days, rather than five or six in a wagon. He was hopeful some would show up, and Amache had sent out numerous invitations to his friends in Dodge City at his request.

•••

After the new year, Matty was realizing Adkin could be back as soon as early February. She was just waiting for Ryan to get the message they were headed back home.

On January, 6, 1873, Donnie came riding hard to the main office, the boy hitting the ground in a cloud of dust before his horse had come to a complete stop.

"Mister Ryan. Mister Ryan. You have news from California," he shouted as he mounted the steps and was immediately on the porch and opening the door.

Matty smiled and hurried to the office. She was sure this was the message she had been waiting for.

As she entered the office, Ryan was still reading the telegram. He looked up and motioned to Matty to have a seat. He looked back down on the paper, as if he was reading it again.

He walked over to Matty and looked at the message, placing a hand on her shoulder.

"It's from J.L., Matty. He says Adkin was arrested for murder and is in jail in Placerville, California …"

Matty jumped up. The words exploded in her mind; "murder" and "in jail."

"What are you saying?" she said as she collapsed back into the chair and started crying.

"Easy Matty. J.L. said he's innocent, but he has to have a hearing in front of the magistrate, and it may take a week to get his hearing," Ryan said, realizing Matty was probably not understanding the language or able to hear while in her state of shock. She kept murmuring and rocking back and forth, "In jail? ... In jail?"

Ryan looked to Donnie and told him to go fetch Missus Amache Prowers and Miss Kanaka and tell them what happened.

"Ask them please come if they can," Ryan pleaded to the boy.

"I'll fetch 'em, Mister Ryan. Don't you worry."

Ryan called to the cleaning woman to go find Dusty and for him to bring his wife, Margarite, to the office to help Matty. The woman asked if Matty was sick?

"Just go, please and be quick," Ryan said. "Matty needs help."

Within a short time, everyone at the ranch knew something was wrong, as Donnie was yelling, "Mister Yates is in jail in California," all the way as he was galloping off the ranch grounds.

Dusty and Margarite arrived soon along with several other women. Ryan related the message to Dusty. He wanted to make sure Matty knew J.L. said Adkin was innocent and there were witnesses, but he would have to wait a week or so in jail until the hearing.

"Tell her not to worry, we need to stay strong and support Adkin," Ryan said.

Amache and Kanaka arrived in a buggy and Matty was very pleased to see them, all hugging each other. They encouraged her to keep faith and all would work out.

Ryan went back to his desk as the women were speaking in Spanish, Kiowa and other languages – soothing Matty. She seemed to be gathering her wits.

Ryan looked over the lengthy telegram again, He didn't tell Matty Adkin had been shot in the ear and bled a lot, but it wasn't serious.

Seems the crew stopped for the night in what had been called Hangtown or Old Dry Diggins on their way to Sacramento to make arrangements to come home.

Shortly after they all gathered at the bar, this drunk stood up at a poker table in the back of the room and yelled, "You won't be cheating anyone again, you son of a bitch."

He then shot his revolver at Adkin's back, nicking his ear and taking out some of those golden locks. By the time Adkin pulled his pistol and turned to see who was shooting, the man got off another shot, which whizzed between Adkin and J.L. into bottles behind the bar. J.L. knew from the sound, the bullet came very close. He also knew his hearing was going to be bad for the rest of the day. His ears were ringing from the blasts.

At that second, Adkin shot from the hip and hit the man right under his chin – dead center. The man's spine was severed, and he was dead before he hit the dusty planks of the saloon's floor. There was about a three-foot circle of blood spray on the wall behind the man from where the .44 had exited the back of his neck.

Witnesses, even a friend of the dead man, said a somewhat smaller and older mountain man who dressed like Adkin, with the buckskin shirt and pants with leather tassels, along with lengthy reddish curls hanging to his shoulders and a similar leather hat, had beat the dead man out of several hundred dollars the night before.

The dead man had accused the man of cheating and challenged him to a fight, but the mountain man backed out and wasn't seen again. They said the dead man had been drinking all day and was looking for the man, saying he was going to kill him. He apparently thought Adkin was him, even though he didn't really see Adkin's face.

He tried to kill Adkin by shooting him in the back. Luckily for Adkin, his aim was bad. Unfortunately for the dead man, Adkin was fast and deadly accurate, even at about 20 paces.

The town's Marshall was called, and he said he had no option but to hold Adkin until the area magistrate cleared him. So, Adkin was being held in the Placerville Jail, a place where vigilante justice was infamous. Adkin and J.L. were hoping the dead man didn't have family or close friends around.

Ryan decided to keep most of the story from Matty for the time being. He figured the important message was Adkin was innocent of murder because it was a self-defense shooting.

The women calmed Matty down, and Matty told Ryan she was fine, she would travel to California if she needed to. Ryan assured her everything would be fine, it was just a matter of time.

Amache asked Ryan if they could take Matty back to their place for the night?

"We'll bring her back tomorrow morning, Ryan, if you don't mind?" Amache said. Ryan agreed and Kanaka squeezed his hand tightly as Amache turned away, and Kanaka gave him a secret smile.

•••

After a flurry of telegrams back and forth and more details from J.L., it was apparent Adkin should have the charges dropped as soon as the magistrate got to town. They just didn't know where he was.

J.L. said Adkin was the talk of the entire area. Word spread about his pistol skills and everyone was calling him the Colorado Englishman, or the British Gent.

An Englishman's Adventures on the Santa Fe Trail (1865-1889)

Sanderson also said a Marshall from El Dorado County came to visit Adkin in the jail on Day 4 and offered Adkin the job of Sheriff of Diamond Springs for $100 a month.

It was quickly discovered the dearly departed had no family in California nor, apparently, any "dear" friends. When Adkin found out, he offered to pay the burial costs, which only added to the sudden myth of this British gunfighter from Colorado who was a true Gent – and a dead-eye pistol shot.

On Day 8, J.L. telegraphed that the magistrate heard the witnesses that morning and cleared Adkin of all charges, but fined him $15 for court costs.

The crew telegraphed the next day, saying they were in Sacramento and had paid rail passage to Cheyenne. Adkin asked Ryan to tell Matty, "Everything is fine, I am well, but my heart aches for you. I love you."

"He's a real poet – if not a Gent, too," Ryan thought to himself, laughing inside.

•••

Donnie came riding into the ranch grounds on February, 11. but in no particular hurry. He delivered a telegram to Ryan. After reading it quickly, Ryan sent Donnie over to Adkin and Matty's little one-room house to fetch Matty.

Within a few minutes, Matty and Donnie came into the office.

"Great news Matty, Adkin and the crew got into Cheyenne yesterday," Ryan said as Matty stood there smiling. "Adkin is well and they were planning to depart today for Denver and then on home. Should be here in about 15 days.

"That's cutting it close to the wedding, and he's supposed to be Best Man," Ryan continued. "He definitely lives on the edge.

"J.L. said everyone had to get off the train and shovel snow that was blocking the tracks in the Rockies – for three days," Ryan added, laughing.

Matty laughed a little, then she thanked Ryan.

"You have been very kind in helping me not to worry so much about my husband," she said softly. "I have to remember I am Kiowa and should not behave like an old lonely squaw who is afraid she will be put out of the tribe at any moment.

"I am stronger and should not be so afraid," she added, walking out the door before Ryan could actually say anything.

"Any answer to the telegram Mister Ryan?" Donnie asked, smiling and still waiting for his tip.

"No, thank you Donnie," Ryan said while flipping Donnie a nickel. "See you next time."

"Thanks, Mister Ryan – see ya."

•••

On the afternoon of February 26, 1873, Ryan, Uribe and a few of the crew arrived with much fanfare. Ranch hands were riding in front of them yelling about their arrival. Little Donnie was among them, having seen them cross the bridge in north Las Animas.

As people started gathering around the main office, Matty stepped up on the porch and grabbed Ryan's hand.

"They are actually home," she said as Ryan said, "I told you everything would be fine."

She smiled then walked back down the steps as the horsemen neared the office. She wanted to hug her husband right away.

"Welcome home, you troublemakers," Ryan yelled as they neared.

"Ees not me, Señor Ryan, ees this Colorado gunfighter," Uribe said laughing as Adkin gave him a frowning look.

"Welcome my husband," Matty said as Adkin bounced out of his saddle and grabbed his Kiowa Princess. Ryan forgot how big a man Adkin was until he saw him hoisting his little wife up in his arms and giving her a kiss.

"I've missed you Matty," he said as he put her back on the ground. She just had her arms around him, hugging hard as she rested her cheek on his side while his huge arm was around her shoulders.

She looked up and suddenly noticed most of his right ear lobe was missing and looked farely raw, like a scab had recently fallen off.

"What happened to your ear?"

"Oh, don't worry about that, it's okay," Adkin answered her. "The man that shot at me trimmed a little hair and took a piece of my ear off."

"Did you know, Mister Ryan?" she looked up at Ryan.

Adkin immediately realized Ryan hadn't told her.

"I asked him not to mention it, Matty. It was no big problem at all," Adkin said, bending down to hug her again. "I'm home, and I promise I will never leave you again, my Kiowa Princess."

She smiled and hugged him back as they started up the steps to the porch. Ryan embraced Adkin and Uribe, after Matty finally let Uribe loose. She thanked him for taking care of Adkin.

Uribe insisted it was Adkin who looked after him, but he told Matty not to tell that to Adkin. She smiled, knowing Uribe liked making believe he was Adkin's protector.

"Oye Señors, ees time for some brandy, si?" Uribe spoke out. Everybody within earshot started yelling in agreement. One man said, "Si, cerveza or whisky will also do."

"Let's head to the dining hall," Ryan shouted. "Drinks on the house."

Matty wouldn't let go of Adkin, even as they sat at the long table with friends and ranch hands and all the women serving up various refreshments and liquors.

Adkin asked for tea, and Matty finally let go long enough to go into the kitchen and make his special English tea and bring it back.

Adkin was glad to see Weldon Campbell was still part of the crew, embracing each other as if they had been friends for life.

Adkin asked Campbell to sit on the other side of them as he continued getting updates from Ryan.

Ryan started telling Adkin about news of the railroads, how the Santa Fe Railroad was now near the Old Granada site at the Colorado-Kansas border. He also mentioned one railroad called the Katy or KT, that had reached down from Kansas city to Fort Gibson southeast of Tulsa, Okla.

The mention of Oklahoma stirred Matty to tell Adkin Mary Catherine and Sam had another baby.

"It was another boy," Matty said smiling. "They named him Oscar – that's four babies now."

"That's Sam's middle name," Adkin said. "When I met him, I remember him distinctly saying, 'Lieutenant Samuel Oscar Phillips at your service, sir,' and saluting."

"Knowing those two, they will have many more children, God willing," Adkin said.

•••

Although preparations for the March 1 wedding had been well under way, Ryan informed Adkin about how many old friends he had heard from.

"The biggest group is coming from Dodge City," Ryan said. "Their travel time has been cut down to about four days total with the railroad. There's even some names I've never heard of, but Matty said she knew them – they had helped with the Dream Home or you and she travelled with them during part of their buffalo hunting trips.

"Even got a telegram from Conrado Aguirre, who said he's coming," Ryan continued. "He has some business in Denver after stopping here."

"Sounds like fun," Adkin said. "You going to have enough liquor for this party?"

"Between my orders, John's and Thomas Boggs, we should have plenty," Ryan said, laughing. "We've even added another fire spit for cooking beeves."

Don Diego came up to Ryan and Adkin, telling them the Velasquez' from Pueblo and La Junta had arrived with two wagons full of family members. The brothers, Mello and Ablo had been station mangers for years since Ryan and Adkin first signed them up.

"Put them in the southwest corner, like our plans – they can set up camps there," Ryan said. "Make sure you show them where the water supply is and get them over here if they're hungry."

"How many are you planning on – its only Wednesday and the wedding isn't until Saturday?" Adkin asked.

"Probably more than 200 folks," Ryan said. "We had some station managers from as far as Trinidad and from Manitou Springs, Colorado, come in already.

"Should start seeing a bunch coming in tomorrow and Friday," he continued. "Locals won't be camping out here, and they'll just come Saturday morning for a full day of events – and Sunday's events as well."

"Events? Saturday and Sunday?" Adkin asked wide-eyed.

"John and Amache have horse races lined up, wrestling matches, stick-ball tournaments, a turkey-shoot – all kinds of stuff," Ryan said, shaking his head in disbelief. "There's even going to be dances Friday and Saturday nights – they're bringing in a band from Bent's Fort."

"Sounds more like a July 4th celebration," Adkin said smiling.

"It should be fun – and Saturday, I believe, will be the best day of my life, Adkin," Ryan said. "I can't wait to get everything over with."

"I'll bet," Adkin said, looking to Matty. "Much more hoopla than standing in Satanta's tipi with Black Horse, si?"

Matty nodded her head and smiled.

"I will be happy it is finished, too," she said smiling.

•••

After a big breakfast Thursday morning, Adkin was just starting to get his ranch feet back under him, feeling like his night getting to snuggle with Matty was only a dream.

Ryan, Adkin and the men got up and headed for their chores while Matty and the women hurried into the kitchen area. The next few days would prove to be a total team effort to feed and take care of several hundred people, and their animals, which Don Diego, Francisco and Peg-Leg Pete were overseeing.

Ray Dee, Tom Marcellus and Campbell were supervising a wild-game hunt, meat butchering and the open cooking pits and their crews.

Dusty and Margarite would work with Matty to oversee the kitchen operations

Uribe appointed himself to be the greeter.

"I will meet la gente and make the peoples feel welcome to our home," Uribe said with those pearly white teeth smiling under that big black mustache. "We want them to see a pretty face and a happy face."

That was met with several guffaws.

As Ryan, Adkin and several of the crew approached the office, a rider raced up to the hitching rail.

"Señors, we have the first of some of the Dodge City amigos coming across the Las Animas Bridge. "There's six wagons and about two-dozens riders."

"Park them where we planned, Don Diego,' Ryan said as Don Diego and Francisco took off for the main gate. Pete said he would update the plat he was drawing to keep track of every party once they had set up camp.

Adkin strained to see back east along the roadway and noticed a small cloud of dust on the horizon, indicating they would be arriving in about 15 minutes.

"Sitler and Wright telegraphed they were going to try to be here early today," Ryan said. "They must've got off the train Tuesday and rode on in. More are going to come in Friday – they had some things to take care of."

"Great, It will be good to see old friends," Adkin said.

Uribe quickly mounted his steed and raced out to the gate to "greet" them.

Sure enough, Henry Sitler and Robert "Bob" Wright were riding side-by-side as the men and wagons came through the front gate.

"That's Chris Rath behind Sitler and Bob," Adkin said. "Who's that beside him?"

"I don't know – don't recognize him, but that's Major Kirk behind him, in civilian dress," Ryan said. "I wonder if Charles Rath is coming, too. I haven't heard from him. Chris will know."

Everyone pulled up and while people came up on the porch to greet the Barlow & Sanderson group, as well as the YR&R Freight crew, Don Diego was showing wagon drivers where their camping area would be while at the ranch.

After embracing Chris, Adkin asked if Charles was coming or if he was off starting more stores somewhere.

"He had business to attend to, so he's coming tomorrow," Chris said. "Charles just moved his family to Dodge City about six months ago."

"Family? He had just married when I saw him two years ago," Adkin said.

"He's got a boy that's just walking – about a year-and-a-half, I think," Chris said.

Wright, Kirk and Sitler couldn't wait to tell Adkin how much his lots in Dodge City were worth now.

"You could get $50 to $100 for those lots on the hill, right now," Wright said, with Sitler agreeing.

"I got $150 each for two lots on the west side near the rails," Sitler added.

"I told you it would be a good investment," Kirk said, laughing.

"What happened to your Army career?" Adkin asked Kirk.

"Dodge City is what happened," Kirk replied while they all laughed. "So I took my retirement and decided Dodge City is where I want to live and be a part of."

"Major Kirk is one of our founding fathers," Sitler said.

Adkin assured them he was going to hang onto his lots, telling them he eventually wants to build a house up there with a view.

"I just have to sell it to Matty," Adkin said, "She's pretty happy just having our Dream House down on the Cimarron, which I still can't express how grateful we are to your help in getting that house built.

"We're going to spend next winter there again," Adkin added. "I'll be dragging her along the lots up on the hill for sure when we come through — showing her the vista if she had a house up there, too."

They all laughed, and then the men started visiting with Ryan, asking him about Kanaka and teasing him about settling down. Matty showed up and greeted everyone — she had met most all of them.

Adkin found out Hoo Doo Brown, Charley Bassett and several others were out hunting buffalo, but Reighard would be on the same train as Charles Rath, a man Adkin had built a strong fondness for. He knew Charles Rath was a very special man of the High Plains.

Wright introduced the man Adkin and Ryan didn't know.

"Gentlemen, I would like you to meet one of our fine citizens and merchants, Frederick C. Zimmermann," Wright said. "He may be the finest gunsmith this side of the Mississippi."

"Nice to meet you Mister Zimmermann," Ryan said.

"Please, call me Fred," Zimmermann interrupted, pumping Ryan's hand.

As he reached for Adkin's hand, Adkin asked. "German? Or Polish?"

"Prussia, Mister Yates, Province of Saxony, near the Polish border," he said smiling. "Northern England? Maybe Vales?"

"The Midlands of Britain, the Village of Olney," Adkin said. "Raised in a coach inn — a blacksmith."

"Ah-ha," Zimmermann said. "Raised in Prussia, but learned gunsmithing there, and in Paris and London."

"Nice to meet you, Fred," Adkin said shaking hands and both smiling. "You can call me Adkin."

"Do you not prefer Adam here in America?"

"No, my mother would thrash my backside — if she were here — if I took the name Adam."

Adkin felt he had connected with a new friend — a man of the world and an accomplished gunsmith. They had a lot in common.

He was also an impressing figure, tall and strong looking with a friendly smile beneath a black mustache that grew into his black sideburns, which had grown out like side beards. It was unique, but he wore his facial hair gentlemanly.

The dining hall filled up with people and Marcellus came in with Campbell and asked if any of the men would like to be a part of a game-hunting party the next morning.

"We need to find some buffalo, if possible, or elk, deer, antelope — you know," Marcellus said. "We need plenty of meat — we've got the beeves."

About a dozen hands flew up.

"Meet us at 6 in the morning at the stables, and we'll head out," Marcellus said. "There will be hot coffee and some biscuits and molasses here at 5 if you want to get a little food and coffee in you – or bring your own cache. We could be out all day. Bring your own water canteens."

"I'm definitely going out on that," Zimmermann said. "I love hunting."

"We'll ride together, if that's okay with you?" Adkin said.

"Wunderbar," the big German shouted slapping Adkin on the back. Adkin liked this man.

They found out Fred had moved to Dodge City with a pile of lumber when the Santa Fe finished rails to Spearville in July last year – 1872.

"Fred has been a gunsmith his whole life – and he's 39 – came to America in 1863," Wright said. "His wife, Matilda came in September to Spearville with their two babies. They used a wagon for the last 16 miles to Dodge City."

The more Adkin learned, the more he was impressed with Fred. The man had practiced his trade in New York City, New Jersey and even Laramie, Wyoming.

"An experienced gunsmith is a valuable addition to Dodge City," Wright continued. "He built his store on Front Street next to George Hoover's store."

"He seems to be a good fellow," Adkin said.

"He's great, and he has a good sense for business and a good sense of humor," Sitler spoke up. "Wait til you see some of the new guns he has – especially the ones from New Haven Arms – the old Henry factory."

"He's got several of the new Winchester lever actions in that new caliber, the centerfire .44-40 cartridge," Wright said. "It's probably the most powerful rifle built nowadays."

With the arrival of the Dodge City men, the party was officially started. People were drinking around the campfire and the cooking fires. Matty and the women were kept busy putting out tongue and ham sandwiches, raw vegetables and biscuits and cookies and bread and cheeses.

Adkin had to find Matty to gather her up and head for bed.

"You can keep working tomorrow, but we need to sleep tonight," Adkin said. "It's going to get real hectic tomorrow, and you'll need your strength."

Matty smiled and took Adkin's hand as they excused themselves from the revelry.

•••

At least a dozen men came to the stables Friday morning interested in hunting for wild game for the wedding. Ray Dee spoke up and said there would be three parties – about five men per group. He immediately asked Adkin and Zimmermann to be in his party, while Campbell and Marcellus picked out other men.

"We will ride south, west of the Purgatoire," Ray Dee said. "Once we reach a place called Little Mound, we will spilt into three parties. One headed back to the west, one southwest and the last back southeast along the river.

"If you kill a buffalo, send a rider to the closest group, and then be back to the ranch by noon if at all possible," Ray Dee continued. "If we can, it would be great if everyone could be back by noon."

"We'll take anything you can get, antelope, elk, turkeys – just make sure its capable of feeding more than just one man."

Everybody laughed.

As they headed out, Zimmermann handed Adkin one of his new Winchesters, the Model 1873.

"If you vant, you can use dis gun," Zimmermann said. "It is very accurate and has good range to 300 to 400 yards, maybe vetter vith good eye."

"Thank you, I will try it," Adkin said. "I'm honored."

Their group was headed due west, an area Adkin hadn't explored since they first moved the headquarters here. Word was buffalo had been sighted about 15 miles west of Las Animas City, moving south. With luck, they may intercept some.

As they came over a slight grassy rise, Ray Dee threw up his arm.

"Antelope, about a dozen," he said as he dismounted and pointed due west of their location and bent over, using his arm to pump downward to the men.

The others dismounted with their long guns and kept bent over as Ray Dee whispered their exact location.

"There's some scrub brush due west in a shallow dry creek bed. They're milling around," he said. "As we spread out and ease up, each man try to get on one from left to right – got it?"

Everyone nodded their head and started up the low rise. Adkin and Zimmermann were on the left side. Adkin saw them as soon as Zimmermann and the others did.

"I'll take the buck on the far left," Adkin whispered to Zimmermann. Everybody seemed to be getting a bead on the animals – they were about 100 yards out.

Suddenly a shot rang out then another. Adkin's buck jumped to his left, and as it stopped to see what was happening, Adkin squeezed the trigger on the Model 1873. The buck dropped.

He heard Zimmermann follow up with a shot and saw another buck not far from his fall down. It was trying to drag itself along. It had been hit in the hindquarters. Zimmermann hastily jacked another bullet into the Winchester and killed the animal with his second shot.

"I got too excited, I tink," he said. "It vas a bad first shot."

"You got him with the second," Adkin said smiling. "That's what is important."

The men started yelping and laughing. Four animals had been killed as the rest of the pronghorns didn't stick around long after a few rounds were fired. But it was very successful.

"Men, we're finished here," Ray Dee shouted to the clapping approval of the others. "We'll head straight back to the ranch, rather than go back to the trail we came out on."

They spread out and had the antelopes gutted and tied across the rumps of four horses, including Diablo's. The big black stallion had carried many animals across his rump throughout the years.

They didn't see any more wildlife, but Adkin still enjoyed the scenery: To the west the snow-covered mountain tops could be seen and the rest was slow rolling long grass hills scattered amongst raw prairies with yucca, cactus and sage brush. It was beautiful in his eyes.

"It is very beautiful land, yes?" Zimmermann spoke up.

"It truly is," Adkin said smiling to the big German.

Their hunting party was back at the ranch by 10 a.m. Their success gave them bragging rights, but there were two groups still out. Adkin took Zimmermann to the side and ask if they could go over to the shooting range and put a few more rounds through the new Winchesters.

'No problem, Adkin," Zimmermann answered. "Let us go."

Adkin learned the whole history of lever-action rifles. Fred knew his business.

The first patented lever-action rifle was invented in 1848, and was called the Volition Repeating Rifle, according to Zimmermann.

"It vas too complicated of a design and never made it to produck-shun," Zimmermann said. "Another party, de Robbins and Lawrence Company, bought de patent and produced a few rifles, but de business was not successful. Dhay collapsed in 1852."

He then went on to say, "Horace Smith and Daniel Vesson bought the patent and, vith several investors, formed the Volcanic Repeating Arms Company in 1855."

You're talking about Daniel Wesson?" Adkin asked.

"Ya, Vesson," Zimmermann answered with that German accent eliminating the letter W and replacing it with a V.

"Von of dhose investors vas Oliver Vinchester," Zimmermann said.

"You mean Winchester?"

"Ya, ya, Vinchester," Zimmermann said, looking a little annoyed that Adkin was trying to correct his words.

"I've heard stories that the Volcanic, though not successful, was the basis for the Henry Repeating rifle," Adkin said.

"Vell, sort of," Zimmermann said, hesitating a moment. "Ven de Volcanic gun failed, Smith and Vesson decided to leave the partnership. Oliver Vinchester bought out de other stockholders and changed de name of de company to de New Haven Arms Company.

"Oliver then hired another gunsmith, Benjamin Henry, to improve de Volcanic, and de result vas de Henry rifle released in 1860," Zimmermann said. "It was used in de var, and de Spencer was developed in dat time, but it, too, vas complicated.

"After de var, New Haven Arms became de Vinchester Repeating Arms Company, and an improved version of the Henry became the first Vinchester repeating rifle, the Model 1866," Zimmermann said. "And now de best of de best, vee have de new Model 1873."

Adkin put about 20 rounds through the rifle, and was impressed. The lever-action reloading was smooth and fast. It didn't kick quite as much as his old Henry. And he learned the new .44-40 bullet was faster, and had more knock-down power than the Henry .44.

"Is this new .44-40 caliber hard to find?" Adkin asked

"No, Vith the release of the new 1873, de ammunition was already being produced by the thousands," Zimmermann said. "I've got thousands of rounds and six of dees new Vinchesters."

Zimmermann said the gun was available in three barrel lengths – a 20-inch, a 24-inch and a musket.

"I only buy dis 24-inch barrel," Zimmermann said.

"I really like it. How much would it cost me if you were to be gracious enough to let me purchase one?" Adkin asked in his full English gentleman's accent.

"They are varry expensive, Adkin," he answered smiling. "But for you, I vould de honored to sell you dat one – and 200 rounds – for $75."

"I will give you $100 – if you throw in 1,000 rounds," Adkin responded smiling.

"I only bring 500 rounds with me," Zimmermann said. "But I vill send telegraph to Dodge City and have 500 more rounds sent to you very soon – maybe one veek at most."

Adkin laughed, "You have a deal Fred," and they shook hands. Zimmermann pumped hands like he was at a water well hand pump that had air locked. Adkin liked it, Fred was a genuine person.

"I vill throw in a bonus, if you like," Zimmermann said. "I vill etch your name into da receiver by tomorrow."

Adkin shook his hand again.

"I'd like that very much, thank you."

•••

As they headed back to the cooking pits, where the men had quickly skinned the four antelopes and salted them and hung them in the shade of the blacksmith's shop, Adkin noticed Uribe was coming through the front gate leading another train of wagons, buggys and ambulance. It looked as if another 50 people had just arrived.

Uribe was waving his arms and yelling, "Bienvenidos, more amigos coming for the wedding."

One of the first to ride up was Charles Rath, who jumped off his mount and gave Adkin a big hug and then embraced Ryan just as hard.

"It's good to set eyes on you rascals," Charley said. "Did my brother tell you I've moved to Dodge City? Goin' start me a store and plan to get rich huntin' buffalo."

They all laughed.

"If there is money to be made killing buffalo, you will find a way for sure," Adkin said chuckling.

"You got that right," Ryan said as he patted Charles on the back.

"Sure glad to see you still have your hair, Charley," Ryan said, laughing.

"I'm not planning any more trips across the Llano Estacado, that's for sure," Charles said.

"Have you heard any news of Charles Goodnight?" Adkin asked.

"Actually, I just recently heard he and his wife, Molly, might be moving to Pueblo, Colorado, where he wants to start a big cattle ranch."

"That would be great," Ryan interrupted. "Parker County, Texas, is too damn far to go to visit an old friend."

"He'd be a close neighbor if they moved to Pueblo," Adkin added.

George Reighard walked up. He had been driving a wagon near the rear of the small train. They all embraced.

"What have you been up to, George?" Adkin asked.

"Been killin' buffalo for a living," Reighard said, laughing. "About everyone in Dodge City is making money from buffalo hides and meat – in one way or another.

"I've set up a hunting camp in Clark County, just west of Bluff Creek, about 20 miles north of the Territories."

"You're not far from our Cimarron House, are you?" Adkin asked.

"That's right," Reighard said. "In fact, that's how I found this place – when we came down to help build your house."

"I'll be," Adkin said. "We'll be back down there for the winter. Probably move down there in early September. We'll have to come see you, or you can come down and visit if you get the time."

Ryan started telling Carles Rath about his investment in White Faced Herefords, and they walked away discussing cattle and the different breeds.

Reighard wanted a beer and Adkin and several others headed for the dining hall, Reighard said there were some folks who had only heard about Adkin and Ryan, but some had been part-time workers for either the stagecoach line or the freighting business. They all appreciated the crews running both organizations, according to Reighard.

Just as Don Diego was moving wagons into the camping area, another set of wagons came through the front gate. Uribe was caught off guard and quickly jumped in his saddle and rode out.

There were four horsemen, and as Uribe got near them, Adkin turned when he heard Uribe yell, "Ees Señor Sanderson, J.L. Sanderson."

"Did you hear that Ryan? It's J.L." Adkin said, amazed.

"He never did answer my invitation," Ryan said. "I just figured he was too busy."

They broke away from the others and hurried back to the office where the horsemen were approaching. J.L. dismounted and embraced Adkin and then grabbed Ryan.

"I wanted to surprise you, Ryan," Sanderson said. "I wouldn't have missed my top hand's wedding for anything in the world."

"Thank you, Boss," Ryan said as he and Sanderson held each other's shoulders. "It's means the world to me – and Kanaka – that you came."

"You've been with me a long time, Tyler Ryan, and I care for you like a brother."

Adkin could see this meant a lot to Ryan. The man had tears in his eyes, and that alone caused tears to well up in Adkin's eyes.

"Well, where's the brandy – before we all start crying like old women," Sanderson said, slapping both men on the shoulders.

About then, Ray Dee walked up and got a long hug from Sanderson as well. The four turned and went into the office for some special brandy, as Don Diego and Uribe led the others who were accompanying Sanderson to the camping area.

As they clinked glasses and toasted each other, Sanderson said he had some bad news.

"I got a wire from Junction City two days ago" he started. "I'm sorry to tell you, but Carl Long got killed last week while loading cattle into a rail car – it was an accident."

"Oh no, no, no,' Ryan said sitting down and holding his head. "What happened, Boss?"

"It appears a cow got a leg stuck through the slats on the side, and he squeezed back there to free it," Sanderson began. "Several other steers got spooked and stomped up the area and caught Carl in there, smashed him and knocked him down, and they stomped him to death."

"Oh my God," Ryan said, then silence filled the room for a minute or so. "I guess that old cowboy probably would have chosen that way before anything else."

"It's sad. He didn't have any family we knew of, so they buried him there in the town cemetery," Sanderson said. "They said he had written a will to give his money to a younger local woman there who he saw a lot of. After his burial, she got close to $5,000."

"Five Thousand dollars?" Ryan asked. "He must have loved her a bunch."

"He did, but she finally broke down and admitted she was Carl's younger sister," Sanderson said, "She had a baby out of wedlock that died, and she got shunned by the family down in Texas. He moved her to Junction City a couple of years ago once he found out she had been barely hanging on for some years down there.

"But he never told people who she was – she didn't want him to tell – she didn't want to shame him or the family name," he added.

"That's Carl, a heart of gold – and he apparently saved a lot of money," Ryan said. "Is Darrell still there, working for the company?"

"Yes, Holmes is doing fine," Sanderson said. "He's managing the office there – he and Carl were doing great. We'll have to see if Darrell can find someone to replace Carl – he did a lot of work for one man."

"That's a shame, Carl will be sorely missed," Ryan said. "We had some good times back there in Leavenworth in the old days."

"We sure did, he was like a rock, never did get all upset like most men when they had a little too much to drink," Ray Dee said. "He saved me a few times when I got a little frisky."

"He saved you more than a few times, Ray Dee," Ryan said, smiling.

"I know," Ray Dee said as he hung his head. "I'll miss Carl, too."

Adkin remained mum. His thoughts floated back to his little sister's death.

When they came out of the office, Uribe rode up shouting. He had yet to hear about Carl. Adkin and Ryan whispered they would tell him after this new excitement calmed down.

"Señors, Don Conrado Aguirre is pulling in with his ambulance orito – at this momento," he shouted smiling.

Conrado's ambulance was followed by three covered freight wagons, at least a dozen outriders and a small herd of horses and mules.

Uribe shouted his greetings to Conrado and said he would visit later. He then signaled Don Diego, and they showed the others where they would camp for the festivities.

Conrado embraced all the men, he was very familiar with Sanderson, as well as Adkin, Ryan, Uribe and Ray Dee, too.

"Welcome, Don Conrado, Adkin shouted as Conrado was hugging Sanderson.

They all went back into the office for a drink and to catch up with Conrado.

He reminded them his brother, Epifanio, was killed by Indians back in 1870, but he and his other brothers, Pedro and Jose Yjinio were still in the freighting business and ran stagecoaches down to Sonora, Mexico – throughout New Mexico and much of Arizona.

"When I saw your invitation to attend the wedding, "I said, 'Conrado, you must make plans to see Señor Tyler Ryan say, 'I do,'" he said laughing. "When an old Indian and Comanchero fighter decides to settle down, it is important. I have not known many who did. And you still have your hair.

"Where is my old friend "Peg-Leg" Pete?" he asked chuckling. "That man is one of the toughest hombres and best stage drivers I have ever known. How he is alive is testament to sheer guts and a will to live. He should make his tribe proud."

"He's hopping around here somewhere, working as hard as any two-legged man," Ryan said. "And twice as mean if you try to push him very hard."

They all laughed and toasted Conrado and Ryan again.

•••

Shortly after noon, the two other hunting parties came in and quickly took the bragging rights away from Adkin's group. They had bagged and quartered a young bull buffalo, two elk and two deer. One of the men also shot three turkeys while he was searching a brushy area for one of the wounded deer. There was going to be more than enough meat.

Many of the men teased Ryan as he had to spend most of Friday evening getting his wedding suit finished, a nip here and a tuck there. He turned red after returning from John and Amache's place where the tailor and seamstresses were working.

The wedding was set to start at 3 p.m. Saturday, and here it was Friday evening and Adkin had only got quick glimpses of Matty. She was buried in work, mainly making sure trays and trays of food and refreshments were on the dining hall tables throughout the day.

A dinner of fowl was planned for Friday evening, and someone said the kitchen was full of every kind of feather imaginable: Chickens, quail, pheasant, ducks and geese, even doves and grouse.

Adkin finally saw his wife as she was toting a large tray of roasted birds out the kitchen doors. She smiled, but Adkin could see she looked a little frazzled – some strands of her long hair had escaped from her beaded bun holder.

He motioned to her and she came over, where he made her sit down and rest.

"They can serve without you being in the middle of it all," he said as she smiled. She realized it did feel nice to sit and catch her breath.

"Okay, I will eat with my husband, who I have not seen all day," she said. "Did your hunt go well?"

"Yes, very well. Let us eat some of this fine cooking," Adkin said chuckling. "I bought a new rifle today."

"White Men not so different than Indian men – always want new guns or new knives or new bows and arrows – a new lance," she said. He shook his head in agreement.

That evening, while Matty was helping tidy up, Adkin got to visit with many of the people who had showed up. Of course, he wished Sam Phillips and Mary Catherine could be there, as well as James Meade.

Fond memories of Kit Carson, William Bent, Jesse Chisholm, General Harney popped up out of nowhere, and Adkin smiled to himself – grateful and honored for getting to know those men.

Those days travelling to the Little Arkansas Treaty seemed years ago, yet in reality, it was only eight years past. Time on the High Plains was in its own dimension. You had to live it to understand it.

Adkin decided to turn in when the fiddler and banjo players started the dance music around the fire pits where they had brought in plank boards for a dance floor surrounded with torches on posts burning kerosine.

Adkin finally ran down Matty and told her again, they needed to get some sleep, for tomorrow was "The Day." She agreed and they walked over to their little home.

•••

The next morning, Adkin noticed a few late party goers were still sleeping around the fire pits and the dance floor, where no lamps were now burning bright. Several of the men had buffalo quarters and a beeve on the spits, probably starting about 2 in the morning in order to have everything ready by 6 or 7 that evening.

There were going to be several events before lunch: Wrestling and the turkey shoots – which was going to be divided into a shotgun challenge and a rifle contest. Adkin would like to try his hand with his new Winchester, but Zimmermann was still engraving his name on the receiver.

The big horse races were scheduled for Sunday. Adkin knew he was going to enter Diablo in the long-distance race. Though the big black steed was 9 or 10 years old, Diablo had the heart of a colt – and he ran harder after the first mile. The race was going to be a 10-mile cross-country, and Adkin liked his chances.

The short sprints were where the action was though, and most of the betting took place with the sprints. There would be a quarter-mile race, a half-mile and a one-mile. The two shorter courses were straightaways while the miler was down and back, turning around at a hay wagon and finishing back at the starting line.

Matty had left the house before Adkin awoke. She had told him the night before the women would be making trays of cornbread and biscuits, as well as boiling, baking and frying all sorts of vegetables. Adkin was looking forward to the sweet yams. He liked to mash them down with a fork and smear on some butter then sprinkle sugar over them.

Much of the women's work would be under control by 1 when they would all then begin washing, bathing, primping, doing their hair with all the decorations and their best dresses. Matty would be wearing her elk-toothed dress which she had altered and added additional elk teeth, beading and designs.

Adkin had actually pulled out an old brown suit he had tailored in Denver the first trip he made there. It fit well for his size, but he had for some reason purchased a brown beaver skin derby to go with it. He thought it was a good idea until he actually looked in a mirror back at the hotel.

"What was I thinking?" he had asked himself. But when Matty saw it back in Las Animas City, she liked the overall look.

"You look like important businessman who makes lots of money," she had said. Little did she understand just how accurate she was. While looking like a mountain man most of the time, Adkin was very wealthy. Even he – let alone Matty – had no idea to the extent of his wealth.

Adkin wasn't interested in the turkey shoots. He was an excellent shot with his old Henry, even with his father's old Sharp's he had brought with him from Olney, but Adkin had practiced with that survival gun that had to be used in close quarters, the revolver. He had put more lead through his Colts and his Remington belly gun, than all the rifles combined.

Adkin's excitement when it came to the events was the long-distance horse race riding his beloved Diablo.

Adkin paced through the dining hall at the barracks for lunch, but didn't see Matty. She was probably in the kitchen, but he managed to grab some biscuits and a few chunks of bacon he wrapped in paper and took out to watch the final shooting contests.

Around 1, he decided to go get dressed in his suit. He couldn't find anyone else around. Seems all the folks were trailing off to get ready. He went to their house and he was walking out about 30 minutes later. Still no sight of Matty. He was hoping she didn't lose track of time, which she did often.

Little did he know but the Prowers had sent over a buggy and whisked her away around 12:30 to their place. After all, Matty was going to be a bridesmaid, and she would arrive fully dressed with the wedding party.

Adkin made his way over to the main office, where Ryan and Ray Dee had rooms on the second floor. They were known as the bachelor quarters, and there were actually several cots in each one where extra guests could bunk.

Adkin felt naked walking over as Matty had asked him to not wear his Colt. While agreeing to eliminating the gun belt and holster, that didn't mean he couldn't wear his Remington belly gun in his waistband, which he patted through his suit coat at the thought of it.

Adkin was sitting at the desk with his new boots resting atop when Ryan came down the stairs. He was wearing a navy-blue suit with a ruffled top shirt covering his breast and a big white cumber bund at the waist. His pleated pants were the same coat material and color, and he had on black cowboy boots and a black, silk top hat.

"Well, if it isn't old Honest Abe," Adkin said teasing Ryan's top hat. Adkin had seen drawings of Abe Lincoln and always admired the way the man could wear a top hat with great distinction. Adkin wasn't sure if Ryan would be able to pull off the same look.

"Never did take to these top hats, but John and Kanaka says it looks 'Gentlemanly,'" Ryan said. "I need a shot of whisky, Adkin, now please."

•••

A temporary stage had been erected on the east end of the barrack's dining hall, where a local priest and Tom Boggs were going to conduct the ceremony.

When the two ambulances pulled up and everybody started unloading, little Donnie came running over to Ryan and Adkin. He was in a small suit with a bow tie that he kept pulling at his neck and new cowboy boots.

As John and Amache stepped out, they were dressed to the top, Amache's scarlet veil covering her face and her matching dress with several stripes of yellow and tan sewn into her hem in the Cheyenne style of decoration. Adkin was sure it meant something, but he hadn't any idea.

John held out his hand to Matty who stepped out into the sunlight in her nearly white deerskin dress decorated with elk teeth at the top and new colorful beads along the hem. Her hair was parted and her long braids on each side were wrapped in strips of brown mink held in place with leather thongs.

She wore reddish-orange Copper Mallow Flowers atop each braid at her ears. They were native to Colorado and also called Cowboy's Delights. Amache probably grew them in her huge hot-house in Boggsville. The color complimented Amache's dress.

Adkin suddenly saw her in a new light, as beautiful as she ever has been and lit up with sheer joy in her eyes. He just took her in, awed by her sight.

Then Kanaka moved out on the ambulance's step. John held her hand as she hopped to the ground. She was wearing a traditional Cheyenne dress of bright reddish-orange calico cloth ornamented with elk eye-teeth.

There were black borders on the ends of her three-quarter length sleeves, her neck and the bottom hem. The elk teeth were in rows starting at her neck and continuing in 10 rows to her waist and down her sleeves. She had white deerskin tasseled leggings and beaded moccasins.

Adkin would find out later many of the beads had belonged to her grandfather, Cheyenne Peace Chief Ochinee – Lone Bear – who was murdered in 1864 in the Sand Creek Massacre along with her mother. Chief Ochinee was her mother's and Amache's father.

Adkin noticed Ryan was just staring, his mouth agape in a huge smile.

"Close your mouth, you old teamster," Adkin said as he elbowed Ryan. Suddenly a fiddler started playing the "Bridal Chorus," also known as "Here Comes The Bride" to many, and John was waving for Ryan and Adkin and the groom's entourage to come up and walk to the temporary altar together.

They did, as others were still filling the dining hall as they all marched to the altar. Once there, John held Kanaka's arm on his right, Adkin stood to the left of Ryan, who was next to John. Then Matty, Amache and a distant cousin stood to Kanaka's right. Ray Dee, Uribe and Dusty made up Ryan's side.

Boggs began by telling how he met Ryan and Adkin, as well as how they had called upon John Prowers to see if he had property to sell so they could relocate the companies' Santa Fe Trail location to the new Las Animas City.

He spoke eloquently about his affection for Ryan and Ryan's strong character, and that Ryan was a good-standing member of the community. Adkin could see these people really did appreciate his partner greatly. He felt proud.

He then stepped back and the priest, Father Vargas came forward and asked, "Who giveth this woman in marriage?"

After a somewhat lengthy service, in Adkin's mind, Ryan finally said "I do," and Kanaka said the same. They were pronounced man and wife and Ryan gave Kanaka a quick peck on the cheek.

"Ladies and gentlemen, myself and Missus Tyler Ryan invite you to participate in our wedding reception," Ryan shouted. "Which starts right now!"

The guests broke out in cheers and started yelping like a bunch of Indians, which Adkin realized they were, mostly, along with Mexicans and those who were of mixed blood like Uribe.

The drinks started flowing and Adkin gathered up Matty and gave her a big kiss, lifting her in the air while doing so.

"You are the most beautiful woman in the place," Adkin said smiling. "In Colorado and probably the whole United States, too."

"Maybe my husband has had a few brandies, si?" Matty asked giggling and hugging his huge chest. Her extended arms only reached about half way around him.

An Englishman's Adventures on the Santa Fe Trail (1865-1889)

Ryan had told Adkin he and Kanaka were planning on leaving Monday morning on a honeymoon to St. Louis.

"We're taking the train all the way – first class – and staying in the finest hotels along the way, especially in Kansas City and St. Louie," Ryan had explained to Adkin.

Adkin had assured Ryan he and the men could run things during his honeymoon, even though Ryan had planned a three-month affair. They planned on taking in a lot of sights and side trips along the way up and back. Ryan had mentioned he was going to pay his respects at the grave of their old friend and mentor, William Bent, and his family in Westport.

Once everyone had refreshed themselves, the sun was getting lower in the west and the band, complete with two brass horns, a bass drum and guitar player, along with the usual fiddlers and banjo player, began to play music at the outdoor dance floor. Adkin noticed the torches had yet to be lit, it wasn't dark enough.

"This will be quite a night," he thought to himself.

"C'mon Boss, let us toast our dear amigo, Señor Ryan and his new bride," Uribe said, holding a brandy up to Adkin.

"Why, gracious, mi amigo," Adkin said in his English accent while taking the drink from Uribe and taking a sip. "Very fine Brandy, indeed."

•••

As Adkin walked over to the barracks, there were people laying around all over the place, even on some tables in the dining hall. If he didn't know better, it looked like they had been raided during the night and bodies were everywhere – sans any blood, of course.

After making his tea, Adkin went to the stables. More and more people were waking and trying to find their footing, so to say. When he arrived at Diablo's stall, Uribe was standing in front of Tóngúl's stall, talking Spanish to the red mare.

"What are you doing, Uribe?"

"I'm telling Tóngúl how we're going to win the race today," Uribe answered, while Adkin had a curious gaze on his face.

"Race? What race?" Adkin asked bewildered.

"Señor, Missus Matty not tell you?" Uribe said, with his out-spread hands in the air. "She asked me to race her red baby in the long-distant race.

"Missus Matty say the men would not let her race Tóngúl because she is a woman."

"Well, hope she – and you – don't mind coming in second behind me and Diablo," Adkin said, boldly with a smile.

"Ees posible," Uribe said laughing.

Adkin watched some of the wrestling, and Tom Marcellus won the final after besting four other men through the preliminaries. Adkin wasn't sure if he could even beat Big Tom.

"Way to go, Marcellus," Adkin said as he slapped Marcellus on the back along with other fans crowding around them and shouting Tom's name.

In the short sprints, most of those were being won by Indian ponies. Donnie Boggs won the half-mile on his "telegram" horse as everyone was calling it.

Nobody had seen Ryan or Kanaka yet, they had stayed in Ryan's office room. Some said Ryan had drank quite a bit, but was in a good mood when they finally retired.

Adkin and Uribe mounted their horses when the starter blew his bugle announcing the 10-mile overland race.

"Five-minutes men, get your rides to the starting line now," he yelled and blew the bugle again. "Five minutes."

Adkin caught sight of Ryan off to the side.

"You not racing that nag of yours?" Adkin asked teasingly.

"No way," Ryan said, shaking his head and chuckling. "I don't think I could stay in the saddle for 100 yards."

The bugle went off again, and Adkin and Uribe made their way over to the wagons where the start/finish banner was waving overhead between the wagon tongues that had been stood upright.

"C'mon men, steady those horses and get them up here in line," the starter shouted from a wagon bed. "Ready … set …" Boom, the pistol exploded, startling several of the steeds, but Adkin and Uribe got a solid start.

There were at least two dozen horses and the cloud of dust was immense. Those in the back were almost riding over each other, horses and saddles were slamming into one another.

The track was marked with small posts with white rags tied atop. It took off southeast toward the Purgatoire River south of Boggsville. Adkin and Uribe were about three or four horses back, spreading out more as they settled into a steady pace.

Adkin could feel Diablo beneath him and knew the big stallion was just getting into a rhythm. Uribe and Tóngúl were running steady as well. Two of the horses in front of them started racing when they saw the turn wagon about a half-mile ahead, with people standing in the wagon waving and shouting encouragement.

Adkin held Diablo back as the stallion instinctively wanted to stay up with the other horses. Adkin didn't want to give Diablo his head this early and tire him. Uribe seemed to be dropping back a little.

As the first two men reached the wagon and turned their mounts back home, Adkin had caught the third-place rider and went into his turn with only the two others ahead and racing hard.

An Englishman's Adventures on the Santa Fe Trail (1865-1889)

As Adkin completed the turn he passed Uribe who was just getting to the turn, about six or seven horse lengths behind. Adkin figured that was probably the end of Tóngúl, she looked tired and sweaty already, and there were five more miles.

Within about a mile from the finish, Adkin had reached the second-place rider as his horse was running out of steam. Adkin started pushing Diablo a little more with his hands on Diablo's neck. The other leading horse was slowing, too.

"Too much racing, too soon," Adkin thought to himself as he was pulling alongside the lead horse. There was only about a quarter of a mile remaining, and the crowd was going crazing, waving their arms and yelling and screaming.

"Take it away big boy," Adkin whispered in Diablo's ear as he released any pressure on the reins to the bit. Adkin kicked him gently in the flanks. Diablo was cruising, the banner was only about 100 yards ahead.

Suddenly, movement on Adkin's left side came into his peripheral vision. He looked over. It was Tóngúl, her head thrusting back and forth with foam flying from her mouth. Uribe looked over with that big smile under that big, black mustache as Tóngúl pulled ahead about half-a-horse length and finished first.

The crowd went wild. Adkin couldn't believe Matty's little red mare had ran so hard and so strong. Of course, Tóngúl was an Indian pony, and most trained well can run for 100 miles before stopping. Tóngúl had been trained as a colt by Cheyenne nearby and was of very old genetics of fine horse flesh.

As people swarmed around them after the remaining horses came in, Matty sneaked up behind Adkin and tickled his sides. He knew it was her and twisted around quickly and shouted, "What?"

She jumped back and then smiled, started laughing and jumping up and down like a Mexican jumping bean and clapping her hands.

"We won, my husband," she said giggling. "We won. We won."

"I know my Kiowa Princess," he said as he hoisted her and kissed her.

Adkin found out Diablo was the favored horse and had heavy betting placed on him. Tóngúl was only at about 5 to 1, but Adkin wasn't sure if Uribe had bet on himself. He knew Matty wouldn't be betting, but he kind of wished he had. Trouble was, he never looked at the racing sheet to see who was racing.

As they were being congratulated and everyone was yelling and saluting the racers, Uribe walked up with Tóngúl, and handed Matty the reins.

"Este caballo es muy bueno, Señora, muy bueno," Uribe said as Matty hugged him and thanked him. She even gave him a peck on his cheek and he turned red as he looked to Adkin. Adkin simply smiled.

"You ran a very good race, Uribe," Adkin said. "You held her back going around the turn. That fooled me, because I thought maybe she was already tired."

"I had to hold her nearly all the way, Boss," Uribe said. "She could run more miles, she's strong – like Missus Matty."

They all laughed, and Ryan came over and suggested some refreshments.

"I think I need a little hair of the dog," Ryan said, chuckling.

"I'll cool the horses down and put them up," Uribe said. "I'll come later."

They made their way to the dining hall, where people were imbibing at will.

"How much you spending on beverages?" Adkin asked Ryan, who was waving at Kanaka and Amache sitting at a table near the kitchen.

"Between five of us, we've put in $100 each for refreshments, and will cover any additional if needed," Ryan said, smiling. "Let's go over to Kanaka."

They sat down, and John Prowers came to the table. He had been over at the office sending a message with Donnie about some cattle they were going to buy. Ryan had told Adkin the Hereford cattle were doing good, most made it through the winter, even though it was a fairly mild winter this season.

After talking and having some drinks and coffee, Uribe walked up to Adkin and Matty.

"Here you are, Missus Matty," Uribe said, handing Matty a leather money purse. "I've taken my share, y muchas gracias Señora, muchas gracias."

He then sat down a few chairs away and grabbed a beer. Matty looked at Adkin sheepishly and held the little leather bag in front of her.

"What's that, Matty?" Adkin asked.

She just sat there, almost paralyzed. Finally she looked around and everyone was staring at her, waiting for an answer.

"Well, I was hoping my Tóngúl could win the race, so I ask mi amigo, Uribe, to ride her – and she won," Matty said softly, barely audible.

"The bag?" Adkin asked, starting to realize his wife may be a betting woman after all. He smiled at her, letting her know it would be okay.

She sat the bag down and untied the thong. She then lifted it and poured the contents in her little palm. Gold pieces, gold coins and silver pieces fell out all over the table. She looked up with eyes as big as coffee cup saucers.

Everyone started laughing.

"I only gave Uribe a few gold pieces of mine to wager," she said with a look of a child who has been caught with its hand in the taffy jar.

"Goodness," Adkin said as he started gathering up the coins and such. "That looks like a fairly good return on investment, my dear."

'It's close to $200, Boss," Uribe said with a big smile. "I invested some, too."

"You mean you and Matty won $400 for that race?" Adkin asked, astounded. The others were stunned and began mumbling among themselves.

"And two ponies – yearlings," Uribe added with a smile.

"A business woman after my own heart," Amache stood and shouted, then started laughing. "She is a strong, smart Kiowa Princess, Adkin Yates."

Everyone was laughing, and Matty started grinning, still not sure she did the right thing – racing and betting were part of a man's world. But she had been raised around betting – Indian warriors bet on everything, nearly everyday.

"You are wonderful, Matty," Adkin said as he bent over and kissed her cheek.

•••

Later in the evening, Adkin caught Ryan as he was walking away from a few friends.

"When are you leaving tomorrow?"

"We're heading out shortly after daybreak," Ryan answered. "We're taking an ambulance to the Granada Depot, then it's trains, trains and more trains."

"Why St. Louis?" Adkin asked.

"I've got an uncle and some cousins over there somewhere, and I want to see if I can find them," Ryan said, motioning to Adkin to take a chair at a dining table. "I don't think I ever told you, but I was born and raised on the Missouri River near where Mill Creek flows into it – a stone's-throw east of Kansas City.

"My pappy was a share cropper, and Jack-of-All-Trades," he continued. "I've farmed, fished, hunted, lumberjacked, you name it.

"But as I got into my middle teens, I kept seeing those steamers, barges, sail boats of every make going up and down that river. And, I often dreamed and made up games wondering where they were going. Not knowing fascinated me.

"By the time I turned 17, I knew I had to follow that river west, into the wild lands – and the Santa Fe Trail," Ryan said. "My pappy's brother, Uncle Kitch, had moved east back to St. Louie to take a mill job. He had three boys and one girl, my cousins, and I ain't laid eyes on 'em since I was 17 – 20 years ago.

"Hell, I may have more cousins since then," he added, chuckling.

Adkin just smiled. He understood more about his dear friend – they both had that urge to go find adventure – to dive into the unknown.

"Well, I hope you and Kanaka find them and have a wonderful time," Adkin said as he rose and patted Ryan on the shoulder.

"Thanks, friend," Ryan said as he stood and turned to go find his new wife.

Adkin whirled around to go catch up with Matty. He was sure she was supervising people in the kitchen and found her there. He grabbed her arm and escorted her into the dining hall.

"Please come sit with us, my beautiful wife," he said, smiling.

"I was, I just wanted to make sure …" she started.

"I know. I know, dear," he said as he urged her toward the Prowers and Ryan and Kanaka. They visited with people all night, with the Dodge City friends, Sanderson and the freighters, or about the cattle business and irrigation.

"When are you going to the Cimarron House?" Sanderson asked Adkin.

"Well, we haven't talked about it with the wedding and all. I haven't been home a week yet,"

Adkin said as he looked to Matty. "When do you want to go?"

"Tomorrow," she said, breaking into laughter. "No, really just so we can spend our winter there, when you don't have so much work."

Adkin laughed and looked to Sanderson.

"I was thinking around early September," Adkin said to Sanderson. "Our business slows down once the caravans stop coming through, plus there seems to be less and less wagon trains with the rails advancing more and more."

"That's what we've talked about for the last five years," Sanderson said. "I understand you just got back, but where are the best opportunities to expand in this area of the High Plains?"

"We might be able to expand throughout northern New Mexico and into Arizona with stage service," Adkin said. "With rail service reaching further west, settlers and businessmen are coming like bees to honey.

"Also, the more mines that are opening in Colorado will be needing stages and freighters, especially here in southern Colorado."

"That's keeping us busy in central and northern Colorado, as well," Sanderson said. "We're doing well into Wyoming and side-trails off the Oregon and Mormon Trails. "I think we can move into Utah off those."

"You, Ray Dee and I will check with Ryan later this evening and get his input and produce a written plan before you leave Friday, if that's okay?" Adkin suggested. "I'll also have better details on my plans to go to the Cimarron House, too."

"Great, that sounds good," Sanderson said.

•••

After dinner, Sanderson, Adkin, Ray Dee and Ryan met in the office and bounced ideas and proposals about expanding services in the West. Ryan also brought up expansion plans with YR&R Freight coinciding with Barlow and Sanderson Company.

Both companies were doing well, despite critiques the railroads would put them out of business. It was seen by Sanderson five years earlier how to expand as the railroads brought more and more people out west. He knew they wanted to branch off the Santa Fe Trail and build communities, needing lumber, household goods and the comforts of home from back east.

They all agreed on most of the ideas, and Adkin assured Sanderson he would have it all written up before Sanderson headed back to Denver in five days.

Sanderson had asked Uribe to take him up the Purgatoire River for a little rest and relaxation time. Plus, Sanderson had discovered fishing with a fly rod and reel while living in Denver.

He wanted to try this on the Purgatoire, and Uribe was full of teasing Sanderson, but he was looking forward to the outing. They were going to take a wagon, tents and spend two nights out fishing and hunting.

"I will like this holiday time," Uribe told Adkin. "Sanderson ees bringing two men, and asked if I would like to invite mis amigos."

"Ees okay to take Dusty and Peg Leg with us, Boss?" Uribe asked.

"Es bueno con mio, mi amigo," Adkin said in his British accent.

"Hey Boss, you're learning Spanish better," Uribe said, chuckling.

"Have a good time, Uribe," Adkin said. "We'll have plenty of work when you get back. We have to clean up this place and get everything back in good condition."

Early Monday, Ryan and Kanaka took off for Dodge City. John and Amache came out to see them off. Four riders were escorting them and would bring back the ambulance after the couple caught the train in Old Granada.

All the women cried, but Matty's tears were happy tears. She was ecstatic two of her closest friends were married and taking off on an adventure. Adkin thought he had never seen Ryan so happy. His smile was huge as they rode out of the ranch waving.

About mid-morning, Sanderson and his fishing and hunting crew were assembled and they headed out. Uribe and Dusty assured Sanderson they knew where plenty of fish were hiding in the Purgatoire. Adkin was happy Sanderson was taking some time to relax.

"And J.L. hasn't seen anything like the canyons up the Purgatoire," he thought to himself, as he knew the canyons were as beautiful as anywhere in the world, he imagined.

•••

After checking the ranch grounds once everybody was off either on a honeymoon or a fishing and camping trip, Adkin realized it would take a few days to clean up the place. Animals that were kept at the camps had left quite a mess of manure and some of the guests had been a little sloppy containing their trash, with bags and sack pieces everywhere.

He decided to go back and take an afternoon nap, like he did often at the Cimarron House. He placed his new Winchester with his name emblazoned on the receiver above the fire place. As soon as he laid down, Matty crept in the door and surprised him. As he rolled over, she had slid out of her deerskin smock and crawled up next to him. Her soft, warm skin and her fragrance nearly made him pass out.

"What a woman," he thought to himself, "And what a blessing."

That evening, Matty was in shock only cooking for about two dozen people remaining at the ranch. The meal was brought out by the women in about 30 minutes, and it was delicious; leftover roasted meats and a few fresh vegetables. Adkin decided to ask Matty for some sugar and ate some raw wild onions like Quanah did, dipping the white end into sugar and then biting it off and eating it.

"This is really unique and different," Adkin said to Matty who just smiled, a smile that showed satisfaction. "And good."

Sanderson and Uribe and their crews got back on the third day after departing. J.L. was in heaven, raving and bragging about how many wild Cutthroat trout he had caught with his new fly rod and reel equipment.

"And those canyons up the Purgatoire are some of the most beautiful places to fish anywhere," Sanderson said. "Colorado has places any man could find peace and beauty to live in for a lifetime."

"Except for those Indians that don't like people in their lands," Uribe said, grinning.

"Don't be so negative Uribe," Sanderson scolded. "I know what you mean, but it's just I've seen remarkable sights; rivers, canyons, valleys, mountains, lakes, all in this state."

"It's part of the beauty and uniqueness of the West and its Frontier," Adkin said. "And, unfortunately, the Indian fighting will end sometime in the near future, and the Indians will be getting the short shrift."

Uribe spoke up, "What is dis short shrift, Boss?"

"Well, it means the soldiers will give little consideration to the Indians' wants or needs," Adkin tried to put it simply.

'Oh, like now, soldiers and Washington don't care how they make Indians stop fighting," Uribe said.

"Si, y no bueno," Adkin said, trying to break the mood.

"Well, all I know is your men showed me one hell of a time," Sanderson said. "We had fun in glorious locations."

"Si, mucho bueno, Boss," Uribe echoed.

"All I know, is it's going to take a few days to get this place back in order – lots of cleaning to do and gathering and burning of trash," Adkin said. "And then we're going to have to make a supply run to Bent's Fort."

Sanderson pulled Adkin to the side once the greeting was finished and men started heading to their camp or the barracks.

"I'll be leaving in the morning, back to Denver, but if your supplies are low, I'll get some in Pueblo," he said to Adkin.

"We have enough to get you back on the trail, J.L., if it's all we have, it's yours – don't you worry."

"Thanks."

About that time, little Donnie came racing through the main gate, apparently in a hurry. He ran right up nearly to the rail, and hit the ground in a dust cloud.

"Mister Yates, news for ya and important." Donnie wheezed, nearly out of breath.

Adkin took the telegram and started reading aloud.

To: Yates and Sanderson. Stop.

Barlow & Sanderson stagecoach robbed by armed bandits March 3, 1873, east of Fort Garland. Stop.

One guard killed, thieves got gold shipment worth about $3,000. Stop.

4 bandits, 2 were white, one identified as Jim Catron. Sheriff posse looking for them still. Stop.

From: Mello Velasquez. Stop.

"I was wondering when it would finally happen?" Sanderson said sadly. "I've been praying no one would get hurt. We've fought off a couple of robberies, but the thieves know we're helping the mines with their shipments.

"I hate we've lost a family member like this," he added. "I wonder who it was, Harry or Walt? They ride messenger cause they're tough fighters and damn good shots."

"I've been afraid this could happen, too, J.L." Adkin said. "It's like we all feared it but wouldn't discuss it – like that might keep it from happening."

"Will you send Mello back a message I should be there in about four or five days, and we'll hurry," Sanderson said. "Hell, I'll help chase that bastard down if they don't have him caught by the time I get there."

"I'll take care of it, J.L. You just have your men come over and get what supplies you need from the warehouse, okay?" Adkin said. "Come in Donnie, I will write out a reply."

Sanderson headed toward the barracks and Adkin and Donnie went into the office. It wouldn't take long until the news got to everybody remaining at the ranch.

Adkin made his way to the dining hall and Sanderson was surrounded by most of the men still at the ranch explaining what had happened with the robbery. He was telling them about how important it was to protect themselves and the coach. Several had ridden shotgun messenger or driven teams on scheduled routes.

"Its following those instincts and reacting at a moment's notice," Sanderson said. "If you hesitate, it could cost you your life."

Adkin made his way to the kitchen where all the women had been standing near the swinging doors trying to find out more details of what happened. Adkin gathered them around him, while holding Matty close with one arm.

"Ladies, one of our shotgun riders out of Pueblo has been killed in a stagecoach robbery a few days ago near Fort Garland," Adkin explained. "We're not sure who it was that died, yet, but he is one of our family, and we must pray for his soul and his family."

Matty translated for those not fluent in English. Several women made the sign of the cross, as Catholicism was a major religion in the region.

"Did they catch the thieves?" Matty asked.

"No, not yet, but they are looking for them."

About that time, a voice from the dining hall shouted near the door to the kitchen.

"Mister Yates, Sheriff Allen is here and wants to talk with you right away."

Adkin strode into the hall and there stood Sheriff L.A. Allen, looking mad.

"Yates, can you tell me more about this robbery?" Allen asked. "I've heard one of your men was killed. Do you have any more information?"

"Yes, Sheriff. Our people tell us the leader of the four thieves was identified as Jim Catron," Adkin said pulling out the telegram from his pocket. "Two looked to be Comancheros and two were white."

"I know of this Catron," Allen said. "He's robbed two other stages before up near Denver, but he hasn't killed anyone, yet."

"Our people said they have a posse looking for them," Adkin said.

"Okay, I'll telegraph the authorities up there in Pueblo and see if I can assist in any way," Allen said while patting Adkin on the shoulder. "If I have any chance, I'll hunt this dog down and either arrest him or shoot him down like the mangy coyote he is."

"Thanks Sheriff."

Several of the men started mumbling about what they'd do if they could get their hands on this Catron.

Adkin was ready to go looking for him, too, but he knew it would be futile at this time. Maybe if they got word Catron and his gang were riding toward their country, Adkin would get in the chase himself.

"Hopefully, they've caught them or killed them already," Adkin thought to himself.

Uribe caught Adkin as he was walking back toward the kitchen.

"Everyone was afraid dis may happen, Boss," Uribe said. "Do not blame yourself, we all know the risks. And we all know that more and more people coming west will bring the outlaw trash, too.

"We just have to stress being more cautious and to shoot first and don't wait til you get shot," he added.

"I know Uribe," Adkin said. "I just know whoever got killed had a family that will never be the same. Its' sad."

"Si, Boss, mi siento triste – very sad," Uribe said as he walked away.

•••

The Las Animas crew learned a few days later that Walt Walker was the hand that got shot by the stage robbers. Adkin filled them in on more details.

"Mello says one of the witnesses in the stage, who were made to get out and had all their valuables stolen, said he recognized Catron's eyes and voice – they wore bandanas covering their lower faces. The man had played poker with Catron numerous times before in Pueblo saloons.

"Walker got shot by two or three of them when he raised his shotgun after they told him to throw it down," Adkin said. "That's important to know – when stopped by armed bandits, shoot first and try to drive the team through. Don't stop and then give them the advantage."

Seems Walker was married and had two sons, 14 and 16, and Adkin told the crew Mello said the oldest was riding with the posse, but the robbers have disappeared, and the posse has been out five days.

"You know, Boss, not only are coaches in more danger, it won't be long until railroad trains get robbed, too," Uribe said. "We've heard stories that trains are carrying gold and silver, too."

"You're probably right, Uribe," Adkin said. "We're just going to have to be more aware of newcomers and people who might want to harm us or steal from us."

•••

In the first week of June, Ryan and Kanaka returned from their honeymoon right on time. They had telegraphed from St. Louis and then Dodge City on their way home.

It was another excuse to have a fiesta, or what they called a fandango, and much of the communities of Las Animas and Boggsville attended. Sheriff L.A. Allen also came over.

"They still haven't caught Jim Catron, yet," he told Adkin. "Someone thought they had seen him in a bordello in Cañon City, a place close to the mines in South Park.

"But, nothing came from it, the Sheriff there couldn't find him," he added. "But we'll keep our ears open in case we hear he's headed down this way again."

"Thanks Sheriff, keep me informed, Please," Adkin said, shaking the old lawman's burley hand.

The day after the newlyweds arrived, the area was hit by another dirt storm. High winds coming off the Rockies stirred up sand and dust until visibility dropped to about a quarter of a mile or less in places.

Men and animals took refuge in houses, barns and stables. When someone had to go out, they had to cover their nose and face with bandanas to keep from breathing the dirt. After two days, calm returned and men had to shovel sand from doorways, gates and forage troughs.

In late July, the wires lit up with news that robbers had stopped a moving train on the evening of July 21, 1873, a mile and a half west of Adair, Iowa.

The thieves were identified as the James Gang, which included Jesse James and his brother, Frank, and two or three Younger brothers.

"Uribe gave Adkin that look of 'I told you so,' when Adkin read the telegram to the crew. It scared everyone. There were people saying if trains start getting robbed, the railroad companies might slow down development of western rails.

Others pointed out the train was robbed in Iowa and the James Gang had started robbing banks years earlier. They learned Jesse James shot and killed a bank teller in 1869 in Missouri, where the James clan called home.

"Those kind of characters wouldn't dare come out here on the Frontier, they'd get their asses shot off – or hung," Sheriff Allen had told several of the ranch crew when they were in a Boggsville saloon. "We don't tolerate thieves and murderers."

When Adkin heard that, he told Uribe he wasn't so sure if it was true.

"I think with the rails and stagecoach services, more and more people, traders, ruffians will be moving out here, and there will be some trash among them," Adkin said, with Uribe nodding in agreement.

"I worry about some of those Rebs that are coming out here," Uribe said. "They look dangerous, and they're always wanting to fight any person who looks at them wrong."

"I know what you mean, they're not through fighting, even though they got whipped in the war," Adkin said.

•••

By mid-August, Matty was counting down the days til departure for the Cimarron House. Her excitement was contagious.

"We'll go to Bent's Fort next week and get whatever supplies you need so we can take them with us," Adkin promised. "We will plan on leaving September 1."

The Santa Fe Railroad had reached old Granada, Colorado, which was only about 55 miles east of Las Animas City.

Adkin figured they could load their supply wagon and team plus their four saddle horses there and be in Fort Dodge in two days. Four days to Dodge instead of the old eight to 10 days.

"Nice way to travel," Adkin thought to himself.

Adkin made sure Sanderson was well aware of his plans, and reported to J.L. that Ryan, Ray Dee and the crew were ready for his departure, with the knowledge Adkin would be gone until late March of '74.

When Adkin took Matty to Bent's Fort for supplies, her biggest purchase was beads, every assortment of color and size they had in the general store. She kept saying she had plenty money from winning horse race.

"I have to make things for all the babies – Mary Catherine's and Margarite's," she said giggling when Adkin just shook his head back and forth. She also asked decided she would buy three of the cured and dressed sheep skins.

"This is new to me, the Kiowas, and I want to make coat for you so you have more than just one buffalo coat," she said. Adkin hadn't thought about sheepskins being somewhat foreign to some Plains Indians, as most their clothing, and all other things, were from wild animals of the Plains – mostly the buffalo.

He, of course, agreed with Matty, although he knew nothing could be better than the buffalo coat she made him several years ago.

The crew had a big celebration the night before they headed out for the Cimarron House. Several friends came over from Boggsville and shared a big meal with plenty of refreshments. Adkin was beginning to wonder why he wasn't in the alcohol trade, these big ranches spent plenty of money on "refreshments."

"Must be plenty of profits to be made," he thought to himself, laughing inside.

•••

The trip to Dodge City was remarkable and quick compared to the old days of driving a wagon or riding in the saddle and all the camps with meals, etcetera. Adkin welcomed train travel any time.

"Wish we could have travelled the desert Dry Route of the Santa Fe Trail like this," he thought.

Someone called his name as he and Matty were helping unload their wagon and animals in Dodge City.

"Yates. Hey Yates, is that you?"

Charles Bassett was waving his arm as he got closer to the train. "How are you, Missus Yates?" Bassett said to Matty as he shook her hand.

"Very good Mister Bassett," she said ever smiling.

How are you getting along Charles?" Adkin said. As he shook hands he noticed a big badge on Bassett's cow-hide vest.

"What's this?" Adkin asked as he lightly touched the badge.

Well, I was chosen the first Sheriff of Ford County on June 5th, 1873. Can you believe it?" he answered.

"I sure can," Adkin said grinning. "They couldn't have found a better man to watch over this wild place."

"I've also went in with a partner and opened a saloon. It's called the Long Branch Saloon. You'll have to see it when you can,

"Guess who my Undersheriff is?" Bassett asked.

"Who?"

"Young Bat Masterson," Bassett said. "He was introduced to you as Bill Masterson at the camp on Mulberry Creek when we were headed to Central Kansas to hunt buffalo. Remember? Everybody now just calls him Bat."

"I sure do, that's great," Adkin said. "If I remember, he was the taller and bigger Masterson brother – but the younger of the two. Ed was his elder brother, yes?"

"That's right," Bassett said. "Looks like y'all are headed to the Cimarron House."

"That we are Charles, but first, I want to talk with some of you about building a house up on one of my lots on the ridge," Adkin said.

"Henry or Reighard can help you with that," Bassett said. "I've given up the construction business. Between keeping the peace, the saloon and our buffalo hunting partnership, I'm staying pretty busy."

"I can imagine," Adkin said. "Henry still live out on the west side?"

"He does, but he might be down at Reighard's land office on Front Street. It's about three blocks from here."

Bassett helped Adkin hook the team up to their wagon and to saddle Diablo and Tóngúl. He also gave Adkin Reighard's office address.

"He's got his name on a shingle hanging out front. You can't miss it."

"Thank you Char... er, Sheriff Bassett," Adkin said as he shook Bassett's hand again. "I'm happy for you and wish you the best of luck – and be safe."

As they turned north one block, then left, they found Reighard's office in the second block. Adkin couldn't believe how much the town had grown. He had noticed all the new corrals spread out south of the railroad yard. They looked like they could hold thousands of cattle. There were several hundred in the pens now.

As Adkin helped Matty off the wagon, Reighard and Sitler walked out on the porch. Following them was Major Kirk.

"If it isn't the Yates," Sitler said as they all greeted each other with embraces and hand shakes. Each of the men tipped their hats to Matty, who was enjoying all the praise of how well she looked.

"The prettiest smile on the Great Plains," Kirk said, laughing.

They were invited into the office and Adkin told them he was interested in building a nice house on the ridge. Matty sat there unimpressed with the discussion. As far as she was concerned, the Cimarron House was the only house she needed – or wanted.

"I want to take Matty up there and show her the vista," Adkin said. "She's not too excited, but I'm looking for a place where we could live if ever the companies decided to move the Santa Fe Trail headquarters to Dodge City.

"I'm not saying that is happening, but it may be a possibility in the future," he continued. "And it's a good investment to make improvements to the property, si?"

"Si, Yates," Sitler said as they all started laughing. "Ees bueno."

They all laughed – except Matty.

"Well lets ride up there. It'll only take a few minutes," Kirk said, adding he and Reighard were running their land office and handling building permits and helping with construction in the city.

•••

When the wagon reached the top of the ridge, Adkin pulled the team's reins to turn them left and stopped looking west.

"Matty, come, let's stand," Adkin said, as she had been mainly watching her hands and saying she had crossed this ridge many times in her life. They stood and Adkin turned her to the south. "Look at this view of the great Arkansas River and Valley."

She looked as Adkin moved his arm across the vista. One could see the train and the huge stock yards and corrals. Buildings and houses had sprouted all over the side of the ridge and all along about three miles of the rails. Matty didn't say a word, as she looked east and west and back again.

Suddenly, she started smiling and then looked at Adkin.

"So this is what you call 'civilization' to Whites?" she asked. "I think it is a fine sight to see so much civilization, my husband."

They hugged and Adkin asked her if he could build a house there for her.

"Not to stay long – our special place will always be the Cimarron House, I promise," he said.

"This good place to have another lodge – very beautiful to see from here," she said, grinning her approval.

The others finally took a breath and started congratulating them and shaking Adkin's hand.

"We'll build you a beautiful house, Matty," Kirk said.

All five of them went back to Reighard's office. Adkin asked if they had any house plans he could look at.

"I won't be able to oversee this, and I'm hoping I can contract with you men to build this house," he said.

"We have blueprints of some that have been built so far, but I'm sure you don't want a house that looks like any others," Sitler said.

Adkin told them he had seen a house in California he loved. He took a pencil and paper and started sketching a two story home with sharp roof angles on top but half the angles for the main floor, which was much larger and had a covered veranda the entire length of the south side.

"Money is no concern men, I want something very special for my Matty," Adkin said in a serious tone. "I want modern equipment – a large kitchen with the biggest and newest cooking stove with one of those ovens. I want rooms with modern beds – plenty rooms for our friends, and oil lamps, lots of lamps.

"Maybe a large room for us and four or five more on the ground floor and four or five rooms for beds upstairs," he continued. "A large entryway with half-circular stairs to the top floor and a crystal chandelier in a high-beamed ceiling entryway."

The men were glancing back and forth at each other, realizing Adkin was serious about grandeur.

"What would you guess a maximum budget would be, Adkin?" Kirk asked.

"Maybe around $10,000 would cover it," he said without blinking.

They all gasped.

"You're saying you want the biggest, most grandest house in Dodge City, Adkin," Reighard spoke up. "An eight- to 10-bedroom house?"

"Now you're talking, and with a water well and indoor pumps and plumbing and a couple of baths upstairs and downstairs."

"A grand house for the Yates," he said, smiling.

"By God ... er goodness, we'll do it," Kirk said. "Sitler, get started trying to get plans worked up or send off for blueprints for mansions, 'cause, men, we're going to build the Yates the biggest mansion in Dodge City. You know, Adkin, Bob Wright can help us, too – if you don't mind him being involved."

"Not at all," Adkin said. "Men, let's do this in the grand manor of the West."

Several "Yays" went up and everybody started laughing and patting Adkin on the back. Matty just smiled and didn't look as if she really understood everything.

Reighard pulled out a bottle of whisky and gave each of the men a shot that they used to toast the Yates.

Adkin told the men he and Matty would spend the night at Sitler's invitation and asked Reighard to write up a contract making Reighard, Sitler, Wright and Kirk as powers of attorneys to design and build this house and identify a bank account where needed funds could be deposited.

"I'll transfer, say, $12,000 to this account immediately, tomorrow, and within 35 to 40 days be travelling back to Dodge City to inspect the progress and cover any additional expenses deemed necessary to order more materials and equipment to build and furnish this house," Adkin said. "Can you have that drawn up by tomorrow morning, George?"

"No problem, Adkin," Reighard said.

Adkin and Matty rode out to Sitler's place in the evening and were surprised how nice it turned out, as it was somewhat unfinished the last time they saw it. Amazingly, he built a complete wood framed house, but had adobe attachments and outbuildings. His stables and corral were rock fence posts and cross timber fencing. It was beautiful.

"This is a very, very impressive ranch house," Adkin said. "I want to build something as nice but a city house, like some I've seen in New Orleans, St. Louis or Westport – know what I mean, Henry?"

"I sure do, and I'll be very proud to help you do that. And it will be a real statement to western Kansas that Dodge City has arrived, as well as we're here to stay."

Matty was still unaware of what a mansion was, but she did like the vista from the top of the ridge. Adkin believed the growing town had something to do with that analysis, as the Kiowa had travelled across that ridge throughout hundreds of years – but there was no White "civilization" there.

...

The following morning, Adkin had worked out a few details of the house contract and telegraphed for money to be transferred to Reighard's account to get them started. He reminded them he would be back in about five to six weeks for supplies and any amendments to the contract could be made then. When the men asked if he and Matty would like to go to lunch, Adkin politely refused.

"Gentlemen, I want to get my wife on the trail to our Cimarron House. All this business has delayed her joy of spending time at our special place," Adkin said, looking to Matty who smiled broadly. "We will stop at the Mulberry Creek camp, and have our lunch there."

"Plus I want to stop by Zimmermann's and get some more bullets for my 'Vinchester,'" Adkin said in his best German accent. They all laughed.

Matty squeezed Adkin's arm, full of happiness and grinning from ear to ear.

"We'll see you gentlemen next month and use your imagination on the house, I trust your judgements," Adkin said as they waved bye and snapped the reins on the wagon team.

Two days later, they were rolling up to their Cimarron House, having a quiet and peaceful trip down Crooked Creek. Adkin was telling Matty that Reighard's men had a camp east of them at Bluff Creek as they pulled up to the Cimarron House.

Matty leapt from the wagon bench before Adkin had completely stopped the team and whipped open the front door.

"We're here," she squealed and ran inside.

Adkin set the brake and got down and followed her into the house. She was opening the windows and tying the sashes back to let fresh air and sunlight in. Adkin checked the guest book on the table and there were three Xs with a roughly scribbled sign of the Comanches. Adkin could only guess. If it had been Quanah, he would have made his KP.

"Maybe Ten Bears came back through," he said to Matty.

"I'm so happy to be here, my husband," Matty said. "Thank you."

Things looked fairly undisturbed, though about five or six tins of pemmican were missing, but that was it.

"I'm going to get the animals comfortable and in the corral," Adkin said as he went out and jumped back into the wagon.

...

As fall was changing leaves to golden and yellow splashes of color, Adkin felt as at peace with himself as ever. He and Matty so enjoyed the lazy days of cooler weather with bright sunshine.

Matty loved trying to accumulate all her buds, remaining flowers, roots and bark for her healing and cooking needs.

Adkin was amazed she could spend the entire morning scavenging around the river bottom, come eat some lunch, then hit the valley slopes and pick and sack items all afternoon.

"You seem happy as the Meadow Lark, my Kiowa Princess," he told her.

"I am my Great Chief," she said while jumping up and reaching behind his neck and kissing him. Then she whistled, mimicking the song of the Meadowlark nearly identical to the yellow-breasted bird with its identifying black V on its chest.

It was a talent he had discovered slowly – her ability to mimic numerous birds of the prairie. Initially, she seemed to be embarrassed when she would make the sounds.

•••

While they were making plans to head to Dodge City to re-supply on October 12, 1873, Adkin noticed two wagons with mule teams and six riders were coming up the south side of the Cimarron from the east.

Adkin grabbed his Winchester by the front door and told Matty to stay inside.

"Riders coming in. Get the shotgun ready and stay inside," he ordered.

As they crossed the river about 300 yards downstream – the usual crossing for people that knew the area – Adkin could tell the men were Whites, except for maybe one. The wagon looked overloaded with buffalo hides.

"Hail there, Adkin Yates," a voice boomed as they were nearing. "It is me Billy Dixon, we're with Charley Reighard's crew."

"Yes. Yes. Welcome men," Adkin said as he laid his rifle against the door frame. "Is that Ed Masterson with you?"

"Yes sir, and Tom Nixon and "Prairie Dog" Morrow – you've met them, too."

"Come on in here, gentlemen," Adkin said, smiling and turning to Matty. "It's okay, come on out, you know most these men."

They rolled to a stop and Adkin and Matty greeted them. Ed spoke up and introduced another Masterson, his brother, Jim.

"Bat is busy being a lawman in Dodge City, if you haven't heard," Ed said.

"I have heard," Adkin said. "I actually saw him in Dodge City about five weeks ago, – Undersheriff to Sheriff Bassett. Who would have guessed it?"

"I know, but he still hunts with us when he can," Ed said.

"What brings you men over this way," Adkin asked. "Reighard told me you had a camp on Bluff Creek."

"We do," Dixon said. "But we've set up another camp on Kiowa Creek, about 30 miles northeast of here."

Ed spoke up, "We chased a small herd of buffalo over this way and decided to come on over since we were close," he said. "Wasn't sure if you and the Missus would be here, but we're glad you are."

Adkin invited them to spend the night and have supper with them, and they accepted.

"I just wanna get down in that river and clean up," Nixon said.

"All of us need that, if you know what I mean?" Ed said. "We've been killin' and skinnin' about 20 head of buffalo a day for three straight days."

"Need any soap?" Adkin asked, and they all laughed.

"We have our own, but thanks," Ed answered, still laughing as they all had some clean clothes gathered from their supply wagon and were headed to the Cimarron.

About 30 minutes later, the men returned to the Cimarron House. Adkin could tell they needed bathing, because he thought Jim was a Comanchero at first sight, with so much buffalo fat and grime on the kid.

Matty had already nearly finished bringing a buffalo stew to a boil with potatoes and onions.

"Give it about 20 more minutes, and we'll have hot biscuits with molasses, too," Matty told the men who had sat down out front on the stump chairs Adkin had made the last time they were at the Cimarron House.

They ate outdoors as the sun neared the western horizon behind the cliffs of their home. They discussed business, how buffalo hunting had turned very profitable once the railroad got to Dodge City.

"I imagine Zimmermann is making money, too," Adkin said, smiling. "Just selling ammunition."

They chuckled, asking how he knew Fred. Adkin explained how he had come to Las Animas for Ryan's wedding.

"He even sold me a Model 1873 Winchester, which I really like – smooth and fast," Adkin said. "Or should I say, a 'Vinchester?'"

They laughed, understanding immediately.

"I bought one, too, just about a month ago when we were in Dodge," Dixon said. "They're nice, but they still don't reach out there like my old Sharp's."

"I know what you mean," Adkin said. "Where are you men headed next?"

"Well, we were thinking about either heading back to the Kiowa Creek Camp or Dodge City," Ed said.

Adkin interrupted, "We're going to Dodge City ourselves to get supplies for the next few months – need sugar, salt, essentials, you know."

"And to see our new lodge," Matty spoke up. "My husband like to have many lodges."

Adkin explained his plans to build a "nice home" on a couple of his lots on the ridge above the railroad and the Arkansas River.

"If you're going to Dodge City, why don't we tag along with them, men" Ed suggested. "We need supplies, too – gotta see Zimmermann."

"That sounds fine," Dixon said, while the others nodded approval.

"Great with me," Nixon said.

"We' were planning on leaving in two days, but we could be ready by 10 tomorrow morning, if that will work with your plans," Adkin said.

"Let's do it – here we come Dodge City," Ed said.

•••

On the trip, Dixon explained to Adkin thousands of buffalo hides were being brought into Dodge City.

"There's days when hides are stacked all along the tracks awaiting shipment," Dixon said. "I tell ya, we're getting $2.50 to $4 apiece, depending on who the buyers are. There's another team working with us, and they're bringing in several wagon loads a week, too.

"And your right, Zimmermann can't hardly keep enough inventory of ammunition on the shelves," he continued. "What's great for now is we're hunting within 60 to 70- miles of Dodge, but I don't thank that's going to be able to be maintained.

"Sooner or later, we're going to have to look elsewhere to find the big herds, and that's in Texas – a dangerous place right now," Dixon added.

"Could be a dangerous place in the future, too," Adkin said.

Ed was interested in Adkin's house in Dodge City. He asked where, and when Adkin told him how many lots he owned on the ridge, Ed wanted to buy one sight unseen.

"I'll have to think about that, but I'll show you when we get there, if you want to take the time," Adkin said. "The team should have a good start on my house – it's been about six weeks."

"I'd love to see it and the lots, maybe we could work out a deal," Ed said, laughing.

When they crossed the bridge where Hoover's Saloon was located, Adkin could see rows of wagons full of buffalo hides while men were stacking them in piles for loading onto rail cars.

Adkin made planes with Ed to meet him at Reighard's land office at 2 p.m., which gave them both time to take care of immediate business – like Adkin sending several telegrams and checking with the quartermaster to ensure more funds would be available to Adkin and to Reighard for the house.

After Adkin and Matty put in their order to the fort's Sutler, they saddled up Diablo and Tóngúl and left the wagon at the warehouse to be loaded. They then rode over to Reighard's.

While they were tying the reins to the hitching rail, Ed rode up with his brothers, Bat and Jim.

"I see you brought back up," Adkin said. "Must want one of those lots pretty bad."

They laughed, and all shook hands. All of them tipped their hats to Matty, who had her ever-lovely smile.

"Hello. Hello. Hello."

About that time, Reighard walked out on the porch.

"Well, the Yates and the Mastersons," he shouted. "What did I do wrong?"

They went inside and Reighard gave Adkin a brief report on the progress of the house in front of the Mastersons, with Adkin's nod of approval. Reighard explained they had ordered four porcelain baths, with sinks and pumps with faucets, the chandeliers, lighting fixtures, windows, a huge Dwyer cooking stove from Detroit, etcetera, etcetera.

The Mastersons sat there with mouths agape, realizing this house was going to be a mansion, not just a "nice home" as Adkin put it.

"I told you the foundation and framing was huge," Bat said to his brothers.

Adkin told Reighard he would go over the financing details after he took Ed up to the ridge to see the house and to look at lots.

"What are lots up there going for now?" Adkin whispered in Reighard's ear.

"One hundred dollars to $200, which you're front and east side lots should get easily," Reighard whispered back.

"Well men – and Matty – let's saddle up and ride up to the ridge," Adkin said.

Once they got there, Adkin stopped next to the foundation and looked back to the river.

"I knew this place was perfect for a house," he said. Matty smiled genuinely. "Now, this is taking shape."

They got off the horses and followed Adkin as he and Matty began walking around the scene. Men were working everywhere, carrying fresh-cut lumber from wagons into the site. Another crew were in the back – about 40 feet away digging a water well, pulling up loads of dirt in pails with ropes.

"With this size of home, Adkin, we had to use four of your lots," Reighard said. "We figured you would want gardens and not be too close to neighbors – should you sell the lots at some time."

"That's fine, this is coming together nicely, George, I like it," Adkin said. "What do you think, Matty?"

"Mucho wood. Mucho grande for a lodge, si?" she said.

"Yes, very large, but it will be beautiful, like my Kiowa Princess," Adkin said, while Matty lit up and giggled softly.

"I'll be damned, Yates. This is something else," Ed said. "I don't know if I'd want to be your neighbor living in a small little house with a mansion sitting right here."

They laughed.

"I could sell you a lot or two north along Second Street here," Adkin said. George says the going price is $200 a lot, but if you want two together, I'll let 'em go for $300."

"Wow, I tell you what, Yates. You have a deal," Ed said and both men shook hands.

"Can you make that happen, George?" Adkin asked Reighard.

"No problem, Adkin," he said smiling and shaking Ed's hand. "What about you two?"

"Not me right now," Bat said. "I'm happy living at the hotel. 'Sides, Bassett keeps me busy – or actually, it's these crazy cowboys that keep me busy."

"Nah, I'm just trying to save my money from buffalo hunting," Jim said. "I'm too young to be building a house and settling down."

Adkin was pleased the house was going up, and Ed was very happy to buy the lots. George assured him it was a great investment.

"Dodge City is the fastest growing city in Kansas right now, Ed," Reighard said.

"I wouldn't doubt it, George," Ed said.

When they got back to Reighard's, the Mastersons rode off to take care of their chores. Adkin found out Reighard and the team needed about $2,000 more into the house account, but Reighard told Adkin the total budget may only be about $11,000.

"Prices are fluctuating mightily," Reighard said. "With the strong growth here, prices swing tremendously depending on what's on order from other mercantile stores and lumber wholesalers."

Adkin interrupted, "Don't worry George, you men just get the best, whatever it costs, okay?"

"Okay, Adkin, we'll get 'er done, and we're sure you'll be proud," Reighard said.

"I'm already very proud, it looks great," Adkin said. "We better go get the wagon and our supplies. Tell the others I'm sorry I missed them, but we want to get back to the Cimarron House."

"Will we see you and Matty in another six to seven weeks?" Reighard asked.

"Yes, we should be back before Christmas."

"Well be careful and we'll see you then," Reighard said.

As Adkin helped Matty get in the saddle and he reached for Diablo, there was a sound coming up through the valley – seemingly from the southeast.

"What's that?" Adkin asked Reighard.

"It's another one of those cattle herds coming up from Texas – look back there," he said, pointing south.

The entire side of the Arkansas valley was covered with cattle, hundreds of them. To Adkin it looked like some of the huge buffalo herds, but these cattle were of various colors and many had huge wide horns.

"Are those the longhorns I've heard about?" Adkin asked Reighard.

"That's them alright, they're big and mean if they want to be," Reighard said. "But I guess they can smell water when men can't even see any. That's what they say anyway."

"Well Matty., we're going to have to ride around all that after we go get the wagon," Adkin said. "See you later George. God bless."

"See ya, be careful," Reighard said. "Your Dodge City mansion should be finished by the time you get back."

•••

Adkin and Matty pulled up at the Cimarron House on October 10, 1873, and no one had stopped or signed the guest book. Nothing had been disturbed. Adkin was wondering if most the Indians had settled back on reservation lands for the winter or, more likely, in the Llano Estacado.

The night temperatures during their trip home had been dropping and then the days were still warm. In a way, Adkin was looking forward to snow. He enjoyed how beautiful things looked with snow covering them. In Olney, snow was rare and only lasted a day or two. Olney's winters were mostly rainy and cold.

"I think we should start stacking fire wood, winter's coming," Adkin said to Matty, who agreed.

"We can begin tomorrow, my husband," she said smiling. "This evening, we rest in the feather bed."

He knew what she meant by "rest," and a big smile crept across his face.

•••

Adkin spent several days hooking up a horse and dragging old deadfall logs up to the house. Though he urged Matty not to swing the axe so much, when he went down to the river, she'd chop as much wood as she could before he returned. She'd be covered in sweat when he'd get back. She even tried using the big two-man saw.

"I've told you Matty, I'll saw up the logs, you should just relax and enjoy this beautiful time of the year," he said.

"Maybe we should go "rest," you think," she said, smiling that look of innocence that he couldn't resist, no matter how much work needed to be finished for winter.

"You're a Diablo, my Princess – the Devil that makes me "rest" too much," he said as she ran to the house giggling.

It finally snowed November 15, but it was just a tease for Adkin. Maybe about four inches, and it was melted within the week. It did help him track the deer in the bottoms though.

He managed to harvest two, which made Matty very happy. She could tan and cure the hides and make children's smocks, moccasins and coats. Adkin salted the strips of venison and hung them in the stables to dry.

When he was writing in his diary, he suddenly remembered Thanksgiving and how Mary Catherine told them of its importance – how President Lincoln had declared that day a special day for all Americans. It was only one day away.

"Matty, I'm going to saddle Diablo and go looking for turkeys, for tomorrow is a very special day. He briefly told her the story Mary Catherine had told him about Thanksgiving.

"We can have turkey to roast if I find them," Adkin said.

"I would like to have the feathers, too, very beautiful for decorations," Matty said, smiling. "When you get back, maybe we 'rest.'"

"Okay, my Kiowa Princess."

Adkin was maybe a mile west of the house along the river bottom walking Diablo softly through the bushes and cottonwoods. He saw several turkey tracks and they were also moving west. He figured they had seen him, and he knew turkeys could run for miles before flying. He only had a Colt and his Henry, so he needed to see them on the ground in order to shoot one.

Suddenly, he heard the blast of a gun shot behind him. He knew that sound, it was his old Remington coach shotgun. Matty wouldn't shoot that gun just for fun. Maybe it was a wolf – or something.

He spun Diablo around and started racing home. He didn't want to think about what that "something" could be. As he crested a small knoll before the ravine that ran by the house and into the Cimarron, he saw several horses milling around the front – at least five, and they were not Indian ponies.

Then he heard Matty's blood curdling scream. He reined Diablo up short of the stump chairs and hit the ground running to the open door with his Colt in hand.

"Matty. Matty," he yelled as he entered the house.

All of a sudden, a rifle barrel hit him in the side of his head – hard. He stumbled and fell into the table that held the guest book, losing his grip on the Colt. He saw it slide across the wood-plank flooring.

"Hit that bastard again, Lew," he heard a man's voice.

Then someone kicked him in the ribs and another was using his rifle butt to hit him in the head and neck area as he was face down. He pushed one backward and tried to stand. He only made it to one knee when he felt a blade slash his left wrist he had held up to protect his head. He saw the knife, it just missed his face.

"This son of a bitch won't stay down, Dog," another voice said as Adkin could hear Matty crying and screaming. He could see through the bedroom door two men had Matty down, one using his knife to shred her buckskin smock from her body.

"Matty! Matty!"

Adkin was kicked and rolled toward the fire place hearth and then received another blow to the head. Then something very hot tore into his side, just below the ribs.

He realized he had heard a gunshot, and it had hit him. He faded into blackness and passed out.

•••

He could hear the crackling of low embers – the smoky stench burning his nostrils. He couldn't open his eyes, but the metallic taste of blood and dirt in his mouth hinted he was still alive.

"I'm sure this is my home, but what is happening?" he thought to himself.

Then it hit him.

He immediately sat upright but fell over to one side on his elbow. His eyes tried focusing through the cloud-like haze as he glanced from side to side.

"Matty?" he creaked, his lungs full of ashes and smoke. "Matty, can you hear me?"

The scenes started rushing back in his mind: The two men hitting him with their rifle butts, another also putting his boots to his rib cage. The other two men had Matty down, one using his knife to shred her buckskin smock from her body, and her terrified screams filled his head.

"Matty, where are you?" he yelled again, this time sounding more like himself as he tried crawling over on his knees – his left wrist unable to hold his weight. He could see tendons and raw muscle sticking out of the knife slash, but he didn't sense the bone was broken. He grabbed his neckerchief and tied it off above the cut, using his teeth as another hand.

As he tried to push himself up with the other arm, he slipped in the huge pool of blood on the old stone base of the fireplace hearth.

His vision was clearing as he crawled toward where the front door had been, as there was no roof.

"God, please don't let them take Matty," he whispered.

"Matty, please Matty, talk to me," he cried out.

He reached over to what remained of the front wall, a three-foot tall burned out section – there was no door. In fact, as he looked around, there were only pieces of the house here and there.

He couldn't believe the fire had burned almost everything down to the ground, especially considering the back half of the home was a dugout. Only the stone fireplace at the back of the house stood with the pool of blood at its base where he had been left for dead.

His eyes shifted to his left where the bed had stood. Everything was charred and smoke wafted from the ashes. He stumbled over to it and froze as he realized the ashes were his beloved Matty.

She had been stripped naked and there were burnt rope strands around her ankles and wrists. They had tied her to the bed posts after he had passed out from the blows. Part of her belly and chest had been cut out, as if they were cleaving apart a buffalo looking for its liver.

Adkin Yates fell to his knees and started weeping.

"Oh God, Matty. I'm so sorry, but I will find those who did this to you – so help me, God Almighty."

He suddenly was hit by the pain in his left side below his ribs. It was where he had been shot. As he grabbed the bullet hole, he realized there was not much blood.

As he tried to step toward where the front door had been, he passed out into agony and darkness.

•••

As Quanah splashed fresh cold water into Adkin's face, Adkin's eyes started fluttering open.

"I think he is alive, yet," Quanah said. "Let us put him on a travois. We will take him to Fort Dodge."

Adkin heard a voice he thought he knew, but it sounded far away, as if it was coming through a cave. Suddenly, his eyes opened and the brightness made him blink several times as his eyes adjusted.

He heard, "We will take him to Fort Dodge." He suddenly realized it was Chief Quanah Parker.

"Is that you Quanah?" he asked.

"Just be calm, Yates, we will take you to White Medicine Man. We have stopped your bleeding, but you have a bullet near the skin on your back hip. It has to be taken out."

"Matty is dead, isn't she?" Adkin asked while starting to weep. "I thought I was dreaming, but this is true now, isn't it?"

'Yes, Mat-tee is dead, Yates. I am very sorry," Quanah said. "But we must save you now. Do you understand?"

"Yes, I guess," Adkin said as he slipped into unconsciousness again.

Quanah had Adkin placed on a travois and made sure he was tied down well if he awakened and tried to move. He picked out about a dozen warriors and his

Medicine Man, Isa-tai, to travel with him to Fort Dodge. He instructed the rest of the tribe to head west to Cedar Springs.

Quanah and his men hauled Adkin for about seven hours until the sun was nearing the horizon. They made camp, and Isa-tai checked Adkin's wounds and put more Yarrow paste in many of them. He also changed the cloths he had carefully wrapped Adkin's wrist and around his waist, covering the bullet hole.

As Isa-tai was finishing Adkin's wrist wrapping, Adkin awoke. He thought he knew who was above him. He blinked several times.

"Who are you?" Adkin asked, startling Isa-tai who didn't see Adkin's eyes open.

"I am Isa-tai, we have met before at your lodge on the Cimarron," he said. "I am Medicine Man of Chief Quanah."

"Oh yes, I remember now."

Isa-tai shouted out to Quanah and said something in Comanche. Quanah came over and leaned over Adkin.

"How are you feeling, Adkin Yates?" he asked.

"I'm in pain in several places," Adkin said. "How did it come you found me, Great Chief Quanah?"

"We were coming to your lodge, the soldiers chased us out of the Llano Estacado," Quanah said. "We saw little smoke when we crossed the ridge and knew your lodge had been on fire."

"There were five White men who attacked Matty while I was hunting," Adkin said. "They knocked me down before I could do anything."

"Don't think so much about it now, Yates. We will take you to Fort Dodge," Quanah said. "You need to be calm and go back to sleep, si?"

"I guess so," Adkin said. "But you cannot go to Fort Dodge, the soldiers will ..."

Quanah interrupted, lightly placing his hand on Adkin's mouth, "Do not worry, we will be careful to not cause fighting."

The next morning, while Adkin slept, the party headed north again. Quanah made sure he travelled about a mile away from the regular trail the traders and settlers used. It was slightly rougher pulling a travois, but they took their time. When they stopped near noon to eat, Adkin awoke, and asked for Quanah.

"You need something, Yates?" Quanah asked.

"I could use some water, please, water," Adkin said, as Quanah waved a hand and spoke Comanche. A warrior ran up with a U.S. Army canteen. Adkin thought that strange in a way.

"I remember two of the men," Adkin said. "I remember two names, as well. I will find them, and I will kill them."

Quanah didn't respond. He saw that look in Adkin's eyes that said Adkin had finally realized the savagery he had seen with Matty's remains there at the house.

Quanah had yet to tell Adkin they had gathered her remains and carefully wrapped them tightly in cloth and then wax paper and a tarp. Her remains had been laid across the haunches of one of the ponies.

"They took my Diablo, too, didn't they?" Adkin asked. "They didn't kill him did they?"

"No, Diablo wasn't there. The trail going away showed maybe 10, 11 horses, all with iron shoes," Quanah said. "They also took a wagon with harness and a team."

"Yes, we had six horses in all and the wagon," Adkin said. "Did you find any guns?"

"Actually, we did," Quanah said. "An old carpet bag was under the end of the bed that didn't burn. It had an old Sharp's rifle and another new Colt pistol. Also, next to the bag was the bow I gave you with the arrows. It lived through the fire – that may be a good sign from the great spirits.

"There was nothing else," he added. "They even burned your stables."

"Do you know which way they travelled?" Adkin asked.

"It looked that they were headed north, maybe back to Dodge City," Quanah said, realizing Adkin's mind was already planning revenge. He could see the darkness overcoming Adkin Yates. It worried him, as he felt Yates was a decent man who could be trusted.

"You must not think about this hate now, Yates. We need to make sure you live," Quanah said.

"Thank you Great Chief Quanah for saving me. I will forever be your friend and brother," Adkin said as he closed his eyes, turned his head away and started silently weeping again, the tears running down his cheeks.

Quanah was afraid Adkin Yates could turn into a vengeful killer. He had seen that kind of hate in men's eyes before.

About noon the third day, Quanah eased up behind a small grove of cottonwoods on the valley ridge about half a mile from the Arkansas River. He got off his horse and went to Adkin, who had his arms freed the day before but was still tethered to the travois full of hides and furs. It was warm, but Adkin still had severe pains all over his body.

"What we are going to do Yates is pull you down to the river. Fort Dodge is on the other side," Quanah said. "We will shoot our guns in the air to make the soldiers in the towers see us. Then we will ride away, but leave you for them to come for you.

"I want to you to keep the pony that has your travois is tied to – and the travois," he continued. "Your bag with guns and the bow are tied to your travois. And, you will need hides and furs for winter. These are small gifts. Oh, and the pony is named Peta, after my father because he is strong and fast."

The horse was a beautiful paint, with white and brown colors splashed haphazardly on him.

"I thank you Great Chief Quanah, I hope to one day return your kindness," Adkin said.

"One more thing, Adkin Yates. I know Whites have different ceremony for death, so we careful to take the remains of Mat-tee and placed them in calico, then wrapped her in wax cloth and then bundled her in canvas tarp," Quanah said, while Adkin was silent with more tears coming from his eyes. "She has been placed over the back of Peta so you can have your own special ceremony."

Adkin was silent, closing his eyes tightly, but the tears still flowed.

Quanah then waved to several warriors. He gave them instructions in Comanche. Quanah himself grabbed the lead rope on Peta and four other warriors were beside him. Isa-tai and five others waited behind the trees.

"Ayeeee," Quanah yelled as they took off, Adkin bouncing hard as they raced down the side of the valley slope. After just a few minutes, they stopped and Quanah leaned over and handed Adkin the lead rope that was attached to a bridle, while the others were firing their repeating rifles into the air and whooping like warring Indians.

"Be well, Adkin Yates," Quanah said as a bullet flew past them from a shot by a tower soldier. They all turned and left Adkin lying there and trying to keep Peta calmed.

It seemed to take a long time to Adkin, but finally about 20 calvary troopers rode up slowly, looking worried maybe the Comanches were hiding in the trees on the ridge.

"My name is Adkin Yates," Adkin tried to yell, but it came out weak.

"Who?" a voice asked nearby.

"Adkin Yates. I have been injured and shot by bandits," he said, starting to tear up again. "They also killed my wife, Matty."

"Oh my God," the voice said. "Troopers, get this man to the infirmary immediately."

•••

"He's got a terrible cut to his left wrist, a gash above his right ear, a cut above his left eye in the hairline, broken ribs and a bullet that entered his left side and is just left of his backbone. That has to come out now," the voice said. "We're going to put him out right away."

"Well get to it Doc," someone said.

Adkin remembered a soft cotton wad was placed over his mouth and nose and he was told to breath in slowly. He drifted into darkness again. He learned later it was chloroform to knock him out so they could cut the bullet out and stitch his cuts and slashes.

"How are you Yates?" a voice asked. Adkin was trying to focus on the face above him. "It's me, Charles Bassett."

"Oh Charles, how long have I been out?" Adkin asked.

"Nearly two days. Doc was worried he gave you too much chloroform, but it was just your body needing solid sleep, too," Bassett said. "Can you tell me what happened?"

"I'm not sure, please give me some water, and let me think about it a moment, please." Adkin said. A man dressed like a Post Surgeon handed Charles a glass of water, and he held it up to Adkin's lips and lifted his head forward for a sip.

"First, where are Matty's remains? I know they had them tied to the horse that pulled me," Adkin said.

"They have her here at the fort, don't worry," Bassett said.

"Second, I need to have you telegraph my partners in Las Animas and tell them they killed Matty, please Charles …"

"I already have Adkin, just a few hours after you were brought in here – they're on their way," Bassett said. "Do you know who did this?"

"I remember someone saying the name Lew," Adkin said. "Also, the name Dog was said.

"They butchered her like a buffalo, Charles, butchered her," he added while starting to weep again. "I'm sorry, but I can't help it, this agony is killing me. I was supposed to take care she never got hurt."

Charles teared up.

"I understand, Adkin. I just want to find these men, and I need your help," Bassett said.

"I'm going find them and kill them, no matter how long it takes," Adkin said. "I'm going to kill each one of them."

Bassett put his hand on Adkin's right arm, "We'll find them, but you don't think Dog could have meant Prairie Dog, the buffalo hunter, do you?"

"No. No. I know him, he was at our place last month – he's a decent man, plus he's probably out hunting with Reighard's men right now," Adkin said. "I did see one man's face fighting with Matty, and two of them holding her down – and the one that shot me.

"If I ever see that face again, I'll know it; big brown mustache with two bottom teeth missing and brown scraggly hair – long and dishevelled – like a mad man.

"I've heard of a Lew Bush, a Reb who's been in trouble with the law out here in western Kansas," Bassett said. "But I'd have to telegraph some people for more information. I'll look into that.

"You get some rest, Adkin," Bassett said. "I'll be back tomorrow morning. If you think of something, have them come and get me right away, okay?"

"Okay, Charles," Adkin said. "But I'm telling you, I'm going to find them, and nothing on this Earth will stop me.

"If you want to hang them, you better get to them before I do," he added with a look in his eyes that made Bassett feel uneasy."

Later, Captain Fitzgerald, the Post Surgeon at Fort Dodge, told Adkin the details of his injuries.

"We tried to stitch several of your tendons back together," he began. "But we're not sure if the smaller ones will actually grow back together. This could affect your fingers and your hand, but we'll just have to wait and see.

"It's a miracle your major vein to the hand wasn't hit. You would've bled to death in a matter of hours.

"You have a concussion, and we've stitched up several head wounds," Fitzgerald continued. "Now the bullet. It doesn't look like it hit anything critical, there were no other fluids when we removed it, say like urinary fluid from the kidney.

"But we will have to watch your urine for any signs of blood," he continued. "If you're interested, the bullet we removed was a .58-caliber, which usually comes from a Springfield muzzle loading Minie rifle musket that was used in the war. I sill own one that I had in the war.

"It could have been some Rebs that attacked y'all," he added. "And don't worry about Matty's remains. We'll take care of her so you can have a Christian burial at a later day.

Adkin asked how long he would be in the infirmary.

"Most likely another two weeks at least," Fitzgerald said. "We have to make sure to keep your bandages changed to prevent infections. Plus, we have to see how well that left arm heals and how much damage has been done to that left hand.

Adkin was laying there with bandages completely around his midsection, his head was completely bandaged down to the eyes and his left arm from the elbow down looked like club from so many bandages. He couldn't even feel his fingers, and there was no way to move them if he could.

He suddenly realized, his bracelet from Ten Bears was gone. It must have been cut off during the attack. He instinctively reached up to his neck, relieved his necklace from Satanta was still with him.

"Also, this is Lieutenant McGhee, he wants to talk with you," Fitzgerald added.

"Sorry to bother you, Yates, but we're interested in who brought you here to safety and treatment," McGhee said. "Did you know the Indians that helped you?"

Adkin paused for a moment.

"No sir, I awoke at our burned out house, and they said they would bring me to Fort Dodge," he said.

"The tower guard who thought we were under attack said he believed the Indians looked to be Comanches," McGhee said.

"I wasn't sure," Adkin said. "I was going in and out."

"How did you communicate with them?"

"Well, my wife is Kiowa, and I basically used sign," Adkin said, realizing he was getting boxed in.

"How do you sign Fort Dodge? Can you show me?" McGhee asked.

"Look, it was mostly sign – but one did say in English, 'Fort Dodge.'" Adkin said, losing patience with the young officer.

"I see, Mister Yates," he said. "If you think of anything else, would you please let me know?"

Adkin knew he didn't want the Army to know it was Quanah who brought him to Fort Dodge, they would start scouring the area and possibly catch up with him and his band. He was determined he would not tell them it was the War Chief they hated and wanted to kill.

•••

Adkin had been attacked and Matty murdered on November 26, 1873. He had been delivered to Fort Dodge on the 29th, and he didn't want to see any visitors, except Bassett for the five days he had been at the fort.

On December 4, visitors from Las Animas City arrived, and they forced their way into his room.

Adkin awoke to see Ryan, Ray Dee and Uribe walking into his room.

"How you feeling, Boss," Uribe spoke first, grabbing Adkin's right hand with both of his hands.

"Not so good," he said as he looked at everybody. "Who's watching the office?"

"Don't worry about that Adkin, Ryan said. "We came as fast as we could. Do you know who did this?"

"No. Bassett is the Sheriff here now, and he's chasing down some names I heard while they were butchering Matty.

"Oh, Boss, please don't talk about our Matty," Uribe said as he started sniffling. "I can't take it."

He stepped over by the door, wiping away his tears.

"She's dead, and I'm going to see to it they all pay," Adkin said to all of them. "I'm going to track down every one of them and kill them. I swear."

"We're really sorry for your loss Adkin," Ray Dee said. "The doctor said they have her remains here. We were thinking you might want to take her back to Las Animas for her burial."

"No. I've had eight days to think about this, and I'm going to take her back to where our Cimarron House was and bury her nearby at a place only I will know – much like Black Horse was buried," Adkin said.

"God bless her soul," Uribe said, making the sign of the cross.

"God doesn't have anything to do with this," Adkin barked. "He let me get too far away from her and then punished me by killing her – He didn't help her, at all."

"Oh, Señor, don't talk that way," Uribe said. "You don't mean that. You can't turn away from God at dis time. Please Boss."

"You're wrong this time, Uribe …"

Ryan interrupted sharply, "Adkin! Don't take it out on Uribe. He loved Matty, too. We all did."

Adkin then started weeping and turned his head away.

The men just looked back and forth at each other, not knowing what to say.

"Well, we're going to stay in Dodge until you're healed up enough to be released," Ryan said. "We'll work with Charles and Bat Masterson to see what we can do. We'll help you find these men – I swear – you hear me."

They all turned and walked out of the room without another word. When they got outside, Uribe broke the silence.

"I never thought I would see such a strong, brave man now like dis," Uribe said. "Es muy malo – Adkin ees broken."

•••

Adkin's mood changed a little after the Las Animas crew had talked with him. He realized he had a right to turn against his God, but he couldn't turn against his friends – his family.

Henry Sitler, Bob Wright and Reighard wanted to see him the following day. He welcomed them. They gave their sincere condolences, which was what was the hardest for Adkin. He felt each time her name was mentioned it tore his heart a little more, and he didn't know if his heart would survive.

"Your house is complete," Sitler said. "I know that probably isn't important right now, but it's something to look forward to, a beautiful home."

Reighard added, "It's the most beautiful house in Dodge City, and we came in under budget. The total was $10,424 – and it's a true mansion."

Adkin didn't say anything. He just stared at the window, seemingly lost in his own thoughts.

"Well, we're here for you Adkin," Wright said. "Everybody in the area is trying to figure out who and where these ruthless killers are."

That got Adkin's attention.

"If you hear anything, and I mean anything, come tell me – please?" he pleaded.

"We will, we promise," Sitler said, as they made their way to the door. "See you later."

The nurse and a male aide came in and changed his bandages again. When they took all the wrapping from his left hand, he studied it.

It was ugly, with a stitched slash starting about 5 inches above his thumb on the top of his arm and wending its way down to the right side of his palm under the thumb. It then streaked across the base of his palm and stopped right at the bottom of his palm below his little finger. Doctor Fitzgerald walked in about that time.

"Not pretty, is it?" Fitzgerald said. "The swelling is down and the purple and black coloring should be clearing up soon.

"Why don't we see if you can move those fingers."

Adkin tried closing his fist, but it seemed the fingers were not getting the message, Then his first and middle fingers curled some, but the other two didn't. His thumb was a little numb as well, but it moved a piece.

"That's enough for now, we'll try more next time we change the bandages – tomorrow," Fitzgerald said, as he looked at the wound above Adkin's right ear. "That's looking good, too.

"Can you lay on your left side yet?"

Adkin nodded he could.

"Good, we'll probably have you out of here in another week to 10 days, Yates," he continued. "I still don't know how much use you're going to get out of that hand.

"I don't believe it will ever be back to normal – too much damage to those small tendons," he added.

"Just as long as it can support a rifle or a shotgun," Adkin said matter of factly. "I can pull the trigger with my right hand."

Fitzgerald shook his head, while the nurse and the aide looked back to the surgeon. They looked frightened.

•••

A week after the Las Animas crew dropped in, they returned with Bassett to Adkin's room. They looked happy, and Adkin was hoping it was news about the killers.

"Well, we got some information that may narrow down who did this," Bassett said, while the others smiled. "Lew may be that Lew Bush I heard about. His full name is Amos Lew "Brushy" Bush. He's wanted for pistol whipping a man in Trinidad, Colorado, and stealing his horse.

"Word is he travels with some Reb outlaws who steal horses and rustle cattle from Council Bluff to Santa Fe, New Mexico," Bassett continued. "Some of his known accomplices are Alfonso "Dog" Sill – a Mexican half breed that comes from Texas and fought for the South.

"There's also Marcus 'Marky' Hall and David 'Hairless' Harrison – both thieving Rebs, too," Bassett continued. "Hairless is bald except for the hair on his sides and back, and he's only about 25 or so. He hates the name 'Baldy' so they call him 'Hairless.' And sometimes, William "Billy Boy" Jones rides with them.

"The last anyone heard was Lew sometimes sets up a liquor tent among the tent bordellos during this time of year at Jacob's Well at Big Basin. Many of the Texas cattle drives stop there before driving them on into here for sale, and it's just south of us," Bassett added.

Adkin spoke up, "I know exactly where it is, just off the trail down to our Cimarron House."

Everybody caught the reference to "our Cimarron House." A quiet went over the men.

"We could ride down there and scout the area to see if dis Lew Bush ees there, Boss," Uribe broke the silence.

"No, I wouldn't want to spook him off to somewhere else," Adkin said. "I'll be out of here in about a week.

"Ryan, you're like a brother to me – you all are actually," Adkin began. "But I'm going to have to quit Barlow and Sanderson Company to pursue these murderers. I've been doing a lot of thinking about this

"I would like to still be a partner in YR&R Freight, but a silent partner. I will sign over all decision making to y'all and freeze any further profits to be invested in my share account," he continued.

"Are you sure that's the way you want it, Adkin?" Ryan asked. "We can help if we all stay together."

"No. It's not your burden to hunt these men down and kill them – it's solely mine, and I intend to start the day I get out of here," Adkin said.

"But Boss, you don't have your Diablo or Tóngúl," Uribe said

"I have my Indian pony, Peta," Adkin said, then realizing he shouldn't have said the horse's name. "I have a good horse."

"That's the one the Indians led to haul you here on a travois, right?" Ryan asked. "Who brought you here, Adkin?"

"I can't tell you right now, Ryan. Please don't ask me, it could mean death to the ones who saved me," Adkin said, pleadingly. "I will tell you in time, I promise."

"Okay, but you are going to have to wire J.L. I'm not going to do that," Ryan added.

"I will," he said. "Charles, would you write down those names for me and any information you have about any of them, like family or where they're from?"

"I suppose so. You seem damned determined to do this, and I'm telling you now, if you kill any of these men, I might have to hang you, Adkin," Bassett said, adding, "If it's not a fair fight."

"I understand," Adkin said. "Could I talk with you men later, I'm getting tired."

•••

A few days later, Adkin wrote out a message for J.L. and ask Uribe to take it to Western Union. He told him to tell the office manager to keep track of Adkin's telegraph charges, and he would get paid when Adkin was released by the doctor.

Uribe came by every day and would bring Adkin small gifts, like chocolate candies or English tea he found at the Charles Rath & Company Store. Uribe said Rath was not in Dodge City, he had asked.

Sanderson answered right away and said he understood, but wished Adkin would not quit, though he could come back whenever he wanted. He said his stock account was, of course, available to Adkin whenever he needed any amount – just wire Sanderson where to send it.

Sanderson also sent his condolences about Matty. It was another unintentional arrow into Adkin's heart.

The Western Union deliveryman also brought Adkin a telegram from Sam and Mary Catherine; Sam said Mary Catherine's heart broke when she heard the news. He wanted to let Adkin know that Mary Catherine said her heart would always have a hole that could never be filled without Matty.

Another painful arrow.

Adkin couldn't seem to get away from the agony of losing her. His hatred grew like weeds near a creek, unchecked and reckless. He couldn't wait to start hunting and killing. It had overwhelmed him.

The Las Animas crew helped Adkin get money transferred to Reighard. Reighard agreed to turn the wires into cash but he was unsure what Adkin wanted to do with his new mansion.

"Do you want to stay in your new home while you're putting your supplies together to go after these men," Reighard asked.

"Not really, George. Do you still have that little room behind your office?" Adkin asked.

"Yes, but it's basically a tack room," Reighard said.

"Would you let me use it for awhile? I could put a cot in there – I noticed it had a wood stove."

"Sure, Adkin. Sure," Reighard said. "What about the new house?"

"Sell it," Adkin said, changing the subject.

"I'm going to need a wagon and a team, harnesses, and a good saddle with tack, small wood stove with wood and two weeks of food supplies," Adkin told Reighard, Ryan, Uribe and Ray Dee. "If one of you could contact Fred Zimmermann and have him lay out the newest Colt .44, a new Winchester 1873, his best skinning knife and extra ammunition for them, I'll come by in a few days and pay him cash."

Reighard had a horrible expression on his face.

"Sell the new house?" he mumbled.

"Yes, George, sell it," Adkin said, looking perturbed. "It was for Matty anyway."

After going over more details, the four men walked outside the surgeon's office.

"I can't believe he wants to sell his mansion we've been working on for nearly three months," Reighard said. "He hasn't even stepped inside it."

Ryan stopped and turned to Reighard.

"Don't sell it for now, George," Ryan said. "If he asks later, tell him it's the most expensive home in Dodge City and you're having trouble selling it for what he has into it.

"It is paid for, yes?" Ryan asked.

"Yes, he paid for it all in advance. In fact, he has about $2,000 coming back to him. I have all the paperwork. I'll see to it he gets that."

"I do like that plan," Reighard said. "He may change his mind in time. It's a beautiful house."

"We know, we went up there and saw it," Ray Dee said. "Unreal. It's a true mansion."

The crew wasn't sure how to proceed. Adkin was due to be released in two days, on December 12. He had spent 14 days in the infirmary.

"I wish he would let me go with him," Uribe said.

"Me, too," Ray Dee said. "This is insanity."

"We know how stubborn he can be, but he's usually level headed and will listen to reasoning," Ray Dee said. "But, I'm afraid Uribe was right – he's a broken man."

"Si. I am afraid for him when he turns against God," Uribe said. "No bueno por nada."

•••

Adkin's friends had gathered December 14, 1873, to help him load his wagon, make sure his guns and ammunition were handy from the wagon bench. He had given his father's Sharps and Quanah's bow and arrows to Ryan and asked him to keep them for him.

Adkin had dressed strangely, in the crew's opinion. He wore black woolen pants with black, cowskin cowboy boots.

He wore a checkered black and red shirt with a black sheepskin vest and a long black wool overcoat which he didn't button. It had a split up the back for horseback riding.

His new black gun belt held his old Colt in a holster low on his right hip, while the new Colt stuck in his gun belt toward his left hip with the grip situated so he could reach across and grab it with his right hand. His gun belt was full of bullets around the back. His new Winchester rested next to the brake handle.

His hat was a black wool Bowler, almost identical to the one like Bat Masterson wore. His blondish curls were still long and reached down into his collar and his full-face, reddish-blond mustache and beard reached down to the top button of his shirt.

With his new high-heeled cowboy boots, and the derby, Adkin looked 6-feet, 7-inches at least with shoulders as wide as a bear's. Only his neckless from Satanta proved he wasn't a mean-looking banker.

"Quite a change from your traditional wardrobe," Ryan said.

"Exactly why I chose it," Adkin said. "Word will get around quick enough that I survived, and I don't want those killers seeing me a half a mile away like I looked before."

His friends watched as Adkin led the team of his loaded wagon east out Military Avenue to Fort Dodge. He had his pony, Peta, tethered behind and saddled, while he was prepared to go hunting. Hunting the killers of his beloved Matty. He had one more stop before heading south to their Cimarron House.

When Post Surgeon Fitzgerald came out the side door of the infirmary, the tarpaulin bundle he held was no more than about 4-feet long. He walked up to Adkin, who was standing next to his wagon. Fitzgerald handed the bundle to Adkin, who held out both arms.

When Adkin took it, it seemed to weigh no more than about 40 pounds, like the weight of the heavy canvas cinched with ropes in four places.

Then … it was like a charge of lightning shot through him. It hit him this was all there was remaining of his beautiful Kiowa Princess – his Matty.

He started silently weeping as he laid her in the wagon behind the bench, not saying a word. Fitzgerald was speechless, as well.

Adkin got on the bench and laid his coat over his Winchester. Still silently crying, he drove his wagon back through Dodge City and down Front Street to the bridge heading south.

He never once wiped away any tears. They flowed steadily until he reached Mulberry Creek, 13 miles away.

The Las Animas crew watched him cross the bridge, unsure if they would ever see their dear friend again.

"I know who saved him and brought him to Fort Dodge," Ryan said.

"Who?" Uribe asked.

"Chief Quanah Parker.," Ryan answered, smiling. "Quanah's father was named Peta Nocono. Who else would name a horse Peta?"

•••

By the time Adkin got within sight of the rock chimney, his heart had hardened further. He was coming to the conclusion he may never be able to shed tears again. He was spent, a hollow tearless shell of a man full of hatred and nightmares.

He walked around the ruins of the house in a daze. He could see the end of the bed that didn't burn all the way to the floor. He now understood how his Fathers's bag, the Sharp's and Quanah's bow survived.

Over by the rock wall where the kitchen was adjoined, he found the charred old cigar box that held his tea. He opened it and there was still a bag of tea leaves within. He slipped it into his coat pocket.

Matty clothes box was totally burned. He could see elk teeth and colored beads among the ashes. He smiled, knowing he was through crying. It was his hatred that swelled up not tears.

Down by the stables, the only remnants were iron pieces such as bridles, rings, small chains and buckles – and, of course, his anvil. He must tell his friends in Dodge where they could find a Yates-made anvil, still of use to someone.

Adkin strode to the wagon and dug out a shovel. He then searched along the rock outcroppings west of the house. He had already determined not to place Matty's remains near any chance of flooding rain waters.

He found a place where there was about a 4-feet wall of limestone and scrabble below it. He decided this was the place. If weather caused the rock to crumble, it would only place more cover on her grave.

He started digging and scratching through the gravel. It was painstakingly slow digging.

Once she had been placed in the deep hole, he covered her with sand, dirt and scrabble. He stood there, unable to even try to pray, which was his way – before.

"There is nothing I can say to you Lord. You have betrayed not just me, but the most wonderful person I should ever know on this earth," he said, as he fell to his knees.

His legs seemed so weary and his head was swimming as he spun out of control and fell across her grave, unconscious. He had feinted.

He started blinking his eyes, trying to focus on where he was. Tiny pieces of ice or sand were hitting his face, stinging his skin. The light was low, shortly after sunset. He got to his hands and knees, realizing where he was.

He looked around and there was a fine dusting of snow and sleet covering the ground, including him. He rose and dusted the sleet from his clothes. He was cold. He backed up and kicked more rocks and sandstone gravel around the surface of her grave. It was not apparent.

He looked back east, and knew she was within 100 paces of their "Special Place." Plus she was near her favorite Black Gum tree and its crooked branches. He then got back in the wagon and turned back east toward Crooked Creek. He wanted to get as far away as possible, even if it meant travelling at dark.

•••

Adkin had made arrangements to return the YR&R wagon and team to Dodge City, after visiting Reighard's buffalo camps at Kiowa Creek and Bluff Creek. He wanted to check with the hunters to see if they had heard of any of the names he had. Bassett had talked him out of going to the Big Basin at Jacob's Well as most cattle drives were through for the year, so the possibility of bordello and liquor tents were minimal.

But the hunting camps were close and any news of the men he was hunting could be vital.

He ran into Dixon and Nixon at Kiowa Creek, but they had heard nothing of the men Adkin asked about. They were shocked about the news of Matty's death. In fact, they didn't know who was approaching them until Adkin had hailed them and identified himself.

They would both tell friends later in Dodge City that the man that came upon them at Kiowa Creek wasn't the Adkin Yates they had known.

They told Adkin the Mastersons and Prairie Dog would not be at the Bluff Creek camp as they had returned to Dodge City for the winter, where they would be following in a couple of days themselves.

Adkin drove on to Dodge City and returned the wagon on December 22, 1873. He made arrangements to travel with a pack horse with pack boards, because he was headed to Santa Fe, New Mexico, where it was warmer and outlaws chased easy money. The Las Animas Crew had already returned home.

Adkin caught the train December 23 to Granada, but he, Peta and his pack horse snuck through Las Animas at night without seeing any of his old crew. He didn't want to fight them over his determination to seek deadly revenge. Plus, he didn't think he could pay the emotional price of all of Matty's loved ones there.

He became painfully aware that riding a horse instead of a wagon was much harder on his ribs. Since mounting Peta at Granada, both sides of his torso were hurting. He was going to have to find a safe place to sleep for a few hours until daylight. No fire, just his bedding and a small hidden ravine or creek bed.

This was the worst for Adkin. He would lay there, not being able to sleep, remembering the scenes that day. His anger and agony would not let him drift off into sleep like he did in his life before.

"Nothing will ever be like before again," he told himself over and over.

He awoke at daylight, the sun higher than he would have liked, but he got back on the trail to La Junta. The hunt was on.

Later that day, Adkin rode into Ablo Velasquez' yard and met with Ablo. Of course, he wanted to know if Ablo had heard of any of the men he was looking for, and second, he was looking for a Buffalo coat. He discovered his buffalo hide was good to lay on, but his woolen overcoat was not that warm, at all.

Ablo told Adkin he had heard of a "Dog' Sill, but he couldn't remember what for.

"All I remember is it was not good, Señor," Ablo said. "You need to talk with our Marshal, Zedidiah Warszawski."

"War-ah-scha... what?" Adkin asked?

"He's Polish, and we just call him Marshal Zed," Ablo said grinning that he could pronounce Zed's last name, and he was Mexican. "He's tough, came out here a couple of years ago from Illinois – was a sheriff back there."

Ablo gave him directions to the Marshal's office, and a general store in town that should have some buffalo coats. It was after their business, that Ablo brought it up.

"We were so sorry to hear of your misfortune and Miss Matty, Señor," he said.

"Don't worry about it, Ablo," Adkin said. "I'm gong to get rid of that pain as soon as I find these men."

The pain and rage surged through him just at the mention of her name. He couldn't see it ever ceasing either.

"Oh, by the way," Ablo said as Adkin was walking toward the door. "Merry Christmas, Señor Yates."

Adkin didn't realize it was December 25, and he wasn't praising Christmas anytime soon. He headed to the general store Ablo told him about.

He bought a buffalo-hide coat. It was the only one that was large enough for him, and it was well made.

"Apparently made by an Indian," Adkin thought to himself.

Sheriff Zed knew of "Dog" Sill. He said he ran with a man named "Hairless" Harrison.

"Petty thieves and card cheats," Zed said. "They got ran out of here about a year ago for cheating a man in cards. If I hadn't dropped in there that evening, I believe they may have killed that man."

"They all three stood up from their chairs just as I walked in," he continued. "Both "Dog" and "Hairless" had their pistols pulled and were yelling at the man. He didn't even have a gun on him."

"I haven't heard anything about them recently, though," Zed said.

Adkin thanked the Sheriff and got back in the saddle. As he headed out of town, he saw Ablo walking down the side street to the Western Union Office.

He kind of smiled to himself. He figured Ablo was going to report to Ryan and the crew Adkin's whereabouts.

He thought of that before arriving in La Junta, but thought it might be wise if the crew knew his locations, just in case something bad happened to others he loved. They could at least telegraph and, hopefully, leave word for him.

...

Adkin made his way on down the Santa Fe Trail. It brought him comfort knowing he had travelled this trail and what it meant to his existence – his whole life in America. He didn't know if it would ever be the same, but he hoped once he killed these men, it would be easier to find that sense of adventure again.

But now, he realized that old Adkin Maxwell Yates was no longer in existence.

He had a good stay and visit with Uncle Dick Wootton, and then made his way to Las Vegas and then onto Santa Fe.

When he tied off Diablo in front of the Aguirre Hotel, Jose Yjinio Aguirre, the youngest brother came our hurriedly and welcomed Adkin.

"Bueno Señor Yates, bienvenidos," Jose said. "Dick Wootton telegraphed and said you may be coming our way."

There you have it, Adkin thought, no sense trying to hide his route or whereabouts.

"How are you Jose?" Adkin asked.

"Muy bien," he answered. "Come in, por favor."

They went into the hotel and straight to the bar. Jose ask for a brandy, and Adkin said that would work for him, too. Jose then suggested they take a table to visit.

"Are you hungry – want something to eat?" Jose asked.

"No. No. Gracias."

"You just missed our Nuevo Ano fandango two nights ago. We celebrate the new year of 1874," he said.

Adkin shrugged and explained he was on the trail. But he did want to go over the names of the men he was seeking, and Jose said he knew of "Billy Boy" Jones and had heard of a Lew Bush.

"I think Bush and a gang held up a stagecoach down near El Paso last year," Jose said. "I'm pretty sure it was Bush … or maybe Brush."

"Sometime he goes by Lew "Brushy" Bush," Adkin said.

"Si. Si. Probably the same man," Jose said.

He went on to explain stage hold-ups were getting to be a serious problem south of Santa Fe.

"All the way down to El Paso and over to Tucson, Arizona," Jose said. "You know Conrado lives south of there in the State of Sonora, Mexico.

"Anyway, we've had several stages robbed between El Paso and Tucson recently," he added. "And with the new mines, thieves follow the oro y dinero.

"There is not so much law officers down there – never has been really," Jose added.

They then started discussing other issues, and Adkin brought it up he had to buy a buffalo coat in La Junta for warmth. Jose said their trading post had received an inventory of the latest overcoats from Texas.

"They are of heavy canvas with a riding cut in the back," Jose said. "They are very great for riding long distances in cold or rain.

"They were developed for the Texas Rangers, and it's all they wear now," he continued. "It is called a Ranger Duster – for some reason."

Jose took Adkin next door to the trading post. The whole complex looked grander than ever to Adkin. The Aguirre Brothers were astute businessmen.

Out of about 20 of these dusters, only two would fit Adkin. He liked the thick, tough feel of the canvas. He understood why Cowboy or Ranger Duster was chosen for the name – it would protect cowboys on the trail from rain, cold, cow horns, cactus and yuccas with its long length down below the knees.

Adkin gladly paid $15 for his. The clerk rolled it up and tied twine around it to keep it bundled. Then Adkin asked Jose for a room for the night, which was arranged immediately after they returned to the entrance of the hotel.

"Would you like to have supper with me, Señor," Jose asked.

Adkin wasn't sure if he could enjoy an evening with Jose – not that Jose was the issue – but because he knew Matty would come up.

But on the other hand, Jose may be able to give him more information about people, outlaws and Sheriffs further south. He had already decided he was going to head that direction for the time being, as that offered his best chances.

"Yes, Jose," Adkin answered. "Would 8 be good for you?"

"Si, si, Señor. "I'll meet you here in the dining hall at 8," Jose said, as he walked away smiling.

After ordering their meals, Adkin started quizzing Jose about people to contact south to El Paso and over to Tucson. He actually took a small writing pad and pencil from his pocket.

"You don't mind if I take notes, do you?" Adkin asked Jose, who told him that was fine.

Once Adkin was feeling he had very valuable information, an idea came to him.

"Let me ask you something, Jose," he started. "The Aguirre Stagecoach line runs the entire routes to El Paso and on west to Tucson, correct?"

"Even further west, Señor," Joe said.

"Would it be possible if I was to work on your stages as the shotgun messenger – your security man?" Adkin asked.

Jose sat there with a worried look on his face.

"I could ride as a shotgun messenger on all your stages going south to El Paso and then travel on to Tucson and back again to here, if I'm still looking for these men," Adkin said. "And I would do it for free – no cost to the Aguirre Brothers."

"This is very interesting proposal, Adkin," Jose said. "I think it very good for you to find these outlaws, but are you suited to ride as a messenger? Have you done this kind of work?"

"Jose, I was riding shotgun with my father when I was 10 years old driving a coach to and from London, England," Adkin said smiling. "I did that until I left for America when I was 18."

"Oh yes, I remember now you came from a coach family – and a blacksmith, too," Jose said. "I would really like to telegraph Conrado and Pedro to get their approval. We are partners, si?"

"I understand," Adkin said, somewhat let down. "How long would that take, Jose?"

"Well, the telegraph lines reached Tucson about five months ago – Pedro lives there now – and it reached Nogales a month ago, where Conrado lives," Jose said. "It should only take tomorrow to ask them."

"That would be muy bueno, Jose," Adkin said with relief in his voice. "Gracias, mi amigo."

Adkin went on to explain by riding shotgun, he could possibly find out valuable information if they stopped thieves and coach robbers. He assured Jose he would be as vigilant as a law man.

"And I'm a very good shot with pistols, rifles and shotguns," Adkin said. "In fact, I'm also looking for an old Remington shotgun – a coach gun – that my father gave me to bring to America. Those outlaws beat me with it, and I intend to get it back if at all possible. They also took my new engraved Winchester."

"I've heard of your pistol skills," Jose said grinning. "I think you make great shotgun messenger on our stagecoaches, too."

Adkin spent the next morning looking at all the goods in the Aguirre Trading Post. They had everything and then some, Adkin thought to himself. He even saw some Indian-made leggings, which brought back the memories of the ones he had bought there years before and the new ones Matty had made him.

Those were so stained by blood they were unwearable and Adkin threw them away – just like his deerskin shirt and pants, too.

He did find two more pairs of woolen pants that fit, and he bought them, as well as four more high-collar shirts; two light blue; one red, gray and brown checkered and one a light green – all with white collars and white cuffs.

After having his clothing bundled and paid for, he noticed plenty of ammunition sitting in front of a counter where long guns were stacked the length of the wall. He asked the clerk if he had any coach guns.

"You know, the short barrel, and I need a 12 gauge," Adkin said.

"Right over here," the clerk said. "I've got a couple of Remingtons in 12 gauge, and I have this 10 gauge made by William Moore and Company from England. It's a real bruiser, if you know what I mean."

"I'll take it if you have plenty of 10 gauge shells," Adkin said.

"I have, let me check first," the clerk stuttered as he bent under the gun cabinet. "I've got one case of 10 gauge – that's 240 total shells, 24 boxes of 10 shells in each box."

"Sold," Adkin said.

"But I haven't told you how much that 10 gauge costs." he said nervously. "It's fairly expensive, Sir."

"I'll take all of it, the gun and all the shells. And I need a saddle scabbard for it, too," Adkin said as he reached for his money bag. "How much for it all?"

The clerk was beside himself as he quickly went and found a couple of leather scabbards to try for a fit of the 18-inch side-by-side, double-barreled coach gun. One was just right, if a little longer than necessary. He laid in on the counter next to the gun and reached down and grabbed the case of shells.

'Now let's see. The gun is $50," he said, pausing to see if Adkin blinked or balked. Adkin was preoccupied with holding the shotgun up at the shoulder position as well as snapping it up to a waist position.

Seeing nothing, the clerk continued. "The scabbard is $15 and the shells are $2 a box, times 24 equals $48.

"That would come to $113, sir," he said.

Adkin laid out several gold coins and a couple of silver coins.

"There's $120 U.S. – keep the balance for yourself for being a gracious host in this wonderful establishment," Adkin said in his best English accent.

•••

At lunch, Jose told Adkin he had sent the telegraphs at 8, when the Western Union Office opened.

"If they are not out travelling, I should hear back sometime today," he said. "Do you have all the supplies you need for travelling?"

"Si Jose," Adkin said. "I found pants as well as shirts I needed at your trading post, and I bought a new 10-gauge coach shotgun. You have so many trade goods. I am mucho impressed."

"We have goods from eastern U.S., Texas, Mexico and even California," Jose said, beaming with pride. "Plus all the wonderful goods made by area Indians."

"Muy bueno, Jose, muy bueno," Adkin said as he patted Jose on the shoulder.

Just as the Mexican woman was removing their lunch dishes, a boy wearing a serape and a large sombrero came running in.

"Señor Aguirre. Yo tengo un mensaje para usted," he wheezed and handed the telegram to Jose.

Jose handed the boy a coin and said, "Gracias."

"It is from Pedro," Jose began. "By chance, Conrado is visiting Pedro and his wife in Tucson and they both agree it is a good idea to help you find these outlaws by being a stagecoach messenger.

"They also send their sincere condolences for your loss of Matty," he added, looking sheepishly at Adkin.

"It will never end until I kill these heathens," Adkin said to himself.

"Wonderful, Jose," Adkin said. "Just great. When can I start?"

Jose went over when the next stage would depart for Socorro and who to talk with.

"You may want to write these things down, Señor," Jose said as Adkin reached for his pad and pencil.

Jose gave him the names of station managers at the various stops all the way to Tucson.

"The hub for our east-west routes is at Las Cruces. It's where our jaunts to El Paso and Juarez split off," Jose said. "I will be sending telegraphs to all the stations where service is available. News of you're coming will be ahead of you."

The stage to Socorro was departing at daybreak the following morning, January 4, 1874. It would make four stops – two overnight – and would arrive in Socorro around noon the 7th.

...

The stage driver, a weather-worn older man of Mexican heritage, spoke broken English, but was able to tell Adkin there were mucho saloons in Socorro and mucho bad men. "Muy malo," he said and Adkin understood.

Seems silver had been discovered about 10 years earlier and was still being mined from the Magdalena District west of Socorro and freight wagons and stages had been robbed around there for several years. Plus, Socorro was full of hotels with gambling, bordellos and outlaws. That was exactly what Adkin was looking for.

Adkin was hoping the fact they were carrying payroll for one of the larger mines in Socorro County would attract thieves, despite being told it had been a very secretive job.

The trip wasn't too eventful, and the overnight coach inns were accommodating, if a little rough. All the men, including passengers, had to sleep on old Army cots in the same small room at the inns, but the food was good at both stops.

They passed the north-bound stage the third day before arriving in Socorro. The drivers stopped to talk with each other. They rattled off in Spanish, with Adkin only catching a few words here and there. After bidding farewell, the driver told him no outlaws had been seen in over a month, and it was down near Las Cruces. The man didn't know the names of the thieves, though.

So, the next morning they were off to Las Cruces. Adkin was hopeful if not impatient. In two long days, they arrived January 9 in Las Cruces without any incidences.

Adkin was somewhat disappointed the stage hadn't been approached by robbers, but he was glad nobody under his watch got hurt. He couldn't hardly believe he was hoping to get robbed, but he wanted to find these men that ruined his life.

After dropping off the passengers, a wagon with five armed guards pulled up and the strongbox was passed over to the men. They were from a mining operation.

Adkin was told he could stay at the coach station for the night, but he decided to take a room at one of the hotels. It would the following day for the next stage to head south. He had all afternoon and evening to roam the streets searching for clues.

He left his packhorse at the coach station stables but saddled Peta, stuck his new 10-gauge into its scabbard and rode around looking for a fleabag hotel. He found one only about two blocks away, and there were beer halls and gambling houses the whole length of the street.

He stopped at the hitching rail, and two Indian boys came running over saying they would rub down his horse and protect it from thieves for 25 cents. He tied the reins to the rail and gave the boys a coin. He grabbed his 10 gauge from one side and the Winchester from the other side and walked into the hotel carrying one in each hand.

He got a room, and the door lock looked fairly secure. He rattled it and pulled it hard, but it was solid. He put his long guns under the fleece-filled mattress and pulled the top cover tight.

He then walked down the stairs and out onto the planked boardwalk. The Indian boys were actually combing Peta with a curry comb and rubbing him with a piece of sheepskin with its wool on one side. Peta looked happy.

He stopped in several establishments and spoke to a few bar keeps and saloon girls that approached him asking about names on his list, trying to seem discrete. No answers.

After walking three blocks, he noticed a horse rearing its head up and down between about a dozen tied to the rails. As he walked up, the horse neighed and stomped its front leg several times.

It was Tóngúl!

And she recognized Adkin right away!

He touched the horse's nose and she got quiet. He squeezed between her and another while rubbing her shoulder, her back, the haunches, and he got to that long red tail. Even with pieces of brush stuck in her tail, it was Matty's horse. There were no other markings on Tóngúl, she was all glorious red with four gray hooves. Her saddle he didn't recognize. There was a Winchester in a saddle scabbard, though, and Adkin slipped it out far enough to see his name engraved on the side of the receiver. He slid it back in.

"Oh Tóngúl, I'm so pleased to see you," he whispered in her ear. His heart started racing. It felt like it was in his throat.

"Hey, what you doing with them horses?" a voice boomed, startling him momentarily.

"Just looking," he answered, continuing to stroke the animal as he came back to the rail. "Do you know who owns this fine looking mare?"

The man on the walkway shook his head, "No."

"Sorry, but that's my horse next to her, and I'm heading home for supper," the man said untying the reins. "Whoever owns her is probably right in there."

"Thanks," Adkin said, as he walked up the steps and through the glass-paned doors and the swinging doors inside those.

Adkin gazed over the crowd, trying to use his hazy memory of who he saw at the Cimarron House. He was sure he had seen the faces of two and maybe a third, but it was a fuzzy memory.

He didn't immediately recognize anyone. There were about six or seven card tables with six to eight men at each one. As he reached the bar, a saloon girl came up to him, reaching her hand up to his shoulder asking him if he would buy her a drink.

"Sure, of course," Adkin said, trying to use a southern Louisiana accent like he did outside and at the hotel. He didn't want anyone to take him for an Englishman.

She ordered a Cactus Wine, a popular drink made from a mix of tequila and peyote tea. Adkin knew that would put a person out after only a few.

"You know who owns that sorrel mare at the rail right there?" he asked.

"Oh, I think that's the horse Dog rides now," she said taking a sip from her drink. "Why? You lookin' for 'im?"

"No, I just love sorrels and thought I'd see iffin' the man would want to sell 'er."

"That's him over there in the corner sitting at the back of the table with that gray Reb's hat," she said.

"Fine, thank you, Maam," Adkin said. "Think I'll see if I can sit in and play some poker."

She started chugging the drink down and gave out a harrumph. He handed her a silver coin for the drink.

He made his way through the tables, trying to see the man's whole face. He instinctively checked his Colt in its holster, making sure it wasn't tied down, and reached over to adjust the other Colt in his left waist belt under his duster.

There were two empty chairs at the table. He reached for the one exactly across from Dog. He knew it was Dog, with the long scraggly hair.

"Mind iffin' I sit in, fellas," Adkin asked. As Dog raised his head and looked up, Adkin knew without a doubt it was him – the one who kicked him and shot him – and one of them who butchered his Matty. And he had two teeth missing in his lower jaw in front.

An Englishman's Adventures on the Santa Fe Trail (1865-1889)

He was speechless and was ready to draw if Dog recognized him, They all said, "okay" or "have a seat, Mister." He pulled out the chair and slowly sat down.

"We're playin' straight draw poker, Mister, no wildcards and $1 ante and a $50 raise limit," said the man dealing who was sitting two chairs away from Dog. Adkin slowly checked out the other men, seven in all, while smiling. He didn't recognize anyone else except for Dog – Alfonso "Dog" Sill. Adkin could almost smell him.

As they played the hands, Adkin was checking out all the others at the various tables. He didn't want to be obvious and wanted to keep an eagle eye on Dog without totally staring.

He was asked where he was from and he said he had lived his early life in New Orleans, but moved to the Fort Leavenworth area about 10 years ago. He said he was looking for steady work, maybe on a ranch. One of the men mentioned he was wondering where that strange accent came from.

Adkin's mind was steadying, and his tenseness was replaced with a deadly focus. He figured he would accuse Dog of cheating and see if he could get him to fight. First, he wanted to know about Tóngúl.

"Who owns that beautiful sorrel mare out there?' Adkin asked the table. "I've been looking for a horse like that for some time. She's a beaut, alright."

Dog looked up and said, "She's mine, Mister, and she ain't for sale."

"Hey, just asking. I'm stuck with an old Indian paint that a Comanchero traded for a buffalo I killed last fall," Adkin said.

"Well forget that one," Dog said. "She's a special horse with good memories."

That did it. Adkin's blood was racing through his body, but he had to wait a few more hands. He had been losing anyway, but he wanted to set it up.

About 20 minutes later, it was nearing 6 o'clock and some would be wanting to eat. It was Dog's turn to deal. After checking their cards, and Dog started dealing out replacements after throwing away cards, Adkin slid his chair back about another foot from the table.

"Hey, you, I just saw you palm a card after dealing – you slipped it up your shirt sleeve," Adkin said.

Dog gave him a deadly glare.

"Mister, I don't know what you're talking about, but no one calls me a cheat," Dog said. "Nobody."

"Well, I saw you cheating, so I guess I can call you a cheat," Adkin said, just sitting there calmly.

"Mister, you say that one more time, and you're a dead man," Dog said loud enough for the closer tables to hear.

The other men started backing away from their table. One man urged calm, but nobody listened.

"Actually, you're not only a card cheat, you're a cowardly bastard that likes to rape and butcher Indian women," Adkin said in a perfectly British accent. He still just sat there. "Like that Indian woman you cut open along the Cimarron the day before last Thanksgiving."

Suddenly Dog's eyes widened, realizing who was challenging him. He started rising kicking back his chair and just as he got his pistol cleared of his holster.

"You son of a …," Dog started.

Boom. Boom.

Two shots from Adkin who had whipped his gun out from his sitting position hit Dog in the right shoulder and his right side, probably through his lung. Dog had got off a shot but it was into the ceiling.

Dog fell backward, dropping his gun while a card slid out of the cuff of his shirt face down near the pistol. Adkin immediately noticed a thin man with a black hat and chaps run out the front doors. He had been playing cards three tables over, near the door.

"You better get out of here Marky," someone said to the running man. People were squeezing out the doors and yelling, "Get the Sheriff."

Dog was moaning as Adkin stood and walked around the now empty table.

"Marky. Marky. Where are you? Shoot this bastard," Dog moaned.

"I think Marky ran off – ran like the coward he is," Adkin said. "Like the coward you are, Dog."

Adkin stood over him and holstered his Colt. Dog's pistol was on the floor to his right about a foot away from Dog's hand, a hand that didn't seem to be working too well.

Adkin intentionally aimed to not kill him immediately. He wanted to try to get more information from Dog.

"Where's Lew Bush, Dog?" Adkin asked. "Is he riding with 'Billy Boy' Jones?"

"I wouldn't tell you if I knew," Dog spit out with blood in his mouth. It was also pouring out of his right side and pooling.

The chaos in the saloon was loud, and Adkin noticed only about a dozen people were still standing around watching, the rest had scurried out the doors.

Adkin noticed Dog kept looking to his pistol. Adkin figured if he turned his back, maybe Dog would reach for it. Sure enough, as Adkin turned toward the bar, saying, "You're going to bleed to death in about five more minutes anyway."

Someone yelled "look out" about the time Dog got his hand on his pistol. He tried pulling it up and squeezed off a shot just as Adkin wheeled around, quickly pulling his Colt and shooting Dog in the face.

Blood splattered across the floor and both lower walls of the corner. Most of the top of Dog's skull was gone.

An Englishman's Adventures on the Santa Fe Trail (1865-1889)

Adkin walked to the bar. The bar keep had his shotgun in his hands, but didn't point it directly at Adkin, who was laying both his pistols on the bar.

"Would you be kind enough to ask someone to gather up the Sheriff?" Adkin asked. "I could use a brandy, too, if you have any, please."

"Sure do Mister," the bar keep said, laying his shotgun on the wall counter behind the bar. "Someone go fetch Sheriff Armijo, hurry."

•••

The Sheriff arrived shortly, right as Adkin was finishing his brandy. Adkin introduced himself and who Dog was. He pointed to the bystanders and explained he had witnesses who would verify it was a fair fight.

Several stepped forward explaining Dog stood and drew first and was aiming his gun at Adkin – who was sitting – and Adkin shot Dog twice as Dog shot errantly.

"Then when this stranger turned away from Dog, Dog got his hand on his pistol on the floor," one of the men said.

"I saw that, too, Sheriff, "the bar keep said. "As someone yelled out Dog had his gun, this man turned, pulled and shot him dead. Dog's' shot is up there somewhere."

Several people said it was all true. Armijo wrote it on a pad he carried, asked several times for correct movements and other details, and then he asked those who would swear to it in court to sign his report.

Nine people signed, while about that many also refused because they didn't want to have to go to a court hearing. Armijo assured them they wouldn't have to go to court if the magistrate refused to make charges.

"This is a pure case of self defense, and this man will not be charged, I'm sure," the Sheriff said. "I'm not even going to arrest him."

Four more then stepped forward to sign the report.

"Very good," Armijo said. "And you Yates, can you wait until the magistrate comes to town? He works between here and El Paso – should be back in a few days."

"Sheriff, I'm working for Aguirre Stagecoach Line as a shotgun messenger, and the stage is supposed to depart in the morning. But I'll ask if they could replace me until this matter is settled. Will that do?"

"Yes, you're free to move around town, just stay out of trouble," Armijo said.

"Three more things Sheriff," Adkin said. "First, that sorrel mare out there was stolen from me and my wife. Her name is Tóngúl, and she will follow me like a pup if you need for me to show you.

Second, that Winchester on that mare is mine," Adkin continued. "My name was engraved by Fred Zimmermann of Dodge City, whom I purchasd it from. You an read it your self.

659

"And third, I'd like to search Dog for a Remington pocket pistol that was stolen from me, too," he continued. "It has a chipped grip on it where I dropped it once and a small piece of wood broke off the left side grip."

"The sheriff told him to go ahead with a search of Dog while he watched. Adkin bent down and patted around his waist and his torso. Sure enough, he reached in the left pocket of Dog's vest and pulled out a Remington pocket pistol with the chipped grip.

"Go ahead, keep it. It's yours alright," Armijo said. "And the horse and the rifle, too. I'm sure you're telling the truth."

"May I go talk to the stagecoach station manager?" Adkin asked, looking at his pocket watch. "I'm staying at the Hotel Arroyo down the street if you need me."

Armijo agreed and he asked for men to help get Dog's body to the undertaker a few blocks away. And the whispering and stories started spreading about this Englishman and his fast draw – and his deadly aim, again.

...

Adkin found the station manager and told him what happened, and he wouldn't be able to ride as security on the morning coach. He had left some belongings on the coach and asked if he could remove them and take them to the hotel.

"Also, this man had stolen a horse I owned, and I would like to keep her here at your stables while this issue is settled – as well as my pack horse," Adkin said. "I will gladly pay for their upkeep and feed."

The station manager agreed and assured Adkin he had a replacement to ride messenger, and the horses would be no problem. But Adkin could tell the manager was cool to him and had a worried look about him, as if he feared Adkin. Adkin said he'd have Tóngúl to him in about 20 minutes and to store the saddle.

"Sheriff Armijo is stripping the saddle of the man's belongings; scabbards, saddle bags and then I can bring her over," Adkin said. "She's a beautiful sorrel and as fast as the wind. She belonged to my wife …"

His voice trailed off into the wind. He has to keep from digging her up memory. He had killed one of the butchers, and he had plenty of satisfaction at that thought.

"This might be easier than I believed," he told himself. "I'm pretty sure that Marky is the one who ran out of the saloon. I can track him down in no time. I don't care if he gets a five-day start, he's a dead man."

Adkin had a strange smile on his face as he turned away and got back on Peta. The station manager just stared at Adkin as he rode off.

The next morning, people were whispering and pointing at Adkin as he walked out of the hotel. People on the walkway moved aside as he passed. He had noticed as small cafe the afternoon before and made his way there. He was able to get some breakfast, even fresh eggs and a beef steak. But he had to drink dark coffee, no tea available.

He spent the rest of the morning writing in his diary back at his room. He couldn't believe how satisfied he was killing a man. It was as different as different could be compared to the man he killed with his fist in St. Augustine back in '65.

He had a little lunch in the hotel dining room, but decided he needed to get out and dig for more information.

He wanted to talk with the bar keep and some of the patrons of the saloon to see if he could fine out more about Marcus "Marky" Hall and where he may be headed. Adkin was fairly sure Marky wouldn't be staying long in Las Cruces.

He stopped first at the Sheriff's office and asked him about Marky. Armijo said he and Dog were drifters, they had come through Las Cruces a couple of times a year. Adkin asked about David "Hairless" Harrison or "Billy Boy" Jones or Lew Bush.

"Bush I know of, and he rides with Billy Jones, I remember that," Armijo said. "I don't recall Harrison.

"I think these men usually go on over to Tucson or Silver City because of the mines around Silver City," Armijo said. "These kind of men feed off the miners when they get paid or rob stages carrying mine payrolls."

"I thank you Sheriff," Adkin said. "I'll be around, call me when the magistrate arrives."

He walked back to the saloon and visited with several saloon girls and the bar keep. He's the one who knew Marky.

"Marcus does what Dog tells him to do," the bar keep said. "He followed Dog around like a puppy, a real weasel. I caught him trying to steal a man's saddle bags that were laying near the man's feet – here at the bar – last year. Told him if he tried anything like that again, he'd be going to jail.

"I've heard them talk that there's more money to be made in Tucson, more gambling with the miners and such," he added. "Where'd you learn to shoot like that?"

"Never mind," Adkin said, asking about the others. The bar keep heard of Bush and Jones but not Harrison. Adkin was starting to believe Harrison may not have anything to do with this bunch.

Then he met Sue, a chubby, dark haired woman who looked to be mixed Indian and Mexican blood. She wore her blouse off her shoulders and low enough in front to show off her cleavage.

"Si, I know Marky and Dog," she said. "They cheap banditos, no want to buy me drinks or not want to pay for sugar time, either.

"They talk about robbing stagecoach near Socorro next month with another man," Sue said.

"Do you know his name?" Adkin asked.

"No, but when he take off his hat, he have no hair – hair only around ears and back of head," she said giggling.

"When was this" When did they talk?" Adkin pushed on.

"Maybe two or three weeks ago," she answered, "You buy me drink, Señor – or want some sugar?"

"I don't have the time right now, but thank you anyway," he said as he handed her a silver dollar. She was ecstatic and hugged him.

Adkin went directly to the stage station and found the manger and told him what he discovered from the soiled dove.

"Yes, I will notify the stations between here and Santa Fe about a possible robbery, but I have some bad news for you Señor," he said, looking as scared as ever. "Jose send message that maybe it best for you and Aguirre Company that you no ride messenger any more."

Adkin's excitement fell through his feet. The manager had telegraphed Jose what had happened, and Jose is looking out for his stagecoach business.

"This man probably didn't tell Jose the whole story or, possibly, not even the truth," Adkin thought to himself. "Time for another plan."

"Thanks," Adkin said, dropping his head a little. "May I still keep my animals here until the magistrate frees me? And declares I'm innocent?"

The man nodded but hurried away, full of fear.

Once Adkin was cleared of any charges, he needed to go back to Socorro. If he could not ride messenger, he could follow the stagecoach closely as a private person with no association with the stage company. That would maybe get him near some more of these killers.

•••

Four days later, the area magistrate arrived in Las Cruces, and Armijo sent a boy to tell Adkin he was wanted at the Sheriff's Office. Adkin followed the boy and had his short, direct meeting with the magistrate.

Adkin was asked to give his side of the story. Armijo then read his scribbled report and additionally told the magistrate what everybody was saying about the shooting that were partly detailed in the report. He also showed him all the names that agreed to testify if needed.

The magistrate quickly cleared Adkin, signed a brief note stating so, and Adkin walked out a free man. Now it was time to put his plan into play. He had been packed and ready to ride as soon as he got the word.

He jumped on Peta and dropped by the stage station, saddled up Tóngúl, got his pack board situated and put a tether on her and the pack horse and stopped briefly at the hotel. With the help of a couple of Indian boys, they carried his bags and belongings out to the horses, and Adkin lashed them down securely on the pack horse.

He checked his pocket watch. He was ready to ride 30 minutes after being cleared, and he was only about two hours behind the stage to Socorro. He calculated it would only take about four hours to get close to the stage. He wanted to ride about a half mile behind it.

Adkin had told the station manger about his plans, and he had no problem with Adkin trailing the stage. Adkin knew if Jose was worried in Santa Fe, Jose hadn't told the manager anything or Adkin would have heard about it before now.

On time, Adkin caught sight of the Aguirre Brothers' stage around 2 p.m. He knew it would stop for the night in Las Palomas, a vibrant little village along the Rio Grande River. The trail ran along the Rio Grande the entire length, not only to Socorro, but to Albuquerque, too.

Adkin had to admit the country was beautiful, and it also offered plenty of sites where ambushes could be possible. Hillocks, trees, small buttes and cliffs gave thieves numerous places to attack a stagecoach. He had to stay within sight or earshot.

Is was nearing sunset when the stage reached Las Palomas. Adkin wasn't far behind. He actually pulled up to the station, as it also had the small rooming house where passengers or travellers stayed.

He had been there about 10 days earlier, and the place had good meals and took well care of the animals. His horses needed that, it had been a hard day's work catching and staying up with the stage.

He decided to introduce himself to the passengers at supper as Tyler Maxwell, and he tried hiding his accent. There were two general store owners from Albuquerque who had been in Las Cruces seeking a place to open a new mercantile store and expand their business. One man and his wife were going back to St. Louis because of a death in the family. The couple had moved to El Paso two years earlier – he was a dentist.

And one man was very quiet and a loner. He finally said he was a cattle rancher from Colorado, but he didn't say where in Colorado. He dressed more like a cowboy, not a ranch owner.

When the people were meeting Mister Maxwell, the cowboy said his name was Davy Harrison. Adkin almost dropped his soup spoon. He bit his tongue and only said, "Nice to meet you, Mister Harrison."

Then he understood why Harrison hadn't removed his hat in the building or while eating at a dining table, even though the other men had done so – even Adkin.

He was sitting at the table with David "Hairless" Harrison.

"You haven't lived in the Dodge City area, have you Mister Harrison?" Adkin asked slowly and politely. "You look somewhat familiar."

Harrison looked up startled.

"No," he said sharply.

"My mistake," Adkin said smiling. "I live there in Doge City, and I'm headed back after a miserable six months looking for silver and gold down here."

"Well, I have passed through Dodge City several times, being in the cattle business," Harrison said, sounding more relaxed. "Maybe you saw me then. But I can tell you, we've never met."

"Yes, I see," Adkin said.

"Dodge City has really grown in the last two years," one of the store owners said. "It's a wild time there, I can tell you."

"When was the last time you visited my fine city?" Adkin asked Harrison. "Do you sell cattle at the railroad yards there?"

"Yes, we do," Harrison said, looking at Adkin in a weary way. "In fact, we sold a herd right there – me and my partners – a few days after Thanksgiving."

That was good enough for Adkin. He was sure Harrison was one of the five that attacked him and butchered Matty the day before Thanksgiving. But what was Harrison doing taking the stage to Socorro? And spending the night at the station and rooming house?

It was a plan to rob the stage, had to be. But why wait two days out of Las Cruces?

"There must be a reason to rob it tomorrow," Adkin thought to himself. And Adkin was sure Marky and maybe others were with the gang that was planning to hit this stagecoach tomorrow.

It was all Adkin could do to keep from standing a putting six .44 bullets into this coward across the table from him.

After the meal, Harrison excused himself, saying he needed his rest. Adkin stood shortly after Harrison headed for the stairs.

"Excuse me, I'll be back shortly," Adkin told the others.

Adkin quietly followed Harrison up the stairs and saw him enter his room. The room was only two doors down from Adkin's. He turned and went back to the table and visited with the others for awhile more.

•••

Back in his room later, Adkin laid in his bed trying figure out what Harrison was up to. He pulled out his map. It was another full day to Socorro and plenty of places to ambush the stage.

Suddenly, he noticed Socorro was only about 60 miles from Silver City, which was almost due west of Las Palomas. A mine operator might prefer loading up silver in Las Palomas than the larger town of Las Cruces.

Maybe that was it, but nobody came by this evening with a strongbox or bag that could hold silver. Something was going to happen tomorrow, and Adkin was going to stop it and kill Harrison and likely whoever was helping him.

He was about to go to sleep when a thought came to him.

It was late, and he took off his boots, kept his Colt holstered and quietly walked down the hall. He gently and slowly tried Harrison's door nob, but it was locked.

"Naturally," Adkin thought to himself.

He crept on down to the door leading outside, the fire escape door. There were stairs going to the street below, and there was a walkway veranda around the rooms of the rooming house on the second floor. He slowly sneaked down the walkway and found Harrison's window.

He couldn't believe his eyes. The window was open about an inch, Adkin guessed to get in fresh air, because the rooms were well heated with the fire place and the heating stove on the ground floor.

He raised the window slowly, softly so as large enough he could bend over and look inside. His eyes were fully adjusted to the darkness, mainly because it was moon bright. He could see Harrison was solidly asleep. Harrison's gun belt was sitting there right next to the window on a wooden chair.

Adkin quietly slid the pistol out of its holster and stood up outside. He removed the six bullets from the revolver and then put it back in the holster. He quietly closed the window to exactly the way it was when he found it.

He wasn't sure if that would help, but he knew if Harrison didn't discover it, an empty gun might save some lives.

"But it won't save your life, 'Hairless,'" Adkin thought to himself, as he slipped back into the hallway and into his room. He would sleep a little better, but he kept a Colt beside him and not in a holster.

Early next morning, as Adkin was checking his long guns and making sure they were fully loaded and ready. He heard a wagon and a team pull up front. It was barely light gray in the eastern sky and he heard several voices whispering, one softly giving orders.

He looked out the window and saw two men sliding a strongbox out the back of the wagon then carrying it under the veranda into the stables where the stagecoach was parked to keep it out of the weather. There were four others in the wagon all carrying repeating rifles – guards. One was standing with the reins in his hands.

"Hurry up men, get that loaded so we can vamoose," he whispered loudly.

The puzzle became clear to Adkin. These men were with a mining operation probably from Silver City and delivering silver or gold in secrecy before any passengers or citizens were awake. Adkin was lucky he always woke early.

"So, Harrison's other gang members are going to rob the silver shipment," Adkin thought to himself. It all made sense now. Harrison was probably put on the stage to confirm there was going to be a shipment and if it's onboard when the stage reaches the ambush spot.

"I presume Harrison is watching this all unfold two doors down, too," Adkin thought. "He can now signal the others the strongbox is on the stage. I'll have to stay close but out of sight."

•••

As passengers were preparing to depart, several of them recommended Mister Maxwell purchase a seat on the stage and ride with them in comfort. Harrison was quiet, not saying anything.

"I would, but I have to watch what little money I have," Adkin pleaded. "That mining scheme cost me nearly everything."

"Nice meeting you folks, but I may stay here and see if I can find a little work," Adkin added, waving as they pulled away.

Once they were out of sight, Adkin saddled Peta and shoved the long guns in their respective scabbards. He tethered Tóngúl and the pack horse and rode off in a trot.

About an hour out of Las Palomas, Adkin could see Elephant Butte, a large mound some said was an old volcano. He thought this area of buttes and ravines would be a good ambush sight, he kicked Peta in the haunches and came to a gallop to ensure he was closer to the stage.

He could see it ahead of him, and then the signal came. Harrison was waving his hat out the window of the coach. Adkin put Peta into a full run. Just as he was about 100 yards away, three riders came out from behind a mound, all firing shots into the air.

Adkin ducked behind some cedars just out of sight. He saw the messenger throw his shotgun down, then two pistols hit the dirt – the messengers' and the driver's. Adkin stayed mounted on Peta, but tied the tether on the other horses to a cedar limb.

Harrison had jumped out of the stage and was ushering the passengers out waving his pistol. He was telling them to keep their hands up. A man on horseback to the side told the two others to get the strongbox.

Adkin couldn't believe his eyes. The man was sitting atop Diablo.

As the men got off their horses and ran back to the rear boot, Adkin noticed Harrison was fighting with the woman over her jewelry, and Harrison knocked her on the side of her head with his pistol. She screamed and fell to the ground holding her head.

Her husband tried to interfere and he, too was hit in the head with the gun and staggered back against the stage. Adkin raised the Winchester and decided to take out the man on Diablo first, as he had a rifle in his hands.

Boom.

The man in the saddle fell off Diablo, who reared up and backed away. Adkin levered in another round as Harrison was looking around and then tried shooting the passengers. His gun was clicking but no shots were being fired. He looked dumbfounded as Adkin put a round into his side and knocked him down.

The other two dropped the strongbox and pulled their pistols, not knowing where the shots were coming from. Adkin slammed his Winchester into the scabbard as he kicked Peta in the haunches and was tearing down on the two still holding guns. He pulled out his shotgun.

One had grabbed the reins of his horse, but the other's horse had spooked and was trotting into the ravine, away from the chaos.

The horseless man shot twice at Adkin as Adkin raced in while the other was swinging into his saddle as his horse was twirling in circles.

The shooter was wearing the black hat and the chaps Adkin had seen at the saloon where he killed "Dog" Sill. Adkin rode closer and lifted his 10 gauge and shot him right in the middle of his chest.

He fell backwards – lifted completely off his feet – as the last bandit was riding away on a beautiful buckskin palomino.

Adkin slid Peta to a stop and jumped from the saddle as the messengers and driver had climbed down. Adkin quickly went to the woman, and helped her up. She had a cut over her left eye, and he grabbed her handkerchief and pressed it against the cut and tole her to keep pressure on it.

He heard a gurgling sound behind him on the ground. It was Harrison, trying to say something and squirming a little on his back, trying to stem the pink blood spewing from his left side. The bullet had torn open his lung and the oxygen bubbles in his blood turned it bright pink.

Adkin knelt down next to him.

"Who was that who rode away, Hairless?" Adkin asked.

Harrison gurgled he didn't know.

"Help me," Harrison eked out.

"For your information 'Hairless,' I was the one you left for dead after you savaged and butchered my Kiowa wife on the Cimarron last Thanksgiving eve," Adkin said. "Now who got away?"

He gurgled again, saying he didn't see who got away.

Adkin walked a few steps over and grabbed the man wearing the black hat and chaps. He drug him by the back of his shirt over to Harrison.

"Is this Marcus Hall?"

Harrison nodded yes.

Adkin did the same with the man he shot off Diablo, who had trotted up the ravine with the other horse. The man had been hit in front of his left shoulder and exited under his right arm. He was dead before he hit the ground.

"Who is this?" Adkin asked. "You may as well tell me, you're dying 'Hairless.'"

He sputtered something, and Adkin knelt down closer.

"Billy..., it's 'Billy Boy,'" Harrison said, as his eyes froze staring into the sky, and his head rolled over. He was dead.

The passengers were mumbling, and the man who's wife had been hit thanked Adkin.

"You sure came along at the right time, Mister Maxwell," he said rubbing his head and holding an arm around his wife. "I'm sure glad that Harrison feller had misfires with his pistol."

The thanks were coming from everybody.

"Please, listen folks," Adkin said raising his arm and in his usual accent. "My name is actually Adkin Maxwell Yates, and I have been hunting these men after they killed my wife and left me for dead. They also burned our home down trying to destroy everything.

"I'm asking your help in getting these men to Socorro and telling the Sheriff there what happened,' Adkin said, smiling. "Can I count on you to just tell the truth?"

They all assured him he could.

Adkin knelt next to Hall and removed the bracelet Ten Bears had given him, telling the passengers he would explain later.

"Now, I need to find my horse, Diablo," he said. "They stole him, too, after the attack on us."

•••

He rode up into the ravine while the men on the stage dragged the three thieves up to the stage. They put the strongbox back in the boot and gathered up the two horses that stayed nearby.

They were pushing the bodies up over the saddles and tying them down when Adkin came out of the ravine with three horses, one being the big black steed.

"They had Harrison's getaway horse tied up back in the ravine," And I found my Diablo," Adkin said.

He got off Peta and had him tethered with all the other horses off the back of the coach.

"You sure you don't want to ride in here, Mister ... Mister Yates?" One of he passengers asked.

"I will a little later, it's just that I haven't had my Diablo in quite awhile."

They headed for Socorro, which they should reach by dark. Adkin was happy to be sitting on Diablo again. He kept rubbing the animal's neck and talking to him while he stroked his mane.

Adkin sensed Diablo was happy as well. When Adkin found him up the ravine with the other horses, Diablo could hardly stop neighing, snapping his head up and down and pawing the ground. He came right to Adkin.

Adkin was happy, too. He had also taken his revenge – legally – against four of the five he was hunting. Only Lew "Brushy" Bush was remaining.

"I will find you Lew Bush – and see to it you go to hell," he whispered to himself.

The stage, Adkin and Diablo rode north for a couple of hours when the stage driver stopped at a well-known watering hole along the Rio Grande River. It was a scenic sight with the Magdalena Mountains to their west.

After talking with the passengers about the attempted stage robbery, Adkin decided to tie Diablo off on a tether with the other horses and ride in the coach. The two store owners had been taking turns riding messenger on the driver's bench.

Adkin decided it was worthwhile to answer as many questions as possible to ensure he had these witnesses on his side in the upcoming inquiry about the shootout.

He explained how he determined Harrison had been the one attacking him and his wife. He then told them of taking the bullets out of his gun during the night.

"I was wondering how he could have had three or four misfires," the married man said. "He was aiming at me and my wife after your first shot."

"That's the kind of coward he was," Adkin said. "He didn't have any problem beating down women, ravaging them and killing them."

The woman swooned and nearly feinted at hearing that. Adkin felt he had to tell them more details than he wanted, but it would be useful. He explained how he retrieved Tóngúl and killed Alfonso "Dog" Sill in Las Cruces.

"We heard some talk of that, but we didn't know that was you," one of the men said. "Where you from?"

Adkin explained his dreams of coming to America and travelling the Santa Fe Trail, and how he ended up with Barlow and Sanderson Stagecoach Company.

"We've travelled on those stages before," the married man said. "Do you work out of Denver?"

He told them he had resigned in order to find the killers of his wife, and that he had been stationed out of Las Animas City.

After saying the name – Las Animas City – Adkin got a pang of homesickness. He thought maybe he should stop there and visit with his friends, but it hit him that he had one more job to do.

Kill Lew Bush.

•••

Once in Socorro, they handed over the bodies of Harrison, Sill and Jones to the Sheriff and gave their versions of the attempted robbery. The Sheriff checked the dead over, and proclaimed all their belongings and animals would be taken by the county and sold to pay their fines and burials.

The news about Adkin's heroics went through the town like wildfire. Adkin knew if Bush was near, he would hear the rumors and try to disappear. Then, too, Bush was heading north and Adkin thought he may go hundreds of miles before stopping.

The Sheriff didn't press any charges or set a hearing with the magistrate. He said six witnesses who had proved the case completely, and it was closed. The banker and his men were glad to get their silver and thanked Adkin immensely for his actions.

Adkin telegraphed Jose and told him the news – as did the station manger in Socorro and his driver – and Jose took him back as a messenger to come to Santa Fe.

Within three days of the robbery shootout, Adkin and his horses were in Santa Fe. He and Jose celebrated.

"You know Adkin, You have avenged Matty's death," Jose said. "I realize, but with only one remaining, I think your mission is actually complete.

"Maybe now you go see sus amigos in Las Animas Cuidad. They miss you very much," he added.

"I think maybe you are correct, Jose," Adkin said, feeling good from about six brandys and a couple of snorts of tequila.

Jose had never seen Adkin drink so much, ever. Adkin had the reputation of hardly ever drinking. He would, but only a few. Jose was seeing a drunk Adkin Yates. He helped Adkin stumble to his room and pulled off his boots before tugging the blankets over him.

"Buenas noche, mi amigo," Jose said as he closed the door.

•••

Adkin awoke with a slight headache – but it wasn't severe. He was hungry though and ran into Jose in the dining hall.

"I remember what you said, Jose, about going to Las Animas," Adkin began. "That's exactly what I'm going to do. It would be a good home to the horses. Do you know how valuable these horses are?

"Diablo was a gift from Black Horse, Satanta's Medicine Man," he continued. "Tóngúl was born to a Cheyenne Chief's daughter; the paint, Peta, was a gift from Quanah, the Comanche War Chief who saved my life."

"Muy valuable horse flesh, Señor," Jose conceded. "Las Animas will be good home for them."

"You are correct, mi amigo," Adkin said. "That's my next stop. I will telegraph Tyler Ryan before I leave this morning."

Adkin did send a telegraph to Ryan, but he failed to mention he had killed four of the five he suspected of butchering Matty. He only said he expected to be arriving Las Animas City in about 8 to 10 days.

Adkin made sure his supplies were ample at the Aguirre store and then bid farewell to Jose.

"Send my respects to Conrado and Pedro," he said as he rode out on Diablo with a string of horses behind him.

Shortly after Adkin rode out of Santa Fe, Jose telegraphed nearly all the stage stations to Pueblo – and to Las Animas – about the rumors spreading throughout New Mexico.

The vengeful pistolero Adkin Yates, an Englishman with a quick draw, had killed four known thieves and murderers in less than two weeks; one in Las Cruces and three outside Socorro.

It was this kind of word-of-mouth, rumor mongering that was fodder for dime-store novels. In fact, by the time Adkin reached La Junta, a newspaper journalist from Denver was looking for him. Ablo said the writer was wanting to interview him about the gang he killed single-handedly in southern New Mexico.

"He said you killed a dozen stage robbers in a week," Ablo said to Adkin. "He wants to write a book about you. Someone told him you were my friend, and he comes by every day for five days wanting to know if you come here."

"Just tell him it's all a lie and not true," Adkin said. "Tell him you heard I got killed in Raton Pass – fell off a cliff. That will stall him."

Adkin took off east feeling uneasy about all these rumors. He knew his friends would have heard in Las Animas. He would have to tell them the truth, and that he had one more murderer to kill. It wouldn't be easy to listen to their arguments about dropping this hunt for Bush, but he had to do it.

It was a promise he made to Matty.

•••

Adkin had butterflies in his stomach. It reminded him of the feeling he had right before charging into the camp of Comancheros with the Army and Uribe by his side. There it was, right across the meadow about a mile. The headquarters for Barlow and Sanderson, as well as YR&R Freight Company. It looked inviting, but Adkin's feelings were swirling like a Plains cyclone.

It was January 30, 1874.

He kicked Diablo and started toward the gate. He didn't make it to the gate before someone spotted him and started shooting into the air and screaming, "Adkin's here!"

As he neared the main office, he could see Ryan, Uribe, Ray Dee, Campbell and Big Tom all walking out on the porch. Some tears rolled out of Adkin's eyes at seeing his other family.

All of them were down the steps as Adkin dismounted. They all took turns embracing him, and nearly every man had tears streaking their weather-worn faces.

Only words like, "Welcome home" and "We missed you," were said as he was herded into the office.

"Brandy?" Ryan asked Adkin as he stood there wiping his eyes.

"Of course, old friend, fill it to the top," Adkin answered.

They all filled goblets of something and Ryan toasted Adkin.

"Here's to our dear friend, and welcome home," he said, raising his glass. The men shouted, "Here, Here."

Ryan explained Dusty and Fransisco were out on the trail fixing stagecoaches.

"We miss your talents with an anvil," Ryan said smiling.

Adkin remembered and told them there was a good Yates Anvil at the old remains of the Cimarron House if anyone goes near there and wants it.

About that time, Kanaka came down the stairs. She looked pregnant. He glanced back to Ryan with his mouth open.

"Yes, we're going to have a baby this summer," Ryan said. "Look who's home, Kanaka."

She gave Adkin a hug and welcomed him home. Having the smell of a woman hugging him almost made him cry.

"How could these wounds be so close to the surface that the feel and smell of a woman crushes me?" he asked himself.

"Congratulations, Kanaka," he said as he held his hat in his hand.

She made her greetings and then excused herself.

"When is the baby due?" Adkin asked Ryan. "You didn't say anything in Dodge City."

"It's due in June, and you never asked about Kanaka in Dodge City," Ryan answered with a bit of disappointment in his voice.

"I'm sorry, Tyler," Adkin said, knowing that was not enough. He had been Ryan's best man but once he lost Matty, it appears to the others he didn't value their relationships anymore.

"If I could use your smitty shop to re-shoe Diablo, I'll be on my way in a few days," Adkin said. "Sure, you can stay in your house in the yard," Ryan said coldly. "It hasn't been touched."

"Come on Boss, I'll help you get situated," Uribe said happily.

"One other favor," Adkin halted. "Would you take care of Tóngúl and Peta for me?"

"Peta was a gift from Quanah, wasn't he?" Ryan asked. "He's the one who found you and brought you to Fort Dodge, yes?"

"Yes he was, and I didn't want to not tell you, it's just I didn't want the Army going after him right at the moment."

"That's what we figured," Ryan said. "We'll be glad to keep the horses for you."

Uribe was chattering away while walking to the little house that belonged to Adkin and Matty. The crew had built it for Matty, after moving most of it from the Fort Lyon headquarters. As Adkin got near, he stopped and just stared at it.

"I can't stay there, Uribe," Adkin said. "Too many memories. May I stay in the barracks?"

"Si, Señor, I understand."

That evening, Adkin decided to tell the crew the details of what happened after he got to Santa Fe and how Jose helped him by allowing him to ride as a stage messenger.

He explained he believed it was fate he ran into Alfonso "Dog" Sill in a Las Cruces saloon. And then, to get solid information about "Dog" and "Marky's" plans to rob a stage was like a gift.

When he got to the part about sneaking Harrison's gun out and emptying the cylinder, Uribe shouted, "Caramba." Adkin made sure he stressed that move did save the passengers lives. He didn't want the crew to think he was endangering innocent people needlessly.

Adkin asked about everybody, feeling the pain he caused Ryan when his selfishness blinded him from asking about Ryan's wife in Dodge City.

Ryan then told him about the news of Satanta.

"The Army finally agreed to parole Satanta and Big Tree because of the good behavior of the Kiowa bands," Ryan said. "Satanta and Big Tree were returned to their people in October while you were at the Cimarron House, though you apparently didn't get the word.

"They're living down in the Wichita Mountains," he added, knowing mentioning the place he and Matty were married would stir memories.

But Ryan was close to telling his best friend that this vengeance and hatred was not the way to live, whether Adkin liked it or not.

"How long are you going to be chasing this one man down?" Ryan blurted out.

"I'm not sure," Adkin said. "I hope it's not long, but I have to get this out of my blood. I realize it's kind of crazy, but I can't help it. I feel like if I don't get rid of it, it will kill me."

"Or, maybe the hate will kill you first – before you find this man," Ryan said.

Adkin looked around the room, nobody said a word. Finally, Uribe spoke up.

"Would you allow me to ride with you, Boss?" he asked. "We've been through many fights and close calls, Señor. I am begging to help."

Adkin was near tears thinking about everything the two of them had been through – all the things all of them had encountered. He looked to Ryan, who nodded his approval for Uribe going with him.

"Let me sleep on it, okay, Uribe," Adkin said. "If you men don't mind, I'm going to get some sleep."

•••

The next morning, Adkin was first to the blacksmith shop and had the coals burning making coke when Uribe walked in.

"Can I help you with that beautiful stallion, Boss?" he asked, ignoring his request to ride with Adkin. "I have missed Diablo – and Tóngúl, our race horse champion."

"Sure, let's get him over here and start filing those hooves clean."

By the time they finished shoeing Diablo, Adkin leaned back against the anvil and crossed his arms.

"Uribe, my old friend. You sure you want to ride with me to kill this man, Lew Bush?" Adkin asked. "It may require long trips in the saddle, little rest or water or food – through snow and ice and cold?"

"No problem, Boss," Uribe said with that huge set of white teeth flashing through that black, bushy mustache. "We've done that already, no problema con mio. Plus, that man, he killed my Matty, too.

"One request, Boss," Uribe said, looking a little uneasy. "Would it be okay with you if I rode Tóngúl on this hunt? Con su permiso?"

"If you want, it's fine with me, but we should get her over here and check her shoes, too," Adkin said, smiling.

Adkin then reached out and shook Uribe's hand.

"Bueno amigo, bueno," Adkin said. "We ride mañana."

Adkin discussed his plans with the crew. He knew they didn't approve, but he felt obligated to be more open with them.

"We're heading to the Wichita Mountains first," Adkin said. "I want to see Chief Satanta. I need to tell him about Matty, and he may be able to help me."

"Just watch out for Uribe, please," Ryan said with a cynical smile. "I know you're suicidal, but don't get him killed – please?"

"He will more than likely keep me from being shot," Adkin said.

Uribe walked in the office with Ray Dee, and when Adkin started talking about supplies for travel, he was reminded about the railroads and that supplies could be found about every place along the rails and the Santa Fe Trail now.

"We will be better off to travel to Dodge City, down to Fort Supply and then on to Fort Sill," Uribe said.

"Good trails and trading posts all over," Ray Dee added.

Adkin agreed, acknowledging times had changed the country.

They agreed to take only one pack horse with a small tent for protection against winter storms if they got caught out on the trail.

"I have a pack mule that is stronger and quicker than most all horses," Uribe bragged. "He ees muy grande, can carry anything."

•••

After a short and tense goodbye to the crew, Adkin and Uribe took off for the railhead at Granada. Then the trip to Dodge City was so quick they could hardly believe it. Almost 200 miles in three days. Arriving February 4, 1874, Adkin immediately headed to the Sheriff's Office to see Bassett.

"Charlie is over at the Long Branch," a man sitting on the porch said. "It's three blocks that way."

They rode down to the saloon and tied off their horses. Once inside, they stopped to look around the place. It was shortly after noon, and the saloon was full.

"Yates, over here," a voice shouted above he murmur. It was Bassett.

When they got to the table, Bassett embraced them both.

"Haven't seen you in a piece," Bassett said to Uribe. "Y'all sit down and have a drink."

Charlie introduced the others at the table, who still had some lunch plates sitting about.

"This here is my partner in the saloon here, the Long Branch, Alfred J. Peacock," Bassett said. "This is Ed Jones and Mister J. Wright Mooar, Josiah, and his brother, John Mooar – all successful local businessmen.

"Ed here is getting into the freighting business, Yates. Y'all might be able to do some work together," Bassett said. "Yates is a partner in YR&R Freight Company, Ed."

"Oh yeah, I've heard of you and know your wagons well. I used a few not long ago to help me move some equipment to Fort Supply," Jones said.

Jones was a man of small stature with slight shoulders but a large head. He wore a big mustache and had a large dark scar on his face.

"And these brothers have a dandy buffalo hunting business," Bassett said. "J. Wright was among those who supplied Charlie Rath with his first buffalo hides shipped to England for tanning.

"Our father immigrated here from England in the 1840s," John said. "We had some connections in London to see how it would go."

Bassett interjected, "When J. Wright sent 57 buffalo hides to John, who was living in New York City in early '72, John sold the hides to a tanning firm that judged them of sufficient quality to order 2,000 more."

"Now John has moved here last year, and they're setting up a hunting camp in the Texas Panhandle on the Llano Estacado," Bassett added, raising his eyebrows in a questioning manner.

"The Llano Estacado can be a very dangerous place at times," Adkin said, looking to Uribe. "Uribe and I were with Rath and Charley Goodnight, and few others when the Comanches ran us out of and off the Llano Estacado."

"We must talk more later about England," Adkin continued. "I, myself, came to this country from England in the summer of 1865."

Bassett spoke up, "J. Wright is working with Ed here to haul in goods and supplies to build stores and a stockade. Rath is planning on building a store there at Adobe Walls, and soon."

"That's a surprise. Rath was with us when we were attacked by comanches just east of old Adobe Walls," Adkin said. "Anyway, I'm sure YR&R can help you with wagons and men if you need them Mister Jones."

"What I'm wondering Sheriff is have you any word about Lew Bush?" Adkin asked Bassett.

"No, is he supposed to be in this area?" Bassett asked. "I've already heard about your incidents in New Mexico."

"I only know last I saw him he was headed north toward Santa Fe," Adkin said. "Just curious if you have heard anything about him."

"No, but I wouldn't be surprised if he was back in these parts – or down in the Texas Panhandle," Bassett said. "This buffalo hunting is making people a lot of money. Everybody is getting in on it."

"There's hunters setting up camps all around Adobe Walls preparing for the buffalo migration north from Mexico and West Texas," Bassett added.

"We've heard Satanta was released from prison and is living back in the Wichita Mountains," Adkin said. "Have you heard anything different?"

"No, that's what the word is – that he's back with his band in the Wichita Mountains," Bassett said.

"Great, I need to speak with him," Adkin said. "Uribe and I should be on our way."

"Before you go. I hear your house hasn't sold, yet," Bassett said. "Have you seen Reighard?"

"No, but I'm not concerned with the house right now," Adkin said. "Tell George I'll see him when I return to Dodge City – hopefully soon."

After the farewell pleasantries, Adkin and Uribe headed south on the Military Road to Fort Supply.

•••

Adkin and Uribe had few problems on the Military Road. They encountered the Army which had built an earthen redoubt on Bear Creek, about 30 miles south of Dodge City. They were warned word was Indian tribes were getting restless in the reservations and heading out onto the Llano Estacado – and raiding any settlers they could find along the way.

A day later, they came across the Army's Cimarron Redoubt, with walls built of flour bags full of sand and dirt, similar to some they had seen at Bear Creek. The quarters and barracks were of sod.

Again, there were stirrings that Indians were wanting to fight and raid. Several soldiers claimed their post was known as Deep Hole and was 3 miles below the Oklahoma line and within the Reservations that were established at the Medicine Lodge Creek Peace Treaty.

Adkin laughed to himself, knowing the government wasn't going to keep to the treaty. There were too many Whites now wanting to hunt buffalo in the Texas Panhandle, and if not enough food is delivered to the reservations, Indians were going hunting in the Panhandle, as they had done for centuries.

Within seven days, they had made it to Fort Supply, which was quite a sight since it had grown so much. There must have been 500 tipis around the fort with markings of Kiowa, Comanche, Cheyenne and Arapahoe, that Adkin could make out.

"Looks very peaceful here, Boss," Uribe said as they rode up to the gate. "Mucho Indians living quietly, si?"

"Until they run out of food," Adkin quipped with a dour look on his face.

They discovered even Fort Supply had been attacked several times recently. Adkin made his customary inquiries about Lew Bush, but nobody seemed to have heard of him. All they heard was warnings about restless Indians.

Adkin and Uribe decided to get a few supplies, like Uribe's tobacco, and get back on the trail. Uribe agreed it was probably safer to be out alone and hidden on the trail.

They went through the Washita Battle area, remembering the bodies of dead horses and the stench of death at every step when they went through there in '68 – the year he and Matty were married by Black Horse.

Adkin had too take deep breaths at the thought. God he missed Matty, and why did God allow this to happen? Why was he being punished so? They were only together five years, yet it seemed to be his entire life. She had been his life.

They rode on in silence. Uribe believed the area was haunted by the spirits of the dead. He wanted to get through the area as fast as possible.

•••

On February 18, Adkin and Uribe stopped briefly on a hill crest where they could see the beginnings of he Wichita Mountains.

"We should be in Satanta's camp before dark," Adkin said, as he kicked Diablo and started riding down the low valley.

Adkin knew the little ravine to enter and soon enough, a voice asked who was riding in. Adkin yelled his name and said he wants to speak with his friend Chief Satanta.

Two riders came down from the cliff and greeted them and led them to Satanta's lodge. Many Indians didn't know Adkin from his dress, and he could see Uribe was getting nervous.

They had slid out of their saddles just as the tipi flaps opened and there stepped out Satanta. He looked thinner and sad to Adkin.

"Hachó Chief Satanta, it is I, Páhy-Chí, I have come to tell you about Mah-ah-Tay," Adkin said as he removed his bowler and stuck it on his saddle horn.

They greeted each other holding out their arms and grasping them in an embrace.

"Come, Adkin Yates, come into my lodge," Satanta said, "Hachó Uribe, come."

Once inside, Satanta insisted they smoke to honor the spirits first. Adkin was dreading the story he had for Satanta, but Uribe loved smoking the pipe. Adkin decided to first ask about Satanta's troubles.

"I am pleased you are back with your people," Adkin said.

"It is good to be with my people, but it is not the same," Satanta said looking weary. "I am tired of the troubles Sheridan has brought upon me and Big Tree. They made untrue stories about us and put us in prisons, where one seldom got to stand in the sunlight, feel the clean air and listen to the songs of the birds.

"Many Chiefs are getting angry that no food or guns have been given to us to hunt, and they promised," Satanta said. "I fear this will be a bad winter, and if there is no food or guns and bullets, many will leave here and go find food and guns.

"I am an old man, Yates, and if I can no longer roam the prairies like my fathers before me, I shall die soon," he added. "What is this news about Mah-ah-Tay?"

"Oh great Chief Satanta, it breaks my heart to tell you ... she is dead," Adkin said, as tears welled up in his eyes. "We were attacked by White outlaws at our Cimarron House, and they butchered her and left me for dead – burned down our lodge."

Adkin was nearly crying, the tears rolling steadily down his cheeks and into his beard.

"I have avenged her death by killing four of the men, but I seek one more before I can try to live without her."

Uribe, now close to tears himself, noticed a tear slide down Satanta's cheek as he spoke up.

"My dear fiend, It saddens me deeply that Mah-ah-Tay is gone," Satanta said. "Like her father, I loved her very much – just as she were my own. I held her up to the spirits the night she came into this world not far from here."

An Englishman's Adventures on the Santa Fe Trail (1865-1889)

He bowed his head and said nothing more for several minutes. All the men were wiping away tears and then, Satanta spoke.

"Who is this man you seek?" he asked, as he finally looked up.

"His name in Lew Bush, sometimes called "Brushy" Bush," Adkin said. "He had a gang of southern Rebels – Alfonso Sill, Billy ..."

Satanta stopped him with a hand raised.

"Wait, I want to get my people in here," he said.

He rose and went out the flap, within a few minutes, he came back in with three warriors. He asked Adkin to go through the names, as these warriors were very good with English, and he wanted them to spread word through the tribe to see if anyone has heard of these men or Lew Bush.

Adkin went through the names of those dead and who had ridden with Bush. Satanta made him go over the names again so the warriors could repeat them correctly and remember them. They then headed out of the tipi.

Satanta insisted they spend a night or two so his people could check with everyone for news. He had several squaws set up a small lodge beside his and fill it with furs and a small fire pit. Within an hour, they were eating in Satanta's lodge with four of his Chiefs, including Big Tree and Lone wolf, who seemed very angry at the soldiers.

Satanta translated for the Chiefs, and they were worried about supplies that had not come from the soldiers. The women and children were running out of food.

"I will not fight or raid anymore, as I have been beat down like the old wolf who has no more teeth, but many of my Chiefs want to go find supplies where ever they are," Satanta said. "That means raiding, fighting and killing."

Lone Wolf interrupted, "We will join the Quahadis if we need to and kill soldiers to get their food, their bullets and their horses."

"Is Chief Quanah among the Quahadis you speak of?" Adkin asked.

"Yes, Quanah and many Cheyenne are starving and have no food – or no more buffalo to hunt – even if they had more bullets," Lone Wolf said, through Satanta's translation.

Adkin looked to Uribe, both of them knowing if Quanah was getting angry and started working with other tribes, troubles would be deadly. Lone Wolf seemed ready to follow anybody that wanted to leave the reservation and attack soldiers – or anyone in their way. He was looking for trouble.

Adkin and Uribe stayed with the Kiowa for two nights. Late on the second night, a band of about 50 men, warriors all, rode into the camp. They had been staying at Fort Sill but had heard that many tribes on the reservation were getting restless because of the hard winter and not enough food from the forts.

They had left their families at Fort Sill to see if Satanta and their Kiowa warriors were going to seek revenge and go after the buffalo hunters who had swarmed all over the Texas Panhandle killing their buffalo, according to Satanta.

He, again, told Adkin and the other Chiefs he no longer would speak for the tribe.

"I'm too old and weary to fight anymore," he told Adkin after speaking to the Council of Chiefs who were quickly assembled that night. "I'm not going to fight, but I'm afraid Lone Wolf and some others may go to Texas and fight. It will not be good for the People or for any tribes."

Satanta asked Adkin and Uribe into his lodge.

"I have news for you, several of the warriors who came in said they had heard of this Lew Bush at Fort Sill," he said as they sat down. "They think he works with the Tonkawa scouts, but he also sells whiskey to Indians when the fort commander is not looking.

"Maybe you go speak with Colonel 'Black Jack' Davidson," Satanta said, reaching out and putting his hand on Adkin's shoulder. "I hope if you kill this man, you start to live again, Páhy-Chí.

"I will carry all your sorrow for Mah-ah-Tay if you will live a full life, my friend," he continued. "You should leave early tomorrow. It' is less than a day to ride. Speak to the commander."

With that, Adkin and Uribe stood and gave their honors to Great Kiowa Chief Satanta and went to their tipi to prepare for their early morning ride.

•••

When they arrived at Fort Sill, they noticed hundreds of Indian lodges, each with trails of smoke whisking away into the icy-cold blue sky surrounding he fort's walls. They soon learned Colonel Black Jack was only a nickname, and the Colonel's name was John Davidson.

He got the nickname by becoming commander of the Army's 10th Calvary which included the Buffalo Soldiers, freed blacks who enlisted with the U.S. Army.

They waited about 30 minutes before getting an audience with the Colonel, and he assured Adkin and Uribe, he didn't know any Lew Bush. When Adkin mentioned he may have worked with the fort's scouts, the Colonel told his aide to take them to his head of the Tonkawa Scouts, Lieutenant Richard H. Pratt.

Adkin found Colonel Davidson a fierce looking man with a bushy mustache and a pointed chin beard. His high cheekbones and deep set eyes, made his angular face seem angry. His aide took them to the barracks to meet Lieutenant Pratt.

Pratt immediately knew of Lew Bush.

"Yeah, he claimed he was a scout and knew this area and West Texas as well as anyone," Pratt said. "We never got to find out, as I caught him selling liquor to the Indians, including a few of my Tonks.

"I ran him off about two weeks ago," Pratt continued. "And I didn't bother the Colonel about it, Bush had only been with us but a few weeks. A real con man, in my opinion. I tried to find out who supplied him with whisky, but he said it was from Comancheros who had come out of Texas."

"You look awful familiar to me, Mister Yates," Pratt said. "Have we met?"

"I was about to say the same, Lieutenant," Adkin said. "Have you ever been stationed out of Fort Supply?"

"That's it," Pratt said, laughing. "It was Camp Supply, and we were joined with the Seventh Calvary under Colonel Custer – I was with the 10th Calvary. I, unfortunately, was involved with the Washita campaign.

"Dreadful stuff, that was," he added, shaking his head.

Adkin asked if he knew where Bush was headed, not wanting to test Pratt's memory about Adkin being arrested for hitting a soldier back then.

"Really don't know, but word is every man with a rifle is going into Texas to hunt buffalo on their spring migration," Pratt said. "Wouldn't surprise me if he didn't hook up with some hunters or whisky runners."

Adkin asked what Bush was wearing, and wanted a current description of how he looked. Pratt wanted to know why Adkin was so interested in every detail of Bush. When Adkin told him Bush was one of several men who killed his wife, Pratt eagerly told him everything.

Bush wore a dirty old light gray Rebel officer's hat with the grubby gold braids and the brim turned up right in the middle of the front and a cowboy's duster like Adkin's but it wasn't canvas, but a cotton fabric and was black. He wore black Reb's boots and dark gray wool pants, with a pistol belt with the holster on his right side.

As Adkin and Uribe were thanking Pratt and saying farewell, he said he also remembered Bush rode a gold palomino mare with a black mane, tail and socks.

"She had a strange name that stuck with me," Pratt said. "He called her Dithol. (Die-thawl) Beautiful horse – he probably stole 'er.

"I don't wanna know what you're goin' do to him iffin' you find him, but I'm sure he's got it comin'," Pratt added. "Good luck."

Adkin remembered that beautiful palomino – it was the horse the only stage robber rode away on. And the black coat tails flying up behind him.

After they refreshed a few supplies with the sutler, Uribe asked Adkin what was next?

"It's February 20 and buffalo hunters are setting up camps in the Texas Panhandle," Adkin began. "Maybe we should go back to Dodge City and see if we can't get in with one of the hunting crews we know well – Rath or Bob Wright, you know some of those men.

"I don't think it wise if we take off into Texas on our own, especially if warring Indian bands are leaving the reservations – hungry and angry," Adkin said. "It is probably wiser to travel into Texas with a band of hunters, where arms and ammunition are aplenty."

"Sound good, Boss," Uribe said. "We can be back in Dodge in a couple of weeks – faster if we pick up a couple of saddle horses and ride harder."

They found Pratt who led them to some horse traders outside the fort. Adkin and Uribe selected two saddle horses and paid in gold. They tethered them to a tow line behind Diablo while Uribe led his favorite mule behind he and Tóngúl.

...

When Adkin and Uribe arrived in Dodge City, it was March 3, 1874. They had rode hard, changing horses about every six hours or so. The two hours they spent in Fort Supply provided no further information about Lew Bush, so Adkin had to rely on Lieutenant Pratt's belief Bush may have headed into Texas.

One of the first people Adkin and Uribe ran into was George Reighard, who started stuttering, explaining why Adkin's mansion hadn't sold yet. Adkin assured him he wasn't worried or troubled with it not selling.

He asked who was putting hunting parties together, and Reighard told him Rath was organizing a wagon train with Ed Jones to haul building supplies and enough merchandise to build a general store.

They hurried over to the Rath Mercantile Store, which was next to the railroad freight yard and went inside.

Rath was there and pleased to see Adkin and Uribe.

"Men, you're just in time for another adventure," Rath said.

Adkin interrupted.

"Charley, we're hunting the last of Matty's killers, a man called Lew Bush, and we want to hook up with a buffalo hunting team going into Texas."

"I may be the answer to your dreams, Adkin Yates," Rath said. "Me, A.C. Myers and several others are headed to the upper Canadian River in the area of old Adobe Walls to build another hide yard and build my supply store. I started planning it last month with Bob Wright, but now I have the supplies to make it come true.

"It's not at the original Adobe Walls where we met Sheriff Allen back when, but Myers said it's in that area where he's interested," Rath continued. "We'll see, and you can't believe how many hides we got out of that area last winter. I had them stacked up in heaps out there in the yard waiting for shipment back east.

'There are probably about 400 hunters headed out into that country right now, setting up hunting camps," Rath said. "Then they will bring the hides to us, and we freight 'em back here to the railroad.

"If you're man is out there, he'll be coming to trade soon enough once the buffalo get moving," he added with a big smile that Adkin knew well – the smile when Charley was thinking about making money.

Rath told them Weldon Campbell was working with Ed Jones to put together the supply train, which was scheduled to depart Dodge City in a few days.

"Hey Charley, could you keep it quiet about what Uribe and I are actually doing – other than hunting buffalo," Adkin said. "I don't want everybody talking about me gunning for Lew Bush. It might scare him off if he heard about us."

Charley smiled and said he understood. Then Adkin asked if he and Uribe could tag along.

"Hell yes," Rath said. "You two could make up to $100 a day shooting buffalo – I know you're both good shots. I'll stake you with supplies, and you pay me back when you bring in the hides."

Uribe flashed a huge grin to Adkin, who said, "We'll see, but we definitely want to go with you.

"Now where can we find Campbell or Jones?" Adkin asked.

They were given directions down Front Street to stables and a blacksmith's shop where Campbell had been working on some wagons.

Sure enough, Weldon Campbell was there hammering a piece he was ironing for a wagon axle.

"Hey, you're pretty good at that," Adkin said. "Where did you learn that?"

Campbell looked up to see Adkin and Uribe standing there smiling. They all embraced and Campbell finally said, "Dusty and Fransisco taught me that, and they said they learned it from you."

They were laughing when Ed Jones rode up in another freight wagon with a bench and four mules tethered to the back.

"Yates, Uribe, good to see y'all," Jones said. "Good ol' YR&R Freight is helping us settle the Panhandle. We're taking another supply train down to the new Adobe Walls – probably tomorrow or the next day.

"I hope you plan on going with us," he added.

"Indeed, Mister Jones, we do," Adkin said.

"Please call me Ed," Jones said, laughing.

"We're going to finish building a saloon down there – James Hanrahan is building it, mainly of sod – and Myers has built a general store and hide yard, and I'm going to be paid for hauling cottonwood logs from the river bottom to build the stockade," Jones said as he climbed down and shook hands. "Myers and

Rath hired me to haul 30 wagons of building supplies and store products to Rath's supply store and the saloon.

"Do you know Tom O'Keefe? He's building a smitty's shop there, too," Jones continued, barely taking a breath.

"With this load, I figure more than $70,000 worth of goods is being hauled down there," he continued. "Imagine that, and it's, basically, unsettled and as isolated as you can get."

Adkin winked at Uribe who between them knew all too well about Adobe Walls and the isolation of the upper Canadian River – or desolation was more apt.

"But the buffalo hunters bring their hides there and buy supplies – I have three wagons that will be completely filled with just rifles and ammunition – three."

"I've made good money just hauling supplies down and bringing back loads of hides," Jones added.

"Well, we plan on getting in on the action," Adkin said, not bringing up his hunt for Lew Bush. Jones and a few others knew about Bush, but they hadn't mentioned him since their meeting in the Long Branch Saloon.

"Great," Jones said.

"I'm going down, too," Campbell said. "At least for as long as Ed stays down there. I'll help him get the hides back. My brother is down here, too. James Campbell, he's a buffalo hunter who's been living out of Hays for a couple of years.

"In fact, Myers is offering all hunters a good wage for hauling freight down there to build a camp and then sell him hides," Weldon continued. "James has hooked up with a couple of friends, hunters he knows – Billy Dixon and a man they call "Frenchy."

"I know a Billy Dixon, was a freighter back on the Military Road when it first opened up to Camp Supply," Adkin said.

"That's him," Weldon said. "Heck, even Bat Masterson is going down, too."

•••

The supply train for the new Adobe Walls departed Dodge City March 5, with an expected arrival at its destination by March 19 at the latest. When everyone was assembling, that's when Adkin saw Dixon.

"Hey, you old teamsters, what's with this buffalo hunting?" Adkin yelled as he rode up to Billy.

'Adkin, how in the world are you," Dixon asked. "Long time."

"Yes, but I've been bitten by the buffalo money, too," Adkin said, feeling a little guilty about the white lie. "We'll catch up tonight at camp, okay?"

"You got it Adkin," Dixon said smiling. "Looking forward to it."

Adkin also waved and spoke to Bat, telling him they would talk later, too.

Jones and Campbell led out the train of 30 wagons with extra mules, horses and some cattle. Myers and most of the others were riding horseback. Rath said because of the dangers of hunting in Indian territory, every man was told to find the best saddle horse they could afford.

"Just in case," Rath had said.

Adkin wasn't worried. He had Diablo, and Uribe had Tóngúl.

Adkin found out the train carried numerous cases of new "Big 50s" Sharps rifles.

Rath had told Adkin and Uribe the "Big 50s" had proven last winter to be the buffalo hunters' most trusted and accurate buffalo gun for them. The .50 caliber 600-grain bullet powered by 125 grains of powder could knock down a 2,000 pound buffalo easily at 1,000 yards.

Rath said "Dirty Face" Jones had hunted down there last winter and shot 107 buffalo by himself – before breakfast – with a Sharps "Big 50."

Rath also explained how Jones got the black splotch on his face. Adkin had assumed it was a birth mark.

"Oh no, he was in a fight with a Indian when the Injun fired off a gun so close to his face, he suffered a severe powder burn – that powder is still under his skin," Rath said. "Many still call him '"Dirty Face"' Jones, but he's one tough son-of-a-bitch."

Adkin was feeling better and better about the bunch of men he and Uribe had hooked up with. Toughs and seasoned Indian fighters all. He knew Rath, Myers, the Mooar brothers, Jones and Campbell could all handle themselves.

In Adkin's mind, they would need it trying to establish a large hunting supply camp at the edge of the Llano Estacado – the secreted escape spot for the Great Plains Indians for decades, if not centuries.

Adkin didn't think it a solid plan for the long run, but he was more interested in finding Bush. He knew if Bush was greedy enough, he may try this buffalo hunting, and as Rath said, "All those hunters need supplies – especially ammunition."

Rath had told him quietly that more than a wagon-and-a-half load was nothing but ammunition. He said he and the gunsmith, Fred Zimmermann, had become partners in an arms deal.

Rath was grinning that grin when he said it, too. Adkin couldn't help but laugh at Rath and slap him on the back.

It wasn't until they were about a day out when Adkin learned there was a woman in the supply train. When he asked Rath, Charley said, "Oh, yeah, it's the wife of cook William Olds. Missus Olds is going to help him. I'm going to build a cafe – to cook meals for the hunters."

Adkin and Uribe just shook their heads in disbelief.

•••

After the supply train crossed Mulberry Creek just out of Dodge City, it veered southwest toward Meade County and Crooked Creek. It was uncomfortable for Adkin when they crossed Crooked Creek and kept southwest to cross the

Cimarron River. They were passing within 20 miles of their burned out Cimarron House and Matty's grave.

Passing the Cimarron was noted as the "Deadline," where Indians didn't allow Whites to enter their territory in the Texas Panhandle – especially to kill their buffalo.

That first night, everyone got reacquainted or introduced to those they had yet to meet.

"I see you wear that curly black hair down onto your shoulders now, Billy," Adkin said in a teasing voice. "Looks mighty tempting to me – if I was a collector of scalps."

Everyone nearby laughed, even though about half had the same lengthy hair. Must be something about it being a "Buffalo Hunter," Adkin was thinking.

Billy told Adkin and Uribe he had been trapping and hunting since last seeing them at Camp Supply.

"We were trapping out of Fort Hays area but kept working south following the furs," Dixon said. "Then the buffalo hide market opened up, and we discovered we could make a lot more money with buffalo hides and tongues.

"But, the buffalo are getting very rare around the Arkansas now, so we're all gambling things will be much better down here in the Panhandle," he added.

"And a little more dangerous, eh?" Adkin asked laughing.

Many in the caravan were on edge during the trip into the Panhandle, especially once they got to the Canadian River Valley and started following it upstream. Everyone seemed to be watching the valley ridges looking for Indians.

After about four hours travelling along the Canadian River, Adkin and Uribe recognized the place they all fled up the valley wall to escape attacking Comanches. They both nodded, knowing they killed a few of those Indians just over the top while the Whites were hiding behind rock mounds.

Within a couple of more hours, they sighted an area where West Adobe Walls Creek flowed into the Canadian. It was a wide open place right down to the river bank which was a clear swift stream at its mouth. They later discovered it was about a mile downstream of the old Adobe Walls ruins.

They were instinctively drawn to this beautiful spot as many had been during the years. They felt immense relief, as they had not been attacked. It was March 18, and nearly two weeks on the trail.

Rath had introduced Adkin and Uribe to several of the men in the wagon train, including John Wesley, Jim and Bob Cator and Jim Lane. J. Wright Mooar was there, too. Adkin had carefully looked around in the first few days of travel, but he didn't see anyone who fit the description by Lieutenant Pratt of Lew Bush.

Adkin only spotted Missus Olds once. It was apparent Mister Olds kept her well hidden.

Adkin felt sure if Bush had joined up with a buffalo hunting group, they would eventually come to this new settlement – it would make a perfect place for outlaws, skinners, freighters, gamblers and alcoholics.

They settled in helping Rath and the businessmen start and finish construction of the stores, the saloon and the stockade. It was strange seeing so much industry in the middle of nowhere.

Adkin was more relieved when he saw how the buildings were being constructed. They had cottonwood log ridgepoles and corner stands with sod walls about 2-feet thick and mainly sod roofs. A few wooden window shutters, which were brought in by Jones were of very thick wood with gun slots – horizontal and vertical – cut in them. Other windows were just small openings through the thick adobe walls.

Rath's mercantile store was going to be one long sod room with dividers where in the back area about a dozen men could sleep and there were three water barrels immediately set out, which were filled by "mandatory volunteers" of whomever had the privilege to sleep under roof, according to Rath. He immediately told Adkin and Uribe they could place their belongings in that area.

Rath said it was apparent his place may not be completed until April, as he was already planning another supply train from Dodge City with Ed Jones.

The stores were going to be aligned in a straight line from the river, with Rath's on the south end closest to the river,. The Hanrahan's place was about finished. His front door would face east while Rath's was looking west.

About 500 yards north of Hanrahan's, Myers & Leonard were building their store. A small mess house was on the southwest side of the stockade, where Myers sat on the northeast corner of that. Also, the blacksmith's place was just on the north side of Hanrahan's place – all facing east except for Rath's. The whole area was nice and flat.

Charley's first priority was to complete that mess hall shanty where Mister and Missus Olds could set up a kitchen to provide meals – for a handsome price, naturally.

A few days after arriving, several hunters wanted to go out and set up hunting camps they could utilize later to hunt from: Bat Masterson, Billy Dixon, Tom Nixon and "Prairie Dog," were among them.

One thing Adkin did enjoy, while always trying to keep an eye and an ear out for Lew Bush, was drinking in Hanrahan's Saloon with his friends when not working. Hanrahan was selling whisky before a roof was completed and everyone was still sleeping under the stars.

Bat had explained Sheriff Bassett allowed him "hunting time" of up to two weeks every now and then.

"I can make as much money in a week of hunting than several months as Undersheriff," Bat said laughing.

Adkin had found a rye whisky at Hanrahan's he took a particular liking to. Of course, every man – and even Missus Olds – drank every evening.

Many of the hunters that rolled into Adobe Walls were already selling hides to Myers, Rath, Lee Reynolds, who had an interest in Rath's place, and J. Wright Mooar. What better way to spend any excess money than to drink and gamble – after re-supplying ammunition and the necessary staples?

Rath and the regulars estimated by the 1st of April, there were probably 250 to 300 buffalo hunters in the Texas Panhandle.

After Jones had pulled several huge cottonwood trunks to the settlement for ridgepoles, he, Rath, the Mooars and others were packing up to go back for more supplies.

Adkin and Uribe helped Rath and Hanrahan with some carpentry work, as well as loading some hides and salted buffalo tongues into wagons for a return trip to Dodge City. The hunters had taken to leaving nearly all the meat to rot. The money was in the hides and the tongues.

With the help of Jones and Campbell, the stockade was completed with a few stables and O'Keefe's blacksmith shop was completed. Someone said this was happening faster than Dodge City's boom.

Once the day's work was finished, Uribe would often go take care of the animals, but Adkin went straight to the bar. It was beginning to concern Uribe, but he didn't think it was worth mentioning. After all, he had trusted Adkin's judgement for more than nine years.

By late April, Rath had returned and completed his place. Dixon had been hunting a few weeks and was surprised when he came back to Adobe Walls that Rath's was open for business. Dixon told Adkin about how many buffalo were around – that the big herds would be moving in from the south.

Adkin and Uribe had started going out with a couple of other hunters on day-trips and shooting buffalo when found. They would shoot up 15 to 20, but would have to stop so they could get them skinned and the hides stacked in a wagon. They didn't have a team of skinners.

It wasn't very profitable to hunt like that, but Adkin and Uribe wanted something to break up the monotony. Uribe got back and cleaned up with soap and a water bowl, but Adkin again, hit the bar to drink and laugh with the men. They now were allowed to sleep in Rath's place with a couple of others.

Uribe came to Hanrahan's one evening and walked up next to Adkin. The odor was obvious.

"Hey Boss, there's some fresh water and soap at Rath's," he said chuckling.

Adkin turned and gave him a piercing look. Uribe could tell Adkin had quite a lot of rye whiskey in him. He'd seen that look before in the past six weeks. It was out of character, and Uribe knew it. He decided to keep quiet and made his way to a poker table.

In early May, Rath and a few of his hunters decided to head back to Dodge City again for more supplies and goods. Adkin had wanted to stay longer at Adobe Walls, positive if Bush was in the Panhandle, he would eventually show up at Adobe Walls.

But, Adkin was running out of money and though Rath gave him an open line of credit, Adkin wanted to get more gold or silver for he and Uribe, who he was now responsible for.

"I need to go to Dodge City and get us some money, Uribe," he said. "Do you want to go, or stay here? I plan on turning right around and coming back."

"I'll stay, but por favor, buy me some of that good tobacco – and it's cheaper than the stores here." Uribe said, laughing. "And a couple of bottles of good tequila, si?"

"Si, mi amigo," Adkin said as he turned to go tell Rath he would be travelling back with him and the wagons full of hides. James Campbell decided to stay; Rath had asked him to help keep up the store and cafe. Jones wasn't sure yet how many wagons would be needed on a return trip from Dodge with more goods.

Uribe was just hoping Rath would convince Adkin to clean up and find some clean clothes. Adkin was turning into one of the filthy, smelly buffalo crowd.

"Maybe returning to civilization would set him straight," Uribe thought to himself.

•••

Rumors were swirling in Dodge City that the Indians were getting restless. Several small raids had occurred south of Dodge and down in the Territories, but nobody had been killed yet. Word was Colonel Ranald MacKenzie and his Fourth Calvary was back in the northern parts of Texas. He had been ordered to south Texas the winter before, but was back now.

Adkin was informed of this when he encountered former Major Kirk, who still had contacts at Fort Dodge.

Kirk said Sheridan had given MacKenzie unbound powers to chase down Indians and either lead them to their reservations or destroy them.

MacKenzie, by all accounts, had learned how to fight Indians by adapting their strengths, like shooting under a horse's neck at a full run. All his troopers carried the newest Colt revolvers and were trained marksmen, even with the pistols.

MacKenzie had learned the hard way where the escape routes were in the Llano Estacado, having been led in circles by such Chiefs as Quanah in the Palo Duro Canyon back in 1872.

Kirk said that last December, MacKenzie's Lieutenant Hudson had intercepted a Kiowa raiding party that had been killing and taking captives and horses in Mexico at Kickapoo Springs in West Texas.

The troopers ended up killing nine of the 15 warriors and capturing 70 horses. They found out that one of the dead was the son of Kiowa Chief Lone wolf. His name was Tau-ankia and Lone Wolf's nephew was killed as well – Gui-tain.

"Rumor is Lone Wolf is so disturbed his family members have been killed by White soldiers, that he cut off all his hair, burned his tipi, his wagon and all his buffalo hides and – get this – he killed all his horses, too," Kirk said, wide-eyed. "He swore revenge, but a few weeks later, Lieutenant Hudson got killed by a friend who was cleaning his rifle when it went off in their tent."

After that victory, MacKenzie's patrol found a raiding party of Comanches on the Brazos and killed 11 of them" Kirk continued. "Then two weeks after that, another Indian party was caught, and 10 Indians were killed.

"I'm telling you, MacKenzie has the Injuns stirred up and afraid," he added. "You and your friends at Adobe Walls should be vigilant."

Adkin thanked Kirk for the update and then went and told Rath. Rath acknowledged he had heard some of the stories, and he was hoping MacKenzie kept up the good work.

It didn't damper Rath's enthusiasm, at all. He ordered more supplies, and Jones got to work organizing another supply train for the new Adobe Walls.

Adkin was about to transfer money to the quartermaster at Fort Dodge, but Bob Wright ran into him and convinced Adkin he was handling banking services now in Dodge City. He said George Hoover was doing the same.

Adkin trusted Wright and telegraphed the Kansas City bank to transfer $2,000 to Bob, who once he saw the telegram, asked Adkin how much he needed to go back to Adobe Walls?

"How about $500 in gold?" Adkin asked.

"Would you take most of that in silver?" Wright asked.

Adkin agreed.

They walked over to Wright's Store and back to his office. As he counted out the gold and silver for Adkin, placing it in a couple of leather pouches, he mentioned he had a hot water bath in the back if Adkin was interested.

"We also have some wash maids if you want to clean any clothes," Wright said grinning.

Adkin gave him a frown at first, then looked down at his clothes, which were covered with buffalo fat and dried blood. He realized he must smell pretty bad.

"Let me pick out some new clothes out front first, then the women can start on these when I jump in a bath," he said, chuckling. "Sorry about my manners – been too long in Adobe Walls."

"You're not the first," Wright said laughing with Adkin. "I'll get the women heating the bath water now."

A couple of hours later, Adkin was refreshed and standing at the bar in the Long Branch Saloon. He decided he would have one rye and then ride down to

Hoover's Liquor Store and get Uribe's tequila and tobacco. Hoover had the best tobacco around.

After that, he would enjoy the band and entertainment – and rye whisky – at the Long Branch. In the morning, he would check with Rath and Ed Jones to see what supplies were heading back and how soon. Adkin wanted to get to Adobe Walls as soon as possible. He didn't want to miss Lew Bush should he come into the camp needing supplies.

When Adkin found "Dirty Face" Jones the next morning, he discovered Jones wasn't going back to Adobe Walls for maybe a week or 10 days, Ed wasn't sure.

Adkin decided he could ride alone and probably make it back to Adobe Walls in four or five days. It would be hard on Diablo, but he could rest once they got back.

Just as Adkin was making his farewells, Bassett rode up with three other men who had two wagons with four-mule teams and supplies. He introduced them to Adkin.

"This here is Joe Plummer, a wellknown local hunter, and he's teamed up with David Dudley here," Bassett said while still in the saddle. "He's hunted with the Mastersons and with them is another experienced hunter, this is Tommy Wallace.

"They're heading off to the Panhandle to set up a hunting camp. Thought y'all might want to ride together for safety reasons," he added.

"Nice to meet you gentlemen, but I'm planning on travelling fast and hard," Adkin said.

They all agreed they'd like to travel as fast as possible, too. So, Adkin mounted Diablo and said, "Okay, men, let's head out."

They all took off on May 15, 1874, for Adobe Walls.

• • •

On this trip, Plummer showed Adkin a smoother and quicker way to go to Adobe Walls. They headed out the same way – southwest crossing Mulberry Creek – but they then skirted a little further west around Crooked Creek and then hooked straight south to cross the Cimarron at a good location and then to the Beaver River.

Once they hit the Canadian, it was the same trail into Adobe Walls, heads twisting back and forth looking for hostiles.

During the trip, Adkin learned Plummer and his crew were headed on further southeast about 40 miles.

"We're going to a place we hunted last fall on Red Deer Creek," Plummer said. "It dumps into the Salt Fork of the Red River – lots of water spread around sand bars, like a delta of sorts."

"Aren't you concerned about getting too far from Adobe Walls? Adkin asked.

"Oh no, there's hunters already northeast of us on Sweetwater Creek, they found the area last fall, and they've set up a hunters' camp there now, just the last few months," Plummer said. "They call it Hidetown."

"What I hear is the Indians are getting restless and looking for revenge against the Army," Adkin said. "I suspect any White man might be a good target nowadays."

"Yep, that's probably correct," Plummer said as they rode on. They were making camp late, riding into the darkness, but they all seemed to know the trail well. And they only slept about six hours and were then back rolling along.

They made it to Adobe Walls in five days, not bad, Adkin thought, since it was 150 miles and with two wagons. They were greeted like hometown heroes, everyone was glad to see another White man and buffalo hunters – each with a "Big 50."

The arrivals, including Adkin, couldn't believe their eyes seeing nearly every building up and completed.

Adkin saw Uribe immediately and jumped from Diablo. He embraced his good friend. Adkin admitted to Uribe he didn't like travelling without him – even to and fro from Dodge City. Uribe smiled, a little red flushing in that brown, weathered face.

Uribe said he hadn't seen any man of Lew Bush's description, but he did meet a man who spoke up when Uribe asked several of them at the saloon, "Does Lew Bush ever come down here to hunt – he's an old friend of mine?

"This one man, definitely a hunter and skinner, said he thought Bush had hunted down in Hidetown, maybe in late February," Uribe said. "He said he couldn't really remember exactly, because he didn't know Bush well, just met him with some other men in Dodge City."

That confirmed what Pratt had guessed – that Bush might be trying to make money hunting. At least someone saw him in Dodge City, and this spring, everybody in Dodge was figuring ways to make their fortunes with buffalo hides.

Rath greeted and embraced Plummer, Dudley and Wallace, knowing them well, he told Adkin and Uribe. He invited them to squeeze into the guest room if they could fit, but Plummer said they had their tent and would stay outside, where most of the hunters slept each night – if there were more than a dozen or so hunters at the settlement.

The next day, March 21, Plummer and his crew headed southeast to Red Deer Creek and bid farewell.

People were coming in and out of Adobe Walls, some going on to Hidetown or other areas to find buffalo. All were expecting the bigger herds, in the thousands, to be moving into the Panhandle from Mexico very soon. They planned on being rich by August or September.

Many hides had already been brought in and sold to Rath and J. Wright and Reynolds and Myers. Jones and Campbell had carried 27 wagon loads of hides and tongues back on their latest trip. There was no telling how many loads were taken directly to Dodge City by area hunters like Plummer and his crew.

"Dirty Face" Jones made it back the day after the Plummer crew departed. He quickly unloaded supplies and checked with who needed what and quickly made a decision because of a request by Myers to head back alone to Dodge City for an emergency load of, naturally, ammunition.

Adkin asked Rath about Hidetown, and Rath said he had been there and was working on building a mercantile store there as well. He was counting on some of his profits from his business in Adobe Walls to finance his expansion into Hidetown in a few months.

"I even ran into Charles Goodnight down there last fall. He's wanting to start some cattle ranching down there," Rath said. "If we can count on the Army to keep things under control."

"I might have to check Hidetown out next month or so," Adkin said. "Bush might be working that area."

•••

About a week after Plummer and his crew headed out, J. Wright's brother, John Mooar, rode into Adobe Walls with several more hunters, skinners and freighters, including Bat Masterson, who wanted to make some quick money again. Along with them was a man called "Dutch Henry" and James "Bermuda" Carlyle. The Mooars, Rath and Myers and Reynolds were buying all the buffalo hides that came into camp.

About a week later, a team of surveyors with Gunter & Munson, which also had an Army escort of nearly 20 troopers arrived. Adkin never did find out what kind of survey they were doing – he still spent his nights drinking Hanrahan's special blend of whisky Hanrahan called "rye."

He would learn later Hanrahan did buy some excellent whisky, a bourbon they called it, but he watered it down and added molasses, reheated it briefly then put it in his own unlabeled bottles.

It was around June 2 or 3 when Plummer had come back for more supplies in one of his two wagons. He had only been gone about 15 days. He said he left Dudley and Wallace looking after their camp on Red Deer Creek.

Plummer didn't even spend the night, turning around with his wagon in the same afternoon. It would only take him a day-and-a-half to get back to their camp.

Three days later, J. Wright and his crew headed out to hunt southeast of Adobe Walls in an area between Red Deer Creek and Saltwater Creek. Adkin and

Uribe volunteered to hunt with them. Uribe was glad to get them out of Adobe Walls, as Adkin was drinking more and more.

About 10 miles out, they came upon Plummer. He was bedraggled, dusty and walking along slowly, his "Big 50" in his hand and leading a lone worn-out horse. The animal only had a blind bridle, and it still had its collar on from when it was part of a team pulling a wagon. It looked close to death.

Plummer was exhausted and they sat him down and gave him and his horse water. Then he began telling what he found when he got back to their Red Deer Creek camp the evening before.

"When I rode in, I saw our wagon full of hides burnt up and David Dudley and Tom Wallace had been killed," Plummer said. "David had been tied up in a sitting position, and the Indians had cut off one of his seeds and tied it in his hand, then drove a stake out front and tied his hand to that so he could see it.

"They also cut a hole in his gut and drove a stake down and into the ground," he continued. "He was just butchered up. And Wallace, he was scalped like David, but he wasn't cut up, as far as I could tell.

"I jumped down off the wagon and took my pocket knife and cut the belly band off this lead horse and jumped on bareback and with my rifle and took straight off," Plummer continued. "I didn't turn back, and that's what saved my life, and the grace of God. I rode straight into the brush and bullets started flying all around me.

"It was nearly sunset and they had figured I'd turn around and then they would ambush me," he said. "There must have been a hundred bullets pass me by. I rode up Red Creek and cleared the breaks. I guess their horses were tied up back the way I came in. Once it was dark, I turned around and rode hard trying to get back to Adobe Walls. Nearly killed my horse.

"I'm shore glad to see you men ride up," Plummer added.

They all headed back to Adobe Walls and Joe's story had the camp stirred up like an angry bee hive. Many of the men, including Adkin and Uribe, and the surveyors and the troopers rode back with Plummer to gather up the bodies of Dudley and Wallace.

Billy Dixon was travelling among them. As soon as they neared the camp, Dixon shouted out the three remaining horses in the team were standing there, still in harness.

They determined only the hides on top in the other wagon were damaged, and the ones beneath might be saved. Once back in Adobe Walls, J.Wright hired a crew with an oxen team to go back and fetch the good hides.

The difficulty was seeing what they did to Dudley, cutting that hole in the pit of his stomach and driving a big stake down through him and into the ground. All his long hair was scalped, and both ears were missing, too.

Once they gathered the bodies, the surveyors and Army escort decided they were riding straight east to Fort Supply. The others went back to Adobe Walls, but J. Wright sent out riders to tell other hunters in the area what had happened. Some of those who were warned immediately headed directly to Dodge City, never to return. Others broke camp and went to Adobe Walls.

Back in camp, the Mooars and many of his crew decided to go back to Dodge City with Plummer, as he had been ruined financially. Hanrahan tried to talk the Mooars out of quitting, but J. Wright said they were through – for awhile anyway.

The next day, "Dirty Face" Jones arrived with a wagon full of ammunition for Myers. He looked worn out.

"I ran into the Mooars and heard of what happened to Dudley and Wallace," Jones said. "Terrible news. They told me to turn back, but I told them I'd been driving that mule team for 90 miles without sleep and never once even unharnessed them. Plus, I had made Myers a promise I would get his supplies to him.

"Besides, like I always say, If you were born to be killed by Indians, you would be killed by Indians if you went to New York. That wouldn't make a difference," he said with a crooked grin. The others laughed.

Jones was tough – mentally and physically, Adkin thought to himself. But Jones' talk didn't last long. After he unloaded his wagon, he was snapping the reins on that eight-mule team to hurry and catch J. Wright and his heavily armed crew.

"I can catch up with them at Palo Duro Creek if I hurry," he said as he waved on his way out of Adobe Walls.

About a week later, three filthy men that looked like Indians but claimed they were Comancheros – and tried dressing the part – made their way into Adobe Walls. They soon found Hanrahan's Saloon and started drinking. They said they were looking for work. Hanrahan later told Adkin he told them there was no work, especially after Dudley and Wallace's killings.

"Another thing is no Comancheros would ever travel with only three men," Hanrahan said. "They are like a pack of wolves, they travel with a dozen or more men – and they don't 'work.'"

The Comancheros drank heavily and were soon staggering drunk. A few men eventually helped them get in the saddle and they rode out of camp heading east.

A few nights later, on the night of June 26, a loud shot rang out in Hanrahan's place, well after it had closed for the night. The men sleeping in the saloon as well as men camping out front were all awakened by the loud sound and others scampered about.

Hanrahan told everybody the loud crack was that of the ridgepole – the center beam that was holding up the ceiling of the sod roof.

"We've got to fix that men," Hanrahan shouted out as he woke men and got everybody started reinforcing the ridgepole. Plus he gave away plenty of free alcohol to all the helpers. They had to cut several new poles and brace the old one to keep it up, so they thought.

Several others in the mercantile stores went back to sleep, but not for long.

As they worked though the early morning hours, all the men who had been staying in Hanrahan's were awake and had little idea what was approaching at sunrise on June 27, 1874.

Except for James N. Hanrahan.

•••

Adkin and Uribe were on one end of the ridgepole with numerous others as posts were fastened along its side with hammers and nails. Most everyone in camp was helping Hanrahan re-enforce the ridgepole he claimed had cracked shortly before midnight.

"I still say that sound was from a rifle," Uribe said to Adkin as they finished and dusted off their hands. "I know we was at Rath's, but I was not full sleeping, Boss. I know my guns."

"I don't doubt you, but I think I'll have a rye now that we're through," Adkin said as he walked to the bar where everybody was downing free drinks.

It was about 6 a.m. and some men outside came running into the Hanrahan's.

"Injuns!" they shouted. Nearly everyone came running outside looking up the valley walls to the east. Hundreds of mounted Indians were driving down upon Adobe Walls, whooping and chanting. Dust was climbing into the gray sky.

The Whites started scrambling to their quarters and back into Hanrahan's, reaching for their long guns and slamming shutters and doors closed. Adkin and Uribe made it into Rath's and Wright's store and helped close every opening they could find. They also used sacks of flour and sugar to help barricade the openings and doors.

It would later be reported that the men caught in Hanrahan's were Hanrahan, Billy Ogg, "Bat" Masterson, Billy Dixon, James McKinley, "Bermuda" Carlisle, Mike Welsh, Shepard and Hiram Watson.

Trapped in Myers store were, "Dutch Henry," Billy Tyler, Mike McCabe, Edward Trevor, Harry Armitage, Old Man Keeler, "Frenchy," Henry Lease, Fred Leonard, Frank Brown and James Campbell.

Adkin, Uribe and the others, including Mister and Missus Olds were caught in Rath's place.

Adkin grabbed his Henry and Uribe got his new Sharp's Big 50 out. Everybody was picking up boxes of ammunition and throwing them to each other. The Indians were circling the buildings.

Adkin saw several braves thrown from their horses when they ran into the prairie dog field east of them and their horses tumbled end-over-end. It was still about 30 minutes away from sunrise, but getting lighter.

The men realized the Shadler brothers had been killed immediately as they were asleep in their wagon outside. Both were dragged out and scalped. They Indians even cut a slice of hair off their big Newfoundland dog after they killed him.

The bullets were flying – and flying everywhere. All the men ducked and took cover. Bullets were getting through in several places, like the gun slots and open windows. Adkin looked over to Uribe who was pressed flat against the wall while bullets zinged through.

"There must be a thousand of them," Uribe shouted, still with his face pressed against the wall.

Adkin took a quick peek and guessed there were probably 500 Indians out there swarming the valley. Inside, the men were still stacking grain sacks around windows, and Adkin was happy the sod walls were about 2-feet thick. Luckily, gunners in Hanrahan's had flanking fire against the Indians attacking Rath's place. And Indians were everywhere.

When Adkin looked back out, he was startled. Quanah Parker was sitting on his horse and backing it into the front door of Myer's store, trying to bust it in.

"Look, it's Chief Quanah," Adkin yelled to nobody in particular.

Uribe shouted back, "I see him."

They wold find out later, Quanah was leading the Comanches, Lone wolf was fighting with his Kiowas, and Stone Calf and White Shield led the Cheyennes.

As they watched with mouths agape, several of the men inside finally started firing back at their attackers. They turned to their pistols as the fighting was too close for long guns.

One of the warriors near Quanah fell from his horse, wounded and was trying to stand.

Quanah, having no success at breaking down he door, heeled his horse around by the man and reached down and picked him off the ground with one arm and slung the brave behind him.

"Did you see that?" Adkin screamed at Uribe.

"Si, si," he is muy strong, Boss," Uribe said. Uribe had leaned his Sharp's against the wall and was using his Colt, as Adkin had done. The fighting was close quarters.

The Indians tried throwing lit torches on the roofs, but the sod wouldn't burn. But that didn't mean their wasn't smoke.

The guns being fired inside the buildings filled them with fumes and there were still bullets screaming through the air all around them. It seemed the Indians would back off a little and regroup and attack at close quarters again and again.

Adkin thought to himself if he could walk out under a white flag, maybe he could negotiate with Quanah because of their friendship. But he had recognized there were other tribes fighting – braves with different head decorations and horses painted with stripes and different colors. He had to consider if Quanah didn't see him with a white flag, he could be in trouble – or killed.

After he told Uribe what his thoughts were, Uribe said, "They put mucho holes in you, Boss."

As the shooting lulled for a bit, Adkin saw several braves crawling along in a shallow ravine toward the corral at the stockade. Quanah was one of them. They finally stood, there was six of them, and they ran to the stockade house, trying to beak down the door. They failed, and ran back to the ravine.

Whenever the Indians rode off away from the buildings, the buffalo hunters would let loose with their "Big 50s" and drop Indians dead at several hundred yards. The Indian's carbines wouldn't hit the buildings from those ranges.

That's when they started noticing all the animals in the corral or tied to wagons had been killed. Dixon's saddle horse had been tied to a wagon next to the corral and was lying there full of arrows.

Adkin immediately wondered if Diablo and Tóngúl had been killed or stolen. Uribe was worried about his mule. They had been turned out with a bunch of other horses and mules, including the bell mule, down by the river in the woods and brush. It had become a custom to let them graze down there. It had been safe to do so up until the attack.

Around 10 a.m., a bunch of braves were around 500 yards out, and Adkin and Uribe saw Quanah again with them. All of a sudden, Quanah's horse fell down after a shot rang out, and they both hit the ground. Quanah wasn't hit, but his horse had been killed.

Quanah crawled along and hid behind a buffalo carcass. Someone shot at him and he flinched and crawled lower. Adkin was sure he had been wounded.

The "Big 50s" in the hands of these buffalo hunters was holding off at least more than 500 warriors, in Adkin's mind.

It was about this time they realized one of the men in their building had been killed. Shouts were coming from other buildings reporting on who had been hit or killed. Some of the men even came outdoors and grabbed a few trinkets and guns from the Indian bodies that were nearby.

One of the men ran from Hanrahan's to Rath's store and hastily carried back a case of ammunition to the saloon.

The Indians were moving even further away, but three-quarters of a mile still wasn't far enough. The "Big 50s" kept picking them off one-by-one. They then moved out even further.

That's when Adkin and Uribe saw Isa-tai, Quanah's Medicine Man on a butte overlooking the valley. He was painted totally yellow, as was his whole horse.

He looked naked at that range. As the mid-morning sunlight hit him, his ochre glow stood out brightly for all to see.

The Indians tried scaring the hide men several times by charging down at them from afar and firing carbines that wouldn't reach the buildings. But when the big guns let loose, they would retreat again out of range. This went on for several days, but on the third day, a remarkable shot changed the Indians' minds of killing off the White hunters.

A band of 15 braves had assembled on a ridge about 1,500 yards out. As Billy Dixon told Adkin, Uribe and the others later after the Indians had departed, "Some of the boys suggested that I try the 'Big 50' on them ... I took careful aim and pulled the trigger. We saw an Indian fall from his horse."

Dixon had been in Hanrahan's Saloon, and Adkin and Uribe had been in Rath's place.

Ironically, Billy's shot would result in the last Indian killed at what became known as the Second Battle of Adobe Walls.

The hunters lost three men total, but one of those had accidently shot himself after falling off a ladder – it was William Olds.

In fact, Masterson asked Missus Olds if he could use the cook's "Big 50" for the rest of the siege, as Bat's rifle was only a Winchester. She allowed it but took possession afterward at a later date, threatening legal action against Masterson if he didn't give it back.

On the fifth day, all the warriors cleared out of the area, some headed further into the Llano Estacado, others back downstream of the Canadian.

They had carried away their wounded and dead, but their killed warriors' bodies that were close to the soddies were gathered up by the hunters.

When the men went down to the area where their animals had been loose and grazing, nearly every one was killed – including Tóngúl and Uribe's mule. But Diablo was not found.

Adkin and Uribe were initially happy thinking Diablo may be alive somewhere with the Indians. But when Adkin noticed Uribe standing there staring at Tóngúl, a tear slid down Uribe's leathery face.

Seeing that, Adkin lost control. He fell to his knees and starting sobbing as he stroked the mare's swollen neck. She had bullet and lance holes in her and at least a dozen arrows. Uribe's mule fared no better, and he just turned and slowly walked away as Adkin knelt there crying by himself.

The hunters were now sitting at Adobe Walls with not one live animal to ride out for help. Every saddle horse, mule or donkey had been killed by the savages – even the few dogs.

Fortunately, word had quickly spread of the attack throughout the Panhandle and by the time the Indians had skedaddled, more than 100 buffalo hunters, skinners and freighters had gathered at the settlement to rescue the 28 men – and Missus Olds – at Adobe Walls.

The Whites had found 13 Indian bodies and decided to cut off the heads and stick them on stakes outside the walls. They took the reeking headless bodies and put them on buffalo hides and dragged them off down the river – along with the dead horses that had been shot.

They decided there had been Arapahoe warriors, as well as Cheyenne, Kiowas and, of course, Comanches. Estimates varied from 300 to 1,500 Indians had been held off. Adkin guessed about 500. Dixon estimated about 700, but even 500 experienced warriors against 28 men and one woman wasn't very good odds – for the Whites.

Hanrahan finally let it out that the loud crack that woke everyone the night before the attack was from a rifle he shot into the roof.

"One of those drunk Comancheros a few days before the attack was whispering – very loudly – to his partner they would take care of all of us in three days," Hanrahan said. "I wanted everybody awake just in case he was telling the truth – and he was."

The men cheered and whooped it up at how sneaky Hanrahan had been, but it proved to be their survival. Men were talking about what would have happened if they were all asleep before sunrise that morning.

Naturally, there was whisky for everybody that had battled for five days. Dixon became an immediate hero and celebrity. Adkin could never imagine how fast Billy's feat swept across the Plains – and even to the newspapers back east.

•••

Though the hide men had escaped death, the Indians decided to take out their revenge on settlements from Colorado to the Territories and West Texas.

A few days after leaving Adobe Walls, Quanah and his Comanches struck east and attacked a wagon train of hunters, stealing their horses and burning wagons. He then turned southwest and hit settlements in Texas.

Smaller groups of Cheyenne and Arapahoes hit settlements in all directions from Colorado to Texas. Lone Wolf took his Kiowa braves and regrouped in Oklahoma and then crossed the border back into Texas, raiding at will. There were even raids as far north as Medicine Lodge in Kansas.

The bands may have been forced out of the Canadian River Valley, but they scattered and terrorized wherever they went. All this resulted in official reports later that Indian depredations across the plains that summer and fall of 1874 left 190 White people dead and many more wounded.

One result was hide hunting in the Texas Panhandle was over – for the time being. All the hunters and merchants returned to Dodge City and then scattered.

The "war" destroyed any negotiations between the Army and the Bureau of Indian Affairs.

Grant gave Sherman the authority to place all the reservations under military control on July 26, 1874. Sherman ordered Lieutenant "Black Jack" Davidson at Fort Sill to make all the friendlies come to the fort to register and enroll by August 3. The Indians would then have to make daily roll call thereafter.

All restrictions on the Army were lifted, and Grant said the Army was to pursue the Indians to the front porch of Fort Sill if they had to and to kill them there. There was no longer a safe harbor for warring Indians on the reservations. The Army was going to hunt down all those who refused authority or resisted in any way.

It was open warfare.

Adkin and Uribe found themselves stuck in Dodge City for a few days. Their first chore was finding the best saddle horses they could find. Word was Sitler had some fine quarter horses.

They were very fast in short distances, but were not like Indian ponies that could run for miles. They went ahead and bought two, Adkin selecting a dark brown horse but with white stockings and a white diamond on its chest.

Uribe picked out a large, light brown palomino with black mane and tail. Sitler said its name was Santa Fe, which pleased Uribe immensely, making Adkin somewhat jealous.

"Your horse, a fine two-year-old is called Dodger," Sitler said. "But you could train him by something else if you wanted to."

"No, Henry, Dodger is just fine," Adkin said. "He's beautiful."

•••

No hunters or merchants would travel to Hidetown on the Sweetwater Creek, where Adkin wanted to look for Lew Bush. So if nobody was down there, Bush may have ended up in Dodge City.

Adkin hit all the saloons and bordellos looking for Bush. Uribe always tagged along, but he seldom drank alcohol. Uribe wanted his wits if they found Bush.

Some of the hunters let it be known they were never going back to the upper Canadian or Adobe Walls ever again. After all the hunters had left the settlement, Indians had torched everything there that would burn.

But, there was "Dirty Face" Jones determined to make more money in the Panhandle.

Ed Jones decided he and Emanuel Dubbs were going to gather up a bunch of armed hunters, skinners and freighters – for security – and go back into the Panhandle to hunt. Adkin offered to help, much to the chagrin of Uribe. When the men gathered, Jones explained to Adkin and Uribe why he was involved.

"Tom Nixon talked Dubbs into putting together a large enough party to protect us," Jones said with a chuckle. "We're tired of waiting for the Army to clear the area of hostiles. So, you know me, I told Dubbs, what the hell? If you're meant to be killed by Indians you will be."

So once they signed up about 30 heavily armed men, 28 exactly, and supplied 14 wagons, off they went.

Within a week, Jones and Dubbs realized their hunting party was too large to hunt successfully, so they split into two groups. Dubbs asked Ed to be his second in command and they headed out in another direction from the other group with seven wagons in each group. Adkin and Uribe ended up riding with Dubbs and Jones.

When the party reached the breaks at upper Wolf Creek, they saw a herd of animals moving across the flats. Someone shouted it was antelope, but Dubbs said he believed it was a herd of Indian horses.

He was correct.

Then the Indians herding the ponies saw the hunters, and they turned to attack. Jones, Dubbs and Adkin, who were on horseback, whirled around and went back to the wagons and told them to turn around. They rode up beside the teams and whipped the teams urging them to go faster.

Uribe was riding behind them on Santa Fe waving his hat and yelling to the teams, too. Then the bullets started flying. A hail of lead was buzzing through the air, and Dubbs realized they would never reach the flats since they were on a ridge.

One of the scouts got shot out of the seat of the wagon he was driving. The team tangled up after he fell off, and it took an extra few minutes to gather that team. That's when Dubbs and Jones decided to form the wagons in a defensive formation, pushing them together as tightly as possible.

Bullets were whizzing everywhere, and then the hunters began returning fire and the Indians fell back a little, thinking they were out of range.

But, just as Adkin had seen at Adobe Walls, the hunters started picking off Indians at great distances with their "Big 50s."

While they were unhooking teams and forming the wagons, five horses got killed by Indian bullets. One man was shot through the hand, but he would be okay.

The shots from both sides got sporadically less and less. Adkin never figured out what band of Indians were attacking. Uribe later said he thought they were Cheyenne.

Around 3 in the afternoon, they saw 15 Indians trying to cross a clearing from one hollow to another.

"Men, set those sights at 500 yards and wait for my command," Dubbs yelled.

The Indians were moving slowly, fully convinced they were clear of any danger. When they got about half way across the clearing, Dubbs gave the order.

"Fire, men," he shouted, as the "Big 50s" roared.

The hunters killed 12 horses and 10 Indians in the melee. Several wounded braves hid behind their dead mounts, and two crawled to the safety of trees across the hollow – only three had made it across on their ponies.

This ended the attack for awhile. Dubbs and Jones gathered the men to decide the best way to escape. They had lost about half their stock, but Jones said they could use their riding horses as part of the teams and pull the wagons with only two horses because they didn't have all that many hides.

They would wait until dark, and someone reminded them they would have to wait for the moon to set, too. So around 9 o'clock, they quietly harnessed their animals and hooked up the teams. They rode out and headed back to the main base where Tom Nixon and the other hunters were camped.

They made it back without problems and told Nixon what had happened. Several of the hunters thought they should hightail it back to Dodge City immediately, but Nixon had an idea.

"Why don't we mount a counter attack," Nixon said. "I'm tired of fleeing from these heathens. They would never in a hundred years think we would attack."

His argument carried the majority, especially when Dubbs told them the Indians had about 100 horses. He was sure they would be camped near where their party had been attacked.

"They'll be in those breaks at Wolf Creek, and we can sneak up and hit them before daylight," Dubbs said. "We'll be able to spot their fires easily."

Adkin wasn't too sure 28 men could take 30 or 40 warriors, but the advantage of surprise might be just the edge they needed for success.

"Make sure those pistols are loaded, Uribe," Adkin said as they headed out. "This is like when we attacked the Comancheros in New Mexico. Remember?"

"Si Señor, I remember Diablo got stabbed, but we did well. Si? Uribe said smiling. "I pray Diablo is still alive."

The attack was almost anticlimactic. The Indians were caught completely unguarded and took off like scared jack rabbits when the hide men started shooting up their camp just as the sky got gray. The warriors didn't even take most of their gear, and the hunters found and captured 79 head of horses, mules and ponies.

The men were ecstatic, and while driving back to Dodge City, Dubbs and Jones decided to split the animals evenly and allow the men to sell whatever they wanted or to replace stock that had been killed. Overall, Dubbs and Jones figured the expedition had broke even.

Once in Dodge City, Adkin and Uribe laughed that at least they still had their hair. The only profits they made were several cases of ammunition, and Jones saw to it to give Adkin a new Sharp's "Big 50."

Then Jones told Adkin and Uribe another adventure was in the works. He related that Fort Dodge's Colonel Nelson Miles had received orders to form the Indian Territorial Expedition to capture or kill Indians from the Washita River drainage to Antelope Hills then west to the upper Red River.

"It's going to made up of eight companies of the Sixth Calvary and four companies from the Fifth Infantry," Jones said. "That's more than 1,000 men. It's going to be all out war."

Jones went on to tell them that Nelson's Lieutenant Frank Baldwin was going to lead an advance scouting force for preparations of battle.

"They're asking for volunteers and there's going to be a sign-up after they check out your shooting skills – if you can hit their targets," Jones laughed. "Several of the men from the Adobe Walls fight are going to sign up."

'Do you think they'll head through Hidetown?" Adkin asked.

Jones looked at him funny.

"I would imagine they'll hit every camp along those rivers in that country," Jones said. "We'll probably even end up at Adobe Walls again – or what's left of it."

•••

When the sign-up day came, Adkin and Uribe showed up and there were several men they knew and had fought along side with. They greeted Bat Masterson and Billy Dixon. Then Joe Plummer rode up. He wanted to go, too. There were numerous other buffalo hunters they had met or seen at Adobe Walls.

Nearly every man had known Dave Dudley and wanted revenge against the Indians for the way they mutilated him. And when it came time for the mandatory rifle test, the Army set up targets at 100 yards, 200 yards and 500 yards.

All the hunters passed easily, and several were teasing soldiers to move that target out to 1,500 yards – "We have Billy Dixon here," someone shouted. They all hooted and laughed, even the soldiers. They, too, had heard about his feat at Adobe Walls – as had about every person on the Great Plains.

The day ended with 20 friendly Delaware Indian scouts and 17 plainsmen and buffalo hunters signing up for scouting duty.

Jones wasn't very fond of Lieutenant Baldwin, and he let it be known. He had met him in Dodge City when Baldwin was off duty and drinking.

"He thinks he's the greatest soldier the world has ever seen," Jones whispered to several of the men. "Watch him, he'll try to bully us when he gets the chance."

The advance scouting party took off from Fort Dodge on August 11, 1874. The men didn't know it yet, but it would be the beginning of what became known as the Red River War. A war that changed the West forever.

Once on the trail, the men found out other Army units were leaving Fort Union, "Black Jack" Davidson's Tenth Calvary from Fort Sill, Fort Richardson and MacKenzie from Fort Concho and Colonel Price from Fort Bascom in New Mexico – all to converge on the Texas Panhandle.

"This is goin' be fun, men," Jones laughed as they rode along. "MacKenzie knows how to fight these savages.

'Word is there's going to be more than 3,000 men taking the field against the Indians," Jones added. "And MacKenzie knows the caprock better than any Army officer alive."

On August 17, they encountered a horrible wind storm after the men had bedded down. Baldwin ordered all men out to keep their horses and mules from stampeding. The animals had to be hobbled. However, Jones and Plummer didn't get out of their bedrolls until Baldwin actually walked into their tent and told them to get up – a second time – or else.

Both men weren't particularly happy with Baldwin's threats and mumbled obscenities behind the Lieutenant's back. This kind of disrespect seemed to be worsening to Adkin and Uribe. It was apparent Plummer and Jones and a few others didn't like orders or "Army Brass," as they called Baldwin.

The following day, Baldwin marched the scouting party 50 miles and camped on West Adobe Walls Creek.

"I told you, he's going to kill us one way or a nuther," Jones complained.

The very next morning, as they were approaching Adobe Walls stockade and stores, several bands of Indians were starting an attack on the remains of the stockade, where a few buffalo hunters had gathered. Baldwin ordered his party to mount arms and attack, which they did. They charged headlong into the Indians which were trying to circle the hunters.

Again, lead was flying everywhere and several Indians fell dead from their ponies as they banded together and rode off down the valley and across the Canadian River. Baldwin's men pursued them until the Indians had crossed the river. He then halted the attack, and they headed back to the stockade and the grateful hunters.

Once they met up with Baldwin's party, the hunters talked amongst themselves and decided they would join Baldwin, who was destined to travel to Fort Supply.

Baldwin tried to dissuade them and encouraged them to head back to Dodge City. But in the end, he was glad to have 35 additional armed hunters. He was now commanding a patrol of 75 men armed to the teeth.

The next day, they surprised a small band of Indians and killed one and wounded another. They travelled on to where Dudley and Wallace were killed. Baldwin named the small creek that emptied into Red Deer Creek there at their old camp, Chicken Creek, because he had sighted a bunch of prairie chickens as they rode up.

They all stopped and men started dismounting. Masterson took off his hat, at which time the others followed suit, and spoke aloud a small prayer asking that

Dudley and Wallace's souls would be taken in by the Lord. All said an amen and then remounted their horses.

Adkin recounted the horrible scene that day they rode up with Plummer to find Dudley and Wallace. It was burned into his mind like that of finding Matty's body. He now burned to find Lew Bush, the last piece in a puzzle that Adkin didn't even understand.

But his will was dampening, especially after seeing Matty's beloved mare lying dead with arrows all over her. And he missed Diablo. His impulse to kill Bush was costing him dearly, and he was wondering was it worth it. But on he trudged.

On August 24, they joined up with Colonel Miles just west of the Antelope Hills on the Canadian River at the Oklahoma State line.

Baldwin's first action was to call Jones, Plummer and two other men to Miles' tent. The four were immediately relieved of duty from Baldwin's scouts.

They had been kicked out.

Naturally, they were angry at being discharged, but they were also let go out in the middle of nowhere, some 150 miles, they figured, from Dodge City. After gathering their belongings and saddling up their horses and recovering a wagon and team Jone's had volunteered, the four bid farewell to the others.

It was apparent to Adkin and Uribe, Baldwin didn't tolerate insubordination, even from scouts.

•••

While organizing the campaign, Miles and the officers talked among the troops and scouts very little. What word got out was they were headed to Palo Duro Canyon. This scuttlebutt was not good news to Adkin's ears, but he would stay with the scouts hoping they would eventually get to Hidetown.

Departure was planned for the next morning, but word got out that Satanta had been arrested again by "Black Jack" Davidson from Fort Sill for violating his pardon agreement. Even though Satanta had claimed he didn't cross into Texas to fight, the fact Lone Wolf and his son did, was held against the old Chief.

They arrested him in his village located in the Wichita Mountains, a place Adkin knew well. Satanta was sent back to Huntsville, Texas, and imprisoned again. Adkin felt sorry for him. He thoroughly believed Satanta had stayed on the reservation and had given up fighting. He was a tired and worn out Chief – having seen fighting was never going to stop the Whites from moving in and killing all their buffalo. It made Adkin very sad.

On August 25, orders were for all men in Miles' command were to fall in for orders from the man himself. As everybody got in formations, the scouts were placed off to the side like sheep at a cattle sale. They were told to have their mounts with them and be prepared for marching.

Miles rode out of the crowd on his horse and walked it along the front lines, yelling so all could hear.

"Men, we're about to take part in an all-out attack on warring Indians with the help of five mounted columns, numerous infantry and more than 3,000 men marching into the Texas Plains and the Llano Estacado," Miles shouted, as he walked his mount slowly up and down the line. "General Sheridan has demanded we end Indian depredations by whatever means necessary.

"We have been summoned forth to hunt, engage and destroy what's left of the horse Indians," he continued. "They will be given no quarter, no rest, no freedom to hunt and be starved out. Their villages will be found, burned out and their horses taken from them or killed.

"Does every man agree with this plan?" Miles asked, stopping his horse facing the troops.

The men all raised their arms and screamed approval, whooping and yelling at the top of their lungs. Everybody was wanting blood, Adkin thought to himself.

"If not, fall out now, or face my personal wrath if you fail to prosecute this plan during enemy encounters," Miles added loudly. "Now prepare to march – Lieutenant."

Lieutenant Baldwin had his ragtag bunch of scouts come to attention and started the parade by having them mount up and marching their horses two-by-two west along the north trail on the Canadian River.

Dixon happened to fall in next to Adkin. He winked at Adkin and laughed. Adkin laughed, too, not knowing what they were getting into. But that had been his lot since leaving England. Adkin looked back and saw Uribe was right behind him.

Word was all the detachments had orders to stay in the field throughout the fall and winter. Sheridan had situated forts and supply lines that would allow units to pursue Indians four or five months without rest.

Miles and Baldwin pushed men and animals hard marching to Prairie Dog Town Fork, which was south of Adobe Walls. The unit made it 100 miles in three days.

About mid-morning on August 30, several Delaware scouts rode back to the column with news they had spotted a large body of Cheyenne warriors near Palo Duro Canyon, which started only a few miles ahead of them.

Miles formed up and attacked their camps which Miles later reported was 400 to 600 warriors. Adkin and several other frontiersmen knew it was only about 200 at most. But it was a victory for Miles – and them.

The men had discovered that Miles was a big rival of MacKenzie's, who had polished his Fourth Calvary as the most fearsome and seasoned Indian fighters in the West. This, to them, explained the exaggerated numbers of hostiles Miles reported.

A few days later, they discovered a large number of Indians were ahead of them up the canyon, and pursued them. In a running 12-mile, four-hour fight, Miles' troopers managed to kill 25 Indians and wounding more. His troops only suffered two wounded. And they did burn down a large village of lodges.

Both Adkin and Uribe knew they had dropped Indians off their ponies during the chase. And Adkin had heard the "whizz" of a bullet passing deadly close. It made him realize this was war and to take it much more serious than just chasing Lew Bush.

Again, Miles reported he had burned a village and chased 3,000 Indians into the upper Prairie Dog Town Fork.

As reports and rumors got to the men, it was apparent to many this entire campaign was a hit and run affair, with soldiers fighting small groups and killing them or accepting their surrender. Messengers were constantly being sent out to other units and Miles was also receiving dispatches from other commanders.

Supposedly, word was the command was being sent to Hidetown and then down to McClelland Creek to look for Cheyenne and Arapahoe bands. This brought a smile to Adkin. He was hoping against hope Lew Bush would be there.

When they rode into Hidetwon, Adkin was amazed it had two rudimentary mercantile stores and a stockade, much like Adobe Walls. Then Adkin saw several men step out of the larger soddy and understood.

"Well if it isn't my favorite Englishman and his friend, Uribe," Charley Rath said. He was standing there with Bob Wright and Lee Reynolds – all prominent merchants from Dodge City.

They embraced while Baldwin kept a sharp eye on Adkin and Uribe. Baldwin didn't like his scouts doing things outside his purview. Adkin related they were signed on with Lieutenant Baldwins Scouts for Colonel Miles out of Fort Dodge.

"I remember you told me you were interested in signing up, but I never heard back from you," Rath said. "Find any Indians?"

Uribe rolled his eyes, and Adkin spoke up.

"Plenty. We had skirmishes at Adobe Walls and then a hell of a fight in Palo Duro Canyon," he said. "Then chased a village up Prairie Dog Town Fork. We've only had a couple wounded though."

"Just can't stay out of the Texas Panhandle, eh?" Adkin asked the men.

"Too much money down here – it's where the buffalo are, Adkin," Wright said. "Word is the Army is going to build a fort here before next year. That will help with our security."

"I hope so, there's 3,000 Army soldiers roaming this Panhandle and stirring up every Indian from every corner," Adkin said.

"I think Sheridan is kicking a swarm of rattlesnakes," Uribe added.

Several of the scouts like Dixon, Nixon and Masterson came over to say hello as the scouts were put at ease.

An Englishman's Adventures on the Santa Fe Trail (1865-1889)

Rath wanted to know which way they were headed, but Masterson spoke up. "Sorry, but we're not to discuss any plans of Colonel Miles," Masterson said, changing the subject. "How is my brother doing?"

"He's fine," Wright said. "Still has the young ladies of Dodge City chasing him around."

They all laughed, then caught up on news of friends and colleagues. Bassett had won re-election as Sheriff, Rath was still a county commissioner and said he and his partners would have a real store and trading post completed in Hidetown by year's end. They were apparently headed back to Dodge City with seven wagons of hides and tongues the following day.

They related how Plummer, "Dirty Face" Jones and two others got kicked out of the scouts. Rath laughed saying that was Jones alright, that he wouldn't take orders from an Army officer.

Baldwin came around telling all the scouts that had scattered about that they would bivouac overnight and be departing at sunrise.

"Now get started setting those tents," be bellowed."

The scouts told Rath and his partners they would talk with them after setting camp that evening. Masterson said he wanted to write a quick letter to brother, Ed.

That evening, they all gathered, and Adkin quizzed Rath about Lew Bush as the others were talking amongst themselves. Rath reported he hadn't heard a word about Bush – not even his name, let alone where he was. Adkin was let down, frustrated there was no word about his quarry.

They had a good visit and found out the trail from Fort Supply to Hidetown had been well travelled by traders, hunters – and especially the Army – and was now a good trail, even for wagons. They were also near Fort Sill to the southeast and only about 30 miles from the Wichita Mountains.

That reminded Adkin of his old friend, and best man, Chief Satanta. He made a promise to himself as soon as he dispatched Bush, Adkin would go visit Satanta in prison. He wasn't sure where Huntsville was, but he would find it.

•••

An hour before sunrise, Baldwin and some of his Delawares were rousting men from their bedrolls and preparing them for travel. As the sky turned gray, the whole company was mounted or in wagons and rode out of Hidetown to the southwest.

"Deeper into the Texas Panhandle," Adkin sighed to himself. He remembered he and Rath and Goodnight had entered the Texas Panhandle years earlier from the New Mexico side much further south, and they survived that trip.

On September 9, 1874, they rode up McClelland Creek after crossing the North Fork of the Red River. A few Delaware scouts found trails made by a large herd of horses and suspected there might be a band of Indians further up the creek. Adkin, Uribe and Masterson had been scouting south of McClelland Creek and found no such trails.

While in consultation with Baldwin and Miles, Miles believed it important to look for the supply train he had ordered for additional supplies before going further.

The supply train was supposed to be delivered by Captain Wyllys Lyman, but little did they know that the train had been attacked that very day by Kiowa Chief Lone Wolf the Elder and Comanches just north of Sweetwater Creek.

Miles asked for two volunteers from the scouts. Baldwin recommended Billy Dixon and Amos Chapman.

Both men stepped forward, gladly volunteering. Dixon was capable as any man in the command, knowing the country very well, especially the trail to Fort Supply. Miles then suggested they pick out a dozen or more enlisted men to accompany them.

Dixon and Chapman both respectfully argued against a large scouting party to carry the dispatches while looking for Lyman, fearing being sighted more easily than a small group.

Miles finally agreed, and the scouts picked Sergeant Z. T. Woodhall and Privates George W. Smith, Peter Rath and John Harrington. Dixon had worked with Smith before Smith enlisted in the Army.

They knew these men to be hardy soldiers with grit and perseverance. And Dixon and Chapman had been at Adobe Walls together – they were dead-eye shots.

They departed September 10 with Miles' dispatches requesting additional food rations and ammunitions.

They would not find out about Lyman's supply train being attacked until Major William Price showed up on September 13 at McClelland Creek and told Miles his scouting party had been attacked in the morning the day before between Gageby Creek and the Washita River, just south of where he had to fight off Indians that were attacking Lymen's supply train.

Price told Miles five men were wounded and one dead when he found a man named Dixon firing shots by himself. Price said they took Dixon's directions and found five others in a buffalo wallow.

"One of the bastards killed the horse of my surgeon's aide," Price said. "They thought we were Indians."

"Where are the men?" Miles yelled in front of at least three dozen men standing around.

"They're at the wallow. I told them I'd send help once I got here," Price said.

"You left them there?" Miles asked in a loud voice.

"I don't have an ambulance or extra horses," Price answered, but before he could say another word, Miles exploded.

"You, Sir, are the bastard," Miles shouted. "Better yet, you're a son-of-a-bitch for leaving my wounded men in the middle of nowhere. And you better get out of my sight before I forget I'm an officer."

He immediately turned to the men, as Price backed out of the gathering.

"I need a platoon to volunteer to go get Dixon and the men and render what aid is necessary," Miles yelled. "And Lieutenant Baldwin, volunteer a Sergeant who can make decisions and take command of this rescue party – immediately."

Adkin, Masterson and Uribe quickly raised their hands, and Baldwin nodded approval. Numerous enlisted men had their hands up and Baldwin went through them patting their shoulders until he had at least 20 men, including one of Miles' surgeons and two Delaware scouts.

Sergeant Dan Bowler volunteered and was accepted. The men only took about 15 minutes, and they were ready to head out. They had a wagon with a four-mule team and five extra horses and medical supplies, including a large bottle of laudanum. They had also thrown in heavy blankets and several buffalo hides into the wagon.

A mile out from their encampment, they ran into Lyman's supply train carrying the vital rations and ammunition Miles' troops were needing.

One of Price's men had volunteered to lead the rescuers to the wallow. It was midnight September 13, and after blowing the company bugle several times, they heard gun shots and rode out of the darkness up to the wallow.

•••

When they rode up, Sergeant Bowler ordered several troopers to break out the oil lamps.

"And you men, gather all those blankets and furs," Bowler shouted as the mounted scouts jumped from their saddles. "And you, get the medical bag."

"Thank God, you got here," Dixon said. "We were sure we'd die by freezing before daylight."

Adkin, and the others who knew Dixon well, assured him and the others they would be okay now, even though they hadn't fully diagnosed the situation, yet.

"Take special care of Chapman, his knee was shattered by a shot early in our fight," Dixon said to the surgeon. "And Woodhall and Harrington are wounded, too."

"I can't believe Major Price just left y'all here," Masterson said.

"Not only that, he refused to give us food or ammunition," Dixon said. "His surgeon just looked at us and said, 'Yep, they're wounded for sure.'"

"He was mad because Woodhall thought his aide was an Indian when they rode up and shot his horse out from under him," Dixon said. "They wouldn't take us along or give us a horse to ride.

"If it hadn't been for some of his troopers throwing us hardtack and jerky on their way by, we would still be starving," he added. "The man is heartless."

"You should've heard Miles set upon him," Adkin said. "Miles called him a bastard then said, no 'you're a son-of-a-bitch.'"

"You won't get no argument from us," Dixon said as soldiers were giving the wounded laudanum, especially Chapman."

"Hey, Dixon here is wounded, too," Harrington said.

"It's not that bad, just a calf wound," Dixon said. "It was a clean shot all the way through. It'll heal okay."

"Poor George Smith here is dead," Dixon added.

As the wounded were being tended to, they helped Dixon and Rath dig a small grave in the bottom of the wallow and buried Private George W. Smith. The rescuers noticed both Rath and Dixon wiped away some tears after a brief prayer for their heroic comrade in arms.

The wounded were feeling fine by daylight with laudanum and a few slugs of whiskey. They kept the warm, wool blankets tightly wrapped around them.

It was then decided by the surgeon and Bowler that Chapman, Harrington and Woodhall should be taken to the Post Surgeon at Fort Supply. Peter Rath and Dixon were wanting to go back to their unit and pursue warring Indians.

So on the morning of September 14, 1874, a wagon with the three wounded men and 10 troopers headed northeast for Fort Supply, the others were going back to McClelland Creek.

It was during that short trip – the scouts had originally only made it about 15 miles from the encampment before being sighted and attacked – that Dixon filled in the details of his and his comrades' harrowing fight against certain death.

All ears were on Dixon as he strolled along on one of the extra horses they took – Peter was off to his side, with Adkin, Uribe, Masterson and the troopers crowded nearby. The only other sounds were from the horses' hoof thuds.

"We made most of our travels during that first night," he started, "That second day, we were nearing a divide between the Washita River and Gageby Creek. Riding to the top of a little knoll, we found ourselves almost face-to-face with a large band of Kiowa and Comanche warriors.

"They saw us at the same time and quickly circled, surrounding us. We were in a trap," Dixon continued. "We knew the best thing to do was make a stand and fight for our lives – rather than making a run for it, where we might get separated and killed off one-by-one.

"We also realized we could do better work on foot," he said, as the soft clop-clops continued. "So we dismounted and placed our horses in care of Smith. In a moment, poor George was shot down, and the horses stampeded.

"When he fell, he landed face down on his stomach, and his gun fell from his hand far beyond his reach," he continued. "No Indian was ever able to capture that gun in the entire fight, though."

Dixon went on to explain he realized he was in the closest quarters he had ever been in and was grateful he wasn't disabled.

"I did get wounded with a bullet in my calf, but I could get by," Dixon said. "And look at this blouse I'm wearing. I never saw a shirt so riddled with bullet holes and how a man could not be hit.

"They could've run us down and killed us at once, but they played with us like a cat will play with a mouse before killing it," he continued. "We saw there was no show for us to survive on that little hillside and decided our best fighting ground was a small mesquite flat several hundred yards distant.

"Before we could shift our position, I was looking at Amos when he was hit. Amos said, 'Billy, I am hit at last,' and eased himself down," Dixon said.

He explained the bullets were flying everywhere, and he didn't have time to ask Chapman how bad his would was. He found out a few moments later, Amos Chapman was disabled – his knee had been shattered by the bullet.

"Every man save Peter and myself had been wounded," Dixon said, as every man in the rescue party was leaning toward him, hanging on every word. "Our situation was growing more desperate. In a short while, we would be dead or in the hands of the Indians who would torture us in the most inhuman manner before taking our lives."

He said he then noticed a spot where buffaloes had pawed and wallowed out a depression, or a buffalo wallow.

"I ran for it at top speed, with bullets whizzing by me at every jump, but I got through unharmed," Dixon said.

The wallow was about 10-feet across, according to Dixon, but it did offer a little better protection. He shouted at the others to come to him, which all of them, save Smith and Chapman, commenced trying to do.

Dixon said as each man made it to the wallow, they were using their knives and hands building up dirt around the edge of the circle.

"We were making good headway, though constantly interrupted by the necessity of firing at Indians as they dashed within range," Dixon said. "It was probably about noon before we all reached the wallow."

"Many times that terrible day did I think that my last moment was at hand," Dixon said as Peter, mumbled, "For sure."

"But then when one of the boys raised up and said, "It's no use boys, we might as well give it up," a bullet hit the soft bank of fresh dirt in front of him and completely filled his mouth with dirt," Dixon continued. "I was so amused that I laughed, though in a sickly way, for none of us felt much like laughing."

There it was again, Adkin thought: Men turning their fear of certain death into laughter, even if just for a moment.

"By this time, I had got past the first excitement of battle and felt perfectly cool, as did the others," he continued. "We decided to aim perfectly and were picking off an Indian at almost every round."

He explained they tried to all sit upright while fighting as to not look wounded but full of vigor and fight.

"Somebody called out to Chapman to come to us, and then found out his leg was shattered when he yelled back 'bout his condition," Dixon said. "It took several efforts to reach him but I finally succeeded. I told him to climb on my back; my plan being to carry him as I would a little child.

"I carried him to the wallow," he said. "It taxed my strength to carry him."

He said they were then all in the wallow, except for Smith's body, and they didn't feel it was worth getting killed just to try moving the body at that moment. They then started digging like gophers with their knives and hands to make their little wall of dirt higher and higher. They then felt more protected, even though their danger was hardly lessened.

Dixon said many times Indians would ride toward them with lances uplifted, ready to spear them, but they managed to shoot the leaders of such groups off their horses and the others would retreat.

"Thus all that long, hot day, the Indians circled round us or dashed past, yelling and cutting all kinds of capers," Dixon continued. "All morning we had been without water, and the wounded were sorely in need of it."

He explained their tongues and lips were soon dry as a whetstone after all the excitement and stress of such an encounter. Even in the despair, he said they all showed courage, knowing what would befall them should they be captured alive.

"We had seen too many naked and mangled bodies of White men who had been spread-eagled and tortured with steel and fire to forget what our own fate would be," Dixon said. "So we were determined to fight to the end, not unmindful of the fact that every once in a while there was another dead or wounded Indian."

He related around 3 o'clock, a dark cloud came up in the west and quickly turned to thunder and lightning. Sheets of rain quickly started and was drenching them to the skin, just as the wind shifted to the north and was then chilling them to the bone.

"Water gathered quickly in the buffalo wallow, and our wounded men eagerly bent forward and drank from the muddy pool," Dixon began after a moment of silence. "It was more than muddy – that water was red with their own blood that had flowed from their wounds and had laid clotting and dry earlier in the day's hot sun."

He said they knew Indians hated heavy, cold rain, and they could see many of them in the distance sitting on horseback with blankets pulled up around their shoulders and over their heads.

Within an hour after the rain started the wind turned very cold, and the men were without coats as all their belongings were tied behind their saddles when the horses stampeded off, never to be seen again.

Dixon said the most dearest treasure in his life was a photo of his mother which he kept in his coat pocket. Adkin knew Billy lost his mother when he was but 12. Billy was never able to recover the photo.

Water finally reached about two inches in the wallow and every man was freezing cold.

"The wounded were shivering as if they had ague," Dixon said.

They realized they were running low on ammunition and that "appalled them," to use Billy's words. They decided to only shoot when they were sure of a good hit. Dixon said someone suggested they go out and get Smith's six-shooter and gun belt, which would be fully loaded with cartridges.

"Peter offered to go and soon returned with the gun and ammunition but also with word that Smith was still alive," Dixon said, adding that made them feel very badly, as if they had neglected him, even though it was in ignorance of his condition.

Dixon and Rath decided they would go get Smith, and they did. They carried him under each arm to the wallow. Smith was even trying to walk most of the distance.

"We could see that there was no chance for him," Dixon said. "He was shot through the left lung and when he breathed, the wind sobbed out of his back under the shoulder blade."

They found a thin willow horse switch dropped by an Indian and broke off the end and used it to stuff a silk handkerchief into the gaping bullet hole in Smith's back.

The night was getting blacker and cold winds were hard on the men. They knew Indians were still around them, and there was no way anyone could sleep. Dixon said he and Rath decided to gather tumbleweeds nearby and get enough to make a springy, somewhat drier bedding for all the men in the wallow.

By the time heavy darkness set in with only a thin new moon above, every Indian had disappeared, but no man dared sleeping. Dixon used the willow switch to clean every gun they had, and they decided somebody needed to go for help.

Rath and Dixon both wanted to go, but Rath insisted and took off. After about two hours, he returned, saying he could not find the trail to Fort Supply.

"By this time Smith had grown much worse and was begging us in piteous tones to shoot him and put an end to his terrible sufferings," Dixon said with tears starting to drip down his cheeks. "We had to keep close watch on him so he couldn't take his own life."

Dixon noted it broke their hearts not being able to ease Smith' pain, but around 10 that night, he fell asleep and later in the night, one of the boys felt him.

"He was cold in death," Dixon said, taking a deep breath and slowly sighing. "Men commonly think of death as something to be shunned. There are times, however, when its hand falls as tenderly as the touch of a mother's hand, and when its coming is welcomed by those to whom hopeless sufferings has brought the last bitter dregs of life."

Those words stung Adkin's whole being. He thought he could actually feel the pain in Dixon's heart and soul.

They placed Smith outside the wallow on the grass and covered his face with a silk handkerchief. At daylight, with no Indians in sight, Dixon took off looking for the trail, moving slowly – wary of being discovered.

"I had travelled scarcely more than half a mile when I struck the plain trail leading to Camp Supply," Dixon said, adding he hurried as quickly as possible keeping a constant lookout for Indians.

Suddenly, he said he spotted the sight of an outfit a couple of miles to the northwest. He couldn't discern whether it was troops or Indians at first and hid. He then decided to go back and look again, and he was able to see it was troops.

"I never felt happier in my life," Dixon said. "I whanged loose with my rifle to attract the attention of the soldiers."

He said he fired an additional shot which brought two soldiers to his location. He told them of the attack and his boys' conditions, and they rode back to the commander.

The command was under Major Price of the 8th Calvary with a troop accompanying General Miles supply train.

"Major Price rode over to where I was waiting bringing his surgeon with him," Dixon said, adding Price sent the surgeon and two soldiers ahead, which was about a mile distant, to see what could be done for the wounded. Price, Dixon said, wanted a full report from him about the fight.

As Dixon was reporting to Price, Billy heard the roar of a gun and a puff of smoke rise from the wallow.

"One of the boys fired at what they thought were Indians and killed the horse of one of the soldiers," Dixon said. "Well, they heard my two shots and thought the Indians had found me and shot me. They were taking no chances."

He said he actually ran toward the wallow yelling it was him and that soldiers were with him.

"Despite the sad plight of the wounded men, about all the surgeon did was to examine their injuries," Dixon said. "Major Price refused to leave any men with us. He would not even provide us with firearms."

An Englishman's Adventures on the Santa Fe Trail (1865-1889)

Price had told Dixon their arms were of different calibers and thus he was unable to leave ammunition with them. Price said he would report their position to General Miles when he reached Miles encampment.

"At the time, we were glad just to have seen these men and did not think much about how they treated us," Dixon said. "Luckily, the soldiers turned over a few pieces of hardtack and some dried beef which happened to be tied behind their saddles as they marched off and left us alone.

"We've been watching and waiting until you rode close and we heard your bugle," he said. "Our nerves were getting jumpy, so strong were our emotions. We were sure that help would come the moment General Miles heard the news."

•••

Back at General Miles' encampment, Dixon's story was making its way to every tent and every man there. If it hadn't been for Miles' vocal public tantrums and guarantees he'd see that Major Price "Will be severely and justly censured by the U.S. Army," Price might have been murdered that next day along McClellan Creek – by the men.

Within a few days, Miles submitted his report to Washington – to headquarters – deeming his opinion that the five survivors and Private Smith, men of the Buffalo Wallow Fight, should be awarded the Medal of Honor.

Not only did the men earn that award, but Dixon received his Medal of Honor from then-General Miles himself when he pinned it on Dixon while on duty in late January 1875 encamped at Carson Creek, which was ironically located about five or six miles west of the original Adobe Walls site.

The men learned in a few weeks that Harrington and Woodhall were recovering well from their wounds, but Amos Chapman had his leg amputated above the knee, but was doing quite well, though.

But Adkin and Uribe wouldn't be there to see their old friend, Billy Dixon, get his Medal of Honor, for things had dramatically changed for Adkin and Uribe right after they returned Dixon to camp from the Buffalo Wallow Fight.

The following morning, Uribe asked Adkin to walk with him down by McClellan Creek, as the unit was preparing to move again.

"Señor, you know I follow you anywhere and will die for you," Uribe started. "I feel love for you as if you are mi hermano. But Adkin Yates, at this time my heart tells me to go home and see my family."

Uribe stopped and wiped tears from his weathered cheeks.

"I don't want to die fighting these Indians all over this God-forsaken Llano Estacado," Uribe said slowly. "I am half Ute, and I know how horrible Indians can torture and kill.

"But I cannot continue. I fear I will always dream of how Private Smith died and how cruel it was for Billy and the ones that lived," Uribe said. "I am going to tell General Miles I have to go home – that I cannot continue.

"No puedo continuar, Señor," Uribe added with tears streaming down his face.

Adkin embraced his dear friend and started crying, too.

"Yo comprende, mi amigo," Adkin whispered. "I feel exactly the same thing. Let us go home together."

Uribe stood back and looked at his friend, wiping away tears on his shirt sleeve.

"Do you mean that, Boss?" he asked, as Adkin still had his hands on Uribe's shoulders

"Yes, Uribe, I mean it," Adkin said, cleaning his own face with his sleeve. "That story by Billy and the Buffalo Wallow fight will never leave my memory. I will go with you to General Miles."

They slowly walked to Miles' tent and ask to see the General. He welcomed them and could see their red, swollen eyes. They both started at the same time., and Miles held up a palm.

"One at a time, gentlemen," he said.

Adkin took charge and told Miles they had both been away from home and did not now have it their heart to continue the fight. Adkin apologized profusely, and Uribe did the same, but Miles didn't ask any questions and gave them his sincere approval for their resignation and thanked them for their service as scouts.

"You have served well, fought very well, and I hope God will bless you," Miles said as he shook their hands. "I'll see to it the quartermaster forwards your pay. Just give him an address."

"Good luck, men, and God bless," Miles added.

As Adkin and Uribe gathered what little they owned, they told their tent mates about their resignations. They were told several other scouts had resigned late the night before.

"Dixon's survival opened a lot of eyes," a scout said. "It's a razor edge we walk out here, and we don't think any less of you, honest."

"In fact, I'm heading back to Dodge City myself by way of Camp Supply," Masterson said as he walked into the tent. "I heard you've resigned, and I have, too. There's plenty of soldiers and scouts out here to secure the country, and they can do it without me, too."

They all laughed and bid farewell to each other. Adkin and Uribe decided to head to Dodge City first and let the family in Las Animas City know their plans and to regroup and resupply. Masterson headed off with two other men to Camp Supply and would return to Dodge City a few months into 1875.

An Englishman's Adventures on the Santa Fe Trail (1865-1889)

•••

Uribe felt like a new man. He couldn't explain it, even to himself, how good it felt that Adkin was going home and not trying to kill Lew Bush. He was thrilled beyond belief. He knew it was really happening when Adkin sent the telegraph to Ryan.

Date: September 22, 1874

To: Tyler Ryan

Las Animas City, Colo.

From: Adkin Yates

Me and Uribe arriving home around Sept. 25 or 26.

Uribe was smiling from ear to ear as Adkin read the telegraph.

"Send it like it is," Adkin told the clerk and turned to Uribe. "Now let's go buy some travelling clothes and plenty of ammunition."

They laughed as they walked out of the Western Union Office and headed down Front Street. They didn't make it a block until they ran into Sheriff Bassett, who insisted he buy them a drink.

They caught up on all the gossip, and Bassett told Adkin Reighard had sold his mansion.

"It's not the biggest any more," Bassett said with a laugh. "A cattleman from Texas built a bigger house about three blocks away, just to spite your house."

They all laughed and Adkin told Uribe they had some cash now. In reality, Adkin still wasn't aware of his wealth. He had been chasing bad guys and Indians since December of 1873 and spent nearly zero. He had been a messenger on stagecoaches for nothing, and he had been a paid scout for about three months at $50 a month.

But Adkin told Uribe and Bassett he would have to go find Reighard to get some cash – or Charley Rath if he was in town. Bassett assured him Rath was somewhere in the Panhandle setting up mercantile stores.

Bassett asked if they had heard Jones and Plummer had gone into business together and constructed a buffalo hide station down in the Panhandle. They said "no," and asked how that came about, telling Bassett both had been mustered out of the Army scouting crew while riding with Baldwin and Miles.

"They told, me," Bassett said laughing. "Well, on the trip back to here, they formed a partnership, knowing men would be returning down there to hunt once some of this Indian trouble had eased.

"They built a dugout down there to keep their stores in, and they even have a bar," Bassett said. "Their store is at the head of Wolf Creek, with a coral made out of cottonwood pickets, too."

Hard to believe, Adkin thought to himself. He looked at Uribe who just shrugged his shoulders.

As they walked out of Hoover's, several screaming children came running up the street while a lone Indian was riding over the bridge into town carrying a tall white flag and leading a large black stallion. Adkin took a second look, blinked several time to clear his eyes and realized the horse looked exactly like Diablo.

As the Indian got closer, Adkin stepped into the street and started saying "Diablo?" "Diablo?" louder and louder and started walking toward the Indian in haste.

"Diablo? Is that you, Diablo?" Adkin shouted.

The big steed started shaking his head and neighing, prancing sideways and pawing the soil – finally rearing up and striking out with both front feet. The Indian let go of the lariat tether and Diablo trotted up to Adkin as he raced to his steed. Adkin hugged the horse's neck and Diablo halted and succumbed to his touch.

The Indian proceeded up to Adkin, still holding the white flag.

"I am of the Quahadis," the Indian started. "My Chief, Chief Quanah, captured this horse at Adobe Walls fight. He say the horse's name is Diablo, and he know you. Call you friend, Adkin Yates.

"I bring you this horse. Quanah say he hope you not fight Comanches any more," he added and started to turn away.

"Please tell Great Chief Quanah I no longer will fight Comanche," Adkin said. "Tell him I am very happy to see my Diablo again. Give Quanah my best wishes for long life."

The Indian nodded, seeming to know exactly what Adkin had said and slowly rode back over the bridge and galloped away toward Mulberry Creek. The gathering citizens just stared in awe of what they had just seen. A real wild Comanche just slowly riding into town and then back out.

Adkin was rubbing Diablo's neck and talking softly to him when the others walked up in disbelief.

"Quanah knew Diablo when they ran off our horses and mules at Adobe Walls, Boss," Uribe said. "He wouldn't let the warriors kill him like Tóngúl – he didn't know her."

"I can't believe it," Adkin said. "My old friend, Diablo, has been returned from the dead. I had already woefully mourned his loss, and now this. Maybe God does work in mysterious ways."

Uribe said amen and was hoping God had reached back into Adkin's heart. He prayed it was so.

"Uribe. We are going to take Diablo to Las Animas and let him live the remainder of his life on beautiful pasture – and have many, many colts," Adkin said, laughing. "Many colts, eh?"

"Si Señor," Uribe said laughing with all those nearby.

"He's only – let's see – only about 11 or 12 years old," Adkin said, hugging Diablo's neck again. "Yes, put out to pasture and have many colts."

•••

Before departing Dodge City via rail to Old Granada, Reighard told Adkin the money from his house sale had been sent to YR&R Freight account in Las Animas City, and Adkin had netted about $2,000 profits on the overall cost of the home, which had been paid in advance. So Reighard had wired $12,500 to Adkin.

Adkin was able to visit with many of his old friends who now lived in Dodge City or owned mercantile stores there. He was going to ask Sitler if he wanted to buy back Dodger, but Adkin had taken a liking to the strong quarter horse and would keep him. Besides, he would only ride Diablo again for sheer enjoyment around Las Animas once in a while.

On September 22, he and Uribe left Dodge City on the Atchison, Topeka & Santa Fe Railroad headed on a two-and-a-half-day ride to Granada and a day's ride on horseback, the old fashioned way, to Las Animas City. Adkin felt a certain anxiety inside as if he was going to have to apologize for something – or everything.

The most important part of the trip was being able to make sure Uribe got back to his freighting family and his Mendosa family, who had established another village a few miles upstream of Las Animas on the Purgatoire River.

When Uribe told Adkin he had to go home when they were down on McClellan Creek, it was the moment Adkin realized he had exposed one of his most dearest friends to the brink of death – all in his selfish obsession to kill Lew Bush – and had exposed Uribe numerous other times.

What would he do if he got Uribe killed?

How would he live with himself?

He couldn't, and he knew it immediately at that time and place. They were going home, and Adkin was finished hunting for Bush. He had killed four of the five. He now felt it was up to God to take care of Bush.

Adkin finally realized within his heart that life doesn't go on forever, but love does.

As they rode the rails, they found out the town of Boggsville had died, as Las Animas City was named the county seat in late 1873. Thomas Boggs was said to be close to moving and Prowers was thinking of doing the same.

"What are you going to do, Boss, once we get back?" Uribe asked as the passenger car tilted left and right while the rails were clicking their steady but endless beat.

"I'm really not sure, Uribe," Adkin said. "I am going to put Diablo out to stud, because he is the greatest horse on the Great Plains."

After a laugh between him and Uribe's agreement about Diablo, Adkin said he was going to have to think about it.

"With the rails going everywhere now, there's few places we haven't established stage stations on and off the Santa Fe Trail," Adkin said. "Those routes will continue to grow outward from the trail and our stations with settlers, cattlemen and pioneers looking for free land.

"You know Uribe, my whole life was to come to America and seek adventure on the Santa Fe Trail," Adkin said wistfully. "By whole life, I mean since I heard of the trail when I was but 11 or 12. It was my dream, and I made it come true.

"And you can attest, old friend, we have had our fair share of adventures together on the trail," he said, patting Uribe on the shoulder as they both chuckled.

"Si, Señor, mucho adventures."

"We keep hearing about the Indian Wars, and I believe General Sheridan will clean up things in a couple of years – maybe five at best, for the Indians that is," he continued. "The wiser Chiefs are seeing how futile warring and raiding is – in the cost of lives of their warriors. The buffalo are disappearing faster than a snow in May.

"I am going to have to search my soul to discover what I want to do," Adkin said. "What does life have for me now? That is the question."

They sat there in silence for quite awhile, each with their own thoughts on what the future would bring. It was glorious for Uribe. He felt his old friend Adkin Yates had come back to Earth – and God.

"I thought the devil had him for good," Uribe thought to himself, then smiling broadly. He suddenly saw his big grin in the reflection in the train window as he looked out. It nearly startled him. But he grinned again, liking his smile, indeed.

•••

The railroad now reached all the way to Granada. They were excited to ride in a train seat rather than a saddle.

Adkin smiled to himself after the train arrived at the Granada Depot when they went to the cattle cars and unloaded the horses.

There was Diablo again. The big stallion walked right to Adkin and nosed him softly in Adkin's chest in greeting. Uribe was still amazed at the sight of Diablo, and he could still see the love between the two.

As they were saddling Dodger and Santa Fe, they heard a voice that sounded familiar but ominous.

"You two are under arrest, hold up your hands," the voice boomed, and just as Adkin and Uribe stopped and started moving their arms out, the voice barked. "You're under arrest for making your loved ones worry so …"

"Ryan, you old dog you," Adkin said as he twirled around and rushed to embrace Ryan.

"caramba, Don't do that to my heart, Señor," Uribe said as he hugged Ryan, too.

"Your favorite little German is here, too," Ray Dee said as they all hugged and shook each other as dear friends do. "We came carrying handcuffs to take you home before you changed your mind."

"It is so great to see you men," Adkin said. "I can't put into words what I feel like seeing you two varmints."

"Is there something wrong with Diablo?" Ryan asked. "You're not saddling him."

"It's a long story, and I will tell you all of it in due time," Adkin said, slapping his friends backs over and over. "Let's get to Las Animas and have a drink."

"Bueno por mio," Uribe spoke up.

•••

Once back home, the crews of the businesses started coming to the main office wanting to greet Adkin and Uribe when they arrived. The crew's welcoming was unimaginable to the two men. Kanaka, Missus Tyler Ryan, looked as beautiful as ever,. She walked out on the porch carrying a baby.

"Who is this," Adkin smiled as he dismounted and walked up the steps to Kanaka.

"That's our son, Adkin," Ryan said, as he tied up his mount to the hitching rail. "His name is Cheyenne Yates Ryan, and he's two months and … about three weeks old.

"He was born July 4, believe it or not," Ryan added. "Started to name him fire-cracker."

Kanaka turned the swaddled youth so Adkin could see his face and his long black curls. His little button eyes were black as coal, and he actually smiled when Adkin asked, "How are you, Boss?" while removing his hat and placing his face near the child.

"He's great," Adkin said as he looked at Kanaka. "You must be very proud Missus Ryan."

"Si, Adkin," she said grinning effusively. "And we are very happy – happy, too, you come home to see us and little Cheyenne.

"Will you be staying long?" she asked innocently.

"Adkin looked to Ryan and back to Kanaka. A tear ran down his cheek as he looked back to Ryan.

"Yes, I am home for good," Adkin said. "I want to be with my family and friends and hope they will help me rid myself of these demons which have besieged me."

There was an awkward silence. Adkin quickly spoke up.

"That's a fairly dangerous middle name for a Cheyenne, don't you think?" Adkin asked trying to change the subject and not start bawling like a lost calf.

"He'll be tough enough to carry it," Ryan said as he slapped Adkin on the back.

Once back in the main office and after a couple of drinks and small talk, catching up on family and the businesses, Ryan did bring up how he allowed Dusty and his wife, Margarite and their two kids to use Adkin and Matty's old house at the yard.

Adkin was genuinely happy Ryan did that and said, "It's their's, with my blessings."

All day long, Adkin and Uribe were visiting with the old hands, Fransisco, Dusty and his family, Peg-Leg Pete was still running things and bossier then ever.

Ryan explained Weldon Campbell had quit and moved to Dodge City. Adkin explained they had seen and visited with Campbell several times while hunting in the Panhandle. Don Diego still handled any extra job that came along, Ryan said.

Tom Marcellus almost broke Adkin's ribs when he picked him up and hugged him.

Ryan said Darrell Holmes was working out of the Junction City yard, still, and J.L. had a full crew at the Denver headquarters now. Coach service was ongoing in California and doing very well financially.

During a break before supper preparations, Ryan asked Adkin if he wanted his old job back with Sanderson – or did he also want to take back co-operations of YR&R Freight? Adkin asked Ryan if he could have a few weeks to try and settle his feelings and what he thought would be best for himself and the family businesses.

"I understand, Adkin," Ryan said. "We all do, and we're just glad you're back home.

"Are you ready for a feast tonight?" he continued. "Everybody has been eager for this. And, of course, everyone is waiting to hear of your's and Uribe's adventures – you know that – starting after we eat."

"There's a few not fit for women or children," Adkin said with his eyebrows uplifted and chuckling.

"I'm going to walk around and look over the place, if you don't mind," Adkin said. "Lots of new outbuildings and an expanded corral."

"No problem, Adkin. Take your time," Ryan said. "Peta is out there in the corral with Diablo. I can't believe you found him."

"That's not the half of it, Ryan. I've found him twice, and I don't intend to ever lose him again."

"Twice?"

An Englishman's Adventures on the Santa Fe Trail (1865-1889)

"I'll tell you the story this evening, I promise," Adkin said as he walked out on the porch.

As he approached the coral, there were about 40 horses and mules in there. Out in the grounds, which were fenced a few years ago by Campbell, Adkin could hear a bell mule and there were at least about 60 mules out there.

When he walked up to the corral fencing, he saw Diablo start moving through the others and coming straight to him. Adkin whistled loudly. Diablo snorted and shook his head up and down several times as if asking Adkin how he was doing when he stepped forward.

Adkin stated petting his face, cheeks and neck and talking to him, like he always did from the first day he had him. When Peta heard his voice, Peta came to him, too. Both horses snorted at each other and Diablo pawed the ground.

But when Adkin started talking and stroking Peta, too, it was like the big steed knew there was something between Adkin and Peta. He stood there momentarily, but pushed his head into Adkin's shoulder as Adkin was standing on the first rail of the fence in order to reach over and let his horses know he cared.

Adkin laughed and said aloud, "I can see you're jealous, Diablo, but you'll have to share me with Peta, too. He is our friend."

Adkin decided right then and there, he was going to go into the horse breeding business. He had two Indian horses; one who was large-boned, strong and fast like a quarter horse. The other was a medium sized horse that was sturdy as any mountain man's ride, plus Peta could run all day long.

"I could start crossbreeding their mare's ponies and develop a saddle horse that would be perfect for the Great Plains," he thought to himself, knowing a great saddle horse was the most valuable tool of every man – and woman – on the Plains.

He bid farewell to the horses and walked through the yard to the outer fencing Campbell had designed and built. He leaned against a top crossbeam and gazed down to the small creek that dumped into the Arkansas – whenever heavy rains hit the area. It's flow was actually diverted by the Consolidation Ditch the town had constructed to irrigate crop lands around Las Animas.

Adkin remembered meeting John Prowers out here on this land when they decided to buy the property from him and build the current headquarters.

"I'll bet John still owns all this land west of the yard," Adkin thought to himself, chuckling. "Probably all the way to New Mexico."

He could look back to his right – north across the Arkansas and see the low rising hills of pasture and grass was covered in spots with White-Faced Hereford cattle. He imagined John, Amache and Ryan were making money or they wouldn't be out there.

That evening after supper, most of the men went to the office for brandy and cigars. Uribe pulled out his trusty little pipe with the red granite stone bowl.

They commenced telling their harrowing adventures in Adobe Walls and how after five days, Diablo was gone and Tóngúl and Uribe's big mule had been killed, as well as all the other animals owned by the men there.

They then told of their friend's fight in the Buffalo Wallow, as they had heard it first hand from Billy Dixon.

"If ever there were proof that man can stare death right in the face and keep cooly fighting, determined to never succumb, that story is for the ages," Adkin said. "A grand story of perseverance, true heroism and never giving up the desire for life.

"It was instrumental in changing my life and discovering my life's priorities," he added, looking down, trying to keep from crying.

"We were blessed to be fighting along side these brave men on the Canadian and the Texas Panhandle," Uribe added.

When Adkin told of how a Comanche rode into Dodge City under a white flag and leading Diablo, the men were in awe.

"Well, how did you find Diablo after … after your near death at the Cimarron House?" Ryan asked softly, worried Adkin would close up.

Adkin started slowly, but told them all the truth: His hunting, the investigations, riding with a killer part of the way in a stagecoach. How the robbery was diverted and three got killed – all the grisly details.

"Then I recognized Diablo right before I blew his rider out of the saddle," Adkin said, matter of factly.

Adkin changed gears and asked his friends what they thought about raising quality horses – using Diablo and Peta as top studs.

"Of mi amigo, raising caballos ees muy bueno," Uribe said. "I could manage the business as good as anyone."

Everybody started laughing, but agreed raising good horses can be profitable.

"You, know, we've been talking about expanding the yard here to the west, and the Prowers still own all that land west of here for miles. Ryan said. "Maybe we should talk to him and see if he would part with a few more acres."

"You're reading my thoughts, Ryan," Adkin said chuckling. "I was thinking about buying land adjacent to this and building myself a house and having enough grasslands to graze a couple of hundred horses."

"We'll go talk to John and Amache tomorrow," Ryan said. "And we can soften up Amache by taking Kanaka and Cheyenne with us. If Amache is sold, John is sold."

Again, laughter spread among the men, with several comments of, "That's right," being heard

•••

After the oohing and aahing over Cheyenne the next morning by Amache, John invited everyone into his study. He had built another house in Las Animas, since all the businesses had moved there as well. Not much was left at old Boggsville.

"You come along, Mother – and bring Kanaka and that baby, too – this is business for us all," John said.

"Now what land are you speaking of?" Amache asked as she sat down.

Ryan spoke up first explaining his desire to add about another 40 acres for expansion, mainly because of the number of animals they were accumulating.

"I want to plant and irrigate forage on about half of that so there's plenty of good feed for the animals in winter," Ryan said.

Then Adkin said he was looking for about double that as he was going to start a horse breeding outfit – and he wanted to build himself a house. Horse breeding got Amache's attention right away. She loved horses – good horseflesh – as she put it, and she owned quite a few grand horses of her own.

When Adkin said he was going to start with breeding Diablo and Peta, she immediate had a couple of mares she said would make "beautiful ponies," as she put it.

John kept rubbing his chin, as if he was separating all the information and aligning it for his input. He then suggested Ryan add the grassland due south of the current place instead of westward.

"We could make it another 50 acres, as long as you don't need additional river front," John said. "And, we could sell Adkin a about 100 acres on the west side of the YR&R yard with the same amount of river frontage YR&R has now."

"What do you think, Mother?" John asked.

"I love it," Amache said, grinning. "I have one mare, she comes from an Indian pony and a wild Mustang. The Mustang was a big beast, and this mare is large and can run all day and night."

"Well, there you have it," John said. "We'll put together a proposal with the plat and bring it over in a few days."

Riding back to the yard in the buggy, Adkin and Ryan were giggling like girls, discussing plans for breeding horses, building a new, "… but small house," according to Adkin. Kanaka smiled to herself, happy her husband had re-connected with Adkin. They were as close as real brothers could ever be.

"Who would've thought that day you stepped into Barlow & Sanderson Stagecoach Company, you'd become a horse breeder, and I'd become a cattleman?" Ryan chuckled. "I've been meaning to tell you how successful John, Amache and our White-Face Hereford business has been doing.

"It's great – beyond our wildest dreams," Ryan added.

•••

It was about a week after they had signed the sales contracts and bought the land from the Prowers that news of the Indian Wars would make its way to Las Animas.

Colonel Ranald S. Mackenzie had been chasing Comanches who had earlier attacked his command when he cut them off by leaving the Tule River Canyon and crossing north to the Palo Duro Canyon.

From the top of the ridge of this yawning, six-mile wide chasm, he found them in September of 1874 – five Indian villages stretching about three miles along the stream consisting of at least two hundred lodges and a large herd of horses.

The only problem was the enemy was at the bottom of the cliffs which fell away about 900-feet straight down. He finally found a place where his men dismounted and slid and crawled down a goat trail single file dragging their horses along to the bottom of the cliff to attack. It took his seven companies of the Fourth Calvary – more than 500 men – nearly an hour to reach the bottom.

It was September 28 and most had got to the stream when the Indians finally saw them and started their furious defense to allow time for their women and children to escape up the canyon.

MacKenzie charged the warriors while their families were discarding all their goods trying to escape. The four-mile running fight ended successfully with MacKenzie routing them, though not killing many.

His big reward was capturing around 1,500 head of horses, which they took back out of the canyon and upon the plains where they headed south again and reached their Tule Canyon camp at 1 p.m.

MacKenzie then cut out a few horses for his own use, allowed the scouts to pick out the best horses and then ordered a little more than 1,000 to be shot and killed. This was the start of the end for the horse tribes of the Great Plains.

This loss, mainly for the Comanches, spawned a legend that a phantom herd can be seen galloping through the Tule Canyon to this day with their manes flying in the wind – and running riderless.

The horses' sun-bleached bones at the head of Tule Canyon became a landmark for decades to come.

•••

One day, when Adkin was going over plans to fence his new property and build a house, Ryan remembered Adkin's gun.

"I forgot, I have your gun and several crates of things from your old house that you and Matty shared," Ryan said. "That old Sharps of your father's is still a great gun.

"They're being stored in the northwest corner of the guest room upstairs," he added. "There's also a few of your old journals wrapped in oil cloth.

An Englishman's Adventures on the Santa Fe Trail (1865-1889)

Adkin had been staying in the barracks with the others and was happy at that. He didn't say anything but went up the stairs in the office and to the guest room Ryan had been talking about.

He slowly opened the first crate, and it contained most of Matty's sewing utensils; hook needles, bone needles and steel White man's needles, spools of thread, beads, porcupine quills, feathers of every stripe.

A couple of deerskin dresses were unfinished and there were a small pair of brightly beaded baby shoes, probably for one of Mary Catherine's children, Adkin thought. He took them out. He was sure little Cheyenne could wear them, if not now, in the near future.

He almost teared up when holding the shoes, but then he was overwhelmed with pride. His woman made them with love, and her life with him was nothing but love. He was determined to rid his heart of hate and fill it back up with the love he had for her and their life.

He smiled as he put the little shoes into his coat pocket. He looked through the other things, little items such as antlers she was going to use as clothing hangers or something, a small mirror that once sat on their table where she would check her braids.

Then he found the old Sharps rifle he had learned to shoot in Olney, England. Then he saw the deerskin bundle tied in two places and rolled it out. It was the bow Quanah had given him with its quiver and handmade arrows.

He nearly cried looking at the letters etched into the bow: K.P. – meaning Kwih-nai Parker, Quanah's Penateka name he was born under. It was the Quahadis who raised him after his father was killed and his mother recaptured by Texas Rangers. Few White men ever knew that, and Adkin felt honored.

He grabbed the gun and tied the bow bundle together and went back downstairs.

"I want Kanaka to have all Matty's things – her sewing items and trinkets. Plus our things that were in the cabin, if she wants," Adkin said. "And, I would be proud if little Cheyenne would get these shoes Matty made."

He held them out and smiled at Ryan.

"We can't have Cheyenne dressing like an old mountain man, can we?" Adkin added chuckling. "He's Chief material."

Plans went on expanding YR&R's fencing. The style was great for animals, too, but Campbell's saw mill was now in Dodge City. Adkin sent a telegraph and asked Campbell if he was interested in a contract for the spring of '75 of building more fencing for his 100 acres and adding to YR&R's new 50 acres.

It didn't take but three days, and Campbell was asking the dimensions and saying he would start milling posts and cutting what trees he could find east of Dodge City. He asked Adkin how much timber was west on his place and asked if he could start shipping to Las Animas by the end of March.

"He never even asked what we'd pay," Adkin said to Ryan, who told him of a local man who was a great house builder and could get planked wood easily from Pueblo.

"With us and him working together, we could probably have your house built by Christmas," Ryan said.

"I've been meaning to tell you, but I'm going to take a few weeks around Thanksgiving and go pay my respects at Matty's grave on the Cimarron," Adkin said. "It's something I have to do. I hope you understand."

"Of course, Adkin."

Once construction began on Adkin's new house, he surprised Ryan with another decision he had made.

"I know this sounds like vain glory, but I'm going to write out my life's story from when I was a small child," Adkin said. "Not that's it's overwhelmingly heroic, but that my family – here and in England – may know how fateful events converged to create the man I am."

"Adkin, you're only 29 years old," Ryan said, astonished. "You have decades more to live. Plus, you still have some old journals."

"Indeed, but if I wait til I'm older, the memories of my early life will have deserted me," he said, smiling. "If I start now, I only have to add small bits as the years go by."

"No arguments about that," Ryan said, laughing.

Next time Ryan saw Adkin, he was coming back from the mercantile store in Las Animas with a ream of lined note pads and a two boxes of pencils.

Ryan noticed Adkin had been riding back and forth to the Western Union office for several days. He finally asked Adkin one day as he rode up to the office what he was up to.

Adkin took an large brown folder from his saddle bag and had a strange stare. He seemed to be unhearing and blind.

"I can't believe it," he mumbled. "I can't believe it."

"Believe what?" Ryan asked as he followed Adkin into the office.

Adkin sat down at the table and then looked at Ryan.

"Ryan, I'm a wealthy man," he said while tapping his folder. "I checked with J.L. on my company stock, and he had his bookkeeper finally send me the details over several days."

"With my profits from stock and interest and dividends re-invested all this time, I've accumulated around $85,000," he said with a numb look on is face. "That doesn't include my personal account I've been building, like with the profits from my house sale in Dodge City. That's around $14,000 now. That alone made me feel very comfortable.

"I'm afraid to ask you what my interest in YR&R Freight Company is worth, even when I retired as an operating stock holder in December last year," Adkin continued, turning to look at Ryan.

"I've been wondering when you would get around to asking," Ryan said, grinning. "I don't think 'afraid' is a word I would use, but your holdings in YR&R Freight Company stock and the company's stock re-investment plan from quarterly profits is quite handsome.

Ryan stopped there and let Adkin squirm. He pulled out a small folder from his desk drawer and slid a piece of paper out.

"It's worth close to $100,000, my friend," Ryan said. "With at least more than $60,000 in cash right now."

Adkin's mouth fell wide open. A burrow owl could start a nest in such a gape.

"You're jesting me," Adkin finally said.

"No, Adkin. You are quite right, my fellow, you are very, very wealthy," Ryan said trying to use an English accent, but he started laughing. "It's true."

Adkin just sat there and shook his head. He was still mumbling as Ryan walked out on the porch. Ray Dee was walking up, and Ryan stopped him.

"I just told Adkin what his share of YR&R is worth," Ryan said. "He needs a moment for it to soak in. He was still mumbling when I left him."

They both started laughing.

•••

Adkin had decided when he took his trip to visit Matty's grave, that he wanted to see once more Chief Satanta. So he planned a side trip to Huntsville, Texas, via a grave visit to pay homage to his Matty. His trip would take him several train trips, stagecoaches and a good saddle horse.

He was happy with the way his house was coming along, even if the builder was over-engineering it, to Adkin's thinking.

So, on November 18, 1875, Adkin departed Las Animas by himself, despite Uribe's pleadings. He was taking the eastbound train with his clothes bag and a carpet bags full of travelling items. He was headed to Dodge City and the would go south to the ruins of their Cimarron House.

He spent two days in Dodge City, meeting with friends and making arrangements to open a bank account with Bob Wright, who said he was close to getting federal approval as a banking institute. Adkin said he would transfer $50,000 to him via wire. Wright nearly feinted, but said, "Fine."

Adkin then went to the Western Union office and wired money from the Westport Bank Sanderson had told him to contact with the correct account number. Adkin said to identify the amount was to be paid to Adkin Maxwell Yates, resident of Las Animas City, Colorado.

Adkin arrived at the former site of their Cimarron House two days before Thanksgiving. He often remembered it was Mary Catherine who taught he and the other men in the freighting crew what Thanksgiving Day was about.

He found the area where he had buried Matty, It was covered by more slate and sandstone from the sides of the cliffs sloughing off into the crevice. He thought it would probably be forever lost in time, but removed his hat, laid down and rolled on his back with his hands behind his head – looking to the sky.

He thought he would probably tear up, but a calm seemed to come over him. He felt like Matty was now flying free with the spirits through the hackberries, cottonwoods, the China Berry trees and plum bushes. Her spirit would never lay still in one spot.

He accidentally fell asleep and didn't wake until nearly dark. He quickly found his horse nearby and put out a lean-to tarp against the rock wall. He went and gathered some firewood and started a small fire. He wasn't sure if Indians still haunted these small ravines along the Cimarron, but he didn't want a glaring fire to attract attention, just in case.

He ate some jerked buffalo meat and made some tea. While enjoying the cold air and a sky full of stars galore, he talked to Matty. He wanted her to know he took care of four of her murderers and ask forgiveness for not hunting down the last one.

He told her killing the last one seemed like wasting time and energy. That God would take care of him. He explained how hearing a friends' story of raw survival against all odds, and while they were wounded with one lying dead next to them – had changed his idea of life versus revenge.

"I hope you will understand, Matty," Adkin said. "This will be my final goodbye – not as a sad farewell but with a smile on my face knowing you are among the spirits and the clouds. Happy and free from all Earthly sufferings.

"I will always love you, Mah-aht-Tay."

Adkin fell asleep watching small bright embers flying off into the darkness, disappearing like tiny red ghosts dancing on the wind. He felt enveloped in peace and calm.

•••

It was five days later Adkin was back in Dodge City and taking a train east. He was excited but wary, too. He loved seeing new places, and he was sure southcentral Texas would be exciting. But he also knew Indians hated anyone in Texas.

His saddle horse was safe in a cattle car, but he carried two Colt .44 revolvers, a hidden belly gun on his body and his Winchester '73 close at hand in the passenger car, just in case.

It was a long trip, going across much of Kansas then taking the KATY Railroad down into the Indian Territories through Oklahoma. The vehicle he loved, the Concord Stagecoach, was even welcomed.

There were plenty of places in Oklahoma where water and timber abounded. He thought with that much wood and water, there would be far more farm houses and small towns. He guessed they were probably scarce due to much of the land having been given to the Indian tribes for surrendering.

He finally arrived in Huntsville on December 14, a little over two weeks from the Cimarron.

"Not bad," he thought to himself, knowing it would have taken three to four weeks on horseback and sleeping on the ground in winter. He was beginning to like these new modes of transportation.

When Adkin arrived at the prison, he felt it an imposing place indeed. It was a fully-walled prison, similar to some forts in a way. He had to go talk to the prison's Officer of the Guard since the Superintendent was away on business.

He related his wish to visit with Satanta, and pulled his coat back and lifted his short beard to show the man his necklace. He told the man he was – in an Indian way – a relative of Satanta's.

They took him down a hallway to a small waiting room and removed his weapons, his coat and vest, his boots, hat and gloves, patted him down and left him in the room alone for nearly an hour.

He was about ready to get up and leave as he was getting cold when the door latch clicked and a guard led Satanta into the room followed by another guard.

They sat Satanta in a chair on the other side of a table from Adkin and stood on each side behind the two men.

"Hacho, Great Chief," Adkin said, raising his palm.

"Hacho, my friend," Satanta responded in same. "My eyes welcome the sight of Adkin Yates, my friend. But I no longer Great Chief."

"You will always be Great Chief to me, Satanta."

"Why you come to see me?"

"I just want to visit and tell you about the time since my … since our Mah-aht-Tay was killed," Adkin said. "I did manage to find four of those who murdered her – and I shot them dead – legally, for they were outlaws, too."

"Yes, I think I remember that, Adkin Yates," Satanta said. "Men who have no honor should die and the People be rid of them."

Satanta gave a look back and forth to the guards as he finished his statement. They stood still with no changes in their faces.

Adkin noticed Satanta had seemed to have shrunk from his former barrel-chested figure, and his face seemed thinner with his cheeks bony and his eyes more sunken. He was a shell of the Great Chief who would fight any man with any weapon or with bare hands – and win.

They discussed Adkin's return to Las Animas City, where he detailed the building activity and how the little town had developed. Satanta told him he and his band camped there many times through the seasons chasing buffalo, when there was no town, no White man and plenty buffalo.

Satanta said they were treating him as well as others in prison. Everybody had to work, but he refused many jobs and was put in isolation, which he didn't care.

He said people were speaking on his behalf to get the Great White Father, President Grant, to parole him. He didn't think that was possible, but he admitted he didn't think his last pardon would happen, either.

Adkin told him he had come to peace with Matty's death and had visited her grave site on the Cimarron. Satanta reminded him her father, Black Horse, was secretly buried nearby, too.

"They fly together on the wings of the Great Spirit," Satanta said wistfully.

They visited for about 30 minutes and then the guards said their time was finished. As Satanta rose and walked around the table, he turned quickly to Adkin and hugged him to his bosom like a child. Adkin hugged back with both arms and said "goodbye." Satanta stepped back raising his palm and said, "Hacho, Adkin Yates."

After he and the guards departed the room, another guard stepped in and threw all Adkin's belongings on the floor at his feet, gun belt and all.

"Here's your stuff Indian lover," he said.

Adkin grabbed his arm and yanked him toward him. He lifted the scared guard onto his tip toes by his shirt front and placed his face about an inch away from his.

"That man has more grit, toughness and honor than you'll ever see in your lifetime, Mister," Adkin growled, and pushed the man back. "Satanta is one of the greatest Chiefs whoever roamed the Great Plains."

The guard quickly scurried away, and Adkin dressed and headed out, down the hall and out to Dodger – a tear or two had slid down his cheeks.

It would be the last time Adkin would see Satanta. He got the news in less than three years of his visit that: "On October 11, 1878, Satanta had slashed his wrists. As he was taken to the second floor of the prison hospital, he jumped off the landing. The fall killed him."

There were theories that he had been murdered as many of his relatives and followers said Satanta didn't believe in suicide. But Adkin felt it probably happened that way.

"They had his corpse, but not his subservience," Adkin thought to himself. "And for a warrior, that was an honorable death."

•••

Adkin arrived in Las Animas City on January 3, 1875, just before sunset. "He celebrated the new year with other train passengers somewhere around old Fort Zarah. He was astonished how many people stayed awake til midnight and how much liquor there was in the three passenger cars during the celebrations, which included singing and dancing in the aisles.

When he sat back down, as someone was saying they were passing Pawnee Rock, he started flashing through the times since leaving England. He drifted off to a shallow sleep when he heard a loud boom, then realizing it was a gun shot, quickly followed by another, he was sure. He jumped up and had both his pistols in his hands looking behind him.

It seems the revelry continued a few hours into the new year, and a freighter heading to Dodge City was shot dead at the back of the car by a jealous gambler who was travelling with an attractive "Wife?"

The men were both drinking heavily, and the gambler claimed when he told the teamster to quick talking with his "Wife?" the man reached for his gun.

The problem for the gambler was the man didn't have a gun on him. The Conductor, a large burly man, took the gambler's gun away and took him to another car after putting him in hand cuffs, telling his "Wife?" he would be turned over to Sheriff Bassett in Dodge City later that morning.

Adkin had asked the Conductor if he needed any help, but was told, "No thanks, Sir. Please get out of the way."

Adkin had no intention of arguing with the tough looking man. He sat down, and stayed awake until they reached Dodge City, which was only about two hours later.

Watching the landscape roll by so quickly didn't halt the joy of a brilliant and glorious sunrise on the Great Plains – a sight that always evoked the feelings of total awe in Adkin. He would have to remember his feelings when he next wrote in his diary.

But, he would always remember what Billy Dixon said late that night after he had been rescued and asked if he was giving up the Plains and going back east. He, naturally, said no, and explained his love of the Great Plains as thus – or something as near to Adkin's recollection:

"There is something beyond description that clutches a man's heart and imagination in the Plains country. Whether it be a long sweep of the horizon, with its suggestion of infinity, touching upon melancholy or that wide-arching expanse of sky, glittering by night and glorious by day, may not be determined – yet no man is ever quite his former self after he has felt deeply the bigness, the silence and the mystery of this region," Dixon had said.

"Amen," Adkin said, whispering to himself. That was why he connected so well with Billy, his ability to put into words what Adkin and all those who went before him into the wilderness that love of the expanse between the Missouri and the Rocky Mountains.

When he saw how Billy had fought with everything he had – and then some more – to stay alive in that buffalo wallow, it changed Adkin's life from that moment on. And Adkin was happy again. He smiled as they rolled into Dodge City and slowed to a stop.

"The train will pull out in 30 minutes, folks," the Conductor yelled as he strolled between the three cars. "Those heading to Las Animas City must be back in 30 minutes."

The Conductor grabbed one of the Mexican boys looking for handouts from the passengers and put a coin in his hand.

"Go get Sheriff Bassett right away," he said, as the boy started to turn away. The Conductor pulled the boy back and smiling said, "Come back with Bassett, and I'll give you more silver, eh?"

Adkin had stepped off the train and was stretching his legs. He was still amazed at how this little area which once had a tent and dugout fort, was a bustling little town with stores and services everywhere. The stock yards alone were the size of large cities it was said.

He glanced up the hills north of town and saw some large houses among the smaller ones. He really couldn't even remember what his former house looked like. He saw several church steeples up there and a water tower, besides the water tanks along the railway.

He was trying to remember: It was the summer of 1872 when the railroad reached Dodge City, nearly a year after he bought his lots up on the hill. He made a mental note to check with Reighard or Sitler what those lots would be worth now, though he wasn't sure he really wanted to sell them. He had already sold two to Ed Masterson.

There was a small rail station platform with the Depot near the tracks, where stacks of crates and bundles of wool, barbed wire, chicken or pig fencing lay waiting. Adkin walked over and into the attached cafe and ordered a coffee. He knew tea would not be available.

As he sat near the window, he saw the arrival of Sheriff Bassett, a deputy and the Mexican boy who smiled delightedly when the Conductor had given him another coin. The Conductor had already retrieved the gambler and was discussing him with Bassett when Adkin stepped out on the landing.

The gambler's "Wife" had met them and was chirping like a magpie and Bassett told her something, and she stomped away and got into a buggy with a driver and headed south across the tracks.

As the Conductor walked away, Adkin shouted at Bassett, who immediately handed over the gambler to his deputy and walked toward Adkin.

"Adkin Yates, How are you fairing?" Bassett asked as he shook hands with Adkin.

"Fine Sheriff," Adkin said. "That gambler is guilty of one thing for sure. His gun shots woke me as I was just starting to dream."

"We'll take that into consideration of charges," he said laughing. "What brings you to Dodge City?"

"Just passing through, going home to Las Animas," Adkin said grinning. "Went to see my old friend Satanta at Huntsville – and stopped at Matty's grave to pay my respects."

Bassett smiled.

"I'm happy for you, Adkin," Bassett said. "Me and all your friends here – and you have more than you know – were worried for you. We didn't want to see you get killed by any of those worthless saddle tramps you were chasing."

"What ya doin' in Las Animas?" he asked.

"I've bought some property next to YR&R Freight, and I am going to raise horses," Adkin said smiling.

"That's great," Bassett said. "Well, I better get back to business. It's become a tough place down here south of the tracks, but we keep it pretty quiet and safe up on the north side."

"And if every stranger that came to Dodge City behaved himself, he would be treated with politeness," Bassett said, shaking his head. "But woe be unto the man who comes seeking a fight. He will soon be accommodated in any way, shape or form that he desires."

"I've got to go find an undertaker to fetch this body off the train, but we've got three undertakers within six blocks now," Bassett said, chuckling.

Adkin told Bassett to be safe and patted him on the back as he turned toward Front Street, as his office and jail were only two blocks away.

Back on the train, Adkin was looking forward to seeing Diablo and Peta and all the family. The Conductor had said it as only going to be about 6 hours to get to Las Animas.

"Over 180 miles in 6 hours," Adkin thought to himself. He still couldn't get over how railroads were changing the Plains. "It won't be long until the Santa Fe Trail will be obsolete."

He found it unbelievable, but there were still the Great Plains. And those were changing, too, especially for the nomadic horse Indians.

•••

When Adkin rode over the bridge at Las Animas and looked west, he could see the little ranch house on the other side of YR&R's main office building. It looked complete from where he was, and as he neared, there were no workers on the roof or other men in wagons around.

"It must be finished," Adkin thought to himself.

When he rode Dodger into the freight yard, several people were running out to greet him. He noticed they had dug out another extension of the road to his house further west and filled it with gravel, too. He couldn't believe how comfortable it looked sitting there with a high-pitched roof about a quarter of a mile from the main office.

"Como esta, Boss," Uribe hollered as he rode up on an unsaddled pony. He reached out and shook Adkin's hand.

"I've missed you, you old rascal," Adkin said laughing.

"Come. Come. Let Señor tell you about your new house," Uribe said. "Ees ready for you, Boss. Ees muy bueno, tambien."

They dismounted at the main office and Ryan stepped out on the porch.

"Good to see you still have your hair, Adkin," he said chuckling. "Hope you had good travels."

"I did, but I missed all this foolishness around here," Adkin said. "Do any of you people work?"

"Look who ees asking – the long traveller on holiday," Uribe said. They all laughed.

Once inside, Ryan told Adkin about finishing the house. How it had a special library for him, a new book case and a new desk with oil lamps everywhere he might want. A complete guest room to the side of his.

"It has four rooms, like your drawing, yet it is small like you requested," Ryan said. "After you wash up, let's go over and take the tour before supper. What do you say?"

"Can't I wash up over there?" Adkin asked with mischief in his voice.

"Damn right you can," Ryan said. "Let's go men."

They went outside where there were five horses tied up, including Adkin's Dodger. Ryan, Ray Dee and Dusty mounted up, with Uribe already on his horse – bareback.

They trotted down to the gate, turned right and started down Adkin's roadway.

"I might have to make me a fancy entrance gate later," Adkin said. They all agreed.

Adkin had two hitching rails in front of his house, one on each side of the steps going up to his planked front porch which ran the entire length of the house front with hand rails around except for the wide opening of the steps.

While riding up, he noticed two rock chimneys. Ryan explained one was between his library area and his bedroom and the other was in the living room not far from the dining table and guest room.

Ryan urged him to enter and Adkin twisted the brass door latch and walked in. He was speechless. He had noticed it looked to have a high-pitched roof, and now he knew why. The entire middle of the house had several timber cross beams the whole length – about 20-feet up.

He could tell the rooms and cooking areas were under the back slope of the house.

"How long is this house, it looks like it goes on forever?" Adkin asked.

"It's 60-feet long and 30-feet wide, just a bit more than your drawing – but not that big in today's standards for men of the English Gentry," Ryan tried in his English accent.

"You need to practice that more – mucho mas, Señor," Uribe said to Ryan, and they all laughed hard.

Ryan could see his library area on the west end and a large glass window on that end looking west and north to the Arkansas River. There was a door off to the right of the fireplace. Ryan hurried him down there, explaining that was his bedroom.

"You set a fire here and leave your door open and you'll be warm as a baby lamb under her mother," Ryan said, opening the door to the room.

Adkin stepped in. It had a wash basin area next to a cedar armoire for storing his clothes, a coat and hat stand was next to it, and of course, a honey pot. The bed was at the back, or north wall, with a large rough-hewn pine headboard. The bed was covered in beautiful furs of wolf, fox and mink. Above it were a set of elk antlers – big and beautiful.

"It's a feather bed, too," Ryan said excitedly.

On the east wall, there was another half-wardrobe with drawers. A small table with note pad and a chair sat next to the door on that side. A hand-woven Ute wool shawl was stretched out and pinned to the wall. It had all the glorious colors of fall. Adkin smiled. It was beautiful.

But Adkin's head turned back to the wash bowl area and the round-framed large mirror over it with a razor strop hanging to the side. Above the mirror, two large eagle feathers stuck out behind the frame. He walked over and touched the feathers gently. He recognized them – they belonged to his dear Matty. She would wear them on special occasions.

Ryan glanced anxiously to the other men.

"We could remove those if you don't care for the location," Ryan said softly.

"No. They are perfect right there," he said softly – then louder, he said, "I can look to them for true guidance to happiness every morning I awake. Don't know how much shaving I'm going to do, though.

"Are you boys trying to tell me something?' he asked while stroking his beard and laughing. They joined in, relieved the feathers didn't depress him in the least.

Ryan took him down toward the dining table. On the left between the guest room and the dining table, another smaller fireplace was situated.

The dining table was large and made from a split deadfall cottonwood trunk about 6-feet in diameter, or wide, and about 15-feet long. It had 10 chairs around it. Off to the left, or south side, was an open entry to a cooking area that had more than Adkin would probably use, but the cooking stove was a new style with numerous heating plates atop and an oven.

When they walked back out, Adkin looked up to the center piece of the whole open room from the dining table at the east end with two huge glass windows looking back to YR&R and north to the river and the sand hills and pasture grasses to the north.

On the back wall between Adkin's room and the guest room and the cooking area at the end – a huge buffalo bull head was taxidermied and hanging just above a man's head at the bottom of its beard with it horns nearly touching the roof eight feet higher.

"That is remarkable," Adkin said, looking up at the beast and stroking its wooly beard. "I didn't know what to think at first, that's why I didn't ask. How in …"

Ryan interrupted, "That's a very special house warming gift from everyone in your YR&R family.

"When you made plans in early October to build this place, we secretly went out and found the biggest bull we could, with a full winter hide. Uribe and the boys hunted several days to find him," Ryan continued. "We then shipped his head and salted front skin across the Atlantic to your homeland.

"We had the famous James Rowland Ward, the British taxidermist and founder of the firm Rowland Ward Limited of Piccadilly, London, fix it for you," Ryan said. "It only made it back one week ago – we've been a nervous bunch waiting for it."

"It barely arrived in time, Boss," Uribe said, making the sign of the cross. 'Thank God for the railroads."

"I adore it," Adkin said as he reached for Uribe and hugged him til all the breath was squeezed out of him.

"Easy Boss, You might break my ribs," Uribe coughed out, while everybody clapped and laughed. Adkin hugged everyone there.

One thing else he noticed was that about every 10 feet, oil lamps with engraved glass globes and brass tanks were hanging on the walls. There were even four larger ones sitting on tables throughout the big room. They had glass lamp shades sitting atop the globes.

"This place will light up as bright as a summer day with all these lamps," Adkin said.

"There's at least two each in the bedrooms, too," Ryan said. "Tell you what. Why don't we take leave and let you wash up, maybe get a little rest and meet us for supper about 7.

"Will that work for you?" Ryan added.

"It sure will," Adkin said. "I can't thank you men with the right words. This means very much to me. Y'all and the builder worked it out even better than my original drawings. It's wonderful."

They all shuffled out, murmuring, trying not to shed any tears, being rough frontiersmen and everything.

"See you at 7," Adkin said, smiling.

•••

An Englishman's Adventures on the Santa Fe Trail (1865-1889)

It wasn't long until Adkin's stables had been completed. He made sure there were a dozen horse stalls with a front roof out over the stalls for weather and sun protection, and each stall having full doors and outward half doors for the horses to look over during daylight hours.

By the end of March, Amache Prowers had four filly's brought over for breeding purposes. She made a deal with Adkin for half-ownership of any colts, less one share, which gave Adkin a majority right to sell the colt and split the proceeds or one-half plus one share if he bred the colt to another stud or mare.

Amache was happy with the agreement, telling Adkin she trusted him more than "All those White Generals in Washington put together." Adkin took that as quite a compliment.

By late May, three of her mares would be pregnant, two by Diablo and one by Peta. Amache sent over another mare to try and get impregnated by Peta.

Ryan walked in around the first of March and said J.L. Sanderson was planning a trip to Washington in late April and would be stopping a few nights at Las Animas on his way. Planning began at once, and Uribe was wanting to turn it into a fandango, inviting the whole town of Las Animas.

"Why not, we should honor all those who help us and provide services," Ryan said. "We are the town's biggest employers, besides Prowers cattle operations, but those cowboys help us in the winter."

Adkin agreed, knowing J.L. since landing in St. Louis back in 1865. He was easy to work for – as long as you tried your best to better the company's goals and profits. And he was generous with compassion and understanding, but a hard-nosed task master. He wouldn't ask any of his crew to do something he hadn't already done or wouldn't do himself.

Sanderson arrived May 10 amid real fanfare. J.L. was a "Big Boss" to many of the stagecoach team.

Uribe helped organize the fandango, with extra tables set up in the bunkhouse dining hall. Anyone and everyone in Las Animas and the surrounding area was invited. Adkin was surprised how many people came he hadn't met or known.

He also got caught in his own house most of the day as friends wanted to see his new abode – made of saw-milled wood and no adobe present anywhere – except for a cooking pit out back where a whole beeve could be put on a spit. And the outhouse.

Sanderson spent two days, encouraging everyone to look at these "feeder routes" off the Santa Fe Trail. He used P.G. Reynolds of Dodge City as an example of starting with mail service to Camp Supply, then adding stagecoach service to the Camp and areas beyond.

"I've heard there is a new trail down to Wolf Creek in the Panhandle and on to Mobeetie, where Fort Elliot is going up," Sanderson said. "Anyone familiar with this Jones and Plummer Trail?"

Adkin and Uribe laughed.

"We've worked with both those rascals," Adkin said. "We were scouts with them for General Miles advance command. They didn't make it but a couple of weeks and were sent packing."

"But that 'Dirty Face' Jones is a tough nut to crack," Uribe spoke up. "He's as tough as a rattle snake, but full of mischief. He makes me laugh."

"I've heard they started a partnership with a hide station and mercantile store down on Wolf Creek, but was unaware that they opened a good trail down that way," Adkin said. "Makes sense, settlers and traders will fill up that Texas Panhandle once the Indians are all moved out or killed."

"That's what we need to look for, those areas where settlers are going to want to travel and homestead or ranch," Sanderson said. "By the way, Sam Phillips and the Jarvis boy are making good profits down in Oklahoma. They've added a few routes and have four coaches working the area now.

"You know they had another child, named him Oscar," Sanderson said.

"Yes, we've heard that," Ryan said. "I'm sure happy Sam and Mary Catherine are doing well."

"They are wonderful people," Adkin chimed in.

"Have you heard anything about James Mead?" Adkin asked.

"You wouldn't believe what that man has accomplished," Sanderson said. "Well, knowing him, you probably would."

"You know he formed that town of Wichita, and it's growing like an ant hill," Sanderson continued. "He bought a railroad, and they're working with the Santa Fe Railroad to go to Medicine Lodge. He's the vice president of the Wichita Bank, he remarried, and he's in the cattle business, too."

"He's always been restless – and successful," Ryan said. "I'm glad for him."

"Me, too," Adkin said. "He's a fine, fine man."

After a few days of catching up on news and rumors, Sanderson made plans to catch the train to Washington the next morning. Sanderson had said Barlow's name was mentioned in a report to Congress about mail contractors.

"There are insinuations that Bradley Barlow has been erroneously mentioned as part of an illegal scheme to pay out profits to those officials permitting U.S. Mail contracts, which we have been one of the largest in the nation, and for nearly 20 years," Sanderson had said about Barlow. "I have never heard of any improprieties, personally, even once during that time.

"I'm sure Bradley hasn't either. I trust the man totally," he added, saying he was going to work with Barlow to go through all those years of contracts to determine and protect his good name and that of the company's.

An Englishman's Adventures on the Santa Fe Trail (1865-1889)

News came through that MacKenzie had been sent to Fort Sill a few weeks later to take command of the bands of Indians that were being forced onto the reservations around the fort. It was rumored one of MacKenzie's peace emissaries found Comanche Chief Quanah Parker and his Quahadi band, and the White-hating Chief were thinking of total surrender after a parlay.

Sanderson departed Las Animas May 13, 1875, and Adkin was still breeding Diablo and Peta, looking for wild Mustangs and large Indian Ponies.

Adkin hired a horse man who once worked for Amache Prowers, but had been fired for drinking. The man, Hector Ruiz, promised Adkin he had given up the evil snake oil.

Ruiz claimed it had been his Cheyenne wife who drove him to drink, and Amache believed everything the woman told her.

"Señor, I never touch my wife to harm her," he explained. "It was she who would beat me with firewood and whips if I came home drunk. She once broke my arm, and she told Señora Prowers I broke it hitting her. She hit her face with firewood to make me look bad. She ees loco.

"Once I was put my wife out, she vamoose to Nebraska to live with her tribe," he said, smiling. "I have never drinked no more since that day. God saved me when she quit me."

Adkin believed the man. He was too gentle and even meek looking, and Adkin had heard he was one of he best horse handlers and trainers in that part of Colorado. Ruiz told him he loved horses; that his mother was an Arapahoe and his father a Mexican teamster and freighter from Las Vegas, Old Mexico, before the war.

"Mi padre, he teach me mucho about taking care of horses, mules and oxen," he said.

Adkin asked him to go to the stables with him and meet Diablo and Peta. Diablo whinnied his approval immediately, shaking his head a little, but allowing Ruiz to stroke his face and his ears, which Diablo was a little touchy about.

"He is an Indian pony?" Ruiz asked while petting Diablo.

"Si, he was raised by Kiowa, and given to me when he was but 2 years old maybe. He's now about 12, give or take," Adkin said.

"He ees muy hermoso, beautiful caballo," Ruiz said.

As they headed for Peta, Adkin explained Peta was raised by Comanches, Quahadis to be exact.

When they walked down to Peta's stable, Peta moved to the back of the stall, wary of a stranger, it seemed to Adkin.

"Ven a mi grande caballo, seremos amigos," Ruiz said, extending his arm into the stall, holding his palm open.

"Peta snorted a few times and dropped his head and slowly moved over to Ruiz and smelled his hand and moved closer. Ruiz petted his neck and his face with his other hand.

"What did you say to him?" Adkin asked, hearing a couple of words he knew.

"I just told him to come to me great horse, we will be friends," Ruiz said. "Comanches train their ponies in several tongues, especially Spanish."

"I know he does well with English, too," Adkin said, smiling.

"Si, he ees smart caballo," Ruiz said grinning. "He probably speak more tongues than me."

Adkin was sold on the man, and hired him, explaining these two stallions were going to be his main breeding steeds. He later told Ryan that Ruiz was too gentle and compassionate to be a wife beater.

"Just don't tell Amache you hired him unless she backs you into a corner," Ryan said, laughing. "She won't be having that man touching her mares – afraid he'll beat them with firewood."

They laughed hard, Ryan slapping his thighs.

•••

In late June of 1875, Adkin was surprised when Charles Goodnight stopped for a visit. Charles was leading a small caravan of two wagons, an ambulance and his famous chuckwagon. He had a dozen heavily-armed cowboys on saddle horses with him and a small herd of horses and a few mules.

"Great to lay eyes on you, Charles," Adkin said as he embraced Goodnight.

"Same to you, Adkin,

Goodnight said. "You look well."

Adkin showed Goodnight his new house, and they sat down to talk. Goodnight explained he was moving a herd of yearling cattle from his Colorado Ranch west of Pueblo to start a new ranch in the Texas Panhandle at Palo Duro Canyon.

"I told you back when we made out trek through there I thought it would be a perfect place for a cattle ranch," Goodnight said. "Well I started a partnership with John Adair, and we're going to start the JA Ranch, right there north of the canyon where we crossed – all that beautiful grassland on the Llano."

"But before John goes in whole hog, I have to prove it will work," Goodnight said. "So, I'm going to get some cattle going and breeding down there and show 'im it can be done."

He told Adkin he was having troubles with rustlers where the cattle were out of Pueblo. He figured it would be better financially going down to the Panhandle.

"What about the Indians?" Adkin asked.

"You haven't heard?"

"I guess not, what's happened," Adkin asked.

"Well, Quanah and Isa-Tai were talked into surrendering, and on May 6, they started for Fort Sill from the Caprock," Goodnight said. "Their poor old ponies were starving – along with his people – and it took them until June 2 to make it to Signal Station, just a couple of miles west of Fort Sill.

"Quanah and 400 Quahadis surrendered, along with 1,500 horses and all their arms," he continued. "They say it was quite a sight, those Indians being so poor and starved they could hardly walk or even ride."

"I can see why you would feel safer now going to Palo Duro Canyon," Adkin said. "That is a beautiful place there on the Caprock of the Llano Estacado.

"You will do well, Charles, I'm positive," Adkin added, while he poured them a brandy.

They talked for several hours, and Adkin met several of his foremen, and they took a short tour of Adkin's new place. The men were very impressed with Diablo and Peta, especially when Goodnight made Adkin tell the stories surrounding his "gifts." The herd was behind them and being moved around the Las Animas area.

They all went to the YR&R Yard for supper, visiting with all the freighters and cowpokes. Everyone had stories to tell. Adkin made a mental note to start writing down some of those adventures in his diary. He knew one day, this life on the trail and surviving the frontier on the Great Plains would be over.

When Quanah Parker surrenders and moves to a reservation, the end is near, in Adkin's thinking. Quanah was another Chief Adkin was determined to see again. And he would in time. They would even become good friends.

Since the railroad had reached Las Animas City. Everyone was excited except Thomas Boggs. He felt it would be the end of the area's importance of providing the major amount of grain, fodder, vegetables and other food crops for the region. He looked to be moving out soon.

•••

In July, Henry Sitler had sent a telegram to Adkin saying he had traded for a large, 4-year-old breeding mare – a full-blooded Quarter Horse, with fancy papers guaranteeing her lineage. He wanted to sell her because she was a little large for the horses Sitler was wanting to raise. He was breeding for race horses mainly.

Adkin sent back word he might be interested, and after numerous telegrams back and forth, Adkin agreed to pay $1,000 for her. Adkin couldn't wait to tell Ryan of his deal.

"You won't believe I paid $1,000 for a horse?" Adkin said. "She's originally from a rancher in The Pueblo. Henry Sitler bought her and wants to sell her to me."

"I've always known a fool and his money are soon parted," Ryan said, laughing.

"What sealed the deal – she's a blue-blood Quarter horse with papers and all that – but get this," Adkin said, sounding as excited as Donnie when he had important telegrams. "Her name is Angelica de Domingo – but they call her Angel.

"Get it, we're going to breed Diablo to an Angel. What does a devil crossed with an angel produce?"

"I have no idea," Ryan answered. "What?"

"I don't know, but I'm dying to see it."

Adkin was beside himself, explaining Henry was going to have two men deliver her in about four days.

"I've got to get a stall prepared for her," Adkin said.

"What color is she?" Ryan asked.

Adkin stopped in his tracks. His head just stared down at the dirt. All was quiet. He dropped his arms to his side.

"I said, what color is she – any distinct markings?" Ryan asked again.

Adkin slowly turned to him.

"You know what? I don't know. I never asked, and Henry didn't say."

Adkin turned toward the office where Dodger was tied to the hitching post and walked away.

It was all Ryan could do to not breakout in laughter. He had tears in his eyes and was choking back giggles as he walked over to the bunkhouse. When he was out of earshot, Ryan almost fell down laughing so hard. He was holding his stomach.

It soon got around the yard Adkin had spent a whopping $1,000 dollars for a mare he had never seen, and he didn't even know what color she was.

"What if she's an albino?" was the biggest joke making the rounds.

On the fourth day of making the deal, two cowboys rode up with a big mare on a tether lead. She was snorting and dancing sideways as they came up the road. All the laughing ended that day.

Adkin walked out on the porch as they stopped at the YR&R gate and saw the boys point to his house. Many people were gathering around the main office and watching. On the cowboys came. The mare didn't seem to settle down much.

As she came into full view, she was beautiful; an inky, all-black mare. Her coat shone like silk in the sunlight. She had four white socks and a snow-white diamond on her chest about two-feet long and eight-or-so-inches wide.

Then Adkin saw the small white diamond – no, it was more like a white cross – on her forehead. What a horse, he thought to himself. Her long, black mane waving in the breeze.

"You must be Mister Adkin Yates?" one of the men asked. "We have Angel here for ya, she's pretty spunky for a saddle horse.

"Want us to take her over to the stables there?" he added.

Adkin slowly walked down the steps and toward Angel, not saying a word. He halted about six feet from her and cocked his head looking at her, trying to catch her eyes. She stopped dancing and skittering about and looked directly at Adkin.

He slowly approached and gently asked, "How was the trip Miss Angel. You are one beautiful lady." He reached out and petted her nose. She rolled her lips up and licked his hand, where he slipped a sugar crystal onto her tongue.

She crunched it slightly, and he stroked her neck and face. He kept stroking her – now with both hands – down her shoulders, down her back and over her haunches. She never moved, just a slight muscle twitch here and there, like she was shooing away a fly.

"I'll take her boys," Adkin said as he reached for the tether. "Follow me, and I'll return your lead."

Adkin led her to the stall he had prepared with fresh hay and some oats in a feed bag. She gave sturdy glances at Diablo and Peta while walking down the stables. The other mares took at look at her, too. She entered her stall without a whimper and started eating oats.

"Thanks gents, anything I need to sign?" Adkin asked, as he handed them their lead rope.

"No Sir, here's your papers on her, including your receipt from Mister Sitler," one said, handing Adkin a brown folder.

"I never saw anyone calm a frisky filly like that before, Mister Yates," the other said with eyes wide open. "She' a fine horse and supposed to have a fine blood line, too."

"Well we better get going."

"You boys want to freshen up first?" Adkin asked.

"Thanks for the offer, but we freshened up at the livery stable there near the train depot in Las Animas. But thanks just the same."

They turned and slowly rode back down the roadway.

"Miss Angel, welcome to your new home," Adkin said as he petted her cheeks again while she was dipping into the oat bag. Adkin realized she was nearly as big as Diablo. She had to be about 15 hands or a little better. Diablo was 16 hands tall. He smiled just thinking of the possibilities of what colts they could produce.

He couldn't wait to show everybody his "albino" horse.

•••

When Ruiz saw Angel, he immediately fell in love with her, too. Everyone – men, women and children – at the yard were mightily impressed with the beautiful mare, gushing with compliments and saying they couldn't wait til she had colts with Diablo.

It might take a little time, but Ruiz was a master of taking care of all the horses – the pregnant mares and those preparing to mate. He would introduce them to Peta or Diablo across a fence and then calm the mares, getting them comfortable around the stallions.

Diablo and Peta seemed to fall into the program quite well and needed little training or supervision.

Angel had only been there about three weeks and she came into season and they started breeding Diablo to her for several days.

•••

In late February 1876, one of Amache's mares, a feisty dark brown filly gave birth to a male colt sired by Diablo. The pony had a chocolate brown body darkening into black leggings and mane and tail like a dark palomino. He was a little scrawny having been born at 325 days, or a little early.

He was the first colt of Adkin's and he named him D-Boy – meaning Diablo's Boy. Amache was fine with that and wanted to sell him right away. Adkin wasn't so sure. He finally decided to wait and train D-Boy and agreed to sell him once he became a good saddle horse.

In the back of Adkin's mind, he was thinking this colt's future may end up in breeding service, for he was somewhat thin but frisky and smart right away. Ruiz said he would make a great saddle horse, but it would take someone special to handle him consistently.

Ryan and the crew could see Adkin had really took to his horses. He, Ruiz and Uribe were constantly caring for them and dealing with all their ailments or muscle cramps.

Adkin had ordered books about doctoring horses and what medicines were perfected at the time. He was teaching himself and Ruiz how to use science with common sense to keep their herd safe – how to be veterinarian.

Adkin had ordered all kinds of salves and ointments, powders, liquid medicines and even hypodermic needles for shots against worms and other ailments.

He was always ordering more books via telegraph. Poor Donnie was still a delivery specialist of the Western Union, but he was a little lankier now that he was about 10 or 11. Adkin couldn't remember. He often had to ride out to Adkin's house with only one thin book to deliver.

"They are like two old women looking after the babies," Uribe said one day, as he often went down and helped with the feeding and training. Uribe was no fool when it came to handling horses, either. He had learned from his father, who as a soldier depended on a horse for his life. Uribe learned that lesson well.

But Uribe, too, was pleased that Adkin was happy and seemed to have emptied his heart of hate and darkness. He was very much like his old trusted and compassionate self.

⋯

In early February, they had received word that Bat Masterson had killed a man and a saloon dancer in Sweetwater, Texas. Adkin was confused initially until he was told that was the second name of Hidetown on Sweetwater Creek. Once a new fort, Fort Elliot, was built they renamed the town Sweetwater, then it came to be re-named Mobeetie.

Anyway, Bat took off for parts unknown and was wanted for murder in Sweetwater. Adkin couldn't believe Bat would kill anybody unless he was threatened and protecting himself. Bat was old-school frontiersman, give you the shirt off his back if you needed help, but wouldn't take threats from anyone.

Last he saw Rath, he was building a mercantile store in Hidetown to buy hides and provide food and ammunition to the hunters crazy enough to go down into the Panhandle. He imagined more and more people had headed that way once Quanah surrendered his 400 people.

He remembered his most recent visit with Goodnight. Goodnight said he had wanted to start a ranch around the headwaters of Sweetwater Creek, but that Hidetown was less than inviting to serious businessmen.

He described Hidetown, or Sweetwater or now Mobeetie, that it, "... was patronized by outlaws, thieves, cut-throats and buffalo hunters, with a large percent of prostitutes. Taking it all, I think it was the hardest place I ever saw on the frontier except maybe Cheyenne, Wyoming."

If it was too rough for Charles Goodnight – Texas Ranger, Indian fighter, cattle drover and true frontiersman – it was too rough for Adkin, he thought to himself. He just hoped his old friend Bat would get these charges straightened out. He knew personally the anguish of being charged with murder.

The next colt born in March of 1876 was sired by Peta, who's mother was one of Amache's Indian ponies which was mainly white with brown splotches and spots. The colt turned out similar, but with brown and black splotches. It had a beautiful range of contrasts and was long legged.

Adkin asked Amache to name the filly. She thought about it for more than a week. She finally settled on Petita, meaning small little Peta. Adkin was agreeable, and so Petita started getting Ruiz's and Adkin's care and handling.

Adkin kept his eye on Angel, for they were sure about last September she was pregnant and therefore due August or September this year.

While the colts were growing, Adkin got the biggest thrill watching them playing with their mothers out in the pasture and grassland. He could watch their antics all day long. They were a true delight, and Amache even came over often to watch them when they were released into the pasture.

Ruiz always ran off and hid when they would see Amache's buggy coming down the roadway She loved those colts and the horses running wild through Adkin's acres, and would show up unannounced.

"Oh, Adkin, they are so much pleasure," Amache said beaming.

"I wish Matty was here to see them, she would be so proud."

Her face froze immediately as her last words came out.

"I'm so sorry, Adkin, I didn't mean to …"

Adkin interrupted and cut her off.

"That's okay Amache. I wish she were here, too. She loved horses as much as anybody I ever met," he said. "Well, maybe not as much as you, my dear friend."

Amache put her arm around Adkin's waist and gave him a squeeze. She didn't say anything, but a few tears were sliding down her cheeks behind her Spanish laced veil.

"Look how high D-Boy can jump already," Adkin said, chuckling.

•••

Later in 1876, he learned Wyatt Earp had been hired as a policeman in Dodge City. He remembered how nice young Wyatt was when he was hunting buffalo in Charlie Bassett's crew years earlier. That crew was where he first met the Masterson boys, too – Bat and Ed. They were hunting the Bluff Creek and Kiowa Creek areas.

He had also heard late that year that settlers were moving into the Bluff Creek area and down from Mulberry Creek, as well as further down into Mead County along Crooked Creek and even to the Cimarron. They were staking out cattle ranches for grazing.

He wondered when someone would discover he had filed on that 160 acres where he and Matty's house had been. His stone markers were still there, if they could be found.

He imagined some rancher or dirt farmer would be wanting to buy it. What would he do? He couldn't hang on to it forever, but he might try, he smiled to himself. One thing for sure, Matty's grave would never be disturbed. That ravine was impossible to ever build in.

He was also getting pressure to sell his house lots on the hill in Dodge City. Offers were up to $300 a lot. Adkin had only paid $10 a lot, and he still had 44 lots remaining. As he calculated the worth, he just shook his head. He began to think of those lots as his safety net. But then he would think of all the small boom towns west of the Mississippi to the Rockies that went boom – then bust.

He decided he would sell 10 lots and use the money to seek some more bloodline horses. The following six to eight months would be time to be looking to sell yearlings, especially saddle-broke yearlings that were well trained to voice and body-language commands.

It was going to be hard to start selling any. If Adkin had his choice, which he did, he would keep them all. He loved going out and riding Diablo and Peta around the pasture, getting them their exercise.

He would also use some of the funds for the reorganization that Ruiz and Uribe recommended for the pasture groupings. It had originally been divided up into three sections fairly even in size. But Ruiz suggested fencing a very large area for running of many of the herd together, with smaller spaces for pregnant mares near birthing.

He also recommended fencing off the training circle where Ruiz and Uribe taught the colts to trot, canter and take orders and get familiar with the bridles and eventually saddles.

Then they needed a securely fenced area to ride or break the colts.

He sent Reighard orders to sell 10 of the lots and keep them together. He said he wanted to wait to sell any of the remaining ones. He also ordered more fencing posts.

He needed expansion here and there, as Peta had mated with three of Amache's mares in April. By late May, two looked like they may have conceived.

•••

It was late June 1876, when Adkin and the whole town of Las Animas City heard the news about Colonel George Armstrong Custer, 36.

John Prowers rode out with the news he had received via telegrams and soldiers on the train from Dodge City. He had been taking care of some business there and just got back home.

"Custer got killed June 25 or 26, by the Sioux and several other tribes on the Little Bighorn River," Prowers said. He had decided to attack a large village and split his command into three columns and surrounded them. He was rounding up Indians to force them onto the reservation.

"Word is he was trying to come to the aid of one of his units that had to retreat or something, and he swooped down on the Indians from the north not realizing Lakota holy man Sitting Bull had called together the largest ever gathering of Plains Indians for a meeting in Montana – at the Little Bighorn.

"People are saying more than 2,000 Indians, including Chief Crazy Horse – who forced Custer's men up the side of the hill from the river and cut them to shreds," Prowers said. "There were Lakota Sioux, Cheyenne and Arapahoes who got in on the attack.

"Custer's whole battalion of 208 men were killed – not one got away," he continued. "Between the two other units and the pack train, an additional 276 men were killed. When General Terry with the main column arrived two days later, they found most of the soldiers' corpses stripped, scalped and mutilated. Custer's body had two bullet holes, one in the left temple and one just above the heart.

"Can you imagine that?" Prowers said. "Four-hundred and eighty-four men killed in one day?"

Adkin and the others sat there quiet as mice. Prowers looked around, not quite understanding the silence. He was outraged, but he didn't know Adkin and several others were there after the Washita River battle site where Custer had massacred women and children. And killed hundreds of horses and mules.

"Whatsoever a man soweth, that shall he also reap," Adkin said softly. "It's a shame so many brave men were under his command."

They all just sat there. Prowers stood and said his goodbyes, still not understanding. He stomped out of the main office and rode away.

"I'll explain our feelings of Custer with Kanaka and Amache," Ryan said. "They will understand and tell John. Custer's ego was bigger than his brain."

•••

In August, Angel was big with her colt. They weren't sure how close she was to giving birth, but Adkin wanted to get her into this new fangled portable branding chute, where she couldn't move around and try this new procedure where he would reach into her birth canal and ensure the front legs and head were where they were supposed to be.

Ruiz, Uribe and several hands were ready to start the procedure, but the first problem was she was too fat to get into the branding chute when trying to close the side squeeze gate.

They had to take out the two bottom bolts on the swivel side gate, pin them back with extension chains added which allowed the bottom to be moved out about a 20 inches.

They then led her into it and slowly lifted the squeeze gate and it worked. It latched, and she wasn't pressed on her sides, and she was calm as Ruiz was at her head, talking and stroking her face.

She was doing fine until Adkin lathered up his arm with lard and started into the birth canal. She nearly tipped the whole chute over, but it held, and she quickly calmed down.

"The legs are right there aside its head," Adkin announced proudly. "She's due any day boys."

Everyone whooped it up and laughed with joy. Uribe had never seen Adkin as happy since he first met the man at Bent's Fort – with exception to his love with Matty. He could tell Adkin was excited to finally see what you get when you cross the devil with an angel.

Angel was led to her stall with no problems, she acted as if nothing had happened at all.

"She is so beautiful," Adkin said to himself. "Even if she looks like a water tank with legs right now."

He went to bed that night struggling to come up with a name for this new colt, whether it was a stallion or a mare. He finally drifted off with absolutely nothing decided.

•••

One problem Adkin did decide on was what to call his operation. Uribe and Ruiz both pressured him saying his ranch needed a name so buyers and sellers could get the word out easier.

He decided it would be simply Yates Ranch. He even designed a large entrance gate and a brand. He made plans to design his own expanse to be placed over the gate.

Naturally, two tall pine logs would be needed to set on each side a few yards from where the roadway turned to enter the YR&R yard. There would be two small but long wrought iron pieces bowed upward, looking like a small rainbow. They would be nailed into the tops of the pine posts.

In the middle he and some of the boys; Don Diego, and Fransisco, made a large "Y" with "ates" going out to the top right of the Y, and a small "R" came off the bottom leg of the "Y" and "anch" was to the right of that in smaller letters.

Once they secured that in the middle of the wrought iron arches, he used chiseled horse head silhouettes to be placed on each side of the "Y"ates "R"anch – both horse heads facincing inward to the brand – and all of it painted black. He even had them paint the pine posts black with warm tar mixed in for weather proofing

Adkin amazed his boys when he did most the iron work, and showed them how to use a chisel on sheet iron. He drew a pattern of the horse head silhouette, carefully chiseled it out, then traced an identical one the same way, and used small twisted wrought iron to secure the two horse heads to the archway.

When it was finished, everyone was fairly impressed, except for Amache. Ruiz ran off when they spotted her coming up the lane in her buggy. She was driving herself this time. She stopped briefly and looked up.

"Is that all you boys have the time to do is make frilly gate entrances?" she barked. "Now how are my babies doing?"

Adkin hopped in the buggy beside her and put his arm around her shoulder.

"Well, let's just go see how those colts of ours are doing, what do you say, Amache?"

She grinned ear-to-ear and snapped her jip and headed to the stables. She really liked this Englishman – he had manners, and he was a charmer.

•••

A new stallion was born to mare Angelica Domingo, sired by Diablo, on September 1, 1876. The colt was amazing; big, strong – he stood within minutes and was coal-black with the exception of two white socks on his back feet. Plus, he had a wonderful white cross on his face. It was even more perfect in the shape of a cross than Angel's cross.

Angel, too, got up to nurse him right away after he staggered a few steps toward her and then started looking for milk. Adkin and Ruiz had been up with her all night. She finally gave birth at 3 in the morning, and she was up about the same time the colt made his steady stance.

Adkin had discussed the name with everybody, and even if the boy wasn't a full-blooded quarter horse, Adkin decided his name would be chosen after he saw fully what the colt looked like.

"Señor Hector Ruiz, mi amigo, I name this caballo, Colorado de la Cruz Blanca," Adkin said proudly, after eyeing the colt.

"Oh, Señor, el llama es perfecto," Ruiz said, grinning. "He ees a wonderful bambino. With his white cross, he has been blessed para mi dios."

"I agree, Ruiz, he is blessed, and we are blessed to have him," Adkin said laughing.

Adkin's chuckle started out of nowhere, probably just the release of angst, anxiety and sleep depredation. Ruiz quickly started laughing, too, They both hugged and jumped up and down like school boys – laughing into the night as Colorado suckled.

Adkin knew at that moment, he would never sell this horse at any cost. This was Diablo's first son with Angel, and Adkin would keep him til death of one or the other. And he figured Colorado of the White Cross was as apt a name as ever.

•••

Naturally, Colorado was a big hit with the families, especially the children. There must had been a couple of dozen boys and girls that ran to Adkin's stable to see the colt – nearly every afternoon.

"How many children live out here with us now, Uribe?" Adkin asked one day while about a dozen kids were peering into the small corral Ruiz put Angel and Colorado in for exercise.

"I don't know, but YR&R and the stagecoach business probably employs about 35-40 people now, Boss," Uribe said with that mischievous grin. "And many like making babies."

An Englishman's Adventures on the Santa Fe Trail (1865-1889)

Amache was the first to say she wanted to buy the colt.

"I will give you $1,000 for him right now, Adkin – even without training," Amache said standing at the stall watching Colorado and Angel. "$2,000."

"I'm sorry, Amache," Adkin said. "I knew a few moments after I saw him I would never sell him. I hope you understand?"

She patted Adkin on the back and said she knew exactly how he felt, as she had watched several birth's of some of her horses and knew that feeling – that immediate bond.

"Well I had to try, si?" she said chuckling.

Ryan and Uribe were amazed the colt kept most all his mother's traits, except only two white socks and just the rear two feet.

"It must be a good sign, Boss," Uribe said, starting to laugh. "Maybe he will have many talents – or none at all."

"I don't want to hear from you, Uribe," Adkin said laughing, too. "Just tell me how my albino looks, eh?"

"Maybe that is what his name should be – Albino – not Colorado," Uribe said. They all started laughing. Adkin looked around and was so happy to be with his family. He thought about that. It was his American family, but he had a family across the Atlantic, too. He hadn't heard from them in a couple of years.

"It is time for me to go home for a visit," he told himself. "I have the money – and the time."

•••

Once Adkin made up his mind, he tried planning everything Uribe, Ruiz and the others would need to do to handle the horses; the breeding, the foaling, the training, exercising. The boys finally told him make his travel plans, and they would handle the operations.

"We know how to run a ranch with horses, Boss," Uribe finally shouted at Adkin one day. He relented and laughed at his obsessive planning.

He telegraphed Sitler, Bob Wright and Reighard to ask around about sailing out of New Orleans or the east coast. They had made contacts with friends in Saint Louis, Philadelphia and Washington.

After about a month and a big Western Union bill, Adkin decided to sail from Philadelphia, and to sail out in early spring. He decided to catch a steamer, with sails, on the Inman Line in March 1877 – only about six months away. The formal name for much of Inman's history was the Liverpool, Philadelphia and New York Steamship Company Line.

One thing he wanted was to visit with Chief Quanah on his way east. He would make a side trip to Fort Sill, even if it took a month to accomplish the round trip from Dodge City. He would plan on five weeks, just to give himself some slack on timing to Philadelphia.

One advantage was once he got back to Dodge City, all his travel to the east coast would be on rails. It was amazing to find out the trip of about 1,500 miles from Dodge City to Philadelphia via rail would only take about two weeks or so, with much of that for stops at train stations.

He was excited about that upcoming adventure. But first, he had to visit with Quanah. He felt obliged; Quanah saved his life after Matty's murder, and he saved his Diablo at Adobe Walls.

"Ryan, I've moved $1,000 into the YR&R Freight account under my name for feed, tack, things like that and any emergencies that might arise while I'm gone," Adkin said, as they sat around the table in the main office with Uribe, Ruiz, Ray Dee and Tom Marcellus listening to Adkin's plans.

"I'm departing here January 3, 1877," Adkin continued. "When I arrive at Dodge, I'm taking Reynolds' stagecoach services as far as they go down into Oklahoma – they may have their route to Fort Sill established by then, that's what they tell me anyway.

"After visiting with Quanah, I'll be headed back by stage to Dodge City to catch the trains east. I should arrive Philadelphia by mid March at latest, whereupon I will purchase passage to Liverpool, England," he added. "I have sent by U.S. mail my intentions to my family in Olney and for them to expect me by last week of April at latest.

"How long are you going to stay with su familia, Boss?" Uribe asked.

"I'm really not sure," Adkin said. "I've been gone so long – in my mind – it may take some time for them to accept me back into the family circle."

"Don't be silly, Adkin," Ryan spoke up. "Knowing your values and seeing the way you were brought up, they'll be happy to shower you with love again."

"That's right, Boss," Uribe echoed while Tom and Ruiz agreed.

"What I will do is telegraph you right before I depart and the day that I return to Philadelphia," he said smiling now. "With no side trips on my return, I should only take about three weeks to be back in Las Animas with my American family – and, hopefully, some new colts."

They all laughed, knowing he would be worried about his pregnant mares and the new colts.

"We take care of the horses, Señor, you just have muy bueno tiempo con sus familia," Ruiz said.

•••

The stagecoach services did make it to Fort Sill, as advertised by old friend P.G. Reynolds in Dodge City. Adkin's stage was actually only the third stage to go to Fort Sill, the route was that new.

Reynolds had been offering service and mail contracts to Camp Supply since early in the camp's founding. He beat Adkin and Ryan to the punch, plus he had inside contacts with military big wigs at the time.

But Adkin was happy to see Reynolds was using the Concord coaches, the most reliable – and comfortable – on the market. He arrived at Fort Sill January 19, 1877, earlier than expected.

He asked the guard at the front gate to see the commander Colonel Ranald S. MacKenzie, a man he had never met but had heard wonderous things about. He was told MacKenzie had been promoted to duty in Nebraska and the current commander was absent.

The officer took Adkin to the garrison commander, a Lieutenant named Todd, Daniel Todd. On the way, he noticed a large tipi near a row of wooden houses, probably officers' quarters, Adkin thought. But why this large tipi while the others were about a half-mile away? He took note there were no walls, per say.

"Lieutenant, my name is Adkin Yates. I worked for Barlow and Sanderson Stagecoach line for years, and I'm a co-founder of YR&R Freight Company of Las Animas City, Colorado," Adkin said. "I am on friendly terms with Comanche Chief Quanah Parker, and I would like to visit with him."

"First, it's a pleasure to meet you Mister Yates, I have heard of you and know those outfits," Todd started. "Second, this is a reservation, not a prison, and I, too, am a friend of Quanah's. He is a remarkable man."

Adkin was taken aback by Todd using the term man and not Indian. He could tell in the Lieutenant's voice he had an admiration for Quanah. This is good, Adkin thought to himself.

"I will send an aide and have Quanah come here if he is not engaged in other affairs," Todd said. "His tipi is next to the Commandant's quarters."

After talking with an aide at the doorway, Todd offered Adkin coffee which he accepted. As the Lieutenant was pouring their cups and setting them on the table, the door swung open. It was Quanah.

He was in good shape, his huge arms the same, but he wore a top hat like Lincoln's photos – but it did have an eagle feather out of the side of the hatband. He wore White man's clothes and a cowskin vest. He had to bow to get through the door.

"If I can believe my eyes, it is Adkin Yates of England," Quanah said, as Adkin rose and they embraced by holding each other's shoulders.

"I am very happy to see my friend Great Chief Quanah Parker," Adkin said. "I am happy we are both still living in this land we love."

Todd had the three take a seat and began to tell Adkin how well Quanah had learned English from Colonel MacKenzie and other ways of the agency and the reservation.

Quanah spoke highly of MacKenzie, telling Adkin he came close to being killed by MacKenzie many times, now they are good friends.

"You maybe try to kill Quanah at Adobe Walls, too, si?" Quanah asked Adkin, who knew this would be coming up between them, and he would have to explain.

"When I saw Quanah at Adobe Walls fight, I did not shoot at Quanah ever," Adkin said. "I did shoot at others, but it was survival. I was not there to hunt buffalo, I got caught there accidentally."

Quanah's head was cocked, seeming to want to hear more. Todd was, too. He had heard, like all of America, about the second Adobe Walls fight.

"I went there with my friend Uribe, you know him, as we were hunting for Lew Bush, an outlaw who murdered my Matty at our Cimarron House and nearly killed me. Where you saved me." Adkin said. "Bush is the last man of five I had yet to kill to avenge her death – I thought he might be in Texas hunting buffalo."

"That is why I was at Adobe Walls – not to seek fight with my friend, Quanah," he added.

"I knew that in my heart, Adkin Yates," Quanah said. "That is why I stopped my warriors from shooting Diablo. I knew that was your horse, a gift from Kiowa Chief Black Horse."

"That is another reason I am here – to thank you for giving Diablo back to me," Adkin said, grinning. "He and Peta are now the stallions at my horse ranch in Colorado."

"Is Peta well?" Quanah asked, smiling.

"He is very well and has sired two beautiful Indian ponies with a third mare carrying his colt as we speak."

"Very good. Very good," Quanah said chuckling.

"Wow, you to must tell me more about how you came to know each other and the adventures you shared," Todd said, wide-eyed.

They went through seeing each other at the second Medicine Lodge Creek Peace Treaty and how Quanah met Adkin's Kiowa wife, and Diablo, all of it – with the exception Adkin and Uribe were with Colorado Sheriff L.A. Allen when they escaped old Adobe Walls by scaling out of the Canadian River Valley, then ambushing some of Quanah's warriors after topping the canyon edge and hiding in the huge boulders.

After about an hour of riveting stories for Todd, Quanah asked if Adkin would like to see his lodge next door. Adkin, naturally, accepted the invitation.

Once in Quanah's tipi, Quanah wanted to smoke the pipe first, then talk. He explained he learned Whites do not like to smoke first, but they do after eating.

"But I don't like those big cigars they smoke," Quanah said. "Looks like coyote dung."

They both broke out laughing.

Quanah said it was MacKenzie's pursuit of him and his people that forced Quanah to look to the future and surrender.

"All through the hot, dry season of '75, MacKenzie or many of his troops chased us all over the Caprock, up on the Llano Estacado and back into the canyons," Quanah said. "There was never enough time to hunt the buffalo – if we could find any – and we were starving, even our animals were hungry.

Finally, in May, we surrendered, but it took us a month to get to Fort Sill – our animals had to be walked, we could not ride them they were so weak," he continued. "My people were same, starving and weak. It was sad, but I had no choices."

Adkin asked how was life so far at the reservation. Quanah explained he has understood certain ways to get beeves from Texas herds coming through the reservation lands.

"I charge them five fat cows and money for each cow crossing our lands the government gave us," he smiled.

Adkin understood exactly. Quanah would exploit others in the name of the government that made him live on the reservation lands. Quanah was smart, and it sounded like his close relationship with MacKenzie had been well utilized, too. He also said he had another lodge a few miles away where most of his band lived.

One thing Quanah was grateful to MacKenzie for was trying to find Quanah's mother, Cynthia Ann Parker. Though she was dead, as well as his little sister who was captured with Cynthia, he had tried making contacts with the Parker family.

"They will have nothing to do with me," Quanah said. "I am just a heathen Indian to the Parkers, even though half my blood comes from them."

Quanah explained during the winter that he got permission to go on three hunts off the reservation into the Texas Panhandle because of MacKenzie's "understanding."

"I told him my people were restless and longed for a buffalo hunt to do the old things the old way," Quanah said. "I gave my word we would not disturb any Whites. They were not very good hunts."

The most depressing buffalo hunt was when Quanah talked MacKenzie in allowing him and a hunting party to go as far as Prairie Dog Canyon. The Comanches and other Indians called the canyon where the Prairie Dog Fork of the Red River flowed through after the river.

The Whites called it Palo Duro Canyon.

Not only did they discover there were no buffalo herds around, a White man told them it was his country now.

"It was a cold day with snow on the ground, and all we find is beeves," Quanah said. "So we start killing cows. A White man rides to us alone and says he owns the cows and the canyon. My warriors placed him with one who speaks good English and surround him in a circle.

"We are not happy him telling us the sacred canyon now belongs to him. We tell him it belongs to us," Quanah continued. "We ask him what he doing there, and he say, 'raising cows.' We tell him the land belongs to us, and he say, 'he had heard the Indians claim the country but the Great Texas Captain also claims it.'

"He is not afraid, and he tells us he came from Colorado. We ask many questions about creeks, rivers and valleys in Colorado to prove he from there," he said. "He know that country well, so he ask for parlay with Chief.

He asked me my name, and I say two names … Mister Parker or Quanah. He not surprised. I think he saw me and know I was Quanah."

'Who was this man?" Adkin asked, having an uneasy feeling he knew.

"His name Charles Goodnight," Quanah spit it out, confirming his fears. He knew Charles would recognize Quanah, too, and certainly didn't want to say he was a Texan, or they would have probably killed him on the spot. They hate Texans.

"Do you know this man?" Quanah asked.

Now Adkin was in a quandary, he couldn't admit he knew this Texan, per say.

"I have heard of him," Adkin skirted the question. "I think I heard in Dodge City he was a cattleman starting a ranch in the Texas Panhandle. I hear he is a fair man and good businessman."

"Well, once I know he not a Tejano, I said, 'We ready to talk business. What you got?' He say, 'I got plenty good men, they are good shots, plenty guns and bullets – but that he not want to fight unless we force him to fight.

"He say, 'You behave and not make trouble, and I will give you two beeves every other day until you find the buffalos,'" Quanah said. "I agree, and we make treaty. He tell me I have good manners. I tell him Colonel MacKenzie teach me White man's manners.

"A few days after, a White officer and 25 Black soldiers arrived, and Goodnight and me tell them all is well. We not afraid of Buffalo soldiers – their hair is not even worthy of scalping.

"We stay camped there for three more weeks, but no buffalos anywhere. We come back to reservation," Quanah added.

Adkin was amazed that nobody through the years, including Colonel MacKenzie, had told Quanah that it was Goodnight, the Texas Ranger, the lead scout, who led the attack on his camp on the Pease River where his father was killed, and his mother and sister were captured.

Adkin could not tell Quanah, either. It would mean death to Goodnight, maybe, and possible death by hanging for Quanah. In reality, Adkin could see no benefit for either man – only harm and danger.

...

After nearly three hours, Quanah asked Adkin to sup with him.

"I've only beeves to pick from, but our roasting has improved, probably because of more White man's seasonings," Quanah said, chuckling.

They had a good meal with help from Quanah's aids, two wives. He bragged he had three wives now that he was on the reservation. It drove certain Army officers "crazy as old women," when he took more wives.

"I told them, there was nothing in our treaty to come to reservation and not have many wives," he explained to Adkin.

They laughed, and Adkin told him he would have to go. He was going to catch a stage early the following morning.

They said their farewells and embraced. Adkin had told him he was going to England to see his family. Quanah was impressed and said he wished he could make such a trip one day.

"Maybe you will," Adkin said. "If not, maybe next year, you come to Las Animas and see Peta and his colts."

Quanah's eyes widened and he gave out a yelp and claimed he would do just that. He was sure he could negotiate such a trip to see Adkin and Peta.

With that, Adkin departed. He had made arrangements to stay the night in a boarding house about a mile from the fort.

•••

The trip back to Dodge City was uneventful. The weather, though, was bad one day, as abnormal rains hit and slowed the stage to a crawl in places where the red clay of Oklahoma bogged the wheels and horses down.

In Dodge, he saw numerous old friends and made his plans for heading to Philadelphia. Bassett, Reighard and Sitler saw him off the day he departed.

They laughed at how passengers stared at the tall man, carrying a Colt in his holster, another in his gun belt and his Winchester in one hand and his father's old carpet bag in the other. It was in good enough shape to still utilize, and his 10 gauge coach gun was inside it with some clothes.

"You can never carry enough arms on the Plains," Adkin said, laughing. "Passengers will have to look the other way, I guess, because I'll never cross Kansas without being loaded for bear."

The others laughed with him and waved as he hung in the doorway as the train started slowly rolling away with its chugging and steam hissing away.

"Off on another adventure," Adkin thought to himself. "I will be happy to see my family."

•••

761

It wasn't but four days and Adkin was in Westport. He couldn't believe his eyes at its growth, especially along the riverfront and all the shipping docks and warehouses with huge yards full of cranes, crates and pipe, fencing, you name it.

He saw most of this from the railroad yard where he was changing trains to get to Saint Louie. If someone had told him it would look like this when he passed through there in 1865, he wouldn't have believed them.

His next train took him to Indianapolis, where he was struck at how many farms and small towns populated Indiana. Parts of the landscape reminded him of Kansas and Oklahoma.

Within a week, he was pulling up in a station in Columbus, Ohio, an industrial looking town from the railroad line. They had built an impressive railroad bridge across the Scioto River, though.

He was noticing more and more people scowled at him, especially mothers with children in hand. He figured it was from his guns. He noticed almost nobody carried firearms on their person – in plain view anyway.

Another six days and he would arrive in Philadelphia, that would put him there on February 21, a little early, but he would prefer that rather than being late. He started listing things he would do to pass a couple of weeks.

He had been told the Liberty Bell was there. It was Prowers who told him the history, or what he knew of it. That it supposedly cracked the first time they rang it. When exactly, Prowers was not too sure. Adkin made up his mind he would find out the truth once there.

He was also interested in seeing Independence Hall and learn more about that. He knew it was where America's Founding Fathers came up with the Declaration of Independence and other famous documents.

From childhood in England, most of the people Adkin met and knew loved bragging about how "The Colonies" came up with such an important documents as its Constitution.

Of course, Adkin also knew the elders in England who resented America and proposed The Monarchy was the superior style of government. Adkin was leaning more toward total freedom than from the rule of monarchs. Monarchs had never seen such sights as the Great Plains.

He had also heard tall tales about the survival of Colonial Troops at Valley Forge. He would seek out that location and find out its truthful history.

He finally decided to do as he did in New Orleans when arriving there – find someone trustworthy and who knew the area well. But as old Captain Jean Carbeauneaux taught him – beware of those who would turn on you and rob you or kill you.

One thing Adkin relished thus far on is trip was the different meals and food he found along the numerous cafes at all the depots and kitchens where the train stopped. Ham, eggs and bread in St Louis were not served the same way in Springfield, Ohio.

Every station seemed to prepare known foods a little different, but the additional herbs and seasonings as well as what was locally produced influenced every meal. He loved the variety. It was like going over another hill and seeing something different every time.

"It's a culinary adventure, as well," Adkin thought to himself, smiling.

Once the train arrived in Philly, as many were calling it, Adkin found buggys for hire lined up at the station to wheel people around the bustling town for a fee. Adkin hailed one and jumped in with his carpet bag and his Winchester in his hands. The driver looked surprised at the rifle but asked, "Where to Mister?"

Adkin told him he wanted to stay at a hotel or boarding house of good repute. The driver said he had just the place and used his jip on a stout old Murphy pulling the buggy. On the way, Adkin asked the driver how big was Philadelphia? The driver wasn't sure how many people were there, but he knew it was the second largest town in America.

"New York City is the sole place larger than Philly," the driver said. "But we is known as the 'Cradle of Democracy.'"

After heading north on Front Street, they turned west down a Macadam road posted as Walnut, it passed a large park area with walkways and benches and a large covered patio, which the driver called a gazebo.

"In the summer, our city band plays music there every Sunday afternoon while people picnic after church," he explained.

He also informed Adkin the huge parkway was called Fairmont Park.

"We's hosted the country's first international exposition last year, to celebrate the 100th birthday of the Declaration of Independence," the driver said. "It went on for about seven months, and the exposition displayed industries from 50 countries.

"It was quite an affair," he added.

They pulled up in a horseshoe gravel drive to the left at a plantation-style building. The small sign off to the right of the wide steps said, "Independence Hotel." It looked elegant to Adkin with its four colonnades reaching up to the second story veranda.

He liked it immediately, even though he knew it would be expensive. But he had already decided to throw expense to the wind on this trip. He was going to enjoy himself and live a different life for awhile.

When he saw the doorman hand a silver coin to the driver, Adkin knew it was expensive – probably the best in Philly – and that was okay. Plus he loved the fact it was located next to the city's biggest central park. He could see the small steeple on Independence Hall at the end of the park in the northwest corner – the driver had pointed it out.

He was about to ask the driver if he would be his guide for a couple of weeks, but decided against it. He would talk with workers at the hotel and find out interesting sights, he was sure.

"The large Black doorman would be a good place to start," Adkin thought.

•••

He had been making friends with Jackson, the Black doorman, who told him of several people who worked at the hotel that were very knowledgeable of the area's history. One man, a valet who was in his early 50s, bothered Adkin with his ways, but he knew the area well and its history.

Adkin had learned early in his stay in Philadelphia from one of the hotel managers that wearing gunbelts with holsters in public was not common, and in some establishments, it was not accepted at all. So Adkin had put his gunbelt and holster away, but still stuck a Colt in his pants' waistband on his the left side of his stomach – and his belly gun in a vest pocket.

It was an enjoyable time for Adkin – learning American history he had only heard parts of, and how the country's founders quarreled, but came up with the Declaration of Independence and its amendments. He was thoroughly enthralled, and really was humbled by the Independence Hall and Valley Forge stories and their meanings to America's founding.

After purchasing his tickets for passage with Inman's Liverpool, Philadelphia and New York Steamship Company Line, he mentioned it to the valet at the bar that evening. He had not told the man his intentions to travel to England. He had simply been acting as a tourist from Colorado.

Once his departure date was known, Adkin took a buggy to the Western Union Office and sent a telegram to the boys in Las Animas, letting them know when he was leaving. He explained he didn't know when he would return but he would telegraph them on his arrival back in Philly.

The night before he was to depart, Adkin decided to eat early at a place down by the wharf that served roasted fish – not as good as he had eaten in New Orleans, but well cooked and tasty.

When he got back to the hotel, he didn't go to the bar, he wanted to get a fresh start the following morning and make sure all his packing was complete. He had bought a shipping trunk a few days earlier where all his belongings could be stowed away safely on the ship. He had purchased a lot more clothes while in Philly, too. And two new Bowlers – a black one and one brown.

As he keyed his door, it slowly swung open, unlocked. It was semi-dark as his window's curtains were open and the lights of the city and moonlight dimly lit the room. As his eyes quickly adjusted, he eased his right hand on the grip of the Colt in his waistband, the adrenaline was surging through his body, a dark shadow was suddenly swinging something at him.

He instinctly turned to his right and raised his left arm, catching the blow near his elbow while simultaneously pulling his Colt and swinging it from right to left at the dark figure. He heard and felt the thud from the Colt and the man's grunt just before hearing a body fall to the floor like a sack of flour.

Adkin turned toward the door and lit the oil lamp. The body on the floor was groaning. As he took the lamp out of the wall hanger, and turned toward the man, the figure was on his hands and knees trying to stand up. Adkin kicked him with all he had right in his face as his head was bent over.

The man flew about three feet and hit the wall. Adkin walked over and held the lamp close. It looked like Mister Strange One, the hotel valet that concerned him, but he was face down.

The man was not moving or making any sounds, but Adkin could see he was breathing. Adkin stepped into the hallway and saw a couple heading toward the stairs.

"Would you people mind asking a hotel manager to come up here when you get to the reception area?" he asked. "There is probably a policeman there, too. Tell them I have incapacitated a burglar in my room, and he needs a doctor right away."

The woman put her kerchief to her mouth, but the man shouted, "I certainly will, Mister. Right away," he said as he dragged his wife hurriedly down the stairs. Adkin re-entered his room and lit several more lamps.

Within a few minutes, a hotel manager, two other valets and a police officer came through the open door. They halted as they saw Adkin rolling the man over on the floor. He was still "incapacitated."

"Know this man?" Adkin asked, pointing down. "I caught him going through my things in the dark. He tried knocking me out with this coat rack, but I whacked him with my Colt. He also got a boot to the head as he tried to stand up."

"Oh my Goodness," the manager said, putting his hands to his cheeks. "I can't believe it's James Ricer – Jim's been with us for 10 years or better."

The man's nose was certainly broken, bleeding badly, and the knot on the left side of his cheek bone was a large as a hen's egg, turning purple as he lay there. Both eyes were blackening, too.

The copper grabbed the water pitcher near the wash bowl and poured some in Mister Ricer's face, which started him moving a little. More water had him gasping for air.

When he saw who was in the room, it hit him he had been caught. Adkin could see the wheels turning as the man laid there.

"This man tried to kill me when I came in the room," he pleaded while reaching for his nose. "I want him arrested."

Adkin kicked him in the ribs – hard – causing him to squeal like a pig.

"You better start with the truth or I will kill you," Adkin said as he raised his Colt and slowly aimed it right between his eyes – then cocked the hammer.

"Okay. Okay. I'm wrong. Please don't shoot me Mister. Please," he said as he started whimpering and raising an arm to the policeman. "Please save me."

A valet had retrieved a towel and handed it to the man so he could stem the bleeding. He and the manager helped him to his feet.

The manager then went into a tizzy asking Adkin not to sue the hotel and that he would give him his room at no cost for the entire two weeks.

"We didn't know Mister Yates, honest," the manager said. "We sincerely apologize, we really do."

"If you want to press charges, come by in the morning at the 12th Street Precinct and sign the papers," the policeman said gruffly. "I'll get him to a doc and get him patched up first."

"I don't want to press charges," Adkin said as he spoke to the crook. "I think he's paid enough thus far. Don't you?"

The man nodded rapidly an assent.

"You are lucky you didn't try this in Dodge City – you would have had several bullets in you right now as we speak," Adkin added as the valet was led out the door, helped by the policeman.

"And, I'll gladly pay my bill," Adkin said to the manager. "I've had a wonderful time in your fair city. Though it is a shame some of these crooks infiltrate such an elegant hotel."

•••

While checking out the following morning, word of the incident had spread all over the hotel and everyone was whispering and pointing at Adkin at the reception counter. The morning manager was just as sniveling as the night manager with his apologies and thanking Adkin for not pursuing claims against the hotel.

"We've experienced a spate of thefts in the last year here, and they were from customer's staterooms, but we and the police thought it a burglar working the area," he said quietly. "The officer last night said the valet, Mister Ricer, admitted to him he had been going through customers belongings in the last year – as many clients were from out of country and here for the International Exposition and said little or nothing about the thefts.

"We're sure we've nipped it in the bud," he said, smiling. "Or you have, actually."

"Don't worry, I won't spread bad words about this place," Adkin said. "And I'll be back in about six months to a year. I like it here.

"Me and Mister Colt are not worried about thieves," he added while patting his holster.

On the buggy ride to the port area, Adkin smiled to himself, thinking of how his instincts developed on the Great Plains to survive actually saved him from harm or worse last night.

"Thank you Santa Fe Trail," he said to himself.

Now, it was time to think about life in general and try to enjoy every moment on crossing the Great Atlantic for the next month. He wondered what kind of people he would meet on board. He had discovered he wasn't too impressed with big-city dwellers after two weeks in Philly.

"But the food was extraordinarily good," he said to himself. "Wonder what we'll eat on this ship?"

As they pulled up to the loading gangplank, Adkin was impressed by the ship. She was huge, looking to be about 200-feet long with four sailing masts and two belching steam engine stacks mid-ship. And she had an iron hull. Adkin smiled as he walked the plank upward. He had two porters carrying his trunk.

"Welcome aboard," a uniformed man said as he reached the ship's main deck. "May I see your tickets, please."

Adkin sat his bag down and pulled out his papers with the tickets and handed them to the man.

"I don't think you'll be needing that rifle, Sir, on this voyage," he said smiling.

"You never know," Adkin said, smiling back, too. "It is one of those tools a man finds he needs sometimes – just in case."

He was given instructions to his stateroom on the second deck of this double-decker. He gave the porters each a silver dollar after they placed his trunk in the room.

It was lovely. A nice large bed and washroom area. A small table with four steel wrought-iron chairs. Three oil lamps with large crystal globes with sea gulls etched into the glass.

There was a small deck area through a glass-paned door with two small chairs where one could sit outside and watch the rolling seas. Two port holes were on each side of the door where one could open them and smell the sweet salt-water breezes.

Adkin was in awe of ships. He thought it might be because he was raised near the Midlands where no shoreline was closer than a couple of hundred miles. "Aye," he thought, "Iffin' I'd be born along the sea coast, I'd be a matey on a great sailing ship." He laughed at himself.

On March 6, 1877, The HRMS Kingsdown steamed out of the Philadelphia docks down the Delaware River on her voyage to Liverpool, England.

•••

Adkin knew he would be at sea for 25 to 30 days, so he bought several books to read during any monotony he may encounter. One was on the history of how the Declaration against the rule of King George came about, and who were the particular leaders who argued and prevailed into garnering the votes to pass it with the Continental Congress.

He also had one written supposedly by Benjamin Franklin himself, his autobiography it was called. He had heard Franklin was a writer of words, an inventor and a prominent man in writing the Declaration and the country's Constitution.

One of Adkin's fears of the long journey was gastronomic satisfaction. If his first supper aboard the HRMS Kingsdown was any indicator, his trip was going to include very fine food indeed.

That first evening as the ship had navigated well out of the Delaware Bay and into the Atlantic, the meal was roasted oysters in cream sauce, broiled Dover sole with tomatoes and fresh green onions or a Beef ribeye with navy beans and cornbread. Adkin had the fish, and it was wonderful.

The vegetable trays on the dining tables had every one known to Adkin. A few he was not even aware of what they were.

"They are surely native greens and roots to the area," he thought to himself. "And not poisonous, hopefully."

The following morning validated Adkin's opinion of the cooks aboard. It was a glorious breakfast and included numerous types of teas: English, East Indian and Chinese. He was in heaven.

Adkin started on his first book that first morning, sitting on his room's deck while gliding through the deep blue waters. He was fascinated with the men. He felt an affinity with them – adventurous and fearless, as a whole. They dared rebuke a King of England and were willing to place everything they owned in the belief of individual freedom and self governance.

It was on the third evening they had the Captain's Supper, where all passengers passed through a greeting line to meet the ship's Captain and his top officers. It reminded him of how Lords and Ladies lined up to greet the King of England. He had heard the stories when he was young from Lord Colchester, who preferred countrymen over royalty.

Adkin finally met the man and chuckled to himself – another short, squat German. His name was Captain Alex Rutz, "with a Z" he would say each time he said his name. He pronounced it "Roots."

He would love for Ray Dee to see this German and his pompous attitude. Adkin figured he would give him the benefit of doubt and just presume it had something to do with Germans – a certain manner, maybe.

The ship was solid, only one day did they encounter seas that were rougher than normal. Word of fellow passengers Adkin would meet said sailing eastward was more difficult than westward. Adkin wasn't sure, all he knew is he enjoyed the slow rolling of the ship. It soothed him, yet many passengers were hanging off the rails the first week with upset stomachs.

An Englishman's Adventures on the Santa Fe Trail (1865-1889)

The trip went well, Adkin finished his first book and had started the second by Franklin, who he was really interested in hearing from after the first book. It was April 9, 1877, when deck hands were walking around the ship shouting it would be docking the following day.

Adkin stood and went forward, checking the horizon. There it was just topping the edge of the sky – gray mounds of land. By his guess, they were the shores of Ireland jutting into the sky. He was amazed. It seemed a short trip in many ways, even though it would be about a 36-day voyage.

Suddenly, butterflies started flittering though his gut. He soon would be seeing his Mum and Father, brothers George and Charles. He was sure they had families now. He had to do some calculations to remember their exact ages during the planning of his trip back in Las Animas.

His father was only 52, his mum was a year younger, 51, and George was now 29 and Charles 27. Poor little Eliza would be 24 if she had survived. Adkin still felt the pain of losing his baby sister.

His brothers were now grown men, Adkin realizing he was only 31 himself. Yet, he knew nothing of what his brothers did for a living – nor did they have any idea of what his life had been like since 1865.

"Only 12 years on the Plains?" Adkin asked himself. "It sure seems longer."

There is that time dichotomy again. It has a different value on the Santa Fe Trail – or it used to. Time lingered slowly at times, yet flew by in dangerous and deadly seconds at other times.

"There's no way to explain it," Adkin finally said to himself.

That day of April 10, Adkin rented a two-horse Pantheon Carriage once the driver said he could handle a large shipping trunk, too. Adkin finally saw his trunk being unloaded and asked a ship's porter to fetch it for him.

The porter was a large man and grabbed the trunk and hefted it upon his back and leaned over and delivered it to the carriage, where he and the driver lashed it down on the back boot. Adkin gave the man a silver U.S. Dollar, and he let out a whoop like an east Indian, which he may very well had been.

Adkin asked the driver how far could he take Adkin into the Midlands, as he wanted to go to a village north of London. The driver said he could take him to Northwich – about 25 kilometers down the road. Adkin agreed and off they went. It would take at least five days to get to Olney from the northwest shores of England.

At Northwich, the driver took him to a stagecoach inn that evening where he made arrangements to travel to Olney, about 140 kilometers away. The Inn manager said Adkin would have to take three different stages, and it would take four days.

Adkin had seen telegraph poles and wires coming into Northwich, and he asked the innskeeper about them, because there was a pole outside his inn with wires coming into the lodge.

"Why yes, we have telegraph service — it's over most of the larger villages in Britain now," he said, looking at Adkin, wondering where he was from. "Let me check and see if Olney is on the line.

"Why yes, it's right here," he said looking up from his book. "Would you like to send a telegraph to friends or family there?"

"Please, to family," Adkin said. "I've been away for a long time and want to let them know I'm near."

The man gave Adkin another strange look as he handed Adkin a piece of paper and a pen to write out his telegram.

"You do write, eh?" he asked politely. He isn't sure where this man was from, but in his mind, four days of travel is not "near." Plus he's wearing these pointed boots and carries a gun and holster."

"Yes, I write – and read," Adkin said, a little peeved.

Adkin sent a telegraph to Arthur Yates, Bull Inn, Olney, Buckinghamshire.

"I should arrive Olney around noon on April 15."

"From: Your Son, Adkin Yates," he added.

"Oh, been away from home, are ya?" the man asked.

"About 12 years," Adkin said.

"Where's ya been?"

"In the heart of America," Adkin said with pride. "Workin' the Santa Fe Trail."

"Santa what …?" the man muttered as Adkin turned away.

•••

On the day he departed – with his next stop, Olney. Adkin was fairly nervous. Not so much as how he would be accepted but how much should he tell his father of his exploits. If he couldn't tell his father, how could he say those things to his mother.

He fought with that, knowing they may take some of his actions as evil or not accepted by God. In truth, some were not. But, he finally decided lying about them or deleting them would be worse. He would have to tell his family everything and let them, hopefully, decide whether or not to judge him.

It was near noon and Adkin finally caught sight of the steeple of the church where he was raised, St. Peter and St. Paul Angelican Church. It made his heart beat faster with excitement. He was only a few kilometers from the Bull Inn.

As he came down Yardley Street and turned onto High Street coming into the Market Place, there was a crowd of maybe 100 people surrounding both sides of the roadway. They started waving and yelling. The Bull Inn was directly across the road from the open Market Place – the village's center.

"What is going on," Adkin asked himself. Then he heard "Adkin, Adkin," being shouted and "Welcome home." All those people were there to welcome him? He couldn't believe it.

As the coach slowed due to the people in the street, Adkin saw his father standing above most of the others waving and smiling. His mother, Annag, was standing beside him, his other arm holding her tight next to him as the crowd jostled them.

"When the stage stopped in front of the Bull Inn, the crowd started applauding and still yelling greetings. Adkin was looking around, astounded and somewhat scared. He didn't even realized he knew this many people in Olney.

He stepped out the door and halted as a whoop went up, and he found the faces of his parents. He jumped off and hugged them both, his mother already crying, which brought tears to his eyes as well.

Someone was slapping him on the back and he turned to see George and Charles. They hugged, too. Someone in the crowd started shouting, "Speech. Speech. Speech," and soon all were yelling it.

"Go ahead, son, say something to these people. They have been waiting to see you back home," Arthur said.

Adkin turned toward the Market Place, and yelled at the crowd, "Thank you all. Thank you."

He looked back at his family, not sure what to say.

"I appreciate you welcoming me home. I have missed Olney and all my old friends," he shouted. "I have especially missed my Mum and Father – and my two brothers."

He felt loved beyond comprehension. He winked at his Father and then yelled loudly, "Drinks on the house at the Bull Inn."

His father's jaw dropped, as the crowd screamed and his mother had both hands over her mouth, looking paralyzed. His father started laughing with Charles and George following suit.

"Don't worry, Father, I have it covered, and it may be the only way to rid ourselves of them," he said laughing.

The revelry started immediately as people crowded into the Bull, spreading throughout the dining areas after filling the pub area. The crowd made room for the Yates though, and they squeezed into the pub area.

"Barkeeps, drinks for all our friends," he said pausing and pulling his watch out and flipping it open, "... drinks for all until 8 O'clock – and put it on Adkin Maxwell Yates' bill."

They all hollered louder it seemed.

"Adkin, dear, that will be foolishly expensive, please don't," Anna pleaded.

"Oh Mother, let me be frivolous today. I have missed you so, and I made a little money in America, too," he said hugging her again. Her hair had quite a bit of gray strands, but her face looked as pretty as ever. There might be a few more lines around her eyes, but as they say, they looked to be laugh lines. She wore her hair in a bun atop her head.

He hugged Arthur again, his gray was situated around his temples only. He looked as rugged as Adkin remembered and as strong. Charles had a woman with him that was a lovely, fair-haired blond and tiny. Charles introduced her as Maggie, short for Margaret. He looked much more mature and actually looked older than George, though he was younger.

Adkin met George's wife, Victoria. She was tall and brown haired but very pretty. She looked to be rather young in Adkin's view. He later found out she was but 20.

A man made his way through the crowd and pulled on Arthur's arm sleeve. He said he had left Adkin's trunk and bag at the side door on the north side of the Bull Inn. It was in the stable area. Arthur handed the man some coins.

He then grabbed George and pulled him away, and they went to the north door into the stables and saw the bag and trunk. They brought them inside and locked the door. Once back in the pub area, Arthur told Adkin his belongings were safe.

The merriment continued, with some of the crowd leaving after only a drink or two. As it thinned out, Adkin's family pushed two tables together and seated themselves. They couldn't get over how big and wide Adkin had gotten. Plus the men really liked his long locks and reddish-blond beard down to his collar button. Anna wasn't so sure.

"I want to see that handsome face again," she said pulling at his beard.

George was really impressed with his Philadelphia Bowler and tried it on. It fell to his ears.

"You always did have a big head," he said, and they all laughed.

Adkin found out George and Victoria had one child, a 2-year-old boy named Adam. Charles and Maggie had three children, two girls and one boy, ages 2, 4 and 7. The boy, Maxwell, was 7.

"I will meet them all, my nephews and nieces, and I can't wait," he said. "But there is plenty of time."

"Are you home for good, Adkin?" Anna blurted out.

He sat there a moment, knowing this was coming. He had hoped it wouldn't jump out and bite him so quick. But it did.

"No Mother, but I can stay a long time if you like," he said, knowing that probably hurt her again. She wasn't that keen on him leaving in the first place back in '65.

"Oh dear, I was just …"

"I know Mother, and I'm sorry to hurt your feelings in any way. You know that," he said. "It's just I have made a life for myself in America. We'll discuss it more later.

"Let's celebrate this evening and the blessings of our friends, because there are people here that don't even know me – they are here for you," he added, putting his arm around Anna and pulling her close.

"Yes, let's celebrate," Arthur said, patting Adkin's shoulder. Adkin noticed his Father was enjoying a brandy. He had never in his life seen Arthur drink alcohol. He toasted his father with his dark ale. They drank to each other.

•••

Most of the people had left the Bull Inn by 8, but a few hung in there. Adkin noticed a lot of people ended up asking for a dining table and ordered supper as well. He was hoping it was a good night for the Bull, financially.

The brothers and their brides went home, all still living in the Olney area. They had to get home to the children, who were in friends' care for the special occasion. Their buggys were in the stables.

"We have your old room above the stables ready for you, my dear," Anna said. She noted she was tired and at 8:30, kissed Arthur and Adkin goodnight and went back to their bedroom.

Adkin reminded his father to tabulate the bar bill and he would go to the bank in the Market Place "on the morrow," and exchange some U.S. currency into pounds.

"And don't short change me, either Father," he said. "I really have done very well in America, I promise."

They stood and hugged again. Adkin always remembered his father's hug while they were standing over Eliza's grave. It was the first time his father had hugged him as an adult, in Adkin's mind. He treasured it – even now."

"Can you find your way to your room?" Arthur asked.

"I'm sure I can."

"Well good night son, welcome home."

When Adkin entered his old room, his mother had already lit a lamp for him. He smiled as he looked it over. It was much larger when he was a child. It seemed so small, yet warm and friendly.

He kicked off his boots and removed his hat, coat and vest and laid on the small bed. His feet hung off the end quite a bit. He laughed, knowing he would have to rearrange the blankets to make sure his feet weren't exposed to cold air. He laughed out loud.

He looked up to the book shelf, and there was still the blank space where his Bible once rested for so long. It now rests on a shelf in Las Animas.

"I need to read more from my Bible when I get back. And, I need to start going to church with the gang, too," he said to himself.

Thinking about the church, he couldn't wait to go to his beloved church in Olney. He wanted to hear the huge brass bells chiming in the steeple and the thunderous old pipe organ, which had been there for years and years. Its pipes were 12-feet tall dropping down to about 6-feet. Brightly shining brass pipes and so loud they could rattle the decades-old stained glass windows. It was a marvelous place to talk with God.

He fell asleep with the fond memories of the old church, forgetting to fix the blankets. That fact woke him about 1 in the morning. He laughed at himself while finishing the chore and went back to sleep with a smile on his face – and blankets over his feet.

•••

Adkin enjoyed that smell of Olney in the damp spring air. It was brisk but not cold like in Kansas or Colorado, where the windswept ground felt as hard as rock and the chill could cut you to the bone. Olney was full of trees, bushes and grasses surrounding everything and was sweet smelling and broke up a chilly breeze.

He enjoyed just walking about for his first several days, especially down by the River Great Ouse and the grain mill behind the church. He visited Eliza's grave every day.

On his first Saturday home, the Market Place filled with farmers and local craftsmen and women who put out their vegetables or meat pies, cookies, fudges and candies. There were great varieties of flowers, carvings, paintings, locally made lace, you name it.

It was festive. The Market Place was an open triangle in the middle of the village, as some villages in America had town squares. And it filled every weekend in good weather.

It finally got to Sunday and the family went to services. He saw several people he knew who welcomed him home. He got to see his Vicar whose presided when he departed for America. Vicar John Piercy Langley had taken over when his father, Vicar David Baxter Langley stepped down in 1856. Adkin was only 10 when John Piercy became Vicar. Adkin enjoyed seeing the man again.

Then as services were over, the family was standing among the headstones of the ancient cemetery around the church visiting with people when Adkin glimpsed the Byrnes, the parents of Devon, the sweetheart he left behind.

He didn't get to talk with them, as they didn't see him and walked down the lane. He asked later, though, what happened to Devon. They were back at the Bull, sitting in the living room, and his parents glanced back and forth and nodded to George.

"Could we talk, Adkin? Privately?" George asked, and they went outside and into the blacksmith shop.

"Devon and I married," he said. "She was my first wife."

Adkin just stood there, not knowing what to say. George broke the silence.

"It happened accidentally, in a way," George continued. "She would come by about every two weeks or so that winter after you left asking if we had news from you. By Spring, I had grown very attached to her and she to me.

"We still had not heard a word from you that first year, and I asked her to marry," he said. "We were but children, I 17 and she 18, and I look back now and realize her pining for you was what it was all about. We misunderstood her loneliness and my sympathy for her. We both felt abandoned – by you, I suppose.

"We realized quickly it wasn't true love between us and divorced within a year," George continued. "We had no children, and she eventually met a fine man – a saddle maker and butcher. They married and live in Emberton, you know across the river south of here? They have two children now.

"I didn't marry Victoria until three years ago," he said. "I didn't trust myself – or marriage – for some time. And then I met Victoria and truly fell in love."

Adkin was quiet for a moment. Then he reached out and took his brother in his arms and hugged him.

"I'm sorry you felt abandoned, George," he whispered. "I don't blame you but it wasn't because I didn't love you. I did and still do, very much.

"I wasn't very good in explaining this longing inside me to go to America and travel the Great Plains," he continued as he stepped back, still holding George's shoulders. "I still can't explain it in the way my heart feels it – even after 12 years.

"But I'm happy you and Devon didn't ruin your lives – and that you found your true love," he added. "I've had that wonderful experience myself."

They turned and went back into the living area with the children running wild and Anna at the cooking stove with Maggie and Victoria. His boys were smiling, which pleased Arthur immensely.

Adkin slowly told the family, first the men and then something a little less to his mother, about his trip to America, his problems in Saint Augustine, Florida.

He explained his excitement going up the Mississippi River on a steamer, but the problem with the German engineer, his meeting J. L. Sanderson in Saint Louis, and how fate brought them together.

He slowly, over about a whole month, told them everything. His difficulty came explaining how he first met, Matty, their marriage and her death. He shed more than one tear through those times.

He was glad he had started writing his diary again, as it had refreshed his memory about lots of events, especially his dread when travelling the old Dry Route and, initially, finding no water at Wagon Bed Springs.

His brothers got the most excitement when he told of fights with Comancheros and Indians. They were spellbound and in disbelief at times. Adkin had to assure them they were, indeed, true stories.

By the time he had got to finding Billy Dixon and his boys at the Buffalo Wallow Fight, it was nearing Christmas. Many of his exploits he had to repeat, as

George was working for Arthur, and was gone several days a week driving stages to and from London.

His father said George really took to the business and felt comfortable it would be in good hands when Arthur got too old to handle things. Charles was in a different vein. He had took to law.

After his local schooling, Charles wanted to go to Northhampton College and earn a law degree. Fortunately, the Bull Inn's business was doing well enough for Arthur to help pay for Charles' schooling. Within three years, Charles was back in Olney, establishing his own business as Charles Yates, Esq. Barrister.

He was only 27, but he was doing quite well for himself. Arthur told Adkin, "The boy is making as much money as me."

Adkin looked forward to Christmas, as his mother liked the holiday and went all out. She liked setting out special candles, lace everywhere, which was a staple of Olney's industries. She also put out evergreen branches throughout the house, which radiated with the sweet smell of the evergreens.

The cooking plans started several days before, and Anna even got some of her grandchildren into making the scones and candies. Adkin enjoyed hearing, "Happy Christmas," as Brits called it.

When February came around, Adkin began thinking about when he should return to Las Animas and his horses. Arthur sensed it, too.

"Will you be going back soon, son" he asked.

"I probably will start looking to set a date, father," Adkin said. "I do want to get back to my horses and friends – they're like my family, too, you know?"

"I understand," Arthur said. "It's just it will be hard on your mother. You have no idea how much she wishes you would stay here in Olney."

"I know, father, and I hate that I cause her – or any of you – any pain,' he said. "It's just I've made a life away from home – albeit it's on another continent. And I can't live it differently. Does that make sense, father?"

"Yes, I suppose," Arthur sighed. "We teach our children to learn how to make a living, to support themselves to be happy and successful. Then they fly away.

"I understand it, that's the way it is supposed to be, even if it hurts some. Your mother will put on a stone face for awhile, but it will get emotional when you leave, Adkin," Arthur said.

"All I ask for – no I beg – is tell her you will write more and then actually do it. She cherishes any letter she gets from you. Let us know what your doing in your life. It helps us feel we are still a part of you."

"Of father, you and the family are a part of me every time I take a breath, or walk a step or watch a sunrise," Adkin said. "But I will write more, and I give you my word as a Yates."

The men hugged.

•••

In late February, George returned from London with a newspaper he brought back for Adkin. One of the headlines on the front page was that "American Inventor Thomas Edison Patents Phonograph Machine."

Adkin got a kick out of the fact an American made the front page of the London Daily Times. They all laughed, but had to read the story several times to understand what a phonograph machine actually does. Arthur wasn't impressed, but his sons were.

Adkin decided he would have to contact Inman Lines and see when the next sailing to Philadelphia would be. He telegraphed them and found out the Kingsdown would be arriving April 2 or through the 5th and was scheduled to depart April 10, regardless of her exact arrival at Liverpool. He asked for a reserved stateroom and gave them his ticket number so they could verify his paid return passage.

Adkin told the family he would be departing Olney April 4 to give himself enough time in case a stage broke down or had a mishap. Arthur insisted George take him in their brougham carriage. It was covered and fairly comfortable for only two people.

"I can't afford to send any of the coaches, their tied up with our schedules," Arthur said. "But I can get by with George gone awhile, right Georgie?"

"I would love to, But father, we've talked about 'Georgie.' George said chuckling and a fake scowl. "Let me take you, Adkiin. It will give us a chance to know each other better, and I would cherish that."

"Okay, I would, too," Adkin said. 'We'll depart April 4."

Adkin spent the next few days making sure his mother understood how much he loved her, and that it was her love of learning that gave him the urge to seek adventure in America. She said she understood, and then asked if he cared for Dawn?

Adkin couldn't help but guffaw. Anna had been introducing him to every available woman in Buckinghamshire trying her best to play cupid. She had told him several times, "Love is around every corner, yee have but to seek it."

"Mother, Dawn is a lovely woman, but I do not love her, and she doesn't love me," Adkin said while chuckling. She is simply intrigued with someone who has visited America."

On the day of his departure, several friends and most of the family came out onto the street to the brougham. Even Vicar Langley came, just as he had in 1865, with his blessing. Adkin thanked him sincerely, feeling as close to God as he had in many a year. It was invigorating.

He held his mother tight and promised he would write every month, at least, with news of his horse ranch and his American family, as he called them. She cried, he shed some tears, and they all laughed and waved with wet eyes as he and George headed off to Liverpool.

His father had whispered in his ear when embracing him, "Keep God close to your heart, my son." It reminded Adkin of when he left for America in '65.

"I am going to keep God close to my heart again, and never let it wane for any reason," he said to himself as they trotted up High Street.

...

They arrived east of Liverpool April 8, crossed the River Mersey and found an inn not far from the Royal Albert Docks. George knew the area, and he took Adkin to a fine cafe along the Mersey where they had kidney pie and cabbage in cheese sauce. It was delicious.

George only stayed that one night, having business to take care of in Olney. But he and George did get closer, especially when Adkin told him the long story about how he came to love Matty.

"It wasn't like a bolt of lightening – I was just going to take care of her," Adkin said. "But watching her smile and laugh at life, and they way she looked at all the White man's ways – she was so positive.

"She grew on me without trying, and then it was, 'Boom.' I was so in love it scared me to death," he said.

"That's how Victoria affected me," George said. "I felt a failure at love and marriage and wasn't interested in this silly child I met at the Carlton House Club. Her father owns the club, and I made it my second home after divorcing Devon.

"She was just one of the children that played around there, and I never took any notice of her until she was about 16 and working as a serving waitress," he continued. "She was so mature in my eyes and was warm and personal and a straight talker. She would tell me of men making ungentlemanly remarks, and she said she would tell them to go to hell and find the kind of women they were looking for there – in hell.

"She was remarkable, and I never thought of her in a romantic way whatsoever, until shortly after she turned 17," George said, lowering his head, looking embarrassed. "I saw her one day at the bank, and asked where she had been, because I had noticed she hadn't been helping her father. She said she just completed finishing school and was looking for a real man.

"I was flabbergasted and said, 'What?'" he continued. "She said, 'I'm looking for a man that has ignored my affections for two years. I've been infatuated with your since I was 15. When are you going to see me as a grown woman?'"

"That had to be scary," Adkin said with a chuckle.

"It was, but I suddenly saw her in a womanly way." George went on. "She was beautiful – and infatuated – and with me of all people. I walked away dumbfounded and she yelled, 'If you like, you should ask my father if you can call on me. I won't wait two more years.'"

George said he went crazy for about a week, but ended up calling on her father and asking to court her. He said her father was more than happy to approve.

"He told me he had great admiration for me and my family. He said he couldn't understand why I hadn't asked earlier.

George said her father told him, 'She loved your kindness and manners for a long time, always talked about you and your father and mother, what good people you were.'

"I felt the same in so many ways, but hadn't seen it until we started seeing each other and our similar backgrounds in service businesses," George explained. "I fell hard within three or four months and asked for her hand in marriage from her father – and her, of course. He happily approved, and though I am 9 years her senior, we are as happy as I can imagine. And we have a wonderful child."

Through that last evening together, Adkin and George shared numerous stories of their lives. Adkin enjoyed it thoroughly and knew it was something he would cherish forever. They didn't go to their room until 2 in the morning, and George wanted to get up at 6 to depart.

"Maybe I'll wait til 8 or 9 to depart for home," he said as they got to the room. They both laughed.

They did sleep in late, and George got on the road at 9. That left Adkin with two more days until the Kingsdown set sail. He had a buggy driver take him to the docks and the Inman Line ticket house. They checked his papers and his ticket and stamped "PAID" on it for his return passage.

The HRMS Kingsdown was sitting a few piers down and looked as grand as ever. Adkin was excited again. It would be more fun knowing the ship's layout and where everything was. He was especially looking forward to the meals. They were excellent in his opinion.

•••

The voyage to Philadelphia was enjoyable. They only had rain storms a few days, but no heavy seas or wind storms. Adkin finished his book by Franklin. He decided with men like him having composed the most famous documents of freedom and individual rights, America's future was on a great course in the history of mankind. He treasured the thinking of this Benjamin Franklin fellow immensely.

They arrived May 8 – just 28 days at sea. "Maybe sailing east to west was faster and quieter," Adkin thought to himself. He caught a carriage to the closest Railroad office and booked passage to Las Animas, Colorado.

The ticket man asked him if Las Animas was close to Dodge City, the cowboy town of shootouts.

"Depends on what you call near?" Adkin said smiling. "It's about 130 miles. We go over there every weekend just to watch the shootouts."

He took the ticket, leaving the man looking befuddled and then asked the carriage driver to take him to the nearest Western Union Office. There he telegraphed Ryan that he was leaving Philly on the morrow, May 9, 1878, and should be home around May 26 or 27.

"Will you please take me to the Independence Hotel?" Adkin asked the driver, who snapped the reins and took off.

On arrival at the hotel, the same huge Black doorman, Jackson, was there and immediately recognized Adkin. He sang out his name, "Mister Yates. Welcome, welcome," and took Adkin's trunk with one hand, and hefted it up and around on his back and took it to the reception counter.

"Look who's here," he said to the manager. "It's Mister Yates, returned to our fine hotel."

It was the same night manager from a year earlier. He almost started shaking.

"Mister Yates, so good to see you again," he said. "Will you be needing a room?"

"You betcha," Adkin said in his so-called western accent. "I can only stay one night, but I'm looking forward to it."

He leaned over to the manager and whispered, "Don't have any more sneak thieves, do ya?"

The man stood back, "Of course not, Mister Yates. That man was let go last year – right away, I might add."

"I'm just foolin' with ya. I really do like this place, truly. Both me and Mister Colt simply love it here," he said, chuckling and patting his holster, which was nestling Mister Colt.

The manager gave him a key, and Adkin and Jackson went down the hall to his room. This one was on the ground floor. Adkin gave Jackson a silver dollar and laid back on the bed, throwing his hat on the desk and giggling to himself.

"I'm sorry Lord for overplaying that incident last year with that manager just now, but he needs to dig a little deeper before he hires men like that," Adkin said to himself.

He hired a buggy that evening and went to the wharf and ate at the same cafe he did last year. It was just as good, and he added some boiled lobster to his choices. He was well satiated.

When he got back to the hotel, he decided to walk around the park there to help digest that big meal he just had. It was pleasant. Philadelphia was a fine town, it seemed to him. It was large, but most everyone he met was kindly and helpful. It was just many were inflicted with city living, having never been exposed to a "frontier" per say.

He looked at Philly differently since reading about Franklin and Franklin's love of the city. Adkin thought it ingenious the way Franklin started the University

An Englishman's Adventures on the Santa Fe Trail (1865-1889)

of Pennsylvania – by organizing trustees and getting them to come up with the cash. He did the same thing to start the first library there.

"Amazing fellow," Adkin whispered to himself as he walked – what he now considered – hallowed ground. "Franklin walked these same grounds – in this same park – as well as George Washington."

•••

The miles to Las Animas City went by faster than Adkin could imagine. It did give him enough time to make his Yates family more prominent in his life than he had before. He promised himself he would write his mother more, much more. He realized it was her love and support that gave him the courage to seek the unknown and dare to go where other men might hesitate. He wanted to stay up with his brothers' lives, as well.

Rumors filled the passenger cars somewhere in Indiana that train robbers, such as the likes of the James Gang were hitting trains. The robbers were not satisfied with gold boxes but stole every valuable they could find from passengers.

When someone would vocalize such a rumor, Adkin laughed to himself as he watched men and women start taking off rings or removing pocket watches and trying to hide them. He saw one woman whose bosom was misshapened from a large pocket watch and several rings and wrist bands it seemed. He almost laughed out loud at the foolishness.

He wondered how these people were going to survive in the West. He would simply reach down and make sure his Colt was untied and would slip it smoothly in and out of its holster several times.

"These people need to make friends with Misters Colt and Winchester," he'd think to himself. No trains he rode for three weeks were robbed.

The train pulled into Dodge City May 23, 1878, and it was only going to stop for 30 minutes to refill the water tank, bring more wood and coal on board and load merchandize. Two men, one wearing a star, were on the platform, expecting someone it seemed. Suddenly Adkin recognized the one wearing a star on his lapel. It was Wyatt Earp.

"Wyatt, is that you?" Adkin asked as he stepped toward him.

"Why, Adkin Yates. Yes it is me. How are you Mister Yates?" Earp asked, shaking Adkin's hand. "It's been awhile since we last seen each other. Down on the Cimarron when I was a buffalo hunter."

"Yes, I remember it well, you were with Bassett's group hunting Bluff and Kiowa Creeks, I believe," Adkin said. "What's this star? I heard you were hired as a policeman in '76."

"It was '75 and '76 actually, but I'm a deputy town marshal now," he said proudly. "I'd like you to meet a good friend of mine, Doc Holliday."

They shook hands and Adkin realized this Doc fellow looked frail in a way, and mighty thin. But he carried two pistols in holsters and carried a coach gun, a double-barrel 12 gauge.

"I just came back from Texas a few weeks ago to take this job," he said. "Bat asked me to come to help out ... That's right, you probably don't know.

"You wouldn't have any way of knowing, but Bat's brother, Ed, got killed last month," Earp said solemnly. "Bat has had a rough go since being elected Sheriff last year. Ed had been made Dodge City Marshall before he got murdered.

"How did it happen?" Adkin asked, feeling really disturbed Ed had been killed. He really liked Ed, who was kind and mild-mannered.

"He had just got over a gunshot wound he got last year and was finally back to work," Earp began. "He heard gun shots and went to the saloon and told these five cowboys – only two were armed – they had to turn over their guns to the saloon barkeep until they were ready to leave Dodge. We have a policy of no guns in town.

'The two boys did, and Ed left the saloon," he continued. "Then he heard steps behind him. The cowboys had collected their guns and were following him. He confronted them and one put the barrel of his pistol in his chest and blew a hole in him.

"It caught Ed's clothes on fire, and as he stumbled down the street. He still made it to Hoover's Saloon – Ed rented a room upstairs at Hoovers. His clothes were still smoking from this huge hole in him, and they took him to his bed. Bat came and talked with him briefly. The Doctor said there was nothing he could do.

"So Bat went looking for the cowboys and found them," Earp continued. "Well the two with guns took aim at Bat who was going straight at 'em and started shooting at Bat. Bat pulled both his pistols and blasted away. He killed one instantly, the other died later.

"He was so angry, he aimed at the other three but held his fire. He decided to arrest them as participants and didn't kill them because they were unarmed," Earp said.

"No one would have blamed him if he did kill the others," Holliday said. "And I surely would have."

"After putting them in jail, Bat went back to Ed's room, he was unconscious then, and Bat held his hand for hours until Ed finally took his last breath," Earp said.

"That's when he got in contact with me, he needed help in the city with his hands full handling the county business," he added.

Adkin was speechless for a few minutes. They stood there in quietness. Finally, Adkin asked how the city's founders were getting along.

Earp filled him in on how Wright, Rath, Reynolds, Myers, Kirk, Sitler, Reighard and other founders were making money and doing well.

"Last year, the census put Dodge City's population at 1,200 citizens," Earp said.

"And we have 19 businesses that are licensed to sell liquor," Holliday added.

"Last time I was through here and talked with Bassett, he also said you had three undertakers within six blocks."

"Oh, I'm sure there are more today," Holliday said smiling. "And Bassett is now the county's undersheriff helping Bat."

Suddenly the train whistle blew and the Conductor started shouting to get aboard. Adkin shook hands again, and said his goodbyes. Earp and Holliday wished him well. Adkin stepped back up into the train.

It was depressing thinking about how Ed died, but death has never been pretty, and Adkin knew that all too well. He felt he was back in the West again. The wild West for sure.

•••

Adkin actually found himself enjoying sitting in a train travelling the Santa Fe Trail with the next stop – Las Animas City. He was getting excited again. How many colts are there now? How are Diablo, Peta and Angel doing?

When he rolled up at the Las Animas Depot, he saw Uribe sitting in a buggy waiting for him. His dear friend. It was great to see him.

"Oh Uribe, how good it is to see you, mi amigo," Adkin said as he hugged the man and lifted him off his feet.

"Don't kill me, Boss, I'm too young to die," Uribe said as they laughed. "Let's get that trunk loaded on the boot and vamoose. Whatcha say?"

'Let's go."

Adkin had Uribe pull into the YR&R yard first, Adkin wanted to go to the main office and see everyone, which were ready for him. As soon as he walked through the office door, a scream of "Welcome home" erupted. There must have been 40 people in that office standing shoulder-to-shoulder and hollering to Adkin.

Someone started singing "For he's a jolly good fellow," and Adkin loved seeing all his American family. He felt blessed he had two families. He knew men who had none.

One of the first pieces of news was when Ryan told Adkin Thomas Boggs – and Donnie – had all moved to somewhere in New Mexico.

"There's some court filings going on whether Tom and Ramalda own which or what land. Tom's tired of it and simply left," Ryan said.

"He was sure Las Animas would die anyway," Adkin said. "With the railroads competing, it might, but I'm going to make hay in the meantime."

Ryan and Kanaka, naturally, had planned a fandango for Adkin's coming home party. Kanaka was standing next to Ryan holding little Cheyenne. Adkin noticed he was wearing Matty's handmade beaded moccasins. He and Kanaka smiled at each other.

Friends and neighbors commingled throughout the evening eating, drinking and dancing. Adkin felt like a King, a benevolent one anyway.

There was only one hiccup, though. That was when Amache Prowers saw Hector Ruiz at the party. She pulled Adkin aside and told him that man was worthless. Adkin then told Amache what he found out about Ruiz and his crazy wife and how violent she was.

"Amache, I hired Ruiz because he was honest with me, and he hasn't had a drink since his wife took off for Nebraska to live with her tribe," Adkin said. "I'm sorry not to tell you sooner, we've been hiding him. But I decided I cannot keep the truth from you, my dear friend and partner.

"Please trust me, Amache," he continued. "He's not the man his wife portrayed him to be. Give him a chance and talk with him again. You will see he's a good man – and one hell of a horse trainer, too."

She stepped back and studied Adkin.

"You have always inspired my faith and trust, Adkin Yates," she said. "If what you tell me is what you believe, then I, too, will believe Ruiz. I will talk with him about our ponies, I promise."

"I will have him come to your table right away," Adkin said. "Is that okay?"

She nodded her approval.

He turned and went over to the end of the barracks and whispered to Ruiz for several minutes. Ruiz looked scared, but he finally nodded, and walked over to Amache. Adkin saw him remove his hat, bow and kiss her hand. She swung her arm around and patted the chair seat, encouraging him to sit next to her.

Ryan walked up to Adkin.

"I saw that," Ryan said. "I was wondering why you ordered Ruiz to attend tonight. He wasn't too happy about it earlier.

"It was time," Adkin said, smiling. "To every thing there is a season, and a time to every purpose under the heaven."

"Amen," Ryan said.

Adkin received a complete update about the horses; Angel was pregnant again with a colt by Diablo; Diablo had impregnated about seven other mares, three from Amache and several others from locals. They had 13 colts, four of them yearlings or close to it.

Peta had about five colts now, all beautiful paints with one having a completely white back half from his haunches down to both hooves – even his long tail, and then mottled white and brown spots throughout his torso, shoulders and head. Adkin told them Quanah wanted to come see Peta and his colts someday.

"If Quanah comes, I'll have to give him one of Peta's colts," Adkin had said. "Seriously."

An Englishman's Adventures on the Santa Fe Trail (1865-1889)

There was talk of the "Lincoln County Wars," down in southeast New Mexico. The county was about a fifth of New Mexico, land wise. Seems some bankers and ranchers were having constant gunfights there over cattle ranges. One of them, an Englishman, got killed.

One of his hands, a youngster called Billy the Kid, was getting the reputation as a deadly gunslinger, a new term to Adkin, and was a true killer, going after the men who had killed his boss. He and his side of the ranchers called themselves "Regulators." That seemed to Adkin another new term for gunslingers.

He wondered if Goodnight was involved in any way. Charles had cattle ranches nearly everywhere nowadays.

In the following days, Adkin was happy to ride Diablo and Peta around the pasture and watch the colts. D-Boy was a yearling now, and he and Amache made plans to meet and see what to do with the colt – sell him or use him for breeding.

Adkin also got news about his old friend Billy Dixon. Seems he was still with Nelson Miles and was present at the rescue of the White German sisters from the Cheyenne Indians on McClellan Creek.

He was also with the party that selected the site of Fort Elliott and was attached to that post for duty when he guided the Nolan expedition in pursuit of Comanche warriors in August, 1877.

His knowledge of the country saved the whole command when he led the men to water at Double Lakes on the Llano Estacado.

"If anyone knows the Llano Estacado now, it's Billy Dixon and Colonel Ranald MacKenzie," Adkin said.

"MacKenzie is back down in south Texas," Ryan said. "He's chasing Indian raiders out of Fort Clark again. He actually chased 'em down into Mexico, and the Mexican government got all huffed about his incursion. But, it prompted the Mexicans to act, and they decided to fight the Indians just to keep MacKenzie out of Mexico."

"He's a warrior," Adkin said.

As summer was fully underway, Adkin and Amache decided they needed more breeding stallions for growth. There were plenty of good mares, but they needed stallions. Therefore, they decided to breed D-Boy and Colorado. There was one of Peta's stallions they would keep, too.

Meanwhile, Uribe and Ruiz had saddled trained nearly half a dozen yearlings, and they set September 1, 1878, for a sale date. The Yates Ranch would host a yearling sale. They printed up pamphlets and sent them all over. Amache was like a child, excited because she, too, would sell some of her horses and split profits with her interests in the Yates Ranch.

•••

The horsemen and Amache, made a little more than $6,500 off the sale of a dozen horses, and they had traded a few for two more stallions. Henry Sitler came from Dodge City and brought along a stallion that he traded for one of Diablo's mare colts.

The horse ranch was growing fast, and Adkin and his crew couldn't be happier. The holiday Thanksgiving neared and Adkin went into a funk for a few days up to the holiday. Ryan knew it was because it was the fifth anniversary of Matty's murder.

But on Thanksgiving Day, Adkin received a lengthy letter from Sam and Mary Catherine in Oklahoma. She had five children now; James "Adam," Anna, Rosa, Oscar and Charles. Plus she lost one during a miscarriage. They were doing very well financially.

But she wanted to tell Adkin how much they missed he and Matty. Mary Catherine told Adkin, Matty was the woman who made her see the beauty in human beings, regardless if they were Indians or Whites.

She also added they would enjoy seeing him when he could make it down their way.

"Those words about Matty's humanity straightened me right up," Adkin told Ryan. "I've got to quit feeling sorry for myself and reinforce that positive attitude.

"I need to bring that up with Preacher Reid next Sunday," Adkin added.

Ryan was smiling to himself. He knew it was always easier for those who hadn't lost someone they loved so much to say, "get over it," but it was very difficult to those who had to keep going. He admired Adkin's strength and perseverance. It had to be tough. And he was glad Adkin had started going to their Evangelical Methodist Church with The Reverand Rex Reid.

Christmas came and went, and a snow storm hit the first day of 1879. It seemed appropriate to Adkin that everything just came to a stop for a couple of days of rest to prepare for a busy new year. But feeding horses and all the other animals was a chore when three-feet of snow was drifted up everywhere.

They were all looking to Spring, when the mares started coming into season. "It is going to be a great breeding season," Adkin whispered to himself.

"It is said that a mare is at her most fertile on Midsummer Day," Ruiz said one day. "It's best when foaling happens in Spring and Summer when these bambinos don't freeze to death, si?"

They received a telegram from J.L. who said Barlow had been charged with bribing U.S. officials for receiving mail contracts, then accused of bribing Congress to stop the first investigation. He recommended all those employees not to panic and sell their stock. He was sure with the company's business beyond the mail contracts under scrutiny were sufficient to withstand the scandal.

"But, I don't know if Barlow will survive it altogether," he added in the telegram.

"I'm not selling," Adkin said matter-of-factly.

"Me either," were Ryan's and Ray Dee's remarks.

"All of our business west of Kansas City is not involved with this in any way," Ryan said. "It will continue to grow as long as we're all working for new expansion routes out here."

Ray Dee interrupted, "And, the sky is the limit out here – literally – and all the way to California."

"Amen," Adkin said.

•••

In early November, they received news of the Earp brothers. They had all moved to Tombstone, Arizona. The town was booming after a silver rush. Anyway, there was some kind of feud going on with a man named Clanton and his kin.

Virgil, Morgan and Wyatt Earp and Doc Holliday faced off against the Clanton gang on October 26, 1881 at the O.K. Corral, and killed two of them, while Morgan, Virgil and Holliday were all wounded, but survived.

They took Earp to trial, but he didn't get convicted. Word was he took off and killed several more of the gang after they killed Virgil a few months later in an ambush.

Adkin said a little prayer for Wyatt, hoping the young man wouldn't be harmed or killed chasing these men. Adkin had known the angst and hate of chasing people who murdered a loved one. He had walked in Wyatt's boots.

•••

Adkin's only disappointment in breeding came in the fall of 1882. Ruiz came running into the house that morning screaming.

"Señor, please come, hurry, hurry. Diablo is sick," Ruiz said.

Adkin grabbed his hat and they went to his stall. Adkin swung open the door and Diablo was laying there, wheezing with blood coming from his mouth. Adkin fell to his knees and started talking and rubbing his neck.

Diablo looked Adkin in the eyes as he tried to raise his head, and Akin could tell he was in pain. Just as Adkin was about to tell Ruiz to go get a pistol, Diablo raised his head again and exhaled loudly, blood splattering everywhere. He dropped his head and was instantly dead.

Adkin and Ruiz started weeping. Adkin felt lost as he fell to his knees. This horse was his last living connection with his Matty.

Later, the town's veterinarian confirmed what Adkin was believing. Diablo probably had an enlarged heart or an aneurysm in a vein and it burst.

Diablo was about 20 years old. Adkin buried him in the northwest corner of the yard – with a stone marker engraved with his name. He fenced it off and put Diablo there so he could see the mighty Arkansas and the pastures beyond.

It was a sad and hard week for everyone associated with Adkin and the ranch. Adkin's only solace was he still had D-Boy and Colorado.

•••

Within a few months, Adkin was back to being happy working with his horses, learning to be a very good but unlicensed veterinarian and getting closer and closer to his God. It hit him one day the months had been just running together, then the years. The West was filling up with settlers, ranchers, some trying farming in the baked, dusty sand.

A town called Fowler had popped up south of Dodge City, with a big hotel and everything. Towns were starting up everywhere in western Kansas and southeastern Colorado, while Las Animas was getting smaller and smaller.

Suddenly, it was 1884, and John Prowers died at the age of 46. He and Amache had nine children together and all that lived to adulthood went to college, even after John's death.

With that long, bushy beard, John looked older than his age. He was surely smarter than his age as he and Amache had enclosed 80,000 acres of land in one body, and owned 40 miles of river frontage, controlling 400,000 acres of range.

His success in the cattle business was extraordinary. He started with a cash capital of $234 in 1862. By the time of his death, his herd numbered more than 10,000 head, many of which are of the best blood – mainly White-faced Herefords.

Amache was heart-broken, but her eldest son, John Jr., stepped in to help. And she knew she had to be herself, because she had been at John's side though all his business ventures. She was the most astute female businessman in the West at that time.

Ryan and John Jr. maintained the growing Hereford herd. Ryan was a partner, and a working one at that. He spent all his spare time helping Amache and John Jr. And Amache made it clear to everyone, she was staying in Las Animas forever.

They still had an old house down in Boggsville, which had been turned into a place where people stopped to see where Kit Carson had been buried for awhile, in fact, and only at L.A. Allen's house. The Prowers old place and Tom Boggs house remained.

Amache organized a society of women who dedicated their time to keeping those old places in shape. They had a "Visitors' Jar" for donations set out by a plaque to help maintain the houses and Kit's old grave site.

Adkin learned Billy Dixon retired from military scouting and returned to civilian life in 1883, settling in Hutchinson County, Texas, where he worked on the Turkey Track Ranch.

Dixon ended up building a home near the site of the original Adobe Walls, where he planted an orchard and 30 acres of alfalfa that he irrigated from Bent's Creek. Adkin knew the area well, but he had seen a lot of blood soaking in the sand in those areas, too.

When the government established a post office at Adobe Walls in August 1887, Dixon became the first postmaster. Adkin was happy Dixon was still alive. If any man was "hard to kill," it was Billy Dixon that took the top prize.

The years were flying by, and most news wasn't about Indian raids anymore, it was gunfights. Every man carried a pistol it seemed, and it was, "Treat me well or we'll settle it with guns." And there were hangings by mobs and vigilantes where law wasn't close by.

It was really bad in the Neutral Strip of the Oklahoma Panhandle. It was often called No Man's Land because it wasn't a state and there was no "Official" lawmen. In fact, outlaws ran to hide in No Man's Land for that reason.

•••

In the year 1889, Charles Goodnight stopped to visit with Adkin and the crew. He arrived two days after their fourth of July celebration, Goodnight was preparing to sell his cattle ranch outside of Pueblo, as he needed the cash.

He needed funds because he had dissolved his alliance with John Adair, his partner in the JA Ranch first settled at Palo Duro Canyon, where he was confronted by Quanah and his band from Fort Sill.

"In 1879, I moved the ranch headquarters to Turkey Creek, farther east, to be closer to the railroad," Goodnight said. "I built a new ranch, a log home, and later, a stone house for the Adairs to live in. Things were good until we started gettin' hit hard by rustlers.

"By 1880, the area was suffering badly, and I warned the Texas Rangers that if they couldn't handle the problem, that I would," he continued. "Well, I established the Panhandle Stockman's Association, and we located it in Mobeetie – old Sweetwater – to take care of the cattle rustling problems. We started applying vigilante justice to the area's outlaws and cattle thieves.

"Well, that's going to end up with troubles so I decided to quit my association with the JA Ranch and took what money I got from John and bought a place down southeast of Amarillo," Goodnight said. "That's the reason I need more funds, I'm going to start another big cattle ranch there."

"Sounds like you've been busy, Charles," Adkin said. "Need any good horses?"

"Actually, I do, and I want to see your operation," Goodnight said. "I've heard about it already, but I have other news you may be interested in.

"I know it's been a long time, but I was down in Liberal, Kansas, a couple of months ago. Do you know it? It was a shanty town, brand new, but its about a year old now."

Adkin shook his head "no."

"Well, last year, the Rock Island Railroad built a line to what they thought was the Oklahoma line," he continued. "Well it was in nowhere because the towns of Fargo Springs and Springfield kept fighting over the railroad's line and wouldn't support the Rock Island by selling bonds for the right away acres.

"Anyway, they stopped it a mile or so from where this man Seymour Rogers had a hand-dug water well and had a post office and general store," he said. "The Rock Island sold more than $180,000 worth of right-a-way lots in about two days. They called the town Liberal, because old man Rogers always gave out water for free to travellers. They'd say, "That's mighty Liberal of ya."

"Well, I went there because that's a place one could sell cattle and ship 'em out on rails. It would be closer to me than Dodge City," Goodnight continued. "I heard some men talking about going to Beer City, about 2 miles south across the Kansas line into Oklahoma on Sunday to drink and gamble. You can't buy beer on Sunday's in Kansas, but in No Man's Land, anything goes.

"I passed on the invite, but I heard them warning some others about the outlaw sheriff they have in Beer City," he said, looking sternly at Adkin. "Get this, they said his name is Lew 'Brushy' Bush. They say he'll rob you at gunpoint just to protect you while you're in his city."

Adkin dropped his chin to his chest, like the wind had been kicked out of him.

"Are you sure it was Lew Bush?" he asked softly.

"I'm sure, Adkin. It rang a bell and jostled my memory. I knew you were – at one time – obsessed in finding that man," Goodnight said.

"How do you get to Liberal?" Adkin asked, with his head still down.

"You can ride the train from here to Garden City, it's a new town west of Dodge," Goodnight said. "Liberal is about 55 miles due south of Garden City – it's a good trail once you get out of the sand hills south of the depot, and you have to cross the Cimarron."

Adkin just sat there. Finally he stood and went out on the porch and yelled for Ruiz, who came running at once.

"Would you mind, Charles, if Ruiz here shows you the horses that are for sale?" Adkin said as he sat back down with his brow furrowed.

"Not at all, Adkin," Goodnight said. "I'm sorry if what I told you upsets your feelings."

"No-no, Charles, not at all. You have nothing to apologize for. I appreciate your information very much," Adkin said, smiling at Goodnight. "Go look at some of those yearlings with Ruiz."

He sat there, his head spinning like a coach wheel with a run-away team. Lew "Brushy" Bush is a thieving sheriff in a place with no real lawmen. It's too tempting.

An Englishman's Adventures on the Santa Fe Trail (1865-1889)

Adkin's prayers and perseverance to forget this man and remove hate from his life was teetering on the edge of Hell in his mind. What was he going to do? It was nearly 16 years ago that Bush and the others slaughtered his Matty, the only love of his suddenly miserable life.

This darkness spread like fire through Adkin's mind. His heart was telling him to forget it. His mind was saying end this darkness once and for all.

His mind won.

•••

He tried to keep his composure as Goodnight came back in and said he'd take three of the saddle horses. He needed some that could be taught cattle herding right away, and a good saddle horse was a lot easier to deal with. He paid the $200 each price and was happy with the deal.

Goodnight wanted to get to the railroad depot in Las Animas and see when the next western train was coming through. Ruiz volunteered to ride over there and find out. Goodnight accepted the offer, and he and Adkin went back into the house and had a rye.

Goodnight noticed Adkin emptied the first glass and then filled it up with more for the second shot. He started regretting telling Adkin about Bush.

Ruiz came back and told Adkin and Goodnight the next train west was going to arrive at 4 p.m. and depart at 4:20 for La Junta and on to Pueblo. Goodnight stood and asked Ruiz to put tethers on his new horses. Adkin gave Charles the lead harnesses. It was 3 p.m., July 6, 1889, and they said their goodbyes, as Goodnight and Ruiz headed to the railroad depot leading three horses behind Adkin's buggy.

Adkin made up his mind he was leaving Las Animas July 7. He was taking Dodger with him in a cattle car to Garden City and then riding south to No Man's Land.

•••

The following morning, Adkin told Ryan bluntly where he was going and why. Ryan asked him to reconsider, but Adkin had that evil in his eyes again. He had Uribe helping him tie off his bedroll, a small tarp on his saddle, and hard tack and jerky and some clothes in the saddle bags. These would be thrown in the cattle cars that were always attached to the few passenger cars.

It took the train three days to get to Garden City – a total of 136 miles. It should have taken only two days, but they hit a dust storm just east of Granada and had to slow to almost a crawl because visibility was about 100 feet. They slowed to about 5 miles an hour, and it was five hours of dirt – everywhere.

They had to close all the windows in the passenger cars and it got to about 100 degrees inside. People were sweating like field hands using a one-horse plow. That slowed them, but it cleared off by the time they stopped in Garden City.

Adkin had heard about this place before, even though Goodnight called it a new town. He asked the conductor about the town, and he said he thought it was founded about 10 years ago. It seemed like every town Adkin had seen on the Plains.

Garden City's advantage was, of course, it lay along the great Arkansas River, the thread of life west of the Great Bend on the Santa Fe Trail.

Adkin brought Dodger out of the cattle car, and saddled him up. It was late in the afternoon and Adkin had two choices. Either stay in a local hotel or boarding house and try to make 55 miles in one day to Liberal; or ride til dark and sleep under a tarp in this wind for the night, shortening the ride to Liberal.

He decided to spend the night in Garden City and found a small hotel near the depot with a livery stable next to it. He got a room and turned over Dodger to the manager of the livery stable. He charged a full $5 for one night for the horse, which included a rub down, curry combing and hay and oats for supper.

Adkin was tempted to stay with Dodger, except he didn't like oats. The rest was okay with him. Besides, the hotel was $5, too, but he had to pay for his own food and drink. He told the man he was departing very early the next day.

Sure enough, Adkin had to knock on the livery stable office and wake the manager to get Dodger saddled up and ready to ride. He galloped out at 5:30 a.m., and it was barely getting gray on the eastern horizon.

Goodnight had been right about the sand hills just south of Garden City. They were hard on Dodger, but he maintained a good pace – for about 35 miles. Then he started showing signs of weariness, but Adkin caught a glimpse of the Cimarron valley ahead and decided to stop there and refresh Dodger and himself with some cool water from the Cimarron.

At the river, he noticed a large house built on the south side ridge of the valley, far enough up from any flooding waters, which the Cimarron was notorious for. It was a nicely built house, planked with two stories and a corral off to the west side. He didn't see any people, but it was at least 1 mile away.

He gave Dodger his head while he laid down and washed his whole head in the cool clear water. He was sure there was extra sand in his scalp from a day earlier in the dust storm on the train.

He loved the Cimarron when it cleared up in certain areas and certain times. It could be clear and slow moving one day and a raging muddy – and deadly – menace the next day. It was the epitome of the Great Plains – contrary at any moment.

He led Dodger to a small grove of cottonwoods and he laid down in the cool grass while Dodger nibbled his way around, staying close to Adkin. Adkin fell asleep, and it was totally unintended. He awoke startled, unsure how long he was out.

He checked his pocket watch, and it was only about an hour.

"It must be my age," he chuckled to himself. "Going to be 43 on July 30. I hope this trip will be a safe birthday gift."

He then started wondering how his draw was and his aim. He hadn't really shot his Colts much in the last few years, Only a snake or a coyote that gets too close – usually around foals' birth sacks.

He thought about practicing now, but if there were folks at the house up there, they might start shooting at him in fear. Plus, it was 6 in the evening, and there was about 15-18 miles to go in his estimation. And three hours of daylight.

He gathered up Dodger and jumped in the saddle. He would find a place in or near Liberal to practice with his Colts. He rode up and out of the valley – he had made 2 miles by the time he reached the top of the ridge.

"The valley must be 3 to 3-and-a-half miles across here," he said to himself. "It's pretty. I have a real affinity for the Cimarron River."

He reached Liberal at 9, just as it was getting dark. There were several mercantile stores, and several saloons, a livery stable down the street. Folks out on the plank walkways were studying him like a hawk watches a kangaroo rat.

Adkin stopped at a saloon where lights were glaring out into the dirt street. He tied off Dodger and walked past several men standing outside the door smoking pipes and cigars.

"Good evening gentlemen," Adkin said as he went through the swinging doors. They were caught off guard and said nothing.

At the bar, Adkin ordered a rye whisky and a beer. When the barkeep set them on the bar, he asked if there was a hotel in Liberal. The man said there was one, it was called the Rock Island Hotel and Depot next to the Grier Eating House.

"It's three blocks down before you cross the railroad tracks," he said.

"Thank you. My name is Adkin Yates of Las Animas City, Colorado," he said as he reached out to shake hands with the man. "And you are …?"

"Oh, I'm called Sandy," he said a smile spreading across his face. "Nice to meet you Mister Yates."

Adkin smiled and picked up his rye. He drank the shot, set down the glass and sipped some beer.

Sandy went on down the bar, whispering to everyone Adkin's name and where he was from. Adkin was sure by the time he got to the last man drinking down there, he and Sandy had been friends for years. Adkin smiled.

When Sandy came back to see if Adkin wanted another drink, Adkin told him he was going to make sure he got a room before it was too late.

"But, I will be back soon, Sandy," Adkin said. "You're rye is quite good. By the way, I raise horses. Is there any good grasslands around here?"

"Why there sure is," Sandy exclaimed, "There's grasslands around here as far as the eye can see – except south. It's only two miles to Beer City in Oklahoma. Not many folks like to fight for land rights down there below the line."

"I see. Well, we'll talk more when I get back," Adkin said as he turned away and walked back out.

Adkin figured by the time he got a room, unloaded his stuff, took Dodger to the livery stable just north of the depot, most folks in Liberal would know all about the Englishman looking for ranch land. He would be welcomed by most.

He checked into the hotel above the depot in Liberal, Kansas, on Wednesday, July 10, a hot breezy night. He went back to the saloon around 10 p.m. There were about 20 people in there and several women were now working the crowd.

It didn't take long for a soiled dove named Cheryl to ask Adkin to buy her a drink. He agreed, and she ordered something called a Mule Skinner. She said it was made with whiskey and blackberry liquor. Sandy smiled at him and winked. Adkin knew Sandy had already told her about this rancher from Colorado. He had to have money to burn.

Adkin was pleasant with Cheryl, but he let her know he wasn't interested in a poke.

"Not tonight, Cheryl," he explained. "I've been in the saddle all day, and I'm tired and dusty ... maybe tomorrow night, eh?"

She bought it, laughing and hugging his arm, but when her Mule Skinner was empty, she excused herself immediately and went to working the crowd again.

Adkin didn't want anybody to know what he was up to, where he was going or one iota of his plan. That was worrying him, as well. He would have to figure a plan, and back up plan, and his escape if needed.

All he knew for sure while standing there enjoying another rye was he was leaving unannounced before noon; riding west of town and circling back south to Beer City. It couldn't be that hard to find it.

He thought it best to go in late rather than early the next morning, as he figured Bush probably drank lot and slept late, as most drunks do. He would get there around noon or shortly thereafter and go to a saloon and get as much info on the "Sheriff" as he could and then decide how to challenge him to a fight.

First, when he got out of earshot of Liberal, he was going to have to practice a few rounds to make sure his draw and aim were still what it used to be. He never bragged, but he knew he could handle a Colt as well as any man he had personally seen.

•••

Adkin slept late himself, not getting up and dressed until 8. He went and checked Dodger and told the keeper to have him saddled by 10. He didn't tell him why, either. He didn't want to say he was going to look at land and have riders following him so they could tell others what land he was checking.

He then went to the Grier House and had breakfast. They had ham, fresh eggs and biscuits. The biscuits were really good, especially with some of the honey they served with them.

Again, Adkin made small talk and learned the Rock Island had stopped here a year earlier and didn't have any plans to set rail any further, that anyone knew of. The townsfolk were building large cattle pens on the northeast side of town along the track.

One of the men working at the Grier House said Liberal had about 800 people now. It was growing fairly quick. Adkin asked what was this Beer City?

The man really got going, about how gamblers, madams and prostitutes were everywhere, empty beer barrels sat on the edge of town drawing flies and stinking.

He said there were several plank houses but most of the town was tents. There were gunfights, the Sheriff wasn't elected, just used his gun to appoint himself Sheriff.

"He carries a sawed off shotgun, and pistols and beats or shoots anyone that gets in his way," the man said. "In fact, they had a big celebration last week for July 4. They had brought in two big-time wrestlers and boxers to have a big match, then they were going to have a Masked Ball after the fight that night.

"I know a man that was there all day, and he saw this madam, she's well known, called Pussy Cat Nell. She was giving Bush a rough time cause she had a bunch of her bet on the fight stolen by Bush. He called it a percentage for holding her stakes, which she never wanted him to hold," he continued. "Anyway, he pulled a pistol and beat her down until you couldn't see her face for the blood.

"They had to carry her to her house and she couldn't make the Masked Ball. She almost died," he added. "That's the kind of scum that lives down in Beer City."

"Mercy, this Bush sounds like pure trouble to me," Adkin said, feeling better about his plans. More confirmation this man doesn't deserve to live.

"He is, but don't anybody make them go down there," he said. "It's just some men have to have that liquor and no-good women."

Adkin walked a few blocks up and down Main Street in Liberal. They had a drug store on the main corner of downtown. There were stores offering the latest styles in women's dresses and shoes, a Star Lumber Yard down the street which took up a big lot with milled planks and lots of farming and ranching supplies.

Adkin could tell it was a nice little town, but he couldn't understand how it would survive with no big river nearby. He discovered the Cimarron ran north and northeast of Liberal, and it was about the same distance away – about 15-16 miles. Most big cities were always right along a big waterway.

Around 10, Adkin first went and got Dodge from the livery and rode him to the depot. He then went to his room, gathered his things and went downstairs, tied off his bedroll, put on his saddle bags and started out this Second Street heading west out of town.

About a mile from the depot, he saw the post office Goodnight had told him about. He decided to stop briefly and meet the man that gave this town its name. When he dismounted, a tall wiry man came out of the post office – it was a few yards from his main house. He looked a little past middle age but healthy and strong.

"Are you the gentleman that gives water freely to passersby?" Adkin asked.

"That's me. Seymour Rogers is the name," he said as he reached out to shake hands.

"Adkin Yates, Mister Rogers," I'm from Las Animas, Colorado. I'm a horse rancher by trade."

"I see. Are you here for a drink of water?" Rogers asked waving his hand toward the well behind the post office.

"No Sir, I just wanted to meet the man who gives away free water out here where it's a very valuable resource," Adkin said. "I'm pleased to meet a man who shares his bounty and blessings. It's very admirable, Mister Rogers."

"Thank you, Mister Yates."

"How far down did you have to dig before hitting water?" Adkin asked.

"About 88 feet," Rogers said. "See that mule over there? She was my lifeline the whole time and pulled every bucket of sod from that hole. And, of course, me at the end of day.

"She was, and is, my real blessing," he said laughing. Adkin chuckled, too.

"Well Mister Rogers, it's been a treat to meet you." Adkin said. "I'm just down here looking around a little. Might see you again."

"You're welcome any time," Rogers said. "Come back when my Missus, Addie, is here and we'll have lunch or supper. She's in town with the wagon buying some supplies."

"I thank you. Thanks again," Adkin said as he rode on westward out of sight of Roger's place.

He kept westward, but then saw a house off to the north about five miles out, and he wanted to get a little further away from people who may mistake his shooting practice. He turned and went south, sure he was in Oklahoma after a couple of miles. Then he saw the shanty town of Tyrone City. He had heard the state had issued some laws that Texas cattle could no longer come across the state line because of disease, so the Rock Island laid track about four miles southwest to the Oklahoma surveyed line and ended the track there. Immediately, Tyrone City sprung up just like Beer City did. But it was in its infancy as far as saloons and bordellos were concerned. Adkin tuned back southeast and out of earshot of Tyrone.

He got in his practice with the Colts, and soon it was noon, so he headed due east. He figured he was maybe about 7 or 8 miles from Beer City.

After about an hour, he could see a few two-story wood buildings or houses and some tent tops on the horizon. He was sure that had to be Beer City, he had to head a little northeast as he had gone to far south after seeing Tyrone City.

He was about a half-mile away, and he heard the sound of a big gun, either a large caliber rifle like a Sharp's "Big 50" or a short barreled shotgun. He halted Dodger a moment, listening.

Boom, boom, boom … six more shots, but from a pistol or small-bore rifle. "What was going on?" he thought to himself. Maybe a robbery or a shootout. Wouldn't it be ironic if someone shot Bush before he could get to him. He chuckled to himself. Not very good odds considering Bush was a murdering bastard.

Then more gunshots, and then more, and more. This sounded like a turkey shoot. He kicked Dodger in the flanks and came to a gallop. The gunfire wasn't decreasing, it actually sounded like war – guns going off over and over.

By the time Adkin pulled up on Dodger at the edge of a dirt road leading east into the center of this shanty town, the gunfire was becoming less. Finally after another six rapid shots, it was total quiet. Adkin walked Dodger slowly into the main intersection.

People were everywhere and crowding into the middle of the street in front of a two-story building. Some were clapping their hands and some were whooping it up. He heard someone say, "The son of a bitch had it coming."

Adkin tied Dodger to the hitching post of the building, which had a saloon sign on the front. Then he noticed a body laying in the dirt face down. As he pushed his way closer, blood was covering the body from head to toe. It was pooling all around him.

He could see a short-barreled shotgun lying next to the man. His hat was a few feet away – a gray Reb's hat. He was wearing a double holster gunbelt and both pistols were still holstered.

The people were getting more and more excited and cheering. Goodness, Adkin thought, they were happy.

Adkin asked a man next to him who was clapping, "Who is that?"

"That, my friend, is the worthless coyote named 'Brushy' Bush."

Adkin froze.

Was it true?

Was this Lew "Brushy" Bush?

The murderer of his Matty?

Someone yelled, "Drinks on the house, Pussy Cat Nell wants to celebrate." A scream went up and everybody headed for the saloon.

Adkin was swept up in the crush of men headed into swinging doors only big enough for a couple of men to squeeze through. Inside, he made it to the bar.

The bar keep had three women helping him pour whisky in every glass and mug the girls set out. People were grabbing them and downing them right away.

"To hell with Bush," someone yelled. That brought out more whooping and applauding. Adkin snatched up a tin cup full of whisky. He took a sip, then held it up and said softly, "Yes, to hell with Amos Lew 'Brushy' Bush," and drank til his cup was empty – he coughed several times afterward.

After several drinks, Adkin made his way through the crowd and looked in the road. The body was still there and several children were checking it out. One of them kicked the body, then had to kneel down and clean the blood off his shoe with sand. Adkin just had to have a look to make sure he wasn't dreaming.

The blood surrounding Bush and covering his whole body was astonishing. Adkin made his way back to the bar, having to muscle his way in close enough to order a whisky. It was unbelievable.

He stood there with a whisky in his hand, among people he didn't know at all, and feeling a weight had been lifted from his soul. The folks here had shot Lew Bush to death. Adkin thought it appropriate; gamblers, cut throats, thieves, rustlers and outlaws killed one of their own who had abused too many of his own kind. The irony was not lost on Adkin.

After about 30 minutes, Pussy Cat Nell came down the stairs to great applause and screams of approval.

"Way to go, Pussy Cat. Way to show him who's not going to take his shit any more," a man who was standing on the bar yelled. The men went wild.

Adkin noticed the woman had been beaten badly. Her face was black and purple all over. Both her eyes were dark blue and black, She had stitches over her left eye and a cuts on her lower lip and chin. She was using a cane to come down the stairs.

"Speech. Speech," someone yelled. She stopped a few steps from the main floor.

"I want to thank my friends for wanting to protect me and wishing me well this week," she shouted above the crowds' murmurs. "But first, I want that bag of shit removed from our streets so we can celebrate."

Everyone went crazy with glee and sheer joy. They all stumbled into the street. One man tried lifting one of Bush's legs and it looked like a piece of limp rope. His arm was the same.

Someone yelled, "Get a flour sack – the big one that holds 100 pounds."

It soon showed up, and it took six or seven men to pick up what was remaining of Bush to put him in the sack. Even his backbone was shattered in many places, making him look like mush.

As he was rolled over while they were wrestling with his body, Adkin stepped closer to see if that face was familiar. It was completely gone. He had been shot so many times in the back of the head, all the exiting bullets had destroyed any resemblance of a man. It actually made Adkin's stomach wretch a few times.

Once they got him into the bag, which was only about 4-feet long, he was thrown in the back of a wagon. Adkin watched as they headed west out the road he came in on. Everybody then returned to drinking.

Later, the burial detail came back and proudly announced they had buried Lew "Brushy " Bush among Beer City's trash pile of beer bottles, tin cans and garbage in a shallow, unmarked grave.

The whooping was as loud as Adkin could believe. He experienced the fact he was not the only person who despised and hated this man. At 7 p.m., he finally decided to get Dodger and head back to Liberal. It was only 2 miles, and he could check back into the hotel at the Depot.

As he was leaving the bar, he heard a man say he believed everybody in town unloaded their guns into Bush after "Pussy Cat" Nell hit him – first – in the back of the neck with both barrels of her 12 gauge shotgun from her second-floor bedroom window as Bush walked by.

"I saw one fella who emptied his pistol, reloaded and put six more rounds into him," he said laughing. "I'll bet he was shot 300 times, and there can't be one bone in his body that wasn't shattered."

Adkin walked out and slid into the saddle of Dodger, who had been sitting there watching the melee. Adkin rode slowly back into Liberal and went to the hotel. After putting Dodger away for the night, Adkin went to bed and slept like a baby that was full of its mother's milk.

•••

When Adkin rode into the YR&R yard, he was a new man. Everyone noticed how happy he was, a grin across his face at all times. When he went into the office and told his dearest friends what had happened, they were in disbelief – except for Uribe.

"It ees the work of the Lord, yes Boss," he asked.

"Yes Uribe. It is God's hand that lifted this stone from around my neck. My … our … Matty is flying higher now among the clouds and stars knowing this man paid the price for his evil ways.

"He was killed around 1 o'clock on July 11, 1889, and I heard every shot and saw his body dragged off to an unmarked grave."

•••

Adkin stayed in Las Animas, even though most of the town died off and was abandoned. His horse ranch was very successful through the years, and Amache, who also stayed with a few of her children, sold him more land so he could expand.

When Adkin died in 1916, at the ripe old age of 70, he had amassed 1,200 acres and nearly 400 head of "Fine Horseflesh."

He had seen the coming of flight with the Wright Brothers, the invention of the automobile, electricity being produced and lighting bulbs. He had a Bell's telephone in his home, and he couldn't believe the roads and towns all over the land he first saw when it was barren, untamed and wild.

He saw his old friend Quanah become the last great Chief of the Comanches – and fairly wealthy, too. He had built a huge "Star House" in Oklahoma and even entertained a President in his dining hall. Quanah died Feb. 24, 1911, in his Star House.

Adkin attended his burial at Fort Sill near Lawton, Oklahoma, on a knoll called Chiefs Knoll. He rested near Chief Satanta, Chief Ten Bears, Chief Little Raven and about a dozen other Chiefs.

It broke Adkin's heart to think of how many freighters, settlers, soldiers and warriors died along the Santa Fe Trail and across the Great Plains.

"The whole of that country was fertilized with blood – and the blood was all red," Adkin thought to himself.

Adkin ended up selling his property where he and Matty's Cimarron House had been located a few years before his death. He regretted he couldn't save Matty's grave, but he knew it would never be found or uncovered. That gave him peace of mind.

Adkin never remarried or had a serious relationship with another woman. He called on a few, but companionship was all he was interested in. He did become very close with Cheyenne, Ryan and Kanaka's son.

Cheyenne called him Uncle Adkin, and stayed with Adkin when Ryan and Kanaka moved the YR&R Freight Yard and Barlow & Sanderson's operations to Dodge City.

Ryan convince Kanaka that Cheyenne was old enough at 17 to stay and work with Adkin. Plus, he went to school in La Junta, Adkin paying his train transportation.

Hector Ruiz stayed with Adkin, eventually living in quarters Adkin had built for Ruiz and Uribe next to the stables.

Uribe stayed, too. His remaining family living in their village in the Purgatoire Valley til 1895, when they migrated to La Junta. Uribe lived and worked with Ruiz, who between the two, made thousands of dollars as horse trainers and breeders. Adkin shared most of his horse operations with his two loyal friends.

When Adkin died, the doctor said it was heart failure, his estate and stock was worth a little more than $355,000. The cash, bonds and stock all went to his family in Olney, England, but the horses, ranch holdings and property was split up between Uribe, Ruiz and Cheyenne Ryan.

Those three continued their partnership for decades, becoming known throughout the Great Plains as breeders of excellent horses. Uribe and Ruiz lived several more years after Adkin's death and were called Dons.

Adkin's diary was finally turned into a book by Amache and her children. It was entitled, "An Englishman's Adventures on The Santa Fe Trail."

Adkin had asked to be buried in the old Boggsville Cemetery, near where Kit Carson and his wife had been originally interred.

His oldest friend in America, Tyler Ryan, had a brass plaque made to go on Adkin's granite tombstone:

"Here lies Adkin Maxwell Yates, an Englishman by birth but a proud American in life. He came to this country in 1865. He was a master blacksmith and became a stagecoach driver, a teamster, an Indian fighter, a frontiersman, a horse breeder and married a Kiowa Princess. He was friends with the most famous Chiefs on the Great Plains, but was also a close friend to all who worked and lived near him. He will be terribly missed by all who knew him."

b. July, 30, 1846
d. August 30, 1916.

Printed in the United States
By Bookmasters